PENGUIN CLASSICS

THE COUNT OF MONTE CRISTO

ALEXANDRE DUMAS was born in 1802 at Villers-Cotterêts. His father, the illegitimate son of a marquis, was a general in the Revolutionary armies, but died when Dumas was only four. He was brought up in straitened circumstances and received very little education. He joined the household of the future king, Louis-Philippe, and began reading voraciously. Later he entered the *cénacle* of Charles Nodier and started writing. In 1829 the production of his play, *Henri III et sa cour*, heralded twenty years of successful playwriting. In 1839 he turned his attention to writing historical novels, often using collaborators such as Auguste Maquet to suggest plots or historical background. His most successful novels are *The Count of Monte Cristo*, which appeared during 1844–5, and *The Three Musketeers*, published in 1844. Other novels deal with the wars of religion and the Revolution. Dumas wrote many of these for the newspapers, often in daily instalments, marshalling his formidable energies to produce ever more in order to pay off his debts. In addition, he wrote travel books, children's stories and his *Mémoires* which describe most amusingly his early life, his entry into Parisian literary circles and the 1830 Revolution. He died in 1870.

ROBIN BUSS is a writer and translator who contributes regularly to *The Times Educational Supplement, The Times Literary Supplement* and other papers. He studied at the University of Paris, where he took a degree and a doctorate in French literature. He is part-author of the article 'French Literature' in *Encyclopaedia Britannica* and has published critical studies of works by Vigny and Cocteau, and three books on European cinema, *The French through Their Films* (1988), *Italian Films* (1989) and *French Film Noir* (1994). He is also part-author of a biography, in French, of King Edward VII (with Jean-Pierre Navailles, published by Payot, Paris, 1999). He has translated a number of other volumes for Penguin, including Jean Paul Sartre's *Modern Times*, Zola's *L'Assommoir* and *Au Bonheur des Dames*, and Albert Camus's *The Plague*.

ALEXANDRE DUMAS (PÈRE)

The Count of Monte Cristo

Translated and with an Introduction and Notes by
ROBIN BUSS

PENGUIN BOOKS

PENGUIN BOOKS

Published by the Penguin Group
Penguin Books Ltd, 80 Strand, London WC2R ORL, England
Penguin Group (USA) Inc., 375 Hudson Street, New York, New York 10014, USA
Penguin Group (Canada), 90 Eglinton Avenue East, Suite 700, Toronto, Ontario, Canada M4P 2Y3
(a division of Pearson Penguin Canada Inc.)
Penguin Ireland, 25 St Stephen's Green, Dublin 2, Ireland (a division of Penguin Books Ltd)
Penguin Group (Australia), 250 Camberwell Road, Camberwell, Victoria 3124, Australia
(a division of Pearson Australia Group Pty Ltd)
Penguin Books India Pvt Ltd, 11 Community Centre, Panchsheel Park, New Delhi – 110 017, India
Penguin Group (NZ), cnr Airborne and Rosedale Roads, Albany, Auckland 1310,
New Zealand (a division of Pearson New Zealand Ltd)
Penguin Books (South Africa) (Pty) Ltd, 24 Sturdee Avenue,
Rosebank, Johannesburg 2196, South Africa

Penguin Books Ltd, Registered Offices: 80 Strand, London WC2R ORL, England

www.penguin.com

First published 1844–5
This translation first published 1996
Reissued with new Chronology and Further Reading 2003
This anniversary edition published 2006

1

Copyright © Robin Buss, 1996, 2003
All rights reserved

The moral right of the translator has been asserted

Set in 9.75/11.75 pt PostScript Adobe Sabon
Typeset by Rowland Phototypesetting Ltd, Bury St Edmunds, Suffolk
Printed in England by Clays Ltd, St Ives plc

ISBN-13: 978-0-140-45532-8
ISBN-10: 0-140-45532-9

Contents

Chronology

1802 Alexandre Dumas is born at Villers-Cotterêts, the third child of Thomas-Alexandre Dumas. His father, himself the illegitimate son of a marquis and a slave girl of San Domingo, Marie-Cessette Dumas, had had a remarkable career as a general in the Republican, then in the Napoleonic Army.

1806 General Dumas dies. Alexandre and his mother, Elisabeth Labouret, are left virtually penniless.

1822 Dumas takes a post as a clerk, then in 1823 is granted a sinecure on the staff of the Duke of Orléans. He meets the actor Talma and starts to mix in artistic and literary circles, writing sketches for the popular theatre.

1824 Dumas' son, Alexandre, future author of *La Dame aux camélias*, is born as the result of an affair with a seamstress, Catherine Lebay.

1829 Dumas' historical drama, *Henri III et sa cour*, is produced at the Comédie-Française. It is an immediate success, marking Dumas out as a leading figure in the Romantic movement.

1830 Victor Hugo's drama *Hernani* becomes the focus of the struggle between the Romantics and the traditionalists in literature. In July, the Bourbon monarchy is overthrown and replaced by a new regime under the Orléanist King Louis-Philippe. Dumas actively supports the insurrection.

1831 Dumas' melodrama *Antony*, with its archetypal Romantic hero, triumphs at the Théâtre de la Porte Saint-Martin.

1832 Dumas makes a journey to Switzerland which will form the basis of his first travel book, published the following year.

1835 Dumas travels to Naples with Ida Ferrier (whom he will later marry), has a passionate affair in Naples with Caroline Ungher and falls in love with Italy and the Mediterranean.

1836 Triumph of Dumas' play *Kean*, based on the personality of the English actor whom Dumas had seen performing in Shakespeare in 1828.

1839 *Mademoiselle de Belle-Isle*. Dumas' greatest success in the theatre.

1840 Dumas marries Ida Ferrier. He travels down the Rhine with Gérard de Nerval and they collaborate on the drama *Léo Burckart*. Nerval introduces Dumas to Auguste Maquet who will become his collaborator on many of his subsequent works.

1841 Spends a year in Florence.

1844 The year of Dumas' two greatest novels: *The Three Musketeers* starts to appear in serial form in March and the first episodes of *The Count of Monte Cristo* follow in August. Dumas starts to build his Château de Monte-Cristo at St-Germain-en-Laye. He separates from Ida Ferrier.

1845 *Twenty Years After*, the first sequel to *The Three Musketeers*, appears at the beginning of the year. In February, Dumas wins a libel action against the author of a book accusing him of plagiarism. Publishes *La Reine Margot*.

1846 Dumas travels in Spain and North Africa. Publishes *La Dame de Monsoreau*, *Les Deux Diane* and *Joseph Balsamo*.

1847 Dumas' theatre, the Théâtre Historique, opens. It will show several adaptations of his novels, including *The Three Musketeers* and *La Reine Margot*. Serialization of *The Vicomte de Bragelonne*, the final episode of the *The Three Musketeers*.

1848 A revolution in February deposes Louis-Philippe and brings in the Second Republic. Dumas stands unsuccessfully for Parliament and supports Louis-Napoléon, nephew of Napoleon I, who becomes President of the Republic.

1849 Dumas publishes *The Queen's Necklace*.

1850 Dumas is declared bankrupt and has to sell the Château de Monte-Cristo and the Théâtre Historique. Publishes *The Black Tulip*.

1851 In December, Louis-Napoléon seizes power in a coup d'état, effectively abolishing the Republic. A year later, the Second Empire will be proclaimed. Victor Hugo goes into exile in Belgium where Dumas, partly to escape his creditors, joins him.

1852 Publishes his memoirs.

1853 In November, returns to Paris and founds a newspaper, *Le Mousquetaire*. Publishes *Ange Pitou*.

1858 Founds the literary weekly, *Le Monte-Cristo*. Sets out on a nine-month journey to Russia.

1860 Meets Garibaldi and actively supports the Italian struggle against Austria. Founds *L'Independente*, a periodical in Italian and French. Garibaldi is godfather to Dumas' daughter by Emilie Cordier.

1861–1870 Dumas continues to travel throughout Europe and to write, though his output is somewhat reduced. None the less in the final decade of his life, he published some six plays, thirteen novels, several shorter fictions, a historical work on the Bourbons in Naples and a good deal of journalism. He had a last love affair, with an American, Adah Menken, and indulged his life-long passions for drama, travel and cookery.

1870 Alexandre Dumas dies on 5 December in Dieppe.

Introduction

'Ah, a children's novel,' a Russian film-maker remarked when I told her that I was translating *The Count of Monte Cristo*. The comment was not intended to be disparaging, merely descriptive; and many people, in different cultures, would tend to agree with the categorization. Most will derive their idea of the novel, not from having read it, but because a kind of abstract of the storyline exists as part of the common culture: innocent man imprisoned, meets fellow-prisoner who directs him to a buried fortune, escapes and plots revenge. It has been adapted for film, television and the theatre, as well as being translated, abridged and imitated in print. It has supplied material for cartoons and comedy: the Irish comedian Dave Allen used to do a series of sketches around the theme of a young man (Dantès) breaking through a dungeon wall and encountering an old, bearded prisoner (Abbé Faria). Some events in the story are so well-known that they exist apart from the novel, like Robinson Crusoe's discovery of Man Friday's footprint, or incidents and characters from *Treasure Island* and *Frankenstein*. *The Count of Monte Cristo* is one of the great popular novels of all time and, like other popular novels, it has suffered the fate of being treated as not fully 'adult' fiction; like children's fiction, it seems to inhabit a realm outside its creator's biography and the period when it was written.

On the other hand, there are not many children's books, even in our own time, that involve a female serial poisoner, two cases of infanticide, a stabbing and three suicides; an extended scene of torture and execution; drug-induced sexual fantasies, illegitimacy, transvestism and lesbianism; a display of the author's classical learning, and his knowledge of modern European history, the customs and diet of the Italians, the effects of hashish, and so on; the length would, in any case, immediately disqualify it from inclusion in any modern series of books for children. Most important of all, perhaps, is the fact that the author himself never thought of this as 'a children's novel'. Yet already in the earliest translations into English, with their omission or subtle alteration of material that might be considered indelicate by Victorian readers, and of some passages (for example, references to classical literature) that might be thought to hold up the story, one can see the start of a process of transformation, from 'novel' to 'genre novel' – which means, ultimately, almost any kind of genre novel: 'adventure', 'romance', 'thriller' and, if you like, 'children's novel'. This is the usual fate of books that fail to meet the criteria for serious, 'literary' fiction.

Dumas himself must bear some of the responsibility. During his most productive decade, from 1841 to 1850, he wrote forty-one novels, twenty-three plays, seven historical works and half a dozen travel books. The nineteenth century was an age of mass production, which is precisely why Art felt the need to distinguish itself by its individuality and craftsmanship: 'Alexandre Dumas and Co., novel factory', was the contemptuous title given to one critical pamphlet, published at the same time as this novel, in 1845. Moreover it was known that Dumas wrote for money, at so much a line, and that he used at least one collaborator, Auguste Maquet, who would make chapter outlines for him and do research. There was a vast difference between this industrial labour and the monastic devotion to the cause of art that kept Gustave Flaubert at his desk for seven hours a day as he wrote and rewrote *Madame Bovary* (1857). In the history of the novel, Dumas and Flaubert stand near the head of divergent streams.

Alexandre Dumas was born on 24 July 1802; or, rather, since the Republican Calendar was still in force, on 5th Thermidor, Year x, in the little town of Villers-Cotterêts, near Soissons. His father was a general in the revolutionary armies, himself the illegitimate son of a marquis, Antoine-Alexandre Davy de la Paillerie, and a black slave from the island of Santo Domingo, Marie Dumas. In 1806, General Dumas died, leaving his family virtually without resources. The child had little education, enough however to allow him to read *Robinson Crusoe* and *The Arabian Nights*, and to cultivate his handwriting. In 1823, thanks to the second of these, he found employment in Paris, copying documents for Louis-Philippe, Duke of Orléans.

The 1820s were a marvellous time for an aspiring young writer in Paris. The two rival literary ideologies, of Classicism and Romanticism, were engaged in a mock-heroic combat for the soul of French literature. Classicism stood for universal themes, refinement, purity of language, clear division of literary genres and (despite its debt to the literature of the classical world) the peculiarly French ethos of the dramatist Racine. Romanticism meant energy, modern subject-matter, mixing genres and openness to foreign influences, particularly that of Shakespeare, the Romantic dramatist *par excellence*. It was in the theatre that the confrontation would chiefly take place.

Racine had based his plays on stories from classical Greece or on biblical history, both of which offered 'universal' events and characters. Shakespeare, like the German playwright Schiller, had dealt with subjects from modern history, which were national and particular rather than universal. In France, especially, the period that followed the great upheavals of the Revolution, the Empire and the Restoration was one which had an urgent need to make sense of the past. Shakespeare's history plays – and, still more, the historical novels of Walter Scott – were models of how this could be done, drawing on the imagination as well as on scholarship. In 1828, Dumas, who had already tried his hand at a couple of plays and some short stories, submitted a historical drama to the Comédie Française entitled *Henri III et sa cour*. It was a typically Romantic work, ignoring the 'unities' of time, place and action, and written in prose, rather than the conventional medium of verse. It underwent the usual ritual of a public reading and, at its first night on 10 February 1829, scored a triumphant success and was warmly applauded by the author's employer, Louis-Philippe. In the following year, Louis-Philippe became king, after a liberal revolution that was supposed to bring in a constitutional monarchy. Dumas welcomed it; so did the former ultra-monarchist, Victor Hugo.

During the next twenty years, Dumas was (with Hugo and Alfred de Vigny) the leading dramatist of the new movement – and, of the three, easily the most prolific. Perhaps too much so: overnight, after the first performance of *Christine* in 1830, while Dumas was asleep, Hugo and Vigny rewrote the play, reducing it to a more manageable size. Despite this, Dumas' play *Antony* (1831) is an essential work of the Romantic period, as representative as Hugo's *Hernani* or Vigny's *Chatterton*, and more successful with its audiences than either. But the theatre is the very opposite of a monastic cell or an ivory tower. Collaboration is not only the norm, but inevitable, feedback from the public is instantaneous, work has to be produced to satisfy demand, and there is an immediate relationship between the author's output and what comes in through the box office. In the theatre, Dumas learned the rudiments of literary production.

On one occasion, Charles-Jean Harel, director of the Odéon theatre, is supposed to have locked Dumas into a room, away from his mistress, for a week, until he had completed the manuscript of *Napoléon* (1831). The huge growth in the periodical press during the 1820s saw the invention of the *feuilleton* – not in the sense of a regular column by one writer, but of a novel published in instalments; Dumas claimed to have invented the *roman feuilleton* with *La Comtesse de Salisbury*, published in *La Presse* in 1836. By the early 1840s he was writing more novels than plays, mainly (but by no means exclusively) historical fiction which, as I have already mentioned, was one of the most popular genres; it was also taken seriously as a means of exploring the past. He did, incidentally, write a book for children at this time: *Le Capitaine Pamphile* (1839).

Travel, to which he was addicted, helped to stave off boredom, providing the material for travel books, while translation filled in the remaining gaps in the working day. Like Balzac, he was a man of huge appetites: food, sex, work, sleep, pleasure, leisure, movement, excitement. In Italy, he found love, opera, colour and the Mediterranean: he visited Naples and Palermo in 1835, stayed a year in Florence in 1841 and returned in 1843 for a visit that included Sicily. The following year saw the publication of his first great historical novel, *Les Trois Mousquetaires/The Three Musketeers*, and on 28 August 1844 *Le Journal des Débats* began publication of *The Count of Monte Cristo*. It was an immediate success, translated, adapted, pirated . . . in short, a popular novel.

It was also, very clearly, a work of its time. The plot was inspired by the true-life story of François Picaud, which Dumas found in Jacques Peuchet's *Police dévoilée: Mémoires historiques tirés des archives de Paris* . . . (1838), a collection of anecdotes from the Parisian police archives.[1]

Briefly, the story is this: Picaud, a young man from the south of France, was imprisoned in 1807, having been denounced by a group of friends as an English spy, shortly after he had become engaged to a young woman called Marguerite. The denunciation was inspired by a café owner, Mathieu Loupian, who was jealous of Picaud's relationship with Marguerite.

Picaud was eventually moved to a form of house-arrest in Piedmont and shut up in the castle of Fenestrelle, where he acted as servant to a rich Italian cleric. When the man died, abandoned by his family, he left his money to Picaud, whom he had come to treat as a son, also informing him of the whereabouts of a hidden treasure. With the fall of Napoleon in 1814, Picaud, now called Joseph Lucher, was released; in the following year, after collecting the hidden treasure, he returned to Paris.

Here he discovered that Marguerite had married Loupian. Disguising himself, and offering a valuable diamond to Allut, the one man in the group who had been unwilling to collaborate in the denunciation, he learned the identity of his enemies. He then set about eliminating them, stabbing the first with a dagger on which were printed the words: 'Number One', and burning down Loupian's café. He managed to find employment in Loupian's house, disguised as a servant called Prosper. However, while this was going on, Allut had fallen out with the merchant to whom he had resold the diamond, had murdered him and had been imprisoned. On coming out of jail, he started to blackmail Picaud. Picaud poisoned another of the conspirators, lured Loupian's son into crime and his daughter into prostitution, then finally stabbed Loupian himself. But he quarrelled with Allut over the blackmail payments and Allut killed him, confessing the whole story on his deathbed in 1828.

It is obvious both how directly Dumas was inspired by Peuchet's account of this extraordinary tale, and how radically he transformed it; incidentally, he used another chapter of Peuchet's book as the basis for the story of Mme de Villefort. One important step in the transformation from 'true crime' to fiction was to shift the opening of the tale from Paris to Marseille, giving the novel its Mediterranean dimension. Though most of the action still takes place in Paris (apart from a few excursions elsewhere, all the novel between Chapters XXXIX and CIV is set in Paris), the sea is always present as a figure for escape and freedom, while the novel uses the southern origins of its characters as a means to evoke that exotic world of the Mediterranean littoral that had so fascinated French writers and artists since the 1820s. The Mediterranean is the point where the cultures of Europe meet those of the Orient, and the region had been in the forefront of people's minds since the 1820s, because of the Greek struggle for independence and the French conquest of Algeria.

Both of these are directly present in the novel: one of its young characters is a soldier who has just returned from Algeria, another sets off to fight in the colony. As for Greece, which rebelled against the Turks in the 1820s, it inspired much fervour among European Romantics, most famously Lord Byron. The story of Ali (1741–1822), Pasha of Janina (Jannina) in Albania, plays a direct part in the novel and also takes us into the Oriental world that fascinated the French Romantics. 'The Orient,' Victor Hugo wrote in the preface to his early collection of poems, *Les Orientales* (1829), 'both as an image and as an idea, has become a sort of general preoccupation for people's minds as much as for their imaginations, to which the author has perhaps unwittingly succumbed. As if of their own accord, Oriental colours have come to stamp their mark on all his thoughts and reveries . . .' – as they also marked the paintings of Ingres and Delacroix. When we meet Haydée in Chapter XLIX, she is lying on a heap of cushions, wearing her native Albanian costume, smoking a hookah and framed in a doorway, 'like a charming painting'.

Italy was another Mediterranean land that held a powerful appeal for the Romantics, and in particular for Dumas. All the components of this appeal are in the novel: the classical world (the night visit to the Colosseum), the excitement of travel (Chapter XXXIII, 'Roman Bandits'), the cruel justice of the Papal states (Chapter XXXV, 'La Mazzolata'), colourful spectacle (Chapter XXXVI, 'The Carnival in Rome'), the Christian past (Chapter XXXVII, 'The Catacombs of Saint Sebastian'). The story of Luigi Vampa could have come directly from one of Stendhal's *Italian Chronicles*, the description of the Colosseum at night from one of Byron's or Shelley's letters. There is also a good deal of wit – and the fruit of personal experience – in Dumas' portrayal of the modern Romans and the day-by-day experience of the Grand Tour. Like all the most skilled popular writers, he offers his readers a mixture of the unfamiliar and the expected: references to places, people and events that will conjure up a whole complex of images and ideas – we have here the notion of Italy as it was perceived in France in the 1840s, through literature and art – combined with those intimate touches that allow readers to experience the sensations of being there. Reading Dumas, we know how it felt to be swept up in the crowd at the Carnival, to travel in a carriage through the Roman streets, to stay in a *pensione*. We can easily recognize the proud bandit, the bustling hotelier, the alluring woman in the Carnival crowd.

All these are described with as much economy as possible in order to avoid holding up the narrative. This is one reason why the popular novel tends to reinforce rather than to challenge prejudices – although, in one case, Dumas' novel reversed a prejudice, namely that Marseille was, in the words of Murray's *Handbook for Travellers in France* (1847), 'a busy and flourishing city . . . [but one that] has few fine public buildings or sights for strangers'. *The Count of Monte Cristo*, on the contrary, with its intimate topography of the area around the old port and its dramatization of Marseille as the focus of mercantile activity, the meeting-place of Mediterranean cultures and the gateway to the Arab Maghreb, is a good deal more flattering than Murray's *Handbook*. Dumas was allegedly thanked by a Marseillais cab-driver for promoting the city.

Apart from this novel depiction of France's major sea-port, however, Dumas offers his readers a Rome, and an Orient, that are very much what they would expect: the first colourful, tuneful, proud and cruel, the second decadent and opulent. But he adds those little details that compel belief in what he is describing: the precise information about Carnival etiquette, the street-by-street itinerary of a drive round the walls of Rome, the horrifying description of a Roman execution, sketches of character or scenery that he has culled from his own memories of staying at Signor Pastrini's hotel when he visited Rome in 1835. His passages on sailing ships spare us none of the technicalities of sails and masts; his descriptions of the effects of opium convince us that he had experienced them. And, in much the same way, he adds touches of erudition: a quotation from Horace, a reference to *Hamlet* – all of which are meant to reassure us that we are in reliable hands. At times he even allows himself the luxury of a longer purple passage (perhaps a sunset over the Mediterranean) to show that he can do that, too.

All this helps to justify his claim that he has transformed Peuchet's material into something infinitely more valuable. Peuchet's account of the Picaud case, he wrote, was 'simply ridiculous . . . [but] inside this oyster, there was a pearl. A rough, shapeless pearl, of no value, waiting for its jeweller.' And, of course, the essential transformation that the jeweller makes to Peuchet's story lies in the character of the Count.

To begin with, we have Edmond Dantès, a man who could well be first cousin to the shoemaker, François Picaud. Betrayed by a jealous rival and an ambitious colleague, sent to the fortress prison of If by a magistrate who cannot afford to let the facts come out, Dantès goes through a kind of burial and resurrection. Educated by Abbé Faria and possessor of a limitless fortune, he can re-emerge into the world, not as the cobbler Picaud, content to stab or poison those responsible for his misfortune, but as an instrument of divine justice. Dumas' first, vital departure from Peuchet is to make Monte Cristo only indirectly the avenger: his 'victims' are all, in reality, destroyed by their own past misdeeds which Monte Cristo uncovers.

As the man who brings the truth to light and uses the discovery to punish the wrongdoer, Monte Cristo is the forerunner of the detective, that central figure in modern popular fiction. In fact, there is more than one reference in the novel to deductive methods that resemble those pioneered by Edgar Allan Poe ('A Manuscript Found in a Bottle', 'The Gold Bug', 'The Murders in the Rue Morgue') – for example, in the way in which Abbé Faria deciphers the will showing where the treasure was hidden, Dantès' own analysis of where exactly it is concealed on the island and, earlier, Faria's explanation of Dantès' imprisonment. Note that, like the intellectual exercises of Monte Cristo's opium-taking successor later in the century, Sherlock Holmes,[2] these deductions at first amaze those who have not been able to follow the logic behind them or who do not have the expertise to know, for example, when something has been written with the left hand by a right-handed person. But, of course, Faria is not really a Holmesian detective: the stereotype in Dumas' mind is that of the eighteenth-century *philosophe*, a believer in the power of reason and a student of human nature. What Faria lacks (ironically, since everyone around thinks him mad, insanely obsessed with his fictitious treasure) is the Holmesian neuroses: the brooding violin and the opium stupor. These come from a different fictional archetype.

So does Monte Cristo, even though he is not averse at times to applying Faria's deductive logic (and shares Holmes's talent for disguise). Having emerged in 1829 from his entombment, found his treasure, discovered the fate of his father and Mercédès, and repaid his debt to Morrel, Dantès then disappears for another nine years, about which the reader is told virtually nothing. This second period of latency is not strictly a remaking but an effacement:

the character who re-emerges in the novel as the Count of Monte Cristo is shrouded in mystery; we only assume, at first, that he is identical to Edmond Dantès on the slender evidence of their using the same pseudonym: 'Sinbad the Sailor'. He is a dark, brooding figure, pale-faced, with an aversion to food and apparently devoid of some human feelings: he takes an evil delight in terrifying his young friends, Albert and Franz, with the spectacle of an execution. He is also, as they learn later, on good terms with the bandit, Luigi Vampa.

The appearance of this deathly-white apparition in a box at the Roman opera immediately evokes two other personalities who played a major role in popular mythology in France in the Romantic era. The first is Lord Byron, a real-life character who very early was confused with his fictional creations, Childe Harold, Manfred and Don Juan – all the more so in France, where the poetry might be known only in translation. The image was that of a young but world-weary hero, tormented by nameless despairs. The second figure was that of the vampire, associated with the first through the story *Lord Ruthwen, or The Vampire*, which was attributed to Byron (though in fact written by his companion, Polidori). This was not by any means the only vampire to be found in France at the time: the theatre, notably during the 1820s, was haunted by the Undead: English vampires, comic vampires, female vampires . . . The nature of the vampire was perhaps not so precisely codified as it was to be later, especially by Bram Stoker in that tale of another mysterious count: garlic, stakes, crosses, Transylvania, the vampire's native soil in the coffin which he keeps in the basement, these are not yet firmly established in the mythology. But the figure is there, and elements of the legend are specifically ascribed to the Byronic figure of Monte Cristo.

What I would like to suggest is that Dumas' novel stands at a crucial point in the development of modern popular fiction, drawing into the genre elements from Romantic literature, popular theatre, history and actuality, and wrapping them up in a narrative carefully enough constructed and dramatic enough to hold the attention of a growing reading public with a great appetite for fiction. They would satisfy it not only with books, but also with the newspaper serials which had brought fame and fortune to Dumas' precursor in the genre, Eugène Sue.

Monte Cristo owes its existence directly to Sue's *Mystères de*

Paris (1842–3): it was precisely the success of Sue's tales that made Dumas' publishers demand a novel, rather than the historical guide to Paris that they had originally commissioned. Sue's appeal to the public was the ability to suggest the existence of a sinister underworld of crime and intrigue behind the façade of a Paris that was familiar to most of his readers. The growth of the nineteenth-century metropolis led to a whole literature of the urban life, later exploited on film, in which the city is no longer seen as a place of civilized, 'urbane' living and safety from attack, but as a menacing sub-world, in which human beings prey on one another or suffer fearful bouts of loneliness, alienation and ennui. A machine devised to supply every need of civilized humanity in one place has become a monster enclosing every form of vice and depravity. Only in England did murder continue to take place in country houses.

As noted earlier, Paris is the setting for the greater part of the book, but the episodes in Marseille and Rome enrich it enormously. We do have, at the very centre, a very Parisian murder story, joined to a rather trite Parisian romance, and Dumas locates every event precisely on the city map, so that all the addresses are real; but the overall impression left by the novel is of something far larger in scope than a tale of Parisian wrongdoing and revenge. The episodes in Marseille and Rome may have been added after the book was begun – it was Dumas' collaborator, Maquet, who suggested actually recounting Dantès' arrest and imprisonment, instead of starting the novel in Rome and then transferring the action rapidly to Paris; yet the first section proves absolutely crucial. Where the count, in himself, descends at times to the level of a melodramatic stage avenger, Dantès is a compelling character, and it is the figure of Edmond Dantès (whom we feel obscurely present in his later incarnation) which gives the latter depth and weight.

The re-emergence of the other characters after the latency period of Dantès' imprisonment is more of a problem. Caderousse is essentially unchanged, Danglars more or less unrecognizable. Fernand offers the least plausible transformation of all, from the brave and honest Spaniard with a sharp sense of honour, whom we meet in the early chapters, to the Parisian aristocrat whose life seems to have been dedicated to a series of betrayals. Fernand/Morcerf seems to confirm a criticism of Dumas and of popular novels in general, namely that they tend to sacrifice character to plot.

In some respects, though, in Dumas' novel the reverse is true:

Dumas' novel is dictated by character. But it is character viewed
more as an imaginative construct than as a psychological novelist
would conceive it. The count himself is a poetic character, a creature
of the imagination who draws on elements from myth as much as
from everyday psychological observation. And, while Madame de
Villefort, Valentine, Morrel and some others in Dumas' huge cast
may be 'flat' characters, performing a largely functional role in the
development of the story, there are several secondary figures to
whom this does not apply, notably Eugénie Danglars and Albert
de Morcerf. In many ways, Eugénie is Valentine's twin. Both women
are heiresses to large fortunes, both are presented with the alterna-
tives of subjecting themselves to their father's will and marrying
men whom they do not love or being confined to a convent. But
where Valentine is willing to submit, Eugénie is not. Her lesbianism
may be a trait of personality, but it is also an expression of her
desire for independence.

There is far more to *The Count of Monte Cristo* than merely a
tale of adventure and revenge. None the less, it is a book that many
people first encounter and enjoy during their teens. Not long after
Dumas' death, Victor Hugo wrote a letter to his friend's son,
Alexandre Dumas *fils*, in which he praised Dumas as a writer of
universal appeal and added 'He creates a thirst for reading.' After
more then 150 years, *The Count of Monte Cristo* remains one of
the most popular and widely read novels in world literature; its
longevity singles it out as almost unique among 'popular' novels.
For many of its readers, despite its length, it seems all too short; we
want to spend more time with the count and the other characters
in the book, more time in its bustling world of drama and passion.
Creating that thirst for more is among Dumas' great contributions
to literature.

Notes

1. Peuchet's text is reprinted in the edition of the novel by Claude Schopp
(Robert Laffont, Paris, 1993).
2. The link with Conan Doyle is actually strengthened by the more obvious
similarities in the field of historical fiction (for example, between Doyle's
The White Company and Dumas' *The Three Musketeers*). Conan Doyle
may have consciously followed Dumas in his historical novels and unconsciously in creating Holmes.

Further Reading

Hemmings, F. W. J., *The King of Romance*, Hamish Hamilton, London, 1979.

Maurois, André, *Three Musketeers. A Study of the Dumas Family*, translated by Gerard Hopkins, Jonathan Cape, London, 1957.

Schopp, Claude, *Alexandre Dumas. Genius of Life*, translated by A. J. Koch, Franklin Watts, New York, 1988.

Stowe, Richard, *Dumas*, Twayne Publishers, Boston, 1976.

A Note on the Text

The Count of Monte Cristo began publication in parts, in the *Journal des Débats*, in August 1844; this continued until January 1846, by which time the first, 18-volume edition had been published by Pétion (1845–6). The second, third and fourth editions appeared in 1846, and there were several pirate editions in the 1840s. The book continued to be re-published throughout the century, the last edition in Dumas' lifetime being that published by Michel Lévy in 1865.

The novel was rapidly translated into English (in England, in *Ainsworth's Magazine*, 1845, and by Emma Hardy, 1846; and in America in 1846); and into: Danish (1845–6); Swedish (1846); Italian (by Oreste Ferrario, 1847); Spanish (1858); Norwegian (1881–2); and German (1902). The first stage adaptation was the one made by Dumas and Maquet themselves (in 1848, in two parts; in 1851, in two parts; finally shown as one single performance, in five acts and 12 tableaux, in 1862). Long before this, however, there had been a stage parody by Deforges and Claireville, *Le Comte de Monte-Fiasco* (1847) – a further tribute to the notoriety of the work.

The most recent stage version was a new adaptation performed in England in 1994. There have been condensed editions, children's editions and a comic-book version. There were film adaptations in 1908 (USA), 1913 (USA), 1914 (France), 1934 (USA), 1942 (France), 1953 (France), 1961 (France), 1975 (USA) and 2001 (USA), as well as television versions. The strength of the story is enough to explain why the novel has proved so adaptable to other media, despite its length: the central themes of betrayal, wrongful imprisonment and revenge are clear enough to allow many of the sub-plots to be discarded for reasons of time or space.

Inevitably, something will be lost: there is simply so much there;

and, from the earliest days, the process undergone by Dumas' novel was one of reduction, as if the original was too vast to stand by itself. There is also the matter of the historical moment at which *The Count of Monte Cristo* appeared.

The mid-nineteenth century saw a continuing struggle to establish the credentials of the literary novel, by giving it the dual aims that Stendhal had helped to pioneer, which were those of exploring the enduring features of human psychology and analysing a particular state of human society. In contrast to such enterprises, fiction which involved larger-than-life characters and implausible situations, Gothic horrors, melodramatic incidents and so on appeared mere entertainment. The gradual emergence of realism in the European novel was not altogether to the advantage of Dumas, whose image was less that of the austere priest than the jolly friar, and whose novels poured out of a factory, the purpose of which was to create entertainment and sell it for money.

This explains why, though Thackeray admitted finding the book impossible to put down, English novelists like George Eliot considered that 'the French' – Dumas, Hugo and Balzac – were mistakenly tempted to deal with the exception rather than the rule: to look for melodramatic situations and characters, when they should be exploring the everyday life that revealed what is enduring in human nature. It is not hard, anyway, to guess that the author of *Middlemarch* and *The Mill on the Floss* would not find much to please her in *The Three Musketeers* or *The Count of Monte Cristo*.

There is also the question of Dumas' style, which is usually unremarkable; and the fact that he wrote his great novels in collaboration with Maquet, which does not accord with the idea of the author as sole creator. No wonder people have thought they could treat *Monte Cristo* as a treasure-trove rather than a sacred text, or that the many adaptations, abbreviations and reworkings of it have been done with a good deal less reverence (and consequently, more often than not, a good deal more success) than, say, Claude Chabrol brought to his film version of *Madame Bovary*. In the main, its fate has been that of most nineteenth-century 'adventure' novels: it has been treated as mere entertainment for adults or literature for the young.

The truth is that, more because of the subject-matter than because of its length, the novel has had to be tampered with before it can be offered to young readers; or, as one may conjecture, to readers in mid-Victorian England. And, because this is merely a 'popular' novel, as well as one which represents a huge amount of work for a translator, there has been little enthusiasm in the English-speaking world for re-translating it.

Claude Schopp's edition (Robert Laffont, 1993), which lists the main foreign translations, records nothing into English since 1910. The most readily available edition in Britain at the moment reproduces the anonymous translation first published by Chapman & Hall in 1846. Its editor for the Oxford World's Classics series (1990), David Coward, writes that 'with one or two exceptions, the small number of "new" translations since made have drawn heavily upon . . . this classic version'.

Anyone who has read *The Count of Monte Cristo* only in this 'classic version' has never read Dumas' novel. For a start, the translation is occasionally inaccurate and is written in a nineteenth-century English that now sounds far more antiquated than the French of the original does to a modern French reader: to mention one small point in this connection, Dumas uses a good deal of dialogue (he wrote by the line), and the constant inversions of 'said he' and 'cried he' are both irritating and antiquated. There are some real oddities, like the attempt to convey popular speech (which does not correspond to anything in Dumas), when the sailor in Chapter XXV says: 'that's one of them nabob gentlemen from Ingy [*sic*], no doubt . . .' Even aside from that, most of the dialogues in this nineteenth-century translation, in which the characters utter sentences like: 'I will join you ere long', 'I confess he asked me none' and 'When will all this cease?', have the authentic creak of the Victorian stage boards and the gaslit melodrama.

It can be argued that this language accurately conveys an aspect of Dumas' work, but not even his worst detractors would pretend that there is nothing more to it than that. Still less acceptable, however, than the language of this Victorian translation is the huge number of omissions and bowdlerizations of Dumas' text. The latter include part of Franz's opium dream at the end of Chapter XXXI, some of the dialogue between Villefort and Madame Danglars in Chapter LXVII, and several parts of Chapter XCVII, on Eugénie and Louise's flight to Belgium. In some cases the changes are so slight as to be quite hard to detect. In the description of Eugénie at the opera (Chapter LIII) for example, Dumas remarks that, if one could reproach her with anything, it was that, both in her upbringing and her appearance, 'she seemed rather to belong to another sex'. The English translator renders this: 'As for her attainments, the only fault to be found with them was . . . that they were somewhat too erudite and masculine for so young a person' (p. 542)! At the end of Chapter XCVII, the translation (p. 950) simply omits the few lines of dialogue where Dumas has Eugénie say that *'le rapt est bel et bien consommé'* – where the word *rapt* ('abduction') has a rather too overtly sexual connotation. Similarly, earlier in the same chapter, where Eugénie jokes that anyone would think she was 'abducting' (*enlève*) Louise – another word used almost exclusively of a man with a woman – the translator prefers the more neutral phrase 'carrying me off' and omits altogether Louise's remark that Eugénie is 'a real Amazon'. Another anonymous translation (Dent, 1894) refers to 'the escape' rather than 'the abduction' – which makes nonsense of Louise's reply that it is not a true abduction since it has been accomplished without violence.

What may be more surprising than these concessions to the prudery of the age is that the Victorian translators left in as much as they did. And the omissions are by no means all to do with sexual matters. At the start of Chapter XXXIV, for example, the translator decides to spare us the description of the route taken through Rome by Albert and Franz on their way to the Colosseum (though the 1894 translator restores it). A whole paragraph analysing the character of M. de Villefort at the start of Chapter XLVIII is cut out; almost a whole page of dialogue between Albert and Monte Cristo, on horses, in Chapter LXXXV is cavalierly omitted (part was restored by the translator of 1894); and so on. This is only a tiny sample of what is, in reality, a vast number of phrases omitted, and occasionally mistranslated.

What we see here, interestingly enough, is a stage in the process of transforming Dumas' text into something simpler, less complex, less rich in allusions, but more concentrated in plot and action. The 1846 translator already has an idea of what kind of novel this is, and that dictates what he, or she, can afford to omit: travelogue, classical references, sexual and psychological analysis, and so on. None of these is essential to the plot of a thriller, and if some of them will embarrass English readers, then why leave them in? The only problem is that, nearly 150 years later, we do not have quite the same idea of what is and what is not important. It was high time to go back to Dumas, entire and unexpurgated.

As the basis for my translation, I have used the edition by Schopp, quoted above, and the three-volume edition in the *Livre de Poche* (1973). Both of these use an arrangement of chapters which differs slightly from that in the nineteenth-century English translations. I have followed the *Livre de Poche* in not changing Dumas' 'errors' of chronology etc. in the text as Schopp does; instead I have pointed out the more important ones in the notes. I owe a debt to Schopp and to Coward's edition in the World's Classics series for some of the information in the notes.

On the broader question of translation, I have tried above all to produce a version that is accurate and readable. A great deal of nonsense is written about translation, particularly by academics who approach it either as a terrain for theoretical debate or, worse still, as a moral issue: 'the translator must always be faithful to his original,' Leonard Tancock wrote, oddly assuming that translation is a masculine activity, even though on this occasion he was prefacing Nancy Mitford's translation of *La Princesse de Clèves* (Penguin, 1978). '. . . he has no right whatever to take liberties with it . . . Nor has he any right to try to smooth the reader's path by the omission of "dull" bits, short-circuitings, explanatory additions, radical transferences or changes of order.' Why? And who says? Is it the reader who is demanding this perfection, this absence of explanatory additions, and so on?

Such academic theorists insist that a translation must read like a translation – it is somehow immoral to conceal the process that has gone into making it. 'Ordinary' readers usually demand the opposite, and reviewers in quite respectable papers sometimes show little appreciation of what the process means and involves: 'Not all of this material works in translation,' said one serious review of a book by Umberto Eco; and another: '. . . the stories [of Viktoria Tokareva] are well served by their translator, who hardly ever gets in the way'.

In philosophical terms I am quite willing to admit the impossibility of translation, while still having in practical terms to engage in it and to believe that everything must, to some extent, be translatable. I feel no obligation to avoid smoothing the reader's path and none, on the other hand, to 'getting in the way' from time to time. Above all, I want to convey some of the pleasure of reading Dumas to those who cannot do so in the original language and, through my one, particular version (since no translation can ever

be definitive), to reveal aspects of his work that are not to be found
in any of the other existing versions. This is a new translation and
consequently a new interpretation of a great – and great popular –
novel. If nothing else, most people would surely agree that it is long
overdue.

The Count of
Monte Cristo

Contents

MARSEILLE – ARRIVAL

On February 24, 1815, the lookout at Notre-Dame de la Garde signalled the arrival of the three-master *Pharaon*, coming from Smyrna, Trieste and Naples. As usual, a coastal pilot immediately left the port, sailed hard by the Château d'If, and boarded the ship between the Cap de Morgiou and the island of Riou.

At once (as was also customary) the terrace of Fort Saint-Jean[1] was thronged with onlookers, because the arrival of a ship is always a great event in Marseille, particularly when the vessel, like the *Pharaon*, has been built, fitted out and laded in the shipyards of the old port and belongs to an owner from the town.

Meanwhile the ship was drawing near, and had successfully negotiated the narrows created by some volcanic upheaval between the islands of Calseraigne and Jarre; it had rounded Pomègue and was proceeding under its three topsails, its outer jib and its spanker, but so slowly and with such melancholy progress that the by-standers, instinctively sensing some misfortune, wondered what accident could have occurred on board. Nevertheless, those who were experts in nautical matters acknowledged that, if there had been such an accident, it could not have affected the vessel itself, for its progress gave every indication of a ship under perfect control: the anchor was ready to drop and the bowsprit shrouds loosed. Next to the pilot, who was preparing to guide the *Pharaon* through the narrow entrance to the port of Marseille, stood a young man, alert and sharp-eyed, supervising every movement of the ship and repeating each of the pilot's commands.

One of the spectators on the terrace of Fort Saint-Jean had been particularly affected by the vague sense of unease that hovered among them, so much so that he could not wait for the vessel to come to land; he leapt into a small boat and ordered it to be rowed out to the *Pharaon*, coming alongside opposite the cove of La Réserve. When he saw the man approaching, the young sailor left his place beside the pilot and, hat in hand, came and leant on the bulwarks of the ship.

He was a young man of between eighteen and twenty, tall, slim, with fine dark eyes and ebony-black hair. His whole demeanour possessed the calm and resolve peculiar to men who have been accustomed from childhood to wrestle with danger.

'Ah, it's you, Dantès!' the man in the boat cried. 'What has happened, and why is there this air of dejection about all on board?'

'A great misfortune, Monsieur Morrel!' the young man replied. 'A great misfortune, especially for me: while off Civita Vecchia, we lost our good Captain Leclère.'

'And the cargo?' the ship owner asked brusquely.

'It has come safe to port, Monsieur Morrel, and I think you will be content on that score. But poor Captain Leclère . . .'

'What happened to him, then?' the shipowner asked, visibly relieved. 'So what happened to the good captain?'

'He is dead.'

'Lost overboard?'

'No, Monsieur, he died of an apoplectic fever, in terrible agony.' Then, turning back to his crew, he said: 'Look lively, there! Every man to his station to drop anchor!'

The crew obeyed. As one man, the eight or ten sailors of which it was composed leapt, some to the sheets, others to the braces, others to the halyards, others to the jib, and still others to the brails. The young sailor glanced casually at the start of this operation and, seeing that his orders were being carried out, prepared to resume the conversation.

'But how did this misfortune occur?' the shipowner continued, picking it up where the young man had left off.

'By heaven, Monsieur, in the most unexpected way imaginable: after a long conversation with the commander of the port, Captain Leclère left Naples in a state of great agitation. Twenty-four hours later, he was seized with fever and, three days after that, he was dead . . . We gave him the customary funeral and he now rests, decently wrapped in a hammock, with a thirty-six-pound cannon-ball at his feet and another at his head, off the island of Giglio. We've brought his medal and his sword back for his widow. Much good it did him,' the young man continued, with a melancholy smile, 'to fight the war against the English for ten years – only to die at last, like anyone else, in his bed.'

'Dammit, Monsieur Edmond, what do you expect?' said the shipowner, who appeared to be finding more and more to console him in his grief. 'We are all mortal. The old must give way to the young, or else there would be no progress or promotion. As long as you can assure me that the cargo . . .'

'All is well with it, Monsieur Morrel, I guarantee you. If you take my advice, you will not discount this trip for a profit of 25,000 francs.'

Then, as they had just sailed past the Round Tower, the young sailor cried: 'Furl the topmast sails, the jib and the spanker! Look lively!'

The order was obeyed with almost as much dispatch as on a man-o'-war.

'Let go and brail all!'

At this last command, all the sails were lowered and the progress of the ship became almost imperceptible, driven only by the impetus of its forward motion.

'And now, if you would like to come aboard, Monsieur Morrel,' Dantès said, observing the owner's impatience, 'I see your super-cargo,[2] Monsieur Danglars, coming out of his cabin. He will give you all the information that you desire. As for me, I must see to the mooring and put the ship in mourning.'

The owner did not need asking twice. He grasped hold of a line that Dantès threw to him and, with an agility that would have done credit to a seaman, climbed the rungs nailed to the bulging side of the ship, while Dantès went back to his post and left the conversation to the man he had introduced as Danglars: the latter was indeed emerging from his cabin and coming across to the shipowner.

This new arrival was a man, twenty-five to twenty-six years old, somewhat sombre in appearance, obsequious towards his superiors and insolent to his subordinates; hence, even apart from the label of supercargo, which always in itself causes aversion among sailors, he was generally as much disliked by the crew as Dantès was loved by them.

'Well, Monsieur Morrel,' said Danglars, 'you have heard the bad news, I suppose?'

'Yes, yes, poor Captain Leclère! He was a fine and upright man!'

'And above all an excellent sailor, weathered between the sea and the heavens, as was proper in a man responsible for looking after the interests of so important a firm as Morrel and Son,' Danglars replied.

'Even so,' the shipowner replied, watching Dantès while he searched for his mooring. 'Even so, I think one need not be a seaman of such long experience as you say, Danglars, to know the business: there is our friend Edmond going about his, it seems to me, like a man who has no need to ask advice of anybody.'

'Indeed,' said Danglars, casting a sidelong glance at Dantès with a flash of hatred in his eyes. 'Yes, indeed, he is young and full of self-confidence. The captain was hardly dead before he had taken command without asking anyone, and made us lose a day and a half on the island of Elba, instead of returning directly to Marseille.'

'As far as taking command of the ship is concerned,' said the owner, 'that was his duty as first mate. As for losing a day and a half at Elba, he was in the wrong, unless there was some damage to the ship that needed repairing.'

'The ship was in as good shape as I am, and as good as I hope you are, Monsieur Morrel. That day and a half was lost on a whim, for nothing other than the pleasure of going ashore.'

'Dantès,' the owner said, turning towards the young man. 'Would you come here.'

'Your pardon, Monsieur,' Dantès said. 'I shall be with you in an instant.' Then, to the crew, he called: 'Drop anchor!'

The anchor was immediately lowered and the chain ran out noisily. Dantès stayed at his post, even though the pilot was there, until the last operation had been carried out, then ordered: 'Lower the pennant and the flag to half-mast, unbrace the yards!'

'You see,' Danglars said. 'I do believe he thinks himself captain already.'

'So he is, in effect,' said the owner.

'Yes, apart from your signature and that of your partner, Monsieur Morrel.'

'By gad, why shouldn't we leave him in the job?' said the owner. 'He is young, I grant you, but he seems made for it and very experienced in his work.'

A cloud passed across Danglars' brow.

'Excuse me, Monsieur Morrel,' Dantès said as he came over. 'Now that the ship is moored, I am entirely at your disposal: I think you called me?'

Danglars took a step back.

'I wanted to ask why you stopped on the island of Elba.'

'I don't know, Monsieur. It was to carry out a last order from Captain Leclère, who gave me, on his deathbed, a packet for Marshal Bertrand.'[3]

'Did you see him, Edmond?'

'Whom?'

'The Grand Marshal.'

'Yes.'

Morrel looked about him and drew Dantès aside.

'And how is the emperor?' he asked, earnestly.

'He is well, as far as I can judge by my own eyes.'

'So you saw the emperor, too, did you?'

'He came to visit the marshal while I was there.'

'And did you speak to him?'

'It was he, Monsieur, who spoke to me,' Dantès said, smiling.

'And what did he say?'

'He asked me about the ship, the time of its departure for Marseille, the route it had taken and the cargo we were carrying. I think that, had it been empty and I the master of it, he intended to buy it; but I told him that I was only the first mate and that the ship belonged to the firm of Morrel and Son. "Ah, yes!" he said. "I know them. The Morrels have been shipowners from father to son, and there was Morrel who served in the same regiment as I did, when I was garrisoned at Valence."'

'By heaven, that's a fact!' the shipowner cried, with delight. 'It was Policar Morrel, my uncle, who later made captain. Dantès, tell my uncle that the emperor remembered him, and you will bring tears to the old trooper's eyes. Come, come, now,' he went on, putting a friendly arm across the young man's shoulders, 'you did well to follow Captain Leclère's instructions and stop on Elba; even though, if it were known that you gave a packet to the marshal and spoke to the emperor, you might be compromised.'

'How could it compromise me, Monsieur?' said Dantès. 'I don't even know what I was carrying, and the emperor only asked me the same questions that he would have put to anyone else. But please excuse me,' he continued. 'The health authorities and the Customs are coming on board. With your permission?'

'Of course, of course, my dear Dantès, carry on.'

The young man went off and, as he did so, Danglars returned.

'So,' he asked, 'it appears that he gave you good reason for stopping off at Porto Ferrajo?'

'Excellent reason, my dear Danglars.'

'I am pleased to hear it,' the other replied. 'It is always distressing to see a comrade fail in his duty.'

'Dantès did his duty,' the shipowner answered, 'and there is no more to be said. It was Captain Leclère who ordered him to put into port.'

'Speaking of Captain Leclère, did he not give you a letter from him?'

'Who?'

'Dantès.'

'Not to me! Was there one?'

'I believe that, apart from the packet, Captain Leclère entrusted him with a letter.'

'Which packet are you referring to, Danglars?'

'The same that Dantès delivered when we stopped at Porto Ferrajo.'

'And how did you know that he had a packet to deliver at Porto Ferrajo?'

Danglars blushed. 'I was passing by the door of the captain's cabin, which was partly open, and I saw him handing the packet and a letter to Dantès.'

'He did not mention it,' said the owner. 'But if he has such a letter, he will give it to me.'

Danglars thought for a moment.

'In that case, Monsieur Morrel,' he said, 'I beg you to say nothing about it to Dantès. I must have been mistaken.'

At that moment the young man came back and Danglars left them.

'Now, my dear Dantès, are you free?' the owner asked.

'Yes, Monsieur.'

'It did not take long.'

'No, I gave the Customs a list of our cargo; as for the port authorities, they sent a man with the coastal pilot, and I handed our papers over to him.'

'So you have nothing more to do here?'

Dantès cast a rapid glance about him. 'No, everything is in order,' he said.

'Then you can come and take dinner with us?'

'Please, Monsieur Morrel, I beg you to excuse me, but the first thing I must do is to visit my father. Nonetheless, I am most grateful for the honour you do me.'

'That's proper, Dantès, very proper. I know that you are a good son.'

'And . . .' Dantès asked, somewhat hesitantly, 'as far as you know, he's in good health, my father?'

'I do believe so, my dear Edmond, though I have not seen him.'

'Yes, he stays shut up in his little room.'

'Which at least proves that he lacked nothing while you were away.'

Dantès smiled.

'My father is a proud man, Monsieur, and even if he were short of everything, I doubt if he would have asked for help from anyone in the world, except God.'

'Now, when you have done that, we can count on your company.'

'I must beg you once more to excuse me, Monsieur Morrel, but after that first visit, there is another that is no less important to me.'

'Ah, Dantès, that's true; I was forgetting that there is someone in Les Catalans who must be expecting you with no less impatience than your father – the lovely Mercédès.'

Dantès smiled.

'Ah, ha,' said the owner, 'now I understand why she came three times to ask me for news of the *Pharaon*. Dash it, Edmond! You're a lucky fellow, to have such a pretty mistress.'

'She is not my mistress, Monsieur,' the young sailor said gravely. 'She is my fiancée.'

'It sometimes amounts to the same thing,' the owner said, with a chuckle.

'Not for us, Monsieur,' Dantès replied.

'Come, come, my dear Edmond,' the other continued. 'Don't let me detain you. You have looked after my business well enough for me to give you every opportunity to look after your own. Do you need any money?'

'No, Monsieur, I have all my salary from the trip – that is, nearly three months' pay.'

'You manage your affairs well, my boy.'

'You might add that my father is a poor man, Monsieur Morrel.'

'Yes, indeed, I know you are a good son to him. So: go and see your father. I, too, have a son and I should bear a grudge against the man who kept him away from me, after a three-month voyage.'

'May I take my leave, then?' the young man said, with a bow.

'Yes, if you have nothing more to say to me.'

'No.'

'When Captain Leclère was dying, he did not give you a letter for me?'

'It would have been impossible for him to write one, Monsieur. But that reminds me: I wanted to ask you for a fortnight's leave.'

'To get married?'

'Firstly, then to go to Paris.'

'Very well! Have as much time as you want, Dantès. It will take us a good six weeks to unload the vessel and we shall hardly be ready to put to sea again within three months . . . In three months' time, however, you must be there. The *Pharaon*,' the shipowner continued, putting a hand across the young sailor's shoulders, 'cannot set sail without its captain.'

'Without its captain!' Dantès cried, his eyes lighting up with joy. 'Be very careful what you are saying, Monsieur, because you have just touched on the most secret of my heart's desires. Can it be that you intend to appoint me captain of the *Pharaon*?'

'If it was up to me alone, I should grasp your hand, my dear Dantès, and say to you: "the matter is settled!" But I have a partner, and you know the Italian proverb: *chi ha compagno, ha padrone*.[4] But, at least, we are half-way there, since you already have one of the two votes you need. Leave it to me to get you the other, and I shall do my best.'

'Oh, Monsieur Morrel!' the young sailor cried, with tears in his eyes, grasping the shipowner's hands. 'Monsieur Morrel, I thank you, on behalf of my father and of Mercédès.'

'Fine, Edmond, fine! There is a God in heaven who looks after honest folk. Go and see your father, go and see Mercédès, then when that's done, come and see me.'

'But don't you want me to accompany you back to land?'

'No, thank you. I shall stay here to settle my accounts with Danglars. Were you happy with him during the voyage?'

'It depends on what you understand by that question, Monsieur. If you mean, as a good companion, no, because I think that he has not liked me since the day when I had the folly, after a trifling dispute between us, to suggest that we should stop for ten minutes on the isle of Monte Cristo to settle the matter. It was wrong of me to propose that, and he was right to refuse. If you are asking me about him as a supercargo, I think there is nothing to say, and that you will be satisfied with the manner in which his duties have been carried out.'

'Come now, Dantès,' the shipowner asked, 'if you were captain of the *Pharaon*, would you be pleased to keep Danglars?'

'Whether as captain or as first mate, Monsieur Morrel,' Dantès replied, 'I shall always have the highest regard for those who enjoy the confidence of my owners.'

'Well, well, Dantès, you are clearly a fine lad, in every respect. Let me detain you no longer, for I can see that you are on tenterhooks.'

'I may take my leave?' asked Dantès.

'Go on, I'm telling you.'

'Will you permit me to use your boat?'

'Take it.'

'Au revoir, Monsieur Morrel, and thank you a thousand times.'

'Au revoir, dear Edmond, and good luck!'

The young sailor leapt into the boat, seated himself in the stern and gave the order to row across to the Canebière. Two sailors immediately bent over their oars and the vessel proceeded as fast as it could, among the thousand small boats that obstruct the sort of narrow alleyway leading, between two lines of ships, from the harbour entrance to the Quai d'Orléans.

The shipowner looked after him, smiling, until the boat touched land and he saw him leap on to the cobbled quay, where he was instantly lost in the variegated crowd that, from five in the morning until nine in the evening, throngs the famous street known as La Canebière: the modern inhabitants of this old Phocean colony are so proud of it that they proclaim, with all the seriousness in the world, in that accent which gives such savour to everything they say: 'If Paris had the Canebière, Paris would be a little Marseille.'

Turning, the shipowner saw Danglars standing behind him, apparently awaiting orders but in reality, like him, watching the young sailor's departure. Yet there were very different expressions in these two pairs of eyes following the one man.

II

FATHER AND SON

We shall leave Danglars, gripped by the demon of hatred, trying to poison the shipowner's ear with some malicious libel against his comrade, and follow Dantès who, after walking along the Canebière, took the Rue de Noailles, entered a small house on the left side of the Allées de Meilhan and hastened up the four flights of a dark stairway. There, holding the banister with one hand, while the other repressed the beating of his heart, he stopped before a half-open door through which he could see to the back of a small room.

In this room lived Dantès' father.

News of the arrival of the *Pharaon* had not yet reached the old man who was standing on a chair, engaged with trembling hands in pinning up some nasturtiums and clematis that climbed across the trellis outside his window. Suddenly, he felt himself grasped around the waist and a well-known voice exclaim behind him: 'Father! My dear father!'

The old man cried out and turned around; then, seeing his son, fell into his arms, pale and trembling.

'What is it, father?' the young man exclaimed, with concern. 'Are you unwell?'

'No, no, dear Edmond, my son, my child. No, but I was not expecting you – and the joy, the shock of seeing you like this, unexpectedly . . . Oh, heavens! It is too much for me!'

'Now, then, father, calm yourself! I am really here! They always say that joy cannot harm you, which is why I came in without warning. Come now, smile; don't look at me like that, with those wild eyes. I am back and there is happiness in store for us.'

'I'm pleased to hear it, my boy,' the old man continued. 'But what happiness? Are you going to stay with me from now on? Come, tell me about your good fortune!'

'God forgive me,' the young man said, 'for rejoicing at good fortune which has brought grief to the family of another. But, God knows, I never wished for it; it has happened, and I do not have the heart to grieve at it. Our good Captain Leclère is dead, father, and it seems likely that, thanks to Monsieur Morrel's support, I shall have his command. Do you understand, father? A captain at twenty! With a salary of a hundred *louis*[1] and a share in the profits! Isn't that better than a poor sailor like myself could expect?'

'Yes, my son, yes,' said the old man. 'This is indeed a stroke of luck.'

'So I want you to have a little house, with the first money I earn, and a garden to grow your clematis, your nasturtiums and your honeysuckle . . . But what's wrong, father? You look ill!'

'An instant, don't worry! It is nothing.' And, his strength failing him, he leant back.

'Father!' cried the young man. 'Come, have a glass of wine; it will revive you. Where do you keep your wine?'

'No, thank you, don't bother to look for it; there is no need,' he replied, trying to restrain his son.

'Yes, indeed there is, father. Show me it.' He opened one or two cupboards.

'It's a waste of time . . .' the old man said. 'There is no wine left.'

'What! No wine!' Dantès said, paling in turn as he looked from the old man's sunken and livid cheeks to the empty cupboards. 'What! You have no wine left? Have you been short of money, father?'

'I am short of nothing, now that you are here,' said the old man.

'But I left you two hundred francs,' Dantès stammered, wiping the sweat from his brow, 'two months ago, as I was leaving.'

'Yes, yes, Edmond, so you did; but when you left you forgot a small debt to my neighbour Caderousse. He reminded me of it and said that if I did not settle it on your behalf, he would go and reclaim it from Monsieur Morrel. So, you understand, I was afraid that it might do you some harm.'

'And?'

'And I paid it.'

'But,' Dantès exclaimed, 'I owed Caderousse a hundred and forty francs!'

'Yes,' the old man mumbled.

'And you paid them out of the two hundred francs that I left you?'

His father nodded.

'Which means that you lived for three months on sixty francs!' the young man exclaimed.

'You know how small my needs are.'

'Oh, heaven, heaven, forgive me!' Edmond cried, falling on his knees in front of the old man.

'What are you doing?'

'Ah! You have broken my heart!'

'Pah! You are here,' the old man said, with a smile. 'All is forgotten, because all is well.'

'Yes, here I am,' said the young man. 'Here I am with a fine future and a little money. Here, father,' he said, 'take it, take it and send out for something immediately.'

He emptied the contents of his pockets on the table: a dozen gold coins, five or six five-franc pieces and some small change.

Old Dantès' face lit up.

'Whose is that?' he asked.

'Mine! Thine! Ours, of course! Take it, buy some food and enjoy yourself. There will be more tomorrow.'

'Gently, gently,' the old man said, smiling. 'If you don't mind, I shall go easy on your money: if people see me buying too many things at once, they will think that I had to wait for you to come back before I went shopping.'

'Do as you think best, but first of all, father, get yourself a housemaid: I don't want you to live on your own from now on. I have some contraband coffee and some excellent tobacco in a little chest in the hold. You will have it tomorrow. But, hush! Someone is coming.'

'That will be Caderousse, who has learned of your arrival and is no doubt coming to welcome you back.'

'There's a fellow who says one thing and thinks another,' Edmond muttered. 'No matter. He is a neighbour who has helped us in the past, so let him come in.'

Just as Edmond finished saying this under his breath, the black, bearded head of Caderousse appeared on the landing, framed in the outer door. A man of twenty-five or twenty-six years of age, he was holding a piece of cloth which, being a tailor, he was about to fashion into the lining of a jacket.

'You're back again, then, Edmond?' he said, with a thick Marseille accent and a broad smile, revealing teeth as white as ivory.

'As you can see, neighbour, and entirely at your service,' Dantès replied, this polite formula barely disguising his coldness towards the man.

'Thank you, thank you. Fortunately, I need nothing; in fact, it is sometimes others who need me.' Dantès bridled. 'I am not saying that for you, my boy. I lent you money and you returned it. That's how things are done between good neighbours, and we're quits.'

'We are never quits towards those who have done us a favour,' said Dantès. 'Even when one ceases to owe them money, one owes them gratitude.'

'There is no sense in speaking of that: what's past is past. Let's talk about your happy return, young man. I just happened to go down to the harbour to fetch some brown cloth, when I met our friend Danglars. "You're in Marseille?" I exclaimed. "Yes, as you see." "I thought you were in Smyrna." "It could well be, because I have just come back from there." "And where is young Edmond, then?" "At his father's, I suppose," Danglars told me. So I came at once,' Caderousse concluded, 'to have the pleasure of shaking the hand of a friend.'

'Dear Caderousse,' the old man said. 'He is so fond of us.'

'Indeed, I am, and I hold you in all the greater esteem, since honest people are so rare! But it seems you have come into money, my boy?' the tailor went on, glancing at the handful of gold and silver that Dantès had emptied on to the table.

The young man observed a flash of greed light up his neighbour's dark eyes. 'Heavens, no!' he said casually. 'That money is not mine. I was just telling my father that I was afraid he might have wanted for something while I was away and, to reassure me, he emptied his purse on the table. Come, father,' he continued. 'Put that money back in your pocket – unless, of course, our neighbour needs some for himself, in which case it is at his disposal.'

'Indeed not, my boy,' said Caderousse. 'I need nothing and, thank God, my business holds body and soul together. Keep your money, keep it; one can never have too much. Still, I am obliged for your offer, as much as if I had taken advantage of it.'

'It was well meant,' said Dantès.

'I don't doubt that it was. So, I learn that you are on good terms with Monsieur Morrel, sly one that you are?'

'Monsieur Morrel has always been very good to me,' Dantès answered.

'In that case, you were wrong to refuse dinner with him.'

'What do you mean: refuse dinner?' Old Dantès asked. 'Did he invite you to dinner?'

'Yes, father,' said Edmond, smiling at his father's astonishment on learning of this high honour.

'So why did you refuse, son?' the old man asked.

'So that I could come straight back here, father,' the young man answered. 'I was anxious to see you.'

'He must have been put out by it, that good Monsieur Morrel,' Caderousse remarked. 'When one hopes to be made captain, it is a mistake to get on the wrong side of one's owner.'

'I explained the reason for my refusal and I hope he understood it.'

'Even so, to be promoted to captain, one must flatter one's bosses a little.'

'I expect to become captain without that,' Dantès retorted.

'So much the better! All your old friends will be pleased for you and I know someone over there, behind the Citadelle de Saint-Nicholas, who will not be unhappy about it, either.'

'Mercédès?' the old man said.

'Yes, father,' Dantès resumed. 'And, with your permission, now that I've seen you, now that I know you are well and that you have all you need, I would like to ask your leave to go and visit Les Catalans.'

'Go, child,' Old Dantès said. 'And may God bless you as much in your wife as He has blessed me in my son.'

'His wife!' said Caderousse. 'Hold on, old man, hold on! As far as I know, she's not that yet!'

'No,' Edmond replied, 'but in all probability she soon will be.'

'Never mind,' said Caderousse, 'never mind. You have done well to hurry back, my boy.'

'Why?'

'Because Mercédès is a beautiful girl, and beautiful girls are never short of admirers, especially that one: there are dozens of them after her.'

'Really?' Edmond said with a smile, not entirely concealing a hint of unease.

'Oh, yes,' Caderousse continued, 'and some with good prospects, too. But, of course, you are going to be a captain, so she'll be sure not to refuse you.'

'By which you mean,' Dantès said, smiling, but barely concealing his anxiety, 'that if I were not a captain . . .'

'Ah! Ah!' said Caderousse.

'Come, now,' the young man said. 'I have a better opinion than you of women in general, and Mercédès in particular, and I am persuaded that, whether I were a captain or not, she would remain faithful to me.'

'So much the better! When one is going to get married, it is always a good thing to have faith. But enough of that. Take my advice, lad: don't waste any time in telling her of your return and letting her know about your aspirations.'

'I am going at once,' said Edmond.

He embraced his father, nodded to Caderousse and left.

Caderousse stayed a moment longer, then, taking his leave of the elder Dantès, followed the young man down and went to find Danglars who was waiting for him on the corner of the Rue Senac.

'Well?' Danglars asked. 'Did you see him?'

'I have just left them,' said Caderousse.

'And did he talk about his hope of being made captain?'

'He spoke of it as though he had already been appointed.'

'Patience!' Danglars said. 'It seems to me that he is in rather too much of a hurry.'

'Why, it seems Monsieur Morrel has given him his word.'

'So he is pleased?'

'He is even insolent about it. He has already offered me his services, like some superior personage; he wanted to lend me money, like some banker or other.'

'You refused?'

'Indeed I did, though I could well have accepted, since I am the one who gave him the first silver coins he ever had in his hands. But now Monsieur Dantès has no need of anyone: he is going to be a captain.'

'Huh!' said Danglars. 'He's not one yet.'

'My God, it would be a fine thing indeed if he wasn't,' said Caderousse. 'Otherwise there will be no talking to him.'

'If we really want,' said Danglars, 'he will stay as he is, and perhaps even become less than he is.'

'What do you mean?'

'Nothing, I was talking to myself. Is he still in love with the beautiful Catalan?'

'Madly. He has gone there now; but, unless I am gravely mistaken, he will not find things altogether to his liking.'

'Explain.'

'What does it matter?'

'This is more important than you may think. You don't like Dantès, do you?'

'I don't like arrogance.'

'Well, then: tell me what you know about the Catalan woman.'

'I have no positive proof, but I have seen things, as I said, that make me think the future captain will not be pleased with what he finds around the Chemin des Vieilles-Infirmeries.'

'What have you seen? Come on, tell me.'

'Well, I have observed that every time Mercédès comes into town, she is accompanied by a large Catalan lad, with black eyes, ruddy cheeks, very dark in colour and very passionate, whom she calls "my cousin".'

'Ah, indeed! And do you think this cousin is courting her?'

'I imagine so: what else does a fine lad of twenty-one do to a pretty girl of seventeen?'

'And you say that Dantès has gone to Les Catalans?'

'He left before me.'

'Suppose we were to go in the same direction, stop in the Réserve and, over a glass of La Malgue wine, learn what we can learn.'

'Who would tell us anything?'

'We shall be on the spot and we'll see what has happened from Dantès' face.'

'Let's go then,' said Caderousse. 'But you are paying?'

'Certainly,' Danglars replied.

The two of them set off at a brisk pace for the spot they had mentioned and, when they arrived, called for a bottle and two glasses.

Old Pamphile had seen Dantès go by less than two minutes before. Certain that he was in Les Catalans, they sat under the budding leaves of the plane-trees and sycamores, in the branches of which a happy band of birds was serenading one of the first fine days of spring.

III

LES CATALANS

A hundred yards away from the place where the two friends, staring into the distance with their ears pricked, were enjoying the sparkling wine of La Malgue, lay the village of Les Catalans, behind a bare hillock ravaged by the sun and the mistral.

One day, a mysterious group of colonists set out from Spain and landed on this spit of land, where it still resides today. No one knew where they had come from or what language they spoke. One of the leaders, who understood Provençal, asked the commune of Marseille to give them this bare and arid promontory on to which, like the sailors of Antiquity, they had drawn up their boats. The request was granted and, three months later, a little village grew up around the twelve or fifteen boats that brought these gypsies of the sea.

The same village, built in a bizarre and picturesque manner that is partly Moorish and partly Spanish, is the one that can be seen today, inhabited by the descendants of those men, who speak the language of their forefathers. For three or four centuries they have remained faithful to the little promontory on which they first landed, clinging to it like a flock of seabirds, in no way mixing with the inhabitants of Marseille, marrying among themselves and retaining the habits and dress of their motherland, just as they have retained its tongue.

The reader must follow us along the only street of the little village and enter one of those houses, to the outside of which the sunlight has given that lovely colour of dead leaves which is peculiar to the buildings of the country; with, inside, a coat of whitewash, the only decoration of a Spanish *posada*.

A lovely young girl with jet-black hair and the velvet eyes of a gazelle, was standing, leaning against an inner wall, rubbing an innocent sprig of heather between slender fingers like those on a classical statue, and pulling off the flowers, the remains of which were already strewn across the floor. At the same time, her arms, naked to the elbow, arms that were tanned but otherwise seemed modelled on those of the Venus of Arles, trembled with a sort of feverish impatience, and she was tapping the ground with her supple, well-made foot, revealing a leg that was shapely, bold and proud, but imprisoned in a red cotton stocking patterned in grey and blue lozenges.

A short distance away, a tall young man of between twenty and twenty-two was sitting on a chair, rocking it fitfully on two legs while supporting himself on his elbow against an old worm-eaten dresser and watching her with a look that combined anxiety with irritation. His eyes were questioning, but those of the young woman, firm and unwavering, dominated their conversation.

'Please, Mercédès,' the man said. 'Easter is coming round again; it's the time for weddings. Give me your answer!'

'You have had it a hundred times, Fernand, and you really must like torturing yourself, to ask me again.'

'Well, repeat it, I beg you, repeat it once more so that I can come to believe it. Tell me, for the hundredth time, that you reject my love, even though your mother approves of me. Convince me that you are prepared to trifle with my happiness and that my life and my death are nothing to you. My God, my God! To dream for ten years of being your husband, Mercédès, and then to lose that hope which was the sole aim of my existence!'

'I, at least, never encouraged you in that hope, Fernand,' Mercédès replied. 'You cannot accuse me of having, even once, flirted with you. I've said repeatedly: "I love you like a brother, but never demand anything more from me than this fraternal love, because my heart belongs to another." Isn't that what I have always told you, Fernand?'

'Yes, Mercédès, I know,' the young man replied. 'Yes, you have always been laudably, and cruelly, honest with me. But are you forgetting that it is a sacred law among the Catalans only to marry among themselves?'

'You are wrong, Fernand, it is not a law, but a custom, nothing more; and I advise you not to appeal to that custom on your behalf. You have been chosen for conscription, Fernand, and the freedom that you now enjoy is merely a temporary reprieve: at any moment you might be called up to serve in the army. Once you are a soldier, what will you do with me – I mean, with a poor orphan girl, sad and penniless, whose only possession is a hut, almost in ruins, in which hang a few worn nets, the paltry legacy that was left by my father to my mother, and by my mother to me? Consider, Fernand, that in the year since she died, I have virtually lived on charity!

Sometimes you pretend that I am of some use to you, so that you can be justified in sharing your catch with me. And I accept, Fernand, because you are the son of one of my father's brothers, because we grew up together and, beyond that, most of all, because it would hurt you too much if I were to refuse. But I know full well that the fish I take to the market, which bring me the money to buy the hemp that I spin – I know, full well, Fernand, that it is charity.'

'What does it matter, Mercédès, poor and alone as you are, when you suit me thus better than the daughter of the proudest shipowner or the richest banker in Marseille? What do people like us need? An honest wife and a good housekeeper. Where could I find better than you on either score?'

'Fernand,' Mercédès replied, shaking her head, 'one is not a good housekeeper and one cannot promise to remain an honest woman when one loves a man other than one's husband. Be satisfied with my friendship for, I repeat, that is all I can promise you and I only promise what I am sure of being able to give.'

'Yes, I understand,' said Fernand. 'You bear your own poverty patiently, but you are afraid of mine. Well, Mercédès, with your love, I would try to make my fortune; you would bring me luck and I should become rich. I can cast my fisherman's net wider, I can take a job as a clerk in a shop, I could even become a merchant myself!'

'You can't do any such thing, Fernand: you're a soldier and, if you stay here among the Catalans, it is because there is no war for you to fight. So remain a fisherman, don't dream of things that will make reality seem even more terrible to you – and be content with my friendship, because I cannot give you anything else.'

'You are right, Mercédès, I shall be a seaman; and, instead of the dress of our forefathers which you despise, I shall have a patent-leather hat, a striped shirt and a blue jacket with anchors on the buttons. That's how a man needs to dress, isn't it, if he wants to please you?'

'What do you mean?' Mercédès asked, with an imperious look. 'What do you mean? I don't understand you.'

'What I mean, Mercédès, is that you are only so hard-hearted and cruel towards me because you are waiting for someone who is dressed like that. But it may be that the one you await is fickle and, even if he isn't, the sea will be fickle for him.'

'Fernand!' Mercédès exclaimed. 'I thought you were kind, but I was mistaken. It is wicked of you to call on the wrath of God to satisfy your jealousy. Yes, I will not deny it: I am waiting for the man you describe, I love him and if he does not return, instead of blaming the fickleness that it pleases you to speak of, I shall think that he died loving me.'

The young Catalan made an angry gesture.

'I understand what that means, Fernand: you want to blame him because I do not love you, and cross his dagger with your Catalan knife! What good would that do you? If you were defeated, you would lose my friendship; if you were the victor, you would see that friendship turn to hatred. Believe me, when a woman loves a man, you do not win her heart by crossing swords with him. No, Fernand, don't be carried away by evil thoughts. Since you cannot have me as your wife, be content to have me as a friend and a sister. In any case,' she added, her eyes anxious and filling with tears, 'stay, Fernand: you said, yourself, a moment ago that the sea is treacherous. It is already four months since he left, and I have counted a lot of storms in the past four months!'

Fernand remained impassive. He made no attempt to wipe the tears that were running down Mercédès cheeks, yet he would have given a glass of his own blood for each of those tears; but they were shed for another. He got up, walked round the hut and returned, stopping before Mercédès with a dark look in his eyes and clenched fists.

'Come now, Mercédès,' he said. 'Answer me once more: have you truly made up your mind?'

'I love Edmond Dantès,' the young woman said, coldly, 'and no one will be my husband except Edmond.'

'And you will love him for ever?'

'As long as I live.'

Fernand bent his head like a discouraged man, gave a sigh that was like a groan, then suddenly looked up with clenched teeth and nostrils flared.

'But suppose he is dead?'

'If he is dead, I shall die.'

'And if he forgets you?'

'Mercédès!' cried a happy voice outside the house. 'Mercédès!'

'Ah!' the girl exclaimed, reddening with joy and leaping up, filled with love. 'You see that he has not forgotten me: he is here!' And she ran to the door, and opened it, crying: 'Come to me, Edmond! I am here!'

Pale and trembling, Fernand stepped back as a traveller might do at the sight of a snake; and, stumbling against his chair, fell back into it.

Edmond and Mercédès were in each other's arms. The hot Marseille sun, shining through the doorway, drenched them in a flood of light. At first, they saw nothing of what was around them. A vast wave of happiness cut them off from the world and they spoke only those half-formed words that are the outpourings of such intense joy that they resemble the expression of pain.

Suddenly, Edmond noticed the sombre figure of Fernand, pale and threatening in the darkness. With a gesture of which he was not even himself aware, the young Catalan had laid his hand on the knife at his belt.

'Oh, forgive me,' Dantès said, raising an eyebrow. 'I did not realize that we were not alone.'

Then, turning to Mercédès, he asked: 'Who is this gentleman?'

'He will be your best friend, Dantès, because he is my friend, my cousin and my brother: this is Fernand, which means he is the man whom, after you, I love most in the world. Don't you recognize him?'

'Ah! Yes, indeed,' said Edmond. And, without leaving Mercédès whose hand he held clasped in one of his own, he extended the other with a cordial gesture towards the Catalan. But Fernand, instead of responding to this sign of friendship, remained as silent and motionless as a statue. It was enough to make Edmond look enquiringly from Mercédès, who was trembling with emotion, to Fernand, sombre and threatening.

That one glance told him everything. His brow clouded with rage.

'I did not realize that I had hurried round to see you, Mercédès, only to find an enemy here.'

'An enemy!' Mercédès exclaimed, looking angrily in the direction of her cousin. 'An enemy, in my house, you say, Edmond! If I thought that, I should take your arm and go with you to Marseille, leaving this house, never to return.'

Fernand's eyes lit up with rage.

'And if any misfortune were to befall you, my dear Edmond,' she continued, with the same cool determination, proving to Fernand that she had read the sinister depths of his mind, 'if any misfortune should happen to you, I should climb up the Cap de Morgiou and throw myself headlong on to the rocks.'

The blood drained from Fernand's face.

'But you are wrong, Edmond,' she continued. 'You have no enemies here. The only person here is Fernand, my brother, who is going to shake your hand like a true friend.'

With these words, the girl turned her imperious face towards the Catalan and he, as if mesmerized by her look, slowly came across to Edmond and held out his hand. His hatred, like an impotent wave, had been broken against the ascendancy that the woman exercised over him. But no sooner had he touched Edmond's hand than he felt he had done all that it was possible for him to do, and rushed out of the house.

'Ah!' he cried, running along like a madman and burying his hands in his hair. 'Ah! Who will deliver me from this man? Wretch that I am, wretch that I am!'

'Hey, Catalan! Hey, Fernand! Where are you going?' a voice called to him.

The young man stopped dead, looked around and saw Caderousse at the table with Danglars under a leafy arbour.

'What now,' said Caderousse, 'why don't you join us? Are you in such a hurry that you don't have time to say hello to your friends?'

'Especially when they still have an almost full bottle in front of them,' Danglars added.

Fernand stared at the two men with a dazed look, and did not answer.

'He seems a bit down in the dumps,' Danglars said, nudging Caderousse with his knee. 'Could we be wrong? Contrary to what we thought, could it be that Dantès has got the upper hand?'

'Why! We'll just have to find out,' said Caderousse. And, turning back to the young man, he said: 'Well, Catalan, have you made up your mind?'

Fernand wiped the sweat from his brow and slowly made his way under the vault of leaves: its shade appeared to do something to calm his spirits and its coolness to bring a small measure of well-being back to his exhausted body.

'Good day,' he said. 'I think you called me?'

'I called you because you were running along like a madman

and I was afraid you would go and throw yourself into the sea,' Caderousse said with a laugh. 'Devil take it, when one has friends, it is not only to offer them a glass of wine, but also to stop them drinking three or four pints of water.'

Fernand gave a groan that resembled a sob and let his head fall on to his wrists, which were crossed on the table.

'Well now, do you want me to tell you what, Fernand?' Caderousse continued, coming straight to the point with that crude brutality of the common man whose curiosity makes him forget any sense of tact. 'You look to me like a man who has been crossed in love!' He accompanied this quip with a roar of laughter.

'Huh!' Danglars retorted. 'A lad built like that is not likely to be unhappy in love. You must be joking, Caderousse.'

'Not at all,' the other said. 'Just listen to him sigh. Come, Fernand, come now, lift your nose off the table and tell us: it is not very mannerly to refuse to answer your friends when they are asking after your health.'

'My health is fine,' said Fernand, clenching his fists and without looking up.

'Ah, Danglars, you see now,' Caderousse said, winking at his friend. 'This is how things are: Fernand here, who is a fine, brave Catalan, one of the best fishermen in Marseille, is in love with a beautiful girl called Mercédès; but it appears that, unfortunately, the girl herself is in love with the second mate of the *Pharaon*; and, as the *Pharaon* came into port this very day . . . You follow me?'

'No, I don't,' said Danglars.

'Poor Fernand has got his marching orders,' Caderousse continued.

'So, what then?' said Fernand, lifting his head and looking at Caderousse, like a man anxious to find someone on whom to vent his wrath. 'Mercédès is her own woman, isn't she? She is free to love whomsoever she wants.'

'Oh, if that's how you take it,' said Caderousse, 'that's another matter. I thought you were a Catalan, and I have been told that the Catalans are not men to let themselves be pushed aside by a rival. They even said that Fernand, in particular, was fearsome in his vengeance.'

Fernand smiled pityingly. 'A lover is never fearsome,' he said.

'Poor boy!' Danglars continued, pretending to grieve for the young man from the bottom of his heart. 'What do you expect? He didn't imagine that Dantès would suddenly return like this; he may have thought him dead, or unfaithful. Who knows? Such things are all the more distressing when they happen to us suddenly.'

'In any event,' Caderousse said, drinking as he spoke and starting to show the effects of the heady wine of La Malgue, 'in any event, Fernand is not the only person to have been put out by Dantès' fortunate return, is he, Danglars?'

'No, what you say is true – and I might even add that it will bring him misfortune.'

'No matter,' Caderousse went on, pouring out some wine for Fernand and replenishing his own glass for the eighth or tenth time (though Danglars had hardly touched the one in front of him). 'No matter. In the meantime he will marry Mercédès, the lovely Mercédès. He has come back for that, at least.'

While the other was speaking, Danglars directed a piercing look at the young man, on whose heart Caderousse's words were falling like molten lead.

'And when is the wedding?' he asked.

'Oh, it's not settled yet,' Fernand muttered.

'No, but it will be,' said Caderousse, 'just as surely as Dantès will be captain of the *Pharaon*, don't you think, Danglars?'

Danglars shuddered at this unexpected stab and turned towards Caderousse, studying his face now to see if the blow had been premeditated; but he saw nothing except covetousness on this face, already almost besotted with drink.

'Very well,' he said, filling the glasses. 'Then let's drink to Captain Edmond Dantès, husband of the beautiful Catalan!'

Caderousse lifted his glass to his lips with a sluggish hand and drained it in one gulp. Fernand took his and dashed it to the ground.

'Ha, ha!' said Caderousse. 'What can I see over there, on the crest of the hill, coming from the Catalan village? You look, Fernand, your eyesight is better than mine. I think I'm starting to see less clearly and, as you know, wine is a deceptive imp: it looks to me like two lovers walking along, side by side and hand in hand. Heaven forgive me! They don't realize that we can see them and, look at that, they're kissing each other!'

Danglars marked every single trait of the anguish that crossed Fernand's face, as its features changed before his eyes.

'Do you know who they are, Monsieur Fernand?' he asked.

'Yes,' the other replied dully. 'It's Monsieur Edmond and Mademoiselle Mercédès.'

'There! You see?' said Caderousse. 'I didn't recognize them. Hey, Dantès! Hey, there, pretty girl! Come down for a moment and let us know when the wedding is: Fernand here is so stubborn, he won't tell us.'

'Why don't you be quiet!' said Danglars, pretending to restrain Caderousse who, with drunken obstinacy, was leaning out of the arbour. 'Try to stay upright and let the lovers enjoy themselves in peace. Why, look at Monsieur Fernand: he's being sensible. Why not try and do the same?'

It may be that Fernand, driven to the limit and baited by Danglars like a bull by the banderilleros, would finally have leapt forward, for he had already stood up and appeared to be gathering strength to throw himself at his rival; but Mercédès, upright and laughing, threw back her lovely head and shot a glance from her clear eyes. At that moment, Fernand recalled her threat to die if Edmond should die, and slumped back, discouraged, on his chair.

Danglars looked at the two men, one besotted by drink, the other enslaved by love, and murmured: 'I shall get nothing out of these idiots: I fear I am sitting between a drunkard and a coward. On the one hand, I have a man eaten up by envy, drowning his sorrows in drink when he should be intoxicated with venom; on the other, a great simpleton whose mistress has just been snatched away from under his very nose, who does nothing except weep like a child and feel sorry for himself. And yet he has the blazing eyes of a Spaniard, a Sicilian or a Calabrian – those people who are such experts when it comes to revenge – and fists that would crush a bull's head as surely as a butcher's mallet. Fate is definitely on Edmond's side: he will marry the beautiful girl, become captain and laugh in our faces. Unless . . .' (a pallid smile hovered on Danglars' lips) '. . . unless I take a hand in it.'

Caderousse, half standing, with his fists on the table, was still shouting: 'Hello, there! Hello! Edmond! Can't you see your friends, or are you too proud to talk to them?'

'No, my dear Caderousse,' Edmond replied. 'I am not proud, but I am happy – and happiness, I believe, is even more dazzling than pride.'

'At last, all is explained,' said Caderousse. 'Ho! Good day to you, Madame Dantès.'

Mercédès bowed gravely and said: 'That is not yet my name, and in my country they say it is bad luck to call a young woman by the name of her betrothed before he has become her husband. So, please, call me Mercédès.'

'You must forgive my good neighbour, Caderousse,' Dantès said. 'He so seldom makes a mistake!'

'So, the wedding is to take place shortly, Monsieur Dantès?' Danglars said, greeting the two young people.

'As soon as possible, Monsieur Danglars. Today, everything is to be agreed at my father's house and tomorrow or, at the latest, the day after, we shall have the engagement dinner here at La Réserve. I hope that my friends will join us: you, of course, are invited, Monsieur Danglars, and you, too, Caderousse.'

'And Fernand?' Caderousse asked, with a coarse laugh. 'Will Fernand be there as well?'

'My wife's brother is my brother,' Edmond said, 'and both Mercédès and I should regret it deeply if he were to be separated from us at such a time.'

Fernand opened his mouth to reply, but his voice caught in his throat and he could not utter a single word.

'The agreement today, the engagement tomorrow or the day after: by George! You're in a great hurry, Captain.'

'Danglars,' Edmond said with a smile, 'I shall say the same to you as Mercédès did a moment ago: don't give me a title that does not yet belong to me, it could bring me ill luck.'

'My apologies,' Danglars replied. 'I was merely saying that you seem in a great hurry. After all, we have plenty of time: the *Pharaon* will not set sail for a good three months.'

'One always hurries towards happiness, Monsieur Danglars, because when one has suffered much, one is at pains to believe in it. But I am not impelled by mere selfishness. I have to go to Paris.'

'Ah, indeed! To Paris. And will this be your first visit, Dantès?'
'Yes.'
'You have business there?'
'Not of my own, but a final request that I must carry out for our poor Captain Leclère. You understand, Danglars, the mission is sacred to me. In any event, don't worry. I shall be gone only as long as it takes to go there and return.'

'Yes, yes, I understand,' Danglars said aloud; then he added, under his breath: 'To Paris, no doubt to deliver the letter that the marshal gave him. By heaven! That letter has given me an idea – an excellent idea! Ah, Dantès, my friend, your name is not yet Number One on the register of the *Pharaon*.'

Then, turning back to Edmond who was leaving, he shouted: '*Bon voyage!*'

'Thank you,' Edmond replied, turning around and giving a friendly wave. Then the two lovers went on their way, calm and happy as two chosen souls heading for paradise.

IV

THE PLOT

Danglars' eyes followed Edmond and Mercédès until the two lovers had vanished round one corner of the Fort Saint-Nicholas; then, turning at last, he noticed Fernand who had slipped back on to his chair, pale and trembling, while Caderousse was mumbling the words of a drinking song.

'So, my good sir,' Danglars told Fernand, 'not everyone, I think, is happy about this marriage.'

'I am in despair,' said Fernand.

'You're in love with Mercédès?'

'I adore her!'

'For a long time?'

'Ever since I've known her; I've always loved her.'

'And all you can do is sit there and tear your hair out, instead of finding some way out of the dilemma! By God! I didn't know that this was how people of your country behaved.'

'What do you expect me to do?' Fernand asked.

'How do I know? Is it any of my business? As I see it, I'm not the one who's in love with Mademoiselle Mercédès; you are. Seek and ye shall find, the Gospel says.'

'I had found already.'

'What?'

'I wanted to put my knife into the creature, but the girl said that if her fiancé was harmed, she would kill herself.'

'Pah! People say such things, but they don't do them.'

'You don't know Mercédès, Monsieur. If she threatens to do something, she will.'

'Idiot!' Danglars muttered. 'What does it matter whether she kills herself or not, provided Dantès does not become captain.'

'And before Mercédès dies,' Fernand went on, in firmly resolute tones, 'I should die myself.'

'There's love for you!' Caderousse said, in a voice increasingly slurred by drink. 'There's love, or I don't know it.'

'Come now,' said Danglars. 'You seem an agreeable enough lad to me and – by Jove! – I'd like to ease your sorrow, but . . .'

'Yes,' said Caderousse. 'Come now.'

'My good friend,' Danglars remarked, 'you are three-quarters drunk: go the whole way and finish the bottle. Drink, but don't interfere with our business, because you need a clear head for what we're doing.'

'Me? Drunk?' said Caderousse. 'Never! I could take another four of your bottles, which are no bigger than bottles of eau de Cologne. Père Pamphile! Bring us some wine!'

And, to make the point, Caderousse banged his glass on the table.

'You were saying, Monsieur?' Fernand asked, impatient to hear what else Danglars had to tell him.

'What was I saying? I don't remember. This drunkard Caderousse has put it quite out of my mind.'

'Drunkard if you like. A curse on those who fear wine: it's because they have evil thoughts and they are afraid that wine will loosen their tongues.'

Caderousse began to sing the last two lines of a song which was much in vogue at the time:

> The Flood proved it beyond a doubt:
> All wicked men do water drink.[1]

'You were saying, Monsieur,' Fernand continued, 'that you'd like to ease my sorrow, but you added . . .'

'Ah, yes. But I added that . . . to give you satisfaction, it is enough for Dantès not to marry the one you love. And this marriage, it seems to me, could very well not take place, even if Dantès does not die.'

'Only death will separate them,' said Fernand.

'You have the brains of an oyster, my friend,' said Caderousse.

'And Danglars here, who is a sharp one, crafty as a Greek, will prove you wrong. Do it, Danglars. I've stuck up for you. Tell him that Dantès doesn't have to die. In any case, it would be a pity if he died. He's a good lad, Dantès. I like him. Your health, Dantès.'

Fernand rose impatiently to his feet.

'Let him babble,' Danglars said, putting a hand on the young man's arm. 'And, for that matter, drunk as he is, he is not so far wrong. Absence separates as effectively as death; so just suppose that there were the walls of a prison between Edmond and Mercédès: that would separate them no more nor less than a tombstone.'

'Yes, but people get out of prison,' said Caderousse, who was gripping on to the conversation with what remained of his wits. 'And when you get out of prison and you are called Edmond Dantès, you take revenge.'

'What does that matter!' said Fernand.

'In any event,' Caderousse continued, 'why should they put Dantès in prison? He hasn't stolen anything, killed anyone, committed any murder.'

'Shut up,' said Danglars.

'I don't want to shut up,' said Caderousse. 'I want to know why they should put Dantès in prison. I like Dantès. Dantès! Your health!'

He poured back another glass of wine.

Danglars assessed the extent of the tailor's drunkenness from his dull eyes, and turned towards Fernand.

'So, do you understand that there is no need to kill him?' he said.

'No, surely not if, as you said a moment ago, there was some means of having Dantès arrested. But do you have such a means?'

'If we look,' Danglars answered, 'we can find one. But, dammit, why should this concern me? What business is it of mine?'

'I don't know why it should concern you,' Fernand said, grasping his arm. 'What I do know is that you have some private animosity against Dantès: a man who feels hated cannot be mistaken about that feeling in others.'

'I? Have some reason to hate Dantès? None, I swear. I saw that you were unhappy and took an interest in your unhappiness, that's all. But if you are going to imagine that I am acting on my own behalf, then farewell, my good friend. You can manage for yourself.' Here Danglars himself made as if to get up.

'No, stay!' said Fernand. 'When it comes down to it, it's of no matter to me whether you have some bone to pick with Dantès or not; I do, and I freely admit it. Find the means and I shall carry it out, as long as there is no murder involved, for Mercédès said that she would kill herself if anyone killed Dantès.'

Caderousse, who had let his head fall on the table, lifted it and turned his dull, drink-sodden eyes on Fernand and Danglars.

'Kill Dantès!' he said. 'Who's talking about killing Dantès? I don't want him killed. He's my friend. This morning, he offered to share his money with me, as I shared mine with him. I don't want anyone to kill Dantès.'

'Who said anything about killing him, idiot?' Danglars went on. 'It's nothing more than a joke. Drink to his health and leave us be,' he added, filling Caderousse's glass.

'Yes, yes. To Dantès' health,' said Caderousse, emptying his glass. 'His health! His health! Like that!'

'But the means, what about the means?' Fernand asked.

'You haven't thought of any yet?'

'No, you said that you would do that.'

'That's true,' said Danglars. 'A Spaniard is inferior to a French-man in one respect: your Spaniard thinks things over, but your Frenchman thinks them up.'

'Well, think up something, then,' Fernand said impatiently.

'Waiter!' Danglars called. 'A pen, ink and paper!'

'A pen, ink and paper,' Fernand muttered.

'Yes, I am an accountant: pens, ink and paper are the tools of my trade, and without them I can do nothing.'

'A pen, some ink and some paper!' Fernand repeated to the waiter.

'What you need is over there on the table,' the waiter said, indicating the items they had requested.

'Give them to us, then.'

The waiter brought the paper, some ink and a quill pen, and put them on the table in the arbour.

'When you think,' Caderousse said, letting his hand fall on to the paper, 'that what you have here can kill a man more surely than if you were to hide in the woods to murder him! I have always been more afraid of a pen, a bottle of ink and a sheet of paper than of a sword or a pistol.'

'This clown is not yet as drunk as he seems,' said Danglars. 'Pour him another drink, Fernand.'

Fernand filled Caderousse's glass and he, like the true drunkard he was, took his hand off the paper and moved it to his glass. The Catalan watched him until Caderousse, almost floored by this new assault, put his glass back – or, rather, let it fall – on to the table.

'Well?' the Catalan asked, seeing that the last traces of Caderousse's wits had begun to disappear in this final draught of wine.

'As I was saying,' Danglars continued, 'for example, after a voyage such as the one Dantès has just made, in the course of which he put in at Naples and the island of Elba, if someone were to denounce him to the crown prosecutor[2] as a Bonapartist agent . . .'

'I'll denounce him, I'll do it!' the young man said eagerly.

'Yes, but in that case you would have to sign your declaration and be confronted with the man you accused: I could give you proof to support your accusation, I know; but Dantès cannot stay in prison for ever; one day he will come out, and on that day, woe betide the one who put him there!'

'Oh, I couldn't ask for anything better,' said Fernand. 'Let him come and challenge me.'

'Yes, but what about Mercédès? Mercédès who will hate you if you are unfortunate enough to leave even a scratch on her beloved Edmond!'

'That's true,' said Fernand.

'No, no,' Danglars continued. 'You see, if we were to make up our minds to such a thing, it would be far better simply to do as I am doing now, and take this pen, dip it in the ink and, with one's left hand – to disguise the writing – make out a little denunciation in these terms.'

To illustrate his meaning, Danglars wrote the following lines, with his left hand, the writing sloping backwards so that it bore no resemblance to his usual handwriting, then passed it to Fernand, who read it in a hushed voice:

The crown prosecutor is advised, by a friend of the monarchy and the faith, that one Edmond Dantès, first mate of the *Pharaon*, arriving this morning from Smyrna, after putting in at Naples and Porto Ferrajo, was entrusted by Murat[3] with a letter for the usurper and by the usurper with a letter to the Bonapartist committee in Paris.

Proof of his guilt will be found when he is arrested, since the letter will be discovered either on his person, or at the house of his father, or in his cabin on board the *Pharaon*.

'So there we have it,' Danglars continued. 'In this way your revenge would be consistent with common sense, because it could in no way be traced back to you and the matter would proceed of its own accord. You would merely have to fold the letter – as I am doing now – and write on it: "To the Crown Prosecutor". That would settle it.' And Danglars wrote the address with a simple stroke of the pen.

'Yes, that would settle it,' cried Caderousse, who had made one final effort to muster his wits and follow the reading of the letter, and understood instinctively all the misfortune that such a denunciation could bring. 'Yes, that would settle it, except that it would be a vile act.' And he reached over to take the letter.

'Which is why,' said Danglars, pushing it beyond the reach of his hand, 'which is why what I am saying and doing is simply in jest; and I should be the first to be upset if anything were to happen to Dantès – dear Dantès! So, watch . . .'

He took the letter, crumpled it in his hands and threw it into a corner of the arbour.

'That's right,' said Caderousse. 'Dantès is my friend and I don't want anyone to harm him.'

'The devil take it! Whoever would think of doing him harm? Certainly not I or Fernand!' said Danglars, getting up and looking at the young man, who had remained seated but who had his covetous eye fixed sideways on the accusing letter where it had fallen.

'In that case,' Caderousse went on, 'bring us more wine: I want to drink to the health of Edmond and the lovely Mercédès.'

'You have had enough to drink already, you tippler,' said Danglars. 'If you go on, you will have to sleep here, because you won't be able to stand up.'

'Me?' said Caderousse, rising with the ridiculous movement of a drunken man. 'Me! Not be able to stand up! I wager I could go up the belfry of Les Accoules, and without wavering.'

'Well, if you wish,' said Danglars. 'I accept the wager, but for tomorrow. Today it is time to go home, so give me your arm and we'll get started.'

'Let's go,' said Caderousse, 'but I don't need your arm for it. Are you coming, Fernand? Come with us to Marseille.'

'No,' said Fernand. 'I'm going back to Les Catalans.'

'Don't be silly. Come with us to Marseille. Come on.'

'I have no business in Marseille and I don't want to go there.'

'What did you say? You don't want to, my lad! Well, do as you wish. Everyone can do as he wishes. Come on, Danglars, and let this gentleman go back to the Catalans, since that's what he wants.'

Danglars took advantage of Caderousse's momentary amenability to drag him towards Marseille; but, to leave a shorter and easier way free for Fernand, instead of going back via the Quai de la Rive-Neuve, he went through the Porte Saint-Victor. Caderousse followed, swaying and gripping his arm.

When he had gone some twenty yards, Danglars turned around and saw Fernand grab the piece of paper and put it in his pocket. Then, running out of the arbour, the young man immediately went in the direction of Le Pillon.

'There, now! What's he up to?' said Caderousse. 'He lied to us. He said he was going to Les Catalans, and he's headed into town. Hey, Fernand, my boy! You're going the wrong way!'

'It's you who can't see properly,' said Danglars. 'He has gone straight down the road to the Vieilles-Infirmeries.'

'Has he?' said Caderousse. 'Well, now, I could have sworn that he turned to the right. Wine really is a deceiver.'

'Come on, come on,' Danglars muttered. 'I think that the matter is properly under way now, and all we have to do is to let it take its course.'

V

THE BETROTHAL

The next day, the weather was fine. The sun rose, brilliant and clear, and its first purple rays glistened like rubies on the foamy crests of the waves.

The meal had been set out on the first floor of the same inn, La Réserve, with the terrace of which we are already acquainted. It was a large room, lit by five or six windows, above each of which (for some inexplicable reason) was inscribed the name of one of the great towns of France. A gallery – of wood, like the rest of the building – ran the whole length of the room under the windows.

Although the meal was due to begin only at noon, this gallery was crowded with impatient onlookers from eleven o'clock in the morning. These were a few chosen sailors from the *Pharaon* and some soldiers who were Dantès' friends. All of them were in their Sunday best, in honour of the engaged couple.

The rumour circulating among these expectant guests was that the owners of the *Pharaon* were to honour its first mate's betrothal feast with their presence, but this would have been to do such a great honour to Dantès that no one yet dared believe it. However, Danglars, when he arrived with Caderousse, confirmed the news: he had seen M. Morrel himself, that morning, and M. Morrel had said that he would be dining at La Réserve.

Indeed, a moment later, M. Morrel made his entrance into the room and was saluted by the crew of the *Pharaon* with a unanimous burst of applause and shouts of 'Hurrah!' The owner's presence was seen by them as confirmation of a rumour, already going about, that Dantès was to be appointed captain; and, since Dantès was much liked on board, the men took this way of thanking the owner because, for once, his choice was concordant with their wishes. Hardly had M. Morrel entered than Danglars and Caderousse were, by general agreement, dispatched to find the fiancé, with orders to advise him of the arrival of this important person whose appearance had caused such a stir, and to tell him to hurry.

Danglars and Caderousse set off at full speed, but had hardly gone any distance before they saw the little band approaching, just coming past the powder magazine. It was made up of four young women, friends of Mercédès and Catalans like her, who were accompanying the fiancée while Edmond gave her his arm. Next to her walked Old Dantès and behind them came Fernand, with his sour smile.

Neither Mercédès nor Edmond could see the smile on Fernand's face. The poor children were so happy that they saw nothing except one another and the pure, clear sky that showered its blessing on them.

Danglars and Caderousse discharged their diplomatic mission, then exchanged a warm and energetic handshake with Edmond, and took up their places, Danglars next to Fernand and Caderousse beside Old Dantès, who was the general centre of attention.

The old man was wearing his fine coat of fluted taffeta, decorated with large-faceted steel buttons. His lanky but vigorous legs were clothed in a splendid pair of spotted stockings that cried out English contraband. A mass of white and blue ribbons hung from his three-cornered hat. Finally, he was supported by a stick of twisted wood, bent at the top like a classical staff or *pedum*. He looked like one of those dandies who used to parade in 1796 in the newly re-opened gardens of the Luxembourg or the Tuileries.

As we said, Caderousse had slipped into step beside him – Caderousse, entirely reconciled with the Dantès by the prospect of a good meal, Caderousse whose mind retained some vague memory of what had happened the previous day, as one's brain on waking in the morning may hold a shadow of the dream that it experienced in sleep.

As he came up to Fernand, Danglars searched deep into the disappointed lover's soul. He was walking behind the engaged couple, entirely forgotten by Mercédès, who, with the childlike and endearing egoism of love, had eyes only for her Edmond. Fernand was pale, then his colour would heighten suddenly, only to give way again to a deepening pallor. From time to time he looked towards Marseille, and an involuntary nervous tremor would shake his limbs. He seemed to be expecting, or at least to anticipate the possibility of, some important event.

Dantès was dressed simply. Since he belonged to the merchant marine, his clothes were halfway between military uniform and civilian dress; in this habit, his evident good health, set off against the happiness and beauty of his fiancée, was perfect.

Mercédès was as lovely as one of those Greek women of Cyprus or Chios, with jet-black eyes and coral lips. She stepped out with the frankness and freedom of an Arlésienne or an Andalusian woman. A city girl might perhaps have tried to conceal her joy under a veil or at least beneath the velvet shade of her eyelids, but Mercédès smiled and looked at all those around her; and her look and her smile said as plainly as she could have in words: if you are my friends, rejoice with me, because I am truly happy!

As soon as the couple and those accompanying them were in sight of La Réserve, M. Morrel came down and set out to meet them, followed by the sailors and soldiers: he had stayed with them to renew the promise he had already made to Dantès himself, that he would succeed Captain Leclère. Seeing him approach, Edmond let go of his fiancée's arm, which he placed under M. Morrel's. Thus the shipowner and the young woman gave a lead by going first up the wooden stairs leading to the room where dinner was served, and the staircase groaned for five minutes under the heavy feet of the guests.

'Father,' Mercédès said, stopping at the middle of the table, 'you go on my right, I pray you; and on my left, I shall place the one who has been a brother to me.' She spoke with such softness that it struck Fernand to the depth of his soul like a blow from a dagger. His lips paled and, under the tanned colouring of his masculine features, you could once more see the blood draining bit by bit as it flooded into his heart.

Meanwhile Dantès had done the same: on his right, he placed M. Morrel, and on his left Danglars. Then he signalled to everyone to sit down wherever they wished.

Already the guests were passing round the strong-smelling Arles sausage with its brown flesh, crayfish in their dazzling armour, pink-shelled clams, sea-urchins looking like chestnuts in their spiny cases, and *clovisses*, those shellfish that gourmets from the South claim are more than an adequate substitute for the oysters of northern waters; in short, all the delicate hors-d'oeuvres that are washed up by the waves on these sandy shores and to which grateful fishermen accord the general appellation of *fruits de mer*.

'Why this silence?' the old man exclaimed, sipping a glass of a wine as yellow as topaz, which Père Pamphile in person had just set down in front of Mercédès. 'Who would imagine that there are thirty people here who ask nothing better than to be merry?'

'Huh! A husband is not always merry,' said Caderousse.

'The fact is,' Dantès said, 'that I am too happy at this moment to be merry. If that's what you mean, neighbour, you are right. Joy may sometimes produce strange effects and be as oppressive as sorrow.'

Danglars was watching Fernand, whose impressionable nature absorbed and reflected his every feeling.

'Come now,' he said. 'Have you anything to fear? It seems to me, on the contrary, that everything is working out as you would wish.'

'That is precisely what terrifies me,' said Dantès. 'I cannot think that man is meant to find happiness so easily! Happiness is like one of those palaces on an enchanted island, its gates guarded by dragons. One must fight to gain it; and, in truth, I do not know what I have done to deserve the good fortune of becoming Mercédès' husband.'

'Husband! Husband!' Caderousse said, laughing. 'Not yet, Captain. Try behaving like her husband right now and you'll see how she treats you.'

Mercédès blushed.

Fernand was shuffling on his chair, starting at the slightest noise and, from time to time, wiping large beads of sweat from his forehead, which seemed to have fallen there like the first drops of rain before a storm.

'By heaven, neighbour,' said Dantès, 'you have no need to give me the lie for so little. It's true, Mercédès is not yet my wife, but . . .' (he took out his watch) '. . . in an hour and a half, she will be!'

There was a gasp of surprise from everyone, except Old Dantès, who exhibited his fine set of teeth in a broad laugh. Mercédès smiled and was no longer blushing. Fernand made a convulsive lunge towards the handle of his dagger.

'In an hour!' said Danglars, himself going pale. 'How is that?'

'Yes, friends,' Dantès replied. 'Thanks to an advance from Monsieur Morrel, the man to whom – after my father – I owe the most in the world, all our difficulties have been overcome. We have paid for the banns and at half-past two the Mayor of Marseille is expecting us at the Town Hall. Now, since it has just sounded a quarter past one, I think I am not much mistaken in saying that in one hour and thirty minutes Mercédès will be Madame Dantès.'

Fernand closed his eyes. A fiery cloud was burning behind their lids and he grasped the table to keep himself from fainting; but, despite his efforts to do so, he could not repress a deep groan that was drowned by laughter and the congratulations of the guests.

'That's the way to do it, no?' Old Dantès said. 'What would you say? Has he wasted any time? Disembarked yesterday morning, married today at three o'clock! Trust a sailor to get the job done without messing around.'

'But,' Danglars put in timidly, 'what about the other formalities: the contract, the settlement?'

'The contract!' Dantès said with a laugh. 'The contract is already made: Mercédès has nothing, and neither have I! We shall be married under a settlement of common estate, that's all. It took little time to write out and won't be expensive.'

This sally brought a further round of applause and hurrahs.

'So, what we thought was a betrothal is nothing less than a wedding feast,' said Danglars.

'Not so,' said Dantès. 'Don't worry, you won't be missing

anything. Tomorrow morning, I leave for Paris: four days to travel there, four days to return and a day to carry out my errand conscientiously. On March the first I shall be back; on March the second, then, we shall have the real wedding feast.'

The prospect of a second meal increased the level of hilarity to such a point that Old Dantès, who had complained of the silence at the start of the dinner, was now making futile efforts, in the midst of the general hubbub, to propose a toast to the prosperity of the happy couple.

Dantès guessed what was in his father's mind and replied with a smile full of filial love. Mercédès had started to watch the time on the cuckoo clock in the room, and she made a sign to Edmond.

Around the table reigned the noisy merriment and freedom of manners that, among people of the lower orders, are common accompaniments to the end of a meal. Those who were dissatisfied with their places had got up from the table and gone to find new neighbours. Everyone had started to speak at once, and no one was bothering to listen to what the person next to him was saying, but was concerned only with his own thoughts.

Fernand's pallor was almost reflected on the cheeks of Danglars; as for Fernand himself, all life appeared to have left him and he was like one of the damned in a lake of fire. He had been among the first to get up and was striding backwards and forwards across the room, trying to block his ears to the sound of songs and clinking glasses.

Caderousse went over to him, just as Danglars, whom he had apparently been trying to avoid, caught up with him in a corner of the room.

'I must say,' Caderousse remarked, the last remnants of the hatred which Dantès' unexpected good fortune had sowed in his mind having succumbed to Dantès' joviality and, above all, to Père Pamphile's excellent wine. 'Dantès is a good fellow and when I see him like this beside his fiancée I feel that it would have been a pity to play the unkind trick on him that you were plotting yesterday.'

'Well, then,' Danglars replied, 'you can see that the matter went no further. Poor Monsieur Fernand was so upset that, at first, I felt sorry for him; but now that he has made up his mind to accept the situation, to the point of allowing himself to become his rival's best man, there is nothing more to be said.'

Caderousse looked at Fernand. He was deathly pale.

'The sacrifice is all the greater,' Danglars went on, 'as the girl is so decidedly pretty. Dammit! My future captain is a lucky dog: I wish I could be in his shoes for just half a day.'

'Shall we go?' Mercédès said softly. 'It is striking two and we are expected at a quarter past.'

'Yes, yes, let's go,' Dantès exclaimed, leaping to his feet.

'Let's go!' all the guests repeated in unison.

At that moment Danglars, who had not taken his eyes off Fernand where he was sitting on the window-ledge, saw him look up frantically, rise as though with a convulsive start, then fall back on to his seat in the casement. At almost the same moment a dull sound echoed through the stairway, the sound of heavy footsteps and confused voices, mingled with the clanking of weapons, which rose above the exclamations of the guests (loud though these were) and instantly attracted everybody's attention, creating an uneasy hush.

The sounds drew closer. Three knocks sounded on the door, and all those in the room looked at their neighbours in astonishment.

'Open, in the name of the law!' cried a voice, in a resounding tone. No one answered. At once the door flew open and a commissioner of police,[1] wearing his sash, strode into the room, followed by four armed soldiers under the command of a corporal.

Uneasiness gave way to terror.

'What is wrong?' the shipowner asked, going over to the commissioner, whom he knew. 'Monsieur, there must undoubtedly be some mistake.'

'If there is a mistake, Monsieur Morrel,' the commissioner replied, 'you may be sure that it will soon be put right. In the meanwhile, I have a warrant here; and though I do it with regret, I must fulfil my duty. Which of you gentlemen is Edmond Dantès?'

All eyes turned towards the young man who, preserving his dignity despite his astonishment, stepped forward and said: 'I am, Monsieur. What do you want with me?'

'Edmond Dantès,' the commissioner said, 'I arrest you in the name of the law.'

'Arrest me!' Edmond said, paling slightly. 'Why are you arresting me?'

'I have no idea of that, Monsieur, but you will be informed of it in your first interrogation.'

M. Morrel realized that there was no sense in trying to argue in the circumstances: a commissioner wearing his sash is no longer a man but a statue of the law, cold, deaf and dumb. But the old man rushed over to the officer: it is impossible, in some situations, to reason with the heart of a parent.

He begged and prayed: prayers and tears were ineffectual, but his despair was so great that the commissioner was moved by it.

'My dear sir,' he said, 'calm yourself. Perhaps your son has forgotten some formality to do with the Customs or the health authorities; and, as likely as not, when he has given them the information they require, he will be released.'

'Well, I never! What does this mean?' Caderousse asked Danglars quizzically, while Danglars feigned surprise.

'How can I tell?' he replied. 'Like you, I can see what is happening, but I am at a loss to understand it.'

Caderousse looked around for Fernand, but he had vanished. At that moment, the whole of the previous evening's events flashed before his eyes with terrifying clarity. It was as though the catastrophe had lifted the veil that drunkenness had cast over his memory of the day before.

'Oh! Oh!' he exclaimed hoarsely. 'Can this be a consequence of the joke you were speaking about yesterday, Danglars? If that is the case, damnation take the perpetrator, for it is a cruel one.'

'Nothing of the sort!' muttered Danglars. 'Far from it: you know very well that I tore up the paper.'

'That you did not,' said Caderousse. 'You merely threw it into a corner.'

'Hold your tongue. You were drunk, you saw nothing.'

'Where is Fernand?' Caderousse asked.

'How do I know?' replied Danglars. 'About his business, no doubt. But instead of worrying about that, why don't we go and comfort these poor people.'

While this conversation was taking place, Dantès had in effect been shaking the hands of all his friends, with a smile to each, and relinquished himself into captivity, saying: 'Stay calm. The mistake will doubtless be explained and it is quite probable that I shall not even go as far as the prison.'

'Certainly not, I guarantee it,' Danglars said, coming across at that moment to the group, as he had indicated.

Dantès went down the stairs, following the commissioner of police, with the soldiers surrounding him. A carriage, its door wide open, was waiting outside. He got in. Two soldiers and the commissioner got up behind him, the door closed and the carriage set out on the road back to Marseille.

'Farewell, Dantès! Farewell, Edmond!' cried Mercédès, leaning across the balustrade.

The prisoner heard this last cry, wrung like a sob from his fiancée's tormented heart. He leant out of the carriage window and called: 'Goodbye, Mercédès!' as he disappeared round one corner of the Fort Saint-Nicholas.

'Wait for me here,' said the shipowner. 'I shall take the first carriage I can find, hurry to Marseille and bring the news back to you.'

'Yes!' everyone cried. 'Go on, and come quickly back.'

After this double departure there was a dreadful moment of stunned silence among all who remained behind. For a time, the old man and Mercédès stayed apart, each immured in grief. But at length their eyes met. Each recognized the other as a victim stricken by the same blow and they fell into each other's arms.

Meanwhile Fernand returned, poured himself a glass of water, drank it and sat down on a chair. By chance, this happened to be next to the chair into which Mercédès sank when she parted from the old man's embrace. Fernand instinctively moved his own chair away.

'He's the one,' Caderousse told Danglars, not having taken his eyes off the Catalan.

'I doubt it,' Danglars replied. 'He was not clever enough. In any case, let whoever is responsible take the blame.'

'You are forgetting the person who advised him.'

'Pah! If one were to be held to account for every remark one lets fall . . .'

'Yes, when it falls point downwards.'

Everyone else, meanwhile, had been discussing every angle of Dantès' arrest.

'And you, Danglars?' someone asked. 'What do you think about what has happened?'

'My view is that he must have brought back some packets of prohibited goods.'

'But if that was the case, you should know about it, Danglars, since you were the ship's supercargo.'

'That may be so, but the supercargo doesn't know about any goods unless they are declared to him. I know that we were carrying cotton, that's all, and that we took the cargo on at Alexandria, from Monsieur Pastret, and at Smyrna, from Monsieur Pascal. Don't expect me to know anything more than that.'

'Yes, I remember now,' Dantès' poor father muttered, clutching at this straw. 'He told me yesterday that he had brought me a cask of coffee and one of tobacco.'

'You see,' said Danglars. 'That's it: while we were away, the Customs must have gone on board the *Pharaon* and discovered the contraband.'

Mercédès did not believe any of this; and, having up to then contained her distress, she burst into a fit of sobbing.

'Come, come! Don't lose hope,' Old Dantès said, though without really knowing what he was saying.

'Hope!' Danglars repeated.

'Hope,' Fernand tried to mutter. But the word stuck in his throat, his lips trembled and no sound emerged from them.

'Gentlemen!' cried one of the guests, who had been keeping watch from the balcony. 'Gentlemen, a carriage! Ah, it's Monsieur Morrel! Come now, he must surely be bringing good news.'

Mercédès and the old man ran out to greet the shipowner, who met them at the door. M. Morrel's face was pale.

'Well?' they all cried at once.

'Well, my friends,' the shipowner replied, shaking his head. 'The matter is more serious than we thought.'

'But, Monsieur!' cried Mercédès. 'He is innocent!'

'I believe him to be so,' M. Morrel replied, 'but he is accused . . .'

'What is he accused of?' Old Dantès asked.

'Of being an agent of Bonaparte.'

Those readers who lived through the period in which this story takes place will recall what a dreadful accusation it was that M. Morrel had just pronounced in those days.

Mercédès gave a cry, and the old man sank into a chair.

'So,' Caderousse muttered. 'You lied to me, Danglars: the trick was played after all. But I do not intend to let this old man and this young woman die of grief, and I shall tell them everything.'

'Hold your tongue, wretch!' Danglars exclaimed, grasping Caderousse's hand. 'Otherwise I can't answer for what may happen to you. How do you know that Dantès is not in fact guilty? The ship did call in at the island of Elba, he landed there and stayed a day in Porto Ferrajo. If he has been found with some compromising letter on his person, anyone who takes his part will look like an accomplice.'

Caderousse was rapidly informed of the full strength of this argument by the dictates of self-interest, and he looked at Danglars with an expression deadened by fear and grief. Having just taken one step forward, he proceeded to take two back.

'So, let's wait and see,' he muttered.

'Yes, we'll wait,' Danglars answered. 'If he is innocent, he will be freed; if he is guilty, there is no sense in compromising oneself for the sake of a conspirator.'

'Let's go, then. I can't stay here any longer.'

'Yes, come on,' said Danglars, delighted at having someone to accompany him out of the room. 'Come, we shall let them extricate themselves as best they may.'

They left; and Fernand, resuming his former role in support of the young woman, took Mercédès' hand and led her back to Les Catalans. For their part, Dantès' friends took the old man, in a state of near-collapse, back to the Allées de Meilhan.

The news that Dantès had just been arrested as a Bonapartist agent soon spread through Marseille.

'Would you have believed it, my dear Danglars?' M. Morrel said, catching up with his supercargo and Caderousse (for he was also heading for town as fast as he could, to have some first-hand news of Edmond from the crown prosecutor, M. de Villefort, who was a slight acquaintance of his). 'Would you believe it?'

'Well, now, Monsieur!' Danglars replied. 'I told you that Dantès put into Elba, for no apparent reason, and that this call seemed suspicious to me.'

'But did you tell anyone else of your suspicions?'

'I was careful not to do any such thing,' Danglars assured him, lowering his voice. 'You know very well that, on account of your uncle, Monsieur Policar Morrel, who served under you-know-whom and makes no secret of his feelings, you are suspected of hankering after the old regime. I would have been afraid I might harm Dantès and also yourself. There are some things that a subordinate has a duty to tell the owner, and to keep well hidden from anyone else.'

'Well done, Danglars, well done. You're a good fellow. I had already thought about you, in the event of poor Dantès becoming captain of the *Pharaon*.'

'How so, Monsieur?'

'Well, you see, I did ask Dantès what he thought of you and if he would have any objection to my leaving you in your post; I don't know why, but I thought I had noticed some coldness between you.'

'And what was his reply?'

'He told me that he did indeed feel that he had some grievance against you, though in circumstances that he would not explain; but that anyone who enjoyed the shipowner's confidence also had his own.'

'Hypocrite!' muttered Danglars.

'Poor Dantès,' said Caderousse. 'He was an excellent fellow, and that's a fact.'

'Yes, but meanwhile,' M. Morrel said, 'the *Pharaon* has no captain.'

'Oh, we must hope,' said Danglars, 'that, since we cannot sail again for three months, Dantès will be freed before then.'

'Of course, but in the meanwhile?'

'Well, Monsieur Morrel, in the meantime, I am here. As you know, I can manage a ship as well as the first ocean-going captain who may come along. It may even benefit you to use me, because when Edmond comes out of prison you will not have to dismiss anybody: he will quite simply resume his post and I mine.'

'Thank you, Danglars,' said the shipowner. 'That arranges everything. I therefore authorize you to take command and supervise the unloading: whatever disaster may befall an individual, business must not suffer.'

'Have no fear, Monsieur. But can we at least go and visit him? Poor Edmond!'

'I'll let you know as soon as I can, Danglars. I shall try to speak to Monsieur de Villefort and intercede with him on the prisoner's behalf. I know that he is a rabid Royalist; but, dammit, though he's a Royalist and the crown prosecutor, he is also a man and not, I believe, a wicked one.'

'No,' said Danglars. 'Though I have heard it said that he is ambitious, which is much the same.'

'Well, we shall find out,' M. Morrel said, with a sigh. 'Go on board and I'll join you there.'

He left the two friends, to make his way towards the law courts.

'You see how things are turning out?' Danglars said to Caderousse. 'Do you still want to go and speak for Dantès?'

'No, indeed not. But it is dreadful that a trick should have such dire consequences.'

'Pah! Who played the trick? Not you or I. You know very well that I threw the paper into a corner. I even thought I had torn it up.'

'No, no,' Caderousse insisted. 'As far as that goes, I am certain. I can see it in the corner of the arbour, screwed up in a ball – and I wish it were still in the place where I saw it.'

'What do you expect? Fernand must have picked it up, copied it or had it copied; perhaps he did not even take that trouble; which means . . . Good Lord! Suppose he sent my own letter! Luckily I disguised my handwriting.'

'But did you know that Dantès was a conspirator?'

'Did I know? I knew nothing at all. As I told you, I was making a joke, that's all. It seems that, like Harlequin, I spoke a true word in jest.'

'No matter,' said Caderousse. 'I'd give a great deal for this not to have happened, or at least not to be involved in it. You wait and see, Danglars! It will bring us misfortune!'

'If it brings misfortune, it will be to the guilty party, and the real responsibility lies with Fernand, not with us. What ill do you suppose could befall us? All we have to do is to keep quiet and not breathe a word of this, and the storm will blow over without striking us.'

'Amen!' Caderousse said, waving goodbye to Danglars and making his way towards the Allées de Meilhan, shaking his head and muttering to himself, as people are inclined to do when they have a good deal on their minds.

'Good!' Danglars exclaimed. 'Everything is working out as I expected. I am now captain *pro tem* and, if only that idiot Caderousse can keep his mouth shut, captain for good. So, the only other eventuality is that the Law may release Dantès? Ah, well,' he added, with a smile, 'the Law is the Law, and I am happy to put myself in her hands.'

Upon which, he leapt into a boat and gave the boatman the order to row him out to the *Pharaon* where the shipowner, as you will recall, had arranged to meet him.

VI

THE DEPUTY CROWN PROSECUTOR

That same day, at the same time, in the Rue du Grand-Cours, opposite the Fontaine des Méduses, a betrothal feast was also being celebrated, in one of those old buildings in the aristocratic style of the
architect Puget. However, instead of the participants in this other
scene being common people, sailors and soldiers, they belonged to
the cream of Marseillais society. There were former magistrates who
had resigned their appointments under the usurper, veteran officers
who had left our army to serve under Condé, and young men
brought up by families which were still uncertain about their security, despite the four or five substitutes that had been hired for them,
out of hatred for the man whom five years of exile were to make a
martyr, and fifteen years of Restoration, a god.[1]

They were dining and the conversation flowed back and forth,
fired by every passion – those passions of the time that were still
more terrible, ardent and bitter in the South where, for five
centuries, religious quarrels had seconded political ones.

The emperor, king of the island of Elba after having been ruler
of part of the world, exercising sovereignty over a population of
500 or 600 souls, when he had once heard the cry 'Long Live
Napoleon!' from 120 million subjects, in ten different languages,
was treated here as a man lost for ever to France and to the throne.
The magistrates picked on his political errors, the soldiers spoke
of Moscow and Leipzig, the women discussed his divorce from
Joséphine.[2] This Royalist gathering, rejoicing and triumphing not
in the fall of the man but in the annihilation of the idea, felt as
though life was beginning again and it was emerging from an
unpleasant dream.

An old man, decorated with the Cross of Saint-Louis,[3] rose and
invited his fellow-guests to drink the health of King Louis XVIII.
He was the Marquis de Saint-Méran.

At this toast, recalling both the exile of Hartwell[4] and the king
who had brought peace to France, there was a loud murmur.
Glasses were raised in the English manner, the women unpinned
their bouquets and strewed them over the tablecloth. There was
something almost poetical in their fervour.

'If they were here, they would be obliged to assent,' said the Marquise de Saint-Méran, a dry-eyed, thin-lipped woman with a bearing that was aristocratic and still elegant, despite her fifty years. 'If they were here, all those revolutionaries who drove us out and whom we, in turn, are leaving alone to conspire at their ease in our old châteaux, which they bought for a crust of bread during the Terror – they would be obliged to assent and acknowledge that the true dedication was on our side, since we adhered to a crumbling monarchy while they, on the contrary, hailed the rising sun and made their fortune from it, while we were losing ours. They would acknowledge that our own king was truly Louis le Bien-Aimé, the Well-Beloved, while their usurper, for his part, was never more than Napoléon le Maudit – the Accursed. Don't you agree, de Villefort?'

'What was that, Madame la Marquise? Excuse me, I was not following the conversation.'

'Come, come, let these children be, Marquise,' said the old man who had proposed the toast. 'They are to be married and, naturally enough, have other things to discuss besides politics.'

'I beg your pardon, mother,' said a lovely young woman with blonde hair and eyes of velvet, bathed in limpid pools. 'I shall give you back Monsieur de Villefort, whose attention I had claimed for a moment. Monsieur de Villefort, my mother is speaking to you.'

'I am waiting to answer Madame's question,' said M. de Villefort, 'if she will be so good as to repeat it, because I did not catch it the first time.'

'You are forgiven, Renée,' said the marquise, with a tender smile that it was surprising to see radiate from those dry features; but the heart of a woman is such that, however arid it may become when the winds of prejudice and the demands of etiquette have blown across it, there always remains one corner that is radiant and fertile – the one that God has dedicated to maternal love. 'You are forgiven ... Now, what I was saying, Villefort, is that the Bonapartists had neither our conviction, nor our enthusiasm, nor our dedication.'

'Ah, Madame, but they do at least have one thing that replaces all those, which is fanaticism. Napoleon is the Mohammed of the West. For all those masses of common people – though with vast ambitions – he is not only a lawgiver and a ruler, but also a symbol: the symbol of equality.'

'Napoleon!' the marquise exclaimed. 'Napoleon, a symbol of equality! And what about Monsieur de Robespierre? It seems to me that you are appropriating his place and giving it to the Corsican. One usurpation is enough, surely?'

'No, Madame,' said Villefort, 'I leave each of them on his own pedestal: Robespierre in the Place Louis XV, on his scaffold, and Napoleon in the Place Vendôme, on his column. The difference is that equality with the first was a levelling down and with the second a raising up: one of them lowered kings to the level of the guillotine, the other lifted the people to the level of the throne – which does not mean,' Villefort added, laughing, 'that they were not both vile revolutionaries, or that the 9th Thermidor and the 4th April 1814[5] are not two fortunate dates in the history of France, and equally worthy to be celebrated by all friends of order and the monarchy. However, it does explain why, even now that he has fallen (I hope, never to rise again), Napoleon still enjoys some support. What do you expect, Marquise: even Cromwell, who was not half the man that Napoleon used to be, had his followers.'

'Do you realize that there is a strong whiff of revolution in what you are saying, Villefort? But I forgive you: the son of a Girondin[6] is bound to be tarred with the same brush.'

Villefort's face flushed a deep red.

'It's true, Madame, that my father was a Girondin, but he did not vote for the death of the king. He was proscribed by the same Terror by which you yourself were proscribed, and narrowly escaped laying his head on the same scaffold as that on which your father's fell.'

'Yes,' the marquise replied, this bloody recollection not having produced the slightest alteration in her expression, 'but, had they both stepped on it, it would have been as men inspired by diametrically opposed principles. The proof is that my family remained loyal to the princes in exile, while your father hastened to rally to the new regime. After Citizen Noirtier was a Girondin, Comte Noirtier became a senator.'

'Mother, mother!' said Renée. 'You know we agreed that we should not mention these unfortunate matters again.'

'Madame,' Villefort replied, 'I join with Mademoiselle de Saint-Méran in humbly begging you to forget the past. What is the sense in recriminations about things over which the will of God itself is powerless? God can change the future, He cannot alter even an instant of the past. As for us, all we can do, since we are unable to repudiate it, is to draw a veil across it. Well, for my part, I have cut myself off not only from my father's opinions but also from his name. My father was, and perhaps still is, a Bonapartist named Noirtier; I am a Royalist, and am called de Villefort. Let the last remnants of the revolutionary sap perish in the old stem and see only the young shoot, Madame, which grows away from the trunk, though it is unable – I might almost say unwilling – to break with it altogether.'

'Bravo, Villefort,' said the marquis. 'Bravo! Well said! I, too, have always urged the Marquise to forget the past, but always in vain; I hope that you will be more successful.'

'Yes, yes, that is very well,' the marquise replied. 'Let us forget the past; I ask nothing better. But let Villefort at least be unyielding for the future. Remember, Villefort: we have answered for you to His Majesty and, on our insistence, His Majesty was willing to forget – just as . . .' (she offered him her hand) '. . . as I am, at your request. However, should any conspirator fall into your hands, remember that all eyes will be fixed upon you, the more so since it is known that you belong to a family which might perhaps have dealings with such conspirators.'

'Alas, Madame!' Villefort exclaimed. 'My office and, most of all, the times in which we live, require me to be harsh. I shall be so. I have already had some political cases to deal with and, in that respect, I have shown my mettle. Unfortunately, we are not finished yet.'

'You think so?' asked the marquise.

'I fear so. Napoleon is very close to France on the island of Elba, and his presence almost within sight of our coast sustains the hopes of his supporters. Marseille is full of officers on half pay who daily seek quarrels with the Royalists on some trivial pretext: this leads to duels among the upper classes and murders among the common people.'

'Yes,' said the Comte de Salvieux, an old friend of M. de Saint-Méran and chamberlain to the Comte d'Artois. 'Yes, but, as you know, he is being moved away by the Holy Alliance.'

'We heard speak of this as we were leaving Paris,' said M. de Saint-Méran. 'Where is he being sent?'

'To Saint Helena.'

'Saint Helena! What is that?' asked the marquise.

'An island lying two thousand leagues[7] from here, on the far side of the Equator,' the Comte replied.

'And about time! As Villefort says, it was a fine folly to leave such a man between Corsica where he was born, and Naples where his brother-in-law is still king, overlooking Italy, the country that he wanted to offer as a kingdom to his son.'

'Unfortunately,' said Villefort, 'there are the treaties of 1814, and Napoleon cannot be touched without breaching them.'

'Why, then, they shall be breached,' said M. de Salvieux. 'Was he himself so scrupulous, when it came to shooting the poor Duc d'Enghien?'[8]

'Yes,' the Marquise said. 'It's agreed. The Holy Alliance will cleanse Europe of Napoleon and Villefort will cleanse Marseille of his supporters. Either the king reigns or he does not: if he does, his government must be strong and its agents unyielding: that is how we shall prevent wrongdoing.'

'Unfortunately, Madame,' Villefort said, smiling, 'a deputy prosecutor to the Crown always arrives on the scene when the wrong has been done.'

'Then it is up to him to repair it.'

'To which I might again reply, Madame, that we do not repair wrongs, but avenge them, that is all.'

'Ah, Monsieur de Villefort,' said a pretty young thing, the daughter of the Comte de Salvieux and a friend of Mlle de Saint-Méran, 'do please try to have a fine trial while we are in Marseille. I have never been to a court of assizes, and I am told it is most interesting.'

'Most interesting, indeed, Mademoiselle, since it is a veritable drama and not an invented tragedy, real sorrows in place of ones that are merely feigned. The man that you see there, instead of returning home, once the curtain is lowered, to dine with his family and go peacefully to bed before starting again the next day, is taken into a prison, there to meet his executioner. You may well understand that, for nervous people who wish to experience strong sensations, no spectacle can equal it. Don't worry, Mademoiselle; if the opportunity arises, I shall present it to you.'

'He makes us shudder – yet he is laughing,' said Renée, going pale.

'What did you think? It is a duel. I have already five or six times asked for the death penalty against those accused of political crimes, or others. Well, who can tell how many daggers are at this very moment being sharpened in the shadows, or are already pointed at me?'

'Heavens!' Renée exclaimed, feeling increasingly faint. 'Are you really serious, Monsieur de Villefort?'

'I could not be more serious, Mademoiselle,' the young magistrate said with a smile. 'And the situation can only get worse with these fine trials that the young lady requires to satisfy her curiosity and which I require to satisfy my ambition. Do you imagine that all these soldiers of Napoleon's, who are accustomed to walk blindly in the direction of the enemy, pause to think before firing a shot or marching forward with fixed bayonets? And, in that case, will they hesitate to kill a man whom they consider their personal foe, any more than they would to kill a Russian, an Austrian or a Hungarian whom they have never set eyes on? In any case, you understand, this is as it should be, because without it there would be no excuse for my profession. As for me, when I see a bright spark of hatred shining in the eye of an accused man, I feel encouraged, I rejoice: it is no longer a trial, but a duel. I go for him, he ripostes, I press harder, and the fight ends, like all fights, in victory or defeat. That is what advocacy means! That is the risk run by eloquence. If a defendant were to smile at me after my speech, he would make me feel that I had spoken poorly, that what I had said was bland, inadequate and lacking in vigour. Imagine the feeling of pride a crown prosecutor experiences when he is convinced of the defendant's guilt and sees the guilty man go pale and bend under the weight of his evidence and the blast of his oratory! The head is lowered; it will fall.'

Renée gave a little cry.

'That's oratory for you,' said one of the guests.

'There's the man we need in times like these,' said another.

'And in your last case,' a third remarked, 'you were magnificent, my dear Villefort. You know: that man who murdered his father. Well, you literally killed him before the executioner had laid a hand on him.'

'Ah, if it's a matter of parricide,' Renée said, 'then I'm not bothered. There is no torture bad enough for such men. But those unfortunate political prisoners . . .'

'They are even worse, Renée, for the king is the father of the nation, so wishing to overthrow or kill the king is the same as wanting to kill the father of thirty-two million men.'

'Ah, but even so, Monsieur de Villefort,' said Renée, 'will you promise me to be indulgent towards those I commend to you?'

'Have no fear,' said Villefort, with his most charming smile. 'We shall prepare my speeches together.'

'My dearest,' said the marquise, 'you look after your little birds, your spaniels and your ribbons, and let your fiancé get on with his work. Nowadays, the sword has been put aside and the gown is supreme: there is a wise Latin tag to that effect.'

'*Cedant arma togae*,' Villefort said, with a bow.

'I did not dare attempt it in Latin,' the marquise replied.

'I think I should rather that you were a physician,' Renée went on. 'The exterminating angel may be an angel, but he has always terrified me.'

'My sweet!' Villefort murmured, enfolding her in a loving glance.

'Daughter,' the marquis said, 'Monsieur de Villefort will be the moral and political physician of our region. Believe me, that is a fine part to play.'

'Which will serve to obliterate the memory of the one played by his father,' added the incorrigible marquise.

'Madame,' Villefort replied with a sad smile, 'I have already had the honour of remarking to you that my father renounced the errors of his past; or, at least, I hope he did, and that he became an ardent friend of religion and order, perhaps a better Royalist than I am myself, since he was fired by repentance, whilst I am fired only by passion.'

After which well-turned phrases, Villefort looked at the guests to judge the effect of his oratory, as he might have looked up from the court towards the public gallery at the end of a similar declaration.

'Just so, my dear Villefort,' said the Comte de Salvieux. 'This is precisely what I replied to the Minister of the King's Household, two days ago in the Tuileries, when he asked me how I might explain this singular union between the son of a Girondin and the daughter of an officer in Condé's army; and the minister fully understood. This policy of alliances is that of Louis XVIII. Hence the king, who had been listening to our conversation without our knowing it, interrupted us in the following terms: "Villefort . . ." – observe that the king did not pronounce the name of Noirtier, but on the contrary stressed that of Villefort – "Villefort", he said, "has a bright future before him. He is a young man who is already mature, and one of us. I was pleased to see that the Marquis and Marquise of Saint-Méran were taking him as their son-in-law, and I should have recommended the match to them if they had not themselves come to ask my permission for it." '

'The king told you that, Comte?' Villefort exclaimed with delight.

'I give you his very words; and if the Marquis so wishes, he will frankly admit that what I am now telling you accords precisely with what the king told him when he himself spoke with His Majesty, six months ago, about the proposed marriage between you and his daughter.'

'That is true,' said the marquis.

'Ah! But this means I owe everything to that worthy monarch. What would I not do to serve him!'

'At last,' said the marquise. 'That is what I want to hear: let a conspirator come here now, and he will be welcome.'

'Speaking for myself, mother,' said Renée, 'I beg God that He does not listen to you, but sends Monsieur de Villefort only petty thieves, puny bankrupts and faint-hearted swindlers; in that case, I shall sleep easy.'

Villefort laughed: 'That is as if you were to wish on the physician nothing but migraines, measles and wasp stings, only ailments that are skin-deep. If, on the contrary, you wish to see me as crown prosecutor, you should wish on me those fearful illnesses that bring honour to the doctor who cures them.'

At this moment, as though chance had merely been waiting for Villefort to express the wish for it to be fulfilled, a valet entered and whispered something in his ear. Villefort excused himself and left the table, to return a few moments later with a smile and a delighted expression. Renée responded with a look of love, for the young man was truly elegant and handsome like this, with his blue eyes, his smooth complexion and the dark side-whiskers framing his face, so that she felt her whole being was hanging on his lips, waiting for him to explain the reason for his brief disappearance.

'Well, Mademoiselle,' said Villefort, 'a moment ago you wished to have a physician for your husband: I have this at least in common with the disciples of Aesculapius'[9] – they still spoke in such terms in 1815 – 'that my time is never my own and I may even be interrupted when I am beside you, celebrating our betrothal.'

'And for what reason were you interrupted, Monsieur?' the young woman asked, with slight misgiving.

'Alas, for a patient who, if I am to believe what I am told, is at the last extremity: this time it is a serious case, and the illness is on the verge of the scaffold.'

'Heaven preserve us!' Renée cried, paling.

'Truly!' the whole company exclaimed together.

'It seems that a little Bonapartist conspiracy has been uncovered, nothing less.'

'Can that be?' said the marquise.

'Here is the letter of denunciation.' And Villefort read:

The crown prosecutor is advised, by a friend of the monarchy and the faith, that one Edmond Dantès, first mate of the *Pharaon*, arriving this morning from Smyrna, after putting in at Naples and Porto Ferrajo, was entrusted by Murat with a letter for the usurper and by the usurper with a letter to the Bonapartist committee in Paris.

Proof of his guilt will be found when he is arrested, since the letter will be discovered either on his person, or at the house of his father, or in his cabin on board the *Pharaon*.

'But, this letter,' said Renée, 'which is, in any case, anonymous, is addressed to the crown prosecutor, and not to you.'

'Yes, but the crown prosecutor is away and in his absence the missive reached his secretary, who is entitled to open his letters. He opened this one and sent for me; when he did not find me, he gave orders for the arrest.'

'So the guilty man has been arrested,' said the marquise.

'You mean, the accused man,' said Renée.

'Yes, Madame,' Villefort replied. 'And, as I have just had the honour to tell Mademoiselle Renée, if the letter in question is found, the patient is indeed sick.'

'Where is this unfortunate man?' Renée asked.

'He is at my house.'

'Go, my friend,' said the marquis. 'Do not neglect your duty by staying with us, when the king's service demands your presence elsewhere: go where duty requires you.'

'Oh, Monsieur de Villefort,' Renée said, clasping her hands together. 'Have pity! This is the day of your betrothal.'

Villefort walked round the table and, coming to the girl's chair, rested his hand on the back of it and said:

'I should do whatever I could to spare you any anxiety, dear

Renée. But if the evidence is correct, if the accusation is true, then this Bonapartist weed must be cut down.'

Renée shuddered at the word *cut*, for the weed that was to be cut down had a head.

'Pah, pah!' said the marquise. 'Don't listen to this little girl, Villefort, she will get used to the idea.' And she offered him a dry hand which he kissed, while giving Renée a look that said: 'This is your hand I am kissing; or, at least, that I should like to be kissing.'

'Here is an ill omen!' Renée murmured.

'Mademoiselle,' said the marquise, 'your childishness is truly exasperating: what, may I ask, can the destiny of the State have to do with your sentimental fantasies and the mawkish movements of your heart?'

'Oh, mother!' Renée murmured.

'Be indulgent with her lack of royalist zeal, Madame la Marquise,' said de Villefort. 'I promise that I shall do my duty as the crown prosecutor's deputy conscientiously – that is to say, I shall be utterly pitiless.'

But, even as the magistrate was addressing these words to the marquise, the fiancé was surreptitiously giving his betrothed a look that said: 'Have no fear, Renée: for the sake of our love, I shall be merciful.' Renée replied to that look with her sweetest smile, and Villefort went out with heaven in his heart.

VII

THE INTERROGATION

Hardly had de Villefort left the dining-room than he put off his joyful mask to take on the serious mien of one called upon to exercise the supreme office of pronouncing on the life of his fellow man. However, despite the mobility of his expression, something which the deputy had studied more than once, as a skilled actor does, in front of his mirror, on this occasion it was an effort for him to lower his brow and darken his features. In reality, apart from the memory of his father's choice of political allegiance (which, if he did not himself completely renounce it, might affect his own career), Gérard de Villefort was at that moment as happy as it is possible for a man to be. At the age of twenty-six, already wealthy in his own right, he held a high office in the legal profession; and he was to marry a beautiful young woman whom he loved, not with passion, but reasonably, as a deputy crown prosecutor may love. Apart from her beauty, which was exceptional, his fiancée, Mlle de Saint-Méran, belonged to a family which was among those most highly thought of at court in this time; and, besides the influence of her mother and father (who, having no other children, could reserve it entirely for their son-in-law), she was in addition bringing her husband a dowry of fifty thousand *écus* which, thanks to her 'expectations' – that dreadful word invented by marriage brokers – might one day be increased by a legacy of half a million.

Hence, the addition of all these elements amounted for Villefort to a dazzling sum of felicity, to such an extent that he thought he was seeing sunspots when he had turned the eyes of his soul for any length of time on the contemplation of his inner life.

At the door, he found the police commissioner waiting for him. The sight of this sombre personage immediately brought him back from seventh heaven to the solid earth on which we all walk. He composed his features, as we mentioned, and approached the officer of the law: 'Here I am, Monsieur. I have read the letter, and you did well to arrest this man. Now tell me everything you know about him and the conspiracy.'

'As far as the conspiracy is concerned, Monsieur, we know nothing as yet. All the papers that we seized on him have been tied in a single bundle and deposited, sealed, on your desk. As for the detainee, you know from the letter denouncing him that he is one Edmond Dantès, first mate on board the three-master *Pharaon*, trading in cotton with Alexandria and Smyrna, and belonging to the house of Morrel and Son, of Marseille.'

'Did he serve in the Navy before joining the merchant marine?'

'No, Monsieur, he is quite a young man.'

'How old?'

'Nineteen . . . twenty, at most.'

At this moment, as Villefort was going down the Grande-Rue and had reached the corner of the Rue des Conseils, a man, who seemed to have been waiting there for him, came over. It was M. Morrel.

'Ah, Monsieur de Villefort!' the good man exclaimed. 'I am so pleased to see you. Can you imagine! The strangest, the most unheard-of mistake has been made: they have just arrested the first mate of my ship, Edmond Dantès.'

'I know, Monsieur,' said Villefort. 'I have come to question him.'

'My good sir,' said M. Morrel, carried away by his friendship for the young man. 'You do not know the person who is being accused; but I know him. He is the mildest, most honest man you could imagine, I might almost say the man who knows his job best of any in the merchant marine. Monsieur de Villefort, I commend him to you most sincerely and with all my heart!'

As we have seen, Villefort belonged to the nobility of the town and M. Morrel to the plebeian part of it: the former was an extreme Royalist, the latter suspected of harbouring Bonapartist sympathies. Villefort looked contemptuously at Morrel and answered coldly: 'You know, Monsieur, that one can be mild in one's private life, honest in one's business dealings and skilled in one's work, yet at the same time, politically speaking, be guilty of great crimes. You do know that, I suppose, Monsieur?'

He emphasized these last words, as if intending to apply them to the shipowner himself, while his enquiring look seemed to search right into the innermost soul of a man who had tried to intervene on behalf of another, when he should have realized that he was himself in need of indulgence.

Morrel blushed, for his conscience was not altogether clear on the point of his political opinions. In any case, his mind was slightly troubled by the confidential information that Dantès had given him about his talk with the marshal and the few words that the emperor had addressed to him. However, he added in tones of the most urgent pleading: 'I beg you, Monsieur de Villefort, be just, as it is your duty to be, and generous, as you always are, and soon restore poor Dantès *to us*.'

This *restore to us* had a revolutionary ring to the ears of the crown prosecutor's deputy.

'Well, well!' he muttered to himself. '*To us* . . . Can this Dantès be a member of some sect of *carbonari*,[1] for his protector to employ that collective expression without being aware that he was doing so? I seem to understand from the commissioner that he was arrested in a cabaret, and he added, in a large gathering: this was some kind of *vente*.'

Then, in reply, he said aloud: 'Monsieur, you may rest entirely assured and you will not have appealed to me in vain if the detainee is innocent; but if, on the contrary, he is guilty ... We live in difficult times, Monsieur, when impunity would be the worst of examples: I shall thus be obliged to do my duty.'

Upon that, having arrived at the door of his house, which backed on to the law courts, he stepped majestically inside, after giving an icy bow to the unhappy shipowner, who remained as if rooted to the spot where Villefort had left him.

The anteroom was full of gendarmes and police officers; and in the midst of them, under close arrest, surrounded by faces burning with hatred, the prisoner stood, calm and motionless.

Villefort crossed the anteroom, gave a sidelong glance in the direction of Dantès and, taking a dossier that was handed to him by one of the officers, vanished, saying: 'Let the prisoner be brought in.'

Swift though it was, the glance had been enough to give Villefort an idea of the man whom he would have to question: he had recognized intelligence in that broad forehead, courage in that firm eye and knitted brow, and candour in those full lips, half-parted to reveal two rows of teeth as white as ivory.

First impressions had been favourable to Dantès, but Villefort had often heard it said, as a profound political maxim, that one must beware of first impulses, even when they were correct, and he applied this rule on impulses to his impressions, without taking account of the difference between the two terms. He thus stifled the good instinct that was attempting to invade his heart and from there to attack his mind, settled his features in front of the mirror into their grandest expression and sat down, dark and threatening, behind his desk.

A moment later, Dantès entered.

The young man was still pale, but calm and smiling. He greeted his judge in a simple but courteous manner, and looked around for somewhere to sit, as though he had been in the shipowner, M. Morrel's drawing-room.

It was only then that he met Villefort's dull gaze, that look peculiar to men of the law who do not want anyone to read their thoughts, and so make their eyes into unpolished glass. The look reminded him that he was standing before Justice, a figure of grim aspect and manners.

'Who are you and what's your name?' Villefort asked, leafing through the notes that the officer had given him as he came in and which, in the past hour, had already become a voluminous pile, so quickly does the mound of reports and information build up around that unfortunate body known as detainees.

'My name is Edmond Dantès, Monsieur,' the young man replied in a calm voice and ringing tones. 'I am first mate on board the vessel *Pharaon*, belonging to Messrs Morrel and Son.'

'Your age?' Villefort continued.

'Nineteen.'

'What were you doing at the time of your arrest?'

'I was celebrating my betrothal, Monsieur,' Dantès said, his voice faltering slightly, so sharp was the contrast between those moments of happiness and the dismal formalities in which he was now taking part, and so much did the sombre face of M. de Villefort enhance the brilliance of Mercédès' features.

'You were at your betrothal feast?' said the deputy, shuddering in spite of himself.

'Yes, Monsieur. I am about to marry a woman whom I have loved for the past three years.'

Though usually impassive, nevertheless Villefort was struck by this coincidence; and the emotion in the voice of Dantès, whose happiness had been interrupted, sounded a sympathetic chord with him: he too was to be married, he too was happy, and his own felicity had been disturbed so that he might help to destroy that of a man who, like himself, was on the very brink of happiness.

This philosophical analogy, he thought, would cause a great stir when he returned to M. de Saint-Méran's salon; and, while Dantès waited for his next question, he was already mentally ordering the antitheses around which orators construct those sentences designed to elicit applause, but which sometimes produce the illusion of true eloquence.

When he had worked out his little interior discourse, Villefort smiled at the effect of it and returned to Dantès: 'Continue, Monsieur.'

'How do you wish me to continue?'

'In such a way as to enlighten Justice.'

'Let Justice tell me on which points it wishes to be enlightened, and I shall tell it all that I know. However,' he added, smiling in his turn, 'I must warn it that I know very little.'

'Did you serve under the usurper?'

'I was about to be enrolled in the Navy when he fell.'

'Your political opinions are reported to be extreme,' said Ville-fort, who had not heard a word about this but was not averse to putting the question in the form of an accusation.

'My political opinions, Monsieur? Alas, I am almost ashamed to admit it, but I have never had what you might call an opinion: I am barely nineteen, as I had the honour to tell you. I know nothing and I am not destined to play any public role. The little that I am and shall be, if I gain the position to which I aspire, I owe to Monsieur Morrel. So all my opinions – I would not say political, but private opinions – are confined to three feelings: I love my father, I respect Monsieur Morrel and I adore Mercédès. That, Monsieur, is all I can tell Justice: you see that there is little to interest it there.'

While Dantès was speaking, Villefort examined his face, at once so mild and so frank, and recalled the words of Renée who, without knowing the prisoner, had begged indulgence for him. The deputy already had some acquaintance with crime and with criminals; so, in every word that Dantès spoke, he saw proof of his innocence. This young man, one might even say this child, plain, unaffected, eloquent with the heartfelt eloquence that is never found by those who seek it, full of affection for everyone, because he was happy and happiness makes even wicked men good, was so effectively spreading the warmth that overflowed from his heart that the accuser himself was not immune to it. Rough and stern though Villefort had been towards him, Edmond's look, tone and gestures expressed nothing but kindness and goodwill towards his interrogator.

'By heaven,' Villefort thought, 'this is a charming young man; and I hope I shall not have great difficulty in putting myself on the right side of Renée, by carrying out the first request that she has made of me. It should earn me a warm clasp of the hand in front of everyone and a delightful kiss in a more secluded corner.'

This pleasurable expectation lit up Villefort's face, so that, when he turned away from his thoughts and back to Dantès, the latter, who had been following every movement across his judge's face, reflected his thoughts in a smile.

'Monsieur,' said Villefort, 'do you know of any enemies you may have?'

'Enemies!' said Dantès. 'I am fortunate enough to be too unim-portant to have any. As to temperament, I may perhaps be a trifle quick-tempered, but I have always tried to restrain it towards my subordinates. I have ten or a dozen sailors under my orders: let them be questioned, Monsieur, and they will tell you that they like and respect me, not as a father – I am too young for that – but as an elder brother.'

'But, if you have no enemies, you may have inspired envy: you are about to be made captain at the age of nineteen, which is a distinction for someone of your class; you are about to marry a pretty girl who loves you, which is a rare fortune for someone of any class at all. Fortune having favoured you in these ways, you may have aroused jealousy.'

'Yes, you are right. You must know human nature better than I do, and what you say is possible. But I confess that if these envious men were to be among my friends, I should rather not know who they are, so as not to be obliged to hate them.'

'You are wrong, Monsieur. One must always see clearly how one stands, as far as possible; and, frankly, you seem to me such a worthy young man that in your case I am going to depart from the normal procedure and help you to throw light on this by showing you the denunciation that has led to your being brought here. This is the accusing letter: do you recognize the writing?'

Villefort took the letter from his pocket and offered it to Dantès, who examined it. His face clouded and he said:

'No, Monsieur, I do not know this handwriting. It is disguised, yet it has an appearance of sincerity. In any case, the writing is that of an educated hand.' He looked at Villefort with gratitude. 'I am happy to find myself dealing with a man such as you, because my rival is indeed a true enemy.'

From the flash that passed through the young man's eyes as he spoke these words, Villefort was able to perceive how much violent energy was hidden beneath his mild exterior.

'Come, then,' said the deputy prosecutor, 'answer my questions honestly, not as an accused man to his judge, but as one wrongly accused might answer another who had his interests at heart. How much truth is there in this anonymous accusation?'

And Villefort threw the letter, which Dantès had just given back to him, on to the desk with a gesture of distaste.

'Everything and nothing, Monsieur: that is the absolute truth, on my honour as a sailor, on my love for Mercédès and on my father's life.'

'Carry on,' Villefort said, adding under his breath: 'If Renée could see me, I hope she would be pleased and no longer call me an executioner.'

'When we left Naples, Captain Leclère fell ill of a brain fever. As we had no doctor on board ship and, because of his haste to reach Elba, he did not want to drop anchor at any point along the coast, his illness worsened until, after three days, realizing that he was dying, he called to see me.

'"My dear Dantès," he said, "swear on your honour to do what I ask of you. This is a matter of the highest importance."

'I swore to do as he asked.

'"Very well. As second-in-command, responsibility for the vessel will fall on you after my death, so I wish you to take command, set course for Elba, disembark at Porto Ferrajo, ask for the marshal and give him this letter. It may be that you will be given another letter and be told to carry out some mission. That mission, which I should have accomplished, Dantès, you will perform in my stead and the honour will be yours."

'"I shall do it, Captain; but it may be more difficult than you think for me to see the marshal."

'"Here is a ring," the captain said. "Make sure that he gets it and all barriers will be removed."

'On this, he gave me a ring. It was none too soon: two hours later, he lapsed into a delirium and, on the next day, he died.'

'Then what did you do?'

'What I had to do, Monsieur, and what anyone would have done in my place. In all events, a dying man's wishes are sacred, but to a sailor the wishes of a superior officer are orders which must be carried out. So I set sail for Elba, arriving there the next day, when I confined everyone to the ship and disembarked alone. As I had foreseen, there was some difficulty in gaining an audience with the marshal, but I sent him the ring which was to serve as a token for me, and all doors were opened. He received me, questioned me on the circumstances of poor Leclère's last hours and, as the captain had predicted, gave me a letter which he told me to take, in person, to Paris. I promised to do so, since these were my captain's final wishes. I made land and quickly settled everything that had to be done on board; then I went to see my fiancée, whom I found more lovely and more loving than ever. Thanks to Monsieur Morrel, we were able to circumvent all the formalities of the Church and at last, as I told you, Monsieur, I was celebrating my betrothal. I was to be married in an hour and expected to leave for Paris tomorrow, when I was arrested, on the basis of this denunciation that you seem to despise as much as I do.'

'Yes, yes,' Villefort muttered. 'I am convinced by your story and, if you are guilty, it is only of imprudence. Even that is excused by your captain's order. Let me have the letter that was entrusted to you on Elba, give me your word that you will appear at the first summons and you can rejoin your friends.'

'So I am free to go!' Dantès exclaimed.

'Yes, provided you give me the letter.'

'It must be in front of you, Monsieur, because it was taken with my other papers, some of which I recognize in that bundle.'

'Wait,' the lawyer told Dantès, who was picking up his hat and gloves. 'To whom was it addressed?'

'To Monsieur Noirtier, Rue Coq-Héron, in Paris.'

If a bolt of lightning had struck Villefort, it could not have done so with greater suddenness or surprise. He fell back into the chair from which he had half-risen to reach over to the bundle of papers that had been taken from Dantès; and, hastily going through them, drew out the fatal letter, on which he cast a look of unspeakable terror.

'Monsieur Noirtier, Rue Coq-Héron, number 13,' he muttered, the colour draining from his face.

'Yes, Monsieur,' Dantès replied in astonishment. 'Do you know him?'

'No!' Villefort answered emphatically. 'A faithful servant of the king does not know conspirators.'

'Is this a matter of conspiracy, then?' Dantès asked, starting to feel even greater anxiety than before, having just thought he would be free. 'In any event, Monsieur, as I told you, I had no idea what was in the dispatch that I carried.'

'Perhaps not,' Villefort said grimly, 'but you did know the name of the person to whom it was addressed!'

'In order for me to give it to him myself, Monsieur, I had to know his name.'

'And you have not shown this letter to anyone?' Villefort asked, reading and growing paler as he read.

'To no one, Monsieur, on my honour!'

'Nobody knows that you were the bearer of a letter from Elba addressed to Monsieur Noirtier?'

'Nobody, Monsieur, except the person who gave it to me.'

'That is one too many, even so,' Villefort muttered, his brow clouding as he read towards the end. His pale lips, trembling hands and burning eyes excited the most painful anxiety in Dantès' mind.

After reading, Villefort put his head in his hands and stayed like it for an instant, overcome.

'Heavens, Monsieur, what is it?' Dantès asked fearfully.

Villefort did not reply but remained like that for a short time, then he looked up, with pale and troubled features, and read the letter once more.

'You say that you have no idea what is in this letter?' he asked.

'I repeat, on my honour, Monsieur,' said Dantès, 'that I do not know. But for goodness' sake, what is wrong with you? You must be feeling unwell. Would you like me to ring, would you like me to call someone?'

'Certainly not,' said Villefort, rising abruptly. 'Don't move or say a word. I am the one who gives orders here, not you.'

'Monsieur,' Dantès said, hurt, 'I wanted to help you, that's all.'

'I don't need any help. I felt dizzy for a moment, nothing more. Look to yourself, not to me. Answer me.'

Dantès was expecting this request to be followed by further questioning, but none came. Villefort slumped into his chair, passed an icy hand across a brow dripping with sweat, and began, for the third time, to read the letter.

'Oh, if he does know what is in this letter,' he thought, 'and if he should ever learn that Noirtier is Villefort's father, I am lost – lost utterly!'

From time to time he glanced at Edmond, as if his look might pierce the invisible barrier that holds secrets in the heart so that they do not pass the lips.

'Ah! Let there be no further doubt!' he exclaimed suddenly.

'But, in heaven's name, Monsieur!' the unfortunate young man cried. 'If your doubts are on my score, if you suspect me, then question me, I am ready to answer you.'

Villefort made a violent effort to control himself and said, in a voice that he tried to keep firm: 'Monsieur, your interrogation has brought up the most serious charges against you, so I am no longer able, as I had first hoped, to set you free immediately. Before I can take that step, I must consult the examining magistrates. Meanwhile, you have seen how I have treated you.'

'Oh, yes, Monsieur,' Dantès exclaimed, 'and I thank you, because you have been more of a friend to me than a judge.'

'Well, I must keep you prisoner a little while longer, but for as short a time as I can. The main charge against you is the existence of this letter, and you see . . .'

Villefort went over to the fireplace, threw the letter into the fire and waited until it was reduced to ashes.

'. . . and you see, I have destroyed it.'

'Monsieur!' Dantès exclaimed. 'You are more than justice, you are goodness itself!'

'But listen to me,' Villefort continued. 'After seeing me do that, you realize that you can trust me, don't you?'

'Order me, Monsieur, and I shall obey you.'

'No,' Villefort said, coming across to the young man. 'No, I shall not give you any orders, you understand: I shall give you some advice.'

'Do so, and I shall follow it as though it were an order.'

'I am going to keep you until evening, here, at the Palais de Justice. Someone else may come and question you: tell him everything you told me, but don't say a word about the letter.'

'I promise not to, Monsieur.'

It seemed as though it was Villefort who was begging and the prisoner who was reassuring his judge.

'You understand,' he went on, looking towards the ashes which still retained the shape of the paper. 'Now that the letter has been destroyed, only you and I know that it ever existed. You will never see it again, so deny it if anyone mentions it to you; deny it boldly and you will be saved.'

'Have no fear, Monsieur, I shall deny it,' Dantès said.

'Good, good!' Villefort exclaimed, reaching for a bell-pull. Then he stopped as he was about to ring and said: 'Was that the only letter that you had?'

'The only one.'

'Swear to me.'

Dantès held out his hand. 'I swear.'

Villefort rang and the police commissioner came in. Villefort went up to the officer and whispered a few words in his ear. The commissioner answered with a nod.

'Follow this gentleman,' Villefort told Dantès.

Dantès bowed, gave Villefort a last look of gratitude and went out. No sooner had the door shut behind him than the strength drained out of Villefort's body and he fell, almost unconscious, into a chair. Then, after a moment, he muttered: 'Oh, my Lord! On what slender threads do life and fortune hang . . . ! If the crown prosecutor had been in Marseille or if the examining magistrate had been called in my place, I should have been lost: that paper, that accursed piece of paper would have plunged me into the abyss. Father! Will you always be an obstacle to my happiness in this world, and shall I always have to contend with your past!'

Then, suddenly, it seemed as though a light had unexpectedly passed through his mind and lit up his face. A smile rose to his still clenched lips, while his distraught look became a stare and his mind appeared to concentrate on a single idea.

'That's it,' he said. 'This letter, which should have destroyed me, might perhaps make my fortune. Come, Villefort, to work!'

After making sure that the prisoner was no longer in the antechamber, the deputy prosecutor also went out and began to make his way briskly towards his fiancée's house.

VIII

THE CHÂTEAU D'IF

Crossing the antechamber, the commissioner of police gestured to two gendarmes, who took up their positions on either side of Dantès. A door leading from the chambers of the crown prosecutor to the law courts was opened, and they went along one of those long dark corridors that inspire a shudder in all who enter them, even when they have no cause to fear.

Just as Villefort's chambers gave access to the Palais de Justice, so the Palais de Justice gave access to the prison, a sombre pile overlooked by the bell-tower of Les Accoules, which rises opposite and examines it with curiosity from every gaping aperture.

After several twists and turns in the corridor down which they went, Dantès saw a door with an iron wicket open before him. The police commissioner knocked on it with a little hammer, and the three blows sounded to Dantès as though they had been struck against his heart. The door opened and the two gendarmes gently pushed their prisoner forward, for he still hung back. Dantès crossed the awful threshold and the door closed noisily behind him. He now breathed a different atmosphere, where the air was heavy and sulphurous: he was in prison.

He was taken to a cell that was quite clean, despite the bars and locks; the appearance of his surroundings consequently did not arouse too much fear in him. In any case, the deputy prosecutor's words, spoken in tones that seemed to Dantès to express such concern, still echoed in his ears like a sweet promise of hope.

It was already four o'clock when Dantès was led into his cell. As we have already mentioned, it was March the first, so the prisoner would soon be in darkness. His hearing became more acute as his sight dimmed and, at the slightest sound which reached him, convinced that they were coming to set him free, he leapt up and took a step towards the door; but the noise soon faded as it vanished in another direction, and Dantès slumped back on to his stool.

Finally, at around ten o'clock in the evening, just as he was starting to lose hope, he heard a new sound that, this time, really did seem to be coming towards his cell. And, indeed, there were steps in the corridor that halted in front of his door. A key turned in the lock, the bolts creaked and the huge mass of oak moved open, suddenly filling the room with the dazzling light of two torches, in which Dantès could see the shining sabres and muskets of four gendarmes.

He had taken two steps forward, but stopped in his tracks at the sight of this increased force.

'Have you come for me?' he asked.

'Yes,' one of the gendarmes replied.

'On behalf of Monsieur the deputy crown prosecutor?'

'I suppose so.'

'Very well,' Dantès replied. 'I am ready to go with you.'

Certain that it was M. de Villefort who had sent for him, the unfortunate young man had no apprehension and went out calmly, with easy steps, to station himself between the soldiers who formed his escort.

A carriage was waiting at the street door, the driver was on his seat and there was a police officer sitting beside him.

'Has this carriage come for me?' Dantès asked.

'It's for you,' one of the gendarmes replied. 'Get in.'

Dantès wanted to say something, but the door opened and he felt a shove. He had neither the opportunity to resist nor any intention of doing so. At once he found himself seated inside the carriage between two gendarmes, while the two others took their place on the bench at the front and the heavy vehicle began to move forward with a sinister rumble.

The prisoner looked at the windows, which were barred: he had merely exchanged one prison for another, with the difference that this one was moving and taking him to some unknown destination. However, through the bars which were so closely set that a hand could barely pass between them, Dantès could observe that they were proceeding down the Rue Caisserie, then the Rue Saint-Laurent and the Rue Taramis, heading towards the port.

Soon, through his own bars and those of the monument beside which they had stopped, he saw the bright lights of the Detention Barracks.

The carriage stopped, the police officer got down and went across to the guardroom. A dozen soldiers emerged and formed ranks. Dantès could see their rifles shining in the reflection from the dockside lamps.

'Can it be for me,' he wondered, 'that they are deploying all these men?'

The officer unlocked the door and, in doing so, answered his question without speaking a word, for Dantès could see that a path had been opened for him between the two lines of soldiers, leading down to the quayside.

The two gendarmes who were sitting on the front bench got out first; then he himself was taken out, followed by those who had been sitting beside him. They set off towards a dinghy that a boatman of the Customs was holding against the quay by a chain. The soldiers watched Dantès go past with a look of dumb curiosity. In an instant he was placed in the stern of the boat, still between the four gendarmes, while the officer stood in the bow. With a violent shudder, the boat was pushed away from the quay and four oarsmen began to row vigorously towards the Pillon. At a cry from the boat, the chain across the entrance to the port was lowered and Dantès found himself in the area known as the Frioul, that is to say, outside the harbour.

The prisoner's first reaction at finding himself outside had been one of joy. The open air was almost freedom. He drew deep breaths,

to fill his lungs with the sharp breeze that carries on its wings all
the unknown perfumes of the night and the sea. Soon, however, he
sighed: they were rowing in front of the same Réserve where he
had been so happy that very morning in the hour before his arrest;
and, through two brightly lit windows, he could hear the merry
sounds of a ball drifting towards him.

He clasped his hands together, raised his eyes to heaven and
prayed.

The boat continued on its way. It had passed by the Tête du
Maure and was opposite the cove of the Pharo. It was about to
round the Battery, and this Dantès could not understand.

'But where are you taking me?' he asked one of the gendarmes.

'You will know soon enough.'

'But, even so . . .'

'We are not allowed to tell you anything.'

Being half a soldier himself, Dantès knew that it was ridiculous
to ask questions of subordinates who had been forbidden to reply,
so he kept silent. However, the strangest ideas crowded through
his brain. Since they could not go far in a boat of this size, and
there was no ship at anchor in the direction towards which they
were heading, he thought that they must be going to put him ashore
on some distant part of the coast and tell him he was free. He was
not bound, and no attempt had been made to handcuff him: this
seemed like a good sign. In any case, had not the deputy prosecutor
told him that, provided he did not mention the dread name of
Noirtier, he had nothing to fear? Had not Villefort, in his very
presence, destroyed the dangerous letter which was the only proof
they had against him?

So he waited, silent and deep in thought, trying to penetrate the
blackness of night with his sailor's eye, accustomed to darkness
and familiar with space.

On their right, they had left behind the Ile Ratonneau, with its
lighthouse, and, almost following the line of the coast, they had
arrived opposite the bay of the Catalans. Here, the prisoner looked
with still greater intensity: here Mercédès lived and he felt at every
instant that he could see the vague and ill-defined shape of a woman
on the dark shore. Was it possible that Mercédès had been warned
by some presentiment that her lover was going by, only three
hundred yards away?

There was only one light burning in the Catalan village. By

studying its position, Dantès realized that it came from his fiancée's room. Mercédès was the only person still awake in the whole of the little colony. If the young man were to shout loudly, his fiancée might hear him. But a false feeling of shame prevented him. What would these men who were watching him say, if he cried out like a madman? So he stayed silent, staring at the light. Meanwhile the boat continued on its way; but the prisoner was not thinking about the boat: he was thinking of Mercédès.

The light disappeared behind a small hill. Dantès turned around and noticed that they were making for the open sea. While he had been looking ashore, taken up with his thoughts, sails had been substituted for the oars and the boat was now being driven before the wind.

Despite his reluctance to ask the gendarme any further questions, Dantès moved over to him and took his hand.

'Comrade,' he said, 'in the name of your conscience and as a soldier, I beg you to have pity on me and to give me an answer. I am Captain Dantès, a good and loyal Frenchman, even though I have been accused of I-know-not-what act of treason. Where are you taking me? Tell me, and I swear as a sailor that I will answer to the call of duty and resign myself to my fate.'

The gendarme scratched his ear and looked at his fellow. The latter made a sign that roughly indicated: since we have gone this far, I see no objection; and the gendarme turned back to Dantès.

'You are a Marseillais and a sailor, and you ask me where we are going?'

'Yes, because, on my honour, I don't know.'

'You haven't guessed?'

'Not at all.'

'That's not possible.'

'I swear by all that is most sacred to me in the world. I beg you, tell me!'

'What about my instructions?'

'Your instructions do not forbid you to inform me of something that I shall know in ten minutes, or half an hour, or perhaps an hour. Yet, between now and then, you can spare me centuries of uncertainty. I ask this of you as though you were my friend. Look: I am not trying to resist or to escape. In any case it would be impossible. Where are we going?'

'Unless you are blindfolded, or you have never been outside the port of Marseille, then you must surely guess where you are going.'

'No.'

'But look around you . . .'

Dantès got up and naturally turned his eyes to the point towards which the boat appeared to be heading: some two hundred yards in front of them loomed the sheer black rock from which, like a flinty excrescence, rises the Château d'If.[1]

To Dantès, who had not been thinking about it at all, the sudden appearance of this strange shape, this prison shrouded in such deep terror, this fortress which for three centuries has nourished Marseille with its gloomy legends, had the same effect as the spectacle of the scaffold on a condemned man.

'My God!' he cried. 'The Château d'If! Why are we going there?'

The gendarme smiled.

'You can't be taking me to incarcerate me there?' Dantès continued. 'The Château d'If is a state prison, meant only for major political criminals. I haven't committed any crime. Are there examining magistrates or any other sort of judges in the Château d'If?'

'As far as I know, only a governor, jailers, a garrison and solid walls. Come now, my friend, don't be so surprised, or I'll think you are showing your gratitude for my indulgence by making fun of me.'

Dantès grasped the gendarme's hand with crushing force.

'Are you telling me, then, that I am being taken to the Château d'If to be imprisoned there?'

'It seems like it,' said the gendarme. 'But, in any case, my friend, it won't do you any good to grip my hand so tightly.'

'Without any further enquiry or formalities?' the young man asked.

'The formalities have been gone through and the enquiry made.'

'Like that, despite Monsieur de Villefort's promise?'

'I don't know what Monsieur de Villefort promised you,' said the gendarme. 'All I do know is that we're going to the Château d'If. Hey, there! What are you doing? Hold on! Give me a hand here!'

With a movement as swift as lightning, though not swift enough, even so, to escape the gendarme's practised eye, Dantès tried to leap overboard but was held back just as his feet left the planks of the boat, into which he fell back, screaming furiously.

'Fine!' the gendarme exclaimed, kneeling on his chest. 'Fine! So that is how you keep your word as a sailor. Still waters run deep! Well now, my good friend, make a single movement, just one, and I'll put a shot in your head. I disobeyed my first instruction, but I guarantee you that I shall not fail to abide by the second.'

He gave every indication of his intention to carry out his threat, lowering his musket until Dantès could feel the barrel pressing against his temple.

For an instant he considered making the forbidden movement and so putting a violent end to the misfortune that had swooped down and suddenly seized him in its vulture's grip. But, precisely because the misfortune was so unexpected, Dantès felt that it could not be long-lasting. Then he remembered M. de Villefort's promises. And finally, it must be admitted that death in the bilge of an open boat at the hands of a gendarme struck him as ugly and grim. So he fell back on to the planks of the vessel with a cry of rage, gnawing at his fists in his fury.

Almost at the same moment, the boat shook violently. One of the oarsmen leapt on the rock that had just struck against its prow, a rope groaned as it unwound from a pulley, and Dantès realized that they had arrived and the skiff was being moored.

His guards, holding him simultaneously by his arms and the collar of his jacket, forced him to get up, obliged him to go ashore, and dragged him towards the steps leading up to the gate of the fortress, while the officer took up the rear, armed with a musket and bayonet.

In any case, Dantès did not attempt to struggle pointlessly: his slowness was the result of inertia rather than resistance. He stumbled dizzily like a drunken man. Once more he could see soldiers lined up along the steep embankment. He felt the steps obliging him to lift his feet and noticed that he was passing beneath a gateway and that the gate was closing behind him, but all of this in a daze, as if through a mist, without clearly perceiving anything. He could no longer even distinguish the sea, that vast sorrow of prisoners who stare into space with the awful feeling that they are powerless to cross it.

There was a momentary pause, during which he tried to gather his wits. He looked around him: he was in a square courtyard, enclosed within four high walls. He could hear the slow, regular footfalls of the sentries and, each time they passed in front of the two or three reflections cast on the walls by the light of as many lamps burning inside the castle, it reflected on the muzzles of their guns.

They waited there for about ten minutes. Certain that Dantès could not escape, the gendarmes had released their hold on him. They appeared to be waiting for orders, which eventually came.

'Where is the prisoner?' asked a voice.

'Here,' one of the gendarmes replied.

'Let him follow me, I'll conduct him to his cell.'

'Come on,' the gendarmes said, shoving Dantès forward.

The prisoner followed his guide, who led him into a room that was nearly underground, its bare, dripping walls seemingly impregnated with a vapour of tears. A species of lamp, on a wooden stool, its wick drowning in fetid oil, lit the shining walls of this appalling abode and showed Dantès his guide, a sort of subordinate jailer, poorly dressed and coarse-featured.

'Here is your room for tonight,' he said. 'It is late and the governor has gone to bed. Tomorrow, when he wakes up and can examine his instructions concerning you, he may move you elsewhere. Meanwhile, here is some bread, you have water in that jar and straw over there in the corner. That is all a prisoner can want. Good night to you.'

Before Dantès could open his mouth to reply, let alone see where the jailer was putting the bread or the place where the jar stood, and look over to the corner where the straw was waiting to make him a bed, the jailer had taken the lamp and, shutting the door, denied the prisoner even the dim light that had shown him, as though in a flash of lightning, the streaming walls of his prison. So he found himself alone in the silence and darkness, as black and noiseless as the icy cold of the vaults which he could feel pressing down on his feverish brow.

When the first rays of dawn started to bring a little light into this den, the jailer returned with orders to leave the prisoner where he was. Dantès had not moved. An iron hand seemed to have nailed him to the very spot where he had stopped the night before: only his deep-set eyes were now hidden behind the swelling caused by the moisture of his tears. He was motionless, staring at the floor. He had spent the whole night in this way, standing, and not sleeping for an instant.

The jailer came over to him and walked round him, but Dantès appeared not to notice. He tapped him on the shoulder, and Dantès shuddered and shook his head.

'Haven't you slept?' asked the jailer.

'I don't know,' Dantès replied. The jailer looked at him in astonishment.

'Aren't you hungry?'

'I don't know,' Dantès replied again.

'Do you want anything?'

'I want to see the governor.'

The jailer shrugged his shoulders and went out. Dantès looked after him, stretched his hands out towards the half-open door, but it was closed again. At this his chest seemed to be torn apart by a profound sob. The tears that filled it burst out like two streams, he fell down, pressed his face to the ground and prayed for a long time, mentally going through the whole of his past life and wondering what crime he had committed in so brief a span that could merit such cruel punishment.

So the day was spent. He ate hardly more than a few mouthfuls of bread and drank a few drops of water. At times he remained seated, wrapped in thought; at others, he paced around his prison like a wild animal trapped in an iron cage.

One thought struck him with particular force. It was this: that during the crossing when, not knowing where they were taking him, he had remained so calm and docile, there had been a dozen times when he could have jumped overboard and, once in the water, thanks to an ability that made him one of the most skilful divers in Marseille, have vanished beneath the waves, evaded his captors, reached the shore, fled, hidden in some deserted bay, waited for a Genoese or Catalan ship, gone to Italy or Spain, and from there written to Mercédès to join him. As for a livelihood, he had no misgivings in any country: good sailors are everywhere in short supply. He spoke Italian like a Tuscan and Spanish like a son of Old Castile. He would have lived in freedom, happy, with Mercédès and with his father – because his father would come to join them. Yet here he was, a prisoner, shut up in this impregnable fortress, in the Château d'If, not knowing what had become of his father or what had become of Mercédès, and all because he had trusted Villefort's word. Dantès thought he would go mad, and he rolled in fury on the fresh straw that his jailer had brought him.

The following day, at the same hour, the jailer came in.

'Well,' he asked, 'are you in a more reasonable frame of mind than yesterday?'

Dantès did not answer.

'Come now, pull yourself together! Is there anything you need that I can get you? Tell me.'

'I want to speak to the Governor.'

'Pah!' the jailer said impatiently. 'I've already told you that's impossible.'

'Why is it impossible?'

'Because, under the prison regulations, a prisoner is not allowed to make that request.'

'And what is allowed here?' Dantès asked.

'Better food, if you pay; walks; and sometimes books.'

'I have no need of books, I have no desire to walk and my food suits me well; so there is only one thing I want, which is to see the Governor.'

'If you get on my nerves by repeating the same thing over and over,' said the jailer, 'I shall stop bringing you any food at all.'

'Well, then,' said Dantès, 'if you do not bring me anything to eat, I shall starve.' The tone of Dantès' voice as he said this showed the jailer that his prisoner would be happy to die; and, as every prisoner, when all is said and done, represents roughly ten sous a day for his jailer, the man considered the loss that he would suffer from Dantès' death and continued in milder vein:

'Listen, what you want is impossible, so don't ask for it again: it is unheard of for the governor to come into a cell at a prisoner's request. But behave well and you will be allowed to exercise; and one day, while you are in the exercise yard, the governor may go by. Then you can talk to him. It is his business whether he wishes to reply.'

'But how long,' Dantès asked, 'am I likely to wait before this occurs?'

'Who knows? A month, three months, six . . . perhaps a year.'

'That's too long,' said Dantès. 'I want to see him at once.'

'Oh! Don't get obsessed by one single thing that is impossible to obtain, otherwise in a fortnight you'll be mad.'

'Do you think so?'

'Quite mad. That is always how madness begins. We have an example right here: it was because he kept on offering a million francs to the Governor if he would set him free, that the abbé[2] who occupied this cell before you went off his head.'

'How long is it since he left this cell?'

'Two years.'

'And was he freed?'

'No, put in a dungeon.'

'Listen,' Dantès said, 'I am not an abbé, nor am I mad. Perhaps I shall become so, but alas for the moment I have all my wits. I want to make another suggestion to you.'

'What?'

'I won't offer you a million because I could not give it to you; but if you want, I shall offer you a hundred *écus* so that, next time you cross to Marseille, you will go to the Catalans and give a letter to a young woman called Mercédès; not even a letter, just a couple of lines.'

'If I were to carry two lines and I was caught, I should lose my job, which is worth a thousand *livres* a year, without food and bonuses. So you can see I would be a fine fool if I were to risk losing a thousand *livres* to make three hundred.'

'Well,' Dantès said, 'listen to me, and mark what I say: if you refuse to carry two lines to Mercédès, or at least to let her know that I am here, I shall wait for you one day, hiding behind my door, and, as soon as you enter, crack your head open with this stool.'

'Threats!' the jailer exclaimed, taking a step back and putting himself on his guard. 'You really are losing your mind. The abbé started the same way. In three days you will be raving mad, as he is. Luckily there are dungeons in the Château d'If.'

Dantès took the stool and swung it around his head.

'Very well! Very well!' said the jailer. 'Since you insist, it will be reported to the governor.'

'At last!' Dantès said, putting the stool down on the floor and sitting on it, wild-eyed, hanging his head, as if he had truly become insane.

The jailer left and, a moment later, returned with three soldiers and a corporal.

'By order of the governor,' he said, 'take this prisoner to the floor below.'

'You mean to the dungeons,' said the corporal.

'To the dungeons. The mad must go with the mad.'

The four soldiers seized Dantès, who fell into a sort of catatonia and followed them without trying to resist. He was led down fifteen steps and they opened the door of a dungeon which he entered, muttering: 'Quite correct: the mad must go with the mad.'

The door closed and Dantès walked straight ahead, his arms outstretched, until he touched the wall. Then he sat down in a corner and remained motionless, while his eyes, gradually becoming accustomed to the gloom, started to make out his surroundings.

The jailer had been right: Dantès was very close to madness.

IX

THE EVENING OF THE BETROTHAL

Villefort, as we mentioned, had set out to return to the Place du Grand-Cours and, on arriving back at the house of Mme de Saint-Méran, discovered that the guests he had left at table were now taking coffee in the drawing-room. Renée was waiting for him with an impatience shared by the rest of the company and he was greeted with general acclaim.

'How now, head-cutter, pillar of the state, royalist Brutus!' cried one. 'Tell us what's up!'

'Yes, are we threatened with a new Reign of Terror?' asked another.

'Has the Corsican Ogre come forth from his cave?' asked a third.

'Madame la Marquise,' said Villefort, going over to his future mother-in-law, 'I have come to ask you to excuse me for being obliged to leave you in this way . . . Marquis, could I beg the favour of a word or two in private?'

'Oh! So it really is serious?' the marquise asked, seeing the cloud that had settled on Villefort's brow.

'So much so that I have to take leave of you for a few days.' He turned towards Renée. 'So you can understand that the matter must be serious indeed.'

'You're going away?' Renée exclaimed, unable to hide her feelings at this unexpected news.

'Alas, Mademoiselle, I must,' Villefort replied.

'And where are you going?' the marquise asked.

'That, Madame, must remain a secret under the law. However, if anyone here has some message for Paris, one of my friends is leaving for there tonight and will be delighted to undertake the errand.'

Everybody exchanged glances.

'You asked for a moment of my time?' the marquis said.

'Yes. If you please, let us go to your study.'

The marquis took Villefort's arm and they went out.

'Now, tell me what this is about,' he asked when they reached the study.

'Something that I believe to be of the utmost importance, which requires my immediate departure for Paris. Marquis, excuse my bluntness and indiscretion, but do you have any government stock?'

'My whole fortune is in bonds, around six or seven hundred thousand francs.'

'Then sell them, Marquis, sell them, or you are ruined.'

'But how can I sell them from here?'

'You have a broker, don't you?'

'Yes.'

'Give me a letter for him, so that he can sell without losing a minute or even a second. Even so, I may be too late.'

'Damn!' the marquis exclaimed. 'Let's not waste time.'

He sat down at a table and wrote a letter to his broker, instructing him to sell at any price.

'Now that I have this letter,' Villefort said, folding it and putting it carefully into his pocket-book, 'I need another.'

'For whom?'

'For the king.'

'The king?'

'Yes.'

'But I dare not take it upon myself to write to His Majesty.'

'I am not asking you to do so yourself, but to request it of Monsieur de Salvieux. He must give me a letter that will allow me to approach His Majesty without having to go through all the formalities of requesting an audience, which might waste valuable time.'

'What about the Lord Chancellor, who has free access to the Tuileries? Through him, you could contact the king at any time of the day or night.'

'No doubt, but why should someone else share the credit for

the news that I carry? Do you follow me? The chancellor would naturally relegate me to a subordinate role and deprive me of any benefit I might obtain in the matter. I can tell you only one thing, Marquis: my career is guaranteed if I can arrive first at the Tuileries, because I shall have done the king a service that he will be unable to forget.'

'In that case, dear boy, go and pack. I shall call de Salvieux and ask him to write a letter that will act as your passport to His Majesty.'

'Pray lose no time, for I must be in my chaise within a quarter of an hour.'

'Have the carriage draw up in front of the door.'

'Of course. Please make my excuses to the marquise. And to Mademoiselle de Saint-Méran – from whom, today of all days, I part with the profoundest regret.'

'They will both be waiting in the study for you to make your own farewells.'

'Thank you a hundred times. Look after my letter.'

The marquis rang and a servant appeared.

'Tell the Comte de Salvieux that I am expecting him . . . Now, you must go,' he added, to Villefort.

'I shall be back immediately.'

Villefort ran out but, on reaching the door, realized that the sight of a deputy crown prosecutor in such a hurry could upset the tranquillity of an entire town, so he slowed to his normal pace, which was quite magisterial.

At his front door he saw a pale, ghost-like figure waiting for him, upright and motionless in the shadows. It was the lovely young Catalan who, having no news of Edmond, had slipped out of the district around the Pharo at nightfall to come in person and see if she could discover the reasons for her lover's arrest.

When Villefort approached, she stepped out of the shadow of the wall against which she was leaning and barred his path. Dantès had told the prosecutor about his fiancée, and Villefort recognized Mercédès without her giving her name. He was surprised at the beauty and dignity of the woman and, when she asked him what had become of her lover, he felt as though he was the defendant and she was the judge.

'The man of whom you speak,' he replied brusquely, 'is a major criminal and I can do nothing for him, Mademoiselle.'

Mercédès could not repress a sob and, as Villefort tried to go past, stopped him again.

'At least tell me where he is, so that I can find out if he is alive or dead.'

'I don't know, he is no longer my responsibility,' Villefort replied. And, embarrassed by her keen look and attitude of entreaty, he pushed Mercédès aside and went in, slamming the door as though to shut out the sorrow that she had brought him.

But sorrow is not so easily put aside. The stricken man carried it with him like the fatal stamp of which Virgil speaks.[1] Villefort went in and closed the door, but when he reached the living-room, his legs too gave way beneath him, he let out a sigh that was more like a sob, and slumped into a chair.

Now, in the depths of that sick heart the first seeds of a mortal abscess began to spread. That man whom he was sacrificing to his own ambition, that innocent man who was paying the price for the guilt of Villefort's father, appeared before him, pale and menacing, clasping the hand of a fiancée who was no less pale, and bearing remorse in his train: not the remorse that makes its victims leap up like a Roman raging against his fate, but that bitter, muffled blow that intermittently chimes on the soul and sears it with the memory of some past action, an agonizing wound that lacerates, deeper and deeper until death.

Even now, there was a moment's hesitation in his heart. Many times before he had called for the death penalty, with no more emotion than that aroused by the contest between the accuser and the accused; and these convicts, who had gone to their deaths because of the thundering eloquence with which he had convinced the judges or the jury, had left no shadow on his brow: they had been guilty; or, at least, so Villefort believed.

This time, however, it was a different matter. He had just condemned a man to perpetual incarceration, but an innocent man, poised on the brink of good fortune, depriving him not only of freedom, but also of happiness. He was not a judge this time, but an executioner. And when he thought of that, he felt the muffled blow that we described, something that he had not previously experienced, sounding in the depths of his heart and filling his breast with a vague feeling of apprehension. Thus a wounded man will be put on his guard by a powerful and instinctive prescience of pain and tremble whenever his finger approaches the site of an open, bleeding wound, for as long as it remains unhealed.

But the wound that Villefort had suffered was one that would not heal; or one that would close, only to re-open, more bloody and painful than before.

If at that moment Renée's sweet voice had sounded in his ear calling for clemency, or if the lovely Mercédès had come in and said: 'In the name of the God who sees us and judges us, give me back my betrothed,' then, surely, that brow, already half prepared to submit to the inevitable, would have bent altogether, and he would no doubt have taken the pen in his numbed fingers and, despite the risk to himself, signed the order to set Dantès free. But no voice spoke in the silence and the door opened only to Villefort's *valet de chambre*, who had come to tell him that the post-horses were harnessed to his barouche.

He got up or, rather, leapt up, like a man resolving some inner struggle, ran across to his writing desk, emptied the gold from one of its drawers into his pockets, paced distractedly around his room for a moment, with his hand on his forehead, muttering incomprehensibly, then at last, feeling the coat which his valet had just put across his shoulders, went out, sprang into his carriage and snapped out the order to stop off at M. de Saint-Méran's in the Rue du Grand-Cours.

The sentence on the unhappy Dantès was confirmed.

As M. de Saint-Méran had promised, Villefort found the marquise and Renée in the study. The young man shuddered on seeing Renée, thinking that she might once more ask him to free Dantès. But, alas, it must be said, to the discredit of self-centred humankind, that the beautiful young woman was concerned with only one thing: Villefort's departure.

She loved Villefort, and he was leaving at the very moment when he was about to become her husband. He could not tell her when he would return, and Renée, instead of feeling pity for Dantès, was cursing the man whose crime was the cause of her separation from her lover.

So there was nothing that Mercédès could say!

On the corner of the Rue de la Loge, poor Mercédès had met Fernand, who was following her. She had returned to Les Catalans and thrown herself on her bed in an extremity of desperation. Fernand knelt beside the bed and, clasping an icy hand that

Mercédès did not think to take from him, covered it with ardent kisses that Mercédès did not even feel.

So she spent the night. The lamp went out when the oil was exhausted, but she no more noticed the darkness than she had noticed the light. When day returned, she was unaware of that also. Sorrow had covered her eyes with a blindfold that showed her only Edmond.

'Ah, it's you,' she said finally, turning towards Fernand.

'I have not left your side since yesterday,' he replied, with a pitiful sigh.

M. Morrel would not admit defeat: he had learned that Dantès had been taken to prison, after being questioned, so he hastened to see all his friends and visit anyone in Marseille who might have some influence there. But already the rumour was spreading that the young man had been arrested as a Bonapartist agent. Since at that time even the most daring considered any attempt by Napoleon to recover the throne as an insane fantasy, M. Morrel was greeted everywhere with indifference, fear or rejection, and returned home in despair, admitting that the position was serious and that no one could do anything about it.

Caderousse, for his part, was deeply disturbed and troubled. Instead of following M. Morrel's example, going out and attempting to do something for Dantès (which was, in any case, impossible), he shut himself in with two bottles of *cassis* and tried to drown his anxiety in drunkenness. But such was his state of mind that two bottles were not enough to extinguish his thoughts; so he remained, too drunk to fetch any more wine, not drunk enough to forget, seated in front of his two empty bottles, with his elbows on a rickety table, watching all the spectres that Hoffmann[2] scattered across manuscripts moist with punch, dancing like a cloud of fantastic black dust in the shadows thrown by his long-wicked candle.

Danglars was alone, but neither troubled nor disturbed. Danglars was even happy, because he had taken revenge on an enemy and ensured himself the place on board the *Pharaon* that he had feared he might lose. Danglars was one of those calculating men who are born with a pen behind their ear and an inkwell instead of a heart. To him, everything in this world was subtraction or multiplication, and a numeral was much dearer than a man, when it was a numeral that would increase the total (while a man might reduce it). So Danglars had gone to bed at his usual hour and slept peacefully.

Villefort, after receiving the letter from M. de Salvieux, had embraced Renée on both cheeks, kissed the hand of Mme de Saint-Méran and shaken that of the marquis, and was travelling post-haste along the road for Aix.

Dantès' father was perishing from grief and anxiety.

As for Edmond, we know what had become of him . . .

X

THE LITTLE CABINET IN THE TUILERIES

Let us leave Villefort going hell for leather down the road to Paris, having paid for extra horses at every stage, and precede him through the two or three rooms into the little cabinet at the Tuileries, with its arched window, famous for having been the favourite study of Napoleon and King Louis XVIII, and today for being that of King Louis-Philippe.[1]

Here, seated in front of a walnut table that he had brought back from Hartwell (to which, by one of those foibles usual among great men, he was especially partial), King Louis XVIII was listening without particular attention to a man of between fifty and fifty-two years, grey-haired, with aristocratic features and meticulously turned out, while at the same time making marginal notes in a volume of Horace, the Gryphius[2] edition (much admired, but often inaccurate) which used to contribute more than a little to His Majesty's learned observations on philology.

'You were saying, Monsieur?' the king asked.

'That I feel deeply disquieted, Sire.'

'Really? Have you by any chance dreamt of seven fat and seven lean cows?'

'No, Sire, for that would presage only seven years of fertility and seven of famine, and, with a king as far-sighted as Your Majesty, we need have no fear of famine.'

'So what other scourge might afflict us, my dear Blacas?'

'I have every reason to believe, Sire, that there is a storm brewing from the direction of the South.'

'And I, my dear Duke,' replied Louis XVIII, 'think you are very ill-informed, because I know for a fact that, on the contrary, the weather down there is excellent.'

Despite being a man of some wit, Louis XVIII liked to indulge a facile sense of humour.

'Sire,' M. de Blacas continued, 'if only to reassure his faithful servant, might Your Majesty not send some trusty men to Langue-doc, to Provence and to the Dauphiné, to give him a report on the feeling of these three provinces?'

'*Canimus surdis*,'[3] the king replied, carrying on with the annota-tion of his Horace.

The courtier laughed, to give the impression that he understood the phrase from the poet of Venusia: 'Your Majesty may well be perfectly correct to trust in the loyalty of the French, but I think I may not be altogether wrong to anticipate some desperate adventure.'

'By whom?'

'By Bonaparte or, at least, those of his faction.'

'My dear Blacas,' said the king, 'you are interrupting my work with your horrid tales.'

'And you, Sire, are keeping me from my sleep with fears for your safety.'

'One moment, my good friend, wait one moment; I have here a most perspicacious note on the line *Pastor quum trahiret*.[4] Let me finish it and you can tell me afterwards.'

There was a brief silence while Louis XVIII, in handwriting that he made as tiny as possible, wrote a new note in the margin of his Horace; then, when the note was written, he looked up with the satisfied air of a man who thinks he has made a discovery when he has commented on someone else's idea, and said: 'Carry on, my dear Duke, carry on. I am listening.'

'Sire,' said Blacas, who had briefly hoped to use Villefort to his own advantage, 'I have to tell you that this news that troubles me is not some vague whisper, these are no mere unfounded rumours. A right-thinking man who has my entire confidence and was required by me to keep a watch on the South . . .' (the duke hesitated as he said this) '. . . has just arrived post-haste to tell me that there is a great danger threatening the king. And so, Sire, I came at once.'

'*Mala ducis avi domum*,'[5] Louis XVIII continued, making another note.

'Is Your Majesty ordering me to say no more on this topic?'

'No, my dear Duke, but stretch out your hand.'

'Which one?'

'Whichever you prefer, over there, on the left.'

'Here, Sire?'

'I tell you the left and you look on the right. I mean my left. There, you have it. You should find a report from the Minister of Police with yesterday's date . . . But here is Monsieur Dandré himself . . . You did say Monsieur Dandré, didn't you?' Louis XVIII remarked, turning to the usher who had indeed just announced the Minister of Police.

'Yes, Sire, Monsieur le Baron Dandré,' the usher repeated.

'That's it, Baron,' Louis XVIII continued, with a faint smile. 'Come in, Baron, and tell the duke your most recent news about Monsieur de Bonaparte. Conceal nothing from us, however serious the situation may be. Let's see: is not the island of Elba a volcano, and shall we see war burst from it, bristling and blazing: *bella, horrida bella*?'[6]

M. Dandré leant elegantly against the back of a chair, resting both hands upon it, and said: 'Was Your Majesty good enough to consult my report of yesterday's date?'

'Yes, of course, but tell the duke what was in this report, because he is unable to find it. Let him know everything that the usurper is doing on his island.'

'Monsieur,' the baron said to the duke, 'all His Majesty's servants should applaud the latest news that we have received from Elba. Bonaparte . . .'

M. Dandré turned to Louis XVIII, who was busy writing a note and did not even look up.

'Bonaparte,' the baron continued, 'is bored to death. He spends whole days watching his miners at work in Porto-Longone.'

'And he scratches himself, as a distraction,' said the king.

'He scratches himself?' the duke said. 'What does Your Majesty mean?'

'Yes indeed, my dear Duke. Have you forgotten that this great man, this hero, this demi-god is driven to distraction by a skin ailment, *prurigo*?'[7]

'There is more, Monsieur le Duc,' said the Minister of Police. 'We are almost certain that the usurper will shortly be mad.'

'Mad?'

'Utterly: his head is softening; sometimes he weeps bitterly, at others he laughs hysterically. On some occasions, he spends hours sitting on the shore playing at ducks and drakes, and when a pebble makes five or six leaps, he seems as satisfied as though he had won another battle of Marengo or Austerlitz. You must agree that these are signs of folly.'

'Or of wisdom, Monsieur le Baron, or of wisdom,' said Louis XVIII, with a laugh. 'The great captains of Antiquity used to replenish their spirits by playing at ducks and drakes; see Plutarch's *Life of Scipio Africanus*.'

M. de Blacas was left speechless between these two forms of unconcern. Villefort, who had not wished to tell him everything, in order to prevent anyone else from taking away all the advantage that he might gain from his secret, had none the less told him enough to make him very anxious.

'Go on, Dandré, go on,' said Louis XVIII. 'Blacas is not yet convinced. Tell him about the usurper's conversion.'

The Minister of Police bowed.

'The usurper's conversion!' muttered the duke, looking from the king to Dandré, who were speaking their parts alternately like two Virgilian shepherds.[8] 'Has the usurper been converted?'

'Absolutely, my dear Duke.'

'To the right principles. Explain it, Baron.'

'Here's the truth of the matter, Duke,' the minister said, with the greatest gravity in the world. 'Napoleon recently reviewed his men and when two or three of his old *grognards*,[9] as he calls them, expressed a wish to return to France, he gave them leave and urged them to serve their good king: those were his own words, Monsieur le Duc, I am assured of it.'

'So, now, Blacas, what do you think?' the king asked triumphantly, turning his attention for a moment from the scholarly tome that lay open beside him.

'I say, Sire, that either the Minister of Police is mistaken or I am. But since it is impossible for it to be the Minister of Police, who is responsible for preserving Your Majesty's safety and honour, then I am probably the one who is wrong. However, Sire, in Your Majesty's place I should wish to question the person about whom I spoke. I would even insist that Your Majesty do him this honour.'

'Certainly, Duke, at your insistence I shall receive whomever you wish, but I should like to do so fully armed. Minister, do you yet have a more recent report than this one: this is dated February the twentieth, and it is now already March the third!'

'No, Sire, but I have been expecting one at any minute. I have been out since early this morning and it may have arrived in my absence.'

'Go to the Prefecture and if there is not one there,' Louis XVIII continued, laughing, 'make one. Isn't that the procedure?'

'Oh, Sire,' the minister exclaimed, 'thank heaven, on that score there is no need to invent anything. Each day brings the most circumstantial denunciations pouring into our offices, the work of a host of miserable wretches who are hoping for a little gratitude for services that they do not render – much as they would like to. They wager on chance, in the hope that one day an unexpected event will give some sort of reality to their predictions.'

'Very well, then go, Monsieur,' Louis XVIII said, 'and remember that I shall be awaiting your return.'

'I shall not tarry, Sire. I shall return in ten minutes.'

'And I, Sire, shall go to fetch my messenger,' said Blacas.

'Wait, wait,' Louis XVIII said. 'Blacas, I really must change your coat of arms: I shall give you an eagle with wings extended, grasping in its claws a prey that is trying in vain to escape; with this device: *Tenax.*'

'I am listening, Sire,' said M. de Blacas, wringing his hands in impatience.

'I should like to consult you about this text: *Molli fugiens anhelitu.*[10] You know: it concerns the stag fleeing the wolf. You are a great huntsman, I believe, and an expert on wolves. In both those capacities, what do you think of this *molli anhelitu?*'

'Admirable, Sire; but my messenger is like the stag that you mention, for he has just covered two hundred leagues by road, in barely three days.'

'He has expended a lot of energy and a lot of trouble, my dear Duke, when we have the telegraph that only takes three or four hours, and does so without making one in the slightest bit out of breath.'

'Sire! This is meagre reward for a poor young man who has come so far and with such ardour to give Your Majesty some important news. If only for the sake of Monsieur de Salvieux, who has recommended him to me, I beg you to receive him well.'

'Monsieur de Salvieux, my brother's chamberlain?'

'The same.'

'But he is in Marseille.'

'He writes to me from there.'

'Does he too speak to you of this conspiracy?'

'No, but he recommends Monsieur de Villefort to me and instructs me to bring him into Your Majesty's presence.'

'Monsieur de Villefort?' cried the king. 'Is this messenger called Monsieur de Villefort?'

'Yes, Sire.'

'And he is the one who has come from Marseille?'

'In person.'

'Why did you not tell me his name at once?' the king asked, a faint shadow of anxiety appearing on his face.

'Sire, I thought that Your Majesty would not know the name.'

'Not so, Blacas, not so. He is a serious young man, well-bred and above all ambitious. And, heavens – you do know his father's name?'

'His father?'

'Yes, Noirtier.'

'Noirtier, the Girondin? Noirtier the Senator?'

'Precisely.'

'And Your Majesty has given employment to the son of such a man?'

'Blacas, my friend, you understand nothing. I told you that Villefort was ambitious: to make his way, Villefort will sacrifice everything, even his father.'

'So, should I let him enter, Sire?'

'This very moment, Duke. Where is he?'

'He must be waiting for me below in my carriage.'

'Go and fetch him.'

'Immediately.'

The duke left with the vivacity of a young man, the warmth of his sincere royalism taking twenty years off his age. Left alone, Louis XVIII turned back to his half-open Horace and murmured: '*Justum et tenacem propositi virum.*'[11]

M. de Blacas came back up the stairs as fast as he had gone down them, but in the antechamber he was obliged to appeal to the king's authority. Villefort's dusty coat and his general appearance, bearing no relation to the dress of the court, had offended the sensibilities of M. de Brézé, who was astonished that any young man should have the audacity to appear in such clothing before the king. But the duke brushed aside his objections with a single phrase: His Majesty's orders; and, though the master of ceremonies continued to mutter his objections, for form's sake, Villefort was ushered into the royal presence. The king was sitting exactly where the duke had left him. On opening the door, Villefort found himself directly opposite him, and the young lawyer's first impulse was to stop dead.

'Come in, Monsieur de Villefort,' the king said. 'Come in.' Villefort bowed and took a few steps forward, waiting for the king to question him.

'Monsieur de Villefort,' the king went on, 'the Duc de Blacas claims that you have something important to tell us.'

'Sire, the duke is right and I hope that Your Majesty will acknowledge the same.'

'Firstly, before anything else, Monsieur, is the problem as serious, in your opinion, as I have been led to believe?'

'Sire, I believe that it is urgent, but I hope that, thanks to my efforts, it will not be irreparable.'

'Take as long as you wish, Monsieur,' said the king, who was starting to succumb to the feelings that he had seen on M. de Blacas' face and which he heard in the strained tones of Villefort's voice. 'Speak and, above all, begin at the beginning. I like order in all things.'

'Sire,' said Villefort, 'I shall give Your Majesty a faithful account, but I beg you to excuse me if, in my eagerness, I am unable to give as clear an account as I should wish.'

A rapid glance at the king after this ingratiating preface reassured Villefort of the benevolence of his august listener and he continued:

'Sire, I have driven post-haste to Paris to inform Your Majesty that, in the course of my duties, I have discovered not one of those commonplace and inconsequential plots, the like of which are hatched daily in the lower ranks of the people and of the army, but a veritable conspiracy, a whirlwind that threatens the very throne on which Your Majesty sits. The usurper is fitting out three ships. He is contemplating some adventure that may perhaps be senseless, but none the less fearsome for all that. At this very moment, he has surely left Elba – to go where? I do not know, but certainly with the intention of landing either at Naples, or on the coast of Tuscany, or even in France. Your Majesty must know that the ruler of the island of Elba has kept in contact both with Italy and with France.'

'Yes, Monsieur, I do know,' said the king, deeply troubled. 'Quite recently, we have been informed that meetings of Bonapartists have taken place in the Rue Saint-Jacques. But pray continue: how did you obtain this information?'

'Sire, it is the result of an interrogation that I carried out on a man from Marseille whom I have had under surveillance for some time and arrested on the day of my departure. This man, a rebellious sailor whose Bonapartist sympathies I suspected, went secretly to the island of Elba. There, he met the Grand Marshal, who entrusted him with a verbal message for a Bonapartist in Paris, whose name I was not able to make him divulge. However, the message was that the Bonapartist was ordered to prepare his supporters for a return – you understand, these are the words of the interrogation, Sire – for a return that cannot fail to take place shortly.'

'And where is the man?' Louis XVIII asked.

'In prison, Sire.'

'You believe the matter to be serious?'

'So much so, Sire, that although this event interrupted a family celebration, on the very day of my betrothal, I left everything, my fiancée and my friends, putting all aside to hasten to see Your Majesty, both to inform you of my fears and to assure you of my loyal devotion.'

'That's right,' said Louis XVIII. 'There was some plan that you should marry Mademoiselle de Saint-Méran, wasn't there?'

'The daughter of one of Your Majesty's most faithful servants.'

'Yes, yes, but let us return to the plot, Monsieur de Villefort.'

'Sire, I fear that this is no longer merely a plot; I fear we are dealing with a conspiracy.'

The king smiled. 'A conspiracy nowadays is an easy matter to contemplate, but harder to put into practice, precisely because, having been recently restored to the throne of our ancestors, we have our eyes fixed on the past, the present and the future. In the past ten months, my ministers have been doubly vigilant, to ensure that the Mediterranean coast is well protected. If Bonaparte were to land at Naples, the entire Coalition would be mobilized against him even before he reached Piombino. If he were to land in Tuscany, he would step on to an enemy shore. If he were to land in France, it would be with a handful of men and we should easily overcome him, hated as he is by the people. So have no fear, Monsieur; but be assured, none the less, of our royal gratitude.'

'Ah, here is Monsieur Dandré!' the Duc de Blacas exclaimed.

At that moment, as he spoke, the Minister of Police appeared at the door, pale, trembling and staring vacantly, as if dazed by a blinding flash of light.

Villefort made to retire from the room, but M. de Blacas clasped his hand to restrain him.

XI

THE CORSICAN OGRE

Louis XVIII, on seeing this ravaged face, thrust away the table before which he was sitting.

'What is wrong with you, Baron?' he cried. 'You seem thunderstruck. Do your troubled appearance and hesitant manner have anything to do with what Monsieur de Blacas was saying and what Monsieur de Villefort has just confirmed to me?'

Meanwhile M. de Blacas had made an urgent movement towards the baron, but the courtier's terror got the better of the statesman's pride: in such circumstances, it was far preferable for him to be humiliated by the Prefect of Police than to humiliate him, in view of what was at stake.

'Sire . . .' the baron stammered.

'Come, come!' said Louis XVIII.

At this, the Minister of Police gave way to an onrush of despair and threw himself at the king's feet. Louis XVIII stepped back, raising his eyebrows.

'Won't you say something?' he asked.

'Oh, Sire, what a terrible misfortune! What will become of me! I shall never recover from it!'

'Monsieur,' Louis XVIII said, 'I order you to speak.'

'Sire, the usurper left Elba on February the twenty-eighth and landed on March the first.'

'Where?' the king asked urgently.

'In France, Sire, in a little port on the Golfe Juan, near Antibes.'

'The usurper landed in France, near Antibes, on the Golfe Juan, two hundred leagues from Paris, on March the first, and it is only today, March the third, that you inform me of it! Well, Monsieur, what you are telling me is impossible: either you have been misinformed, or you are mad.'

'Alas, Sire, it is only too true!'

Louis XVIII made a gesture of inexpressible anger and alarm, leaping to his feet as though a sudden blow had struck him simultaneously in the heart and across the face.

'In France!' he cried. 'The usurper in France! But was no one watching the man? Who knows, perhaps you were in league with him!'

'Sire, no!' the Duc de Blacas cried. 'A man like Monsieur Dandré could never be accused of treason. We were all blind, Sire, and the Minister of Police was as blind as the rest of us, nothing more.'

'But . . .' Villefort said, then he stopped dead in his tracks. 'I beg your forgiveness, Sire,' he said, with a bow. 'My ardour carried me away. I beg Your Majesty to forgive me.'

'Speak, Monsieur, speak without fear. You alone warned us of the disease, help us to find the cure.'

'Sire,' Villefort said, 'the usurper is hated in the South. It appears to me that, if he risks his chances there, we can easily rouse Provence and Languedoc against him.'

'No doubt we can,' said the minister, 'but he is advancing through Gap and Sisteron.'

'Advancing, advancing,' said Louis XVIII. 'Is he marching on Paris then?'

The Minister of Police said nothing, but his silence was as eloquent as a confession.

'What about the Dauphiné?' the king asked Villefort. 'Do you think we could raise resistance there as in Provence?'

'Sire, I regret to inform Your Majesty of an unpalatable truth: feeling in the Dauphiné is not nearly as favourable to us as it is in Provence and Languedoc. The mountain-dwellers are Bonapartists, Sire.'

'So, his intelligence is good,' Louis XVIII muttered. 'How many men does he have with him?'

'I do not know, Sire,' said the Minister of Police.

'How do you mean, you don't know! Did you forget to find out that detail? It is a trivial matter, of course,' he added, with a disdainful smile.

'I was unable to learn it, Sire. The dispatch contained only the news of the landing and the route taken by the usurper.'

'And how did you come by this dispatch?'

The minister hung his head and blushed brightly. 'By the telegraph, Sire,' he stammered.

Louis XVIII stepped forward and crossed his arms, as Napoleon would have done.

'You mean,' he said, going pale with rage, 'that seven armies overthrew that man; a divine miracle replaced me on the throne of my fathers after twenty-five years of exile; and during those twenty-five years I studied, sounded out and analysed the men and the affairs of this country of France that was promised to me, only to attain the object of all my desires and for a force that I held in the palm of my hand to explode and destroy me!'

'It is fate, Sire,' the minister muttered, realizing that such a weight, though light in the scales of destiny, was enough to crush a man.

'So is it true, what our enemies say about us: nothing learned, nothing forgotten? If I had been betrayed as he was, then that might after all be some consolation; but to be surrounded by people whom I have raised to high office, who should consider my safety more precious than their own, because their interests depend on me – people who were nothing before me, and will be nothing after – and to perish miserably through inefficiency and ineptitude! Oh, yes, Monsieur, you are right indeed: that is fate.'

The minister was crushed beneath the weight of this terrifying indictment. M. de Blacas wiped a brow damp with sweat and Villefort smiled to himself, because he felt his own importance swelling.

'To fall,' Louis XVIII continued, having immediately realized the depth of the gulf above which the monarchy was tottering, 'to fall and to learn of one's fall through the telegraph! Oh, I should rather mount the scaffold like my brother Louis XVI, than to descend the steps of the Tuileries in this way, driven out by ridicule . . . Monsieur, you do not know what ridicule means in France; and yet, if anyone ought to know . . .'

'Sire,' the minister mumbled, 'Sire, for pity's sake!'

The king turned to the young man who was standing, motionless, at the back of the room, following the progress of this conversation on which hung the fate of a kingdom: 'Come here, Monsieur de

Villefort, come; and tell this gentleman that it was possible to have foreknowledge of everything, despite his ignorance of it.'

'Sire, it was materially impossible to guess at plans which that man had hidden from everybody.'

'"Materially impossible"! Those are grand words, Monsieur. Unfortunately, grand words are like grand gentlemen: I have taken the measure of both. "Materially impossible" – for a minister, who has his officials, his offices, his agents, his informers, his spies and fifteen hundred thousand francs of secret funds, to know what is happening sixty leagues off the coast of France! Come, come: here is this gentleman who had none of these resources at his disposal, this gentleman, a simple magistrate, who knew more than you did with all your police force, and who would have saved my crown if, like you, he had the right to operate the telegraph.'

The Minister of Police turned with an expression of profound acrimony towards Villefort, who lowered his head with the modesty of triumph.

'I am not saying this for you, Blacas,' Louis XVIII went on. 'Even though you discovered nothing, you did at least have the good sense to persevere in your suspicions: anyone else might have thought Monsieur de Villefort's revelations insignificant, or else the product of some self-serving ambition.'

The last was an allusion to what the Minister of Police had said with such confidence an hour earlier.

Villefort understood the king's strategy. Another person might have been carried away, intoxicated by this flattery, but he was afraid of making a mortal enemy of the minister, despite knowing that the man was doomed; because even though, at the height of his power, the minister had been unable to guess Napoleon's secret, in the final death throes of his fall he might discover Villefort's; he had only to question Dantès. So Villefort came to the man's aid instead of adding to his misery.

'Sire,' Villefort said, 'the swiftness of the events proves to Your Majesty that only God, by raising a storm, could have forestalled them. What Your Majesty attributes to profound perspicacity on my part is purely and simply the outcome of chance. All I have done is to use what chance put in my way, as a devoted subject. Do not give me more credit than I deserve, Sire, and you will never have to revise your first opinion of me.'

The Minister of Police thanked the young man with a look, and

Villefort knew that his plan had succeeded: having lost none of the king's gratitude, he had just made a friend on whom he could count, should need be.

'Very well,' said the king; then, turning to M. de Blacas and the Minister of Police: 'Now, gentlemen, I have no further need of you. You may go. What has to be done from now on falls within the province of the Minister of War.'

'Thankfully, Sire, we can count on the army,' said M. de Blacas. 'Your Majesty knows that every report speaks of its devotion to Your Majesty's government.'

'Don't speak to me of reports, Duke; I know now how much faith I should put in them. But, on that subject, Monsieur le Baron, what further news do you have about the matter of the Rue Saint-Jacques?'

'The matter of the Rue Saint-Jacques!' Villefort exclaimed, unable to contain himself. Then he stopped short and said: 'Forgive me, Sire, my devotion to Your Majesty continually makes me forget, not the respect that I feel for you, which is too deeply engraved on my heart, but the rules of etiquette.'

'You may speak out, Monsieur,' said Louis XVIII. 'Today you have earned the right to ask questions.'

'Sire,' the Minister of Police replied, 'I was on the point of giving Your Majesty the new information that I have gathered about this, when Your Majesty's attention was distracted by the terrible disaster on the coast. This information can be of no further interest to His Majesty.'

'On the contrary, Monsieur, this affair seems to me to relate directly to the one uppermost in our minds, and General Quesnel's death may perhaps put us on the trail of an important internal conspiracy.'

Villefort shuddered at this mention of General Quesnel.

'Indeed, Sire,' the Minister of Police continued, 'everything suggests that he was the victim, not of suicide, as first thought, but of murder. It appears that General Quesnel was coming out of a Bonapartist club when he disappeared. A stranger had visited him the same morning and made an appointment with him in the Rue Saint-Jacques. Unfortunately, the valet, who was doing the general's hair at the time when the stranger was shown into his dressing-room, clearly heard him mention the Rue Saint-Jacques, but could not remember the number.'

While the Minister of Police was giving this information to the king, Villefort, who appeared to hang on his every word, blushed red, then went pale.

The king turned to him. 'Don't you agree with me, Monsieur de Villefort, that General Quesnel, who might have been thought a supporter of the usurper, but who was in reality entirely loyal to me, was the victim of an ambush by the Bonapartists?'

'It seems probable, Sire,' said Villefort. 'Is nothing more known?'

'We are tracking down the man who made the appointment with him.'

'Tracking him down?' Villefort repeated.

'Yes, the servant gave us a description. He is a man of between fifty and fifty-five years old, with dark eyes overhung by bushy eyebrows, and a moustache. He was dressed in a blue frock-coat and wore the rosette of an officer of the Legion of Honour in his buttonhole. A man who precisely answers to this description was followed yesterday, but my agent lost him at the corner of the Rue de la Jussienne and the Rue Coq-Héron.'

Villefort had leant against the back of a chair and, while the Minister of Police was speaking, he felt his legs give way beneath him; but when he heard that the stranger had evaded his pursuer, he breathed again.

'You must track this man down, Monsieur,' the king told the Minister of Police. 'If, as everything leads me to believe, General Quesnel, who has been so helpful to us at this time, was a victim of murder, whether or not by Bonapartists, I wish his assassins to be cruelly punished.'

Villefort needed all his self-control to avoid showing the terror he felt on hearing the king's words.

'How odd it is!' the king continued, with a gesture that expressed his irritation. 'The police consider they have said the last word on the matter when they announce that a murder has been committed; and that they have done everything when they add: "We are tracking down the people responsible."'

'On this, at least, I hope that Your Majesty will have satisfaction.'

'Very well, we shall see. I shall keep you no longer, Baron. Monsieur de Villefort, you must be tired after your journey; go and rest. You are doubtless staying with your father?'

A cloud passed in front of Villefort's eyes.

'No, Sire, I am staying at the Hôtel de Madrid, in the Rue de Tournon.'

'You have seen him, I suppose?'

'I asked to be taken directly to the Duc de Blacas, Sire.'

'But you will see him, nonetheless?'

'I think not, Sire.'

'Ah yes, of course,' Louis XVIII said with a smile, indicating that there had been a motive behind this repeated questioning. 'I was forgetting the coldness in your relations with Monsieur Noirtier, and that this is another sacrifice you have made to the royal cause, for which I must compensate you.'

'Sire, the expression of Your Majesty's goodwill is a reward that so far exceeds my ambitions, and I can have nothing further to ask of my king.'

'No matter, Monsieur; have no fear, we shall not forget you, and meanwhile . . .' The king unpinned the cross of the Legion of Honour which he normally wore on his blue coat, next to the Cross of Saint-Louis and above the medal of the order of Notre-Dame du Mont Carmel et de Saint-Lazare, and, giving it to Villefort, said: 'Meanwhile, take this cross.'

'But, Sire,' Villefort said, 'Your Majesty is mistaken: this is the cross of an officer of the Legion.'

'So be it, Monsieur,' said Louis XVIII, 'take it for what it is. I have no time to request another. Blacas, ensure that the certificate is delivered to Monsieur de Villefort.'

Villefort's eyes moistened with a tear of happiness and pride. He took the cross and kissed it.

'And now,' he asked, 'what orders do I have the honour to receive from Your Majesty?'

'Take the rest that you need and consider that, while you have no power to serve me in Paris, you can be of the greatest service to me in Marseille.'

Villefort bowed. 'Sire, in an hour I shall have left Paris.'

'Go then, Monsieur; and if I should forget you – for the memory of kings is short – do not hesitate to make yourself known to me . . . Monsieur le Baron, give the order to fetch the Minister of War. Blacas, stay here.'

'Monsieur,' the Minister of Police said to Villefort as they were leaving the Tuileries, 'you have come through the right door: your fortune is made.'

'How long will it last?' Villefort murmured, taking leave of the minister, whose career was finished, and looking around for a cab to take him home. One passed along the quay, Villefort waved it down and the cab drew over. He gave his address to the driver and leapt inside, where he abandoned himself to his ambitious dreams. Ten minutes later he was home. He ordered his horses to be prepared for him to leave in two hours and asked for dinner to be served.

He was about to sit down at the table when a firm, clear ring sounded at the door. The valet went to open it and Villefort heard someone speak his name.

'Who can know that I am here so soon?' he wondered.

At that moment, the valet returned.

'What is it?' Villefort answered. 'Who was that ringing? Who is asking for me?'

'A stranger who will not give his name.'

'What anonymous stranger is that? What does he want?'

'He wishes to speak to Monsieur.'

'To me?'

'Yes.'

'He asked for me by name?'

'Certainly.'

'And what does this stranger look like?'

'He is a man of around fifty, Monsieur.'

'Short? Tall?'

'About the same size as Monsieur.'

'Fair or dark?'

'Dark, very dark, with black hair, black eyes and black eyebrows.'

'And dressed?' Villefort demanded urgently. 'How is he dressed?'

'In a long blue frock-coat buttoned from top to bottom, with the decoration of the Legion of Honour.'

'It is he,' Villefort murmured, going pale.

'By heaven!' The person whose description we have twice given appeared on the doorstep. 'This is a fine way to treat a man. Is it the custom in Marseille for a son to keep his father waiting at the door?'

'Father!' Villefort exclaimed. 'So I was not wrong: I guessed that it must be you.'

'If you guessed as much,' the newcomer remarked, putting his cane in a corner and his hat on a chair, 'then permit me to remark, my dear Gérard, that it is most unfriendly of you to keep me waiting like this.'

'Leave us, Germain,' said Villefort. The servant went out with obvious signs of astonishment.

XII

FATHER AND SON

M. Noirtier (for this was the man who had just entered) kept an eye on the servant until the door had closed. Then, doubtless fearing that he might be listening in the antechamber, he went and opened it again behind him. This was no vain precaution, and the speed of Germain's retreat proved that he was no stranger to the sin that caused the downfall of our first parents. M. Noirtier then took the trouble to go himself and shut the door of the antechamber, returned and shut that of the bedroom, slid the bolts and went over to take Villefort's hand. The young man, meanwhile, had been following these manoeuvres with a surprise from which he had not yet recovered.

'How now! Do you know, dear Gérard,' Noirtier said, looking at his son with an ambiguous smile, 'that you do not appear altogether overjoyed at seeing me?'

'On the contrary, father,' said Villefort, 'I am delighted. But your visit is so unexpected that I am somewhat dazed by it.'

'My dear friend,' Noirtier continued, taking a seat, 'I might say the same myself. How is this! You tell me that you are getting engaged in Marseille on the twenty-eighth of February, and on March the third you are in Paris?'

'If I am here, father,' said Gérard, going across to M. Noirtier, 'do not complain about it. I came for your sake and this journey may perhaps save your life.'

'Indeed!' said M. Noirtier, casually leaning back in the chair where he was sitting. 'Indeed! Tell me about it, Monsieur le Magistrat; I am most curious.'

'Have you heard about a certain Bonapartist club that meets in the Rue Saint-Jacques?'

'At Number fifty-three? Yes, I am its vice-president.'

'Father! I am amazed by your composure.'

'What do you expect, dear boy? When one has been proscribed by the Montagnards, left Paris in a hay-cart and been hunted across the moorlands of Bordeaux by Robespierre's bloodhounds, one is inured to most things. So continue. What has happened in this club in the Rue Saint-Jacques?'

'What has happened is that General Quesnel was called to it and that General Quesnel, having left home at nine in the evening, was pulled out of the Seine two days later.'

'And who told you this fine story?'

'The king himself.'

'Well now, in exchange for your story, I have some news to tell you.'

'Father, I think I already know what you are about to say.'

'Ah! So you already know about the landing of His Majesty the Emperor?'

'I beg you not to say such things, father, firstly for your own sake, then for mine. I did know this piece of news; I knew it even before you did, because over the past three days I have been pounding the road between Marseille and Paris, raging at my inability to project the thought that was burning through my skull and send it two hundred leagues ahead of me.'

'Three days ago! Are you mad? The emperor had not landed three days ago.'

'No matter, I knew of his plans.'

'How did you know?'

'From a letter addressed to you from the island of Elba.'

'To me?'

'To you. I intercepted it in the messenger's wallet. If that letter had fallen into another's hands, father, you might already have been shot.'

Villefort's father burst out laughing.

'Come, come, it seems that the Restoration has taken lessons from the Empire in how to expedite matters . . . Shot! My dear boy, you are being carried away! So where is this letter? I know you better than to imagine you would leave it lying around.'

'I burned it, to make sure that not a scrap remained. That letter was your death-warrant.'

'And a death-knell to your future career,' Noirtier replied coldly.

'Yes, I understand that; but I have nothing to fear, since you are protecting me.'

'I have done better still, Monsieur. I have saved you.'

'The devil you have! This is becoming more dramatic still. Explain what you mean.'

'I am again referring to the club in the Rue Saint-Jacques.'

'The gentlemen of the police seem most attached to this club. Why did they not look more carefully: they would have found it.'

'They have not yet found it, but they are on the trail.'

'That's the usual phrase, I know. When the police are at a loss, they say they are on the trail – and the government waits patiently until they come and whisper that the trail has gone cold.'

'Yes, but they have found a body. General Quesnel was killed and, in every country in the world, that is called murder.'

'Murder, you say? But there is nothing to prove that the general was murdered. People are found every day in the Seine, where they threw themselves in despair, or drowned because they could not swim.'

'Father, you know very well that the general did not drown himself in despair and that no one bathes in the Seine in January. No, no, make no mistake, his death has indeed been attributed to murder.'

'Who made the attribution?'

'The king himself.'

'The king! I thought him enough of a philosopher to realize that there is no such thing as murder in politics. You know as well as I do, my dear boy, that in politics there are no people, only ideas; no feelings, only interests. In politics, you don't kill a man, you remove an obstacle, that's all. Do you want to know what happened? I'll tell you. We thought we could count on General Quesnel. He had been recommended to us from the island of Elba. One of us went round to his house and invited him to attend a meeting in the Rue Saint-Jacques where he would be among friends. He came and was told the whole plan: departure from the island of Elba, the intended landing place. Then, when he had listened to everything and heard everything, and there was no more for him to learn, he announced that he was a Royalist. At this, we all looked at one another. We obliged him to take an oath and he did so, but truly with such little good grace that it was tempting God to swear in that way. In spite of all, however, we let him go freely, quite freely. He did not return

home: what do you expect, my dear? He left us and must have
taken the wrong road, that's all. A murder! Really, Villefort, you
surprise me – you, a deputy crown prosecutor, making an accusation founded on such poor evidence. Have I ever told you, when
you have done your job as a Royalist and had the head cut off one
of our people: "My son, you have committed murder"? No, I
have said: "Very well, Monsieur, you have fought and won, but
tomorrow we shall have our revenge."'

'Father, beware, our revenge will be terrible when we take it.'

'I don't understand.'

'Are you counting on the usurper's return?'

'I confess I am.'

'You are wrong, father; he will no sooner have got ten leagues
into France than he will be pursued, hunted down and captured
like a wild animal.'

'My good friend, the emperor is at this moment on the road for
Grenoble. On the tenth or the twelfth, he will be in Lyon, and on
the twentieth or the twenty-fifth in Paris.'

'The people will rise up . . .'

'To march before him.'

'He has only a handful of men with him and they will send armies
against him.'

'Which will provide an escort for him to return to the capital.
The truth, my dear Gérard, is that you are still only a child. You
think you are well informed because the telegraph told you, three
days after the landing: "The usurper has landed at Cannes with a
few men. He is being pursued." But where is he? What is he doing?
You have no idea. He is being pursued, that's all you know. Well,
they will pursue him as far as Paris, without firing a shot.'

'Grenoble and Lyon are loyal cities which will offer an invincible
barricade against him.'

'Grenoble will open its doors and acclaim him; the whole of
Lyon will march in his van. Believe me, we are as well informed as
you are and our police are at least the equal of yours. Do you want
proof? Here it is: you tried to hide your journey from me, yet I
knew about your arrival half an hour after you had entered Paris.
You gave your address to no one except your postilion, yet I know
your address, and to prove it I arrived here at the very moment
when you were sitting down to eat. So ring for your servant to set
another place and we shall dine together.'

'I have to admit,' replied Villefort, looking at his father with astonishment, 'you seem very well informed.'

'Heavens, it's simple enough. You people, who hold power, have only what can be bought for money; we, who are waiting to gain power, have what is given out of devotion.'

'Devotion?' Villefort laughed.

'Yes, devotion. That is the honest way to describe ambition when it has expectations.'

Villefort's father stretched out his own hand towards the bell-pull to call for the servant, since his son would not do it.

Villefort restrained him: 'Father, wait. Another word.'

'Say it.'

'However incompetent the Royalist police may be, they do know one dreadful thing.'

'Which is?'

'The description of the man who visited General Quesnel on the day of his disappearance.'

'Ah, the fine police know that, do they? And what is the description?'

'Dark in colouring, black hair, side-whiskers and eyes, a blue frock-coat buttoned up to the chin, the rosette of an officer of the Legion of Honour in his buttonhole, a broad-brimmed hat and a rattan cane.'

'Ah, ha, so they know that?' said Noirtier. 'In that case, why do they not have their hands on this man?'

'Because they lost him, yesterday or the day before, on the corner of the Rue Coq-Héron.'

'Didn't I tell you your police were idiots?'

'Yes, but at any moment they may find him.'

'Yes,' Noirtier said, looking casually around him. 'Yes, if the man is not warned. But,' he added, smiling, 'he has been warned and he will change his appearance and his clothing.'

At these words, he got up, took off his coat and cravat, went over to a table on which everything was lying ready for his son's toilet, took a razor, lathered his face and, with a perfectly steady hand, shaved off the compromising side-whiskers which had provided such a precious clue for the police. Villefort watched him with terror, not unmixed with admiration.

Once he had finished shaving, Noirtier rearranged his hair. Instead of his black cravat, he took one of a different colour which was lying on top of an open trunk. Instead of his blue buttoned coat, he slipped on one of Villefort's which was brown and flared. In front of the mirror, he tried on the young man's hat, with its turned-up brim; seemed to find that it suited him and, leaving his rattan cane where he had rested it against the fireplace, he took a little bamboo switch – that the dandyish deputy prosecutor would use to give himself that offhand manner which was one of his main attributes – and twirled it in his wiry hand.

'How's that?' he said, turning back to his astonished son after completing this sort of conjuring trick. 'Do you think that your police will recognize me now?'

'No, father,' stammered Villefort. 'I hope not, at least.'

'My dear Gérard, I rely on your prudence to dispose of all these objects that I am leaving in your care.'

'Oh, father, have no fear,' said Villefort.

'Indeed, I shall not. And now I believe you are right and that you may indeed have saved my life. But rest assured, I shall shortly repay the service.'

Villefort shook his head.

'Don't you believe me?'

'I hope, at least, that you are mistaken.'

'Will you see the king again?'

'I may.'

'Do you wish him to think you have the power of prophecy?'

'Those who prophesy misfortune are unwelcome in court, father.'

'Yes, but they are more justly treated in the long run. Suppose there is a second Restoration: then you will be considered a great man.'

'So, what must I tell the king?'

'Tell him this: "Sire, you have been deceived about the mood of the country, opinions in the towns and the spirit of the army. The man whom you in Paris call the Corsican ogre and who is still called the usurper in Nevers, is already hailed as Bonaparte in Lyon and as emperor in Grenoble. You think he is being hunted down, hounded and fleeing, but he is marching, as swiftly as the eagle which he brings back with him. His soldiers, whom you believe to be dying of starvation, exhausted and ready to desert, are increasing in numbers like snowflakes around a snowball as it plunges down a hill. Sire, leave – leave France to her true master who acquired her not for gold, but by conquest. Leave, Sire, not because you are in any danger – your adversary is strong enough to spare you – but because it would be humiliating for a grandson of Saint-Louis to owe his life to the man of Arcole, Marengo and Austerlitz."[1] Tell him that, Gérard; or rather, no, tell him nothing; conceal your journey; don't boast of anything that you intended to do or have done in Paris; take the coach and, if you pounded the road in coming, fly like a bird as you return; go back into Marseille at night, enter your house by the back door and stay there, quietly, humbly, secretly and, above all, harmlessly; because this time, I promise you, we shall act as determined men who know their enemies. Go, my son, go, my dear Gérard, and provided you are obedient to your father's orders – or, if you prefer, respectful of the wishes of a friend – we shall allow you to keep your office.' Noirtier smiled. 'This will give you an opportunity to save me for the second time, should the political seesaw one day raise you up again and put me down. Farewell, my dear Gérard. On your next visit, stay with me.'

At this, Noirtier left, as calm as he had been throughout the length of this difficult interview.

Villefort, pale and troubled, ran to the window, parted the curtains and saw him go by, tranquil and unmoved, between two or three sinister-looking men who were stationed by the boundary posts or at the corner of the street and who may well have been there to arrest a man with black whiskers, wearing a blue coat and a broad-brimmed hat.

He remained standing where he was, holding his breath, until his father had vanished beyond the Carrefour Bussy. Then he rushed to the things that Noirtier had left behind, thrust the black cravat and blue frock-coat into the bottom of his trunk, twisted the hat and concealed it in the bottom of a cupboard, and broke the rattan cane into three pieces, which he threw on the fire. Then he put on a travelling cap, called his valet, giving him a look that forbade him to ask any of the thousand questions that were on his lips, settled his account with the hotel, leapt into the carriage which was waiting for him, with the horses ready harnessed, learnt in Lyon that Bonaparte had just entered Grenoble and, in the midst of the turmoil that he found throughout the whole length of the road, arrived in Marseille, a prey to all the agonized feelings that enter a man's heart when he has ambition and has been honoured for the first time.

XIII

THE HUNDRED DAYS

M. Noirtier was a good prophet and events moved quickly, as he had said. Everyone knows about the return from Elba, that strange and miraculous return, with no earlier precedent and probably destined to remain unique for all time.

Louis XVIII made only feeble efforts to ward off this terrible blow: his lack of confidence in men deprived him of any confidence in events. Kingship or, rather, the monarchy, which he had barely rebuilt, was already trembling on its uncertain foundations and a single gesture from the emperor brought the entire edifice crashing down, a shapeless compound of old prejudices and new ideas. So Villefort received nothing from his king except gratitude, and that was not only useless for the time being, but actually dangerous; and the cross of the Legion of Honour which he was wise enough not to display, even though M. de Blacas had done as the king required and duly sent him the certificate.

Villefort would surely have been dismissed by Napoleon, had it not been for the protection of Noirtier, who had become all-powerful at court under the Hundred Days,[1] both for the danger that he had run and for the services he had rendered. So, as promised, the Girondin of '93 and the Senator of 1806 protected the man who had earlier protected him. Consequently, all Villefort's efforts during this reincarnation of the empire – which, it was not difficult to predict, would fall again – consisted in suppressing the secret which Dantès had been on the point of divulging. The crown prosecutor alone was dismissed, suspected of lack of enthusiasm for Bonapartism.

The imperial regime was re-established, which meant that the emperor moved into the Tuileries that Louis XVIII had just left, and began to issue a host of different orders from the little study into which, hard on the heels of Villefort, we recently introduced our readers, and from the walnut table on which he found Louis XVIII's snuffbox, wide open and still half full. And, no sooner had this happened than Marseille, despite the attitude of its judiciary, began to feel the warmth of those smouldering fires of civil war that are never entirely extinguished in the South. The reprisals threatened to exceed the occasional rowdy outburst against the houses of Royalists who decided to stay indoors, or public insults hurled at those who ventured outside.

Naturally, the turn of events meant that the worthy shipowner, whom we have already described as a supporter of the people's party, found himself in these circumstances, if not exactly all-powerful – since M. Morrel was a cautious and slightly timid man, like all those who have made their fortunes in trade by their own laborious efforts – at least able to stand up and lodge a complaint, even though he was dismissed as a moderate by Bonapartist fanatics. And his complaint, as one may easily imagine, concerned Dantès.

Villefort had remained on his feet, despite his superior's dismissal, but his wedding, though still agreed in principle, had been postponed until more propitious times. If the emperor should keep his throne, then Gérard would need to marry into another family and his father would find a suitable match for him. If Louis XVIII returned to France under a second Restoration, M. de Saint-Méran's influence and his own would be greatly increased, and the union become more favourable to him than ever. So, for the time being, the deputy crown prosecutor was the principal magistrate in Marseille; and, one day, his door opened and M. Morrel was announced.

Anyone else would have hastened to greet the shipowner, betraying his own weakness in his haste. But Villefort was a man of superior intelligence who, though he had little experience of the world, had an instinct for it. He kept M. Morrel waiting, as he would have done under the Restoration, not because he had anyone with him, but simply because it is normal for a crown prosecutor to keep people waiting; then, after a quarter of an hour which he spent reading two or three newspapers of various persuasions, he gave the order for the shipowner to be shown in.

M. Morrel expected to find Villefort dejected; but he found him as he had seen him six weeks earlier, that is to say calm, firm and full of the distant good manners that make up the most impenetrable of barriers separating a well-bred man from one of the people. He had entered Villefort's chambers convinced that the magistrate would tremble at the sight of him, only to discover that, on the contrary, he was himself overcome with nervousness and anxiety when confronted with this man who was waiting for him with an enquiring look and his elbows resting on his desk.

He paused at the door. Villefort examined him, as though he could not quite remember who he was. At last, after studying him in silence for some seconds, during which the good shipowner twisted and untwisted his hat in his hands, Villefort said: 'Monsieur Morrel, I believe?'

'Yes, Monsieur, I am he,' the shipowner replied.

The magistrate gestured protectively with his hand. 'Come over here and tell me to what I owe the honour of this visit.'

'Have you no idea, Monsieur?' M. Morrel asked.

'Not the slightest; but that does not in any way prevent me from wishing to serve you, if it is in my power to do so.'

'It depends entirely on you, Monsieur,' said Morrel.

'So please explain.'

'Monsieur,' continued the shipowner, gaining in confidence as he spoke, and further strengthened by the justice of his case and the clarity of his position, 'you remember that, a few days before the news of His Majesty the Emperor's landing, I came to beg your indulgence for an unfortunate young man, a sailor, who was second mate on board my brig. You will recall that he was accused of being in contact with the island of Elba: this connection, though a crime in those days, is now a recommendation. At that time, you served Louis XVIII and you did so unreservedly, Monsieur – that was your duty. Today, you are serving Napoleon, and you should protect him – that, too, is your duty. So I have come to ask you what became of him.'

Villefort struggled to contain his feelings.

'What is the man's name?' he asked. 'Please be so good as to tell me his name.'

'Edmond Dantès.'

Of course, Villefort would have been as happy to confront an armed adversary in a duel at twenty-five paces as to have this name fired at him point blank, yet he did not raise an eyebrow.

'In this way,' he thought, 'no one can accuse me of having any purely personal interest in the arrest of this young man.'

'Dantès?' he asked aloud. 'Edmond Dantès, you say?'

'Yes, Monsieur.'

Villefort opened a large register housed in a pigeon-hole near his desk, then crossed to a table and, from the table, went over to some files, before turning back to the shipowner.

'Are you sure that you are not mistaken, Monsieur?' he asked, in the most natural tone of voice.

If Morrel had been more sharp-witted or better informed about the matter, he would have found it odd that the deputy crown prosecutor even deigned to answer him on a subject which was entirely outside his competence; and he might have wondered why Villefort did not send him to consult the prison registers, prison governors or the prefect of the *département*. But Morrel, who had looked in vain for any sign of fear in Villefort, as soon as the man appeared to have none, perceived only a desire to oblige: he was no match for Villefort.

'No, Monsieur,' Morrel said, 'I am not mistaken. In any case, I have known the poor lad for ten years and he has served under me for four. Don't you remember? I came to see you six weeks ago, to ask for clemency on behalf of this unfortunate young man, just as today I am asking for justice. In fact, your manner was quite offhand and you spoke to me as though displeased by my enquiry. Oh, Bonapartists could expect harsh treatment from Royalists in those days!'

Villefort parried this thrust with his usual agility and cool-headedness. 'Monsieur, I was a Royalist as long as I considered the Bourbons not only the rightful heirs to the throne but also the choice of the nation. However, the miraculous turn of events that we have just witnessed proved to me that I was wrong. Napoleon's genius has triumphed: the legitimate monarch is the one who has the love of the people.'

'Pleased to hear it, at last!' Morrel exclaimed, with bluff sincerity. 'When you speak in that way, it augurs well for Edmond.'

'Wait,' Villefort continued, leafing through another register. 'He was a sailor, isn't that right . . . who was marrying a Catalan girl? Yes, yes, I remember now: it was a very serious matter.'

'How, serious?'

'You know that when he left here he was taken to the prison at the Palais de Justice.'

'So?'

'Well, I made my report to Paris and sent the papers that were found on him. That was my duty: what else could I do? A week after his arrest, the prisoner was transferred.'

'Transferred!' M. Morrel exclaimed. 'What can have been done with the poor boy?'

'Don't worry. He would have been taken to Fenestrelle, in Pignerol, on the Iles Sainte-Marguerite, which is officially described as transportation. One fine day you will see him return to take command of his ship.'

'He can come whenever he likes, the post will be kept for him. But why is he not back already? I should have thought that the first priority of Bonapartist justice would have been to release those who were imprisoned under the Royalist regime.'

'Don't be too eager to make accusations, my dear Monsieur Morrel,' Villefort replied. 'Due process of law must be observed in everything. The order for his incarceration came from the highest authority and the order for his release must do likewise. Napoleon has only been back for a fortnight, so the annulments can only just have been sent out.'

'But is there no way of expediting the formalities, now that we are back in power? I have some friends and some influence: I could have the judgement reversed.'

'There was no judgement in this case.'

'The detention order, then.'

'In political cases there is no register of detainees. It is sometimes in the interest of governments to make a person disappear without trace: detention orders would help to find him.'

'Perhaps that's how things were under the Bourbons, but now . . .'

'That's how things are at all times, my dear Monsieur Morrel: one regime follows another and resembles its predecessor. The penitentiary system established under Louis XIV still applies, apart from the Bastille. The emperor was always stricter than even the Sun King himself when it came to the management of his prisons: the number of prisoners whose names do not figure on any register is incalculable.'

Even certainty would have been misled by such benevolent concern, and M. Morrel did not even feel suspicion.

'So finally, Monsieur de Villefort,' he said, 'what advice would you give me to hasten poor Dantès' return?'

'Just this, Monsieur: make a petition to the Minister of Justice.'

'Yes, but we know what happens to petitions. The minister gets two hundred a day and doesn't read four of them.'

'Certainly,' Villefort agreed, 'but he will read a petition that is sent by me, certified by me and personally addressed by me.'

'Would you undertake to send such a petition?'

'With the greatest pleasure. Dantès might have been guilty then, but he is innocent now and it is my duty to have him released, just as it was once my duty to have him imprisoned.'

In this way, Villefort could avoid running the risk, small though it might be, of an enquiry that would certainly prove his undoing.

'How does one go about writing to the minister?'

'Sit here, Monsieur Morrel,' Villefort said, giving the shipowner his chair. 'I shall dictate the letter.'

'Would you really be so kind?'

'Of course. Let's lose no more time, we have wasted enough already.'

'Yes, Monsieur. Consider how the poor lad must be waiting, suffering and perhaps giving way to despair.'

Villefort shuddered at the idea of the prisoner cursing him in the darkness and silence, but he had gone too far to retreat. Dantès would have to be broken between the cogs of his ambition.

'I am ready,' the shipowner said, sitting in Villefort's chair and taking up a pen.

So Villefort dictated a request in which, undoubtedly with the best of intentions, he exaggerated Dantès' patriotism and the service he had rendered to the Bonapartist cause. In it, Dantès became one of the most significant figures in ensuring Napoleon's return: clearly, when he saw the document, the minister must immediately see that justice was done, if it had not been done already.

When they had completed the petition, Villefort read it out.

'That's it,' he said. 'Now, count on me.'

'Will the petition be sent soon, Monsieur?'

'This very day.'

'Certified by you?'

'The finest apostil I can put on it is to certify that all you have said in this request is true.'

Villefort resumed his place and stamped his certification on a corner of the petition.

'So, what do we have to do now?' asked Morrel.

'Wait,' Villefort replied. 'I shall look after everything.'

Morrel's hopes were raised by this assurance; he left the deputy prosecutor's office delighted with himself and went to tell Dantès' father that he would be seeing his son before long.

As for Villefort, instead of sending the request to Paris, he put it carefully aside for safekeeping, knowing that what might save Dantès in the present would become a disastrously compromising document in the future, in the event – which the situation in Europe and course of affairs already allowed him to predict – of a second Restoration.

So Dantès remained a prisoner. In the depths of the dungeon where he was buried, no sound reached him of the resounding crash of Louis XVIII's throne or of the still more dreadful collapse of the empire.

Villefort, however, had watched all this closely and listened to it attentively. On two occasions during the brief reappearance of the emperor known as the Hundred Days, M. Morrel had renewed his efforts, always demanding that Dantès be released, and each time Villefort had reassured him with promises and expectations. Finally, Waterloo. Morrel was not again seen at Villefort's: the shipowner had done everything humanly possible for his young friend and, if he were to make any further attempt under this second Restoration, he would compromise himself, to no useful end.

Louis XVIII returned to the throne. For Villefort, Marseille was full of memories that were soured with remorse, so he requested and obtained the vacant post of crown prosecutor in Toulouse. A fortnight after moving into his new home, he married Mlle Renée de Saint-Méran, whose father was more in favour at court than ever.

So it was that Dantès, during the Hundred Days and after Waterloo, remained under lock and key, forgotten, if not by men, at least by God.

When Danglars witnessed Napoleon's return to France, he realized the full effect of the blow he had directed against Dantès: his denunciation had been accurate and, like all men with a certain natural aptitude for crime and only average understanding of ordinary life, he described this strange coincidence as 'a decree of Providence'. But when Napoleon had returned to Paris and his voice, imperious and powerful, was heard once more in the land, Danglars knew fear. At every moment he expected Dantès to reappear, a Dantès who knew everything, a Dantès who was strong and who threatened every kind of vengeance. So he gave M. Morrel notice of his desire to renounce seafaring and obtained a reference from him to a Spanish trader, whose service he entered as accounts clerk towards the end of March, that is to say ten or twelve days after Napoleon's return to the Tuileries. He left for Madrid and nothing more was heard of him.

As for Fernand, he understood nothing. Dantès had gone away; that was enough. What had happened to him? Fernand did not try to find out. Throughout the reprieve that this absence gave him, he strove, partly to mislead Mercédès about the reasons for it, and partly to devise plans for emigration and abduction. From time to time – these were the dark moments in his life – he also sat at the extremity of the Cap Pharo, at the point from which you can see both Marseille and the Catalan village, sad, motionless as a bird of prey, watching in case he might see, returning by one or other of these routes, the handsome young man who walked freely, with his head held high; and who, for Fernand also, had become the messenger of a cruel revenge. In that event, Fernand was decided: he would break Dantès' skull with his gun and then, he thought, afterwards kill himself, to disguise the murder. But Fernand was mistaken: he would never kill himself, because he lived in hope.

While this was happening, among all these painful changes, the empire called for a final muster of soldiers and every man who was capable of bearing arms marched across the frontier of France in obedience to the emperor's resounding call. Fernand set off with the rest, leaving his hut, leaving Mercédès, devoured by the dark and dreadful thought that, when he had gone, his rival might return and marry the woman he loved. If ever Fernand meant to kill himself, he would have done so on leaving Mercédès.

His attentions to the young woman, the pity which he appeared to feel for her in her misfortune and the care that he took to anticipate the least of her wishes, had produced the effect that an appearance of devotion inevitably produces on a generous heart: Mercédès had always loved Fernand as a friend and now her friendship towards him was increased by a new feeling: gratitude.

'My brother,' she said, fastening his conscript's bag across the Catalan's shoulders, 'my only friend, do not let yourself be killed, do not leave me alone in the world, where I weep and where I shall be entirely alone if you leave it.'

These words, spoken on his departure, gave Fernand new hope. If Dantès did not return, then Mercédès might be his.

Mercédès remained alone in that bare landscape, which had never appeared to her more arid, bounded by the vastness of the sea. Bathed in tears, like the madwoman whose painful story we have heard, she could be seen wandering continually around the little Catalan village, now pausing beneath the burning southern

sun, standing motionless and silent as a statue, looking towards
Marseille; now seated on the shore, listening to the moaning of the
sea, as endless as her sorrow, and ceaselessly wondering if it would
not be better to lean forward, sink beneath her own weight into the
abyss and let herself be swallowed up, rather than to suffer all the
cruel uncertainties of hopeless expectation.

It was not the fact that Mercédès lacked the courage to carry out
this intention, but the succour of religion that saved her from
suicide.

Caderousse was called up as Fernand had been; but, being eight
years older than the Catalan and married, he was not recruited
until the third wave of conscription and sent to guard the coast.

Old Dantès, who had been sustained only by hope, lost hope
when the emperor fell. Five months to the day after being separated
from his son, and almost at the very hour when Dantès was arrested,
he breathed his last in Mercédès' arms.

M. Morrel undertook to pay all the expenses of the funeral and
settled the trifling debts that the old man had run up during his last
illness. It took more than benevolence to do this: it took courage.
The South was ablaze, and to assist the father of a Bonapartist as
dangerous as Dantès, even on his deathbed, was a crime.

XIV

THE RAVING PRISONER AND THE MAD ONE

Approximately one year after the return of Louis XVIII, the Inspector General of Prisons paid a visit.

Dantès heard all the trundling and grinding of preparations from
the depth of his cell: there was a great deal of commotion upstairs,
but the noise would have been imperceptible below for any ear
other than that of a prisoner who was accustomed to hearing,
in the silence of night, the sound made by a spider spinning its web
or the regular fall of a drop of water which took an hour to gather
on the ceiling of his dungeon.

He guessed that among the living something exceptional was
taking place; he had lived so long in the tomb that he might
justifiably have considered himself dead.

In the event, the inspector was visiting the rooms, cells and dungeons, one after the other. Several prisoners were questioned – those who had earned the goodwill of the governors by their mild manner or sheer stupidity. The inspector asked them how they were fed and any demands that they might have to make.

They replied unanimously that the food was execrable and that they demanded their freedom.

The inspector then asked if they had anything else to say to him.

They shook their heads. What can any prisoner have to ask for, apart from his freedom?

The inspector turned around with a smile and said to the governor: 'I can't think why they oblige us to make these pointless visits. When you have seen one prisoner, you have seen a hundred; when you have heard one prisoner, you have heard a thousand. It's always the same old song: badly fed and innocent. Have you got any others?'

'Yes, we have the mad or dangerous prisoners, whom we keep in the dungeons.'

'Very well,' the inspector said, with an air of profound weariness. 'We had better do the job properly. Let's go down to the dungeons.'

'One moment,' said the governor. 'We should at least get a couple of men to go with us. Sometimes the prisoners, if only because they are sick of life and wish to be condemned to death, commit vain and desperate acts; you might be a victim of such an attempt.'

'Then take some precautions,' said the inspector.

They sent for two soldiers and began to go down a flight of stairs that was so foul-smelling, so filthy and so mildewed that even to pass through the place simultaneously offended one's sight, hampered one's breathing and assaulted one's nostrils.

'Who in hell's name can live here?' the inspector asked, stopping half-way.

'The most dangerous of conspirators, against whom we have been warned as a man capable of anything.'

'He is alone.'

'Indeed he is.'

'How long has he been here?'

'For about a year.'

'Was he thrown into this dungeon as soon as he arrived?'

'No, Monsieur, only after he had attempted to murder the turnkey who brought him his food.'

'He tried to kill a turnkey?'

'This same one who is holding the lamp. Isn't that so, Antoine?' the governor asked.

'He did want to kill me for sure,' the turnkey answered.

'Well, I never! Is the man mad?'

'Worse than that,' said the turnkey. 'He's a devil.'

'Would you like me to make a complaint about him?' the inspector asked the governor.

'There is no need, Monsieur, he is being punished enough as it is. In any case, he is already close to madness and, judging by what we have observed, in another year he will be quite insane.'

'Well, so much the better for him,' said the inspector. 'When he is altogether mad, he will suffer less.' As you can see, this inspector was a man of the utmost humanity and altogether worthy of the philanthropic office with which he had been entrusted.

'You are right, Monsieur,' said the governor. 'Your remark proves that you have given the matter a good deal of thought. As it happens, in a dungeon not more than twenty feet away from this one which is reached by another staircase, we have an old abbé, a former leader of a faction in Italy, who has been here since 1811 and who lost his wits around the end of 1813. Since then, he has been physically unrecognizable: he used to weep, now he laughs; he was growing thin, now he is putting on weight. Would you like to see him instead of this one? His madness is entertaining; it won't depress you.'

'I'll see them both,' replied the inspector. 'We must be conscientious about our work.' He was carrying out his very first tour of inspection and wanted to make a good impression on the authorities.

'Let's go in here first,' he added.

'Certainly,' said the governor, indicating to the turnkey that he should open the door.

Dantès was crouching in a corner of the dungeon where he had the unspeakable happiness of enjoying the thin ray of daylight that filtered through the bars of a narrow window; hearing the grating of the massive locks and the screech of the rusty doorpost turning in its socket, he looked up. At the sight of a stranger, lit by two turnkeys with torches, who was being addressed by the governor, hat in hand, together with two soldiers, Dantès guessed what was going on and, seeing at last an opportunity to petition a higher authority, leapt forward with his hands clasped.

The soldiers immediately crossed their bayonets, thinking that the prisoner was rushed towards the inspector with some evil intent. The inspector himself took a step backwards.

Dantès realized that he had been depicted as someone dangerous; so he summoned up a look that expressed the utmost leniency and humility and spoke with a kind of pious eloquence that astonished everyone, in an attempt to touch the heart of his visitor.

The inspector listened to what Dantès had to say until he had finished; then, turning to the governor, he whispered: 'He has the makings of a religious devotee; already he is inclined to more benevolent feelings. You see, fear has had an effect on him. He recoiled from the bayonets, while a madman recoils at nothing: I have done some interesting research on the subject in Charenton.'

Then, turning back to the prisoner, he said: 'Tell me briefly, what do you want?'

'I want to know what crime I have committed, I am asking for judges to be appointed to my case and for a trial to be held; finally, I am asking to be shot, if I am guilty; but equally to be set free if I am innocent.'

'Are you well fed?' asked the inspector.

'Yes, I think so, I don't know. It is of little importance. What is important, not only for me, a wretched prisoner, but also for all those officials who administer justice and for the king who rules us, is that an innocent man should not be the victim of an infamous denunciation and die behind bars, cursing his tormentors.'

'You are very submissive today,' said the governor. 'You were not always like this. You spoke in quite a different manner, my good friend, the day when you tried to beat the life out of your warder.'

'That is true, Monsieur,' Dantès said, 'and I humbly ask the forgiveness of this man, who has always been kind to me. But what do you expect? I was mad, I was raging.'

'Not any longer?'

'No, Monsieur, captivity has bowed me, broken me, demolished me. I have been here for so long!'

'So long? When were you arrested?' asked the inspector.

'On the twenty-eighth of February, 1815, at two in the afternoon.'

The inspector made a calculation.

'It is now July the thirtieth, 1816. So what do you mean? You have been a prisoner for only seventeen months.'

'Only seventeen months!' Dantès repeated. 'Oh, Monsieur, you do not know what seventeen months are in prison: seventeen years, seventeen centuries; above all for a man like myself, who was on the brink of happiness, for a man like myself, who was about to marry a woman whom he loved, for a man who could see an honourable career ahead of him and who was deprived of it all in a moment; who, from the most glorious day, was plunged into the deepest night, who saw his career destroyed, who does not know if the woman who loved him does so still, who cannot tell if his old father is alive or dead. Seventeen months of prison, for a man accustomed to the sea air, to a sailor's independence, to space, immensity, infinity! Monsieur, seventeen months of prison is more than enough punishment for all the crimes reviled by the most odious names known to the tongues of men. Have pity on me, Monsieur, and beg for me, not indulgence, but firmness; not a pardon, but a verdict. A judge, Monsieur, I ask only for a judge: an accused man cannot be refused a judge.'

'Very well,' the inspector said, 'we shall see.' Then, turning to the governor: 'Truly, I feel sorry for the poor devil. When we go back upstairs, you must show me his detention order.'

'Certainly,' said the governor, 'but I think that you will find some dreadful charges against him.'

'Monsieur,' Dantès continued, 'I know that you cannot your-self make the decision to have me released, but you can pass on my request to the authorities, you can start an enquiry, you can have me brought to judgement: all I ask is to be judged; let me be told what crime I have committed and what sentence I have been given; because, you understand, uncertainty is the worst of torments.'

'Enlighten me,' said the inspector.

'Monsieur,' Dantès exclaimed, 'I can see from the sound of your voice that you feel for me. Please tell me to hope.'

'That I cannot do,' the inspector replied. 'All I can promise is that I shall examine your dossier.'

'Oh! In that case, Monsieur, I am free, I am saved.'

'Who ordered your arrest?' the inspector asked.

'Monsieur de Villefort,' Dantès replied. 'You may see him and consult with him.'

'Monsieur de Villefort has not been in Marseille for the past year, but in Toulouse.'

'Ah, that does not surprise me now,' Dantès murmured. 'My sole protector has left.'

'Did Monsieur de Villefort have any reason to hate you?' the inspector asked.

'None at all, Monsieur; he was well-disposed towards me.'

'So I can rely on any notes he may have left on your case, or which he may give me?'

'Fully.'

'Very well. Be patient.'

Dantès fell to his knees, raising his hands to heaven and asking God to protect this man who had descended into his prison like Our Saviour going down to deliver the damned from hell. The door closed, but the hope that the inspector had brought with him remained locked in Dantès' dungeon.

'Do you wish to see the committal records straightaway,' the governor asked, 'or to go on to the abbé's dungeon?'

'Let's have done with the dungeons at once,' the inspector replied. 'If I were to go back into daylight, I might lose the resolve to carry on with this dreary task.'

'This prisoner is not like the last one: you will find his folly makes you less melancholy than the other's reason.'

'What kind of folly is it?'

'A rare one, indeed: he believes himself to be the owner of a vast fortune. In the first year of his imprisonment, he made the government an offer of a million francs, if they would set him free; the second year, it was two million; the third, three, and so on upwards. He is now in his fifth year of imprisonment, so he will ask to speak to you privately and offer you five million.'

'Well, well, that certainly is curious,' said the inspector. 'What is the name of this millionaire?'

'Abbé Faria.'

'Number twenty-seven!' said the inspector.

'This is it. Open up, Antoine.'

The turnkey obeyed and the inspector strained to see into the dungeon of the 'mad abbé', as the prisoner was usually known.

A man was lying in the middle of the room, in a circle drawn on the ground with a piece of plaster from the wall, almost naked, his clothes having fallen into tatters. He was drawing very precise geometrical lines in the circle and appeared as absorbed in solving his problem as Archimedes when he was killed by one of Marcellus' soldiers.[1] He did not even look up at the noise made by the opening of the cell door, but only appeared to become aware of something when the beams of the torches cast an unfamiliar light on the damp ground where he was working. Then he turned around and was astonished to see that a group of people had just come down into his dungeon.

He immediately leapt to his feet, took a blanket from the foot of his miserable bed and hurriedly wrapped it round him, to appear more decently dressed in front of these strangers.

'What requests do you have?' the inspector asked, not varying his set question.

'I, Monsieur?' the abbé replied in astonishment. 'I have no requests.'

'You do not understand,' the inspector continued. 'I am a representative of the government with responsibility for visiting prisons and listening to the prisoners' demands.'

'Ah! In that case, it's another matter,' the abbé exclaimed, livening up. 'I hope we shall come to some understanding.'

'You see,' the governor whispered. 'Isn't it just as I predicted?'

'Monsieur,' the prisoner continued, 'I am Abbé Faria,[2] born in Rome, twenty years secretary to Cardinal Rospigliosi. I was arrested early in 1811, I'm not quite sure why, and since then I have demanded my freedom from the Italian and French authorities.'

'Why from the French authorities?' the governor asked.

'Because I was arrested in Piombino and I assume that, like Milan and Florence, Piombino is now the capital of some French *département*.'

The inspector and the governor looked at one another and laughed.

'Well, I never!' the inspector said. 'My friend, your news of Italy is rather stale.'

'It dates from the day of my arrest. But since His Majesty the Emperor had just created the kingdom of Rome for the son that heaven had sent him, I assume that he has pursued his conquests to realize the dream of Machiavelli and Cesare Borgia, and united the whole of Italy in one single kingdom.'

'Fortunately,' the inspector said, 'providence has somewhat modified that ambitious plan, though you appear to me to support it quite enthusiastically.'

'It is the only means by which Italy can become a strong, independent and prosperous state,' the abbé replied.

'Perhaps so,' said the inspector. 'But I have not come to debate ultramontane politics with you. I am here to ask, as I have already done, whether you have any complaints about your food and conditions.'

'The food is like that in all prisons,' the abbé answered. 'In other words, vile. As for my lodging, you can see for yourself: it is damp and unhealthy, but nonetheless quite acceptable for a dungeon. However, all that is beside the point; I have something of the greatest significance and the most vital importance to reveal to the government.'

'Here it comes,' the governor whispered to the inspector.

'That is why I am pleased to see you,' the abbé went on, 'even though you have disturbed me in a most important calculation which, if it were to succeed, might alter the Newtonian system. Could you grant me the favour of a private interview?'

'There! What did I tell you?' the governor asked the inspector.

'You know your man,' the latter answered, smiling. Then, turning to Faria, he said: 'Monsieur, what you ask is impossible.'

'Even so, Monsieur,' the abbé insisted, 'what if it were a matter of the government gaining a huge sum of money; a sum of five million francs, for example?'

'Well, well!' the inspector said, turning to the governor. 'You even guessed the amount!'

'One moment,' the abbé went on, seeing the inspector make a movement towards the door. 'It is not necessary for us to be entirely alone. The governor could hear what I have to say.'

'My dear friend,' the governor said, 'unfortunately we already know by heart what you will tell us. You are thinking of your treasure, aren't you?'

Faria looked at the scornful man with eyes in which any disinterested observer would surely have seen the light of reason and truth.

'Of course,' he said. 'What else should I talk about, if not that?'

'My dear inspector,' the governor continued, 'I can tell you the story as well as the abbé himself, after hearing it over and over during the past four or five years.'

'That only goes to show, governor,' the abbé said, 'that you are like those men in the Scriptures who have eyes, but see not, and who have ears, but will not hear.'

'Monsieur,' the inspector said, 'the government is rich and, thank heavens, has no need of your money. Keep it for the day when you get out of prison.'

The abbé's eyes dilated and he grasped the inspector's hand: 'But if I don't get out of prison . . . Suppose that, contrary to all notions of justice, they should keep me in this dungeon and I should die here without bequeathing my secret to anyone, then the treasure will be lost! Isn't it better for the government to profit by it, and for me to do so? I shall go up to six million, Monsieur. Yes, I would give away six million and be satisfied with the remainder, if they would set me free.'

'I swear that if one did not know this man was mad,' the inspector said, under his breath, 'he speaks with such conviction that you would believe he was telling the truth.'

'I am not mad, Monsieur, and I am telling the truth,' Faria replied, having picked up every word that the governor said, with that acuteness of hearing that is peculiar to prisoners. 'The treasure I mention really does exist and I am ready to sign an agreement with you, under which you will take me to a place that I shall designate, have the earth dug up in our presence and, if I am lying, if nothing is found, if I am mad, as you say, then you can bring me back to this same dungeon where I shall remain for ever, and die without asking for anything further from you or from anyone else.'

The governor burst out laughing.

'Is it a long way to your treasure?' he asked.

'About a hundred leagues from here,' Faria said.

'It's a clever idea,' said the governor. 'If every prisoner was to take his warders on a wild-goose chase for a hundred leagues, supposing the warders agreed to it, there is a good chance that the prisoner would manage to take to his heels as soon as he had the opportunity, which would no doubt occur in the course of such a journey.'

'It's an old trick,' said the inspector, 'and this gentleman cannot even claim to have invented it for himself.'

Then he turned back to the abbé. 'I asked you if you were well fed?'

'Monsieur,' Faria replied, 'swear to me in Christ's name to set me free if what I have told you is the truth, and I shall tell you the place where the treasure is buried.'

'Are you well fed?' the inspector insisted.

'But in this way, you take no risk: you can see that it is not in order to contrive some opportunity to escape, since I shall remain in prison while the journey is made.'

'You haven't replied to my question,' the inspector repeated impatiently.

'And you haven't replied to my request!' cried the abbé. 'Then be damned, like the other idiots who refused to believe me. You don't want my gold, then I shall keep it. You deny me my freedom, then God will give it to me. Go, I have nothing more to say.'

Throwing off his blanket, he picked up his scrap of plaster and once more sat down in the middle of his circle, where he went back to his lines and his sums.

'What is he doing?' the inspector asked, at the door.

'Counting his treasure,' the governor answered.

Faria's reply to this sarcastic remark was a look of the most sovereign contempt. They went out and the jailer locked the door behind them.

'Perhaps he did have some treasure, after all,' the inspector said, on his way up the stairs.

'Or dreamed about it,' the governor replied, 'and woke up the next morning, mad.'

'Of course,' the inspector remarked, with the naïvety of the corrupt, 'if he had really been rich, he would not be in prison.'

For Abbé Faria, that was the end of the adventure. He remained a prisoner and, following the inspector's visit, his reputation as an entertaining imbecile was greater than ever.

Those great treasure-hunters, Caligula and Nero, searchers after the unattainable, would have listened to the poor man's words and given him the opportunity that he wanted, the space that he valued so highly and the freedom for which he was ready to pay so great a price. But kings today, confined within the limits of probability, no longer possess the audacity of willpower. They are afraid of the ears that listen to their orders and the eyes that watch whatever they do. They no longer have any sense of the superiority of their divine being: they are men who wear crowns, nothing more. At one time they would have believed themselves (or, at least, have claimed to be) the sons of Jupiter, and their manners would somehow have reflected those of their father, the god: what happens beyond the clouds is not so easily controlled, but nowadays kings are well within reach. And, as despotic governments have always been loath to exhibit the effects of prison and torture in broad daylight – just as there are few instances of a victim of the Inquisition emerging with broken bones and bleeding wounds – so folly, that ulcer conceived in the mire of dungeons as a result of moral torture, almost always remains carefully hidden in the place of its birth, or else, if it should emerge, does so only to be buried once more in some dark hospital whose doctors can recognize neither the man nor his ideas in the shapeless wreck entrusted to them by its tired jailer.

Abbé Faria had gone mad in prison and was condemned, by his very madness, to perpetual confinement.

As for Dantès, the inspector was as good as his word. On returning to the governor's lodgings, he asked to be shown the committal order. The note on the prisoner was couched in the following terms:

EDMOND DANTES:
Fanatical Bonapartist. Played an active role in the return from Elba.
To be kept in solitary confinement, under the closest supervision.

This note was in a different handwriting and ink from the rest of the order, proving that it had been added after Dantès' imprisonment.

The accusation was too precise to allow any latitude for discussion, so above the words, which were bracketed together, the inspector wrote: 'No action.'

The visit had in a sense revived Dantès. Since his arrival at the prison he had forgotten to count the days, but the inspector had given him a new date, which Dantès had not forgotten. Behind him, with a piece of plaster that had fallen from his ceiling, he wrote on the wall: July 30, 1816. From that time on, he made a mark every day, so that he would no longer lose track of the passage of time.

The days went by, then weeks, then months. Dantès waited. He had begun by setting a limit of a fortnight on his release: if the inspector were to devote half the concern that he had appeared to feel to pursuing the matter, then a fortnight should be enough. When that time had expired, he decided that it had been ridiculous of him to think that the inspector would have taken up his case before returning to Paris. Since he could not return to Paris until the end of his tour of inspection, which might last a month or two, he gave himself three months instead of a fortnight. When the three months had passed, he found consolation in a different argument, with the result that he allowed six months; but when the six months were over, adding up all the days, it appeared that he had waited for ten and a half months. Nothing, in these ten months, had changed in the conditions of his imprisonment; he had received no encouraging news and when he questioned his jailer the man remained silent, as usual. Dantès began to doubt the evidence of his senses – to think that what he had taken for a memory was nothing more than a hallucination and that the ministering angel who had appeared to him in his prison had flown in on the wings of a dream.

A year later, the governor was transferred: he had been appointed to manage the fort at Ham, and took with him several of his subordinates, including Dantès' jailer. A new governor arrived. It would have taken him too long to learn the names of his prisoners, so he asked only to be told their numbers. There were fifty furnished rooms in this frightful lodging-house. Its inhabitants were called by the number of the one that they occupied, and the unfortunate young man was no longer called by his first name, Edmond, or his family name, Dantès. He became Number 34.

XV

NUMBER 34 AND NUMBER 27

Dantès went through all the stages of misery endured by prisoners who are left entombed in prison. He started with pride, which is the product of hope and the knowledge of one's innocence. Then he came to doubt his own innocence, which did a great deal to justify the governor's ideas on mental derangement. Finally, he fell from the summit of his pride and prayed, not to God, but to men; God is the last refuge. Such unfortunates, who should begin with Our Lord, only come to trust in Him after exhausting all other sources of hope. So Dantès prayed to be removed from his dungeon and put in another, even one that was deeper and darker: any change, albeit for the worse, would be a change, and would provide some relief for a few days. He begged to be allowed exercise, fresh air, books or implements. None of these requests was granted, but he continued to make them for all that. He had become accustomed to talk to his new jailer, even though the man was (if that was possible) more uncommunicative than his predecessor: it was still a pleasure to speak to another human being, however dumb. Dantès talked to hear the sound of his own voice; he had tried talking to himself when he was alone, but that frightened him.

Often, in the days of his freedom, Dantès had been alarmed at the idea of the obscure revels and terrifying camaraderie of those prison cells where vagabonds, bandits and murderers share their base pleasures. But he came to wish that he might be thrown into one of those holes, so that he could catch sight of some other face apart from that of his impassive jailer who refused to speak; and he dreamed of a convict's life: the shameful uniform, the ankle chain, the branded shoulder. At least men in the galleys enjoyed the company of their fellows, they breathed fresh air and could see the open sky. Convicts were lucky.

One day he begged the jailer to ask for him to be given a cell-mate: anyone, even the mad abbé he had heard about. However rough a jailer's skin, there is always something human beneath. Although he had never shown any sign of it, the jailer had often, in the depth of his heart, pitied this unfortunate young man whose captivity was so harsh; so he passed on Number 34's message to the governor. The latter, cautious as a politician, concluded however that Dantès wanted to start a riot among the prisoners, devise some plot or have a friend to help him in an escape attempt. He turned down the request.

Dantès had exhausted every human resource. Inevitably, as we said earlier, he turned to God. Every pious notion ever sown in the world and gleaned by some wretch, bowed beneath the yoke of destiny, now came to refresh his soul. He recalled the prayers that his mother had taught him and discovered a significance in them that he had not previously understood: to a happy man, a prayer is a monotonous composition, void of meaning, until the day when suffering deciphers the sublime language through which the poor victim addresses God.

So he prayed, not with fervour, but with fury. Praying aloud, he was no longer frightened by the sound of his own words; he fell into a sort of ecstasy, he saw God radiant in every word he uttered and confided every action of his humble and abandoned life to the will of this powerful Deity, deriving instruction from them and setting himself tasks to perform. At the end of every prayer he added the self-interested entreaty that men more often contrive to address to their fellows than to God: 'And forgive us our trespasses, as we forgive them that trespass against us.'

Despite his fervent prayers, Dantès remained a prisoner.

So his mind darkened and a cloud formed in front of his eyes. Dantès was a simple, uneducated man; to him, the past was covered by a murky veil that can be raised only by knowledge. In the solitude of his dungeon and the desert of his thoughts, he could not reconstruct ages past, revive extinct races or rebuild those antique cities that imagination augments and poeticizes so that they pass before one's eyes, gigantic and lit by fiery skies, as in Martin's Babylonian scenes.[1] All he had were: his own past, which was so short; his present – so sombre; and his future – so uncertain: nineteen years of light to contemplate, in what might be eternal darkness! There was consequently nothing to help distract his mind. His energetic spirit, which would have wished for nothing better than to take flight through the ages, was forced to remain trapped like an eagle in a cage. He clung to one idea: that of his happiness, which had been destroyed, for no apparent reason, by an unprecedented stroke of fate. He refused to release this thought, turning it over and over, as it were consuming it ravenously, like the pitiless Ugolino[2] devouring Archbishop Roger's skull in Dante's *Inferno*. His faith had been transient and he lost it, as others do when they achieve success. The difference was that he had not gained by it.

Fury followed asceticism. Edmond's curses made his jailer start back in horror. He dashed himself against the walls of his prison and raged against everything around him, himself first of all, at the slightest discomfort caused by a grain of sand, a straw or a draught. Then it was that he recalled the denunciatory letter that he had seen, that Villefort had shown him, that his hands had touched. Every line blazed on the cell wall like the *Mene, Mene, Tekel, Upharsin* at Belshazzar's feast.[3] He decided that it was human hatred and not divine vengeance that had plunged him into this abyss. He doomed these unknown men to every torment that his inflamed imagination could devise, while still considering that the most frightful were too mild and, above all, too brief for them: torture was followed by death, and death brought, if not repose, at least an insensibility that resembled it.

He often told himself, thinking of his enemies, that tranquillity was death and that other means, apart from death, were needed by whoever wished to inflict a cruel punishment, until eventually he fell into the melancholy quietude of thoughts of suicide. Woe to the man who, sliding into misfortune, is drawn by such dark thoughts! This is one of those dead seas that seem to offer the inviting blue of pure waters, but where the swimmer's feet are sucked into a bituminous mire which draws him, drags him down and swallows him up. Once caught, he is lost if God does not come to his aid, and every effort that he makes pulls him nearer to death.

However, this state of moral agony is less fearful than the suffering that precedes it or the punishment that may follow: it is a kind of dizzying comfort to contemplate the open abyss when, at the bottom of that abyss, lies nothingness. Reaching this point, Edmond found some consolation in the idea; all his sufferings, all his sorrows and the procession of spectres that follow in their train seemed to take wing and fly from the corner of his prison where the angel of death might rest his silent foot. Dantès looked with equanimity at his past life, with terror at what was to come, and chose the mid-point that appeared to offer a refuge.

'Sometimes,' he thought at such moments, 'in my distant voyages, when I was still a man – and when that man, free and powerful, gave orders to others that they carried out – I used to see the sky open, the sea tremble and groan, a storm brewing in some part of the sky and thrashing the horizon with its wings like a giant eagle; then I would feel that my vessel was nothing but a useless refuge, itself shaking and shuddering, as light as a feather in the hand of a giant. Soon the appearance of some sharp rocks and the awful thundering of the waves against them spoke to me of death, and death appalled me. I strove to escape it, uniting all my strength as a man and all my skill as a sailor in the struggle against God! . . . All this, because I was happy then; to return to life was to return to happiness; because I had not asked for death, I had not chosen it; because finally sleep on a bed of seaweed and pebbles seemed hard to me – I, who believed myself to be a creature made in the image of God, rebelled at the idea of serving, after my death, as nourishment for seagulls and vultures. But today it is different: I have lost everything that could make me love life and now death smiles at me like a nursemaid to the child she will rock to sleep. Today I die at my own pleasure and go to sleep, tired and broken, as I used to fall asleep after one of those evenings of despair and fury when I had counted three thousand circuits of my room, that is to say thirty thousand paces, or almost ten leagues.'

As soon as this thought had taken root in the young man's mind he became milder and more amenable. He was more ready to accept his hard bed and black bread, he ate less, no longer slept and found this remainder of a life more or less bearable, being sure that he could cast it off when he wanted to, like a discarded suit of clothes.

There were two ways for him to die. The first was simple: it involved fixing his kerchief to one of the bars on the window and hanging himself. The alternative was to pretend to eat and allow himself to die of hunger. Dantès was very loath to adopt the first course. He had been brought up with a horror of pirates, people who are hanged from the yardarm, so he saw hanging as an ignominious method of execution which he did not want to apply to himself. Consequently he chose the second way and began to carry out his decision that very day.

Almost four years had passed while his mood fluctuated in the way we have described. At the end of the second, Dantès had ceased to count the days and lapsed back into the unawareness of time from which the inspector's visit had roused him.

Having said 'I wish to die' and chosen his own death, Dantès had given thought to the implications and, afraid that he might change his mind, had sworn to himself that he would die in this way. 'When they bring me my morning and evening meals,' he thought, 'I shall throw the food out of the window, and so appear to have eaten it.'

He did as he had promised. Twice a day, he threw his food out of the little barred opening which gave him no more than a glimpse of the sky, first joyfully, then thoughtfully and finally with regret. He had to remind himself of the oath he had sworn to find the strength to pursue his awful resolution. Seen with the eyes of hunger, this food, which had formerly disgusted him, appeared appetizing to look at and smelled exquisite. Sometimes he held the plate containing it for an hour in his hand, staring at the piece of rotten meat or repulsive fish, and the mouldy black bread. The last instinct of survival struggled within him and occasionally defeated his resolve. At such times, his dungeon seemed less dark and his situation less desperate. He was still young, he must be about twenty-five or twenty-six, so he had roughly fifty years left to live, that is to say twice as long as he had lived so far. In this vast expanse of time, how many different events might unlock the doors and break down the walls of the Château d'If, and set him free! At such times he put his lips towards the meal that, like a deliberate Tantalus, he was snatching from his own mouth. But then he would remember the oath which his nature was too generous to break for fear that he might end by despising himself. So, firm and implacable, he summoned up the little remnant of life that remained to him, until the day came when they brought him his supper and he was too weak to get up and throw it out of the window.

The next day he was unable to see and could hardly hear.

The jailer thought he was seriously ill. Edmond hoped for a quick death.

So the day passed. Edmond felt himself overtaken by a numbing sense of drowsiness, which was not altogether unpleasant. The cramps in his stomach had died down and his burning thirst had calmed. When he closed his eyes, he saw a host of brilliant lights like those will-o'-the-wisps that hover at night over marshlands: this was the twilight of that unknown country known as death. Suddenly, in the evening at about nine o'clock, he heard a dull sound on the wall beside which he was lying.

So many verminous creatures used to make noises in the prison that Edmond had gradually become accustomed to sleeping through them; but this time, either because his senses were heightened by abstinence or because the noise really was louder than usual, or because at this final moment everything acquires some importance, Edmond raised his head so that he could hear better.

It was a regular scratching that seemed to suggest a huge claw or powerful teeth, or else the tapping of some implement on the stones. Weak as he was, the young man's brain was struck by an ordinary notion which is constantly present in a prisoner's mind: freedom. This noise came so aptly at the moment when, for him, every noise was about to cease, that he felt God must finally be taking pity on his suffering an sending him this noise to warn him to stop on the edge of the grave above which his foot was already poised. Who knows? Perhaps one of his friends, one of those beloved beings about whom he had thought so much that his mind was worn out with it, might be concerned for him at this moment and trying to lessen the distance between them.

No, Edmond must surely be mistaken: this was one of the hallucinations that hover around the doors of death.

However, he kept listening to the noise. It lasted about three hours, then he heard a sort of crumbling sound and the noise ceased.

A few hours later, it resumed, louder and nearer. Edmond was already interested in this burrowing that kept him company. Then, suddenly, the jailer came in.

In the week since he had decided to die and for the four days since he had begun to carry out his plan, Edmond had not spoken a word to the man, had not replied when he asked what Edmond thought was the matter with him, and had turned his face to the wall when he was too closely observed. But today the jailer might hear the dull grating sound, become alarmed by it and take steps to end it, thus perhaps upsetting that flicker of hope, the very idea of which delighted Dantès in his last hours.

The jailer was bringing his lunch.

Dantès raised himself on his bed and, in as loud a voice as he could muster, began to talk about everything: about the poor quality of the food he was given and the coldness of his dungeon, muttering and complaining so that he would have an excuse to speak louder. He tried the patience of the jailer, who had actually requested clear broth and fresh bread that day for his sick prisoner and was bringing them to him.

Fortunately, he imagined that Dantès was delirious. He put the food down on the miserable rickety table where he usually left it, and went out.

As soon as he was free to do so, Edmond joyfully went back to listen. The noise had become so clear that the young man could now hear it easily.

'There's no doubt about it,' he thought. 'Since the noise is continuing, even by day, it must be some unfortunate prisoner like myself who is trying to escape. Oh, if only I was beside him! How willingly I would help!'

Then, suddenly, a dark cloud passed across this first light of hope, in a mind accustomed to misfortune and unable easily to revert to feelings of joy: the idea struck him that the noise was caused by some workmen whom the governor was employing to repair one of the neighbouring cells.

It would be easy to find out, but how could he risk asking? Of course, he could just wait for the jailer to come, ask him to listen to the noise and judge his reaction; but if he were to satisfy his curiosity in this way, might he not sacrifice some more precious interest for a very short-lived gain? Unfortunately, Edmond's head was an empty vessel, deafened by the buzzing of a single idea; he was so weak that his mind drifted like a whiff of smoke and could not fasten on a single thought. He could see only one way to sharpen his wits and recover the lucidity of his judgement: he turned towards the still-steaming broth that the jailer had just put down on the table, got up, staggered over to it, took the cup, raised it to his lips and drank down the liquid that it contained with an unspeakable sensation of well-being.

He had the resolution to leave it at that: he had heard that when unfortunate, shipwrecked mariners had been picked up in the last extremity of starvation, they had died after gorging themselves on too much solid food. Edmond put the bread – which he was already raising to his lips – back on the table and returned to his bed. He no longer wished to die.

He soon felt that some light was once again penetrating his brain: all his vague and almost indefinable ideas resumed their place on that marvellous chessboard where perhaps a single extra square is enough to ensure the superiority of men over animals. He was able to think and to strengthen his thoughts by reasoning.

So he told himself: 'I must carry out a test, but without compromising anyone. If the person I can hear is an ordinary workman, I have only to knock against the wall and he will immediately stop what he is doing to try and guess who is knocking and why. But since he will not only be working legitimately, but also to orders, he will soon resume what he was doing. If, on the contrary, he is a prisoner, he will be alarmed by the noise that I make. He will be afraid of being found out, so he will stop work and only come back to it this evening, when he imagines everyone to be in bed and asleep.'

Edmond got up again. This time his legs were steady and his eyes could see clearly. He went over to a corner of the cell, took out a stone that had been loosened by the damp, and came back in order to tap it against the wall at the very point where the echoing sound was loudest.

He knocked three times.

At the first knock, the noise stopped, as if by magic.

Edmond listened intently. An hour passed, then two, but no further sound could be heard. He had created a total silence on the far side of the wall.

Full of hope, he ate a few crumbs of the bread, swallowed some mouthfuls of water and, thanks to the powerful constitution with which nature had endowed him, was more or less restored to himself.

The day went by and the silence continued. Night came, and the noise had still not resumed.

'It's a prisoner,' Edmond thought, with inexpressible joy. At this, his mind began to race and life returned to him, with all the more force for having something to exercise it upon.

The night passed without him hearing the slightest sound. That night, Edmond did not close his eyes.

Daylight returned and the jailer came in with more food. Edmond had already eaten his previous meal and he devoured this one, continually listening out for the noise, which did not come, fearful that it might have ceased for ever. He walked ten or twelve leagues around his dungeon, spending whole hours shaking the iron bars on his window to restore to his limbs the strength and elasticity that they had lost over a long period without exercise, in short preparing himself for the struggle with whatever fate had in store for him, like a wrestler flexing his arms and rubbing his body with oil before he enters the ring. Then, between these periods of feverish activity, he listened to hear if the sound had returned, growing impatient with the caution shown by this prisoner who had not guessed that it was another like himself who had disturbed him in his efforts to escape – another prisoner whose eagerness to be free was at least as great as his own.

Three days went by, seventy-two deadly hours which he counted, minute by minute.

Finally, one evening when the jailer had just paid his final visit, when Dantès pressed his ear to the wall for the hundredth time, he thought that a barely perceptible scratching echoed in his head as it rested against the silent stones.

Dantès moved back to compose his whirling brain, walked a few times round the room, then put his ear again to the same spot.

There was no doubt: something was happening on the other side. The prisoner had recognized the danger of his earlier method and had changed it: certainly, in order to carry on the work in greater security, he was using a lever instead of a chisel.

Encouraged by the discovery, Edmond decided to come to the assistance of this indefatigable workman. He began by moving his bed, behind which he judged that the burrowing was taking place, and looked around for some object which he could use to chip away at the wall, dig out the damp cement and eventually dislodge a stone. But he could see nothing. He had no knife or other cutting implement, no metal except iron bars, and he had tested these bars often enough to know that they were firmly set and that it was not even worth the effort of trying to loosen them.

His only furniture was a bed, a chair, a table, a bucket and a pitcher.

Certainly, there were iron brackets on the bed, but they were fixed to the wood with screws; it would take a screwdriver to turn these and take off the brackets.

There was nothing on the table and chair. The bucket had once had a handle, but it had been removed.

Only one thing remained for Dantès to do, which was to break the pitcher and set to work with one of the earthenware fragments shaped to a point. He swung the pitcher against a stone and it shattered.

He chose two or three pointed fragments and hid them in his mattress, leaving the rest scattered around on the floor: the breaking of the pitcher was too natural an occurrence for it to arouse any comment.

Edmond had the whole night to work, but he made little progress in the dark because he had to feel his way and he realized that he was blunting his crude implement against a piece of stone harder than it. So he put his bed back and waited for daylight. Recovering hope, he had recovered patience.

Throughout that night he listened, hearing the unknown miner continue his subterranean burrowing.

Day came and the jailer entered. Dantès told him that, the evening before, while he was taking a drink straight from the pitcher, it had slipped out of his hands and broken on the ground. The jailer went off, grumbling, to get a new pitcher, without even bothering to take away the pieces from the previous one. He returned a few moments later, told the prisoner to be more careful and then left.

Dantès was overjoyed at hearing the sound of the bolt which previously used to make his heart sink every time it slammed shut. He listened to the noise of footsteps fading and, when it died away, hurried over to his bed and pulled it aside. By the dim light of day that entered the dungeon, he could see that he had achieved nothing by his efforts the night before, because he had attacked the stone itself, instead of the plaster around it.

This plaster had been softened by damp. With a thrill of joy, Dantès saw that fragments of it could be removed. Admittedly, these fragments were so small as to be almost invisible, but after half an hour, even so, Dantès had scraped away roughly a handful. A mathematician could have calculated that after some two years' work, provided he did not encounter the solid rock, it would be possible to dig out a passage two feet across and twenty feet deep.

Realizing this, the prisoner regretted not having devoted the long hours that had already passed, ever more slowly, to this task, instead of wasting them in hope, prayer and despair. However slow the work, how much would he have achieved in the six or so years that he had spent buried in this dungeon! The idea fired him with renewed enthusiasm.

Over the next three days, taking extraordinary care to avoid discovery, he managed to remove all the plaster and expose the stone. The wall was composed of rubble which had been strengthened in places by blocks of hewn stone. He had almost loosened one of these blocks, and he now had to shift it in its socket. He tried to do so with his nails, but made no impression, and the fragments of the pitcher which Dantès pushed into the gaps, in the hope of using them as a lever, broke when he tried to do so.

After an hour of fruitless effort, he got up, perspiring with anguish. Was he to be defeated at the very start? Would he have to wait, helpless and inactive, for his neighbour to do everything – when the man himself might become discouraged?

Then an idea occurred to him, and he stood there, smiling. Of its own accord, the sweat dried on his forehead.

Every day the jailer brought Dantès his soup in a tin pot. This pot contained soup for him and for another prisoner, because Dantès had noticed that it was always either full or half empty, depending on whether the turnkey had started his rounds, giving out the food, with Dantès or with his fellow-prisoner.

The pot had an iron handle: it was this iron handle that Dantès coveted – and would have paid for it, if required to do so, with ten years of his life.

The jailer poured the contents of the pot into Dantès' plate. After eating his soup with a wooden spoon, Dantès would wash the plate, so that it could serve the same purpose each day.

In the evening, Dantès put his plate on the floor, half-way between the door and the table. As he came in, the jailer stepped on the plate and broke it into a thousand pieces.

This time, he had nothing to reproach Dantès with: he had been wrong to leave his plate on the floor, admittedly, but the jailer had been wrong not to look where he was walking. So he merely grumbled. Then he looked around to see where he could pour the soup. As Dantès had only that one plate, there was no alternative.

'Leave the pot,' Dantès said. 'You can collect it when you bring me my dinner tomorrow.'

This advice appealed to the jailer, since it saved him the trouble of going back upstairs, then down and back up again. He left the pot. Dantès shuddered with joy.

This time, he eagerly ate the soup and the meat which, as is customary in prisons, was put in with the soup. Then, after waiting for an hour, to make sure that the jailer did not change his mind, he moved his bed, took the pot, slipped the end of the handle between the stone block which he had scraped clean of plaster and the surrounding rubble, and began to lever it. A slight movement in the stone proved to him that he was succeeding; and indeed, after an hour, the stone had been removed from the wall, leaving a gap more than one and a half feet in diameter.

Dantès carefully swept up all the plaster, distributed it around the corners of the cell, scraped at the greyish earth with a splinter from his jug and covered the plaster in earth.

Then, wanting to take full advantage of this night in which chance – or, rather, the ingenuity of the scheme that he had dreamt up – had delivered so precious an implement to him, he continued to dig eagerly. At dawn, he replaced the stone in its hole, pushed his bed against the wall and lay down on it.

His breakfast consisted of a piece of bread. The jailer came in and put it on the table.

'What? Aren't you bringing me a new plate?' Dantès asked.

'No,' said the turnkey. 'You break everything. You smashed your jug and it's your fault that I broke your plate. If all the prisoners were responsible for as much damage, the government couldn't keep up with it. We are leaving you the pot and your soup will be poured into that. In this way, perhaps you won't destroy everything around here.'

Dantès raised his eyes to heaven and joined his hands in prayer under the blanket.

This piece of iron which he had been allowed to keep aroused a more profound wave of gratitude towards heaven in his heart than he had experienced, in his previous life, from the greatest blessings that had descended upon him.

However, he had noticed that, since he himself had started to work, the other prisoner was no longer digging.

No matter. This was no reason to give up his efforts. That evening, thanks to his new implement, he had extracted more than ten handfuls of stone filling, plaster and mortar from the wall.

When the time came for the jailer's visit, he straightened out the twisted handle of the pot and put the receptacle back in its usual place. The turnkey poured out the standard ration of soup and meat; or, rather, of soup and fish, because this happened to be a fast day: three times a week the prisoners were given a meatless diet. That would have been another way of counting time, if Dantès had not long ago given up measuring it.

Then, after pouring out the soup, the turnkey went out.

This time Dantès wanted to ascertain whether his neighbour had in fact stopped working. He listened. All was as silent as it had been during the three days when the work was interrupted. Dantès sighed. His neighbour was clearly suspicious of him.

However, he did not give up and continued to work throughout the night. But after two or three hours of digging, he came up against an obstruction. The iron had ceased to cut, but slid across a flat surface.

Dantès felt the object with his hands and realized that he had hit a beam. It ran across – or, rather, entirely blocked – the hole that Dantès had started to dig.

Now he would have to dig over or under. The poor young man had not foreseen this obstacle.

'Oh, my God, my God!' he cried. 'I have prayed so often to You that I hoped You might have heard me. My God! After having deprived me of freedom in life, oh, God! After having deprived me of the calm of death. Oh, God! When you had recalled me to life, have pity on me! God! Do not let me die in despair!'

'Who is it that speaks of God and despair at one and the same time?' asked a voice which seemed to come from beneath the earth and which, muffled by the darkness, sounded on the young man's ears with a sepulchral tone. Edmond felt his hair rise on his head and shuffled back, still kneeling.

'Ah!' he exclaimed. 'I can hear a man's voice!'

For the past four or five years, Edmond had heard no one speak except his jailer; and, to a prisoner, a jailer is not a man but a living door added to the oak door of his cell and a bar of flesh joined to his bars of iron.

'In heaven's name!' Dantès cried. 'Whoever spoke, speak again, even though your voice terrified me. Who are you?'

'Tell me who you are,' the voice demanded.

'An unfortunate prisoner,' Dantès said, not at all unwilling to reply.

'Of what country?'

'France.'

'And your name?'

'Edmond Dantès.'

'Profession?'

'Seaman.'

'How long have you been here?'

'Since February the twenty-eighth, 1815.'

'What was your crime?'

'I am innocent.'

'But what were you accused of?'

'Conspiring for the return of the emperor.'

'What! The return of the emperor! Is he no longer on the throne, then?'

'He abdicated in Fontainebleau in 1814 and was exiled to the island of Elba. But what of yourself? How long have you been here, if you know nothing of all that?'

'Since 1811.'

Dantès shuddered. This man had been four years longer in prison than he had.

'Very well. Do not dig any more,' the voice said, speaking rapidly. 'Just tell me at what level is the hole that you have dug?'

'At ground level.'

'How is it concealed?'

'Behind my bed.'

'Has your bed been moved since you were in the cell?'

'Not once.'

'What is outside your cell?'

'A corridor.'

'Which leads where?'

'To the courtyard.'

'Alas!' the voice exclaimed.

'Heavens above, what is the matter?' Dantès cried.

'The matter is that I have made a mistake, that the inaccuracy of my drawings led me astray, that I am lost for not having a compass, that a deviation the thickness of a line on my plan was equal to fifteen feet on the ground and that I mistook the wall where you have been digging for that of the castle!'

'But then you would have come out on the sea.'

'That is what I wanted.'

'Suppose you had succeeded.'

'I should have plunged into it and swum for one of the islands in the vicinity of the Château d'If, either the Ile de Daume or the Ile de Tiboulen, or even the coast itself; and then I should have been saved.'

'Would you have managed to swim so far?'

'God would have given me strength. But now all is lost.'

'Lost?'

'Yes. Seal up your hole carefully, stop working on it, take no notice of anything and wait for me to contact you.'

'Who are you? At least tell me who you are!'

'I am . . . I am Number 27.'

'Don't you trust me, then?' Dantès asked.

He thought he heard a bitter laugh make its way through the stonework towards him.

'Oh, I'm a good Christian,' he called, guessing instinctively that the man was thinking of leaving him. 'I swear on Christ's name that I would allow myself to be killed rather than give away a hint of the truth to your jailers and mine. But, in heaven's name, do not deprive me of your presence, do not deprive me of your voice or – I swear it – I shall dash my head against the wall, and you will have my death on your conscience.'

'How old are you? Your voice sounds like that of a young man.'

'I do not know my age, because I have had no means of measuring time since I have been here. All I know is that I was approaching nineteen when I was arrested, on February the eighteenth, 1815.'

'Not quite twenty-six,' the voice muttered. 'Very well, then: at that age, men are not yet traitors.'

'No, no! I swear it,' Dantès said again. 'I have already told you, and I repeat, that I would let myself be cut into pieces rather than betray you.'

'You did well to talk to me, and you did well to beg me, because I was about to change my plans and have nothing to do with you. But I am reassured by your age. I shall join you. Expect me.'

'When?'

'I must calculate the risks. I shall give you a signal.'

'But you won't abandon me, you won't leave me alone, you will come to me or allow me to go to you? We shall escape together and, if we cannot escape, we shall talk: you of those you love, I of those who are dear to me. You must love someone?'

'I am alone in the world.'

'Then you shall love me. If you are young, I shall be your friend; if you are old, your son. I have a father who must be seventy years old, if he is still alive. I loved only him and a young woman called Mercédès. My father has not forgotten me, I am sure; but as for her – God knows if she still thinks of me. I shall love you as I loved my father.'

'Very well,' said the prisoner. 'Until tomorrow.'

These few words were said in tones that convinced Dantès. He asked nothing more, but got up, took the same precautions as before with the rubble he had removed from the wall, and pushed his bed back against it.

And then he gave himself over entirely to his feelings of happiness. He was certainly no longer going to be alone, he might perhaps even be free. The worst case, should he remain a prisoner, was to have a companion: captivity shared is only semi-captivity. Sighs united together are almost prayers; prayers coming from two hearts are almost acts of grace.

Throughout the day, Dantès came and went in his cell, his heart leaping with joy. From time to time this joy stifled him. At the least noise in the corridor, he leapt on to his bed, clasping his chest with his hands. Once or twice his thoughts turned to the fear that he might be separated from this stranger, whom he already loved as a friend. So he had made up his mind: at the moment when the jailer pushed his bed aside and bent over to examine the opening in the wall, he would crack his head open with the stone on which his jug stood. He knew quite well that he would be condemned to death; but was he not about to die of boredom and despair when that miraculous sound had brought him back to life?

In the evening the jailer came. Dantès was on his bed, feeling that there he was better able to guard the unfinished opening. He must have looked at this unwelcome visitor in a peculiar manner, because the man said: 'Come, come, are you going mad again?'

Dantès did not answer, fearing that the emotion in his voice might betray him.

The jailer left, shaking his head.

When night came, Dantès thought that his neighbour would take advantage of the silence and darkness to resume their conversation, but he was wrong. The night passed but no sound came to relieve his feverish expectation. But the following day, after the morning visit, when he had just moved his bed away from the wall, he heard three knocks, equally spaced. He fell to his knees.

'Is that you?' he said. 'I am here!'

'Has your jailer left?' the voice asked.

'Yes,' Dantès said. 'He will not be back until this evening. We have twelve hours' freedom.'

'So it is safe for me to act?' asked the voice.

'Yes, yes; don't delay, do it now, I beg you.'

Dantès was half inside the opening and, at this moment, the portion of ground on which he was resting his two hands seemed to give way beneath him. He plunged back, while a mass of earth, rubble and broken stones fell away into a hole that had opened up beneath the opening which he himself had made. Then, in the bottom of this dark hole, the depth of which he was unable to assess, he saw a head appear, then some shoulders and finally a whole man, who emerged, with a fair degree of agility, from the pit they had dug.

XVI

AN ITALIAN SCHOLAR

Dantès embraced this new friend for whom he had waited so long and with such impatience, and drew him over to the window, so that the faint light that seeped from outside into the cell would illuminate his face.

He was short in stature, with hair whitened by suffering more than by age, a penetrating eye hidden beneath thick, grizzled brows, and a still-black beard that extended to his chest. The leanness of his face, which was deeply furrowed, and the firm moulding of his features implied a man more accustomed to exercise his spiritual than his physical faculties. This newcomer's brow was bathed in sweat.

As for his clothes, their original form was impossible to make out, for they were in tatters.

He appeared to be at least sixty-five, though some agility in his movements suggested that he might be younger than he appeared after his long captivity.

He showed a kind of pleasure on receiving the young man's effusions: for a moment, a soul chilled to its depth seemed to be heated and to melt in contact with the other's ardour. He thanked him with some warmth for his cordiality, though he must have been deeply disappointed at finding another dungeon where he had expected to find freedom.

'First of all,' he said, 'let us see if we can disguise the traces of my entry from your jailers. All our future peace of mind depends on their not knowing what has happened.'

He bent down towards the opening, took the stone, which he lifted easily despite its weight, and put it back into the hole.

'This stone was very crudely cut out,' he said, shaking his head. 'Don't you have any tools?'

'Do you have any?' Dantès asked in astonishment.

'I have made myself a few. Apart from a file, I have everything I need: chisel, pliers, a lever.'

'I should be most curious to see these products of your patient efforts,' Dantès said.

'Well then, to start with, here is a chisel.' He showed him a strong, sharpened blade fixed in a beechwood handle.

'How did you make that?' Dantès asked.

'From one of the pegs from my bed. This is the tool with which I dug almost the whole of the passage that brought me here – roughly fifty feet.'

'Fifty feet!' Dantès cried, in a kind of terror.

'Keep your voice down, young man, keep your voice down. They often listen at the prisoners' doors.'

'They know that I am alone.'

'No matter.'

'You are telling me that you dug fifty feet to reach me here?'

'Yes, that is approximately the distance between my cell and yours. But I miscalculated the curve, not having any geometrical instrument with which to draw up a relative scale: instead of a forty-foot ellipse, the measurement was fifty feet. As I told you, I was expecting to reach the outer wall, break through it and throw myself into the sea. I followed the line of the corridor that runs outside your room, instead of going underneath it – and all my labour is in vain, because this corridor leads to a courtyard full of guards.'

'True,' said Dantès. 'But this corridor only touches on one wall of my room, and there are four of them.'

'Of course – but, to start with, one of them is solid rock: it would take ten miners, fully equipped, ten years' work to cut through it. This one here must be contiguous with the foundations of the governor's quarters: we should break into cellars, which are clearly locked, and be recaptured. The other wall . . . Wait a moment, what is beyond the other wall?'

This side of the dungeon was the one with the tiny window through which the daylight shone: the opening narrowed progressively as it went towards the light. Even though a child could not have passed through it, it was furnished with three rows of iron bars, which would have reassured the most distrustful jailer as to the impossibility of escape.

As he asked the question, the newcomer pulled the table over to the window.

'Climb up here,' he told Dantès.

Dantès obeyed, climbed on to the table and, guessing his companion's intentions, pressed his back against the wall and held out his cupped hands. The man who had taken the number of his cell – and whose true name Dantès still did not know – climbed up with more agility than one might have expected from a man of his age, like a cat or a lizard, first on to the table, then from the table on to Dantès' hands, then from his hands on to his shoulders. Bent double, because the roof of the dungeon prevented him from standing upright, he thrust his head between the first row of bars and in that way could see outside and downwards.

Immediately, he drew his head back sharply.

'Oh, oh!' he said. 'I guessed as much.'

And he slipped down past Dantès on to the table and from there jumped to the ground.

'What did you guess?' the young man asked anxiously, jumping down after him.

The old prisoner thought for a while, then said: 'Yes, that's it. The fourth wall of your dungeon overlooks a gallery on the outside of the castle, a sort of walkway along which patrols can march or sentries keep watch.'

'Are you sure?'

'I saw the shako of a soldier and the tip of his rifle: I jumped back quickly because I was afraid he might see me.'

'Well?' Dantès asked.

'You can clearly see that it is impossible to escape through your cell.'

'So, what now?'

'So, let God's will be done,' said the old prisoner, a look of profound resignation crossing his face.

With a mixture of astonishment and admiration, Dantès looked at this man who, with such philosophical resignation, could give up the hope that he had nurtured for so long.

'Now, tell me who you are,' Dantès said.

'Why, yes, I will if you like and if it still interests you, now that I can no longer be of any use to you.'

'You can console me and support me, because you seem to me a person of exceptional strength.'

The abbé smiled sadly.

'I am Abbé Faria. I have been a prisoner in the Château d'If since 1811, as you already know, but I spent three years before that in the fortress of Fenestrelle. In 1811 I was transferred from Piedmont to France. Then it was that I learned that Fate – who at the time appeared to be his servant – had given Napoleon a son and that while still in his cradle this child had been named King of Rome.

At that time I could never have guessed what you told me a moment ago: that four years later the colossus would be overturned. So who rules in France? Napoleon II?'

'No, Louis XVIII.'

'Louis XVIII, brother of Louis XVI! Heaven's decrees are shrouded in mystery. Why did Providence choose to bring down the one whom she had raised up, and raise the one she had brought down?'

Dantès looked at this man, who had momentarily forgotten his own fate so that he might contemplate that of the world.

'Yes, indeed, yes,' he went on. 'It is just as in England: after Charles I, Cromwell; after Cromwell, Charles II. Then perhaps after James II, some son-in-law or other, some relative, some Prince of Orange, a *Stathouder* who will appoint himself king. And then: new concessions to the people, a constitution, liberty! You will see all this, young man,' he said, turning to Dantès and examining him with deep, shining eyes, like those of a prophet. 'You are still young enough, you will see this.'

'Yes, if I ever get out of here.'

'That's true,' said Abbé Faria. 'We are prisoners. Sometimes I forget it and, because my eyes penetrate the walls that enclose me, think myself at liberty.'

'But why are you imprisoned?'

'Me? Because in 1807 I dreamed up the plan that Napoleon tried to carry out in 1811; because, like Machiavelli, I wanted a single, great empire, solid and strong, to emerge from all those petty principalities that make Italy a swarm of tyrannical but feeble little kingdoms; because I thought I had discovered my Cesare Borgia in a royal simpleton who pretended to agree with me, the better to betray me. This was the ambition of Alexander VI and Clement VII. It will always fail, because they tried in vain, and even Napoleon could not succeed. Without any doubt, Italy is accursed.'

He bowed his head.

Dantès could not understand how a man could risk his life in such a cause. He did, indeed, know Napoleon, since he had seen and spoken to him, but on the other hand he had no idea who Clement VII and Alexander VI were. He was beginning to share the opinion of his jailer, which was that generally held in the Château d'If.

'Aren't you the priest who is said to be . . . ill?'

'You mean, who is thought to be mad?'

'I didn't like to say it,' Dantès replied, smiling.

'Yes,' Faria went on, with a bitter laugh. 'Yes, I am the one they think is mad. I am the one who has for so long entertained visitors to the prison and who would amuse the little children if there were any in this sojourn of hopeless agony.'

For a short time Dantès did not move or speak.

'So, you have abandoned any idea of escape?'

'I can see that escape is impossible. It is a rebellion against God to attempt something that God does not wish to be achieved.'

'But why be discouraged? It would be asking too much of Providence if you were to expect to succeed at the first attempt. Why not start out again in a different direction?'

'Can you imagine what I have done so far, you who speak about beginning again? Do you realize that it took me four years to make the tools that I have? Do you realize that for the past two years I have been digging and scraping in earth as hard as granite? Do you know that I have had to lay bare stones that I would never previously have thought I could shift, that whole days were spent in these titanic efforts and that, by the evening, I was happy when I had removed a square inch of the old mortar, which had become as hard as the stone itself? Do you realize that to accommodate all the soil and all the stones that I dug up, I had to break through into a stairway and bury the rubble bit by bit in the stairwell; and that the well is now full so that I could not fit another handful of dust into it? Finally, do you realize that I thought my labours were at an end, that I felt I had just enough strength to complete the task, and that God has now not only set back my goal but removed it, I know not where? Oh, let me tell you, and repeat it: I shall not take another step to try and regain my freedom, since God's will is for me to have lost it for ever.'

Edmond lowered his head, so that the man would not perceive that the joy of having a companion was preventing him from sympathizing, as he should, with the prisoner's torment at his failure to escape. Abbé Faria slumped down on Edmond's bed, while Edmond remained standing.

The young man had never thought about escape. There are things that seem so impossible that one instinctively avoids them and doesn't even consider attempting them. To dig fifty feet beneath the ground, to spend three years on this task, only to arrive – if you were successful – at a sheer precipice above the sea; to descend fifty, sixty, perhaps a hundred feet, only to fall and crush your head against the rocks – if the sentries had not already shot you; and, even supposing you managed to evade all these dangers, to be faced with swimming a distance of a league – all this was too much for one not to resign oneself; and, as we have seen already, Dantès had almost resigned himself to the point of death.

But now that he had seen an old man clasping on to life with such energy and giving him the example of such desperate resolve, he started to reflect and to measure his courage. Another man had attempted to do something that he had not even thought of doing; another, less young, less strong and less agile than himself, had succeeded, by sheer skill and patience, in acquiring all the implements he needed for this incredible task, which had failed only because of a failure of measurement; someone else had done all this, so nothing was impossible for Dantès. Faria had dug fifty feet, he would dig a hundred; Faria, at the age of fifty, had spent three years on the work; he was only half Faria's age, he could afford six; Faria, the priest, the learned churchman, had not shrunk from the prospect of swimming from the Château d'If to the islands of Daume, Ratonneau or Lemaire; so would he, Edmond the sailor, Dantès the bold swimmer, who had so often plunged to the bottom of the sea to fetch a branch of coral – would he shrink from swimming a league? How long did it take to swim a league: one hour? And had he not spent whole hours on end in the sea without setting foot on shore? No, Dantès needed only to be encouraged by example. Anything that another man had done or could have done, Dantès would do.

He thought for a moment. 'I have found what you were looking for,' he told the old man.

Faria shivered, and looked up with an expression that announced that if Dantès was telling the truth, his companion's despair would be short-lived. 'You?' he asked. 'Come, now, what have you found?'

'The tunnel that you dug to reach here from your own cell extends in the same direction as the outer gallery. Is that so?'

'Yes.'

'It can only be some fifteen feet away from it?'

'At the most.'

'Well, around the middle of this tunnel we will dig another at right-angles to it. This time, you will take your measurements more carefully. We will come out on to the exterior gallery. We shall kill the sentry and escape. All we need, for this plan to succeed, is resolve, and you have that; and strength, which I have. I say nothing of patience: you have demonstrated it already and I shall do the same.'

'One moment,' the abbé replied. 'My good friend, you do not realize the nature of my resolve or the use that I intend to make of my strength. As for patience, I have been patient enough, in resuming every morning the work that I left the night before, and, every night, that which I left in the morning. But you must understand this, young man: I thought that I was serving God by freeing one of His creatures who, being innocent, had not been condemned.'

'Well, then,' said Dantès. 'What is different now; have you found yourself guilty since you met me?'

'No, and I do not wish to become so. Up to now, I thought I was dealing only with things, but you are suggesting that I deal with men. I can cut through a wall and destroy a staircase, but I shall not cut through a man's breast and destroy his life.'

Dantès made a small gesture of surprise and said: 'Do you mean that, when you might be free, you would be deterred by such considerations?'

'What of you?' asked Faria. 'Why have you never bludgeoned your jailer one evening with the leg of your table, then put on his clothes and tried to escape?'

'I never thought of doing it.'

'Because you have an instinctive horror at the idea of such a crime, to the point where it has never even entered your head,' the old man continued. 'For, in simple and permitted matters, our natural appetites warn us not to exceed the boundaries of what is permissible for us. The tiger, which spills blood in the natural course of things, because this is its state of being, its destiny, needs only for its sense of smell to inform it that a prey is within reach; immediately it leaps towards this prey, falls on it and tears it apart. That is its instinct, which it obeys. But mankind, on the contrary, is repelled by blood. It is not the laws of society that condemn murder, but the laws of nature.'

Dantès was struck dumb: this was indeed the explanation of what had gone on, without him knowing it, in his mind – or, rather, in his soul: some thoughts come from the head, others from the heart.

'Moreover,' Faria went on, 'in the course of nearly twelve years that I have spent in prison, I have mentally gone over all famous escapes; only very rarely do they succeed. Fortunate escapes, those which succeed fully, are the ones that have been prepared carefully and over a long period of time. That is how the Duc de Beaufort escaped from the Château de Vincennes, Abbé Dubuquoi from the Fort-l'Evêque, Latude from the Bastille.[1] There are also some opportunities that occur by chance; those are the best. Let us await such an opportunity and, believe me, if it comes, let us take advantage of it.'

'You were able to wait,' said Dantès, sighing. 'This long labour occupied your every moment and, when you did not have that to distract you, you were consoled by hope.'

'I did other things as well.'

'What were they?'

'I wrote or I studied.'

'Do they give you paper, pens and ink, then?'

'No,' said the abbé, 'but I make them for myself.'

'You make paper, pens and ink?' Dantès exclaimed.

'Yes.'

Dantès looked admiringly at the man, but found it hard to credit what he was saying. Faria noticed this shadow of a doubt.

'When you come to visit me,' he said, 'I shall show you a whole book, the product of the thoughts, the research and meditations of my entire life, which I contemplated writing in the shadow of the Colosseum in Rome, beneath the column of St Mark's in Venice, on the banks of the Arno in Florence – and which I never suspected that my jailers would one day leave me ample time to complete between the four walls of the Château d'If. It is a *Treatise on the Prospects for a General Monarchy in Italy*. It will make one large in-quarto volume.'

'You have written it?'

'On two shirts. I have invented a preparation that makes linen as smooth and even as parchment.'

'So you are a chemist . . .'

'A little. I knew Lavoisier and I am a friend of Cabanis.'[2]

'But, for such a work, you must have needed to do historical research. Do you have any books?'

'In Rome, I had nearly five thousand volumes in my library. By reading and re-reading them, I discovered that one hundred and fifty books, carefully chosen, give you, if not a complete summary of human knowledge, at least everything that it is useful for a man to know. I devoted three years of my life to reading and re-reading these hundred and fifty volumes, so that when I was arrested I knew them more or less by heart. In prison, with a slight effort of memory, I recalled them entirely. So I can recite to you Thucydides, Xenophon, Plutarch, Livy, Tacitus, Strada, Jornadès, Dante, Montaigne, Shakespeare, Spinoza, Machiavelli and Bossuet; I mention only the most important . . .'

'But that must mean you know several languages?'

'I speak five living languages: German, French, Italian, English and Spanish. I can understand modern Greek with the help of Ancient Greek, but I speak it poorly; I am studying it now.'

'You are studying it?' Dantès exclaimed.

'Yes, I have compiled a vocabulary of the words that I know and have arranged them, combined them, turned them one way, then the other, so as to make them sufficient to express my thoughts. I know about one thousand words, which is all I absolutely need, though I believe there are a hundred thousand in dictionaries. Of course I shall not be a polished speaker, but I shall make myself understood perfectly, which is good enough.'

Increasingly astonished, Edmond began to consider this man's faculties almost supernatural. He wanted to catch him out on some point or other, so he went on: 'But if they did not give you a pen, with what did you manage to write this huge treatise?'

'I made very good pens, which would be found superior to ordinary ones if the substance was known, out of the soft bones from the heads of those big whiting that they sometimes serve us on fast days. In this way, I always looked forward to Wednesdays, Fridays and Saturdays, because they offered me at least a hope of increasing my stock of pens. I have to admit that my historical work is my favourite occupation. When I go back to the past, I forget the present. I walk free and independently through history, and forget that I am a prisoner.'

'But ink?' Dantès asked. 'How did you make ink?'

'There used to be a chimney in my dungeon,' Faria said. 'This chimney was doubtless blocked up some time before my arrival but, previously, fires had been built there for many years, so the whole of the inside was coated with soot. I dissolve the soot in part of the wine that they give me every Sunday, and it makes excellent ink. For particular notes which must stand out from the text, I prick my fingers and write with my blood.'

'And when can I see all this?' Dantès asked.

'Whenever you wish,' Faria replied.

'At once! At once!' the young man exclaimed.

'Then follow me,' said the abbé; and he disappeared down the underground passage. Dantès followed him.

XVII

THE ABBÉ'S CELL

After passing through the underground passage, bent over but still without too much difficulty, Dantès arrived at the far end of the tunnel where it entered the abbé's cell. At this point it narrowed to allow just enough room for a man to squeeze through. The floor of the abbé's cell was paved and it was by lifting one of the stones, in the darkest corner, that he had begun the laborious tunnelling that had brought him to Dantès.

As soon as he was inside and standing up, the young man studied the room carefully. At first sight there was nothing unusual about it.

'Good,' said the abbé. 'It is only a quarter past twelve, so we still have a few hours ahead of us.'

Dantès looked around, to find the clock on which the abbé had been able to tell the time so precisely.

'Look at that ray of sunlight shining through my window,' said the abbé. 'Now look at the lines I have drawn on the wall. Thanks to these lines, which take account of the double movement of the earth and its course round the sun, I know the time more accurately than if I had a watch, because the mechanism of a watch may be damaged, while that of the earth and the sun never can.'

Dantès understood nothing of this explanation: he had always thought, seeing the sun rise behind the mountains and set in the Mediterranean, that it moved, and not the earth. He considered almost impossible this 'double movement' of the earth which he did not perceive, even though he inhabited it, and he saw contained in each of the other man's words the mysteries of a science that would be as exciting to explore as the mines of gold and diamonds he had visited while still almost a child on a journey that he had made to Gujarat and Golconda.

'Come, now,' he said to the abbé. 'I am impatient to see your treasures.'

The abbé went over to the chimney and, with the chisel which he still had in his hand, moved the stone that had once formed the hearth of the fire, behind which there was a fairly deep hole. In this, he concealed all the objects he had mentioned to Dantès.

'What do you wish to see first?' he asked.

'Show me your great work on the monarchy in Italy.'

Faria took three or four linen rolls out of the precious cupboard, wound over on themselves like rolls of papyrus: these were bands of cloth, about four inches wide and eighteen long. Each one was numbered and covered with writing which Dantès could read, because it was in the abbé's mother-tongue, Italian, and, as a Provençal, Dantès understood it perfectly.

'See,' the abbé told him, 'it is all there. It is now about a week since I wrote the word "end" at the foot of the sixty-eighth roll. Two of my shirts and all the handkerchiefs I had have gone into it. If ever I should regain my freedom and find a printer in Italy who dares to print the work, my reputation will be made.'

'Yes,' said Dantès, 'I can see. And now, please show me the pens with which you wrote this work.'

'Look,' said Faria, and showed the young man a small stick, six inches long and as thick as the handle of a paintbrush, at the end of which one of the fishbones that the abbé had mentioned was tied with thread; still stained with ink, it had been shaped to a point and split like an ordinary pen-nib.

Dantès studied it and looked around for the implement that could have served to sharpen the nib so finely.

'Ah, yes. The penknife?' said Faria. 'This is my masterpiece. I made it, as I did this other knife, out of an old iron candlestick.'

The penknife cut like a razor. As for the other, it had the advantage of being able to serve both as a cutting implement and as a dagger.

Dantès examined these various objects as closely as – in curiosity shops in Marseille – he had sometimes studied the tools made by savages, brought back from the South Seas by captains on long-haul voyages.

'As for the ink,' said Faria, 'you know how I manage. I make it as and when I need it.'

'Now, only one thing still puzzles me,' said Dantès, 'which is that the days were long enough for you to accomplish all this.'

'I had the nights,' Faria replied.

'The nights! Are you a cat? Can you see in the dark?'

'No, but God has given mankind enough intelligence to compensate for the inadequacies of his senses. I found light.'

'How?'

'I separate the fat from the meat that they bring me, melt it and obtain a kind of solid oil from it. Look: this is my candle.'

He showed Dantès a sort of lamp, like those they use to illuminate public places.

'How did you light it?'

'Here are my two flints and some scorched linen.'

'But what about a match . . . ?'

'I pretended to have a skin disease and asked for sulphur, which they gave me.'

Dantès put all the objects he was holding on the table and bowed his head, overawed by the perseverance and strength of this spirit.

'That is not all,' said Faria. 'One should not hide all one's treasure in a single place. Let's close this one.'

They put the stone back, the abbé spread a little dust over it, ran his foot across it to disguise any evidence of unevenness on the surface, went over to his bed and pushed it to one side. Behind the head of the bed, hidden beneath a stone that formed an almost perfectly hermetic lid, was a hole, with inside it a rope ladder of between twenty-five and thirty feet in length. Dantès examined it; it was strong enough to sustain any weight.

'Who supplied you with the rope for this wonderful contrivance?' he asked.

'First of all, some shirts that I had, then the sheets from my bed which I unpicked, in my three years' captivity in Fenestrelle. When I was transported to the Château d'If, I found the means to bring the threads with me and I carried on working after I arrived here.'

'Did no one notice that your bed-linen no longer had any hems?'

'I resewed it.'

'What with?'

'With this needle.'

The abbé, parting a shred of his clothes, showed Dantès a long, sharp fishbone, still threaded, which he carried with him.

'Yes,' he continued. 'At first I thought of loosening the bars and escaping through this window, which is a little wider than yours, as you can see; I should have widened it still further during my escape. But I noticed that the window gives access only to an inner courtyard, so I abandoned the plan as being too risky. However, I kept the ladder in case some opportunity should arise for one of those escapes I mentioned, which are the outcome of chance.'

Dantès appeared to be examining the ladder, while his mind was actually on something else; an idea had entered his head. It was that this man, so intelligent, so ingenious and so deep in understanding, might see clearly in the darkness of his own misfortune and make out something that he had failed to see.

'What are you thinking about?' the abbé asked with a smile, imagining that Dantès' silence must indicate a very high degree of admiration.

'Firstly, I am thinking of one thing, which is the vast knowledge that you must have expended to attain the point that you have reached. What might you not have done, had you been free?'

'Perhaps nothing: the overflowing of my brain might have evaporated in mere futilities. Misfortune is needed to plumb certain mysterious depths in the understanding of men; pressure is needed to explode the charge. My captivity concentrated all my faculties on a single point. They had previously been dispersed, now they clashed in a narrow space; and, as you know, the clash of clouds produces electricity, electricity produces lightning and lightning gives light.'

'No, I know nothing,' said Dantès, ashamed of his ignorance. 'Some of the words that you use are void of all meaning for me; how lucky you are to know so much!'

The abbé smiled: 'You said a moment ago that you were thinking of two things.'

'Yes.'

'You have only told me one of them. What is the other?'

'The other is that you have told me about your life, but you know nothing about mine.'

'Your life, young man, has been somewhat short to contain any events of importance.'

'It does contain one terrible misfortune,' said Dantès; 'a misfortune that I have not deserved. And I should wish, so that I may no longer blaspheme against God as I have occasionally done, to have some men whom I could blame for my misfortune.'

'So you claim to be innocent of the crime with which you are charged?'

'Entirely innocent, I swear it by the heads of the two people whom I hold most dear, my father and Mercédès.'

'Well then,' said the abbé, closing the hiding-place and putting his bed back in its place. 'Tell me your story.'

Dantès told what he called his life story, which amounted to no more than a voyage to India and two or three voyages to the Levant, until finally he arrived at his last journey, the death of Captain Leclère, the packet that the captain gave him for the marshal, the interview with the marshal, the letter he was handed, addressed to a certain M. Noirtier; and, after that, his return to Marseille, his reunion with his father, his love for Mercédès, his betrothal, his arrest, his interrogation, his temporary confinement at the Palais de Justice, and then his final imprisonment in the Château d'If. From that point, Dantès knew nothing more, not even the amount of time that he had been a prisoner.

When the story concluded, the abbé was deep in thought; then, after a moment, he said: 'There is a very profound axiom in law, which is consistent with what I told you a short time ago, and it is this: unless an evil thought is born in a twisted mind, human nature is repelled by crime. However, civilization has given us needs, vices and artificial appetites which sometimes cause us to repress our good instincts and lead us to wrongdoing.[1] Hence the maxim: if you wish to find the guilty party, first discover whose interests the crime serves! Whose interests might be served by your disappearance?'

'No one's, for heaven's sake! I was so insignificant!'

'That is not the answer, because that answer is wanting in both logic and common sense. Everything, my good friend, is relative, from the king who stands in the way of his designated successor to the employee who impedes the supernumerary: if the king dies, the successor inherits a crown; if the employee dies, the supernumerary inherits a salary of twelve hundred *livres*. These twelve hundred *livres* are his civil list: they are as necessary to his survival as the king's twelve million. Every individual, from the lowest to the highest on the social scale, is at the centre of a little network of interests, with its storms and its hooked atoms, like the worlds of Descartes;[2] except that these worlds get larger as one goes up: it is a reverse spiral balanced on a single point. So let's get back to your world: you were about to be appointed captain of the *Pharaon*?'

'Yes.'

'You were about to marry a beautiful young woman?'

'Yes.'

'Was it in anyone's interest that you should not become captain of the *Pharaon*? Was it in anyone's interest that you should not marry Mercédès? Answer the first question first: order is the key to all problems. Would anyone gain by your not becoming captain of the *Pharaon*?'

'No, I was well-loved on board. If the sailors could have chosen their own leader, I am sure that they would have picked me. Only one man had a reason to dislike me: a short time before, I had quarrelled with him and challenged him to a duel, which he refused.'

'Really? And what was the man's name?'

'Danglars.'

'What was his position on board?'

'Supercargo.'

'If you had become captain, would you have kept him in his post?'

'No, if the choice had been mine, because I thought I had discovered some irregularities in his accounts.'

'Very well. Now, was anyone present at your last meeting with Captain Leclère?'

'No, we were alone.'

'Could anyone have overheard your conversation?'

'Yes, the door was open and . . . wait! Yes, yes, Danglars went past just at the moment when Captain Leclère gave me the packet to deliver to the marshal.'

'Good,' the abbé said. 'Now we are getting somewhere. Did you take anyone off the ship with you when you anchored on Elba?'

'No one.'

'You were given a letter.'

'Yes, by the Grand Marshal.'

'What did you do with it?'

'I put it into my briefcase.'

'Did you have your briefcase with you? How could a briefcase intended to contain an official letter fit into a sailor's pocket?'

'You are right: my briefcase was on board.'

'So it was only when you returned on board that you put the letter into the briefcase?'

'That is right.'

'What did you do with the letter between Porto Ferrajo and the ship?'

'I held it in my hand.'

'So that when you came back on board the *Pharaon*, anyone could have seen that you were carrying a letter?'

'Yes.'

'Danglars as well as anyone else?'

'Danglars as well as anyone else.'

'Now, listen carefully and concentrate your memory: do you remember the precise terms in which the denunciation was phrased?'

'Indeed, I do. I read it three times, and every word is etched on my memory.'

'Repeat it to me.'

Dantès paused to gather his thoughts, then said: 'Here it is, word for word:

The crown prosecutor is advised, by a friend of the monarchy and the faith, that one Edmond Dantès, first mate of the *Pharaon*, arriving this morning from Smyrna, after putting in at Naples and Porto Ferrajo, was entrusted by Murat with a letter for the usurper and by the usurper with a letter to the Bonapartist committee in Paris.

Proof of his guilt will be found when he is arrested, since the letter will be discovered either on his person, or at the house of his father, or in his cabin on board the *Pharaon*.'

The abbé shrugged his shoulders.

'It is as clear as daylight, and you must have a very simple and kind heart not to have guessed the truth immediately.'

'Do you think so?' Dantès exclaimed. 'Oh, it would be most dastardly.'

'What was Danglars' handwriting like, normally?'

'A fine, copperplate hand.'

'And what was the writing of the anonymous letter?'

'Writing that leant backwards.'

The abbé smiled: 'Disguised, surely?'

'Very firm for a disguised hand.'

'Wait,' he said, taking his pen – or the implement that he called a pen – dipping it in the ink and writing with his left hand, on a ready-prepared piece of cloth, the first two or three lines of the denunciation. Dantès started back and looked at the abbé with something close to terror.

'It's astonishing,' he said. 'That writing is so like the other.'

'That is because the denunciation was written with the left hand. I have noticed something,' the abbé added, 'which is that while all handwriting written with the right hand varies, all that done with the left hand looks the same.'

'Is there anything that you haven't seen or observed?'

'Let's continue.'

'Yes, willingly.'

'What about the second question?'

'I am listening.'

'Was there someone who stood to gain if you did not marry Mercédès?'

'Yes, a young man who was in love with her.'

'Called?'

'Fernand.'

'A Spanish name . . . ?'

'He is a Catalan.'

'Do you think him capable of writing this letter?'

'No! He would have put a knife in me, quite simply.'

'Yes, that is like a Spaniard: a killing, certainly, but a cowardly act, no.'

'In any case,' Dantès went on, 'he knew none of the details which were in the denunciation.'

'You confided them to no one?'

'No one.'

'Not even your mistress?'

'Not even my fiancée.'

'It must be Danglars.'

'Now I am sure of it.'

'Wait: did Danglars know Fernand?'

'No . . . Or . . . Yes: I remember . . .'

'What do you remember?'

'Two days before my wedding, I saw them sitting together at Père Pamphile's. Danglars was friendly and merry, Fernand pale and troubled.'

'Were they alone?'

'No, they had someone else with them, someone I know well, who had no doubt introduced them to each other, a tailor called Caderousse; but he was already drunk. Wait . . . wait . . . How did I forget this? Near the table where they were drinking, there was an inkwell, some paper and pens . . .' (Dantès drew his hand across his brow). 'Oh, the villains! The villains!'

'Do you want to know anything else?' the abbé said, smiling.

'Yes, since you understand everything, since you can see everything clearly, I want to know why I was only interrogated once, why I was not given judges to try me and why I have been condemned unheard.'

'Ah, there now,' said the abbé, 'that is rather more serious. Justice has dark and mysterious ways which are hard to fathom. So far, with your two friends, what we did was child's play, but on this other matter you must be as accurate as you can possibly be.'

'You ask the questions, because you truly seem to see into my life more clearly than I do myself.'

'Who interrogated you? Was it the crown prosecutor, the deputy or the investigating magistrate?'

'The deputy.'

'Young or old?'

'Young: twenty-six or twenty-seven.'

'Good! Not yet corrupt, but already ambitious,' the abbé said. 'What was his manner towards you?'

'Kind rather than harsh.'

'Did you tell him everything?'

'Everything.'

'Did his manner change in the course of the interrogation?'

'For a moment, it changed, when he had read the letter that compromised me. He seemed to be overwhelmed by my misfortune.'

'By your misfortune?'

'Yes.'

'Are you quite sure that it was your misfortune that he felt?'

'He gave me every evidence of his sympathy, at any rate.'

'In what way?'

'He burned the only document that could compromise me.'

'What was that? The denunciation?'

'No, the other letter.'

'Are you sure?'

'I saw it with my own eyes.'

'That's another matter; the man may be a deeper-dyed villain than you imagine.'

'I swear, you are frightening me!' said Dantès. 'Is the world full of tigers and crocodiles, then?'

'Yes, except that the tigers and crocodiles with two legs are more dangerous than the rest.'

'Continue, tell me more.'

'Gladly. You say he burned the letter?'

'Yes, and as he did so said to me: "You see, this is the only proof against you, and I am destroying it."'

'Such behaviour was too good to be true.'

'Do you think so?'

'I am certain. To whom was the letter addressed?'

'To Monsieur Noirtier, 13, rue Coq-Héron, Paris.'

'Have you any reason to believe that your deputy had some reason to want this letter to disappear?'

'Perhaps. He did make me promise two or three times, in my own interests, as he said, not to mention the letter to anyone, and he made me swear not to speak the name that was written on the address.'

'Noirtier?' the abbé repeated. 'Noirtier ... I used to know a Noirtier at the court of the former Queen of Etruria, a Noirtier who was a Girondin during the Revolution. And what was the name of this deputy of yours?'

'Villefort.'

The abbé burst out laughing, and Dantès looked at him in astonishment.

'What's the matter?' he asked.

'Do you see that ray of sunlight?' the abbé asked.

'Yes.'

'Well, everything is now clearer to me than that brightly shining ray of light. My poor child, you poor young man! And this magistrate was good to you?'

'Yes.'

'This noble deputy burned the letter, destroyed it?'

'He did.'

'This honest purveyor of souls to the dungeon made you swear never to speak the name of Noirtier?'

'Correct.'

'This Noirtier, poor blind fool that you are, do you know who this Noirtier was? This Noirtier was his father!'

If a shaft of lightning had fallen at Dantès' feet and opened an abyss with hell in its depths, it would not have produced a more startling or electric or overwhelming effect on him than these unexpected words. He got up and clasped his head in both hands, as if to prevent it from bursting.

'His father? His father!' he cried.

'Yes, his father, who is called Noirtier de Villefort,' the abbé said.

At this, a devastating flash of light burst inside the prisoner's head and the picture that he had not previously understood was instantly bathed in dazzling light. He recalled everything: Villefort's shilly-shallying during the interrogation, the letter he had destroyed, the promise he had elicited and the almost pleading tone of the magistrate's voice – which, instead of threatening him, seemed to be begging. He gave a cry and staggered for a moment like a drunken man; then, rushing to the opening that led from the abbé's cell to his own, he exclaimed: 'Ah! I must be alone to consider this.'

When he reached his dungeon, he fell on the bed and it was there that the turnkey found him that evening, still sitting, his eyes staring and his features drawn, motionless and silent as a statue.

During those hours of meditation, which had passed like seconds, he had made a fearful resolution and sworn a terrible oath.

A voice roused Dantès from his reverie: it was the Abbé Faria who, after being visited in his turn by the jailer, had come to invite Dantès to take supper with him. As a certified madman, above all as an entertaining madman, the old prisoner enjoyed certain privileges, among them that of having bread that was a little whiter than the rest and a small jar of wine on Sundays. This happened to be a Sunday and the abbé was asking Dantès to share his bread and wine.

Dantès followed him. His expression had returned to normal and his features were composed, but with a strength and firmness, as it were, that implied a settled resolve. The abbé looked closely at him.

'I regret having helped you in your investigation and said what I did to you,' he remarked.

'Why is that?' Dantès asked.

'Because I have insinuated a feeling into your heart that was not previously there: the desire for revenge.'

Dantès smiled and said: 'Let us change the subject.'

The abbé gave him a further brief look and sadly shook his head; then, as Dantès had requested, he began to talk of other things.

The old prisoner was one of those men whose conversation, like that of everyone who has known great suffering, contains many lessons and is continually interesting; but it was not self-centred: the unfortunate man never spoke about his own troubles.

Dantès listened to every word with admiration. Some of what the abbé said concurred with ideas that he already had and things that he knew from his profession as a seaman, while others touched on the unknown and, like the aurora borealis giving light to sailors in northern latitudes, showed the young man new lands and new horizons, bathed in fantastic colours. Dantès understood the happiness of an intelligence that could follow such a mind on the moral, philosophical and social peaks where it habitually roamed.

'You must teach me a little of what you know,' he said, 'if only to avoid becoming bored by my company. I now feel that you must prefer solitude to an uneducated and narrow-minded companion like myself. If you agree, I undertake not to mention escape to you again.'

The abbé smiled.

'Alas, my child,' he said, 'human knowledge is very limited and when I have taught you mathematics, physics, history and the three or four modern languages that I speak, you will know everything that I know; and it will take me scarcely two years to transfer all this knowledge from my mind to yours.'

'Two years!' said Dantès. 'Do you think I could learn all this in two years?'

'In their application, no; but the principles, yes. Learning does not make one learned: there are those who have knowledge and those who have understanding. The first requires memory, the second philosophy.'

'But can't one learn philosophy?'

'Philosophy cannot be taught. Philosophy is the union of all acquired knowledge and the genius that applies it: philosophy is the shining cloud upon which Christ set His foot to go up into heaven.'

'Come then,' said Dantès. 'What will you teach me first? I am eager to begin, I am athirst for knowledge.'

'Everything, then!' said the abbé.

So that evening the two prisoners drew up an educational syllabus which they began to carry out the following day. Dantès had a remarkable memory and found concepts very easy to grasp: a mathematical cast of mind made him able to understand everything by calculating it, while a seafarer's poetry compensated for whatever was too materialistic in arguments reduced to dry figures and straight lines. Moreover he already knew Italian and a little Romaic, which he had picked up on his journeys to the East. With those two languages, he soon understood the workings of all the rest, and after six months had started to speak Spanish, English and German.

As he promised Abbé Faria, he no longer spoke of escape, either because the enjoyment of study compensated him for his loss of freedom, or because (as we have seen) he would always keep his word strictly, once he had given it, and the days passed quickly and instructively. After a year, he was a different man.

As for Abbé Faria, Dantès noticed that, though the older man's captivity had been lightened by his presence, he grew more melancholy by the day. One pervasive and incessant thought seemed to plague his mind. He would fall into deep reveries, give an involuntary sigh, leap suddenly to his feet, cross his arms and pace gloomily around his cell.

One day, he stopped abruptly while pacing for the hundredth time around his room, and exclaimed: 'Oh! If only there was no sentry!'

'There need be no sentry, if only you would agree to it,' said Dantès, who had followed the train of thought inside his head as if there were a crystal window in his skull.

'I have told you,' the abbé said, 'I abhor the idea of murder.'

'Yet if this murder were to be committed, it would be through our instinct for self-preservation, through an impulse of self-defence.'

'No matter, I cannot do it.'

'But you think about it?'

'Continually,' the abbé muttered.

'And you have thought of a plan, haven't you?' Dantès asked eagerly.

'Yes, if only we could station a blind and deaf sentry on that walkway.'

'He will be blind, he will be deaf,' the young man said, with a grim resolve that terrified the abbé.

'No, no,' he exclaimed. 'Impossible!'

Dantès wanted to pursue the subject, but the abbé shook his head and refused to say any more about it.

Three months passed.

'Are you strong?' the abbé asked Dantès one day.

Without saying anything, Dantès took the chisel, bent it into a horseshoe and then straightened it again.

'Would you undertake only to kill the sentry as a last resort?'

'Yes, on my honour.'

'Then we can carry out our plan,' said the abbé.

'How long will it take?'

'A year, at least.'

'But we can start work?'

'At once.'

'Look at that!' Dantès cried. 'We have wasted a year!'

'Do you think it was wasted?' the abbé asked.

'Oh! Forgive me, forgive me,' Edmond said, blushing.

'Hush,' said the abbé. 'A man is only a man, and you are one of the best I have ever encountered. Now, here is my plan.'

The abbé showed Dantès a drawing he had made: it was a plan of his own room, that of Dantès and the passageway linking them. From the middle of this he had drawn a side-tunnel like those they use in mines. This would take the two prisoners beneath the walkway where the sentry kept guard. Once they had reached this, they would carve out a broad pit and loosen one of the paving-stones on the floor of the gallery. At a chosen moment this paving-stone would give way beneath the soldier's feet and he would fall into the pit. Dantès would jump on him as, stunned by his fall, he was unable to defend himself; he would tie him up and gag him, and the two of them, climbing through one window of the gallery, would go down the outside wall with the help of the rope ladder, and escape.

Dantès clapped his hands; his eyes shone with joy: the plan was so simple that it was bound to succeed.

That same day, the tunnellers set to work, all the more eagerly since they had been idle for a long time and, quite probably, each had secretly been longing for this resumption of physical labour.

Nothing interrupted their work except the time when they were both obliged to go back to their cells for the jailer's visit. Moreover they had grown accustomed to detecting the almost imperceptible sound of his footsteps and could tell precisely when the man was coming down, so neither of them was ever taken by surprise. The soil that they dug out of their new tunnel, which would eventually have filled up the old one, was thrown bit by bit, with extreme caution, through one or other of the windows in Dantès' or Faria's dungeon: it was ground up so fine that the night wind carried it away without a trace.

More than a year passed in this work, undertaken with no other implements than a chisel, a knife and a wooden lever. Throughout that year, even as they worked, Faria continued to instruct Dantès, speaking to him sometimes in one language, sometimes in another, teaching him the history of the nations and the great men who from time to time have left behind them one of those luminous trails that are known as glory. A man of the world and of high society, the abbé also had a sort of melancholy majesty in his bearing – from which Dantès, endowed by nature with an aptitude for assimilation, was able to distil the polite manners that he had previously lacked and an aristocratic air which is usually acquired only by association with the upper classes or by mixing with those of superior attainments.

In fifteen months the tunnel was complete. They had dug out a pit beneath the gallery and could hear the sentry passing backwards and forwards above them; the two workmen, who were obliged to wait for a dark and moonless night to make their escape more certain, had only one fear: that the floor might give way prematurely under the soldier's feet. To guard against this, they put in place a sort of little beam, which they had found in the foundations. Dantès was just fixing this when he suddenly heard a cry of distress from Abbé Faria, who had stayed in the young man's cell sharpening a peg which was to hold the rope ladder. Dantès hurried back and found the abbé standing in the middle of the room, pale-faced, his forehead bathed in sweat and his fists clenched.

'Oh, my God!' Dantès cried. 'What is it? What is wrong?'

'Quickly,' the abbé said. 'Listen to what I say.'

Dantès looked at Faria's livid features, his eyes ringed with blue, his white lips and his hair, which was standing on end. In terror, he let the chisel fall from his hand.

'But what is the matter?' he cried.

'I am finished,' the abbé said. 'Listen to me. I am about to have a terrible, perhaps fatal seizure; I can feel that it is coming. I suffered the same in the year before my imprisonment. There is only one cure for this sickness, which I shall tell you: run to my room, lift up the leg of the bed, which is hollow, and you will find there a little flask, half full of red liquid. Bring it; or, rather, no, I might be discovered here. Help me to return to my room while I still have some strength. Who knows what might happen while the seizure is on me?'

Dantès kept his head, despite the immensity of the disaster, and went down into the tunnel, dragging his unfortunate companion behind him; and taking him, with infinite care, to the far end of the tunnel, found himself at last in the abbé's room, where he put him on the bed.

'Thank you,' said the abbé, shivering in every limb as though he had been immersed in icy water. 'This is what will happen: I shall fall into a cataleptic fit. I may perhaps remain motionless and not make a sound. But I might also froth at the mouth, stiffen, cry out. Try to ensure that my cries are not heard: this is important, because otherwise they may take me to another room and we should be separated for ever. When you see me motionless, cold and, as it were, dead – and only at that moment, you understand – force my teeth apart with the knife and pour eight to ten drops of the liquid into my mouth. In that case, I may perhaps revive.'

'Perhaps?' Dantès exclaimed, pitifully.

'Help me! Help!' the abbé cried. 'I am . . . I am dy . . .'

The seizure was so sudden and so violent that the unhappy man could not even finish the word. A cloud, rapid and dark as a storm at sea, passed over his brow. His eyes dilated, his lips twisted and his cheeks became purple. He thrashed, foamed, roared. But, as he had been instructed, Dantès stifled the cries beneath the blanket. The fit lasted two hours. Then, totally inert, pale and cold as marble, bent like a reed broken underfoot, he fell, stiffened in one final convulsion and paled to a livid white.

Edmond waited for this semblance of death to invade the whole body and chill it to the very heart. Then he took the knife, put the blade between the man's teeth, prised the jaws apart with infinite care, measured ten drops of the red liquid one after the other and waited.

An hour passed without the old man making the slightest movement. Dantès feared that he might have waited too long and sat, clasping his head in both hands, looking at him. Finally, a slight colour appeared on the old man's lips; the look returned to his eyes, which had remained open, but blank, throughout; he uttered a faint sigh and moved slightly.

'Saved! He is saved!' Dantès cried.

The sick man still could not speak, but with evident anxiety he held out his hand towards the door. Dantès listened and heard the jailer's steps. It was almost seven o'clock and Dantès had not been able to take any account of time. He leapt to the opening, dived into it, pulled the paving-stone back behind him and went back to his cell. A moment later, his own door opened and the jailer, as usual, found the prisoner sitting on his bed.

No sooner was his back turned and the sound of his footsteps receding down the corridor than Dantès left his food uneaten and, a prey to terrible anxiety, went back down the tunnel, pushed up the stone with his head and returned to the abbé's cell.

The abbé had regained consciousness, but was still stretched on his bed, motionless and exhausted.

'I did not expect to see you again,' he told Dantès.

'Why not?' the young man asked. 'Did you expect to die?'

'No, but everything is ready for your escape and I expected you to take this opportunity.'

Dantès reddened with indignation.

'Alone! Without you!' he cried. 'Did you really believe me capable of doing that?'

'I see now that I was mistaken,' said the sick man. 'Oh, I am very weak, broken, finished . . .'

'Take heart. Your strength will return,' said Dantès, sitting on the bed beside Faria and taking his hands.

The abbé shook his head: 'Last time the fit lasted half an hour, and after it I felt hungry and got up by myself. Today, I cannot move my right leg or my right arm. My head is muddled, which proves there is some effusion on the brain. The third time, I shall either remain entirely paralysed, or I shall die at once.'

'No, no. Don't worry. You shall not die. If you do have a third fit, it will be in freedom. We shall save you as we did this time – and better than this time, because we shall have all the necessary help.'

'My friend,' the old man said, 'do not deceive yourself. The blow that has just struck me has condemned me to prison for ever. To escape, one must be able to walk.'

'We shall wait a week, a month, two months if necessary. During this time, your strength will return. Everything is ready for our escape and we are free to choose our own time. When the day comes that you feel strong enough to swim, then we shall carry out our plan.'

'I shall never swim,' said Faria. 'This arm is paralysed, not for a day, but for ever. Lift it yourself, feel its weight.'

The young man raised the arm, which fell back, inert. He sighed.

'You are convinced now, Edmond, aren't you? Believe me, I know what I am saying: since the first attack of this sickness, I have thought about it constantly. I was expecting this, because it is a hereditary illness; my father died on the third attack and so did my grandfather. The doctor who made up this potion for me, who is none other than the celebrated Cabanis, predicted the same fate for me.'

'The doctor was wrong,' Dantès exclaimed. 'As for your paralysis, it does not bother me. I shall take you on my shoulders and support you as I swim.'

'My child,' the abbé said, 'you are a seaman, you are a swimmer, and you must know that a man carrying such a burden could not swim fifty strokes in the sea. You must not let yourself pursue phantoms which do not deceive even your generous heart: I shall remain here until the hour of my deliverance which can no longer be any other than the hour of my death. As for you, flee, begone! You are young, agile and strong. Do not bother about me, I release you from your oath.'

'Very well,' said Dantès. 'Then I, too, shall remain.' And, standing up and solemnly extending his hand above the old man's head: 'I swear by the blood of Christ that I shall not leave you until your death.'

Faria looked at the young man – so noble, so simple, so exalted – and read the sincerity of his affection and the fidelity of his vow on a face that was lit with an expression of the purest devotion.

'Very well,' he said. 'I accept. Thank you.'

Then, holding out his hand, he added: 'You may perhaps be rewarded for your disinterested devotion. But as I cannot – and you will not – escape, we must block the underground passage beneath the gallery. The soldier might notice the hollow sound of the place we have excavated as he walks there, and call for an inspector: in that event we should be discovered and separated. Go and do this; unfortunately I cannot help you. Spend all night at the task if necessary, and do not return until tomorrow morning, after the jailer's visit. I shall have something important to tell you.'

Dantès took the abbé's hand; he was reassured with a smile, and he left, in a spirit of respectful obedience and devotion to his old friend.

XVIII

THE TREASURE

The following morning, when Dantès returned to the cell of his fellow-prisoner, he found him sitting up, his face calm. In the sole ray of light that penetrated through the narrow window of his cell, he was holding something in his left hand – the only one, it will be remembered, that he could still use. It was an open sheet of paper which had been so long tightly rolled up that it was still resistant to being flattened. Saying nothing, he showed it to Dantès.

'What is this?' the young man asked.

'Look carefully,' the abbé said with a smile.

'I am looking as carefully as I can and see nothing except a piece of paper, half-consumed by fire, with Gothic characters written on it in some unusual kind of ink.'

'This paper, my friend . . .' said Faria, 'I can now confess everything to you, since I have tested you . . . This paper is my treasure, and from today half of it belong to you.'

Dantès felt a cold sweat on his forehead. Until now (and for how long!) he had refrained from speaking with Faria about this treasure, the origin of the charge of madness levelled against the poor abbé. With instinctive tact, Edmond preferred not to touch on this tender spot, and Faria, for his part, had said nothing. He took the old man's silence to mean that he had regained his reason; but now, these few words, which had escaped Faria's lips after such a desperate crisis, seemed to imply a serious relapse into a state of mental alienation.

'Your treasure?' Dantès muttered.

Faria smiled and said: 'Yes. Edmond, your heart is noble in every respect and I realize, from your pallor and the shudder that you gave, what you are thinking. No, have no fear, I am not mad. This treasure exists, Dantès, and if I am unable to possess it, you shall. No one wished to listen to me or to believe me because they assumed I was mad. But you, who must know that I am not, listen to me, and afterwards believe me or not as you will.'

'Alas!' Edmond thought. 'He has suffered a relapse indeed! This misfortune is all that we lacked.'

Then, aloud, he said: 'My friend, perhaps your seizure has tired you. Why not rest a little? Tomorrow, if you wish, I shall listen to your story, but today I want to nurse you back to health, nothing more. In any case,' he said, smiling, 'are we in a hurry to find a treasure here?'

'Very much so, Edmond,' the old man replied. 'Who knows if tomorrow, or perhaps the next day, I shall have my third seizure? In that case, all would be finished! Yes, it's true, I have often thought with bitter delight of these riches, which would make the fortune of ten families, knowing that they are beyond the reach of my persecutors: that idea was my revenge, and I savoured it slowly in the darkness of my cell and the despair of my imprisonment. But now, out of love for you, I have forgiven the world, and now that I see you young, with your future before you, now that I think of all the happiness that such a revelation can bring you, I am impatient of delay and tremble at the idea that I might not be able to give all this buried wealth to so worthy an owner as you.'

Edmond turned away with a sigh.

'You persist in your incredulity, Edmond. Do my accents not convince you? I see that you require further proof. Well, read this paper which I have not shown to anybody.'

'Tomorrow, my friend,' Edmond said, loath to participate in the old man's folly. 'I thought we had agreed not to speak of this until tomorrow.'

'We shall speak of it tomorrow, but read the paper today.'

'I must avoid upsetting him,' Edmond thought. And he took the paper, half of which was missing, no doubt as the result of some accident. He read as follows:

> This treasure which may amount to two
> Roman écus in the furthest cor
> of the second opening, which
> to him in full benefice as
> itor
>   April 25, 149

'Well?' said Faria, when the young man had finished reading.

'All I can see here,' said Dantès, 'are broken lines and unconnected words. The letters have been partly burned off and the words are unintelligible.'

'To you, my friend, reading them for the first time; but to me, when I have gone pale bending over them night after night, reconstructing each sentence, completing each thought . . .'

'And you think you have found the intended meaning?'

'I am sure of it. Judge for yourself. But first let me tell you the history of this piece of paper.'

'Hush!' Dantès cried. 'Footsteps! Someone is coming . . . I must go . . . Farewell!'

And, happy at this opportunity to avoid the story and an explanation that would surely have confirmed his friend's malady, he slid like a viper through the narrow passage while Faria, roused to febrile activity by terror, pushed back the stone with his foot and covered it with a cloth, so as to hide the disturbance in the dust which he had not had time to conceal.

His visitor was the governor who, having learned of Faria's accident from the jailer, had come to judge for himself how serious it was. Faria received him sitting down, was careful to avoid any compromising movement and managed to conceal the deadly paralysis that had already stricken one half of his body. He was afraid that the governor might take pity on him and put him in some more healthy cell, thus separating him from his young companion. Luckily this was not the case and the governor left, convinced that his poor madman, for whom in the depths of his heart he felt some degree of affection, was only suffering from a slight indisposition.

Meanwhile Edmond was sitting on his bed with his head in his hands and trying to collect his thoughts. Since he had first met

Faria, everything about the man had spoken of such reasoning, such grandeur, such logical consistency, that he could not understand how this supreme wisdom over all others could be combined with unreason about this one single matter: was it that Faria was wrong about his treasure, or that everyone else was wrong about Faria? Dantès remained in his cell the whole day, not daring to return to his friend's. In this way he was trying to delay the moment when he would learn for certain that the abbé was mad: such a certainty would be appalling to him.

Towards evening, however, after the time of the jailer's customary visit, when the young man did not return, Faria tried to make his way across the space between them. Edmond shuddered on hearing the old man's painful efforts to drag himself along: his leg was immobile and he could not use one of his arms. Edmond was obliged to pull him into his cell, because he could never otherwise have managed to force himself through the narrow opening by his own efforts.

'As you see, I am absolutely pitiless in my pursuit of you,' he said with a radiant smile, full of benevolence. 'You thought you could escape my lavish generosity, but you will not. So listen.'

Edmond saw that there was no backing away, and made the old man sit down on his bed, taking up a place next to him on his stool.

'You know that I used to be the secretary, the intimate and the friend of Cardinal Spada,[1] last prince of that name. To this worthy lord I owe all the happiness that I have tasted in this life. He was not rich, even though his family's wealth was proverbial and I have often heard people say: "As rich as a Spada". But, like the proverb, he lived on this reputation for opulence. His palace was paradise to me. I taught his nephews, who died, and when he was alone in the world, I repaid him for all that he had done for me during the previous ten years by my absolute dedication to fulfilling his every wish.

'The cardinal's house soon held no secrets for me. I had often seen Monseigneur at work consulting ancient books and eagerly hunting through the dusty old family papers. One day, when I reprimanded him for vainly losing sleep and for the exhaustion that followed his late nights, he gave me a bitter smile and opened a book on the history of the city of Rome. There, at the twentieth chapter in the life of Pope Alexander VI, I read the following lines, which I have never forgotten:

*

The great wars in the province of Romagna were ended. Cesare Borgia, having completed his conquests, was in need of money to purchase the whole of Italy. The Pope also needed money if he was to have done with Louis XII, king of France, who was still a threat despite his recent defeats. It was essential for him to speculate successfully and this was no longer easy in the poor, exhausted land of Italy.

His Holiness had an idea. He resolved to create two cardinals.

By choosing two of the leading men in Rome, and above all two wealthy men, the Holy Father could expect the following from his speculation: firstly, he would have at his disposal the high offices and magnificent titles that these two cardinals possessed; and, secondly, he could count on a splendid price for the sale of the two cardinals' hats. There was also a third source of income, which will soon appear.

The Pope and Cesare Borgia first found their two future cardinals: they were Giovanni Rospigliosi, who alone had at his disposal four of the highest offices of the Holy See; and Cesare Spada, one of the richest men, from one of the most noble families in Rome. Both men realized the value of the Pope's favour. They were ambitious. Having decided on them, Cesare soon found purchasers for their offices.

The result was that Rospigliosi and Spada paid to become cardinals and that eight other men paid to become what previously these two newly created cardinals had been. The speculators were the richer by eight hundred thousand *écus*.

The time has now come for us to consider the last part of the speculation. The Pope showered his favours on Rospigliosi and Spada and conferred the insignia of their new office on them; then, certain that, in order to meet the quite substantial debt of gratitude that was imposed on them, they must have consolidated their fortunes and liquidated them, prior to settling in Rome, the Pope and Cesare Borgia invited the two cardinals to dinner.

The Holy Father and his son argued over the matter. Cesare thought that they could employ one of those devices which he always kept at the disposal of his intimate friends, for example, the famous key with which certain people would be asked to go and open a particular wardrobe. The key happened to have a little point of iron negligently left sticking out of it by the locksmith. When anyone pressed it, in order to open the wardrobe – the lock was stiff – he would be pricked by this little pin and would die the following day. There was also the lion's-head ring, which Cesare wore on his finger to shake certain people by the hand. The lion bit the skin of these specially favoured hands and the bite would prove fatal within twenty-four hours.

So Cesare suggested to his father, either that they should send the cardinals to open the wardrobe, or else that each of them should be given a warm handshake. But Alexander VI replied:

Let us not begrudge a dinner when our guests are to be those fine men, Cardinals Spada and Rospigliosi. Something tells me that we shall have our expenses back. In any case, Cesare, you are forgetting that indigestion strikes immediately, while a prick or a bite takes a day or two to work.

Cesare was won over by this argument; so that is how the two cardinals were invited to dinner.

The tables were laid in the vineyard that the Pope owned near San-Pietro-in-Vincula, at a charming residence which the cardinals knew very well by repute.

Rospigliosi, bemused by the dignity of his new office, prepared his belly and his most agreeable countenance. Spada, a cautious man who loved only his nephew, a young captain with the brightest prospects, took paper and a pen to make his will.

He then sent word to his nephew to wait for him close to the vineyard, but it appears that the servant could not find the young man.

Spada knew the significance of such invitations. From the time when Christianity, that great civilizing influence, brought enlightenment to Rome, it was no longer a matter of a centurion who would come from the tyrant and announce: *Caesar wishes you to die*. Now it was a legate *a latere* who arrived, with a smile on his lips, bringing the message from the Pope: *His Holiness wishes you to dine with him*.

Around two o'clock, Spada left for the vineyard where the Pope was expecting him. The first person who met his eyes was his own nephew, elegant and finely dressed, the object of Cesare Borgia's affectionate attentions. Spada paled – and Cesare, casting him a glance full of irony, let him know that he had anticipated everything and that the trap had been carefully set.

They dined. Spada found the opportunity only to ask his nephew whether he had received the message. The nephew replied that he had not, and he fully appreciated the sense of the question; it was too late, for he had just drunk a glass of excellent wine set aside for him by the Pope's vintner. At the same moment, Spada saw another bottle being brought, from which he was offered a liberal quantity. An hour later a doctor declared that both of them had been poisoned by some lethal mushrooms. Spada died at the entrance to the vineyard, while the nephew breathed his last at his own door, making a sign to his wife which she did not understand.

Cesare and the Pope at once hastened to seize hold of the inheritance, under the pretext of looking for some papers left by the dead men. But the inheritance consisted of this: a sheet of paper on which Spada had written: *I bequeath to my well-beloved nephew my coffers and my books, among them my fine breviary with the gold corners, desirous that he should keep this in memory of his affectionate uncle.*

The heirs looked everywhere, admired the breviary, seized the furniture and were astonished that Spada, that rich man, was in fact the poorest of uncles. As for treasure, they found nothing, except the treasures of knowledge contained in his library and his laboratories.

That was all. Cesare and his father hunted, ransacked and kept watch, but found nothing, or at least very little: perhaps a thousand *écus'* worth of plate and perhaps the same amount in silver coin; but the nephew had had time to tell his wife: *Look among my uncle's papers – there is a true will.*

They probably searched even more assiduously than did the noble heirs. All was in vain: all that remained were two palaces and a vineyard behind the Palatine Hill. At that time, landed property was of relatively little value, so the two palaces and the vineyard were left to the family, as being beneath the rapacity of the Pope and his son.

Months and years passed. Alexander VI died, poisoned by a misunderstanding which you know of; Cesare, poisoned at the same time as the Pope, escaped with a change of skin, like a snake, putting on a new covering on which the poison had left stains such as one sees on the fur of a tiger. Finally, forced to leave Rome, he died in an obscure night-time brawl which history has barely troubled to record.

After the death of the Pope and his son's exile, most people expected the family to resume the princely style of life that it had known in the days of Cardinal Spada, but this was not the case. The Spadas continued in an ambiguous state of moderate comfort, and a lasting mystery shrouded this grim affair; the rumour was that Cesare, a more subtle politician than his father, had purloined the fortune of both cardinals from the Pope; I say both, because Cardinal Rospigliosi, who had taken no precautions, was completely dispossessed.

'So far,' Faria said, interrupting with a smile, 'this does not seem to you too devoid of sense, does it?'

'My friend,' said Dantès, 'on the contrary, I feel I am reading a fascinating piece of history. Please continue.'

'I shall do so:

'The family grew accustomed to its obscurity. Years passed and, among the descendants of Cardinal Spada, some became soldiers, some diplomats, some men of the Church, some bankers; some became rich, others ended in poverty. I now come to the last of the family, the Count Spada whose secretary I was.

'I had often heard him complain that his wealth was disproportionate to his rank, so I advised him to invest what little he had in annuities. He did so, and thus doubled his income.

'The celebrated breviary had remained in the family, and it was Count Spada who owned it. It had been passed down from father to son, because the strange clause in the only will that had been found had made this a veritable relic, to be preserved in the family with superstitious veneration. It was decorated with the finest Gothic illuminations and so heavy with gold that a servant always carried it before the cardinal on solemn occasions.

'At the sight of the papers of all sorts – titles, contracts, parchments – which were kept in the family archives, and which all came from the poisoned cardinal, I began to peruse these massive bundles, just as twenty servants, twenty stewards and twenty secretaries had done before me: despite the energy and devotion that I gave to my research, I found nothing. However, I had read – I even wrote one myself – a precise, almost a day-by-day history of the Borgias, for no other reason than to discover whether these princes had acquired any additional fortune on the death of my cardinal, Cesare Spada, and I only noted the addition to their riches of the money belonging to Cardinal Rospigliosi, his companion in misfortune.

'In this way I was almost certain that neither the Borgias nor the family had benefited by the inheritance, but that it had remained ownerless, like those treasures in the *Arabian Nights* which sleep beneath the earth, guarded by a genie. Over and over, a thousand times, I searched, I counted, I calculated the family's income and expenses for the past three hundred years: all to no avail; I remained in my ignorance and the Count of Spada in his poverty.

'My master died. From his annuity he had held back his family papers, his library of five thousand volumes and his famous breviary. He bequeathed all this to me, with a thousand Roman *écus* which he had in cash, on condition that I had a Mass said for him on the anniversary of his death and that I drew up a genealogical

tree and a history of the House of Spada, all of which wishes I
carried out to the letter.

'Be patient, dear Edmond. We are near the end.

'In 1807, a month before my arrest and a fortnight after the
death of the count, on December the twenty-fifth – and you will
shortly understand why the date of that memorable day has
remained in my memory – I was reading these papers for the
thousandth time and setting them in order: since the palace now
belonged to a stranger, I was going to leave Rome and settle in
Florence, taking some twelve thousand books that belonged to me,
my library and my famous breviary ... Worn out by study and
indisposed by the rather heavy dinner that I had eaten, I let my
head fall on my hands and went to sleep. It was three o'clock in the
afternoon.

'I awoke as the clock was striking six.

'I looked up. I was in utter darkness. I rang for a servant to bring
me a light, but no one came, so I decided to fend for myself. In
any case, this was something to which I should have to resign myself
in future. In one hand I took a candle and in the other, knowing
that there were no matches in their box, I looked for a piece of
paper that I could light from the last embers burning in the grate.
But I was afraid that, in the darkness, I would take some precious
leaf of paper instead of a useless one, so I hesitated. Then I
remembered that, in the famous breviary, which was sitting on the
table beside me, I had seen an old piece of paper, partly yellowed
with age, which appeared to serve as a bookmark and which had
been handed down as such through the ages, preserved by the
veneration of Cardinal Spada's heirs. I groped around for this
useless scrap, found it, folded it and thrust it into the dying fire to
light it.

'But, beneath my fingers as the fire took hold, I saw yellowing
characters emerge from the white paper and appear on it, as if by
magic. At this, I was seized with terror. I clasped the paper in my
hands, stifled the flame and lit the candle directly from the hearth.
Then, with feelings I cannot describe, I re-opened the crumpled
letter and realized that there were words on it written by some
mysterious, invisible ink, which became visible only on contact
with heat. About one-third of the paper had been consumed by the
flames. This is the paper that you read this morning. Read it again,

Dantès, and when you have done so, I shall fill in whatever is missing or unclear.'

Faria handed the paper to Dantès who, this time, avidly read the following words, written in a reddish ink like rust:

> This day, April 25, 1498, hav
> Alexander VI, and fearing that, not
> he might wish to inherit my wealth and
> and Bentivoglio, fatally poisoned,
> my sole legatee, that I have con
> having visited it with me, that is
> Isle of Monte Cristo, all that I o
> stones, diamonds, jewels, that I al
> may amount to nearly two mill
> find, on lifting the twentieth
> creek eastwards in a straight line. Two
> these grottoes: the treasure is in the
> which treasure I bequeath and endow
> sole heir.
>   April 25, 1498   CES

'Now,' said the abbé, 'read this other piece of paper.' And he handed Dantès a second sheet with other, partially complete lines: Dantès took it and read:

> ing been invited to dinner by His Holiness
> content with making me pay for my cardinal's hat
> design for me the fate of Cardinals Crapara
> I declare to my nephew Guido Spada,
> cealed in a place that he knows,
> in the grottoes of the little
> wned of gold bars, gold coin, precious
> one know of the existence of this treasure which
> ion Roman écus, and that he will
> rock starting from the little
> openings have been made in
> furthest corner away from the second,
> to him in full benefice as my

ARE SPADA

Faria watched him intently. 'And now,' he said, when he saw that Dantès had reached the bottom line, 'put the two fragments together and judge for yourself.'

Dantès obeyed. When he put the two fragments together, they made up the following:

This day, April 25, 1498, hav . . . ing been invited to dinner by His Holiness
Alexander VI, and fearing that, not . . . content with making me pay for my cardinal's hat
he might wish to inherit my wealth and . . . design for me the fate of Cardinals Crapara
and Bentivoglio, fatally poisoned, . . . I declare to my nephew Guido Spada,
my sole legatee, that I have con . . . cealed in a place that he knows,
having visited it with me, that is . . . in the grottoes of the little
Isle of Monte Cristo, all that I o . . . wned of gold bars, gold coin, precious
stones, diamonds, jewels, that I al . . . one know of the existence of this treasure which
may amount to nearly two mill . . . ion Roman écus, and that he will
find, on lifting the twentieth . . . rock starting from the little
creek eastwards in a straight line. Two . . . openings have been made in
these grottoes: the treasure is in the . . . furthest corner away from the second,
which treasure I bequeath and endow . . . to him in full benefice as my
sole heir.
April 25, 1498   CES . . . ARE SPADA

'Now, finally, do you understand?' asked Faria.

'This was Cardinal Spada's last will and testament that they had been hunting all that time?' said Edmond, still incredulous.

'Yes, a thousand times yes.'

'Who pieced it together in this way?'

'I did: with the help of the remaining fragment, I guessed what was missing by measuring the length of the lines against that of the paper and uncovering the hidden meaning by means of what was plain, as one might be guided in a tunnel by a glimmer of light from above.'

'So what did you do when you were sure of what you knew?'

'I wanted to go there, and I did in fact leave at once, taking with me the start of my great work on the unity of the kingdom of Italy. But I had been under surveillance by the imperial police which, at that time, wanted to divide the provinces – even though later, when his son was born, Napoleon wanted the opposite. The police did not know the reason for my hasty departure, but it aroused suspicion and, just as I was taking ship at Piombino, I was arrested.

'Now,' Faria went on, looking at Dantès with an almost paternal expression, 'now, my friend, you know as much as I do. If we should ever manage to escape together, half of my treasure is yours; if I should die here and you alone escape, all of it belongs to you.'

'But surely,' Dantès asked hesitantly, 'is there not someone in the world who has a more legitimate claim to it than we do?'

'No, have no fear on that point. The family is entirely extinct. In any event, the last Count of Spada made me his heir; by bequeathing me this breviary, he symbolically bequeathed to me also what it contained. No, no, calm yourself: if we can put our hands on this fortune, we can enjoy it without any scruples.'

'And you say that the treasure consists of . . .'

'Two million Roman *écus*, worth around thirteen million of our money.'

'Impossible!' Dantès exclaimed, staggered by the enormity of the sum.

'Impossible? Why impossible?' the old man asked. 'The Spadas were one of the oldest and most powerful families of the fifteenth century. In any event, at a time when there was no speculation and no industry, such collections of gold and jewels were not rare, and there are still today Roman families who are dying of hunger beside a million in diamonds and precious stones handed down in trust, which they cannot touch.'

Edmond thought he must be dreaming; he hovered between joy and disbelief.

'The only reason that I kept this secret from you for so long,' Faria went on, 'was firstly in order to test you, and secondly to surprise you. If we had escaped together before my cataleptic fit, I should have taken you to Monte Cristo. Now,' he added, sighing, 'you will have to take me. Well, Dantès, aren't you going to thank me?'

'This treasure is yours, my friend,' said Dantès. 'It belongs to you alone and I have no right to it. We are not related.'

'You are my son, Dantès!' the old man cried. 'You are the child of my captivity. My priestly office condemned me to celibacy: God sent you to me both to console the man who could not be a father and the prisoner who could not be free.'

And he held out his good arm to the young man, who fell weeping on his breast.

XIX

THE THIRD SEIZURE

Now that the treasure, which had been for so long the object of the abbé's meditations, might ensure the future happiness of the man whom Faria loved truly as a son, it doubled in worth in his eyes. Every day, he dwelt on the amount, explaining to Dantès how much a man could do nowadays, in the way of good to his friends, with a fortune of thirteen or fourteen millions. Then Dantès' face clouded, because he recalled the oath of vengeance that he had taken and he considered how much, nowadays, with a fortune of thirteen or fourteen millions, a man could do in the way of harm to his enemies.

The abbé did not know Monte Cristo, but Dantès knew it. He had often sailed past this island, which lies twenty-five miles from Pianosa, between Corsica and Elba; once he had even dropped anchor there. The island was, had always been and is still utterly deserted: it is a rock of almost conical shape, which appears to have been thrown up by some volcanic cataclysm from the depths to the surface of the sea.

Dantès made a plan of the island for Faria, and Faria gave Dantès advice on the best way to recover the treasure. But Dantès was considerably less enthusiastic and above all less confident than the old man. Admittedly he was now quite certain that Faria was not mad, and the means by which he had arrived at the discovery that had made others believe him insane only added to Dantès' admiration for him. But he could also not believe that the cache, assuming that it had ever existed, existed still; and, while he did not consider the treasure as a chimera, he did at least think of it as absent.

However, as if destiny wanted to deprive the prisoners of their last hope and let them know that they were condemned to prison for life, a new misfortune struck. The gallery beside the sea, which had been crumbling for many years, was rebuilt, the stone courses were repaired and the hole that had already been half excavated by Dantès was filled with huge blocks of stone. Without the precautions that (as the reader will remember) had been suggested to Dantès by the abbé, the misfortune would have been greater still, because the attempted escape would have been discovered and they would certainly have been separated. In any case, a new door, stronger and more impenetrable than the rest, had been closed before them.

'You see,' the young man told Faria wistfully. 'God wishes to deprive me even of the merit of what you call my devotion to you. I promised to stay with you for ever and I am no longer free to break my promise. I shall no more have the treasure than you will: neither one of us will leave this place. Moreover, my true treasure, my friend, is not the one that awaits me under the dark rocks of Monte Cristo, but your presence, and the time that we spend together for five or six hours a day, in spite of our jailers; it is those rays of understanding that you have shone into my brain and the languages that you have implanted in my memory and which now grow there, putting out further branches of language in their turn. The many sciences that you have brought within my grasp by the depth of your own knowledge of them and the clarity of the basic principles which you have derived from them – this is my treasure, my friend, this is what you have given to make me rich and happy. Believe me, and console yourself; this is worth more to me than tons of gold and trunkloads of diamonds, even if they were not uncertain, like those clouds which can be seen in the morning above the sea and which appear to be dry land, but which evaporate, disperse and fade away as one approaches them. Having you close to me for as long as possible, hearing your eloquent voice as it enlightens my mind, re-tempering my soul, making my whole being capable of great and awe-inspiring deeds if ever I should be free, filling my mind and soul so thoroughly that the despair to which I was ready to give way when I met you can no longer find any place in them – this is my fortune. It is not a chimera. I truly owe it to you, and all the sovereigns on earth, were they all Cesare Borgias, could not succeed in taking it away from me.'

For the two unfortunates, these days, if not exactly happy, did at least speed past as quickly as those that followed. Faria, who had kept silent about the treasure for many years, now spoke incessantly about it. As he had predicted, he remained paralysed in the right arm and left leg, and had almost lost any hope of being able to enjoy the fortune himself, but he continually dreamed that his young companion might be freed, or escape, and would enjoy it for him. Fearing that the letter might be mislaid or lost one day, he obliged Dantès to learn it by heart; and, since the first day, Dantès had known it from the first word to the last. Then he destroyed the second half, convinced that if the first was found, no one would be able to understand its true meaning. Sometimes whole hours passed in which Faria gave Dantès instructions, to be carried out when he was free. And, once he was free, from the very day, hour, instant of his freedom, he must have no thought except that of somehow reaching Monte Cristo, remaining alone there under some pretext and, once there, once alone, trying to find the wonderful grottoes and searching the spot indicated in the letter: this, you may remember, was the furthest angle of the second opening.

Meanwhile, the hours passed, if not quickly, at least bearably. Faria, as we said, had not recovered the use of his hand and foot, but his mind was perfectly clear and, apart from the moral precepts which we have mentioned, he had taught his young companion the patient and noble craft of the prisoner, which is to make something out of nothing. So they were constantly occupied, Faria to ward off old age, Dantès in order to forget a past that was now almost extinct, and which only hovered in the furthest depths of his memory like a distant light flickering in the darkness. So time passed, as it does for those lives which have remained untroubled by misfortune and which continue calmly and mechanically under the eye of Providence. But beneath this calm surface, in the young man's heart, and also perhaps in that of the older one, there were many suppressed emotions and stifled sighs, which emerged when Faria was alone and Edmond had gone back to his own cell.

One night Edmond woke up with a start, thinking he had heard a cry. He opened his eyes and tried to penetrate the darkness.

He faintly heard his name; or, rather, a plaintive voice trying to speak his name.

He rose up on his bed, sweat rising to his forehead, and listened. There was no doubt. The cry was coming from his friend's dungeon.

'Good God!' he muttered. 'Could it be . . . ?'

He moved his bed, pushed aside the stone, rushed into the passage and reached the far end; the paving-stone was up.

In the vague, shimmering light of the lamp (which has already been mentioned), Edmond could see the old man: pale, still standing, clinging to his wooden bedpost. His face was already contorted by those fearful symptoms that Edmond now recognized, which had so terrified him when he saw them for the first time.

'So, my friend,' said Faria, in a resigned voice, 'you understand? I don't need to tell you anything.'

Edmond cried out in pain and sorrow, and – completely losing his head – ran to the door, shouting: 'Help! Help!'

Faria still had enough strength to restrain him.

'Silence!' he said. 'Otherwise you are lost. From now on we must think only of you, my child, and of how to make your captivity bearable or your flight possible. It would take you years by yourself to do alone all that I have done here, and it would be destroyed at once if our warders learned about the meetings between us. In any case, be calm, dear friend. The dungeon that I leave will not remain empty for long: some other unfortunate will come to take my place. This other man will look on you as a guardian angel. He may be young, strong and patient like yourself, he may help you in your escape, while I would only hinder you. You will no longer have half a corpse tied to you, impeding all your movements. Decidedly, God is at last doing something for you: he is giving you more than he is taking away. It is time I was dead.'

Edmond could only clasp his hands and exclaim: 'Oh, my friend, be quiet!' Then, recovering himself after the first shock and the old man's dispiriting words, he said: 'I have already saved you once, I can save you again.'

He picked up the leg of the bed and took out the flask, still one-third full of red liquid.

'Look, we still have some of the life-giving draught. Quickly, tell me what I must do this time. Are there any new instructions? Please tell me, my friend, I am listening.'

'There is no longer any hope,' Faria replied, shaking his head. 'No matter; God wants Man, whom he has created and in whose heart he has so profoundly entrenched a love for life, to do all he can to preserve an existence that is sometimes so painful, but always so dear to him.'

'Yes, yes! I shall save you!'

'Well, then, you may try. I am starting to feel cold and can feel the blood rushing to my head. The awful shivering that makes my teeth chatter and seems to unhinge my bones has begun to spread through my body. In five minutes the seizure will strike me, and in a quarter of an hour I shall be nothing but a corpse.'

'Oh!' Dantès cried sorrowfully, his heart smitten.

'Do as you did before, only do not wait so long. All the springs of my life are by now worn out and death' (indicating his paralysed arm and leg) 'will only have half its work left to do. If, after pouring twelve drops – instead of ten – into my mouth, you observe that I am still not coming to, then give me the rest. Now, take me to my bed. I cannot stand up any longer.'

Edmond took the old man in his arms and put him on the bed.

'Now, my friend,' said Faria, 'the only consolation of my un-happy life, you whom heaven has given me – late, but given me none the less – an inestimable present, for which I thank it . . . at this moment when we are to be separated for ever, I wish you all the happiness and prosperity that you deserve: my son, I bless you!'

The young man fell to his knees, pressing his head against the old man's bed.

'But above all, listen to what I am telling you in these final moments: the Spadas' treasure does exist. God has abolished all distance and every obstacle for me: I can see it, at the bottom of the second grotto; my eyes penetrate the depths of the earth and are dazzled by such riches. If you manage to escape, remember that the poor abbé, whom everyone believed mad, was not so. Hasten to Monte Cristo, take advantage of our fortune, enjoy it – you have suffered enough.'

A violent trembling interrupted his words. Dantès looked up and saw the eyes becoming bloodshot: it was as though a wave of blood had flowed up from the chest to the forehead.

'Farewell, farewell,' the old man murmured, convulsively grasp-ing the young one's hand. 'Adieu!'

'Not yet, not yet,' Dantès cried. 'Oh, God, do not abandon us. Help him! Help! Help . . .'

'Be quiet, be quiet,' the dying man muttered. 'If you can save me, we must not be separated.'

'You are right. Oh, yes! Have no fear, I shall save you! And, though you are suffering a great deal, you seem to suffer less than the first time.'

'Do not be deceived: I am suffering less, because I have less strength in me to suffer. At your age, you have faith in life; it is a privilege of youth to believe and to hope. But old men see death more clearly. Here it is! It is coming . . . it is the end . . . my life is going . . . my reason is clouded . . . Dantès, your hand . . . Adieu, adieu!' And rising in one final effort of his whole being, he said: 'Monte Cristo! Do not forget Monte Cristo!'

At this, he fell back on the bed.

The fit was terrible. All that remained on the bed of pain in place of the intelligent being that had lain there a moment before were twisted limbs, swollen eyes, bloody froth and a motionless corpse.

Dantès took the lamp and put it by the head of the bed on a jutting stone, so that its flickering flame cast a strange and fantastic light on these twisted features and this stiff, inert body. Staring directly at it, he waited imperturbably for the moment when he could administer the life-saving medicine.

When he thought it was time, he took the knife, prised apart the lips, which offered less resistance than they had the first time, and counted the ten drops one by one. Then he waited. The phial still contained about twice the amount that he had poured from it.

He waited ten minutes, a quarter of an hour, half an hour: there was no movement. Trembling, his hair standing on end, his forehead bathed in cold sweat, he counted the seconds by the beating of his heart.

Then he thought it was time to try the last resort: he brought the phial to Faria's violet lips and, without needing to prise apart the jaw, which was still open, he emptied it of all its contents.

The medicine produced an immediate effect, galvanizing the old man with a violent shudder through all his limbs. His eyes re-opened with a terrifying expression, he let out a sigh that was closer to a shout, then the whole trembling body relapsed gradually into immobility.

Only the eyes remained open.

Half an hour, an hour, an hour and a half passed. During this hour and a half of anguish, Edmond leant over, with his hand pressed against his friend's heart, and felt the body gradually grow cold and the beating of the heart become more muffled and more dull. At last, nothing remained. The last trembling of the heart ceased and the face became livid; the eyes stayed open but lifeless.

It was six in the morning. Day began to break and its pale light, penetrating the dungeon, dimmed the dying light of the lamp.

Strange shadows passed across the face, at times giving it the appearance of life. While this struggle between day and night continued, Dantès could still doubt, but as soon as day triumphed he knew for certain that he was alone with a corpse.

Then a deep and invincible terror seized him. He no longer dared to hold the hand that dangled outside the bed, he no longer dared to look into those staring white eyes, which he tried several times to close, but in vain; they always reopened. He put out the lamp, hid it carefully and made his retreat, replacing the stone above his head as best he could.

He was just in time. The jailer was about to appear.

This morning, he began his round with Dantès. After his cell, he went to Faria's, bringing breakfast and fresh linen. Nothing in the man's manner indicated that he knew anything about the accident that had occurred. He went out.

Dantès was now seized with an unspeakable impatience to know what would happen in his unfortunate friend's cell; so he went back down the underground passage and arrived in time to hear the turnkey's cries, as he called for help.

The other warders soon entered. Then you could hear the heavy, regular footsteps typical of soldiers, even when they are off duty. Behind the soldiers came the governor.

Edmond listened to the sound of the bed moving as they shook the body, then the governor's voice ordering water to be thrown in its face and, seeing that despite this the prisoner was not coming to, demanding the doctor.

The governor went out and a few words of compassion reached Dantès' ears, mixed with ironic laughter.

'Well, well, then!' one of them said. 'The madman has gone to find his treasure. *Bon voyage!*'

'For all his millions he won't have enough to pay for his winding-sheet,' said another.

'Winding-sheets are not expensive at the Château d'If,' remarked a third voice.

'Since he is a churchman,' said one of the first two voices, 'perhaps they will go to some extra expense for him.'

'In that case he will have the honour of a sack.'

Edmond listened and did not miss a word, but he understood very little of what was said. Soon the voices faded and he decided that the men had left the cell. However, he did not dare go in: they might have left a turnkey to guard the body. So he remained silent and motionless, hardly daring to breathe.

When someone returned, it was the governor, followed by the doctor and several officers. There was a brief silence: obviously the doctor was going up to the bed and examining the body. Then the questions began.

The doctor diagnosed the patient's condition and declared him dead. The questions and answers were delivered with a nonchalance that infuriated Dantès: it seemed to him that everyone should feel at least part of his own affection for the poor abbé.

'I am sad to hear it,' the governor said, in reply to the doctor's confirmation of the old man's death. 'He was a mild and inoffensive prisoner, who delighted us with his follies, and was above all easy to guard.'

'As for that,' said the warder, 'we could not have guarded him at all and I guarantee that this one would have stayed here fifty years without once attempting to escape.'

'However,' the governor continued, 'as I am responsible in this matter, I think that, certain as you are – and I don't doubt your competence – it is important as soon as possible to ensure that the prisoner is truly dead.'

There was a moment of utter silence during which Dantès, still listening, guessed that the doctor must be examining the body for a second time.

'You can set your mind entirely at rest,' he said shortly. 'He is dead, I guarantee it.'

'But as you know, Monsieur,' the governor insisted, 'we are not satisfied in such cases with a simple examination; so, despite all appearances, please complete your duties and carry out the formalities prescribed by law.'

'Let the irons be heated,' said the doctor. 'But, in truth, this is a quite useless precaution.'

The order to heat the irons made Dantès shudder.

He heard steps hurrying back and forth, the door grating on its hinges, some comings and goings inside the cell and, a few moments later, a turnkey returning and saying: 'Here is the brazier with a hot iron.'

There was a further moment's silence, then the sound of burning flesh, emitting a heavy, sickening odour which even penetrated the wall behind which Dantès was listening, horrified. At the smell of burning human flesh, sweat bathed the young man's brow and he thought that he was about to faint.

'You see, governor: he is indeed dead,' said the doctor. 'A burn on the heel is conclusive: the poor idiot is cured of his folly and delivered from his captivity.'

'Wasn't he called Faria?' asked one of the officers accompanying the governor.

'Yes, Monsieur, and he claimed that it was an old family. He was certainly very well educated and even quite reasonable on any matter not touching his treasure; on that, it must be said, he was intractable.'

'It is an affliction which we call monomania,' said the doctor.

'Have you ever had to complain about him?' the governor asked the jailer responsible for bringing the abbé's food.

'Never, governor,' the jailer replied. 'Never, not the slightest! On the contrary: at one time he used to entertain me greatly by telling me stories; and one day, when my wife was ill, he even gave me a recipe which cured her.'

'Ah, ah! I didn't know that he was a colleague,' said the doctor; the he added, with a laugh: 'I hope, governor, that you will treat him accordingly?'

'Yes, yes, have no fear, he will be decently shrouded in the newest sack we can find. Does that satisfy you?'

'Must we carry out this final formality in your presence, Monsieur?' asked a turnkey.

'Of course, but hurry. I cannot stay all day in this cell.'

Dantès heard further comings and goings; then, a moment later, the sound of cloth being rumpled. The bed grated on its springs, there was a heavy step on the paving like that of a man lifting a burden, then the bed creaked again under the weight that was returned to it.

'Until this evening, then,' said the governor.

'Will there be a Mass?' asked one of the officers.

'Impossible,' the governor replied. 'The prison chaplain came to me yesterday to ask for leave to go on a short journey for one week to Hyères, and I told him that I could take care of my prisoners for that time. The poor abbé shouldn't have been in such a hurry, then he would have had his requiem.'

'Pooh!' said the doctor, with the customary impiety of his

profession. 'He is a churchman. God will consider his state and not give hell the satisfaction of receiving a priest.'

This ill-judged quip was greeted with a burst of laughter. And meanwhile the preparation of the corpse continued.

'Till this evening, then,' the governor said, when it was completed.

'At what time?' the turnkey asked.

'Around ten or eleven, of course.'

'Should we guard the body?'

'Why? We shall lock the cell as if he were alive, that's all.'

The footsteps and the voices faded, Dantès heard the groaning lock on the door and its creaking bolts, and a silence more melancholy than solitude, the silence of death, fell over all, penetrating deep into the young man's soul. Then he slowly raised the paving-stone with his head and looked around the cell. It was empty. Dantès emerged from the tunnel.

XX

THE GRAVEYARD OF THE CHÂTEAU D'IF

Stretched out on the bed, weakly outlined by a dusty ray of light from the window, there was a sack of coarse cloth, under the broad folds of which one could vaguely distinguish a long, stiff shape: this was Faria's last winding-sheet which, according to the turnkeys, had cost so little. So all was finished. Between Dantès and his old friend there was already a gulf: he could no longer see those eyes, wide open as if looking beyond death; he could no longer clasp that industrious hand which for him had lifted the veil that covered arcane matters. Faria, that good and valuable companion to whom he had become so strongly attached, now existed only in his memory. He sat down at the head of this awful bed and lapsed into a deep and bitter melancholy.

Alone! He was once more alone! He had fallen back into silence, he was faced once more with nothingness!

Alone, he no longer had even the sight or the sound of the voice of the only human being who still bound him to the earth! Would it not be better for him, like Faria, to go and ask God to explain the enigma of life, even at the risk of passing through the dark gate of suffering? The idea of suicide had been driven away by his friend's presence, but returned like a ghost and rose up beside Faria's corpse.

'If I could die,' he said, 'I should go where he has gone and I should certainly find him again. But how can I die? It is easy,' he added, laughing. 'I have only to remain here, throw myself on the first person who enters and strangle him; they will guillotine me.'

But, as often happens, in great sorrow as in great storms, the abyss lies between the crests of two waves; Dantès shrank from the idea of so dishonourable a death and rapidly went from this feeling of despair to a burning thirst for life and freedom.

'Die! No, no!' he cried. 'It was not worth living so long, and suffering so much, to die now. Death was welcome previously, when I made a resolution to meet it, many years ago. But now it would truly be conceding too much to my miserable fate. No, I want to live, I want to struggle to the end. No, I want to recover the happiness that has been taken away from me. I am forgetting that, before I die, I have my enemies to punish and, who knows? – perhaps a few friends to reward. But now that I am forgotten here, I shall not escape my dungeon except in the same way as Faria.'

At these words, Edmond remained motionless, his gaze fixed, like a man who has suddenly been struck by an idea, but one that appals him. At once he got up, put his hand on his forehead as if suffering from dizziness, walked around the room two or three times and returned to the bed.

'Ah!' he exclaimed. 'Where did that idea come from? From you, God? Since only the dead leave this place freely, let us take the place of the dead.' And, without wasting any time in reconsidering the decision, as if to avoid giving his thoughts the opportunity to annihilate his desperate resolve, he bent over the ghastly sack, opened it with the knife that Faria had made, removed the body, dragged it into his own cell, put it in his bed, covered its head with the scrap of linen that he was accustomed to wear on his own, drew his blanket over it, kissed its icy brow for the last time and tried to close the eyes, which still remained stubbornly open, terrifying because there was no thought behind them. After that, he turned the head to the wall so that the jailer, when he brought the evening meal, would think that he was asleep, as quite often happened;

then he returned to the tunnel, dragged the bed against the wall, went back to the other cell, took the needle and thread out of the wardrobe, threw off his rags so that they would feel naked flesh under the cloth, slipped into the empty sack, lay down in the same position as the body, and sewed it up from inside.

If anyone had unfortunately chanced to come in at that moment, they would have heard his heart beating.

Dantès could easily have waited until after the evening visit, but he was afraid that between now and then the governor might change his mind and take away the body. In that case, his last hope would be gone.

Now, in any case, his plan was fixed. Here is what he intended to do:

If, during the journey out of the cell, the gravediggers realized that they were carrying a living man instead of a corpse, Dantès would not give them time to gather their wits. He would split the sack from top to bottom with a sharp lunge of the knife and take advantage of their terror to escape. If they tried to stop him, he would use the knife.

If they took him to the burial ground and put him in a grave, he would allow himself to be covered with earth; then, since it was night, the gravediggers would hardly have turned their backs before he would tunnel out of the soft earth and escape. He hoped the soil would not be too heavy for him to lift it. If he was wrong and the earth proved to be too heavy, he would suffocate, and so much the better: all would be over!

Dantès had not eaten since the previous day, but he had not thought of his hunger that morning, and he still did not notice it. His position was too precarious for him to waste time on thinking of anything else.

The first danger that threatened was that the jailer, bringing him his supper at seven o'clock, would notice the substitution; luckily Dantès had many times received the jailer's visit lying down, either through misanthropy or fatigue. In such cases the man usually put the bread and soup on the table and left without speaking to him. This time, however, the jailer might lapse from his habitual silence, say something and, when Dantès did not reply, go over to the bed and discover the deception.

As seven o'clock approached, Dantès began to suffer in earnest.

One hand was pressed against his heart, attempting to stifle its beating while the other wiped the sweat from his brow as it streamed along his temples. From time to time, a shudder would run through his whole body and seize his heart in an icy grip; at such moments he thought he would die. The hours passed without bringing any sound of movement in the fortress and Dantès realized that he had escaped the first danger, which was a good sign. Finally, at around the time appointed by the governor, footsteps were heard in the stairway. Edmond realized that the moment had come. He summoned up all his courage, holding his breath; he would have been happier could he have stifled the beating of his pulse in the same way.

The footsteps, two sets of them, stopped outside the door. Dantès guessed that this must be the two gravediggers who had come to fetch him. This suspicion became a certainty when he heard the noise that they made setting down the bier.

The door opened and a muffled light reached Dantès' eyes. Through the cloth covering him he saw two shapes approach the bed. At the door was a third, carrying a lantern. The two who had come over to the bed each grasped one end of the sack.

'He's still pretty heavy, this one, for such a thin old man!' one said, raising the head.

'They do say that each year adds half a pound to the weight of the bones,' the other replied, taking the feet.

'Have you made your knot?' the first asked.

'It would be stupid to carry any unnecessary weight; I'll make it when we get there.'

'Quite right, let's go.'

'What knot is that?' Dantès wondered.

They carried the supposed corpse from the bed to the bier. Edmond stiffened, the better to play dead. They put him down on the stretcher, and the funeral procession, led and lit by the man with the lantern, went up the stairs.

Suddenly, he was bathed in the fresh, sharp air of night. Dantès recognized the mistral and was filled with a sudden feeling of both delight and anguish.

The men carrying him went about twenty paces, then stopped and set the bier down on the ground. One of them went away: Dantès could hear his footsteps on the pavement.

'Where can I be?' he wondered.

'You know something, he's not at all light!' said the one who had stayed behind, sitting down on the edge of the stretcher.

Dantès' first instinct had been to escape, but luckily he resisted it.

'Give us some light, here, you brute,' said the one who had moved away. 'Otherwise I'll never find what I'm looking for.'

The man with the lantern obeyed, even though, as we have seen, the request was couched in rather offensive terms.

'What can he be looking for?' Dantès wondered. 'No doubt a spade.'

A satisfied exclamation indicated that the gravedigger had found whatever it was he needed.

'At last,' the other said. 'You made a hard job of it.'

'Yes, but there's nothing lost by the delay.'

At these words, he went over to Edmond, who heard something heavy and resounding being put down beside him. At the same moment, a rope was bound tightly and painfully around his feet.

'Well, have you done the knot?' asked the gravedigger who had remained idle.

'And done it well,' said the other. 'I guarantee.'

'In that case, let's be going.'

And the bier was lifted and carried forward.

They took about fifty paces, then stopped to open a gate, before carrying on. The sound of waves breaking against the rocks on which the castle was built reached Dantès more and more clearly as they went on.

'The weather is bad,' said one of the men. 'I'd not like to be out at sea tonight.'

'Yes, the abbé runs a serious risk of getting wet,' said the other – and they burst out laughing.

Dantès did not entirely understand this joke, but the hair still rose on his neck.

'Good, here we are!' said the first man.

'Further on, further on,' said the other. 'You remember that the last one stayed behind, caught on the rocks, and the next day the governor told us what lazy devils we were.'

They took four or five steps more, still going up, then Dantès felt them take him by the head and feet and swing him.

'One!' said the gravediggers.

'Two . . .'

'Three!'

At this moment, Dantès felt himself being thrown into a huge void, flying through the air like a wounded bird, then falling, falling, in a terrifying descent that froze his heart. Although he was drawn downwards by some weight that sped his flight, it seemed to him that the fall lasted a century. Finally, with a terrifying noise, he plunged like an arrow into icy water, and he cried out, his cry instantly stifled by the water closing around him.

Dantès had been thrown into the sea – and a thirty-six-pound cannonball tied to his feet was dragging him to the bottom.

The sea is the graveyard of the Château d'If.

XXI

THE ISLAND OF TIBOULEN

Though stunned and almost suffocated, Dantès still had the presence of mind to hold his breath and since, as we have said, his right hand was prepared for any eventuality, holding the open knife, he quickly slit the cloth and put out his arm, then his head. But then, despite his attempts to raise the cannonball, he felt himself being continually dragged down, so he bent over to search for the rope restraining his legs and, with one last despairing effort, cut it just as he was suffocating. Kicking powerfully, he rose, free, to the surface of the sea, while the weight dragged the coarse linen that had almost become his shroud down into the unknown depths.

Dantès stayed no longer than was necessary to take a breath, before diving once more: the first precaution that he had to take was to avoid being seen.

When he emerged a second time, he was already at least fifty yards from the place where he had fallen. Above him, he saw a black, lowering sky, across which the clouds were being rapidly swept by the wind, from time to time revealing a small patch of blue from which a star shone. In front of him was a dark, roaring plain, its waves starting to seethe as at the approach of a storm; while behind him, blacker than the sea, blacker than the sky, like a

threatening phantom, rose the granite giant, its sombre peak like
a hand outstretched to grasp its prey. On the topmost rock was a
lantern lighting two human forms.

It seemed to him that the two forms were bending uneasily over
the sea: the strange gravediggers must indeed have heard the cry
that escaped him as he flew through the air. So Dantès dived again
and swam underwater for a considerable distance; he had once
been quite used to doing this and would formerly, in the cove of
the Pharo, have attracted many admirers around him, who often
proclaimed him the most accomplished swimmer in Marseille.

When he came back to the surface, the lantern had vanished.

Now he must find his bearings. Of all the islands around the
Château d'If, Ratonneau and Pomègue are the nearest; but Ratonneau and Pomègue are inhabited; so is the little island of Daume.
The safest landfall was therefore on either Tiboulen or Lemaire,
and these two islands lie a league away from the Château d'If.

Even so, it was one of these two that Dantès decided to make
for: but how could he find them in the depth of the night that was
deepening moment by moment around him? But then, shining like
a star, he noticed the Planier lighthouse. If he swam directly towards
the light, he would leave Tiboulen a little to his left; so if he were
to swing a small distance to the left, he would be heading for the
island.

However, as we have said, it was at least a league from the
Château d'If to Tiboulen.

Often, in their prison, Faria had told the young man, when he
saw him depressed and languid: 'Dantès, you must not give way to
this debility. If you do manage to escape and you have failed to
keep up your strength, you will drown.'

Beneath the heavy, bitter swell, Dantès once more heard these
words in his ears, and he hurried back to the surface to plough
through the waves and test whether he had indeed lost his power.
He was overjoyed to find that his enforced idleness had deprived
him of none of his strength and agility, and to find that he was still
master of this element in which he had gambolled as a child.

In any event, fear, that swift tormentor, doubled his vigour.
Rising on the crest of the waves, he listened to find out if he could
hear any noise. Each time that he reached the highest point of a
wave, he quickly surveyed the visible horizon and tried to penetrate
the blackness. Every wave that climbed a little higher than the rest

looked to him like a boat pursuing him, so he strove all the harder, which certainly took him further onward but also threatened to exhaust him more quickly.

Yet he did swim; and the fearful fortress had faded somewhat into the mists of night: he could no longer see it, but he felt it still.

An hour passed, during which Dantès, buoyed up by the sense of freedom that had spread through his whole body, continued to drive on through the waves on the course he had set himself.

'Now, let's see,' he thought. 'I have been swimming for almost an hour, but with a contrary wind I must have lost a quarter of my speed. However, unless I have mistaken the direction, I must now be close to the island of Tiboulen . . . But what if I am mistaken?'

The swimmer felt a shudder pass through him. He tried to float for a moment to give himself a rest, but the sea was getting heavier all the time, and he soon realized that such respite, which he had counted on having, was impossible.

'Well, so be it,' he said. 'I shall go on until the end . . . until my arms fail, until cramp seizes my whole body . . . and then I shall sink!' And he began to swim with the energy and urgency of despair.

Suddenly it seemed that the sky, already so dark, grew still darker and that a thick, heavy, impenetrable cloud was coming down over him. At the same time he felt a sharp pain in his knee. His imagination immediately told him that this must be the shock of a bullet and that he would instantly hear the report of a rifle; but there was no explosion. Dantès put out his hand and felt something. He brought up his other leg, and touched solid ground. It was then that he saw what it was he had taken for a cloud.

Twenty yards ahead of him rose a mass of oddly shaped rocks that looked like a vast fire, solidified just at the moment when it was burning most fiercely. This was the island of Tiboulen.

Dantès stood up and took a few steps forward, then he lay down, thanking God, on these points of granite that seemed softer to him at that moment than the softest bed. Then, despite the wind, despite the storm, despite the rain that was starting to fall, exhausted as he was, he fell asleep with that delicious sleep of the man whose body is numbed but whose mind is awake to the knowledge of unhoped-for good fortune.

After an hour, Edmond woke to the sound of an immense clap

of thunder. The storm had broken in the heavens and was beating the air with its flashing flight. From time to time a shaft of lightning shot from the sky like a fiery snake, illuminating the waves and the clouds that plunged headlong after each other like the breakers of a vast abyss.

Dantès, with his sailor's eye, had judged rightly. He had landed on the first of the two islands, which is Tiboulen. He knew that it was a naked rock, open to the elements and shelterless. When the storm was over, he would plunge back into the sea and make for the island of Lemaire, no less deserted but wider and consequently more welcoming.

An overhanging rock did offer him some temporary shelter and he took refuge under it. At almost the same moment the storm broke in all its fury.

Edmond felt the rock beneath which he was hiding tremble and the waves, breaking against the base of the huge pyramid, reached his hiding-place. Safe as he was, in the midst of this shattering noise and these blinding flashes of light, he was seized with a sort of dizziness. He felt as though the very island were shaking beneath him and, from one moment to the next, would break its moorings like a vessel at anchor and drag him down with it into the midst of the huge maelstrom.

At this, he remembered that he had not eaten for twenty-four hours: he was hungry and thirsty. He stretched out his hands and his neck, and drank some rainwater from a hollow in the rock.

As he was lifting his head, a shaft of lightning, which seemed to crack open the heavens as far as the foot of God's radiant throne, lit up the scene. By its light Dantès saw a little fishing boat appear, like a phantom slipping from the crest of a wave into the abyss, driven forward both by the waves and by the storm, between the Ile Lemaire and the Cap Croisille, a quarter of a league away from him. A second later the phantom reappeared on the crest of another wave, coming towards him at fearful speed. Dantès wanted to shout; he looked for a scrap of cloth that he could wave in the air, to show them that they were heading for destruction, but they could see it perfectly well for themselves. In the light of another shaft of lightning the young man saw four men hanging on to the masts and the rigging, while a fifth held the bar of a broken helm. No doubt these men whom he saw could also see him, for desperate cries were carried across to him on the whistling gusts. Above the mast, twisted like a reed, a tattered sail was flapping rapidly over and over against the air. Suddenly, the ropes that still held it broke and it vanished, carried away into the dark depths of the sky, like a great white bird silhouetted against a black cloud.

At the same time he heard a fearful crack and cries of agony. Grasping his rock like a sphinx above the abyss, Dantès glimpsed the little boat in the light of another flash, broken; amid its wreckage, heads with terrified faces and hands reached for the sky. Then darkness returned; the awful scene had lasted the lifetime of a lightning bolt.

Dantès hastened down the slippery rocks, at the risk of himself falling into the sea. He looked, listened, but could hear and see nothing: no more cries, no more human struggle. Only the storm, that great act of God, continued to roar with the wind and to foam with the waves.

Little by little, the wind subsided. Westwards across the sky rolled huge grey clouds which seemed to have been discoloured by the storm. Patches of blue sky reappeared with stars that shone brighter than ever. Soon, in the east, a long reddish band lit up the undulating blue-black line of the horizon. The waves danced and instantly a light sped across their crests; transforming each one into a mane of gold. Day was breaking.

Dantès remained motionless and silent before this great spectacle, as if seeing it for the first time. Indeed, in all the years that he had been at the Château d'If he had forgotten it. He turned back to look at the fortress, sweeping his eyes across the whole arc of the land and the sea. The dark pile rose out of the midst of the waves with the imposing majesty common to all motionless objects which seem at once to watch and to command. It must have been about five o'clock. The sea was growing calmer all the time.

'In two or three hours,' Edmond thought, 'the turnkey will go into my room, find the body of my poor friend, recognize it, look in vain for me and give the alarm. Then they will find the hole and the tunnel. They will question the men who threw me into the sea, who must have heard me cry out. Immediately, ships full of soldiers will set out in pursuit of the unfortunate fugitive, who cannot have gone far. The cannon will be fired to warn everyone on the coast not to give shelter to any man who appears, naked and starving. The spies and alguazils[1] of Marseille will be informed: they will search the coast while the governor of the Château d'If will be searching the sea. So, hunted down at sea, hemmed in on land, what will become of me? I am hungry and thirsty, I have even lost my life-saving knife, because it hampered me while I was swimming. I am at the mercy of the first peasant who wants to earn twenty francs by handing me in. I have no strength, no ideas, no resolve left. Oh, my God, my God! Haven't I suffered enough? Now, can you do more for me than I can do for myself?'

Just as Edmond was uttering this ardent prayer, in a sort of delirium due to his exhaustion and the lightness of his head, and anxiously turning towards the Château d'If, he saw off the point of the Ile de Pomègue, its lateen sail against the horizon like a seagull skimming the waves, a little ship which only the eye of a sailor would have recognized as a Genoese tartan[2] which appeared on the still indistinct line of the sea. It was coming from the port of Marseille and heading out to sea, driving the shining spray in front of a sharp prow that cut the sea ahead of its swelling sides.

'Just think!' Edmond exclaimed. 'In half an hour I could have reached that ship, if I were not afraid of being questioned, recognized as an escaped prisoner and taken back to Marseille! What can I do, what can I say? What story can I invent to deceive them? These people are all smugglers, nearly pirates. Pretending to ply the coast, they scour it for booty; they would rather sell me than do a good deed for nothing.

'Let's wait . . .

'But it is impossible to wait. I am dying of hunger. In a few hours I shall have exhausted the little strength that remains to me. In any case, the time of the warder's rounds is approaching; the alarm has not yet been sounded, so perhaps they will suspect nothing. I can pretend to be one of the sailors from that little boat which sank last night. This is a plausible enough story. No one will be able to contradict me, since the whole crew is drowned. Let's go.'

As he said these words, Dantès looked towards the place where the little ship had foundered, and shuddered. The Phrygian cap[3] of one of the drowned sailors was hanging from the jagged edge of a rock and near it some wreckage from the ship's hull was floating, dead beams that the sea drove against the base of the island which they hammered like powerless battering-rams.

In an instant, Dantès had made up his mind. He plunged back into the sea, swam towards the cap, put it on his head, grasped hold of one of the beams and set a course that would take him to meet up with the boat.

'Now I am saved,' he muttered; and the certainty gave him strength.

He soon saw the tartan which, as it was sailing almost directly into the wind, was tacking between the Château d'If and the Tour de Planier. For a moment, Dantès was afraid that, instead of hugging the coast, the little ship would head out to sea, as it would have done, for example, had it been bound for Corsica or Sardinia. But from the way it was manoeuvring, the swimmer soon realized that it intended to pass between the islands of Jarre and Calseraigne.

However, the ship and the swimmer were gradually converging. As it tacked in one direction, the little ship even came to about a quarter of a league from Dantès. He rose up in the sea and waved his cap as a distress signal, but no one on the ship saw him and it went about to begin tacking in the other direction. Dantès thought of calling out, but he assessed the distance and realized that his voice would not reach the ship, but would be carried away on the sea breeze and covered by the noise of the waves.

Now he congratulated himself for having had the foresight to lie on a beam. Weak as he was, he might not have been able to keep afloat until he reached the tartan; and, certainly, if – as was quite possible – the tartan passed without seeing him, he would not have been able to reach the shore.

Though he was almost certain of the course that the boat had set, Dantès looked anxiously after it until the moment when he saw it tack again and return towards him. Then he swam to meet it. But before their paths had crossed, the boat began to turn.

Immediately, summoning all his strength, Dantès rose almost out of the water, waved his cap and gave one of those pitiful cries of a sailor in distress which sound like the wailing of some genie of the sea.

This time he was seen and heard. The tartan changed course and turned towards him. At the same time he saw that they were preparing to put a boat into the sea. A moment later, the boat, rowed by two men, their oars striking the sea, was coming towards him. Dantès let go of the beam, thinking he would no longer need it, and swam vigorously to halve the distance between himself and his saviours.

However, he had counted on strength that had almost deserted him. Now he realized how much that piece of wood, already floating inertly a hundred yards away, had helped him. His arms began to stiffen, his legs had lost their suppleness, his movements became forced and jerky, and his chest heaved. He let out a great cry; the two rowers increased their efforts and one called out in Italian: '*Coraggio!*'

The word reached him just as a wave, which he no longer had the strength to ride above, broke over his head and drenched him in spray. He reappeared, thrashing the sea with the uneven, desperate movements of a drowning man, cried out a third time and felt himself sinking into the sea, as if he still had the fatal cannonball attached to his legs. The water closed over his head and, above the water, he saw a livid sky, speckled with black.

One last, superhuman effort brought him back to the surface of the sea. Then it seemed to him that someone had grasped him by the hair, and he saw and heard nothing more. He had lost consciousness.

When he next opened his eyes, he was on the deck of the tartan, which was under way again. The first thing he did was to look to see what course it was following; it was still sailing away from the Château d'If.

Dantès was so exhausted that his exclamation of joy was mistaken for a cry of pain.

As we said, he was lying on the deck. A sailor was rubbing his limbs with a woollen blanket, while another, whom he recognized as the one who had shouted '*coraggio!*', was putting the lip of a gourd to his mouth. A third, an old sailor, who was both the pilot and the master, looked at him with the selfish pity that men usually feel towards a misfortune that they escaped only the day before and which might be waiting for them on the following one.

A few drops of rum from the gourd stimulated the young man's heart, while the massage that the other sailor was still giving him with the wool, kneeling in front of him, gave some movement back to his limbs.

'Who are you?' the master asked in broken French.

'I am a Maltese seaman,' Dantès replied, in broken Italian. 'We were sailing from Syracuse, with a cargo of wine and panoline. The squall last night surprised us off Cap Morgiou and we foundered against those rocks that you see over there.'

'And where have you come from?'

'From those same rocks, on which I had the good fortune to wash up, while our poor captain's head was broken against them. Our three companions were drowned. I think I must be the only one left alive. I saw your ship and, fearing that I might have to wait a long time on that isolated desert island, I took my chances on a piece of the wreckage from our boat to try and reach you. Thank you,' Dantès went on, 'you have saved my life. I was exhausted when one of your sailors grasped me by the hair.'

'That was me,' said a sailor with a frank and open face, framed in long side-whiskers. 'It was none too soon; you were going under.'

'Yes,' Dantès said, offering his hand. 'Yes, my friend. I thank you once more.'

'Damn it!' said the sailor. 'I was almost reluctant to do it. With your six-inch beard and your hair a full foot long, you look more like a brigand than an honest sailor.'

Dantès remembered that he had, indeed, not cut his hair or shaved his beard in the whole time he was in the Château d'If.

'Yes,' he said. 'This was a vow that I made to Our Lady of Pie della Grotta, in a moment of danger: to go ten years without cutting my hair or my beard. Today sees the expiation of my vow – and I nearly drowned on the anniversary of it.'

'Now, what are we going to do with you?' asked the master.

'Alas!' Dantès replied. 'You can do what you like. The felucca on which I was sailing is lost, the captain is dead. As you can see, I escaped his fate, but totally naked: luckily I am a fairly good sailor. Put me off at the first port where you make land and I shall always find employment on some merchant vessel.'

'Do you know the Mediterranean?'

'I have been sailing round it since my childhood.'

'You know the best anchorages?'

'There are few ports, even the most difficult, where I could not sail in or out with my eyes closed.'

'Well, how about it, patron?' said the sailor who had cried 'coraggio!' to Dantès. 'If what this comrade says is true, why shouldn't he stay with us?'

'Yes, if it is true,' said the master, looking doubtful. 'But in the present state of this poor devil, one may promise a lot, meaning to do what one can.'

'I shall do even more than I have promised,' said Dantès.

The master laughed. 'We'll see about that.'

'Whenever you wish,' Dantès replied, getting up. 'Where are you headed?'

'To Leghorn.'

'Well, then, instead of tacking and wasting precious time, why don't you simply sail closer into the wind?'

'Because we would be heading directly for the Ile de Riou.'

'You will be more than a hundred and twenty feet away from it.'

'Take the helm, then,' said the master, 'and let's judge your skill.'

The young man sat at the helm, touched it lightly to verify that the boat was responsive; seeing that it was reasonably so, though not of the finest class, he said: 'All hands to the rigging!'

The four members of the crew ran to their posts, while the master looked on.

'Haul away!'

The sailors obeyed quite effectively.

'Now, make fast!'

This order was carried out as the first two had been and the little ship, instead of continuing to tack, began to make for the Ile de Riou, passing near it and leaving it off the starboard side, at about the distance Dantès had predicted.

'Bravo!' said the master.

'Bravo!' the sailors repeated, all looking with wonder at this man whose face had recovered a look of intelligence and whose body possessed a strength that they had not suspected.

'You see,' Dantès said, leaving the helm. 'I might be of some use to you, at least during the crossing. If you want to leave me in Leghorn, you can do so. I shall repay you for my food up to that time, and for the clothes that you will lend me, out of my first month's pay.'

'Very well, then,' said the master. 'We can come to some arrangement if you are reasonable.'

'One man is worth as much as another,' said Dantès. 'Give me what you give to my companions, and we shall be quits.'

'That's not fair,' said the sailor who had pulled Dantès out of the sea. 'You know more than we do.'

'Who the devil asked you? Is this any of your business, Jacopo?' said the master. 'Every man is free to sign on at the rate which suits him.'

'Correct,' said Jacopo. 'I was just commenting.'

'Well, you would do better to lend this poor lad a pair of trousers and a jacket, if you have any to spare; he is stark naked.'

'I haven't,' said Jacopo, 'but I do have a shirt and trousers.'

'That is all I need,' said Dantès. 'Thank you, my friend.'

Jacopo slid down the hatch and returned a moment later with the two articles of clothing, which Dantès was unspeakably happy to put on.

'Do you need anything else?' asked the master.

'A scrap of bread and another draught of that excellent rum that you gave me. I have not eaten for a long time.' It was, in fact, around forty hours.

They brought Dantès a piece of bread, and Jacopo offered him the flask.

'Hard a-port!' the captain cried, turning to the helmsman.

Dantès looked in the same direction as he put the flask to his lips, but it stopped half-way.

'Look there!' the master exclaimed. 'What is going on at the Château d'If?'

A little puff of white smoke, which is what had caught Dantès' attention, had just appeared above the battlements of the south tower of the fortress.

A second later, the sound of a distant explosion reached the tartan. The sailors looked up and exchanged glances.

'What does that mean?' the master asked.

'Some prisoner escaped last night,' said Dantès, 'and they are firing the warning gun.'

The master looked at the young man who, as he spoke the words, brought the flask to his lips. He drank the liquid with such calm and satisfaction that, if the master had felt the shadow of a doubt, it would immediately have been dispelled.

'This rum is devilish strong,' Dantès said, wiping the sweat from his brow with the sleeve of his shirt.

'In any case,' the master thought, looking at him, 'even if it is him, so much the better. I have gained a fine man.'

Pretending that he was tired, Dantès asked if he could sit at the helm. The helmsman, delighted to be relieved of his job, looked at the master, who nodded to let him know that he could hand the bar over to his new companion. From this vantage point, Dantès could remain with his eyes fixed towards Marseille.

'What day of the month is it?' Dantès asked Jacopo, who had come to sit next to him, as they lost sight of the Château d'If.

'February the twenty-eighth,' he replied.

'And what year?'

'What do you mean, what year! Are you asking me what year it is?'

'Yes,' said the young man. 'I am asking you the year.'

'You have forgotten what year we are in?'

'What do you expect! I was so terrified last night,' Dantès said, laughing, 'I nearly lost my mind. As it is, my memory is troubled. So I am asking you: this is the twenty-eighth of February, of what year?'

'Of the year 1829,' said Jacopo.

Fourteen years earlier, to the day, Dantès had been arrested. He had entered the Château d'If at the age of nineteen and was now emerging from it at thirty-three.

A pained smile crossed his lips: he was wondering what had become of Mercédès during this time, when she must have thought him dead. Then a spark of hatred lit up in his eyes, when he thought of the three men who were responsible for his long, cruel captivity. And once more he vowed that same, implacable oath of vengeance that he had already taken in prison against Danglars, Fernand and Villefort.

But now the oath was no longer an empty threat, because the finest fully-manned sailing ship in the Mediterranean could surely not have overtaken the little tartan which was making for Leghorn at full speed.

XXII

THE SMUGGLERS

Dantès had not been a day on board before he realized the sort of people he was dealing with. Without ever having had lessons from Abbé Faria, the worthy master of the *Jeune-Amélie* (as the Genoese tartan was called) was acquainted with more or less every language spoken around the great lake known as the Mediterranean, from Arabic to Provençal. This relieved him of the need to employ an interpreter – a class of people who are always bothersome and sometimes indiscreet – and made it easy for him to communicate, whether with any ships that he might encounter at sea, or with the little boats that he met along the coasts, or finally with those people, without name, nationality or evident profession, who are always to be found on the paved quaysides of seaports, living on mysterious and secret resources which one can only believe must come to them directly from Providence, since they have no other visible means of support: the reader may have guessed that Dantès was on a smugglers' ship.

For this reason the master had been slightly suspicious about taking him on board. He was well known to all the Customs officers along the coast, engaging with these gentlemen in a mutual exchange of stratagems, each more cunning than the last, so he had at first thought that Dantès was an emissary of my lords the excisemen, who were using this ingenious method to root out some of the secrets of his trade. But the brilliance with which Dantès had succeeded in the test of fine navigation had entirely convinced him. Then, at the sight of the puff of smoke rising like a plume over the Château d'If and the distant sound of the explosion, he momentarily guessed that he had just taken on board one of those men – in this respect like kings – whose entrances and exits are honoured by the firing of cannon. This bothered him less, it must be said, than if the newcomer had been a Customs officer, and this new suspicion vanished like its predecessor when he saw how perfectly calm his latest recruit remained.

In this way, Edmond had the advantage of knowing what his master was, while his master did not know the same about him. Whenever the old seaman and his crew questioned him, and on whatever subject, he held firm and confessed nothing, giving a wealth of details about Naples or Malta, both of which he knew as well as he knew Marseille, and sticking to his first story with a consistency that was a credit to his memory. Thus the Genoan, wily as he was, let himself be taken in by Edmond, thanks to the young man's gentle manner, his experience of the sea and, above all, his unusual skill at deception.

But, then, perhaps the Genoan was like those clever men who never know more than they need and believe only what it is in their interests to believe.

This was the situation when they arrived at Leghorn.

Here Edmond had to face a new trial: he had to find out if he would recognize himself, not having seen his own face for fourteen years. He could remember the young man quite clearly; now he would discover what he had become as a mature one. As far as his companions were concerned, he had fulfilled his vow. He had already been twenty times to Leghorn and knew a barber in the Rue Saint-Fernand. That was where he went to have his beard shaved and his hair cut.

The barber looked with astonishment at this man, with his long hair and thick black beard, who resembled one of those fine heads by Titian. At that time it was not yet the fashion to wear one's beard and hair long; nowadays a barber would rather be surprised that a man who could enjoy such physical attributes should wish to deprive himself of them. He said nothing and set about his work. When it was done, when Edmond felt his chin to be clean-shaven and when his hair had been shortened to normal length, he asked for a mirror and looked in it.

Dantès was now thirty-three years old, as we have said, and his fourteen years in prison had brought what might be described as a great spiritual change to his features. He had entered the Château d'If with the round, full, radiant face of a contented young man whose first steps in life have been easy and who looks to the future as a natural extension of the past. All that had changed utterly.

His oval face had lengthened and his once merry lips had adopted a fixed, firm line that spoke of stern resolve. His eyebrows arched under a single, pensive line and his eyes themselves were imprinted with deep sadness, behind which from time to time could be seen dark flashes of misanthropy and hatred. His complexion, kept so long from daylight and the sun, had taken on the dull tones that give such aristocratic beauty to men of the north when black hair frames their faces. Moreover the knowledge that he had acquired gave a look of intelligent self-confidence to his whole face. Though naturally quite tall, his body had taken on the compact vigour of one that has learnt to concentrate all its strength within itself.

The elegance of lean, nervous limbs had been replaced by the solidity of a well-built, muscular man. His voice, accustomed to prayers, sobs and curses, had at times a strangely soft resonance, at others a rough edge that was almost husky. In addition, having been constantly in darkness or half-light, his eyes had acquired the remarkable ability of seeing in the dark, like those of wolves and hyenas.

Edmond smiled when he saw himself. It would have been impossible for his best friend – if he had any friends left – to recognize him; he didn't recognize himself.

The master of the *Jeune-Amélie*, who was very keen to keep someone of Edmond's ability in his crew, had offered him an advance on his share of future profits and Edmond had accepted, so the first thing he did on leaving the barber's where he had undergone this preliminary metamorphosis was to find a shop where he could buy a complete set of seaman's clothes. Of course, this is very simple, consisting of white trousers, a striped shirt and a Phrygian cap.

Edmond returned the trousers and shirt that Jacopo had lent him, and appeared in his new dress before the master of the *Jeune-Amélie*, who asked him to repeat his story. The master could hardly recognize the heavily bearded man, half drowned and with seaweed in his hair, whom he had brought, naked and dying, on to the deck of his ship, in this smartly dressed and stylish sailor. Encouraged by this change in appearance, he repeated his offer to take Dantès on, but Dantès would accept it for only three months; he had plans of his own.

The crew of the *Jeune-Amélie* was a very busy one and subject to a master who was not used to wasting time. They had been hardly a week in Leghorn before the ship's swelling hold was full of coloured muslin, forbidden cotton cloth, English powder, and tobacco on which the state monopoly had forgotten to put its stamp. They had to get all this out of Leghorn, duty paid, and unload it on the Corsican coast, from where certain speculators would take charge of conveying it to France.

They set sail, and Edmond found himself once more crossing the azure sea that had been the first horizon of his youth and which he had seen so often in his prison dreams. Leaving the Gorgone on their right and the Pianosa on their left, they set out for the birthplace of Paoli and Napoleon.

Coming up on deck early the following day, as was his custom, the master found Dantès leaning against the side of the ship with a strange look on his face as he stared out towards a heap of granite that the rising sun was bathing in rosy light: the island of Monte Cristo.

The *Jeune-Amélie* passed, some three-quarters of a league to starboard, and continued to make for Corsica.

As they sailed past this island, the name of which held such significance for him, Dantès was thinking that he had only to leap into the sea and within half an hour he would be in this promised land. But what would he do there, with no tools to recover his treasure and no weapons to defend himself? In any case, what would the sailors say? What would the master think? He must wait.

Waiting, fortunately, was something that he knew how to do. He had waited fourteen years for his freedom and, now that he was free, he could easily wait for six months or a year to obtain his wealth. Would he not have chosen freedom without wealth if he had been offered it? In any case, was the wealth not an illusion, which had been born in poor Abbé Faria's sick brain and died with him? Yet Cardinal Spada's letter was oddly precise – and Dantès repeated it in his head from beginning to end. He had not forgotten a single word.

Evening came. Edmond watched the island pass through all the colours of sunset and dusk, then fade into the darkness for all except himself: his eyes, accustomed to the darkness of a prison cell, doubtless continued to make out the island, since he was the last to leave the deck.

The next day they woke up off Aleria. All day they tacked, backwards and forwards, and in the evening bonfires were lit on shore. The placing of the fires must have shown that it was safe to disembark, because a lantern took the place of the flag on the little ship's yard-arm and they sailed to within gunshot range of the coast.

Dantès had noticed that, approaching land on what he must consider solemn occasions, the master of the *Jeune-Amélie* would set up two little culverines on pivots, of the sort that might be used in defending a rampart and which, without making much noise, would project a quarter-pound shot a thousand paces.

This evening, however, the precaution proved unnecessary. Everything went off as peacefully and as genteelly as might be imagined. Four launches rowed quietly over to the ship which, no doubt to welcome them, put its own launch in the water; and between them the five rowing-boats had laboured so hard that, by two o'clock in the morning, the whole cargo had been transferred from the *Jeune-Amélie* to dry land.

The master of the ship was a man of such well-regulated habits that the very same night the bounty had been divided up. Each man had his share, a hundred Tuscan *lire*, which is about eighty francs in our money. But the voyage was not over. They set course for Sardinia, with a view to reloading the vessel that had just been unloaded. This second operation went as smoothly as the first; the *Jeune-Amélie* was in luck.

The new cargo was destined for the duchy of Lucca. It was almost entirely composed of Havana cigars, sherry and malaga wine.

Here, however, they had a brush with the excise, that eternal enemy of the *Jeune-Amélie*'s master. A Customs officer was laid low and two sailors were wounded; Dantès was one of them: a shot passed through his left shoulder, leaving a flesh wound.

He was almost happy at this skirmish and his wound. These hard tutors had taught him how he viewed danger and bore suffering. He had laughed at danger and, as the shot pierced him, said like a Greek philosopher: 'Pain, you are not an evil.'

Moreover he had looked at the mortally wounded Customs man and – whether because his blood was up or because his feelings were chilled – the sight made very little impression on him. Dantès was on the track that he wished to follow, proceeding towards the end that he wished to attain: his heart was turning to stone in his breast.

Jacopo, seeing him fall, had thought him dead and rushed to his side, raised him up and finally, when he was under cover, tended him like the good friend he was.

In short, could it be that the world was neither as good as Doctor Pangloss[1] pretended, nor as bad as it seemed to Dantès, since this man, who had nothing to expect from his friend except to inherit his part of the bounty, had felt such distress at seeing him fall dead?

Happily, as we have said, Dantès was only wounded. With the help of some herbs picked at special times and sold to the smugglers by old Sardinian women, the wound quickly healed. So Edmond wanted to tempt Jacopo: as a reward for his care, he offered him his share of the bounty, but Jacopo refused indignantly.

As a result of this kind of sympathetic devotion that Jacopo had accorded to Edmond from the first moment that they met, Edmond conceded a certain degree of affection to Jacopo. The latter asked for nothing better: he had perceived in Edmond a great superiority to his present state, something that Edmond had managed to conceal from the others; so the good sailor was satisfied with the little that Edmond gave him.

In this way, during the long days on board, when the ship was safely gliding across an azure sea with a favourable wind swelling its sails and needing no more than the attention of its helmsman, Edmond would take a chart of the coast and make himself Jacopo's instructor as poor Abbé Faria had become Edmond's. He showed him how to take bearings in coastal waters, explained the compass to him and taught him to read in that great open book above our heads which is called the sky and in which God writes on the blue firmament in diamond letters.

When Jacopo asked him: 'What is the use of teaching all these things to a poor sailor like me?', Edmond replied: 'Who knows? One day you may be captain of a ship. Your fellow-countryman Bonaparte became emperor!'

We forgot to mention that Jacopo was a Corsican.

Two and a half months passed in such successive journeys. Edmond had become as skilled in navigating the coastal waters as he had once been on the open sea. He got to know all the smugglers around the Mediterranean and learned the Masonic signs that these semi-pirates used to recognize one another.

Twenty times he had sailed one way or the other past his island of Monte Cristo, but not once had he found an opportunity to land there. So he made a resolution, which was that, as soon as his contract with the master of the *Jeune-Amélie* came to an end, he would hire a little boat on his own account (which he could well do, having saved around a hundred *piastres* on his different voyages) and, on some pretext or other, sail to Monte Cristo.

There he would be free to hunt for his treasure.

Well, not entirely free, since he would no doubt be spied upon by those who had crossed with him. But in this world one must learn to take some risks. However, prison had made Edmond cautious and he would have preferred not to risk anything.

Hard though he tried and fertile though his imagination was, he could not find any other means of reaching the island except to get someone to take him there.

Dantès was still racked by doubt when one evening the master, who had great confidence in him and was very anxious to retain his services as a member of the crew, took his arm and led him to a tavern in the Via del Oglio, where the cream of the smuggling profession in Leghorn was accustomed to meet.

This is where affairs along the coast were usually discussed. Dantès had already been to this maritime exchange two or three times and, at the sight of these bold buccaneers – the product of a coast of some two thousand leagues in circumference – he had wondered what power a man might wield if his will could manage to direct all these divergent or united threads.

This time, an important matter was under discussion. There was a ship loaded with Turkish carpets and cloth from the Levant and Kashmir. They had to find some neutral ground on which the exchange could take place, before bringing these goods to the coast of France. The bounty was so large that, if they were successful, each man should have fifty or sixty *piastres*.

The master of the *Jeune-Amélie* proposed disembarking on the island of Monte Cristo: since it was deserted and there were no soldiers or Customs men on it, it seemed to have been set down in the midst of the sea in the days of the pagan Olympus by Mercury, God of Tradesmen and Thieves – two sorts of people whom we consider separate, if not entirely distinct, but whom Antiquity appears to have classed together.

At the name of Monte Cristo, Dantès trembled with joy. He got up to hide his emotion and paced round the smoke-filled tavern, in which every dialect of the known world was blended into a single lingua franca.

When he returned to the discussion, it had been decided that they would land on Monte Cristo, setting off on this expedition the following night. Edmond was consulted and he confirmed that the island offered the greatest possible security and that, if they were to succeed, great enterprises needed to be undertaken promptly.

So the plan was adhered to, and it was agreed that they would get under way the following evening, meaning, if they had a calm sea and a favourable wind, that the day after next they would find themselves in the waters off the shore of the neutral island.

XXIII

THE ISLAND OF MONTE CRISTO

At last, by one of those unexpected chances which sometimes happen to people on whom misfortune has exhausted its ingenuity, Dantès was going to reach his goal by a simple, natural means and set foot on his island without arousing any suspicion. Only one night separated him from this long-awaited departure.

That night was one of the least restful that Dantès had ever spent. In the course of it he ran over every good and bad eventuality in his mind: if he closed his eyes, he saw Cardinal Spada's letter written in blazing letters on the wall; if he fell asleep for a moment, the most insane dreams raced around his skull. He was going down into caves paved with emeralds, with walls of ruby and diamond stalactites. Pearls fell drop by drop in place of the water that habitually filters through the ground.

Edmond, delighted, wondering, filled his pockets with precious stones, then clambered up into the daylight, only to find them turned into nothing but ordinary rocks. Then he tried to get back into the marvellous caverns which he had only glimpsed, but the path twisted into infinite spirals and the entrance had become invisible. He searched through his tired brain for the mysterious, magic word that had opened the wonderful caves of Ali Baba to the Arab fisherman; but all in vain. The vanished treasure had reverted to the ownership of the genii of the earth, from whom he had momentarily hoped to ravish it.

Daylight found him almost as feverish as he had been at night, but it also brought logic to assist imagination, and Dantès managed to draw up a plan that had, until now, been only vaguely outlined in his mind.

With evening came the preparations for departure. These preparations gave Dantès an opportunity to hide his anxiety. Bit by bit, he had acquired an authority over his companions that allowed him to give orders as though he were the captain of the vessel; and since his orders were always clear, precise and easy to carry out, the crew obeyed him not only promptly but with pleasure.

The old seaman let him do as he pleased: he too had recognized Dantès' superiority both to the others and to himself. He saw the young man as his natural successor and regretted that he did not have a daughter so that he might bind Edmond to him in that way.

At seven o'clock all was ready, and at ten past they rounded the lighthouse, just as it was being lit.

The sea was calm, with a fresh wind from the south-east. They were sailing under a clear sky in which God too was progressively putting on His lights, each another world. Dantès announced that everyone could go to bed and that he would take over the helm. When the Maltese – as they called him – made such an announcement, that was enough for everyone and they all went easily to bed.

This sometimes happened: from time to time, Dantès, driven out of solitude into the world, felt an imperative need for solitude. And what solitude is more vast and more poetic than that of a ship sailing alone on the sea, in the darkness of night and the silence of infinity, under the eye of the Lord?

This time his solitude was peopled with thoughts, the night illuminated by his dreams and the silence riven with his promises.

When the master woke up, the ship was proceeding under full sail; there was not an inch of canvas that was not swollen by the wind. They were travelling at more than two and a half leagues an hour. The island of Monte Cristo was rising before them on the horizon.

Edmond handed the ship back to its owner and went to take his turn in his hammock. Despite a night without sleep, he could not shut his eyes for an instant.

Two hours later, he returned on deck. The ship was just rounding Elba. They were abreast of Mareciana and had just passed the flat green island of La Pianosa. The blazing summit of Monte Cristo could be seen, reaching into the heavens.

Dantès ordered the helmsman to turn to port, so that they would leave La Pianosa on their right. He had reckoned that this manoeuvre would shorten the distance by two or three knots.

Around five in the evening, they could see the whole of the island. Every detail of it was clear, thanks to that clarity of the air which is peculiar to the light of the dying sun. Edmond gazed hungrily on the mass of rocks as they passed through all the colours of sunset, from bright pink to dark blue. From time to time, he flushed warmly, his forehead became congested and a purple haze crossed before his eyes. No gambler whose whole fortune is staked on a single roll of the dice has ever experienced the agony that Edmond did in his paroxysms of hope.

Night fell. At ten o'clock they dropped anchor. The *Jeune-Amélie* was the first to reach the rendez-vous.

Despite his usual self-control, Dantès could not contain himself. He was the first to leap on shore and, if he had dared, he would have kissed the soil like Brutus.

It was pitch black; but at eleven o'clock the moon rose over the sea, throwing a silver light on every crest; then, as it rose higher, its rays began to tumble in white cascades of light over the piled rocks of this other Pelion.[1]

The crew of the *Jeune-Amélie* were familiar with the island; it was one of their usual points of call. Dantès, on the other hand, had recognized it from each of his voyages to the Near East, but had never stopped off here.

He questioned Jacopo.

'Where are we going to spend the night?'

'On board, of course,' the sailor replied.

'Wouldn't we be better in the caves?'

'What caves?'

'The ones on the island.'

'I don't know any caves,' Jacopo said.

A cold sweat broke out on Dantès' forehead.

'There are no caves on Monte Cristo?' he asked.

'No.'

For a moment he was stunned, then he thought that the caves might have been filled in by some accident or even been blocked by Cardinal Spada himself, as an extra precaution.

The main thing, in that case, would be to find the lost entrance. There was no point in looking at night, so Dantès put off his search until the next day. In any case, a signal displayed by a boat some half a league out to sea, to which the *Jeune-Amélie* responded immediately with the same, showed that the time had come to set to work.

The second ship, reassured by the signal which told the late arrival that it was safe to make land, soon appeared, white and silent as a ghost, and dropped anchor, a cable's length from the shore. The transfer of goods began immediately.

As he worked, Dantès thought of the shout of joy that he could have brought from all these men with a single word if he had spoken aloud the thought that hummed incessantly in his ears and in his heart. But, far from revealing the marvellous secret, he was already afraid he might have said too much or that, by his coming and going, his repeated questions, his minute observations and his constant preoccupation, he might have aroused some suspicion. It was fortunate, at least in these circumstances, that an unhappy past had stamped his features with an indelible air of sadness and that one could perceive only brief flashes of the lights of merriment hovering beneath this cloud.

No one suspected anything and when, the next day, Dantès took a gun, some shot and powder, and said he would like to go and shoot one or two of the wild goats that could be seen leaping from rock to rock, his expedition was ascribed purely to love of hunting and a desire for solitude. Only Jacopo insisted on following him. Dantès did not want to object, fearing that any reluctance to take a companion with him might awaken suspicion. But they had gone hardly a quarter of a league when, seizing the opportunity to shoot a kid, he told Jacopo to take it back to the crew, suggesting that they should cook it, then signal to him that it was ready for him to share, by firing a shot. Some dry fruit and a flagon of Montepulciano would complete the meal.

Dantès continued, turning from time to time. Reaching the summit of a rock, he saw his companions a thousand feet below him; Jacopo had just joined them and they were already engaged in preparing a dinner which, thanks to Edmond's skill, now had a main dish. He watched them for a moment with a sad, gentle smile of superiority.

'In two hours,' he said, 'these men will leave, richer by fifty *piastres*, and proceed to risk their lives to gain fifty more. Finally, when they have six hundred *livres*, they will go and squander this fortune in some town or other, as proud as sultans and as arrogant as nabobs. Today, hope means that I despise their wealth, which seems to me like the most abject poverty; tomorrow, perhaps disappointment may mean that I shall be forced to consider that abject poverty as the height of happiness . . . Oh! no,' he cried, 'it cannot be. The wise, the infallible Faria cannot have been mistaken on this one point. In any event, better to die than to go on living this sordid and base existence.'

So Dantès, who three months earlier had wanted nothing except freedom, felt already not free enough, but wanted wealth. It was not the fault of Dantès, but of God who, while limiting the power of man, has created in him infinite desires! Meanwhile Dantès had approached the place where he supposed the caves to be situated, going along a road hidden between two walls of rock and down a path cut by the torrent, which, in all likelihood, no human foot had ever trodden. Following the line of the shore and examining everything minutely, he thought he could see on certain rocks marks which had been made by human hands.

Time casts its mossy mantle over physical objects and a mantle of forgetfulness on non-physical ones, and it seemed to have respected these marks, made with some regularity, probably with the aim of tracing a route; but occasionally they disappeared under great bunches of myrtle, heavy with flowers, or under clinging lichens. Edmond would then have to push aside the branches or lift the moss to discover the clues that led him into this new labyrinth. In any case, these marks had given Edmond hope. Why should it not be the cardinal who had made them, so that, in the event of some misfortune which he could not have imagined so absolute, they could serve to guide his nephew? This solitary place seemed designed for a man who wished to hide a treasure. But could these treacherous marks have attracted eyes other than those for which they were intended; had the dark and wonderful island guarded its marvellous secret faithfully?

Arriving at a point only about sixty yards from the port, but still hidden from his companions by the rocks, Edmond thought that the scratches had come to an end; but they did not lead to any kind of cave. The only point to which they seemed to direct him was a large round rock settled on a solid base. Edmond thought that, instead of having reached the end of the trail, he might, on the contrary, be only at the beginning, so he decided to take the opposite course and retrace his steps.

Meanwhile his companions had been preparing dinner, getting water from the spring, carrying bread and fruit ashore and cooking the kid. Just as they were taking it off its improvised spit, they saw Edmond leaping from rock to rock, as light and daring as a chamois; so they fired a shot as a signal to him. The huntsman immediately changed direction and ran back to them. But, just as they were all watching him as he leapt through the air – and accusing him of pushing his skill beyond the limits of caution – as if to justify their fears, Edmond lost his footing. They saw him totter on the peak of a rock, cry out and disappear.

All of them dashed forward at once, because they were all fond of Edmond, despite his superiority; but it was Jacopo who arrived first.

He found Edmond lying on the ground, covered in blood and almost unconscious: he must have tumbled from a height of twelve to fifteen feet. They put a few drops of rum in his mouth, and this medicine, which had already proved so effective with him, had the same result the second time.

Edmond re-opened his eyes, complained of a sharp pain in the knee, a great weight on his head and an unbearable stabbing in the small of the back. They tried to carry him to the beach, but when they touched him, even though Jacopo was directing operations, he groaned and said that he did not feel strong enough to be moved.

Of course, there was no question of him taking food, but he insisted that the others, not having the same reason as he did to fast, should go back to their dinner. For himself, he declared that he only needed a little rest and that they would find him better when they returned. Old sea-dogs do not stand on ceremony: the sailors were hungry and the smell of kid was wafting up to them, so they did not wait to be asked twice.

An hour later they returned. All that Edmond had managed to do was to drag himself about ten yards so that he was leaning against the mossy rock. But the pain, instead of lessening, actually seemed to have increased. The old master, who was obliged to leave that morning so that he could put off his cargo on the frontier of France and Piedmont, between Nice and Fréjus, insisted that Dantès try to get up. Dantès made a superhuman effort to comply, but every time fell back, pale and groaning.

'His back is broken,' the master whispered. 'No matter, he's a good comrade and we can't abandon him. Let's try to carry him to the tartan.'

But Dantès announced that he would rather die where he was than suffer the terrible pain that he felt at the slightest movement.

'Well, then,' said the master, 'whatever happens, it will not be said that we left a good comrade like yourself without help. We'll delay our departure until this evening.'

This suggestion astonished the sailors, though none of them opposed it; on the contrary. The master was a man of such rigid ideas that this was the first time they had seen him give up a project, or even delay it. But Dantès did not want such a serious breach of the ship's rules to be made on his behalf.

'No, no,' he told the master. 'I was clumsy and it is right that I should suffer for my own carelessness. Leave me a small supply of biscuits, a gun, powder and shot to kill goats – or even to defend myself – and a pickaxe so that I can build some kind of house, in case you are too long in returning to fetch me.'

'You will starve,' said the master.

'Better that,' Edmond answered, 'than to suffer the unspeakable pain that I feel at the slightest movement.'

The master turned to look at the ship, swaying at anchor in the little harbour with its sails partly set, ready to head out to sea as soon as the rest of its canvas had been raised.

'What can we do, Maltese?' he said. 'We cannot abandon you here, but we can't stay, either.'

'Leave, leave!' Dantès cried.

'We'll be gone for at least a week, and even then we shall have to turn off course to pick you up.'

'Listen,' said Dantès, 'if, two or three days from now, you meet some fishing boat or other that is sailing near here, let them know about me and I shall pay them twenty-five *piastres* to take me back to Leghorn. If you don't pass any such vessel, then come back yourselves.'

The master shook his head.

'Listen, Monsieur Baldi,' Jacopo told the master, 'there's a way to settle all this. You leave and I'll stay with the patient and take care of him.'

'Would you give up your share in the bounty,' Edmond said, 'to stay with me?'

'Willingly.'

'You are a fine lad, Jacopo,' said Edmond. 'God will reward you for your goodwill. But I don't need anyone, thank you. In a day or two I shall be rested, and I expect to find some excellent herbs in these rocks which will cure my wounds.'

A strange smile passed over Dantès' face and he shook Jacopo's hand warmly; but he was unshaken in his resolve to remain, and to remain alone.

The smugglers left Edmond what he wanted and walked off, looking back several times and warmly waving goodbye; Edmond replied with only one hand, as though he could not move the rest of his body.

Then, when they had gone, he muttered, with a laugh: 'It's strange that one should find such proof of affection and acts of devotion among men of that kind.'

At this, he cautiously dragged himself to the top of a rock that lay between him and the sea, and from there he could see the tartan completing its preparations, raising anchor, hovering elegantly like a seagull about to take flight, and setting sail.

An hour later, it had completely disappeared: at least, from the place where the wounded man was lying, it had vanished from sight.

Then Dantès got up, lighter and more supple than one of the goats that prance around among the gum-trees and myrtle bushes on these savage rocks, took his gun in one hand and his pick in the other and ran to the rock which represented the end of the trail of notches that he had followed.

'And now!' he shouted, recalling the story about the Arab fisherman that Faria had told him: 'and now – open, Sesame!'

XXIV

DAZZLED

The sun had travelled about one-third of its way across the sky and its invigorating May light fell on rocks that themselves seemed responsive to its warmth. Thousands of cicadas, invisible in the heather, produced a continuous, monotonous murmuring, while there was an almost metallic sound from the quivering leaves of the myrtles and the olive-trees. At each step that Edmond took on the hot granite he startled lizards, the colour of emeralds, and in the distance, on the sloping scree, he could see the wild goats that sometimes drew huntsmen to the place. In short, the island was inhabited, bustling with life; yet Edmond felt himself alone here in the hand of God. He experienced an intangible emotion, close to fear: the suspicion of daylight that makes us assume, even in the desert, that inquisitive eyes are upon us.

The feeling was so strong that, as he was about to start work,

Edmond stopped, put down his pickaxe, picked up the gun and climbed once more to the top of the highest pinnacle on the island, to take a broad, sweeping look at everything around.

It must be said that what attracted his attention was not the poetical island of Corsica, on which he could almost see the individual houses, or the almost unknown Sardinia that lay beyond it, or the isle of Elba with its associations of majesty, or even the barely perceptible line on the horizon on which the sailor's practised eye could sense the presence of proud Genoa and busy Leghorn. No: what he saw were the brig, which had left at daybreak, and the tartan, which had just set sail. The first was about to vanish in the straits of Bonifacio while the other, travelling in the opposite direction, was preparing to sail round Corsica.

The sight reassured Edmond. He began to look at the objects in his more immediate vicinity. He was on this highest point on the conical island, a slender statue on a huge pedestal. Beneath him, not a soul; around him, not a ship: nothing except the blue sea lapping round the base of the island and eternally ringing it in silver.

He hurried down, but cautiously, deeply fearing that he might, at such a moment, have a real accident like the one he had so cleverly and successfully pretended to have.

As we said, Dantès had been retracing the notches in the rocks and had seen that the route led to a sort of little creek, hidden like the bath of an antique nymph; however, it was wide enough at its entrance and deep enough at its centre for a little boat, like a *speronara*, to glide in there and remain hidden. So, by inductive logic, that thread which he had seen in Abbé Faria's hands guide his mind so ingeniously through the maze of probabilities, he considered that Cardinal Spada, who had reasons for not wishing to be seen, had landed in this creek, hidden his little boat, followed the route traced by the notches and, at the end of this trail, buried his treasure.

As a result of this supposition, Dantès returned to the circular rock.

Just one thing bothered Edmond and upset this train of conclusions: how, without using considerable force, could anyone have lifted this rock, which weighed perhaps five or six *milliers*, on to the sort of plinth where it stood?

Suddenly, Dantès had an idea: 'Instead of being lifted,' he

thought, 'it must have been brought down.' And he climbed up above the rock, to find where it had originally rested.

Here, in effect, he saw that a slight slope had been made and that the rock had slid on its own base, before coming to a halt. Another rock, as large as a normal building stone, had served as a wedge. Stones and pebbles had been carefully moved to disguise any interference, and this sort of little dry-stone wall had been covered with soil. Grass had grown there, the moss had spread, some seeds of myrtle and mastic had fallen on it – and the old rock looked as though it was soldered to the ground.

Dantès cautiously removed the soil and recognized, or thought he recognized, all the ingenuity of the work. Then he started to attack this temporary wall, which time had cemented in place, with his pickaxe. After ten minutes' work, the wall gave way, leaving a hole large enough for his arm to pass through it.

Dantès went and cut down the strongest olive-tree that he could find, stripped it of its branches, put it through the hole and used it as a lever. But the rock was too heavy and too solidly wedged against the rock beneath it for any human force, even that of Hercules, to move it. So Dantès decided that it was the wedge itself that had to be attacked.

But how?

He looked around, like a bewildered man, and his eyes lit on a mouflon's horn full of powder that his friend Jacopo had left him. He smiled: the infernal invention would do his work for him.

With his pick Dantès dug a shaft between the upper rock and the one on which it rested, of the kind that sappers make when they want to save effort, then stuffed it with powder; and, finally, tearing his handkerchief into strips and rolling it in saltpetre, he made a fuse.

After setting fire to this fuse, Dantès stepped back.

The explosion soon came. The upper rock was lifted for an instant by this incalculable force and the lower one burst into pieces. Through the little hole that Dantès had first made, a host of fluttering insects escaped and a huge grass snake, the guardian of this mysterious path, rolled over on its bluish coils and disappeared.

Dantès went across. The higher rock, now with nothing to rest against, was poised in space. The intrepid explorer walked all round it, chose the most unsteady point, fixed his lever in one of its cracks and, like Sisyphus, heaved with all his strength.

Already shaken by the explosion, it trembled. Dantès increased his efforts; he seemed like one of those Titans who pick up mountains in order to cast them at the chief of the gods. Finally the rock gave way, rolled, bounced, crashed and disappeared into the sea.

Where it had been was a circular area, in the midst of which could now be seen an iron ring fixed in the middle of a square paving-stone.

Dantès gave a cry of joy and astonishment. No first attempt had ever been crowned with such magnificent success.

He wanted to go on, but his legs were trembling so much and his heart beating so violently that a burning cloud passed in front of his eyes, and he had to pause.

He did so for only an instant. Then he put his lever into the ring and lifted. The stone, now unsealed, opened and revealed a sort of stairway, descending steeply into the increasingly profound darkness of a cavern. Anyone else would have rushed down it, exclaiming with joy. Dantès stopped and paled, full of doubt.

'Come now, be a man!' he thought. 'We are used to adversity; let's not be crushed by a mere disappointment, or else I shall have suffered for nothing. The heart breaks when it has swelled too much in the warm breath of hope, then finds itself enclosed in cold reality. Faria was dreaming: Cardinal Spada buried nothing in this cave, perhaps he never even came here or, if he did, Cesare Borgia, that intrepid adventurer, that dark and tireless robber, came after him, found his tracks, followed the same indications as I did, lifted this stone as I have and went down before me, leaving nothing behind him.'

For a moment he stayed, pensive and motionless, staring at the entrance leading away into the darkness.

'Well, now that I am not counting on anything, now that I have decided it would be senseless to cling to any hope, what happens from now on will merely satisfy my curiosity, nothing more.' But he remained thoughtful and motionless.

'Yes, yes, this is another adventure to be included in the chiaroscuro of that royal bandit's life, in the web of strange events that went to make up the variegated cloth of his existence. This fabulous event must have been inexorably linked to the rest: yes, Borgia came here some night, with a blazing torch in one hand and a sword in the other, while twenty yards away – perhaps at the foot of that rock – two of his henchmen, dark and threatening, searched the earth, the sky and the sea, while their master went forward as I shall do, dispersing the darkness with his terrible flaming arm.

'Yes, but what would Cesare have done with the men to whom he had thus revealed his secret?' Dantès wondered.

'The same as was done,' Dantès said with a smile, answering himself, 'with those who buried Alaric:[1] they were buried in their turn.

'However, if he had come,' Dantès continued, 'he would have found the treasure and removed it. Borgia, the man who compared Italy to an artichoke which he devoured leaf by leaf, knew too much about the value of time to waste his own in replacing that rock on its base . . . Let's go!'

So he went down, smiling sceptically and muttering the final word in human wisdom: 'Perhaps!'

Instead of the darkness that he had expected to find and a dense, fetid atmosphere, Dantès saw a gentle glow that was dispersed into bluish daylight: air and light not only came through the opening that he had just made, but also through fissures in the rocks that were invisible from the surface; through them could be seen the blue of the sky and the shivering branches of green oak-trees against it, with beneath them a tangled mass of brambles.

After spending a few seconds in this cave, where the air was warm rather than dank and sweet-smelling rather than stale, bearing the same relationship to the temperature of the island as the blue light did to the sun, Dantès could see into the furthest depths of the cavern, his eyesight (as we have previously mentioned) being accustomed to darkness. The walls were of granite, spangled and faceted so that they sparkled like diamonds.

'Alas!' Edmond thought, smiling. 'These must be the treasures that the cardinal left behind him. The good abbé, when he saw these sparkling walls, was no doubt confirmed in his high hopes.'

But Dantès recalled the exact words of the will, which he knew by heart: 'In the furthest angle of the second opening,' it said. He had only reached the first cavern; now he must look for the entrance to the second.

He sought to get his bearings. The second cavern should naturally extend towards the centre of the island. He looked closely at the base of the rocks and tapped on the wall in which, he thought, the opening ought to be, having been disguised for reasons of security.

The pickaxe rang for a moment against the rock, sending back a flat sound, the solidity of which brought sweat to Dantès' brow. Finally, the persistent miner thought that one section of the granite wall answered his enquiry with a rounder and deeper echo. He studied it with care and, with the instinct of a prisoner, recognized what someone else might have missed: that there must be an opening here.

However, to avoid wasted effort (having, like Cesare Borgia, learned the value of time), he tapped the other walls with his pick, tried the ground with the butt of his gun and cleared the sand in some suspicious places, until, finding nothing, he came back to the section of wall that had given this encouraging sound. He struck it again, with greater force.

Then he perceived something odd, which was that as he struck it a sort of outer coating, like the plaster that is put on walls before painting a fresco, was breaking off and falling in flakes, to reveal a whitish soft stone, like an ordinary building stone. The opening in the rocks had been closed with a different type of stone and this plaster had been spread over it, then painted to imitate the colour and lustre of granite.

Dantès struck the surface with the sharp end of the pick and it sank about an inch into the wall. This was the point at which he should dig.

Because of a mysterious property of the human organism, the more Dantès should have been reassured by this mounting proof that Faria had not been mistaken, the more his heart gave way to doubt and even to discouragement. This new experiment, which should have given him renewed strength, took away the little that remained: the pickaxe dropped towards the ground, almost slipping out of his hands; he put it down, wiped his brow and went back into the daylight, telling himself that this was because he wanted to make sure that no one was spying on him, but in reality because he needed air, feeling as though he were about to faint.

The island was deserted and the sun, at its zenith, seemed to be gazing down with its fiery eye. In the distance, little fishing boats spread their wings over a sea of sapphire blue.

Dantès had eaten nothing so far, but he could not think of wasting time on food at such a moment; he took a swig of rum and went back into the cavern with renewed vigour. The pick that had seemed so heavy had become light again and he raised it like a feather and eagerly returned to work.

After a few blows he noticed that the stones were not cemented but simply laid one on top of the other and covered with the plaster that we mentioned. He inserted the point of the pick into the gap between them, put his weight on the handle and was overjoyed to see the stone fall down at his feet. After that, he only had to pull each stone towards him with the head of the pickaxe and, one by one, they fell down beside the first.

He could have got through as soon as the gap was opened, but by a few minutes' delay he put off certainty and clung to hope.

Finally, after a last moment of hesitation, Dantès went from the first cavern into the second. It was lower, darker and more frightening than the first. The air, which only came through the opening he had just made, had the musty smell that he had been surprised not to find in the first cavern. Before entering, he allowed the outside air time to freshen this dead atmosphere.

On the left of the opening was a deep, dark corner – though, as we have said, there was no such thing as darkness for Dantès' eyes. He peered into the second cavern; it was as empty as the first.

The treasure, if there was one, was buried in this dark corner.

The agonizing moment had come. There were two feet of soil to dig: that was all that remained to him between the summit of happiness and the depth of despair.

He went over to the corner and, as if driven by a sudden resolve, attacked the soil boldly. At the fifth or sixth stroke of the pick, iron rang against iron.

Never had a funereal tolling or resounding death-knell produced such an effect on the person who heard it. If Dantès had found nothing, he would undoubtedly not have gone any whiter. He dug again in the same place and met with the same resistance, but not the same sound.

'It's a wooden casket, bound in iron,' he said.

At that moment a shadow passed swiftly across the daylight.

Dantès dropped the pick, grasped his gun, returned through the hole and hurried out into the light. A wild goat had leapt above the main entrance to the caverns and was grazing a few yards away. It was a good opportunity to make sure of his dinner, but Dantès was afraid that the gunshot would attract someone's attention.

He thought for a moment, then cut a branch from a resinous

tree, went to light it at the still-smoking fire where the smugglers had cooked their dinner, and returned with this torch. He did not want to miss a single detail of what he was about to see.

He brought the torch down to the rough hole that he had started to make and confirmed that he had not been wrong: his blows had landed alternately on iron and wood. He planted the torch in the ground and resumed his work.

Rapidly he uncovered an area about three feet long by two feet wide and could see an oak chest bound in wrought iron. In the centre of the lid, on a silver plate that the earth had not tarnished, shone the arms of the Spada family: a sword lying vertically across an oval shield (that being the shape of Italian shields), with a cardinal's hat above it. Dantès recognized it at once: Faria had often drawn it for him.

Now there could be no further doubt. This was the treasure. No one would have taken such precautions to hide an empty box in this place.

In a moment he had cleared all round the casket and revealed by turns the lock in the middle, between two padlocks, and the handles at each end. The whole was worked and engraved in the manner of the time, when art made the basest metals precious.

Dantès took the casket by its handles and tried to lift it; it was impossible. He tried to open it; the lock and the padlocks were shut and these faithful guards did not seem to want to give up their treasure.

Finally he put the head of the pickaxe between the box and its lid, and pressed down on the handle. The lid groaned, then broke apart. A wide gap opened in the boards, making the iron bindings unnecessary: they too fell off, though with their tenacious fingers still grasping fragments of the boards. The box was open.

Dantès felt faint. He took his gun, loaded it and placed it beside him. At first he shut his eyes, as children do when they want to count more stars in the shimmering darkness of their imagination than they can in a still light sky; then he opened them and was dazzled.

The casket was divided into three compartments.

In the first were gold *écus*, gleaming with wild radiance. In the second were unpolished ingots, neatly stacked, with nothing of gold about them – except the weight and worth of gold. Finally, in the third compartment, half full, Edmond plunged his hand into fistfuls of diamonds, pearls and rubies, then let them fall in a shimmering fountain which gave off the sound of hailstones on a window-pane.

After touching, feeling and plunging his trembling hands into the gold and precious stones, Edmond got up and ran through the caves with the wild exultation of a man on the brink of madness. He leapt on to a rock from which he could see the sea, but saw nothing. He was alone, entirely alone, with this incalculable, unimagined, fabulous wealth, and it belonged to him. But was he asleep or awake? Was he inside a dream or grappling with reality?

He needed to see his gold again, but he felt that he would not at that moment have the strength to bear the sight of it a second time. For a short while he clasped the top of his head with his hands, as if to hold in his reason. Then he set off across the island, not only running away from the beaten track – there are no beaten tracks on Monte Cristo – but altogether aimlessly, scaring the mountain goats and the seabirds by his cries and gesticulations. Then, by a roundabout route, he came back, still doubting, plunged through the first and second caverns, and found himself confronted by this mine of gold and diamonds.

This time he fell to his knees, convulsively clasping both hands to his beating heart and muttering a prayer that God alone could understand.

At length he felt calmer – and yet happier, because it was only from then on that he started to believe in his happiness.

Then he began to count his fortune. There were a thousand gold ingots, each of two or three pounds. Next to these, he piled 25,000 gold *écus*, each worth perhaps twenty-four francs in today's money, each bearing the head of Pope Alexander VI or his predecessors – and he observed that the compartment was only half empty. Finally, he measured ten times the capacity of his joined hands in pearls, precious stones and diamonds, many of which were in settings made by the finest goldsmiths of the time, giving them great additional value on top of their intrinsic worth.

He saw the sun go down and daylight fade little by little. He was afraid that someone would surprise him if he stayed in the cave, so he came out holding his gun. His supper was a piece of ship's biscuit and a few mouthfuls of wine. Then he replaced the stone and lay down on it, sleeping for a few hours with his body covering the entrance to the cave. This night was both terrible and delicious, a night such as this man of powerful feelings had experienced only once or twice before in his life.

XXV

THE STRANGER

Day broke. Dantès had been waiting for it for a long time. At the sun's first rays, he got up and, as he had done on the previous day, climbed to the highest point on the island to look around. As before, everything was deserted.

Edmond went down, lifted the rock, filled his pockets with precious stones and replaced the boards and the iron bindings of the casket as best he could; then he covered it with earth, which he trampled down and scattered with sand, to make the newly turned soil look similar to the rest. He went out of the cave, replaced the entrance, piled stones of various sizes around it, put earth into the gaps, planted myrtle and heather in them, and watered these new plants to make them seem well established. Finally, he covered the traces of his footprints around the spot and waited impatiently for the return of his companions. There was no sense now in spending his time looking at this gold and these diamonds, and staying on Monte Cristo like a dragon guarding a useless treasure: he must return to life and take his place among men and in society, with the rank, influence and power that are bestowed in this world by wealth – that first and greatest of forces that a human being can control.

The smugglers returned on the sixth day. From afar, Dantès recognized the *Jeune-Amélie* by its cut and its gait: it was limping into port like a wounded Philoctetes. When his companions stepped ashore, Dantès told them that he was considerably better, though he continued to complain. Then in turn he listened to the smugglers' tales. They had certainly been successful, but hardly had the cargo been off-loaded than they learned that a brig of the excise from Toulon had just left harbour and was heading in their direction. They took flight at once, regretting that Dantès, who knew how to get so much greater speed out of the vessel, was not there to guide them. The following boat soon came into view, but they managed to escape under cover of night and by rounding the Cap Corse. In short, the voyage had not been unsuccessful and everyone, particularly Jacopo, expressed regret that Dantès had not been with them, so that he could have his share of the profits they had brought back, a share which amounted to fifty *piastres*.

Edmond remained impassive. He did not even smile when they emphasized how much he would have benefited by leaving the island; and, since the *Jeune-Amélie* had called at Monte Cristo only to pick him up, he embarked the same evening and went with the boat to Leghorn. There he went to visit a Jew and sold four of his smallest diamonds for five thousand francs apiece. The Jew might have enquired how a mere seaman came into possession of such things, but he was careful not to ask; he was making a thousand francs on each diamond.

The next day Dantès bought a new boat which he gave to Jacopo, together with a hundred *piastres* so that he could engage a crew, all on condition that Jacopo went to Marseille and asked for news of an old man called Louis Dantès, living in the Allées de Meilhan, and a young woman from the Catalan village, named Mercédès.

Now it was Jacopo's turn to think he was dreaming. Edmond told him that he had become a sailor on an impulse, because his family would not give him money to support himself; but that on arriving in Leghorn he had received a bequest from an uncle who had made him his sole heir. This story seemed plausible enough, in view of Dantès' superior upbringing, and Jacopo did not for a moment doubt that his former comrade had told him the truth.

In addition, since Edmond's contract of service with the *Jeune-Amélie* had ended, he said farewell to the master, who at first tried to dissuade him but, having learnt the same story as Jacopo about the inheritance, abandoned hope of overcoming his former employee's resolve.

The next day Jacopo set sail for Marseille; he was to pick Edmond up on Monte Cristo. The same day Dantès himself left without saying where he was going, bidding farewell to the crew of the *Jeune-Amélie* with a splendid present and to the master with the promise that he would hear from him again one day.

Dantès was going to Genoa.

He arrived at the moment when they were testing a little yacht ordered by an Englishman who, having heard it said that the Genoese were the best boat-builders in the Mediterranean, had decided to have a yacht built there. He had settled on a price of forty thousand francs; Dantès offered sixty, on condition that the boat was delivered to him that same day. The Englishman had gone on a trip to Switzerland while the boat was being completed. He was not due to return for three weeks or a month, so the boat-builder reckoned he would have time to start building another. Dantès took him to a Jewish banker, who led them behind his shop and counted out sixty thousand francs for the boat-builder.

The latter offered Dantès his services to find a crew, but Dantès thanked him and said that he was used to sailing by himself and that the only thing he wanted was for the man to build him, in the cabin behind the bed, a secret cupboard with three hidden compartments in it. He gave the measurements for the compartments, and they were completed by the following day.

Two hours later Dantès sailed out of Genoa, followed by the stares of a crowd of inquisitive onlookers who wanted to see this Spanish gentleman who was in the habit of sailing on his own.

He succeeded brilliantly: with the help of the rudder, and without needing to leave it, he put his boat through its paces, so that it seemed like an intelligent being, ready to obey the slightest command. Silently, Dantès agreed that the Genoese deserved their reputation as the finest boat-builders in the world.

The crowd looked after the little ship until it was out of sight, then fell to discussing where it was going. Some said Corsica, others Elba; there were those ready to bet that he was heading for Spain, but some argued just as warmly that he was en route for Africa. No one thought to mention the island of Monte Cristo.

Dantès was bound for Monte Cristo.

He reached the island around the end of the second day. The ship handled superbly and he had covered the distance in thirty-five hours. He recognized every inch of the coast and, instead of making for the usual port, he dropped anchor in the little creek.

The island was deserted. No one appeared to have landed there since Dantès was last there. He went to his treasure. Everything was just as he had left it.

By the next day his huge fortune had been transported on to the yacht and shut up in the three secret compartments of the hidden cupboard.

He waited another week. During this time, he sailed his yacht around the island, studying it as a horseman studies his mount; by the end he knew all its qualities and its defects and had promised himself to enhance the former and remedy the latter.

On the eighth day he saw a little ship sailing at full speed towards the island, and recognized Jacopo's vessel. He made a signal, Jacopo replied, and two hours later the ship had drawn alongside the yacht.

There was bad news in reply to both Edmond's questions. Old Dantès was dead; Mercédès had vanished.

Edmond's face remained impassive as he listened to this information, but he immediately disembarked, not allowing anyone to follow him.

Two hours later he returned. Two men from Jacopo's vessel joined him on his yacht to help him sail it and he gave orders to make for Marseille. He was not surprised at the death of his father; but what had become of Mercédès?

Edmond had not been able to give detailed enough instructions to another party without divulging his secret; in any event, there was further information that he wanted to obtain and for which he could rely only on himself. His mirror had informed him in Leghorn that he ran no danger of being recognized and, moreover, he now had at his disposal every means to disguise himself. So one morning the yacht, followed by the little ship, sailed proudly into the port of Marseille and stopped directly in front of the place from which, on that fatal evening, they had set sail for the Château d'If.

Dantès shuddered a little at the sight of a gendarme being rowed out towards him. But, with the perfect self-assurance that he had acquired, he handed over an English passport which he had bought in Leghorn. With this foreign document, far more highly respected in France than our own, he had no difficulty in landing.

The first person he saw when he set foot on the Canebière was a sailor who had served under him on the *Pharaon*, as if placed there to reassure Dantès as to the changes which had taken place in him. He went straight up to the man and asked him a number of questions, to which he replied without the slightest hint in his words or his expression that he recalled ever having seen the man who was talking to him.

Dantès gave the sailor a coin to thank him for the information, only to hear the man running after him a moment later. He turned around.

'Excuse me, Monsieur,' the sailor said. 'You must have made a mistake. You doubtless thought you were giving me forty sous, but in reality this is a double *napoléon*.'[1]

'Yes, indeed, my friend,' said Dantès, 'I was mistaken; but as your honesty deserves a reward, here is a second coin which I beg you to accept, and drink to my health with your friends.'

The sailor looked at Edmond in such astonishment that he did not even consider thanking him, but watched him walk away, saying: 'Here's some nabob straight off the boat from India.'

Dantès carried on, but every step he took brought some new emotion to his heart. All his childhood memories, those memories that are never effaced, but remain ever-present in one's thoughts, lay here, rising up from each street corner, in every square and at every crossroads. When he reached the end of the Rue de Noailles and saw the Allées de Meilhan, he felt his knees give way and nearly fell under the wheels of a carriage. At last he reached the house in which he had lived with his father. The aristoloches and the nasturtiums had vanished from the attic roof where the old man's hands used once to trellis them so carefully.

He leant against a tree and stayed for a while, thinking and looking up at the top floor of the mean little house. Finally he went across to the door, stepped inside and asked if there was no lodging vacant. Even though it was occupied, he insisted on going to visit the one on the fifth floor, until finally the concierge agreed to go up and ask the people living in it whether a stranger could take a look at their two rooms. The little lodging was inhabited by a young man and woman who had been married only a week. When he saw this young couple, Dantès gave a deep sigh.

As it happened, there was nothing to remind Dantès of his father's apartment. The wallpaper had changed and all the old furniture, Edmond's childhood friends, which he recalled in every detail, had disappeared. Only the walls were the same.

He turned towards the bed, which the new tenants had kept in the same place. Involuntarily his eyes filled with tears: this was where the old man must have expired with his son's name on his lips.

The young couple looked in astonishment at this stern-faced man down whose otherwise impassive cheeks two large tears were falling. But as every sorrow inspires some awe, they did not question the stranger, but stepped back to let him weep at his ease. When he left, they went with him to the door and told him that he could come back whenever he wished: there would always be a welcome in their humble abode.

Reaching the floor below, Edmond paused in front of another door and asked if the tailor, Caderousse, lived there. But the concierge told him that the person he mentioned had failed in business and now kept a little inn on the Bellegarde road in Beaucaire.

Dantès went down to the street, asked for the address of the owner of the house in the Allées de Meilhan, went to visit him and was announced as Lord Wilmore – which was the name and title on his passport. He bought the house for twenty-five thousand francs, which was at least ten thousand more than it was worth; but if it had stood at half a million, Dantès would have bought it for that.

The same day, the young couple on the fifth floor were informed by the notary who had drawn up the contract that the new owner was offering them any apartment in the house, at no additional rent, provided they would let him have the two rooms that they then occupied.

These strange events preoccupied all the regulars in the Allées de Meilhan for more than a week and were the subject of a thousand conjectures, none of which proved correct. But what muddled everyone and confused every mind was that, on the same evening, this same man who had been seen going into the house in the Allées de Meilhan was observed walking in the little Catalan village and going into a poor fisherman's house, where he stayed for more than an hour asking for news of several people who were either dead or who had vanished more than fifteen or sixteen years earlier.

Next day, the people among whom he had made these enquiries received a present of a brand-new Catalan boat, with two seine nets and a trawl net. The good people would have liked to thank the generous enquirer, but he had been seen, after leaving them, giving orders to a sailor, mounting a horse and leaving Marseille through the Porte d'Aix.

XXVI

AT THE SIGN OF THE PONT DU GARD

Those who have walked across the south of France, as I have done, may have noticed an inn, situated between Bellegarde and Beaucaire, roughly half-way between the village and the town (though rather closer to Beaucaire than to Bellegarde), outside which hangs a crude painting of the Pont du Gard on a metal plate which creaks at the slightest breath of wind. This little inn, lying parallel to the course of the Rhône, is situated on the left side of the road with its back to the river. It has what in Languedoc is described as a garden: that is to say that the side opposite the one through which travellers enter overlooks an enclosure in which a few stunted olive-trees lurk beside some wild figs, their leaves silvered with dust. Between them, the only vegetables that grow here are some heads of garlic, some peppers and some shallots. Finally, in one corner, like a forgotten sentry, a tall umbrella pine rises in melancholy fashion on its pliable trunk, while its crest, fanned out, blisters under thirty degrees of sunshine.

All these trees, large or small, are naturally bent in the direction of the mistral, one of the three scourges of Provence, the two others, as you may or may not know, being the River Durance and Parliament.

Here and there in the surrounding plain, which is like a great lake of dust, stand a few stalks of wheat that the farmers hereabouts must surely grow out of mere curiosity. There is a cicada perched on every one of these stalks which pursues any traveller who has strayed into this wilderness with its high-pitched, monotonous call.

For perhaps the last seven or eight years this little inn had been kept by a man and woman whose only staff were a chambermaid called Trinette and a stableboy answering to the name of Pacaud. In fact, these two assistants had amply sufficed for the task, since a canal between Beaucaire and Aigues-Mortes had ensured the victory of water over road haulage, and barges had taken the place of the stagecoach.

As if to torment still further the unfortunate innkeeper, who was ruined by it, the canal ran between the Rhône – which supplied it with water – and the road – which it drained of traffic – only some hundred yards from the inn which we have just briefly (but accurately) described.

The innkeeper was a man of forty to forty-five, tall, dry, nervous, a typical Southerner with his deep-set, shining eyes, his hooked nose and his teeth as white as those of some beast of prey. Though his hair had felt the first breath of age, it could not make up its mind to go grey: like the beard that he wore following the line of his jaw, it was thick, curly and spattered with just a few strands of white. His complexion, naturally swarthy, was covered by yet a new layer of brown from the habit he had adopted of standing from morning to night on the threshold of his door to see if some customer might not arrive, either on foot or by carriage. His expectations were almost invariably disappointed; but he stood there still, with no protection against the burning heat of the sun other than a red handkerchief knotted about his head, like a Spanish mule-driver. This man was our old acquaintance, Gaspard Caderousse.

His wife, in contrast, whose maiden name had been Madeleine Radelle, was pale, thin and sickly. She came from the region around Arles and had preserved some traces of the traditional beauty of the women of that area, while seeing her features slowly deteriorate, ravaged by one of those persistent fevers which are so common among the peoples who live near the ponds of Aigues-Mortes and the swamps of the Camargue. In consequence she spent most of her time seated, shivering, in her room on the first floor, either stretched out in an armchair or leaning against her bed, while her husband kept his customary watch at the door. He was all the more happy to spend his time there, since whenever he found himself in the same room as his better – or certainly bitter – half, she would harass him with unending lamentations on her fate, to which her husband would normally only respond with these philosophical words: 'Quiet, La Carconte! It's God's will.'

The nickname derived from the fact that Madeleine Radelle had been born in the village of La Carconte, between Sallon and Lambesc. So, in accordance with local custom, by which people are almost always given a nickname in place of their names, her husband had substituted this for Madeleine, which was probably too soft and pleasant sounding for his rough tongue.

However, it should not be thought that the innkeeper, despite this pretence of resignation to the decrees of fate, was not acutely sensible of the poverty to which he had been reduced by the confounded Beaucaire canal, or that he was proof against the endless complaints that his wife heaped on him. Like all Southerners, he was moderate, needing little for himself, but vain when it came to external matters; so, in the days of his prosperity, he would not let a *ferrade* or a procession of the tarasque[1] go past without appearing in it, La Carconte at his side: he would be dressed in the picturesque costume of a man from the Midi, somewhere between Catalan and Andalusian dress, while she would have on the delightful attire of the women of Arles, suggestive of Greece and Arabia. Little by little, however, watch-chains, necklaces, gaudy belts, embroidered blouses, velvet jackets, elegantly trimmed stockings, multicoloured gaiters and silver-buckled shoes had vanished, until Gaspard Caderousse could no longer appear in his former splendour; so, on his own behalf and that of his wife, he gave up all these worldly exhibitions, though he felt a bitter pang when the happy sounds of some celebration would reach this miserable inn, which he kept much more to have a roof over his head than as a business proposition.

As was his custom, Caderousse had spent part of the morning standing at the door, turning his sad eyes from a little bare patch of grass where some hens were pecking, to each end of the empty road which extended southwards in one direction, northwards in the other. Suddenly his wife's sour voice called him away from his post. He went inside, grumbling, and up to the first floor, while leaving the door wide open as if to persuade travellers not to forget him as they went by.

When Caderousse turned back into the house, the main road down which, as we said, he had been looking, was as empty and lonely as a desert under the midday sun. White and endless, it ran between two lines of slender trees and it was quite reasonable to suppose that no traveller who was free to choose any other hour of the day would wish to venture into this awful Sahara.

However, if he had remained at his post, Caderousse would have seen, defying probability, a horse and rider approaching from Bellegarde with that frank and friendly manner which suggests the best possible understanding between the horseman and his mount. The horse was a gelding which ambled pleasantly along; on its back was a priest, dressed in black and wearing a three-cornered hat, despite the blistering heat of the sun which was now at its zenith. The pair proceeded at a very sensible trot.

When they reached the door, they stopped: it would have been difficult to decide whether it was the horse that stopped the man or the man who stopped the horse. In any event, the rider dismounted and, leading the horse by its bridle, attached it to the knob of a dilapidated shutter that was hanging by a single hinge. The priest then went across to the door, wiping his dripping brow with a red cotton handkerchief, and knocked three times with the iron tip of his cane.

A large black dog immediately got up and took a few steps forward, barking and baring its sharp white teeth; this show of hostility only demonstrated how unused it was to receiving company.

At once, the wooden stairway running along the wall shook with a heavy tread: the landlord of the mean lodging-house at whose door the priest was standing was coming down, bent over and walking backwards.

'Here I am,' Caderousse said in astonishment. 'Here I am! Be quiet, Margottin! Don't worry, Monsieur, he barks but he doesn't bite. Would you like some wine? How hot it is! It's a right little strumpet of a day . . . Oh! I beg your pardon,' he said, when he saw what kind of traveller this was. 'I didn't know whom I had the honour to serve. What can I get you? What would you like, Monsieur l'Abbé? I am at your command.'

The priest looked at the man for two or three seconds with unusual concentration, even appearing to want to draw the innkeeper's attention to himself. Then, since the other's face expressed nothing but surprise at not having an answer to his question, the newcomer decided it was time to put an end to the delay and said, with a very heavy Italian accent:

'Aren't you Monsieur Caderousse?'

'Yes, sir,' the innkeeper said, perhaps even more surprised by the question than he had been by the silence which preceded it. 'I am indeed. Gaspard Caderousse, at your service.'

'Gaspard Caderousse . . . Yes, I think that is the name. Did you once live in the Allées de Meilhan, on the fourth floor?'

'That is correct.'

'Where you exercised the profession of tailor?'

'Yes, but the profession went downhill. It's so hot in that damned

Marseille that I honestly believe in the end people there won't dress at all. But talking of heat, wouldn't you like to take some refreshment, Monsieur l'Abbé?'

'Certainly; bring me a bottle of your best wine, then we can carry on the conversation where we left off, if you would be so good.'

'However you like, Monsieur l'Abbé,' said Caderousse. And, not wishing to miss this opportunity of selling one of the last bottles of Cahors wine that remained to him, he hastened to lift a trapdoor in the boards of this same ground-floor room which served as both dining-room and kitchen.

When he reappeared, five minutes later, he found the abbé sitting on a stool, with his elbow on a long table, while Margottin's scrawny neck rested on his thigh and the dog was looking at him with a languid eye, apparently having made his peace with this unusual traveller when he understood that, contrary to custom, he was going to partake of refreshment.

'Are you alone?' the abbé asked his host, who put a bottle and glass in front of him.

'My God, yes! Or almost, Monsieur l'Abbé. I have my wife who can't help me at all, because she's always ill, poor Carconte.'

'Ah, you are married?' the priest said, with some interest, looking around as if assessing the meagre value of the couple's poor furniture.

'You are thinking that I'm not rich, eh, Monsieur l'Abbé?' Caderousse said with a sigh. 'What do you expect! It is not enough to be honest to prosper in this world.'

The abbé stared hard at him.

'Yes, honest. That I can boast of, Monsieur,' the innkeeper said, returning his stare with one hand on his heart and nodding his head. 'And, nowadays, not everyone can say as much.'

'So much the better, if what you boast of is true,' said the abbé. 'Because I am convinced that, sooner or later, a righteous man is rewarded and a wicked one punished.'

'You're a man of the cloth, Monsieur l'Abbé,' said Caderousse with a bitter look, 'and it's your job to say that. But everyone is free to disbelieve what you claim.'

'You are wrong to say that, Monsieur,' said the abbé, 'for I myself may well be, in your own case, the proof of what I am saying.'

'How do you mean?' asked Caderousse in astonishment.

'I mean that I must first of all ensure that you are the person I think you are.'

'What proof can I give you?'

'Did you in 1814 or 1815 know a sailor called Dantès?'

'Dantès! Yes, I knew poor Edmond! I certainly knew him: he was one of my best friends!' Caderousse exclaimed, his face turning deep purple, while the abbé's clear, confident eyes seemed to dilate and embrace every detail of the man opposite him.

'Yes, I do believe he was called Edmond.'

'He certainly was! I should know, if anyone: Edmond was his name as sure as my name is Gaspard Caderousse. But what happened to him, Monsieur, to poor Edmond?' the innkeeper continued. 'Did you know him? Is he still alive? Is he free? Is he happy?'

'He died a prisoner, more forlorn and despondent than the convicts who wear their shackles in the penal colony in Toulon.'

The redness which had first swept over Caderousse's face was replaced by a deathly pallor. He turned aside and the abbé saw him wipe away a tear with a corner of the red handkerchief that he wore to cover his head.

'The poor boy!' Caderousse muttered. 'Well, that just goes to show what I was saying, Monsieur l'Abbé: the Good Lord is only good to the wicked. Ah,' he went on, with the exaggerated language usual to Southerners, 'the world is going from bad to worse. If only the sky would rain gunpowder for two days and fire for an hour, and we could have done with it all!'

'You seem to have been sincerely attached to the young man, Monsieur,' said the abbé.

'I was indeed,' said Caderousse, 'though I have to confess that for a moment I did envy him his good fortune. Since then, I swear, on the honour of a Caderousse, I truly pitied him his terrible fate.'

There was a moment's silence, during which the abbé continued to direct a penetrating gaze at the innkeeper's changing expression.

'And did you know him, this poor lad?' Caderousse went on.

'I was called to his deathbed to offer him the last rites of the Church,' the abbé replied.

'And how did he die?' Caderousse asked, in a barely audible voice.

'Of prison itself: how else do you die in prison when you are thirty years old?'

Caderousse wiped the sweat off his streaming brow.

'What is odd in all this,' the abbé said, 'is that Dantès, on his deathbed, as he kissed the feet of the crucifix, always swore to me that he did not know the true reason for his imprisonment.'

'That's true, that's true,' Caderousse muttered. 'There was no way he could know. No, Monsieur l'Abbé, the poor young man was not lying.'

'And it was for that reason that he asked me to find out the truth about this misfortune, on which he was himself unable to shed any light, and to rehabilitate his name, if it had been blackened in any way.'

The abbé's gaze became increasingly fixed on the almost grim look that spread over Caderousse's face.

'A rich Englishman,' he continued, 'his companion in misfortune, was released from prison at the Second Restoration[2] and owned a diamond of considerable worth. When he was ill, Dantès had cared for him like a brother and, when he left prison, he wanted to give some token of his gratitude by leaving Dantès this diamond. Instead of using it to bribe his jailers, who might in any case have taken it and afterwards betrayed him, he kept it preciously in the hope that he might be released. If he was, the sale of this single diamond would ensure his fortune.'

'So, you are saying,' Caderousse asked, his eyes lighting up, 'that this was a very valuable stone?'

'Everything is relative,' the abbé answered. 'Very valuable to Edmond: its worth was estimated at fifty thousand francs.'

'Fifty thousand francs!' Caderousse exclaimed. 'It must have been as big as a walnut!'

'Not quite,' said the abbé. 'But you can judge for yourself, because I have it with me.'

Caderousse seemed to be looking straight through the abbé's clothes for the object.

The abbé took a small black shagreen box out of his pocket, opened it and displayed before Caderousse's astonished eyes the shining jewel set on a finely wrought ring.

'This is worth fifty thousand francs?'

'Without the setting, which is itself quite valuable,' said the abbé. And he closed the box and returned the diamond to his pocket, though it continued to shine in Caderousse's head.

'But how did you come into possession of this diamond, Monsieur l'Abbé?' he asked. 'Did Edmond make you his heir?'

'No, but the executor of his will. "I had three good friends and a fiancée," he told me. "I am sure that all four of them must feel my loss bitterly. One of those good friends was called Caderousse."'

Caderousse shuddered.

'"The other",' the abbé went on, appearing not to notice Caderousse's reaction, '" was called Danglars. And the third," he added, "even though he was my rival, also loved me."'

A diabolical smile passed over Caderousse's face and he made as if to interrupt the speaker.

'Wait,' said the abbé, 'let me finish. Then, if you have any remarks to make, you can do so later. "The third, even though he was my rival, also loved me; he was called Fernand. As for my fiancée, her name was . . ." Ah! I don't remember the fiancée's name,' said the abbé.

'Mercédès,' said Caderousse.

'Mercédès! That's it,' the abbé agreed, suppressing a sigh.

'Well?' said Caderousse.

'Give me a jug of water,' said the abbé.

Caderousse hastened to do as he was asked. The abbé poured himself some water and took a few sips.

'Now, where were we?' he asked, putting down the glass.

'The fiancée was called Mercédès.'

'That's right. "You will go to Marseille . . ." – it's still Dantès speaking, you understand?'

'Absolutely.'

'"You will sell this diamond, divide the proceeds into five and share them among these good friends, the only creatures on earth who ever loved me!"'

'Why five shares?' said Caderousse. 'You mentioned only four people.'

'Because the fifth is dead, or so they tell me . . . The fifth was Dantès' father.'

'Alas, yes,' said Caderousse, torn between conflicting feelings. 'Alas, yes, poor man! He died.'

'I learned this in Marseille,' the abbé replied, making an effort to appear unconcerned. 'But the event took place so long ago that I could learn nothing further about it. Do you happen to know anything about the man's end?'

'Who could know better than I?' said Caderousse. 'I lived right next door to him. Heaven help us! It was hardly a year after his son's disappearance that the old man died!'

'What did he die of?'

'The doctors called it ... gastro-enteritis, I think. Those who knew him said he died of grief. But I – and I almost saw him die, myself – I would say that he died ...'

Caderousse paused.

'Died of what?' the priest repeated, anxiously.

'To tell the truth – of starvation!'

'Starvation!' cried the abbé, leaping up from his stool. 'Starvation! The lowest creature does not die of starvation! Even a dog roaming the streets may find a pitying hand to throw it a crust of bread. Yet you say this man, a Christian, died of hunger in the midst of other men who also call themselves Christians! Impossible! It's impossible!'

'I only know what I know,' Caderousse said.

'And you are wrong,' said a voice from the staircase. 'What has it to do with you?'

The two men turned and saw La Carconte's sickly features staring through the banisters. She had dragged herself down to the foot of the staircase and was listening to their conversation, sitting on the stair with her head on her knees.

'And what has it to do with you, wife?' asked Caderousse. 'The gentleman wants some information. It's only polite to give it to him.'

'Yes, and it's only common sense to refuse. Who says what his purpose is in making you talk, you idiot?'

'An excellent purpose, Madame, I promise you,' said the abbé. 'Your husband has nothing to fear, as long as he answers me frankly.'

'Huh! Nothing to fear ... They always start with fine promises, then afterwards tell you that you have nothing to fear; then, off they go, without keeping their word, and one fine morning misfortune comes to poor people, without them knowing where it comes from ...'

'Have no fear, my good woman, no misfortune will come to you from me, I guarantee it.'

La Carconte muttered a few inaudible words, let her head fall back on her knees and continued to shiver feverishly, leaving her husband free to continue the conversation, but seated in such a way that she would not miss a word.

Meanwhile the abbé had taken a few more sips of water and recovered his composure.

'But,' he went on, 'was this poor old man so totally abandoned by everyone that he could die in such a manner?'

'Ah, Monsieur,' said Caderousse, 'it's not that either Mercédès the Catalan or Monsieur Morrel abandoned him, but the poor old man had taken a profound antipathy to Fernand, the very person,' he added, smiling ironically, 'that Dantès told you was one of his friends.'

'He was not?' asked the abbé.

'Gaspard, Gaspard!' the woman muttered from the top of the stairs. 'Mind what you say!'

Caderousse made an impatient gesture and, with no other reply to the woman who had interrupted him, told the abbé: 'Can anyone be the friend of a man whose wife he covets? Dantès, who had a heart of gold, called all those people his friends . . . Poor Edmond! After all, it is better that he knew nothing, he would have found it too hard to forgive them on his deathbed. Whatever anyone says,' Caderousse concluded, with a kind of rough poetry in his speech, 'I am still more afraid of a dead man's curse than of a living man's hatred.'

'Idiot!' said La Carconte.

'Do you know what Fernand did to harm Dantès, then?' asked the abbé.

'Indeed I do.'

'Tell me.'

'Gaspard, you can do as you wish, you are the master here,' said his wife. 'But if you take my advice, you'll say nothing.'

'This time, I think you may be right, woman,' said Caderousse.

'So, you don't want to tell me?' the abbé continued.

'What is the use? If the lad was alive and if he came to me to tell him, once and for all, who were his friends and who his enemies, then I might do it. But he is dead and gone, so you say; he can feel hatred no longer, nor can he take revenge. Let's draw the blind on all this.'

'So, you want me to give these people, who you tell me are unworthy and false friends, a gift that was meant to reward their fidelity?'

'That's true, you're right,' said Caderousse. 'In any case, what would poor Edmond's bequest be to them now? A drop of water in the ocean.'

'Apart from which, those people could crush you with a flick of the hand,' said his wife.

'What do you mean? Have they become rich and powerful then?'

'Don't you know what happened to them?'

'No. Tell me.'

Caderousse seemed to reflect for a short time. Then he said: 'No, in fact the story is too long.'

'You are quite at liberty to keep it to yourself,' the abbé said, with an air of the most profound indifference. 'If so, I shall respect any reservations you may have. Indeed, you are showing yourself to be a truly generous man, so let's say no more about it. The duty that I have to carry out is a mere formality: I shall sell the diamond.'

He took it out of his pocket, opened the box and displayed the shining stone before Caderousse's eyes.

'Come and see it, wife!' the innkeeper said, his voice breaking.

'A diamond!' said La Carconte, getting up and walking quite resolutely down the stairs. 'What is this diamond then?'

'Didn't you hear? It's a diamond that the boy left us: first of all to his father, then to his three friends: Fernand, Danglars and myself, and to his wife Mercédès. It's worth fifty thousand francs.'

'Ah! What a lovely thing!' she exclaimed.

'So, one-fifth of the amount belongs to us?' Caderousse asked.

'Yes, Monsieur. Plus Dantès' father's share, which I feel I have the right to divide among the four of you.'

'But why among four?' asked La Carconte.

'Because the four of you were Edmond's friends.'

'Traitors are not friends,' the woman muttered grimly.

'Yes, just so,' said Caderousse. 'I was only saying as much. It's almost blasphemy, almost sacrilegious to reward treachery, or even crime.'

'That's what you wanted,' the abbé continued calmly, putting the diamond back into his cassock pocket. 'Now, give me the address of Edmond's friends, so that I can carry out his last wishes.'

Sweat was pouring down Caderousse's forehead. He saw the abbé get up and go towards the door, as if to make sure that his horse was waiting, before coming back.

Caderousse and his wife exchanged an indescribable look.

'The diamond would belong to us alone,' Caderousse said.

'Do you think so?' his wife replied.

'A man of the cloth would not try to deceive us.'

'As you wish. I am having nothing to do with it.'

She returned, shivering, to the staircase. Her teeth were chattering, despite the burning heat of the day. On the top step she paused and said: 'Think about it, Gaspard!'

'I've made up my mind,' said Caderousse.

La Carconte went back to her room with a sigh. The ceiling creaked under her feet until she reached her armchair and let herself fall heavily into it.

'What have you decided to do?' asked the abbé.

'To tell you everything.'

'Quite honestly, I think that's best,' said the priest. 'Not that I want to know anything that you want to hide from me; but if you can help me to distribute the bequest in accordance with the wishes of the departed, that will be best.'

'I hope so,' Caderousse replied, his cheeks flushed with greed and expectation.

'I am listening,' said the abbé.

'One moment,' said Caderousse. 'We might be interrupted at the most interesting point, which would be a pity. In any case, it's better that no one knows you have been here.' He went across to the door of the inn and closed it, putting the bolt across it as an extra precaution.

Meanwhile the abbé had chosen a place from which he could listen in comfort. He was sitting in a corner, in such a way as to be in shadow, while the light fell full on the face of whoever was opposite him. His head bowed, his hands folded – or, rather, clasped together – he prepared to give all his attention to the story.

Caderousse drew up a stool and sat down opposite the abbé.

'Remember, I'm not forcing you,' said the quavering voice of La Carconte, as if she had observed the setting of this scene through the floor of the room above.

'Agreed, agreed,' said Caderousse. 'Say no more about it. I take full responsibility.'

And he began his tale.

XXVII

CADEROUSSE'S STORY

'Before we start, Monsieur,' said Caderousse, 'I must beg you to promise me one thing.'

'Which is?'

'Which is that, if you should ever make any use of the information I am about to give you, no one should ever know that it came from me, because the men I am about to speak of are rich and powerful; if they were merely to touch me with the tip of a finger, they would shatter me like glass.'

'Have no fear, my friend,' said the abbé. 'I am a priest and confessions die in my heart. Remember that we have no other purpose than to carry out the wishes of our friend in a proper manner, so speak frankly, but without animosity; tell the truth, and the whole truth. I do not know and probably never shall know the people about whom you are to speak. In any case, I am Italian and not French. I belong to God and not to men: I am going to return to my monastery, having left it only to carry out the last wishes of a dying man.'

This positive promise seemed to reassure Caderousse slightly.

'Well, in that case,' he said, 'I want to tell you the truth – I might even say, I am obliged to tell you about those whom poor Edmond considered his sincere and devoted friends.'

'Let us start with his father, if you would,' the abbé said. 'Edmond spoke a great deal to me about the old man, to whom he was most deeply attached.'

'It is a sad story,' said Caderousse, shaking his head. 'You probably know how it started.'

'Yes, Edmond told me what happened up to the moment of his arrest, in a little cabaret near Marseille.'

'La Réserve! Good Lord, yes! I can see the whole thing as if it were yesterday.'

'Was the occasion not his betrothal feast?'

'Yes: a meal that started in merriment and ended in sorrow. A police commissioner came in, followed by four soldiers, and Dantès was arrested.'

'From this point onwards I know nothing,' said the priest. 'Dantès himself only knew whatever concerned him directly, because he never again saw any of the five people I mentioned to you or heard any news of them.'

'Well, once Dantès had been taken into custody, Monsieur Morrel went to discover what had happened to him, and the news was not good. The old man went back home alone, wept as he folded up his best suit, spent the rest of the day pacing backwards and forwards in his room and did not go to bed that night: I was living directly below and I could hear him walking around from dusk till dawn. I must tell you that I did not sleep, either, because the poor father's grief was so painful to me that each of his steps crashed against my heart as if he had really stamped his foot on my chest.

'The next day, Mercédès came to Marseille to beg Monsieur de Villefort's protection. She obtained nothing from him, but at the same time she went to see the old man. When she found him so sad and depressed, and learned that he had not been to bed that night or eaten since the day before, she wanted him to go with her so that she could take care of him, but the old man would never agree to it.

' "No," he used to say, "I shall never leave the house, because I am the person that my poor child loves above everything; and, if he comes out of prison, I am the one he will come to see first. What would he say if I was not there, waiting for him?"

'I could hear all this from the landing, because I would have liked Mercédès to persuade the old man to go with her: I could not get a moment's rest with his footsteps resounding day after day above my head.'

'But did you not go up to console the old man yourself?' the priest asked.

'Ah, Monsieur,' said Caderousse, 'you can only console those who wish to be consoled, and he didn't. In any case, I don't know why, but it seemed to me that he felt some disgust at the sight of me. Even so, one night when I could hear him sobbing, I could bear it no longer, so I went up. When I reached the door, he had stopped sobbing and was praying. I can't tell you, Monsieur, what eloquent words and what heart-rending pleas he found for his prayer: it was more than piety, it was more than grief. I'm no pious hypocrite myself, and I don't like the Jesuits, and that day I thought: it's as well, after all, that I am alone and the Good Lord never gave me any children, because if I was a father and I felt the same sorrow as that poor old man, I wouldn't be able to find all the words that he had for the Good Lord, either in my memory or in my heart, so I would go straight away and throw myself into the sea, to avoid suffering any longer.'

'Unhappy father!' the priest muttered.

'Day by day, he lived more alone and more isolated. Often, Monsieur Morrel and Mercédès came to see him, but his door was shut and, even though I was quite sure he was at home, he would not answer. One day when, exceptionally, he had invited Mercédès in and the poor girl, who was in despair herself, was trying to comfort him, he told her: "Believe me, my dear, he's dead. Instead of us waiting for him, he is waiting for us; I am happy to think that, being older than you, I shall be the first to see him again."

'However good-hearted one is, you understand, one eventually stops seeing people who depress you, so in the end Old Dantès was all alone. From time to time, from then on, I would see only strangers going up to his room, then coming down again with some packet under their coats. I soon guessed what the packets were: he was gradually selling everything he had in order to stay alive. Finally he came to the end of his miserable possessions. He owed three lots of rent and the landlord threatened to evict him. He begged for another week, which he was allowed – I know all this because the landlord would come in to see me after leaving him.

'The first three days, I heard him walking around as usual, then on the fourth the sounds stopped. I ventured to go up: the door was locked but through the keyhole I could see him, looking so pale and haggard that I thought he must be really ill; so I sent for Monsieur Morrel and went to see Mercédès. They both hurried round. Monsieur Morrel brought a doctor who diagnosed gastro-enteritis and prescribed a diet. I was there, Monsieur, and I shall never forget the old man's smile when he heard that prescription. From then on, he opened his door: he had an excuse for not eating, since the doctor had put him on a diet.'

The abbé gave a sort of groan.

'You are interested in this story, I think, Monsieur?' said Caderousse.

'Yes,' the abbé replied. 'It is touching.'

'Mercédès came back. She found him so changed that once more she wanted to take him to her home. This was also Monsieur

Morrel's advice, and he wanted to take him there by force; but the old man protested so loudly that they were afraid. Mercédès remained at his bedside and Monsieur Morrel went away, indicating to the Catalan that he was leaving a purse on the mantelpiece. But, with the doctor's prescription to back him up, the old man refused to take anything. Finally, after nine days of despair and abstinence, he died, cursing those who were the cause of his misfortune and telling Mercédès: "If ever you see my Edmond again, tell him that I died with a blessing for him."'

The abbé got up, walked twice round the room and brought a trembling hand up to his dry throat.

'And you think that he died . . .'

'Of starvation, Monsieur, of starvation . . .' said Caderousse. 'I swear it, as surely as I am standing here.'

Convulsively the abbé seized the glass of water which was still half full, emptied it at a draught and sat down, red-eyed and pale-cheeked. 'You must admit that was dreadful misfortune!' he said hoarsely.

'All the more so as God had nothing to do with it, and men alone were responsible.'

'So tell me about these men,' said the abbé; then he added, in a tone that was almost threatening: 'but remember that you promised to tell me everything. Who were these men who killed the son with despair and the father with hunger?'

'Two who were jealous of him, one for love, the other for ambition: Fernand and Danglars.'

'So, how did this jealousy manifest itself?'

'They denounced Edmond as a Bonapartist agent.'

'Which of them denounced him – who was the real guilty party?'

'Both of them, Monsieur. One wrote the letter, the other sent it.'

'And where was the letter written?'

'At La Réserve itself, the day before the wedding.'

'That's it, that's it,' the abbé muttered. 'Oh, Faria, Faria! How well you could read the hearts of men and the ways of the world!'

'I beg your pardon, Monsieur?'

'Nothing; continue.'

'It was Danglars who wrote the denunciation with his left hand, so that the writing would not be recognized, and it was Fernand who sent it.'

'But . . .' the abbé exclaimed suddenly, 'you were there!'

'Me?' said Caderousse in astonishment. 'Who told you that?'

The abbé saw that he had gone too far.

'No one did,' he said. 'But, to know all these details, you must have witnessed the events.'

'It's true,' Caderousse said, his voice choking. 'I was there.'

'And you did nothing to stop this outrage? Then you are an accomplice.'

'Monsieur,' said Caderousse, 'they had both made me drink until I was almost senseless. Everything was blurred. I protested as much as a man can in such a state, but they assured me it was a joke they were playing and that nothing would come of it.'

'The next day, Monsieur! You saw plainly that something did come of it, the next day, but still you said nothing. Yet you were there when he was arrested.'

'Yes, I was there and I wanted to speak out, to tell everything, but Danglars stopped me. "Suppose that, by chance, he is guilty," he said. "Suppose he really did stop off at Elba and has a letter to deliver to the Bonapartist committee in Paris: well then, if they find the letter on him, anyone who has spoken out in his favour will be suspected of complicity."

'I was afraid of getting mixed up in politics as they were then, I admit it. I said nothing, which was cowardly, I agree, but not a crime.'

'I understand: you stood idly by, nothing more.'

'Yes, Monsieur,' said Caderousse, 'and I regret it every day of my life. I often ask God to forgive me, I swear, all the more so since this deed, the only act I have ever committed that weighs seriously on my conscience, is no doubt the cause of my present adversity. I am paying for a moment of selfishness; as I always say to La Carconte whenever she complains: "Quiet, woman, it's God's will".'

And Caderousse bowed his head with every sign of genuine remorse.

'Very well, Monsieur,' said the abbé. 'You have been honest. Such a frank confession deserves forgiveness.'

'Unfortunately,' Caderousse said, 'Edmond is dead and he never forgave me.'

'But he did not know . . .'

'Perhaps he does know now: they say that the dead know everything.'

There was a moment of silence. The abbé had risen and was walking around, deep in thought. Then he returned and sat down in his place.

'You spoke to me two or three times of one Monsieur Morrel,' he said. 'Who is this man?'

'The owner of the *Pharaon*, Dantès' employer.'

'What part did he play in this sad business?'

'The part of an honest, brave and feeling man, Monsieur. He interceded twenty times on Edmond's behalf. When the emperor returned, he wrote, begged and threatened – so much so that at the Second Restoration he was persecuted as a Bonapartist. Ten times, as I told you, he came to fetch old Dantès and take him to his own house; and the day before he died – or was it the day before that? – as I told you already, he left a purse on the mantelpiece which served to pay the old man's debts and the expenses of his funeral; so the old fellow could at least die as he had lived, harming no one. I still have the purse, myself, a large one, in red crochet.'

'Is Monsieur Morrel still alive?'

'Yes,' Caderousse replied.

'In that case,' said the abbé, 'he must be a man blessed by God, he must be rich and happy . . . ?'

Caderousse smiled bitterly.

'Yes, happy . . .' he said, 'as I am.'

'Monsieur Morrel is unhappy?' the abbé exclaimed.

'He is on the brink of destitution, Monsieur; worse still, of dishonour.'

'Why?'

'That's how it is,' Caderousse continued. 'After twenty-five years of work, after acquiring the most honourable place among the merchants of Marseille, Monsieur Morrel is utterly ruined. He has lost five vessels in the past two years, suffered three terrible bankruptcies and has nothing to hope for, except that same ship, the *Pharaon* that poor Dantès commanded, which is on its way from India with a cargo of cochineal and indigo. If that fails, as the others did, he is lost.'

'Does this unfortunate man have a wife and children?' asked the abbé.

'Yes, he has a wife who has behaved like a saint through all this, and he has a daughter who was going to marry a man whom she loved, but now his family will not allow him to marry a ruined woman. He also has a son, a lieutenant in the army. But, as you will appreciate, this only increases the poor man's suffering, instead of easing it. If he was by himself, he would blow out his brains and that would be an end to it.'

'This is appalling!' the priest muttered.

'That's how God rewards virtue, Monsieur,' said Caderousse. 'Look at me: I have never done a wicked deed, apart from the one I told you about, and I live in poverty. After watching my poor wife die of fever, unable to do anything for her, I shall die of starvation myself, as old Dantès did, while Fernand and Danglars are rolling in gold.'

'How did this come about?'

'Because everything turned out well for them, while everything turned out ill for honest people like myself.'

'What has happened to Danglars? He is the most guilty, the instigator of it all, is that not so?'

'What happened to him? He left Marseille and, on Monsieur Morrel's recommendation – because Morrel knew nothing of his crime – he went as accounts clerk to a Spanish banker. During the war in Spain he obtained a contract for supplying part of the French army and made a fortune. With this, he gambled on the exchange and tripled or quadrupled his fortune. He married his banker's daughter and, when she died, married a widow, Madame de Nargonne, daughter of Monsieur Servieux, the present king's chamberlain, who enjoys support from the highest quarter. He became a millionaire, and they made him a baron, so that he is now Baron Danglars, with a private residence in the Rue du Mont-Blanc, ten horses in his stable, six lackeys in his antechamber and I don't know how many millions in his coffers.'

'Ah!' the abbé said, in an odd voice. 'And is he happy?'

'That, no one can tell. The secret of happiness and misery is between four walls; walls have ears, but not tongues. If you can be happy with a great fortune, then Danglars is happy.'

'And Fernand?'

'Fernand is another story, too.'

'But how could a poor Catalan fisherman, with no possessions and no education, make his fortune? I have to admit that is beyond me.'

'And beyond everyone else. There must be some strange secret in his life that no one knows about.'

'But by what visible means did he climb to his great fortune, or his high position?'

'Both, Monsieur! Both! He has both fortune and position.'

'This is some wild yarn you are spinning.'

'It may indeed seem so; but listen and you will understand.

'A few days before Bonaparte's return, Fernand was called up to the army. The Bourbons would have left him quietly in the Catalan village, but Napoleon came back and there was a general muster of troops, so Fernand had to go. I, too, had to leave, but as I was older than Fernand and had just married my poor wife, I was merely assigned to the coastal watch. Fernand was called up for active service, went to the frontier with his regiment and took part in the Battle of Ligny.

'The night after the battle, he was on orderly duty at the door of the general, who was secretly in contact with the enemy. That very night, this general was planning to go over to the English. He invited Fernand to accompany him. Fernand agreed, abandoned his post and followed the general.

'Something that would have had him court-martialled if Napoleon had stayed on the throne was an asset for him with the Bourbons. He came back to France with a sub-lieutenant's stripes; and as he remained a protégé of the general, who was much in favour, he was made captain in 1823, at the time of the war in Spain[1] – that is, at the very moment when Danglars was making his first investments. Fernand was a Spaniard, so he was sent to Madrid to report on the mood among his countrymen. He looked up Danglars, got in contact with him, promised his general support from the Royalists in the capital and the provinces, received promises in his turn, entered into agreements, guided his regiment by tracks that he alone knew through gorges under Royalist guard, and in short rendered such services in this short campaign that after the capture of the Trocadero[2] he was appointed colonel and awarded the cross of an officer of the Legion of Honour, together with the title of count.'

'Fate, fate!' muttered the abbé.

'Yes, but listen: that is not all. When the war ended in Spain, Fernand's career seemed to be threatened by the lengthy peace that was about to break out in Europe. Only Greece had risen against Turkey and begun its war for independence. All eyes were on Athens: it was fashionable to feel sympathy for the Greeks and to support their cause. The French government, while not openly taking sides, as you know, turned a blind eye to some active supporters. Fernand asked for permission to go and serve in Greece, which he obtained, while still remaining subject to the discipline of the army.

'Some time later it was learned that the Comte de Morcerf (that was his title) had entered the service of Ali Pasha[3] with the rank of general-instructor.

'As you know, Ali Pasha was killed, but before his death he rewarded Fernand for his services by leaving him a considerable amount of money. With it, Fernand returned to France and his rank of lieutenant-general was confirmed.'

'So, today . . . ?' the abbé asked.

'So today,' Caderousse continued, 'he has a magnificent private residence in Paris, at number twenty-seven, Rue du Helder.'

The abbé opened his mouth to say something but hesitated for a moment; then, making an effort to control his feelings, he asked: 'And Mercédès? They tell me she disappeared?'

'Disappeared?' said Caderousse. 'Yes, like the sun disappears, to rise more glorious the following day.'

'So did she also make her fortune?' the abbé asked, with an ironic smile.

'As we speak, Mercédès is one of the greatest ladies in Paris,' said Caderousse.

'Carry on,' said the abbé. 'I feel as though I were listening to the account of some dream. But I have seen enough extraordinary things myself not to be so much amazed by what you are telling me.'

'At first Mercédès was in despair at the cruel fate that had taken Edmond away from her. I have told you about her efforts to persuade Monsieur de Villefort and her devotion to Dantès' father. In the midst of her despair, she suffered another blow, with Fernand's departure: she knew nothing of Fernand's guilt and considered him as her brother. With him gone, she was alone.

'Three months went by, which she spent weeping. She had no news of Edmond and none of Fernand; nothing to turn to, in fact, but the spectacle of an old man dying of grief.

'One evening, having spent the whole day as she was accustomed to, seated at the crossing of the two roads between Marseille and the Catalan village, she returned home feeling more desolate than ever: neither her lover nor her friend was coming down one or the other of the roads and she had no news of either of them.

'Suddenly, she thought she heard a familiar footstep. She turned around anxiously, the door opened and she saw Fernand appear in his sub-lieutenant's uniform. This was not even half of her sorrow relieved, but at least part of her past life had returned.

'She grasped Fernand's hands with a warmth that he mistook for love, though it was only joy at no longer being alone in the world, at finally seeing a friend after long hours of sadness and solitude. Then, it is true, she had never hated Fernand; it was just that she had never loved him, that's all. Her heart belonged to another, but this other was absent, he had vanished, perhaps he was dead . . . At this last thought, Mercédès burst into tears and wrung her hands in grief; but the notion, which she formerly used to reject when it was suggested to her by someone else, now came spontaneously to her mind. In any case, Old Dantès was constantly telling her: "Our Edmond is dead, because otherwise he would come back to us."

'The old man died, as I told you. If he had lived, then perhaps Mercédès would never have married another, because he would have been there to reproach her with her infidelity. Fernand knew that. When he learned of the old man's death, he came back. By this time he was a lieutenant. On his earlier visit he had not said a word about love to Mercédès, but now he reminded her that he loved her.

'Mercédès asked him for six more months, so that she could wait for Edmond and mourn him.'

'In effect,' the abbé said with a bitter smile, 'that made eighteen months in all. What more could any lover ask of his beloved?' And he muttered the English poet's words: 'Frailty, thy name is woman.'[4]

'Six months later,' Caderousse went on, 'the wedding took place at the Eglise des Accoules.'

'The same church as the one in which she was to marry Edmond,' the priest murmured. 'Only the bridegroom was different.'

'So Mercédès married,' Caderousse continued. 'She appeared to everyone calm but, even so, nearly fainted as she walked past La Réserve where, eighteen months earlier, she had celebrated her betrothal to the man whom she would have recognized that she still loved if she had dared search the bottom of her heart.

'Fernand was happier, but no more at ease, for I saw him at that time and he was constantly afraid that Edmond would return. He immediately set about taking his wife and himself abroad: there were too many dangers and too many memories for him to remain in Les Catalans.

'A week after the wedding, they left.'

'And did you see Mercédès again?' asked the priest.

'Yes, at the time of the war in Spain, in Perpignan, where Fernand had left her. She was occupied in those days in educating her son.'

The abbé shuddered and asked: 'Her son?'

'Yes,' Caderousse replied. 'Little Albert.'

'But if she was educating this child,' said the abbé, 'did she have any education herself? I thought that Edmond told me she was a simple fisherman's daughter, beautiful but untutored.'

'Huh!' said Caderousse. 'Did he know so little of his own fiancée? Mercédès could have been queen, Monsieur, if the crown was only reserved for the most lovely and most intelligent heads. Her fortune was already growing and she grew with it. She learned to draw, she studied music, she learned everything. In any case, between ourselves, I think she only did all this to take her mind off it, to forget: she put all those things into her head to crush what she had in her heart. But now we must tell the truth,' he went on. 'No doubt her wealth and honours consoled her. She is rich, she is a countess, and yet . . .'

He paused.

'And yet . . . ?' said the abbé.

'And yet I am sure that she is not happy,' said Caderousse.

'What makes you think that?'

'Well, when I fell on misfortune myself, I thought that my former friends might help me. I called on Danglars, who would not even receive me. I went to Fernand, and he sent his valet to give me a hundred francs.'

'So you did not see either of them?'

'No, but Madame de Morcerf did see me.'

'How was that?'

'As I was leaving, a purse fell at my feet. There were twenty-five *louis* in it. I looked up quickly and saw Mercédès closing the shutter.'

'And Monsieur de Villefort?' asked the abbé.

'Oh, he was never my friend, I didn't know him. I had no reason to ask him for help.'

'But do you know what became of him, and what part he played in Edmond's misfortune?'

'No. All I know is that, some time after having him arrested, he married Mademoiselle de Saint-Méran and shortly afterwards left Marseille. No doubt fortune smiled on him as it did on the others; no doubt he is as rich as Danglars and as highly thought of as Fernand. Only I have remained poor, as you see, destitute and forgotten by God.'

'You are wrong there, my friend,' said the abbé. 'God may sometimes appear to forget, when his justice is resting; but the time always comes when he remembers, and here is the proof.'

At this, he took the diamond from his pocket and gave it to Caderousse, saying: 'Take this, my friend. Take this diamond, it is yours.'

'What! All mine!' Caderousse exclaimed. 'Ah, Monsieur – you are not teasing me, surely?'

'This diamond was to be divided among his friends. Edmond had only one friend, so there is no need to divide it. Take the jewel and sell it. It is worth fifty thousand francs, as I told you, and I hope that this sum will be enough to rescue you from poverty.'

'Monsieur,' Caderousse said, nervously holding out one hand, while the other wiped the sweat that was beading on his brow, 'Oh, Monsieur, do not jest with a man's happiness and despair!'

'I know what happiness is, and what is despair, and I never jest with feelings. Take it, but in return . . .'

Caderousse's hand had already touched the diamond, but he drew it back.

The abbé smiled. 'In return,' he continued, 'give me that red silk purse which Monsieur Morrel left on old Dantès' mantelpiece, which you told me was still in your possession.'

Increasingly astonished, Caderousse went over to a large oak cupboard, opened it and gave the abbé a long purse of faded red silk, bound with two copper rings that had once been gilded. The abbé took it and in exchange gave Caderousse the diamond.

'You are a man of God, Monsieur!' cried Caderousse. 'Because no one knew that Edmond had given you this diamond and you could have kept it.'

'Yes, indeed,' the abbé murmured to himself. 'And likely enough that is what you would have done yourself.'

He got up and took his hat and gloves.

'Everything that you told me is quite true, isn't it? I can believe every word?'

'Look here, Monsieur l'Abbé,' said Caderousse. 'Here in the corner of this wall is a crucifix of consecrated wood; here, on this sideboard, is my wife's New Testament. Open it and I will swear to you on it, with my hand extended towards the crucifix: I will swear by my immortal soul, by my Christian faith, that I have told you everything just as it was and as the recording angel will whisper it into God's ear on the Day of Judgement!'

'Very good,' said the abbé, convinced by his tone that Caderousse was telling the truth. 'Very good. Let the money benefit you. Farewell, I am going to withdraw far from the haunts of men who do so much ill to one another.'

Escaping with difficulty from Caderousse's expressions of thanks, he went over and himself drew back the bolt on the door, went out, remounted his horse, waved for the last time to the innkeeper, who was pouring out incoherent farewells, and set off in the direction from which he had come.

When Caderousse turned around, he found La Carconte behind him, paler and more unsteady than ever.

'Is it true, what I heard?' she asked.

'What? That he has given us the diamond for ourselves alone?' said Caderousse, almost mad with joy.

'Yes.'

'Nothing could be truer. Here it is.'

The woman looked at it for a moment, then muttered: 'Suppose it is a fake?'

Caderousse went pale and swayed on his feet.

'A fake . . .' he mumbled. 'A fake? Why would this man give me a fake diamond?'

'To learn your secrets without paying for them, idiot!'

For a time Caderousse was stunned by the awfulness of this possibility. Then he said: 'Ah, we shall soon know.' And he took his hat and placed it on the red handkerchief knotted around his head.

'How?'

'The fair is at Beaucaire; there are jewellers from Paris there. I'll show them the diamond. Look after the house, woman. I'll be back in two hours.' And he ran out of the house, taking the opposite road from the one down which the stranger had just ridden.

'Fifty thousand francs!' murmured La Carconte, when she was alone. 'That is a lot of money . . . but it's not a fortune.'

XXVIII

THE PRISON REGISTER

The day after the one on which the scene we have just described took place on the road between Bellegarde and Beaucaire, a man of between thirty and thirty-two years of age, dressed in a corn-flower-blue frock-coat, nankeen trousers and a white waistcoat, whose manner and accent both proclaimed him to be British, presented himself at the house of the mayor of Marseille.

'Monsieur,' he said, 'I am the head clerk of the House of Thomson and French, of Rome. For the past ten years we have had dealings with Morrel and Son of Marseille. We have some hundred thousand francs invested in the business, and we are somewhat uneasy, since the company is said to be on the brink of ruin. I have therefore arrived directly from Rome to ask you for information about its affairs.'

'I do indeed know, Monsieur,' the mayor replied, 'that for the past four or five years Monsieur Morrel seems to have been dogged by misfortune. He lost four or five ships in succession and suffered from three or four bankruptcies. But, even though I myself am his creditor for around ten thousand francs, it is not appropriate for me to give you any information about his financial affairs. Ask me, as mayor, what I think of Monsieur Morrel and I shall tell you that he is a man who is honest to the point of inflexibility and that he has up to now fulfilled all his responsibilities with the utmost nicety. That is all I can tell you, Monsieur. If you wish to know anything further, you must ask Monsieur de Boville, inspector of prisons, residing at number fifteen, Rue de Noailles. I believe he has two hundred thousand francs invested in Monsieur Morrel's firm and, if there is really anything to be feared, as the amount is far greater than mine, you will probably find him better informed than I am about the matter.'

The Englishman appeared to appreciate the delicacy of this reply. He bowed and left, making his way towards the street in question with that stride which is peculiar to the natives of Great Britain.

M. de Boville was in his study. Seeing him, the Englishman started, as if with surprise, suggesting that this was not the first time they had met. As for M. de Boville, he was so desperate that it was obvious that his mind, entirely taken up with its immediate concerns, had no room left for either his memory or his imagination to wander back into the past.

The Englishman, with the phlegm characteristic of his race, asked him more or less the same question and in the same terms as he had just put to the mayor of Marseille.

'Alas, Monsieur!' M. de Boville exclaimed. 'Your fears are unfortunately quite justified and you see before you a desperate man. I had two hundred thousand francs invested in the house of Morrel: that money was my daughter's dowry; she was to be married in a fortnight. It was to be reimbursed, the first hundred thousand on the fifteenth of this month, the remainder on the fifteenth of next month. I advised Monsieur Morrel that I wished to have the money paid in due time; and now he has just been here, Monsieur, barely half an hour ago, to tell me that if his ship the *Pharaon* does not return between now and the fifteenth, he will be unable to reimburse me.'

'But this sounds very like procrastination,' said the Englishman.

'Why not rather say that it sounds like bankruptcy!' M. de Boville cried in despair.

The Englishman seemed to reflect for a moment, then said: 'So you are anxious about the repayment of this debt?'

'More than that: I consider it lost.'

'Very well, I shall buy it from you.'

'You?'

'Yes, indeed.'

'But at a huge discount, I don't doubt?'

'No, for two hundred thousand francs. Our company,' the Englishman said with a laugh, 'does not do that kind of business.'

'And how will you pay?'

'In cash.'

The Englishman took a sheaf of banknotes out of his pocket, probably amounting to twice the sum that M. de Boville was afraid of losing.

A look of joy suffused M. de Boville's face, but he made an effort and said: 'I must warn you, Monsieur, that in all probability you will not recover six per cent of the amount.'

'That does not concern me,' the Englishman replied. 'It concerns the House of Thomson and French; I am only acting for them. Perhaps they wish to hasten the ruin of a rival firm. All that I do know, Monsieur, is that I am prepared to give you this sum in exchange for the transfer of the debt; all I shall want is a brokerage fee.'

'What, Monsieur! This is too scrupulous!' M. de Boville exclaimed. 'There is usually a commission of one and a half per cent. Do you want two? Or three? Do you want five per cent? Or more? Tell me.'

'Monsieur,' said the Englishman with a laugh, 'I am like my firm, which does not do that kind of business. No, my fee is of quite a different kind.'

'Tell me. I am listening.'

'You are the inspector of prisons?'

'I have been for fourteen years.'

'You hold the registers of admissions and discharges?'

'Naturally.'

'And notes concerning the prisoners are attached to these registers?'

'There is a dossier on each prisoner.'

'Well, Monsieur, I was brought up in Rome by a poor devil of an abbé who suddenly disappeared. I later learned that he was held in the Château d'If. I should like to have some information about his death.'

'What was his name?'

'Abbé Faria.'

'Oh, yes! I remember very well!' M. de Boville said. 'He was mad.'

'So it was said.'

'Oh, there's no doubt about it.'

'Quite probably. What was the nature of his madness?'

'He claimed to have knowledge of some huge treasure and would offer vast sums to the government if it would set him free.'

'The poor devil! And he died?'

'Yes, Monsieur, some five or six months ago, last February.'

'You have an excellent memory, Monsieur, to remember the date so precisely.'

'I recall it because something strange happened at the same time as the poor man's death.'

'Can you tell me what that was?' the Englishman asked, with a look of curiosity that a close observer would have been surprised to see on his normally impassive features.

'Why, yes, I can. The abbé's cell was some forty-five or fifty feet approximately from that of a former Bonapartist agent, one of those who did most to assist in the usurper's return in 1815, a very resolute and dangerous fellow.'

'Indeed?' said the Englishman.

'Yes,' said M. de Boville. 'I even had occasion to see the man in 1816 or 1817, and you could only enter his cell with a squad of soldiers. The man made a deep impression on me; I shall never forget his face.'

The Englishman gave a hint of a smile.

'So you say that the two cells . . .' he continued.

'Were about fifty feet apart, but it seems that this Edmond Dantès . . .'

'This dangerous man was called . . .'

'Edmond Dantès. Yes, Monsieur, it appears that this Edmond Dantès had obtained some tools, or made them for himself, because they found a passageway through which the two prisoners used to communicate.'

'The passage was no doubt made with a view to escape?'

'Precisely. But, unfortunately for the prisoners, Abbé Faria had a seizure and died.'

'I understand. That must have put an end to the plans for escape.'

'As far as the dead man was concerned, yes,' M. de Boville replied. 'But not for the one who was left alive. On the contrary, this Dantès saw the means to hasten his escape. No doubt he thought that prisoners who die in the Château d'If are buried in an ordinary cemetery. He moved the dead man into his own cell, took his place in the shroud into which he had been sewn and waited for the body to be buried.'

'That was a risky plan, arguing some courage,' the Englishman said.

'Ah, as I told you, Monsieur, he was a very dangerous fellow; but, fortunately, he himself relieved the government of any fears it may have had on his account.'

'How was that?'

'What? Don't you understand?'

'No.'

'The Château d'If has no cemetery. The dead are simply thrown into the sea after a thirty-six-pound cannonball has been tied to their legs.'

'Which means?' said the Englishman, as if he was finding it hard to follow.

'Well, of course they attached the weight to his legs and threw him into the sea.'

'Really?' the Englishman exclaimed.

'Yes, Monsieur,' the inspector went on. 'You can just imagine the fugitive's amazement when he felt himself falling from the top of the cliff. I should like to have seen his face at that moment.'

'It would have been difficult.'

'No matter!' said M. de Boville, in much better humour, now that he was certain of recovering his two hundred thousand francs. 'No matter! I can still imagine it!' And he burst out laughing.

'So can I,' said the Englishman, starting to laugh in his turn, but in the way that the English laugh, through clenched teeth.

'I suppose that means,' he went on, being the first to regain his composure, 'that he was drowned.'

'Yes. Well and truly.'

'With the result that the prison governor got rid of the maniac and the madman simultaneously?'

'Just as you say.'

'I imagine some sort of report was drawn up about it?'

'Yes, certainly, a death certificate. You understand, Dantès' relatives, if he has any, might wish to know for certain whether he was alive or dead.'

'And now they can rest assured if they have anything to inherit from him. He is definitely dead?'

'Oh, heavens yes, no doubt about it. They will have a certificate whenever they want.'

'So be it,' said the Englishman. 'But to return to the registers . . .'

'Indeed. This story distracted us. Forgive me.'

'For what? For the story? Not at all, it intrigued me.'

'It is intriguing. So, Monsieur, you want to see everything concerning your poor abbé; he was as mild as a lamb.'

'I should very much like to.'

'Come into my study and I shall show it to you.'

They both went into M. de Boville's study, where everything was perfectly in order: each register at its number, each dossier in its box. The inspector asked the Englishman to sit down in the armchair and put in front of him the register and dossier relating to the Château d'If, allowing him to peruse it at his leisure, while he sat in a corner and read the newspaper.

The Englishman had no difficulty finding the dossier concerning

Abbé Faria, but it appeared that he had been greatly interested in the story that M. de Boville had told him because, after studying these first papers, he continued to peruse the file until he came to the bundle concerning Edmond Dantès. Here, he found everything in its place: the denunciation, the interrogation, M. Morrel's petition and M. de Villefort's annotation. He quietly folded the denunciation and put it in his pocket; read the interrogation and observed that it did not mention the name of Noirtier; and read through the petition dated 10 April 1815, in which Morrel, following the advice of the deputy prosecutor, had exaggerated the services rendered by Dantès to the imperial cause – with the best of intentions, since Napoleon was then still on the throne – all of which was confirmed by Villefort's signature. At this, he understood everything. Under the Second Restoration, this petition to Napoleon, which Villefort had kept, became a deadly weapon in the hands of the royal prosecutor. Thus he was not surprised, continuing through the register, to find these sentences bracketed together opposite his name:

EDMOND DANTES:
Fanatical Bonapartist. Played an active part in the return from Elba.
To be kept in solitary confinement, under the closest supervision.

Beneath these lines, in different handwriting, he read: 'In view of the above note, *no action*.'

However, by comparing the writing in the brackets with that on the certificate under M. Morrel's petition, he felt certain that both were in the same hand, and that the hand was Villefort's.

As for the note appended to the note, the Englishman realized that it must have been placed there by an inspector who had taken a passing interest in Dantès' case, but who would have been unable to take any further steps in his favour because of the information that we have just quoted.

As we mentioned, the inspector had placed himself some distance away and was reading *Le Drapeau Blanc*, so as not to inconvenience Abbé Faria's former pupil. This is why he did not see the Englishman fold and pocket the denunciation that Danglars had written in the arbour at La Réserve, which bore the stamp of the Marseille post office for the evening collection at 6 o'clock on 27 February.

We have to admit, on the other hand, that, even if he had seen this, he attached too little importance to this scrap of paper and too much to his two hundred thousand francs to protest at what the Englishman was doing, however improper it might be.

'Thank you,' the latter said, slamming the register shut. 'I have what I need. Now I must keep my side of the bargain. Prepare a transfer of the money you are owed, in which you acknowledge that you have received the full sum, and I shall count it out.'

He got up so that M. de Boville could take his place at the desk, where he sat down and proceeded, as quickly and simply as possible, to draw up the necessary paper, while the Englishman was counting the banknotes on to the edge of the filing cabinet.

XXIX

MORREL AND COMPANY

Someone who had known the interior of the House of Morrel a few years earlier, and who had then returned to Marseille at the period now reached by our narrative, would have found it much changed.

In place of that relaxed atmosphere of life and good cheer that seems to be, so to speak, exhaled by a firm enjoying prosperity; in place of the happy faces looking out of the windows and the busy clerks hurrying down the corridors with pens behind their ears; in place of the courtyard full of boxes, resounding to the shouts and laughter of the delivery men; in place of all this, from the moment he came in, he would have found an indefinable air of sadness and death. The corridor was empty, the courtyard deserted; and, of all the many employees who had once crowded into the offices, only two remained: the first was a young man, aged about twenty-three or twenty-four, named Emmanuel Herbault, who was in love with M. Morrel's daughter and had stayed with the firm despite his relatives' efforts to extricate him; while the other was an old cashier, one-eyed, nicknamed Coclès by the young people who had once populated this vast, busy hive which was now almost uninhabited, a label that had now so completely and utterly replaced any previous ones, that in all probability he would not even have turned around if someone were to have called him by his true name.

Coclès had remained in M. Morrel's service, and the good man's situation had changed in a rather unusual way: he had simultaneously risen to the rank of cashier and fallen to that of a house servant.

He was still the same Coclès for all that, kind, patient and devoted, but immovable when it came to arithmetic, the only point on which he would have challenged the whole world, even M. Morrel, knowing nothing beyond his Pythagorean tables, but having these at his fingertips, whichever way one chose to turn them or however one tried to lure him into error.

In the midst of the general depression that had settled over the firm of Morrel and Son, Coclès was the only one who had remained impassive. There should be no mistake: this impassivity was not due to any lack of feeling, but on the contrary to an unshakeable faith. We have mentioned that the host of clerks and employees who owed their livelihood to the shipowner's firm had gradually deserted the office and the shop, like the rats which, so they say, gradually leave a ship when it has been preordained by fate to perish at sea, with the result that these self-interested guests have entirely abandoned it by the time it sets sail. Coclès had watched all of them depart without even thinking to enquire into the cause of their departure. Everything for Coclès came down to a matter of numbers and, in the twenty years that he had worked for Morrel's, he had always seen payments go through without hindrance and with such regularity that he could no more accept an end to that regularity or a suspension of those payments, than a miller whose wheel is turned by the waters of a plentiful stream would accept that the same stream might cease to flow. Indeed, nothing so far had threatened Coclès' confidence. The previous month's payments had gone through with absolute punctuality. Coclès had noted an error of seventy *centimes* which M. Morrel had made to his own detriment and, the same day, brought the excess fourteen *sous* to M. Morrel, who took them with a melancholy smile and dropped them into an almost empty drawer, saying: 'Coclès, Coclès, you are a jewel among cashiers.'

So Coclès left, more or less satisfied. Praise from M. Morrel, himself a jewel among the best men in Marseille, did more for Coclès' self-esteem than a bonus of fifty *écus*.

However, since achieving this victory over the end-of-month payments, M. Morrel had suffered some moments of agony. It had meant mustering all his resources. Fearful that the rumour concerning his difficulties might spread through the town if he was seen to be turning to such extremities, he had travelled in person to the fair at Beaucaire to sell some jewellery belonging to his wife and daughter, and part of his silver. As a result of this sacrifice, the reputation of the house of Morrel had been spared the slightest hint of a stain, but the cashbox was totally empty. With its usual egoism, all credit had slipped away, terrified by the rumours: the truth was that if he was to meet the hundred thousand francs which he would owe M. de Boville on the 15th of the present month, and the second hundred thousand francs which would fall due on the 15th of the month following, M. Morrel's only hope lay in the return of the *Pharaon*, which had certainly set sail, as they knew from another ship which had weighed anchor at the same time and which had come safely to port. But this ship (coming, like the *Pharaon*, from Calcutta) had arrived a fortnight earlier, while there was as yet no news of the *Pharaon*.

This is how things stood when, the day after concluding the important business we have described with M. de Boville, the agent of the firm of Thomson and French, of Rome, announced himself on his arrival at Morrel and Son.

He was received by Emmanuel. The young man shied away from any unfamiliar face, because each new one meant a new creditor who had come to demand something from the shipowner, and he wished to spare his employer the unpleasantness of this visit; so he questioned the stranger; but the latter declared that he had nothing to say to M. Emmanuel: he wished to speak to M. Morrel in person. With a sigh, Emmanuel called Coclès. Coclès appeared, and the young man asked him to take the stranger to see M. Morrel.

Coclès went ahead, the stranger following. On the staircase they passed a beautiful girl of between sixteen and seventeen, who looked uneasily at the stranger. The latter noticed the look, though it was lost on Coclès.

'Monsieur Morrel is in his study, Mademoiselle Julie?' he asked.

'Yes – at least I think he is,' the girl replied, hesitating. 'Coclès, you go first and see, and if my father is there, announce the gentleman.'

'There is no point in announcing me, Mademoiselle,' the Englishman replied. 'Monsieur Morrel does not know my name. This good man has only to let him know that I am the head clerk of Messrs

Thomson and French, of Rome, with whom your father's firm does business.'

The girl paled and carried on down the stairs, while Coclès and the stranger continued on their way up. She went into the office where Emmanuel was sitting, and Coclès, using a key that had been entrusted to him and which warned the boss of some important arrival, opened a door in a corner of the second-floor landing, showed the stranger into an antechamber, opened a second door, which he then closed behind him and, after momentarily leaving the emissary of Thomson and French on his own, reappeared and signalled to him to enter. The Englishman did so, to find M. Morrel sitting at a table, paling at the awful columns of figures in the register that recorded his debts.

Seeing the foreigner, he closed the register, rose and drew up a chair. Then, when the other man was seated, he sat down.

Fourteen years had profoundly changed the merchant who, thirty-six years old at the beginning of this story, was now about to reach fifty: his hair was grey, his forehead was lined with anxious furrows and his look, which had once been so firm and confident, had become vague and irresolute, as if it were constantly trying to avoid having to settle on a single idea or a single person.

The Englishman looked at him with curiosity and obvious interest.

'Monsieur,' said Morrel, apparently made still more uneasy by this appraisal, 'you wished to speak to me?'

'Yes, Monsieur. You know on whose behalf I am here?'

'The firm of Thomson and French, or so my cashier says.'

'He informed you correctly, Monsieur. The firm of Thomson and French had some three or four hundred thousand francs to pay in France in the course of this month and the following; so, knowing your reputation for scrupulous punctuality, it collected all the bills that it could find with your signature and requested me to cash these bills successively as they came up for payment and to make use of the funds.'

Morrel gave a deep sigh and drew a hand across a forehead covered in sweat.

'So, Monsieur,' he said, 'you have bills of exchange signed by me?'

'Yes, Monsieur, for some considerable amount.'

'For how much?' Morrel asked, in what he hoped was a confident voice.

'Well, first of all,' the Englishman said, taking a sheaf of papers out of his pocket, 'here is a transfer of two hundred thousand francs made out to the benefit of our firm by Monsieur de Boville, inspector of prisons. Do you acknowledge owing this amount to Monsieur de Boville?'

'Yes, I do. It was an investment that he made in my company, some five years ago, at four and a half per cent.'

'To be repaid . . .'

'Half on the fifteenth of this month, half on the fifteenth of next month.'

'That's right.. Then I have here thirty-two thousand francs, for the end of this month: these are bills which you have signed and which have been made out to our order by third parties.'

'I accept that,' said Morrel, blushing with shame at the thought that for the first time in his life he might be unable to honour his signature. 'Is that all?'

'No, Monsieur. In addition, I have these bills, due at the end of next month, assigned to us by the firms of Pascal and Wild and Turner of Marseille: about fifty-five thousand francs. In all, two hundred and eighty-seven thousand, five hundred francs.'

Poor Morrel's suffering as all this was being counted out is impossible to describe.

'Two hundred and eighty-seven thousand, five hundred francs,' he repeated mechanically.

'Yes, Monsieur,' the Englishman replied. Then, after a moment's silence: 'I cannot conceal from you, Monsieur Morrel, that even allowing for your probity, which until now has been beyond reproach, the general rumour in Marseille is that you will not be able to meet your debts.'

At this almost brutally direct approach, the colour drained horribly from Morrel's face.

'Monsieur,' he said, 'so far . . . and it is now more than twenty-four years since I took over this firm from my father, who had himself managed it for thirty-five years . . . so far, not a single bill signed by Morrel and Son has been presented at our counter and gone unpaid.'

'Yes, I know that,' said the Englishman. 'But, as one man of honour to another, tell me honestly: will you be able to pay these as promptly?'

Morrel shuddered and looked at the man opposite him with more confidence than he had shown so far.

'A question which is asked with such frankness,' he said, 'deserves an equally frank answer. Yes, Monsieur, I shall pay if, as I hope, my ship arrives safely to port, because its arrival will restore to me the credit that has been lost to me because of a succession of accidents. But if, by misfortune, the *Pharaon*, which I am counting on as my last resource, were to fail me . . .'

Tears came to the poor shipowner's eyes.

'Well? If this last resource were to fail . . . ?'

'Well, Monsieur, it is hard to say it, but . . . I am already used to misfortune and I must learn to be used to shame . . . I believe that I should be obliged to withhold payment.'

'Have you no friends who could help you in these circumstances?'

Morrel smiled sadly and said: 'In business, Monsieur, as you very well know, one has no friends, only associates.'

'That is true,' the Englishman muttered. 'So you have only one hope left?'

'Only one.'

'Your last?'

'My last.'

'So that if this hope fails . . .'

'I am lost, Monsieur, completely lost.'

'As I was on my way to see you, a ship was coming into port.'

'I know. A young man who has remained loyal to me in my misfortune spends part of his time at a lookout on the top floor of the house, hoping to be able to be the first to bring me good news. He told me of this ship's arrival.'

'But it is not yours?'

'No, it is a ship from Bordeaux, the *Gironde*, also coming from India, but not mine.'

'Perhaps it encountered the *Pharaon* and will bring you news.'

'I must admit, Monsieur, that I am almost as fearful of receiving news of my vessel as of remaining in this uncertainty. At least uncertainty means the continuation of hope.'

And M. Morrel added glumly: 'This delay is not natural. The *Pharaon* left Calcutta on February the fifth. It should have been here more than a month ago.'

'What is that?' the foreigner said, straining his ears. 'What is the meaning of that noise?'

'My God! Oh, my God!' Morrel exclaimed, becoming pale. 'What is it now?'

There was a considerable noise on the staircase: comings and goings, even a cry of distress.

Morrel got up to open the door, but his strength failed and he slipped back into his chair. The two men remained facing one another, Morrel shaking uncontrollably, the foreigner studying him with a look of profound pity. The noise had ceased, but Morrel still appeared to be waiting for something: the noise had a cause and must in turn produce some effect. The foreigner thought he could hear the footsteps of several people coming up the stairs and stopping on the landing. A key turned in the first door and it creaked on its hinges.

'Only two people have the key to that door,' Morrel muttered, 'Coclès and Julie.'

At that moment, the second door opened and the young girl appeared, pale, her cheeks bathed in tears. Morrel got up, trembling, and leant against the arm of his chair, because he could not stand up. He wanted to ask a question, but his voice failed him.

'Oh, father!' the girl said, clasping her hands. 'Forgive your child who is the bringer of bad news.'

The colour drained from Morrel's cheeks and Julie threw herself into his arms.

'Father! Father!' she cried. 'Have courage!'

'The *Pharaon* is lost?' he asked in a strangled voice.

The girl did not reply, but nodded her head, still pressing it against his chest.

'And the crew?' Morrel asked.

'Safe,' said the girl, 'saved by the ship from Bordeaux that has just come into port.'

Morrel raised both hands heavenwards with a sublime look of resignation and gratitude.

'Thank you, Lord!' he said. 'At least you have smitten me alone.'

Phlegmatic though the Englishman was, a tear rose to his eye.

'Come in, come in,' said Morrel. 'I suppose you are all there at the door.'

Indeed, no sooner had he spoken these words than Mme Morrel came in, sobbing, followed by Emmanuel. Behind them, in the antechamber, could be seen the rough features of seven or eight half-naked sailors. At the sight of these men, the Englishman started. He took a step as if to approach them, then thought better of it and stepped back into the darkest, most distant corner of the study.

Mme Morrel went and sat down in the armchair, taking one of her husband's hands in her own, while Julie remained clinging to his breast. Emmanuel had stayed half-way across the room and seemed to link the Morrel family group to the sailors at the door.

'How did it happen?' Morrel asked.

'Come here, Penelon,' said the young man, 'and tell us.'

An old sailor, tanned by the equatorial sun, stepped forward, twisting the remains of a hat between his hands.

'Good day, Monsieur Morrel,' he said, as if he had left Marseille only the day before and had returned from Aix or Toulon.

'Good day, my friend,' the shipowner said, unable to suppress a smile, even through his tears. 'But where is your captain?'

'As far as the captain is concerned, Monsieur Morrel, he stayed behind, ill, in Palma. But, God willing, it was nothing and you will see him home in a few days, as fit as you or I.'

'That's good. Now speak up, Penelon,' said M. Morrel.

Penelon switched his quid of tobacco from the right cheek to the left, put his hand in front of his mouth, turned around and spat a long jet of blackish saliva into the antechamber, then stepped forward and, swaying on his hips, began:

'Well now, Monsieur Morrel, we were near enough between Cape Blanc and Cape Boyador and sailing before a nice south-south-easter after having been well and truly becalmed for a week, when Captain Gaumard came over to me – I should mention I was at the wheel – and said: "Penelon, old boy, what do you think of them there clouds gathering on the horizon?"

'And I'll be blowed if I wasn't looking at them myself.

'"What do I think of them, Captain? What I think is they're coming up a bit faster than they need to and they're a bit darker than well-meaning clouds have any right to be."

'"I'm thinking the same myself," said the captain, "and I'm going to take some precautions. We are carrying too much sail for the wind that's coming. Hey, there! Bring in the royal and furl the flying jib!"

'It was not before time. Hardly had the order been carried out than we had the wind on our heels and the ship was listing.

'"Fair enough!" said the captain. "We're still carrying too much sail. Furl the mainsail!"

'Five minutes later, the mainsail was furled and we had only the foresail, the topsails and the topgallants.

' "So, tell me, old Penelon," said the captain. "Why are you shaking your head?"

' "Because, in your place, I still wouldn't be running ahead like that."

' "I think you're right, old man," he said. "There's a puff of wind coming."

' "If that's how you like to put it, Captain," I said. "Anyone who bought what's down there at the price of a puff would make on the bargain. It's an out-and-out storm, if I've ever seen one."

'By which I mean you could see the wind coming like you can see the dust rising in Montredon.[1] Luckily this storm was up against a man who knew it.

' "Double-reef the topsails!" the captain yelled. "Let go the bowlines, to take in the topsails and weigh the yards!" '

'That was not enough in those waters,' said the Englishman. 'I should have reefed in four times and got rid of the foresail.'

Everyone started at the unexpected sound of this firm, sonorous voice. Penelon shaded his eyes with his hand and looked at the person who was so confidently directing his captain's manoeuvre.

'We did better than that, Monsieur,' the old sailor said, with some respect, 'because we struck the mizzen and turned into the wind to run before the storm. Ten minutes later, we struck the main topsails and went on with bare masts.'

'The ship was rather old to risk doing that,' the Englishman said.

'Yes, it was indeed! That's what did for us. After twelve hours of being tossed this way and that, as if the devil was on our tail, we sprang a leak. "Penelon," the captain told me, "I think we're going under, old chap. Give me the wheel and go down into the hold."

'I gave him the wheel and went below. There was already three feet of water. I came back up, shouting: "All hands to the pump! To the pump!" But it was already too late. We all set to it, but I think the more we put out, the more there was coming in.

' "Dammit!" I said after we'd struggled for four hours. "Since we're sinking, let's sink; you only die once!"

' "Is that how you set an example, Master Penelon?" said the captain. "Well, just you wait there." And he went to fetch a pair of pistols from his cabin. "The first man who leaves the pump," said he, "I'll blow his brains out." '

'That was well done,' said the Englishman.

'Nothing inspires a man like a solid argument,' the sailor went on, 'and all the more so as meanwhile the weather had lightened and the wind had fallen. But, for all that, the water kept on rising, not much, perhaps two inches an hour, but it did rise. You see, two inches an hour may seem like nothing; but in twelve hours it's not an inch short of twenty-four, and twenty-four inches are two feet. Those two feet, added to the three we had already, makes five. And when a ship has five feet of water in it, it's fit to be called dropsical.

' "Come on, then," said the captain. "That's enough. Monsieur Morrel will have nothing to reproach us for: we've done what we could to save the ship; now we must try to save the men. To the boats, boys, and look sharp about it."

'Listen, Monsieur Morrel,' Penelon continued. 'We loved the *Pharaon* but, much as a sailor may love his ship, he loves his hide better. So we didn't wait to be asked twice, especially as the ship itself was groaning as if to say: "Be off with you, be off with you." And it was telling the truth, the poor old *Pharaon*, because you could feel it literally going down under our feet. So in a trice the boat was in the sea and all eight of us were in the boat.

'The captain came down last; or, rather, he didn't come down, because he didn't want to leave the ship. I had to seize him myself and throw him after our shipmates, before jumping in myself. It was not too soon. Just after I jumped, the deck burst with a noise which you would have thought was a volley from a forty-eight-gun man-of-war.

'Ten minutes later, it dipped its bows, then its stern, then started to roll over like a dog chasing its own tail. And finally, heigh-ho, boys! Brrrou . . . ! Down she went, no more *Pharaon*!

'As for us, we were three days with nothing to eat or drink, and we'd even started to talk about drawing lots to see which of us would be food for the rest, when we saw the *Gironde*. We signalled to her, she saw us, made for where we were, put down her boat and picked us up. That's how it happened, Monsieur Morrel, on my word! On the word of a sailor! Isn't that true, you others?'

A general murmur of assent showed that the storyteller had unanimous support for the truth of the basic facts and the picturesque embroidery of the details.

'Very well, my friends,' said M. Morrel, 'you are fine men, and I already knew that no one was responsible for the misfortune that has befallen me other than my own fate. It's God's will and not the fault of men. Let us bow to His will. Now, how much pay are you owed?'

'Oh, no! Let's not talk about that, Monsieur Morrel.'

'On the contrary, let's,' said the shipowner with a melancholy smile.

'In that case, we are owed three months . . .' said Penelon.

'Coclès, pay two hundred francs to each of these good men. At any other time, my friends,' he went on, 'I should have added: "And give each of them two hundred francs bonus." But times are bad, and the little money that remains is not mine to give. So accept my regrets, and don't hold it against me.'

Penelon grimaced with emotion, turned to his companions, said a few words to them and turned back.

'As far as that's concerned, Monsieur Morrel,' he said, shifting his quid of tobacco to the other side of his mouth and sending a second jet of saliva into the antechamber to balance the first, 'as far as that's concerned . . .'

'What's concerned?'

'The money . . .'

'Well?'

'Well, Monsieur Morrel, my comrades say that for the moment they will have enough with fifty francs each, and they can wait for the rest.'

'My dear friends!' exclaimed M. Morrel, deeply moved. 'Thank you, you are all the best of men. But take it! Take it, and if you find a good owner to sail with, join him, you are free.'

This last remark produced a startling effect on the worthy seamen. They looked at one another aghast. Penelon, as if winded by a blow, almost swallowed his quid; luckily he put a hand to his throat in time.

'What, Monsieur Morrel!' he said in a strangled voice. 'What! You are dismissing us! Are you displeased with us?'

'No, my children, not at all,' said the shipowner. 'I am not displeased, quite the opposite. I am not dismissing you. But what do you expect? I have no more ships, I have no further need of seamen.'

'What do you mean, you have no more ships?' said Penelon.

'Well, have some more built. We'll wait. Thank God, we know what it is to ride out a spell of bad weather.'

'I have no money left to build ships, Penelon,' the shipowner replied, smiling sadly. 'I can't accept your offer, generous as it is.'

'Well, if you have no money, don't pay us. We'll just do what the poor old *Pharaon* did: we'll keep our sails furled!'

'Enough, my dear friends, enough!' M. Morrel exclaimed, stifled with emotion. 'Go, I beg you. We shall meet again in better times. You go with them, Emmanuel, and see that my wishes are carried out.'

'At least this is not farewell for ever, is it, Monsieur Morrel?' said Penelon.

'No, my friends – at least, I hope not. Goodbye then.'

He signalled to Coclès, who took the lead; the sailors followed the cashier and Emmanuel followed the sailors.

'Now,' the shipowner said to his wife and daughter, 'please leave us alone for a moment. I have to talk to this gentleman.'

He nodded towards the representative of Thomson and French, who had remained motionless throughout this scene, standing in his corner and intervening only with the few words we mentioned. The two women looked at the stranger, whom they had entirely forgotten, and left the room; but as she went the girl addressed a sublime look of supplication to him, to which he replied with a smile that any disinterested observer would have been astonished to see flowering on that icy face. The two men were left alone.

'Well, Monsieur,' said Morrel, slumping down into a chair. 'You saw and heard everything, so there is nothing for me to say.'

'What I saw, Monsieur,' said the Englishman, 'is that you have suffered a further misfortune, as undeserved as the rest, and this has confirmed me in my desire to oblige you.'

'Oh, Monsieur!' said Morrel.

'Let us see,' said the foreigner. 'I am one of your principal creditors, am I not?'

'You are certainly the one whose bills fall due in the shortest time.'

'Would you like a stay before paying me?'

'A space of time might save my honour and so my life.'

'How long do you need?'

Morrel hesitated.

'Two months,' he said.

'Good. I shall give you three.'

'But do you think that the house of Thomson and French . . . ?'

'Have no fear, Monsieur, I take full responsibility. Today is June the fifth.'

'Yes.'

'Well, reassign all these bills to September the fifth. On that day at eleven in the morning' (the clock showed precisely eleven as he spoke) 'I shall present myself here.'

'I shall be waiting for you, Monsieur,' said Morrel. 'And you shall be paid, or I shall be dead.'

The last words were spoken so softly that the other man could not hear them.

The bills were renewed, the old ones torn up, and at least the poor shipowner found himself with three months to muster his last resources. The Englishman accepted his thanks with the sang-froid peculiar to his nation and took his leave of Morrel, who accompanied him with his blessings as far as the door.

On the staircase he met Julie. The girl was pretending to go down, but in fact had been waiting for him.

'Oh, Monsieur!' she said, clasping her hands.

'Mademoiselle,' the foreigner said. 'One day you will receive a letter signed by . . . Sinbad the Sailor. Do precisely as this letter tells you, however strange its instructions may seem.'

'Yes, Monsieur,' Julie said.

'Do you promise me this?'

'I promise.'

'Very well. Farewell, Mademoiselle. Stay always as good and virtuous as you are now and I truly believe God will reward you by giving you Emmanuel as a husband.'

Julie gave a little cry, blushed as red as a cherry and clasped the banister to stop herself falling. The stranger went on his way, with a wave of farewell. In the courtyard he met Penelon, who was holding a roll of one hundred francs in each hand, apparently undecided whether to take them with him.

'Come with me, friend,' the stranger said. 'We must talk.'

XXX

SEPTEMBER THE FIFTH

The stay granted by the representative of Thomson and French, just when M. Morrel least expected it, seemed to the poor ship-owner like one of those changes of fortune which tell a man that fate has at last tired of hounding him. The same day, he told his daughter, his wife and Emmanuel what had happened, and a modicum of hope, if not peace of mind, descended on the family. But unfortunately Morrel did not only have to deal with Thomson and French, who appeared so well disposed towards him. As he himself said, in business one has associates, but no friends. When he thought seriously about it, he could not even understand the generosity of Messrs Thomson and French. The only explanation he could find was that the firm had made the following self-interested calculation: it is better to support a man who owes us nearly three hundred thousand francs, and have the money at the end of three months, than to precipitate his ruin and have only six or eight per cent of the original sum.

Unfortunately, whether through hatred or blindness, not all M. Morrel's associates thought in that way; some even thought the opposite. The bills that Morrel had signed were consequently presented at the till with scrupulous punctuality but, thanks to the time that had been allowed them by the Englishman, were paid on the nail by Coclès. The latter consequently went on in his state of fateful indifference. Only M. Morrel could appreciate, with horror, that if he had had to reimburse the fifty thousand francs to de Boville on the 15th and, on the 30th, the thirty-two thousand five hundred francs of bills for which (as for his debt to the inspector of prisons) he had obtained a stay, he would have been a lost man that very month.

The conclusion in business circles in Marseille was that Morrel would not be able to ride out the succession of disasters that were befalling him. There was consequently great astonishment at seeing him pay his debts at the end of the month with his habitual promptitude. However, this was not enough to restore confidence, and there was unanimous agreement that the end of the following month would see the unfortunate man bankrupt.

The month passed in extraordinary efforts on Morrel's part to muster all his resources. At one time his paper, whatever the term on it, had been accepted with confidence and even sought out. Morrel tried to issue some bills for ninety days but found the doors of the banks closed. Luckily, Morrel himself had some bills due that he could call in; he did so successfully, and so found himself once more able to meet his obligations at the end of July.

No one, as it happened, had seen the representative of Thomson and French again in Marseille. The day after his visit to Morrel, or the day after that, he had vanished. As he had not been in contact with anyone in Marseille except the mayor, the inspector of prisons and M. Morrel, his stay had left no trace behind it other than the different memories that these three people had of him. As for the sailors of the *Pharaon*, it appeared that they had found another ship to sign on, because they too had vanished.

Captain Gaumard had recovered from the illness that kept him in Palma and returned to Marseille. He was reluctant to go to see M. Morrel, but the shipowner heard of his arrival and went himself to find him. He already knew, from Penelon's story, how courageously the captain had behaved throughout the shipwreck, and it was he who tried to console the other man. He brought him his salary, which Captain Gaumard had not dared to draw.

As he was coming down the stairs, Morrel met Penelon coming up. It appeared that the helmsman had made good use of his money, because he was kitted out in entirely new clothes. He seemed quite embarrassed on meeting his owner; he drew back into the further corner of the landing, shifted his quid of tobacco from left to right and right to left, rolling his eyes and only replying with a feeble handshake to the one that M. Morrel, with his habitual warmth, had offered him. Morrel attributed Penelon's embarrassment to the elegance of his dress: it was clear that the good man had not indulged in such luxury out of his last pay, so he must clearly have signed on with another ship, and his shame must be for not having, so to speak, gone into a longer period of mourning for the *Pharaon*. Perhaps he had even been to tell Captain Gaumard of his good fortune and let him know what his new master was offering.

'Fine men, brave men,' Morrel said as he walked away. 'I hope your new master feels as much affection for you as I did, and enjoys more luck than I do!'

August passed with continued and repeated attempts by Morrel to increase his old credit or open a new account. On 20 August it was learned in Marseille that he had reserved a place on the stage-coach, and as a result they said that it must be at the end of that current month that he would declare his bankruptcy: he had already left, so that he would not have to be present in these awful circumstances, leaving his head clerk, Emmanuel, and his cashier, Coclès, to take care of it on his behalf. But, against all expectations, when 31 August came, the office opened for payment as usual. Coclès appeared behind the grille, as calm as Horace's just man, examined the paper that was presented to him with the same attention as ever and, from first to last, settled the bills with his usual precision. There were even two reimbursements which had been foreseen by M. Morrel, which Coclès paid as scrupulously as the bills which were personally drawn on the shipowner. No one could understand what was happening but, with the usual tenacity of prophets of doom, they postponed the bankruptcy until the end of September.

Morrel returned on the first of the month. His whole family had been waiting anxiously for him, because in this trip to Paris lay his last hope of salvation. Morrel had thought of Danglars, now a millionaire but once indebted to him, because it was on Morrel's recommendation that Danglars had entered the service of the Spanish banker in whose firm he had started to build his vast fortune. Today, it was said that Danglars had six or eight million of his own, and limitless credit. Without taking a single *écu* from his own pocket, Danglars could rescue Morrel: he had only to guarantee a loan and Morrel was safe. Morrel had thought of Danglars a long time ago, but one has certain instinctive and uncontrollable aversions . . . so Morrel had waited as long as possible before turning to this last resort. He had been right to do so, because he returned broken by the humiliation of a refusal.

Despite that, Morrel had not voiced the slightest complaint on his return or the least recrimination. He had wept as he embraced his wife and daughter, proffered a friendly hand to Emmanuel, shut himself up in his study on the second floor and asked for Coclès.

'This time,' the two women said to Emmanuel, 'we are done for.'

Then they put their heads together and quickly agreed that Julie should write to her brother, who was with the army at Nîmes, to tell him to come immediately. Instinctively the poor women felt that they would need all their strength to bear the coming troubles.

In any case, Maximilien Morrel, though barely twenty-two, already had a considerable influence over his father. He was a firm, upright young man. When the time came for him to take up a career, his father had not tried to impose upon him and asked young Maximilien how he felt. The lad replied that he wanted to follow a military career. He had consequently studied successfully, taken the competitive exam to enter the Ecole Polytechnique and graduated from there as a sub-lieutenant in the 53rd regiment of the line. He had been at this rank for the past year, but was promised a promotion to lieutenant at the first opportunity. In the regiment, Maximilien Morrel was often cited as strictly observing, not only all his obligations as a soldier but also all his duties as a man, and he was nicknamed The Stoic. Naturally, many of those who called him by this name repeated it because they had heard it, without knowing what it meant.

This was the young man whose mother and sister were about to call him to their aid, to support them through what they guessed would be difficult times. They were not mistaken about the difficulty. A moment after M. Morrel went into his study with Coclès, Julie saw the cashier come out, pale, trembling, his face expressing utter dismay. She wanted to question him as he went past, but the good man, plunging down the staircase at what was for him an unprecedented speed, only cried out, raising his arms to heaven: 'Oh, Mademoiselle! Mademoiselle! What a terrible disaster! I would never have believed it!'

Shortly afterwards Julie saw him return, carrying two or three thick registers, a pocket book and a bag of money. Morrel examined the registers, opened the pocket book and counted the money.

His entire fortune amounted to six or eight thousand francs, and his expected revenue, up to the fifth, to four or five thousand, making – at the very most – total assets of fourteen thousand francs with which to pay outgoings of two hundred and eighty-seven thousand, five hundred francs. It was not possible even to consider an interim payment.

However, when M. Morrel came down to dinner, he seemed quite calm. The two women were more terrified by this calm exterior than they would have been by the most abject depression.

After dinner, Morrel was accustomed to go out: he went to take coffee at the Cercle des Phocéens, where he read *Le Sémaphore*. That day, he stayed in and went back to his office.

As for Coclès, he appeared totally numb. For part of the day he remained in the courtyard, sitting on a stone, bareheaded, under the blazing sun.

Emmanuel tried to reassure the women, but he could not find the right words. He knew too much about the affairs of the firm not to realize that a great catastrophe was about to descend on the Morrel family.

Night came. The two women had stayed up, hoping that Morrel would come and see them on his way back from his study, but they heard him tiptoe past their door, no doubt fearing that they would call out to him. They listened as he went into his room and locked the door from inside.

Mme Morrel sent her daughter to bed and, half an hour later, got up, took off her shoes and crept out into the corridor to look through the keyhole and see what her husband was doing. In the corridor she saw a shadow moving away: it was Julie who, also worried, had been there before her.

'He's writing,' she said, going up to her mother.

The two women had read each other's thoughts.

Mme Morrel bent over to the keyhole. M. Morrel was indeed writing, but Mme Morrel saw something that her daughter had not noticed, which was that her husband was writing on headed paper. The awful idea came to her that he was making his will. She shuddered uncontrollably, yet had the strength to say nothing.

The next day, M. Morrel appeared altogether calm. He went to his office as usual and came down to lunch as usual; only, today, after dining, he made his daughter sit next to him, took her head in his arms and pressed it for a long time against his breast.

In the evening Julie told her mother that, however calm he might seem on the outside, she had noticed that her father's heart was beating furiously.

The following two days went by in almost the same way. On 4 September, in the evening, M. Morrel once more asked his daughter to give him back the key of his study. She shivered: the request seemed ominous to her. Why should her father ask her to return this key, which she had always held – and which, even when she was a child, he had taken away from her only as a punishment!

She looked at him. 'What have I done wrong, father,' she said, 'for you to take back the study key?'

'Nothing, child,' the unhappy Morrel replied, tears brimming in his eyes at this simple question. 'It is only that I need it.'

Julie pretended to look for the key. 'I must have left it in my room,' she said. She went out but, instead of going to her room, she went down to look for Emmanuel.

'On no account give your father back that key,' he told her. 'And tomorrow morning, as far as is possible, don't leave him alone.'

She tried to question him, but Emmanuel either knew nothing more or else wished to say nothing.

Throughout the night of 4th to 5th September, Mme Morrel stayed with her ear pressed against the panelling. Until three o'clock in the morning she heard her husband pacing nervously around his room. It was only at three o'clock that he threw himself on his bed.

The two women spent the night together. They had been waiting for Maximilien since the previous evening.

At eight o'clock, M. Morrel came into their room. He was calm, but the torments of the previous night could be read on his pale and haggard face. The women did not dare ask if he had slept well.

Morrel was kinder to his wife and more paternal towards his daughter than he had ever been: he could not have his fill of looking at the poor child and embracing her. She recalled Emmanuel's injunction and tried to follow her father when he went out, but he gently pushed her aside.

'Stay with your mother,' he said.

She tried to protest.

'I insist!' said Morrel.

This was the first time that he had ever said 'I insist' to his daughter, but he did so in a voice so full of paternal affection that Julie did not dare take a step forward. She remained standing where she was, motionless and speechless. A moment later the door opened again and she felt two arms enfold her and a mouth pressed against her brow. She looked up and gave a cry of joy.

'Maximilien! Brother!' she exclaimed.

Hearing this, Mme Morrel ran in and threw herself into her son's arms.

'Mother,' the young man said, looking from Mme Morrel to her daughter, 'what has happened? What is wrong? Your letter terrified me; I came straight away.'

'Julie,' Mme Morrel said, motioning to the young man. 'Go and tell your father that Maximilien has just arrived.'

The girl ran out but, at the top of the stairs, found a man with a letter in his hand.

'Are you Mademoiselle Julie Morrel?' he asked, in a strong Italian accent.

'Yes, Monsieur,' she stammered. 'But what do you want of me? I don't know you.'

'Read this letter,' the man said, handing a note to her.

She hesitated.

'Your father's life depends on it,' said the messenger.

She tore the letter from his hands, opened it hastily and read as follows:

Go immediately to the Allées de Meilhan, enter the house at number 15, ask the concierge for the key to the room on the fifth floor, go into this room, take the purse knitted in red silk that you will find on the corner of the mantelpiece and take this purse to your father.

It is essential that he should have it before eleven o'clock.

You promised to obey me unquestioningly, and I am holding you to that promise.

SINBAD THE SAILOR.

The girl cried out for joy and looked around for the man who had given her the letter, to ask him some questions, but he had disappeared. So she looked back again at the paper and noticed that there was a postscript. She read: 'It is important that you should carry out this mission yourself, and alone. If you are accompanied, or if anyone except you comes in your place, the concierge will reply that he knows nothing about it.'

This postscript dampened the girl's happiness. Perhaps there was some risk, perhaps this was a trap? Because of her innocence, she was ignorant of exactly what might threaten a young girl of her age; but one does not need to identify a danger to fear it. Indeed, it is noticeable that it is precisely the danger that is unknown which one fears most.

Julie hesitated and decided to ask for advice. But, for some reason, it was not either to her mother or to her brother that she turned, but to Emmanuel.

She went down, told him what had happened on the day when

the representative of Thomson and French had come to her father's, told him about the scene on the stairs, repeated the promise that she had made and showed him the letter.

'You must go, Mademoiselle,' said Emmanuel.

'Go?' Julie murmured.

'Yes, I shall accompany you.'

'But can't you see where it says I must be alone?'

'And so you shall be. I shall wait for you on a corner of the Rue du Musée. If you are away long enough to give me any anxiety, I shall follow you and, I promise you this, it will be the worse for anyone against whom you may have any complaint.'

'You mean, Emmanuel,' said the girl, still undecided, 'that you think I should do as it says here?'

'Yes. Didn't the messenger tell you that your father's life was at stake?'

'But, Emmanuel, what risk is there to his life then?'

Emmanuel paused for a moment, but the wish to make up the girl's mind at once overcame his hesitation.

'Listen,' he said. 'Today is the fifth of September, isn't it?'

'Yes.'

'And today, at eleven o'clock, your father has nearly three hundred thousand francs to pay.'

'We know that.'

'Well,' Emmanuel said, 'he doesn't have even fifteen thousand in his cashbox.'

'So what will happen?'

'What will happen is that today, if your father has not found someone to help him before eleven o'clock, by midday he will have to declare himself bankrupt.'

'Come, come quickly!' the girl cried, pulling him along with her.

Meanwhile Mme Morrel had told everything to her son. He had known that there had been serious reforms in the economy of the household as a result of his father's misfortunes, but he did not realize that things had reached such a pass. He was completely overwhelmed. Then, suddenly, he rushed out of the apartment and ran up the stairs, thinking his father was in his study, but there was no answer to his knock.

As he was at the door of the study, he heard that of the apartment open and turned around to see his father. Instead of going directly up to his study, M. Morrel had gone into his room, from which he was only now emerging.

He gave a cry of surprise on seeing Maximilien. He did not know that the young man had returned. He stayed motionless on the spot, clasping something hidden under his frock-coat with his left arm. Maximilien quickly came down the stairs and embraced his father but suddenly started back, leaving only his right hand resting on his father's chest.

'Father,' he said, deathly pale, 'why have you a pair of pistols under your coat?'

'This is what I feared!' said Morrel.

'Father, father! In heaven's name!' the young man exclaimed. 'What are these weapons for?'

'Maximilien,' Morrel replied, looking directly at his son, 'you are a man, and a man of honour. Come with me and I shall tell you.'

Morrel walked with a firm step up to his study while Maximilien followed him, his knees trembling.

Morrel opened the door and closed it behind his son. Then he crossed the antechamber, went into the office, placed his pistols on a corner of the table and pointed to the open register. Here was a precise summary of the situation. In half an hour Morrel would have to pay two hundred and eighty-seven thousand five hundred francs.

His total assets amounted to fifteen thousand, two hundred and fifty-seven francs.

'Read it,' he said.

The young man read and for a moment appeared to be crushed. Morrel said nothing: what was there to say that would add anything to the inexorable verdict of the figures?

'Father, have you done everything,' the young man said, after a moment's pause, 'to stave off this misfortune?'

'Yes,' said Morrel.

'You are expecting no funds to be paid in?'

'None.'

'You have exhausted every possible resource?'

'Every one.'

'And in half an hour,' Maximilien said in a dull voice, 'your name will be dishonoured.'

'Blood washes away dishonour,' said Morrel.

'You are right, father. I take your meaning.' Then, stretching his hand out towards the pistols: 'There is one for you and one for me. Thank you!'

Morrel clasped his hand.

'Your mother . . . your sister . . . who will feed them?'

The young man's body shook from head to toe.

'Father,' he said, 'are you asking me to live?'

'Yes, I tell you to. It is your duty. Your mind is calm and strong, Maximilien. You are no ordinary man. I am not ordering you, I am not instructing you, I am just saying: consider your situation as if you were an outsider looking at it, and judge for yourself.'

The young man thought for a moment, then an expression of sublime resignation passed across his eyes. But, with a slow, sad gesture, he took off his epaulettes, the marks of his rank.

'Very well,' he said, offering Morrel his hand. 'Die in peace, father! I shall live!'

Morrel made as if to throw himself at his son's feet. Maximilien drew his father to him, and for a moment these two noble hearts beat, one against the other.

'You know it is not my fault?' said Morrel.

Maximilien smiled.

'I do know, father that you are the most honest man I have ever met.'

'Very well, there is nothing more to say. Now go back to your mother and your sister.'

'Father, give me your blessing!' The young man knelt.

Morrel grasped his son's head between both hands, drew him to him and, kissing him over and over, said: 'Oh, yes, yes! I bless you in my name and in the name of three generations of men of impeccable reputation; listen to what they are saying in my voice: the edifice which misfortune has destroyed, Providence can rebuild. When they see me dead in this manner, even the most inexorable will take pity on you. Perhaps you will be given the time that has been refused me. Try to ensure that the word infamy is not spoken. Go to work, young man, struggle eagerly and bravely: live, you, your mother and your sister, on the basic minimum so that, day by day, the wealth of those in whose debt I am should grow and bear fruit in your hands. Consider that a fine day is coming, a great day, the solemn day when the bankruptcy will be discharged, the day when, in this same office, you will say: "My father died because he could not do what I am doing today; but he died with calm and peace of mind, because he knew as he died that I would do it." '

'Oh, father, father!' cried the young man. 'If only you could live!'

'If I live, everything will change. Concern will change to doubt, pity to implacability. If I live, I shall be no more than a man who failed to keep his word, who could not live up to his promises – in short, a bankrupt. But think: if I die, Maximilien, my body will be that of an unfortunate but honest man. If I live, my best friends will shun my house; if I die, all Marseille will follow me, weeping, to my final rest. If I live, you will be ashamed of my name; if I die, you can hold up your head and say: "I am the son of a man who killed himself because, for the first time, he was obliged to break his word." '

The young man groaned, but he appeared resigned. This was the second time that certainty had descended, not on his heart, but on his mind.

'And now,' Morrel said, 'leave me and try to keep the women away from here.'

'Do you not wish to see my sister?' Maximilien asked.

The young man saw a vague last hope in this meeting, which is why he suggested it. M. Morrel shook his head, saying: 'I saw her and said farewell this morning.'

'Don't you have any particular requests for me, father?' Maximilien asked in a strained voice.

'I do, my son, a sacred request.'

'Tell me, father.'

'The firm of Thomson and French is the only one which, out of humanity, perhaps out of self-interest – but it is not for me to read into the hearts of men – took pity on me. Its representative is the man who in ten minutes will come here to cash a bill for two hundred and eighty-seven thousand five hundred francs, and he – I won't say he granted me, but he offered me three months' grace. Let this firm be repaid first of all, my son; let this man be sacred to you.'

'Yes, father,' said Maximilien.

'And now, once more, adieu,' said Morrel. 'Go now, I need to be alone. You will find my will in the writing-table in my bedroom.'

The young man stayed, not moving, feeling the wish to do so but not the power to carry out the wish.

'Listen, Maximilien,' said his father. 'Suppose I were a soldier like you, and I had received an order to capture a redoubt and you knew that I would be killed in doing so, wouldn't you say to me what you said a short while ago: "Go on, father, because you will be dishonoured if you stay, and death is better than shame"?'

'Yes,' said the young man. 'Yes, yes.' And, clasping his father in his arms with a convulsive movement, he said: 'Farewell, father!' and dashed out of the study.

When his son had left, Morrel remained for a moment standing, staring at the door. Then he reached out his hand, found the rope of a bell-pull and rang. A moment later Coclès appeared.

He was no longer the same man. These three days of certainty had broken him. This thought: the House of Morrel could not meet its obligations, bent him closer to the ground than the weight of another twenty years on his back.

'My dear Coclès,' said Morrel, in an indescribable tone of voice. 'Please remain in the antechamber. When the gentleman who was here three months ago – you know, the representative of Thomson and French – when he arrives, you will announce him.'

Coclès said nothing. He nodded, went into the antechamber and waited.

Morrel fell back into his chair. His eyes turned to the clock. He had seven minutes left, no more. The hand was turning at an incredible speed: he even thought he could see it move.

It is impossible to say what was going on in these final moments in the mind of this man who, still young, perhaps as the result of misguided reasoning, however persuasive it might be, was about to separate himself from all that he loved in the world and leave this existence, which offered him all the joys of family life. In order to gain some idea of it, one would need to see his forehead bathed in sweat, but resigned; his eyes wet with tears, yet raised heavenwards.

The hand moved on, the pistols were loaded. He reached out, took one of them and murmured his daughter's name.

After that he put down the fatal weapon, took a pen and wrote a few words. He felt that he had still not said a sufficient farewell to his dear child.

Then he turned back to the clock. The time could no longer be counted in minutes, but in seconds.

He picked up the weapons again, his mouth half open and his eyes on the hands of the clock. Then he shuddered at the noise he himself made in cocking the gun.

At that moment a colder sweat broke out on his brow and a more terrible agony gripped his heart.

He heard the door to the stairway creak on its hinges.

The door of his study opened.

The clock was about to strike eleven.

Morrel did not turn around. He was waiting for Coclès to say: 'The representative of Thomson and French . . .'

He put the gun to his mouth . . .

Suddenly he heard a cry: it was his daughter's voice.

He turned around and saw Julie. The gun dropped from his hand.

'Father!' the girl cried, breathless and almost fainting with joy. 'Saved! You are saved!'

And she flung herself into his arms, brandishing in one hand a red silk purse.

'Saved, child! What do you mean?'

'Yes, saved! Look, look!'

Morrel took the purse and shivered, because he vaguely recalled it as something that had once belonged to him.

In one side was the bill for two hundred and eighty-seven thousand five hundred francs. The bill was acquitted.

In the other side was a diamond the size of a hazelnut, with these words written on a small piece of parchment: 'Julie's dowry'.

Morrel wiped his brow. He thought he was dreaming.

At that moment the clock struck eleven. It struck for him as if each blow of the hammer was striking on his very heart.

'Come now, my child,' he said. 'Explain this: where did you find this purse?'

'In a house in the Allées de Meilhan, at number fifteen, on the mantelpiece of a poor little room on the fifth floor.'

'But this purse does not belong to you!' he cried.

Julie handed her father the letter she had received that morning.

'And you went to this house alone?' he said, after reading it.

'Emmanuel came with me, father. He agreed to wait for me on the corner of the Rue du Musée. But the strange thing is that, when I came back, he was no longer there.'

'Monsieur Morrel!' cried a voice on the stairs. 'Monsieur Morrel!'

'That's his voice,' said Julie.

At the same moment Emmanuel came in, his face contorted with joy and emotion.

'The *Pharaon*!' he shouted. 'The *Pharaon*!'

'What is this? The *Pharaon*? Are you mad, Emmanuel? You know very well that she is lost.'

'The *Pharaon*, Monsieur! They have signalled the *Pharaon*. She is coming into port.'

Morrel slumped backwards into his chair, drained of all strength, his mind refusing to accept this succession of incredible . . . unheard of . . . fabulous events.

Then his son came in, exclaiming: 'Father, why did you say the *Pharaon* was lost? The lookout has announced its arrival and it is sailing into port.'

'My friends,' said Morrel, 'if this is so, we must believe in a divine miracle. It is impossible, impossible!'

But what was real, but no less incredible, was the purse that he held in his hands, the bill of exchange acquitted and this splendid diamond.

'Oh, Monsieur!' said Coclès. 'What does it mean? The *Pharaon*?'

'Come on, children,' said Morrel, getting up, 'let us go and see; and God have pity on us if this is a false rumour.'

They went down. Mme Morrel was waiting on the stairs; the poor woman had not dared to come up.

In a moment they were on the Canebière.

There was a large crowd in the port, and it parted to make way for Morrel. Every voice was crying: 'The *Pharaon*! The *Pharaon*!' And, indeed, something wonderful, unimaginable: off the Tour Saint-Jean, a ship with these words in white letters inscribed on its prow: '*Pharaon* (Morrel and Son of Marseille)', exactly like the other *Pharaon*, laden like the other with cochineal and indigo, was lowering its anchor and furling its sails. On deck, Captain Gaumard was giving orders and Master Penelon was waving to M. Morrel.

There could be no further doubt: the evidence of his senses was supported by ten thousand witnesses.

As Morrel and his son were embracing on the jetty, to the applause of the whole town which had come to see this extraordinary event, a man, his face half covered by a black beard, who had been hiding behind a sentry box and observing the scene with obvious emotion, muttered the following words: 'Be happy, noble heart. Be blessed for all the good you have done and will yet do. Let my gratitude remain hidden in the shadows like your good deeds.'

With a smile in which joy and happiness mingled, he left his hiding-place, without anyone paying any attention to him, so pre-occupied were they with the events of the day, and went down one of those small flights of steps that serve as a landing-stage, crying three times: 'Jacopo! Jacopo! Jacopo!'

At this, a boat rowed over to him, took him aboard and carried him out to a yacht, superbly fitted out, on to the deck of which he leapt with the agility of a sailor. From there, he looked once again towards Morrel who, weeping with joy, was shaking the hands of everyone in the crowd and vaguely thanking his unknown bene-factor whom he seemed to be searching for in the sky.

'And now,' said the stranger, 'farewell, goodness, humanity, gratitude . . . Farewell all those feelings that nourish and illuminate the heart! I have taken the place of Providence to reward the good; now let the avenging God make way for me to punish the wrongdoer!'

At this, he gave a sign and, as if it had been waiting just for this to set sail, the yacht headed out to sea.

XXXI

ITALY – SINBAD THE SAILOR

Near the beginning of the year 1838, two young men belonging to fashionable Parisian society, Vicomte Albert de Morcerf and Baron Franz d'Epinay, found themselves in Florence. They had agreed that they would meet to spend that year's carnival together in Rome, where Franz, who had lived in Italy for nearly four years, would serve as Albert's guide.

Since visiting Rome for the carnival is no small matter, especially when one does not intend to spend the night in the Piazza del Popolo or the Campo Vaccino, they wrote to Signor Pastrini,[1] proprietor of the Hôtel de Londres in the Piazza di Spagna, to request him to reserve a comfortable suite for them.

Pastrini replied that he could only offer them two rooms and a drawing-room *al secondo piano*, for which he would accept the modest emolument of a *louis* a day. The two young men accepted; and then, wishing to make use of the intervening period, Albert left for Naples, while Franz remained in Florence.

When he had spent some time enjoying life in the city of the Medici, when he had walked back and forth in that Eden which is known as the Casini, when he had been a guest in the houses of those splendid hosts who do the honours of Florence, he took a fancy – having already seen Corsica, the cradle of Bonaparte – to visit the island of Elba, that great staging-post in the life of Napoleon.

So one evening he untied a barchetta from the iron ring that was attaching it to the docks at Leghorn, settled himself in the stern, wrapped in his cloak, and spoke only these words to the sailors: 'To Elba!'

The boat left the harbour like a seabird leaving its nest and the next day put Franz down in Porto Ferrajo.

He crossed the imperial island, following every trace that the giant's footsteps had left there, and embarked at Marciana.

Two hours after leaving land, he touched it again, getting off at Pianosa, where he had been assured that he would find infinite numbers of red partridge.

The hunting proved poor. Franz killed barely a handful of thin birds and, like any huntsman who has tired himself out to no purpose, got back into his boat in rather bad humour.

'Now, if Your Excellency wishes,' said the boatman, 'you could have some good hunting.'

'Where?'

'Do you see that island?' the boatman said, pointing southwards and indicating a conical mass which rose out of the sea, bathed in the loveliest indigo light.

'What is it?' Franz asked him.

'Monte Cristo,' said the Livornan.

'But I have no licence to hunt on that island.'

'Your Excellency does not need permission, the island is deserted.'

'Well I never,' said the young man. 'That's rare: a desert island in the middle of the Mediterranean.'

'But natural, Excellency. The island is a mass of rock; there is perhaps not so much as an acre of cultivable land on all its surface.'

'And to whom does it belong?'

'To Tuscany.'

'What game will I find there?'

'Thousands of wild goats.'

'Which live by licking the rocks, I suppose,' Franz said, with an incredulous smile.

'No, by grazing on the heather, the myrtles and the gum-trees that grow between them.'

'Where could I sleep?'

'On the ground, in the caves, or on board in your cloak. In any case, if Your Excellency wishes, we can leave immediately the hunt is over: as Your Excellency knows, we can sail as well by night as by day and, if the wind fails, we can row.'

As Franz still had some time before he needed to meet his friend, and as he was assured of their lodgings in Rome, he accepted this proposal to compensate for the disappointment of his previous hunt. On his assent, the sailors exchanged a few words in a whisper.

'Well?' he asked. 'What now? Is there some problem?'

'No,' said the master of the boat, 'but we must advise Your Excellency that the island has been designated contumacious.'

'What does that mean?'

'It means that, since Monte Cristo is uninhabited and is sometimes used as a staging-post by smugglers and pirates from Corsica, Sardinia or Africa, if there is any evidence of our having stopped there, we shall be obliged when we return to Leghorn to spend six days in quarantine.'

'The devil we will! That puts a different complexion on it! Six days! The same time that it took God to create the world. It's a bit too long, my friends.'

'But who is to say that His Excellency has been to Monte Cristo?'

'I certainly shan't!' Franz exclaimed.

'And nor will we,' said the sailors.

'In that case, ahoy for Monte Cristo.'

The master ordered them to change course for the island and the boat began to sail in that direction.

Franz waited for the manoeuvre to be completed and, when the new course was set, the wind was filling the sail and the four sailors had resumed their places, three at the bow, one at the rudder, he resumed his conversation with the captain. 'My dear Gaetano,' he said, 'I think you just said that the island of Monte Cristo was a refuge for pirates: this is a rather different game from goats.'

'Yes, Excellency, that's a fact.'

'I knew that there were such people as smugglers, but I thought that since the capture of Algiers[2] and the destruction of the Regency, there were no pirates left outside the novels of Fenimore Cooper and Captain Marryat.'

'Your Excellency is wrong. The same is true of pirates as of bandits, who were supposed to have been exterminated by Pope Leo XII, but who nonetheless stop travellers every day right up to the gates of Rome. Did you not hear that barely six months ago the French chargé d'affaires to the Holy See was robbed, five hundred yards from Velletri?'

'Yes, I did.'

'Now, if Your Excellency were to live in Leghorn, as we do, you would hear from time to time that a vessel laden with merchandise, or a pretty English yacht which was expected in Bastia, Porto Ferrajo or Civita Vecchia, has not made port, and that no one knows what has become of it, except that it has doubtless been wrecked on some rock. Well, the rock that it hit was a low narrow-boat, with six or eight men on board, which surprised it and pillaged it, some dark and stormy night off a wild, uninhabited island, just as bandits stop and pillage a mail coach at the entrance to a wood.'

'But in that case,' said Franz, still lying back in the boat, 'why don't the victims of these accidents complain and bring down the vengeance of the French, Tuscan or Sardinian governments on the head of the pirates?'

'Why not?' Gaetano asked with a smile.

'Yes, why not?'

'Because first of all they unload everything that is worth taking off the ship or the yacht and put it in their boat; then they tie the hands and feet of the crew, tie a cannonball round the neck of each man, make a hole as big as a barrel in the keel of the captured vessel, go back up on deck, batten down the hatches and return to their own boat. Ten minutes later, the ship starts to moan and groan, then bit by bit it founders. First one side, then the other goes under; then it rises up, then dips down again, slipping lower and lower each time. Suddenly, there is a noise like a cannon shot: that's the air bursting the deck. Then the vessel struggles like a drowning man, getting heavier with every movement that it makes. Soon the water, trapped under pressure inside, bursts out of every opening, like the spouting liquid from the air-holes of a gigantic whale. Finally it gives its death-cry, rolls over on itself and goes under, leaving a huge funnel in the deep which spins for an instant, then gradually fills and eventually disappears altogether. The result is that in five minutes only the eye of God Himself could see a trace of the vanished ship beneath the calm surface of the sea.

'Now do you understand,' he added, smiling again, 'why the ship does not return to port and the crew does not lodge a complaint?'

If Gaetano had told him this story before suggesting their expedition, Franz would quite probably have thought twice before agreeing to it; but they were on their way, and he felt it would be cowardly to go back. He was one of those who do not court danger but who, if it presents itself, retain all their composure in confronting it; he was one of those calm-willed men who consider a risk in life as they do an opponent in a duel, measuring his movements, studying his strength, and breaking off long enough to catch their breath, but not enough to appear cowardly. Such men, assessing all their advantages with a single glance, kill with a single blow.

'Huh!' he continued. 'I have crossed Sicily and Calabria, I've sailed around the archipelago for two months, and never yet have I seen a trace of any bandit or pirate.'

'But I did not say that to Your Excellency in order to suggest that you should alter your plans. Your Excellency asked me a question and I replied, nothing more.'

'Yes, my dear Gaetano, and your conversation is most interesting. So, as I want to enjoy it as long as possible, let's go to Monte Cristo.'

However, they were quickly nearing the end of the journey. They had a fresh wind in their sails and the boat was making six or seven knots. At their approach, the island seemed to rise up out of the sea. Through the clear atmosphere of the dying rays of the sun they could see, like cannonballs in an arsenal, the mass of rocks piled up, one above the other, with between them the dark red of the heather and the light green of the trees. Though the sailors appeared perfectly calm, it was clear that they were watchful, scanning the vast mirror across which the boat was slipping, its horizon interrupted only by the white sails of a few fishing boats which hovered like seagulls on the crests of the waves.

They were scarcely more than fifteen miles from Monte Cristo when the sun began to set behind Corsica, the mountains of which rose up to their right, darkly serrated against the sky. The mass of stones rose threateningly in front of the boat, like the giant Adamastor,[3] its crest gilded by the sun which was concealed behind it. Little by little the shadowy figure came up out of the sea and appeared to drive before it the last ray of the dying day, until at last the shaft of light was driven to the very tip of the cone, where it paused for a moment like the flaming plume of a volcano. Finally the darkness, still rising, progressively swept across the summit as it had previously swept across the base, and the island had only the appearance of a mountain, growing constantly a darker shade of grey. Half an hour later, everything was pitch black.

Luckily the sailors were in familiar waters and knew every last rock in the Tuscan archipelago; otherwise, in the midst of this blackness that had enfolded the boat, Franz might not have been altogether easy in his mind. Corsica had vanished entirely and even the island of Monte Cristo had become invisible; but the sailors seemed to have the lynx's faculty of seeing in the dark, and the pilot, sitting at the rudder, did not show the slightest hesitation.

About an hour had passed since sunset when Franz thought he could see a dark shape, about a quarter of a mile to the left. It was so difficult to distinguish what it could be that, rather than risking the sailors' mockery by mistaking some passing clouds for land, he said nothing. But suddenly a great light appeared on the shore: the land might resemble a cloud, but this fire was not a meteor.

'What's that light?' he asked.

'Hush!' said the boatman. 'It's a fire.'

'But you said that the island was uninhabited.'

'I said that it had no permanent inhabitants, but I also mentioned that smugglers sometimes put in there.'

'And pirates?'

'And pirates,' said Gaetano, repeating Franz's words. 'That's why I gave the order to sail past the island: as you can see, the fire is behind us.'

'But surely,' Franz said, 'it seems to me that this fire should reassure us rather than otherwise. People who were afraid of being seen would not have lit a fire like that.'

'Oh, that means nothing,' said Gaetano. 'If you could judge the position of the island in the darkness, you would see that the fire is sited in such a way that it cannot be seen from the coast, or from Pianosa, but only from the open sea.'

'So you suspect that this fire indicates unwelcome company?'

'That's what we must find out,' said Gaetano, keeping his eyes fixed on the terrestrial star.

'How can we do that?'

'You'll see.'

At this, Gaetano had a few words with his comrades and, after they had talked for five minutes, they carried out a manoeuvre which allowed them instantly to reverse their course. In this way they were sailing back in the direction from which they had come and, a few moments later, the fire disappeared, hidden behind some outcrop on the land.

At this, the pilot altered course yet again with the rudder, and the little boat came visibly closer to the island, until it was only some fifty yards off-shore. Gaetano lowered the sail and the boat remained stationary.

All this had taken place in the most profound silence; indeed, since the change of course not a word had been spoken on board.

Gaetano, having suggested the expedition, had taken full responsibility for it on himself. The four sailors kept peering at him, preparing the oars and evidently getting ready to row to shore which, thanks to the darkness, was not difficult.

As for Franz, he was inspecting his weapons with the characteristic sang-froid we have mentioned. He had two double-barrelled guns and a rifle, which he loaded. Then he cocked them and waited.

Meanwhile the master had taken off his shirt and jacket, and secured his trousers around his waist; as he was barefoot, he had no shoes or stockings to remove. Once dressed – or, rather, undressed – like this, he put his finger to his lips to show that they should observe complete silence and, after slipping gently into the sea, swam towards the shore, but so cautiously that they could not hear the slightest sound. His path could be followed only by the phosphorescent trail he left in his wake. Soon even this disappeared, and it was clear that Gaetano had reached land.

For half an hour everyone on the boat remained motionless. Then the same luminous furrow reappeared near the shore and came towards them. In a moment, with two strokes, Gaetano was alongside.

'Well?' Franz and the four sailors asked simultaneously.

'Well,' said Gaetano, 'they are Spanish smugglers, and they only have with them two Corsican bandits.'

'What are two Corsican bandits doing with Spanish smugglers?'

'Bless my soul!' said Gaetano, in tones of the most sincere Christian charity. 'We are here to help one another, Excellency. Bandits are often hard-pressed on land by the gendarmes or the carabinieri, so they find a boat with good fellows like us in it. They come and request the hospitality of our floating house. How can one refuse to succour a poor devil with men on his tail? We take him in and, for greater safety, put out to sea. This costs us nothing and it saves the life – or, at least, the freedom – of one of our fellow men who, as it happens, acknowledges the service we have done him by showing us a good spot to put off our cargo where it is safe from prying eyes.'

'Oh, I see!' said Franz. 'And are you a bit of a smuggler yourself, then, my dear Gaetano?'

'What do you expect, Excellency!' he replied with an indescribable smile. 'One does a bit of everything. A man must live.'

'So you know where you stand with the present inhabitants of Monte Cristo?'

'More or less. We sailors are like freemasons, we recognize one another by certain signs.'

'And you think we shall have nothing to fear if we disembark here in our turn?'

'Nothing at all. Smugglers are not thieves.'

'But what about the two Corsican bandits?' Franz insisted, trying to allow for every possibility.

'Good Lord!' said Gaetano. 'It's not their fault if they're bandits, it's the fault of the authorities.'

'How can that be?'

'Of course! They are being hunted down because they made their bones, nothing more. As if revenge wasn't in a Corsican's nature . . .'

'What do you mean by "making their bones"? Having killed someone?' Franz asked, still curious.

'I mean killing an enemy,' said the master. 'That's quite different.'

'Well then,' the young man said, 'let's go and ask for the hospitality of these smugglers and bandits. Will they welcome us?'

'No doubt at all.'

'How many of them are there?'

'Four, Excellency; with the two bandits, that makes six.'

'Just the same as us, in fact. And if these gentlemen should prove unfriendly, then we are in a position to keep them at bay. So, one last time, let's land on Monte Cristo.'

'Yes, Excellency. But will you allow me to take a few extra precautions?'

'What, my good fellow! Be as wise as Nestor and as cautious as Ulysses. I not only allow it, I beg you.'

'Silence!' said Gaetano; and they all fell silent.

For someone like Franz, who considered everything in its true light, the situation, while not dangerous, still gave pause for serious thought. He was here, in the most profound darkness, in the middle of the sea, with sailors who did not know him and who had no reason to be loyal to him; who, moreover, knew that he had a few thousand francs in his belt and who had ten times examined his guns, at least with curiosity, if not envy: they were fine pieces. In addition to that, escorted by only these men, he was about to land on an island which certainly had a very religious name, but which appeared to offer Franz no greater hospitality than Calvary did to Christ, in view of the smugglers and the bandits. Then those stories of scuttled ships, which he had thought exaggerated by day-light, seemed more believable in the dark. So, caught between this – perhaps imaginary – double danger, he did not take his eyes off the men or his hand off the rifle.

During this time, the sailors had once more raised their sails and resumed their previous course. Through the darkness, Franz, whose eyes were already becoming somewhat accustomed to it, could see the granite giant beside which the boat was sailing; then finally, as they came round a rock for the second time, he saw the fire burning more brightly than ever, and around it five or six seated figures.

The light extended some hundred yards across the sea. Gaetano sailed just outside its reach, keeping the boat in the unlit darkness beyond. Then, when he was directly across from the bonfire, he turned the bow towards it and sailed boldly into the circle of light, singing a fisherman's song and taking the main part himself, while the crew joined in with the chorus.

At the first words of the song the men sitting around the fire got up and walked across to the landing-stage, keeping a close watch on the approaching boat so as to assess its size and intentions. They soon appeared to have satisfied themselves and went back to their places around the fire, where a kid was roasting – apart from one, who remained, standing on the shore.

When the boat was about twenty yards from land, the man on

the shore mechanically gestured with his carbine, like a sentry greeting a returning patrol, and shouted: 'Who goes there?' in Sardinian *patois*.

Franz cocked his repeating rifle unemotionally.

At this, Gaetano exchanged a few words with the man, which Franz could not understand, though they clearly concerned him.

'Does Your Excellency wish to be named,' the master asked, 'or would he prefer to go incognito?'

'My name must be entirely unknown to these men,' Franz said. 'So just tell them that I am a Frenchman who is travelling for his own amusement.'

When Gaetano had communicated this to him, the sentry gave an order to one of the men sitting at the fire; he immediately got up and disappeared among the rocks.

There was a silence. Everyone appeared preoccupied with his own affairs: Franz with the landing, the sailors with their sails, the smugglers with their kid; but, in the midst of this apparent lack of curiosity, they were observing one another.

The man who had gone away suddenly came back, from the opposite direction to the one in which he had gone. He nodded to the sentry, who turned to them and said merely: *'S'accommodi.'*

This Italian *'s'accommodi'* is untranslatable. It means at once: come, come in, welcome, make yourself at home, you are the master. It's like the Turkish phrase in Molière's play which astonished the Bourgeois Gentilhomme[4] by all the meanings that it could contain.

The sailors did not wait to be asked twice. With four strokes of the oars they brought the boat to shore. Gaetano jumped on to the beach, whispered a few more words to the sentry, and his crew then came down one after the other. Finally it was Franz's turn.

He had one of his guns slung across his shoulder, Gaetano had the other and one of the sailors was holding the rifle. His dress had something of both the artist and the dandy, which aroused no suspicion in his hosts, and consequently no unease.

The boat was tied up on the shore and they started to walk around, looking for a suitable place to camp; but the direction in which they were walking was not to the liking of the smuggler who was acting as sentry, because he shouted to Gaetano: 'No, not over there, please.'

Gaetano mumbled some excuse and, without argument, went

over to the other side, while two sailors went to fetch lighted torches so that they could see their way.

They went for about thirty yards then stopped on a little esplanade entirely surrounded by rocks, in each of which a kind of seat had been hollowed, not unlike small sentry-boxes where the guard can sit down. Around them, in patches of soil, grew some dwarf oaks and thick clumps of myrtle. Franz lowered a torch and recognized, from a pile of ashes, that he was not the first person to notice the comfort of this spot, which must be one of the usual stopping-places of random visitors to Monte Cristo.

He stopped worrying about any incident that might occur. Once on dry land, and having seen the mood of his hosts which, if not friendly, was at least one of indifference, all his anxieties had vanished; with the smell of roast kid coming from the nearby camp, anxiety had changed to appetite.

He mentioned this to Gaetano, who said that nothing was easier than to make supper when they had bread, wine and six partridge in the boat, and a fire to prepare them.

'Moreover,' he added, 'if Your Excellency is so tempted by the smell of that kid, I can go and offer our neighbours two of our birds for a slice of their beast.'

'Do it, Gaetano, do it,' said Franz. 'You are a born negotiator.'

Meanwhile the sailors had pulled up handfuls of heather and made firewood from myrtle and green oak branches, then set fire to it, so that they had quite a fine blaze going.

Franz was waiting impatiently, sniffing the smell of roasting kid, when the master came back with an anxious look about him.

'What now?' asked Franz. 'Have they refused our offer?'

'On the contrary,' Gaetano replied. 'Their chief, on learning that you were a young Frenchman, has invited you to dine with him.'

'Well, well,' said Franz, 'this chief is a most civil man and I see no reason to refuse, all the more so as I'm bringing my own contribution to the meal.'

'It's not that: there is more than enough to eat. But he is imposing an unusual condition on your visiting his home.'

'His home! Does he have a house here, then?'

'No, but I am assured that he has a very comfortable home, nonetheless.'

'Do you know this chief?'

'I have heard speak of him.'

'Good things or bad?'

'Both.'

'Well, dammit, what is this condition?'

'That you should let your eyes be bandaged and not remove the blindfold until you are told you can do so.'

Franz read what he could into Gaetano's face to discover what was behind this suggestion. Gaetano read his thoughts.

'The devil!' he said.

'I know, it needs thinking about.'

'What would you do in my place?' the young man asked.

'I've got nothing to lose. I'd go.'

'You would agree?'

'Yes, if only out of curiosity.'

'So this chief can show us something unusual?'

'Listen,' Gaetano said, lowering his voice, 'I don't know if what they say is true . . .' He paused and looked around to make sure they were not overheard.

'What do they say?'

'They say that the chief lives in a subterranean abode beside which the Pitti Palace is a mere trifle.'

'What a dream!' Franz said, sitting down again.

'Oh, it's not a dream, it's a reality! Cama, pilot of the *Saint-Ferdinand*, went in there one day and came out completely dazzled, saying that such treasures only exist in fairy-stories.'

'You know,' said Franz, 'what you are telling me sounds as if you were trying to lure me into the caves of Ali Baba.'

'I am only saying what I was told, Excellency.'

'So you advise me to accept?'

'That I'm not saying! Your Excellency will do as he pleases. I should not like to advise him in such circumstances.'

Franz thought for a few moments, realized that such a rich man could not feel any envy for him, as he had only a few thousand francs with him and, since he could see nothing coming of this but an excellent dinner, accepted. Gaetano went back with his answer.

However, as we mentioned, Franz was prudent, so he wanted to know as much as he could about his strange and mysterious host. Consequently he went back to the sailor who, while the above conversation was going on, had been plucking the partridges with the grave air of a man proud of his job, and asked him what kind of vessel the other men had landed in, since he could not see any *speronara*, tartan or other boat.

'I'm not concerned about that,' the sailor said. 'I know their vessel.'

'Is it a fine one?'

'I wish Your Excellency such a one, should he sail round the world.'

'What is its displacement?'

'A hundred tons, or thereabouts. In any event, it is a pleasure boat – a yacht, as the English call it – but built, you understand, in such a way that it can go to sea in any weather.'

'Where was it built?'

'That I don't know; but I believe in Genoa.'

'And how does the head of a gang of smugglers,' Franz asked, 'dare to have a yacht built for his trade in the port of Genoa?'

'I didn't say that the owner of the yacht was a smuggler,' the sailor replied.

'No, but I believe Gaetano said so.'

'Gaetano had seen the crew from a distance, but he had not yet spoken to anyone.'

'And if the man is not a smuggler, then what is he?'

'A rich aristocrat who travels for his own pleasure.'

'Come now,' Franz thought to himself. 'This man is becoming more and more mysterious, since the stories differ.' Then he said aloud: 'What is his name?'

'When asked, he replies that he is called Sinbad the Sailor. But I suspect this may not be his true name.'

'Sinbad the Sailor?'

'Yes.'

'Where does this gentleman live?'

'At sea.'

'What country does he come from?'

'I don't know.'

'Have you seen him?'

'A few times.'

'What is he like?'

'Your Excellency can judge for himself.'

'And where will he entertain me?'

'Doubtless in the underground palace that Gaetano mentioned.'

'But have you never been curious, when you landed on this island and found it deserted, to try and enter this enchanted palace?'

'Oh, yes indeed, Excellency,' the sailor replied. 'More than once, in fact. But all our efforts have been fruitless. We have looked all round the grotto and not found the smallest passageway. In any case, it is said that the door does not open with a key, but with a magic word.'

'I have definitely stepped off into a tale from the *Thousand and One Nights*,' Franz muttered.

'His Excellency awaits you,' said a voice behind him which he recognized as that of the sentry. He had with him two men from the crew of the yacht. In reply, Franz simply took out his handkerchief and offered it to the man who had spoken.

Without a word, they blindfolded him, taking enough care to show that they were afraid he might commit some indiscretion, then made him swear that he would not try to remove the blindfold. He swore. At that, the two men each took one of his arms and they led him forward, preceded by the sentry.

After some thirty paces, he guessed, from the increasingly appetizing smell of kid, that they were walking past the encampment. They carried on for about fifty paces more, clearly proceeding in the direction that had been forbidden to Gaetano, which explained why they had not wanted him to go there. Soon, from the change in the air, he realized that he was going underground and, after they had walked for a few more seconds, he heard a creaking sound and felt that the air had again changed, to become warm and scented. Finally he felt his feet walking on a thick, soft carpet, and his guides let go of his arms. There was a moment's silence and a voice said, in good French, though with a foreign accent: 'Welcome to my home, Monsieur. You may take off your handkerchief.'

As one may imagine, Franz did not wait to be asked again: he took off his handkerchief and found himself standing in front of a man of between thirty-eight and forty, wearing Tunisian dress, that is to say a red skullcap with a long blue silk tassel; a jacket in black woollen cloth embroidered all over with gold thread; wide, loose, dark-red trousers, with gaiters in the same colour, embroidered in gold like the jacket; and yellow Turkish slippers. Around his waist was a splendid cashmere belt with a sharp little curved dagger hanging from it.

Although his colouring was an almost livid white, the man had a remarkably handsome face. The eyes were bright and penetrating, the nose straight and almost on a level with the forehead, suggesting the purest Greek type; and the teeth, white as pearls, shone splendidly under a dark moustache. It was only the pallor that was strange: the man looked as if he had been shut up for a long time in a tomb and afterwards had been unable to recover the natural rosy complexion of the living.

Though not very tall, he was well-built and had the small hands and feet typical of Mediterranean men.

However, what astonished Franz, who had treated Gaetano's story as a fantasy, was the sumptuousness of the furnishings. The whole room was hung with crimson Turkish hangings, brocaded with gold flowers. In a recess there was a sort of divan, and above it a display of Arab swords with vermeil sheaths and hilts shining with precious stones. From the ceiling dangled a lamp in Venetian glass, delightful in shape and colour, and his feet sank up to the ankles in the Turkish rug underneath them. There were curtains hanging in front of the door by which Franz had entered and in front of another door which led into a second room which seemed to be splendidly lit.

The man allowed his guest a moment to take all this in, while using the opportunity to examine him in turn and keeping his eyes fixed on him.

'Monsieur,' he said finally, 'I beg you to forgive me a thousand times for the precautions that we had to take before showing you into my home, but, since this island is deserted for most of the time, if the secret of where I live were to get out I should no doubt return to find my dwelling in a rather poor state. I should be much displeased at this, not because of any loss that it might occasion, but because I should no longer have the assurance that, whenever I wish, I can separate myself from the rest of the world. Now I shall try to make you forget any slight displeasure I may have caused you, by offering you something that you surely did not expect to find here, namely a decent supper and quite a good bed.'

'My dear host,' said Franz, 'you must not apologize. I know that people who visit enchanted palaces always do so blindfold: look at Raoul in *The Huguenots*.⁵ And I really have no cause for complaint, because what you are showing me is equal to the marvels of the *Arabian Nights*.'

'Alas! I have to say, like Lucullus: if I had known I was going to have the honour of your visit, I should have made some preparation for it. But, in the event, I put my humble retreat at your disposal and invite you to share my supper, such as it is. Ali, are we served?'

At almost that very moment the curtain in front of the door was raised and a Nubian, black as ebony and wearing a simple white tunic, indicated to his master that they could proceed to the dining-room.

'Now,' the stranger told Franz, 'I am not sure whether you agree with me, but I find nothing more irritating than to spend two or three hours with a person and not know by what name or title one should address him. Observe that I respect the laws of hospitality too much to ask you your name or title. I should just like to ask you to suggest some name or other which I might use when speaking to you. As for myself, to put you similarly at ease, I should tell you that people are accustomed to call me Sinbad the Sailor.'

'And I,' said Franz, 'I shall tell you that, as I have everything except the celebrated magic lamp, I see no objection for the moment to your calling me Aladdin. In this way we can stay in the Orient, where I suspect that I must have been transported with the help of some good genie.'

'Well, Aladdin, sir,' said the strange host, 'you heard that we are served, I think? So please be good enough to come into the dining-room. Your humble servant will go first to show you the way.'

At these words, raising the curtain, Sinbad stepped through the doorway.

Franz went from one wonder to another. The table was splendidly laid. Once he had assured himself of this important detail, he looked around: the dining-room was no less magnificent than the boudoir that he had just left. It was entirely in marble, with the most precious antique bas-reliefs. The room was oblong, and at each end there were superb statues carrying baskets on their heads. The baskets contained two pyramids of wonderful fruit: Sicilian pineapples, pomegranates from Malaga, oranges from the Balearics, French peaches and Tunisian dates.

As for the 'supper', it consisted of a roast pheasant sitting on a bed of Corsican blackbirds, a wild boar's ham in jelly, a quarter of a kid *à la tartare*, a magnificent turbot and a huge lobster. Between the main dishes were smaller plates with the various side-dishes.

The serving dishes were silver and the plates of Japanese porcelain.

Franz rubbed his eyes to make sure he was not dreaming.

Only Ali was allowed to wait on them, acquitting himself very well. The guest complimented his host on the fact.

'Yes, yes,' the other replied, continuing to do the honours of his table in the most easy manner. 'He's a poor devil who is most devoted to me and who does his best. He recalls that I saved his life and, as he was attached to his head, apparently, he owes me some gratitude for having preserved it for him.'

Ali went up to his master, took his hand and kissed it.

'It's very simple,' the host replied. 'It appears that the fellow had wandered closer to the harem of the Bey of Tunis than is acceptable for a lad of his colour. In consequence he was condemned by the bey to have his tongue, his hand and his head cut off: the tongue on the first day, the hand on the second and the head on the third. I had always wanted to have a dumb servant. I waited for him to have his tongue cut out, then I went to offer the bey, in exchange for him, a splendid two-stroke repeating rifle which, on the previous day, had appeared to take His Highness's fancy. He hesitated a moment, so keen was he to make an end of this poor devil. But I added to the rifle an English hunting knife with which I had blunted His Highness's yataghan;[6] as a result the bey decided to spare him his hand and his head, on condition that he never again set foot in Tunis. The stipulation was unnecessary. As soon as the miscreant catches sight of the African coast, he flees to the bottom of the hold and cannot be persuaded to come out until we have lost sight of the third quarter of the world.'

For a moment Franz said nothing, considering what he should think of the cruel good humour with which his host had told him this story.

'And, like the honourable sailor whose name you have taken,' he asked, changing the subject, 'do you spend all your time travelling?'

'Yes, this is the result of a vow that I made at a time when I did not expect I should be able to accomplish it,' the stranger said with a smile. 'I have made a few vows of that sort, and I hope to be able to accomplish them all in due course.'

Though Sinbad had spoken these words with the greatest sang-froid, his eyes gave a glance of peculiar ferocity.

'Have you suffered a great deal, Monsieur?' Franz asked.

Sinbad shuddered, and stared closely at him.

'How can you tell that?' he asked.

'Everything speaks of it,' said Franz. 'Your voice, your look, your pallor, even the sort of life that you lead.'

'What! I lead the happiest life of any man I know – the life of a pasha! I am the lord of creation: if I am enjoying myself in a place, I stay there; if I am bored, I leave. I am as free as a bird and, like a bird, I have wings. I have only to make a sign for the people around me to obey me. From time to time I amuse myself in teasing justice by snatching a wanted bandit away from it, or a criminal with the police on his trail. Then I have my own justice, high and low, which suspends no sentences and hears no appeals, which merely condemns or pardons, and concerns nobody. Oh, if you could have tasted my life, you would want no other, you would never return to the world, unless you had some great project to carry out.'

'Some act of revenge, for example,' said Franz.

The stranger held the young man in one of those looks that penetrate to the depths of the soul and the mind. 'Why revenge?' he asked.

'Because,' said Franz, 'you look to me like a man who has been persecuted by society and has a terrible account to settle with it.'

'Well, well,' Sinbad said, laughing his strange laugh and showing his sharp, white teeth, 'you're quite wrong. You might not think it, but I am a kind of philanthropist and perhaps one day I shall go to Paris to rival Monsieur Appert[7] and the Man in the Little Blue Cloak.'

'Would that be your first visit?'

'Certainly, it would. I don't appear very curious, do I? I assure you, however, that it is not my fault if I have not been before, and it will happen one day or another.'

'Do you expect to go soon?'

'I don't know yet; it depends on circumstances that are still uncertain.'

'I should like to be there when you come, so that I could return, as far as I am able, the hospitality that you have been so generous as to offer me on Monte Cristo.'

'I would be most happy to accept your offer,' the host replied. 'But if I do go, unfortunately, it might well be incognito.'

Meanwhile the dinner continued and appeared to have been served purely for Franz, for the stranger had barely nibbled at one or two of the dishes in the splendid feast that he had offered him and on which his unexpected guest had dined handsomely.

Finally Ali brought the dessert; or, rather, he took the baskets from the hands of the statues and placed them on the table. Between the two baskets he set down a little bowl in vermeil, with a lid of the same metal. Franz's curiosity was awakened by the respect with which the servant had brought this bowl. He lifted the lid and saw a sort of greenish paste that he did not recognize, though it resembled a sort of sweet made from angelica. He replaced the lid, as ignorant of the contents of the bowl after lifting the lid as he had been before and, turning back to his host, saw him smile at his disappointment.

'You cannot guess,' he said, 'what kind of foodstuff is in that little container, and it intrigues you, I imagine?'

'I admit it does.'

'I'll tell you. That sort of green sweetmeat is nothing more nor less than the ambrosia that Hebe served at the table of Jupiter.'

'Which ambrosia,' said Franz, 'no doubt, on coming into the hand of man, lost its celestial name to take a human one. What is the name of this substance – to which, I must admit, I feel no great attraction – in ordinary speech?'

'Ah!' cried Sinbad. 'It is precisely in this that we reveal our base material origins. Often we pass beside happiness without seeing it, without looking at it, or, even if we have seen and looked at it, without recognizing it. If you are a practical man and gold is your God, then taste this, and the mines of Peru, Gujarat and Golconda will be open to you. If you are a man of imagination, a poet, then taste this too, and the boundaries of the possible will vanish, the fields of infinity will be open and you will walk through them, free in heart, free in mind, in the limitless pasture of reverie. If you are ambitious and seek earthly glory, then you too can taste this and in an hour you will be a king, not the king of some little kingdom buried away in a corner of Europe, like France, Spain or England, but king of the world, king of the universe, king of creation. Your throne will be raised up on the mountain where Satan took Jesus. And, without having to pay him homage, without having to kiss his claw, you will be the sovereign master of all the kingdoms on earth. Aren't you tempted by my offer? Tell me, is it not an easy thing to do, since there is nothing to do but that? Look.'

With this, he lifted the lid off the little vermeil bowl which contained the substance of which he had spoken so highly, took a coffee-spoon full of the magic sweetmeat, raised it to his lips and slowly savoured it, his eyes half closed and his head leaning back.

Franz gave him as long as he needed to enjoy his favourite food; then, seeing that he had somewhat recovered his attention, said: 'But tell me, what is this precious sweetmeat?'

'Have you heard speak of the Old Man of the Mountain?' his host asked. 'The one who tried to kill Philip Augustus?'

'Of course.'

'Well, you know that he ruled over a rich valley overlooked by the mountain from which he had taken his picturesque name. In that valley were splendid gardens planted by Hassanben-Sabah, and in those gardens were isolated pavilions. According to Marco Polo, he would bring his chosen friends into these pavilions and there make them eat a certain grass which would take them into paradise, in the midst of plants that were always in flower, fruits that were always ripe and women who were always virgins. What these fortunate young men imagined was reality was a dream; but a dream so sweet, so intoxicating, so voluptuous that they would sell themselves, body and soul, to the person who had procured it for them, obey his orders like those of God and strike whatever victim he directed at the furthest end of the earth, dying under torture without a murmur, simply because they believed that the death they would suffer was merely a transition to that life of delights of which the holy grass, which you see before you, had given them a foretaste.'

'In that case,' Franz exclaimed, 'it's hashish! Yes, I do know it, at least by name.'

'Precisely; you have said the word, my lord Aladdin, it's hashish, the best and finest hashish of Alexandria, hashish from Abugour, the great maker, the only man, the man for whom they should build a palace with the following inscription: "To the merchant of happiness, from a grateful world".'

'Do you know,' Franz said, 'I am quite eager to judge for myself as to the truth or otherwise of your commendation?'

'Do so, my dear guest, do so. But do not be content with just one experiment: as with everything, the senses must become accustomed to a new impression, whether it is pleasant or not, happy or sad. Nature wrestles with this divine substance, because our nature is not made for joy but clings to pain. Nature must be defeated in this struggle, reality must follow dreams; and then the dream will rule, will become the master, the dream will become life and life become a dream. What a difference is made by this transfiguration! When you compare the sorrows of real life to the pleasures of the imaginary one, you will never want to live again, only to dream for ever. When you leave your world for that of others, you will feel as if you have travelled from spring in Naples to winter in Lapland, from paradise to earth, from heaven to hell. Try some hashish, my friend! Try it!'

Instead of replying, Franz took a spoonful of the wonderful paste, about as much as his host had taken, and brought it to his mouth.

'Dammit!' he exclaimed, swallowing this divine substance. 'I am not yet sure if the outcome will be as pleasant as you say. But the thing itself doesn't seem to me as delicious as you claim.'

'That is because the nodes of your palate are not yet accustomed to the sublimity of the thing they are tasting. Tell me: the first time, did you like oysters, tea, porter, truffles, all these things that you were later to adore? Can you understand the Romans, who seasoned pheasants with asafoetida, or the Chinese, who eat birds' nests? Of course you can't! Well, it's the same with hashish: just try taking it for a whole week, and no food in the world will seem to you comparable in fineness to this taste which today you find musty and repellent. Now let us go into the next room, which is your bedroom, and Ali will serve us coffee and give us some pipes.'

They both got up and, while the man who called himself Sinbad – the name which we, too, have used from time to time, so that we may be able to designate him in some way – was giving orders to his servant, Franz went through to the other room.

The furnishings were simpler, though no less rich. The room was round and a large divan extended along the walls. But the divan, the walls, the ceiling and the floor were hung with splendid animal-skins, as sweet and soft as the deepest-piled carpet: there were lions' skins from the Atlas Mountains, with great manes; there were tigers' skins from Bengal, warmly striped; there were the skins of panthers from the Cape, as merrily spotted as the one that appeared to Dante; finally, there were bears' skins from Siberia and Norwegian foxes. All these were heaped one upon the other, in such profusion that one would have imagined oneself to be walking on the thickest lawn and resting on the most silken couch.

Both men lay down upon the divan. Chibouks with jasmine stems and amber mouthpieces were within easy reach, all prepared so that they never needed to smoke the same one twice. They each took one. Ali lit them and went out to fetch coffee.

There was a moment's silence in which Sinbad was immersed in the thoughts that seemed continually to occupy him, even in the midst of conversation, and Franz abandoned himself to the silent reverie into which one almost invariably falls when smoking fine tobacco, which seems to carry away all the sufferings of the mind on its smoke and give the smoker in exchange all the dreams of the soul.

Ali brought them coffee.

'How would you like it?' the stranger said. 'A la française or à la turque, strong or weak, with sugar or without, filtered or boiled? You choose. We have it prepared in every manner.'

'I should like Turkish,' Franz replied.

'How right you are!' cried his host. 'This proves that you have a natural disposition for Oriental life. Ah, the Orientals, you understand, are the only people who know how to live! As for me,' he added, with one of those odd smiles that did not escape the young man's observant eye, 'when I have finished my business in Paris, I shall go and die in the East; and then if you want to find me, you will have to look in Cairo, Baghdad or Isfahan.'

'I do believe,' said Franz, 'that it will be the easiest thing, because I think I am growing eagles' wings and with them I shall fly round the world in a day.'

'Ah, ha! That's the hashish working. Well, then, open your wings and fly into regions beyond the reach of men. Fear nothing. You are being watched over and if, like those of Icarus, your wings should melt in the sun, we are there to catch you.'

He said a few words in Arabic to Ali, who signified his obedience and retired, without going too far away.

As for Franz, a strange transformation was taking place in him. All the physical tiredness of the day, all the concerns awakened in the mind by the events of the evening were disappearing as in that first moment of rest when one is still conscious enough to feel the arrival of sleep. His body seemed to acquire the lightness of some immaterial being, his mind became unimaginably clear and his senses seemed to double their faculties. The horizon was constantly receding; it was no longer that dark horizon which he had seen before falling asleep and over which a vague terror loomed, but a blue, transparent and vast horizon, containing all the blueness of the sea, all the sparkle of the sun and all the perfumes of the breezes. Then, in the midst of the songs of his sailors, songs that were so pure and so clear that they would have made the most divine harmonies if one could have noted them down, he saw the island of Monte Cristo appear, no longer like a threatening reef rising out of the waves but like an oasis lost in the desert; and, as the boat approached, the songs swelled in volume, because an enchanting and mysterious harmony rose towards heaven out of the island, as if some fairy, like Lorelei, or some enchanter, like Amphion, wanted to lure a soul towards it or to build a city there.

Finally, the boat reached the shore, effortlessly, with no shock, but as lips touch lips, and he came into the cave, without a pause in the charming music. He went down a few steps, or seemed to do so, breathing a fresh and scented air such as must surround Circe's grotto, composed of perfumes that inspire the soul to dream and warmth such that the senses are inflamed by it; and he saw everything that he had seen before falling asleep, from Sinbad, his fantastic host, to Ali, the dumb servant. Then everything seemed to fade and become confused before his eyes, like the last rays of a magic lantern going out; and he found himself in the room with the statues, lit only by one of those dim antique lights that are kept burning at night to watch over sleep or voluptuous pleasures.

The statues were indeed the same, rich in shape, in sensuality and in poetry, with their magnetic eyes, lustful smiles and opulently flowing hair. Here were those three great courtesans, Phryne, Cleopatra and Messalina; then, like a pure ray in the midst of these immodest shades, like a Christian angel among the gods of Olympus, came one of those chaste countenances, one of those calm shadows, one of those sweet visions that appeared to veil its virginal brow beside all these marble impurities.

At this, it seemed to him that the three statues had combined the love of all three, to offer to a single man, and that that man was himself; that they were approaching the bed where he was dreaming a second sleep, their feet covered by their long white tunics, barebreasted, their hair coursing like water across their shoulders, in those poses which can seduce gods – but not saints – and those burning looks, such as those the serpent turns on a bird, and that he was abandoning himself to these painful expressions as if to an embrace, as voluptuous as a kiss.

Franz felt that he was closing his eyes and that in the last glance he cast around him he noticed the modest statue cover itself entirely with its veil; then his eyes closed on reality and his senses opened to inconceivable feelings.

After that, he felt unremitting sensuality and continual love-making, such as the Prophet promised to the elect. Now all those stone mouths became living ones and those breasts became warm, to such an extent that for Franz, falling for the first time under the domain of hashish, this lust was almost pain and this voluptuous-ness almost torture, as he felt the lips of these statues, supple and cold as the coils of a viper, touching his parched mouth. But the more his arms tried to ward off this unknown embrace, the more his senses fell beneath the spell of this mysterious dream, so that, after a struggle in which he would have given his soul, he abandoned himself unreservedly and eventually fell back, panting, seared with exhaustion, worn out with lust, beneath the kisses of these marble mistresses and the enchantment of this unimaginable dream.

XXXII

AWAKENING

When Franz regained consciousness, the outside world seemed like a continuation of his dream: he felt himself to be in a tomb where barely a single ray of sunshine, like a look of pity, could penetrate. He reached out and felt stone. He sat up and found that he was lying, wrapped in his burnous, on a bed of dry heather, soft and sweet-smelling.

His visions had all ended and the statues, as though they had been no more than mere figments risen from their tombs during his sleep, had fled when he awoke.

He took a few steps towards the point from which daylight was coming; the calm of reality was succeeding to the feverishness of dreams. He saw that he was in a cave, walked towards the opening and through the arched door observed blue sky and azure sea. The air and the water sparkled in the rays of the morning sun; on the shore, the sailors were chattering and laughing where they sat; and, ten yards out to sea, the boat bobbed gracefully at anchor.

For a short while he enjoyed the cool breeze on his forehead, listening to the muffled sound of the waves against the shore, where they left a lace pattern of silvery white foam on the rocks. He abandoned himself, without attempting to analyse it, to the divine charm of natural things, especially when one can enjoy them after a fantastic dream. Then, little by little, this outside life, with its calm, its purity and its grandeur, recalled the improbability of his dream, and memories began to flood back.

He remembered arriving on the island, being introduced to the chief of the smugglers, then an underground palace full of marvels, an excellent dinner and a spoonful of hashish. But, confronted by the reality of daylight, it seemed to him that all this had happened at least a year ago, so large did his dream loom in mind and so immediate did it seem. Thus, from time to time, his imagination took one of the shadow figures who had lit up his night with their kisses, and made her sit amongst the sailors, or walk across a rock or stand in the rocking boat. In any case, his head was quite clear and his body perfectly rested. There was no heaviness in his brain but, on the contrary, a certain general feeling of well-being and an ability to absorb the air and the sun that was greater than ever.

So it was with a light heart that he went down to join his sailors. As soon as they saw him, they rose and the master came across.

'Milord Sinbad,' he said, 'requested us to convey his compliments to Your Excellency, and asked us to express his regret at not being able to bid Your Excellency farewell. He hopes that you will excuse him when you know that he has urgent business in Malaga.'

'So, my dear Gaetano,' Franz said, 'all this is real then: there was a man who welcomed me to this island, treated me royally and left while I was asleep?'

'So real is he that you can see his little yacht speeding off under full sail. If you want to take your spyglass, you will quite probably recognize your host himself in the midst of his crew.'

As he said this, Gaetano pointed towards a little boat steering a course for the southern tip of Corsica.

Franz took out his glass, adjusted the focus and turned it towards the point indicated. Gaetano was quite right. The mysterious stranger was standing on the stern of the boat, facing in his direction and, like Franz, with a spyglass in his hand. His dress was the same as the one in which he had appeared to his guest on the previous evening, and he was waving goodbye with his handkerchief.

Franz pulled out his own handkerchief and returned the greeting by waving it in the same manner. A moment later, a small puff of smoke appeared from the stern of the boat, detached itself from the vessel and rose in a graceful arc towards the sky, after which Franz heard the faint sound of a shot.

'There! Did you hear that?' said Gaetano. 'He is bidding you farewell.'

The young man took his rifle and fired it in the air, but without much expectation that the noise would reach the yacht at that distance from the shore.

'What would Your Excellency like us to do?' said Gaetano.

'Firstly, to light me a torch.'

'Ah, yes! I understand. You want to look for the entrance to the enchanted dwelling. With great pleasure, Excellency: if it amuses you, I shall give you the torch you ask for. I, too, once had the same idea as you, and I gave in to it three or four times, but eventually I abandoned the attempt. Giovanni,' he added, 'light a torch and bring it to His Excellency.'

Giovanni obeyed. Franz took the torch and went into the underground cavern, followed by Gaetano.

He recognized the place where he had woken up by his bed of heather, which was still crumpled. But, however much he ran the torch over the walls of the cavern, he could find nothing except traces of smoke, showing where others had investigated before him in vain.

However, he did not leave a single foot of the granite wall unexamined, even though it was as impenetrable as futurity. He did not notice a single crack without putting the blade of his knife into it, or a lump jutting out of the surface without pressing it, in the hope that it would give way; but all was futile and he spent two hours on this fruitless search. After that, he gave up. Gaetano was triumphant.

When Franz returned to the shore, the yacht was only a little white dot on the horizon. He tried his glass, but even with that it was impossible to make anything out.

Gaetano reminded him that he had come here to hunt the goats, something that he had completely forgotten. He took his gun and began to scour the island like a man accomplishing a duty rather than one enjoying a pleasure; after a quarter of an hour, he had killed a goat and two kids. But, though the goats were as wild and shy as chamois, they bore too great a resemblance to the domestic variety and Franz did not consider them true game.

And anyway, there were far more powerful ideas on his mind. Since the previous evening he had effectively been the hero of a tale from the *Thousand and One Nights*, and he was irresistibly drawn back to the cave. So, even though the first investigation had failed, he began a second one, after telling Gaetano to have the two kids roasted. This second visit must have lasted a fairly long time because, when he returned, the kid was cooked and the meal was ready.

Franz sat down on the spot where, the evening before, they had come to invite him to supper with this mysterious host; and he could still see the little yacht, like a seagull rocking on the crest of a wave, continuing on its path to Corsica.

'But, Gaetano,' he said, 'you informed me that Milord Sinbad was heading for Malaga, while it seems to me that he is going directly towards Porto Vecchio.'

'Don't you remember,' the master said, 'my telling you that, with his crew, there were for the time being two Corsican bandits?'

'Of course! So is he going to put them off on the coast?'

'Just as you say. Ah,' Gaetano exclaimed, 'there's a man who doesn't fear either God or the devil, so they say, and who would go fifty leagues out of his way to help a poor soul.'

'That sort of help could get him into trouble with the authorities of the country where he performs this kind of philanthropic deed,' Franz said.

'Huh! The authorities!' said Gaetano. 'What does he care about the authorities? He couldn't give a damn for them! Let them just try to catch him. To start with, his yacht is not a ship, it's a bird, and he could gain three knots on a frigate for every twelve. Then he has only to put off at the coast himself. He would find plenty of friends of his own there.'

What was most clear in all this was that Milord Sinbad, Franz's host, had the honour to be associated with every smuggler and bandit on every coast around the Mediterranean, which could only make his position seem even more peculiar. As for Franz, there was nothing further to keep him on Monte Cristo, since he had lost all hope of finding the secret of the cavern; so he hastened to finish his lunch, while ordering the men to prepare the boat for when he was ready.

Half an hour later, he was on board.

He cast a final glance at the yacht. It was about to vanish into the Gulf of Porto Vecchio. He gave the signal to depart.

At the moment when his boat set off, the yacht disappeared.

With it vanished the last link with the reality of the previous night: the supper, Sinbad, the hashish and the statues – all were beginning for Franz to merge into a single dream.

The boat sailed all day and all night. The next morning, at sunrise, it was the island of Monte Cristo itself that had disappeared.

Once Franz had landed, he put aside all memory of recent events, at least temporarily, in order to complete his personal and social affairs in Florence and concentrate on joining his friend, who was waiting in Rome. So he left for there, and on the Saturday evening arrived by stage-coach on the Piazza della Dogana.

As we mentioned earlier, the apartment was already reserved, so there was nothing to be done except to repair to Signor Pastrini's establishment. This was less easy than it sounds: the streets were jammed with people and Rome was already a prey to the dull, feverish hum that precedes great events. And in Rome there are four great events in the year: carnival, Holy Week, Corpus Christi and the Feast of Saint Peter.

The rest of the year, the city slumps back into its melancholic apathy, a limbo between life and death, which makes it comparable to a kind of stopping-place between this life and the next; but a sublime stopping-place, full of character and poetry, that Franz had experienced five or six times before, and which each time he had found more marvellous and more fantastic than the last.

At length he managed to make his way through the swelling and increasingly expectant crowd, and reached the hotel. At his first request, he was told, with that impertinence which is peculiar to cab-drivers when they have already been booked and innkeepers whose establishments are full, that there was no more room for him in the Hôtel de Londres, whereupon he sent his card up to Signor Pastrini and asked to be announced to Albert de Morcerf. This tactic succeeded and Signor Pastrini hurried down in person, begging pardon for having kept His Excellency waiting, scolding his staff, snatching the candlestick from the hand of the guide who had already taken charge of the traveller, and preparing to conduct him to Albert, when the latter himself came to meet them.

The apartment they had rented consisted of two little rooms and a study. Both bedrooms overlooked the street, a feature that Signor Pastrini emphasized, as enormously enhancing their worth. The remainder of the floor was rented to a very rich gentleman, believed to be a Sicilian or a Maltese: the hotelier could not say precisely to which of the two nations the traveller belonged. He was called the Count of Monte Cristo.

'Very well, Signor Pastrini,' said Franz, 'but we shall immediately need some kind of supper for this evening and a barouche for tomorrow and the following days.'

'As to the supper,' said the innkeeper, 'you shall have it at once; but regarding the barouche . . .'

'What! What, regarding the barouche?' Albert exclaimed. 'Hold on now, one moment! We are not joking, Signor Pastrini! We shall need a barouche.'

'Monsieur,' said the innkeeper, 'everything possible will be done to procure one for you. I cannot say more than that.'

'And when shall we know?' asked Franz.

'Tomorrow morning,' answered the innkeeper.

'Damnation!' said Albert. 'All this means is that we shall pay dearer for it. You know how it goes: from Drake or Aaron – twenty-five francs on ordinary days, and thirty or thirty-five on Sundays and holidays. Add five francs a day as your own fee, and we are in for a round forty francs.'

'I very much fear that the gentlemen would not be able to find such a vehicle for double that amount.'

'Well, then, find some horses and harness them to my own. It is a little the worse for wear after the journey, but no matter.'

'You won't find any horses.'

Albert looked at Franz like a man who has just been given an incomprehensible answer.

'Do you understand this, Franz? No horses! But what about post-horses, aren't there any of those?'

'All hired a fortnight ago; all that is left are those which are absolutely essential for the mail.'

'What do you say to that?' asked Franz.

'I say that, when something is beyond my comprehension, I am in the habit of not wasting any more time on it, but of turning to something else. Is the supper ready, Signor Pastrini?'

'Yes, Excellency.'

'Well, then, let's dine first of all.'

'But what about the barouche and the horses?' asked Franz.

'Don't worry about them, my dear friend, they will come of their own accord. It is simply a matter of finding a price.'

At which, Morcerf, with that admirable philosophy that believes nothing impossible so long as it feels its purse to be fat and its wallet full, supped, went to bed, fell instantly fast asleep and dreamt that he was prancing through the carnival with a carriage and six horses.

XXXIII

ROMAN BANDITS

The next morning Franz was the first to wake up and, as soon as he was awake, rang. The tinkling of the bell could still be heard when Signor Pastrini in person came in.

'So! It is just as I thought yesterday,' the innkeeper said triumphantly, without even waiting for Franz to put the question to him, 'when I didn't want to promise you anything, Excellency. Your search has begun too late: there is not a single carriage to be had in Rome – for the final three days, of course.'

'Yes,' Franz remarked. 'You mean for the three when it is quite indispensable.'

'What is it?' asked Albert, coming in. 'No barouche?'

'Exactly, my dear friend,' Franz replied. 'You've got it in one.'

'Well, a fine city it is, your Eternal City.'

'By which I mean, Excellency,' Signor Pastrini continued, wishing the visitors to retain some modicum of respect for the capital of the Christian world, 'I mean that there will be no carriage from Sunday morning to Tuesday evening, but that between now and then you can find fifty if you so wish.'

'Ah! That's something anyway,' said Albert. 'Today is Thursday. Who knows what may happen between now and Sunday.'

'Ten or twelve thousand travellers are what will happen,' Franz replied, 'aggravating the problem.'

'My friend,' Morcerf said, 'let's enjoy the present and not let it cloud the future.'

'At least we shall be able to have a window?' said Franz.

'A window, where?'

'Lord love us! Overlooking the Corso.'

'Ah, yes! A window!' exclaimed Signor Pastrini. 'Impossible! Completely impossible! There was one remaining on the fifth floor of the Palazzo Doria, but it was rented to a Russian prince for twenty sequins a day.'

The two young men looked at one another in amazement.

'Damnation, my dear Albert,' Franz said. 'Do you know what we should do? We should go and celebrate the carnival in Venice. At least there, if we don't find a carriage, we'll find a gondola.'

'No, no, no!' Albert cried. 'My mind is set on seeing the carnival in Rome and here I shall see it, even if I have to use stilts.'

'Ah, now!' Franz said. 'That's a brilliant idea, especially for putting out moccoletti;[1] we'll dress up as vampire polichinelli or else as peasants from the Landes. We'll be a roaring success.'

'Do Your Excellencies still wish to have a carriage until Sunday?'

'Yes, dammit!' said Albert. 'Do you expect us to go running round the streets of Rome on foot, like bailiff's clerks?'

'I shall hasten to carry out Your Excellencies' orders,' said Signor Pastrini. 'But I must warn you that the carriage will cost six *piastres* a day.'

'And I, dear Signor Pastrini,' said Franz, 'since I am not our neighbour the millionaire, I must warn you that this is my fourth visit to Rome, and consequently I know the price of a barouche on weekdays, Sundays and holidays. We shall give you twelve *piastres* for today, tomorrow and the day after, and you will still have a very handsome bonus.'

'But, Excellency!' said Signor Pastrini, trying to protest.

'Come, my dear fellow, come,' said Franz, 'or else I'll go myself and bargain with your *affettatore*,[2] who also happens to be mine. We are old friends, he has already stolen quite a bit of money from me in his time and, in the hope of stealing some more, will accept an even lower price than the one I am offering you: so you will lose the difference and it will be your own fault.'

'Do not put yourself to so much trouble, Excellency,' said Signor Pastrini, with the smile of an Italian speculator admitting defeat. 'I shall do my best and I hope that it will be to your satisfaction.'

'Completely! Now we're talking.'

'When would you like the carriage?'

'In an hour.'

'In one hour it will be at the door.'

And, indeed, an hour later the carriage was waiting for the two young men: it was a simple cab which, in view of the solemnity of the occasion, had been elevated to the rank of barouche. But, despite its unassuming appearance, the two men would have been very pleased to have such a vehicle for the last three days of carnival.

'Excellency!' the guide cried, seeing Franz looking out of the window. 'Should we bring the coach to the palace door?'

Even though Franz was accustomed to Italian exaggeration, his first impulse was to look around; but the words were indeed addressed to him. He, Franz, was the Excellency; the hackney cab was the coach; and the palace was the Hôtel de Londres. In that single phrase was contained the whole genius of a nation that knows how to turn a compliment better than any other.

Franz and Albert went out, the coach drove up to the palace, Their Excellencies arranged themselves across the seats and the guide jumped up behind. 'Where do Their Excellencies wish to be driven?'

'First of all to Saint Peter's, of course, then to the Colosseum,' said Albert, like a true Parisian. However, there was one thing that Albert did not know, which is that you need a day to see St Peter's and a month to study it. The day was consequently spent solely in visiting St Peter's.

Suddenly the two friends noticed that the sun was starting to go down. Franz took out his watch: it was half-past four, so they immediately set off back to the hotel. At the door, Franz ordered the driver to be ready at eight. He wanted to show Albert the Colosseum by moonlight, as he had shown him St Peter's in broad daylight. When one is showing a friend round a city that one already knows, one does so with the same coquetry as when showing off a woman who has been one's mistress.

Franz consequently told the driver which route he should take: he was to go out through the Porta del Popolo, follow the outer wall, then come back into the city through the Porta San Giovanni. In this way, the Colosseum would appear before them with no prior rehearsal – that is to say, without the Capitol, the Forum, the Arch of Septimus Severus, the Temple of Antoninus and Faustina and the Via Sacra serving as so many steps on the road, to reduce its magnificence.

They sat down at table. Signor Pastrini had promised his guests a splendid feast. He gave them a passable dinner, so they couldn't complain. At the end of it he came in himself. Franz at first imagined that it was to accept their compliments and he prepared to make them, but he was interrupted after the first few words.

'Excellency,' Signor Pastrini said, 'I am flattered by your approval, but that is not the reason that I came up to see you.'

'Was it to tell us that you have found a carriage?' asked Albert, lighting a cigar.

'Still less – and I suggest, Excellency, that you would do better not to think about this any more, but to accept the inevitable. In Rome, either things can be done, or they cannot. When someone tells you that they cannot, there's an end to it.'

'In Paris, it's much more convenient: when something can't be done, you pay double and immediately you get what you wanted.'

'I hear all Frenchmen say this,' said Signor Pastrini, a trifle stung by it. 'So I don't understand how they manage to travel.'

'But, then,' said Albert, unhurriedly blowing his smoke towards the ceiling and leaning backwards, balancing on the two rear legs of his chair, 'it is only fools and innocents like ourselves who travel. Sensible men stay in their apartments in the Rue du Helder, and don't stray beyond the Boulevard de Gand and the Café de Paris.' It goes without saying that Albert lived in the aforementioned street, took his daily walk down the said fashionable thoroughfare and dined every day in the only café where one does dine – at least, assuming one is on good terms with the waiters.

Signor Pastrini said nothing for a moment, obviously considering this reply and no doubt not finding it altogether clear.

'The point is,' said Franz, interrupting his host's geographical musings, 'that you did come here for some reason, so perhaps you would be good enough to tell us why?'

'Ah, that's right! Here it is: you ordered the barouche for eight o'clock?'

'Just so.'

'You intend to visit the Colosseo?'

'You mean the Colosseum?'

'They are the same place.'

'As you say.'

'You told your coachman to leave by the Porta del Popolo, go round the walls and return through the Porta San Giovanni?'

'My very words.'

'Well: this itinerary is impossible.'

'Impossible?'

'Or, at least, very dangerous.'

'Dangerous! Why?'

'Because of the famous Luigi Vampa.'

'Come, come, my dear fellow, who is this famous Luigi Vampa?' Albert asked. 'He may be very famous in Rome, but I must tell you that he is quite unknown in Paris.'

'What! You don't know about him?'

'I don't have that honour.'

'You have never heard the name?'

'Never.'

'He is a bandit, beside whom Decesaris and Gasparone were mere choirboys.'

'Careful, Albert!' cried Franz. 'Here we have a bandit at last!'

'Be warned, my good host, I shall not believe a word of what you are about to tell us. And, now that that is clear, speak as long as you like, I am listening. "Once upon a time . . ." Off you go, then!'

Signor Pastrini turned towards Franz, who seemed to him the more reasonable of the two young men. We must be fair to the good man: he had put up a considerable number of Frenchmen in his life, but there was a side to their wit that he had never understood.

'Excellency,' he said, very gravely, turning, as we have said, towards Franz. 'If you consider me a liar, there is no sense in my telling you what I intended to tell you. But I can assure Your Excellencies that it would be in your interest.'

'Albert did not say that you are a liar, my dearest Monsieur Pastrini,' said Franz. 'He merely said that he would not believe you. But have no fear, I shall believe you, so you may speak.'

'Nevertheless, Excellency, you must understand that if doubt is to be cast on my veracity . . .'

'Dear man,' said Franz, 'you are more easily offended than Cassandra, even though she was a prophetess and no one listened to her: you at least can be assured of one-half of your audience. Come, sit down and tell us about this Monsieur Vampa.'

'As I told you, Excellency, he is a bandit, the like of which we have not seen since the famous Mastrilla.'

'And what does this bandit have to do with the order I gave my coachman to leave by the Porta del Popolo and to return through the Porta San Giovanni?'

'He has the following to do with it,' Signor Pastrini replied, 'that, while you may well go out by one gate, I very much doubt whether you will return by the other.'

'Why?'

'Because, after nightfall, no one is safe within fifty yards of the gates.'

'Truly?' Albert exclaimed.

'Monsieur le Vicomte,' said Signor Pastrini, still wounded to the very depth of his soul by the doubt Albert had expressed as to his veracity, 'what I am saying is not for you. It is for your travelling companion, who is acquainted with Rome and knows that one does not mock when speaking of such matters.'

'Franz,' said Albert, 'we have here a splendid adventure ready made for us. All we have to do is fill our carriage with pistols, blunderbusses and repeating rifles. Luigi Vampa will try to seize us, and we will seize him. We'll bring him back to Rome, offer him as a token of our respect to His Holiness, who will ask what he can do to recompense us for such a great service. Then all we have to do is ask for a coach and two horses from his stables and we can see the carnival by coach. Apart from which, the people of Rome will probably be so grateful to us that we shall be crowned on the Capitol and proclaimed, like Curtius and Horatius Cocles, saviours of the fatherland.'

The expression on Signor Pastrini's face, while Albert was pursuing this train of thought, would be impossible to describe.

'And where, for a start,' Franz asked Albert, 'would you find these pistols, these blunderbusses and these rifles which you want to cram into our carriage?'

'The fact is I have no such things in my arsenal,' he said, 'because even my dagger was confiscated at Terracina. What about you?'

'The same was done to me at Aquapendente.'

'Well, there now!' Albert said, lighting his second cigar from the stub of the first. 'My dear host, do you realize how convenient this regulation is for thieves – so much so that I suspect it was introduced in collusion with them?'

Signor Pastrini no doubt found the joke compromising, because he answered only obliquely, still addressing himself to Franz as the one reasonable person with whom he might reach a proper understanding.

'His Excellency knows that it is not usual to defend oneself when one is attacked by bandits.'

'What!' Albert cried, his courage rebelling at the idea of being robbed without saying a word. 'What! It's not usual?'

'No, because any resistance would be useless. What can you do against a dozen bandits leaping out of a ditch, from behind a hut or an aqueduct, all of whom have their sights trained on you at once?'

'Well, by all the devils! I'd let myself be killed!' Albert exclaimed.

The innkeeper turned to Franz with a look that meant: Undoubtedly, Excellency, your companion is mad.

'Albert,' Franz continued, 'that is a magnificent reply, almost as good as old Corneille's *"Qu'il morût . . ."*[3] But when Horatius said that, Rome itself was at stake and the sacrifice was justified. But in our case, it is just a matter of satisfying a whim; and it would be folly to risk our lives for the sake of a whim.'

'Ah! *Per Baccho!*' Signor Pastrini cried. 'At last! Someone is talking sense.'

Albert poured himself a glass of Lacryma Christi, which he drank in small sips, muttering unintelligibly.

'So, then, Signor Pastrini,' Franz continued, 'my friend, as you see, has calmed down; now that you have been able to judge of my peaceful temperament, tell us: who is this gentleman, Luigi Vampa? Is he a shepherd or a nobleman? Young or old? Short or tall? Describe him for us so that, if we should chance to meet him in society, like Jean Sbogar or Lara, we shall at least recognize him.'

'You could not have a better informant than I, Excellency, if you want to have the full story, because I knew Luigi Vampa as a young child. One day when I myself fell into his hands while travelling from Ferentino to Alatri, he remembered our earlier acquaintance, luckily for me. He let me go, not only without making me pay a ransom, but even making me a present of a very fine watch, and telling me his life story.'

'Let us see the watch,' said Albert.

Signor Pastrini pulled out of his fob a magnificent Breguet, signed by its maker and marked with the stamp of Paris and a count's coronet. 'Here it is,' he said.

'Dammit!' said Albert. 'I congratulate you. I have one almost the same' – he took his watch out of his waistcoat – 'and it cost me three thousand francs.'

'Let us hear the story,' said Franz, drawing up a chair and signalling to Signor Pastrini to sit down.

'Do Your Excellencies permit?'

'Please!' said Albert. 'You are not a preacher, my dear man, that you must speak on your feet.'

The hotelier sat down, after bowing respectfully to his future listeners, with the intention of letting them know that he was ready to give them any information about Luigi Vampa that they might require.

'Now,' said Franz, interrupting Signor Pastrini just as he was about to open his mouth. 'You say that you knew Luigi Vampa as a young child. This means he must still be a young man?'

'A young man! I should say he is. He's barely twenty-two years old. Oh, don't worry! He's a young man who will go far!'

'What do you say to that, Albert?' said Franz. 'It's a fine thing, is it not, to be famous already at twenty-two?'

'Yes, indeed; and at his age, Alexander, Caesar and Napoleon, who later acquired a certain reputation, had not gone as far as he.'

'So,' Franz continued, turning to the innkeeper, 'the hero whose story we are about to hear is only twenty-two.'

'Barely, as I have just had the honour to inform you.'

'Is he short or tall?'

'Of medium height, much the same as His Excellency,' Pastrini replied, indicating Albert.

'Thank you for the comparison,' the latter said with a bow.

'Carry on, Signor Pastrini,' Franz urged, smiling at his friend's sensitivity. 'And what class of society does he come from?'

'He was a simple herdsman attached to the farm of the Count of San-Felice, lying between Palestrina and the Lake of Gabri. He was born in Pampinara, and entered the count's service at the age of five. His father, himself a shepherd in Anagni, had a little flock of his own and lived on the product of the wool from his sheep and the milk of his ewes, which he brought to Rome to sell.

'While still a child, little Vampa had an unusual character. One day, at the age of seven, he came to see the curé of Palestrina and begged him to teach him to read. This was not easy, because the young herdsman could not leave his flock. But the good curé would go every day to say Mass in a poor little town that was too small to be able to afford a priest; it was too small even to have a name, just being known by that of Il Borgo. He invited Luigi to wait for him on his way at the time when he was returning, when he would give him his lesson, warning him that the lesson would be short and he would have to take full advantage of it. The boy gleefully accepted.

'Every day, Luigi would take his flock to graze on the road between Palestrina and Il Borgo. Every day, at nine in the morning, the curé came past. The priest and the child would sit on the edge of a ditch and the little shepherd learned his lesson from the priest's breviary.

'In three months, he could read.

'This was not all: now he needed to learn to write. The priest had a teacher of writing in Rome make him three alphabets: one in large script, one in medium and the third in small; and he showed Luigi that by tracing the alphabet on a slate with a metal point he could learn to write.

'The same evening, when the flock had returned to the farm, little Vampa ran across to the locksmith's in Palestrina, took a large nail, heated it in the forge, hammered it, shaped it and made a kind of antique stylus.

'The next day he collected some slates and set to work. In three months, he could write.

'The curé, astonished by this intelligence and touched by his aptitude, made him a present of several notebooks, a sheaf of pens and a penknife.

'This required further study, but it was nothing compared to what he had already done. A week later, he could write with a pen as well as he could write with his stylus.

'The curé told the story to the Count of San-Felice, who wanted to see the little shepherd, made him read and write in front of him, ordered his steward to have him eat with the servants and gave him two *piastres* a month. With the money Luigi bought books and pencils.

'In fact, he applied this faculty for imitation that he possessed to everything and, like the young Giotto, he would draw his ewes, the trees and the houses on his slates. Then, with the point of his knife, he began to carve wood, giving it all sorts of shapes: this is how Pinelli, the popular sculptor, began.

'A girl of six or seven, that is to say a little younger than Vampa, was keeping the ewes in a farm next door to Palestrina. She was an orphan called Teresa, born in Valmontone.

'The two children began to meet; they used to sit down together beside one another, let their flocks mingle and graze beside each other, while they would chatter, laugh and play. Then, in the evening, they separated the Count of San-Felice's sheep from those of the Baron Cervetri, and the two children would take leave of each other and go back to their respective farms, promising to meet again the following morning.

'The next day, they would keep their promise, and so they grew up side by side.

'In due course, Vampa was approaching the age of twelve and little Teresa eleven. Meanwhile, their natural instincts were developing.

'Beside the taste for the arts that Luigi had taken as far as it is possible to do in isolation, his nature was fitfully sad, intermittently passionate, capriciously angry, and always derisive. None of the young boys of Pampinara, Palestrina or Valmontone could gain any influence over him, or even become his companion. His wilful temperament, always inclined to demand without ever wishing to make the slightest concession, repelled any friendly advance or demonstration of sympathy. Only Teresa could command this impetuous character with a word, a look or a gesture; he bent beneath the hand of a woman, yet would have stiffened to breaking point beneath that of any man.

'Teresa, in contrast, was vivacious, merry and lively, but excessively coquettish. The two *piastres* that Luigi was given by the Count of San-Felice's steward and the price of all the little carvings that he would sell in the toy markets in Rome went on pearl earrings, glass necklaces and gold pins. Thanks to her young friend's generosity, Teresa was the most beautiful and most elegantly dressed peasant girl in all the country around Rome.

'The two children continued to grow, spending all their days together and abandoning themselves freely to the primitive instincts of their natures. Thus, in their conversations, in their longings and in their dreams, Vampa would always imagine himself the captain of a ship, the general of an army or the governor of a province. Teresa imagined herself rich, wearing the loveliest dresses and attended by servants in livery. Then, when they had spent all day embroidering their futures with these brilliant and foolish patterns, they went their separate ways, each leading the sheep to the appropriate fold, and plummeting from the summits of their dreams to the humble reality of their situation.

'One day the young shepherd told the count's steward that he had seen a wolf coming down from the mountains of La Sabina and prowling around the flock. The steward gave him a gun – which is what Vampa wanted.

'As it happened this gun was a fine Brescia piece which fired as far as an English carbine; but one day the count had broken the butt while bludgeoning a wounded fox, and they had thrown it on the scrap heap.

'This was no problem for a wood-carver like Vampa. He studied the original setting, adjusted the aim to suit himself and made a new butt so splendidly carved that, if he had wanted to sell the wood by itself, he could certainly have got fifteen or twenty *piastres* for it in town.

'But the young man had no interest in doing that: for a long time he had dreamed of having a gun. In every country where independence takes the place of liberty, the first need felt by any strong mind and powerful constitution is to possess a weapon which can serve both for attack and defence; and which, by making its bearer formidable, will mean that he often inspires dread.

'From this time on, Vampa devoted all his spare moments to practising with his gun. He bought powder and shot, and took anything as his target: the trunk of the olive-tree that grows sadly, grey and cringing on the slopes of La Sabina; the fox emerging from its earth at dusk to begin its nightly hunt; the eagle gliding through the air. He soon became so skilled that Teresa overcame the fear that she had originally felt on hearing the gun fire and was entertained at seeing her friend put the shot just where he wanted to, as precisely as if he had placed it with his hand.

'One evening, a wolf did indeed come out of a pine wood near which the young people were in the habit of staying. This wolf had not taken ten steps in the open before it was dead. Vampa, proud of his prowess, slung the body over his shoulders and took it back to the farm.

'All this gave Luigi a certain reputation in the district. A superior being, wherever he may be, always acquires a following of admirers. People spoke of the young shepherd as the most skilful, the strongest and bravest *contadino* for ten leagues around; and even though

Teresa, for her part, was considered over an even greater distance as one of the loveliest girls of La Sabina, no one considered speaking a word to her about love, because everyone knew she was loved by Vampa.

'Despite this, the two young people had never declared their love to one another. They had grown up side by side like two trees, the roots of which mingle beneath the earth, as their branches above it and their scents in the air. Yet their desire to see one another was the same: this desire had become a need, and they could understand death better than a single day's separation.

'Teresa was sixteen and Vampa seventeen.

'At about this time, people began to speak a great deal about a band of brigands that was gathering in the Lepini mountains. Banditry has never been properly eradicated from the countryside around Rome. There may sometimes be a shortage of leaders but, when one appears, seldom does he find any shortage of bandits to lead.

'The celebrated Cucumetto, hunted down in the Abruzzi, driven out of the kingdom of Naples, where he had been carrying on a veritable war, had crossed Garigliano like Manfred and come to take refuge on the banks of the Amasina between Sonnino and Juperno. Here he set about reorganizing a band of outlaws, following in the footsteps of Decesaris and Gasparone, whom he hoped soon to surpass. Several young people from Palestrina, Frascati and Pampinara vanished. At first people were concerned about them, but it was soon learned that they had gone to join Cucumetto's band.

'Cucumetto himself shortly became the focus of everybody's attention. Acts of astonishing daring were attributed to him, as well as disgusting brutality.

'One day, he carried off a young girl, the daughter of the land surveyor in Frosinone. The rule among bandits is clear: any girl belongs to the man who first abducts her, then the others draw lots for her, and the unfortunate creature serves to satisfy the lusts of the whole band until the brigands abandon her or she dies.

'When the parents are rich enough to buy her back, the bandits send a messenger to bargain over the ransom: the prisoner's life serves as a guarantee of the emissary's safety. If the ransom is refused, the prisoner is irretrievably condemned.

'This girl had a lover in Cucumetto's band; his name was Carlini.

When she recognized the young man, she held out her arms to him and imagined that she was saved. But poor Carlini, when he in turn recognized her, felt his heart break, because he knew very well what fate had in store for her.

'However, as he was Cucumetto's favourite, had shared every danger with him for three years and had saved his life by shooting a *carabiniere* whose sabre was already poised above Cucumetto's head, he hoped that the chief would take pity on him. So he took him aside, while the young girl, seated against the trunk of a tall pine growing in the middle of a clearing in the forest, had made a veil from the picturesque head-dress that these Roman peasant women wear, and was hiding her face from the lustful gaze of the bandits.

'He told Cucumetto everything: about his love for the prisoner, their promises of fidelity and how, every night while they had been in the district, they had met in some ruins. That evening, as it happened, Cucumetto had sent Carlini to a neighbouring village, so he had not been able to keep his appointment; but Cucumetto, or so he said, had chanced to go there and this was how he came to abduct the girl. Carlini begged his leader to make an exception for him and to respect Rita, telling him that her father was rich and would pay a good ransom.

'Cucumetto appeared to give in to his friend's prayers and instructed him to find a shepherd whom they could send to Rita's father in Frosinone.

'At this, Carlini went joyfully to the girl, told her she was saved and asked her to write a letter to her father, letting him know what had happened and telling him that her ransom had been fixed at three hundred *piastres*. The father was given a mere twelve hours to comply, that is to say, by the next morning at nine o'clock.

'Once the letter had been written, Carlini immediately took it and ran down into the valley to find a messenger.

'He found a young shepherd who was driving his flock to the pen. Shepherds are natural messengers for bandits, because they live between the town and the mountain, between civilized life and savagery.

'The young shepherd left at once, promising to be in Frosinone within the hour, while Carlini returned happily to find his mistress and tell her this good news.

'He found the rest of the band in the clearing where they were merrily supping on the provisions which bandits would levy on the peasants as a simple tribute. Among the merrymakers he looked in vain for Cucumetto and Rita. He asked where they were, but the bandits replied with a huge burst of laughter. A cold sweat broke out on Carlini's brow and he felt his scalp creep with anxiety.

'He repeated the question. One of the diners filled a glass with Orvieto wine and handed it to him, saying: "To the health of brave Cucumetto and the beautiful Rita!"

'At that moment, Carlini thought he heard a woman's cry. He guessed what had happened. He took the glass, broke it across the face of the man who was offering it to him and ran towards the place from which the cry had come.

'A hundred yards away, on the other side of some bushes, he found Rita, senseless in the arms of Cucumetto. When he saw Carlini, Cucumetto got up with a pistol in each hand. The two bandits stared at each other, one with a lustful smile on his lips, the other with the pallor of death on his brow.

'You would have thought that something terrible was about to happen between the two men; but, little by little, Carlini's features relaxed and the hand which he had brought up to one of the pistols in his belt lapsed back to his side.

'Rita was lying between the two of them and the scene was lit by moonlight.

' "Well?" said Cucumetto. "Did you carry out my orders?"

' "Yes, captain," Carlini replied. "Tomorrow, before nine o'clock, Rita's father will be here with the money."

' "Splendid! Meanwhile, we shall enjoy a pleasant night. This girl is charming and I must congratulate you on your taste, Signor Carlini. So, as I am not selfish, we shall return to our comrades and draw lots to see who will have her next."

' "So you have decided to abandon her to the common law?"

' "Why make an exception in her favour?"

' "I thought that my request . . ."

' "And are you more important than the others?"

' "Correct."

' "Calm yourself," Cucumetto said, laughing. "Sooner or later, you will have your turn."

'Carlini's teeth were clenched to breaking point.

' "Come on," Cucumetto said, taking a step in the direction of the feast. "Will you join us?"

' "I will follow you . . ."

'Cucumetto went off without letting Carlini out of his sight, no doubt fearing that he might strike him from behind. But nothing in the bandit's manner suggested any hostile intention. He was standing, with his arms folded, beside the body of Rita, who had still not regained consciousness.

'For a moment, Cucumetto thought that the young man might take her in his arms and escape with her. Not that it mattered to him very much now: he had had what he wanted of Rita and, as far as the money was concerned, three hundred *piastres* divided among all of them amounted to so little that he hardly cared about it. So he carried on towards the clearing where, to his great astonishment, Carlini arrived almost at the same time as he did.

' "Cast lots! Cast lots!" the bandits cried when they saw their chief. And the eyes of all these men shone with drunkenness and lust, while the flames from the fire threw a red light on the figures around it that made them resemble demons.

'What they asked for was within the regulations, so the chief nodded to show that he agreed to their request. All the names were put into a hat, Carlini's with the rest, and the youngest member of the band drew one of them out.

'The slip of paper bore the name of Diavolaccio.

'Now, this was the same man who had proposed the chief's toast, and Carlini had replied to him by breaking a glass on his face. The blood was still flowing from a long cut, extending from his temple to his mouth. When he saw how fortune had favoured him, Diavolaccio burst out laughing.

' "Captain," he said, "a short while ago, Carlini did not want to drink to your health, so suggest that he drinks to mine. Perhaps he will be more obliging to you than he was to me."

'Everyone expected some outburst from Carlini but, to everyone's surprise, he took a glass in one hand and a flask in the other; and, filling the glass, he announced, in a perfectly calm voice: "To your health, Diavolaccio!"

'He swallowed the contents of the glass without a tremor of the hand then, sitting by the fire, he said: "Where's my share of supper? The errand I have just run has given me an appetite."

' "Long live Carlini!" the bandits cried. "Not before time! That's how to accept the matter like a good companion!"

'They all returned to make a circle around the fire, while

Diavolaccio went off. Carlini ate and drank as if nothing had happened.

'The bandits were looking at one another in astonishment, not understanding this impassivity, when they heard heavy footsteps on the ground behind them. They looked around and saw Diavolaccio carrying the girl in his arms. Her head was thrown back and her long hair hung down to the ground. As the two came closer to the light from the fire, the spectators noticed the pallor of the girl and the pallor of the bandit.

'There was something so strange and so solemn about this apparition that everyone got up, except Carlini, who remained seated and continued to eat and drink as if nothing was happening. Diavolaccio continued to walk forward, surrounded by the deepest silence, and set Rita down at the captain's feet.

'At this, everyone understood the reason for the girl's pallor and that of the bandit: Rita had a knife buried up to the hilt beneath her left breast.

'All eyes turned towards Carlini. The sheath at his belt was empty.

'"Ah!" said the chief. "Now I understand why Carlini stayed behind."

'Any savage nature is capable of appreciating a determined action; perhaps no other of the bandits would have done what Carlini had just done, but all of them understood him.

'"Well?" said Carlini, getting up and walking over to the body, with his hand on the butt of one of his pistols. "Does anyone still want to argue with me over this woman?"

'"No," said the chief. "She is yours."

'Then Carlini himself took her in his arms and carried her out of the circle of light thrown by the flames of the fire.

'Cucumetto placed his sentries as usual and the bandits went to sleep, wrapped in their cloaks, around the fire.

'At midnight the sentry sounded the alarm, and immediately the chief and his companions were on their feet. It was Rita's father coming in person and bearing his daughter's ransom.

'"Here," he said to Cucumetto, handing him a bag of money. "Take it: this is three hundred pistols. Now give me back my child."

'But the chief, without taking the money, motioned to him to follow. The old man obeyed and both went away under the trees, under the moonlight filtering through their branches. Eventually

Cucumetto stopped and pointed out two people sitting together under a tree.

' "There," he said to the old man. "Ask Carlini for your daughter. He will tell you about it."

'And he went back to the group.

'The old man stood there, motionless, staring. He felt that some unknown misfortune, vast and unprecedented, was about to strike him. Finally he took a few steps towards the shapeless group which he could barely make out.

'At the sound of his approach, Carlini looked up and the shape of the two figures began to become clearer to the old man's eyes. A woman was lying on the ground with her head resting on the knees of a seated man who was bending over her. When he looked up the man had revealed the face of the woman which he had been pressing against his chest. The old man recognized his daughter, and Carlini recognized the old man.

' "I was expecting you," the bandit said to Rita's father.

' "Miserable creature!" said the old man. "What have you done?" And he looked in horror at Rita, who was lying, pale, motionless, bloodstained, with a knife in her breast. A ray of moonlight struck her and lit the scene with its wan light.

' "Cucumetto violated your daughter," the bandit said. "And, since I loved her, I killed her, for after him she would have served for the pleasure of the whole band."

'The old man said nothing but went as pale as a ghost.

' "Now," Carlini said, "if I was wrong, avenge her." And he drew the knife from the young girl's breast, got up and offered it to the old man with one hand, while with the other opening his shirt and presenting him with his bared chest.

' "You did well," the old man said in a dull voice. "Embrace me, my son."

'Carlini flung himself, sobbing, into the arms of his mistress's father. These were the first tears that this man of blood had ever shed.

' "Now," the old man told him, "help me to bury my daughter."

'Carlini went to fetch two spades, then the father and lover began to dig under an oak-tree whose dense foliage would cover the young girl's grave. When it was dug, the father kissed her, followed by the lover. Then, one taking her by the feet, the other beneath the shoulders, they lowered her into the grave.

'After that they knelt, one on each side, and recited the prayer for the dead. When that was done, they shovelled the earth back on the body until the grave was full.

'Then, holding out his hand, the old man said: "Thank you, my son! Now, leave me alone."

' "But . . ." said Carlini.

' "I order you to leave me."

'Carlini obeyed and went back to his comrades, wrapped himself in his cloak and soon appeared to have fallen into as deep a sleep as the others.

'The previous day it had been decided that they would move camp. An hour before daybreak, Cucumetto woke up his men and gave the order to leave. But Carlini did not want to leave the forest without finding out what had happened to Rita's father. He went to the spot where he had left him and there found the old man hanging from one of the branches of the oak-tree that overshadowed his daughter's grave.

'So Carlini swore on the body of one and the grave of the other that he would avenge them both.

'However, he was unable to keep his oath for, two days later, in an encounter with the Roman *carabinieri*, Carlini was killed.

'The only surprising thing was that, though he had been facing the enemy, he was shot by a bullet through the back. But no one any longer felt surprised when one of the bandits pointed out to his colleagues that Cucumetto had been standing ten yards behind Carlini when the latter fell.

'On the morning of their departure from the forest of Frosinone, he had followed Carlini in the darkness, heard the oath he swore and, being a cautious man, had decided to strike first.

'There were ten other tales no less extraordinary than that one told about this fearful bandit leader. So, from Fondi to Perugia, everyone trembled at the mere name of Cucumetto.

'These stories were often the subject of conversation between Luigi and Teresa. The girl would be very frightened by them, but Vampa reassured her with a smile and tapped his fine gun which shot so accurately. Then, if she was still not easy in her mind, he would point to some crow perched on a dead branch, take aim at it and fire: the creature would fall at the foot of the tree.

'Time went by. The two young people had agreed to marry when Vampa was twenty and Teresa nineteen. Both were orphans, so they did not need to ask permission except from their masters; they had done so and it was granted.

'One day, when they were discussing the future, they both heard two or three shots. Then, suddenly, a man came out of the wood near which the pair of them were accustomed to graze their sheep and ran towards them. As soon as he was in earshot, he cried: "I am being pursued! Can you hide me?"

'The young couple easily realized that this fugitive must be a bandit of some sort, but there exists an innate sympathy between the peasant and the Roman bandit which means that the former is always ready to help the latter.

'So, saying nothing, Vampa ran to the stone that covered the entrance to their cave, opened it by pushing back the stone, indicated to the fugitive that he should hide in this refuge which no one knew, returned the stone to its place and went back to sit beside Teresa.

'Almost immediately, four *carabinieri* appeared on horseback at the edge of the wood. Three seemed to be hunting the fugitive, the fourth had a bandit as his prisoner and was leading him by a rope around the neck.

'The first three surveyed the scene, saw the two young people, galloped over and began to question them.

'They had seen nothing.

' "That's annoying," said the brigadier, "because the one we are looking for is the leader."

' "Cucumetto?" Luigi and Teresa could not refrain from crying out together.

' "Yes," the brigadier said. "And since there is a price of a thousand Roman *écus* on his head, there would have been five hundred for you if you had helped us to capture him."

'The couple looked at one another. For a moment, the brigadier's hopes rose: five hundred Roman *écus* is equal to three thousand francs, and three thousand francs is a fortune for two poor orphans who want to marry.

' "Yes, it's very annoying," said Vampa, "but we haven't seen him."

'So the *carabinieri* scoured the countryside in different directions, but to no avail. Then, one by one, they left.

'At this, Vampa went to move the stone and Cucumetto came out.

'Through the cracks in his granite door, he had seen the two young people chatting with the *carabinieri* and guessed the tenor of the conversation, reading on the faces of Luigi and Teresa their unshakeable determination not to hand him over; so he drew from his pocket a purse full of gold and offered it to them.

'But Vampa tossed his head proudly. As for Teresa, her eyes shone when she thought of all the rich jewels and fine clothes she could buy with that purse full of gold.

'Cucumetto was an extremely clever tempter: in him Satan had taken the shape of a bandit rather than a serpent. He intercepted the look and recognized in Teresa a worthy daughter of Eve. He went back into the forest, turning around several times, on the pretext of thanking his liberators.

'Several days passed without them seeing or hearing any more of Cucumetto.

'The time of the carnival was approaching. The Count of San-Felice announced that he would be holding a great masked ball to which all the most elegant members of Roman society would be invited. Teresa was very anxious to see this ball. Luigi asked his protector the steward for permission for himself and Teresa to take part in it, concealed among the house servants. Permission was granted.

'The ball was being given by the count chiefly to please his daughter Carmela, whom he adored. Carmela was just the same age and height as Teresa, and Teresa was at least as beautiful as Carmela.

'On the evening of the ball, Teresa put on her finest dress, her most expensive pins, her most brilliant glass beads. She was wearing the costume of the women of Frascati. Luigi had on the picturesque clothes worn by a Roman peasant on feast days. Both mingled, as had been agreed, with the waiters and peasants.

'The feast was splendid. Not only was the villa itself brightly lit, but thousands of coloured lanterns were hanging from the trees in the garden. The guests soon overflowed on to the terraces and then to the alleys in the garden. At each crossroads there was an orchestra, a buffet and refreshments. The strollers paused, a quadrille was formed and they danced wherever the fancy took them.

'Carmela was dressed as a woman from Sonino. She had a bonnet embroidered with pearls, her hairpins were of gold and diamonds, her belt was of Turkish silk embroidered with large flowers, her coat and her skirt were of cashmere, her apron was of Indian muslin and the buttons on her bodice were precious stones.

'Two of her companions were dressed in the costumes of women from Nettuno and La Riccia.

'Four young men from the richest and noblest families in Rome were accompanying them, with that Italian freedom of manner which has no equivalent in any other country in the world; they were dressed as peasants from Albano, Velletri, Civita Castellana and Sora. It goes without saying that their peasant costumes, like those of the women, glittered with gold and precious stones.

'Carmela had the idea of making them into a uniform quadrille, but they were short of a woman. She looked around, but not one of the other guests had a costume similar to hers and those of her companions. Then the Count de San-Felice showed her Teresa, leaning on Luigi's arm among the peasant women.

'"May I, father?" said Carmela.

'"Of course you may," the count replied. "After all, it's carnival!"

'Carmela leant over to a young man who was walking beside her and talking, and said a few words to him, pointing at the girl. He followed the direction indicated by the pretty hand, made a sign of obedience and went across to invite Teresa to join the quadrille led by the count's daughter.

'Teresa felt as if a flame had passed across her face. She looked questioningly at Luigi: there was no way to refuse. Luigi slowly let slip Teresa's arm which he was holding beneath his own, and Teresa went off, trembling, led by her elegant squire, to take her place in the aristocratic quadrille.

'Admittedly, to an artist, there was a great difference between the austere, restrained costume worn by Teresa and those worn by Carmela and her companions; but Teresa was a frivolous and coquettish young girl; she was dazzled by the embroidered muslin, the buckles on the belts, the sheen on the cashmere; she was driven wild by the sparkling of the sapphires and diamonds.

'Luigi, on the other hand, was gripped by a previously unknown emotion: it was like a dull pain, gnawing first at his heart, then quivering as it spread through his veins and took possession of his whole body. His eyes followed every movement made by Teresa and her squire. When their hands touched, he felt a sort of dizziness, his heart thumped and it was as though a bell were chiming in his ears. When they spoke, though Teresa was listening shyly and with lowered gaze to the young nobleman's words, Luigi could read in the man's eyes that they were compliments, and it seemed to him that the earth was spinning beneath his feet, while all the voices of hell whispered ideas of murder and violence. Then, fearing that he might be carried away by his folly, with one hand he clasped the arbour beneath which he was standing, and with the other he grasped convulsively the dagger with the sculpted hilt which he kept in his belt and which, unconsciously, he was drawing from time to time almost entirely out of its sheath.

'Luigi was jealous! He realized that Teresa, carried away by her proud and capricious nature, might one day be lost to him.

'Meanwhile, the young peasant girl, at first shy and almost terrified, had quickly recovered. I said that Teresa was beautiful, but that is not all; she had charm, that savage grace that is so much more powerful than any simpering or affected elegance.

'She almost had the honours of the quadrille and, though she was certainly envious of the count's daughter, it is not altogether impossible that Carmela was jealous of her.

'Her handsome squire led her back, accompanied by many compliments, to the place from which he had taken her, where Luigi was waiting.

'Two or three times, during the contredanse, the girl had cast an eye in his direction and each time had seen him looking pale and drawn. Once, even, the blade of his knife, half drawn out of the sheath, had cast a sinister shaft of light towards her. So she was almost afraid when she returned to her lover's arm.

'The quadrille had been a tremendous success and there was clearly a call for the experiment to be repeated. Only Carmela objected, but the Count of San-Felice begged his daughter so tenderly that she eventually consented.

'One of the young noblemen went across to invite Teresa, without whom the dance could not take place; but she was gone.

'What had happened was that Luigi, not feeling strong enough to be tested any further, had led Teresa partly by force and partly by persuasion into another part of the garden. She had gone very unwillingly; but from the young man's distraught appearance and his silence, broken by nervous twitching, she guessed that something unusual was going on in his mind. She herself was not altogether easy inside and, even though she had not done anything wrong, she understood that Luigi had the right to reproach her. For what? She did not know. Nonetheless she felt that such reproaches would be deserved.

'Yet, to Teresa's great astonishment, Luigi remained silent and not a word passed his lips throughout the rest of the evening. But when the chill of the night had driven the guests from the gardens and the doors of the villa had been closed against them while the ball continued indoors, he took Teresa back home and, as she was about to go in, asked: "Teresa, what were you thinking of while you were dancing opposite the young Countess of San-Felice?"

' "I was thinking," the girl answered in all frankness, "that I should give half my life to have a costume like the one she was wearing."

' "And what did your partner say?"

' "He told me that it was up to me if I should have such a dress, I had only to say one word."

' "He was right," Luigi replied. "Do you want it as desperately as you say?"

' "Yes."

' "Then you shall have it!"

'The young girl looked up in astonishment to ask for an explanation, but his face was so sombre and fearful that the question froze on her lips. In any case, while he was speaking, Luigi had started to walk away. Teresa looked after him until he disappeared into the darkness and, when she could no longer see him, she sighed and went into her house.

'That same night a great accident occurred, no doubt because of the neglectfulness of some servant who had forgotten to put out the lights: the Villa San-Felice caught fire, in the very wing where the beautiful Carmela had her apartments. Woken up in the middle of the night by the glow of the flames, she had leapt out of bed, pulled on her nightgown and tried to escape through the door; but the corridor outside was already enveloped in flames. So she returned to her room, crying loudly for help, when suddenly her window, which was twenty feet off the ground, flew open and a young peasant lad burst into the apartment, took her in his arms and, with superhuman strength and agility, carried her out and down to the lawn, where she fainted. When she regained her senses, her father was standing in front of her, surrounded by all the servants who were trying to help her. A whole wing of the villa had burned down – but what did it matter, since Carmela was safe and sound?

'They looked everywhere for her saviour, but he did not appear. Everyone was questioned; no one had seen him. As for Carmela, she was so overwhelmed by events that she did not recognize him.

'In any event, as the count was immensely rich, apart from the danger that had threatened Carmela – and which appeared to him, thanks to her miraculous escape from it, more like a new sign that fate was smiling on him, rather than a real disaster – the loss caused by the flames mattered very little to him.

'The next day, at the usual time, the two young peasants met on the edge of the forest. Luigi was the first to arrive. He came joyfully to meet the girl, apparently having entirely forgotten what had passed between them the previous evening. Teresa was pensive but, when she saw Luigi's good humour, she adopted the attitude of merry insouciance which was her natural temperament when no greater passion happened to disturb it.

'Luigi took Teresa's arm in his and led her to the door of the cave. There he stopped. The girl, realizing that something extraordinary was up, stared closely at him.

' "Teresa," he said, "yesterday evening you told me that you would give everything to have a costume like that of the count's daughter?"

' "Yes," she replied with amazement, "but I was mad to make such a wish."

' "And I told you: very well, you shall have it?"

' "Yes," the girl said, her astonishment growing with every word that Luigi spoke. "But I suppose you only said that to please me."

' "I have never promised you anything which I have not given you, Teresa," Luigi said proudly. "Go into the grotto, and dress yourself."

'At this, he rolled back the stone and showed Teresa the inside of the cave, lit by two candles burning on each side of a splendid mirror. On a rustic table which Luigi had made were the pearl necklace and diamond pins; on a chair beside them, the rest of the costume.

'Teresa gave a cry of joy and, without asking where the dress had come from or taking the time to thank Luigi, she dashed into the cave which had been transformed into her dressing-room.

'Luigi pulled the stone back behind her, because he had just noticed a traveller on horseback on the crest of a little hill that blocked the view between where he was and the town of Palestrina. The rider had paused as if uncertain of his way and was outlined against the blue sky with the peculiar sharpness given to distant objects by the atmosphere in southern lands.

'When he saw Luigi, the traveller galloped down towards him. Luigi had been right: the man was going from Palestrina to Tivoli and had lost his way. The young man put him on the right track; however, since the road divided again into three paths, when the traveller reached them he might lose his way once more, so he begged Luigi to act as his guide.

'Luigi took off his cloak and put it on the ground, slung his carbine over his shoulder and, free of his heavy shepherd's mantle, walked ahead of the traveller with the rapid pace of a mountain-dweller with which even a walking horse has difficulty in keeping up.

'In ten minutes the two of them had reached the sort of crossroads that the young shepherd had mentioned. Here, with a majestic gesture like that of an emperor, Luigi pointed to the one of the three roads that the traveller should follow.

' "There is your way, Excellency," he said. "You cannot make a mistake from here on."

' "And here is your reward," the traveller said, offering the young shepherd a few small coins.

' "Thank you," said Luigi, withdrawing his hand. "I give services, I don't sell them."

'The traveller seemed used to this difference between the servility of the townsman and the pride of the countryman: "Very well," he said. 'If you refuse payment, at least accept a gift."

' "Ah, that is another matter."

' "Fine! Take these two Venetian sequins and give them to your fiancée to make a pair of earrings."

' "And you, then, take this dagger," said the young shepherd. "You will not find one with a better-carved handle between Albano and Civita Castellana."

' "I accept," said the traveller. "But in that case, it is I who shall be in your debt, because this dagger is worth more than two sequins."

' "To a shopkeeper, perhaps, but to me, who carved it myself, it is hardly worth one *piastre*."

' "What is your name?" asked the traveller.

' "Luigi Vampa," the shepherd replied, in the same accents in which he might have said: Alexander, king of Macedonia. "And yours?"

' "I," said the traveller, "am called Sinbad the Sailor." '

Franz d'Epinay gave a cry of astonishment.

'Sinbad the Sailor!' he exclaimed.

'Yes,' the storyteller answered. 'That was the name that the traveller told Vampa.'

'What do you have against the name?' Albert interrupted. 'It's a very fine one, and the adventures of the gentleman's patron, I must admit, entertained me greatly when I was young.'

Franz did not insist. As one may understand, the name of Sinbad the Sailor had brought back a flood of memories to him, as had the name of the Count of Monte Cristo the previous evening.

'Continue,' he told his host.

'Vampa disdainfully put the sequins into his pocket and slowly returned the way he had come. When he had arrived within two or three hundred yards of the cave, he thought he heard a cry. He stopped, listening to make out where it came from. A moment later, he clearly heard someone calling his name. The sound was coming from the grotto.

'He leapt like a chamois, cocking his gun as he ran, and in less than a minute he had reached the top of the hill opposite the one on which he had seen the traveller. From there, he could hear the cry of "Help, help!" more clearly than ever. He looked down into the hollow below him and saw that a man was carrying Teresa off, just as the centaur Nessus carried off Deianira.

'The man was making his way towards the woods and had already reached the halfway point between there and the cave.

'Vampa measured the distance. They were at least two hundred yards ahead of him; he had no hope of catching them up before they reached the woods.

'The young shepherd stopped as if his feet had grown roots. He put the gun to his cheek, slowly raised the barrel towards the ravisher, followed this moving target for a second and fired. The man stopped in his tracks. His knees buckled and he fell, taking Teresa down with him.

'However, she got up immediately. As for the man, he stayed on the ground, thrashing in agony.

'Vampa at once ran towards Teresa because she had not got ten

paces away from the dying man when her own legs failed her and
she fell to her knees. The young peasant was terrified that the shot
which had just brought down his enemy might have wounded her
at the same time.

'Fortunately this was not the case; sheer terror had deprived
Teresa of strength. When Luigi was quite sure that she was safe and
sound, he turned to the wounded man.

'He had just expired, with his fists clenched, his mouth twisted
in pain and his hair rigid with the sweat of his final agony. His eyes
had remained open and threatening.

'Vampa went across to the corpse and recognized Cucumetto.

'On the day when the bandit had been saved by the two young
people, he had fallen in love with Teresa and had sworn that the
girl would be his. Since that time he had spied on her and, taking
advantage of the moment when her lover left her alone to show the
traveller his way, he had abducted her and already considered her
his own when Vampa's bullet, guided by his unerring aim, went
straight through Cucumetto's heart.

'Vampa looked at him for a moment without showing the slightest sign of emotion, while Teresa, on the contrary, was still trembling and only dared to creep towards the dead bandit and
cautiously take a look at him over her lover's shoulder.

'After a short time, Vampa turned to his mistress and said: "Ah,
good! You are dressed. Now it's my turn to get ready."

'Teresa was indeed dressed from head to foot in the costume
belonging to the daughter of the Count of San-Felice.

'Vampa took Cucumetto's body in his arms and carried it into
the grotto while Teresa remained outside. If at this time a second
traveller had ridden past, he would have seen something odd: a
shepherdess watching her sheep in a cashmere dress, with pearl
earrings and necklace, diamond pins and buttons of sapphires,
emeralds and rubies. He would no doubt have thought he had been
transported back into the age of Florian[4] and on his return to Paris
would have sworn that he had seen the Shepherdess of the Alps
seated at the foot of the Sabine Mountains.

'After a quarter of an hour Vampa came out of the cave. His
costume was no less elegant in its way than Teresa's. He had on
a jacket of garnet-coloured velvet with wrought-gold buttons, a
waistcoat covered in embroidery, a Roman scarf knotted around
his neck and a cartridge-belt picked out in gold leaf and ornamented

with red and green silk. He had sky-blue velvet trousers, fastened above the knee with diamond buckles, richly tooled buckskin gaiters and a hat decorated with ribbons in every colour. Two watches hung at his waist and there was a splendid dagger set in his cartridge belt.

'Teresa cried out in admiration. Dressed in this way, Vampa looked like a painting by Léopold Robert or Schnetz.[5] He had decked himself out in Cucumetto's entire costume.

'He observed the effect of this on his fiancée and a smile of pride crossed his lips. "Now," he said, "are you ready to share my fortune, whatever it may be?"

' "Oh, yes!" the girl exclaimed eagerly.

' "To follow me wherever I lead?"

' "To the ends of the earth."

' "Then take my arm and let's go, for we have no time to lose."

'The girl took her lover's arm without even asking where they were going; for, at that moment, he seemed to her as handsome, as proud and as powerful as a god. In a few moments the couple had crossed into the forest and began to proceed through it.

'It goes without saying that Vampa knew all the mountain tracks, so he went forward into the forest without hesitation, even though there was no path before them, finding his way merely by looking at the trees and bushes. They walked for about an hour and a half.

'After that, they reached the thickest part of the wood. A dry river-bed led into a deep gorge. Vampa took this strange path which, enclosed between two banks and darkened by the thick shade of the pines, resembled in everything but the ease of descent the path of the Avernus[6] of which Virgil speaks.

'Teresa's fears had returned at the sight of this wild and desolate place. She pressed close to her guide, saying nothing; but, seeing that he continued to walk ahead at an even pace with a profound look of tranquillity on his face, she herself found the strength to hide her feelings.

'Suddenly, ten yards ahead of them, a man seemed to appear from the very trunk of the tree behind which he had been concealed, and levelled his gun at Vampa, crying: "Not another step, or you are a dead man!"

' "Come now," said Vampa, raising his hand in a contemptuous gesture, while Teresa clung to him, no longer able to conceal her terror. "Do wolves fight among themselves?"

' "Who are you?" asked the sentry.

' "I am Luigi Vampa, shepherd from the farm of San-Felice."

' "And what do you want?"

' "I wish to speak to your companions who are in the clearing of Rocca Bianca."

' "Then follow me," said the sentry. "Or, rather, as you know where it is, lead the way."

'Vampa smiled contemptuously at this precaution, stepped ahead with Teresa and continued on his way with the same calm, firm step that had brought him this far.

'In five minutes the bandit signalled to them to stop. They did so. The bandit gave the cry of a crow three times, and it was answered by a single cawing.

' "Very well," said the bandit. "Now you can carry on."

'Luigi and Teresa did so; but as they advanced, Teresa trembled and pressed even closer to her lover: through the trees they could see weapons appearing and the sunlight glittering on the barrels of guns.

'The clearing at Rocca Bianca was on the summit of a little mountain which had no doubt previously been a volcano, but one that had become extinct before Romulus and Remus left Alba to come and build Rome. Teresa and Luigi reached the summit and were immediately confronted with about twenty bandits.

' "Here is a young man who has been looking for you and wants to talk to you," said the sentry.

' "And what does he want to say?" asked the man who was acting as captain in their leader's absence.

' "I want to say that I am tired of being a shepherd," said Vampa.

' "Ah, I understand," replied the lieutenant. "You have come to ask to be admitted to our ranks?"

' "Let him be welcome!" several bandits from Ferrusino, Pampinara and Anagni cried, having recognized Luigi Vampa.

' "Yes, except that I am requesting something else, apart from being your companion."

' "What is your request?" the bandits said in astonishment.

' "I want to ask to be your captain," the young man said.

'The bandits burst out laughing.

' "So what have you done to aspire to such an honour?" the lieutenant demanded.

' "I have killed your leader, Cucumetto, whose clothes these are," said Luigi. "And I set light to the villa of San-Felice to give my fiancée a wedding dress."

'An hour later, Luigi Vampa had been elected captain to replace Cucumetto.'

'Well, my dear Albert,' said Franz, turning to his friend. 'What do you think now of Citizen Luigi Vampa?'

'I think he's a myth,' Albert replied. 'He never existed.'

'What is a myth?' Pastrini asked.

'It would take too long to explain, my good friend,' Franz replied. 'So you are telling us that Signor Vampa is currently exercising his profession in the environs of Rome?'

'With a boldness that no previous bandit has ever displayed.'

'So the police have tried in vain to capture him?'

'What do you expect? He is in league with the shepherds of the plain, the Tiber fishermen and the coastal smugglers. If they go looking for him in the mountains, he is on the river; if they hunt him down the river, he is out at sea; then suddenly, when they think he has taken refuge on the islands of Giglio, Guanouti or Monte Cristo, he reappears in Albano, Tivoli or La Riccia.'

'And how does he treat travellers?'

'Very simply. According to the distance from the city, he allows them eight hours, twelve hours or a day to pay their ransom. Then, when the time has elapsed, he gives them an hour's grace. On the sixtieth minute of that hour, if he does not have the money, he blows out the prisoner's brains with his pistol or buries his dagger in his heart, and there's an end to it.'

'Well, Albert,' Franz asked his companion, 'do you still feel like going to the Colosseum via the boulevards outside the walls?'

'Naturally,' said Albert, 'if the route is more picturesque.'

At that moment the clock struck nine, the door opened and the coachman appeared.

'Excellencies,' he said, 'your carriage awaits you.'

'Very well,' said Franz, 'in that case, to the Colosseum!'

'Via the Porta del Popolo, Excellencies, or through the streets?'

'Through the streets, confound it! Through the streets!' said Franz.

'Oh, my dear fellow!' said Albert, getting up and lighting his third cigar. 'I must confess I thought you braver than that!'

Upon which the two young men went down the stairs and got into their carriage.

XXXIV

AN APPARITION

Franz had found a compromise that would allow Albert to reach the Colosseum without passing by any antique ruin, avoiding a gradual approach that might deprive the colossus of a single cubit of its massive proportions. This compromise was to go down the Via Sistina, turn due right at Santa Maria Maggiore and take the Via Urbana, past San Pietro in Vincoli, to the Via del Colosseo.

There was an additional advantage in this route, which was that it would not at all distract Franz from the effects of the story which Signor Pastrini had told them – and in which his mysterious host from the island of Monte Cristo had made an appearance. So he was able to sit, resting, in a corner of the carriage and to consider the endless succession of questions that had arisen in his mind, though without finding a satisfactory reply to any of them.

Something else, as it happens, had brought his friend Sinbad the Sailor to mind: this was the mysterious relationship between bandits and seamen. What Signor Pastrini said about Vampa taking refuge on the fishing boats and smugglers' craft reminded Franz of the two Corsican bandits whom he had found dining with the crew of the little yacht, which had gone out of its way and made land at Porto Vecchio, solely in order to put them ashore. The name which his host on Monte Cristo had given himself, spoken by the proprietor of the Hôtel de Londres, proved that he played the same philanthropic role on the coasts of Piombino, Civita Vecchia, Ostia and Gaeta as on those of Corsica, Tuscany or Spain; and, as far as Franz could remember, he had himself spoken of Tunis and Palermo, proving that he operated over a wide area.

However powerfully all these ideas occupied the young man's mind, they vanished the instant he found himself confronted with the dark and massive spectre of the Colosseum, through the openings of which the moon was casting those long pale rays of light that shine from the eyes of ghosts. The carriage halted a few yards from the Mesa Sudans. The coachman came and opened the door; the two young men jumped out and found themselves confronted by a guide who seemed to have sprung up out of the earth. Since the one from the hotel had followed them, they now had two.

In any case, it is impossible in Rome to avoid this over-provision of guides: apart from the general one who takes charge of you as soon as you step over the threshold of the hotel and who does not release you from his clutches until you step outside the city, there is a special guide attached to every monument; one might almost say, to every fragment of every monument. So you can well imagine that there was no shortage of them at the Colosseum, that is to say at the monument of monuments, the one of which Martial[1] said: 'Let Memphis cease to boast of the barbarous marvels of its pyramids and let them sing no more of the wonders of Babylon; everything must give precedence to the vast labour of the amphitheatre of the Caesars and all the trumpets of praise unite in admiration of this monument.'

Franz and Albert did not try to evade this tyranny of the guides, something that would in any case have been all the more difficult, since only guides have the right to visit the Colosseum by torchlight. So they offered no resistance and yielded to their controllers, as it were bound hand and foot.

Franz knew the walk: he had done it ten times already. But since his less experienced companion was stepping for the first time into the monument of Flavius Vespasian, I must say to his credit that he was highly impressed, in spite of the ignorant chatter of his guides. Anyone who has not seen it can have no idea of the majesty of this ruin, its proportions doubled by the mysterious clarity of the southern moon, the rays of which give a light resembling that of a western sunset.

So, hardly had the thoughtful Franz taken a hundred paces beneath the inner arches than he abandoned Albert to the guides, who were unwilling to give up their inalienable right to show him every inch of the Lions' Pit, the Gladiators' Box and the Imperial Podium, and slipped away by a partly dilapidated staircase. Then, allowing the others to continue the usual course round the ruins, he simply went and sat at the base of a column, facing a hollow depression which allowed him to take in the full extensive majesty of the granite giant.

He had been there for about a quarter of an hour, seated, as I said, in the shadow of a column and lost in the contemplation of Albert who, accompanied by his two torchbearers, had just emerged from a vomitorium at the far end of the Colosseum and with them, like shadows pursuing a will-o'-the-wisp, was descending step by step towards the seats reserved for the Vestal Virgins, when Franz thought he heard a loose stone tumbling into the depths of the building from the staircase opposite the one that he had just taken to reach the place where he was sitting. No doubt there is nothing exceptional here in a stone coming away beneath the foot of time and rolling into the depths; but it seemed to him that on this occasion a man's foot was the cause and that steps were approaching him, even though the person responsible for them was doing his very best to muffle them. And, in effect, a moment later a man appeared, gradually emerging from the shadows as he came up the staircase, the opening of which was in front of Franz and lit by the moon, though its steps receded into the darkness as they went down.

It might be a traveller like himself who preferred solitary meditation to the meaningless chatter of the guides, so there should be nothing surprising in the apparition; but from the hesitant manner in which he came up the last few steps and the way that, once he had reached the landing, he stopped, seeming to be listening for something, it was clear that he had come there for some particular purpose and was expecting someone.

Franz instinctively did his utmost to melt into the shadow behind the column.

Ten feet above the level on which both of them were now standing, there was a round hole in the vaulted roof, like the opening of a well, through which could be seen the sky, bestrewn with stars. This opening had quite probably been letting in the moonlight for a hundred years and around it grew bushes whose delicate green foliage stood out sharply against the soft blue of the sky, while great creepers and huge bunches of ivy dangled down from this upper terrace and hung below the arched roof, like trailing ropes.

The person whose mysterious arrival had attracted Franz's attention was standing in the half-light, so that it was impossible to distinguish his features, but not so much as to prevent one seeing his dress: he was wrapped in a vast brown cloak, one fold of which, thrown over his left shoulder, hid the bottom part of his face, while the upper part was concealed beneath his broad-brimmed hat. Only the outer part of his clothing was lit by the glancing ray of moonlight through the opening in the roof, and it showed a pair of black trousers elegantly framing a polished shoe.

Clearly the man belonged either to the aristocracy or, at least, to the upper realms of society.

He had been there for some minutes and was starting to give visible signs of impatience, when a slight noise was heard on the terrace above. At the same moment a shadow passed in front of the light and a man appeared, framed in the hole, staring intently into the darkness beneath him. Seeing the man in the cloak, he immediately grasped a handful of the dangling creepers and hanging ivy, let himself slide down them and, at about three or four feet above the ground, leapt lightly down. He was dressed in the pure costume of Trastevere.

'Forgive me, Excellency,' he said, in Roman dialect. 'I've kept you waiting. Even so, I am only a few minutes late. Ten o'clock has just sounded at St John Lateran.'

'You are not late; I was early,' the stranger replied, in pure Tuscan. 'So, no apologies. In any event, if you had kept me waiting, I should have guessed that it was for some unavoidable reason.'

'You would have been right, Excellency. I have just returned from the Castel Sant' Angelo, and I found it very hard getting to speak to Beppo.'

'Who is Beppo?'

'Beppo is an employee at the prison, to whom I pay a small sum in exchange for information about what goes on inside His Holiness's castle.'

'Ah, I can see you are a man of foresight.'

'What do you expect, Excellency! One never knows what may happen. I too might one day be caught in the same net as poor Peppino and need a rat to gnaw away the meshes of my prison.'

'So, briefly, what did you learn?'

'There will be two executions on Tuesday at two o'clock, as usual in Rome at the start of an important holiday. One of the condemned will be *mazzolato*: this is some wretch who killed a priest who had brought him up; he deserves no pity. The other will be *decapitato*: that is poor Peppino.'

'What do you expect, my dear fellow? You inspire such terror, not only in the papal government, but even in the neighbouring kingdoms; they are absolutely determined to set an example.'

'But Peppino does not even belong to my band. He is a poor shepherd who has committed no other crime than to supply us with food.'

'Which undeniably makes him your accomplice. But they are showing him some consideration. Instead of being beaten to death, as you would be if they ever caught you, he will merely be guillotined. In any event, this will vary the entertainment and they will have something for everyone to watch.'

'Quite apart from the entertainment which I am planning and which no one expects.'

'My dear friend,' said the man in the cloak, 'forgive me for saying this, but I suspect you may be preparing to commit some act of folly.'

'I shall do everything to prevent the execution of a poor devil who finds himself in this pass because he helped me. By the Madonna! I should consider myself a coward if I were not to do something for the poor boy.'

'And what do you intend to do?'

'I shall deploy twenty men or so around the scaffold and, as soon as they bring him, give a signal; then we shall leap on the escort with daggers drawn and carry him off.'

'This plan seems very risky to me and I honestly believe that mine may be better.'

'And what is your plan, Excellency?'

'I shall give a thousand *piastres* to someone I know and shall succeed in having Peppino's execution delayed until next year. At that time I shall give another thousand *piastres* to another person, whom I also know, and have him escape from prison.'

'Are you sure this will work?'

'*Pardieu!*' said the man in the cloak, in French.

'I beg your pardon?' said the Trasteveran.

'What I mean, my dear fellow, is that I shall do more by myself with my gold than you and all your people with their daggers, their pistols, their carbines and their blunderbusses. So let me do it.'

'Willingly; but if you should fail, we shall still be ready and waiting.'

'Be ready, that's up to you; but you may be sure I shall have him pardoned.'

'Tuesday is the day after tomorrow, so beware. You only have tomorrow.'

'Yes, agreed. But there are twenty-four hours in a day, sixty minutes in an hour and sixty seconds in a minute. A lot can be done in eighty-six thousand four hundred seconds.'

'How will we know if you have succeeded, Excellency?'

'Simple. I have rented the last three windows in the Café Rospoli. If I have obtained a stay of execution, the two corner windows will be hung with yellow damask, but the middle one with a red cross on white damask.'

'Perfect. And how will you deliver the pardon?'

'Send me one of your men, disguised as a penitent, and I shall give it to him. Dressed in that way, he will easily get to the foot of the scaffold and pass the decree to the head of the Order of Penitents, who will give it to the executioner. Meanwhile, have the news given to Peppino. We don't want him to die of fear or go mad, because in that case we would have been to a lot of needless trouble and expense on his behalf.'

'Listen, Excellency,' said the peasant. 'I am deeply devoted to you, you know that, I suppose?'

'I hope so, at least.'

'Well, if you can save Peppino, it will be more than devotion from now on, it will be obedience.'

'Careful what you are saying, my good friend! I may perhaps remind you of this one day, because the day may come when I shall need you in my turn . . .'

'Well, then, Excellency, you will find me in your hour of need as I found you at this moment. Even if you should be in the other end of the earth, you have only to write to me: "Do this!", and I shall do it, by my . . .'

'Hush!' the other man said. 'I can hear something.'

'It's some travellers visiting the Colosseum by torchlight.'

'There would be no sense in letting them find us together. The guides are all informers and they might recognize you; honourable though your friendship is, my dear friend, if people knew that we were as close as we are, I fear that my reputation might suffer from it.'

'So, if you do obtain the stay of execution?'

'The middle window will have a damask hanging with a red cross.'

'And if you fail to obtain it?'

'The yellow hangings.'

'And in that case?'

'In that case, my good fellow, feel free to exercise your dagger: I give you my permission and I shall be there to see it.'

'Farewell, Excellency. I am counting on you. Count on me!'

With these words, the Trasteveran disappeared down the stairway, while the stranger, wrapping his face still more tightly in his cloak, passed within a couple of yards of Franz and went down into the arena by the outside steps. A second later Franz heard his name echoing beneath the vaults: Albert was calling him.

He waited until the two men had got well away before replying, not wishing to let them know that there had been a witness who, even though he had not seen their faces, had not missed a word of their conversation.

Ten minutes later, Franz was driving back towards the Hôtel d'Espagne, listening with quite unmannerly lack of attention to the learned discourse that Albert was making, based on Pliny and Calpurnius, about the nets furnished with iron spikes which used to prevent the wild animals from pouncing on the spectators.

He let him chatter on without arguing. He was anxious to be left alone so that he could give his whole mind to what had just taken place in front of him.

One of the two men had certainly been a stranger to him, and this had been the first time he had seen or heard him; but the same was not true of the other. And, though Franz had not been able to make out the man's face, which was constantly wrapped either in darkness or in his cloak, the sound of that voice had struck him too forcibly the first time he heard it for him ever to hear it again without recognizing it. There was, above all, something strident and metallic in those mocking tones which had made him tremble in the ruins of the Colosseum as before in the caves of Monte Cristo. He was utterly convinced that the man was none other than Sinbad the Sailor.

The curiosity that the man had inspired in him was so great that in any other circumstances he would have made himself known to him; but on this occasion the conversation he had just heard was too personal for him not to be constrained by the very reasonable fear that his appearance would not be welcome. So he had let him depart, as we saw, though promising himself that, if they met again, he would not let another opportunity escape as he had this one.

Franz was too preoccupied to sleep well. He spent the night going over and over in his mind everything he knew about the man in the caves and the stranger in the Colosseum and which would support the idea that they were one and the same. And the more he thought about it, the more convinced he was.

He did not fall asleep until daybreak, which meant that he woke up very late. Albert, like a true Parisian, had already made his plans for the evening. He had sent someone to book a box at the Teatro Argentina. As Franz had several letters to write home, he abandoned the carriage to Albert for the whole day.

At five o'clock, Albert returned. He had taken round his letters of introduction, had received invitations for every evening of his stay and had seen Rome. A day had been enough for him to do all this, and he had still had time to find out what opera was being performed and with which actors.

The piece was called *Parisina*[2] and the actors were named Coselli, Moriani and La Spech. As you can see, our two young men were not especially hard done by: they were going to attend a performance of one of the best operas by the author of *Lucia di Lammermoor*, performed by three of the most renowned artists in Italy.

Albert had never been able to get used to these Italian theatres – to the orchestra pit where you could not walk around and to the absence of balconies or open boxes. All this was hard for a man who had his own stall in the Opéra-Bouffe and a share in the omnibus box at the Opéra; but it did not prevent Albert from dressing up outrageously every time he went to the opera with Franz – a wasted effort; for, it must be admitted to the shame of one of the most deserving representatives of French fashion, in the four months during which he had travelled the length and breadth of Italy, Albert had not had a single romantic adventure.

He sometimes tried to joke about this, but underneath he was deeply mortified. He, Albert de Morcerf, one of the most eligible of young men, was still idly kicking his heels. It was all the more painful since, with the usual modesty of our dear compatriots, Albert had left Paris convinced that he would score the most astonishing triumphs in Italy and, on his return, delight the whole Boulevard de Gand with the story of his successes.

Alas, it had not been so. The charming Genovese, Florentine and Neapolitan countesses had chosen to stick, not with their husbands, but with their lovers, and Albert had come to the painful conclusion that Italian women at least have this over their French sisters – that they are faithful in their infidelity.

By which I do not mean that in Italy, as everywhere, there may not be exceptions.

Yet Albert was not only a most elegant young bachelor, but also a man of considerable wit. Moreover, he was a viscount – of the new nobility, admittedly; but nowadays, when one no longer has to prove one's title, what does it matter if it dates from 1399 or from 1815? Added to all this, he had an income of fifty thousand *livres*: this is more than one needs, as we can see, to be fashionable in Paris. So, all in all, it was slightly humiliating not to have been seriously noticed by anyone in the towns through which they had passed.

However, he fully intended to make up for lost time in Rome, carnival being, in every country on earth where that admirable institution is celebrated, a time of liberty when even the sternest may be led into some act of folly. So, since the carnival was due to start the following day, it was most important for Albert to present his credentials before it began.

With this in mind, he had rented one of the most prominent boxes in the theatre and was impeccably fitted out for the occasion. They were on the first level, corresponding to our balcony; in any event, in Italy the first three floors are all as 'aristocratic' as each other, which is why they are known as the 'noble' parts of the auditorium. And the box, which could comfortably hold a dozen spectators, had cost the two friends a little more than a box for four people at the Ambigu.

Albert had an additional hope, which was that if he managed to find a place in the heart of some beautiful Roman woman, this would automatically lead to the award of a *posto* in her carriage and consequently he would see the carnival from the top of some aristocratic vehicle or from a princely balcony.

All these considerations made Albert more lively than ever before. He turned his back on the actors, leant half out of the box and eyed all the pretty women through a pair of opera-glasses six inches long. All of this did not induce one single woman to reward all Albert's agitation with a solitary glance, even of curiosity.

Instead, the audience was thoroughly absorbed with its own affairs, loves, pleasures, or talking about the carnival which was to begin on the day after the end of Holy Week, without paying a moment's attention either to the actors or to the play, except at certain specific points when everyone would turn back towards the stage, either to listen to a section of Coselli's recitative or to applaud some virtuoso effect by Moriani, or else to cry 'bravo' to La Spech; after which the private conversations would be resumed as before.

Towards the end of the first act, Franz looked across to a box that had until then remained empty, and saw the door open to admit a young woman to whom he had had the honour of being introduced in Paris, but who he assumed was still in France. Albert noticed his friend start at seeing this person and turned to ask him: 'Do you know that woman?'

'Yes,' Franz replied. 'What do you think of her?'

'Charming, my dear fellow, and blonde. Oh, what delightful hair! Is she French?'

'Venetian.'

'And her name?'

'Countess G—.'[3]

'I know the name!' Albert exclaimed. 'Her wit is said to be equal to her beauty. Good heavens! Just think! I could have been introduced to her at Madame de Villefort's last ball, which she attended, but I neglected to do so. What an idiot I am!'

'Would you like me to make up for the omission?'

'Why, do you know her well enough to take me to her box?'

'I have had the honour to speak to her three or four times in my life; but, you know, that's quite enough for us not to be committing any *faux pas*.'

At this moment the countess noticed Franz and gave him a graceful wave with her hand, to which he replied by bowing respectfully.

'Well I never! But it looks to me as if you could be on very close terms with her?' said Albert.

'That's just where you're wrong, and the very thing that is constantly leading us Frenchmen into one blunder or other when we are abroad: we judge everything from a Parisian point of view. In Spain, above all in Italy, you can never tell how intimate people are by the informality of their behaviour together. The countess and I happened to find common ground, nothing more.'

'In the heart?' Albert asked, laughing.

'No, simply in the mind,' Franz replied seriously.

'On what occasion?'

'On the occasion of a walk in the Colosseum very much like the one we took together.'

'By moonlight?'

'Yes.'

'Alone?'

'Almost.'

'And you spoke of . . .'

'The dead.'

'Huh!' Albert exclaimed. 'That is highly diverting. Well, I promise you that if I should ever have the good fortune to accompany the beautiful countess on such a walk, I should only talk to her about the living.'

'You might perhaps be wrong.'

'But until that happens, will you introduce me to her as you promised?'

'As soon as the curtain falls.'

'How devilish long this first act is!'

'Listen to the finale: it's splendid, and Coselli sings it exceptionally well.'

'Yes, but look how he carries himself!'

'No one could act better than La Spech.'

'You know, when you've seen La Sontag and La Malibran . . .'

'Don't you find Moriani's technique excellent?'

'I don't like brunettes who sing blonde.'

'My dear chap,' said Franz, turning around while Albert continued to peer through his opera-glasses, 'you really are too fussy.'

At last the curtain fell, much to the satisfaction of the Vicomte de Morcerf, who took his hat, rapidly adjusted his hair, his cravat and his cuffs, and told Franz that he was waiting.

Franz had exchanged a look with the countess, who indicated that he would be welcome, so he wasted no time in satisfying his friend's eagerness and set off round the semi-circle – followed by Albert, who took advantage of this journey to smooth out some creases that might have appeared in his shirt collar and the lapels of his coat – so that they eventually arrived at box No. 4, which was the one occupied by the countess.

Immediately the young man sitting beside her at the front of the box got up according to the custom in Italy and gave his seat to the newcomer, who must relinquish it in his turn when a new visitor arrives.

Franz introduced Albert to the countess as one of our most

distinguished young people, both for his social standing and for his wit – all of which was true; for, in Paris, and in the society in which Albert moved, he was a model of a young gentleman. Franz added that, desperate at not having been able to take advantage of the countess's stay in Paris to obtain an introduction to her, he had asked him to repair this omission, and he was doing precisely that, while begging the countess to forgive his presumption, since he himself might have been thought to need someone formally to introduce him to the countess.

She replied by greeting Albert in the most charming way and offering Franz her hand.

At her invitation, Albert took the empty seat at the front while Franz sat in the second row behind them. Albert had found an excellent subject of conversation: Paris. He talked to the countess of their mutual acquaintances. Franz realized that things were going well and decided to let them continue in that way; asking for the loan of Albert's gigantic opera-glasses, he began to study the audience for himself.

Sitting alone at the front of a box, at the third level facing them, was a superbly beautiful woman, dressed in Greek costume which she wore with such ease that it was clear that this style of dress was natural to her. Behind her, in the shadows, could be seen the outline of a man, though it was impossible to make out his face.

Franz interrupted the conversation between Albert and the countess to ask the latter if she knew the lovely Albanian woman who so much deserved to attract the attention not only of men but also of women.

'No,' she answered. 'All I do know is that she has been in Rome throughout the season, because when the theatre opened at its start I saw her where you see her now, and in the past month she has not missed a single performance, sometimes in company with the man who is with her at present, sometimes simply attended by a black servant.'

'What do you think of her, countess?'

'Extremely beautiful. Medora must have looked like her.'

Franz and the countess exchanged a smile; she went back to her conversation with Albert, and Franz to examining his Albanian.

The curtain rose for the ballet. It was one of those fine Italian ballets directed by the celebrated Henri, who had acquired an enormous reputation as a choreographer in Italy before losing it in the nautical theatre; one of those ballets where everyone, from the principals to the chorus line, is so actively involved that one hundred and fifty dancers make the same movement at the same time, lifting the same arm or leg in perfect unison.

This ballet was called *Poliska*.

Franz was too preoccupied with his beautiful Greek to take any notice of the ballet, interesting though it was. As for her, she was clearly enjoying the performance, and her pleasure was in the most marked contrast to the profound indifference of the man who accompanied her. Throughout the entire length of this choreographic masterpiece he remained utterly motionless and, despite the infernal racket emanating from the trumpets, bells and cymbals, appeared to be enjoying the celestial delights of a luxurious and untroubled sleep.

At last the ballet ended and the curtain fell, amid frenzied applause from the delighted audience in the stalls.

Because of this custom of dividing up the opera with a ballet, intervals are very short in Italian theatres, as the singers have an opportunity to rest and change their costumes while the dancers are executing their pirouettes and concocting their entrechats. So the overture of the second act began and, at the first touch of the strings, Franz saw the sleeper slowly rise up and come over to the Greek woman, who turned around to speak to him, then returned to her position, leaning against the front of the box. The man's face was still in shadow and Franz could see none of his features.

The curtain rose and Franz's attention was inevitably drawn to the actors, so for a moment his eyes left the box, with the beautiful Greek, and turned to the stage. As we know, the act opens with the dream duet: in her sleep, Parisina lets slip the secret of her love for Ugo in front of Azzo. The betrayed husband goes through all the rages of jealousy until, convinced that his wife is being unfaithful to him, he wakes her up to announce his forthcoming revenge.

This duo is one of the most lovely, most expressive and most powerful to have come from Donizetti's fertile pen. This was the third time that Franz had heard it and, though he had no pretensions to being a fanatical opera-lover, it had a profound effect on him. So he was about to join in with the applause coming from the rest of the theatre when his hands, on the point of meeting, remained frozen opposite one another and the 'Bravo!' that was on the point of emerging from his lips died before reaching them.

The man in the box had stood up entirely and, now that his head was in the light, Franz had just once more recognized the mysterious inhabitant of Monte Cristo, the very same whose figure and voice he had so clearly recognized the evening before in the ruins of the Colosseum. There could no longer be any doubt. The strange traveller lived in Rome.

The expression on Franz's face must have reflected the turmoil that this apparition created in his mind, because the countess looked at him, burst out laughing and asked what was wrong.

'Madame la Comtesse,' Franz replied, 'a moment ago I asked you if you knew that Albanian woman; now I am wondering if you know her husband.'

'No more than I do her.'

'You have never noticed him before?'

'There's a very French question! You must know that for an Italian woman there is no man in the world except the one that she loves!'

'Of course,' said Franz.

'In any case,' she remarked, putting Albert's opera-glasses to her eyes and turning them towards the box, 'someone must have recently dug him out: he looks like a corpse which has just emerged from the tomb with the gravedigger's permission, because he is atrociously pale.'

'He's always like that,' said Franz.

'Do you know him then?' asked the countess. 'In that case I should be asking you who he is.'

'I believe I have seen him before; I think I recognize him.'

'I can certainly understand,' she said, with a movement of her lovely shoulders as if she had felt a chill in her veins, 'that when one had seen such a man once, one would never forget him.' So the feeling that Franz had experienced was not peculiar to him, since someone else also felt it.

'Well, then,' Franz asked the countess, who had decided to take another look at him, 'what do you think of that man?'

'He looks to me like Lord Ruthwen[4] in flesh and blood.'

Franz was struck by this new association with Byron. If any man could make one believe in vampires, this was he.

'I must find out who he is,' Franz said, getting up.

'No, no!' cried the countess. 'Don't leave me! I must keep you to myself because I'm counting on you to take me home.'

'What! Are you serious?' Franz asked, leaning over to whisper in her ear. 'Are you really afraid?'

'Listen,' she said. 'Lord Byron swore to me that he believed in vampires. He even told me that he had seen them and described how they look – and that was it, exactly! The black hair, the large eyes glowing with some strange light, that deathly pallor. Then: observe that he is not with a woman like other women, but with a foreigner – a Greek, a schismatic – and no doubt a magician like himself. I beg you, stay with me. Go and look for him tomorrow if you must, but today I declare that I am keeping you here.'

Franz insisted.

'Listen,' she said, getting up, 'I am going, I cannot stay until the end of the opera because I have guests at home. Will you be so unmannerly as to refuse me your company?'

There was no reply to this, except to take his hat, open the door and offer the countess his arm, which he accordingly did.

The countess was genuinely quite deeply troubled, and Franz himself could not avoid feeling some superstitious terror, all the more natural in that what, with the countess, was the outcome of instinct, with him derived from memory.

He felt her tremble as she got into her carriage. He drove her back home. There were no guests there and no one was expecting her. He reproved her.

'In truth,' she said, 'I am not feeling well and I need to be alone. The sight of that man has quite upset me.'

Franz tried to laugh.

'Don't laugh,' she said. 'I know that you don't really want to. But do promise me one thing.'

'What?'

'Promise.'

'Anything you wish, except to give up my search to discover who that man is. I have reasons, which I cannot tell you, for discovering the answer, and where he comes from, and where he is going.'

'I don't know where he comes from, but I can tell you where he is going: to hell, for certain.'

'So what is the promise that you want to demand of me, countess?'

'It is to go directly back to your hotel and not to try to see that man this evening. There are certain affinities between the people that one meets and those one has just left: don't serve as a conductor between that man and me. Go after him tomorrow if you wish, but never introduce him to me, unless you want me to die of fright. And now, good-night; try to sleep. I for my part know one person who will not.'

With these words, she took her farewell of Franz, leaving him uncertain whether she had been enjoying a joke at his expense or if she had really felt as afraid as she claimed.

On returning to the hotel, he found Albert wearing his dressing-gown and pantaloons, contentedly lounging in an armchair and smoking a cigar.

'Oh, it's you!' he said. 'I swear, I didn't expect to see you until tomorrow.'

'My dear Albert,' Franz replied, 'I am pleased to have this opportunity to tell you once and for all that you have the most erroneous notions about Italian women – though I should have thought that your disappointments in love would have made you relinquish them by now.'

'What do you expect! It's impossible to understand the confounded creatures! They give you their hand, they press yours, they whisper to you, they allow you to accompany them home . . . With only a quarter of all this, a Parisian woman's reputation would be in tatters.'

'Precisely! It's because they have nothing to hide and because they live their lives under the midday sun that women are so easygoing in the lovely land that rings to the sound of *si*, as Dante put it. In any case, you could see that the countess was really afraid.'

'Afraid of what? Of that respectable gentleman sitting opposite us with the pretty Greek woman? I wanted to put my mind at rest when they left, so I crossed them in the corridor. He's a handsome young man, well turned out, who looks as if he dresses in France at Blin's or Humann's; a little pale, admittedly, but of course pallor is a mark of distinction.'

Franz smiled. Albert had pretensions to looking pale.

'I am convinced,' Franz said, 'that there is no sense in the countess's ideas about him. Did he say anything in your hearing?'

'He did speak, but in Romaic. I recognized the language from some corrupted words of Greek. I must tell you, my dear fellow, that I was very good at Greek when I was at school.'

'So he spoke Romaic?'

'Probably.'

'There's no doubt; it's him.'

'What?'

'Nothing. So what were you doing here?'

'Preparing a surprise for you!'

'What surprise?'

'You know it's impossible to get a carriage?'

'Good Lord! We've done everything humanly possible, but in vain.'

'Well, I've had a wonderful idea.'

Franz gave Albert the look of someone who did not have much confidence in his ideas.

'My good fellow,' said Albert, 'you have just favoured me with a look which will oblige me to demand satisfaction.'

'I am ready to give it to you, my dear friend, if your idea is as ingenious as you claim.'

'Listen.'

'I am listening.'

'There is no means of obtaining a carriage, is there?'

'None.'

'Or horses?'

'Or horses.'

'But we could get a cart?'

'Perhaps.'

'And a pair of oxen?'

'Probably.'

'Well, then! That's what we need. I will have the cart decorated, we can dress up as Neapolitan farmworkers and we will be a living representation of the splendid painting by Léopold Robert. If, for the sake of still greater authenticity, the countess wishes to put on the costume of a woman of Puzzoli or Sorrento, this will complete the tableau; and she is beautiful enough to represent the original of the Woman With Child.'

'Why!' Franz exclaimed. 'This time you're right, Monsieur Albert: this is a really inspired idea.'

'And altogether French, coming direct from the Do-Nothing Kings,[5] precisely that! Ah, you Romans! Did you think we would run around your streets on foot like *lazzaroni*, just because you have a shortage of horses and carriages? Not a bit of it! We'll think something up!'

'Have you told anyone of this brilliant scheme yet?'

'Our host. When I got back I called him up and told him what we would need. He assured me that nothing could be simpler. I wanted to have gold leaf put on the horns of the oxen, but he said it would take three days, so we'll have to do without that detail.'

'Where is he?'

'Who?'

'Our host.'

'Looking for the cart. Tomorrow may be too late.'

'So you are expecting his reply this evening?'

'At any moment.'

On this, the door opened and Signor Pastrini put his head round. *'Permesso?'* he said.

'Most certainly it's permitted,' said Franz.

'Tell me then,' said Albert. 'Have you found us the oxen we asked for and the cart that we need?'

'I have found better than that,' came the self-satisfied reply.

'Beware, my dear Signor Pastrini!' said Albert. 'The better is the enemy of the good.'

'Let Your Excellencies trust in me,' said Signor Pastrini, speaking with the voice of competence.

'So what do you have?' asked Franz.

'You know that the Count of Monte Cristo is staying on the same floor as you?'

'We most certainly do know it,' said Albert. 'It's thanks to him that we are housed like two students in the Rue Saint-Nicolas-du-Chardonnet.'

'Very well. But he knows of your difficulty and has required me to offer you two places in his carriage and two places at his windows in the Palazzo Rospoli.'

Albert and Franz looked at one another. Albert said: 'Should we accept this offer from a stranger, someone we don't know?'

'What kind of man is this Count of Monte Cristo?' Franz asked the innkeeper.

'A very important Sicilian or Maltese gentleman, I am not quite sure which, but as aristocratic as a Borghese and as rich as a goldmine.'

'It strikes me,' Franz said, 'that if this man was as well-mannered as our host says, he would have found some other way to deliver his invitation, in writing, or . . .'

At that moment there was a knock on the door.

'Come in,' said Franz.

A servant, dressed in perfectly elegant livery, appeared at the door of the room.

'From the Count of Monte Cristo, to Monsieur Franz d'Epinay and Monsieur le Vicomte Albert de Morcerf,' he said; and handed two cards to the innkeeper which the latter passed on to the two men.

'As their neighbour, Monsieur le Comte de Monte Cristo,' the servant continued, 'asks permission of these gentlemen to visit them tomorrow morning. He begs the gentlemen to be so good as to tell him at what hour they will be able to receive him.'

'The deuce!' Albert exclaimed to Franz. 'There's nothing more to be said.'

'Please inform the count,' Franz replied, 'that it is we who shall have the honour to visit him.'

The servant went out.

'This is what you might call overwhelming us with courtesies,' said Albert. 'You are quite clearly right, Signor Pastrini: this Count of Monte Cristo of yours is a perfect gentleman.'

'So you will accept his offer?'

'Good heavens, yes,' said Albert. 'Though I must admit that I rather regret our peasants on the cart. And if there was not the window in the Palazzo Rospoli to make up for what we shall be losing, I should keep to my original idea. What do you say, Franz?'

'I too say that the windows in the Palazzo Rospoli have made up my mind for me,' he replied.

This offer of two places at a window in the Palazzo Rospoli had reminded Franz of the conversation which he had heard in the ruins of the Colosseum between the stranger and the man from Trastevere, in the course of which the man with the cloak had promised to win a pardon for the condemned prisoner. If, as everything led Franz to believe, the man in the cloak was the same whose appearance in the Sala Argentina had so greatly preoccupied him, he would no doubt recognize the man and nothing would then prevent him from satisfying his curiosity.

He spent part of the night dreaming about his two apparitions and looking forward to the next day. Then everything should become clear; this time, unless his host possessed the ring of Gyges and the power that it confers of making oneself invisible, it was clear that he would not escape. In consequence he was awake before eight o'clock.

As for Albert, who had not the same reasons as Franz to wake up early, he was still fast asleep.

Franz called for the innkeeper, who arrived, behaving with his accustomed obsequiousness.

'Signor Pastrini,' he asked, 'is there not to be an execution today?'

'Yes, Excellency, but if you are asking me to have a window, it is a bit late to start thinking about it.'

'No, no. In any case, if I was really anxious to see this spectacle, I suppose I could find a place on the Monte Pincio.'

'Oh, I assumed that Your Excellency would not wish to mingle with the common herd, which finds that a kind of natural amphitheatre.'

'I shall probably not go,' said Franz. 'But I should like to have a few details.'

'What?'

'I should like to know how many condemned men there are, their names and the nature of the penalty they are to suffer.'

'Perfectly timed, Excellency! I have just been brought the *tavolette*.'

'What are the *tavolette*?'

'*Tavolette* are the wooden tablets which are hung at every street-corner on the day of an execution, with a notice stuck to them giving the names of the condemned, the charge and the method of execution. These notices are intended to invite the faithful to pray that God will make the guilty men truly repentant.'

'And these *tavolette* are brought to you so that you can add your prayers to those of the faithful?' Franz asked dubiously.

'No, Excellency. I have an understanding with the bill-poster and he brings these to me as he does the advertisements for entertainments, so that if any of my guests wish to watch the execution, they can be fully informed.'

'How very thoughtful!' Franz exclaimed.

'Yes,' said Signor Pastrini with a smile, 'I flatter myself that I do all in my power to satisfy the noble foreigners who honour me with their confidence.'

'As I see, Signor Pastrini! I shall mention the fact to whoever wishes to hear it, of that you may be sure. Meanwhile, perhaps I could read one of these *tavolette*?'

'With no trouble at all,' said the innkeeper, opening the door. 'I have had one put on the landing.'

He went out, took down the *tavoletta* and handed it to Franz. Here is a literal translation of the notice:

Let all be informed that on Tuesday, 22 February, the first day of carnival, by order of the Court of La Rota, the sentence of death will be carried out in the Piazza del Popolo on Andrea Rondolo, guilty of murder against the most respectable and venerated person of don Cesare Terlini, Canon of the Church of St John Lateran, and on Peppino, alias Rocca Priori, found guilty of complicity with the abominable bandit Luigi Vampa and his followers. The first will be *mazzolato*, the second *decapitato*.

All charitable souls are requested to pray God for the sincere repentance of these two miserable creatures.

This was precisely what Franz had heard two days earlier in the ruins of the Colosseum, and nothing had changed: the names of the condemned men, the crimes for which they were to suffer and the methods of execution were exactly the same. This meant that, in all probability, the Trasteveran was none other than the bandit Luigi Vampa and the man in the cloak Sinbad the Sailor who, in Rome as in Porto Vecchio and in Tunis, was engaged in yet another philanthropic mission.

However, time was passing and it was nine o'clock. Franz was on his way to wake up Albert when, to his great astonishment, he saw him emerging from his room, fully dressed. The idea of carnival had passed through his head and woken him earlier than his friend could have hoped.

'Very well,' Franz said to the innkeeper. 'Now that we are both ready, do you think, dear Monsieur Pastrini, that we might introduce ourselves to the Count of Monte Cristo?'

'Yes, indeed! The Count of Monte Cristo is in the habit of rising very early and I'm sure that he must have been up for two hours.'

'And you don't think it would be at all indiscreet to go and see him at this hour?'

'Not at all.'

'In that case, Albert, if you are ready . . .'

'Quite ready.'

'Let us go and thank our neighbour for his courtesy.'

'Let's go!'

Franz and Albert had only to cross the landing. The innkeeper preceded them and rang on their behalf. A servant opened. *'I signori francesi,'* said the innkeeper. The servant bowed and ushered them in.

They crossed two rooms, furnished with a degree of luxury that they had not expected to find in Signor Pastrini's establishment, and finally arrived in a supremely elegant drawing-room. A Turkish carpet covered the floor, and there were the most comfortable seats with ample cushions and tilted backs. Fine old-master paintings hung from the walls, with splendid displays of weapons arranged between them, and tapestry hangings covered the doors.

'If Their Excellencies would like to sit down,' said the servant, 'I shall inform Monsieur le Comte.' He went out of one of the doors.

For a moment, when the door opened, the two friends had caught the sound of a *guzla*,[6] but it was immediately extinguished: the door, almost no sooner opened than closed, had as it were allowed this brief gust of music to waft into the drawing-room.

Franz and Albert looked at one another and then round the furniture, the pictures and the armaments. At second glance it all looked even more impressive to them than at first.

'Well?' Franz asked his friend. 'What do you make of this?'

'My dear fellow, what I make of it is that either our neighbour is some stockbroker who gambled successfully on Spanish stock, or else he is a prince who is travelling incognito.'

'Hush!' Franz said. 'We'll soon know. Here he comes.'

The sound of a door opening on its hinges had just reached the two visitors, and almost at once the tapestry parted to make way for the owner of all this wealth.

Albert stepped forward, but Franz remained rooted to the spot. The man who had just entered was none other than the cloaked figure in the Colosseum, the stranger in the box at the theatre and his mysterious host on the island of Monte Cristo.

XXXV

LA MAZZOLATA

'Gentlemen,' said the Count of Monte Cristo as he came in, 'I apologize for allowing you to anticipate my call, but I was afraid that it might have been indiscreet of me to visit you any earlier than this. In any case, you informed me that you would come, so I have kept myself at your disposal.'

'Franz and I must thank you a thousand times, Count,' said Albert. 'You have truly spared us a great deal of irritation: we were inventing the most fantastic sorts of conveyance when we received your most kind invitation.'

'Upon my soul, gentlemen,' the count said, motioning the two young men to sit down on a divan, 'it is only because of that idiot Pastrini that I did not come to your rescue earlier! He told me nothing of your difficulty, even though he must have known that I, alone as I am here, wanted nothing better than to make the acquaintance of my neighbours. As soon as I knew that I could be of service to you, you can see how eagerly I grasped the opportunity to present my compliments.'

The two young men bowed. Franz had not yet said a word; he had not been able to make up his mind and, since nothing indicated that the count either wished to recognize him or to be recognized by him, he did not know whether he should make any allusion to the past or leave time in the future for something new to arise. Moreover, while he was sure that it was the count who had been in the theatre on the previous evening, he could not be so sure that it was also the same person who had been in the Colosseum on the evening before, so he decided to let events take their course without himself making any direct reference to what had occurred. In addition, this gave him an advantage over the count, being the master of his secret, while he could have no hold over Franz, who had nothing to hide. However, he decided to lead the conversation towards a point which might, meanwhile, confirm a few of his suspicions.

'Monsieur le Comte,' he said, 'you have offered us places in your carriage and at your windows in the Palazzo Rospoli; now can you tell us how we might obtain some *posto* – as they say here in Italy – overlooking the Piazza del Popolo?'

'Yes, you are quite right,' the count said in an offhand manner, not taking his eyes off Morcerf. 'Is there not to be something like an execution in the Piazza del Popolo?'

'There is,' Franz said, seeing that the conversation was turning of itself towards the point where he wished to bring it.

'Please wait one moment. I believe that I told my steward yesterday to take care of that. Perhaps I can do you this further small service.'

He reached out for the bell-pull, which he rang three times.

'Have you ever paused to consider,' he asked Franz, 'how to save time and simplify the comings and goings of servants? I have studied the matter. When I ring once, it's for my valet; twice, for my butler; three times, for my steward. In this way, I do not waste time or words. Ah, here he is now.'

A man of between forty-five and fifty years of age came in; to Franz he was the spitting image of the smuggler who had shown him into the cave, but he gave not the slightest sign of recognition. He understood that the man was under orders.

'Monsieur Bertuccio,' the count said, 'I asked you yesterday to obtain a window for me overlooking the Piazza del Popolo; did you take care of it?'

'Yes, Excellency,' the steward answered. 'But we left it very late.'

'What!' the count said, raising an eyebrow. 'Didn't I tell you that I wished to have one?'

'And Your Excellency does have one, the same that was rented to Prince Lubaniev; but I was obliged to pay a hundred . . .'

'Very good, very good, Monsieur Bertuccio, you may spare these gentlemen all the housekeeping details; you managed to obtain the window, which is all that matters. Give the address of the house to the coachman and be ready on the stairs to conduct us there. That's all; you may go.'

The steward bowed and took a step towards the door.

'One moment!' the count said. 'Be so good as to ask Pastrini if he has received the *tavoletta* and if he could send me the programme of the execution.'

'No need,' said Franz, taking his notebook out of his pocket. 'I have seen the tablet myself and copied it down: here it is.'

'Splendid. In that case, Bertuccio, you may go, I shan't need you any more. Just get them to tell us when luncheon is served. Will these gentlemen,' he asked, turning to the two friends, 'do me the honour of taking lunch with me?'

'But, Monsieur le Comte,' said Albert, 'that would really be imposing on you.'

'Not at all, on the contrary, you would oblige me greatly; and one or other, or perhaps both of you, can return the favour one day in Paris. Monsieur Bertuccio, ask them to lay three places.'

He took the notebook from Franz's hand.

'So, we were saying . . .' he continued in the same tone of voice as though he were reading the personal column, 'that "on Tuesday the twenty-second of February, the first day of carnival, by order of the Court of La Rota, the sentence of death will be carried out in the Piazza del Popolo on Andrea Rondolo, guilty of murder against the most respectable and venerated person of don Cesare Terlini, Canon of the Church of Saint John Lateran, and Peppino, alias Rocca Priori, found guilty of complicity with the abominable bandit Luigi Vampa and his followers . . ." Hum! "The first will be *mazzolato*, the second *decapitato*." Yes, this is what was originally intended, but I think that since yesterday there has been a change in the order and conduct of the ceremony.'

'Huh!' said Franz.

'Yes, I spent the evening yesterday with Cardinal Rospigliosi and they were speaking of some kind of stay of execution having been granted to one of the two condemned men.'

'To Andrea Rondolo?' asked Franz.

'No . . .' the count replied casually. 'To the other . . .' (he looked at the notebook as if to remind himself of the name) '. . . to Peppino, alias Rocca Priori. That means you will be denied a guillotining, but you still have the *mazzolata*, which is a very curious form of torture when you see it for the first time – or even the second; while the other, which in any case you must know, is too simple, too unvaried. There is nothing unexpected in it. The *mandaïa* makes no mistakes, its hand doesn't shake, it doesn't miss and it doesn't make thirty attempts before succeeding, like the soldier who beheaded the Comte de Chalais[1] and who had perhaps been particularly chosen for this victim by Richelieu. Ah, come now,' said the count in a scornful tone, 'don't talk to me about Europeans where torture is concerned. They understand nothing about it. With them, cruelty is in its infancy – or perhaps its old age.'

'Truly, Monsieur le Comte,' said Franz, 'anyone would think you had made a comparative study of executions in different parts of the world.'

'There are very few types at least that I have not seen,' the count replied coldly.

'Did it please you to witness these horrible spectacles?'

'My first feeling was repulsion, my second, indifference, and my third, curiosity.'

'Curiosity! The idea is terrible, isn't it?'

'Why? There is only one serious matter to be considered in life, and that is death. So! Isn't it worth one's curiosity to study the different ways that the soul may leave the body and how, according to the character, the temperament, or even the local customs of a country, individuals face up to that supreme journey from being to nothingness? As for me, I can assure you of one thing: the more you have seen others die, the easier it becomes to die oneself. So, in my opinion, death may be a torment, but it is not an expiation.'

'I am not sure that I understand,' said Franz. 'Please explain. I can't tell you how interested I am in what you say.'

'Listen,' said the count, his face flushing with the gall of hatred as another face might be coloured with blood. 'If a man had murdered your father, your mother, your mistress, or any of those beings who, when they are torn from your heart, leave an eternal void and a wound that can never be staunched, and if he had subjected them to unspeakable torture and endless torment, would you consider that society had accorded you sufficient reparation just because the blade of the guillotine had travelled between the base of the murderer's occipital and his trapezius muscles, and because the person who had caused you to feel years of moral suffering had experienced a few seconds of physical pain?'

'I know,' Franz said. 'Human justice is inadequate as a consolation: it can spill blood for blood, that's all. But one must only ask it for what is possible, not for anything more.'

'Moreover, the example that I give you is a material one,' the count went on; 'one where society, attacked by the death of an individual among the mass of individuals which composes it, avenges that death by another. But are there not millions of sufferings which can rend the entrails of a man without society taking the slightest heed of them or providing even the inadequate means of reparation that we spoke of just now? Are there not crimes for which impalement à la turque, or Persian burial alive, or the whips of the Iraqis would be too mild a torment, but which society in its indifference leaves unpunished? Answer me: are there no such crimes?'

'Yes,' Franz replied. 'It is precisely to punish them that we tolerate duelling.'

'Ah, duelling!' exclaimed the count. 'There's a fine way, I must say, to achieve one's end, when the end is vengeance! A man has stolen your mistress, a man has seduced your wife, a man has dishonoured your daughter. He has taken an entire life, a life that had the right to expect from God the share of happiness that He promises to every human being in creating us, and turned it into a mere existence of pain, misery and infamy; and you consider yourself revenged because you have run this man through with your sword or put a bullet in his head, after he has turned your mind to delirium and your heart to despair? Come, come! Even without considering that he is often the one who comes out of this contest on top, purged in the eyes of the world and in some respect pardoned by God . . . No, no,' the count went on, 'if I ever had to take my revenge, that is not how I should do it.'

'You mean, you disapprove of duelling? You mean, you wouldn't fight a duel?' Albert asked, joining the conversation and astonished at hearing anyone express such an odd point of view.

'Oh, certainly!' said the count. 'Make no mistake: I should fight a duel for a trifle, an insult, a contradiction, a slap – and all the more merrily for knowing that, thanks to the skill I have acquired in all physical exercises and long experience of danger, I should be more or less certain of killing my opponent. Oh, yes, indeed! I should fight a duel for any of these things; but in return for a slow, deep, infinite, eternal pain, I should return as nearly as possible a pain equivalent to the one inflicted on me. An eye for an eye, a tooth for a tooth, as they say in the East, those men who are the elect of creation, and who have learnt to make a life of dreams and a paradise of reality.'

'But, with such an outlook,' Franz told the count, 'which makes you judge and executioner in your own case, it would be hard for you to confine yourself to actions that would leave you forever immune to the power of the law. Hatred is blind and anger deaf: the one who pours himself a cup of vengeance is likely to drink a bitter draught.'

'Yes, if he is poor and clumsy; no, if he is a millionaire and adroit. In any case, if the worst comes to the worst, he can only suffer the ultimate penalty which we mentioned just now: the one that the philanthropic French Revolution put in place of quartering and the wheel. Well, then! What does the penalty matter if he is avenged? In truth, I am almost irritated at the fact that, quite probably, this miserable Peppino will not be *decapitato*, as they say; you'd see how long it takes, and whether it's really worth bothering about. But, gentlemen, this is indeed an odd topic of discussion for carnival time. How did we get round to it? Ah, yes, I remember! You asked for a seat at my window. Very well, yes, you shall have one. But first, let's eat: I see that they have come to tell us we are served.'

A servant had opened one of the four doors of the drawing-room and at this pronounced the sacramental words: '*Al suo commando!*' The two young men got up and went through to the dining-room.

During lunch, which was excellent and served with the greatest refinement, Franz tried to read in Albert's eyes the impression that he was sure their host's words would have left on him. But, whether it was that, with his habitual insouciance, he had not paid great attention to them, or that the Count of Monte Cristo's concession on the matter of duelling had reconciled him to the man, or finally that prior events which we have related, and which were known only to Franz, had doubled the effect that the count's theories had on him, he did not perceive that his friend was in the slightest concerned. On the contrary, he was paying the meal the compliment one would expect from a man who has been condemned for four or five months to suffer Italian cooking (which is among the worst in the world). As for the count, he barely touched each dish: one would think that courtesy alone had induced him to sit down with his guests and that he was waiting for them to leave, to have himself brought some rare or special delicacy.

Franz was involuntarily reminded of the terror that the count had inspired in the Contessa G—, and her unshakeable conviction that the man whom he had shown her in the opposite box at the theatre was a vampire.

When lunch was finished, Franz took out his watch.

'What are you doing?' the count asked.

'You must excuse us, Monsieur le Comte,' Franz replied, 'but we still have a thousand matters to attend to.'

'What matters?'

'We have no disguises, and today a disguise is obligatory.'

'Don't worry about that. I believe that we have a private room at the Piazza del Popolo. I shall have any costumes that you require brought there and we shall put on our masks as we go.'

'After the execution?' Franz cried.

'Of course: after, during, before . . . as you wish.'

'In front of the scaffold?'

'The scaffold is part of the entertainment.'

'Excuse me, Count,' said Franz, 'I've been thinking. I am most grateful to you for your generosity to us, and I shall be happy to accept a place in your carriage and a seat at the window of the Palazzo Rospoli, and you can feel free to give my place at the window in the Piazza del Popolo to someone else.'

'But I must warn you, you will be missing something well worth seeing,' the count replied.

'You will tell me about it afterwards,' Franz went on. 'I am certain that the story will impress me almost as much from your mouth as it would if I were to see the events myself. In any case, I have more than once thought about watching an execution, but I have never been able to make up my mind to it. What about you, Albert?'

'I did once,' said the vicomte. 'I saw them execute Castaing,[2] but I think I was a little drunk that day. It was on my last day at school, and we spent the night in some cabaret or other.'

'Come now, just because you have not done something in Paris, that is no reason for not doing it abroad. When one travels, one does so to learn: a change of place should mean a change of scenery. Imagine how you will look when people ask you: "How do they execute criminals in Rome?" and you have to answer: "I don't know." Then, they say that the condemned man is an infamous rogue, a maniac who took a gridiron and beat to death a good priest who had brought him up as his own son. Just think! When you kill a man of the cloth, you should at least use a more appropriate implement than a gridiron, especially when this priest could be your father. If you were travelling through Spain, you would go and see a bullfight, wouldn't you? Well, imagine that we are going to see a fight; imagine the Ancient Romans and their Circus, those wild-beast hunts in which they killed three hundred lions and a hundred men. Remember the eighty thousand spectators clapping their hands, the virtuous matrons who would take their unmarried daughters, and those delightful Vestal Virgins whose pure white hands would give a charming little sign with the thumb that meant: "Come on, don't be lazy! Finish him off, that man who is already three-quarters dead!"'

'Are you going, Albert?' Franz asked.

'Certainly, my dear fellow. I was like you, but the count's eloquence has convinced me.'

'Well, then, let's go, if that's what you want,' Franz said. 'But on my way to the Piazza del Popolo, I want to go by the Corso. Can we do that, Count?'

'On foot we can, but not in the carriage.'

'In that case, I'll go on foot.'

'Do you have to go via the Corso?'

'Yes, there is something there I need to see.'

'Then let's go by the Corso and send the carriage by the Strada del Babuino, to wait for us in the Piazza del Popolo. As it happens, I shall not be sorry to go down the Corso, to see if some orders I gave have been carried out.'

'Excellency,' the servant said, opening the door, 'a man dressed as a penitent has come to see you.'

'Ah, yes,' said the count. 'I know who that is. Gentlemen, pray go back into the drawing-room, where you will find some excellent Havana cigars on the table. I shall join you shortly.'

The two young men got up and went out through one door while the count, after excusing himself again, went out of the other. Albert, who was a keen smoker and considered it no small sacrifice, since he had come to Italy, to have been deprived of the cigars that he smoked in Paris, went over to the table and exclaimed with joy on discovering some genuine puros.

'So,' Franz asked him, 'what do you think of the Count of Monte Cristo?'

'What do I think!' Albert said, clearly astonished that his friend should even ask such a question. 'I think he is a charming man, a wonderful host, someone who has seen a lot, studied a lot and thought a lot, who belongs like Brutus to the Stoic school, and –' he added, allowing a voluptuous puff of smoke to escape from his lips and spiral up towards the ceiling, 'someone who, in addition to all that, has the most excellent cigars.'

This was Albert's opinion; and, since Franz knew that Albert claimed not to form any opinion on either men or things except after giving it deep thought, he did not try to change this one. 'But,' he said, 'have you noticed something unusual?'

'What's that?'

'How closely he looks at you.'

'At me?'

'Yes, at you.'

Albert thought for a moment.

'Ah!' he said, with a sigh. 'There's nothing surprising about that. I have been away from Paris for nearly a year and I must be dressed in the most outlandish fashion. I expect the count mistook me for a provincial: please take the first opportunity, I beg you, to tell him that this is not so.'

Franz smiled.

A moment later the count came back. 'Here I am, gentlemen,' he said, 'entirely at your disposal. I've given the orders: the carriage will go to the Piazza del Popolo by its route and we by ours, along the Corso, if you wish. Please help yourself to some of those cigars, Monsieur de Morcerf.'

'By gad, yes, with great pleasure,' said Albert. 'Because those Italian cigars of yours are even worse than the ones sold by the state monopoly at home. When you come to Paris, I shall have the opportunity to repay you for all this.'

'I shall not refuse your invitation. I hope to go to Paris one day and, since you give me leave to do so, I shall knock on your door. Now, Messieurs, come, we have no time to lose. It is half-past twelve. Let's be going.'

All three went downstairs. There the coachman took his master's latest orders and set off down the Via del Babuino, while the pedestrians went up through the Piazza di Spagna and along the Via Frattina, which led them directly between the Palazzo Fiano and the Palazzo Rospoli. Franz kept looking at the windows of the latter: he had not forgotten the signal agreed in the Colosseum between the man in the cloak and the Trasteveran.

'Which windows are yours?' he asked the count in the most natural manner he could.

'The last three,' he replied, with an entirely unaffected lack of concern, for he could not have guessed the reason for the question.

Franz immediately looked at the windows. Those on each side were hung with yellow damask and the one in the middle in white damask with a red cross. The man in the cloak had kept his word to the other, and there was no longer any doubt: the man in the cloak was the count.

The three windows were still empty.

Meanwhile on all sides preparations were being made, chairs

were being set out, scaffolding put up and windows decorated. The masks could appear and the carriages start to drive around only at the sound of a bell, but you could sense the masks behind every window and the carriages behind every door.

Franz, Albert and the count continued on their way down the Corso. As they approached the Piazza del Popolo, the crowd became more dense and, above the heads of the people, they could see two things: the obelisk, surmounted by a cross, that stands in the centre of the square, and, in front of the obelisk, precisely at the point where the lines of sight of the three streets, Babuino, Corso and Ripetta, meet, the two highest beams of the scaffold with, burning between them, the rounded blade of the *mandaïa*.

They met the count's steward at the corner of the street, waiting for his master. The window that had been hired at what was doubtless an exorbitant price (which the count had not wished to communicate to his guests) was on the second floor of the great palazzo, between the Via del Babuino and the Monte Pincio. It was a sort of dressing-room opening on to a bedroom. By closing the bedroom door, the inhabitants of the dressing-room could be on their own. Clowns' costumes in white and blue satin, most elegantly cut, had been laid across the chairs.

'As you left the choice of costumes to me,' the count told the two friends, 'I had these made for you. Firstly, they are the best that will be worn this year, and then they are the most convenient design for confetti, because flour doesn't show up on them.'

Franz took in what the count was saying only very partially and may not have appreciated this new mark of courtesy at its true value, for all his attention was drawn by the spectacle of the Piazza del Popolo and the awful implement that on this occasion was its chief ornament.

It was the first time that Franz had seen a guillotine – we say guillotine, because the Roman *mandaïa* is constructed on more or less the same pattern as our instrument of death, the only difference being that the knife is shaped like a crescent, cutting with the convex part of the blade, and falls from less of a height.

Two men, seated on the tipping plank on which the condemned person lies, were waiting and eating a lunch that, as far as Franz could make out, consisted of bread and sausage. One of them lifted the plank and brought out a flagon of wine from under it, took a drink and passed it to his companion. These two men were the executioner's assistants!

Just looking at them, Franz felt the sweat burst out at the roots of his hair.

The condemned prisoners had been brought, the previous evening, from the Carceri Nuove to the little church of Santa Maria del Popolo and had spent the night, each attended by two priests, in a chapel of rest, secured with an iron grating and in front of which sentries marched, being relieved every hour.

A double row of *carabinieri* extended from each side of the church door to the scaffold, widening out on reaching it to leave a path some ten feet across and, around the guillotine, a clear space of some hundred yards in circumference. The whole of the rest of the square was carpeted with the heads of men and women. Many of the women had children seated on their shoulders. These children, who were a good head and shoulders above the rest of the crowd, would have an excellent view.

The Monte Pincio seemed like a huge amphitheatre with all of its terraces crowded with spectators. The balconies of the two churches at the corners of the Via del Babuino and the Via di Ripetta were overflowing with privileged onlookers. The steps of the peristyles had the appearance of swelling, many-coloured waves, driven towards the portico by the flow of an unceasing tide. Every protuberance on the wall capable of supporting a man had a living statue attached to it.

So what the count said was true: there is no more interesting spectacle in life than the spectacle of death.

And yet, instead of the silence that the solemnity of the occasion would seem to demand, a great noise rose from the crowd, a noise made up of laughter, booing and joyful cries. It was clear, as the count had also said, that the execution was nothing more for the people than the start of carnival.

Suddenly the noise ceased as if by enchantment; the church door had just opened.

First to appear was a company of penitents, each of them dressed in a grey sack which covered him entirely except for the holes for the eyes, and each holding a lighted candle in his hand. At the front marched the head of the order.

Behind the penitents came a tall man. He was naked except for linen trunks, on the left side of which was attached a huge knife concealed in its scabbard. Over his shoulder he carried a heavy iron mace. This man was the executioner. He also had sandals fastened around the lower part of the leg with thongs.

Behind the executioner, in the order in which they were to be executed, came Peppino, then Andrea. Each of them was accompanied by two priests. Neither of them was blindfolded.

Peppino was walking with quite a firm step. No doubt he had been told what to expect. Andrea was supported under each arm by a priest. From time to time each of them would kiss the crucifix that a confessor held out to him.

At the mere sight of this, Franz felt his legs ready to fold under him. He looked at Albert. The latter had gone as white as his shirt and mechanically tossed away his cigar, even though it was only half smoked.

Only the count appeared impassive. More than that: a faint blush of red seemed to be appearing beneath the livid pallor of his cheeks. His nose was dilating like that of a wild beast at the smell of blood, and his lips, slightly parted, showed his white teeth, as small and sharp as a jackal's. Yet, despite that, his face had an expression of smiling tenderness that Franz had never before seen on it; his black eyes, above all, were compellingly soft and lenient.

Meanwhile, the two condemned men continued to proceed towards the scaffold and, as they approached, one could make out their faces. Peppino was a handsome young man of between twenty-four and twenty-six, with a wild and free look on his sunburnt face. He carried his head high and seemed to be sniffing the wind to see from which direction his liberator would come.

Andrea was short and fat. His face was mean and cruel, of no definite age, though he was probably about thirty. He had let his beard grow in prison. His head was falling over on one shoulder and his legs were giving way beneath him; his whole being appeared to be driven by some mechanical force in which his own will no longer played any part.

'I thought you told me,' Franz said to the count, 'that there would be only one execution.'

'That was the truth,' he replied coldly.

'But there are two condemned men here.'

'Yes – but, of those two, one is at the point of death, while the other has many years yet to live.'

'It would seem to me that, if a pardon is to come, there is not much time to be lost.'

'And it is coming. Look,' said the count.

Just as Peppino reached the foot of the *mandaïa*, a penitent, who seemed like a late arrival, broke through the wall of soldiers without them attempting to stop him and, going up to the head of the order, gave him a sheet of paper folded in four. Peppino's sharp eyes had missed none of this. The head of the order unfolded the paper, read it and raised his hand.

'The Lord be blessed and His Holiness be praised!' he said loudly and clearly. 'There is a pardon for the life of one of the condemned prisoners.'

'A pardon!' the crowd cried in unison. 'There is a pardon!'

At this word, 'pardon', Andrea seemed to stiffen and raise his head. 'A pardon for whom?' he cried.

Peppino remained silent, motionless, panting.

'There is a pardon from the death penalty for Peppino, alias Rocca Priori,' said the head of the order. And he passed the sheet of paper to the captain in charge of the *carabinieri*, who read it and handed it back.

'A pardon for Peppino!' yelled Andrea, entirely roused from the state of torpor into which he had seemed to be plunged. 'Why a pardon for him and not for me? We were to die together. I was promised that he would die before me. You have no right to make me die alone. I don't want to die alone!' And he broke away from the two priests, twisting, shouting, bellowing and making insane efforts to break the ropes binding his hands.

The executioner made a sign to his two assistants, who jumped off the scaffold and seized the prisoner.

'What's wrong?' Franz asked the count.

'What is wrong?' the count repeated. 'Don't you understand? What's wrong is that this human being who is about to die is furious because his fellow creature is not dying with him and, if he were allowed to do so, he would tear him apart with his nails and his teeth rather than leave him to enjoy the life of which he himself is about to be deprived. Oh men! Men! Race of crocodiles, as Karl Moor says,' the count exclaimed, brandishing his two clenched fists towards the heads of the crowd. 'How well I know you by your deeds and how invariably you succeed in living down to what one expects of you!'

Andrea and the two assistant executioners were rolling around in the dust, the prisoner still crying out: 'He must die, I want him to die! You do not have the right to kill me alone!'

'Look, look,' the count continued, grasping each of the two young men by the hand. 'Look, because I swear to you, this is worthy of your curiosity. Here is a man who was resigned to his fate, who was walking to the scaffold and about to die like a coward, that's true, but at least he was about to die without resisting and without recriminations. Do you know what gave him that much strength? Do you know what consoled him? Do you know what resigned him to his fate? It was the fact that another man would share his anguish, that another man was to die like him, that another man was to die before him! Put two sheep in the slaughter-house or two oxen in the abattoir and let one of them realize that his companion will not die, and the sheep will bleat with joy, the ox low with pleasure. But man, man whom God made in His image, man to whom God gave this first, this sole, this supreme law, that he should love his neighbour, man to whom God gave a voice to express his thoughts – what is man's first cry when he learns that his neighbour is saved? A curse. All honour to man, the masterpiece of nature, the lord of creation!'

He burst out laughing, but such a terrible laugh that one realized he must have suffered horribly to be able to laugh in such a way.

Meanwhile the struggle continued, and it was awful to watch. The two assistants were carrying Andrea on to the scaffold, but the crowd had taken against him and twenty thousand voices were crying: 'Death! Death!'

Franz stepped back, but the count seized his arm and kept him in front of the window.

'What are you doing?' he said. 'Is this pity? In faith, it is well placed! If you heard someone cry: "mad dog", you would take your gun, rush out into the street and kill the poor beast by shooting it point blank, without mercy; yet the animal would, after all's said and done, be guilty of nothing more than having been bitten by another dog and doing the same as was done to it. And yet now you are taking pity on a man who was bitten by no other man, but who killed his benefactor and who now, unable to kill anyone else because his hands are tied, wants more than anything to see his companion in captivity, his comrade in misfortune, die with him! No, no! Watch!'

The injunction was almost unnecessary. Franz was, as it were, mesmerized by the horrible scene. The two assistants had carried the condemned man on to the scaffold and there, despite his efforts, his bites and his cries, they had forced him to his knees. Meanwhile the executioner had taken up his position on one side and raised the mace. Then, on a sign, the two assistants stepped aside. The prisoner wanted to get to his feet but, before he had time to do so, the club struck him on the left temple. There was a dull, muffled sound, the victim fell like a stricken bull, face downwards, then on the rebound turned over on his back. At this the executioner dropped his mace, pulled the knife out of his belt, cut open his throat with a single stroke and, immediately stepping on his belly, began as it were to knead the body with his feet. At each stamping of the foot, a jet of blood spurted from the condemned man's neck.

This time, Franz could bear it no longer. He flung himself backwards into the room and collapsed on a chair, half senseless.

Albert, with his eyes closed, remained standing, but only because he was clasping the curtains.

The count stood upright and triumphant like an avenging angel.

XXXVI

THE CARNIVAL IN ROME

When Franz recovered his senses, he found Albert drinking a glass of water, which his pale colour showed he needed urgently, and the count already putting on his clown's costume. He automatically looked into the square. Everything had vanished: scaffold, executioners, victims. Only the people remained, noisy, busy, jovial. The bell on the Monte Citorio, which was rung only for the death of the pope and the beginning of the *mascherata*, was pouring forth its sound.

'What happened?' he asked the count.

'Nothing,' he replied, 'nothing at all, as you see. But the carnival has begun, so let's quickly get dressed.'

'So: nothing is left of that awful scene but the vestige of a dream.'

'Because it was nothing more than a dream or a nightmare that you had.'

'Yes, that's as may be; but what about the condemned man?'

'Also a dream, except that he remained asleep, while you woke up. Who can tell which of you is the more fortunate?'

'And Peppino,' Franz asked, 'what became of him?'

'Peppino is a sensible lad, not at all vain and, unlike most men who are furious when no one is paying attention to them, he was delighted to see that all eyes were turned on his fellow-prisoner. As a result he took advantage of the distraction to slip away into the crowd and disappear, without even thanking the worthy priests who had accompanied him. Man is undoubtedly a most ungrateful and selfish creature ... But you must dress: look, Monsieur de Morcerf is setting you a good example.'

Albert was mechanically drawing on his taffeta trousers over his black trousers and polished boots.

'Well, Albert,' Franz asked, 'are you enjoying these departures from custom? Tell me honestly.'

'No,' he said, 'but I am truly pleased now to have seen such a thing and I understand what Monsieur le Comte said, namely that once one has managed to become accustomed to such a spectacle it is the only one that is still able to arouse any emotion in you.'

'Besides which,' said the count, 'it is only at that moment that one can make a study of character. On the first step of the scaffold, death tears away the mask that one has worn all one's life and the true face appears. It must be admitted that Andrea's was not a pretty sight ... What a horrible scoundrel! Come, gentlemen, let's get dressed!'

It would have been ridiculous for Franz to start putting on airs and not follow the example given by his two companions; so he in turn put on his costume and his mask, which was certainly no whiter than his face.

When they were dressed, they went down. The carriage was waiting at the door, full of confetti and bouquets of flowers. They joined the queue of traffic.

It is hard to imagine a more complete contrast with what had just taken place. Instead of the gloomy and silent spectacle of death, the Piazza del Popolo was the scene of unbridled and garish merrymaking. A crowd of masked figures cascaded forth, bursting out on all sides, pouring through the doors and clambering through the windows. Carriages were emerging from every side-street, laden with pierrots, harlequins and dominos, marquesses and plebeians, grotesques, knights and peasants – all yelling, waving their hands, throwing flour-filled eggs, confetti or bunches of flowers, assaulting friend and foe, stranger and acquaintance with words and missiles, without anyone having the right to object, with not a single reaction permitted except laughter.

Franz and Albert were like men who had been conducted to an orgy to help them forget some awful grief and who, the more they drank and the more they became intoxicated, felt a curtain descend between the past and the present. They could still see – or, rather, they continued to feel inside them – the shadow of what they had witnessed. But little by little they were possessed by the intoxication of the crowd; their minds began to feel unsteady and the power of reason seemed to be slipping away; they experienced a strange need to take part in this noise, this movement, this dizziness. A handful of confetti which struck Morcerf, thrown from a nearby carriage, covered him in dust, as it did his two companions, while stinging his neck and wherever on his face was not covered by the mask, as if a gross of pins had been thrown at him; but it had the effect of driving him into the fray in which all the masks they encountered were already engaged. He rose in turn in the carriage, filled his hands from the sacks and hurled eggs and dragées at his neighbours with all the strength and skill he could muster.

Now, battle was joined. The recollection of what they had witnessed half an hour earlier entirely vanished from the minds of the two young men, so much were they distracted by the many-coloured, ever-moving, demented spectacle before their eyes. As for the Count of Monte Cristo, he had not once, as we have already observed, appeared to be impressed for a moment.

If you were to imagine that lovely and magnificent thoroughfare, the Corso, lined from one end to the other on either side with four- or five-storey mansions, each with its balconies spread with hangings and every window decked with draperies; and at the balconies and the windows, three hundred thousand spectators, Romans, Italians or foreigners from the four corners of the earth – every form of aristocracy brought together: aristocracy of birth, aristocracy of money, aristocracy of talent; charming women who, themselves carried away by the spectacle, are bending over the balconies and leaning out of the windows to shower the carriages passing beneath with a hail of confetti, which is repaid in bunches of flowers – the air thick with falling confetti and rising flowers; and then on the road itself a joyful, unceasing, demented crowd, with crazy costumes: huge cabbages walking along, buffalo-heads roaring on men's bodies, dogs apparently walking on their hind legs; and in the midst of all this, in the midst of this temptation of Saint Anthony as it might have been dreamed by Callot,[1] a mask raised for some Astarte to reveal her delicious features, which you want to follow but from which you are kept back by demons such as might haunt a nightmare ... then you would have a rough idea of what the carnival is like in Rome.

On the second circuit the count had the carriage stopped and asked his companions' permission to leave them, with the carriage at their disposal. Franz looked up: they were opposite the Palazzo Rospoli; and at the middle window, outside which there was a sheet of white damask with a red cross, he saw a blue domino costume under which he had no difficulty imagining the lovely Greek from the Teatro Argentina.

'Gentlemen,' said the count, 'when you are tired of being actors and would like to become spectators again, you know that there are places for you in my windows. Meanwhile, please make use of my carriage, my coachman and my servants.'

We forgot to mention that the count's coachman was dressed soberly in a black bear's skin exactly like the one worn by Odry in *The Bear and the Pasha*;[2] and that the two lackeys standing behind the barouche had green monkey costumes, which fitted them perfectly, and masks on springs with which they were making faces at the passers-by.

Franz thanked the count for his kind offer. As for Albert, he was engaged in flirting with a whole carriage full of Roman peasants which, like the count's, had stopped to take a rest, as vehicles are accustomed to do in traffic; he was showering it with bouquets.

Unfortunately for him, the traffic started to move again and he found himself turning back towards the Piazza del Popolo, while the carriage which had attracted his attention was going up towards the Palazzo di Venezia.

'Oh! I say!' he said to Franz. 'Didn't you see?'

'What?' Franz asked.

'There: that barouche which is going off, full of Roman peasants.'

'No.'

'Well, I'm sure they are charming ladies.'

'What a pity you are masked, my dear Albert,' said Franz. 'This was an opportunity to make up for your disappointment in love.'

'Oh, I hope that the carnival will not end without bringing me some kind of consolation!' he replied, half laughing and half serious.

Despite these hopes, the whole day passed without any other adventure except two or three further meetings with the carriage bearing the Roman peasant women. On one of these occasions, either by accident or by design, Albert's mask fell off. At this, he took the rest of the bouquet of flowers and threw it into the other barouche.

One of the charming women whom Albert perceived under the fetching costume of a peasant from the Romagna must have been touched by this gallantry because, when the two friends' carriage next passed by, she in turn threw them a bouquet of violets.

Albert seized the flowers. As Franz had no reason to think that they were intended for him, he let Albert take them. Albert victoriously fixed the sprig of violets in his buttonhole and the carriage continued its triumphal progress.

'There you are!' said Franz. 'That could be the start of an adventure!'

'Laugh as loud as you wish,' he replied, 'but I really think so. I am not going to let go of this bouquet.'

'Don't dream of it!' said Franz, laughing. 'It will serve as a mark of recognition.'

The joke was soon close to reality because, when Franz and Albert, still carried along by the line of traffic, next passed the carriage with the *contadine*, the one who had thrown the sprig of violets to Albert clapped her hands when she saw it in his buttonhole.

'Bravo, my dear friend! Bravo!' said Franz. 'This is developing splendidly. Shall I go? Would you rather be alone?'

'No, no, let's not rush things. I don't want to be fooled by what is just a first step, a meeting under the clock as we say at the Bal de l'Opéra. If the lovely peasant has any wish to go further, then we'll meet up with her again tomorrow – or, rather, she will meet up with us. Then she can give me some sign of life and I'll see what is to be done.'

'There's no denying it, my dear Albert,' said Franz, 'you are as wise as Nestor and as prudent as Ulysses. And if your Circe is to change you into some beast or other, she will have to be either very clever or very powerful.'

Albert was right. The beautiful stranger had no doubt decided not to carry the intrigue any further that day because, although the two young men made several more circuits, they did not find the carriage they were looking for: it had no doubt disappeared down one of the neighbouring side-streets. So they went back to the Palazzo Rospoli, but the count too had vanished, with the blue domino. The two windows hung with yellow damask continued to be occupied by people who were no doubt his guests.

At that moment the same bell that had announced the opening of the *mascherata* sounded its end. At once the procession of traffic up and down the Corso dissolved and all the carriages quickly vanished into the adjoining streets. Franz and Albert were next to the Via delle Maratte: the coachman turned into it without a word and, travelling past the Palazzo Poli to the Piazza di Spagna, he pulled up next to the hotel.

Signor Pastrini came to the door to welcome his guests.

Franz's first consideration was to find out about the count and express his regret at not having returned to pick him up in time, but Signor Pastrini reassured him by letting him know that the Count of Monte Cristo had ordered a second carriage for himself, which had gone to the Palazzo Rospoli for him at four o'clock. Moreover he had been requested on the count's behalf to offer the two friends the key to his box in the theatre.

Franz asked Albert what he intended to do, but Albert had some important plans to carry out before he could think about going to the theatre; so, instead of replying, he asked if Signor Pastrini could find him a tailor.

'A tailor?' said the hotelier. 'For what?'

'To make us some Roman peasant costumes by tomorrow, as elegant as possible.'

Signor Pastrini shook his head. 'Two costumes by tomorrow!' he said. 'I beg Your Excellencies' pardon, but that is a very French request. Two costumes! You will certainly not find a tailor in Rome during the next week who will agree to sew six buttons on a waistcoat for you, even if you were to pay him an *écu* apiece for them!'

'So we must give up our idea of getting these costumes?'

'Not at all, because we have them ready-made. Let me look after it, and tomorrow when you wake up you will find a collection of hats, jackets and breeches which will meet your requirements.'

'Leave it up to our host,' Franz said. 'He has already shown us that he is a man of resource. So why don't we have a quiet dinner, then go and see *L'Italiana in Algeri*?'[3]

'Very well, let it be *L'Italiana in Algeri*,' said Albert. 'But consider, Signor Pastrini, that this gentleman and I' (indicating Franz) 'attach the highest importance to having the costumes that we asked for tomorrow morning.'

The innkeeper once more reassured his guests that they had nothing to worry about and that their needs would be fully met, so Franz and Albert went upstairs to take off their clowns' costumes. As he was getting out of his, Albert was very careful to put away his sprig of violets, which would serve as a sign of recognition for the next day.

The two friends sat down to dinner; but as they were eating, Albert could not refrain from pointing out the marked difference between the respective merits of Signor Pastrini's cook and the one employed by the Count of Monte Cristo; and indeed, honesty obliged Franz to confess, despite the reservations he still seemed to have on the subject of the count, that the comparison was not to the advantage of Signor Pastrini's chef.

Over dessert, the servant enquired to know the time when the two young men would like their carriage. Albert and Franz exchanged glances, because they were really afraid that they might be taking too many liberties. The servant understood.

'His Excellency the Count of Monte Cristo,' he said, 'has given definite orders that the carriage should remain at the disposal of their lordships for the whole day. Their lordships can therefore make use of it without any compunction.'

They determined to enjoy the count's courtesy to the full and asked for the horses to be harnessed while they went to change out of their daytime clothes into evening ones, the others having been slightly rumpled by the events of the day. After that, they repaired to the Teatro Argentina and took their places in the count's box.

During the first act, Countess G— came into her box. The first place she looked was towards the place where, the previous evening, she had seen the count, so that she saw Franz and Albert in the box of the man about whom she had expressed such a strange opinion to Franz a day earlier. Her opera-glasses interrogated him with such emphasis that Franz realized it would be cruel to leave her curiosity unsatisfied any longer. So, taking advantage of the privilege of spectators in Italian theatres, which allows them to use the playhouses as their reception rooms, the two friends left their box to present their regards to the countess. No sooner had they come into her box than she motioned to Franz to take the place of honour. Albert sat behind them.

'Well, then,' she said, hardly giving Franz time to sit down. 'It appears that you cannot wait to make the acquaintance of this new Lord Ruthwen and that you are now the very best of friends?'

'Although we are not quite as intimate as you imply, I cannot deny, Madame la Comtesse, that we have taken advantage of his hospitality all day.'

'How – all day?'

'That's precisely it: this morning we took lunch from him, we went up and down the Corso in his carriage throughout the *mascherata* and finally, this evening, we are in his box at the theatre.'

'Does this mean that you are now acquaintances?'

'Yes and no.'

'What do you mean?'

'It's a long story.'

'Tell it to me.'

'You would be too frightened by it.'

'All the more reason.'

'At least wait until the story has an ending.'

'Agreed. I do like stories to be complete. Meanwhile, how did you make contact? Who introduced you to him?'

'No one. On the contrary: he had himself introduced.'

'When?'

'Yesterday, after we left you.'

'By what means?'

'Oh, the most banal imaginable: through the intermediary of our landlord.'

'Is he staying at the Hôtel de Londres then, like you?'

'Not only in the same hotel, but on the same floor.'

'What's his name? You must at least know his name?'

'Of course. The Count of Monte Cristo.'

'What kind of a name is that? It's not the name of any family.'

'No, it's the name of an island he has purchased.'

'Is he a count?'

'Yes, a Tuscan count.'

'Huh! We must learn to swallow that,' said the countess, who came from one of the oldest families in the Venezia. 'What kind of a man is he, otherwise?'

'Ask the Vicomte de Morcerf.'

'Do you hear that, Monsieur? I am being referred to you.'

'We would be very hard to please if we were not to find him pleasing, Madame,' said Albert. 'A friend of ten years could not have done more for us than he did, and with the grace, delicacy of feeling and courtesy that betray a genuine man of the world.'

'Come, come,' said the countess, laughing. 'You will find that my vampire is quite simply some *nouveau riche* who wants to be excused for his wealth and who has adopted the mask of Lara so as not to be mistaken for Rothschild. Did you see her?'

'Her?' Franz asked, with a smile.

'The beautiful Greek from yesterday.'

'No. I do believe that we heard the sound of her *guzla*, but she herself remained completely invisible.'

'My dear Franz,' said Albert, 'when you say "invisible", you are quite simply trying to be mysterious. Who do you think was that blue domino we saw in the window hung with white damask?'

'And where was this window with the white damask?' asked the countess.

'At the Palazzo Rospoli.'

'So the count had three windows in the Palazzo Rospoli?'

'Yes. Did you drive down the Corso?'

'Naturally.'

'And did you notice two windows with yellow damask and one with white damask, marked with a red cross? Those were the count's.'

'Well I never! Is the man a nabob? Do you know what it costs to have three windows like those for carnival week in the Palazzo Rospoli, that is to say the best place on the Corso?'

'Two or three hundred Roman *écus* . . . ?'

'Two or three thousand, you should say.'

'The devil it does!'

'Does his island bring in such an income?'

'His island? Not a *baiocco*.'

'So why did he buy it?'

'On a whim.'

'He's an eccentric?'

'The fact is,' said Albert, 'that he did seem quite eccentric to me. My dear man, if he were to live in Paris and go to our theatres, I would say that he was either a hoaxer, or else some poor devil destroyed by literature: there's no denying he made two or three quips this morning worthy of Didier or Antony.'[4]

At this moment a visitor came in and Franz gave up his seat to the newcomer, according to custom. This move and the disturbance changed the subject of conversation.

An hour later the two friends returned to the hotel. Signor Pastrini had already taken care of their disguises for the next day and promised them that they would be pleased with the results of his ingenious efforts.

The next morning at nine he came into Franz's room, accompanied by a tailor carrying eight or ten Roman peasant costumes. The two friends chose two alike, more or less of their size, and requested their host to have about twenty ribbons sewn to each of their hats, and to obtain for them two of those charming striped silk scarves in bright colours that the men of the people are accustomed to tie round their waists on holidays.

Albert was anxious to see how he looked in his new costume: it was a jacket and trousers of blue velvet, embroidered stockings, buckled shoes and a silk waistcoat. Indeed Albert could not do otherwise than look elegant in this picturesque costume; and when the belt was fastened round his slender waist, and his hat, tilted a little to one side, let a shower of ribbons fall over his shoulder, Franz was obliged to admit that dress often has a lot to do with the superior physique that we attribute to some nations. The Turks – so picturesque in the old days with their long, brightly coloured robes – are now hideous in their blue buttoned frock-coats and those Greek hats which make them look like wine bottles with red tops. Don't you agree?

Franz complimented Albert who, moreover, was standing in front of the mirror and smiling at himself with a quite unmistakable air of self-satisfaction. It was at this point that the Count of Monte Cristo came in.

'Gentlemen,' he said, 'since, agreeable though it is to have a companion in pleasure, freedom is more agreeable still, I have come to tell you that I am leaving the carriage that you used yesterday at your disposal today and for the following days. Our host must have told you that I have three or four at livery with him, so you are not depriving me in any way. Feel free to enjoy it, either for pleasure or for business. Our meeting-place, should we have anything to say to one another, is the Palazzo Rospoli.'

The two young friends tried to make some objection, but there was really no good reason to refuse an offer which suited them very well, so eventually they accepted.

The count stayed with them for about a quarter of an hour, conversing fluently on every subject. As we have already been able to observe, he was well acquainted with the literature of every country. A glance at the walls of his drawing-room had shown Franz and Albert that he was a connoisseur of fine art. A few unpretentious words which he let slip in passing proved that he was not without some understanding in science; it appeared that he had particularly concerned himself with chemistry.

The two friends did not presume to repay the count for the luncheon he had given them: it would have been a poor jest to offer him, in exchange for his excellent table, the very mediocre fare that made up Signor Pastrini's table d'hôte. They said as much openly and he accepted their excuses with evident appreciation of their thoughtfulness.

Albert was charmed by the count's manners and was only prevented from recognizing him as a true aristocrat because of his learning. Most of all he was delighted at being able to have full use of the carriage: he had some ideas concerning his graceful peasant girls and, since they had appeared to him in a very elegant carriage, he was not sorry at being able to continue to seem to be on an equal footing with them in this respect.

At half-past one the two friends went downstairs. The coachman and the footmen had had the notion of putting their livery on over their wild animals' skins, which made them look even more grotesque than the day before, and were complimented warmly by Albert and Franz. Albert had sentimentally attached his sprig of fading violets to his buttonhole.

At the first sound of the bell, they set off and hurried into the Corso down the Via Vittoria.

On their second circuit, a bouquet of fresh violets, thrown from a carriage full of young lady clowns into the count's barouche told Albert that, like himself and his friend, the peasant girls from the previous day had changed costume and, whether by accident or by reason of the same feeling that had inspired him, gallantly, to adopt their costume, they had chosen the one that he and Franz had been wearing.

Albert put the fresh flowers in place of the old ones, but kept the faded bouquet in his hand; and, when he once more passed by the barouche, lifted it tenderly to his lips: not only the person who had thrown it to him but also her companions seemed to find this highly amusing.

The day was no less lively than the one before; a careful observer might even have noticed more noise and more merriment. The count was seen for a moment at the window, but when the carriage came round again, he had already gone.

It goes without saying that the flirtatious exchange between Albert and the lady clown with the bunch of violets lasted the whole day.

That evening, when he returned, Franz found a letter from the embassy telling him that he would have the honour of an audience with His Holiness the following day. On every previous occasion when he had visited Rome, he had asked for and obtained the same favour; and, for religious reasons and out of gratitude, he did not want to stop off in the capital of the Christian world without paying a respectful homage to one of the successors of Saint Peter who stands as a rare example of all the Christian virtues.

So he did not intend to go to the carnival the next day; for, despite the benevolence with which he tempers his grandeur, it is always with respect full of deep emotion that one prepares to bow before that noble and saintly old man, Gregory XVI.[5]

Coming out of the Vatican, Franz went straight back to the hotel, deliberately avoiding the Corso. He was carrying with him a treasure of pious thoughts which would have been profaned by the wild merriment of the *mascherata*.

At ten past five, Albert returned. He was overjoyed: the clown had resumed her peasant costume and, while passing by Albert's barouche, lifted her mask. She was enchanting.

Franz sincerely congratulated his friend, who took the compliments as no more than his due. By certain signs of authentic elegance, he claimed to have recognized that the beautiful stranger must belong to the highest ranks of Roman society. He was determined to write to her the next day.

While Albert was confiding in him, Franz noticed that he seemed to have a question he wanted to put but hesitated to ask. He pressed him, declaring that he would promise in advance to make any sacrifice he could for his friend's happiness. Albert allowed himself to be entreated for just as long as good manners required between friends and finally confessed to Franz that he would do him a great service if he were to leave him in sole charge of the carriage on the following day. He attributed the lovely peasant's exceptional kindness in lifting her mask to the absence of his friend.

Naturally Franz was not so selfish that he would hinder Albert in the midst of an adventure that promised to be so satisfactory both for his curiosity and for his self-esteem. He was well enough acquainted with his friend's exceptional lack of discretion to realize that he would be kept informed of the smallest details of his success. And since, in two or three years of travelling the length and breadth of Italy, he had never had the good fortune even to begin such an intrigue on his own account, Franz was not displeased to discover how matters proceeded in such cases. So he promised Albert that on the following day he would be content to watch the scene from the windows of the Palazzo Rospoli.

The next day he saw Albert going past again and again, with a huge bouquet, no doubt acting as the bearer of a love letter. This probability became certainty when Franz saw the same bouquet – immediately identifiable by a circle of white camellias – in the hands of a delightful clown dressed in pink satin.

That evening there was not merely joy, but delirium. Albert had no doubt that the beautiful stranger would answer him by the same means. Franz anticipated his wishes by saying that he found all that noise tiring and had decided to spend the following day looking through his album and making notes.

Albert was not mistaken. The following evening he came leaping in a single bound into Franz's room, holding a sheet of paper by one of its corners and brandishing it in the air.

'Well, was I mistaken?'

'Did she reply?' Franz exclaimed.

'Read it.'

The tone of Albert's voice as he said this would be impossible to convey. Franz took the letter and read:

On Tuesday evening at seven o'clock get out of your carriage at the entrance to Via dei Pontefici and follow the Roman peasant woman who will take hold of your *moccoletto*. When you reach the first step of the Church of San-Giacomo, make sure to tie a pink ribbon on the shoulder of your clown's costume, so that you can be recognized. Between now and then you will not see me again.

                                        Constancy and discretion.

'Well, now,' he asked Franz, when the latter had finished reading, 'what do you think of that, dear friend?'

'I think,' said Franz, 'that the business is taking on the character of a most agreeable adventure.'

'I think the same, and I am very afraid that you may be going alone to the Duke of Bracciano's ball.'

The very same morning, Franz and Albert had received invitations from the celebrated Roman banker.

'Take care, my dear Albert,' said Franz. 'All of high society will be at the duke's; and if your beautiful stranger is really an aristocrat, she will not be able to escape putting in an appearance.'

'Whether she does or not, I shall not alter my opinion of her. Have you read the letter?'

'Yes.'

'Don't you know how poorly educated the women of the *mezzo cito* are in Italy?' This was a term designating the bourgeoisie.

'Yes,' Franz replied again.

'So! Re-read the note, examine the writing, and tell me if there is a single mistake in grammar or spelling?'

The writing was certainly charming, the spelling faultless.

'You are predestined,' Franz said, once more returning the letter.

'Laugh if you wish, joke as much as you like,' Albert went on. 'I am in love.'

'Good Lord! You scare me!' said Franz. 'I can see that not only will I be going alone to the Duke of Bracciano's ball, but I may well also find myself returning on my own to Florence.'

'The fact is that, if my stranger is as agreeable as she is beautiful, then I do declare I shall be settling in Rome for at least six weeks. I adore the city, and in any case I have always had this marked predilection for archaeology.'

'Decidedly. A few more meetings like this one and I feel sure that we shall see you elected to the Académie des Inscriptions et Belles-Lettres.'

Albert looked as though he were about to argue seriously his

THE CARNIVAL IN ROME

claims to the academic chair, but at that moment a servant came
to tell the young friends that dinner was served. Love, for Albert,
was not incompatible with a healthy appetite, so he hurried to sit
down at the table beside his friend, though quite ready to resume
the discussion after dinner.

After dinner, however, the Count of Monte Cristo was
announced. They had not seen him for two days: business, according to Signor Pastrini, had taken him to Civita Vecchia. He had left
the evening before and got back only an hour ago.

He was charming. Whether because he was watching, or because
the circumstances did not strike those acrimonious chords that on
other occasions had charged his utterances with bitterness, he was
more or less like other men. Franz found him truly enigmatic. The
count could not doubt that the young traveller had recognized
him, yet not a single word had fallen from his lips since their
acquaintance was renewed to suggest that they had met before. For
his part, much though Franz would like to have referred to their
previous interview, he was restrained by the fear of displeasing a
man who had shown such consideration towards him and his
friend, so he went on copying the other man's reserve.

The count had learned that the two friends wanted a box in the
Teatro Argentina and had been told that all places were reserved;
so he was once more bringing them the key to his box – at least,
this was the avowed purpose of his visit.

Franz and Albert objected, on the grounds that they did not want
to deprive the count, but he replied that he was going to the Teatro
Palli that evening, so his box at the Argentina would be wasted if
they did not take advantage of it. This made up their minds.

Franz was becoming accustomed to the count's pallor, which
had struck him so forcibly on first meeting. He could not deny the
beauty of the man's stern face, of which the pale colour was either
the only defect or perhaps the chief quality. Franz, a true Byronic
hero, could not see, or even think of, him without imagining those
sombre features on the shoulders of Manfred or under Lara's
head-dress.[6] He had the furrowed brow that spoke of bitter, ines-
capable thoughts; he had those burning eyes that penetrate to the
depths of a soul; he had those haughty, contemptuous lips which
give the words that issue from them a particular bent, so that they
become deeply engraved in the memory of whoever hears them.

The count was no longer young: forty at least;[7] yet one could easily understand that he would prevail over any young men among whom he might find himself. The truth is that he also had this in common with the fantastic heroes of the English poet: that he appeared to possess the gift of spellbinding others.

Albert was constantly remarking how lucky they had been to meet such a man. Franz was less enthusiastic, though he too was susceptible to the influence exercised by any superior being over those around him. He thought about the plan the count had mentioned once or twice of going to Paris and had no doubt that, with his unusual personality, his striking features and his huge wealth, he would make a considerable mark there. Yet he himself would prefer not to be in Paris when the count was there.

The evening passed as most evenings do at the theatre in Italy, not in listening to the singers, but in renewing acquaintances and conversation. Countess G— wanted to discuss the count, but Franz told her that he had something much more novel to tell her and, despite Albert's exhibitions of false modesty, he described the major event that had taken up most of the two friends' thoughts over the previous three days.

Intrigues of this kind are not rare in Italy (at least, if travellers are to be believed), and the countess, far from expressing incredulity, congratulated Albert on the start of an adventure that promised to end in such a satisfactory manner. They parted, agreeing to meet at the Duke of Bracciano's ball, to which all Rome had been invited.

The lady with the bouquet kept her promise to Albert: neither the next day nor the one after did she give him any sign of life.

At last Tuesday came, the last and most rowdy day of the carnival. On Tuesday the theatres are open at ten in the morning because, after eight in the evening, Lent starts. On the Tuesday, everyone who – through shortage of time, money or inclination – has not yet taken part in the festival joins the bacchanalian orgy, is carried away by the revels and contributes a share of noise and movement to the sum of movement and noise.

From two until five Franz and Albert followed the line of carriages, exchanging handfuls of confetti with those in the line opposite and with the pedestrians walking between the feet of the horses and the wheels of the carriages, without a single accident occurring, a single argument erupting or a single fight breaking out in all this appalling chaos. The Italians are supreme in this respect: a festivity for them is a genuine festivity. The author of this story, who lived for five or six years in Italy, can never once remember having seen a celebration interrupted by any of those disturbances that inevitably accompany our own.

Albert was a huge success in his clown's costume. On his shoulder he had a knotted pink ribbon, the ends of which fell down to his knees. To avoid any confusion between them, Franz had kept his Roman peasant's costume.

As the day wore on, so the noise grew greater. On all those pavements, in all those carriages, at all those windows, not a single mouth remained silent, not a single arm remained still. It was a veritable human storm made up of a thunder of voices and a hail of dragées, bouquets, eggs, oranges and flowers.

At three o'clock, the sound of cannon being fired across the Piazza del Popolo and the Palazzo di Venezia, though it could only just be heard through this awful tumult, announced that the races were about to begin.

The races, like the *moccoli*, are a particular feature of the last days of carnival. At the sound of these cannon, the carriages instantly broke ranks and each headed for the side-street nearest wherever they happened to be. All these manoeuvres take place with unbelievable skill and wonderful speed, without the police bothering in the slightest to assign anyone to a post or to show anyone where he should go. Those on foot pressed themselves against the palazzi. Then a great sound of horses' hoofs and rattling of sabres was heard.

A squadron of *carabinieri*, fifteen abreast, galloped the whole length of the Corso, clearing it in readiness for the *barberi*. When the squadron reached the Palazzo di Venezia, the sound of another roll of cannon gave the signal that the road was clear.

Almost at once, in the midst of a vast, universal, inconceivable clamour, they saw seven or eight horses go past like wraiths, driven on by the cheering of three hundred thousand voices and the metal castanets clattering on their backs. Then the cannon in the Castel Sant'Angelo fired three times: this meant that number three was the winner.

Needing no other signal but that, the carriages moved off again, cascading back towards the Corso, flowing out from every street like tributaries that had been dammed for a moment, before simul-taneously pouring back into the bed of the river that they fed, and the huge torrent resumed its course, swifter than ever, between the two granite banks.

Now, however, a new element had added still further to the noise and movement of the crowd. The sellers of *moccoli* had come on to the scene.

Moccoli or *moccoletti* are candles of varying thickness, from an Easter candle to a taper, which excite two contradictory ambitions in the actors of the great finale of the Roman carnival: first, to keep one's own *moccoletto* alight; second, to extinguish everyone else's.

The same is true of the *moccoletto* as of life: mankind has so far found only one way of transmitting it, which he owes to God. But he has found a thousand ways to extinguish it – and here the Devil has surely given him some little help.

A *moccoletto* is lit by bringing it up to another source of light. But who can describe the thousand ways that have been invented to put out a *moccoletto*: great puffs of breath, monstrous bellows, superhuman fans?

Everyone hastened to buy *moccoletti*, Franz and Albert with the rest.

Night was falling fast. Already, at the cry 'Moccoli!', repeated by the strident voices of a thousand manufacturers, two or three stars began to shine above the crowd. This was the signal.

In ten minutes, fifty thousand lights glittered all the way from the Palazzo di Venezia to the Piazza del Popolo, and back up from the Piazza del Popolo to the Palazzo di Venezia. It was like a vast congregation of will-o'-the-wisps, impossible to envisage if you have never seen it: imagine that all the stars in the sky were to come down and dance wildly about the earth, to the accompaniment of cries such as no human ear has ever heard elsewhere on its surface.

This is the time, above all, when class distinctions are abolished. The *facchino* takes hold of the prince, the prince of the Trasteveran, the Trasteveran of the bourgeois, each one blowing out, extinguishing and relighting. If old Aeolus[8] were to appear at this moment he would be proclaimed King of the Moccoli, and Aquilo the heir presumptive to the throne.

This wild, blazing dash lasted some two hours. The Corso was lit as if in broad daylight and the features of the spectators' faces could be distinguished up to the third or fourth storey. Every five minutes Albert took out his watch. At last, it showed seven o'clock.

The two friends had reached exactly the corner of the Via dei

Pontefici. Albert leapt out of the carriage, his *moccoletto* in his hand.

Two or three masked figures tried to come up to him either to put it out or take it away, but Albert was a skilled boxer. He sent them reeling a good ten yards, one after the other, and continued running towards the Church of San Giacomo.

The steps were crowded with bystanders and masked figures struggling to take the candles from each other's hands. Franz watched Albert as he went, and he saw him put his foot on the first step; almost at once a masked figure, wearing the familiar costume of the peasant girl with the bouquet, reached out and took his *moccoletto*, without Albert this time offering any resistance. Franz was too far away to hear what they said, but her words were doubtless reassuring, for he saw Albert and the girl walk off, arm in arm. For a time he followed them through the crowd, but he lost sight of them at the Via Macello.

Suddenly the bell which signals the end of the carnival rang out and at the same moment all the *moccoli* went out simultaneously, as if by enchantment. You would have thought that one single, enormous breath of wind had extinguished them all.

Franz found himself in total darkness.

At the same moment, all the cries ceased, as if the breath of wind that had put out the lights had carried off the noise at the same time. All that could be heard was the rumbling of the carriages as they took the masked figures home. All that could still be seen were the few lights burning behind the windows.

The carnival was over.

XXXVII

THE CATACOMBS OF SAINT SEBASTIAN

Never in his life, perhaps, had Franz ever felt such a sharply defined and rapid transformation from merriment to sadness as he did at that moment. You would have thought that Rome, under the magic wand of some demon of the night, had changed into one vast tomb. By an eventuality which added to the blackness of the night, the moon was waning and not due to rise until eleven o'clock, so the streets through which the young man walked were plunged in utter darkness. But the journey was short. In ten minutes his carriage – that is to say, the count's – stopped at the Hôtel de Londres.

Dinner was waiting for him but, since Albert had warned him that he might not return immediately, Franz sat down to eat without waiting for him.

Signor Pastrini, who was used to seeing them dine together, asked why Albert was not there, but Franz said no more than that his friend had received an invitation two days earlier and had accepted it. The sudden extinction of the *moccoletti*, the darkness that had replaced the light and the silence that had followed the din had left Franz feeling melancholy, and even a little tense; so he dined in total silence, even though Signor Pastrini was as attentive as ever and came in two or three times to ask if he had everything he needed.

Franz was determined to wait up as late as possible for Albert, so he ordered the carriage only for eleven o'clock, asking Signor Pastrini to inform him immediately if Albert reappeared at the hotel for any reason. At eleven Albert had not returned, so Franz dressed and left, telling his host that he would be spending the night at the Duke of Bracciano's.

The Duke of Bracciano's house is one of the most delightful in Rome. His wife, one of the last heirs of the Colonna family, is a perfect hostess. Consequently the duke's entertainments are famous throughout Europe. Franz and Albert had arrived in Rome with letters of introduction to him, so his first question was to ask Franz what had become of his travelling companion. Franz replied that he had left him at the moment just as the *moccoli* were about to be extinguished and that he had lost sight of him in the Via Macello.

'And he has not come home?' said the duke.

'I waited for him until now,' Franz replied.

'Do you know where he was going?'

'Not precisely, but I believe that there was some kind of assignation.'

'Damnation!' said the duke. 'This is a bad day – or, rather, a bad night – to be out late; don't you think, Madame la Comtesse?'

The last words were addressed to Countess G—, who had just arrived, on the arm of M. Torlonia, the duke's brother.

'On the contrary, I think the night is charming,' said the countess.

'Those who are here will only have one thing to complain of, which is that it will go too quickly.'

The duke smiled. 'I am not talking of those who are here, who run no risk except, if they are men, that of falling in love with you and, if they are women, falling ill with jealousy at seeing you so beautiful. I am thinking of those who are in the streets of Rome.'

'Good heavens,' said the countess. 'Whoever would be in the streets at this time of night, unless coming to your ball?'

'Our friend Albert de Morcerf, Countess, whom I left in pursuit of his beautiful stranger at seven o'clock this evening,' said Franz. 'I haven't seen him since.'

'What! And you don't know where he is?'

'I have not the slightest idea.'

'Is he armed?'

'He's wearing clown's dress.'

'You should not have let him go,' the duke said. 'You know Rome better than he does.'

'Perhaps, but it was not so easy: one might as well have tried to stop the number three horse which won today's race,' Franz replied. 'In any case, what could happen to him?'

'Who knows? The night is very black and the Tiber is quite close to the Via Macello.'

Franz felt his blood run cold at seeing the duke and the countess's thoughts running along similar lines to the ones suggested by his own anxieties.

'I informed the hotel that I should have the honour of spending the night at your house, Duke,' he said. 'They are to come and tell me when he returns.'

'There!' said the duke. 'I think this is one of my servants looking for you now.'

He was right. Seeing Franz, the servant came over.

'Excellency,' he said, 'the owner of the Hôtel de Londres wishes to inform you that a man is waiting there with a letter from the Vicomte de Morcerf.'

'A letter from the vicomte!' Franz exclaimed.

'Yes.'

'Who is this man?'

'I cannot tell you.'

'Why did he not bring it to me here?'

'He gave me no explanation.'

'Where is this messenger?'

'He left as soon as he saw me come into the ballroom to speak to you.'

'Oh, my goodness!' the countess exclaimed. 'Go quickly. Poor young man, perhaps he has had an accident.'

'I'm going this moment,' said Franz.

'Will you come back and tell us any news?' asked the countess.

'Yes, if the matter is not serious; otherwise I cannot say where I will be myself.'

'In any case, be prudent,' said the countess.

'Don't worry, I shall.'

Franz took his hat and left hurriedly. He had sent away his carriage, ordering it for two o'clock; but fortunately the Palazzo Bracciano, which faces on to the Corso on one side and the Piazza dei Santi Apostoli on the other, is hardly ten minutes on foot from the Hôtel de Londres. As he approached the hotel, Franz saw a man standing in the middle of the street, and did not for an instant doubt that this was the messenger from Albert. The man was wearing a large cloak. He went over but, much to Franz's surprise, it was the man who spoke first.

'What do you want of me, Excellency?' he said, stepping backwards like a man wanting to keep up his defences.

'Aren't you the person who is bringing me a letter from the Vicomte de Morcerf?' Franz asked.

'Is Your Excellency staying at Pastrini's hotel?'

'I am.'

'And is Your Excellency the viscount's travelling companion?'

'Yes.'

'What is Your Excellency's name?'

'Baron Franz d'Epinay.'

'Then this letter is indeed addressed to Your Excellency.'

'Is there to be any reply?' Franz asked, taking the letter from the man's hand.

'Yes – at least your friend hopes so.'

'Come up, then, and I'll give it to you.'

'I should prefer to wait here,' the messenger said, laughing.

'Why?'

'Your Excellency will understand everything when you have read the letter.'

'So, am I to meet you again here?'

'Certainly.'

Franz went into the hotel and met Signor Pastrini on the stairs.

'Well?' the innkeeper asked.

'Well, what?' said Franz.

'Did you see the man who wanted to speak with you on behalf of your friend?' he asked Franz.

'Yes, I saw him,' he replied. 'And he gave me this letter. Please bring lights to my room.'

The hotelier gave the order to a servant to go ahead of Franz with a candle. The young man had sensed that Signor Pastrini was afraid, and this made him even more anxious to read Albert's letter. He went close to the candle as soon as it was lit and spread out the sheet of paper. The letter was in Albert's hand and was signed by him. Franz read it twice, so unexpected were its contents. This is precisely what it said:

Dear Friend, as soon as you receive this, be so good as to take the letter of credit from my portfolio, which you will find in the square drawer of the writing table. If the amount is not enough, add your own. Go immediately to Torlonia's, draw four thousand *piastres* and give them to the bearer. It is urgent that this amount should reach me without delay.

I shall not insist further: I count on you as you could count on me.

P.S. I believe now the Italian banditti.*

Your friend, ALBERT DE MORCERF

Beneath these lines was written in a strange hand these few words in Italian:

Se alle sei della mattina le quattro mile piastre non sono nelle mie mani, alla sette il conte Alberto avia cessato di vivere.†

LUIGI VAMPA

The second signature explained everything to Franz, who understood the messenger's reluctance to come up to his room: the street would seem safer to him. Albert had fallen into the clutches of the

---

* In English.

† If at six in the morning the four thousand *piastres* are not in my hands, by seven o'clock Vicomte Albert de Morcerf will have ceased to exist.

famous bandit chief in whose existence he had so long refused to believe.

There was no time to be lost. He ran to the writing table and opened it; in the drawer mentioned, he found the portfolio and, in the portfolio, the letter of credit. In all it was for six thousand *piastres*, but Albert had already spent three thousand of them. As for Franz, he had no letter of credit. Since he was living in Florence and had come to Rome for only seven or eight days, he had taken about a hundred *louis* with him and, of these, at the most fifty were left.

This meant that the two of them, Franz and Albert together, were seven or eight hundred *piastres* short of the amount asked for. It is true that in such a case Franz could count on the under-standing of Messrs Torlonia. He was consequently preparing to return to the Palazzo Bracciano immediately, when suddenly he had a brilliant idea. He thought of the Count of Monte Cristo. He was just about to give the order to send for Signor Pastrini when the man appeared in person at the door.

'My dear Signor Pastrini,' he said eagerly, 'do you know if the count is in?'

'Yes, Excellency. He has just returned.'

'Will he have had time to go to bed yet?'

'I doubt it.'

'Then kindly ring at his door and ask his permission for me to pay him a visit.'

Signor Pastrini hurried off to carry out these instructions and returned in five minutes.

'The count is expecting Your Excellency,' he said.

Franz crossed the landing and a servant showed him in to the count, who was in a little study that Franz had not yet seen, with divans around the walls. He came forward to meet him.

'What fair wind brings you here at this hour?' he asked. 'Are you inviting me to take supper with you? That would be very obliging, I must say.'

'No, I have come to speak with you on serious business.'

'Business!' said the count, giving Franz his usual penetrating look. 'What business?'

'Are we alone?'

The count went across to the door, then returned.

'Completely alone,' he said.

Franz gave him Albert's letter. 'Read this,' he said.

The count read it and said only: 'Ah!'

'Did you see the postscript?'

'Yes, certainly I did: *"Se alle sei della mattina le quattro mile piastre non sono nelle mie mani, alla sette il conte Alberto avia cessato di vivere."'*

'What do you say about that?'

'Do you have the amount required?'

'Yes, except for eight hundred *piastres*.'

The count went over to his writing table, opened it and pulled out a drawer full of gold. 'I hope,' he said, 'that you will not insult me by going to anyone else?'

'On the contrary, you see that I came straight to you,' said Franz.

'Thank you. Please take what you need.' And he motioned towards the drawer.

'Is it really necessary to send this money to Luigi Vampa?' the young man asked, staring fixedly at the count in his turn.

'By God! Ask yourself: the postscript is clear enough.'

'It seems to me that, if you were to look for it, you would find a means to simplify the negotiation considerably,' said Franz.

'What means?' asked the count in astonishment.

'For example, if we were to go together to meet Luigi Vampa, I am sure that he would not refuse to grant you Albert's freedom.'

'Me? What influence could I have over this bandit?'

'Have you not just rendered him the sort of service that is not easily forgotten?'

'What service?'

'Didn't you just save Peppino's life?'

'Ah ha! Now who told you that?'

'What does that matter? I know.'

The count stayed silent for a moment, frowning.

'If I went to meet Vampa, would you come with me?'

'If my company was not too displeasing to you.'

'Very well. The night is fair and a walk in the Roman *campagna* can only do us good.'

'Should we arm ourselves?'

'What for?'

'Should we take any money?'

'There is no need. Where is the man who brought this note?'

'Outside, in the street.'

'Is he waiting for an answer?'

'Yes.'

'We must have some idea of where we are going. I'll call him.'

'It is pointless, he does not want to come up.'

'To your apartments, perhaps, but he will not mind coming to mine.'

The count went to the window of the study, which overlooked the street, and whistled in a particular way. The man in the cloak stepped out of the shadows and into the middle of the street.

'*Salite!*' the count said, as if giving orders to a servant. The messenger obeyed at once without hesitation, even eagerly, and, leaping across the four steps at the entrance to the hotel, came in. Five seconds later, he was at the study door.

'Ah, it's you, Peppino!' said the count.

Peppino, instead of answering, fell to his knees, grasped the count's hand and pressed his lips to it repeatedly.

'Well, I never,' said the count. 'You have not yet forgotten how I saved your life. Odd. It was already a week ago.'

'No, Excellency, and I shall never forget,' said Peppino, in a tone of voice that expressed the depth of his gratitude.

'Never is a very long time, but it counts for a lot that you should believe it. Stand up and answer me.'

Peppino looked anxiously at Franz.

'Oh! You can speak in front of His Excellency,' the count said. 'He is a friend of mine.' Then he added, in French, turning to Franz: 'I hope you will allow me to call you that. It is necessary to gain this man's confidence.'

'You may speak in front of me,' Franz said. 'I am a friend of the count's.'

'Fine!' said Peppino, turning back to the count. 'Your Excellency can ask the questions and I shall reply.'

'How did Vicomte Albert fall into Luigi's hands?'

'Excellency, the Frenchman's carriage drove several times past the one with Teresa in it.'

'The chief's mistress?'

'Yes. The Frenchman flirted with her and it amused Teresa to reply. The Frenchman threw her bouquets, she threw some back. All this, of course, was with the chief's consent. He was in the carriage himself.'

'What!' Franz exclaimed. 'Luigi Vampa was in the carriage with the peasant women!'

'He was driving it, disguised as the coachman.'

'And then?' asked the count.

'Well, then the Frenchman took off his mask. Teresa, still with the chief's agreement, did the same. The Frenchman asked for a rendez-vous, and Teresa agreed; however, in place of Teresa, it was Beppo who was waiting on the steps of San Giacomo.'

'What!' Franz exclaimed, interrupting him again. 'The peasant girl who took his *moccoletto* from him . . . ?'

'Was a fifteen-year-old boy,' Peppino answered. 'But there is no shame for your friend in the mistake; Beppo has fooled lots of others, take my word for it.'

'And Beppo took him outside the walls?' asked the count.

'Just so. A carriage was waiting at the end of the Via Macello. Beppo got in and told the Frenchman to follow; he did not need asking twice. He graciously offered the right-hand seat to Beppo and sat beside him. Thereupon Beppo told him he would be driven to a villa a league outside Rome. The Frenchman assured Beppo that he was prepared to follow him to the end of the earth. At this, the coachman went up the Via Ripetta, through the Porta San Paolo and, two hundred yards into the countryside, as the Frenchman was starting to get a little too forward, Beppo stuck a pair of pistols in his throat; upon which the coachman stopped the horses, turned around in his seat and did the same. At the same time four of our men who had been hiding on the banks of the Almo rushed across to the doors. The Frenchman tried his best to defend himself and even, so I heard, half strangled Beppo, but there was not much to be done against five armed men. He had to give up. He was taken out of the coach, along the banks of the stream and eventually to Teresa and Luigi, who were waiting for him in the Catacombs of San Sebastian.'

'Well, what do you say to that?' said the count, turning towards Franz. 'That's not a bad story, I think. You are a connoisseur in such matters; what do you think?'

'I think I would find it most amusing,' Franz replied, 'if it had happened to anyone except poor Albert.'

'The fact is,' said the count, 'that if you had not found me there, your friend's good fortune would have cost him dear. But don't worry: in the event he will get away with a fright.'

'We're still going to find him?'

'Certainly! All the more so since he is in a very picturesque spot. Do you know the Catacombs of Saint Sebastian?'

'No, I have never been into them, but I had promised myself that I would visit them one day.'

'Well, now you have a ready-made opportunity, and it would be hard to find a better one. Do you have your carriage?'

'No.'

'No matter. They invariably keep one ready harnessed for me, day and night.'

'Ready harnessed?'

'Yes, I must tell you, I am a very capricious person. Sometimes I get up from the table at the end of my dinner, in the middle of the night, and have a sudden desire to set off for some part of the world; so I leave.'

The count rang and his valet appeared.

'Bring the carriage out of the coachhouse,' he said, 'and take the pistols which you will find in the pockets. There is no sense in waking the coachman, Ali will drive.'

A moment later the carriage could be heard drawing up outside the door. The count took out his watch.

'Half-past midnight,' he said. 'We could have left at five o'clock in the morning and still arrived in time; but that delay might have meant your friend spending an unpleasant night, so we had better set off at once to rescue him from the clutches of the infidel. Are you still set on accompanying me?'

'More than ever.'

'Well then, come.'

Franz and the count left, followed by Peppino. They found the carriage waiting at the door, with Ali on the box. Franz recognized the dumb slave from the grotto on Monte Cristo.

Franz and the count got into the carriage, a coupé. Peppino sat beside Ali and they set off at a gallop. Ali had had his orders in advance, for he followed the Corso, crossed the Campo Vaccino and drove up the Strada San Gregorio until they reached the Porto San Sebastiano. Here the gatekeeper tried to detain them, but the Count of Monte Cristo showed him an authorization from the governor of Rome allowing him to go in or out of the City at any time of the day or night, so the gateway was raised, the keeper had a *louis* for his trouble and they passed through.

The road that the carriage followed was the old Appian Way, lined with tombs. From time to time, in the light of the newly risen moon, Franz saw what he thought was a sentry gliding out of a ruin; but as soon as a sign had been exchanged between Peppino and this wraith, it vanished back into the shadows.

A little way before the amphitheatre of Caracalla, the carriage halted, Peppino opened the door, and Franz and the count got down. 'In ten minutes,' the count told his companion, 'we shall be there.' He took Peppino aside, whispered some order to him, and Peppino left after taking a torch which they found in the trunk of the coupé.

Five more minutes elapsed, during which Franz saw the shepherd follow a little path through the hillocks, which litter the uneven surface of the Roman plain, and disappear into a clump of that tall, reddish grass which resembles the bristling mane of some gigantic lion.

'Now,' said the count. 'Let's follow him.'

They went along the same path and found that, after a hundred paces, it went down a slope to the bottom of a little valley. Soon they saw two men talking together in the darkness.

'Should we go on,' Franz asked the count, 'or should we wait?'

'Carry on. Peppino must have warned the sentry of our arrival.'

One of the men, as it turned out, was Peppino, and the other a bandit acting as a guard. Franz and the count approached and the bandit greeted them.

'Excellency,' Peppino told the count, 'please be so good as to follow me: the entrance to the catacombs is a short distance from here.'

'Very well,' said the count. 'Lead the way.'

Behind a clump of bushes and hidden among some rocks was an opening through which a man could barely pass. Peppino went through this slit first, but he had hardly advanced more than a step or two before the passage widened; so he stopped, lit his torch and turned around to see that the others were following. The count had been the next to venture into this sort of funnel and Franz came after.

The ground sloped gently downwards and the path widened as they went on, but Franz and the count were obliged to walk bent double and would still have had difficulty in going two abreast. They continued for a further fifty yards like this and were then

stopped by the cry of: '*Who goes there?*' At the same time they saw
the light from their own torch shining on the barrel of a rifle in the
midst of the darkness.

'A friend!' said Peppino. And he went on alone to say a few
words in a low voice to this second sentry who, like the first, greeted
the nocturnal visitors with a sign showing that they could continue
on their way.

Behind the sentry was a staircase of about twenty steps. Franz
and the count went down them and found themselves in a sort of
crossroads of tombs: five paths led off it like the rays of a star and
the walls were carved out with niches, one above the other, in
the form of coffins, indicating that they had at last reached the
catacombs.

In one of the cavities, the depth of which it was impossible to
assess, one could see by day a few chinks of light. The count put his
hand on Franz's shoulder. 'Would you like to see an encampment of
bandits at rest?' he asked.

'Yes, indeed,' said Franz.

'Then come with me. Peppino, put out the light.'

Peppino obeyed, and they found themselves plunged into the
most profound darkness; however, about fifty yards ahead of them,
a few reddish lights continued to play across the walls, made more
visible since Peppino had put out his torch.

They went on in silence, the count guiding Franz as if he had the
unusual ability of being able to see in the dark; and Franz himself
could make out the way more easily, the closer they approached to
the glow that showed them their way. Eventually, they passed
through three arches, the middle one serving as a door.

On one side, these arches opened on the corridor down which
the count and Franz had walked and, on the other, on a large
square room completely surrounded by niches like the ones we
have already mentioned. In the middle of the room stood four
stones which had once served as an altar, as the cross on them still
showed. A single lamp, placed on the shaft of a column, threw a
faint and flickering light on the strange scene that met the eyes of
the two visitors as they watched from the shadows.

A man was sitting, his elbow resting on the column, and reading
with his back turned towards the arches through which the
new arrivals could watch him. It was the chief of the band, Luigi
Vampa.

Around him could be seen some twenty bandits, lying as they chose, wrapped in their cloaks or propped against a sort of stone bench that ran all round the walls of the chamber. Each had his gun within reach. At the far end, hardly visible, like a ghost, a sentry was walking backwards and forwards in front of a sort of opening that could only be made out because the darkness seemed thicker at this point.

When the count decided that Franz had had time to take in this picturesque scene, he put a finger to his lips to ensure his silence, then climbed the three steps leading from the passage to the chamber, went through the middle archway and walked across to Vampa, who was so deeply engrossed in what he was reading that he did not hear the sound of footsteps.

'Who goes there?' cried the sentry, more alert, seeing a sort of shadow growing in the light of the lamp behind his chief.

At this, Vampa leapt to his feet, at the same time drawing a pistol from his belt. Immediately all the bandits were on their feet, and twenty gun-barrels were pointing towards the count.

'Well, well,' he said quietly, in a perfectly calm voice, with a muscle twitching in his face. 'My dear Vampa, there is no need to go to such trouble just to greet a friend.'

'Put down your weapons,' the bandit chief said, with an imperious gesture of one hand, while with the other he respectfully removed his hat. Then, turning to the remarkable figure who dominated the whole of the scene, he added; 'I beg your pardon, Monsieur le Comte. I was not expecting you to honour me with a visit and consequently did not recognize you.'

'It seems that your memory is short in everything, Vampa,' the count said. 'Not only do you forget a man's face, but also the agreement you have made with him.'

'What agreement have I forgotten, Monsieur le Comte?' the bandit asked in a voice that implied that, if he had made a mistake, he asked nothing better than to make amends for it.

'Was it not understood,' said the count, 'that not only my own person but also that of my friends would be sacred to you?'

'How have I failed in this respect, Excellency?'

'This evening you have abducted and brought here Vicomte Albert de Morcerf. Now,' the count continued in a voice that made Franz shudder, 'this young man is one of *my friends*, staying at the same hotel as I am; he rode along the Corso for a week in my own carriage; yet, I repeat, you abducted him, brought him here and . . .' (here the count took the letter out of his pocket) 'you have set a price on his head – like any Tom, Dick or Harry.'

'Why was I not told of this?' the chief asked, turning towards his men, who shrank away from his look. 'Why did you put me in a situation where I might fail in my promise to the count, who holds all our lives in his hands? By the blood of Christ! If I thought that any one of you knew that this young man was a friend of His Excellency, I should blow out his brains with my own hand.'

'You see?' the count said, turning towards Franz. 'I told you that there must be some mistake.'

'You are not alone?' Vampa asked anxiously.

'I am with the person to whom this letter is addressed, and I wanted to prove to him that Luigi Vampa is a man of his word. Come, Excellency,' he said to Franz, 'Luigi Vampa will tell you himself that he is in despair at the mistake he has made.'

Franz came into the chamber. The chief stepped towards him.

'Welcome among us, Excellency,' he said. 'You have heard what the count just said, and my reply. I might add that I would not wish such a thing to have happened for the four thousand *piastres* at which I set your friend's ransom.'

'But where is the prisoner?' Franz asked, looking all around him anxiously. 'I can't see him.'

'I hope no harm has come to him!' the count said, frowning.

'The prisoner is there,' Vampa said, pointing to the recess in front of which the sentry was marching. 'I shall go myself and tell him that he is free.'

The chief went over to the place which he had indicated as Albert's prison, followed by the count and Franz.

'What is the prisoner doing?' Vampa asked the sentry.

'My word, I don't know, Captain,' he replied. 'I haven't heard him stir for more than an hour.'

'Come, Excellency!' Vampa said.

The count and Franz went up seven or eight steps, still following the chief, who slipped a bolt and pushed open a door.

By the light of a lamp like the one burning in the adjoining chamber, they could see Albert, wrapped in a cloak that he had been lent by one of the bandits, lying in a corner and sleeping profoundly.

'Look at that!' the count said, smiling his peculiar smile. 'Not bad for a man who was to be shot at seven tomorrow morning.'

Vampa looked at the sleeping figure with a certain degree of admiration: it was clear that he was not unimpressed by this proof of courage.

'You are right, Monsieur le Comte,' he said. 'This must be one of your friends.' Then, crossing over to Albert and touching him on the shoulder, he said: 'Excellency, would you wake up?'

Albert stretched his arms, rubbed his eyes and opened them.

'Ah, it's you, Captain!' he said. 'Egad, you might have let me sleep. I was having a delightful dream: I dreamed that I was dancing the *gallopade* at Torlonia's with Countess G—!'

He took out his watch, which he had kept so that he could himself keep track of the time.

'But it's only half-past one in the morning!' he exclaimed. 'Why the devil are you waking me up at this time?'

'To tell you that you are free, Excellency.'

'My dear friend,' Albert said, with perfect equanimity, 'in future be so good as to remember this maxim of our great emperor, Napoleon: "Only wake me up when it's bad news." If you had let me sleep, I should have finished my *gallopade* and been grateful to you for the rest of my life ... So, have they paid my ransom?'

'No, Excellency.'

'Then how does it come about that I am free?'

'Someone to whom I can refuse nothing has come to ask for your freedom.'

'Come here?'

'Here.'

'Then, by heaven, he's a most generous someone!'

Albert looked around and saw Franz.

'What! My dear Franz, are you so devoted a friend?'

'No,' Franz replied, 'it is not I, but our neighbour, the Count of Monte Cristo.'

'Well, bless me!' said Albert merrily, adjusting his cravat and his cuffs.

'Monsieur le Comte, you're a precious friend indeed and I hope that you will consider me eternally obliged to you, firstly for the matter of the carriage, and then for this!' He held his hand out to the count, who shuddered as he took it in his own but did return the handshake even so.

The bandit was watching the whole of this scene with stupefaction: obviously, he was used to his prisoners trembling before him, but here was one whose derisive and quizzical mood had not faltered for a moment. As for Franz, he was delighted that Albert had upheld the honour of their nation, even when dealing with a bandit.

'My dear Albert,' he said, 'if you would hurry, we may yet have time to end the night in Torlonia's. You can resume your *gallopade* where you left it off, and in that way you will harbour no grudge against Signor Luigi, who has truly acted as a man of honour in all this business.'

'Certainly!' he said. 'You are right: we could be there at two o'clock. Signor Luigi,' Albert continued, 'are there any other formalities to be completed before we may take leave of Your Excellency?'

'None at all, Monsieur,' the bandit said. 'You are as free as the air.'

'In that case, I wish you a long life and good fortune. Come, gentlemen, come!'

And Albert, followed by Franz and the count, went down the stairs and across the square chamber. All the bandits were standing with their hats in their hands.

'Peppino,' said their leader, 'give me the torch.'

'What are you doing?' asked the count.

'I shall show you the way,' the captain said. 'It's the least I can do for Your Excellency.'

Taking the lighted torch from the hands of the shepherd, he went ahead of his guests, not like a valet who does some servant's work, but like a king leading a group of ambassadors.

Arriving at the entrance, he bowed.

'And now, Monsieur le Comte, I apologize again and hope that you will bear me no ill-will for what has happened?'

'None, my dear Vampa,' said the count. 'In any event, you make up for your mistakes with such gallantry that one is almost grateful to you for having committed them.'

'Gentlemen!' the chief said, turning towards the two young men. 'The offer may perhaps not appear very attractive to you, but should you ever wish to pay me a second visit, you will be welcome wherever I am.'

Franz and Albert bowed. The count went out first, followed by Albert, Franz staying until last.

'Does Your Excellency have something to ask me?' said Vampa, smiling.

'Yes, I admit,' Franz replied. 'I should very much like to know what book you were reading so attentively when we arrived.'

'Caesar's *Commentaries*,' the bandit said. 'It is my favourite reading.'

'Aren't you coming?' Albert called.

'Yes,' Franz replied. 'Yes, here I am.' And he followed the others through the narrow opening. They started off across the plain.

'Oh, one moment!' said Albert, turning back. 'May I, Captain?' And he lit his cigar on Vampa's torch.

'Now, Monsieur le Comte,' he said, 'as quickly as possible! I am very keen to finish the night at the Duke of Bracciano's.'

The carriage was still where they had left it. The count said a single word in Arabic to Ali, and the horses set off at full speed.

It was exactly two o'clock by Albert's watch when the two friends came into the ballroom. Their return caused a sensation; but, as they were coming in together, all anxieties that people may have had about Albert immediately ceased.

'Madame,' the Vicomte de Morcerf said, stepping over to the countess, 'yesterday you had the goodness to promise me a *gallopade*. I am a little late in asking you to fulfil this kind promise, but my friend here, whose trustworthiness you know, will confirm that it is not my fault.'

As at this moment the musicians were striking up a waltz, Albert put his arm round the countess's waist and disappeared with her into the whirlwind of dancers.

Franz, meanwhile, was thinking about the extraordinary shudder that had passed through the whole of the Count of Monte Cristo's body at the moment when he was more or less obliged to give Albert his hand.

XXXVIII

THE RENDEZ-VOUS

The first thing that Albert said on getting up the next day was to suggest that he and Franz went to visit the count. He had already thanked him on the previous evening, but he realized that he deserved to be thanked twice for a service such as the one he had performed for him.

Franz, who was drawn towards the count by an attraction mingled with terror, accompanied Albert because he did not want to let him go to see the man alone. Both of them were introduced into the drawing-room. Five minutes later, the count appeared.

'Monsieur le Comte,' Albert said, advancing towards him, 'allow me to repeat this morning what I could only imperfectly tell you yesterday, which is that I shall never forget the nature of the assistance you gave me and that I shall always remember that I owe you my life, or nearly so.'

'My dear neighbour,' the count replied, laughing, 'you are exaggerating your debt to me. All I did was to save you the sum of twenty thousand francs on the expenses of your trip, nothing more. As you see, it is hardly worth mentioning. For your part,' he added, 'may I congratulate you on your remarkable nerve and coolness.'

'How else could I behave, Count?' said Albert. 'I pretended to myself that I had got into an argument and a duel had resulted. I wanted to demonstrate something to those bandits, namely that while people fight one another in every country in the world, only a Frenchman jests as he fights. However, since my obligation to you is no less great for all that, I have come to ask you if, either myself, or through my friends – or my own acquaintances – I might not be of some service to you. My father, the Comte de Morcerf, who is a Spaniard by origin, holds high positions in both France and Spain, so I have come to put myself, and all those who are fond of me, at your disposal.'

'Well,' said the count, 'I must confess, Monsieur de Morcerf, that I was expecting your offer and that I accept it gratefully. I had already set my heart on the idea of asking a great service of you.'

'What service?'

'I have never been to Paris! I do not know the city . . .'

'Really!' Albert exclaimed. 'Have you managed to live so long without seeing Paris! That is incredible.'

'It is so, nonetheless. But, like you, I feel that it is not possible for me to remain any longer in ignorance of the capital of the intelligent world. There is something more: I might even have made this essential journey a long time ago if I had known someone who could have introduced me into Parisian society; but I have no connections there.'

'What! A man like you!' said Albert.

'You are very kind. But since I would not claim any greater merit for myself than that of being able to compete in wealth with Monsieur Aguado or Monsieur Rothschild,[1] and since I am not going to Paris to invest on the Stock Exchange, this little consideration prevented me. Now, thanks to your offer, I have made up my mind. So, do you promise, dear Monsieur de Morcerf,' (the count smiled in a singular manner as he said these words) 'do you promise, when I go to France, to open for me the doors of that society where I shall be as much a foreigner as a Huron or a Cochin Chinese?'

'Oh, so far as that is concerned, Monsieur le Comte, entirely and most willingly!' Albert replied. 'And all the more so – my dear Franz, do not make too much fun of me! – since I have been recalled to Paris by a letter which I received this morning, which speaks of my alliance with a very fine house, and one that has excellent connections in Parisian society.'

'An alliance by marriage?' Franz asked, laughing.

'Heavens above, yes! So, when you return to Paris you will find me firmly settled down and perhaps even a father. This should suit my natural gravity, don't you think? In any case, Count, I repeat: I and my family are entirely at your disposal.'

'I accept,' said the count. 'I assure you that I was only waiting for this opportunity to carry out some plans that I have been considering for a long while.'

Franz did not doubt for a moment that these plans were the same that the count had mentioned in passing in the caves of Monte Cristo, and he watched him as he was speaking in an attempt to glimpse something in his expression which would indicate what it was that would bring him to Paris; but it was very difficult to probe the man's soul, especially when he veiled it with a smile.

'Come now, Count,' Albert went on, delighted at the idea of being able to exhibit a man like Monte Cristo. 'Isn't this one of those vague plans, like thousands that one makes when travelling, which are founded on sand and which blow away in the first breeze?'

'No, I guarantee that,' said the count. 'I want to go to Paris. I must go there.'

'When?'

'When will you be there yourself?'

'Me?' said Albert. 'My goodness! In a fortnight or three weeks: as long as it takes me to get there.'

'In that case,' said the count, 'I give you three months. You see that I am leaving you considerable latitude.'

'And in three months,' Albert exclaimed joyfully, 'you will knock on my door?'

'Do you want us to make an appointment, day for day and hour for hour?' said the count. 'I warn you, I am fearfully punctual.'

'Day for day, hour for hour,' said Albert. 'That will suit me down to the ground.'

'Agreed, then.' He reached over to a calendar hanging beside the mirror. 'Today is the twenty-first of February . . .' (he took out his watch) '. . . and it is half-past ten in the morning. May I call at half-past ten on May the twenty-first next?'

'Perfect!' said Albert. 'Breakfast will be ready.'

'Where do you live?'

'Number twenty-seven, Rue du Helder.'

'Is that a bachelor apartment? I won't be disturbing you?'

'I live in my father's house, but in entirely separate lodgings at the back of the courtyard.'

'Very well.'

The count took his notebook and wrote: 'Rue du Helder, No. 27, on May 21, at half-past ten in the morning.'

'Now,' he said, returning the notebook to his pocket, 'have no fear: the hand of your clock will not be more punctual than I.'

'Shall I see you before my departure?' asked Albert.

'That depends. When do you leave?'

'Tomorrow, at five in the evening.'

'In that case, I must bid you farewell. I have business in Naples and I shall not return until Saturday evening or Sunday morning. And you, Monsieur le Baron,' the count asked, turning to Franz, 'are you also leaving?'

'Yes.'

'For France?'

'No, for Venice. I shall be staying another year or two in Italy.'

'So we shall not see you in Paris?'

'I fear I shall not have that honour.'

'Very well, gentlemen. *Bon voyage*,' the count said to the two friends, offering each of them a hand.

This was the first time that Franz had touched the man's hand, and he shuddered; it was as icy as the hand of a corpse.

'One last time,' said Albert. 'It's agreed, isn't it, on your word? Number twenty-seven, Rue du Helder, on May the twenty-first at half-past ten in the morning?'

'May the twenty-first, at half-past ten in the morning, at number twenty-seven, Rue du Helder,' the count repeated.

At this, the two young men took their leave of the count and left.

'What's wrong?' Albert asked Franz when they got back to his rooms. 'You seem quite preoccupied with something.'

'Yes,' said Franz. 'I must confess that the count is an odd man and I am worried about the rendez-vous that he made with you in Paris.'

'Worried! About the rendez-vous! I never! Are you mad, my dear Franz?' Albert exclaimed.

'Mad or not, I can't help it.'

'Listen,' Albert said, 'I am happy to have an opportunity to say this to you: I have always thought you behaved rather coldly towards the count, while I think he, on his side, has always been most agreeable towards us. Do you have anything in particular against him?'

'Perhaps.'

'Did you come across him somewhere before meeting him here?'

'Precisely.'

'Where?'

'Do you promise me that you will not say a word of what I am about to tell you?'

'I promise.'

'On your honour?'

'On my honour.'

'Very well. Then I'll tell you.'

Franz described his voyage to the island of Monte Cristo, how he had found a crew of smugglers there and two Corsican bandits among them. He told at great length about the fairy-tale hospitality that the count had offered him in his grotto out of the *Thousand and One Nights*: the supper, the hashish, the statues, reality and dream, and how when he woke up there was nothing left as evidence to recall any of these events except the little yacht sailing over the horizon towards Porto Vecchio.

Then he went on to Rome, to the night in the Colosseum and the conversation that he had heard between the count and Vampa concerning Peppino, in which the count promised to secure a pardon for the bandit (a promise which he had fully kept, as the readers can judge).

Finally he got to the adventure of the previous night, the difficulty he found himself in when he discovered that he was six or seven hundred *piastres* short of the necessary amount; and the idea that he had eventually had of going to the count, an idea that had had such an exotic and, at the same time, satisfactory outcome.

Albert listened attentively.

'Well, now,' he said, when the story was over. 'What do you have to reproach him with in all this? The count is a traveller and he had his own boat, because he is rich. Go to Portsmouth or Southampton and you will see the ports crowded with yachts belonging to rich Englishmen who are indulging the same whim. So that he has somewhere to stop in his travels and so that he does not have to eat this frightful cooking that has been poisoning me for the past four months, and you for the past four years, and so that he does not have to lie in those abominable beds where you can't sleep, he had a pied-à-terre fitted out on Monte Cristo. When it was furnished, he was afraid that the Tuscan government would expel him and that he would lose his money, so he bought the island and took its name. My dear friend, just think: how many people can you remember who have taken the names of properties that they never had?'

'But what about the Corsican bandits in his crew?' Franz asked.

'What about them? What is surprising about that? You know as well as anyone that Corsican bandits are not thieves, but purely and simply outlaws who have been exiled from their town or their village because of some vendetta. Anyone can mix with them without being compromised. Why, I do declare that if ever I go to Corsica, before I am introduced to the governor and the *préfet*, I shall have myself introduced to the bandits of *Colomba*,[2] if they are anywhere to be found. I think they're delightful.'

'But Vampa and his band,' Franz went on, 'are bandits who abduct people to steal from them: you won't deny that, at least, I hope. What do you say about the count's influence over such men?'

'What I say, my dear man, is that since I probably owe my life to it, it's not my place to criticize him. So, instead of treating this influence as a capital offence, as you do, I wonder if you would mind if I excuse him, if not for having saved my life, which might be going a little too far, at least for saving me four thousand *piastres*, which is a good twenty-four thousand *livres* in our money: I should certainly not have had such a high price in France – which only goes to prove,' Albert added, laughing, 'that no man is a prophet in his own country.'

'Precisely, there you have it! What country does the count come from? What is his language? What are his means of support? Where does his huge fortune come from? What was the first half of this mysterious and unknown life, that it has cast over the second half such a dark and misanthropic shadow? That, if I were you, is what I should want to know.'

'My dear Franz,' Albert said, 'when you received my letter and you saw that we needed the count's influence, you went to tell him: "My friend, Albert de Morcerf, is in danger; help me to rescue him from it." Is that not so?'

'Yes.'

'And did he ask you: "Who is that Albert de Morcerf? Where does he get his name? Where does his fortune come from? What are his means of support? What is his country? Where was he born?" Tell me, did he ask you all that?'

'No, he didn't, I admit.'

'He came, quite simply. He helped me to escape from the clutches of Monsieur Vampa in which, despite what you call my air of entire unconcern, I must confess I was in a pretty sorry pass. Well, my dear fellow, when in exchange for such a service he asks me to do what one does every day for the first Russian or Italian prince who passes through Paris, that is to say, to introduce him to society, how could I refuse! You are mad to suggest it!'

It must be admitted that this time, contrary to what was usually the case, Albert had all the arguments on his side.

'Very well,' Franz said, sighing, 'do as you wish, my dear Vic-omte, because I have to agree that everything you have just said is very persuasive. But the fact remains that the Count of Monte Cristo is a very strange man.'

'The Count of Monte Cristo is a philanthropist. He didn't tell you his purpose in coming to Paris, but he is coming to take part in the Prix Montyon;[3] and if he only needs my vote and that of the very ugly gentleman who distributes them to succeed, then I shall give him the first and make sure he has the second. With that, my dear Franz, let's say no more about it, but have lunch and go on a final visit to Saint Peter's.'

It was as Albert said, and the following day, at five in the afternoon, the two young men took their leave of one another, Albert de Morcerf to return to Paris and Franz d'Epinay to go and spend a fortnight in Venice.

But before he got into his carriage, Albert gave the waiter at the hotel a card for the Count of Monte Cristo, so determined was he that his guest should not fail to attend their meeting. On it were the words: 'Vicomte Albert de Morcerf' and, under them, in pencil: 'May 21, at half-past ten in the morning, at 27, Rue du Helder.'

XXXIX

THE GUESTS

On the morning of 21 May, in the house in the Rue du Helder where Albert de Morcerf, while in Rome, had agreed to meet the Count of Monte Cristo, everything was being prepared to honour the young man's word.

Albert de Morcerf lived in a *pavillon*, or lodge, in the corner of a large courtyard, opposite another building containing the outhouses. Only two windows of the lodge overlooked the street, three of the others being in the wall looking across the courtyard and two at right-angles overlooking the garden. Between the court and the garden, built with the bad taste of the Empire style in architecture, was the vast and fashionable residence of the Count and Countess de Morcerf.

The whole extent of the property was surrounded by a wall, abutting on the street, crowned at intervals with vases of flowers and broken in the middle by a large wrought-iron gateway with gilded lances, which was used for formal comings and goings; a little door almost next to the concierge's lodge was intended for the servants or for the masters, if they should be coming in or going out on foot.

One could guess that there was the delicate forethought of a mother behind this choice of the *pavillon* for Albert: while not wanting to be separated from her son, she nevertheless realized that a young man of the viscount's age needed all his freedom. On the other hand, it must be said that one could also recognize in this the intelligent egoism of the young man, the son of wealthy parents, who enjoyed the benefits of a free and idle life, which was gilded for him like a birdcage.

Through the windows that overlooked the street, Albert de Morcerf could explore the outside world: life outdoors is so essential to young men, who always want to see the world pass over their horizon, even if that horizon is bounded by the street! Then, once his preliminary exploration was finished, if it should reveal anything that deserved closer examination, Albert de Morcerf could pursue his investigation by going out through a little door corresponding to the one (already noted) near the porter's lodge, which deserves particular mention.

It was a little door that you would have thought forgotten by everyone on the very day that the house was built and which you would imagine was condemned to eternal neglect, so dusty and well concealed did it seem – except that, on close examination, the lock and the hinges, assiduously oiled, showed it to be in continual and mysterious use. This sly little door competed with its two fellows and cocked a snook at the concierge, escaping both his vigilance and his jurisdiction, to open like the famous cavern door in the *Thousand and One Nights*, like Ali Baba's enchanted Sesame, only by means of some occult phrase or some prearranged tapping, spoken in the softest of voices or performed by the slenderest fingers in the world.

At the end of a wide, peaceful corridor, entered through this little door and serving as an antechamber to the apartments, were two rooms: on the right, Albert's dining-room, overlooking the court, and on the left his little drawing-room, overlooking the garden. Banks of climbing plants, fanned out in front of the windows, hid the interior of these two rooms from the court and the garden; since they were the only ones on the ground floor, they were also the only ones which might be spied on by prying eyes.

On the first floor, the two rooms were repeated with the addition of a third, above the antechamber. The three first-floor rooms were a drawing-room, a bedroom and a boudoir. The downstairs drawing-room was only a smoking-room, like an Algerian *diwan*. The first-floor boudoir led into the bedroom and, by a secret door, to the staircase. One can see that every precaution had been taken.

Above the first floor was a vast studio which had been enlarged by taking down the inner walls and partitions to make a domain of chaos in which the artist battled for supremacy over the dandy. Here was the resting-place in which were amassed all Albert's successive whims: hunting horns, basses and flutes – a full orchestra – because Albert had once conceived, not a taste for music, but a fancy; easels, palettes and pastels, because the fancy for music had been followed by a fad for painting; and, last of all, foils, boxing gloves, swords and sticks of every variety, because finally, in the way of fashionable young men at the time when our story is set, Albert de Morcerf gave infinitely greater application than he had done to music and painting to the three arts that go to make up the education of a member of the dominant class in society, namely fencing, boxing and exercising with the quarter-staff. In this room, designed for all kinds of physical exertion, he would receive successively Grisier, Cooks and Charles Leboucher.[1]

The remaining furniture in this special room consisted of chests dating from the time of François I, full of Chinese porcelain, Japanese vases, faience by Luca della Robbia and plates by Bernard de Palissy; and antique chairs on which Henri IV or Sully, Louis XIII or Richelieu might have sat, for two of them, bearing carved blue shields on which shone the French fleur-de-lis surmounted by a royal crown, clearly came from the collection at the Louvre, or at least from some other royal palace. Across the chairs with their dark upholstery were casually draped rich materials in bright colours, dyed in the Persian sun or brought to light beneath the fingers of women in Calcutta or Chandannagar. It was impossible to say what these fabrics were doing there; they were awaiting some destiny unknown even to their owner, providing sustenance for the eyes and meanwhile setting the room ablaze with their silken and golden lights.

In the place of honour was a piano, made of rosewood by Roller and Blanchet, and designed to fit into a modern drawing-room, yet containing a whole orchestra within its compact and sonorous frame and groaning under the weight of masterpieces by Beethoven, Weber, Mozart, Haydn, Grétry and Porpora.

Then, everywhere, along the walls, above the doors, on the ceiling, were swords, daggers, *kris*, maces, axes, complete suits of gilded, damascened or encrusted armour, as well as herbaria, blocks of mineral samples and stuffed birds spreading their brilliant, fiery wings in immobile flight and opening beaks that were never closed.

It goes without saying that this room was Albert's favourite.

However, on the day fixed for the meeting, the young man, dressed, but wearing casual indoor clothes, had set up his head-quarters in the little ground-floor drawing-room. Here, on a table set some way from the divan that surrounded it and magnificently displayed in the crackled faience pots that the Dutch appreciate so much, were all the known varieties of tobacco, from yellow Petersburg to black Sinai, through Maryland, Puerto Rico and Latakia. Beside them, in boxes of aromatic wood and in order of size and quality, were laid out puros, regalias, Havanas and Manillas. And finally, on an open rack, a collection of German pipes, chibouks with amber bowls, decorated with coral, and nar-giles encrusted with gold, their long morocco stems twisted like serpents, awaited the smoker's preference or whim. Albert himself had supervised the arrangement – or, rather, the systematic disorder that guests at a modern luncheon like to contemplate through the smoke as it escapes from their lips and rises, in long, fantastic spirals, towards the ceiling.

At a quarter to ten, a *valet de chambre* came in. This was a little fifteen-year-old groom, who spoke nothing but English and answered to the name of 'John'. He was Morcerf's only servant. Of course, on ordinary days the cook from the main house was at his disposal – as was also, on grand occasions, his father the count's lackey.

The *valet de chambre*, who was called Germain and who enjoyed his young master's entire confidence, was holding a bundle of newspapers, which he put down on a table, and a packet of letters, which he gave to Albert.

Albert glanced casually at the various missives and chose two, with perfumed envelopes addressed in fine hands; these he unsealed and read with a certain amount of attention.

'How did these letters come?' he asked.

'One came by the post, the other was brought by Madame Danglars' valet.'

'Let Madame Danglars know that I accept the place she is offering me in her box . . . Wait . . . Then, during the day, go to Rosa's and tell her that, in accordance with her invitation, I shall sup with her on leaving the opera; and take her six bottles of different wines, Cyprus, sherry, Malaga . . . and a barrel of Ostend oysters. Buy the oysters from Borel and make sure that he knows they are for me.'

'At what time would Monsieur like to be served?'

'What time is it now?'

'A quarter to ten.'

'Well, serve breakfast at exactly half-past ten. Debray may be obliged to go into his ministry; and in any case . . .' (Albert looked at his notebook) '. . . that was the time that I agreed with the count: May the twenty-first at half-past ten in the morning. Even though I don't set much store by his promise, I want to be punctual. Do you know if the countess is up?'

'If Monsieur le Vicomte wishes, I can find out.'

'Do. Ask her for one of her liqueur cabinets: mine is not fully replenished. And tell her that I shall have the honour to visit her at about three o'clock and should like her permission to introduce her to someone.'

When the valet had left, Albert slumped on to the divan, tore the wrappings off two or three newspapers, looked at the theatre programmes, winced on seeing that they were performing an opera and not a ballet, hunted in vain through the advertisements for cosmetics for an electuary for the teeth that he had heard mentioned, and successively tossed aside two or three of the most read prints in Paris, muttering in the midst of a prolonged yawn: 'Really, these papers do get more and more frightfully dull.'

At that moment a light carriage pulled up in front of the door, and a moment later the valet returned to announce M. Lucien Debray. A tall young man, fair-haired, pale, with a confident grey eye and cold, thin lips, wearing a blue coat with engraved gold buttons, a white cravat and a monocle in a tortoiseshell rim dangling from a silk cord – which, by a co-ordinated effort of the supercilliary and zygomatic arches, he managed from time to time to secure in the cavity of his right eye – came in without smiling or speaking, and with a semi-official bearing.

'Good morning, Lucien, good morning,' Albert said. 'Ah, but you terrify me, my dear fellow, with your punctuality! What am I saying – punctuality! I was expecting you last of all, and you arrive at five to ten, when the invitation was definitely fixed only at half-past! It's a miracle! Can this mean that the government is overthrown, by any chance?'

'No, my dearest fellow,' the young man said, planting himself on the divan. 'Rest assured, we are always unsteady, but we never fall. I am beginning to think that we are becoming utterly unmovable, even without the affairs of the Peninsula, which are going to fix us in place once and for all.'

'Yes, that's right. You are getting rid of Don Carlos of Spain.'[2]

'Not at all, dearest fellow, we must put this straight: we are taking him across the French frontier and entertaining him most royally in Bourges.'

'In Bourges?'

'Yes, and he has no grounds for complaint, dammit! Bourges is King Charles VII's capital. What! You hadn't heard? All Paris has known about it since yesterday, and it had already reached the Stock Exchange the day before that, because Monsieur Danglars – I haven't the slightest idea how that man manages to learn everything as soon as we do – Danglars bet on a bull market and won a million.'

'And you, a new ribbon, apparently. Isn't that a blue band I can see with the rest of your decorations?'

'Huh! They sent me the Charles III medal, y'know,' Debray answered in an offhand manner.

'Come now, don't pretend you're not pleased. Admit that you're glad to have it.'

'Well, yes, so I am. As a fashion accessory, a medal looks quite fine on a high-buttoned black frock-coat. Very elegant.'

'And,' Morcerf said, smiling, 'it makes one look like the Prince of Wales or the Duke of Reichstadt.'

'Which is why you are seeing me at this time in the morning, my dearest fellow.'

'Because you wanted to let me know they had given you the Charles III medal?'

'No, because I spent the night sending out letters: twenty-five diplomatic dispatches. When I arrived home this morning at dawn, I tried to sleep but I was overcome with a headache, so I got up to go out for an hour's ride. In the Bois de Boulogne I was overcome with hunger and boredom, two enemies that rarely attack together but, despite that, were leagued against me in a sort of Carlist–Republican alliance. It was then that I remembered we are feasting with you this morning. So here I am: I am hungry, feed me; I am bored, entertain me.'

'It is my duty as your host to do both, dear friend,' said Albert, ringing for his valet, while Lucien turned over the folded newspapers with the tip of a switch which he held by its gold knob inlaid with turquoise. 'Germain, a glass of sherry and a biscuit. And, while you are waiting for those, dear Lucien, take a cigar – contraband, naturally. I insist that you try one and suggest to your ministry that they sell us the same, instead of those dried walnut-leaves that they condemn conscientious citizens to smoke.'

'Pooh! Certainly not! As soon as you knew they came from the government, you would find them abominable and refuse to touch them. In any case, it's nothing to do with the Home Office, it's a matter for the Inland Revenue. Apply to Monsieur Humann, Department of Indirect Taxes, corridor A, room twenty-six.'

'Well, I never,' said Albert. 'I am amazed at how much you know. But, go on: take a cigar.'

'Ah, my dear Viscount,' Lucien said, lighting a Manilla at a pink candle burning in a silver-gilt candlestick before slumping back on to the divan, 'my dear Viscount, how lucky you are to have nothing to do! You really can't tell how lucky!'

'And what would you do, my jolly old pacifier of kingdoms,' Morcerf asked, with a hint of irony, 'if you had nothing to occupy you? What! The minister's private secretary, engaged simultaneously in the great European cabal and in the petty intrigues of Parisian society; with kings – and, better still, queens – to protect, parties to unite, elections to manage; doing more from your study with your pen and your telegraph than Napoleon did from his battlefields with his sword and his victories; enjoying an income of twenty-five thousand *livres* apart from your salary, and a horse that Château-Renaud offered to buy from you for four hundred *louis*, which you refused to sell, and a tailor who never fails to make you a perfect pair of trousers; being able to go to the Opera, the Jockey Club and the Théâtre des Variétés . . . you have all this, and you are bored? Well, I have got something to entertain you.'

'What's that?'

'I'm going to introduce you to someone.'

'Man or woman?'

'A man.'

'Huh! I already know plenty of those!'

'Not like the one I am speaking about.'

'Where does he come from? The end of the world?'

'Perhaps from even further than that.'

'No! Then I hope he's not bringing our breakfast.'

'Don't worry. Breakfast is being cooked in the kitchens of the maternal home. Are you hungry, then?'

'I am ashamed to confess it, but I am. I had dinner yesterday at the home of Baron Danglars. I don't know if you have noticed, my friend, but one always dines very poorly with these Stock Exchange types. It's as though they had a guilty conscience.'

'Huh! You can afford to disparage other people's dinners, seeing the kind of spread one gets from your ministers.'

'Yes, but at least we don't invite respectable people. If we were not obliged to do the honours for some right-thinking and, above all, right-voting bumpkins, we would shun our own tables like the plague, believe me.'

'In that case, my good fellow, have another glass of sherry and a biscuit.'

'With pleasure. Your Spanish wine is excellent: you see, we were quite right to pacify that country.'

'Yes, but what about Don Carlos?'

'Let Don Carlos drink claret, and in ten years we'll marry his son to the little queen.'

'Which should get you the Golden Fleece if you're still in the ministry.'

'I do believe, Albert, that you are quite set this morning on feeding me with illusions.'

'Ah, you must admit that's the diet that best satisfies the stomach. But wait: I can hear Beauchamp's voice in the antechamber. You can have an argument; that will pass the time.'

'Argument about what?'

'About the newspapers.'

'Oh, my dear man,' Lucien said, with sovereign contempt, 'do you think I read the papers?'

'All the better: then you can argue even more about them.'

'Monsieur Beauchamp!' the valet announced.

'Come in, come in, acid pen!' Albert said, getting up and going to meet the young man. 'I have Debray here, as you see. He hates you without even reading you, apparently.'

'He's quite right,' said Beauchamp. 'I'm just the same. I criticize him without knowing what he does. Good morning, *Commandeur*.'

'So! You already know about that, do you?' the private secretary replied, smiling and shaking hands with the journalist.

'As you see,' said Beauchamp.

'And what are they saying about it out there?'

'Out where? There are a lot of constellations out there in this year of grace 1838.'

'In the critical-political one where you shine so brightly.'

'They say that it is well deserved and that you have sown enough red for a little blue to spring from it.'

'Now then, that's not bad at all,' said Lucien. 'Why aren't you with us, my dear Beauchamp? With your wit you would make your fortune in three or four years.'

'I am quite ready to follow your advice, as soon as I see a government that is guaranteed to last at least six months. Now, one word, dear Albert, because I must give poor Lucien a chance to draw breath. Are we to have breakfast, or lunch? I'm expected in the House: as you see, all is not roses in our profession.'

'Just breakfast. We are waiting for two more guests, and we shall start as soon as they arrive.'

'And what sort of people are these whom you are expecting for breakfast?'

'A nobleman and a diplomat.'

'Then we can expect to be kept waiting barely two hours for the nobleman and fully two hours for the diplomat. I'll come back for the last course. Keep me some strawberries, coffee and cigars. I can take a lamb cutlet at the House.'

'Please, don't do that, Beauchamp, because even if the nobleman were a Montmorency and the diplomat a Metternich, we should still take breakfast at exactly half-past ten. Meanwhile, do what Debray is doing: taste my sherry and biscuits.'

'Very well then, I'll stay. I really must have something to take my mind off things this morning.'

'Well, well, you are just like Debray! I would have thought that when the government is sad, the opposition would be merry.'

'Ah, you don't realize, old man, what is in store for me. This

morning I shall have to sit through a speech by Monsieur Danglars
in the lower house, and this evening, at his wife's, a tragedy by a
peer of the realm. The devil take this constitutional government!
They do say that we had a choice, so what did we choose this one
for?'

'I understand: you need to store up some merriment.'

'Don't say anything against Monsieur Danglars' speeches,' said
Debray. 'He votes for your side; he's in the opposition.'

'Damnation, that's the worst thing about it! That's why I'm
waiting for you to boot him into the Upper House, where I can
laugh at him as much as I like.'

'My dear,' Albert said to Beauchamp, 'it's plain to see that the
Spanish business is settled: you're in a foul temper this morning. So
I shall have to remind you that the gossip columns are talking about
a marriage between myself and Mademoiselle Eugénie Danglars.
For that reason I cannot, in all conscience, allow you to speak ill of
the eloquence of a man who one day could well be saying to me:
"Monsieur le Vicomte, you know that I am giving my daughter a
dowry of two millions."'

'Be serious!' said Beauchamp. 'The marriage will never take
place. The king may have made him a baron, he could make him a
peer of the realm, but he can never make him a gentleman, and the
Comte de Morcerf comes of too aristocratic a line ever to agree to
such a misalliance for a mere two million francs. The Vicomte de
Morcerf must marry a marchioness at least.'

'Two million! It's a pretty sum, even so!' said Morcerf.

'It's the working capital you would invest in a music-hall or a
railway line from the Jardin des Plantes to the Râpée.'

'Take no notice, Morcerf,' Debray said offhandedly. 'Get married. You will be marrying the label on a moneybag, won't you? So
what does it matter? Better that the label should have one more
nought and one less shield on it. There are seven blackbirds on
your own coat of arms: well, you can give three to your wife and
still have four left for yourself. That is one more than Monsieur de
Guise, who was nearly king of France and whose first cousin was
emperor of Germany.'

'Lucien, by gad, I do believe you're right,' Albert replied absent-
mindedly.

'Of course I am! In any case, every millionaire is as noble as a
bastard, or can be.'

'Hush, don't say that, Debray,' Beauchamp replied, laughing. 'Here is Château-Renaud who might well run you through with the sword of his ancestor, Renaud de Montauban, to cure you of the habit of making such quips.'

'Then he would surely be lowering himself,' Lucien retorted, '"for I am low-born and very mean".'

'Huh!' Beauchamp exclaimed. 'Listen to this: the government sings Béranger.[3] What are we coming to, for heaven's sake?'

'Monsieur de Château-Renaud! Monsieur Maximilien Morrel!' cried the *valet de chambre*, announcing the two new arrivals.

'All present and correct,' said Beauchamp. 'Now we can eat! If I'm not mistaken, you were only expecting two more guests, Albert?'

'Morrel!' Albert muttered in surprise. 'Morrel? Who's that?'

Before he could finish, M. de Château-Renaud, a handsome young man of thirty and an aristocrat from head to foot (that is to say, with the face of a Guiche and the wit of a Mortemart), had seized Albert by the hand:

'My dearest, allow me to present Captain Maximilien Morrel, my friend and, moreover, my saviour. In any event, the man presents himself well enough. Vicomte, salute my hero.'

At this, he stood aside to reveal the tall, noble young man with the broad brow, piercing eye and dark moustache whom our readers will remember seeing in Marseille – in such dramatic circumstances that they cannot so soon have forgotten about them. His broad chest, decorated with the cross of the Legion of Honour, was shown off by a rich uniform, part-French and part-Oriental, worn magnificently, which also brought out his military bearing. The young officer bowed with elegant good manners: every one of Morrel's movements was graceful, because he was strong.

'Monsieur,' said Albert, with courteous warmth, 'Monsieur le Baron de Château-Renaud already knew how much it would delight me to meet you. You are one of his friends, Monsieur; please be ours.'

'Very well,' said Château-Renaud, 'and hope, my dear Vicomte, that if the situation should arise, he will do the same for you as he did for me.'

'What was that?' asked Albert.

'Please!' Morrel protested. 'It is not worth mentioning. The baron exaggerates.'

'What do you mean,' said Château-Renaud, '"not worth mentioning"? Life is not worth mentioning? I must tell you that you are sounding a little bit too philosophical about it, my dear Morrel. It is all very well for you, when you risk your life every day, but for me, who does so only once, and by accident . . .'

'If I understand you correctly, Baron, you are saying that Captain Morrel saved your life.'

'By God he did, and that's the long and short of it,' said Château-Renaud.

'On what occasion?' Beauchamp asked.

'Beauchamp, old chap, you must know I'm dying of hunger,' said Debray. 'Let's not start on any long stories.'

'Very well, then,' said Beauchamp. 'I certainly have no objection to sitting down at table. Château-Renaud can tell us about it over breakfast.'

'Gentlemen,' said Morcerf, 'please note that it is still only a quarter past ten, and we are waiting for one last guest.'

'Of course, that's right!' said Debray. 'A diplomat.'

'A diplomat or something else, I don't know what. All I do know is that I entrusted him with a mission on my behalf which he carried out so much to my satisfaction that if I had been king I should have instantly made him a knight of all orders, including the Garter and the Golden Fleece, if I had both to give.'

'So, as we are not yet going in to breakfast,' said Debray, 'pour yourself a glass of sherry, as we have done, Baron, and tell us about it.'

'You know that I got this notion of going to Africa.'

'Your ancestors had already shown you the way, my dear Château-Renaud,' Morcerf remarked elegantly.

'Yes, but I doubt if your purpose was, like theirs, to liberate the tomb of Our Saviour.'

'You are quite right, Beauchamp,' said the young aristocrat. 'It was quite simply to get some amateur pistol-shooting. As you know, I hate duels, since the time when two witnesses, whom I had chosen to settle some dispute, obliged me to break an arm of one of my best friends. Yes, by heaven! It was poor Franz d'Epinay, whom you all know.'

'Of course! That's right,' said Debray. 'You did have a duel once. What was it about?'

'The devil only knows: I can't remember!' said Château-Renaud. 'What I clearly recall is that I felt ashamed at letting a talent like mine go to waste, and, as I had been given some new pistols, I thought I'd try them out on the Arabs. So I set sail for Oran, and from Oran I went on to Constantine[4], where I arrived in time to witness the end of the siege. Like the rest, I joined the retreat. For the first forty-eight hours I was able to put up with the rain by day and the snow by night well enough; then, at last, on the third morning, my horse froze to death. Poor animal! It was used to a blanket and the stove in its stables – an Arab horse, which just happened to find itself a little out of place in Arabia when the temperature dropped to minus ten.'

'That's why you wanted to buy my English horse,' said Debray. 'You thought he would stand the cold better than your Arab.'

'No, you're wrong there, because I have sworn never to go back to Africa again.'

'So you had a really bad fright?' asked Beauchamp.

'Yes, I confess I did,' Château-Renaud replied, 'and I was right to be scared. As I said, my horse died, so I was continuing my retreat on foot when six Arabs bore down on me at a gallop, intending to cut off my head. I shot two with the two barrels of my gun, and another two with my two pistols, all right on target. But there were still two left and I had no other weapons. One of them seized me by the hair (which is why I have it cut short nowadays, because you never know what might happen), and the other put his yataghan[5] against my throat so that I could already feel the cold steel, when this gentleman here charged at them, shot dead with his pistol the one who was holding my hair and used his sabre to crack open the skull of the one who was about to cut my throat. He had taken it upon himself to save a man that day and, as luck would have it, I was the one. When I am rich, I shall have a statue of Luck made by Klagmann or Marochetti.'[6]

'Yes,' Morrel said, smiling. 'It was the fifth of September, which is the anniversary of a day on which my father's life was miraculously saved. So, whenever possible, I celebrate that day with some . . . With some action . . .'

'Some heroic deed, you mean,' Château-Renaud interrupted. 'In short, I was the lucky man. But that is not all. After having saved me from the cold steel, he saved me from the cold itself, not by giving me half of his cloak, as Saint Martin did, but by giving me the whole of it. And then he saved me from hunger, by sharing . . . guess what?'

THE GUESTS
449

'A pâté from Chez Félix?' suggested Beauchamp.

'Not so. His horse: we each ate a piece of it with great relish. It was tough.'

'The horse?' Morcerf asked, laughing.

'No, sacrificing it,' Château-Renaud replied. 'Ask Debray if he would sacrifice his English horse for a stranger.'

'Not for a stranger,' said Debray. 'For a friend, perhaps.'

'I guessed that you would become mine, Baron,' said Morrel. 'In any case, as I already told you, heroism or not, sacrifice or not, on that particular day I owed an offering to ill-fortune as a reward for the favour that good fortune once did for us.'

'The story that Monsieur Morrel refers to,' Château-Renaud continued, 'is a quite admirable one which he will tell you one day, when you know him better. For the present, let's line our stomachs instead of plundering our memories. When do we breakfast, Albert?'

'At half-past ten.'

'On the dot?' Debray asked, taking out his watch.

'Oh, you must allow me the usual five minutes' grace,' said Morcerf, 'for I too am awaiting a saviour.'

'Whose?'

'Why, my own!' Morcerf replied. 'Do you think me incapable of being saved like anyone else? It is not only Arabs who cut off heads, you know. Ours is to be a philanthropic breakfast, and I sincerely hope that we shall have two benefactors of mankind at our table.'

'How shall we manage?' asked Debray. 'There is only one Prix Montyon.'[7]

'Well, we shall just have to give it to someone who has done nothing to deserve it,' said Beauchamp. 'That's how the Academy usually solves the dilemma.'

'Where will he be coming from?' Debray asked. 'Forgive my insisting; I know that you have already answered the question, but so vaguely that I feel entitled to ask it again.'

'To tell the truth,' Albert said, 'I don't know. When I invited him, three months ago, he was in Rome, but, since then, who can tell where he may have been.'

'Do you think he is capable of being punctual?' asked Debray.

'I think he is capable of anything,' Morcerf replied.

'Note that, with the five minutes' grace, we have now only ten minutes left.'

'Then I'll take advantage of it to tell you something about my guest.'

'I beg your pardon,' said Beauchamp, 'but is there the material for an article in what you are going to tell us?'

'Certainly there is, and a very unusual one.'

'Then carry on. I can see that I won't get to the House, so I must make up for it in some way.'

'I was in Rome for the last carnival.'

'We know that much,' said Beauchamp.

'But what you don't know is that I was kidnapped by bandits.'

'There's no such thing as bandits,' said Debray.

'Yes, there are, and some very ugly ones, which means they were good bandits, because I found them pretty terrifying.'

'Come now, my dear Albert,' said Debray. 'Admit it: your cook is late, the oysters have not arrived from Marennes or Ostend, and, like Madame de Maintenon, you want to make up for one course with a story. Carry on with it, old man, we are good enough guests to indulge you and listen to your tale, however incredible it may be.'

'I tell you, incredible though it may be, it is true from beginning to end. The bandits captured me and took me to a very melancholy spot called the Catacombs of Saint Sebastian.'

'I know them,' said Château-Renaud. 'I nearly caught a fever there.'

'I did better than that,' said Morcerf. 'I really caught something. They told me that I was a hostage for a ransom of the trifling amount of four thousand Roman *écus* or twenty-six thousand *livres*. Unfortunately, I had only fifteen hundred left; I was at the end of my journey and my credit was exhausted. I wrote to Franz . . . But of course! Listen, Franz was there, you can ask him if I am not telling the absolute truth. I wrote to Franz that if he did not come before six in the morning with the four thousand *écus*, by ten past six I should have joined the blessed saints and glorious martyrs in whose company I had the honour to find myself. And I can assure you that Monsieur Luigi Vampa – that was the name of my chief bandit – would have kept his word to the letter.'

'So Franz arrived with the four thousand *écus*?' Château-Renaud said. 'Of course he did! You are not short of four thousand *écus* when your name is Franz d'Epinay or Albert de Morcerf.'

'No, he arrived, but accompanied purely and simply by the guest I have promised you and to whom I hope to introduce you.'

'He must be a Hercules killing Cacus, this gentleman, or a Perseus delivering Andromeda?'

'No. He's a man of about my height.'

'Armed to the teeth?'

'He did not have so much as a knitting needle.'

'But he did pay your ransom?'

'He whispered two words to the chief bandit and I was free.'

'They even apologized to him for arresting you,' said Beauchamp.

'Exactly.'

'Well, I never! Was he Ariosto, this man?'

'No, just the Count of Monte Cristo.'

'No one is called Count of Monte Cristo,' said Debray.

'I think not,' Château-Renaud added, in the unruffled tones of a man who has the entire nobility of Europe at his fingertips. 'Does anyone know of a Count of Monte Cristo anywhere?'

'Perhaps he comes from the Holy Land,' said Beauchamp. 'One of his ancestors might have owned Calvary, just as the Mortemarts did the Dead Sea.'

'Excuse me, gentlemen,' said Maximilien, 'but I think I can solve the problem for you. Monte Cristo is a tiny island about which I often heard speak from the sailors who were employed by my father: it is a grain of sand in the midst of the Mediterranean, an atom in infinity.'

'Just so, Monsieur,' said Albert. 'And the person I am telling you about is the lord and king of this grain of sand, of this atom. He must have bought his deeds to the title of count somewhere in Tuscany.'

'Is your count rich, then?'

'By gad, I think he is.'

'But it must show, surely?'

'There's where you are wrong, Debray.'

'I don't understand.'

'Have you read the *Thousand and One Nights*?'

'Heavens! What an extraordinary question!'

'Well then: can you tell if the people in it are rich or poor? If their grains of wheat are not rubies and diamonds? They look like penniless fishermen, don't they? That's how you treat them, and suddenly they open up before you a mysterious cavern in which you find a treasure vast enough to purchase the Indies.'

'So?'

'So my Count of Monte Cristo is one of those fishermen. He even has an appropriate name: he calls himself Sinbad the Sailor and he owns a cavern full of gold.'

'Have you seen this cavern, Morcerf?' asked Beauchamp.

'No, I haven't; it was Franz who saw it. But, hush! Don't say a word about this in front of him. Franz was taken there blindfolded and served by dumb men and women beside whom, it appears, Cleopatra was nothing but a strumpet. However, he is not quite sure about the women, since they only appeared after he had consumed some hashish, so that it could well be that what he took for women were in fact quite simply a group of statues.'

The young men looked at Morcerf as if to say: 'My good fellow, have you lost your wits, or are you teasing us?'

'It's true,' Morrel said pensively, 'that I did hear something similar to what Monsieur de Morcerf is telling us from an old sailor called Penelon.'

'Ah!' Albert exclaimed. 'It's a good thing that Monsieur Morrel has come to my support. You're not pleased, are you, that he has trailed this ball of thread through my labyrinth?'

'Forgive us, dear fellow,' said Debray, 'but what you are saying just seems too improbable . . .'

'Damnation! Just because your ambassadors and your consuls don't tell you anything about it! They don't have time, they're too busy molesting their compatriots whenever they go abroad.'

'Now, now! You're getting angry and taking it out on our poor emissaries. Heavens above, how do you expect them to protect us? Every day the House nibbles away at their salaries, to the point where it is getting impossible to find anyone. Would you like to be an ambassador, Albert? I'll have you appointed to Constantinople.'

'No, thank you! Just so the sultan, the first time I put in a good word for Mehmet Ali,[8] can send round a rope for my secretaries to strangle me.'

'You see,' said Debray.

'But that does not mean that my Count of Monte Cristo does not exist!'

'Everybody exists! What a miracle!'

'No doubt everybody does exist, but not as he does. Not everybody has black slaves, princely galleries, weapons like those in the Casauba,[9] horses worth six thousand francs apiece, and Greek mistresses!'

'Did you see this Greek mistress?'

'Certainly: saw and heard. I saw her at the Teatro Valle and heard her one day when I dined with the count.'

'So he does eat then, your extraordinary man?'

'If he does eat, it is too little to be worth mentioning.'

'You see: he's a vampire.'

'Laugh if you wish. That was precisely the opinion of Countess G—, who, as you know, was acquainted with Lord Ruthwen.'

'Oh, that's fine!' said Beauchamp. 'For a man who is not a journalist, this is the answer to the *Constitutionnel*'s famous sea-serpent: a vampire! The very thing!'

'A savage eye, with a pupil that is dilated or contracted at will,' said Debray. 'Highly developed facial angle, splendid forehead, livid colouring, black beard, teeth white and pointed, manners the same.'

'That's it precisely, Lucien,' said Morcerf. 'You have described him to a "t". Yes: sharp and pointed manners. The man often made me shudder; for example, one day when we were together watching an execution, I thought I would faint, much more from seeing him and hearing him discourse coldly about all the sufferings imaginable than from seeing the executioner carry out his task and hearing the cries of the condemned man.'

'Didn't he take you for a stroll through the ruins of the Colosseum to suck your blood, Morcerf?' asked Beauchamp.

'And after setting you free, didn't he make you sign some fiery coloured parchment, by which you ceded him your soul, like Esau his birthright?'

'Mock, mock as much as you wish, gentlemen!' said Morcerf, a trifle irritated. 'When I look at you fine Parisians, regulars on the Boulevard de Gand, strollers through the Bois de Boulogne, and then remember that man – well, it strikes me that we are not of the same race.'

'Flattered!' said Beauchamp.

'The fact remains,' Château-Renaud added, 'that your Count of Monte Cristo is a gentleman in his spare time, except for his little understandings with Italian bandits.'

'Huh! There are no Italian bandits!' said Debray.

'No vampires!' Beauchamp added.

'And no Count of Monte Cristo,' concluded Debray. 'Listen, my dear Albert: half-past ten is striking.'

'Admit that you had a nightmare, and let's start breakfast,' said Beauchamp.

But the echo of the striking clock had not yet died away when the door opened and Germain announced: 'His Excellency, the Count of Monte Cristo!'

All those present started despite themselves, in a way indicating that Morcerf's story had touched something deep inside them. Even Albert could not avoid feeling faintly shocked. They had heard no sound of a vehicle in the street or a step in the antechamber, and even the door had opened silently.

The count was framed in it, dressed with the greatest simplicity; but the most demanding of dandies would not have found anything to criticize in his appearance. Everything – clothes, hat, linen – was in perfect taste and came from the finest suppliers.

He seemed to be barely thirty-five years of age; and what struck everybody was how closely he resembled the portrait that Debray had sketched of him.

He came forward, smiling, into the middle of the drawing-room, going directly towards Albert who was advancing to meet him and affably holding out his hand.

'Punctuality,' said Monte Cristo, 'is the politeness of kings, or so I believe one of your sovereigns claimed.[10] However, it is not always that of travellers, despite their good intentions. I hope, dear Vicomte, that you will take my good intentions into consideration and forgive me if, as I think, I am two or three seconds late for our rendez-vous. It is impossible to cover five hundred leagues without some small accidents, especially in France, where it appears that it is forbidden to whip a postilion.'

'Monsieur le Comte,' Albert replied, 'I was just announcing your imminent arrival to a few of my friends, whom I invited to join us, in view of the promise that you were kind enough to make me, and whom I should like to introduce to you. They are Monsieur le Comte de Château-Renaud, who traces his noble lineage back to the paladins of Charlemagne and whose ancestors sat at the Round Table; Monsieur Lucien Debray, private secretary to the Minister of the Interior; Monsieur Beauchamp, a fearful journalist and the scourge of the French government – of whom, despite his celebrity here, you may never have heard tell in Italy, since his newspaper is not distributed there; and finally Monsieur Maximilien Morrel, a captain in the regiment of spahis.'

Up to this point the count had bowed courteously, but with a certain English coldness and impassivity; but at the last name he involuntarily stepped forward and a faint touch of red passed like a flash across his pale cheeks.

'Monsieur wears the uniform of the recent French victors,' he said, 'and it is a fine one.'

It was impossible to tell what emotion gave the count's voice such a profoundly vibrant tone and made his eye shine, as if against his will – that eye which was so fine, so calm and so clear when he had no reason to shade it.

'You have never seen our African soldiers, Monsieur?' said Albert.

'Never,' the count replied, entirely regaining control of himself.

'Well, Monsieur, under this uniform beats one of the bravest and noblest hearts in the army.'

'Oh, Monsieur le Comte . . .' said Morrel, interrupting.

'Let me continue, Captain,' Albert said. 'We have just been hearing of such a heroic deed by this gentleman that, even though I met him today for the first time, I would ask him the favour of introducing him to you as my friend.'

Again, at these words, one could detect in Monte Cristo that strangely intense look, that slight blush and barely perceptible trembling of the eyelid that signalled some deep feeling in him.

'Ah, Monsieur has a noble heart,' he said. 'So much the better!'

This sort of exclamation, which responded to the count's own thoughts rather than to what Albert had just said, surprised everyone, most of all Morrel, who looked at Monte Cristo with astonishment. But at the same time the tone was so soft and – for want of a better word – so soothing that, strange though the exclamation was, it would be impossible to be annoyed by it.

'Why should he doubt it?' Beauchamp asked Château-Renaud.

'In truth,' said the latter, who, being accustomed to society and with the sharpness of his aristocratic eye, had seen everything that it was possible to see in Monte Cristo, 'in truth, Albert did not deceive us: this count is an unusual person. What do you think, Morrel?'

'Frankly,' he said, 'he has an honest eye and a pleasing voice, so I like him, despite the odd reflection he has just made regarding me.'

'Gentlemen,' said Albert, 'Germain tells me that you are served. My dear Count, allow me to show you the way.'

They walked silently through into the dining-room, where each took his place.

'Gentlemen,' the count said as he sat down, 'allow me to confess something that will serve as my excuse for any impropriety on my part: I am a foreigner, and so much one that this is the first time I have been in Paris. Consequently, I know absolutely nothing of French manners, having virtually up to now practised only an Oriental style of life, which is the one most opposed to the fine traditions of Paris. I beg you therefore to excuse me if you find anything in my behaviour which is too Turkish, too Neapolitan or too Arabian. Having said that, gentlemen, let us dine.'

'How well he says all that!' Beauchamp muttered. 'He is undoubtedly some noble lord.'

'A noble lord,' Debray repeated.

'A noble lord of all countries, Monsieur Debray,' said Château-Renaud.

XL

BREAKFAST

It will be remembered that the count was an abstemious guest. Albert made the observation, while expressing a fear that, from the start, Parisian life might not displease the traveller with respect to its least spiritual yet, at the same time, most necessary side.

'My dear Count,' he said, 'you see me prey to an anxiety, which is that the cuisine of the Rue du Helder may not please you as much as that of the Piazza di Spagna. I should have enquired about your taste and had some dishes prepared to suit your fancies.'

'If you knew me better, Monsieur,' the count replied with a smile, 'you would not concern yourself with an attention which is almost humiliating for a traveller who has lived in turn with *macaroni* in Naples, *polenta* in Milan, *olla podrida* in Valencia, *pilaff* in Constantinople, curry in India and birds' nests in China. There is no such thing as a cuisine for a cosmopolitan like myself. I eat everything, everywhere, but little. And today, when you reproach me with my abstinence, I am in fact indulging my appetite, for I have not eaten since yesterday morning.'

'What! Not since yesterday morning,' the guests exclaimed. 'You have not eaten for twenty-four hours?'

'No,' Monte Cristo replied. 'I was obliged to make a detour and ask for some information near Naples. This delayed me slightly and I did not want to stop.'

'Did you not eat in your carriage?' asked Morcerf.

'No, I slept, as I am accustomed to do when I am bored but do not have the strength to amuse myself, or when I am hungry without having the desire to eat.'

'Can you control sleep then, Monsieur?' asked Morrel.

'More or less.'

'Do you have a recipe for that?'

'An infallible one.'

'It would be invaluable to us Africans, who do not always have anything to eat and seldom have anything to drink,' said Morrel.

'Yes,' said Monte Cristo. 'Unfortunately my preparation, while excellent for a man like myself who leads a quite exceptional life, would be very dangerous if given to an army, which would not wake up when it was needed.'

'Can we know the recipe?' asked Debray.

'Indeed, yes,' said Monte Cristo. 'There's no secret. It is a mixture of excellent opium which I brought myself from Canton so that I could be certain it was pure, and the best hashish harvested in the East, namely that which comes from between the Tigris and the Euphrates. These two ingredients are mixed in equal proportions and shaped into pills which can be taken when needed. The result follows within ten minutes. Ask Baron Franz d'Epinay; I think he tried it once.'

'Yes,' Morcerf replied. 'He mentioned it to me and has a very pleasant memory of the occasion.'

'And do you always carry this drug with you?' asked Beauchamp who, as a journalist, was very incredulous.

'Always,' said Monte Cristo.

'Would it be indiscreet to ask you to show us these precious pills?' Beauchamp continued, hoping to catch the stranger out.

'Not at all, Monsieur,' said the count; and he took out of his pocket a wonderful pillbox formed out of a single emerald and closed by a gold screw which, when it was loosened, allowed to emerge a small, greenish ball, about the size of a pea. The ball had a pervasive, acrid smell. There were four or five others like it inside the emerald, which might have been able to contain a dozen of them.

This pillbox was passed around the table, but this was much more so that the splendid emerald itself could be examined than to see or sniff the pills that the guests passed from one to another.

'Is it your cook who prepares this delicacy?' asked Beauchamp.

'No, Monsieur. I do not entrust my real pleasures to unworthy hands. I am a good enough chemist to prepare the pills myself.'

'This is a splendid emerald and the largest I have ever seen, even though my mother has some quite remarkable family jewels,' said Château-Renaud.

'I had three like that,' Monte Cristo went on. 'I gave one to the sultan, who had it mounted on his sword. I gave the second to our Holy Father the Pope, who had it encrusted into his tiara opposite an emerald that was more or less similar, though not so beautiful, which had been given to his predecessor, Pius VII, by the Emperor Napoleon. I kept the third for myself and had it hollowed out, thus diminishing its value by half, but fitting it better for the use I wished to make of it.'

Everyone looked at Monte Cristo with astonishment. He spoke so unaffectedly that it was clear either that he was speaking the truth or that he was mad; but the emerald which had remained in his hands naturally inclined one to the first supposition.

'And what did those two sovereigns give you in exchange for this marvellous present?' asked Debray.

'The sultan gave me a woman's freedom,' the count replied. 'His Holiness, the life of a man. In this way, once in my existence, I was as powerful as if God had allowed me to be born on the steps of a throne.'

'It was Peppino that you freed, wasn't it?' Morcerf cried. 'He was the one who benefited from your pardon?'

'Perhaps,' said Monte Cristo, smiling.

'Monsieur le Comte, you have no idea how much pleasure I feel in hearing you say that!' said Morcerf. 'I had already let my friends know in advance that you were a fabulous being, like an enchanter from the *Thousand and One Nights*, or a sorcerer of the Middle Ages; but Parisians are people whose wits are so used to paradoxes that they mistake the most undeniable truths for mere figments of the imagination if these truths do not conform in every respect to the conditions of their daily lives. For example, Debray here reads

and Beauchamp prints day by day that a late-returning member of
the Jockey Club has been stopped and robbed on the boulevards;
that four people have been murdered in the Rue Saint-Denis or the
Faubourg Saint-Germain; and that ten, fifteen or twenty thieves
have been arrested in a café on the Boulevard du Temple, or in the
Thermes de Julien; yet they still deny the existence of bandits in the
Maremma, the Roman Campagna or the Pontine marshes. So tell
them yourself, I beg you, Monsieur le Comte, how I was captured
by those bandits and that, in all probability, without your generous
intervention I should today be awaiting my eternal resurrection in
the Catacombs of Saint Sebastian, instead of giving them dinner in
my unworthy little house in the Rue du Helder.'

'Puh!' said Monte Cristo. 'You promised me never to speak of
that trifle.'

'Not I, Monsieur le Comte!' cried Morcerf. 'That was someone
else to whom you must have rendered the same service and whom
you are confusing with me. Let us, on the contrary, speak of it, I
beg you; for if you decide to talk about the circumstances of this
affair, perhaps you will not only tell me again a little of what I
know, but also a good deal that I do not.'

The count smiled. 'It seems to me that you played a large enough
part in the business to know as well as I do what happened.'

'Will you promise me,' said Morcerf, 'that if I tell you all that I
know, you will tell me, in turn, everything that I do not know?'

'More than fair,' Monte Cristo replied.

'Well, then, even at the expense of my vanity,' Morcerf proceeded, 'for three days I thought myself to be the object of the
coquetry of a masked lady whom I took for some descendant of
Tullia or Poppaea, when in fact I was purely and simply the victim
of the provocative manoeuvres of a *contadina* – and note that I say
contadina, to avoid calling her a peasant. All that I do know is that,
naïve as I was – still more naïve than the person I just mentioned –
I mistook for this same peasant girl a young bandit of fifteen or
sixteen, beardless, narrow waisted, who at the very moment when
I wanted to take the liberty of planting a kiss on his chaste shoulder
put a pistol to my throat and, with the help of seven or eight of
his companions, led me, or dragged me, into the depths of the
Catacombs of Saint Sebastian, where I met a very cultured chief
bandit who, dammit, was reading Caesar's *Commentaries*, but
deigned to interrupt his reading to tell me that if, on the following

morning at six o'clock, I had not put four thousand *écus* into his coffers, then on the same day at a quarter past six I should quite simply have ceased to exist. There is a letter to prove it, in the possession of Franz, signed by me with a postscript by Luigi Vampa. If you doubt my word, I can write to Franz, who will verify the signatures. That is all I know. Now, what I do not know is how you, Monsieur le Comte, managed to inspire so much respect in these Roman bandits who respect so little else. I must admit to you that Franz and I were totally overcome with admiration.'

'Nothing could be simpler, Monsieur,' the count replied. 'I had known the celebrated Vampa for more than ten years. One day, when he was quite young and still a shepherd, I gave him some gold coin or other because he had shown me the way and, so that he would not be indebted to me, he gave me in return a dagger which he had carved and which you must have seen in my collection of weapons. Later, either because he had forgotten this small exchange of presents between us or because he did not recognize me, he tried to arrest me, but I turned the tables on him and captured him myself with a dozen of his men. I might have delivered him to the justice of Rome, which is swift and would have been even more expeditious in his case, but I did not. Instead I let him and his followers go.'

'On condition that they sinned no more,' said the journalist, laughing. 'I am pleased to see that they scrupulously kept their word.'

'No, Monsieur,' Monte Cristo replied. 'On the simple condition that they would always respect me and mine. Perhaps what I am about to say will appear strange to you gentlemen, socialists, progressives, humanitarians as you are, but I never worry about my neighbour, I never try to protect society which does not protect me – indeed, I might add, which generally takes no heed of me except to do me harm – and, since I hold them low in my esteem and remain neutral towards them, I believe that society and my neighbour are in my debt.'

'At last!' Château-Renaud exclaimed. 'Here is the first brave man whom I have heard frankly and unashamedly preaching egoism. This is excellent! Bravo, Monsieur le Comte!'

'At least it is honest,' said Morrel. 'But I am sure that Monsieur le Comte does not regret once at least having acted contrary to the principles that he has just described to us in such a positive manner.'

'How did I act contrary to those principles, Monsieur?' asked Monte Cristo, who had been unable to prevent himself looking from time to time at Maximilien so attentively that the bold young man had already had to lower his eyes before the clear and penetrating gaze of the count.

'It seems to me,' said Morrel, 'that by delivering Monsieur de Morcerf, who is unknown to you, you served both your neighbour and society.'

'. . . of which he is the finest ornament,' Beauchamp said gravely, emptying a glass of champagne in a single gulp.

'Monsieur le Comte!' Morcerf exclaimed. 'Here you are, caught in a logical argument – you, possessor of one of the most rigidly logical minds I have ever encountered; and you will see what is about to be clearly demonstrated to you, namely that, far from being an egoist, you are on the contrary a philanthropist. Oh, Count! You call yourself an Oriental, a Levantine, a Malay, an Indian, a Chinese, a Savage; you use Monte Cristo as your family name and Sinbad the Sailor as your Christian name; and yet, look what happens on the very day you set foot in Paris: instinctively you possess the finest and the worst quality of us eccentric Parisians, which is to lay claim to the vices that you do not have and to hide the virtues that you do!'

'My dear Vicomte,' said Monte Cristo, 'I can see not a single word in all that I have said or done to merit the supposed praise that I have just received from you and from these gentlemen. You were not a stranger to me: I knew you, for I had relinquished two rooms to you, I had given you lunch, I had lent you one of my carriages, we had watched the masks go past together in the Corso and we watched out of a window in the Piazza del Popolo that execution which had such a strong effect on you that you were almost taken ill by it. I appeal to all these gentlemen: could I leave my guest in the hands of those frightful bandits, as you call them? In any case, I had, as you know, a personal interest in saving you, which was to use you to introduce me into polite society in Paris when I came to France. At one time you may have considered that intention as merely a vague and fleeting project; but today, as you see, it is entirely real and you must submit, or else fail to keep your word.'

'I shall keep it,' said Morcerf. 'But I am afraid that you will be very disappointed, my dear Count, accustomed as you are to mountainous terrain, picturesque events and fabulous horizons. Here, you will encounter not the slightest excitement of the kind to which your adventurous life has accustomed you. Our Chimborazzo is Montmartre, our Himalayas, the Mont Valérien, and our Great Desert, the Plaine de Grenelle: indeed, they are digging an artesian well there, for the caravans to have water. We do have thieves, quite a few as it happens, though not as many as people say; but these thieves fear the meanest copper's nark infinitely more than they do the greatest peer of the realm. Finally, France is such a prosaic country and Paris such a highly civilized city that in all our eighty-five *départements*[1] – I say eighty-five, because of course I do not count Corsica as a part of France – in all our eighty-five *départements* you will not find the smallest mountain without its telegraph or a single cave with the least blackness inside it, in which some police commissioner has not put a gaslight. So, my dear Count, there is only one service that I can perform for you, and I am entirely at your disposal: it goes without saying that I shall introduce you everywhere, or have you introduced by my friends. In any case, you have no need of that: your name, your fortune and your wit' (Monte Cristo bowed with a faintly ironic smile) 'will mean that you can present yourself anywhere with no further introduction, and be well received. In reality, there is only one way in which I can serve you. If my experience of Parisian life and its comforts, or my acquaintance with the market, may recommend me to you, then I am at your disposal to find you a suitable house. I would not dare to offer to let you share my lodgings as I shared yours in Rome – I who do not profess egoism but am a perfect egoist; for here there is no room to house even a shadow apart from myself, unless it were the shadow of a woman.'

'Ah! That is a very conjugal exception,' said the count. 'And indeed, Monsieur, I believe you said something to me in Rome about a projected marriage. Should I congratulate you on your future happiness?'

'The matter is under consideration, Monsieur le Comte.'

'Which means "perhaps",' said Debray.

'Not at all,' Morcerf replied. 'My father is anxious for it to take place and I shortly expect to introduce you, if not to my wife, at least to my fiancée, Mademoiselle Eugénie Danglars.'

'Eugénie Danglars!' the count exclaimed. 'One moment: isn't her father Baron Danglars?'

'Yes,' said Morcerf, 'but recently created baron.'

'What does that matter,' Monte Cristo replied, 'if he has rendered the state some service that deserved the distinction?'

'He did, indeed,' said Beauchamp. 'Although a Liberal by instinct, he arranged a loan of six million francs in 1829 for King Charles X, who made him a baron, no less, and knight of the Legion of Honour, which means that he wears the ribbon, not, as you might think, in the buttonhole of his waistcoat, but quite plainly on his coat itself.'

Morcerf laughed: 'Come now, Beauchamp, my good fellow, keep that for *Le Corsaire*, and *Le Charivari* but, in my presence at least, spare my future father-in-law.' Then he turned back to Monte Cristo: 'But you mentioned him a moment ago as if you knew him?'

'I don't,' Monte Cristo said in an offhand manner, 'but it seems likely that I shall shortly make his acquaintance, since I have a credit opened on him by the firms of Richard and Blount of London, Arnstein and Eskeles in Vienna and Thomson and French in Rome.'

As he spoke the last two names, Monte Cristo looked out of the corner of his eye at Maximilien Morrel. Perhaps he expected to produce some effect on the young man and, if so, he was not disappointed. Maximilien shuddered as though he had received an electric shock.

'Thomson and French?' he asked. 'Do you know that firm, Monsieur?'

'They are my bankers in the Eternal City,' the count replied calmly. 'Can I be of service to you regarding them?'

'Monsieur le Comte! Perhaps you might help us to solve a problem that has so far proved insoluble. That firm once did our own a great service and yet, I don't know why, always denies having done so.'

'I shall look into it, Monsieur,' said the count, bowing.

'But the subject of Monsieur Danglars has taken us a long way,' Morcerf said, 'from the matter in hand, which was to find suitable accommodation for the Count of Monte Cristo. Come, now, gentlemen; let's put our heads together. Where shall we house this newly arrived guest of our great city?'

'In the Faubourg Saint-Germain,' said Château-Renaud. 'There the count will find a charming, secluded little private house.'

'Puf! Château-Renaud,' said Debray, 'you know nothing beyond that gloomy and melancholy Faubourg Saint-Germain of yours.

Don't listen to him, Monsieur le Comte; find somewhere in the Chaussée d'Antin – that's the true centre of Paris.'

'The Boulevard de l'Opéra,' said Beauchamp. 'On the first floor, an apartment with a balcony. There, the count can have them bring his cushions embroidered in silver thread and, while he smokes his chibouk or swallows his pills, he can watch the whole city pass before his eyes.'

'Morrel, don't you have any suggestions?' asked Château-Renaud. 'Have you no ideas?'

'Yes, certainly I do,' the young man said, smiling. 'But I was waiting to see if Monsieur was tempted by any of the fine offers that he has just been made. Now, since he has not replied, I think I might venture to offer him an apartment in a charming little house, in Pompadour style, which my sister has been renting for the past year in the Rue Meslay.'

'Do you have a sister?' Monte Cristo asked.

'Yes, Count. The most excellent sister.'

'Married?'

'For the past nine years.'

'Is she happy?' the Count continued.

'As happy as any human creature may be,' Maximilien replied. 'She married the man whom she loved, the man who had remained loyal to us in our times of misfortune: Emmanuel Herbault.'

Monte Cristo gave a faint smile.

'I am staying there while I am on leave,' Maximilien continued, 'and, with that same brother-in-law Emmanuel, I shall be at the count's disposal for any information he might require.'

'One moment,' Albert exclaimed, before Monte Cristo had time to reply. 'Be careful, Monsieur Morrel: you are trying to cage a traveller, Sinbad the Sailor, in the prison of family life. Here is a man who came to see Paris, and you want to make him a patriarch.'

'Not at all,' Morrel replied with a smile. 'My sister is twenty-five and my brother-in-law thirty: they are young, merry and contented. In any case, the count will be free to do as he wishes; he will only meet his hosts when he chooses to come down and do so.'

'Thank you, Monsieur, thank you,' said Monte Cristo. 'It will be enough for me to be introduced to your sister and your brother-in-law, if you wish to do me that honour. But the reason I did not accept the offers of any of these gentlemen is that I have already arranged for somewhere to live.'

'What!' Morcerf exclaimed. 'You are going to stay in a hotel? That would be very gloomy indeed for you.'

'Was I so ill-housed in Rome?' Monte Cristo asked.

'Huh! In Rome,' Morcerf said, 'you spent fifty thousand *piastres* in furnishing an apartment for yourself, but I don't suppose you are prepared to spend that every day.'

'It was not the expense that deterred me,' Monte Cristo replied. 'But I was resolved to have a house in Paris – a house of my own, you understand. I sent my valet on ahead of me and he must have bought me this house and had it furnished.'

'Are you telling us that you have a valet who knows Paris!' Beauchamp exclaimed.

'Like me, he is visiting France for the first time. He is black, and cannot speak,' Monte Cristo replied.

At this, there was general surprise. 'So, it must be Ali?' Albert ventured.

'Yes, Monsieur, Ali himself, my Nubian, my dumb fellow, whom I believe you saw in Rome.'

'Certainly, I recall him very well,' Morcerf replied. 'But why did you make a Nubian responsible for buying you a house in Paris and a dumb man for furnishing it? He will have got everything back to front, the poor fellow.'

'Not at all, Monsieur. I am certain, on the contrary, that he will have chosen everything in accordance with my tastes; because, you know, my tastes are not shared by everyone. He got here a week ago, and he will have criss-crossed the town with the instincts of a good hunting-dog, hunting alone. He knows my whims, my caprices, my needs. He will have arranged everything as I want it. He knew that I would be arriving today at ten o'clock, and since nine he has been waiting for me at the Fontainebleau gate. He handed me this paper, with my new address on it. Here, read it!'

Monte Cristo passed the paper across to Albert, who read: 'Number thirty, Champs-Elysées.'

'That's really novel!' Beauchamp exclaimed involuntarily.

'And very princely,' Château-Renaud added.

'What! You truly don't know your house?' Debray asked.

'No,' said Monte Cristo. 'As I told you, I did not want to miss our appointment. I shaved and dressed in the carriage and got out at the viscount's door.'

The young men exchanged glances. They did not know whether

Monte Cristo was play-acting, but everything that this man said, despite his eccentricity, was delivered in such a simple tone that it was impossible to suspect him of lying. And, for that matter, why should he lie?

'So we must make do,' Beauchamp said, 'with ensuring that the count has all the other little things that we are able to give him. For my part, as a journalist, I offer him all the theatres of Paris.'

'I thank you, Monsieur,' said Monte Cristo, with a smile, 'but my butler has already been ordered to rent me a box in each of them.'

'Is your butler also a dumb Nubian?' Debray asked.

'No, sir, merely one of your compatriots, if a Corsican can be said to be anyone's compatriot; but you know him, Monsieur de Morcerf . . .'

'Not by any chance the good Signor Bertuccio who is so expert at hiring windows?'

'The very same: you met him at my house on the day when I had the honour to invite you to luncheon. He is an excellent fellow who was something of a soldier, something of a smuggler and, in short, a little of all that one can be. I would not swear to it that he has not been in trouble with the police over some trifle – like a knifing, say.'

'And you chose this honest citizen of the world as your butler, Count?' Debray said. 'How much does he steal from you every year?'

'You have my word on it, no more than any other, I am sure. He is just what I need, he never takes no for an answer and I am keeping him.'

'Well, then,' said Château-Renaud, 'you have a household all ready: a mansion on the Champs-Elysées, servants, a butler; the only thing lacking is a mistress.'

Albert smiled, thinking of the beautiful Greek woman whom he had seen in the count's box at the Teatro Valle and the Argentina.

'I have something better than that,' Monte Cristo replied. 'I have a slave. You hire your mistresses at the Théâtre de l'Opéra, at the Vaudeville, at the Variétés. I bought mine in Constantinople. She was more expensive, but I have no further worries on that score.'

Debray laughed. 'You are forgetting that here, as King Charles said, we are Franks by name and frank by nature. As soon as she set foot in France, your slave became free.'

'Who will tell her?' asked Monte Cristo.

'Heavens, anybody who comes along.'

'She only speaks Romaic.'

'Ah, that's another matter.'

'Shall we see her, at least?' asked Beauchamp. 'Or, having already one dumb servant, do you also have eunuchs?'

'No, certainly not,' said Monte Cristo. 'I do not take my orientalism that far. All those around me are free to leave, and will have no further need of me or of anyone else. Perhaps that is why they do not leave me.'

They had long since moved on to the dessert and the cigars.

'My dear fellow,' Debray said, getting up, 'it is half-past two and your guest is charming, but there is no company so good as that one leaves, even sometimes for worse. I must go back to my Ministry. I shall speak of the count to the minister and we must find out who he is.'

'Take care,' said Morcerf. 'Cleverer men have given up the search.'

'Huh! We have a budget of three million for intelligence. Admittedly it is almost always spent in advance; but, no matter, there will still be fifty thousand for this.'

'And when you know who he is, you will tell me?'

'I promise. Au revoir, Albert. Gentlemen, your most humble servant.'

As he left, Debray cried out loudly in the antechamber: 'Bring my carriage.'

'Very well,' Beauchamp told Albert. 'I shall not go to the House, but offer my readers something better than a speech by Monsieur Danglars.'

'I beg you, Beauchamp,' Morcerf said. 'Not a word, I pray. Don't deprive me of the credit for introducing him and explaining him. Isn't he an odd fellow?'

'Better than that,' replied Château-Renaud. 'One of the most extraordinary men I have ever seen. Morrel, are you coming?'

'I must just give my card to Monsieur le Comte, who has kindly promised to visit us at fourteen, Rue Meslay.'

'You may be sure that I shall not fail to do so, Monsieur,' the count said with a bow. And Maximilien Morrel went out with the Baron de Château-Renaud, leaving Monte Cristo alone with Morcerf.

XLI

THE INTRODUCTION

When Albert was alone with Monte Cristo, he said: 'Monsieur le Comte, let me embark on my duties as your guide by showing you this example of a bachelor apartment. Accustomed as you are to Italian palaces, it will be interesting for you to estimate in how few square feet a young man can live in Paris without being counted among those who are the most poorly housed. As we pass from one room to the next, we shall open the windows to allow you to breathe.'

Monte Cristo already knew the dining-room and the downstairs drawing-room. Firstly, Albert conducted him to his attic; this, you will remember, was his favourite room.

Monte Cristo was well able to appreciate all the things that Albert had amassed in the room: old chests, Japanese porcelain, oriental cloths, jewels of Venetian glass and weapons from every country in the world: he was familiar with all these things and needed only a glance to recognize century, country and provenance. Morcerf imagined that he would do the explaining, but on the contrary, under the count's guidance, he found himself taking lessons in archaeology, mineralogy and natural history. They came back down to the first floor and Albert showed his guest into the drawing-room. The walls here were hung with modern paintings: there were landscapes by Dupré, with long reeds, slender trees, lowing cows and wonderful skies; there were Arab riders by Delacroix, dressed in flowing white burnous, with shining belts and damascened weapons, whose horses were biting their own flanks in fury while the riders rent one another with iron maces; there were watercolours by Boulanger illustrating the whole of *Notre-Dame de Paris* with the energy that makes the painter the equal of the poet; there were canvases by Diaz, who makes flowers more lovely than flowers and a sun brighter than the sun; drawings by Decamps, as highly coloured as those of Salvator Rosa, but more poetic; pastels by Giraud and Müller depicting children with angel faces and women with virginal features; pages torn from Dauzat's sketchbook of his journeys to the East, drawn in a few seconds on the saddle of a camel or beneath the dome of a mosque; in short, everything that modern art can offer in exchange and compensation for the art lost and vanished with earlier centuries.[1]

Here, at least, Albert expected to show the stranger something new but, to his great astonishment, the count, without even having to look for the signature (some of those in any case only took the form of initials), instantly put the name of each artist on his work, so that it was easy to see that not only was each of these names already known to him, but that he had also studied and judged each of these talented artists.

From the drawing-room they went into the bedroom. This was at the same time a model of elegance and austere in its taste. Only one portrait here, but by Léopold Robert,[2] magnificent in its burnished gold frame. The portrait at once attracted the Count of Monte Cristo's attention, because he took three rapid paces across the room and stopped in front of it.

It showed a young woman of twenty-five or twenty-six, dark in colouring, her burning eyes veiled beneath languorous lids. She was wearing the picturesque costume of a Catalan fisherwoman, with a red-and-black bodice and her hair held back with gold pins. She was looking at the sea, so that her elegant figure was outlined against the two blues, of the sky and the waves.

Had it not been dark in the room, Albert would have observed the livid pallor that spread across the count's cheeks and noticed the nervous tremor that shook his shoulders and his chest.

There was a moment's silence, in which Monte Cristo remained with his eyes unwaveringly fixed on the painting.

'You have a beautiful mistress there, Vicomte,' he said, in a perfectly calm voice. 'And this costume, no doubt intended for the ball, suits her astonishingly well.'

'Ah, Monsieur!' Albert said. 'I should not forgive you this mistake, if you had seen any other portrait beside this one. You do not know my mother, Monsieur. She is the person in that picture, which she had done six or eight years ago, dressed like this in some imaginary costume, apparently; the resemblance is so good that I feel I can still see my mother as she was in 1830. The countess had the portrait done for herself while the count was away. No doubt she intended to give him a pleasant surprise when he returned, but, oddly enough, the portrait displeased my father and the value of the canvas which, as you can see, is one of Léopold Robert's excellent works, could not overcome the dislike he had conceived

for it. Between ourselves, my dear Count, it is true to say that
Monsieur de Morcerf is one of the most conscientious peers in the
Upper Chamber and a general renowned for his theories, but a very
poor connoisseur of art. The same is not true of my mother, who
paints remarkably well and has too much respect for such a work
to relinquish it altogether and who gave it to me so that in my
house it would be less liable to upset Monsieur de Morcerf. I shall
shortly show you his portrait, painted by Gros.[3] Forgive me if I
seem to chatter on about domestic matters and my family, but as I
shall later have the honour of introducing you to the count I am
telling you this so that you will know not to praise this portrait in
front of him. In any case, it has an unhappy aura. My mother very
seldom comes to my house without looking at it and still less often
does she look at it without weeping. The cloud that entered our
household with the appearance in it of this painting is the only one
that has ever fallen across the count and countess who, though they
have been married for more than twenty years, are still as closely
united as on the very first day.'

Monte Cristo glanced rapidly at Albert as if to discover some
hidden meaning behind his words, but it was clear that the young
man had spoken with all the candour of his simple heart.

'Now that you have seen all my riches, Monsieur le Comte,' he
continued, 'allow me to offer them to you, unworthy though they
are. Consider this your home here and, to put you still more at your
ease, pray accompany me to Monsieur de Morcerf's. I wrote from
Rome to tell him of the service you had done me and to announce
that you had promised to visit me. I may tell you that the count
and countess are impatient to thank you. I know, Monsieur le
Comte, that you are a little blasé about everything, and that Sinbad
the Sailor is little touched by scenes of family life: you have witnessed other so much more exciting ones! However, as your
initiation to Parisian life, allow me to offer you the round of daily
etiquette, visits and introductions.'

Monte Cristo bowed in reply. He accepted the proposal without
enthusiasm or reluctance, as one of those social conventions with
which every well-bred man must comply. Albert called his valet
and told him to go and advise M. and Mme de Morcerf that the
Count of Monte Cristo would shortly wait on them. Albert and the
count followed him.

On reaching the count's antechamber, the visitor could see a shield above the door leading to the reception room which, being extravagantly mounted and made to harmonize with the décor of the room, indicated the importance that the owner of the mansion attached to this coat of arms. Monte Cristo paused in front of it and examined it carefully.

'Azur, seven merlets, or, placed bender. No doubt this is your family's coat of arms, Monsieur? Apart from the knowledge of the elements of the shield that permits me to decipher it, I am very ignorant in matters of heraldry, being myself an accidental count, fabricated by Tuscany with the help of a commandership of Saint Stephen: I should never have passed myself off as a great nobleman were it not that I was repeatedly told this was absolutely necessary for anyone who travels a lot. When it comes down to it, one must have something on the doors of one's coach to dissuade the Customs from searching it. So forgive me for asking.'

'The question is not at all indiscreet, Monsieur,' Morcerf replied in the frank tones of someone who believed what he said. 'You are right: this is our coat of arms, that is to say it bears my father's crest, but attached to a shield that is gules with a silver tower, bearing my mother's crest. On her side I am Spanish, but the Morcerfs are French and, so I am told, one of the oldest families in the south of France.'

'Yes,' said Monte Cristo, 'that is shown by the merlets or black-birds. Almost all the crusaders who conquered, or tried to conquer, the Holy Land took either crosses as their emblems, as a sign of the mission to which they had dedicated themselves, or else migratory birds, as a symbol of the long journey that they intended to under-take and which they hoped to accomplish on the wings of faith. One of your paternal ancestors must have taken part in the Cru-sades; and, if it was only the Crusade led by Saint Louis, that already takes us back to the thirteenth century, which is already a very fine thing.'

'That may be so,' said Morcerf. 'Somewhere in my father's study there is a family tree which will answer these questions for us; I used to have a commentary on it that would have meant a lot to d'Hozier and Jaucourt.[4] Nowadays I don't bother about it, but I should tell you, Monsieur le Comte – and this falls within my scope as your guide – that people are starting to worry a great deal about such things under this popular government of ours.'

'Well then, your government should have chosen something

better from French history than those two placards I have noticed on your public monuments, which are meaningless in heraldic terms. As for you, Viscount,' Monte Cristo continued, turning back towards Morcerf, 'you are luckier than your government, because your coat of arms is truly beautiful and inspiring. Yes, that is it: you come both from Provence and from Spain and, if the portrait you showed me is a good likeness, that explains the fine tan that I so greatly admired on the face of the Catalan.'

One would have needed to be Oedipus or the Sphinx itself to detect the irony that the count put into these words, which were apparently delivered with the finest good manners. Morcerf consequently thanked him with a smile and, going ahead to show him the way, opened the door beneath his coat of arms, which, as we mentioned, led into the reception room.

In the most prominent place on the walls of the room there was another portrait. It depicted a man of between thirty-five and thirty-eight years old, wearing a general's uniform with the twisted double epaulette that indicates the higher ranks and the ribbon of the Legion of Honour around his neck, showing that he was a Commander of the Order. On his chest, to the right, he wore the medal of a Grand Officer of the Order of the Saviour and, to the left, that of the Great Cross of Charles III, demonstrating that the person represented in the portrait must have fought in the Spanish and Greek Wars, or else (this being identical as far as medals were concerned) have carried out some diplomatic mission in those two countries.

Monte Cristo was examining this portrait with no less attention than he had given to the other when a side door opened and he was confronted with the Comte de Morcerf himself.

The count was aged between forty and forty-five but had the appearance of a man of at least fifty. His dark moustache and eyebrows contrasted oddly with almost white hair, cut short in the military manner. He was dressed in the everyday clothes of a man of his class; the different strands of the ribbon that he wore in his buttonhole recalled the various orders with which he had been decorated. He came in with quite an aristocratic step and, at the same time, a sort of condescending alacrity. Monte Cristo watched him approach without taking a step to meet him: it was as though his feet were fixed to the floor and his eyes on the Comte de Morcerf's face.

'Father,' the young man said, 'I have the honour to introduce the Count of Monte Cristo, the generous friend whom I was fortunate enough to meet in the awkward circumstances about which I told you.'

'Monsieur is welcome to my house,' the Comte de Morcerf said, smiling and bowing to Monte Cristo. 'He has done our family such a favour, in preserving its only heir, that it will elicit our eternal gratitude.' As he spoke, the Comte de Morcerf motioned to a chair and, at the same time, took one himself facing the window.

As for Monte Cristo, while he took the chair that the Comte de Morcerf had indicated, he repositioned it in such a way as to remain hidden in the shadow of the great velvet curtains. From there he could read in the count's tired and careworn features a whole history of secret sorrows which lay imprinted there in each of the lines that the years had marked on it.

'Madame la Comtesse was at her toilet,' Morcerf said, 'when the vicomte asked her to be informed that she had the good fortune to receive our guest. She will come down shortly and join us in ten minutes' time.'

'It is a great honour for me,' Monte Cristo said, 'on the very day of my arrival in Paris, to meet a man whose merits are equal to his reputation and whom Fortune, just once, has not been mistaken in favouring. But did she not have a marshal's baton to offer you, somewhere on the plains of Mitidja or in the Atlas Mountains?'

'Oh!' Morcerf exclaimed, blushing slightly. 'I have left the service, Monsieur. I was given my peerage under the Restoration and served under Maréchal de Bourmont. For that reason, I might have hoped for some higher command: who knows what would have happened if the senior branch of the royal family had remained on the throne! But it seems that the July Revolution was glorious enough to afford ingratitude: it behaved thus to all whose service did not date back to the empire. So I resigned because, when a man has won his epaulettes on the battlefield, he does not know how to manoeuvre on the slippery surface of a drawing-room. I put down my sword and devoted myself to politics, to industry; I studied the useful arts. I had wanted to do that during my twenty years' service to my country, but I did not have time.'

'It is things such as these that maintain your people's superiority over others, Monsieur,' Monte Cristo replied. 'You, a nobleman of good family, heir to a large fortune, agreed first of all to make your

way up from the ranks, which is very rare. Then, having become a
general, a peer of the realm and a Commander of the Legion of
Honour, you were willing to undertake a second apprenticeship,
with no other expectation and no other reward than that of one
day being useful to your fellow men. Monsieur! This is truly fine! I
will go further: it is sublime!'

Albert was watching and listening to Monte Cristo with astonishment. He was not accustomed to seeing him fired with such
enthusiasm.

'Alas,' the foreigner went on, no doubt to lift the hardly perceptible cloud that his words had brought to the elder Morcerf's brow,
'we should not behave in that way in Italy. There we grow according
to our genus and our species, keeping the same foliage, the same
height and often the same inutility all our lives.'

'But, Monsieur,' the Comte de Morcerf replied, 'Italy is not a
homeland for a man of your worth and France may not be ungrateful to all: it treats its own children badly, but usually has a magnificent welcome for foreigners.'

'Oh, father,' said Albert, smiling, 'you clearly do not know the
Count of Monte Cristo. He finds satisfaction elsewhere than in the
things of this world and does not aspire to any honours, taking
only those that can fit on his passport.'

'That is the most accurate description of myself that I have ever
heard,' the stranger said.

'Monsieur was able to control his own future,' the Comte de
Morcerf said, sighing, 'and chose a pathway lined with flowers.'

'Precisely, Monsieur,' Monte Cristo retorted, with one of those
smiles that no painter could ever catch and a physiologist would
despair of analysing.

'If I had not been afraid of tiring the count,' said the general,
clearly charmed by Monte Cristo's manners, 'I should have taken
him to the Chamber. Today's sitting will be unusual for anyone
who does not know our modern senators.'

'I should be very grateful to you, Monsieur, if you would be good
enough to renew the invitation at some later date; but today I have
been flattered that I might be introduced to the countess, so I shall
wait.'

'Here is my mother!' the vicomte exclaimed.

Monte Cristo, urgently swivelling on his seat, saw Mme de
Morcerf at the entrance to the room, in the threshold of the door

opposite the one by which her husband had entered: pale and motionless, she let her arm fall, when Monte Cristo turned around, from the gilt door-frame on which, for some unknown reason, she had rested it; she had been there for some minutes, hearing the last words that the southern visitor had spoken.

He got up and bowed deeply to the countess, who formally returned the bow in silence.

'Heavens above, Madame!' the Comte de Morcerf exclaimed. 'What is the matter? Is the heat of the room making you unwell?'

'Are you ill, mother?' the viscount asked, hurrying over to Mercédès.

She thanked them both with a smile. 'No,' she said, 'but I was moved at seeing for the first time the man without whose help we should now be in tears and in mourning. Monsieur,' she went on, coming across the room with the bearing of a queen, 'I owe you my son's life and I bless you for that. Now I must acknowledge the pleasure that you have brought me, in allowing me this opportunity to thank you as I bless you, namely from the depth of my heart.'

The count bowed again, more profoundly than the first time. He was even paler than Mercédès.

'Madame,' he said, 'Monsieur le Comte and you are too generous in rewarding me for a very simple action. To save a man's life, to spare a father's torment and to protect a mother's feelings is not a good deed, it is an act of mere humanity.'

Mme de Morcerf answered these words, which had been spoken with exquisite gentleness and good manners, in tones of profound feeling: 'Monsieur, my son is very fortunate to have you as a friend and I thank God that He has brought this to pass.' And Mercédès raised her lovely eyes to heaven with such infinite gratitude that the count thought he could detect a tear rising in each of them.

M. de Morcerf went across to her.

'Madame,' he said, 'I have already made my excuses to the count for being obliged to leave him. I beg you to repeat them. The sitting began at two o'clock, it is now three, I must leave.'

'Very well, Monsieur, I shall try to make our guest overlook your absence,' the countess said in the same feeling voice. Then, turning to Monte Cristo: 'Monsieur le Comte, will you do us the honour of spending the rest of the day with us?'

'Thank you, Madame. Believe me, I could not be more grateful for your invitation, but I stepped off this morning at your door from my travelling carriage. I have no idea how I am to be lodged in Paris; indeed, I hardly know where. I realize that this is a small cause of anxiety, but an appreciable one, nonetheless.'

'At least you will promise that we shall have the pleasure some other time?' asked the countess.

Monte Cristo bowed, without replying; but the gesture could be taken for one of assent.

'In that case, I shall not detain you, Monsieur, for I should not wish my gratitude to obtrude on your time or to importune you.'

'My dear Count,' said Albert, 'I should like, if you will permit me, to return the favour that you did us in Rome and put my coupé at your disposal until you have had time to arrange a suitable conveyance for yourself.'

'Thank you a thousand times, Vicomte, you are most considerate; but I presume that Monsieur Bertuccio has been making good use of the four and a half hours that I have accorded him, and that I shall find a fully harnessed coach waiting at the door.'

Albert was used to the count's ways and knew that, like Nero, he was in pursuit of the impossible, so nothing surprised him. However, he wanted to judge for himself how well the count's order had been obeyed, so he accompanied him to the door of the house.

Monte Cristo had guessed right. No sooner did he appear in the Comte de Morcerf's anteroom than a footman (the same who in Rome had brought the two young men the count's card and announced that he would visit them) rushed out through the colonnade, so that when the illustrious traveller reached the steps he found his carriage waiting.

It was a coupé from the Keller workshops, harnessed to a team for which, as every dandy in Paris knew, Drake had only the day before refused 18,000 francs.

'Monsieur,' the count said to Albert, 'I will not invite you to accompany me, because I could only show you improvised lodgings – and, as you know, I have my reputation to keep up where improvisation is concerned. Grant me a day and then let me invite you: I shall be more certain that I am not breaching the laws of hospitality.'

'If you are asking me for a day, Monsieur le Comte, then I feel certain that it will not be a house that you show me, but a palace. There's no doubt about it: you have some genie at your command.'

'Please, please, put it around!' said the count, with one foot on the velvet-covered steps of his magnificent carriage. 'It will do me no harm with the ladies.' At this, he leapt into his coach, slamming the door behind him, and set off at a gallop, though not so fast that he failed to notice the barely perceptible movement of the curtains in the drawing-room where he had left Mme de Morcerf.

When Albert rejoined his mother indoors, he found her in the boudoir, slumped in a large velvet armchair. The whole room was deep in shadow, concealing everything except the highlights sparkling on some oriental vase or in the corner of a gilded picture-frame.

Albert could not see the countess's face, which was hidden by a cloud of gauze that she had wrapped around her head like a halo of vapour, but he thought that her voice sounded odd and, above the scent of rose and heliotrope rising from the bowl of flowers, he could distinguish the sharp and bitter smell of sal volatile. Indeed, the young man could observe the countess's phial of smelling-salts, out of its shagreen case, resting on one of the mouldings of the mantelpiece.

'Are you well, mother?' he cried as he came in. 'Did you feel faint while I was away?'

'I? No, Albert. But, you know, in this early heat, before we have had time to become accustomed to it, all these roses, tuberoses and orange flowers give off such a powerful scent . . .'

'In that case, mother,' Morcerf said, reaching for the bell, 'we must have them taken into your dressing-room. You are really unwell: you were already very pale a short while ago when you came in.'

'Do you think I was pale, Albert?'

'A pale complexion suits you wonderfully, mother, but, even so, my father and I were concerned.'

'Did your father remark on it?' Mercédès asked urgently.

'Not to me: you remember, he made the observation to you, yourself.'

'I don't recall,' said the countess.

A valet entered in answer to Albert's summons.

'Take these flowers into the antechamber or the dressing-room,' the viscount said. 'The countess is incommoded by them.'

The valet obeyed. There was quite a long silence, which lasted as long as it took him to complete the task.

'What is this title of Monte Cristo?' the countess asked, when the servant had left with the last vase of flowers. 'Is it the name of a family, a place, or simply a title?'

'I believe it is simply a title, mother, nothing more. The count bought an island in the Tuscan archipelago and, as he told me only this morning, founded a chivalric commandership. You know that the same was done for Saint Stephen of Florence, for Saint George Constantinian of Parma and even for the Knights of Malta. In any case, he has no pretension to nobility and calls himself an accidental count, though the general opinion in Rome is that he is a very noble aristocrat.'

'His manners are excellent,' the countess said. 'At least, as far as one can tell from the short while he stayed here.'

'They are perfect, mother; even so perfect as greatly to surpass those I have found among the noblest members of the three proudest aristocracies in Europe, that is the nobility of England, Spain and Germany.'

The countess thought for a moment, then continued:

'My dear Albert, you have seen . . . You understand, this is a mother's question that I am asking . . . You have seen Monsieur de Monte Cristo at home. You are perspicacious, you know the world and you have more tact than is usual at your age. Do you think that the count is really all that he appears to be?'

'What does he appear to be?'

'You said it yourself a moment ago: a great nobleman.'

'I said, mother, that he was thought to be one.'

'And what do you think, Albert?'

'I must admit that I have no definite view on the matter. I think he is a Maltese.'

'I am not asking about his nationality, I am asking you about the man himself.'

'Ah, that's quite a different matter. I have seen so many strange things to do with him that, if you ask what I think, I would say that I am inclined to consider him as some kind of Byronic figure, branded by Fate's dread seal: some Manfred, some Lara, some Werner . . . In short, one of those rejects of an old aristocratic family, cut off from the paternal inheritance, who made a fortune for themselves by the force of a daring and a genius that put them above the laws of society . . .'

'What do you mean?'

'I mean that Monte Cristo is an island in the Mediterranean, uninhabited, unguarded, the haunt of smugglers of all nations and pirates from every shore. Who knows whether these industrious workers may not pay their lord for giving them asylum?'

'Possibly,' the countess said distractedly.

'No matter,' the young man went on. 'Smuggler or not, you must admit, having seen him, mother, that the Count of Monte Cristo is a remarkable man and one who will be a great success in the drawing-rooms of Paris. Why, this very morning, at my house, he began his progress in high society by astonishing even Château-Renaud.'

'How old do you think the count is?' Mercédès asked, clearly attaching great importance to the question.

'Between thirty-five and thirty-six, mother.'

'So young! It's impossible,' Mercédès exclaimed, replying at once to what Albert was saying and to her own thoughts.

'It is true, even so. Three or four times he said to me, assuredly without any premeditation: at that time I was five; at this other, I was ten; and at another, twelve. I was so curious about the smallest detail that I compared the dates and never found any discrepancy. This remarkable man is ageless, but I can assure you that he is thirty-five. In any case, mother, remember the brightness of his eye, the darkness of his hair and how his brow, though pale, is unfurrowed. This is someone who is not only active, but still young.'

The countess lowered her head as if bowed under a mass of ideas that completely absorbed her.

'And this man has conceived a liking for you, Albert? He wants to be your friend?' she asked, with a nervous shudder.

'I believe so, mother.'

'Do you also like him?'

'I do, in spite of Franz d'Epinay trying to make me believe he was a spectre returning from the Beyond.'

The countess shrank back in terror and said, in a strained voice: 'Albert, I have always warned you against new acquaintances. Now you are a man and old enough to advise me. Yet I repeat: Albert, beware.'

'My dear mother, to profit from your advice, I should need to know in advance what I am supposed to beware of. The count never gambles, the count only ever drinks water, coloured with a little Spanish wine, and the count has declared himself to be so rich that he could not borrow money from me without appearing ridiculous. What can I fear from the count?'

'You are right,' his mother said. 'My anxiety is foolish, especially when directed towards the man who saved your life. By the way, Albert, did your father receive him suitably? It is important for us to be more than polite with the count. Monsieur de Morcerf is sometimes so busy and his work preoccupies him so, that he may involuntarily have . . .'

'My father was perfect, mother,' Albert interrupted. 'I would go further: he seemed greatly flattered by two or three very subtle compliments that the count made – as finely turned and surely aimed as if he had known him for the past thirty years. Each of these eulogistic little darts must have flattered my father so much,' he added, with a laugh, 'that they separated the best friends in the world and Monsieur de Morcerf even wanted to take him to the House so that he could listen to his speech.'

The countess said nothing; she was absorbed in such a profound reverie that her eyes gradually closed. The young man, standing in front of her, watched with that filial love that is more tender and affectionate in children whose mothers are still young and beautiful. Then, after seeing her eyes close, he listened for a moment to her breathing, sweetly still, and then, thinking her asleep, tiptoed away, cautiously opening the door of the room where he left her.

'Damn the man,' he muttered, shaking his head. 'I predicted to him in Rome that he would be a sensation in Parisian society; now I can measure his effect on an infallible thermometer. My mother remarked on him, so he must indeed be remarkable.'

He went down to his stables, harbouring a secret feeling of pique at the fact that, without thinking, the Count of Monte Cristo had obtained a team of horses that would outshine his bays in the eyes of any connoisseur.

'Men,' he said, 'are most certainly not equal. I must get my father to expound this theory in the Upper House.'

XLII

MONSIEUR BERTUCCIO

Meanwhile the count had arrived at his house. The journey had taken him six minutes, and these six minutes had been enough for him to be seen by twenty young men who, recognizing the cost of a team that was well beyond their means, had spurred their mounts to a gallop so that they could catch a glimpse of this noble lord who paid ten thousand francs apiece for his horses.

The residence that Ali had chosen to serve as Monte Cristo's town house was situated on the right as you go up the Champs-Elysées, with a courtyard on one side and a garden on the other. A leafy clump of trees in the courtyard shielded part of the façade and, around it, like two enclosing arms, were two avenues directing carriages to right and left from the front gate towards a double stairway, every step of which supported a vase full of flowers. The house, standing alone in quite ample grounds, had another entrance apart from the main one on the Rue de Ponthieu.

Even before the coachman had called out to the concierge, the huge gate was swinging back on its hinges: the count had been seen approaching and, in Paris as in Rome (as, indeed, everywhere else), his needs were met with lightning rapidity. So the coach entered and described the half-circle without slowing down. The gate had already shut while the wheels were crunching on the gravel of the path.

The carriage stopped on the left-hand side of the stairway and two men appeared at its door. One was Ali, giving his master a smile of joy that was astonishing in its sincerity; it was rewarded with a simple glance from Monte Cristo.

The other man bowed humbly and offered the count his arm to get down from the carriage.

'Thank you, Monsieur Bertuccio,' the count said, lightly jumping over the three steps. 'What about the notary?'

'In the little drawing-room, Your Excellency,' Bertuccio replied.

'And the visiting cards that I asked you to have printed as soon as you knew the number of the house?'

'They are already done, Monsieur le Comte. I went to the finest printer in the Palais-Royal and he engraved the plate in front of

me. The first card struck off from it was sent, as you required, to
Monsieur le Baron Danglars, *député*, at number seven, Rue de
la Chaussée-d'Antin. The others are on the mantelpiece of Your
Excellency's bedroom.'

'Good. What time is it?'

'Four o'clock.'

Monte Cristo gave his gloves, his hat and his cane to the same
French lackey who had sprung out of the Comte de Morcerf's
antechamber to call the carriage; then he went into the smaller
drawing-room, with Bertuccio showing him the way.

'The statues in this antechamber are very poor stuff,' Monte
Cristo said. 'I sincerely hope that they will be removed.'

Bertuccio bowed.

As the steward had said, the notary was waiting in the antechamber – a respectable-looking Parisian assistant solicitor elevated to the insurmountable dignity of a pettifogging suburban
lawyer.

'You are the notary appointed by the vendors of the country
house that I wish to buy?' Monte Cristo asked.

'Yes, Monsieur le Comte,' the notary answered.

'Is the deed of sale ready?'

'Yes, Monsieur le Comte.'

'You have it with you?'

'Here it is.'

'Splendid. And where is this house that I'm buying?' Monte
Cristo asked casually, addressing the question partly to M. Bertuccio
and partly to the notary.

The steward made a sign that meant: 'I don't know.' The notary
stared at Monte Cristo in astonishment. 'What!' he exclaimed.
'Does Monsieur le Comte not even know the location of the house
that he is buying?'

'Why, no,' said the count.

'Monsieur le Comte is not acquainted with the property?'

'How on earth could I be? I arrived from Cadiz this morning. I
have never been to Paris; this is the first time that I have even set
foot in France.'

'That is a different matter,' the notary replied. 'The house that
Monsieur le Comte is buying is located in Auteuil.'

On hearing this, Bertuccio went pale.

'And where is this Auteuil of yours?' Monte Cristo asked.

'No distance at all, Monsieur le Comte,' said the notary. 'A little beyond Passy, charmingly situated in the middle of the Bois de Boulogne.'

'So close!' Monte Cristo said. 'But this is not the country. The devil take it! How did you manage to choose me a house on the outskirts of Paris, Monsieur Bertuccio?'

'I!' cried the steward, with unusual haste. 'No, no! I am not the one whom Monsieur le Comte asked to choose this house. If Monsieur le Comte would be so good as to remember, to rake his memory, to cast his mind back . . .'

'Oh, yes. Quite correct,' said Monte Cristo. 'Now I recall. I read the advertisement in a newspaper and allowed myself to be taken in by the mendacious heading: "country house".'

'There is still time,' Bertuccio said in a lively voice. 'If Your Excellency would like me to look everywhere else, I shall find him the very best, whether in Enghien, Fontenay-aux-Roses or Bellevue.'

'No, no,' Monte Cristo said idly. 'I've got this one, so I'll keep it.'

'And Monsieur is right!' exclaimed the notary, afraid of losing his commission. 'It is a charming property: running streams, dense woodland, a comfortable house, though long abandoned – not to mention the furniture which, old though it is, is valuable, especially nowadays when antiques are so prized. Forgive me, but I would imagine Monsieur le Comte to have fashionable tastes.'

'Carry on,' said Monte Cristo. 'So it's acceptable, then?'

'Oh, Monsieur, much more than that: it's magnificent!'

'Let's not pass up such a bargain, then,' said Monte Cristo. 'Notary, the contract of sale!'

He signed quickly, after glancing at the point on the deed where the position of the house and the names of the owners were marked.

'Bertuccio,' he said. 'Give this gentleman fifty-five thousand francs.'

The steward went out with faltering steps and returned with a sheaf of notes which the notary counted out like a man who is used to receiving his money only after due legal process.

'Now,' said the count. 'Have all the formalities been completed?'

'Every one, Monsieur le Comte.'

'Do you have the keys?'

'They are held by the concierge who is looking after the house. Here is the order that I have made out to him, requiring him to show Monsieur into his property.'

'Very good,' said Monte Cristo, nodding to the notary in a way that meant: 'I have no further need of you. Go!'

'But, Monsieur le Comte,' said the honest pen-pusher. 'I think Monsieur le Comte has made a mistake. It was only fifty thousand francs, *in toto*.'

'And your fee?'

'Included in that amount, Monsieur le Comte.'

'But did you not come here from Auteuil?'

'Yes, indeed.'

'Well, you must be paid for your trouble,' said the count, dismissing him with a gesture.

The notary backed out of the room, bowing to the floor. This was the first time since obtaining his articles that he had ever met such a client.

'Show this gentleman out,' the count said to Bertuccio, who followed the notary out.

No sooner was the count alone than he took out of his pocket a locked wallet and opened it with a little key that he kept always around his neck and which never left him. He looked for a moment, then stopped at a page containing some notes, compared the notes with the deed of sale lying on the table and, searching his memory, said: 'That's it: Auteuil, number twenty-eight, Rue de la Fontaine. Now, am I relying on a confession extracted by religious terror or physical fear? In any event, I shall know all in an hour's time. Bertuccio!' He banged on the table with a sort of little hammer with a folding handle, that gave a high-pitched, resonant sound, like a tom-tom. 'Bertuccio!'

The steward appeared in the doorway.

'Monsieur Bertuccio,' said the count, 'didn't you once tell me that you had travelled in France?'

'In some parts of France, yes, Excellency.'

'So you doubtless know the country around Paris?'

'No, Excellency, no,' the steward replied with a sort of nervous stammer which Monte Cristo, a specialist in the matter of human emotions, rightly attributed to extreme anxiety.

'It is annoying,' he said, 'this fact that you haven't explored the district around Paris, because I wish to go and see my new property this very evening, and you would no doubt have been able to accompany me and give me some useful information.'

'To Auteuil?' Bertuccio cried, his bronzed features becoming almost livid. 'Me! Go to Auteuil!'

'What is it? What is so astonishing about you going to Auteuil, may I ask? When I am living there, you will have to come, since you are part of my household.'

Bertuccio lowered his eyes before his master's imperious gaze and remained silent and motionless.

'Well I never! What's wrong with you? Do you want me to ring again for my carriage?' Monte Cristo said in the tone of voice adopted by Louis XIV to speak the celebrated words: 'I was almost made to wait!'[1]

Bertuccio went in a flash from the little drawing-room to the antechamber and called out in a hoarse voice: 'Prepare His Excellency's carriage!'

Monte Cristo wrote two or three letters. As he was coming to the end of the last of them, the steward reappeared.

'You Excellency's carriage is at the door,' he said.

'Well then, get your hat and gloves,' said the count.

'Am I to accompany Monsieur le Comte?' Bertuccio cried.

'Of course. You must give your orders, for I intend to live in this house.'

It was unheard of to question one of the count's commands, so the steward followed his master, unprotesting. The latter got into the carriage and motioned to him to do likewise. The steward sat respectfully on the front seat.

XLIII

THE HOUSE AT AUTEUIL

Monte Cristo noticed that, as he came down the steps, Bertuccio crossed himself in the manner of the Corsicans, who make a cross in the air with their thumbs; and that when he took his place in the carriage he muttered a short prayer under his breath. A less curious man would have taken pity on the worthy steward in view of the extreme reluctance he had shown to the idea of a drive *extra muros* with the count; but it appeared that the man was too keen to discover the reason why for him to excuse Bertuccio their little journey.

In twenty minutes they had reached Auteuil. The steward's anxiety had increased steadily. As they entered the village, Bertuccio, slumped in a corner of the carriage, began to study each of the houses that they passed with feverish attention.

'Tell them to stop at number twenty-eight, Rue de la Fontaine,' the count said, staring pitilessly at his steward while giving him this order.

A sweat broke out on Bertuccio's face, but he obeyed and, leaning out of the carriage, called to the coachman: 'Rue de la Fontaine, number twenty-eight.'

Number 28 was at the far end of the village. As they travelled, night had fallen; or, rather, a black cloud heavy with electricity gave the premature darkness the appearance and the solemnity of a dramatic event. The carriage stopped and the footman leapt down to open the door.

'Well, now, Monsieur Bertuccio,' said the count, 'won't you get down? Do you intend to stay in the carriage, then? What the devil is up with you this evening?'

Bertuccio hastened to the door and offered the count his shoulder. This time he put his weight on it and took the three steps out of the carriage one by one.

'Knock,' said the count, 'and announce me.'

Bertuccio knocked, the door opened and the concierge appeared.

'What is it?' he asked.

'Your new master, my good man,' said the footman, handing the concierge the letter of recommendation from the notary.

'Is the house sold, then?' asked the concierge. 'And is this the gentleman who will live here?'

'Yes, my friend,' the count replied. 'I shall try to ensure that you do not wish for your former master's return.'

'Oh, Monsieur,' said the concierge. 'I shan't miss him a lot because we see him rarely enough. He has not been here for five years and I think he was right to sell a house that brought him nothing.'

'What was your former master's name?' Monte Cristo asked.

'The Marquis de Saint-Méran. He didn't sell the house for what it cost him, I'll be bound.'

'The Marquis de Saint-Méran!' Monte Cristo repeated. 'Now, I feel sure I know that name: Marquis de Saint-Méran . . .' He appeared to be searching his memory.

'An old gentleman,' the concierge went on. 'A loyal subject of the Bourbons. He had an only daughter whom he married to Monsieur de Villefort, who was the king's prosecutor in Nîmes and later in Versailles.'

Monte Cristo glanced at Bertuccio, to find him whiter than the wall against which he had leant to prevent himself falling.

'And the daughter died, didn't she?' Monte Cristo asked. 'I thought I heard something of the sort.'

'Yes, Monsieur, twenty-one years ago, since when we have not seen the poor dear Marquis more than three times.'

'Thank you, thank you,' said Monte Cristo, judging from his steward's prostrate appearance that he could not stretch that cord any tighter without breaking it. 'Thank you, my good man. Give us some light.'

'Does Monsieur want me to come with him?'

'Don't bother, Bertuccio will light my way.'

Monte Cristo accompanied these words with the gift of two gold pieces, which gave rise to an explosion of blessings and sighs.

'Oh, Monsieur!' said the concierge, after looking in vain on the mantelpiece and the surrounds. 'I'm afraid I have no candles here.'

'Take one of the lanterns from the carriage, Bertuccio, and show me the house,' said the count.

The steward obeyed without a murmur but it was easy to see, from the trembling of the hand which held the lantern, how much it cost him to obey.

They entered a large ground floor consisting of a drawing-room, a bathroom and two bedrooms. Through one of the bedrooms you could reach a spiral staircase which led down to the garden.

'Ah, here's a stairway to the outside,' said the count. 'How convenient. Give me some light, Monsieur Bertuccio; lead the way and let's see where this staircase will take us.'

'Monsieur,' said Bertuccio, 'it goes to the garden.'

'How do you know that, if you please?'

'I mean, that is where it must go.'

'Very well. Let's find out.'

Bertuccio sighed and led the way. The staircase did, indeed, take them into the garden. The steward stopped at the outer door.

'Carry on, Monsieur Bertuccio!' said the count.

But the man to whom this injunction was addressed was dumbstruck, stupefied, crushed. His haggard eyes searched around him as if hunting for the traces of some awful event, and his clenched fists seemed to be warding off some frightful memory from the past.

'Well?' the count insisted.

'No, no!' Bertuccio cried, reaching out to the inside wall. 'No, Monsieur, I will go no further. I cannot!'

'What does this mean?' Monte Cristo's implacable voice demanded.

'But, Monsieur, surely you can understand,' cried the steward. 'It isn't natural! It's not natural that, when you are to buy a house in Paris, you should choose to buy one in Auteuil, and that the one you buy in Auteuil should be number twenty-eight, Rue de la Fontaine! Oh, why didn't I tell you everything before we set out, Sire. You would surely not have insisted that I come. I hoped that Monsieur le Comte's house would be any house other than this one. As if there was no house in Auteuil, except the house of the murder!'

'Ah, now!' Monte Cristo said, stopping short. 'That is an ugly word you have just spoken. By all the devils! Irredeemable Corsican – full of mystery and superstition! Come now, take the lantern and let's have a look at the garden. You will not be afraid while you are with me, I hope.'

Bertuccio obediently picked up the lantern.

When they opened the door, it was to reveal a wan sky in which the moon struggled in vain to hold its own against a sea of clouds which poured dark waves across it, waves which it lit for a moment before they raced on, still darker than before, to lose themselves in the depths of infinity.

The steward tried to make off towards the left.

'No, no, Monsieur,' said Monte Cristo. 'What is the point of following the paths? We have a fine lawn here: let's go straight ahead.'

Bertuccio wiped the sweat from his brow, but he obeyed, while still veering towards the left. Monte Cristo, on the contrary, made for the right. Reaching a group of trees, he stopped. The steward could contain himself no longer.

'Come away, Monsieur,' he cried. 'Come away, I beg you. You are on the very spot!'

'What spot is that?'

'The spot where he fell.'

'My dear Monsieur Bertuccio,' said Monte Cristo, laughing, 'take a hold of yourself, I pray you. We are not in Sartène or Corte. This is not your Corsican bush, but a garden, in the English fashion, poorly enough kept, I grant you, but not to be insulted for all that.'

'Monsieur, don't stay there! I beg you, don't stay there!'

'I think you are going mad, Monsieur Bertuccio,' the count said coldly. 'If that is the case, please inform me and I shall have you confined to some lunatic asylum before any harm is done.'

'Alas, Excellency,' said Bertuccio, shaking his head and clasping his hands in an attitude that would have made the count laugh if he had not been seized by more urgent thoughts at that moment, which made him acutely responsive to the slightest movement of that timorous soul. 'Alas, Excellency! The harm is already done.'

'Monsieur Bertuccio,' the count said. 'I am pleased to tell you that, amid your gesticulations, you are twisting your arms and rolling your eyes like a man possessed of a devil which is unwilling to depart from his body. Now I have always observed that the devil which is least inclined to leave its post is a secret. I knew you to be a Corsican, I knew you to be sombre and I knew that you were always mulling over some old tale of a vendetta; and in Italy I forgave you that, because in Italy such things are acceptable. However, in France people usually consider murder to be in very poor taste: there are gendarmes to look after it, judges to condemn it and scaffolds to avenge it.'

Bertuccio clasped his hands – and since, while he was performing these various movements, he kept hold of the lantern, the light fell on his stricken face. Monte Cristo examined it with the same eye as he had turned, in Rome, on the execution of Andrea. Then, in a voice that sent a new shudder through the whole of the steward's frame, he said: 'So Abbé Busoni lied to me, then, after his journey to France in 1829, when he sent you to me with a letter of recommendation in which he assured me of your exceptional qualities. Well, I must write to the abbé. I hold him responsible for his protégé and he will no doubt tell me what all this business of murder is about. One thing, however, Monsieur Bertuccio: I warn you that when I visit a country, I am accustomed to conform with its laws and I have no wish to become embroiled with French justice for your sake.'

'Oh, don't do that, Excellency. I have served you well, have I not?' Bertuccio cried out in despair. 'I have always been a good man and I have even, as far as I was able, done good deeds.'

'I don't deny it,' said the count. 'So why the devil are you so agitated? It is a bad sign: a clear conscience does not put so much pallor on a man's cheeks or so much fever in his hands.'

'But, Monsieur le Comte,' Bertuccio said, hesitantly, 'did you not tell me yourself that Abbé Busoni, who heard my confession in prison at Nîmes, warned you, when he sent me to you, that I had a grave sin on my conscience?'

'Yes, but since he sent you to me, telling me that you would make an excellent steward, I just supposed that you must have stolen something!'

'Monsieur le Comte!' said Bertuccio, with contempt.

'Or that, being a Corsican, you had been unable to resist the temptation to "make your bones", as they say there – by antiphrasis, when, on the contrary, they unmake some.'

'Yes, Monseigneur! Yes, my good master, that's it!' Bertuccio cried, throwing himself at the count's knees. 'Yes, it was a vendetta, I swear it, a simple act of revenge.'

'I understand. What I do not understand, however, is why this house in particular should have such an effect on you.'

'But, Sire, it's natural,' Bertuccio went on, 'since it was in this house that the revenge was carried out.'

'What! In my house!'

'Well, Sire, it was not yet yours at the time,' Bertuccio replied naïvely.

'Whose was it then? I believe the concierge said it belonged to Monsieur le Marquis de Saint-Méran; so what on earth grudge could you have against the Marquis de Saint-Méran?'

'Not against him, Sire – against someone else.'

'This is an odd coincidence,' Monte Cristo said, as if giving way to his own thoughts, 'that you should find yourself like this, by chance, with no prior knowledge, in a house which was the scene of an event that causes you such terrible remorse.'

'Sire,' said the steward, 'I am sure that Fate is responsible for all this. First of all, you buy a house in Auteuil, and nowhere else, and this house is the one where I committed a murder; then you entered the garden by the very staircase that he came down; you paused at the very spot where he fell. Two steps away, under that plane-tree, was the hole where he had just buried the child. All this is not chance because, if it were, then chance would be too much like Providence.'

'Come now, come now, my Corsican friend, just imagine it was Providence – I always imagine what people ask me to; and in any case, one must make some allowance for a sick mind. So gather your wits and tell me all about it.'

'I have only told the story once, and that was to Abbé Busoni,' Bertuccio said, adding: 'Such things can only be told under the seal of the confessional.'

'In which case, my dear Bertuccio,' said the count, 'you won't mind if I send you back to your confessor. You will become a Carthusian or a Benedictine, and chat about your secrets. However, it makes me anxious, having a guest who is terrified by such ghosts. I don't like it when my people dare not walk around my garden at night. Then, I must admit to you, I should not be delighted by a visit from some police commissioner, because – mark this well, Monsieur Bertuccio – in Italy one only pays justice to keep quiet, while in France, on the contrary, one pays it when it speaks. Damn! I did think you a bit of a Corsican, a good deal of a smuggler and a very able steward, but I see that you have other strings to your bow. You are no longer one of my men, Monsieur Bertuccio.'

'Oh, Monseigneur! Monseigneur!' the steward cried, stricken with terror at this threat. 'If that is the only thing that prevents me from remaining in your service, I shall speak. I shall tell all. Then, if I leave you, it will be to walk to the scaffold.'

'That's a different matter,' said Monte Cristo. 'But if you are thinking of lying to me, consider this: it would be better for you to say nothing at all.'

'No, Monsieur, I swear on my immortal soul, I shall tell you everything! Even Abbé Busoni only knew part of my secret. But first, I pray you, let us come away from this place. Why, the moon is about to come out from behind that cloud – and there, standing as you are, wrapped in that cloak which hides your figure from me and looks like Monsieur de Villefort's . . . !'

'What!' Monte Cristo exclaimed. 'Is it Monsieur de Villefort . . . ?'

'Does Your Excellency know him?'

'The former royal prosecutor in Nîmes?'

'Yes.'

'Who married the daughter of the Marquis de Saint-Méran?'

'Yes.'

'And whose reputation at the Bar was that of the most honest, the strictest and the most inflexible judge?'

'Well, Monsieur!' Bertuccio cried. 'That man, with his unblemished reputation . . .'

'Yes?'

'He is a villain!'

'Pah!' said Monte Cristo. 'Impossible.'

'Yet it is true.'

'Really?' said Monte Cristo. 'Do you have proof of this?'

'I did have it.'

'And you have lost it, you oaf?'

'Yes; but if we look carefully, we can find it.'

'Can we indeed?' said the count. 'Well then, tell me about it, Monsieur Bertuccio, because I am starting to become seriously interested in what you say.' And the count, humming a little tune from *Lucia*, went and sat on a bench, while Bertuccio followed, collecting his memories and his thoughts. He remained standing in front of the count.

XLIV

THE VENDETTA

'Where would Monsieur le Comte like me to begin?' Bertuccio asked.

'Wherever you wish,' Monte Cristo replied, 'because I know nothing.'

'But I thought that Abbé Busoni had told Your Excellency . . .'

'Yes, a few facts, perhaps, but that was seven or eight years ago and I have forgotten.'

'So, not wishing to bore Your Excellency, I can safely . . .'

'Come on, Monsieur Bertuccio, come: you will be my evening newspaper.'

'It all goes back to 1815.'

'Ah!' Monte Cristo exclaimed. 'A long time ago, 1815!'

'Indeed, Monsieur. However, the smallest detail has remained in my memory as clearly as if it happened yesterday. I had a brother, an elder brother, who served the emperor. He had risen to the rank of lieutenant in a regiment entirely composed of Corsicans. My brother was my only friend; we had been left orphans when I was five and he was eighteen, and he brought me up as though I were his son. In 1814, under the Bourbons, he got married. Then the emperor came back from Elba, my brother immediately returned to the army and, after sustaining a slight wound at Waterloo, he retreated with the army beyond the Loire.'

'You are telling me the whole history of the Hundred Days,[1] Monsieur Bertuccio,' the count said. 'It's all over and done with, if I'm not mistaken.'

'Excellency, pray forgive me, but these preliminary details are essential. You promised to be patient.'

'Very well. I did agree.'

'One day we received a letter. I have to tell you that we lived in the little village of Rogliano, at the far end of Cap Corse. The letter was from my brother and informed us that the army had been disbanded and he was returning home, via Châteauroux, Clermont-Ferrand, Le Puy and Nîmes. If I had any money, he begged me to leave it for him in Nîmes, with an innkeeper who was an acquaintance of ours and with whom I had had some dealings . . .'

'By way of contraband . . .'

'For heaven's sake, Monsieur le Comte, one must live.'

'Undoubtedly. Carry on.'

'As I told you, Excellency, I loved my brother dearly, so I decided not to send him the money but to take it myself. I had a thousand francs, so I left five hundred for Assunta – that is, my sister-in-law – and, with the other five hundred, I set off for Nîmes. It was easy. I had a boat and a cargo to pick up on the way, so everything favoured my design. But once I had taken on the cargo, the wind changed and we had to wait for four or five days before we could pass the mouth of the Rhône. Finally, we succeeded in entering the river, and sailed up as far as Arles. I left the boat between Bellegarde and Beaucaire, and set off on the road for Nîmes.'

'We shall get there eventually, I suppose?'

'Yes, sir. Forgive me, but as Your Excellency will appreciate, I am only telling him what is absolutely essential. This was the moment when the celebrated massacres took place in the south. There were two or three brigands called Trestaillon, Truphemy and Graffan who went around cutting the throats of anyone suspected of Bonapartism. Monsieur le Comte has doubtless heard about these killings?'

'Vaguely. I was a long way from France at the time. Go on.'

'When you entered Nîmes, you literally walked in blood; there were bodies lying everywhere. The murderers were organized in gangs to kill, loot and burn.

'When I saw the carnage, I was filled with fear, not for myself: being a simple Corsican fisherman, I had little to fear. On the contrary, that was a fine time for us smugglers; but I was concerned for my brother, a soldier of the empire, returning from the Army of the Loire with his uniform and his epaulettes. He had every reason to feel afraid.

'I hastened to the inn. My foreboding was correct: my brother had arrived in Nîmes the day before and, at the very door of the man from whom he had come to beg hospitality, he had been murdered.

'I made every effort to identify his assassins, but they inspired such fear that no one dared tell me their names. Then I remembered French justice, which I had heard so much about and which was reputed to fear nothing, so I went to the king's prosecutor.'

'Whose name was Villefort?' Monte Cristo asked casually.

'Yes, Excellency. He came from Marseille, where he had been a deputy prosecutor and was promoted as a reward for his dedication. It was said that he had been among the first to warn the government of Napoleon's landing on his return from Elba.'

'So you went to see him,' said Monte Cristo.

'"Monsieur," I told him, "my brother was murdered yesterday in the streets of Nîmes, I don't know by whom, but it is your responsibility to find out. You administer a law that should avenge those it has been unable to protect."

'"Who was your brother?" the prosecutor asked me.

'"A lieutenant in the Corsican battalion."

'"So he was a soldier in the usurper's army, was he?"

'"He was a soldier in the French army."

'"Very well," he replied. "He lived by the sword and he died by the sword."

'"You are wrong, Monsieur. He lived by the sword, but he died by the dagger."

'"And what do you expect me to do about it?" the magistrate asked.

' "I have told you: I want his revenge."

' "On whom?"

' "On his murderers."

' "How do I know who they are?"

' "Have them found."

' "For what purpose? Your brother must have fallen out with someone and got into a fight. All those old soldiers are inclined to intemperance: it worked well enough for them in the days of the empire, but that kind of thing is not appropriate now. Our southerners don't like soldiers and they don't like unruly behaviour."

' "Monsieur," I said, "I am not asking this for myself. If it were just up to me, I should weep or I should take my revenge, nothing more. But my poor brother had a wife. If anything were to happen to me, the poor woman would die of starvation, because it was only my brother's work that kept her. Let her have a small government pension."

' "There are disasters in every revolution," Monsieur de Villefort replied. "Your brother was a victim of this one. It's unfortunate, but it doesn't mean that the government owes your family anything. If we were to try all the cases of reprisals that the supporters of the usurper carried out on those of the king when they were in power, then it could well be that your brother would be condemned to death. What happened was entirely natural, it's the law of retaliation."

' "What, Monsieur!" I exclaimed. "I cannot believe that you, a magistrate, are saying this!"

' "On my word, all these Corsicans are mad!" Monsieur de Villefort replied. "And they still think that their fellow-countryman is emperor. You have missed the boat, my dear fellow. You should have come to me about this two months ago. Now is too late, so be off with you. If you don't leave, I'll have you thrown out."

'I looked at him for a moment to see if there was anything to be gained by begging him further. The man was like granite. I went over to him, and said under my breath: "Well, then, since you know Corsicans, you must know that they keep their word. Because you are a Royalist, you think that it was a good thing to kill my brother, a Bonapartist. Well, I too am a Bonapartist, and let me tell you something: I shall kill you. From this moment on, I declare a vendetta against you, so look after and protect yourself as best you

may, because the next time we are face to face, your last hour will
have come." And, with that, before he could recover from his
surprise, I opened the door and fled.'

'Well, I'll be darned!' said Monte Cristo. 'You, Monsieur Bertuccio, with that honest face of yours! You, do something like that!
And to the crown prosecutor, what's more! Shame on you! I hope
he at least understood the meaning of the word "vendetta"?'

'He understood it well enough to avoid going out alone from
that time onwards, and to hole up in his house, while getting his
people to look everywhere for me. Luckily I was too well hidden
for them to find me. So then he took fright. He was afraid to stay
any longer in Nîmes and asked to be moved. Since he was a person
with influence, he was appointed to Versailles. However, as you
know, no distance is too great for a Corsican when he has sworn
revenge on his enemy, and his carriage, swift as it was, could never
keep more than half a day's journey ahead of me, even though I
was following on foot.

'The main thing was not to kill him; I had a hundred opportunities
to do that: I had to kill him without being identified and, above all,
without being caught. From then on I was no longer my own man:
I had to protect and support my sister-in-law. I stalked Monsieur
de Villefort for three months, and for three months he did not take
a step, go for a walk or take a stroll without my watching where he
went. Finally I discovered that he was paying mysterious visits to
Auteuil. I followed him and saw him enter the house where we are
now; but instead of going in like everyone else through the main
door on the street, he arrived, either on horseback or by carriage,
left his horse or his carriage at the inn and entered the house by the
little door that you see there.'

Monte Cristo nodded to show that, despite the darkness, he could
indeed see the entrance towards which Bertuccio was pointing.

'I had nothing further to do in Versailles, so I settled in Auteuil
and made enquiries. If I was to take him, this was clearly the place
to set my trap.

'As the concierge told Your Excellency, the house belonged to
Villefort's father-in-law, Monsieur de Saint-Méran. He resided in
Marseille, so this property was of no use to him. It was said,
moreover, that he had just let it to a young widow known only as
"the baroness".

'One evening, looking over the wall, I did indeed see a beautiful young woman walking alone in this garden, which was overlooked by no window in any other house. She kept looking towards the little door and I understood that she was waiting for Monsieur de Villefort. When she was close enough for me to make out her features, despite the darkness, I saw a lovely young woman of eighteen or nineteen, tall and fair-haired. As she was dressed in a simple gown, with no belt around her waist, I could see that she was with child, and even quite far advanced in her pregnancy.

'A few moments later the little door opened and a man came in. The young woman ran to him as fast as she could. They threw themselves into each other's arms, kissed tenderly and both turned to look at the house.

'The man was Monsieur de Villefort. I guessed that, when he came out, especially if he came out at night, he would probably walk the whole length of the garden alone.'

'Since then,' asked the count, 'have you learned the name of the woman?'

'No, Excellency,' Bertuccio replied. 'As you will discover, I did not have time to find out.'

'Carry on.'

'That evening,' Bertuccio resumed, 'I might perhaps have been able to kill the crown prosecutor, but I still did not know every nook and cranny in the garden. I was afraid that if I did not kill him stone dead, and if someone ran up in answer to his cries, I might not be able to escape. I put the deed off until the next meeting and, so that no detail would escape me, took a little room overlooking the street that ran beside the wall of the garden.

'Three days later, at around seven o'clock in the evening, I saw a servant riding out of the house and galloping along the pathway leading to the Sèvres road. I assumed he was going to Versailles, and correctly so. Three hours later, the man returned, covered in dust. His message had been delivered.

'Ten minutes later, another man, this time on foot and wrapped in a cloak, opened the little door to the garden, which shut behind him.

'I quickly went down. Though I had not seen Villefort's face, I recognized him by the beating of my heart. I crossed the street and went up to a milestone at one corner of the wall, on which I had stood in order to look into the garden for the first time.

'This time I was not satisfied merely to look. I drew my knife out of my pocket, made sure that the point was sharp, and leapt over the wall. My first thought was to run across to the gate. He had left the key, taking the simple precaution of turning it twice in the lock. So, nothing impeded my flight in that direction. I began to study the place. The garden formed a long rectangle with a lawn of fine English grass running down the middle, at the corners of which were clumps of trees, bushy and mingled with autumn flowers.

'To go from the house to the little gate or from the little gate to the house, according to whether he was coming in or going out, Monsieur de Villefort was obliged to pass beside one of these clumps of trees.

'It was towards the end of September. There was a strong wind blowing and a few pale shafts of moonlight, repeatedly hidden by large clouds racing across the sky, lit the sandy pathways leading to the house, but were too feeble to penetrate the tufts of foliage among the trees, where a man could hide with no fear of discovery.

'I concealed myself in the nearest of those that Villefort had to pass. No sooner had I taken up my position than I thought I heard, between the gusts of wind that bent the trees across my face, some kind of groaning. But as you know, Monsieur le Comte – or, rather, you surely don't know – the person who is poised to commit a murder always thinks he can hear muffled cries in the air. Two hours passed, and several times during them I thought I heard these same groans.

'Midnight struck. The last lugubrious, echoing note was still sounding when I saw a light in the windows looking out from the back stairway which we have just come down.

'The door opened and the man with the cloak reappeared. This was the fatal moment, but I had so long prepared myself for it that I shrank at nothing. I took out my dagger, opened it and waited.

'The man in the cloak came directly towards me, but as he approached across the opened ground I thought that I could discern a weapon in his right hand. I was afraid, not of a struggle, but of failure. When he was just a few yards away from me, I realized that what I had thought was a weapon was nothing more than a spade.

'I had still not managed to guess why Monsieur de Villefort

should be carrying a spade, when he stopped at the edge of the clump of trees and started to dig a hole in the ground. At this point I noticed that he had something wrapped in his cloak which he had put down on the lawn, so as to leave his hands free.

'Now, I must confess, my hatred was tempered by a dash of curiosity. I wanted to see what Villefort was doing there, so I stayed motionless, holding my breath, and waited.

'Then something occurred to me which was confirmed by the crown prosecutor taking a little box out of his cloak, about two feet long and six or eight inches wide.

'I let him place the box in the hole and cover it with earth; then he stamped on this freshly dug soil to cover the traces of his night's work. At that, I leapt out at him and plunged my dagger into his breast, saying: "I am Giovanni Bertuccio! Your death is for my brother, your treasure for his widow: you can see that my revenge is more perfect than I could have hoped."

'I do not know if he heard me. I think not, because he fell without a sound. I felt his hot blood flowing out over my hands and spattering my face; but I was drunk, I was delirious: the blood refreshed me instead of burning. It took me a second to dig up the box with the spade. Then, to disguise the fact that it had gone, I filled the hole in again and threw the spade over the wall. I ran out of the gate, turning the key twice in the door from outside and taking it with me.'

'Fine!' said Monte Cristo. 'It seems you committed a modest little murder, combined with robbery.'

'No, Excellency,' Bertuccio replied. 'It was a vendetta, combined with reparation.'

'It was a decent sum, at least?'

'There was no money.'

'Ah, yes. I remember. You said something about a child?'

'Precisely, Excellency. I hurried down to the river, sat on the bank and, eager to know what was in the box, broke the lock with my knife.

'A newborn baby was wrapped in a child's fine cambric robe. The purple colour of its face and hands showed that it must have succumbed to asphyxiation caused by the umbilical cord wrapped around the neck. However, as it was not yet cold, I felt uneasy about throwing it into the stream by my feet. Then, a moment later, I thought I could feel a faint fluttering near the heart. I unwrapped the cord and, as I used to be an orderly at a hospital in Bastia, I did what a doctor might have done in the circumstances: in other words, I energetically breathed air into its lungs and, after a quarter of an hour of considerable effort, I saw it start to breathe and heard it give a cry.

'I also cried out, but with joy. God had not cursed me, I thought, since he has allowed me to give life back to one human being in exchange for the life that I had taken away from another.'

'So what did you do with this child?' Monte Cristo asked. 'It was quite a tiresome burden for a man who had to escape.'

'That is why I never once considered keeping it. But I knew that there was an orphanage in Paris where they took in such poor creatures. On arriving at the city gates, I claimed to have found the child on the road and asked directions. I had the box, which supported my story, and the cambric linen showed that the child belonged to rich parents. The blood which covered me could as well have come from it as from anyone else. No one protested. I was shown the way to the orphanage, which was at the far end of the Rue d'Enfer and, after taking the precaution of cutting the sheet in half, so that a piece with one of the two letters embroidered on it was still wrapped around the child, I put my bundle down at the gatehouse, rang the bell and fled as fast as I could. A fortnight later I was back in Rogliano and I told Assunta: "Sister, dry your tears. Israel is dead, but I have avenged him." She asked me to explain this, and I told her everything that had happened.

'"Giovanni," she said, "you should have brought the child back. We could have taken the place of its lost parents and we should have called it Benedetto. God would surely have blessed us as a reward for our good deed."

'In reply, I simply gave her the half of the sheet that I had kept, so that I could reclaim the child if we could ever afford it.'

'What letters were on the cloth?' Monte Cristo asked.

'H and N, surmounted by the ordinary of a baron, tortily.'

'I do believe, heaven help us, that you are using terms from heraldry, Monsieur Bertuccio! Where the devil did you study that science?'

'In your service, Monsieur le Comte, where one may learn everything.'

'Carry on. I am curious to know two things.'

'What are they, Monseigneur?'

'What happened to the little boy . . . You did say that it was a little boy, Monsieur Bertuccio?'

'No, Excellency, I do not remember saying that.'

'Ah, I thought you did. I must have been mistaken.'

'Well, you are not mistaken, because it was indeed a little boy. But Your Excellency said that he wished to know two things: what is the other one?'

'The other one is what crime you were accused of when you asked for a confessor, and Abbé Busoni came to you in the prison at Nîmes in response to this request.'

'The tale might be quite long, Excellency.'

'What matter? It is barely ten o'clock. You know that I am an insomniac, and I suppose you too must have little desire for sleep.'

Bertuccio bowed and carried on with his story.

'Partly to drive away the memories that plagued me and partly to provide for the poor widow, I returned eagerly to the profession of smuggling which had been made easier by the relaxation of laws that always follows a revolution. The southern coasts of France, in particular, were badly guarded because of the unending riots that took place, sometimes in Avignon, sometimes in Nîmes, sometimes in Uzès. We took advantage of the sort of truce accorded us by the government to establish relations on all parts of the coastline. Since my brother's murder in the streets of Nîmes, I had been loath to return there; the outcome was that the innkeeper with whom we used to deal, seeing that we no longer came to him, had decided to come to us and set up a companion to his inn on the road from Bellegarde to Beaucaire, at the sign of the Pont du Gard. Near Aigues-Mortes, in Martigues or in Bouc we also had a dozen warehouses where we could deposit our goods and where, if the need arose, we could hide out from the Customs and the gendarmes. Smuggling is a trade that pays well when carried on with a measure of intelligence and some zeal. As for myself, I lived in the mountains, because I now had a double reason to fear the gendarmes and the Customs men, in view of the fact that my arraignment in front of a judge could lead to an enquiry, and every enquiry is an excursion into the past: in my past, now, they might come across something more serious than smuggled cigars or a few barrels of brandy being dispatched without the proper papers. So, preferring death a thousand times to arrest, I accomplished astonishing feats which, more than once, proved to me that our excessive concern with the welfare of our bodies is almost the only obstacle to the success of any of our plans, when these demand rapid decisions and vigorous and determined execution. In reality, once you have made the sacrifice of your life, you are no longer the equal of other men; or, rather, they are no longer your equal, because whoever has taken such a resolution instantly feels his strength increase ten times and his outlook vastly extended.'

'Philosophy, too, Monsieur Bertuccio!' the count interrupted. 'Have you then done a little bit of everything in your life?'

'I beg Your Excellency's pardon.'

'No, no! It's just that ten thirty at night is a little late for philosophy. But I have no other objection, particularly since I agree with your views, which cannot be said of all philosophy.'

'My trips became more and more prolonged, more and more profitable. Assunta was a good housewife and our little fortune grew. One day, when I was setting off on business, she said: "Go, and you will have a surprise when you return." There was nothing to be gained by questioning her; she refused to tell me anything, so I left.

'The trip lasted nearly six weeks. We went to Lucca to take on oil and to Leghorn to load some English cotton cloth. We unloaded it all without any unpleasant incidents, took our profits and came back home, very pleased with ourselves.

'When I entered the house, the first thing I saw, in the place where it was least likely to be missed in Assunta's room, was a child of seven or eight months, in a cot far more luxurious than the furnishings around it. I gave a cry of joy. The only moments of sadness that I had felt since the murder of the crown prosecutor were due to my abandonment of the child. It goes without saying that I suffered no remorse for the murder itself.

'Poor Assunta had guessed everything. She had taken advantage of my absence and, taking the half of the sheet with her, had written down the exact day and time when the child was left in the orphanage, so that she would not forget them. Then she set off for Paris and went herself to reclaim him. No obstacle was put in her way, and the child was entrusted to her.

'Oh, Monsieur le Comte, I have to admit that when I saw the poor little creature in his cot, my heart filled and tears poured from my eyes.

' "Assunta," I cried, "you are without doubt a worthy woman and Providence will bless you." '

'Now that,' said the count, 'is less true than your philosophy. But, then, it's only faith, after all.'

'Alas! Excellency, how right you are!' Bertuccio continued. 'It was the child himself that God appointed to punish me. Never did a more perverse character become evident earlier in life, yet no one can say that he was badly brought up, because my sister-in-law treated him like the son of a prince. He was a handsome boy, with light-blue eyes, like the colour in Chinese porcelain that harmonizes so well with the milky whiteness of the background; but his strawberry-blond hair, which was excessively bright, gave a strange appearance to his face, heightening his vivacious look and roguish smile. Unfortunately a proverb says that redheads are either all good or all bad; it was right in Benedetto's case: he was all bad from childhood on. Admittedly, his mother's sweet nature also encouraged his natural bent. My poor sister-in-law would travel four or five leagues to the town market to buy the earliest fruit and the finest sweetmeats, while the child disdained Palma oranges or Genoese preserves, preferring the chestnuts that he could steal from the neighbours by climbing over the hedge or the apples that were drying out in their loft – when he had all the chestnuts and apples he wanted in our own orchard.

'One day, when Benedetto was about five or six years old, our neighbour Wasilio, who, like all Corsicans, never locked up his purse or his jewellery, because (as Monsieur le Comte knows better than anyone) there are no thieves in Corsica – our neighbour Wasilio complained to us that a gold *louis* had vanished from his purse. We thought he had miscalculated, but he insisted that he was sure of what he said. That day, Benedetto had left the house early in the morning and we were very worried by the time he returned that evening, leading a monkey, which he said he had found chained to the trunk of a tree.

'For the past month, the wicked child, who could not think what to do with himself, had longed for a monkey. No doubt this unfortunate whim was inspired in him by a travelling showman who had passed through Rogliano with several of these animals, whose antics had delighted the boy.

' "There are no monkeys to be found in these woods," I said, "especially not chained ones. Tell me truly how you came by it."

'Benedetto persisted in his lie, supporting it with details that said more for his imagination than for his love of the truth. I became annoyed, and he started to laugh; I threatened him and he stepped back. "You can't hit me," he said. "You have no right: you are not my father."

'We had no idea who had revealed the secret to him, despite our efforts to conceal it. However it may be, this reply, which was entirely characteristic of the child, filled me with something close to fear, and my raised hand fell without touching the guilty boy. He had triumphed and the victory made him so bold that, from then on, Assunta, whose love for him seemed to increase in proportion to his unworthiness, spent all her money on whims that she was unable to combat and follies that she did not have the strength to prevent. When I was in Rogliano, then the situation was still more or less bearable. But as soon as I left, Benedetto became master of the house and everything went wrong. When he had barely reached the age of eleven, all his friends were young men of eighteen or twenty, the worst young hooligans of Bastia and Corte; and already, because of some tricks (which deserved a worse name), the law had warned us about him.

'I was terrified. Any further unfavourable report might have serious consequences: I had shortly to go away from Corsica on an important expedition. I thought carefully and, hoping to ward off disaster, I decided to take Benedetto with me. I hoped that the rough and active life of a smuggler, and the harsh discipline on board ship, would rescue a character on the point of being corrupted, provided it had not already gone too far. So I took Benedetto aside and suggested that he accompany me, dressing the proposal up with every sort of promise that might attract a twelve-year-old boy.

'He let me continue right to the end and, when I had finished, burst out laughing. "Are you mad, uncle?" he said (that was his name for me when he was in a good mood). "Am I to exchange the life I lead for yours: my idleness for the awful toil that you have imposed on yourself! To be cold by night, hot by day and constantly in hiding – or, if you show yourself, to be shot at; and all to earn a little money! I have all the money that I want! Ma Assunta gives me some whenever I ask for it. So you can easily see that I'd be a fool to accept your proposal."

'I was dumbstruck at this shameless argument. Benedetto went back to play with his friends and I could see him, from a distance, pointing me out to them as an idiot.'

'What a delightful child!' Monte Cristo muttered.

'Oh, if he had been mine,' Bertuccio replied, 'if he had been my own son, or at least my nephew, I should soon have brought him back to the straight and narrow, because a clean conscience gives a man strength. But the idea that I would beat a child whose father I had killed made it impossible for me to punish him. I gave good advice to my sister, who always took the miserable child's side whenever we talked about him and, since she confessed to me that she had several times lost quite large sums of money, I showed her a place where she could hide our little fortune. For my part, I had made up my mind what to do. Benedetto knew very well how to read, write and do sums, because when he happened to want to work he could learn in one day what took another child a week. As I said, my mind was made up. I would sign him on as secretary on some ocean-going ship and, without giving him any advance warning, have him picked up one fine morning and carried on board. In this way, if I recommended him to the captain, he would be entirely responsible for his own future. Having taken this decision, I set off for France.

'On this occasion all our business was to take place in the Gulf of Lyon. Smuggling was becoming more and more difficult, because it was now 1829, peace had been entirely restored and consequently the coastguard was operating more regularly and more efficiently than ever. Moreover its vigilance was temporarily intensified by the fair at Beaucaire, which had just opened.

'The start of our expedition went off without a hitch. Our boat had a concealed hold to hide our contraband; we tied up alongside a large number of other boats lining both banks of the Rhône from Beaucaire to Arles. When we arrived there, we began to unload the forbidden goods at night and had them carried into town by associates of ours, or by the innkeepers whom we used to supply. It may be that success had made us careless, or else we had been betrayed, because one evening, around five o'clock, just as we were about to sit down to a light meal, our boy ran up in a state of great excitement to tell us that he had seen a squad of revenue men approaching. What worried us was not the patrol itself – because whole companies of Customs officials would scour the banks of the Rhône, and especially at that time – but the precautions that the boy told us they were taking not to be seen. We instantly leapt up, but it was already too late: our boat, which had clearly been the object of their investigation, was surrounded. Among the Customs men I noticed some gendarmes. Now the sight of these frightened me as much as that of any other militiamen would make me bold, so I went down into the hold and, slipping out through one of the hatches, I let myself slide into the river, then swam underwater, holding my breath for long periods, and escaped detection until I reached a small ditch that had just been dug, joining the Rhône to the canal that runs from Beaucaire to Aigues-Mortes. Once there, I was safe, because I could go down the ditch without being seen. In this way, I reached the canal without incident. I had chosen this route of escape deliberately: I think I told Your Excellency about an innkeeper in Nîmes who had set up a little hostelry on the Beaucaire to Bellgarde road.'

'Yes, you did,' said Monte Cristo. 'I remember it perfectly. If I am not mistaken, this worthy man was your associate.'

'Yes,' Bertuccio replied, 'but seven or eight years before, he had relinquished his business to a tailor from Marseille who had gone bankrupt in his own trade and wished to try his luck at another. It goes without saying that the little arrangement we had with the first owner was continued with the second, so this was the man from whom I intended to ask for shelter.'

'What was his name?' the count asked, apparently taking a renewed interest in Bertuccio's tale.

'He was called Gaspard Caderousse, and he was married to a woman from the village of Carconte whom we never knew except by the name of her village; she was a poor creature, stricken with malaria and languishing. As for the man, he was a sturdy fellow of forty or forty-five; more than once he had given us proof of his presence of mind and his courage in difficult circumstances.'

'And you were saying that all this took place in the year . . .'

'1829, Monsieur le Comte.'

'What month?'

'In June.'

'At the beginning or the end of the month?'

'On the evening of the third.'

'Ah,' Monte Cristo said. 'June the third, 1829. Very well, go on.'

'So I was hoping to ask for shelter from Caderousse. Usually, even in normal circumstances, we did not enter his house by the front door and I decided to follow our established procedure, so I climbed over the garden hedge, crawled past the stunted olive-trees and wild figs and, fearing that Caderousse had some traveller in his inn, I made my way to a kind of hutch in which I had more than once spent the night as comfortably as in the best bed. This hutch or cupboard was only separated from the main parlour on the ground floor of the inn by a wooden wall, in which holes had been drilled for us, so that we could wait there until the time was ripe for us to reveal our presence. If Caderousse was alone, I intended to announce my arrival to him, finish at this table the meal that had been interrupted by the arrival of the Customs men and take advantage of the coming storm to return to the banks of the Rhône and find out what had become of the ship and those on board. So I slipped into the hutch – and it was as well that I did so, because at that very moment Caderousse was returning home with a stranger.

'I kept quiet and waited, not because I wanted to discover my host's secrets, but because I had no alternative. In any case, the situation had already arisen a dozen times before.

'The man with Caderousse was obviously not a native of the south of France: he was one of those fairground tradesmen who come to sell jewellery at the fair in Beaucaire and who, for the month that it lasts, attracting merchants and buyers from all over Europe, sometimes do a hundred or a hundred and fifty thousand francs' worth of business.

'Caderousse hurried in, leading the way. Then, when he saw the downstairs room empty as usual and watched over only by his dog, he called his wife: "Hey, La Carconte!" he said. "The good priest didn't deceive us. The diamond was real."

'There was a shout of joy and almost at once the staircase began to creak under footsteps made heavier by weakness and ill-health. "What did you say?" the woman asked, paler than death.

' "I said that the diamond was real and that this gentleman, one of the leading jewellers in Paris, is prepared to give us fifty thousand francs for it. However, to ensure that the diamond is truly ours, he wants you to tell him, as I did, the miraculous way in which the diamond came into our hands. Meanwhile, Monsieur, please be seated and, as the weather is close, I shall go and find you something to refresh yourself."

'The jeweller looked carefully round the interior of the inn, examining the obvious poverty of this couple who were about to sell him a diamond that might have belonged to a prince.

' "Tell me about it, Madame," he said, no doubt wanting to take advantage of the husband's absence to ensure that the two accounts coincided and avoid Caderousse prompting her in any way.

' "Well, you wouldn't believe it," the woman gushed. "It was a blessing from on high, when we least expected one. To start with, I must tell you, my dear sir, that in 1814 or 1815 my husband was friendly with a sailor called Edmond Dantès. This poor lad, whom Caderousse had entirely forgotten, did not forget him and on his deathbed left him the diamond that you have just seen."

' "But how did he come into possession of the diamond?" the jeweller asked. "Did he have it before going to prison?"

' "No, Monsieur," the woman replied. "But it appears that while in prison he became acquainted with a very rich Englishman; and when his cellmate fell ill, Dantès took the same care of him as if he had been his brother, so the Englishman, on his release, left this diamond to poor Dantès, who was less fortunate than he was and who died in prison, bequeathing it in turn to us as he died and entrusting it to the good priest who came to give it to us this morning."

' "The accounts agree," the jeweller muttered. "And, when all's said and done, the story may be true, however implausible it may seem. Now all that remains is to agree about the price."

' "What do you mean, agree?" said Caderousse. "I thought you had accepted the price I asked."

' "You mean, I offered you forty thousand francs," said the jeweller.

' "Forty thousand!" exclaimed La Carconte. "We certainly can't let it go at that price. The abbé told us it was worth fifty thousand, even without the setting."

' "What was this abbé's name?" the tireless questioner asked.

' "Abbé Busoni," she replied.

' "A foreigner then?"

' "An Italian from near Mantua, I think."

' "Show me the diamond," the jeweller said. "I'd like to examine it again. One often estimates a jewel wrongly at first sight."

'Caderousse got a little bag of black shagreen out of his pocket, opened it and passed it to the jeweller. At the sight of the diamond, which was as fat as a small walnut – I remember it as well as if I could still see it – La Carconte's eyes shone with greed.'

'And what did you think of all that, eavesdropper?' Monte Cristo asked. 'Did you believe the fine tale?'

'Yes, Excellency. I did not consider Caderousse a wicked man. I felt he was incapable of committing a crime, or even pilfering.'

'That does more honour to your heart than to your experience, Monsieur Bertuccio. Did you know the Edmond Dantès they mentioned?'

'No, Excellency. I had never before heard his name and I have never heard it mentioned since, except once by Abbé Busoni himself when I saw him in prison in Nîmes.'

'Very well. Continue.'

'The jeweller took the ring from Caderousse and brought a little pair of steel pliers and a little copper balance out of his pocket. Then, removing the stone from the gold clamps that held it in the ring, he lifted the diamond from the bezel and weighed it with the utmost care in the scale.

' "I can go to forty-five thousand francs," he said, "but not a *sou* more. In any case, since that was the value of the diamond, that is all the money I have brought with me."

' "Oh, don't worry about that," said Caderousse. "I'll come back to Beaucaire with you to fetch the other five thousand francs."

' "No," the jeweller said, returning the ring and the diamond to Caderousse. "No, it's not worth more; and I'm sorry to have offered that much, since there is a defect in the stone which I did not notice at first. However, it's too bad. I've given my word. I said forty-five thousand and I won't unsay it."

' "Well, do at least put the diamond back in the ring," said La Carconte sourly.

' "That's fair," said the jeweller, replacing the stone in its setting.

' "Very well, very well," Caderousse said, putting the bag back in his pocket. "We'll sell it to someone else."

' "Do," the jeweller said, "though he may not be as easy as I am. Someone else might not be satisfied with the explanation you gave me. It is not normal for a man like you to have a diamond of fifty thousand francs. This other person will probably inform the magistrate, Abbé Busoni will have to be found – and it's not easy to find an abbé who gives away diamonds worth two thousand *louis*! Then they would start by arresting him, they would send you to prison and, even if you were found innocent and released after three or four months inside, the ring would have been mislaid in the clerk of the court's office, or else they would give you a piece of glass worth three francs instead of a diamond worth fifty thousand, or at best fifty-five – but which, as you must admit, my good fellow, represents a risk to the buyer."

'Caderousse and his wife exchanged looks. "No," he said. "We are not rich enough to lose five thousand francs."

' "As you wish, friend," said the jeweller. "But, as you can see, I have brought the sum in cash." And he took a handful of gold from one pocket and held it, shining, before the dazzled eyes of the innkeeper, and a bundle of banknotes from the other.

'It was clear that there was a battle going on inside Caderousse: obviously the little shagreen bag which he was turning over and over in his hands did not appear to him to correspond in value to the huge sum of money which mesmerized him. He turned back to his wife.

' "What do you think?" he whispered.

' "Go on, give it to him," she said. "If he returns to Beaucaire without the diamond, he will report us! And, as he says, no one knows whether we shall ever be able to put our hands on Abbé Busoni again."

' "Very well, agreed," said Caderousse. "Take the diamond for forty-five thousand. But my wife wants a gold chain and I a pair of silver buckles."

' "The jeweller took a long flat box out of his pocket containing several examples of the required objects. "Go on," he said. "I do business fairly. Choose what you want."

'The woman chose a gold chain that was possibly worth five *louis* and her husband a pair of buckles worth around five francs.

' "I hope you're satisfied," said the jeweller.

' "The abbé said it was worth fifty thousand," Caderousse muttered.

' "Come, come, now. Give over! What a terrible creature!" the jeweller said, taking the diamond from his hands. "I am giving him forty-five thousand francs and two thousand five hundred in kind, all of which adds up to a fortune that I wouldn't mind having myself, and he still isn't satisfied."

' "And what about the forty-five thousand francs?" Caderousse demanded hoarsely. "Where are they?"

' "Here," said the jeweller, and he counted out fifteen thousand francs on the table in gold and thirty thousand in banknotes.

' "Just wait while I light the lamp," said La Carconte. "It's getting dark and we might make a mistake."

'Night had indeed fallen while they were discussing this and, with it, the storm that had been threatening for the past half-hour. In the distance you could hear the dull rolls of thunder, but neither the jeweller, nor Caderousse, nor La Carconte seemed to be bothered by it, all three being possessed by the demon of greed. Even I felt a strange fascination at the sight of all that gold and all those banknotes. It seemed to me that I was dreaming; and, as happens in dreams, I felt rooted to the spot.

'Caderousse counted and re-counted the gold and the notes, then passed them to his wife, who counted and re-counted them in her turn.

'Meanwhile the jeweller was turning the diamond in the rays of the lamp, and the diamond gleamed with flashes that outshone those, heralding the storm, that were starting to light up the window.

' "Is it all there?" the jeweller asked.

' "Yes," said Caderousse. "Give me the portfolio and look for a bag, Carconte."

'La Carconte went to a wardrobe and came back carrying an old leather portfolio, out of which they took a few greasy letters which they replaced with the notes, and a bag in which there were two or three *écus* of six *livres*, which probably represented the unfortunate couple's entire fortune.

' "There," said Caderousse. "Even though you may have under-paid us by about ten thousand francs, would you like to take supper with us? You're welcome."

' "Thank you," said the jeweller, "but it must be getting late and I have to return to Beaucaire. My wife will be worried." He took out his watch. "Heavens above!" he exclaimed. "It's nearly nine. I won't be in Beaucaire before midnight. Goodbye, my children. If any more Abbé Busonis happen to drop by, think of me."

' "In a week, you will no longer be in Beaucaire," said Caderousse. "The fair ends next week."

' "No, but that doesn't matter. Write to me in Paris: Monsieur Joannès, at the Palais-Royal, number forty-five, Galerie de Pierre. I'll come down here specially if it's worth my while."

'A peal of thunder sounded, with a bolt of lightning so bright that it almost dimmed the light from the lamp.

'"Oh, ho," said Caderousse. "Are you going out in this weather?"

'"I'm not afraid of thunder," said the jeweller.

'"Or thieves?" asked La Carconte. "The road is never quite safe when the fair's in town."

'"Huh! As far as thieves are concerned, here's my answer to them." And he took a pair of little pistols, fully loaded, out of his pocket. "These are dogs that bark and bite at the same time, and I'm keeping them for the first two men who want to get their hands on your diamond, Caderousse."

'Caderousse and his wife exchanged a dark look: they both appeared to have the same frightful idea.

'"Very well, *bon voyage*!" said Caderousse.

'"Thank you," the jeweller replied.

'He took his cane, which he had set down, leaning against an old sideboard, and went out. As soon as he opened the door, there was such a gust of wind that it almost put out the lamp.

'"Ho, ho!" he said. "Lovely weather . . . And I have two leagues to travel in it."

'"Don't go," said Caderousse. "You can sleep here."

'"Yes, stay," said La Carconte in a quivering voice. "We'll take good care of you."

'"No, I can't. I must sleep in Beaucaire. Farewell."

'Caderousse walked slowly over to the doorway.

'"You can't see an inch ahead," said the jeweller, already outside. "Should I go to the right or the left?"

'"Right," said Caderousse. "You can't miss your way. The road is lined with trees on each side."

'"Very well, I'm there," said the voice, hardly audible in the distance.

'"Shut the door," said La Carconte. "I don't like leaving the door open when there's thunder."

'"Or when there's money in the house, you mean," said Caderousse, turning the key twice in the lock.

'He came back, went over to the cupboard, took out the bag and the portfolio, and both of them started to count over their gold and their banknotes for the third time. I have never seen an expression like the one on those two faces, with the dim light of the lamp shining on their cupidity. The woman, above all, was frightful to see. Her limbs trembled feverishly, twice as much as usual, her pale face was livid and her hollow eyes blazed.

'"And why did you offer to let him sleep here?" she muttered.

'Caderousse started. "Well, of course, so that he would not need to go back to Beaucaire . . ."

'"Ah," the woman said, with an indescribable expression. "I thought it might be for some other reason."

'"Wife, wife!" Caderousse cried. "Where do you get such ideas? And, if you have them, why not keep them to yourself?"

'"No matter," La Carconte said, after a moment's silence. "You are not a man."

'"What do you mean?" asked Caderousse.

'"If you had been a man, he would not have left here."

'"Wife!"

'"Or else he would never reach Beaucaire."

'"Wife!"

'"He must follow the road, which has a bend in it, but there is a short-cut along the canal."

'"Woman, you are offending the Good Lord. Listen . . ."

'Indeed, as he spoke there was a fearful crash of thunder, while at the same time a bluish shaft of lightning lit up the whole room, and the thunder, fading in the distance, seemed unwilling to go away from the accursed house.

'"Jesu!" said La Carconte, making the sign of the cross.

'At the same moment, in the awed silence that habitually follows a loud burst of thunder, they heard a knocking on the door. Both Caderousse and his wife shuddered and looked at one another.

'"Who goes there?" Caderousse shouted, getting up and pushing the gold and the notes, which had been spread out over the table, into a single pile and covering it with both hands.

'"It's me!" said a voice.

'"Who are you?"

'"Who do you think? Joannès, the jeweller."

'"What were you saying?" La Carconte said, with an awful smile. "That the Good Lord was offended? Well, look: the Good Lord has sent him back to us."

'Caderousse slipped back, white and breathless, on his chair. But La Carconte, on the other hand, got up and walked with a determined step over to the door, then opened it. "Come in, dear Monsieur Joannès," she said.

'"I'll be darned," the jeweller said, dripping with rain. "It seems that the devil does not want me to go back to Beaucaire this evening. The best follies are the shortest-lived, my dear Caderousse. You offered me your hospitality; I accept and I have come back to stay the night with you."

'Caderousse muttered a few words, wiping the sweat from his brow. La Carconte double-locked the door behind the jeweller.'

XLV

A SHOWER OF BLOOD

'As he came in, the jeweller looked around enquiringly, but nothing seemed to arouse his suspicions, if he had none so far, or to confirm any that he might have had. Caderousse was still holding his banknotes and his gold in both hands. La Carconte smiled at her guest as pleasantly as she could.

'"Ah! I see," said the jeweller. "It appears you were afraid of having been underpaid, so you were counting your wealth after I left."

'"Not at all," said Caderousse. "But the events that brought us this fortune were so unexpected that we still cannot believe in it, and when we do not have the actual proof under our eyes we imagine that we may still be dreaming."

'The jeweller smiled.

'"Do you have any travellers in your inn?" he asked.

'"No," Caderousse replied. "We do not let rooms. We are too close to the town and no one stops here."

'"In that case, will I be a terrible nuisance to you?"

'"You! A nuisance! My dear sir," La Carconte said amiably, "not at all, I assure you."

'"But where will you put me?"

'"In the upstairs room."

'"That is your own room, isn't it?"

'"Don't worry! We have a second bed in the room next door to this one."

'Caderousse looked at his wife in astonishment. The jeweller hummed a little tune while warming his back at a log which La Carconte had just lit in the fireplace so that he could dry his clothes. Meanwhile she put the meagre remnants of a dinner on one corner of the table where she had laid a cloth, adding two or three fresh eggs.

'Caderousse had once more shut the notes up in his wallet, the gold in his bag and both of these in his cupboard. He was walking back and forth, grim and pensive, casting an occasional glance at the jeweller who stood steaming in front of the hearth and, when he started to dry on one side, turned to the other.

' "There you are," said La Carconte, putting a bottle of wine down on the table. "Supper is ready, when you want it."

' "What about you?" asked Joannès.

' "I'm not having anything," Caderousse said.

' "We had a very late dinner," La Carconte hastened to add.

' "Will I have to eat alone, then?"

' "We'll serve you," said La Carconte, with an eagerness that would have been exceptional in her, even with one of her paying guests. From time to time Caderousse gave her a rapid glance.

'The storm continued.

' "Do you hear that?" La Carconte said. "My word! You did well to come back."

' "Despite which," said the jeweller, "if the wind does drop while I am eating my supper, I shall set out again."

' "It's the mistral," Caderousse said, shaking his head. "We've got it now until tomorrow." And he sighed.

' "Well I never," said the jeweller, taking his place at the table. "Bad luck on anyone who's outside."

' "Yes," said La Carconte. "They will have a rough night."

'The jeweller began to eat and La Carconte continued to fuss over him like an attentive hostess. Usually so crabby and ill-tempered, she had become a model of consideration and good manners. If the jeweller had known her earlier he would surely have been astonished by the change, which could not help arousing his suspicions. As for Caderousse, he said nothing but went on walking up and down and seemed unwilling even to look at his guest.

'When supper was over, Caderousse himself went to the door.

' "I think the storm has passed," he said. But at that moment, as if to contradict him, the house was shaken by an enormous clap of thunder, and a gust of rain and wind came in, blowing out the lamp. Caderousse shut the door and his wife lit a candle at the dying fire.

' "Here," she said to the jeweller. "You must be tired. I have put clean linen on the bed. Go on up, and sleep well."

'Joannès waited for a moment longer to see whether the storm would abate, and when he was sure that the thunder and rain were only increasing in strength he said goodnight to his hosts and went up the stairs.

'He passed right above my head. I could hear each stair creak beneath his feet. La Carconte looked after him hungrily, while Caderousse turned his back and did not even glance in his direction.

'All these details, which I have recalled since the events, did not strike me while they were taking place before my eyes. When it comes down to it, everything that had happened was quite normal and, apart from the story of the diamond, which struck me as somewhat improbable, everything was perfectly consistent. As I was dropping with tiredness and intended myself to take advantage of the first break in the weather, I decided to sleep for a few hours, then make off while it was still dark.

'In the room above my head I could hear the jeweller going about his preparations for spending as comfortable a night as he could. Shortly afterwards, the bed creaked under him: he had just got into it.

'I felt my eyes closing despite myself and, as I had no suspicion of what was to come, I did not try to fight against sleep. I took one last look around the kitchen. Caderousse was sitting, beside a long table, on one of those wooden benches which they use instead of chairs in village inns. His back was turned to me, so that his face was hidden – though, even if he had been sitting on the opposite side of the table, it would still have been impossible for me to see his face, because his head was buried in his hands.

'La Carconte looked at him for a time, shrugged her shoulders and went to sit opposite him.

'At that moment the dying embers of the fire caught a piece of dry wood that until then had remained unconsumed, and a brighter light flared up, illuminating the dark interior of the inn. La Carconte was staring at her husband and, since he remained in the same position, I saw her reach out towards him with her gnarled hand and touch his forehead.

'Caderousse started. I thought I could see the woman's lips move, but either she was speaking in a very low voice or else I was already dulled by sleep, because the sound of her words did not reach me. In fact, I saw everything through a kind of mist, in that period of uncertainty that precedes sleep, when we feel that we are starting to dream. At length my eyes closed and I was no longer aware of my surroundings.

'I was slumbering profoundly when I was awoken by a pistol-shot, followed by a dreadful cry. Someone staggered a few steps across the floor of the bedroom and an inert mass crashed on the stairs, directly above my head.

'I was still not entirely master of my senses. I heard groans, then stifled cries, like those that might accompany a struggle. A final shout, lasting longer than the rest and ending in a series of moans, forced me entirely from my lethargy.

'I sat up on one elbow, opened my eyes, which could see nothing in the darkness, and put my hand to my forehead, where I thought I felt a heavy shower of warm rain dripping through the boards of the stairway.

'The horrid sounds had given way to the most profound silence. Then I heard a man's footsteps above my head and the creak of the stairs. He came into the downstairs room, went across to the fireplace and lit a candle. It was Caderousse. His face was livid and his nightshirt covered in blood. Once he had lit the candle, he hurried back upstairs and I heard him moving about there again, with rapid and uneasy steps.

'After a short while he came back. He was holding the box in his hand and making sure that the diamond was inside. Then he paused for a moment, trying to decide which of his pockets to put it in. Finally, having no doubt concluded that his pocket was not a secure enough hiding-place, he wrapped it in the red kerchief around his neck.

'Then he hurried across to the cupboard, took out his banknotes and the gold, putting the first in the fob pocket of his trousers and the second in his jacket, seized two or three shirts and, running across to the door, disappeared into the darkness. It was only now that everything became clear to me. I felt responsible for what had happened, as though I were really the guilty party. I thought I could hear someone moaning. Perhaps the unfortunate jeweller was not dead and it was within my power to go to his aid and make up for some of the evil that I had, if not done, at least allowed to be done . . . I thrust my shoulder against one of the ill-fitting planks which separated the sort of cubby-hole, in which I was hiding, from the downstairs room. The planks gave way and I was inside the house.

'I hastened to pick up the candlestick and ran to the stairs. A body was lying across them: it was La Carconte.

'The pistol-shot that I heard had been fired at her. Her throat was shot through and, as well as this double wound that was bleeding copiously, there was blood coming from her mouth. She was stone dead. I stepped over the body and went upstairs.

'The bedroom was a shambles. Some of the furniture had been overturned and the sheets, which the unfortunate jeweller had clasped on to, were spread across the room. He himself was lying on the floor, his head resting against the wall and bathed in a pool of blood still flowing from three gaping wounds in his chest. In a fourth was embedded a long kitchen knife, of which only the handle could be seen.

'I went over to the second pistol, which had not been fired, probably because the powder was damp.

'Then I approached the jeweller. In fact he was not yet dead. Hearing the sound that I made and, still more, the shaking of the floor, he opened his wildly staring eyes, managed to focus them on me for a moment, moved his lips as though to speak, and expired.

'At this frightful scene, I almost fainted. Now that there was no assistance I could give anyone, I felt only one need, which was to be away from there. I plunged down the stairs, grasping my hair with my hands and giving a roar of terror.

'In the lower room there were five or six Customs men and two or three gendarmes: a small squad of armed men.

'They seized me. I made no attempt to resist, because I was no longer in command of my senses. I merely tried to speak and gave some inarticulate cries. Then I saw that the officers were pointing at me. I looked down and saw that I was covered in blood. The warm shower that I had felt rain down on me through the boards of the staircase was La Carconte's blood.

'I pointed to the place where I had been hiding.

' "What is he trying to say?" a gendarme asked.

'One of the customs men went to look.

' "He's telling us that he came through here," he answered, pointing to the hole which had indeed been my means of entry.

'On this, I realized that they thought I was the assassin. I recovered my voice and my strength and broke away from the two men who were holding me, shouting: "It wasn't me, it wasn't me!" '

'Two gendarmes levelled their carbines at me: "Don't move," they said, "or you're dead!" '

' "But I tell you, it wasn't me!" I cried.

' "You can tell your little story to the judges in Nîmes," they replied. "For the time being, follow us – and, we warn you, don't try to resist."

'I had no intention of doing so; I was overwhelmed with amazement and terror. They put handcuffs on me, attached me to the tail of a horse and led me into Nîmes.

'I had been followed by a Customs man. He had lost sight of me somewhere near the inn and guessed that I would spend the night there. He went to fetch his comrades, and they arrived just in time to hear the pistol-shot and to arrest me, amid all that evidence of guilt. I realized at once how hard it would be to convince anyone of my innocence.

'For this reason, I clung to just one thing: my first request from the examining magistrate was to beg him to have them search everywhere for a certain Abbé Busoni who had stopped during the day at the inn of the Pont du Gard. If Caderousse had made up the story and the abbé did not exist, I was clearly lost, unless Caderousse himself was arrested and confessed everything.

'Two months passed in which – be it said to the magistrate's credit – every effort was made to find the witness I had requested. I had already lost all hope. Caderousse had not been caught. I was to be tried at the next assizes when, on September the eighth, that is to say three months and five days after the event, Abbé Busoni, of whom I had quite given up hope, presented himself at the prison, saying that he had been told a prisoner wanted to speak to him. He said that he had learned of this in Marseille and hastened to comply with my request.

'You can imagine how eagerly I welcomed him. I told him everything that I had witnessed. I was reluctant to embark on the story of the diamond but, against all my expectations, it proved to be true, point by point, and – also to my surprise – he gave complete credence to everything that I told him. Whereupon, encouraged by his sweet and forgiving nature, recognizing that he entirely understood the customs of my country and feeling that from such charitable lips I might perhaps receive absolution for the only crime I had ever committed, I told him, under the seal of the confessional, all about what had happened in Auteuil. What I did on impulse had the same effect as if I had contrived it: by confessing this first murder, even though nothing compelled me to do so, I proved to him that I had not committed the second. He left me with an injunction to have faith, promising to do all that was in his power to convince the judges of my innocence.

'I had evidence of his actual efforts on my behalf when I observed that the prison regime was gradually lightened and when I learned that my case would be held over until the next assizes following those that were due to convene.

'Meanwhile, as luck would have it, Caderousse was arrested abroad and brought back to France. He confessed everything, blaming his wife for planning and initiating the crime. He was sentenced to the galleys for life and I was freed.'

'So that was the time,' Monte Cristo said, 'when you arrived at my door bearing a letter from Abbé Busoni?'

'Yes, Excellency. He had taken a distinct interest in me.

'"Smuggling will be the end of you," he told me. "If you are released from here, give it up."

'"But, Father," I asked, "how shall I live and keep my poor sister?"

'"One of my penitents," he replied, "esteems me greatly and has asked me to find him a reliable assistant. Would you like the post? I shall send you to him."

'"Father!" I exclaimed. "How good you are to me!"

'"Swear to me that I shall never have cause to regret it."

'I raised my hand to swear the oath, but he said: "That will not be necessary: I know what you Corsicans are like, and love you for it. Here is my letter of recommendation."

'He wrote the few lines that I gave you, as a result of which Your Excellency was good enough to take me into his service. Now, I ask Your Excellency with pride, have you ever had cause to complain of me?'

'No,' the count replied. 'I am pleased to admit it. You are a good servant, Bertuccio, though you have shown too little trust in me.'

'I, Monsieur le Comte?'

'Yes, you. How is it that you have a sister-in-law and an adoptive son, yet you have never mentioned either of them to me?'

'Alas, Excellency, I have still to tell you of the saddest part of my life. I set off for Corsica. As you can imagine, I was in a hurry to see my poor sister again and to console her. But when I arrived at Rogliano, I found the house in mourning. There had been a terrible drama, which the neighbours remember to this day. Benedetto had wanted my poor sister-in-law to give him all the money in the house and she, on my advice, had resisted his demands. One morning he threatened her and vanished for the whole day. She wept, dear Assunta, because she felt like a mother towards the wretch. When evening came, she waited up for him. At eleven o'clock he came back with two of his friends, the usual companions of all his follies, and she held her arms out to him. But they seized her and one of the three – I fear it could have been that infernal child – shouted: "Let's play at torture; she will soon confess where her money is."

'The neighbour, Wasilio, happened to be in Bastia; only his wife had stayed at home and she alone could hear or see what was going on in my sister's house. Two of them held poor Assunta. She, unable to believe that such a criminal act was possible, smiled at the men who were to become her tormentors. The third went to barricade the doors and windows, then returned, and the three of them, stifling the terrified cries elicited from her by these more serious preparations, dragged Assunta's feet towards the brazier on which they were relying to make her reveal where our little treasure was hidden. But as she struggled, her clothes caught fire. They let her go, to avoid being burned themselves, and she ran to the door, a mass of flames. However, the door was locked.

'She turned to the window, but that was barricaded. At this, the neighbour heard frightful screams: Assunta was begging for help. Soon her voice was stifled, the screams became moans. The next day, when Wasilio's wife, after a night of terror and anxiety, dared to emerge and had the judge open the door of our house, they found Assunta half burned, though still breathing, the cupboards broken into and the money stolen. As for Benedetto, he had left Rogliano, never to return. I have not seen him since that day, or even heard speak of him.

'It was after hearing this sad news,' Bertuccio continued, 'that I came to Your Excellency. I had no further occasion to mention

Benedetto to you, since he had vanished, or my sister-in-law, since she was dead.'

'What did you conclude from all this?' Monte Cristo asked.

'That it was a punishment for my crime,' Bertuccio replied. 'Ah, those Villeforts are a cursed breed!'

'I think you are right,' the count muttered grimly.

'Now, surely,' Bertuccio went on, 'Your Excellency will understand why this house, which I have not seen since that time, this garden in which I suddenly found myself and this spot on which I killed a man, were enough to cause those disturbing emotions which you observed and wanted to know the cause of. Even now I do not know whether Monsieur de Villefort is not there, at my feet, in the grave that he dug for his own child.'

'Anything is indeed possible,' Monte Cristo said, rising from the bench where he had been sitting; and he added, under his breath: 'including that the crown prosecutor may not be dead. Abbé Busoni did well to send you to me. You were right to tell me your story, because I shall not have any suspicions about you. As for Benedetto, that ill-named youth, have you never tried to find him, or to discover what became of him?'

'Never! Had I known where he was, instead of going to find him, I should have fled him like a monster. No, fortunately, I have never heard anyone mention him. I hope he is dead.'

'Don't hope too much, Bertuccio,' said the count. 'The wicked do not die in that way: God seems to take them under his protection to use them as the instruments of his vengeance.'

'Indeed,' said Bertuccio. 'All I ask Heaven is that I shall never see him again. Now,' the steward said, bowing his head, 'you know everything, Monsieur le Comte. You are my judge here below as God will be there above. Will you not say a few words to console me?'

'Yes, indeed: I can tell you what Abbé Busoni would tell you. The man you struck down, that Villefort, deserved punishment for what he had done to you and perhaps for other things as well. Benedetto, if he is still alive, will (as I told you) serve the purpose of some divine vengeance, then be punished in his turn. As for you, you have in truth only one thing to reproach yourself with: ask yourself why, having saved that child from death, you did not return it to its mother. That was the crime, Bertuccio.'

'Yes, Monsieur. That was the crime, and a true crime, for I was a coward in this. Once I had revived the child, there was only one thing for me to do, as you say, which was to send it back to its mother. But to do that I should have had to make enquiries, attract attention and perhaps give myself away. I did not want to die: I was attached to life because of my sister-in-law and because of that innate vanity which makes us want to remain whole and victorious after a vendetta; and, then, perhaps I was attached to life simply for the love of it. Oh, I am not a brave man like my poor brother!'

Bertuccio hid his face in both hands and Monte Cristo stared long and enigmatically at him. Then, after a moment's silence that was made more solemn by the hour and the place, he said with an unusual accent of melancholy: 'Monsieur Bertuccio, to bring this conversation to a worthy end – because it will be the last we shall have about these events – listen to me carefully, because I have often heard these words from Abbé Busoni himself. There are two medicines for all ills: time and silence. Now, Monsieur Bertuccio, let me walk awhile in this garden. The feelings that are so powerful for you, who took part in the drama, will be for me almost a sweet sensation and one that will add to the value of my property. You understand, Monsieur Bertuccio: trees only give us pleasure because they give shade, and shade itself only pleases us because it is full of reveries and visions. I bought a garden, imagining that I was purchasing a simple space enclosed in walls; but it was not so at all: suddenly the space has become a garden full of ghosts, which were nowhere mentioned in the deed of sale. I like ghosts. I have heard it said that the dead have never done, in six thousand years, as much evil as the living do in a single day. So go back inside, Monsieur Bertuccio, and sleep in peace. If the confessor who gives you the last rites is less compassionate towards you than Abbé Busoni, fetch me, if I am still of this world, and I shall find the words that will gently soothe your soul as it prepares to start out on that rough voyage that they call eternity.'

Bertuccio bowed respectfully to the count and went off, sighing. Monte Cristo remained alone and, taking four steps forward, said: 'Here, beside this plane-tree, is the grave where the child was placed. Over there, the little gate by which one might enter the garden. In that corner, the back stairway that led to the bedroom. I don't think I need to take all that down in my notebook. Here before my eyes, around me, beneath my feet, in relief, is the living map of it.'

After a last walk round the garden, the count went to look for his carriage. Bertuccio, seeing that he was preoccupied with his thoughts, got up on the seat beside the coachman without saying anything, and the carriage set off for Paris.

That same evening, on arriving at the house on the Champs-Elysées, the Count of Monte Cristo inspected the whole residence as a man might have done who had been familiar with it for many years. Not once, even though he went ahead, did he open one door in mistake for another, or go up a staircase or down a corridor which did not lead directly to where he wanted it to take him. Ali accompanied him in this night-time inspection. The count gave Bertuccio several orders for the embellishment or rearrangement of the apartments and, taking out his watch, told his assiduous Nubian: 'It is half-past eleven. Haydée will soon be here. Have the Frenchwomen been told?'

Ali pointed towards the suite intended for the beautiful Greek, which was so separate from the rest that, when the door was concealed behind a tapestry, one could visit the whole house without realizing that anyone was living here in a drawing-room and two bedrooms. Ali, as we said, pointed to the suite, indicated the number three with the fingers of his left hand and, opening the same hand out flat, put his head on it and closed his eyes as if asleep.

'Very well,' Monte Cristo said, used to this sign-language. 'There are three of them in the bedroom, then?'

'Yes,' Ali indicated, nodding his head.

'Madame will be tired this evening,' Monte Cristo continued. 'She will no doubt want to sleep. She should not be obliged to talk. The French servants must simply greet their new mistress and then retire. Make sure that the Greek servant does not communicate with the French ones.'

Ali bowed. Shortly afterwards there was the sound of someone calling to the concierge. The outer gate opened, a carriage drove along the path and stopped beneath the steps. The count came down to find the carriage door already open. He offered his hand to a young woman wrapped in a green silk mantle embroidered in gold and covering her head. She took his hand, kissed it with a degree of love mingled with respect. A few words were exchanged, tenderly on the part of the young woman and with gentle gravity on that of the count, in that sonorous language which antique Homer put into the mouths of his gods.

Then, following Ali, who was carrying a torch of pink wax, the young woman, who was none other than the beautiful Greek who habitually accompanied Monte Cristo when he was in Italy, was shown into her apartments and the count retired to the wing that he had reserved for himself. At half-past midnight, all the lights in the house went out, and you might have thought that all its inhabitants were asleep.

XLVI

UNLIMITED CREDIT

The next day at about two in the afternoon, a barouche drawn by two splendid horses pulled up in front of Monte Cristo's door and a man in a blue jacket, with silk buttons of the same colour, a white waistcoat crossed by a huge gold chain and hazel-coloured trousers, with a head of such black hair, worn so low above the eyebrows that it seemed hardly natural, being so inconsistent with those wrinkles on the forehead that it was unable to disguise; in short, a man of between fifty and fifty-five, trying to look forty, put his head out of the window of a coupé with a baron's crown painted on its door, and sent his groom to enquire of the concierge whether the Count of Monte Cristo was at home.

As he waited, the man examined the exterior of the house, what could be seen of the garden and the livery of a few servants who might be observed coming and going – and did so with such close attention as to amount almost to impertinence. His eye was sharp, but with more cunning in it than wit or irony. His lips were so thin that they vanished inside the mouth instead of protruding from it. Finally, the breadth and prominence of the cheekbones (an infallible sign of shrewdness), the retreating forehead, the bulging occiput which extended well beyond his wide and not in the least aristocratic ears, all contributed to give this gentleman (whom any ordinary person would have thought very respectable in view of his magnificent horses, the enormous diamond he wore in his shirt and the red ribbon that stretched from one buttonhole to another on his coat), a face which to a trained physiognomist betrayed an almost repulsive character.

The groom hammered on the concierge's window and asked: 'Does the Count of Monte Cristo live here?'

'His Excellency does live here,' the concierge replied, 'but . . .' And he looked at Ali, who nodded in reply.

'But?' asked the groom.

'But His Excellency is not receiving guests,' the concierge said.

'In that case, here is the card of my master, Baron Danglars. You will give it to the Count of Monte Cristo and tell him that my master made a detour while on his way to the House, in order to have the honour of seeing him.'

'I don't talk to His Excellency,' said the concierge. 'The *valet de chambre* will take the message.'

The groom went back to the carriage.

'Well?' said Danglars.

The boy, somewhat crestfallen at the lesson he had just been given, delivered the concierge's reply to his master.

'Huh!' the latter remarked. 'The gentleman is a prince, is he, calling himself Excellency and only allowing his *valet de chambre* to speak to him. No matter. Since he has a credit on me, he will have to see me when he wants money.' And he slumped back into his carriage, shouting to the coachman in a voice that could be heard on the far side of the street: 'To the Chambre des Députés!'

Informed of his arrival, Monte Cristo had seen the baron and been able to study him through the shutters of his house, thanks to a fine lorgnette, with as much attention as M. Danglars himself had given to the house, the garden and the servants.

'Undoubtedly,' he said, with a gesture of disgust as he closed the binoculars in their ivory case, 'undoubtedly that man is an unprepossessing creature. How can anyone fail at first sight to recognize in him the serpent with its flattened head, the vulture with its bulging skull and the buzzard with its rapacious beak?'

'Ali!' he cried, then struck the copper gong. Ali appeared. 'Call Bertuccio.'

At the same moment, Bertuccio entered. 'Your Excellency called for me?' he said.

'Yes, sir,' said the count. 'Did you see the horses that just drew up at my door?'

'Indeed, Excellency. I might say they were very fine.'

'How is it,' Monte Cristo said quizzically, 'when I asked you for the two finest horses in Paris, that there still remain in Paris two other horses equally as good which are not in my stables?'

At the sharp tone of voice and the raised eyebrow, Ali bent his head.

'It is not your fault, my dear Ali,' the count said in Arabic, with a softness that one would never have thought to hear in that voice. 'You are no expert when it comes to English horses.'

Ali's features resumed their accustomed serenity.

'Monsieur le Comte,' said Bertuccio, 'the horses that you refer to were not for sale.'

Monte Cristo shrugged his shoulders. 'Bertuccio, everything is always for sale when you know the price to put on it.'

'Monsieur Danglars paid sixteen thousand francs for them, Monsieur le Comte.'

'Then you should have offered him thirty-two thousand. He is a banker, and a banker never misses an opportunity to double his money.'

'Is Monsieur le Comte serious?' Bertuccio asked.

Monte Cristo looked at his steward like a man astonished that anyone should dare to question his seriousness. 'This evening,' he said, 'I have a visit to make. I wish to have those two horses draw my carriage, with a new harness.'

Bertuccio retired, bowing. Reaching the door, he paused and said: 'At what time does His Excellency intend to pay this visit?'

'At five o'clock.'

'I might venture to point out to Your Excellency that it is now two o'clock,' the steward said, gingerly.

'I know,' was Monte Cristo's only reply. Then, turning to Ali, he said: 'Have all the horses paraded in front of Madame, so that she can choose the team that suits her best; and ask her to let me know if she will dine with me. In that case, we shall be served in her apartments. Now, go and as you do, send me the *valet de chambre*.'

Ali had hardly disappeared when the *valet de chambre* entered.

'Monsieur Baptistin,' said the count, 'you have been in my service for a year. This is the probationary period that I usually give to my servants. You suit me.'

Baptistin bowed.

'It remains for you to say if I suit you.'

'Oh! Monsieur le Comte!' Baptistin said unhesitatingly.

'Hear me out. You earn fifteen hundred francs a year, which is the stipend of a fine, brave army officer who risks his life every day. You enjoy meals that many a head clerk, a poor slave who is far busier than you, would envy. Though a servant, you yourself have servants who take care of your laundry and your belongings. Over and above your fifteen hundred francs in wages, you are taking a cut on the toiletries and similar purchases that you make for me, and stealing nearly an additional fifteen hundred francs every year.'

'Oh! Excellency!'

'I am not complaining, Monsieur Baptistin, it's a reasonable amount. However, I wish it to stop forthwith. Nowhere will you find a position comparable to the one that good fortune has given you here. I never beat my servants, I never swear, I never lose my temper, I always forgive a fault, but never negligence or forgetfulness. My orders are usually brief, but clear and precise: I prefer to repeat them twice or even three times, rather than for them to be carried out incorrectly. I am rich enough to know everything that I wish to know and – be warned – I am very curious. So if I were ever to learn that you had spoken either good or ill of me, that you had commented on my actions or watched over what I do, you would leave my house immediately. I never give my servants more than one warning. You have had yours. You may go!'

Baptistin bowed and took three or four steps towards the door.

'By the way,' the count continued, 'I forgot to tell you that, every year, I invest a certain sum for each of my people. Those whom I dismiss inevitably lose this money, which reverts to those who remain and who will be able to collect it after my death. You have been a year with me, your fortune has begun to grow: let it continue.'

This homily, delivered in front of Ali who remained impassive, since he did not understand a word of French, produced an effect on M. Baptistin which will be understood by anyone who has studied the psychology of the French domestic servant.

'I shall try to conform in every respect to Your Excellency's wishes,' he said. 'Indeed, I shall model myself on Monsieur Ali.'

'Oh! Do no such thing!' Monte Cristo said, as cold as marble. 'Ali has many faults, as well as qualities. Don't follow his example, because Ali is an exception. He receives no wages, he is not a servant, he is my slave, he is my dog. If he were to fail in his duty, I should not dismiss him. I should kill him.'

Baptistin's eyes bulged.

'Do you doubt it?' And the count repeated the same words to Ali that he had spoken in French to Baptistin. Ali listened, smiled, went over to his master, knelt on one knee and respectfully kissed his hand. This little epitome of the lesson left Baptistin utterly dumbfounded.

The count motioned to Baptistin to leave them, and Ali to come with him. He led the way into his cabinet and they spent a long time talking there.

At five o'clock the count knocked three times on the gong. One strike was for Ali, two for Baptistin and three for Bertuccio. The steward entered.

'My horses!' Monte Cristo demanded.

'They are ready, with the carriage, Excellency,' Bertuccio replied. 'Shall I be accompanying Monsieur le Comte?'

'No, just the coachman, Baptistin and Ali.'

The count came downstairs and saw, harnessed to his carriage, the horses that he had admired that morning in Danglars' barouche. He glanced at them as he went past.

'They are very fine, indeed,' he said. 'You did well to buy them, even though you were a little late.'

'Excellency,' said Bertuccio, 'it took a great deal of trouble to get them and they were very expensive.'

'Are they any the less attractive for that?' the count asked, shrugging his shoulders.

'If Your Excellency is content,' Bertuccio said, 'then all is well. Where is Your Excellency going?'

'To the rue de la Chaussée d'Antin, to Baron Danglars'.'

This conversation took place at the top of the front steps. Bertuccio made as if to go down the first step.

'One moment, Monsieur,' Monte Cristo said, holding him back. 'I need an estate near the seaside, in Normandy for example, between Le Havre and Boulogne. As you see, I am giving you room to manoeuvre. The property must have a little harbour – a small creek or bay, where my corvette can enter and moor. It has a draught of only fifteen feet. It will always be kept ready to put to sea, at any hour of the day or night when I choose to give the signal. You will enquire of all the notaries about a property of this kind and, when you have found one, you will visit it and, if you are satisfied, buy it in your name. The corvette must be sailing towards Fécamp, I suppose?'

'I saw it put to sea on the very evening when we left Marseille.'

'And the yacht?'

'The yacht was ordered to remain at Les Martigues.'

'Very well. From time to time you must keep in touch with their two captains, so that they do not fall asleep at their posts.'

'What about the steamship?'

'Which is in Chalon?'

'Yes.'

'The same orders as for the two sailing ships.'

'Very good.'

'As soon as the property has been acquired, I shall have relays of horses ready every ten leagues on the roads to the north and to the south.'

'Your Excellency can count on me.'

Monte Cristo gave a nod of satisfaction, went down the steps and leapt into his carriage, which was borne forward at a trot by the superb team of horses and did not stop until it reached the banker's mansion.

Danglars was chairing a commission, which had been appointed for a railway company, when they came in to announce the Count of Monte Cristo. In any case, the meeting was almost finished. At the mention of the count's name, he got up.

'Gentlemen,' he said, addressing his colleagues, several of whom were honourable members of one House or the other, 'I apologize for leaving you in this way, but I must ask you to believe that the firm of Thomson and French, in Rome, has sent me a certain Count of Monte Cristo and opened a limitless credit for him with me. This is the most ludicrous joke any of my correspondents abroad has yet played on me. As you may well imagine, I was – and still am – consumed by curiosity. This morning, I went to visit the so-called count; if he was a real one, you will agree, he would not be so rich. Monsieur was not at home to me. What do you think? It seems our Monte Cristo has the manners of a princeling or a prima donna, doesn't it? Aside from that, the house on the Champs-Elysées, which he owns, I enquired about that, appeared respectable enough. But – unlimited credit!' Danglars repeated, smiling one of his odious smiles. 'That's something that makes the banker with whom such a credit is opened rather fussy about his man. So I was keen to see him. I think they are trying to lead me up the garden path, but he who laughs last . . .'

M. le Baron ended, stressing the last words with an expressive flourish that made his nostrils flare, then left his guests and went into a reception room, done up in white and gold, that had made the tongues wag on the Chaussée d'Antin. He had asked the visitor to be brought here, to impress him right from the start.

The count was standing, inspecting some copies of Albano and Fattore[1] which had been passed off on the banker as originals and which, copies though they were, clashed with the beading in every shade of gold decorating the ceiling. On hearing Danglars come in, the count turned around.

Danglars nodded in greeting and gestured to the count to sit down on an armchair of gilded wood upholstered in white satin and embroidered in gold thread. The count did so.

'I have the honour of speaking to Monsieur de Monte Cristo?'

'And I,' the count replied, 'to Monsieur le Baron Danglars, Knight of the Legion of Honour and member of the Chamber of Deputies?'

The count was repeating all the titles to be found on the baron's visiting card. The baron took the hint and bit his lip.

'Forgive me, Monsieur,' he said, 'for not addressing you at the start by the title under which you were introduced to me. But, as you know, we live under a government of the people and I am a representative of the interests of the people.'

'With the result,' Monte Cristo replied, 'that, while retaining the custom of having yourself called "Baron", you have abandoned that of calling other men "Count".'

'Oh, I'm not even bothered about it for myself, Monsieur,' Danglars replied casually. 'They granted me the title and made me a Knight of the Legion of Honour for some services rendered, but . . .'

'But you abdicated your titles, as formerly Monsieur de Montmorency and Monsieur de Lafayette did? You offer a fine example to your fellow men, Monsieur.'

'Well, not altogether,' Danglars replied, with some embarrassment. 'You understand, for the servants . . .'

'Ah, so you call yourself "monseigneur" for your staff, "monsieur" for journalists and "citizen" for your agents. These nuances are quite appropriate in a constitutional regime; I understand perfectly.'

Danglars clenched his teeth. He could see that on this ground he

was no rival for Monte Cristo, so he tried to return to terrain that
was more familiar to him.

'Monsieur le Comte,' he said, bowing, 'I have received a letter
from the firm of Thomson and French.'

'I am delighted, Monsieur le Baron. Oh! Permit me to address
you as your servants do: it's a bad habit I picked up in countries
where they still have barons, precisely because they are not making
them any more. As I say, I'm charmed. I have no need to present
myself, which is always embarrassing. So, you have received a
letter?'

'Yes,' said Danglars, 'but I have to admit that I did not entirely
take its meaning.'

'Really?'

'I even had the honour to visit you to ask for an explanation.'

'Very well, Monsieur, I am here, ready and listening.'

'I have the letter,' Danglars said, '. . . on my person, I believe.'
He rummaged around in his pocket. 'Yes, here we are. This letter
opens an unlimited credit on my bank on behalf of the Count of
Monte Cristo.'

'So, Monsieur le Baron, what needs explaining in that?'

'Nothing, Monsieur. Only, the word "unlimited" . . .'

'It is a French word, is it not? You must understand, the letter
comes from an Anglo-German firm . . .'

'Oh, yes, Monsieur, indeed. There is no problem in respect of
the syntax, but the same is not true of the arithmetic.'

'Are you trying to tell me,' Monte Cristo asked, with the most
innocent air that he could manage, 'that the firm of Thomson and
French is not absolutely reliable, in your opinion, Monsieur le
Baron? I should be most sorry to hear it, for I have some money
invested with them.'

'Oh, perfectly reliable,' Danglars replied, with a smile almost of
mockery. 'But the meaning of the word "unlimited", in financial
terms, is so vague . . .'

'As to be unlimited, perhaps?' said Monte Cristo.

'Just so, Monsieur, that is precisely what I meant. Now, where
something is vague, there is doubt and, as the wise man says, when
in doubt – don't!'

'In other words,' Monte Cristo remarked, 'you mean that while
the firm of Thomson and French may be inclined to folly, that of
Danglars is unwilling to follow its example.'

'How do you mean, Monsieur le Comte?'

'Just this: Messrs Thomson and French engage in unlimited business, but Monsieur Danglars does put a limit on his. As he was saying only a moment ago, he is a wise man.'

'Monsieur,' the banker replied haughtily, 'no one has yet found my funds to be wanting.'

'So, it seems that I shall be the first,' Monte Cristo replied coldly.

'Who says that you will?'

'All these explanations you require of me, Monsieur, which seem to me very much like cold feet . . .'

Danglars bit his lip: this was the second time that the man had worsted him, and this time on his own ground. His condescending politeness was only an affectation and he was getting close to an extremity very similar to condescension, which is impertinence.

Monte Cristo, on the other hand, was smiling with the best grace in the world. When he wished, he could adopt an air of innocence that was extremely favourable to him.

'To come to the point, Monsieur,' said Danglars, after a moment's silence. 'I shall try to make myself plain by asking you yourself to state the amount that you intend to draw on us.'

'But, my good sir,' said Monte Cristo, determined not to lose an inch of ground in the debate, 'if I asked for unlimited credit from you, that was precisely because I did not know what amount I should require.'

The banker felt that the moment had at last come to regain the upper hand. He sat back in his chair and, with a broad and supercilious smile, said: 'Oh, Monsieur! Do not be afraid to ask. You will then be able to satisfy yourself that the funds of Danglars and company, limited though they may be, can meet the largest requirements. Even if you were to ask for a million . . .'

'I beg your pardon?' said Monte Cristo.

'I said, a million,' Danglars repeated, with idiotic self-satisfaction.

'What use would a million be to me?' said the count. 'Good heavens, Monsieur! If all I wanted was a million, I should not have bothered to open a credit for such a paltry sum. A million? But I always carry a million in my portfolio or my wallet.' And, opening a little box where he kept his visiting cards, he took out two bonds for five hundred thousand francs each, drawn on the Treasury and payable to bearer.

A man like Danglars needed to be bludgeoned, rather than

pricked. The blow had the desired effect: the banker reeled and felt faint. He looked at Monte Cristo with amazement, the pupils of his dazed eyes terrifyingly dilated.

'Come now,' said Monte Cristo, 'admit it! You have no faith in the firm of Thomson and French. Well, that's no problem. I anticipated it and, though I know little about business, I took the necessary precautions. Here are two other letters like the one addressed to you. The first comes from the firm of Arnstein and Eskeles, in Vienna, drawn on the Baron de Rothschild, the other from the house of Baring in London, drawn on Monsieur Laffitte. Just say the word, Monsieur, and I shall relieve you of any anxiety by going to one or other of those two firms.'

That was it: Danglars was defeated. With hands visibly trembling, he opened the letter from Vienna and the other from London, which the count was holding out to him, verified the signatures with a degree of attention that would have been insulting to Monte Cristo if he had not made allowance for the banker's bewilderment.

'Ah, Monsieur, here are three signatures that are worth many millions,' Danglars said, rising to his feet, as though to salute the power of gold personified in the man seated before him. 'Three unlimited credits on our three firms! Excuse me, Monsieur le Comte, but, while I am no longer suspicious, I may at least be allowed to feel astonishment.'

'Oh, a firm like yours would not be astonished by such a thing,' said Monte Cristo, with all the condescension he could muster. 'So, you can send me some money, I assume?'

'Name the sum, Monsieur le Comte. I am at your orders.'

'Very well, then,' Monte Cristo continued. 'Now that we are agreed . . . we are agreed, aren't we?'

Danglars nodded.

'And you are no longer at all suspicious?'

'Monsieur le Comte, please!' the banker exclaimed. 'I was never suspicious!'

'No, you simply wanted some proof, nothing more. Very well, now that we are agreed and you no longer have any suspicion, let us settle on a broad amount for the first year; say, six million?'

'Six million! Very well then,' said Danglars, choking.

'If I should need more,' Monte Cristo continued, 'we can increase the amount; but I am only expecting to stay a year in France, and during that year I do not think I shall exceed that amount . . . Well, we shall see . . . So, for a start, please have five hundred thousand francs sent round to me tomorrow. I shall be at home until midday and, in any case, if I were to go out, I should leave a receipt with my steward.'

'The money will be with you tomorrow at ten in the morning, Monsieur le Comte,' Danglars replied. 'Would you like gold, bank-notes or coin?'

'Half gold and half notes, if you please.'

He got up to leave.

'One thing I must confess, Monsieur le Comte,' Danglars said. 'I thought that I was rather well acquainted with all the great fortunes in Europe; but I have to admit that yours, though it seems to be considerable, had entirely escaped my notice. Is it recent?'

'No, Monsieur,' Monte Cristo replied. 'On the contrary, it dates back a long way. It is a sort of family treasure which was not allowed to be touched; the accumulated interest tripled the capital sum. The period allotted under the will only elapsed a few years ago, so I have only been drawing on the money for a short time and your ignorance in the matter is entirely natural. In any event, you will shortly be better informed.'

The count accompanied these last words with one of those faint smiles that so terrified Franz d'Epinay.

'With your taste and your intentions, Monsieur,' Danglars continued, 'you will exhibit in Paris a degree of extravagance before which we shall pale into insignificance, we poor millionaires. However, as you strike me as a connoisseur – I did notice you looking at my pictures when I entered – I beg your permission to show you my collection. All guaranteed old masters. I do not like the modern school.'

'You are quite right, Monsieur. On the whole, they have one great shortcoming, which is that they have not yet had time to become old masters.'

'Could I show you some statues by Thorwaldsen, Bartolini or Canova?[2] All foreigners: I don't favour French artists.'

'You have the right to be unjust towards them, Monsieur, since they are your fellow-countrymen.'

'But all that can come later, when we know one another better. For the time being, with your permission, of course, I shall be content to introduce you to Baroness Danglars. Forgive my eagerness, Count, but a client such as yourself is almost one of the family.'

Monte Cristo bowed, indicating that he would accept the honour that the financier was offering to accord him.

Danglars rang and a footman appeared, dressed in brightly shining livery.

'Is the baroness at home?' Danglars asked.

'Yes, Monsieur le Baron,' the footman replied.

'Is she alone?'

'No, Madame has company.'

'It would not be indiscreet of me to introduce you when someone else is present, Count? You are not travelling incognito?'

'No, Baron,' Monte Cristo said, smiling. 'I do not allow myself that privilege.'

'Who is with madame? Is it Monsieur Debray?' Danglars asked, with a good humour that made Monte Cristo smile to himself, informed as he already was about the financier's domestic secrets.

'Yes, Baron, Monsieur Debray,' the footman replied.

Danglars nodded, then turned to Monte Cristo.

'Monsieur Lucien Debray,' he said, 'is an old friend of the family and the private secretary to the Minister of the Interior. As for my wife, she had to give up a title when she married me, for she belongs to an old family. She is a Mademoiselle de Servières, the widow from her first marriage, to the Marquis de Nargonne.'

'I do not have the honour of knowing Madame Danglars, but I have already met Monsieur Lucien Debray.'

'Huh!' Danglars exclaimed. 'Where was that?'

'At Monsieur de Morcerf's.'

'Oh, so you know the little viscount?' said Danglars.

'We found ourselves in Rome at the same time, during the carnival.'

'Oh, yes, indeed,' said Danglars. 'Did I not hear a rumour about something like a strange adventure with bandits and robbers in the ruins? He escaped by a miracle. I think he told my wife and daughter something about that when he returned from Italy.'

'Madame la baronne is expecting Your Lordships,' said the footman, coming back into the room.

'I shall lead the way,' Danglars said with a bow.

'And I shall follow you,' said Monte Cristo.

XLVII
THE DAPPLE-GREYS

Followed by the count, the baron led the way through a long succession of apartments characterized by tedious ostentation and expensive bad taste, until they reached Mme Danglars' boudoir, a small octagonal room hung with red satin and trimmed with Indian muslin. The chairs were in antique gilded wood and covered in old fabrics. Above the doors were paintings of shepherds and shepherdesses in the style of Boucher. Two pretty pastels, in oval frames, complementing the rest of the décor, made this little room the only one in the house with some individuality. Admittedly, it had been overlooked in the general design agreed between M. Danglars and his architect, one of the most famous and eminent members of his profession under the empire, so only the baroness and Lucien Debray were involved in doing it up. Danglars, a great admirer of Antiquity – as interpreted by the Directoire[1] – consequently had nothing but contempt for this charming little cubbyhole to which, in any case, he was usually admitted only on condition that he brought someone with him to excuse his presence. So in reality it was not Danglars who introduced visitors, but he himself who was introduced, to be received well or ill, depending on how much the visitor's face pleased or displeased the baroness.

Mme Danglars, who could still be described as beautiful despite her thirty-six years, was at the piano, a little masterpiece of cabinet-making, while Lucien Debray was sitting at an embroidery table, leafing through an album.

Before their arrival, Lucien had had time to tell the baroness several things about the count. The reader knows what an impression Monte Cristo made on Albert's guests over luncheon; though Debray was not easily susceptible to such impressions, this one had not yet faded, but left its mark on the details he gave to the baroness. Mme Danglars' curiosity, excited some time before by what she had learned from Morcerf, and now by Lucien, was consequently at its apogee. The tableau with the piano and the album was just one of those little social ruses which help to disguise one's preparations, and the baroness greeted M. Danglars with a smile, which was unusual on her part. As for the count, he received a solemn but graceful curtsey in exchange for his bow, while Lucien gave him a nod, acknowledging the brevity of their acquaintance-ship, greeting Danglars in more intimate fashion.

'Baroness,' Danglars said. 'Allow me to introduce the Count of Monte Cristo, who has been highly recommended to me by my business associates in Rome. I have only one thing to say about him, but it is one that will instantly make him the darling of all our lovely ladies: he has come to Paris, intending to stay here for a year, and in that time to spend six million francs, so we can expect a series of balls, dinners and feasts, in which I hope the count will not forget us, any more than we shall forget him in our own humble entertainments.'

The flattery in this introduction was fairly gross; however, it is so rare for a man to come to Paris, meaning to spend a prince's fortune in a single year, that Mme Danglars cast a glance at the count which was not devoid of interest.

'When did you arrive, Monsieur?' she asked.

'Yesterday, Madame.'

'And you have come, as I am told is your custom, from the ends of the earth?'

'This time quite simply from Cadiz, Madame.'

'You find us at an abominable season. Paris is frightful in summer: there are no more balls, no gatherings, no parties. The Italian opera is in London, the French opera is everywhere except in Paris and, as for the Théâtre Français, I suppose you know that it is no longer anywhere. So we have nothing to entertain us except a few miserable races at the Champ-de-Mars and Satory. Will you be racing your horses at all, Monsieur le Comte?'

'I shall be doing everything, Madame,' the count said, 'that is done in Paris, if I am fortunate enough to find someone who can reliably inform me on the customs of the country.'

'Do you like horses, Monsieur?'

'I have spent part of my life in the East, Madame, and, as you know, Orientals prize only two things in the world: the nobility of horses and the beauty of women.'

'My dear Count,' said the baroness, 'you might have been gallant enough to put women first.'

'You see, Madame: I was right a moment ago when I said that I needed a tutor to guide me in the ways of the country.'

At this, Mme Danglars' favourite chambermaid came in, went

over to her mistress and whispered a few words in her ear. The baroness paled.

'Impossible!' she exclaimed.

'It is the plain truth, Madame, for all that,' the chambermaid replied.

Mme Danglars turned to her husband.

'Is this true, Monsieur?'

'What, Madame?' asked Danglars, visibly uneasy.

'What this girl has just told me . . .'

'Which is?'

'She tells me that when my coachman went to harness my horses, they were not in the stable. I ask you, what can this mean?'

'Madame,' said Danglars, 'please listen to me . . .'

'Oh, I am listening, Monsieur, because I am curious to know what you have to tell me. I shall let these gentlemen judge between us, and I am going to start by explaining the situation to them. Gentlemen,' she said, turning to them, 'Baron Danglars has ten horses in his stables. Among these ten, there were two which belong to me, delightful creatures, the finest horses in Paris. You know them, Monsieur Debray: my dappled greys. Well, just when Madame de Villefort is to borrow my carriage, which I promised to her so that she could go in it tomorrow to the Bois, the two horses suddenly cannot be found! I presume that Monsieur Danglars saw the opportunity to make a few thousand francs, and sold them. Oh, God! What a vile breed they are, these speculators!'

'Madame,' Danglars replied, 'those horses were too lively. They were barely four years old and I was constantly afraid for your safety.'

'So, Monsieur?' said the baroness. 'You very well know that for the past month I have had the services of the finest coachman in Paris – unless, that is, you sold him with the horses.'

'My dear friend, I shall find a pair for you that are precisely the same, or even finer, if that is possible; but this time they will be mild-mannered and calm, and not make me so worried for you.'

The baroness shrugged her shoulders with a look of profound contempt. Danglars appeared not to notice these less than wifely manners and turned to Monte Cristo, saying: 'Sincerely, I am sorry that we did not meet earlier, Monsieur le Comte. Are you setting up your house?'

'Indeed, I am,' said the count.

'I should have offered them to you. Believe me, I gave them away for nearly nothing; but, as I said, I wanted to be rid of them. They are a young man's horses.'

'Thank you,' said the count. 'But I bought some this morning which are serviceable and not too expensive. Come, Monsieur Debray, you are a connoisseur, I think? Take a look.'

While Debray was going over to the window, Danglars went to his wife.

'You'll never guess,' he whispered to her. 'Someone came and offered me a ridiculous price for the horses. I don't know who the madman can be who is determined to ruin himself by sending his steward to me this morning, but the fact is that I made sixteen thousand francs on the deal. So don't sulk. I'll give you four thousand and two to Eugénie.'

Mme Danglars gave him a withering look.

'Bless my soul!' Debray exclaimed.

'What is it?' asked the baroness.

'If I am not mistaken, those are your horses – your very own – harnessed to the count's carriage.'

'My dappled greys?' Mme Danglars cried, running over to the window. 'Yes, undoubtedly!'

Danglars was astonished.

'Is it possible?' said Monte Cristo, feigning astonishment.

'Incredible!' the banker muttered.

The baroness whispered something to Debray, who came across to Monte Cristo. 'The baroness would like to ask you for how much her husband sold you the team.'

'I really don't know,' said the count. 'My steward meant it as a surprise to me . . . which cost me, I believe, thirty thousand francs.'

Debray conveyed this reply to the baroness.

Danglars was so pale and disconcerted that the count pretended to try to console him.

'You see how ungrateful women are,' he said. 'The baroness is not in the slightest touched by your consideration for her safety. Indeed, the word is not ungrateful, but mad. Then, what do you expect? They always like what is harmful to them. So, the simplest answer, my dear Baron, believe me, is to let them have their heads; then, if they break them, they have only themselves to blame.'

Danglars did not answer. He could foresee a disastrous quarrel looming on the horizon: already the baroness's eyebrow was raised and, like that of Olympian Jove, it presaged a storm. Hearing the first rumble, Debray made some excuse and left. Monte Cristo, not wanting to compromise the position that he hoped to gain by staying any longer, bowed to Mme Danglars and retired, leaving the baron to his wife's rage.

'Very well, then!' he thought as he left. 'I have achieved my aim. I now hold the domestic bliss of this household in my hands, and I am simultaneously about to win the heart of the baron and that of his wife. How fortunate! But, in the meantime,' he added, 'I have not yet been introduced to Mademoiselle Eugénie Danglars, whom I should have been very pleased to meet. However,' he continued, with a little smile that was all his own, 'we are in Paris, and we have lots of time before us . . . It can wait!' And, at this, he stepped into his carriage and returned home.

Two hours later, Mme Danglars received a charming letter from the Count of Monte Cristo, in which he told her that he did not wish to make his entry into Parisian society by upsetting a beautiful woman, and so begged her to accept her horses. They came in the same harness that she had seen on them that morning, except that the count had had a diamond sewn into the centre of each of the rosettes that they wore on their ears.

Danglars also had a letter. In it, the count asked his permission to convey this millionaire's whim to the baroness and begged him to excuse the Oriental gesture that accompanied their return.

That evening, Monte Cristo left for Auteuil, accompanied by Ali.

The next day, at around three o'clock, Ali was summoned by a ringing of the bell. He came into the count's study.

'Ali, you have often told me of your prowess with a lasso.'

Ali nodded and proudly drew himself up to his full height.

'Very well! With a lasso, could you bring down a bull?'

Ali nodded.

'A tiger?'

Again, Ali nodded.

'A lion?'

Ali imitated the motions of a man throwing a lasso and produced a strangled roar.

'Yes, I understand,' said Monte Cristo. 'Have you ever hunted a lion?'

Ali nodded proudly.

'But could you stop two horses in their tracks?'

Ali smiled.

'Good. Then listen to me. In a short while, a carriage will go by, drawn by two dapple-grey horses, the same ones that I had yesterday. Even at the risk of being run over, you must stop that carriage in front of my door.'

Ali went down into the street and drew a line on the cobbles. Then he came back and showed the line to the count, who had been watching him. The count tapped him gently on the shoulder, which was his way of expressing his thanks. Then the Nubian went to smoke his chibouk on the corner-stone between the house and the street, while Monte Cristo paid no further heed to the matter.

However, at about five o'clock, which was the time when the count expected the carriage to arrive, one might have observed in him some almost imperceptible signs of impatience. He walked up and down in a room overlooking the street, listening out from time to time and occasionally going across to the window, through which he could see Ali expelling puffs of smoke with a regularity that showed he was entirely absorbed in the important business of smoking his chibouk.

Suddenly there was a distant sound of rumbling, which approached at thunderous speed, then a barouche appeared, drawn by horses which the coachman was vainly trying to restrain as they dashed wildly forward, bristling and lunging madly this way and that.

In the barouche was a young woman, clasping a child of seven or eight years old in such an excess of terror that she had even lost the strength to cry out. A stone under the wheel or the branch of a tree would have been enough to smash the coach to pieces. It was already disintegrating as it drove down the middle of the street, and you could hear the terrified shouts of the onlookers as it approached.

Suddenly Ali put down his chibouk, took the lasso out of his pocket, threw it and wrapped it three times round the front legs of the left-hand horse. He was pulled three or four yards by the shock but, after these few yards, the lassoed horse came down, falling against the shaft, which it broke, thwarting the efforts of its companion to continue racing forward. The coachman took advantage of the momentary pause to leap off his box, but Ali had already grasped the nostrils of the second horse in his iron fingers and the animal, whinnying in pain, had dropped, shuddering, to the ground beside its fellow.

All this was accomplished in the time that it takes a bullet to find its mark.

The interval was enough, however, for a man to rush out of the house opposite which the accident happened, followed by several servants. Just as the coachman was opening the door of the coach, the man lifted out the lady, one of whose hands was grasping the upholstery of the seat while the other clasped her son, who was senseless with fear. Monte Cristo carried both of them into the drawing-room and set them down on a sofa, saying: 'Have no fear, Madame. You are safe.'

The woman recovered her senses and, in reply, indicated her son, with a look more eloquent than any entreaty. The boy was still unconscious.

'Madame, I understand you,' the count said, examining the child, 'but rest assured, he is unhurt, and fear alone has left him in this state.'

'Oh, Monsieur!' the mother cried. 'Perhaps you are just saying this to reassure me? Look how pale he is. Edouard, my son, my child! Answer your mother! Oh, please, Monsieur, send for a doctor. My fortune to the man who can save my son!'

Monte Cristo made a reassuring gesture to calm her and, opening a chest, took out a flask of Bohemian glass, encrusted with gold. It contained a blood-red liquid, a single drop of which he put on the child's lips. Although still pale, the boy immediately opened his eyes.

At this, the mother became almost delirious with joy. 'Where am I?' she cried. 'To whom do I owe such happiness after so frightful an ordeal?'

'Madame, you are in the house of a man who could not be more delighted to have relieved you of your woe,' the count replied.

'Accursed curiosity!' the lady said. 'All Paris was speaking about those magnificent horses of Madame Danglars, and I was crazy enough to wish to try them out.'

'What!' the count exclaimed, making a splendid appearance of surprise. 'Are those the baroness's horses?'

'Yes, Monsieur. Do you know her?'

'Madame Danglars? Yes, I have had the honour; and I am all the more delighted at seeing you safe from the danger in which these horses put you, since you might have blamed me for it. I bought them yesterday from the baron, but the baroness seemed to regret losing them so much that I sent them back to her the same day, begging her to accept them as a present from me.'

'This means that you must be that Count of Monte Cristo about whom Hermine spoke so much to me yesterday?'

'Yes, Madame,' said the count.

'And I, Monsieur, am Madame Héloïse de Villefort.'

The count bowed, like a man on hearing a name that was completely unknown to him.

'Oh, how grateful Monsieur de Villefort will be to you!' Héloïse continued. 'He owes you the lives of both of us: you have given him his wife and his son. Assuredly, without your noble-hearted servant, both this dear child and myself would have been killed.'

'Alas, Madame, I still shudder to think of the danger you were in.'

'I do hope you will allow me to give a suitable reward to the man for his determined action.'

'Please, Madame,' said Monte Cristo, 'don't spoil Ali for me, either with praise or with gifts. I don't want him to learn bad ways. Ali is my slave. In saving your life, he was merely serving me, which it is his duty to do.'

'But he risked his own life,' said Mme de Villefort, much impressed by the count's masterful tone.

'He owes me that life,' the count replied. 'I saved it, so it belongs to me.'

Mme de Villefort said nothing. Perhaps she was thinking about this man who made such a strong first impression.

In the momentary silence, the count had time to look at the child, whom the mother was smothering in kisses. He was small and lanky, with a whiteness of skin more common in redheads. However, an unruly forest of black hair covered his domed forehead and, falling across his shoulders on each side of his face, doubled the light of juvenile cunning and spitefulness that shone from his eyes. His broad mouth and slender lips were just recovering their colour; this eight-year-old's features were those of a child of twelve, at least. His first movement was brusquely to shake himself free of his mother's arms and to go across to the chest from which the count had taken the phial of elixir. Immediately he opened it and, without asking permission, like a child used to having his every whim satisfied, began to take the stoppers off the bottles.

'Don't do that, my young friend,' the count said sharply. 'Some of those liquids are dangerous, not only to drink, but even to breathe in.'

Mme de Villefort paled and clasped her son's arm, pulling him back to her. Yet the count noticed that, once relieved of her fear, she cast a brief but significant glance at the chest. At that moment, Ali came in.

Mme de Villefort made a gesture of joy and drew her son even closer to her.

'Edouard,' she said. 'Look at this good servant. He is most brave, because he risked his own life to stop the horses that were bolting with us and the carriage, which was about to crash. So, thank him, because it is probable that without him we should both be dead at this moment.'

The child pouted and scornfully turned away. 'He's too ugly,' he said.

The count smiled as if the child had just done precisely what he hoped. As for Mme de Villefort, she rebuked her son with a moderation that would surely not have pleased Jean-Jacques Rousseau,[2] if little Edouard had been called Emile.

'You see, now,' the count said in Arabic to Ali. 'This lady asked her son to thank you for saving both their lives, and the child answered that you were too ugly.'

For a moment Ali's intelligent head turned away and he looked blankly at the boy, but a slight trembling of his nostril told Monte Cristo that the Arab had suffered a mortal wound.

'Tell me, Monsieur,' said Mme de Villefort, getting up to leave, 'is this house your usual home?'

'No, Madame,' the count replied. 'This is a sort of pied-à-terre that I have bought. I live at number thirty, Avenue des Champs-Elysées. But I see that you have entirely recovered and would like to leave. I have just ordered these same horses to be harnessed to my carriage. This ugly boy, Ali,' he said, smiling at the child, 'will have the honour of driving you back home, while your coachman will stay here to arrange for the repairs to your barouche. As soon as the necessary work has been done, one of my own teams will take it back to Madame Danglars.'

'But I shall never dare to set off with those same horses,' said Mme de Villefort.

'Oh, wait and see, Madame,' Monte Cristo said. 'In Ali's hands they will be as mild as a pair of lambs.'

Ali had indeed gone over to the horses, which had with great difficulty been helped back to their feet. In his hand he carried a little sponge dipped in aromatic vinegar, and with this he rubbed the nostrils and temples of the horses, which were covered in sweat and foam. Almost at once they began to snort loudly and for a few seconds trembled in all their limbs.

Then, in the midst of a large crowd, attracted to the street outside the house by the remains of the carriage and the rumour of what had happened, Ali had the horses harnessed to the count's coupé, took up the reins, got on the box and, to the great astonishment of those present who had seen these same horses rushing forward as though driven by a tornado, was obliged to make good use of the whip before they would set off. Even then, the best he could obtain from these famous dappled greys, now stunned and petrified, was such a listless and uncertain trot that it took Mme de Villefort nearly two hours to return to her home in the Faubourg Saint-Honoré.

Hardly had she arrived and reassured her family than she sat down to write the following letter to Mme Danglars:

DEAR HERMINE,

I have just been miraculously saved, together with my son, by that same Count of Monte Cristo about whom we spoke so much yesterday evening, but whom I never thought I should see today. Yesterday you spoke to me of him with such enthusiasm that it took all the strength of my feeble spirit to refrain from mockery, but today I find your enthusiasm falls well below the man who inspired it. On reaching the Ranelagh,[3] your horses bolted as if touched by madness and we should probably have been dashed to pieces, poor Edouard and I, against the first tree on the road or the first village signpost, when an Arab, a Negro, a Nubian, in short, a black man, one of the count's servants, I believe, at a sign from the count, stopped the horses in their tracks, though at the risk of being run down himself; indeed, it is a miracle that he was not. The count ran out and had us carried into his house, Edouard and me, where he brought my son back to life. I returned home in his own carriage; yours will be sent back to you tomorrow. You will find your horses much enfeebled after the accident. It is as though they were stunned: one would think they could not forgive themselves for having been tamed by a man. The count asks me to tell you that two days' rest on straw and no food except barley will restore them to as healthy – that is to say, as terrifying – a state as before.

Farewell! I do not thank you for my ride; yet, on reflection, it is ungrateful of me to blame you for the capriciousness of your horses, because I owe them the opportunity of meeting the Count of Monte Cristo and, apart from his millions, this illustrious foreigner seems to me so odd and so interesting an enigma that I intend to study him at any price, even if it means another ride in the Bois with your horses.

Edouard bore the ordeal with extraordinary courage. He fainted, but before that did not make a sound and afterwards not a tear. You will tell me again that I am blinded by maternal love, but there is an iron will in that frail and delicate little body.

Dear Valentine sends her best wishes to your dear Eugénie. I embrace you with all my heart.

HÉLOÏSE DE VILLEFORT

P.S. Arrange it so that I can meet the Count of Monte Cristo at your house. I am determined to see him again. In any case, I have just got M. de Villefort to agree to pay a visit to him; I do hope it will be returned.

That evening, the accident at Auteuil was the subject of every conversation. Albert spoke of it to his mother, Château-Renaud at the Jockey-Club and Debray in the minister's drawing-room. Even Beauchamp paid the count the tribute, in his paper, of a twenty-line news item which presented the noble foreigner as a hero to all the women of the aristocracy. Several people went to leave their cards at Mme de Villefort's so that they would be able to pay a second visit at the appropriate time and hear the details of this exotic event from her own lips.

As for M. de Villefort, as Héloïse said, he took a black frock-coat, white gloves and his finest livery, then got into his coach which, that same evening, drew up in front of the door of number thirty, Avenue des Champs-Elysées.

XLVIII

IDEOLOGY

If the Count of Monte Cristo had lived longer in Parisian society, he would have been able to appreciate the full significance of M. de Villefort's gesture towards him. In favour at court, regardless of whether the reigning monarch belonged to the senior or junior branch of the royal family,[1] and whether the government of the day was doctrinaire, liberal or conservative; considered able by all, as people usually are when they have never suffered a political reverse, hated by many but eagerly protected by a few, though not loved by anyone, M. de Villefort occupied a high position in the judiciary and remained at that height by the same means as a Harlay or a Molé.[2] His salon, though enlivened by a young wife and a daughter from his first marriage who was barely eighteen years old, was nonetheless one of those strict Parisian salons which worship tradition and observe the religion of etiquette. Frigid good manners, absolute fidelity to the principles of the government in power, a profound contempt for theory and theoreticians, and a deep hatred of ideologues made up the elements of his public and private life that M. de Villefort exhibited to the world.

He was not only a magistrate, he was almost a diplomat. His connection with the old court, about which he always spoke with dignity and deference, gained him the respect of the new regime; he knew so much that not only was he always treated with tact but was even asked for his advice from time to time. Things might have been different, had it been possible to get rid of M. de Villefort, but – like a feudal baron in revolt against his monarch – he occupied an impregnable fortress. This was his post as crown prosecutor; he exploited all the advantages of his position and would have left it only to go into parliament, thus replacing neutrality with opposition.

On the whole, M. de Villefort made and returned few visits. His wife visited on his behalf: this was accepted in society, where it was attributed to the amount and gravity of the lawyer's business – when it was, in reality, deliberate arrogance, an extreme example of aristocratic contempt, in short, the application of the maxim: 'Admire yourself and others will admire you', a hundred times more useful in our days than the Greek one: 'Know thyself', which has now been replaced by the less demanding and more profitable art of knowing others.

To his friends M. de Villefort was a powerful protector; to his enemies, a silent but relentless adversary; to those who were neither, he was the statue of the law made flesh. Haughty in manner, impassive in expression, with eyes that were either dull and lifeless, or insolently penetrating and enquiring: this was the man whom four revolutions,[3] neatly stacked one on top of the other, had first elevated, then cemented to his pedestal.

M. de Villefort had the reputation of being the least curious and the least trivial-minded man in France. He gave a ball every year, showing his face in it for a mere quarter of an hour, that is to say, forty-five minutes less than the time the king spends in his balls. He was never seen at the theatre, at a concert or in any public place. Sometimes (but rarely) he would play a hand at whist, and on such occasions they were careful to choose players worthy of him: some ambassador or other, an archbishop, a prince, a president or some dowager duchess.

This was the man whose carriage had just drawn up before Monte Cristo's door. The valet announced M. de Villefort at the moment when the count was bending across a large table and tracing on a map the itinerary of a journey from St Petersburg to China. The crown prosecutor entered with the same heavy, measured tread that he would adopt on entering court. This was indeed the same man or, rather, the continuation of the same man, whom we met earlier as a *substitut* in Marseille. Nature, consistent with its principles, had changed nothing in the course laid down for him: once slim, he was now thin; once pale, he was now yellow. His deep-set eyes were hollow and his gold-rimmed spectacles, resting in the sockets, seemed to be part of the face. Apart from his white tie, the remainder of his dress was entirely black and this funereal colour was broken only by the fine strip of red ribbon imperceptibly threaded through his buttonhole, like a line of blood painted with a brush.

Though he gave no sign of any other emotion in returning his greeting, Monte Cristo examined the magistrate with visible curiosity. The other man, habitually cautious and, above all, incredulous where fashionable marvels were concerned, was more inclined to see in the Noble Foreigner (as people had already started to call

Monte Cristo) some knight of industry who had come to expand into new realms, or an outlaw creeping back into society, than a prince of the Holy See or a sultan of the *Thousand and One Nights*.

'Monsieur,' he said, with that hectoring tone that advocates adopt for addressing the courtroom, and which they are unable or unwilling to set aside in normal conversation, 'the notable service that you performed yesterday for my wife and son has put me under an obligation to thank you. I have therefore come to accomplish this duty and to express my gratitude to you.'

As he spoke these words, the judge's strict gaze lost none of its usual arrogance. He had articulated the words in his public prosecutor's voice, with the inflexible stiffness of the neck and shoulders that, as we have already mentioned, made his flatterers describe him as the living statue of the Law.

'Monsieur,' the count replied, in a voice of icy coldness, 'I am very happy at having been able to preserve a son for his mother, for they say that the feeling of maternal love is the holiest of all; and my enjoyment of this happiness released you, Monsieur, from the necessity of fulfilling a duty, the accomplishment of which undoubtedly flatters me, knowing as I do that Monsieur de Villefort is not prodigal with the honour that he does me, but which, precious though it may be, is less valuable to me than my sense of inner satisfaction.'

Villefort was astonished by this unexpected sally and winced like a soldier feeling a sword-thrust beneath his armour. A scornful curl of his lip showed that he did not henceforth consider Monte Cristo a very civil gentleman. He looked around for something on which to anchor the lapsed conversation (which seemed to have broken apart as it lapsed), and saw the map that Monte Cristo had been studying when he entered.

'Do you take an interest in geography, Monsieur?' he asked. 'It is a rich field of study, especially for someone like yourself who, we are assured, has seen as many countries as are marked in the atlas.'

'Yes, Monsieur,' the count replied. 'I have tried to subject the human race in general to the same analysis you daily apply to the exceptions, that is to say, a physiological one. I considered that it would eventually be easier to move from the whole to the part, than from part to whole. There is an axiom in algebra that requires us to proceed from the known to the unknown, and not the contrary ... But, sit down, I beg you, Monsieur.'

Monte Cristo directed the crown prosecutor to a chair so positioned that he had to take the trouble to bring it forward himself, while the count needed only to sit back in the one on which he had been kneeling when the prosecutor entered. In this way the count found himself half turned towards his visitor, with his back to the window and his elbow leaning on the map which, for the time being, was the object of their conversation – a conversation which was taking, as it had done with Morcerf and Danglars, a turn that was analogous, if not to the situation, at least to the persons involved.

'I see you are a philosopher,' said Villefort, after a momentary silence in which he had been gathering strength like a wrestler meeting a powerful opponent. 'Well, Monsieur, I do declare, if, like you, I had nothing to do, I should look for a less melancholy pastime.'

'Very true, Monsieur,' said Monte Cristo. 'Mankind is an ugly worm when you look at it through a solar microscope. But I think you said I have nothing to do. Now, Monsieur, I ask you, do you imagine you have anything to do? Or, to put it more clearly, do you believe that what you do deserves to be called something?'

Villefort's amazement was only increased by this second blow smartly delivered by his strange adversary. It was a long time since the judge had heard anyone deliver such a powerful paradox; or, more precisely, this was the first time he had heard it. He struggled to find a reply.

'Monsieur, you are a foreigner and, as I believe you admit yourself, part of your life has been spent in the East; so you may not know the prudence and formality that here surrounds judicial proceedings, which are so expeditiously dealt with in the East.'

'Very true, Monsieur, very true: the *pede claudo*[4] of Antiquity. I know all that, because my particular study in every country has been justice, assessing the criminal proceedings of every nation against natural justice; and, Monsieur, I have to tell you that the law of primitive peoples, that is to say, an eye for an eye, seems to me in the end closest to God's will.'

'If such a law were to be adopted,' the prosecutor said, 'it would greatly simplify our system of laws and the result would be that our judges, as you said a moment ago, would not have very much to do.'

'It may happen,' said Monte Cristo. 'You know that all human inventions progress from the complex to the simple and that perfection is always simplicity.'

'In the meantime,' said the judge, 'we have our laws, with their contradictory provisions, some reflecting the usages of the Gauls, others the laws of the Romans, and still others the customs of the Franks. You must admit that a knowledge of all those laws can only be had by years of toil, so one must study long and hard to acquire the knowledge and have a good brain, once it has been acquired, not to forget it.'

'I quite agree, Monsieur. But everything that you know, with respect to the French legal system, I know, not only with respect to that, but also to the laws of every country: the laws of the English, the Turks, the Japanese and the Hindus are as familiar to me as those of the French, so I was right to say that relatively – you know that everything is relative, Monsieur – relative to all that I have done, you have very little to do, and relative to what I have learned, you still have very much to learn.'

'To what end did you learn all this?' Villefort asked in astonishment.

Monte Cristo smiled.

'Very well, Monsieur,' he said. 'I can see that, despite your reputation as a superior being, you see everything from the vulgar and material point of view of society, beginning and ending with man, that is to say, the most restricted and narrow point of view that human intelligence can adopt.'

'I beg you to explain yourself, Monsieur,' said Villefort, more and more astonished. 'I don't entirely follow . . .'

'What I am saying, Monsieur, is that your eyes are fixed on the social organization of nations, which means that you only see the mechanism and not the sublime worker who operates it. I am saying that you only recognize in front of you and around you those office-holders whose accreditation has been signed by a minister or by the king and that your short-sightedness leads you to ignore those men whom God has set above office-holders, ministers and kings, by giving them a mission to pursue instead of a position to fill. This weakness is inherent in humans, with their feeble and inadequate organs. Tobias[5] mistook the angel who had just restored his sight for an ordinary young man. The nations mistook Attila, who would annihilate them, for a conqueror like other conquerors.

It was necessary for both to reveal their celestial missions for them to be recognized – for one to say: "I am the angel of the Lord", and the other: "I am the hammer of God", for their divine essence to be revealed.'

'Does this mean,' Villefort said, increasingly amazed and thinking he must be speaking to a visionary or a madman, 'that you consider yourself to be like one of these extraordinary beings you have just mentioned?'

'Why not?' Monte Cristo asked coldly.

'Please forgive me, Monsieur,' Villefort continued, in bewilderment, 'if when I called on you I was not aware that I was to be introduced to a man whose understanding and mind extend so far beyond the ordinary knowledge and usual cast of thought of mankind. It is not common among us, unfortunate victims as we are of the corrupting effects of civilization, for gentlemen who, like yourself, possess a vast fortune – at least, that is what I am told; but please do not think that I am prying, only repeating – as I say it is not customary for those who enjoy the privilege of wealth to waste their time in social speculation and philosophical dreams, which are rather designed to console those whom fate has deprived of the goods of the earth.'

'Well, well, Monsieur,' the count replied, 'have you reached your present eminent position without admitting that there may be exceptions, or even without encountering any? Do you never exercise your mind, which must surely require both subtlety and assurance, in trying to guess in an instant what kind of man you have before you? Should a jurist not be, not the best applier of the law or the cleverest interpreter of legal quibbles, but a steel probe for the testing of hearts and a touchstone against which to assay the gold that every soul contains in greater or lesser amounts?'

'Monsieur,' said Villefort, 'I have to admit, I am bewildered: on my word, I have never heard anyone speak as you do.'

'That is because you have constantly remained enclosed in the realm of general conditions, never daring to rise up on beating wings into the higher spheres that God has peopled with invisible and exceptional beings.'

'Are you saying that such spheres exist and that these exceptional and invisible beings mingle among us?'

'Why not? Do you see the air that you breathe, without which you could not live?'

'So we cannot see these beings of whom you speak?'

'Indeed we can, we can see them when God permits them to take material form. You touch them, you rub elbows with them, you speak to them and they answer you.'

'Ah!' Villefort said with a smile. 'I must confess that I should like to be told when one of these beings was in contact with me.'

'You have your wish, Monsieur. You were told a moment ago and I am telling you again.'

'You mean that you . . . ?'

'Yes, Monsieur. I am one of those exceptional beings and I believe that, before today, no man has found himself in a position similar to my own. The kingdoms of kings are confined, either by mountains or rivers, or by a change in customs or by a difference of language; but my kingdom is as great as the world, because I am neither Italian, nor French, nor Hindu, nor American, nor a Spaniard; I am a cosmopolitan. No country can claim to be my birthplace. God alone knows in what region I shall die. I adopt every custom, I speak every tongue. You think I am French, is that not so? Because I speak French as fluently and as perfectly as you do. Well, now. Ali, my Nubian, thinks me an Arab. Bertuccio, my steward, takes me for a Roman. Haydée, my slave, believes I am Greek. In this way, you see, being of no country, asking for the protection of no government and acknowledging no man as my brother, I am not restrained or hampered by a single one of the scruples that tie the hands of the powerful or the obstacles that block the path of the weak. I have only two enemies: I shall not say two conquerors, because with persistence I can make them bow to my will: they are distance and time. The third and most awful is my condition as a mortal man. Only that can halt me on the path I have chosen before I have reached my appointed goal. Everything else is planned for. I have foreseen all those things that men call the vagaries of fate: ruin, change and chance. If some of them might injure me, none could defeat me. Unless I die, I shall always be what I am. This is why I am telling you things that you have never heard, even from the mouths of kings, because kings need you and other men fear you. Who does not say to himself, in a society as ridiculously arranged as our own: "Perhaps one day I shall come up against the crown prosecutor"?'

'But, Monsieur, you too might say that yourself because, as long as you live in France, you are automatically subject to French law.'

'I know that,' Monte Cristo replied. 'But when I have to go to a country, I begin by studying, by methods peculiar to me, all those persons from whom I may have something to hope or to fear. I get to know them quite well, perhaps even better than they know themselves. The result of this is that the crown prosecutor with whom I had to deal, whoever he might be, would certainly be more put out by it than I would be myself.'

'By which you mean,' Villefort said hesitantly, 'that, in your view, human nature being weak, every man has committed some . . . error or other?'

'Some error . . . or crime,' Monte Cristo replied casually.

'And that you alone, among these men whom, as you yourself said, you do not recognize as your brothers . . .' (Villefort's voice sounded slightly strained) 'you alone are perfect?'

'Not perfect,' the count replied. 'Just impenetrable. But let us change the subject, Monsieur, if this one displeases you. I am no more threatened by your justice than you are by my second sight.'

'No, no!' Villefort said quickly, doubtless afraid that he might appear to be abandoning the field. 'Certainly not! With your brilliant and almost sublime conversation, you have elevated me above ordinary matters: we were no longer merely chatting, but discoursing. Well, now, you know theologians lecturing at the Sorbonne or philosophers in their disputations must sometimes tell one another painful truths. Imagine that we were debating social theology or theological philosophy, and I would say this, brutal though it is: brother, you are giving in to pride. You are above other men, but above you is God.'

'Above everything, Monsieur!' Monte Cristo replied, in a voice of such deep emotion that Villefort shuddered involuntarily. 'I have my pride for men, those serpents always ready to rise up against anyone who overtakes them, without crushing them beneath his foot. But I lay down that pride before God, who brought me out of nothingness to make me what I am.'

'In that case, Monsieur le Comte, I admire you,' Villefort said – for the first time in this strange dialogue addressing the foreigner, whom he had until then called simply 'Monsieur', by his aristocratic title. 'Yes, I say, if you are really strong, if you are really a superior being, really holy or impenetrable – you are quite right, the two amount virtually to the same thing – then revel in your magnificence

– that is the law of domination. But do you have some kind of ambition?'

'Yes, I do have one.'

'What is it?'

'Like every other man, at least once in his life, I too have been carried up by Satan to the highest mountain on earth. Once there, he showed me the whole world and, as he did to Christ, said to me: "Now, Son of Man, what do you want if you are to worship me?" So I thought for a long time, because in reality a terrible ambition had long been devouring my soul. Then I answered him: "Listen, I have always heard speak of Providence, yet I have never seen her or anything that resembles her, which makes me think that she does not exist. I want to be Providence, because the thing that I know which is finest, greatest and most sublime in the world is to reward and to punish." But Satan bowed his head and sighed. "You are wrong," he said. "Providence does exist, but you cannot see her, because, as the daughter of God, she is invisible like her father. You have seen nothing that resembles her because she proceeds by hidden means and walks down dark paths. All that I can do for you is to make you one of the agents of this Providence." The deal was concluded. I shall perhaps lose my soul,' Monte Cristo continued. 'But, what matter? If the deal had to be struck over again, I should do it.'

Villefort looked at him with sublime amazement.

'Do you have any relatives, Count?' he asked.

'None, Monsieur. I am alone in the world.'

'So much the worse!'

'Why?' asked Monte Cristo.

'Because you might have a spectacle capable of breaking your pride. You fear nothing but death, I think you said?'

'I did not say that I feared it. I said that it alone could prevent me.'

'And old age?'

'My mission will be accomplished before I am old.'

'And madness?'

'Once, I did almost become mad – and you know the saying: *non bis in idem*.[6] It is an axiom of the criminal law, so it falls within your province.'

'There are other things to fear, Monsieur,' Villefort said, 'apart from death, old age and madness. For example, apoplexy, that lightning bolt which strikes you down without destroying you, yet after which all is finished. You are still yourself, but you are no longer yourself: from a near-angel like Ariel you have become a dull mass which, like Caliban, is close to the beasts. As I said, in human language, this is quite simply called an apoplexy or stroke. Count, I beg you to come and finish this conversation at my house one day when you feel like meeting an opponent able to understand you and eager to refute what you say, and I shall show you my father, Monsieur Noirtier de Villefort, one of the most fiery Jacobins of the French Revolution – which means the most splendid daring put to the service of the most rigorous organization; a man who may not, like you, have seen all the kingdoms on earth, but who helped to overthrow one of the most powerful; a man who did not, like you, claim to be one of the envoys of God, but of the Supreme Being, not of Providence but of Fate. Well, Monsieur, the rupture of a blood vessel in the brain put an end to all that, not in a day, not in an hour, but in a second. One day he was Monsieur Noirtier, former Jacobin, former senator, former *carbonaro*,[7] who scorned the guillotine, the cannon and the dagger; Monsieur Noirtier, manipulator of revolutions; Monsieur Noirtier, for whom France was only a vast chessboard from which pawns, castles, knights and queens were to vanish when the king was mated. The next day, this redoubtable Monsieur Noirtier had become "poor Monsieur Noirtier", a paralysed old man, at the mercy of the weakest being in his household, his granddaughter Valentine. In short, a silent, icy corpse who only lives without suffering to allow time for the flesh to progress easily to total decomposition.'

'Alas, Monsieur,' Monte Cristo replied, 'this spectacle is not unknown to my eyes or to my thoughts. I have some training in medicine and, like my colleagues, I have more than once sought the soul in matter, living and dead; and, like Providence, it remained invisible to my eyes, though present in my heart. A hundred writers, from Socrates onwards, or Seneca, Saint Augustine or Gall, have made the same remark as you, whether in prose or in verse; yet I can understand that the sufferings of a father can accomplish great changes in the mind of his son. Since you are good enough to invite me, Monsieur, I shall come and observe this sad spectacle, which must bring great sorrow to your house and will incite me to humility.'

'The household would indeed be sad were it not that God has given me ample compensation. To counterbalance the old man who is thus delayed in his descent towards the grave, there are two whose lives have just begun: Valentine, daughter of my first marriage to Mademoiselle de Saint-Méran, and Edouard, the son whose life you saved.'

'What do you conclude from this compensation?' Monte Cristo asked.

'I conclude that my father, led astray by his passions, committed some of those sins that fall within the sphere of divine rather than human justice, and that God, wishing to punish only one person, struck him down alone.'

Monte Cristo had a smile on his lips, but he gave a roar in the depth of his heart that would have put Villefort to flight, could he have heard it.

'Farewell, Monsieur,' said the judge, who had risen to his feet some time ago and was standing as he spoke. 'I must leave you, taking away an esteem for you that, I hope, you will appreciate when you know me better, for I am not an insignificant person, far from it. In any case, you have made a friend for life in Madame de Villefort.'

The count bowed and accompanied Villefort only to the door of his study. The judge was conducted from there on to his carriage by two lackeys who, on a sign from their master, had rushed to open the door for him. Then, when the king's prosecutor had gone, Monte Cristo forced himself to smile despite the weight on his soul and said: 'Come, come. Enough of poison. Now that my heart is full of it, let us go and find the antidote.'

He struck the bell and, when Ali appeared, told him: 'I am going up to Madame. Have my carriage ready in half an hour!'

XLIX

HAYDÉE

The reader will remember the new – or, rather, the old – acquaintances of the Count of Monte Cristo, living in the Rue Meslay: Maximilien, Julie and Emmanuel.

Anticipation of the pleasure of this visit, of these few happy moments and of this celestial light breaking through into the hell which he had chosen to inhabit, had spread a look of utter serenity across the count's face as soon as Villefort was out of sight; and Ali, who had hurried to answer the ring of the bell, seeing his face radiant with such unaccustomed joy, had tiptoed out, holding his breath, as if to avoid scaring away the happy thoughts that he could see fluttering around his master.

It was midday. The count had put aside a time to go and see Haydée; it seemed as though joy could not penetrate all at once into a soul so deeply wounded but that it had to prepare itself for tender feelings, as the souls of others need to be prepared for violent ones.

The young Greek woman lived, as we have said, in a suite entirely separate from that of the count. It was completely furnished in the Oriental manner: that is to say, the floors were covered in thick Turkish carpets, brocade hangings were spread across the walls and, in each room, a broad divan ran all the way round the room, piled with cushions which those using them could arrange as they wished.

Haydée had three French maids and a Greek one. The three Frenchwomen remained in an outer room, ready to answer the sound of a little gold bell and obey the orders of the Romaic slave-girl, who knew enough French to pass on her mistress's wishes to the three maids, who had been instructed by Monte Cristo to show the same consideration towards Haydée as they would to a queen.

The young woman herself was in the most distant room in her suite, that is to say a sort of round boudoir, lit only from above, into which daylight only penetrated through panes of pink glass. She was lying down on blue satin cushions trimmed with gold, half leaning backwards across the divan, her head framed in the soft curve of her right arm, while the left hand held to her lips a coral mouthpiece inserted into the flexible pipe of a hookah, from which her gentle breath drew the smoke, obliging it to pass through benzoin water so that none would arrive unperfumed to her mouth.

Her pose, quite natural for a woman of the East, might perhaps, in a Frenchwoman, have suggested slightly affected coquetry.

As for her dress, it was that of a woman of Epirus: white satin trousers embroidered with pink flowers, displaying a child's feet which seemed carved out of Parian marble, except that they were toying with two tiny sandals, studded with gold thread and pearls, and with curled toes; a blue-and-white striped jacket, with wide slit sleeves, gold buttonholes and pearl buttons; and finally a sort of bodice, low cut across the heart, leaving the neck and upper part of the bosom bare, and buttoned across the breasts with three diamond buttons. The bottom part of this bodice and the top part of the trousers were concealed by one of those brightly coloured belts with long silken fringes that are so much admired by our elegant Parisian women.

On her head she wore a little skullcap, also in gold, studded with pearls, tipped to one side; and over this cap, on the side towards which it was leaning, a lovely purple-coloured rose emerged from hair so black that it seemed blue.

The beauty of her face was Grecian beauty in the full perfection of the type, with luscious black eyes, straight nose, coral lips and pearl-white teeth. In addition, this charming whole was crowned with the flower of youth in all its brilliance and sweetness: Haydée would have been around nineteen or twenty years old.

Monte Cristo called the Greek maid and had her ask Haydée's permission for him to go in to her. In reply, Haydée merely gestured to her maid to lift up the tapestry hanging over the door – the square outline of which framed the young woman on the divan like a delightful painting. Monte Cristo came into the room. Haydée rose on the elbow nearest to the hookah and offered the count her hand, greeting him with a smile and asking, in the resonant tongue of the daughters of Sparta and Athens: 'Why do you ask my permission to come in? Are you not my master, am I not your slave?'

Monte Cristo also smiled and said: 'You know, Haydée . . .'

'Why do you not say *tu* to me,[1] as usual?' the young woman interrupted. 'Have I done something wrong? In that case, I must be punished, but don't say *vous* to me.'

'Haydée,' the count said, reverting to the familiar form of address, 'you know that we are in France and that, consequently, you are free.'

'Free to do what?'

'Free to leave me.'

'To leave you . . . Why should I leave you?'

'How do I know? We are going to meet people.'

'I don't want to meet anyone.'

'And among the handsome young men whom you will meet, you may find one whom you like. I would not be so unjust as to . . .'

'I have never seen any man more handsome than you, or loved any man except my father and you.'

'Poor child,' said Monte Cristo. 'That is because you have only ever spoken to your father and to me.'

'What need have I to speak to anyone else? My father called me "my sweet", you call me "my love", and you both call me "my child".'

'Do you remember your father, Haydée?'

The girl smiled and put her hand on her eyes and her heart: 'He is here . . . and here . . .' she said.

'And where am I?' Monte Cristo asked with a smile.

'You are everywhere.'

He took Haydée's hand to kiss it, but the innocent girl drew it back and offered him her forehead.

'Now, Haydée,' he said, 'you know that you are free, that you are your own mistress, that you are queen. You can keep your native costume, or change it as you wish. You can stay here whenever you like, and go out when you want to go out. There will always be a carriage harnessed and ready for you. Ali and Myrto will accompany you everywhere and be at your orders. I ask only one thing.'

'Tell me.'

'Keep the secret of your birth and do not say a word about your past. At no time must you give the name of your illustrious father or that of your poor mother.'

'My Lord, I have already told you: I shall not meet anyone.'

'Listen to me, Haydée: this Oriental style of seclusion may not be possible in Paris. Carry on learning about life in these northern countries, just as you did in Rome, Florence, Milan and Madrid. It will always be useful to you, whether you continue to live here or you return to the East.'

The girl looked at the count with her wide, moist eyes and asked: 'If we return to the East, you must surely mean, my Lord?'

'Yes, child,' said Monte Cristo. 'You know very well that it will never be I who will leave you. It is not the tree that forsakes the flower, but the flower that forsakes the tree.'

'And I shall never leave you, my Lord,' said Haydée. 'For I am sure that I could not live without you.'

'Poor child! In ten years I shall be old and in ten years you will still be young.'

'My father had a long white beard, but that did not stop me loving him. My father was sixty years old and he seemed to me more beautiful than any of the young men I saw.'

'But tell me, do you think you could get used to living here?'

'Shall I see you?'

'Every day.'

'So, my Lord, why are you asking me?'

'I am afraid you may be bored.'

'No, Lord, for in the morning I shall be thinking that you will come and in the evening I shall recall your visit. In any case, when I am alone I have marvellous memories, I see huge landscapes and vast horizons, with Pindus and Olympus in the distance. Then I have in my heart three feelings with which one can never be bored: sadness, love and gratitude.'

'You are a worthy daughter of Epirus, Haydée, graceful, poetic ... One can see that you are descended from that family of goddesses to which your country gave birth. So have no fear, my child, I shall ensure that your youth will not be wasted; for, if you love me as though I were your father, I love you as my child.'

'You are mistaken, Lord. I did not love my father as I love you. My love for you is a different kind of love. My father is dead, and I am alive, while if you were to die, I should die also.'

The count held out his hand to the young woman with a smile of deep tenderness and she, as usual, kissed it.

In this way, prepared for the interview that he was about to have with Morrel and his family, the count left, murmuring these verses from Pindar: 'Youth is a flower of which love is the fruit ... Happy the vintager who picks it after watching it slowly mature.'

As he had ordered, the carriage was ready. He stepped into it and the horses, as always, set off at a gallop.

L

THE MORRELS

In a few minutes the count reached No. 7, Rue Meslay. It was a cheerful white house with a front garden with two small banks full of quite lovely flowers.

The count recognized the concierge who came to open the gate to him: it was old Coclès. But the latter, as you may recall, had only one eye, and even this eye had considerably weakened over the past nine years, so he did not recognize the count.

To reach the front door, carriages had to drive round a little fountain of water, set in the middle of a rocky pool: this ostentation had excited much jealousy in the district and accounted for the house being called 'Little Versailles'. The pool, needless to say, was full of red and yellow fish. The house had a basement with kitchens and cellars, above which, apart from the ground floor, there were two full storeys and attics. The young people had bought it with its appurtenances: a huge workshop, two lodges in the garden, and the garden itself. On first visiting the property, Emmanuel had seen that this arrangement might be the opportunity for a little speculative venture. He had set aside the house and half the garden for himself and had drawn a line across it: that is to say, he built a wall between himself and the workshops, which he leased out with the outbuildings and the part of the garden surrounding them. In this way, he had a home for a quite modest sum and was as tightly enclosed in his own home as the most fastidious householder of a private mansion on the Faubourg Saint-Germain.

The dining-room was in oak, the drawing-room in walnut and blue velvet, and the bedroom in lemonwood and green damask. In addition, there was a study for Emmanuel, who did not study, and a music room for Julie, who did not play any music.

The second floor was entirely devoted to Maximilien. It was the precise replica of his sister's apartment, except that the dining-room had been converted into a billiard room where he brought his friends. He was himself overseeing the grooming of his horse and smoking a cigar at the entrance to the garden when the count's carriage drew up in front of the gate.

As we said, Coclès opened the gate and Baptistin, leaping down from his seat, asked if M. and Mme Herbault and M. Maximilien Morrel would receive the Count of Monte Cristo. 'The Count of Monte Cristo!' Morrel exclaimed, casting aside his cigar and running down to meet the visitor. 'I should say we will receive the Count of Monte Cristo! Thank you, thank you a hundred times, Count, for not forgetting your promise.'

The young officer shook the count's hand so warmly that he could not mistake the sincerity of the gesture and understood that he had been awaited with impatience, to be greeted with enthusiasm.

'Come, come,' said Maximilien. 'I want to introduce you myself. A man like you should not be announced by a servant. My sister is in her garden, pruning the roses. My brother is reading his two newspapers, the *Presse* and the *Débats*[1] – a few feet away from her; because, wherever you see Madame Herbault, you have only to search in a radius of four yards around her to find Monsieur Emmanuel – and reciprocally, as they say at the Ecole Polytechnique.'

Their footsteps attracted the attention of a young woman of between twenty and twenty-five, wearing a silk robe, who was concentrating on pruning a reddish brown rose bush. This was little Julie. As the emissary of the firm of Thomson and French had predicted, she was now Mme Emmanuel Herbault. She looked up and gave a cry on seeing a stranger. Maximilien began to laugh.

'Don't worry, sister,' he said. 'The count has only been in Paris for two or three days, but he already knows what to expect from a lady with a private income in the Marais. If he doesn't, you will show him.'

'Oh, Monsieur,' said Julie. 'This is treachery on the part of my brother, bringing you here without the slightest regard for how his sister looks . . . Penelon! Penelon!'

An old man who was digging a bed of Bengal roses stuck his spade in the ground and came over, cap in hand, doing his best to hide a quid of tobacco which he had temporarily pushed to the back of his cheek. His hair was still thick, though streaked with a few while strands, while his sunburnt complexion and his sharp, fearless eyes betrayed the old sailor, tanned by the equatorial sun and weathered in the storm.

'I think you called me, Mademoiselle Julie. Here I am.'

Penelon still called his boss's daughter 'Mademoiselle Julie', never having managed to accustom himself to call her 'Madame Herbault'.

'Penelon,' Julie said, 'go and inform Monsieur Emmanuel of our visitor's welcome arrival, while Monsieur Maximilien is showing the count into the drawing-room.' Then, turning to Monte Cristo, she added: 'You will permit me to retire for a moment, I hope?' and, without waiting for the count's consent, she set off briskly behind a bank of flowers, taking a side-path into the house.

'Oh, now, my dear Monsieur Morrel!' Monte Cristo said. 'It pains me to see that I am turning your whole house upside down.'

'Come, come,' Maximilien said, laughing. 'Look: there is the husband, who is also changing his jacket for a frock-coat! You are known in the Rue Meslay and, I beg you to believe me, your arrival was announced.'

'It appears to me that you have a happy family here,' said the count, following his own train of thought.

'Yes, indeed, you may be assured of that. What do you expect? They have all that they need to be happy. They are young, merry, in love and, with their income of twenty-five thousand *livres* a year, even though they have rubbed shoulders with vast fortunes, they think themselves as wealthy as Rothschild.'

'Yet, it is a small sum, twenty-five thousand *livres* a year,' said Monte Cristo with such softness that it found a path to the depths of Maximilien's heart like the voice of a loving father. 'But these young people will not stop there. They will be millionaires in their turn. Is your brother-in-law a lawyer . . . a doctor . . . ?'

'He was a merchant, Count. He took over my poor father's business. Monsieur Morrel died leaving five hundred thousand francs. There were only two children, so I had one half and my sister the other. Her husband, who had married her with no other fortune except his unflinching honesty, his outstanding intelligence and his spotless reputation, wanted to match his wife's patrimony. He worked until he had saved two hundred and fifty thousand francs; six years were enough. I assure you, Count, it was touching to see these two young people, so hardworking, so devoted to one another, destined by their talents to enjoy the greatest good fortune, desirous of changing nothing in the customary methods of the family firm: they took six years to accomplish what an innovator could have done in two or three, and all Marseille resounded with praise for such brave self-denial. Finally, one day, Emmanuel came to his wife, who had just made the final payment.

' "Julie," he told her, "here is the last bundle of one hundred francs that Coclès has just given me, completing the two hundred and fifty thousand francs that we set as the limit to our profits. Will you be content with this small sum on which we shall have henceforth to survive? Listen, the firm has a turnover of a million a year and can bring in a profit of forty thousand francs. If we wish, we can sell our clientele within the hour for three hundred thousand francs: here is a letter from Monsieur Delaunay, offering us that in exchange for our assets, which he wants to merge with his own. Consider what we should do."

' "My dear," my sister answered, "the firm of Morrel can only be run by a Morrel. Is it not worth three hundred thousand francs, to save our father's name for ever from the mischances of fortune?"

' "I had reached the same conclusion," Emmanuel said, "but I wanted to know your opinion."

' "Now you know it, my dear. All our accounts are up to date, all our bills are paid. We can draw a line under the balance sheet for this fortnight and put up the shutters: let's do it." And they did, immediately. It was three o'clock. At a quarter past, a customer came in to insure two ships for a voyage, which would have meant a clear profit of fifteen thousand francs.

' "Monsieur," Emmanuel said, "please be so good as to take your business to our colleague, Monsieur Delaunay. We are no longer in business."

' "Since when?" the customer asked in amazement.

' "Since a quarter of an hour ago."

'And that, Monsieur,' Maximilien continued, with a smile, 'is how my sister and my brother-in-law come to have an income of only twenty-five thousand *livres*.'

Maximilien had barely finished his story – the count's heart had swelled progressively as it proceeded – when Emmanuel re-appeared, properly fitted out with a hat and frock-coat. He gave a bow that acknowledged the visitor's importance, then, after showing the count round the little flower garden, he led him back to the house.

The drawing-room was already redolent of the flowers that burst out of a huge, wicker-handled Japanese vase. Julie, tidily dressed and her hair prettily done (she had achieved this *tour de force* in ten minutes), was waiting to receive the count as he came in.

Birds could be heard singing in a nearby aviary, and the blue velvet curtains were bordered with clusters of laburnum and pink acacia branches: everything in this charming little retreat spoke of tranquillity, from the song of the birds to the smile of the owners.

From the moment he entered the house, the count had been filled with this happiness. He remained silent and meditative, forgetting that the others were waiting for him to resume the conversation, which had halted after the first exchange of greetings. Finally, becoming aware of this silence, which was on the point of becoming embarrassing, and forcing himself out of his reverie, he said: 'Madame, forgive me. Accustomed as you are to the atmosphere of happiness that I find here, my feelings must astonish you. But, for me, the sight of contentment on a human face is so novel that I cannot resist looking at you and your husband.'

'We are, indeed, very happy, Monsieur,' Julie replied. 'But we had to suffer for a long time, and few people have bought their happiness as dearly as we have.'

The count's face expressed his curiosity.

'Oh, there is a whole family history here, as Château-Renaud told you the other day,' Maximilien remarked. 'You, Monsieur le Comte, accustomed as you are to notorious misfortunes and illustrious joys, will find little to interest you in this domestic scene. Yet, as Julie says, we have suffered much pain, even though it was confined to a small stage . . .'

'And did God give you consolation for your sufferings, as He does for all of us?' Monte Cristo asked.

'Yes, Count,' Julie said. 'We can say that, indeed, for He did something for us that He does only for the chosen few: He sent us one of his angels.'

The count blushed and he coughed, to give himself an excuse to put a handkerchief to his mouth and hide the evidence of his feelings.

'Those who are born with a silver spoon,' Emmanuel said, 'those who have never needed anything, do not understand what happiness is, any more than those who do not know the blessing of a clear sky and who have never entrusted their lives to four planks tossing on a raging sea.'

Monte Cristo got up and started to pace up and down the

room, but said nothing, because his voice would have betrayed his emotion.

'You are smiling at the splendour of our apartments, Count,' said Maximilien, watching him.

'No, not at all,' replied Monte Cristo, pale, holding one hand across his chest to repress the beating of his heart and pointing with the other to a crystal globe under which a silk purse was carefully preserved, lying on a black velvet cushion. 'I was just wondering what was the purpose of this purse which, it seems to me, holds on one side a piece of paper and on the other a rather fine diamond.'

'That, Monsieur le Comte, is the most precious of the family treasures.'

'The diamond is indeed rather fine,' the Count replied.

'Oh, my brother is not referring to the value of the stone, Monsieur, though it is estimated at a hundred thousand francs. He merely wishes to tell you that the objects in this purse are the relics of the angel about whom we spoke a moment ago.'

'I do not understand what you can mean, yet I have no right to question you about it, Madame,' Monte Cristo said, with a bow. 'Pray forgive me. I did not mean to be inquisitive.'

'What do you mean, inquisitive? Please, Count, allow us the pleasure of this opportunity to talk about it. If we wished to conceal this fine deed and keep secret the story behind this purse, then we should not exhibit it in this way. But we wish, on the contrary, to publish it throughout the world, so that our unknown benefactor might give a sign which would betray his presence to us.'

'Indeed!' Monte Cristo exclaimed in a muffled voice.

Maximilien lifted the crystal dome and piously kissed the silk purse. 'Monsieur,' he said, 'this has been touched by the hand of a man who saved my father from death, us from ruin and our name from ignominy – a man thanks to whom we, poor children destined for poverty and tears, can today hear people rhapsodize about our happiness and good fortune. This letter' (Maximilien took it out of the purse and handed it to the count) 'was written by him on a day when my father had taken the most desperate decision and this diamond was given to my sister by this generous stranger as her dowry.'

Monte Cristo opened the letter and read it with an indescribable expression of happiness: it was the note that the reader will already know: the one addressed to Julie and signed by 'Sinbad the Sailor'.

'A stranger, you say? So you have never discovered the identity of the man who did this for you?'

'No, Monsieur, we have never had the pleasure of shaking his hand. It is not through want of praying God for the opportunity to do so,' Maximilien continued, 'but there was a mysterious purpose behind all this adventure that we cannot yet understand: it was entirely controlled by an invisible hand, powerful as that of an enchanter.'

'Oh!' Julie exclaimed. 'I have not lost all hope that I may one day kiss that hand as I now kiss the purse that it touched. Four years ago Penelon was in Trieste – Penelon, Count, is the honest sailor whom you saw with a spade in his hand and who, once a bosun, is now a gardener. As I say, Penelon was in Trieste where he saw an Englishman on the quayside about to embark on a yacht and recognized the man who came to my father's on June the fifth, 1829, and wrote me that note on September the fifth. He assures me it was the same man, but that he did not dare speak to him.'

'An Englishman!' Monte Cristo said thoughtfully, growing more anxious whenever Julie glanced at him. 'You say it was an Englishman?'

'Yes,' Maximilien replied. 'An Englishman who presented himself to us as an emissary from the firm of Thomson and French in Rome. That is why you saw me start the other day, at Monsieur Morcerf's, when you mentioned that Messrs Thomson and French are your bankers. As we said, this happened in 1829: in heaven's name, Monsieur, did you know this Englishman?'

'I thought you also told me that Thomson and French consistently denied having performed this service for you?'

'Yes, they do.'

'So the Englishman might well be a man who, in gratitude to your father for some good deed that even your father had forgotten, used this as a pretext to do him a favour?'

'In the circumstances, everything is possible, even a miracle.'

'What was his name?' Monte Cristo asked.

'He left no name,' Julie replied, looking very closely at the count, 'except the one with which he signed the note: Sinbad the Sailor.'

'Which is evidently not a name, but a pseudonym.' Then, as Julie was looking still more attentively at him and was trying to catch something in his voice and place it, the count continued: 'Come now: was it perhaps a man of about my height, perhaps a little taller, somewhat slimmer, wearing a high cravat, buttoned up, tightly corseted, who always had a pencil in his hand?'

'You do know him!' Julie cried, her eyes gleaming with joy.

'No,' the count replied, 'it was just a supposition. I did know a Lord Wilmore who would perform such acts of generosity.'

'Without revealing himself!'

'He was an odd man who did not believe in gratitude.'

'In that case,' Julie cried, in sublime tones, clasping her hands, 'what did he believe in, the poor man?'

'He certainly did not believe in it at the time when I knew him,' Monte Cristo said, moved to the very depths of his being by her soulful voice. 'Since then, he may perhaps have had some proof that gratitude does exist.'

'Do you know this man?' Emmanuel asked.

'Oh, Monsieur, if you do know him,' Julie exclaimed, 'tell me, please; if you cannot bring him to us, show him to us, tell us where he is! If we should ever find him, he would surely have to believe that the heart does not forget, is that not so, Emmanuel? Maximilien?'

Monte Cristo felt two tears gather in his eyes and paced once more up and down the room.

'I beg you, Monsieur,' said Maximilien, 'if you do know anything of this man, please tell us what you know.'

'Alas!' Monte Cristo exclaimed, repressing the emotion in his voice. 'If Lord Wilmore is indeed your benefactor, I am very much afraid that you will never find him. I left him two or three years ago in Palermo and he was about to set off for the most fabled shores; indeed, I gravely doubt if he will ever return.'

'Oh, Monsieur! It is cruel of you to say so!' said Julie, horrified, tears springing to her eyes.

'Madame,' Monte Cristo said gravely, his gaze fixed on the two liquid pearls running down her cheeks, 'if Lord Wilmore could witness what I have just seen here, he would still love life, because your tears would reconcile him to the human race.' And he held out his hand to Julie, who gave him hers, finding herself captivated by the count's look and the tone of his voice.

'But,' she said, clasping at one last straw, 'this Lord Wilmore: he must have had a country, a family, relatives – in short, he was known? Could we not . . . ?'

'Don't even try, Madame,' said the count. 'Do not build some sweet hope on the foundation of a word that slipped from my lips. No, Lord Wilmore is probably not the man you are looking for. He was my friend, I knew all his secrets and he would have told me that one.'

'But he said nothing to you?' Julie asked.

'Nothing.'

'Not a word that might have suggested . . . ?'

'Never a word.'

'Yet his was the name that immediately sprang to your lips.'

'Oh, you know: in such cases, one makes a guess . . .'

'Sister, dear sister,' said Maximilien, coming to his aid, 'the count is right. Remember what our good father so often told us: "It was not an Englishman who did us this great service." '

Monte Cristo shuddered. 'Your father said . . . what, Monsieur Morrel?' he asked sharply.

'My father saw this act as a miracle. He believed that our benefactor was someone who had come back from the dead. Oh, Monsieur, it was a touching superstition and, while I did not believe it myself, I certainly had no wish to destroy the belief in his noble heart! How many times did he mutter the name of a dear, dear friend, a friend whom he had lost; and when he was on the point of death and the prospect of eternity might have given his mind some illumination from beyond the grave, this idea, which until then had been no more than a suspicion, became a certainty, and the last words that he spoke before he died were these: "Maximilien, it was Edmond Dantès." '

The colour had been draining from the count's face as Maximilien spoke and, at these words, his face became awful in its pallor. All the blood had rushed to his heart and he was speechless. He took out his watch as if he had forgotten the time, grasped his hat, brusquely muttered an embarrassed farewell to Mme Herbault and said, clasping the hands of Emmanuel and Maximilien: 'Madame, allow me to come from time to time to pay my compliments to you. I love your house and I am most grateful to you for your hospitality, because this is the first time for many years that I have been able to forget my troubles.' And he left, striding out of the house.

'An odd fellow, this Count of Monte Cristo,' Emmanuel said.

'Yes,' Maximilien replied, 'but I think he has a good heart and I am sure that he likes us.'

'So am I!' Julie exclaimed. 'His voice touched me deeply and two or three times I thought that this was not the first time I had heard it.'

LI

PYRAMUS AND THISBE

Two-thirds of the way down the Faubourg Saint-Honoré, behind a magnificent private mansion (remarkable even among the many remarkable residences in this rich district), there is a huge garden surrounded by walls as high as ramparts. From here, in springtime, the tufted chestnuts drop their pink-and-white flowers into two fluted stone vases, placed opposite one another on two quadrangular pilasters, between which is set an iron gateway from the time of Louis XIII.

Despite the splendid geraniums growing in the two vases which tossed their marbled leaves and purple flowers in the wind, this grandiose entrance had been condemned since the time – and it was some time earlier – when the owners of the mansion confined themselves to possession of the house itself, the tree-lined courtyard opening into the Faubourg and the garden behind the gateway we have mentioned, which formerly gave access to a magnificent vegetable garden, an acre in size, adjoining the property. But the demon of speculation drew a line, in the form of a street, along the side of the vegetable garden; the street, before it even existed except as a line, received a name, thanks to a polished-iron plaque; and someone had the idea that the vegetable garden could be sold for buildings along the street, to compete with the major Parisian thoroughfare called the Faubourg Saint-Honoré.

However, where speculation is concerned, man proposes and money disposes. The street was baptized and died in its cradle. The purchaser of the vegetable garden, having paid the full amount for it, could not resell at the price he wanted; so, while waiting for a rise in prices that was bound, sooner or later, to more than compensate him for past losses and the capital which he had tied up, he made do with renting the plot to some market gardeners for the sum of five hundred francs a year. This was money invested at half a per cent, which is not much nowadays when so many people invest it at fifty and still complain that the returns are poor.

However, as we said, the garden gate, which used at one time to look over the vegetable garden, has been condemned and rust is eating into its hinges. Worse still: so that the low-born market gardeners shall not sully the interior of the aristocratic property with their vulgar gaze, a wall of planks has been affixed to the bars of the gate up to a height of six feet. Admittedly these planks are not so tightly juxtaposed as to prevent a furtive glance slipping between them; but the house is a forbidding house and not afraid of indiscreet eyes.

In the vegetable garden, instead of cabbages, carrots, radish, peas and melons, the only growing things to show that this otherwise abandoned site is still sometimes tended are tall alfalfa plants. A low door, opening on the proposed line of the street, allows entry to the place, which is surrounded by walls. The tenants have, in the past week, abandoned it because of its barrenness, and now, instead of the previous half a percent, it is bringing in no per cent at all.

On the side nearest to the mansion, the chestnut-trees which we mentioned crown the wall, though this does not prevent other luxuriantly flowering rivals from insinuating their branches between them in search of air. At a corner where the growth is so thick that the light can hardly penetrate, a wide stone bench and some garden seats mark a meeting place or favourite retreat of an inhabitant of the large house, which can hardly be seen through the protective wall of greenery around this spot, even though it is only a hundred yards away. Apart from that, the position of this mysterious shelter could have been dictated by: the absence of sun, giving a permanent chill to the air, on even the hottest summer days; the singing of the birds; and the distance from the house and from the street, that is to say from bustle and noise.

On the evening of one of the warmest days that Paris had so far enjoyed that spring, the stone bench carried a book, a sunshade, a work basket and a lawn handkerchief, partly embroidered. Not far from the bench, beside the gate, looking through a gap in the planks, was a young woman whose attention was directed towards the deserted vegetable garden which we have just described.

Almost at the same moment as she was looking out across it, the little doorway into the site closed silently and a young man came through it, tall, energetic, wearing an undyed cotton smock and corduroy cap – though his well-tended moustache, beard and black hair did not harmonize with this lower-class attire. He looked quickly around to ensure that he was not being watched, came through the door, closed it behind him and strode rapidly towards the iron gate.

Seeing the man she was expecting, if not necessarily in that dress, the young woman was taken aback and started. But the man, with a sharpness of perception that belongs only to a lover, had already seen, through the gaps in the planks, the fluttering of her white dress and long blue belt. He ran across to the gate and, pressing his lips against the opening, said: 'Don't worry, Valentine. It's me!'

The girl came back.

'Oh, Monsieur,' she said, 'why are you so late today? Do you realize that it will soon be dinner and that I needed a great deal of diplomacy and a great deal of rapid thinking to get rid of my stepmother who watches me, my chambermaid who spies on me, and my brother who teases me, before I could manage to come down here and work on this embroidery which, I fear, will not be finished for a long while yet? Then, when you have explained and asked forgiveness for your lateness, you can tell me what is this new style of dress that you have decided to adopt, which almost prevented me from recognizing you.'

'Dear Valentine,' said the young man, 'you are too far above my love for me to dare speak of it to you, yet every time that I see you I need to tell you that I adore you, so that the echo of my own words will gently caress my heart when I am no longer with you. Now, let me thank you for your scolding; it charms me, because it proves that . . . I dare not say that you were waiting for me, but at least that you thought of me. You wish to know the reason for my late arrival and for my disguise. I shall tell you and I hope you will forgive them. I have chosen a trade . . .'

'A trade! What do you mean, Maximilien? Are we fortunate enough for you to jest about what matters so much to us?'

'Heaven forbid that I should jest when my life depends on it,' said the young man. 'But I have grown tired of being a runner through fields and a climber of walls; and I was seriously worried by the idea you suggested to me the other evening, that your father

might one day have me hauled up as a thief, which would be a blow
to the honour of the entire French army. Apart from which, I feared
people might find it odd for a captain in the spahis to be constantly
hovering around this plot of land, where there is not a single fortress
to attack or blockhouse to defend; so I have become a market
gardener and put on the clothing of my profession.'

'What idiocy is this!'

'None at all but, I think, the most sensible thing I have done in
my life, because it gives us complete security.'

'Explain what you mean.'

'Well, I went to find the owner of this plot of land and, since the
lease with the old tenants had run out, I took it over from him
myself. All this alfalfa that you see is mine, Valentine. Nothing
prevents me from building a cabin in the stubble and from henceforth living twenty yards away from you. Oh, happiness and joy –
I can hardly contain myself. Do you think that those two things
can be bought, Valentine? Impossible, isn't it? Well, all this happiness and joy, for which I would have given ten years of my life, are
costing me . . . guess how much? Five hundred francs a year, in
quarterly instalments. You see, from now on we have nothing to
fear. I am at home here. I can put a ladder against my wall and look
over it. I am entitled to tell you that I love you, without fearing that
the night watch will disturb me, provided your pride is not wounded
at hearing this word on the lips of a poor day-labourer dressed in
a smock and wearing a cap.'

Valentine gave a little cry of joyful surprise; then, as if a jealous
cloud had suddenly come between her and the ray of sunshine
that had lit up her heart, she remarked sadly: 'Alas, Maximilien,
now we shall be too free and our happiness will tempt fate. We
shall misuse our freedom and a false sense of security will destroy
us.'

'Can you say that to me, my dearest; to the man who, since he
has known you, has proved every day that he subordinates his own
thoughts and his own life to yours? Was it not my happiness that
gave you confidence in me? When you told me that some vague
instinct had convinced you that you were running a great danger,
I devoted myself to serving you, and asked for no reward save the
happiness of being able to do so. Since that time, have I given any
indication that would make you repent of having chosen me from
among all those who would have been happy to die for you? Poor

child, you told me that you were engaged to Monsieur d'Epinay, that your father had decided that this match would take place and that, consequently, it was certain to do so, since everything that Monsieur de Villefort wants is bound to happen. Well, I stayed in the background, not expecting anything from my own will or yours, but everything from events and from Providence; and yet you love me, you took pity on me, Valentine, and you told me so. Thank you for those sweet words: all I ask is that you should repeat them from time to time, and I shall forget everything else.'

'This is why you have become so bold, Maximilien; this is why my life is at once very sweet and very unhappy, to the point where I often ask myself which is better for me: the sorrow that I once endured because of my stepmother and her blind preference for her own child, or all the perils of the happiness that I feel when I see you.'

'Perils!' Maximilien exclaimed. 'How can you say such a hard and unjust word? Have you ever seen a more submissive slave than I? Valentine, you permitted me occasionally to speak to you, but forbade me to follow you. I obeyed. Since I discovered the means to break into this plot of land and speak to you through this door – in short, to be so close to you without seeing you – have I ever asked to touch even the hem of your dress through the gate? Tell me. Have I ever taken a step towards climbing over the wall, a trivial obstacle to one as young and as strong as I am? Not a single rebuke for your harshness towards me, not a single desire spoken aloud. I have kept my word as scrupulously as a knight of old. At least admit that, so that I may not think you unjust.'

'It is true,' Valentine said, slipping the tip of one of her slender fingers between two planks for Maximilien to kiss it. 'It's true, you are a trustworthy friend. But, in the end, you only acted out of self-interest, my dear, because you know very well that, on the day when the slave becomes too demanding, he must lose everything. You promised me the friendship of a brother – I who have no friends, I who am ignored by my father, I who am persecuted by my stepmother and who have no other consolation but a motionless, benumbed old man, whose hand cannot press my hand and who can speak to me only with his eyes, though his heart no doubt beats with some trace of warmth for me. What a bitter irony of fate that I should be the enemy and victim of all those who are stronger than I am, having only a corpse as my supporter and friend! Oh,

Maximilien, I say it again, I am truly unfortunate, and you are right to love me for myself and not for you.'

'Valentine,' the young man said, deeply moved, 'I cannot say that you are the only person that I love in the world, because I also love my sister and my brother-in-law; but my love for them is tranquil and calm, quite unlike the feeling that I have for you. When I think of you, my blood churns, my chest swells, my heart flows over; but I shall direct all this strength, all this ardour, all this superhuman power to loving you only as long as you tell me to devote them to your service. They say that Monsieur Franz d'Epinay will be away for another year yet. What good fortune might not befall us in a year, what favourable turn might events not take! So let us hope, because it is so good and so sweet to hope. Meanwhile you, Valentine, you who accuse me of egoism, how have you behaved towards me? Like the beautiful and cold statue of some prudish Venus. In exchange for my devotion, my obedience and my restraint, what have you promised me? Nothing. What have you given me? Very little. You talk to me of Monsieur d'Epinay, your fiancé, and you sigh at the thought that you might one day belong to him. Come, Valentine, is that the only idea on your mind? What! I offer you my life, I give you my soul, I dedicate the slightest beat of my heart to you; and, while I am all yours, while I whisper to myself that I should die if I were to lose you, you, on your side, are not appalled at the very idea of belonging to another man! Oh, Valentine, Valentine! If I was what you are, if I felt myself to be loved as you may be sure that I love you, I should already have put my hand a hundred times through the bars of this gate and grasped poor Maximilien's, saying: "Yours, yours alone, Maximilien, in this world and in the next."'

Valentine made no reply, but the young man heard her sighing and weeping. The effect on him was immediate.

'Oh, Valentine, Valentine!' he cried. 'Forget what I said. Something in my words must have upset you!'

'No,' she replied. 'You are right. But can you not see that I am a poor creature, abandoned virtually in a stranger's house – because my father is almost a stranger to me – whose will has been broken for ten years, day by day, hour by hour, minute by minute, by the iron will of the masters who are set over me? No one can see what I suffer and I have told no one except you. In appearance, in the eyes of everyone, all is well with me, all is goodness and affection

– when in reality all is hostility. The outside world says: "Monsieur de Villefort is too serious and strict to be very gentle with his daughter, but at least she has had the good fortune of finding a second mother in Madame de Villefort." Well, the outside world is wrong. My father abandons me, with indifference, and my step-mother hates me with an unremitting hatred that is all the more frightful for being hidden beneath an eternal smile.'

'She hates you! You, Valentine! How can anyone hate you?'

'Alas, my friend,' Valentine said, 'I have to admit that her hatred towards me comes from what is almost a natural feeling. She adores her son, my brother Edouard.'

'So?'

'So, while it may seem strange to bring money into the question that we are discussing, I do believe, my dear, that her hatred derives from that. Since she has no wealth on her own side, and I am already rich, thanks to my mother, with a fortune that will even be more than doubled by that of Monsieur and Madame de Saint-Méran which is due one day to revert to me, well, I think she is envious. Oh, my God, if I could give half that fortune and feel in Monsieur de Villefort's house as a daughter should in the house of her father, I would do it in an instant.'

'Poor Valentine!'

'Yes, I feel like someone bound, and at the same time so weak that it seems to me that my chains support me and I am afraid to break them. In any case, my father is not the sort of man whose orders can be disregarded with impunity. He is powerful in his opposition to me, he would be powerful against you: he would be the same against the king, protected as he is by an irreproachable past and an almost unassailable position. Oh, Maximilien! I swear it, if I do not struggle, it is because I fear you would be broken as much as I would in the fight.'

'But Valentine, why despair, why always paint the future in such sombre hues?' Maximilien asked.

'Because, my friend, I judge it by the past.'

'Come now: while I may not be an outstanding match from the aristocratic point of view, I still belong, in many ways, to the same world as the one in which you live. The time when there were two nations in France has passed. The leading families of the monarchy have melted into the families of the empire and the aristocracy of the lance has married the nobility of the cannon.[1] Well, I belong to the latter: I have a fine future in the army, I possess a small but independent fortune and, finally, the memory of my father is venerated in our part of the country as that of one of the most honest merchants who ever lived. I say, our part of the country, Valentine, because you almost come from Marseille.'

'Don't mention Marseille to me, Maximilien. The name alone recalls my dear mother, that angel, mourned by everyone, who watched over her daughter during her brief sojourn on earth and, I hope, still watches over her during her eternal sojourn in heaven. Oh, if my poor mother were alive, Maximilien, I should have nothing to fear. I should tell her that I love you and she would protect us.'

'Alas, Valentine,' Maximilien said, 'if she was alive I should certainly not know you; for, as you said, you would be happy if she were alive – and a happy Valentine would have looked down on me in contempt.'

'Oh, my dear friend, now you are being unfair in your turn,' Valentine exclaimed. 'But tell me . . .'

'What do you want me to tell you?' Maximilien asked, seeing that Valentine was hesitating.

'Tell me: was there ever, at one time, in Marseille, some matter of dispute between your father and mine?'

'No, not as far as I know,' Maximilien replied, 'except that your father was an utterly devoted supporter of the Bourbons and mine was devoted to the emperor. I assume that that was the only bone they ever had to pick between them. Why do you ask?'

'I shall tell you, because you ought to know everything. It was on the day when your nomination as officer of the Legion of Honour was published in the newspaper. We were all visiting my grandfather, Monsieur Noirtier, and Monsieur Danglars was there: you know, the banker whose horses nearly killed my mother and my brother two days ago? I was reading aloud from the newspaper to my grandfather while these gentlemen were talking about Mademoiselle Danglars' marriage. When I got to the paragraph concerning you, which I had already read, because you had told me the good news on the previous day, I was very happy, but also very uneasy at having to speak your name aloud. I should certainly have left it out, were it not that I feared that my silence might be misinterpreted. So, I plucked up all my courage and read.'

'Dearest Valentine!'

'Well, as soon as I spoke your name, my father turned around. I was so certain – you see what a silly goose I am! – that everyone would be struck by your name as if by a bolt of lightning, that I thought I saw my father, and even Monsieur Danglars, shudder at the sound of it; but in his case I am sure it was an illusion.

'"Morrel," my father said. "Wait!" And he raised an eyebrow. "Would that be one of those Morrels of Marseille, one of those Bonapartist fanatics who gave us so much trouble in 1815?"

'"Yes," Danglars replied. "I even think it may be the son of the former shipowner."'

'Indeed!' said Maximilien. 'What did your father say?'

'Something dreadful that I dare not repeat.'

'Repeat it anyway,' Maximilien said with a smile.

'"Their emperor," he said contemptuously, "knew how to put all those fanatics in their place: he called them cannon-fodder, and that was the only name they deserved. I am delighted to see that the new government has restored this salutary principle. I should congratulate it on keeping Algeria, if only for that reason, even though the cost is a little excessive."'

'Admittedly, that is rather brutal, as a policy,' Maximilien said. 'But, my darling, you have no need to blush at what Monsieur de Villefort said, because my good father was a match for yours in this respect: he said repeatedly: "Why does the emperor, who has done so many fine things, not enrol a regiment of judges and lawyers, and put them in the forefront of the battle?" So you see, my dear, that the two deserve one another, both in kindness of thought and sweetness of expression. But what did Monsieur Danglars say to this remark by the king's prosecutor?'

'Oh, he started to laugh with that peculiar sly laugh that he has, which I find savage. Then, a moment later, they got up and left. Only then did I see that something had upset my grandfather. I must tell you, Maximilien, that I am the only person who can tell how he feels, because no one else takes any notice of the poor, paralysed old man; and I guessed that the conversation might have impressed him, since they had been speaking ill of his emperor and it appears he was a fanatical Bonapartist.'

'Certainly,' said Maximilien. 'He was one of the leading figures of the imperial era. He was a senator and, whether you realize it or not, Valentine, he was close to all the Bonapartist conspiracies under the Restoration.'

'I have sometimes heard whispers about that, and was surprised by them: a Bonapartist grandfather and a Royalist father. Anyway, what do you expect? I turned back to him and his eyes indicated the paper.

'"What is it, papa?" I asked. "Are you pleased?"

'He nodded.

'"At what my father has just said?" I asked.

'He shook his head.

'"At what Monsieur Danglars said?"

'Again, he shook his head.

'"So, you are pleased that Monsieur Morrel" (I did not dare say, Maximilien) "has been appointed officer of the Legion of Honour?"

'He nodded.

'Can you believe that, Maximilien? He was pleased that you had been appointed to the Legion of Honour, even though he does not know you. It may perhaps be folly on his part, because people say he is entering a second childhood; but I love him, even so.'

'That's odd,' Maximilien meditated. 'Your father hates me, while your grandfather . . . How peculiar these political loves and hatreds are!'

'Hush!' Valentine suddenly exclaimed. 'Hide! Quickly! Go away, someone is coming!'

Maximilien grasped a spade and began to dig pitilessly into the alfalfa.

'Mademoiselle!' cried a voice behind the trees. 'Madame de Villefort is looking everywhere for you and asking after you. There is a visitor in the drawing-room.'

'A visitor!' Valentine said, in an anxious voice. 'Who is visiting us?'

'A great lord, a prince, they say. The Count of Monte Cristo.'

'I'm coming,' Valentine said loudly.

On the other side of the gate, the man to whom Valentine's 'I'm coming!' served as a farewell at the end of every meeting, started on hearing the name of her visitor.

'Well, well,' Maximilien said to himself, leaning thoughtfully on his spade. 'How does the Count of Monte Cristo happen to know Monsieur de Villefort?'

LII

TOXICOLOGY

It really was the Count of Monte Cristo who had just arrived at the Villeforts', intending to repay the crown prosecutor's visit. As one may imagine, the whole household had been put into a state of great excitement at the announcement of his name.

Mme de Villefort, who was in the drawing-room, immediately called for her son, so that he could repeat his thanks to the count. Edouard, who for the past two days had heard tell of nothing except this great man, hurried down – not out of any desire to obey his mother or to thank the count, but from curiosity and to make some remark which would allow him the opportunity for one of those jibes that his mother always greeted with: 'Oh, the wicked child! But you have to forgive him, he's so witty!'

When the usual greetings had been exchanged, the count asked after M. de Villefort.

'My husband is dining with the chancellor,' the young woman replied. 'He has just left and will be very sorry, I am sure, at having been deprived of the pleasure of seeing you.'

Two visitors who had arrived in the drawing-room before the count, and who could not take their eyes off him, left after the period of time needed to satisfy good manners and curiosity.

'By the way,' Mme de Villefort asked Edouard, 'what is your sister Valentine doing? Someone must go and fetch her so that I can present her to Monsieur le Comte.'

'You have a daughter, Madame?' the count asked. 'But she must be a little girl?'

'She is Monsieur de Villefort's daughter,' the young woman replied, 'by his first marriage, a tall, handsome girl.'

'But melancholic,' little Edouard interrupted, pulling the tail-feathers out of a splendid macaw to make a plume for his hat while the bird, on its gilded perch, cried out in pain. Mme de Villefort said only: 'Be quiet, Edouard!', before continuing: 'The young rascal is almost right: he is repeating what he has often heard me say, regretfully, because Mademoiselle de Villefort, despite all our efforts to amuse her, has a sad nature and taciturn character, which often contradict the impression given by her beauty. But where is she? Edouard, go and see why she is not coming.'

'I know: because they are looking in the wrong place.'

'Where are they looking?'

'With Grandpa Noirtier.'

'And you don't think she's there?'

'No, no, no, no, no, she's not there,' Edouard chanted.

'Where is she then? If you know, tell us.'

'She is under the chestnut,' the naughty child said, offering the parrot (despite his mother's protests) some living flies, a species of game which the bird seemed to appreciate very much.

Mme de Villefort was reaching out for the bell, to let the chamber-maid know where she could find Valentine, when the latter came in. She did, indeed, appear sad and if one examined her closely one could even see traces of tears in her eyes.

Carried forward by the rapidity of the narrative, we have merely introduced Valentine to the reader without making her better known. She was a tall, slim girl of nineteen, with light-chestnut hair, dark-blue eyes and a languid manner, marked by that exquisite distinction that had been characteristic of her mother. Her slender, white hands, her pearl-white neck and her cheeks, marbled with transient patches of colour, gave her at first sight the appear-ance of one of those beautiful English girls whose walk has been somewhat poetically compared to the progress of a swan mirrored in a lake.

She came in and, seeing the stranger about whom she had already heard so much at her stepmother's side, she greeted him with none of the simpering of a young girl and without lowering her eyes, with a grace that made the count take even more notice of her. He got up.

'Mademoiselle de Villefort, my stepdaughter,' Mme de Villefort told him, leaning across her sofa and pointing at Valentine.

'And Monsieur le Comte de Monte Cristo, King of China, Emperor of Cochin China,' the juvenile wit said, giving his sister a sly look.

This time, Mme de Villefort went pale and was on the point of losing her temper with this domestic pest answering to the name of Edouard; but the count, on the contrary, smiled and seemed to regard the child with such indulgence that the mother's joy and enthusiasm were full to overflowing.

'But Madame,' the count continued, picking up the conversation and looking from Mme de Villefort to Valentine, 'have I not already had the honour of seeing you somewhere, you and mademoiselle? It already occurred to me a moment ago and, when mademoiselle came in, it cast a further light on a memory which – you must forgive me – is confused.'

'It seems hardly likely, Monsieur. Mademoiselle de Villefort does not like being in company and we seldom go out,' the young mother said.

'So perhaps it was not in company that I saw the young lady, and yourself, Madame, and this delightful young scamp. In any case, I am entirely unacquainted with Parisian society for, as I think I had the honour to inform you, I have only been in Paris for a few days. No, if you would allow me to search my memory . . . Wait . . .'

The count put a hand to his forehead, as if to concentrate his memory.

'No, it was outside . . . It was . . . I don't know . . . but I think the memory involves some kind of religious ceremony . . . Mademoiselle had a bunch of flowers in her hand, the boy was running after a fine peacock in a garden and you, Madame, were sitting under an arbour . . . Do help me, please: does what I am saying not remind you of anything?'

'No, I must confess it does not,' Mme de Villefort replied. 'Yet I am sure, Monsieur, that if I had met you somewhere, I should not have forgotten the occasion.'

'Perhaps the count saw us in Italy,' Valentine suggested timidly.

'There you are: in Italy . . . It could be,' Monte Cristo said. 'You have travelled in Italy, Mademoiselle?'

'Madame and I went there two years ago. The doctors feared for my chest and suggested that the Neapolitan air might be beneficial. We went via Bologna, Perugia and Rome.'

'But there we are, Mademoiselle!' Monte Cristo exclaimed, as though this simple hint had been enough to clarify his memory. 'It was in Perugia, on the day of Corpus Christi, in the garden of the hostelry of the Post, that chance brought us together – you, Mademoiselle, your son and I. I remember having been fortunate enough to see you.'

'I remember Perugia perfectly well, Monsieur, and the hostelry and the festival that you mention,' said Mme de Villefort. 'But, though I am racking my brains and feel ashamed at my poor memory, I do not remember having had the honour of seeing you.'

'That's strange! Neither do I,' Valentine said, turning her lovely eyes on Monte Cristo.

'I remember though!' said Edouard.

'Let me help you, Madame,' said the count. 'It had been a burning hot day and you were waiting for some horses that had not arrived because of the religious festival. Mademoiselle went away into the furthest part of the garden and your son ran off after the bird.'

'I caught it, Mama, you know,' said Edouard. 'I pulled three feathers out of its tail.'

'You, Madame, remained under the arbour. Do you not recall, while you were sitting on a stone bench and, as I say, Mademoiselle de Villefort and your son were absent, you spoke for quite a long time with someone?'

'Yes, indeed, I do,' the young woman said, blushing. 'I remember. It was a man wrapped in a long woollen cloak, a doctor, I believe.'

'Precisely, Madame. I was that man. I had been living in that hostelry for a fortnight; I cured my valet of a fever and the innkeeper of jaundice, so I was regarded as a great doctor. We spoke for a long time, Madame, of various things – of Perugino, of Raphael, of the manners and customs of the place, and about that celebrated *aqua tofana*, the secret of which, I believe you had been told, was still kept by some people in Perugia.'

'That's true!' Mme de Villefort said, energetically but with some signs of unease. 'I do recall.'

'I am not sure of precisely everything that you told me, Madame,' the count continued, in a perfectly calm voice, 'but I do remember that, making the same mistake as others about me, you consulted me on the health of Mademoiselle de Villefort.'

'But, Monsieur, you really were a doctor,' said Mme de Villefort, 'since you cured the sick.'

'Madame, Molière or Beaumarchais would reply that it was precisely because I am no doctor that my patients were cured – not meaning that I cured them. I shall simply say that I have made a profound study of chemistry and natural science, but only as an amateur . . . you understand . . .'

At this point, the clock chimed six.

'It's six o'clock,' Mme de Villefort said, visibly agitated. 'Won't you go, Valentine, and see if your grandfather is ready to have dinner?'

Valentine got up, took her leave of the count and went out of the room without uttering a word.

'Oh, dear! Is it because of me, Madame, that you sent Mademoiselle de Villefort away?' the count said when she had gone.

'Not at all,' the young woman replied emphatically. 'This is the time when we give Monsieur Noirtier the sad meal that sustains his sad existence. You know, Monsieur, of the unhappy state to which my husband's father is reduced?'

'Yes, Madame, Monsieur de Villefort did mention it to me. A paralysis, I believe?'

'Alas, yes! The poor old man is quite incapable of moving; his soul alone remains alive in that human mechanism, and even that is pale and quivering, like a lamp about to go out. But forgive me, Monsieur, for telling you of our family misfortunes. I interrupted you just as you were saying that you are a skilled chemist.'

'Oh, no, I didn't say that, Madame,' the count replied, smiling. 'On the contrary, I studied chemistry because, having made up my mind to live mainly in the East, I wanted to follow the example of King Mithridates.'

'*Mithridates, rex Ponticus,*'[1] said the little pestilence, cutting the illustrations out of a splendid album. 'The one who breakfasted every morning on a cup of poison *à la crème*.'

'Edouard! You wicked child!' Mme de Villefort exclaimed, seizing the mutilated book from her son's hands. 'You are unbearable, you're driving us mad. Leave us alone; go to your sister Valentine and dear Grandpa Noirtier.'

'The album . . .' said Edouard.

'What about the album?'

'I want it.'

'Why did you cut out the pictures?'

'Because it amuses me.'

'Go away! Off with you!'

'I shan't go unless you give me that album,' the child said, settling into a large armchair and pursuing his usual policy of never giving way.

'There you are. Take it and leave us in peace,' said Mme de Villefort. She gave Edouard the album and walked to the door with him. The count looked after her.

'Let's see if she closes the door after him,' he muttered.

Mme de Villefort closed the door with the utmost care behind the child; the count pretended not to notice. Then, with one final glance around her, the young woman came back to her chair.

'I hope you will forgive me, Madame,' said the count in that good-natured way we have already noticed in him, 'for remarking that you are very strict with that delightful little scamp.'

'He needs a strong hand, Monsieur,' Mme de Villefort replied, with what was truly a mother's imperturbability.

'Monsieur Edouard was reciting his Cornelius Nepos when he spoke about Mithridites,' the count said. 'You interrupted him in a quotation which proves that his tutor has not been wasting his time and that your son is very advanced for his age.'

'The fact is, Monsieur le Comte,' the mother replied sweetly, 'that he is very quick and can learn whatever he wants. He has only one fault: he is very wilful. But, on the subject of what he was saying, do you think, Count, that Mithridates really did take such precautions and that they can be effective?'

'So much so, Madame, that I myself took the same measures to avoid being poisoned in Naples, in Palermo and in Smyrna, on three occasions when I might otherwise have lost my life.'

'And you were successful?'

'Perfectly so.'

'That's right: now I remember you telling me something of the sort in Perugia.'

'Really!' the count said, admirably feigning surprise. 'I don't recall it.'

'I asked you if poisons acted equally and with similar force on men from the north and those from the south, and you answered that the cold lymphatic temperaments of northerners made them less susceptible than the rich and energetic nature of those from the south.'

'Quite so,' said Monte Cristo. 'I have seen Russians untroubled as they devour substances which would surely have killed a Neapolitan or an Arab.'

'So you think the method would be even more effective here than in the East, and that, in the midst of our fogs and rains, a man would more easily become accustomed to this gradual absorption of poison than in a warm climate?'

'Yes, indeed; though of course one would only be protected against the poison to which one had become accustomed.'

'I understand. And how would you, yourself, obtain this immunity; or, rather, how did you do so?'

'It is very easy. Suppose you know in advance what poison is to be used against you . . . Suppose this poison to be, for example . . . brucine . . .'

'Brucine is obtained from the nux vomica, I believe,' said Mme de Villefort.

'Precisely, Madame,' Monte Cristo replied. 'But I think I have very little to teach you. Let me compliment you: such learning is rare in a woman.'

'I must confess,' said Mme de Villefort, 'that I have an all-consuming passion for the occult sciences, which speak like poetry to the imagination and yet in the end come down to figures like an algebraic equation. But please continue. I am extremely interested in what you tell me.'

'Well then, suppose this poison to be brucine, for example, and that you take a milligram the first day, two milligrams the second, and so on. After ten days you would have a centigram; and, increasing the daily dose by a further milligram, you would have three centigrams after twenty days; in other words, a dose that you would support with no ill-effects but which would be very dangerous for anyone who had not taken the same precautions. Finally, after a month, you could drink water from the same jug and kill a person who had taken it with you, while feeling no more than a slight discomfort to tell you that the water contained a poisonous substance.'

'You know of no other antidote?'

'None.'

'I often read and re-read that story of Mithridates,' Mme de Villefort said pensively, 'and always thought it was a myth.'

'No, Madame, unlike most things in history, it is true. But what you are telling me, your question, is not just idle curiosity, is it, since you have been considering this matter for two years already and you tell me that the story of Mithridates has been in your mind for a long time?'

'That's true, Monsieur. When I was young, my two favourite subjects were the study of botany and of mineralogy. Later, when I realized that one could often explain all the history of the nations and all the lives of individuals in the East by their use of herbs and simples, just as flowers explain all their concepts of love, I regretted not being a man so that I could follow the example of Flamel, Fontana or Cabanis.'²

'All the more so, Madame,' Monte Cristo continued, 'since the Orientals are not content, like Mithridates, to make a shield of poison, but also use it as a dagger. In their hands, this science becomes not only a defensive weapon but often an offensive one. The one serves to protect them against physical suffering, the other against their enemies. With opium, belladonna, strychnine, *bois de couleuvre* or cherry-laurel, they put to sleep those who would rouse them. There is not one of those Egyptian, Turkish or Greek women whom you call here wise women or spaewives, who does not know enough of chemistry to astound a doctor and of psychology to appal a confessor.'

'Really!' Mme de Villefort exclaimed, her eyes shining with a strange light as she listened.

'Yes, indeed, Madame!' Monte Cristo continued. 'This is how the secret dramas of the Orient are woven and unwoven, from the plant that induces love to the one that kills, from the draught that opens the heavens to the one that plunges a man into hell. There are as many subtle distinctions of all kinds as there are whims and peculiarities in the moral and physical nature of man. I would even say that the art of these chemists can admirably supply the ill and the cure to his need for love or desire for revenge.'

'But, Monsieur, are these countries in which you have spent part of your life really as fantastic as the tales that come out of them? Can a person be disposed of there with impunity? Are Baghdad and Basra truly as Monsieur Galland³ described them? Are you seriously telling me that the sultans and viziers who rule those peoples, making up what we here in France call the government, are like Haroun al-Rashid or Giaffar – men who not only forgive a poisoner, but will even appoint him prime minister if his crime is ingenious enough and, in that case, have the story set down in gold letters to amuse them in their idle moments?'

'No, Madame, the marvellous no longer exists even in the East. There, too, disguised under other names and concealed in different costumes, they have police commissioners, investigating magistrates, crown prosecutors and other experts. Criminals there are very pleasantly hanged, decapitated or impaled; but, being clever fraudsters, they have managed to outwit human justice and ensure the success of their designs by skilful plotting. In our country, when some fool is seized with the demon of hatred or greed, when he has an enemy to destroy or a grandparent to obliterate, he goes to a grocer, gives a false name (that will identify him more surely than his real one) and, pretending that the rats are keeping him awake, he buys five or six grammes of arsenic. If he is very clever, he goes to five or six grocers, so he will be five or six times more easily detected. Then, once he has his medicine, he administers a dose of arsenic to his enemy or his grandparent that would kill a mammoth or a mastodon, and this, without rhyme or reason, causes the victim to emit cries that put the whole district into a turmoil. At that, a crowd of policemen and gendarmes arrives. They send for a doctor who cuts the dead man open and takes arsenic by the spoonful out of his stomach and his entrails. The next day, a hundred newspapers report the matter with the name of the victim and the murderer. The very same evening, the grocer – or grocers – come and announce: "I sold this gentleman the arsenic." They would identify twenty purchasers, rather than not identify this one. So the foolish criminal is caught, imprisoned, interrogated, confronted, confounded, condemned and guillotined. Or, if it is a woman of some status, then she is sentenced to life imprisonment. This is the understanding you northerners have of chemistry, Madame; though I must admit Desrues[4] was better than that.'

'What do you expect, Monsieur!' the young woman said with a laugh. 'We do what we can. Not everyone knows the secrets of the Medici or the Borgias.'

The count shrugged his shoulders: 'Would you like me now to tell you the cause of all this ineptitude? It is because in your theatres, as far as I can tell by reading the plays that they put on there, you always see people swallowing the contents of a flask or biting the bezel of a ring, then dropping, stone dead: five minutes later, the curtain falls and the audience leaves. No one knows the consequences of the murder, one never sees the police commissioner with his scarf, or the corporal of the guard with his four men, and as a result a lot of weak brains imagine that this is the way that things happen. But if you just go a step outside France, to Aleppo or Cairo, or even no further than Naples or Rome, you will see people walking along the street, upright, fresh-faced and ruddy with health, of whom the devil, were he to touch you with his cloak, could tell you: "This man has been poisoned for three weeks and he will be completely dead in a month."'

'In that case,' Mme de Villefort said, 'they have rediscovered the secret of that famous *aqua tofana* which was said to have been lost in Perugia.'

'Come, come, Madame, is anything ever lost to mankind? The arts and sciences travel around the world, things change their name, that's all, and ordinary people are deceived by it; the outcome is always the same. Poisons will particularly affect one organ or another: the stomach, the brain, the intestines. Well, then: a poison can give rise to a cough and that cough, in turn, to a pneumonia or some other illness recognized by medical science – which does not prevent it from being quite deadly; or, if it was not already, from becoming so thanks to the remedies administered by ignorant doctors, who are generally very poor chemists, remedies that will favour the illness or impede it, as you wish. The result: a man artistically killed in accordance with the rules, about whose death the law has nothing to discover, in the words of one of my friends, that fearful and excellent chemist Abbé Adelmonte of Taormina, in Sicily, who had made an exhaustive study of these phenomena.'

'That's terrifying, but wonderful,' said the young woman, riveted to the spot. 'I must admit that I had always thought such things to be inventions from the Middle Ages.'

'So they are, but perfected in our own time. What do you suppose is the point of time, encouragement, medals, awards and the Prix Montyon, except to bring society closer to perfection? Mankind will not be perfect until it can create and destroy like God. It can already destroy: that's half the battle.'

'What you mean,' Mme de Villefort continued, always coming back to what interested her, 'is that the poisons of the Borgias and the Medicis, the Renés, the Ruggieris and probably later the Baron de Trenk,[5] so badly treated in modern drama and novels . . .'

'Were simply works of art, Madame, nothing more,' said the count. 'Do you think the true scientist is crudely concerned with the individual himself? Not so. Science loves the oblique approach, *tours de force*, imagination if you like. Take the worthy Abbé Adelmonte, whom I mentioned a moment ago: he made some astonishing experiments in this field.'

'Really!'

'Yes. Let me give you just one example. He had a splendid garden, full of vegetables, flowers and fruit. From among his vegetables he would choose the least exotic, most digestible of all: say, a cabbage.

For three days he would water this cabbage with a solution of arsenic. On the third day, the cabbage would fall sick and wither: this was the moment to cut it. Everyone saw it as ripe and healthy, only Abbé Adelmonte knew it was poisoned. So he took the cabbage home, got a rabbit – he had a collection of rabbits, cats and guineapigs as magnificent as his collection of vegetables, flowers and fruit – and made the rabbit eat a leaf of the cabbage. The rabbit died. What investigating magistrate would dare question this; what crown prosecutor would ever draw up a petition against Monsieur Magendie or Monsieur Flourens[6] for the rabbits, guinea-pigs and cats that they have killed? Not one. So the rabbit is now dead, and the law has no reason to ask questions about it. Abbé Adelmonte gets his cook to gut the rabbit and throws the intestines on a dungheap. On the dungheap there is a hen, which pecks at the intestines, falls ill in its turn and dies the following day. Just as it is in its final, convulsive agony, a vulture flies past – there are a lot of vultures in Adelmonte's country – dives at the body and carries it off to a distant crag to eat it. Three days later the poor vulture, having felt constantly ill since its meal, is seized with a fainting fit several hundred feet up. It falls out of the sky and plummets into your fishpond. Pikes, eels and moray eels are greedy fish, as you know, so they bite the vulture. Well, suppose that on the following day this eel or this pike is served up at your table, poisoned at four removes, and your guest is poisoned at the fifth and dies after a week or ten days from a pain in the guts, vomiting and an abscess on the duodenum. There will be a post-mortem and the doctors will say: "The patient died of a tumour on the liver, or of typhoid fever." '

'You link all these events together,' said Mme de Villefort, 'but the slightest accident might break the chain. The vulture might not fly over at the right moment, or it might fall a hundred yards away from the fishpond.'

'That's precisely where the art lies: to be a great chemist in the East, you must direct chance. It can be done.'

Mme de Villefort listened thoughtfully.

'But arsenic is ineradicable,' she said. 'However it is absorbed, if there is enough to kill, it will remain in the man's body.'

'Just so!' cried Monte Cristo. 'Just so! That is precisely what I told my good friend Adelmonte. He thought a while, smiled and replied with a Sicilian proverb which, I believe, is also a French one: "My child, the world was not made in a day, but in seven. Come back on Sunday."

'The following Sunday I returned. Instead of watering his cabbage with arsenic, he had watered it with a solution of salts of strychnine, *strychnos colubrina*, as scientists call it. This time, the cabbage seemed altogether healthy, so the rabbit had no suspicion of it. Five minutes later the rabbit died, the hen ate the rabbit, and the following day it was dead. So then we played the part of the vultures, took off the hen and opened it up. This time all specific symptoms had vanished and only general symptoms remained. There was no specific indication in any organ – irritation of the nervous system, that's all, and evidence of cerebral congestion, nothing more. The hen had not been poisoned, it had died of apoplexy. This is a rare condition in hens, I know, but very common among human beings.'

Mme de Villefort seemed more and more preoccupied with her thoughts. 'It's fortunate,' she said, 'that such substances can only be prepared by chemists, or else one half of the world would be poisoning the other.'

'By chemists, or people who are interested in chemistry,' said Monte Cristo offhandedly.

'But then,' said Mme de Villefort, making an effort to rouse herself from her own thoughts, 'however cleverly engineered it may be, crime is still crime. It may evade the human investigator, but it cannot escape from the eye of God. Orientals are less sensitive than we are on points of conscience and they have wisely got rid of hell, that's all.'

'Ah, Madame, such scruples would naturally arise in a soul as honest as yours, but might soon be eradicated by reasoning. The worse side of human thought will always be summed up in that paradox of Jean-Jacques Rousseau[7] – you know the one: "The mandarin whom one can kill from a distance of five hundred leagues just by raising a finger". Man's life is spent doing such things and his intelligence is exhausted in dreaming about them. You will find very few people who would go, brutally, and stick a knife in the heart of their fellow man or who, to make him disappear off the face of the earth, would administer the amount of arsenic that we mentioned a short time ago. That is really either eccentricity or stupidity. One can only reach that point if the blood is heated up to thirty-six degrees, the pulse is racing at ninety beats a minute and the mind is driven outside its ordinary limits. But if, as though advancing like a philologist from a word to its near synonym, you make a mere "elimination" ... Instead of committing a base murder, you purely and simply remove from your path the person who bothers you, without any clash, or violence, or all that paraphernalia of suffering which, becoming a torment, makes the victim into a martyr and the person responsible into a butcher, in the full force of the word ... If there is no blood, no cries, no contortions and, above all, none of that horrible and compromising instantaneousness of the event, then you will evade the weight of the human law that tells you: "Don't upset the social order!" This is what Orientals do and that is how they succeed: serious and phlegmatic people, they are little troubled by matters of time when something of any importance is to be resolved.'

'There is still conscience,' said Mme de Villefort in a strained voice, stifling a sigh.

'Yes,' said Monte Cristo. 'Yes, fortunately there is still conscience, because without it we should be in a fine mess. After any slightly energetic action, conscience saves us, because it supplies us with a thousand good excuses, which we alone are left to judge: these excuses, effective as they may be in ensuring our sleep, might perhaps be rather less so before a court where they had to protect our lives. So Richard III, for example, was wonderfully well served by his conscience after the elimination of Edward IV's two children. He could say to himself: "These two children, sons of a cruel tyrant, had inherited the vices of their father, though I alone was able to detect this in their juvenile dispositions. These two children stood in the way of my efforts to bring happiness to the English people, to whom they would certainly have brought misfortune." In the same way, Lady Macbeth was served by her conscience: her desire, whatever Shakespeare says, was to give a throne to her son, not to her husband. Oh, maternal love is such a great virtue and powerful impulse that it can excuse many things. Hence, without her conscience, Lady Macbeth would have been a very unhappy woman after the death of Duncan.'

These frightful axioms and horrid paradoxes were delivered by the count with his own peculiar brand of ingenuous irony. Mme de Villefort received them avidly.

There was a moment's silence.

'Do you know, Count,' she said, 'that you are a terrible reasoner and that you see the world in a somewhat lurid light! Is it because you have viewed mankind through alembics and retorts that you see it in this way? For you are right, you are a great chemist, and the elixir which you gave my son, which so quickly brought him back to life . . .'

'Oh, don't trust it, Madame,' said Monte Cristo. 'A drop of that elixir sufficed to bring the child back to life when he was dying, but three drops would have driven the blood into his lungs in such a way as to give him palpitations of the heart. Six would have interrupted his breathing and caused him a much more serious fit than the one he was already suffering. Ten would have killed him. You recall, Madame, how I hastened to pull him away from those phials which he had been rash enough to touch?'

'Was that some frightful poison?'

'Good heavens, no! Firstly, let's forget this word "poison", because doctors use the most deadly poisons which, according to the way in which they are administered, become very effective medicines.'

'So what was it?'

'A subtle preparation made by my friend, Abbé Adelmonte, which he showed me how to use.'

'Oh, it must be an excellent antispasmodic.'

'A sovereign remedy, Madame, as you saw,' the count replied. 'I often use it – with all due caution, of course,' he added with a smile.

'I imagine so,' Mme de Villefort replied, in the same tone. 'I myself, nervous as I am and subject to fainting fits, I need a Doctor Adelmonte to discover a remedy that will help me to breathe easily and overcome my fear of one day suffocating to death. Meanwhile, as such things are hard to find in France and your abbé would probably not be willing to come to Paris for me, I made do with Monsieur Planche's antispasmodics, and I frequently use the mint and drops from Hoffmann. Look, here are some pastilles that I had made up for me. They contain a double dose.'

Monte Cristo opened the tortoiseshell pill-box that she handed to him and sniffed the pastilles with the air of a specialist able to appreciate the preparation.

'They are exquisite,' he said, 'but unfortunately they need to be swallowed, which is often not possible for an unconscious person. I prefer my specific.'

'Of course, I agree, having seen it at work. But no doubt it is a secret and I shall not be indiscreet enough to ask for it.'

'But I, Madame,' Monte Cristo said, getting up, 'am gallant enough to offer it to you.'

'Oh, Monsieur!'

'Just remember one thing: in small doses this is a cure, in large ones, a poison. One drop may restore life, as you have seen; five or six would certainly kill, and all the more frightfully because, if dissolved into a glass of wine, they would not alter the taste in the slightest. But I must stop, Madame, or I shall seem to be giving you advice.'

The clock had just struck half-past six and the maid announced a friend of Mme de Villefort's who was to dine with her.

'If I had the honour to be meeting you for the third or fourth time, instead of the second, Monsieur le Comte,' said Mme de Villefort, 'if I had the honour to be your friend, instead of having merely the pleasure of being indebted to you, I should insist that you stay to dinner and I should not accept your first refusal.'

'Thank you a thousand times, Madame,' Monte Cristo replied, 'but I do myself have an engagement from which I cannot escape. I have promised to take a Greek princess, a friend of mine, to the theatre. She has not yet seen grand opera and is counting on me to introduce her to it.'

'Go, then, Monsieur, but do not forget my recipe.'

'What, Madame! Were I to do so, I should also have to forget the hour I have just spent in conversation with you – and that would be quite impossible.'

Monte Cristo bowed and went out, leaving Mme de Villefort absorbed in her thoughts. 'That is a strange man,' she said to herself. 'And one who, I would guess, was baptized Adelmonte.'

As for Monte Cristo, the visit had succeeded beyond his expectations. 'Well, indeed,' he thought, as he went out, 'this is fertile soil, and I am certain that the seed that falls in it will not remain barren.'

The next day, as he had promised, he sent the recipe she had asked for.

LIII

ROBERT LE DIABLE

The excuse of the opera had been all the more appropriate since there was that evening a formal soirée at the Royal Academy of Music. Levasseur had long been indisposed but was returning in the role of Bertram and, as ever, the work of the fashionable maestro had attracted the cream of Parisian society.

Morcerf, like most rich people, had his own orchestra stall, plus ten people whom he knew, in whose boxes he could request a seat, without counting his place in the lions' box. Château-Renaud's stall seat was next to Morcerf's. Beauchamp, being a journalist, was king of the theatre and could sit where he wished.

That evening, Lucien Debray had the minister's box at his disposal and had offered it to the Comte de Morcerf who, on Mercédès' refusal, had sent it to Danglars with a message that he would probably go and visit the baroness and her daughter in the course of the evening, if those ladies would like to accept the box that he offered them. Those ladies were sure not to refuse. No one likes a free box as much as a millionaire.

As for Danglars, he had declared that his political principles and his position as a *député* for the opposition would not permit him to go into the minister's box. As a result, the baroness wrote to Lucien to take her, since she could not go to the opera alone with Eugénie.

True, if the two women had gone alone, people would surely have considered this very bad behaviour; while no one could object to Mlle Danglars going to the opera with her mother and her mother's lover. One must take the world as it is.

The curtain went up, as usual, on an almost empty house. It is fashionable among Parisians to arrive at the theatre when the show has begun, with the result that the first act is spent, by those members of the audience who have arrived, not in watching or listening to the play, but in watching the entry of those spectators who are arriving, so that nothing can be heard except the sound of doors banging and voices in conversation.

'Look!' Albert suddenly exclaimed, seeing the door open in a side box in the dress circle. 'Look! Countess G—.'

'Who or what is Countess G—?' Château-Renaud asked.

'Come, now, Baron! You can't be forgiven for asking that. Who is Countess G—!'

'Oh, that's right,' said Château-Renaud. 'Isn't it that charming Venetian woman?'

'Exactly.'

At that moment, Countess G— noticed Albert and greeted him with a wave and a smile.

'Do you know her?' asked Château-Renaud.

'Yes. Franz introduced me to her when we were in Rome.'

'Could you do the same for me in Paris?'

'Of course.'

'Hush!' cried the audience.

The two young men continued their conversation, not appearing to take the slightest notice of the fact that the stalls seemed to want to listen to the music.

'She was at the races in the Champ-de-Mars,' said Château-Renaud.

'Today?'

'Yes.'

'Well, now. I'd forgotten about the races. Were you in for anything?'

'A mere trifle. Fifty *louis*.'

'Who won?'

'Nautilus. I was betting on him.'

'But there were three races?'

'Yes: the Prix du Jockey-Club, a gold cup ... Something quite odd happened.'

'What was that?'

'Be quiet!' shouted the audience.

'What was that?' Albert repeated.

'The winners of that race were an entirely unknown horse and jockey.'

'What?'

'Yes, egad! No one took any notice of a horse entered under the name of Vampa and a jockey entered under the name of "Job", when suddenly a superb chestnut appeared, with a jockey the size of your fist. They had to give him a handicap of twenty pounds of lead in his saddle, and it still didn't stop him getting to the post three lengths ahead of Ariel and Barbaro, who were running against him.'

'And no one knew whom the horse and jockey belonged to?'

'No.'

'You say the horse was entered in the name of . . .'

'Vampa.'

'In that case,' Albert said, 'I'm a step ahead of you, because I do know the owner.'

'Silence!' the stalls yelled.

This time the outcry was so great that the two young men finally realized that they were the object of the audience's appeals. They turned around for a moment, looking for a man in the crowd who would take responsibility for what they regarded as an impertinence, but no one repeated the invitation, so they turned back towards the stage.

At that moment the door to the minister's box opened and Mme Danglars, her daughter and Lucien Debray took their seats.

'Ah, ha!' said Château-Renaud. 'There are some people you know, Viscount. Why on earth are you staring to the right; someone is trying to catch your eye.'

Albert turned and his eyes did meet those of Baroness Danglars, who gave a little greeting with her fan. As for Mlle Eugénie, her large black eyes would scarcely deign to look down to the stalls.

'In truth, my dear friend,' said Château-Renaud, 'I do not understand, apart from the misalliance – and I don't suppose that bothers you very much . . . As I say, I cannot understand, apart from the misalliance, what you can have against Mademoiselle Danglars. She really is a very fine-looking creature.'

'Very fine, indeed,' said Albert, 'but I must confess that, as far as beauty is concerned, I should prefer something softer, smoother and, in short, more feminine.'

'That's the younger generation for you,' said Château-Renaud who, as a man of thirty, took on a paternal air with Morcerf. 'Never satisfied. What, my dear fellow! They find you a fiancée built like Diana the Huntress, and you are not happy!'

'Precisely. I should have preferred something like the Venus de Milo or the Venus of Capua. This Diana the Huntress, always surrounded by her nymphs, frightens me a little. I'm afraid she might treat me like Actaeon.'

A glance at the girl might have gone some way to justify the feelings to which Morcerf had just admitted. Mlle Danglars was beautiful but, as Albert said, her beauty was somewhat strict: her hair was a lustrous black, but there was a certain rebelliousness in its natural wave. Her eyes, as black as her hair, were framed in magnificent eyebrows that had only one defect, which was that from time to time they were quizzically raised, and the eyes were exceptional above all for their determined expression, which it was surprising to find in a woman. Her nose had the precise proportions that a sculptor would have given to Juno; only her mouth was a little too large, but it exhibited fine teeth which highlighted the excessive redness of lips that did not harmonize with the pallor of the complexion. Finally, a beauty-spot at the corner of the mouth, larger than is usual with these freaks of nature, completed the look of resolution in the face that somewhat dismayed Morcerf.

For that matter, the rest of Eugénie's person was of a piece with the head that we have just attempted to describe. As Château-Renaud said, she was Diana the Huntress, but with something even firmer and more muscular in her beauty.

As for her upbringing, if there was anything to be said against it, it was that, like some traits of her physiognomy, it seemed more appropriate to the other sex. She spoke two or three languages, had an innate talent for drawing, wrote verse and composed music; this last was her great passion, which she studied with one of her school-friends, a young woman with no expectations but (one was assured) with everything needed to become an outstanding singer. It was said that a great composer took an almost paternal interest in this girl and encouraged her to work in the hope of eventually finding a fortune in her voice.

The possibility that Mlle Louise d'Armilly (this was the name of the talented young person) might one day appear on the stage meant that Mlle Danglars, although she received her at home, did not appear with her in public. Despite this, while she did not have the independent position of a friend in the banker's house, Louise did enjoy a higher status than that of an ordinary governess.

A few seconds after Mme Danglars entered her box, the curtain came down and, because the length of the intervals allowed the opportunity to walk around the foyer or to pay visits for some half an hour, the stalls were more or less emptied.

Morcerf and Château-Renaud were among the first to go out. For a moment Mme Danglars thought that Albert's haste was owing to his desire to pay her his compliments, and she had leant over to her daughter to warn her of this visit, but the girl was content to shake her head, with a smile. At the same time, as if to prove how well founded Eugénie's denial was, Morcerf appeared in a side box in the dress circle. This box belonged to Countess G——.

'Ah, traveller! There you are!' she said, offering him her hand with all the cordiality of an old acquaintanceship. 'It is most kind of you to have recognized me and, more especially, to have given me preference for your first visit.'

'Believe me, Madame,' Albert replied, 'had I been informed of your arrival in Paris and known your address, I should not have waited so long. But permit me to introduce Monsieur le Baron de Château-Renaud, my friend and one of the few gentlemen left in France, who has just told me that you were at the races on the Champ-de-Mars.'

Château-Renaud bowed.

'You were at the races then, Monsieur?' the countess enquired, examining him with interest.

'Yes, Madame.'

'Very well,' she asked. 'Can you tell me whose was the horse that won the Prix du Jockey-Club?'

'I regret not, Madame,' said Château-Renaud. 'I was just asking Albert the same question.'

'Do you insist, Countess?' asked Albert.

'On what?'

'On knowing the owner of the horse?'

'Absolutely. I must tell you . . . But would you happen to know, Viscount?'

'Madame, you were about to begin a story. "I must tell you . . .", you said.'

'Well, I must tell you that that charming chestnut horse and the pretty little jockey in his pink cap appealed to me so much from the first moment I saw them that I was making a wish for them both, just as though I had bet half my fortune on them. So, when I saw them pass the post three lengths ahead of the other runners, I was so happy that I started to clap my hands like a madwoman. Imagine my astonishment when, on arriving home, I met the little pink jockey on the staircase! I thought that the winner of the race must chance to live in the same house as I, when, on opening the door of my drawing-room, the first thing I saw was the gold cup, the prize won by the unknown horse and jockey. Inside it was a little scrap of paper with the following words: "To Countess G—, Lord Ruthwen".'

'Precisely!' said Morcerf.

'What do you mean, "precisely"?'

'I mean, it was Lord Ruthwen himself.'

'What Lord Ruthwen?'

'Ours, the vampire, the one from the Teatro Argentina.'

'Really!' the countess exclaimed. 'Is he here?'

'Indeed he is.'

'And you see him? You receive him? You visit him?'

'We are close friends; even Monsieur de Château-Renaud here has the honour of knowing him.'

'What makes you think that he was the winner?'

'His horse ran under the name Vampa.'

'So?'

'Don't you remember the name of the famous bandit who took me prisoner?'

'Of course!'

'From whose hands the count miraculously saved me?'

'Indeed . . .'

'His name was Vampa. So, you see, it must be him.'

'But why did he send me the cup?'

'First of all, Countess, because I often mentioned you to him, as you may well imagine. Then, because he was delighted at finding a compatriot and pleased by the interest that this compatriot took in him.'

'I hope you never told him of the silly things we used to say about him!'

'I can't swear it . . . And, in fact, this idea of giving you the cup under the name of Lord Ruthwen . . .'

'This is terrible! He will be fearfully angry with me.'

'Is he behaving as if he was?'

'No, admittedly . . .'

'Well, then!'

'So, you're telling me he's in Paris?'

'Yes.'

'And what sort of a stir has he caused?'

'Oh,' said Albert, 'they did talk about him for a week. Then there was the coronation of the Queen of England and the theft of

Mademoiselle Mars' diamonds, and no one talked about anything else.'

'My dear fellow,' said Château-Renaud, 'one can see that the count is your friend and you treat him accordingly. Don't believe what Albert is saying, Countess, because the truth is that no one in Paris is talking about anything except the Count of Monte Cristo. The first thing he did was to send Madame Danglars some horses worth thirty thousand francs. Then he saved Madame de Villefort's life, and now it appears he has won the Jockey-Club race. Despite what Morcerf says, I maintain that people are still talking about the count at the moment and that they will talk about him even more a month from now, if he carries on behaving in this eccentric manner – which appears, in the event, to be his normal way of carrying on.'

'Maybe,' said Morcerf. 'Meanwhile, who has taken up the Russian ambassador's box?'

'Which?' the countess asked.

'The one between the columns, in the first tier. It looks as though it has been entirely done up.'

'So it does,' said Château-Renaud. 'Was there someone there in the first act?'

'Where?'

'In that box?'

'No,' said the countess. 'I didn't see anyone.' Then, returning to the original subject of the conversation: 'You think that your Count of Monte Cristo won the prize?'

'I'm certain of it.'

'And sent me the cup?'

'No doubt about it.'

'But I don't know him,' said the countess. 'I'm quite tempted to send it back.'

'Oh, don't do that! He would send you another, carved out of sapphire or rubies. He does those things. One must take him as he is.'

At that moment the bell rang to announce that the second act was about to begin. Albert got up to return to his place.

'Shall I see you?' the countess asked.

'In the intervals, if you permit, I may come and find out if I can be of some use to you while you are in Paris.'

'Gentlemen,' the countess said, 'I am at home to my friends every

Saturday evening at number twenty-two, Rue de Rivoli. So now you know.' The two young men bowed and went out.

As they came back into the theatre, they saw everyone standing in the stalls, all eyes turned towards a single point in the room. They turned their own eyes in the same direction and stopped at what had once been the Russian ambassador's box. A man in black, aged between thirty-five and forty, had just entered with a woman in oriental dress. The woman was strikingly beautiful and her costume so ornate that, as we said, all eyes were immediately fixed on her.

'Well, well!' said Albert. 'It's Monte Cristo and his Greek!' It was indeed the count and Haydée.

A moment later the young woman was the object of attention not only from the stalls but throughout the theatre. Women were leaning out of their boxes to see the cascade of diamonds shining in the light of the chandeliers.

The second act was played against that dull murmuring which is the response of a large crowd to some great event. No one thought of shouting: 'Silence!' The woman, so young, so beautiful and so dazzling, was the most interesting spectacle to be had.

This time, a sign from Baroness Danglars clearly indicated to Albert that she wished him to call on her in the next interval. Morcerf was too well bred to keep someone waiting when they had shown that they wanted to speak to him, so, when the act ended, he hurried up to the box in the front of the house. There he greeted the two ladies and held out his hand to Debray. The baroness welcomed him with a charming smile and Eugénie with her habitual icy indifference.

'My good fellow,' said Debray, 'you see before you a man at the end of his tether, begging you to assist him. Madame has been deluging me with questions about the count: what he is, where he comes from, where he is going . . . Dammit, I'm not Cagliostro! So, to get out of it, I said: "Ask Morcerf, he knows his Monte Cristo like the back of his hand." That's why we called you.'

'Isn't it incredible,' said the baroness, 'that someone with half a million in secret funds at his disposal can be so ill-informed?'

'Madame,' Lucien said, 'please believe me when I tell you that, if I had half a million at my disposal, I should use it for some other purpose than making enquiries about Monsieur de Monte Cristo, who has no merit as far as I can see apart from being twice as rich as a nabob. But I am handing over to my friend Morcerf. Settle it with him, it's no longer my business.'

'A nabob would certainly not have sent me a pair of horses worth thirty thousand francs, with four diamonds at their ears, each worth five thousand francs.'

'Ah, diamonds!' Morcerf said, laughing. 'He has a passion for them. I think that, like Potemkin, he always has some in his pocket and spreads them along his path as Tom Thumb did with his pebbles.'

'He must have found a diamond mine,' said Mme Danglars. 'Do you know that he has unlimited credit with the baron's bank?'

'I didn't know,' Albert replied. 'But it doesn't surprise me.'

'And that he told Monsieur Danglars that he meant to stay a year in Paris and spend six millions?'

'He must be the Shah of Persia travelling incognito.'

'The woman, Monsieur Lucien,' said Eugénie; 'have you noticed how beautiful she is?'

'Really, Mademoiselle, you are the only woman I know who is so generous in speaking about others of your own sex.'

Lucien put his eye-glass to his eye. 'Delightful!' he said.

'Does Monsieur Morcerf know who she is?'

'Mademoiselle,' Albert said, in reply to this almost direct question, 'I do know, more or less, as I more or less know everything relating to this mysterious personage. The young woman is Greek.'

'It is easy to see that by her dress, so you're telling me nothing that all the rest of the theatre doesn't already know.'

'I much regret,' said Morcerf, 'that I am such an ignorant guide, but I have to admit that my information goes no further than that – though I do also know that she is a musician, because one day, when I was lunching with the count, I heard the sound of a *guzla* which only she could have been playing.'

'So he gives lunch, does he, your count?' asked Mme Danglars.

'Magnificently, believe me.'

'I must urge Danglars to offer him a dinner or a ball; then he will invite us back.'

'What! You would visit him?' Debray said, laughing.

'Why not? With my husband.'

'But he is a bachelor, this mysterious count.'

'Not at all, as you can plainly see,' the baroness said, laughing in her turn and indicating the beautiful Greek.

'The woman is a slave, as he told us himself. Do you remember, Morcerf, at your breakfast?'

'You must admit, Lucien,' said the baroness, 'that she looks more like a princess.'

'From the *Thousand and One Nights*.'

'Agreed: from the *Thousand and One Nights*. But what makes a princess, my dear? Diamonds, and she's covered in them.'

'Too much so, in fact,' said Eugénie. 'She would be more beautiful without them, because you could see her neck and her wrists, which are delightfully shapely.'

'There speaks the artist!' said Mme Danglars. 'See what an enthusiast she is!'

'I love everything beautiful,' said Eugénie.

'So what do you think of the count?' said Debray. 'He strikes me as not too bad himself.'

'The count?' said Eugénie, as if she had not previously considered looking at him. 'He's very pale, your count.'

'Precisely,' said Morcerf. 'The secret we are looking for lies in that pallor. You know, Countess G— claims he is a vampire.'

'Countess G—? Is she back, then?' asked the baroness.

'In that side box,' Eugénie said. 'Look, mother, almost opposite us: she's that woman with the magnificent blonde hair.'

'Oh, yes,' said Mme Danglars. 'Morcerf, do you know what you should do?'

'I am at your command, Madame.'

'You should go and visit your Count of Monte Cristo and bring him back here.'

'Why?' asked Eugénie.

'So that we can talk to him. Aren't you curious to see him?'

'Not at all.'

'Peculiar child!' the baroness muttered.

'Look!' said Morcerf. 'He'll probably come of his own accord. He's seen you, Madame, and is bowing to you.'

The baroness returned the count's greeting, together with a charming smile.

'Very well, then,' said Morcerf. 'It's up to me. I must leave you while I go and see if there is not some way of talking to him.'

'Simple: go into his box.'

'But I haven't been introduced.'

'To whom?'

'To the beautiful Greek.'

'Didn't you say she was a slave?'

'Yes, but you claim she is a princess . . . No, I hope that when he sees me go out, he will do the same.'

'Perhaps. Off you go then.'

'I am going.'

Morcerf bowed and left. As predicted, when he walked past the count's box, the door opened. The count said a few words in Arabic to Ali, who stood in the corridor, and took Morcerf's arm.

Ali shut the door and stood in front of it. People gathered around the Nubian in the corridor.

'Really,' Monte Cristo said, 'Paris is an odd city and you Parisians an odd people. Anyone would think that this was the first time they had seen a Nubian. Look at them crowding round poor Ali, who doesn't know what to make of it. I guarantee one thing, however, which is that a Parisian could go to Tunis, Constantinople, Baghdad or Cairo, and no crowd would gather around him.'

'That is because your Orientals are sensible folk who only look at something when it is worth looking at. But I can assure you that Ali is enjoying this popularity for no reason except that he belongs to you, because you are the man *à la mode* just now.'

'Really? To what do I owe that distinction?'

'To yourself – what else? You give away horseflesh to the value of a thousand *louis*, you save the life of the king's prosecutor, you dub yourself Major Brack to race thoroughbreds ridden by jockeys no bigger than marmosets and, finally, you win gold cups and send them to beautiful women.'

'Who the devil told you of all these follies?'

'Why, the first comes from Madame Danglars, who is dying to see you in her box – or, rather, for people to see you there; the second I had from Beauchamp's newspaper; and the third I worked out for myself. Why do you call your horse Vampa, if you wish to remain incognito?'

'True, true!' said the count. 'That was unwise of me. But tell me, does the Comte de Morcerf never come to the opera? I looked around for him but could not find him anywhere.'

'He will be here this evening.'

'Where?'

'In the baroness's box, I think.'

'And the enchanting young lady with her is her daughter?'

'Yes.'

'I compliment you.'

Morcerf smiled.

'We must speak of that later, and at length,' he said. 'How do you find the music?'

'What music?'

'The music you have just heard.'

'I think it's very good for music composed by a human composer and sung by birds with two feet and no feathers, as the late Diogenes remarked.'

'My dear Count, you speak as though you could, at will, call up the seven choirs of paradise.'

'That's more or less the case. When I want to listen to fine music, Vicomte, music such as mortal ear has never heard, I sleep.'

'Well, this is the perfect place. Sleep away, my dear Count, sleep away. The Opera was designed for no other purpose.'

'No, I can't: your orchestra is making too much noise. For me to enjoy the kind of sleep I mean, I need calm and silence; and a particular kind of preparation . . .'

'Ah, the famous hashish?'

'Precisely. Viscount, when you want to hear some music, come and take supper with me.'

'But I have already heard it at lunch,' said Morcerf.

'In Rome?'

'Yes.'

'Of course! That was Haydée's *guzla*. The poor exile sometimes amuses herself by playing me some of her native airs.'

Morcerf did not press the matter, and the count, for his part, fell silent. At that moment the bell rang.

'Will you excuse me?' said the count, going back towards his box.

'What?'

'My best wishes to Countess G— from her vampire.'

'And the baroness?'

'Tell her that I should be honoured, if she would allow me to present my compliments to her in the course of the evening.'

The third act began. During it, the Comte de Morcerf came, as he had promised, to join Mme Danglars. Morcerf was not one of those people who cause a commotion in the auditorium, so no one noticed his arrival except the others in the box where he took his seat. However, Monte Cristo saw him, and a hint of a smile hovered on his lips. As for Haydée, she saw nothing from the moment when the curtain rose. Like all primitive natures, she adored everything that appealed to her eyes and her ears.

The third act followed its usual course. Mlles Noblet, Julia and Leroux[1] executed their accustomed entrechats; the Prince of Grenada was challenged by Robert-Mario; and finally the magnificent king (already familiar to you) strode round the theatre showing off his velvet cloak and leading his daughter by the hand. Then the curtain fell, and the audience immediately repaired to the foyer and the corridors.

The count came out of his box and a moment later appeared in that of Baroness Danglars. The baroness could not restrain a cry of surprise, in which there was a hint of joy.

'Come in, Count, come in!' she exclaimed. 'I have been anxious to add my verbal thanks to those I had already conveyed to you in writing.'

'Oh, Madame,' said the count, 'do you still remember that trifle? I had forgotten it.'

'Perhaps, but what cannot be forgotten, Monsieur le Comte, is that the very next day you saved my good friend Madame de Villefort from the danger she was in with those same horses.'

'Once again, Madame, I do not deserve your thanks. It was my Nubian servant, Ali, who was fortunate enough to be able to perform this service for Madame de Villefort.'

'Was it also Ali,' asked the Comte de Morcerf, 'who rescued my son from the Roman bandits?'

'No, Count,' said Monte Cristo, shaking the hand that the general offered him. 'No, this time I will take the thanks for myself. But you had already offered them, I had received them and, in truth, I am embarrassed to find you still so grateful. Please do me the honour, Madame la Baronne, of introducing me to your daughter.'

'You are already introduced, at least in name, for we have spoken of nothing except you over the past two or three days. Eugénie,' the baroness went on, turning to her daughter, 'the Count of Monte Cristo!'

The count bowed and Mlle Danglars gave a slight nod of the head.

'You are accompanied by a splendid young woman, Monsieur le Comte,' said Eugénie. 'Is she your daughter?'

'No, Mademoiselle,' Monte Cristo replied, astonished at what was either great naïvety or amazing insolence. 'She is a poor Greek; I am her guardian.'

'And her name?'

'Haydée,' Monte Cristo replied.

'A Greek!' the Comte de Morcerf muttered.

'Yes, Count,' said Mme Danglars. 'But tell me if you have ever seen in the court of Ali Tebelin,[2] at which you served with such distinction, as admirable a costume as that.'

'Ah!' said Monte Cristo. 'You served in Janina, Count?'

'I was inspector-general to the pasha's troops,' Morcerf replied. 'I do not disguise the fact that I owe my fortune, such as it is, to the generosity of the illustrious Albanian leader.'

'Look at that!' Mme Danglars urged.

'At what?' muttered Morcerf.

'Well, well!' said Monte Cristo, wrapping his arm round the count and leaning out of the box.

At that moment Haydée, who had been looking around for the count, saw his pale features beside those of M. de Morcerf, whom he was clasping. The sight produced the same effect as a Medusa on the girl. She started forward as if to devour both of them with her eyes, then, almost immediately, leapt back with a weak cry – which was, however, heard by those closest to her and by Ali, who at once opened the door.

'Well, I never!' said Eugénie. 'What has just happened to your ward, Monsieur le Comte? She seems to be feeling ill.'

'Yes, she does,' said the count. 'But don't worry. Haydée is very nervous and consequently very sensitive to smells. A perfume that she does not like is enough to make her faint. However,' he added, taking a medicine bottle out of his pocket, 'I have the remedy here.'

Then he saluted the baroness and her daughter with a single bow, shook hands one final time with Morcerf and Debray, and left Mme Danglars' box. When he reached his own, Haydée was still very pale. No sooner did he appear than she grasped his hand and said: 'To whom were you talking, my Lord?'

'The Comte de Morcerf,' Monte Cristo replied, 'who served under your illustrious father and admits owing him his fortune.'

'The miserable wretch!' Haydée cried. 'He it was who sold him to the Turks and the fortune was the price of his treachery. My dear master, did you not know that?'

'I did hear some talk of this story in Epirus,' said Monte Cristo, 'but I am not familiar with the details. Come, child, you will tell me. It must be a curious tale.'

'Oh, yes, come with me, and I shall. I think I shall die if I stay any longer facing that man.'

Haydée leapt to her feet, wrapped herself in her white cashmere burnous embroidered with pearls and corals, and ran out just as the curtain was rising.

'Look at that man: he does nothing like anyone else!' Countess G— told Albert, who had gone back to her box. 'He sits religiously all the way through the third act of *Robert le Diable*, then leaves just as the fourth act is about to begin.'

LIV

RISE AND FALL

A few days after this encounter, Albert de Morcerf visited the Count of Monte Cristo in his house on the Champs-Elysées; it had already taken on the palatial appearance that the count, thanks to his vast fortune, gave to even the most temporary accommodation. Morcerf had come to reiterate Mme Danglars' thanks, already conveyed in a letter signed 'Baroness Danglars, née Herminie de Servieux'.

Albert was accompanied by Lucien Debray, who added to his friend's words some compliments that were no doubt not official – though, with his sharp instincts, the count could be quite sure of their source. It even appeared that Lucien had come to see him partly out of a feeling of curiosity, half of which came from the Rue de la Chaussée d'Antin. Indeed, he might safely have guessed that Mme Danglars, being unable to use her own eyes to explore the interior of the home of a man who gave away horses worth thirty thousand francs and who went to the opera with a Greek slave wearing a million francs' worth of diamonds, had instructed the eyes through which she was accustomed to see such things to inform her about this interior. But the count gave no sign of suspecting that there was any connection between Lucien's visit and the baroness's curiosity.

'Are you in almost continual contact with Baron Danglars?' he asked Albert de Morcerf.

'Yes, Monsieur le Comte. You know what I told you.'

'It still applies?'

'More than ever,' said Lucien. 'The matter is settled.'

Whereupon Lucien, doubtless judging that this word thrown into the conversation gave him the right to retire from it, put his tortoiseshell monocle into one eye, chewed the gold pommel of his cane and began to walk round the room, looking at the shields and the pictures.

'Ah,' said Monte Cristo, 'listening to you, I should not have believed in such a rapid solution.'

'What do you expect? Things proceed in ways that one does not suspect. While you are not thinking about them, they are thinking about you and, when you turn round, you are surprised at the distance they have covered. My father and Monsieur Danglars served together in Spain, my father in the army, Monsieur Danglars in supplies. My father was ruined by the Revolution, and Monsieur Danglars had never had any inheritance, so that is where both of them laid the foundations – in my father's case of his fine political and military career, and in Monsieur Danglars' of his admirable political and financial one.'

'Yes, indeed,' said the count. 'I think that, during the visit I paid him, Monsieur Danglars spoke to me of that. And,' he continued, glancing at Lucien, who was leafing through an album, 'Mademoiselle Eugénie is pretty, isn't she? I seem to remember her name is Eugénie.'

'Very pretty; or, rather, very beautiful,' Albert replied. 'But it is a type of beauty that does not appeal to me. I am not worthy of her!'

'You already speak as if you were her husband!'

'Oh!' said Albert, looking around in his turn to see what Lucien was doing.

'Do you know . . .' Monte Cristo said, lowering his voice, 'you don't seem to me very enthusiastic about this marriage.'

'Mademoiselle Danglars is too rich for me,' Morcerf said. 'It scares me.'

'Huh!' Monte Cristo exclaimed. 'That's no reason. Aren't you rich yourself?'

'My father has an income of something like fifty thousand *livres* and he might give me ten or twelve, perhaps, when I marry.'

'I admit, that is a modest sum,' said the count, 'especially in Paris. But money is not everything in this world, and a fine name and good social standing count for something, too. Your name is famous, your position is magnificent; and, in addition to that, the Comte de Morcerf is a soldier and it is a pleasure to see the integrity of Bayard allied to the poverty of Du Guesclin. Disinterestedness is the finest ray that can shine from a noble sword. I must say that, on the contrary, I find this match as appropriate as may be: Mademoiselle Danglars will enrich you and you will ennoble her!'

Albert shook his head and remained thoughtful. 'There is something more,' he said.

'I admit,' Monte Cristo continued, 'that I find it hard to understand your repugnance for a rich and beautiful young girl.'

'Oh, good Lord!' said Morcerf. 'The repugnance, if there is any, does not only come from me.'

'From whom, then? You told me that your father was in favour of the marriage.'

'From my mother, and she has a prudent and unfailing eye. Well, she does not favour the match. I don't know what she has against the Danglars.'

'It's understandable,' said the count, in a slightly unnatural voice. 'The countess, who is the epitome of distinction, aristocracy and good taste, might have misgivings about embracing a family that is low-born, coarse and ignoble. It's only natural.'

'I don't know if that is it,' said Albert. 'What I do know is that I feel that, if this marriage takes place, she will be unhappy about it. We should have met six weeks ago to talk business, but I had such migraines . . .'

'Real ones?' the count asked, smiling.

'Oh, quite real . . . no doubt caused by fear. So the appointment was delayed for two months. You understand, there is no hurry. I am not yet twenty-one and Eugénie is only seventeen; but the two months are over at the end of next week. We shall have to go through with it. You cannot imagine, Count, how much it bothers me . . . Oh, how lucky you are to be free!'

'Then be free yourself. What is stopping you, I want to know?'

'My father would be too disappointed if I did not marry Mademoiselle Danglars.'

'Then marry her,' said the count, with an odd shrug of the shoulders.

'Yes,' said Morcerf. 'But for my mother that would not be a disappointment, but a pain.'

'Don't marry her, then,' said the count.

'I shall see, I shall try. You will advise me, won't you? And, if possible, get me out of this trap. I do believe that, to avoid causing pain to my dear mother, I would fall out with the count.'

Monte Cristo turned away. He seemed moved. 'Well, now,' he said to Debray, who was sitting in a deep armchair at the far end of the room, holding a pencil in his right hand and a notebook in the left. 'What are you doing? A drawing from Poussin?'

'I?' he answered calmly. 'A drawing? No, I love painting too much for that. No, I am doing the very opposite of painting: arithmetic.'

'Arithmetic?'

'Yes, I am calculating. It concerns you, indirectly, Viscount. I am calculating what the firm of Danglars made on the last rise in Haitian stock: from 206, the fund rose to 409 in three days, and the provident banker bought a lot at 206. He must have made three hundred thousand *livres*.'

'That's not his best coup,' said Morcerf. 'Didn't he make a million this year with Spanish bonds?'

'Listen, my dear fellow,' said Lucien. 'The Count of Monte Cristo here will tell you, as the Italians do,

Danaro e santità
Metà della Metà[1]

And that's a lot. So when I hear stories like that, I shrug my shoulders.'

'You were talking about Haiti?' said Monte Cristo.

'Oh, Haiti is something else; Haiti is the écarté of French speculation. You may like bouillotte, be attached to whist, be mad about boston, and yet tire of them all; but one always comes back to écarté: it is in a class of its own. So yesterday Monsieur Danglars sold at 406 and pocketed three hundred thousand francs. If he had waited until today, when the rate fell to 205; instead of gaining three hundred thousand francs, he would have lost twenty or twenty-five thousand.'

'Why did the rate fall from 409 to 205?' Monte Cristo asked. 'I must apologize, but I am very ignorant when it comes to all these manoeuvrings on the exchange.'

'Because,' Albert said with a laugh, 'news comes in dribs and drabs, and one piece is unlike another.'

'The devil!' said the count. 'Monsieur Danglars plays to win or lose three hundred thousand francs in a day. He must be immensely rich?'

'He's not the one who gambles!' Lucien exclaimed. 'It's Madame Danglars. She is really daring.'

'But you are reasonable, Lucien, and you know how news changes, since you are at the source of it, so you should stop her,' said Morcerf.

'How could I, if her husband can't?' Lucien asked. 'You know what the baroness is like. No one has any sway over her; she does precisely as she wishes.'

'If I was in your place . . .' Albert said.

'What?'

'I should cure her; it would be a service to her future son-in-law.'

'How?'

'Dammit, man, it's quite easy. I'd teach her a lesson.'

'A lesson?'

'Yes. Your position as the minister's secretary gives you great authority as a source of news. As soon as you open your mouth, stockbrokers are hurrying to telegraph what you have said. Let her lose a hundred thousand francs or so straight off, and it will make her more cautious.'

'I don't follow you,' Lucien stammered.

'But it's as clear as daylight,' the young man replied with a naïvety that was entirely unaffected. 'Tell her one fine morning about something quite unheard of: news from the telegraph that you alone can know; for example, that Henri IV was seen at Gabrielle's yesterday. It will mean that stock prices will go up, she will hazard her money on it and certainly lose when Beauchamp writes the following day: "Well-informed people are quite wrong to say that King Henri IV was seen at Gabrielle's yesterday. The report is entirely unfounded. King Henri IV has not left the Pont Neuf." '[2]

Lucien forced a laugh, while Monte Cristo, though apparently not at all interested in the conversation, had not missed a word of it. His penetrating eye even thought it detected a secret behind the private secretary's embarrassment. This embarrassment had altogether escaped Albert, but it resulted in Lucien cutting his visit short. He clearly felt ill at ease. The count, seeing him to the door, whispered a few words to him, and he replied: 'Very well, Count, I agree.'

The count came back to young Morcerf.

'Don't you think,' he said, 'on reflection, that you were wrong to speak in that way about your mother-in-law in front of Debray?'

'Please, Count,' Morcerf said. 'I beg you, don't use that word in anticipation.'

'Really, and without exaggerating, is the countess so strongly opposed to the match?'

'So much so that the baroness rarely comes to the house and my mother, I believe, has not been twice in her life to Madame Danglars'.'

'What you say emboldens me to be frank with you,' said the count. 'Monsieur Danglars is my banker and Monsieur de Villefort has been showering me with attention in gratitude for a service which a fortunate chance allowed me to perform for him. Behind all this I can anticipate an avalanche of dinners and balls. Well, to avoid all this ostentation and, so to speak, to recapture the advantage, I thought I might invite Monsieur and Madame Danglars, together with Monsieur and Madame de Villefort, to my country house in Auteuil. If I invite you to this dinner, with the Count and Countess de Morcerf, won't it seem rather like a sort of matrimonial gathering, or, at least, might not the Countess de Morcerf see things in that way, especially if Baron Danglars does me the honour of bringing his daughter? So your mother might shun me, which I certainly don't want; on the contrary – and I hope you'll tell her so at every opportunity – I want her to think well of me.'

'My dear Count,' said Morcerf, 'thank you for speaking to me so frankly. I accept your suggested non-invitation. You say that you want my mother to think well of you, and she already does.'

'You think so?' Monte Cristo asked, with interest.

'I'm sure of it. When you left us the other day, we spoke about you for an hour. But, to get back to what we were saying, if my mother could know that you were concerned for her – and I shall tell her about it – I am sure that she would be very grateful to you. It is true that, for his part, my father would be furious.'

The count laughed. 'Well,' he told Morcerf, 'you have been warned. But I think it is not only your father who would be furious. Monsieur and Madame Danglars would consider me a very ill-mannered person. They know that you and I are friends, and even that you are my oldest acquaintance in Paris – and they won't see you at my house. They will ask why I didn't invite you. At least think some prior engagement that will be more or less plausible, and write a little note informing me of it. You know: with bankers, nothing is valid unless it is in writing.'

'I shall do better than that, Count,' said Albert. 'My mother wants to take the sea air. What day is your dinner?'

'Saturday.'

'It is Tuesday today. Very well, we'll leave tomorrow evening and, the day after, we'll be in Le Tréport. Count, do you know how charming it is of you to put people at their ease in this way?'

'No! You imagine me to be something more than I am. I just want to please you, that's all.'

'When did you send out your invitations?'

'Today.'

'Fine! I'll go straight round to Danglars and announce that my mother and I are leaving Paris tomorrow. I have not seen you, so I know nothing about your dinner.'

'Are you crazy? What about Monsieur Debray, who has just seen you here?'

'Oh! You're right!'

'On the contrary, I saw and invited you here, and you quite simply replied that you could not be my guest, because you were leaving for Le Tréport.'

'Well then, that's settled. But will you come and see my mother before tomorrow?'

'It will be difficult so soon; and I would interfere with the prep-arations for your departure.'

'Well, do better than that. You were only a charming man, but you could be an adorable one.'

'What must I do to achieve that distinction?'

'What must you do?'

'That's what I asked.'

'Well, today you are free as air. Come and dine with me. We shall make an intimate little party: just you, my mother and I. You have hardly glimpsed my mother: you could see her properly. She

is a very remarkable woman, and I only regret one thing, which is
that there's no one like her who is twenty years younger. If that
were so, there would soon be a Viscountess as well as a Countess
de Morcerf, I assure you. As far as my father is concerned, he won't
be there: he is on duty this evening and will be dining with the
public auditor. Come along, we can talk about travel. You have
seen the whole world, and you can tell us of your adventures. You
can tell us about the beautiful Greek who was with you the other
evening at the opera, whom you call your slave and treat like a
princess. We can talk Italian or Spanish. Come on, accept. My
mother will thank you.'

'A thousand thanks,' said the count. 'Your invitation is most
gracious and I deeply regret not being able to accept. I am not as
free as you think and, on the contrary, I have a very important
appointment.'

'Ah, be careful! A moment ago you taught me how one discharges
an unpleasant responsibility where dinners are concerned. I need
proof. I am fortunately not a banker like Monsieur Danglars, but
I warn you that I am as hard to convince as he is.'

'I shall prove it,' said the count; and he rang the bell.

'Huh!' said Morcerf. 'This is the second time you have refused to dine with my mother. There is some prejudice here,
Count.'

Monte Cristo shuddered. 'Please don't think such a thing,' he
said. 'In any case, here is my proof.'

Baptistin came in and stood, waiting, at the door.

'I was not warned of your visit, was I?'

'Dammit! You're such an extraordinary man that I can't be
certain of that.'

'Well, at the very least, I could not guess that you would invite
me to dinner, could I?'

'That, I must admit, is probable.'

'Well, listen . . . Baptistin, what did I tell you this morning when
I called you into my study?'

'To have Monsieur le Comte's door closed when five o'clock
struck.'

'Then?'

'Oh, Monsieur le Comte . . .' said Albert.

'No, no. I am quite determined to get rid of this mysterious
reputation that you have given me, my dear Viscount. It is too hard

to have to play Manfred the whole time. I want to live in a house of glass. Then . . . Carry on, Baptistin.'

'Only to admit Major Bartolomeo Cavalcanti and his son.'

'Do you hear: Major Bartolomeo Cavalcanti, a gentleman from the oldest noble family in Italy, for whom Dante acted as d'Hozier[3] – I don't know if you remember: in the tenth canto of the *Inferno*. In addition, his son, a charming young man of about your age, Viscount, with the same title as you, who is making his debut in Parisian society with his father's millions. This evening, the major will be bringing me his son Andrea, the *contino*, as we call him in Italy. He is entrusting him to me. I shall advance him, if he has any merit; and you will help me, won't you?'

'Of course. So is this Major Cavalcanti an old friend of yours?' Albert asked.

'Not at all. He's a worthy aristocrat, very polite, very unassuming and very discreet, as there are many in Italy – descendants of old families who have descended a very long way. I have seen him several times, in Florence, or in Bologna, or in Lucca, and he told me he was coming here. Acquaintances made on journeys are demanding. They require of you, in any place whatsoever, the same friendship that you showed them once, by chance; as if a civilized man, who can pass an hour with anyone, did not always have some reservations! The good Major Cavalcanti wants to revisit Paris, which he has only seen once, during the empire, when he passed through on his way to catch a cold in Moscow. I shall give him a good dinner, he will leave me his son. I shall promise to look after the boy, then I'll let him commit whatever folly he wishes and we shall be quits.'

'Perfectly so!' said Albert. 'I can see that you are a fine tutor. Farewell, then, we shall return on Sunday. Oh, by the way, I have heard from Franz.'

'Really!' Monte Cristo said. 'Is he still enjoying Italy?'

'I think so. However, he misses you. He says that you were the sunshine of Rome and without you the skies are grey. I think he may even have said that it's raining there.'

'So, he has changed his opinion of me, your friend Franz?'

'On the contrary, he insists on thinking you a highly fantastic creature, that's why he misses you.'

'What a delightful young man!' said Monte Cristo. 'I felt a liking for him the first evening I met him, looking for a supper, when he was good enough to accept mine. He is, I believe, the son of General d'Epinay?'

'Precisely.'

'The one who was so disgracefully assassinated in 1815?'

'By the Bonapartists.'

'That's it! By heaven, I like him! Is there not also some marriage planned for him?'

'Yes, he is to marry Mademoiselle de Villefort.'

'Is that true?'

'As true as that I am to marry Mademoiselle Danglars,' Albert said with a laugh.

'Did you laugh?'

'Yes.'

'Why?'

'Because I think there is as much enthusiasm for that marriage as there is from here for the match between Mademoiselle Danglars and me. But, honestly, my dear Count, we are speaking about women as women speak about men. That's unforgivable!' And Albert got up.

'Are you leaving?'

'What a question! I have been boring you for the past two hours, and you are kind enough to ask if I'm leaving! Really, Count, you are the most civil man on earth! And your servants, how well trained they are! Above all, Monsieur Baptistin! I have never been able to find one like that. Mine always seem to model themselves on the ones in the Théâtre Français who, just because they have only one word to say, always come and say it in front of the footlights. So, if you ever want to get rid of Monsieur Baptistin, please give me first refusal.'

'Agreed, Vicomte.'

'Wait, that's not all. Convey my compliments to your discreet Luccan, Signor Cavalcanti dei Cavalcanti; and if by chance he wants to settle his son, find him a woman who is very rich and very noble, at least on her mother's side, and a baroness on her father's. I'll willingly help.'

'Dear, oh dear!' the count replied. 'Are things really that bad? You can never tell.'

'Oh, Count,' Morcerf cried. 'What a favour you would do me and how I would love you a hundred times more if, thanks to you, I were to remain a bachelor, if only for ten years.'

'Nothing is impossible,' Monte Cristo replied gravely. And, having said goodbye to Albert, he came back inside and rang three times. Bertuccio appeared.

'Monsieur Bertuccio,' the count said. 'You know that on Saturday I am having guests at my house in Auteuil.'

Bertuccio shuddered slightly. 'Very well, Monsieur,' he said.

'I need you,' the count went on, 'to get everything ready. The house is very beautiful, or might be so.'

'A lot of changes will have to be made to achieve that, Monsieur le Comte; all the materials are worn.'

'So, change it all, except for one thing: the bedroom with the red damask. That must be left exactly as it is.'

Bertuccio bowed.

'And don't touch the garden. But do what you like in the courtyard, and so on. I shall even be glad if it is unrecognizable.'

'I shall do everything I can to please Monsieur le Comte. However, I should be easier in my mind if Monsieur le Comte will tell me what he intends by this dinner.'

'Really, my dear Monsieur Bertuccio,' the count said, 'I find that since we have been in Paris you are nervous and seem out of place. Don't you know me by now?'

'But Your Excellency might tell me who is to be invited!'

'I don't know yet, and you have no reason to know either. Lucullus dines with Lucullus, that's all.'

Bertuccio bowed and went out.

LV

MAJOR CAVALCANTI

Neither the count nor Baptistin had lied when they told Morcerf that the major from Lucca was to visit, which was Monte Cristo's excuse for refusing the invitation to dinner.

The clock had just struck seven – M. Bertuccio, as instructed, having left for Auteuil at two o'clock – when a cab drew up at the door, then hurried off, in what looked like shame, immediately after depositing at the gate a man of around fifty-two, wearing one of those green frock-coats, frogged in black, which seem in Europe to belong to an undying breed of garment. Wide blue trousers; boots still clean, although their polish was questionable and their sole a trifle too thick; suede gloves; a hat, in shape close to a gendarme's; and a black collar edged in white which, if its owner were not wearing it by choice, might have been mistaken for an iron yoke: such was the picturesque costume worn by the person who rang the outer bell, asking if it was not here, at number 30, Avenue des Champs-Elysées, that the Count of Monte Cristo lived; and who, on receiving the answer 'Yes', closed the gate behind him and walked towards the front steps.

The man's small, angular head, his greying hair and his thick, grey moustache identified him to Baptistin, who had a precise description of the visitor and was waiting for him in the hall. So, no sooner had he announced his name to the intelligent servant than Monte Cristo was informed of his arrival. The stranger was introduced into the simplest drawing-room, where the count was waiting and came to greet him with a welcoming smile.

'My dear sir,' he said. 'Welcome. I was expecting you.'

'Really?' said the Luccan. 'Your Excellency was expecting me?'

'Yes, I was informed that you would be arriving this evening at seven.'

'You were informed of my arrival?'

'Precisely.'

'I'm so glad. I must admit, I was afraid that they had forgotten to take that little precaution.'

'Which one?'

'That of informing you in advance.'

'No, not at all.'

'But are you sure you are not mistaken?'

'Quite sure.'

'I am really the person that Your Excellency was expecting today at seven?'

'Yes, you are. In any case, we can make sure.'

'Oh, if you were expecting me, there is no need,' said the Luccan.

'Yes, there is!' said Monte Cristo. The man looked faintly uneasy.

'Now, let's see,' said Monte Cristo. 'Aren't you the Marquis Bartolomeo Cavalcanti?'

'Bartolomeo Cavalcanti,' the Luccan repeated, joyfully. 'That's right.'

'Formerly a major in the service of the Austrian army?'

'Was I a major?' the old soldier asked timidly.

'Yes, a major,' said Monte Cristo. 'That is the name we give in France to the rank that you held in Italy.'

'Very well, I ask nothing better, you understand.'

'In any event,' said Monte Cristo, 'you have not come here on your own initiative.'

'No, no, certainly not.'

'You were sent by someone.'

'Yes.'

'By the good Abbé Busoni?'

'That's right!' the major exclaimed delightedly.

'Do you have a letter?'

'Here it is.'

'So, you see! Give it to me.' And Monte Cristo took the letter, opened it and read it. The major watched him, his eyes wide with astonishment, then looked curiously at every part of the room, though always eventually turning back to its owner.

'Here we are . . . the dear abbé . . . "Major Cavalcanti, a worthy physician of Lucca, descendant of the Cavalcantis of Florence,"' Monte Cristo said, reading, '". . . who possesses a fortune of half a million in income."' The count looked up from the paper and bowed. '"Of half a million . . ." I say! My dear Monsieur Cavalcanti . . .'

'Does it say half a million?' the Luccan asked.

'In so many words. And it must be true, because Abbé Busoni is the man who knows most about the great fortunes of Europe.'

'Let it be half a million, then,' said the Luccan. 'But, on my word, I didn't think it was such a sum.'

'That's because you have a steward who robs you. What do you expect, dear Monsieur Cavalcanti, we must all go through it.'

'You have just shown me the light,' the Luccan said gravely. 'I shall dismiss him.'

Monte Cristo continued reading: '". . . and who only needs one thing for his happiness . . ."'

'Yes, my God! Yes, one thing,' said the Luccan with a sigh.

'". . . To find the son he adores."'

'The son he adores!'

'". . . who was abducted in his youth either by an enemy of his noble family or by gypsies."'

'At the age of five, Monsieur,' said the Luccan, sighing deeply and raising his eyes towards heaven.

'Poor father!' said Monte Cristo; then continued: ' "I am giving him hope, I am restoring him to life, Monsieur le Comte, by telling him that you may be able to find this son, whom he has sought in vain for fifteen years." '

The Luccan looked at Monte Cristo with an indefinable expression of anxiety.

'I can,' said Monte Cristo.

The major drew himself up to his full height. 'So!' he said. 'So! The letter was true then from beginning to end?'

'Did you ever doubt it, my dear Monsieur Bartolomeo?'

'No, never. How could it be! A serious man like Abbé Busoni, a man with that aura of sanctity, could not allow himself to joke on such a matter. But you have not read everything, Excellency.'

'True! There is a postscript.'

'Yes,' the Luccan repeated. 'There is . . . a postscript.'

' "To spare Major Cavalcanti the trouble of having to transfer funds to his banker, I am sending an order of two hundred thousand francs for his travelling expenses and a credit on you in the sum of forty-eight thousand francs which you still owe me." '

The major followed this postscript anxiously.

'Good,' the count said.

'He said "good",' the Luccan muttered. 'So, Monsieur . . .'

'So?' Monte Cristo asked.

'The postscript . . .'

'What about the postscript?'

'You welcome it as favourably as the rest of the letter?'

'Certainly. We have an arrangement, Abbé Busoni and I. I don't know if it is exactly forty-eight thousand *livres* that I owe him, but we are not going to quarrel about a few banknotes. Come, come! Did you attach such importance to that postscript, my dear Monsieur Cavalcanti?'

'I must confess,' the Luccan replied, 'that, full of confidence in Abbé Busoni's signature, I did not take any other funds with me so that, if this letter had failed, I should have been greatly embarrassed here in Paris.'

'Is a man like yourself ever embarrassed anywhere?' said Monte Cristo. 'Come now!'

'Heavens, not knowing anyone!' said the Luccan.

'But you are known . . .'

'Yes, I am known, so that . . .'

'Carry on, Monsieur Cavalcanti!'

'So that you will give me the forty-eight thousand *livres*?'

'As soon as you request it.'

The major's eyes opened wide in astonishment.

'But sit down,' said Monte Cristo. 'I really don't know what can have come over me. I have kept you standing for a quarter of an hour.'

'Please don't mention it.' The major drew up a chair and sat down.

'Now,' said the count, 'would you like something to drink: a glass of sherry, port or alicante?'

'Alicante, since you offer it. It is my favourite wine.'

'I have some excellent alicante. With a biscuit, perhaps?'

'With a biscuit, since you insist.'

Monte Cristo rang and Baptistin appeared. The count went over to him and whispered: 'Well?'

'The young man is there,' the valet answered, in the same manner.

'Good. Have you brought him in?'

'In the blue drawing-room, as Your Excellency ordered.'

'Perfect. Bring some alicante and biscuits.' Baptistin went out.

'I really am embarrassed at the trouble I am giving you.'

'Oh, come now!' said Monte Cristo. Baptistin returned with the glasses, the wine and the biscuits.

The count filled one glass and, into the second, poured only a few drops of the ruby liquid from the bottle, which was covered in cobwebs and all the other signs that indicate the age of a wine more surely than wrinkles do that of a man. The major followed the pouring out of the wine, and took the full glass and a biscuit.

The count ordered Baptistin to put the tray within reach of his guest's hand and the Luccan began by taking a sip of the alicante, giving a look of satisfaction, then gently dipping the biscuit into the glass.

'So, Monsieur,' Monte Cristo said, 'you live in Lucca, you are rich, you are noble, you enjoy universal respect: you have everything that might make a man happy.'

'Everything, Excellency,' the major said, devouring his biscuit. 'Absolutely everything.'

'There was only one thing needed to complete your happiness?'

'Only one thing.'

'Which was to recover your child?'

'Ah!' said the major, taking another biscuit. 'But it was a desperate need.' He looked up and tried to sigh.

'Now, then, dear Monsieur Cavalcanti,' Monte Cristo said. 'Who was this much-loved son? Because I have been told that you remained a bachelor.'

'So people thought, Monsieur,' said the major. 'And I myself . . .'

'Yes,' Monte Cristo continued. 'You gave credence to that belief. A youthful error that you wanted to hide from everyone.'

The Luccan drew himself up and adopted the calmest and most dignified air that he could, at the same time modestly lowering his eyes, either to keep up appearances or to assist his imagination, all the while looking from under his eyebrows at the count, the fixed smile on whose lips expressed the same unfailing, benevolent curiosity.

'Yes, Monsieur,' he said. 'I wanted to hide my error from everyone.'

'Not for your sake,' said Monte Cristo. 'A man is above such things.'

'Oh, no, certainly, not for my sake,' the major said with a smile and a shake of the head.

'But for the child's mother,' said the count.

'For his mother!' the Luccan exclaimed, taking a third biscuit. 'For his poor mother!'

'Have another glass, dear Monsieur Cavalcanti,' said Monte Cristo, pouring him some more alicante. 'The emotion is stifling you.'

'For his poor mother!' the Luccan muttered, trying to find out whether an effort of will might not act upon the lachrymal duct and dampen the corner of his eye with a false tear.

'Who belonged to one of the leading families in Italy, I believe?'

'A patrician lady from Fiesole, Monsieur le Comte; a patrician from Fiesole.'

'Whose name was?'

'You want to know her name?'

'But of course!' said Monte Cristo. 'No need to tell me. I know it.'

'Monsieur le Comte knows everything,' said the Luccan, with a bow.

'Olivia Corsinari, if I'm not mistaken?'

'Olivia Corsinari.'

'A marchesa?'

'A marchesa.'

'Whom you did eventually marry, despite the opposition of the family?'

'Yes, eventually!'

'So, you have got your papers,' said Monte Cristo. 'All signed and sealed?'

'What papers?' the Luccan asked.

'Well, your marriage certificate and the child's birth certificate.'

'The child's birth certificate?'

'The birth certificate of Andrea Cavalcanti, your son. He was called Andrea, I believe?'

'I think so,' said the Luccan.

'What do you mean: you think so?'

'Well, by God, I can't be sure. It's so long since he disappeared.'

'Quite so,' said Monte Cristo. 'And you do have all these papers?'

'Count, I regret to say that, not having been told to obtain these documents, I forgot to bring them with me.'

'Oh, the devil!' said Monte Cristo.

'Were they absolutely essential?'

'Quite indispensable!'

The Luccan scratched his head. 'Ah, *per Bacco*!' he said. 'Indispensable!'

'Of course. If anyone here should raise any doubt as to the validity of your marriage or the legitimacy of your child . . . !'

'That's right,' said the Luccan. 'Doubts might be raised.'

'It would be troublesome for the young man.'

'It might be fatal.'

'It could spoil a splendid match for him.'

'*O peccato!*'

'You realize that in France the authorities are strict. It is not enough, as in Italy, to go and find a priest and say: "We are in love, marry us!" There is civil marriage in France and, to be married in the eyes of the state, you must have papers to prove your identity.'

'There's the rub. I don't have the papers.'

'Luckily, I do,' said Monte Cristo.

'You do?'

'Yes.'

'You have them?'

'I have them.'

'Well I never!' the Luccan exclaimed, having seen the object of his journey threatened by the absence of his papers and fearing that the omission might put some barrier between him and his forty-eight thousand *livres*. 'Well I never! How fortunate! Yes,' he continued, 'how very fortunate, because I should never have thought of it myself.'

'Good Lord, I suppose not. One cannot think of everything. But, luckily, Abbé Busoni thought of it for you.'

'You see: the dear abbé!'

'A cautious man.'

'An admirable one,' said the Luccan. 'Did he send the papers to you?'

'Here they are.'

The Luccan clapped his hands in admiration.

'You married Olivia Corsinari in the Church of Santa Paula at Monte Catini. Here is the priest's certificate.'

'Yes, by gad! There it is!' the major said, looking at it.

'And here is the certificate of baptism of Andrea Cavalcanti, issued by the priest in Saravezza.'

'All in order,' said the major.

'So, take these papers, which are of no use to me, and give them to your son who will keep them carefully.'

'He certainly will! Because if he were to lose them . . .'

'If he were to lose them?' Monte Cristo asked.

'Well, we would have to write off to Italy,' said the Luccan. 'It would take a long time to get replacements.'

'Difficult, in fact,' said Monte Cristo.

'Almost impossible,' said the major.

'I can see that you appreciate the value of these papers.'

'I consider them priceless.'

'Now,' said Monte Cristo, 'regarding the young man's mother?'

'The young man's mother . . .' the major said anxiously.

'Marchioness Corsinari?'

'Good Lord!' said the Luccan, who seemed to see new pitfalls constantly opening in front of his feet. 'Will we need her?'

'No, Monsieur,' Monte Cristo replied. 'In any case, is she not . . .'

'Yes, yes,' said the major. 'She did . . .'

'Pay her debt to nature?'

'Alas, yes!' the Luccan said eagerly.

'As I knew,' said Monte Cristo. 'She died ten years ago.'

'And I mourn her still, Monsieur,' said the major, taking a check handkerchief from his pocket and dabbing the left eye, then the right.

'There is nothing to be done about it,' said Monte Cristo. 'We are all mortal. Now, my dear Monsieur Cavalcanti, you understand that it is not necessary for anyone in France to know that you have been separated from your son for fifteen years. All those stories of gypsies who steal children are not fashionable here. You sent him to be educated in a provincial college and you want him to finish his education in Parisian society. That is why you left Via Reggio, where you have been living since the death of your wife. That's all you need say.'

'You think so?'

'Certainly.'

'Very well, then.'

'If anyone found out about the separation . . .'

'Oh, yes! What should I say then?'

'That a faithless tutor, paid by the enemies of your family . . .'

'The Corsinari?'

'Yes, certainly . . . had abducted the child to ensure the death of the name.'

'That is plausible, since he is an only child.'

'Well, now that we have settled everything and your memory has been refreshed, so that it will not let you down, you will no doubt have guessed that I have a surprise for you?'

'A pleasant one?' asked the Luccan.

'Ah!' said Monte Cristo. 'I can see that one cannot deceive either the eye or the heart of a father.'

'Hum!' said the major.

'Someone has revealed something to you indiscreetly, or else you guessed that he was there.'

'Who was there?'

'Your son, your child, your Andrea.'

'I guessed so,' the Luccan replied, with the greatest coolness imaginable. 'So, he is here?'

'In this very house,' said Monte Cristo. 'The valet informed me of his arrival when he came in a moment ago.'

'Good! Oh, very good! Very, very good!' the major said, grasping the frogging on his coat with each exclamation.

'My dear sir,' said Monte Cristo, 'I understand your feelings. You must take time to compose yourself. I should also like to prepare the young man for this long-awaited interview, because I should imagine he is as impatient as you are.'

'I imagine so,' said Cavalcanti.

'Well, then; we shall join you in a quarter of an hour.'

'You will bring him to me then? Does your generosity extend to introducing him to me yourself?'

'No, I should not like to stand between a father and his son. You will be alone, major. But have no fear, even should the call of blood itself be silenced, you cannot be mistaken: he will come through this door. He is a handsome, fair-haired young man, with delightful manners. You will see.'

'By the way,' the major said, 'you know that I only brought with me the two thousand francs that the good Abbé Busoni gave me. They paid for my journey and . . .'

'You need money . . . Of course you do, dear Monsieur Cavalcanti. Here, for a start, are eight thousand-franc notes.'

The major's eyes shone like emeralds. 'In that way I still owe you forty thousand francs,' said Monte Cristo.

'Would Your Excellency like a receipt?' the major asked, slipping the notes into the inner pocket of his greatcoat.

'For what purpose?' said the count.

'To settle your debt with Abbé Busoni?'

'Well, then, give me a general receipt when you have the last forty thousand francs. Between honest men such precautions are unnecessary.'

'Of course,' said the major. 'Between honest men.'

'Now, one last thing, Marquis.'

'What?'

'Would you permit me to make a small suggestion?'

'What is it? Just tell me.'

'It might not be a bad idea to take off your greatcoat.'

'Really!' said the major, looking at the garment with some affection.

'Yes, though it may still be worn in Via Reggio, in Paris that style of dress, elegant though it may be, has long since gone out of fashion.'

'How annoying,' said the Luccan.

'Oh, if you are really attached to it, pick it up on your way out.'

'But what can I put on?'

'You will find something in your luggage.'

'What do you mean: in my luggage? I only have a portmanteau.'

'With you, of course. Why weigh oneself down? In any case, an old soldier likes to travel light.'

'Which is precisely why . . .'

'But you are a careful man, so you sent your trunks on in advance. They arrived yesterday at the Hôtel des Princes, in the Rue Richelieu. That is where you are booked in.'

'And in the trunks?'

'I assume you took the precaution of getting your valet to pack everything you need: city clothes, uniform. On important occasions, you will wear your uniform: it makes a good impression. Don't forget your cross. People sneer at it in France, but they always wear it.'

'Yes, very well, very well!' the major said, mounting from one level of astonishment to another.

'And now,' Monte Cristo said, 'when your heart has been strengthened against any too violent emotion, prepare, Monsieur Cavalcanti, to see your son Andrea.' At which, giving a delightful bow to the Luccan, enchanted, ecstatic, Monte Cristo disappeared behind the hangings.

LVI

ANDREA CAVALCANTI

The Count of Monte Cristo went into the neighbouring room which Baptistin had dubbed the blue drawing-room; he had been preceded there by a young man with a casual air and quite elegantly dressed, whom a cab had set down half an hour before at the door of the house. Baptistin had not had any difficulty in recognizing him. He was the tall young man, with blond hair and a reddish beard and black eyes, whose rosy colouring and fine white skin had been described to him by his master.

When the count entered the room, the young man was stretched out on a sofa, idly tapping his boot with a slender, gold-topped cane. When he saw Monte Cristo, he leapt to his feet.

'Is Monsieur the Count of Monte Cristo?' he asked.

'Yes, Monsieur,' the latter replied. 'I think I have the honour of addressing Viscount Andrea Cavalcanti?'

'Viscount Andrea Cavalcanti, at your service,' the young man repeated, with an extremely offhand bow.

'You must have a letter accrediting you to me?'

'I did not mention it to you because of the signature, which seemed strange.'

'Sinbad the Sailor, I believe?'

'Precisely; and as I do not know any Sinbad outside the *Thousand and One Nights* . . .'

'It's one of his descendants, a very rich friend of mine, a most eccentric, almost mad Englishman, whose real name is Lord Wilmore.'

'That explains everything,' Andrea said. 'That's perfect. It is the same Englishman I met in . . . Yes, very good! Monsieur le Comte, at your service!'

'If what you do me the honour to say is true,' the count replied with a smile, 'I hope that you will be good enough to let me have some details about yourself and your family.'

'Happily, Monsieur le Comte,' the young man said, with a volubility that demonstrated how reliable his memory was. 'As you said, I am Viscount Andrea Cavalcanti, son of Major Bartolomeo Cavalcanti, a descendant of the Cavalcantis whose name is written in the golden book of Florence. Our family, though still very rich, since my father possesses an income of half a million, has suffered greatly down the years and even I, Monsieur, was carried off at the age of five or six by a treacherous tutor, so that it is now fifteen years since I saw my parents. Since reaching the age of reason, and being free and my own master, I have been looking for him, but in vain. Finally, a letter from your friend Sinbad informed me that he was in Paris, and suggested that I address myself to you for news.'

'Well, well, Monsieur, everything you tell me is most interesting,' said the count, looking with sombre satisfaction at the man's relaxed features, which were stamped with a beauty similar to that of the fallen angel. 'You have done well to follow my friend Sinbad's suggestion precisely, because your father is here and looking for you.'

Since coming into the room, the count had not taken his eyes off the young man. He had admired the self-assurance in his look and the firmness of his voice; but at these quite natural words: 'your father is here and looking for you', young Andrea started violently and exclaimed: 'My father? My father . . . here?'

'Of course,' Monte Cristo replied. 'Your father, Major Bartolomeo Cavalcanti.'

Almost at once, the look of terror that had spread across the young man's features disappeared. 'Oh . . . oh, yes. Of course,' he said. 'Major Bartolomeo Cavalcanti. And, Monsieur le Comte, you tell me he is here, my dear father?'

'Yes, Monsieur. I might add that I have just left him, and that the story he told me, about his dear long-lost son, moved me deeply. In truth, there is a most touching poem in his agonies, his fears and his hopes on the subject. Finally, one day, he received news that his child's abductors had offered to return him, or to state where he was, for a rather large sum of money. But nothing was too much for the good father. The money was dispatched to the frontier of Piedmont, with a passport and visas for Italy. You were in the south of France, I believe?'

'Yes, Monsieur,' Andrea replied, with a slightly uneasy air. 'Yes, I was in the south of France.'

'A carriage was to wait for you in Nice?'

'That's right, Monsieur. It took me from Nice to Genoa, from Genoa to Turin, from Turin to Chambéry, from Chambéry to Pont-de-Beauvoisin, and from Pont-de-Beauvoisin to Paris.'

'Perfectly! He kept hoping to meet you on the way, because he followed the same route himself; that is why you were given the same itinerary.'

'But if he had met me,' said Andrea, 'this dear father of mine, I doubt whether he would have recognized me. I have changed somewhat since I lost touch with him.'

'Ah, but the call of blood!' said Monte Cristo.

'Yes, that's true. I didn't think of the call of blood.'

'Now,' said Monte Cristo, 'there is just one last thing troubling the Marquis Cavalcanti, which is what you did while you were separated from him, how you were treated by your persecutors, whether they treated you with all the consideration due to your noble birth and, finally, whether the moral torments to which you have been subjected, torments which are a hundred times worse than those caused by physical suffering, have not left you with some weakening of the faculties with which you were so generously endowed by nature, and if you yourself feel ready to take up the rank in society that belongs to you and to maintain it worthily.'

'Monsieur,' the young man stammered, stupefied, 'I hope that no false rumour . . .'

'I insist that I heard speak of you for the first time by my friend Wilmore, the philanthropist. I learned that he had discovered you in difficult circumstances, I don't know what precisely, and I did not question him about it. I am not curious. Your misfortunes interested him, so you were interesting. He told me that he wanted to restore you to the position in society that you had lost, that he was looking for your father and that he would find him. He looked, and apparently he found, since he is here. Finally, he advised me yesterday of your arrival, giving me some other instructions concerning your fortune. That's all. I know that my friend Wilmore is an eccentric, but at the same time, as he is a reliable man, rich as a gold mine and, consequently, one who had indulged his eccentricities without ruining himself, I promised to follow his instructions. Now, Monsieur, please do not be offended if I ask you one question: as I shall be obliged to sponsor you to some extent, I should like to know if the misfortunes you have suffered – misfortunes for which you were not responsible and which in no way diminish my respect for you – have not made you something of an outsider in this world where your fortune and your name should entitle you to shine?'

'Monsieur,' said the young man, who had been regaining his composure as the count spoke, 'have no worries on that score. The abductors who took me away from my father – and who, no doubt, intended eventually to sell me back to him, as they have done – judged that, if they were to profit by me, they must conserve all the value of my person and even, if possible, enhance it. I consequently received quite a good education and I was treated by the robbers more or less as slaves were in Asia Minor, whose masters turned them into grammarians, doctors and philosophers, so that they might get a better price for them in the market in Rome.'

Monte Cristo smiled. He had not expected so much, apparently, of M. Andrea Cavalcanti.

'In any event,' the young man continued, 'if my education – or, rather, my familiarity with the ways of society – were deficient in some respects, I suppose people would be good enough to forgive it, in view of the misfortunes surrounding my birth and my youth.'

'Ah, now,' the count said casually, 'you must do as you wish, Viscount, because this is your business and you are in charge; but I must say that in your place I should say nothing of all these adventures. Your life story is a novel; and people, though they love novels bound between two yellow paper covers, are oddly suspicious of those which come to them in living vellum, even when they are as gilded as you are capable of being. Allow me to point out this difficulty to you, Monsieur le Vicomte, which is that no sooner will you have told your touching story to someone, than it will travel all round society, completely distorted. You will have to play the part of Antony,[1] and Antony's day has passed somewhat. You might perhaps enjoy the reputation of a curiosity, but not everyone likes to be the centre of attention and the butt of comment. It might possibly fatigue you.'

'I think you are right, Count,' the young man said, going pale in spite of himself under Monte Cristo's unwavering gaze. 'It would be very inconvenient.'

'Oh, but not to be exaggerated, either,' said the count. 'For, to avoid a folly, one might commit an error. No, there is just a simple plan of conduct to be settled on and, for a man as intelligent as you are, the plan will be all the easier to follow since it is in your own interests. You must do all you can, through the evidence of witnesses and through cultivating honourable friends, to overcome everything that may seem obscure in your past.'

Andrea was visibly unsettled by this.

'I should willingly offer myself as your guarantor,' said Monte Cristo, 'but it is an ingrained habit with me to doubt my best friends and a necessity for me to try to instil doubt in others. So I should be playing a role outside my range, as tragic actors say, and risk being booed, which is pointless.'

'However, Monsieur le Comte,' Andrea said boldly, 'considering that Lord Wilmore recommended me to you . . .'

'Yes, indeed,' said Monte Cristo. 'But Lord Wilmore did not disguise from me, my dear Monsieur Andrea, that you had had a somewhat tempestuous youth. Oh!' he exclaimed, seeing Andrea's reaction to this. 'I am not asking you for a confession. In any case it was to ensure that you had no need of anyone that we brought your father, the Marquis Cavalcanti, from Lucca. You will see: he is a little formal, a bit starchy; but that is a matter of the uniform and, when people know that he served in the Austrian army for eighteen years, everything will be forgiven. In short, he is a very adequate father, I assure you.'

'You are indeed reassuring me, Monsieur. It is so long since I last saw him that I have no memory of him.'

'And, you know, a large fortune excuses a lot of things.'

'Is my father really very rich, Monsieur?'

'A millionaire . . . an income of five hundred thousand *livres*.'

'So,' the young man asked anxiously, 'I shall find myself . . . comfortably off?'

'Very comfortably, my dear sir. He will give you an income of fifty thousand *livres* just as long as you stay in Paris.'

'In that case, I shall always stay here.'

'Ah, but who can ever know what may happen, my dear fellow? Man proposes, God disposes . . .'

Andrea sighed and said: 'But as long as I remain in Paris and nothing forces me to leave, this money that you just mentioned is guaranteed?'

'Oh, yes, absolutely.'

'By my father?' Andrea asked uneasily.

'Guaranteed by Lord Wilmore who, at your father's request, has just opened a credit of five thousand francs a month for you with Monsieur Danglars, one of the most reliable bankers in Paris.'

'And does my father intend to stay in Paris long?' Andrea asked, still uneasy.

'Only a few days,' said Monte Cristo. 'His obligations will not allow him to be absent for more than two or three weeks.'

'Oh, the dear man,' said Andrea, visibly delighted at this early departure.

'Which being the case,' Monte Cristo said, pretending to mistake the tone in which these words were uttered, 'I do not wish to delay your reunion for a moment longer. Are you ready to embrace the worthy Monsieur Cavalcanti?'

'I hope you do not doubt that I am.'

'Very well, then: come into the drawing-room, my dear friend, and you will find your father waiting for you.'

Andrea bowed deeply to the count and went into the drawing-room. The count looked after him and, seeing him disappear, pressed a catch next to one of the pictures which, opening away from the frame, allowed one to look through a cleverly designed crack in the panelling, into the drawing-room. Andrea had shut the door behind him and was walking over to the major, who got up immediately he heard the sound of footsteps.

'Monsieur! My dear father!' Andrea said loudly, so that the count could hear him through the closed door. 'Is it really you?'

'Greetings, my dear son,' the major said gravely.

'After so many years' separation,' Andrea said, still looking back towards the door, 'what happiness to meet again!'

'The separation was indeed long.'

'Should we not embrace, Monsieur?' Andrea asked.

'As you wish, my son,' said the major.

The two men embraced as people embrace in the Théâtre Français; that is to say, each putting his head over the other's shoulder.

'We are reunited again!' said Andrea.

'Reunited,' said the major.

'Never again to separate?'

'Indeed so! I think, dear son, that you now consider France a second home?'

'The fact is,' the young man said, 'that I should despair were I to leave Paris.'

'And I, you understand, could not live outside Lucca. So I shall return to Italy as soon as I can.'

'But before you leave, my dearest father, you will no doubt give me the papers I need to prove my origins.'

'Of course; this is the very reason I have come; and I had too much trouble in finding you, in order to give you these papers, for us to start looking for one another again. It would take the last part of my life.'

'So, the papers?'

'Here they are.'

Andrea avidly grasped his father's marriage certificate and his own baptismal certificate and, after opening the packet with the eagerness natural in a good son, perused the two documents with a speed and facility that suggested both a lively interest and a highly practised eye.

When he had finished, an indefinable expression of joy crossed his face and, looking at the major with a strange smile, he said: 'Well, I'll be damned! Are there no galleys in Italy?'

The major drew himself up. 'Why do you ask?' he said.

'Can one manufacture such documents with impunity? For half such an offence in France, my dearest father, they would send us on holiday to Toulon for five years.'

'I beg your pardon?' the Luccan said, trying to manage a dignified look.

'My dear Monsieur Cavalcanti,' Andrea said, grasping the major's arm, 'how much are they giving you to be my father?'

The major tried to reply.

'Hush!' Andrea said, lowering his voice. 'Let me set you an example by showing my trust in you. They are giving me fifty thousand francs a year to be your son, so you understand that I am hardly likely to deny that you are my father.'

The major looked around anxiously.

'Have no fear!' said Andrea. 'We are alone. In any case, we are speaking Italian.'

'Well,' said the Luccan. 'I am getting a single payment of fifty thousand francs.'

'Monsieur Cavalcanti, do you believe in fairy tales?'

'I didn't, but I have to now.'

'You have proof?'

The major took a fistful of gold out of his pocket. 'Palpable proof, as you see.'

'So you think I can trust the promises I have been made?'

'I believe you can.'

'And that the good count will keep his word?'

'In every respect. But, you understand, for that we must play our parts.'

'What?'

'I as the doting father . . .'

'And I as the dutiful son.'

'Since they want you to be my descendant . . .'

'Who: *they*?'

'Truly, I don't know. The people who wrote to you.'

'Didn't you get a letter?'

'Yes.'

'From whom?'

'One Abbé Busoni.'

'Who is unknown to you?'

'I have never seen him.'

'What did your letter say?'

'You will not betray me?'

'It is hardly likely. Our interests are identical . . .'

'Then read it.'

The major passed a letter to the young man, who read it out in a low voice:

You are poor and an unhappy old age awaits you. Would you like to become rich, or at least independent?

Leave for Paris immediately, and go to the Count of Monte Cristo at number thirty, Avenue des Champs-Elysées to claim the son you had by the Marchionesse di Corsinari, who was abducted from you at the age of five.

This son is called Andrea Cavalcanti.

To ensure that you entertain no doubt about the undersigned's desire to serve you, you will find herein: 1. An order for 2,400 Tuscan lire, payable at Signor Gozzi's in Florence; 2. A letter of introduction to the Count of Monte Cristo in which I accredit you for the sum of 48,000 francs.

Be at the count's house on 26 May at seven o'clock in the evening.

Signed: ABBÉ BUSONI

'That's it.'

'What do you mean, that's it?' the major asked.

'I mean that I had an almost identical letter.'

'You did?'

'Yes, I did.'

'From Abbé Busoni?'

'No.'

'From whom?'

'From an Englishman, a certain Lord Wilmore, who uses the name "Sinbad the Sailor".'

'But you are no more acquainted with him than I am with Abbé Busoni?'

'Yes, there I am further ahead than you.'

'You have seen him?'

'Yes, once.'

'Where?'

'Ah, that's just what I cannot tell you. You would know as much as I do and there would be no sense in that.'

'And the letter told you . . .'

'Read it.'

' "You are poor and your future looks bleak. Would you like to have a name, to be free and to be rich?" '

'Huh!' the young man said, rocking back on his heels. 'What a question!'

Take the post chaise which you will find ready harnessed on leaving Nice via the Genoa gate. Go via Turin, Chambéry and Pont-de-Beauvoisin. Present yourself to the Count of Monte Cristo, in the Avenue des Champs-Elysées, on 26 May at seven o'clock in the evening and ask to see your father.

You are the son of Marquis Bartolomeo Cavalcanti and his wife, Olivia Corsinari. This will be confirmed in the papers that will be handed to you by the marquis and which will allow you to present yourself under this name in Parisian society.

An income of 50,000 francs a year will allow you to live in a style appropriate to your rank.

Enclosed is an order for 5,000 livres payable at Monsieur Ferrea's, banker, in Nice, and a letter of introduction to the Count of Monte Cristo, who is instructed by me to supply all your needs.

SINBAD THE SAILOR

'Hum,' said the major. 'Very fine!'

'Isn't it?'

'Have you seen the count?'

'I have just left him.'

'And he confirmed this?'

'All of it.'

'Do you understand what's going on?'

'Good heavens, no.'

'All this is designed to fool someone.'

'But not you or me, in any case?'

'No, surely not.'

'So, what's to be done?'

'Why worry?'

'Exactly. Let's go through with it and not show our hand.'

'Agreed. You will see that I'm a worthy ally.'

'I never doubted it for a moment, my dear father.'

'I am honoured by your trust, my dear son.'

Monte Cristo chose this moment to come into the room. Hearing his footsteps, the two men threw themselves into each other's arms, and the count came in to find them enlaced.

'Well, Marquis,' he said, 'you seem happy with the son you have found?'

'Oh, Monsieur le Comte, I am overcome with joy.'

'And you, young man?'

'Oh, Monsieur le Comte, I am overwhelmed with happiness.'

'Fortunate father! Fortunate child!' said the count.

'Only one thing makes me sad,' said the major. 'And that is that I have to leave Paris so soon.'

'Oh, my dear Monsieur Cavalcanti,' said Monte Cristo, 'I hope you will not leave before I have had time to introduce you to a few friends.'

'I am at Monsieur le Comte's disposal,' the major said.

'Now, young man, make your confession.'

'To whom?'

'To your father, of course. Tell him about the state of your finances.'

'Oh, dear me,' said Andrea. 'That's a sore spot.'

'You hear, Major?'

'Of course I hear.'

'Yes, but do you understand?'

'Perfectly.'

'The dear child says he is in need of money.'

'What can I do about it?'

'Well, give him some, for heaven's sake!'

'Me?'

'Yes, you.'

Monte Cristo walked between the two men.

'Here!' he told Andrea, slipping a sheaf of banknotes into his hand.

'What's that?'

'Your father's reply.'

'My father's?'

'Of course. Didn't you just tell him that you needed money?'

'Yes. So?'

'Well, he has asked me to give you this.'

'An advance on my income?'

'No, to cover the cost of settling in.'

'Oh, my dear father!'

'Ssh!' Monte Cristo said. 'Can't you see that he doesn't want me to tell you that it comes from him?'

'I appreciate such delicacy,' said Andrea, thrusting the banknotes into the pocket of his trousers.

'Very well,' said Monte Cristo. 'Now, go!'

'When will we have the honour of seeing Monsieur le Comte again?' Cavalcanti asked.

'Yes, indeed,' said Andrea. 'When will we have that honour?'

'On Saturday, if you like . . . Yes, let's see . . . Saturday. I have invited several people to dine with me at my house in Auteuil, at number twenty-eight Rue de la Fontaine, including Monsieur Danglars, your banker. I will present you to him. He must know you both if he is to pay you your money.'

'Formal dress?' whispered the major.

'Formal dress: uniform, medals, breeches.'

'And for me?' asked Andrea.

'Oh, you . . . Very simple: black trousers, polished boots, white waistcoat, black or blue jacket, long cravat. Get Blin or Véronique to dress you. If you don't know their addresses, Baptistin will give them to you. The less pretentious your manner of dressing, being rich as you are, the better impression it will give. If you buy horses, get them from Devedeux. If you buy a phaeton, go to Baptiste.'

'At what time should we arrive?' asked the young man.

'Around half-past six.'

'We shall be there,' said the major, reaching for his hat. And the two Cavalcantis bowed to the count and left.

The count went across to the window and saw them crossing the courtyard, arm in arm. 'Good Lord!' he said. 'There go two miserable creatures. What a shame they aren't really father and son!' Then, after a moment of grim reflection, he added: 'Time to go to the Morrels. I do believe that disgust makes me sicker than hatred.'

LVII
THE ALFALFA FIELD

Our readers must allow us to take them back to the patch of ground next to M. de Villefort's house where, behind the fence overhung by chestnut trees, we shall find some people we know.

This time, Maximilien has arrived first. He is the one with his eye pressed to the gap in the board, waiting for a shadow to slip between the trees from the far end of the garden and the crunch of a silk shoe on the gravel path.

At last, it came, this long-awaited sound, but, instead of one shadow, two approached. Valentine had been delayed by a visit from Mme Danglars and Eugénie, which had continued beyond the time of Valentine's rendez-vous. So, not to miss the meeting, the girl had suggested to Mlle Danglars that they take a walk in the garden, hoping in this way to show Maximilien that she was not to be blamed for the wait that he had to endure.

The young man understood all this with the rapid intuition peculiar to lovers, and his heart was eased. In addition, while not coming within earshot, Valentine arranged her walk so that Maximilien would be able to see her go back and forth, and each time that she did so, a glance – unobserved by her companion, but tossed beyond the gate and caught by the young man – told him: 'Be patient, my friend; you see that it is not my fault.'

Maximilien was, indeed, patient and meanwhile admired the contrast between the two girls: the blonde with the languid eyes and willowy figure, and the brunette with the proud eyes and stance as upright as a poplar. Needless to say, the comparison between these two opposite natures was, in the heart of the young man, entirely favourable to Valentine.

After half-an-hour's walk, the two girls disappeared. Maximilien understood that Mme Danglars' visit was coming to an end; and, sure enough, an instant later, Valentine reappeared by herself. Fearing that some inquisitive eyes might be following her, she walked slowly and, instead of going directly to the fence, she went and sat down on a bench, after unobtrusively scrutinizing each tuft of greenery and looking all the way along every path.

Having done that, she ran across to the gate.

'Greetings, Valentine,' a voice said.

'Greetings, Maximilien. I kept you waiting. I hope you saw why?'

'I recognized Mademoiselle Danglars. I didn't think you were a friend of hers.'

'Who said we were friends, Maximilien?'

'No one, but that is how I interpreted the way that you were walking, arm in arm, and talking: one would have thought you were two boarding-school girls telling each other their secrets.'

'We did confide in one another, as it happens,' Valentine said. 'She told me how disgusted she was at the idea of marrying Monsieur de Morcerf and I admitted how little I want to marry Monsieur d'Epinay.'

'Dear Valentine!'

'That, my friend, is why you saw that apparent intimacy between me and Eugénie: while I was talking about the man I cannot love, I was thinking of the man whom I do love.'

'How perfect you are in every respect, Valentine. You have something that Mademoiselle Danglars will never have: an indefinable charm which is to a woman what its scent is to a flower and its flavour to a fruit; for it is not enough for a flower to be beautiful or for a fruit to be fine-looking.'

'It is love that makes you see things in this way, Maximilien.'

'No, Valentine, I promise you. Come, I was watching both of you just now and, on my honour, while paying due tribute to Mademoiselle Danglars' beauty, I cannot understand how a man could fall in love with her.'

'As you said, Maximilien, that is because I was there and my presence made you judge unfairly.'

'No . . . Tell me . . . just out of curiosity, something that was suggested to me by certain ideas I have about Mademoiselle Danglars.'

'Oh, I'm sure they are very unjust, even without knowing for certain what they are. When you men judge us poor women, we cannot expect much sympathy from you.'

'Meaning that you are very fair among yourselves when you criticize each other!'

'Because there is almost always passion in our judgments. But come back to your question.'

'Is it because Mademoiselle Danglars loves someone else that she does not want to marry Monsieur de Morcerf?'

'I told you, Maximilien: I am not a friend of Eugénie's.'

'Pah! Young ladies confide in one another, whether they are friends or not. Admit that you did probe her on it. There! I can see a smile.'

'In that case, Maximilien, there's no sense in our having this fence between us.'

'Come, now: what did she tell you?'

'She told me that she was not in love with anyone,' said Valentine. 'That she detested marriage; that her greatest joy would be to lead a free and independent life; and that she almost wished her father would lose his fortune so that she could become an artist like her friend, Mademoiselle Louise d'Armilly.'

'You see!'

'What does that prove?' asked Valentine.

'Nothing,' Maximilien replied, smiling.

'So why are you smiling now?'

'There!' said Maximilien. 'See! You're looking too, Valentine.'

'Would you like me to go away?'

'Oh, no! No, no. But let's get back to you.'

'Yes, certainly, because we have barely ten minutes together.'

'Heavens!' said Maximilien in dismay.

'Yes, Maximilien, you are right,' Valentine said sadly. 'What a poor friend you have in me. What a life I lead you, when otherwise you possess everything needed for happiness. Believe me, I do bitterly reproach myself.'

'Why does it matter to you, Valentine, if I am happy as I am, if my eternal waiting seems to me fully compensated for by five minutes with you, by two words from your lips and by the deep, enduring conviction that God has not created any two hearts as well suited as ours, and has certainly not almost miraculously brought them together, only to separate them again.'

'Very well. And thank you, Maximilien. Hope for both of us. I am half-happy if you can hope.'

'So what has happened this time, Valentine, to make you hurry away from me again?'

'I don't know. Madame de Villefort sent a message for me to go and see her so that she could tell me something, they said, on which part of my fortune depends. Oh, God! Let them take my fortune! I am too rich. When they have it, then let them leave me in peace and free. You would love me as much if I were poor, wouldn't you, Morrel?'

'I shall always love you. What would riches or poverty matter to me if my Valentine was by my side and I was sure that no one could take her away! But aren't you afraid that this news she has for you may be something to do with your marriage?'

'I don't think so.'

'Listen to me, Valentine, and don't be scared, because as long as I live I shall not belong to anyone else.'

'Do you think that reassures me, Maximilien?'

'Forgive me! You are right, I am too blunt. Well, I meant to tell you that the other day I met Monsieur de Morcerf.'

'So?'

'Monsieur Franz is his friend, as you know.'

'Yes. What of it?'

'So, he has had a letter from Franz, announcing that he will soon be back.'

Valentine went pale and leant against the gate.

'Oh, my God!' she said. 'Suppose that were it! But, no, it would not be Madame de Villefort who told me.'

'Why not?'

'Because . . . I don't know . . . I just feel that Madame de Villefort, while not openly opposed to the match, does not favour it either.'

'Do you know, Valentine, I think I may like this Madame de Villefort.'

'Don't be in too much of a hurry, Maximilien,' said Valentine with a melancholy smile.

'Well, if she is opposed to this match, if only enough to prevent it going ahead, she might be open to other suggestions.'

'Don't think that, Maximilien. It is not husbands that Madame de Villefort rejects, but marriage itself.'

'What? Marriage! But if she hates marriage so much, why did she herself marry?'

'You don't understand, Maximilien. When, a year ago, I spoke of retiring to a convent, despite some remarks that she felt she should make, she welcomed the proposal. Even my father agreed, though at her insistence, I'm sure. Only my poor grandfather restrained me. You cannot imagine, Maximilien, the expression in the eyes of that poor old man, who loves only me in the world and who – God forgive me if this is blasphemy – is loved only by me. If you knew how he looked at me when he learned what I had decided, how reproachful that look was and how desperate were the tears that coursed down his motionless cheeks, unaccompanied by any moan or sigh! Oh, Maximilien! I felt something close to remorse. I fell at his feet, begging him: "My father, my father, forgive me! Let them do what they will to me, I shall never leave you!" At that, he raised his eyes to heaven. Maximilien, I may suffer a great deal, but that look on my grandfather's face has already compensated me for whatever I have to suffer.'

'Dear Valentine! You are an angel and I really don't know what I have done to merit your unburdening yourself to me, unless it is by cutting down a few Bedouin whom God considered as infidels. But, Valentine, I ask you, what interest can Madame de Villefort have in your not getting married?'

'Didn't you hear me tell you a moment ago that I am rich – too rich, Maximilien? From my mother, I have an income of nearly fifty thousand *livres*; my grandmother and grandfather, the Marquis and Marquise de Saint-Méran, should leave me the same amount; and Monsieur Noirtier clearly intends to make me his sole heir. The result is that my brother Edouard, who can expect no fortune from Madame de Villefort's side, is poor in comparison with me. Yet Madame de Villefort loves that child to distraction and if I were to have taken the veil, all my fortune, concentrated on my father who would then inherit from the marquis, the marquise and me, would eventually revert to her son.'[1]

'How strange, such cupidity in a beautiful young woman!'

'You must admit, it is not for herself, but for her son; and what you blame as a defect in her is, from the point of view of maternal love, almost a virtue.'

'But what if you were to cede part of your inheritance to her son, Valentine?'

'How can one suggest such a thing, especially to a woman who is constantly talking about disinterestedness?'

'Valentine, my love has always been sacred to me and, like anything sacred, I have shrouded it in the veil of respect and locked it in my heart. No one in the world, not even my sister, suspects my feelings, because I haven't confided them to anyone. Valentine, would you allow me to mention them to a friend?'

Valentine started back. 'To a friend?' she said. 'Oh, heaven, Maximilien, I shudder to hear you say that! A friend? Who is this friend?'

'Tell me, Valentine, have you ever experienced an irresistible liking for someone which means that, although you are seeing this person for the very first time, you feel that you have known him for a long time and wonder where and when you may have seen him; so much so that, unable to recall either the place or the time, you come to think that it must have been in a world before our own and that the attraction is a reawakened memory?'

'Yes.'

'Well, that is what I felt the first time I met this extraordinary man.'

'An extraordinary man?'

'Yes.'

'Whom you have known for a long time, then?'

'For barely a week or ten days.'

'And you call this man your friend, when you have known him for a week? Oh, Maximilien! I thought you less generous in attributing such a title.'

'Logically, Valentine, you are right; but, say what you may, nothing will alter this instinctive feeling in me. I think that this man will be involved in everything good that happens to me in the future: sometimes his deep gaze seems to have foreknowledge of that and his powerful hand to control it.'

'Is he a fortune-teller, then?' Valentine asked, smiling.

'In truth, I often believe that he does tell ... good fortunes, above all.'

'Oh,' Valentine said sadly, 'let me know who this man is, Maximilien, and I can ask him if I am well enough loved to compensate me for all that I have suffered.'

'My poor love! But you know him!'

'I do?'

'Yes. He's the man who saved your stepmother's life and that of her son.'

'The Count of Monte Cristo?'

'The very same.'

'Oh, no!' Valentine exclaimed. 'He can never be my friend, he is too much a friend of my stepmother's.'

'The count is a friend of your stepmother's? Valentine, my instincts cannot be so unreliable. I am sure you are wrong.'

'If only you knew, Maximilien! It is no longer Edouard who rules in that house, it is the count. The count – sought out by Madame de Villefort, who sees him as an encyclopedia of human wisdom;

admired – do you hear? – admired by my father, who says he has never heard such lofty ideas expressed so eloquently; and worshipped by Edouard who, despite his fear of the count's great black eyes, runs to him as soon as he comes in and opens his hand, where he always finds some admirable toy. When Monsieur le Comte de Monte Cristo is here, he is not in my father's house; when Monsieur le Comte is here, he is not in Madame de Villefort's; the Count of Monte Cristo is at home.'

'Well, then, dearest Valentine, if what you say is true, then you must already be feeling the effects of his presence; or you soon will feel them. When he met Albert de Morcerf in Italy, he rescued him from brigands. When he saw Madame Danglars for the first time, it was to make a regal gift to her. When your stepmother and your brother came past his door, his Nubian servant saved their lives. The man obviously has the power to influence events. I have never seen such simple tastes allied to such magnificence. His smile is so sweet, when he turns it on me, that I forget how bitter others find it. Tell me, Valentine, has he smiled at you in that way? If he does, you will be happy.'

'Me?' the girl said. 'Oh, heavens, Maximilien, he doesn't even look at me; or, rather, if I happen to go by, he looks away from me. Come, he is not generous, admit it! Or else he does not have that ability to penetrate to the depth of another's heart, as you wrongly suppose. For otherwise, if he had been generous, seeing me alone and sad in the midst of that household, he would have protected me with the influence he enjoys there; and, since you claim that he plays the role of a sun, he would have warmed my heart with his rays. You say that he likes you, Maximilien. But, in heaven's name, what do you know? Men show their best side to an officer like you, who is five feet six inches tall, has a long moustache and carries a broad sabre, but they think they can crush a poor weeping girl with impunity.'

'Valentine, you are wrong, I swear.'

'If it were otherwise, Maximilien, if he treated me diplomatically, that is to say as a man would who is trying in some way or other to curry favour in the house, admit that he would at least once have honoured me with that smile which you admire so much. But no: he has seen me unhappy, he realizes that I cannot be of any use to him and he doesn't even notice me. Who knows? Perhaps in his eagerness to ingratiate himself with my father, Madame de Villefort or my brother, he may join them in persecuting me as far as it is within his power. Frankly, you must agree that I am not a woman to be despised for no reason; you said so yourself. Oh, forgive me!' she went on, seeing the impression that these words produced on Maximilien. 'I am wicked, and I have told you things about that man that I was not even myself aware of thinking. Come, I don't deny that he may have the influence that you spoke of, or that he may exercise it over me; but, if so, as you see, it is in a harmful way, which corrupts my good thoughts.'

'Very well, Valentine,' Morrel said with a sigh. 'Let's say no more about it. I shall tell him nothing.'

'Alas, my friend! I can see I have upset you. Oh, how I wish I could clasp your hand to ask your forgiveness! But I ask nothing better than to be convinced. Tell me, what has this Count of Monte Cristo done for you?'

'What has he done for me? I must admit, that is a very difficult question. Nothing tangible, I know. But, as I told you, my affection for him is entirely instinctive, not reasoned. Has the sun done something for me? No. It warms me and by its light I can see you, that's all. Has this or that scent done anything for me? No. Its smell pleasantly refreshes one of my senses. I can't say anything other than that when someone asks me why I praise that perfume; my friendship for him is as strange as his for me. A secret voice tells me that there is more than chance behind this reciprocal and unexpected friendship. I find a correlation between his merest action, or his most secret thought, and my actions, my thoughts. You will laugh at me again, Valentine, but since meeting this man I have the absurd idea that everything good that happens to me emanates from him. However, I lived for thirty years without needing this protector, didn't I? And yet . . . Let me take an example. He has invited me to dine with him on Saturday, which is natural at this stage in our acquaintance, I think. Well, what have I learned since? Your father has been invited to this dinner and your mother will be coming. I shall meet them – and who knows what might come of that meeting, in the future? The circumstances are apparently very simple, yet I perceive something astonishing in it and it gives me a strange sense of optimism. I feel that the count, that remarkable man who guesses everything, wanted to bring me together with Monsieur and Madame de Villefort; and sometimes, I promise you, I try to read in his eyes to see whether he has guessed our love.'

'My dear friend,' said Valentine, 'I should take you for a visionary and I should be seriously concerned for your wits, if all I heard from you were ideas of this kind. What! You imagine that this meeting is something other than a coincidence? Seriously, just think about it. My father, who never goes out, was ten times on the point of refusing to let Madame de Villefort go, while she, on the other hand, could not contain her desire to see this extraordinary nabob in his own home; she had great difficulty in getting him to agree to accompany her. No, no, believe me, apart from you, Maximilien, I have no one to turn to except my grandfather, who is a corpse; and no other support except my poor mother, who is a ghost!'

'I expect you are right, Valentine, and that reason is on your side. But today your sweet voice, which usually has such power over me, has not convinced me.'

'Any more than yours has convinced me,' said Valentine. 'I must say that if you have no more evidence to offer . . .'

'I do have some,' Maximilien said hesitantly, 'but I must say, I am forced to admit it myself, this piece of evidence is even more absurd than the last.'

'Too bad,' said Valentine, smiling.

'Yet I find it no less convincing, being a man of inspiration and feeling who has sometimes, in his ten years' service, owed his life to one of those inner flashes that tell you to move forward or back, so that the bullet that should have struck you flies harmlessly past.'

'Dear Maximilien, why don't you attribute some of the warding off of those bullets to my prayers? When you are over there, I no longer pray to God for myself or my mother, but for you.'

'Yes, since I have known you,' Morrel said, smiling in his turn. 'But what about before, Valentine?'

'Huh! Since you do not wish to be indebted to me for anything, you scoundrel, give me this evidence which you yourself admit to be absurd.'

'Well, then, look through the barrier and you will see the new horse on which I rode here, over there, by the tree.'

'Oh, what a splendid creature!' Valentine exclaimed. 'Why didn't you bring him close up to the gate? I could have spoken to him and he would have heard me.'

'He is indeed, as you can see, quite a valuable animal. And, as you know, my income is limited and I am what is called a "reasonable" man. Well, I saw this splendid Médéah, as I call him, at a place where they sell horses. I asked the price and was told four thousand five hundred francs, so, as you may well imagine, I was obliged to abstain from admiring him much longer; though I must admit that I left with a heavy heart, because he had looked at me tenderly, nuzzled me with his head and pranced about under me in the most captivating and lively way. That same evening, I had some friends at my house: Monsieur de Château-Renaud, Monsieur Debray, and five or six other ne'er-do-wells with whom it is your good fortune to be unacquainted, even by name. Someone suggested bouillotte. I never play, because I am not rich enough to afford to lose or poor enough to want to win. But being the host, you understand, I was obliged to send for some cards, which I did.

'As we were sitting down, the count arrived. He took his place, we played and I won. I hardly dare to tell you this, Valentine, but I won five thousand francs. We separated at midnight. I could wait no longer; I took a cab and ordered it to drive me to the stables. Feverish and shivering, I rang the bell. The man who came to open up must have thought I was mad. I dashed through the door, as soon as it was open, and into the stable, where I looked in the stall. Happiness! Médéah was munching his oats. I grabbed a saddle, put it on his back myself and slipped the bridle over his head. Médéah accepted all this with the best grace in the world! Then, pressing the four thousand five hundred francs into the hands of the astonished merchant, I came back – or, rather, I spent the night riding along the Champs-Elysées. And I saw a light at the count's window; I even thought I saw his shadow behind the curtains. Now, Valentine, I would swear that the count knew I wanted that horse and lost deliberately so that I could have it.'

'My dear Maximilien,' Valentine said, 'your imagination really is running away with you . . . You will not love me for very long. A man who makes such poetry will never be happy, languishing in such a banal passion as ours . . . But, can you hear? They are calling me!'

'Oh, Valentine!' Maximilien said through the little gap in the barrier. 'Your smallest finger . . . let me kiss it.'

'Maximilien, we said that we would be only two voices and two shadows for one another, nothing more!'

'As you wish, Valentine.'

'Will you be happy if I do as you ask?'

'Yes! Oh, yes!'

Valentine got up on a bench and put, not her little finger but her whole hand through the opening in the fence.

Maximilien gave a cry and, rushing to the spot, grasped the adored hand and covered it with burning kisses; but at once the little hand slipped between his and the young man heard Valentine run off, perhaps alarmed by her own feelings!

LVIII

MONSIEUR NOIRTIER DE VILLEFORT

Here is what had happened in the crown prosecutor's house after the departure of Mme Danglars and her daughter, and during the conversation that we have just recorded.

M. de Villefort had gone to see his father, followed by Mme de Villefort (as for Valentine, we know where she was). Both of them greeted the old man and, after sending away Barrois, his servant for more than twenty-five years, sat down beside him.

M. Noirtier was sitting in a large wheelchair where they put him from morning till evening, in front of a mirror which reflected the whole apartment and allowed him to see who was coming in or going out, and what was happening around him, without attempting any movement: this was something that had become impossible for him. Motionless as a corpse, he greeted his children with bright, intelligent eyes, their ceremonious bows telling him that they had come unexpectedly on some official business.

Sight and hearing were the only two senses which, like two sparks, still lit up this human matter, already three-quarters remoulded for the tomb. Moreover, only one of these two senses could reveal to the outside world the inner life which animated this statue, and the look which disclosed that inner life was like one of those distant lights which shine at night, to tell a traveller in the desert that another being watches in the silence and the darkness.

Consequently, in old Noirtier's black eyes, under their black brows – black, while all the rest of the hair, which he wore long and resting on his shoulders, was white – in his black eyes (as usually happens with any human organ which has been exercised at the expense of the others) were concentrated all the activity, all the skill, all the strength and all the intelligence once distributed around this body and this mind. The gesture of the hand, the sound of the voice and the attitude of the body may indeed have gone, but these powerful eyes made up for all: he commanded with them and thanked with them. He was a corpse with living eyes and, at times, nothing could be more terrifying than this marble face out of which anger burned or joy shone. Only three people could read the poor man's language: Villefort, Valentine and the old servant whom we mentioned. But Villefort rarely saw his father (indeed, only when it was unavoidable) and, when he did see him, made no effort to please him by understanding, so all the old man's happiness derived from his granddaughter: Valentine had succeeded, by devoted effort, love and patience, in understanding all Noirtier's thoughts in his looks. She replied to this language, incomprehensible to anyone else, with all her voice, all her expression and all her soul, setting up lively dialogues between the girl and this apparently dead clay, almost returned to dust; and which, despite that, was still a man of immense learning, unparalleled perception and a will as powerful as any can be when the soul is trapped in a body that no longer obeys its commands.

Thus Valentine had managed to solve the enigma of understanding the old man's thoughts in order to make him understand her own, to such an extent that it was now very rare, in normal circumstances, for her not to hit precisely on what this living soul desired or the needs of this near-insensible corpse. As for the servant, he had (as we mentioned) been serving his master for twenty-five years and knew all his habits, so it was not often that Noirtier needed to ask him for anything.

However, Villefort did not need the help of either one of them to engage his father in the strange conversation that was to follow. As we said, he was perfectly well acquainted with the old man's vocabulary; only boredom or indifference prevented him from using it more often. So he let Valentine go out into the garden and he sent Barrois away, taking the servant's place on his father's right, while Mme de Villefort sat on his left.

'Monsieur,' he said, 'do not be surprised if Valentine has not come up with us and I have sent Barrois away, because the discussion that we are about to have is one that could not take place in front of a young girl or a servant. Madame de Villefort and I have something to tell you.'

Noirtier's face stayed impassive during these preliminaries, but Villefort's, on the contrary, might have been trying to penetrate to the depths of the old man's heart. He continued, in those icy tones that seemed to brook no contradiction: 'Madame de Villefort and I are sure that what we have to say will be agreeable to you.'

The old man's eyes remained blank. He was listening, nothing more.

'Monsieur,' Villefort continued, 'we are going to have Valentine married.'

A wax figure could not have remained more indifferent to this news than the old man's face.

'The marriage will take place within three months,' Villefort continued.

The old man's face still showed no emotion.

Now Mme de Villefort spoke, and she hastened to add: 'We thought that you would want to know this news, Monsieur. In any case, Valentine has always seemed to enjoy your affection. All that remains is for us to tell you the name of the young man we intend for her. He is one of the finest matches to which Valentine could aspire, bringing her a fortune, a good name and sure guarantees of happiness, given the manners and tastes of the man whom we have chosen for her. His name is not unknown to you. He is Monsieur Franz de Quesnel, Baron d'Epinay.'

While his wife was speaking, Villefort had been concentrating still more closely on the old man's face. When Mme de Villefort spoke Franz's name, Noirtier's eyes, which his son knew so well, fluttered, and their lids, opening as lips might do to allow the voice to pass, let out a flash of light. Knowing the public hostility that had existed between his own father and Franz's, the crown prosecutor understood this flame and the agitation it betrayed. But he pretended not to have noticed and, continuing where his wife had left off, said: 'You must accept that it is important for Valentine to be settled, as she is now nearly nineteen. However, we have not forgotten you in these negotiations and we have been assured in advance that Valentine's husband, while he might not agree to live near us – that could be awkward for a young couple – but that you at least might live with them, since Valentine is so fond of you and you seem to return her affection. In this way, you will not have to change any of your habits, except that you will henceforth have two children instead of one to care for you.'

The light in Noirtier's eyes was savage. Something frightful must surely be taking place in the old man's heart; and surely a cry of pain and anger was rising to his throat where, unable to escape, it suffocated him, because his face became purple and his lips turned blue.

Villefort calmly opened the window, remarking as he did so: 'It is very hot in here and the heat is making Monsieur Noirtier uncomfortable.' Then he came back but did not sit down.

'Both Monsieur d'Epinay and his family are pleased with the match,' Mme de Villefort continued. 'In any case, his only family is an uncle and an aunt. His mother died giving birth to him, and his father was murdered in 1815, when the child was barely two years old, so he is responsible only to himself.'

'A mysterious business,' said Villefort. 'The murderers have never been identified, although many people were suspected.'

Noirtier made such an effort that his lips almost contracted into a smile.

'However,' Villefort went on, 'the guilty parties, those who know that they committed the crime and who may be subject to human justice in their lives and divine justice when they are dead, would be happy indeed to be in our place, with a daughter whom they could offer to Monsieur Franz d'Epinay, to extinguish even the merest glimmer of suspicion.'

One might have thought it impossible for Noirtier's broken frame to achieve such self-control. 'Yes, I understand,' his eyes replied, with a look that simultaneously expressed both profound contempt and contained rage.

Villefort interpreted the meaning of this look perfectly and answered it with a slight shrug of the shoulders. Then he motioned to his wife to get up.

'Now, Monsieur,' Mme de Villefort said, 'please accept my regards. Would you like Edouard to pay his respects to you?'

It was understood that when the old man meant 'yes', he would close his eyes, when he meant 'no' he would blink them repeatedly and, when he needed something, he would raise them upwards. If he wanted Valentine, he closed only the right eye; if he wanted Barrois, he closed the left. At Mme de Villefort's suggestion, he blinked vigorously.

At this blatant refusal, Mme de Villefort pursed her lips.

'So, shall I send you Valentine?' she asked.

'Yes,' the old man said, shutting his eyes tightly.

M. and Mme de Villefort took their leave of the old man and went out, giving orders for Valentine to be called. She already knew that she would have to attend M. Noirtier during the day. She came in behind them, still flushed with emotion. It took only a glance for her to realize how much her grandfather was upset and how much he wanted to speak to her.

'Oh, grandfather!' she exclaimed. 'What is wrong? Someone has upset you, haven't they? You're angry?'

'Yes,' he said, closing his eyes.

'Who has made you angry? My father? No. Madame de Villefort, then? No. Are you angry with me?'

The old man indicated: 'Yes.'

'With me?' Valentine said in astonishment.

The old man again closed his eyes.

'My dearest grandfather, what have I done?' Then, getting no reply, she went on: 'I have not seen you all day. Has someone told you something about me?'

'Yes,' the old man's eyes said, emphatically.

'Let me think. In God's name, I swear . . . Ah! Monsieur and Madame de Villefort have just left, haven't they?'

'Yes.'

'So it was they who told you whatever has made you angry. What can it be? Do you want me to go and ask them, so that I can apologize?'

'No, no,' said the eyes.

'You are frightening me. Heavens, what can they have said?'

She thought for a while, then she exclaimed: 'Ah! I've got it!' and, lowering her voice and coming close to the old man: 'They spoke about my marriage, perhaps?'

'Yes,' the eyes replied angrily.

'I understand. You are cross with me because I did not tell you. Oh, but you must understand, they insisted that I keep it from you, because they did not say anything to me themselves: I stumbled on the secret as it were by chance. That explains my reserve with you. But forgive me, dear Papa Noirtier.'

The eyes became fixed and expressionless, seeming to reply: 'It is not only your silence that pains me.'

'What, then?' the girl asked. 'Do you think I would abandon you, grandfather, and that marriage would make me forgetful?'

'No,' said the old man.

'So they told you that Monsieur d'Epinay agreed that we could still live together?'

'Yes.'

'So why are you angry?'

A look of infinite pain entered the old man's eyes.

'I understand,' said Valentine. 'Because you love me?'

'Yes.'

'And you are afraid I shall be unhappy?'

'Yes.'

'You do not like Monsieur Franz?'

Three or four times the eyes said: 'No, no, no . . .'

'And this causes you great sorrow, grandfather?'

'Yes.'

'Well, then, listen to me,' said Valentine, kneeling in front of Noirtier and putting her arms round his neck. 'I, too, am very unhappy about it, because I do not love Monsieur Franz d'Epinay either.'

The old man's eyes lit up with joy.

'Do you remember how angry you were with me when I wanted to retire to a convent?'

A tear moistened the dry lid of the old man's eye.

'The reason,' Valentine went on, 'was to escape from this marriage which was driving me to despair.'

Noirtier began to breathe more rapidly.

'So, you are unhappy at the prospect of this match? Oh, God, if only you could help me, grandfather; if only we could join forces to undermine their schemes! But you are powerless against them, even though your mind is so sharp and your will so strong. When it comes to a fight, you are as weak, or even weaker than I am. Alas! In the days when you had your strength and your health, you would have been such a powerful protector for me. But now, all you can do is to sympathize, and either rejoice or mourn with me. That you can still do so is one last blessing that God has forgotten to take away with the rest.'

At these words the depths of Noirtier's eyes were lit with such malice that the girl thought she could hear them say: 'You are wrong: I can still do a lot for you.'

'You *can* do something for me?' she translated.

'Yes.'

Noirtier looked upwards. This was the sign that meant he wanted something.

'What do you want, grandfather? Let's see.' She racked her brains for a moment, expressing her ideas aloud as they came to her, but found that, whatever she said, the old man answered 'no'.

'Very well,' she said. 'We'll have to take more extreme measures, since I am so stupid!' And she began to recite all the letters of the alphabet, one after another, starting with 'a', until she got to 'n', smiling and watching the invalid's face; at 'n', Noirtier indicated: 'Yes.'

'So!' Valentine said. 'Whatever you want starts with "n". We are dealing with the letter "n"? And what do we want after "n"? Na, ne, ni, no . . .'

'Yes, yes, yes,' the old man said.

'So it's "no" . . . ?'

'Yes.'

Valentine went to fetch a dictionary, which she put on a reading stand in front of Noirtier. She opened it and when she saw that he was looking attentively at the pages, she ran her finger up and down the columns. Over the six years during which Noirtier had been in his present unhappy state, the exercise had become so easy that she guessed the invalid's thoughts as quickly as though he had been able to use the dictionary himself.

At the word 'notary', Noirtier signalled to her to stop.

'Notary,' she said. 'Do you want a notary, grandfather?'

The old man indicated that this was the case.

'So, shall I ask for them to fetch a notary?' Valentine asked.

'Yes.'

'Ought my father to be told?'

'Yes.'

'Are you in a hurry to see this notary?'

'Yes.'

'Then I shall send for him at once, dear grandfather. Is that all you need?'

'Yes.'

Valentine ran to the bell, called a servant and told him to ask M. or Mme de Villefort to come to her grandfather.

'Are you happy?' she asked. 'Yes . . . Yes, I think you are, aren't you? Wasn't that quite easy, after all?' And she smiled at the old man as she might have done to a child.

M. de Villefort came in, having been fetched by Barrois.

'What do you want, Monsieur?' he asked the invalid.

'Monsieur, my grandfather would like to see a notary,' said Valentine.

At this odd and unexpected request, M. de Villefort looked at the invalid, whose eyes said 'yes' with a firmness that indicated that, with the help of Valentine and his old servant, who now knew what he wanted, he was ready to hold his own.

'You are asking for a notary?' Villefort repeated.

'Yes.'

'Why?'

Noirtier did not answer.

'What need can you have of a notary?' Villefort asked.

The invalid's eyes remained motionless and, consequently, dumb, which meant: I am sticking by what I have said.

'You want to do us a bad turn?' Villefort said. 'Is it worth it?'

'But, after all,' Barrois said, and, with the obstinacy characteristic of some old servants, he was prepared to argue the point, 'if Monsieur wants a notary, that means he must need one. So I shall go and get a notary.'

Barrois recognized no master but Noirtier, whose wishes he would never allow to be challenged in any way.

'Yes, I want a notary,' the old man said, closing his eyes with a defiant air, as if to say: refuse me, if you dare.

'Since you are determined to have a notary, Monsieur, you shall have one. But I shall apologize to him on my behalf and you will on yours, because the scene will be quite ridiculous.'

'No matter,' said Barrois. 'I shall fetch him even so.' And he left the room in triumph.

LIX

THE WILL

As Barrois went out, Noirtier looked at Valentine with a malicious interest that promised trouble to come. The girl understood the meaning of the look; so did Villefort, whose brow clouded with a dark frown. He took a seat, settled down in the invalid's room and waited. Noirtier watched him with total indifference; but, out of the corner of his eye, he had told Valentine to wait, and not to worry.

Three-quarters of an hour later, the servant returned with a notary.

'Monsieur,' Villefort said, after the usual exchange of greetings, 'you have been requested by Monsieur Noirtier de Villefort, here present. A general paralysis has deprived him of the use of his limbs and his voice. Only we are able, with the greatest difficulty, to grasp a few fragments of his thoughts.'

'No, Monsieur. I understand everything my grandfather says.'

'That's right,' said Barrois. 'Everything, absolutely everything, as I told this gentleman on our way here.'

'Monsieur,' said the notary, turning to Villefort, then to Valentine, 'and you also, Mademoiselle, allow me to say that this is one of those cases where a lawyer cannot proceed, regardless, without assuming a dangerous degree of responsibility. For an act to have legal force, the first requirement is that the notary should be entirely convinced that he has faithfully interpreted the wishes of the person making such an act. Now, I cannot myself be sure of the approval or otherwise of a client who does not speak. And since, in view of his silence, I cannot be clearly persuaded that he wants something or that he does not want it, my functions would be exercised to no avail, indeed, illegally.'

The notary made to leave, and a faint smile of triumph appeared on the lips of the crown prosecutor. But Noirtier was looking at Valentine with such an expression of anguish that she went and placed herself between the notary and the door.

'Monsieur,' she said, 'the language in which I communicate with my grandfather can easily be learnt and, just as I myself understand it, so in a matter of minutes I can teach you to do so. Tell me, what do you need to satisfy your conscience?'

'Whatever is necessary for our acts to be legally valid,' the notary replied. 'That is to say, certainty of the client's approval or disapproval. A person may attest when physically sick, but he must be mentally healthy.'

'Well, then, Monsieur, two signs will show you for certain that my grandfather has never been in greater command of his mental faculties than he is at this moment. Being deprived of voice and movement, Monsieur Noirtier closes his eyes when he means "yes" and blinks them several times when he means "no". You now have all you need to converse with Monsieur Noirtier. Try it.'

The look that the old man gave Valentine was so brimming with tenderness and gratitude that even the notary could follow it.

'Have you heard and understood what your granddaughter has just said, Monsieur?' the notary asked.

Noirtier gently closed his eyes, re-opening them a moment later.

'And you approve of what she says? That is to say, that the signs mentioned by her are truly those by which you make yourself understood?'

'Yes,' the old man repeated.

'You asked for me to come?'

'Yes.'

'To make your will?'

'Yes.'

'And you do not wish me to leave without making this will?'

The invalid blinked energetically several times.

'Very well, Monsieur,' the girl asked, 'do you now understand and will your conscience be clear?'

Before the notary could reply, Villefort drew him aside.

'Monsieur,' he said, 'do you think that a man can endure a physical assault as severe as that experienced by Monsieur Noirtier de Villefort, without also suffering some grave mental damage?'

'It is not exactly that which concerns me,' the notary replied. 'However, I do wonder how we shall be able to guess his thoughts in order to elicit a reply.'

'You see, it is impossible,' said Villefort.

Valentine and the old man could hear this conversation. Noirtier was staring at Valentine so fixedly and with such determination that he clearly expected her to respond in some way.

'Monsieur,' she said, 'don't worry about that. However difficult it may be, or may seem to you, to discover my grandfather's thoughts, I shall show you how it may be done, in such a manner as to dispel all your doubts on this head. I have been with Monsieur Noirtier for six years; let him tell you himself if, in those six years, a single one of his wishes has remained buried in his heart for want of making me understand.'

'No,' the old man answered.

'Well, let's try, then,' said the notary. 'Do you accept the young lady as your interpreter?'

The invalid gave an affirmative sign.

'Good. Now, Monsieur, what do you want of me and what is the act that you would like to perform?'

Valentine went through all the letters of the alphabet down to 't'. At that letter, Noirtier stopped her with an expressive look.

'The gentleman wants the letter "t",' said the notary. 'That's obvious.'

'Wait,' said Valentine. Then, turning back to her grandfather: 'Ta . . . Te . . .'

He stopped her at the second of these syllables, so Valentine took the dictionary and, under the watchful eye of the notary, turned the pages.

'Testament,' her finger said, instructed by Noirtier's eyes.

'Testament!' the notary exclaimed. 'This is quite clear. The gentleman wants to make his will.'

'Yes,' Noirtier indicated several times.

'You must admit, Monsieur, this is wonderful,' the notary said in astonishment to Villefort.

'Yes, indeed,' the latter replied. 'The testament itself will be still more wonderful, because I really don't think that the articles of this last will and testament will put themselves down on paper, word by word, without the clever inspiration of my daughter. And it could be that Valentine will have rather too direct an interest in the will to act as a suitable interpreter for Monsieur Noirtier de Villefort's nebulous desires.'

'No, no!' the invalid said.

'What! Valentine has no interest in your will?' M. de Villefort asked.

'No,' said Noirtier.

The notary was delighted by the results of the test and determined to dine out on this picturesque anecdote. 'Nothing, Monsieur,' he said, 'now seems simpler to me than this task which a moment ago I considered impossible. This will quite simply be a "mystical", that is to say, one allowed for under the law provided it is read before seven witnesses, approved by the testator in their presence and sealed by the notary, also in their presence. As for the time involved, it will scarcely take longer than an ordinary will. There are, first of all, the usual formalities which are always the same; as for the details, most of these will be supplied by the state of the testator's affairs themselves and by you who, having managed his estate, are acquainted with it. At the same time, to make this will unchallengeable, we shall make sure that everything is signed and sealed: one of my colleagues will serve as my assistant and, contrary to the usual practice, be present when the will is dictated. Does that satisfy you, Monsieur?' he continued, turning to the old man.

'Yes,' Noirtier said, delighted at having been understood.

'What is he going to do?' wondered Villefort, whose eminent position did not allow him to show his feelings and who, in any event, could not guess what his father had in mind.

He turned around to look for the second notary whom the first had mentioned, but Barrois, having heard everything and anticipated his master's wishes, had already left. So the prosecutor sent for his wife. A quarter of an hour later, everyone was assembled in the invalid's room and the second notary had arrived.

The two officials quickly agreed. Noirtier was read a vague and commonplace form of last will and testament; then, to begin probing his intelligence so to speak, the first notary turned to him and said: 'When one makes a will, Monsieur, it is in favour of someone.'

'Yes,' said Noirtier.

'Do you have some idea of the amount of your fortune?'

'Yes.'

'I am going to mention several figures, in ascending order. Stop me when I get to the one you think is correct.'

'Yes.'

There was a kind of solemnity in this interrogation. Never had the struggle of mind against matter been more clearly visible, and the resulting spectacle, if not sublime (as we were inclined to call it), was at least curious.

They formed a circle around Noirtier. The second notary was seated at a table, poised to write. The first stood in front of him and asked the questions.

'Is your fortune greater than three hundred thousand francs?' he asked.

Noirtier indicated that it was.

'Do you have four hundred thousand francs?' the notary asked.

Noirtier remained impassive.

'Five hundred thousand?'

Still no movement.

'Six hundred? Seven hundred? Eight hundred? Nine hundred?'

Noirtier indicated: 'Yes.'

'You have nine hundred thousand francs?'

'Yes.'

'In property?' the notary asked.

Noirtier said, 'No.'

'In government bonds?'

Noirtier said, 'Yes.'

'And do you have these bonds in your possession?'

A glance at Barrois sent the old servant hurrying out, to return a moment later with a small box.

'Will you allow us to open this box?' asked the notary.

Noirtier said, 'Yes.'

The box was opened to reveal government bonds to the amount of 900,000 francs. The first notary passed them, one by one, to his colleague. The amount stated by Noirtier was exact.

'Correct,' the notary said. 'It is clear that the man's intelligence is unimpaired.' Then he turned to the invalid and said: 'So, you have a capital of nine hundred thousand francs which, invested in this way, must bring you an income of around forty thousand *livres*?'

'Yes,' said Noirtier.

'To whom do you wish to leave this fortune?'

'Oh!' Mme de Villefort said. 'There can be no doubt on that score. Monsieur Noirtier only loves his granddaughter, Mademoiselle Valentine de Villefort. She has looked after him for six years and this dedicated care has managed to win her grandfather's affection, I might even say his gratitude. So it is only fair that she should have some reward for her devotion.'

Noirtier's eyes flashed, as if to show that he was not taken in by this false consent that Mme de Villefort was giving to what she supposed to be his intentions.

'Do you then wish to leave these nine hundred thousand francs to Mademoiselle Valentine de Villefort?' the notary asked, thinking that he had only to write this provision into the will, but wanting, even so, to have Noirtier's consent and to let it be noted by all the witnesses to this unusual scene.

Valentine had stepped back and was weeping, her eyes lowered. The old man looked at her for a moment with an expression of profound tenderness, then turned back to the notary and blinked his eyes in the most emphatic way.

'No?' the notary asked. 'Do you mean that you do not wish to name Mademoiselle Valentine de Villefort as your sole heir and legatee?'

Noirtier said, 'No.'

'Are you sure that you are not making a mistake?' the notary exclaimed. 'Are you really saying "no"?'

'No!' Noirtier repeated. 'No.'

Valentine looked up. She was astonished, not at being disinherited but at the feeling which usually dictates such an action. But Noirtier was looking at her with such an expression of tenderness that she exclaimed: 'Oh, grandfather, I can see that you are only depriving me of your fortune, while leaving me your heart!'

'Oh yes, indeed,' said the invalid's eyes, closing with an emphasis that Valentine could not fail to understand.

'Thank you, thank you!' she murmured.

However, the old man's emphatic 'No' had awakened an unexpected hope in Mme de Villefort's heart. She came closer to him and asked: 'So, dear Monsieur Noirtier, are you leaving your money to your grandson, Edouard de Villefort?'

There was a fearful blinking of the eyelids, almost expressive of loathing.

'No,' said the notary. 'Then is it your son, here present?'

'No,' the old man answered.

The two notaries exchanged looks of astonishment, while Villefort and his wife felt the blood rise to their cheeks, one in shame, the other in fury.

'But what have we done to you, grandfather?' said Valentine. 'Don't you love us any more?'

The old man's eyes swept rapidly past his son and daughter-in-law, to rest, with an expression of deep tenderness, on Valentine.

'Well, then,' she said. 'If you love me, my dearest grandfather, try to associate that love with what you are doing at the moment. You know me, you know that I have never considered your fortune. In any event, they say that I am rich on my mother's side . . . too rich. So explain yourself.'

Noirtier stared eagerly at Valentine's hand.

'My hand?' she said.

'Yes,' said Noirtier.

'Her hand!' everyone exclaimed.

'There, gentlemen!' said Villefort. 'Now you can plainly see that this is useless and that my poor father is ill.'

'Ah! I understand!' Valentine exclaimed suddenly. 'You mean my marriage, don't you, grandfather?'

'Yes, yes, yes,' the invalid said, three times, his eyes flashing each time the lid was raised.

'You reproach us, concerning the marriage?'

'Yes.'

'But this is absurd,' said Villefort.

'On the contrary, Monsieur, if I may say so,' said the notary, 'but all this is very logical and seems to me to hang together quite perfectly.'

'You don't want me to marry Monsieur Franz d'Epinay?'

'No, I don't want you to,' said the old man's eyes.

'And you are disinheriting your granddaughter because she is engaging in a match of which you do not approve?' the notary exclaimed.

'Yes,' said Noirtier.

'Meaning that, without this marriage, she would be your heir?'

'Yes.'

At this, a profound silence fell over everyone.

The two notaries looked questioningly at each other. Valentine, her hands clasped, gave her grandfather a grateful smile. Villefort bit his thin lips. Mme de Villefort could not repress a feeling of joy which, in spite of herself, showed on her face.

Villefort was the first to break the silence. 'But,' he said at length, 'it seems to me that I alone am able to assess the advantages of this union. I alone am master of my daughter's hand and I want her to marry Monsieur Franz d'Epinay. So she will marry him.'

Valentine let herself fall, weeping, on to a chair.

'Monsieur,' the notary said, speaking to the old man, 'what do you intend to do with your fortune, in the event of Mademoiselle Valentine marrying Monsieur Franz?'

The old man did not budge.

'You do, however, intend to bequeath it to someone?'

'Yes,' said Noirtier.

'Someone in your family?'

'No.'

'To the poor, then?'

'Yes.'

'But you do realize that the law will not permit you to deprive your son altogether?'

'Yes.'

'So you will only bequeath the share that the law authorizes you to dispose of outside your family?'

Noirtier did not move.

'You still want to dispose of the whole amount?'

'Yes.'

'But after your death the will will be contested!'

'No.'

'My father knows me, gentlemen,' M. de Villefort said. 'He realizes that his wishes will be sacred to me, and, in any case, he knows that in my position I cannot argue my case against the poor.'

Noirtier's eyes wore an expression of triumph.

'What are you going to do, Monsieur?' the notary asked Villefort.

'Nothing. This decision has been taken by my father and I know that he does not change his mind. Consequently, I am resigned. The nine hundred thousand francs will leave our family and go to enrich some charitable foundation; but I will not give in to an old man's whim. I shall follow my conscience.'

At this, Villefort and his wife left, leaving Noirtier free to make his will in whatever way he desired.

The last will and testament was drawn up the same day. The witnesses were sent for and the old man gave his approval of the document, which was sealed in the presence of the witnesses and deposited with M. Deschamps, the family lawyer.

LX

THE TELEGRAPH

When M. and Mme de Villefort returned to their own apartments, they learned that the Count of Monte Cristo, who had come to pay them a visit, had been shown into the drawing-room and was waiting for them there. Mme de Villefort was too upset to go in directly but went first to her bedroom, while the crown prosecutor was more sure of himself and proceeded at once towards the drawing-room. But, however successful he was in controlling his feelings and not letting them show on his face, M. de Villefort was unable entirely to dispel the cloud from his brow, so the count, greeting him with a radiant smile, could not help noticing his sombre air of preoccupation.

'Good Lord, Monsieur de Villefort!' Monte Cristo said, after the first greetings had been exchanged. 'What is wrong? Have I come at a moment when you were compiling rather too capital an indictment?'

Villefort tried to smile. 'No, Count,' he said. 'I am the only victim here. I am losing my own case, and the indictment was drawn up as a result of chance, obstinacy and folly.'

'How do you mean?' Monte Cristo asked, with a perfect show of sympathetic curiosity. 'Have you really suffered some serious misfortune?'

'Oh, Monsieur le Comte,' Villefort said, with icy bitterness, 'it is not worth mentioning. It is nothing, simply a financial loss.'

'Agreed,' said Monte Cristo. 'A financial loss is a trivial matter to someone who possesses a fortune and a philosophical outlook which are both as broad as yours.'

'Yes,' Villefort replied. 'It is not the money that bothers me – though, when all's said and done, nine hundred thousand francs may be worth a sigh, or at least a snort of irritation. But I am chiefly vexed by the turn of fate, of chance, of destiny . . . I don't know what to call the force behind the blow that has just struck me, destroying my financial expectations and, perhaps, my daughter's future, because of the whim of a senile old man.'

'My goodness! What is this?' the count exclaimed. 'Did you say nine hundred thousand francs? Even a philosopher might regret the loss of such a sum. Who has brought this upon you?'

'My father, whom I mentioned to you.'

'Really? Monsieur Noirtier? But I thought you told me that he was totally paralysed and deprived of all his faculties?'

'Yes, his physical faculties, for he cannot move or speak; yet, as you see, despite that, he thinks, wills and acts. I left him five minutes ago and at this moment he is dictating his last will to two notaries.'

'So he must have spoken?'

'He did better than that: he made himself understood.'

'How?'

'With a look: his eyes still live and, as you see, their look can kill.'

'My friend,' Mme de Villefort said, coming into the room, 'perhaps you are exaggerating the situation?'

'Madame . . .' the count said with a bow. In return, Mme de Villefort gave him her most gracious smile.

'What is Monsieur de Villefort telling me, then?' Monte Cristo asked. 'And what incomprehensible change of heart . . . ?'

'Incomprehensible! That's the word,' the prosecutor repeated with a shrug of the shoulders. 'An old man's whim!'

'And there is no way of making him change his mind?'

'Yes, there is,' said Mme de Villefort. 'It is entirely within my husband's power to ensure that the will, instead of being made to Valentine's disadvantage, is in her favour.'

The count, seeing that the couple were starting to speak in parables, took on an absent-minded air, and began to give the most profound attention and the most marked approval to Edouard, who was pouring ink into the birds' drinking dish.

'Now, dearest,' Villefort said, in answer to his wife, 'you know that I do not enjoy playing the tyrant in my own home and that I have never thought the fate of the world hung on my nod. However, it is important that my decisions should be respected in my family, and that the folly of an old man and the whim of a child should not be allowed to upset a plan that has been settled in my mind for several years. The Baron d'Epinay was my friend, as you know, and a match with his son is entirely suitable.'

'Do you think,' Mme de Villefort asked, 'that Valentine might be in league with him? Consider: she has always been opposed to this match and I should not be surprised if all we have just seen and heard were not the result of a plan agreed between the two of them.'

'Believe me, Madame,' said Villefort, 'no one gives up a fortune of nine hundred thousand francs just like that.'

'She would have given up the world, since a year ago she wanted to go into a convent.'

'No matter,' Villefort persisted. 'I insist, Madame, that this marriage should take place.'

'Despite your father's wishes?' Mme de Villefort said, changing to another tack. 'That is serious.'

Monte Cristo pretended not to be listening, but he heard every word that was being said.

'I have to tell you that I have always respected my father because, as well as natural filial feeling, I had an awareness of his moral superiority; and because a father is doubly sacred, both as our creator and as our master. But today I can no longer recognize any intelligence in an old man who is transferring on to the son what is nothing any more except a memory of hatred for the father. It would be ridiculous for me to subject my behaviour to his whims. I shall continue to have the greatest respect for Monsieur Noirtier. I shall accept the financial punishment that he is imposing on me without complaint. But I shall remain inflexible in my resolve and the world will recognize that common sense is on my side. Consequently, I shall marry my daughter to Baron Franz d'Epinay because, in my view, this marriage is good and honourable; and, when it comes down to it, because I wish to marry my daughter to whomsoever I please.'

'What!' said the count, to whom the prosecutor had constantly been looking for approbation. 'What! Do I understand that Monsieur Noirtier is disinheriting Mademoiselle Valentine because she is going to marry Baron Franz d'Epinay?'

'Yes, by heaven! Yes, yes, Monsieur: that's the reason,' Villefort said, shrugging his shoulders.

'At least, as far as one can see,' Mme de Villefort added.

'The real reason, Madame. Believe me, I know my father.'

'Can you imagine such a thing?' the young woman replied. 'I ask you, how can Monsieur Noirtier find Monsieur d'Epinay any less acceptable than anyone else?'

'Indeed,' said the count. 'I have met Monsieur Franz d'Epinay, the son of General de Quesnel, I think, who was created Baron d'Epinay under King Charles X?'

'Precisely,' Villefort replied.

'He seems to me to be a charming young man!'

'So it must be an excuse, I am sure of it,' said Mme de Villefort. 'Old men are jealous of their affections. Monsieur Noirtier does not want his granddaughter to marry.'

'But is there some cause for this hatred?'

'Good Lord, who can tell?'

'Perhaps some political antipathy?'

'As it happens, my father and Monsieur d'Epinay's did live through those stormy times, of which I only experienced the final days,' said Villefort.

'Wasn't your father a Bonapartist?' Monte Cristo asked. 'I seem to remember you telling me something like that.'

'My father was a Jacobin more than anything else,' Villefort said, driven to abandon his usual caution. 'The senator's cloak that Napoleon threw over his shoulders only served to disguise the man, without changing him. When my father plotted, it was not for the emperor but *against* the Bourbons, because he had this fearsome quality of not struggling for some unattainable Utopia, but only for what was achievable; and, to attain that, he would apply the terrible doctrines of the Montagne,[1] which would shrink from nothing.'

'There you are, then,' said Monte Cristo. 'Monsieur Noirtier and Monsieur d'Epinay must have met in the political field. I believe that General d'Epinay, even though he served under Napoleon, remained a Royalist at heart. Is he not the same who was assassinated one evening on his way home from a Napoleonic club, which he had been persuaded to visit by some who thought he shared their opinions?'

Villefort looked at the count with something akin to terror.

'Am I mistaken?' Monte Cristo asked.

'Not at all, Monsieur,' said Mme de Villefort. 'On the contrary, quite correct. And it is because of what you have just mentioned, and to extinguish this old animosity, that Monsieur de Villefort considered uniting in love two children whose fathers had been divided by hatred.'

'What a sublime thought!' said Monte Cristo. 'A generous thought and one that the world should applaud. It would indeed be fine to see Mademoiselle Noirtier de Villefort become Madame Franz d'Epinay.'

Villefort shuddered and looked at Monte Cristo as if trying to read the deeper impulse that had inspired these words. But the count's face wore only the same benevolent smile fixed on it and, try as he might, the crown prosecutor could not see what lay beyond that.

'So,' Villefort resumed, 'although it is a great misfortune for Valentine to lose her grandfather's legacy, I do not see this as any reason to annul the marriage. I do not think Monsieur d'Epinay will be discouraged by this financial setback. He may realize that I am worth more than the money, since I am prepared to sacrifice it to keep my word. In any case, he will realize that Valentine has her mother's wealth, which is administered by Monsieur and Madame de Saint-Méran, her maternal grandparents, both of whom love her dearly.'

'And who deserve to be loved and cared for as much as Valentine has done for Monsieur Noirtier,' said Mme de Villefort. 'As it happens, they will be coming to Paris in a month, or less, and after such an affront she will be relieved of any obligation to stay constantly with Monsieur Noirtier, as she did before.'

The count listened indulgently to the discordant cries of all these wounded vanities and damaged interests. Then, after a moment's silence, he said: 'It seems to me ... And I beg you in advance to forgive me for what I am about to say ... but it seems to me that while Monsieur Noirtier may be disinheriting Mademoiselle de Villefort because she is marrying a man whose father he hated, he cannot find the same fault with your dear Edouard.'

'Absolutely, Monsieur!' Mme de Villefort exclaimed, in a voice that defies description. 'Is it not unjust, horribly unjust? Poor Edouard is as much Monsieur Noirtier's grandchild as Valentine, yet if Valentine had not been engaged to Franz, Monsieur Noirtier would have left everything to her. What is more, Edouard bears the family name, but that does not alter the fact that, even supposing her grandfather really does disinherit her, she will still be three times as rich as he will.'

Having turned the knife in this wound, the count listened in silence.

'Come, Count,' said Villefort, 'come, I pray you, let us say no more about these family troubles. Yes, my fortune will go to enrich the poor: it is they who truly have the wealth nowadays. Yes, my father has denied me my legitimate expectations, and for no good reason. But I shall have acted like a man of sense and a man of heart. I promised Monsieur d'Epinay the income from that money and he shall have it, however much I may have to put up with ...'

'However,' said Mme de Villefort, returning to the one idea constantly hovering at the back of her mind, 'perhaps it might be better to confide all this in Monsieur d'Epinay, who can release us from the engagement.'

'Oh, that would be a disaster!' Villefort exclaimed.

'A disaster?' Monte Cristo repeated.

'Of course,' Villefort said, in softer tones. 'A broken engagement, even when money is the cause, reflects very badly on a young woman. And then the old rumours, which I have tried to suppress, would become more plausible. But it won't happen. Monsieur d'Epinay, if he is a gentleman, will feel himself more firmly engaged than before by Valentine's loss of prospects, or else he would seem to be acting out of pure avarice. No, it's impossible.'

'I agree with Monsieur de Villefort,' said Monte Cristo, looking intently at Mme de Villefort. 'And if I were a close enough friend to venture to offer some advice, I would suggest that he reinforces the engagement to the point where it cannot be undone, since Monsieur d'Epinay, as I understand, is about to return to Paris. In short, I should arrange for this marriage, which will do such honour to Monsieur de Villefort, to take place.'

Villefort got up, visibly overwhelmed with delight, while the colour drained from his wife's cheeks.

'Very well,' he said, offering Monte Cristo his hand. 'That is all I was asking for; I shall take advantage of your excellent advice. So, let everyone consider that what has happened here today is irrelevant. Nothing in our plans has changed.'

'Monsieur,' the count said, 'unjust though people are, they will thank you for your resolve, I promise you. Your friends will be proud of you. As for Monsieur d'Epinay, even if he were obliged to accept Mademoiselle de Villefort without any dowry at all – which cannot be the case – he would be delighted to join a family whose members can rise to such a sacrifice to keep their word and do their duty.' With this, he got up and prepared to depart.

'Are you leaving us, Monsieur le Comte?' asked Mme de Villefort.

'Madame, I must. I came only to remind you of your promise for Saturday.'

'Were you afraid that we might forget?'

'You are too kind, Madame. But Monsieur de Villefort has such grave and sometimes such pressing obligations . . .'

'My husband has given his word, Monsieur,' said Mme de Villefort. 'You have just seen that he will keep it even when he has everything to lose; so how much more when he has everything to gain . . . ?'

'Are we to meet at your house in the Champs-Elysées?' Villefort asked.

'No,' said Monte Cristo. 'This is what makes your compliance all the more praiseworthy: in the country.'

'In the country?'

'Yes.'

'But where? Near Paris, I hope?'

'Just outside, half an hour from the gates, in Auteuil.'

'In Auteuil!' Villefort exclaimed. 'Of course, I'd forgotten. Madame told me that you lived in Auteuil because she was taken into your house. Where in Auteuil?'

'In the Rue de la Fontaine.'

'The Rue de la Fontaine!' Villefort repeated, in a strangled voice. 'What number?'

'Number twenty-eight.'

'So you have bought Monsieur de Saint-Méran's house?' Villefort cried.

'Monsieur de Saint-Méran?' said the count. 'Did that house belong to Monsieur de Saint-Méran?'

'Yes,' Mme de Villefort said. 'And can you believe this . . .'

'What.'

'You found it a pretty house, I imagine, Monsieur le Comte?'

'Delightful.'

'Well, my husband has never wanted to live there.'

'Oh! I must say, Monsieur, that I cannot imagine what your objection can be.'

'I do not like Auteuil, Monsieur,' the prosecutor replied, making an effort to control his feelings.

'I hope that this dislike will not deprive me of the pleasure of receiving you?' Monte Cristo asked anxiously.

'No, Count . . . I hope . . . I shall do all in my power . . . believe me,' Villefort stammered.

'Oh, I can accept no excuses,' said Monte Cristo. 'I shall be expecting you on Saturday at six o'clock. If you don't come, I shall start to imagine that there must be – how shall I say? – some dark superstition or some blood-stained tale connected with a house that has been uninhabited for more than twenty years.'

'I shall be there, Monsieur le Comte, I shall be there,' Villefort said, hurriedly.

'Thank you,' said Monte Cristo. 'And you must please permit me to take my leave.'

'Now, now, you did tell us that you have to leave us, Monsieur

le Comte,' said Mme de Villefort. 'And I think you were even going
to tell us why, when your train of thought was interrupted.'

'In truth, Madame,' said Monte Cristo, 'I am not sure that I dare
tell you where I am going.'

'Come, come! Tell us!'

'I am an idle fellow, I confess, but I am going to visit a thing that
has often made me stop and stare for hours.'

'And what is that?'

'A telegraph.[2] There you are: I've said it.'

'A telegraph!' Mme de Villefort repeated.

'Yes, indeed, the very thing: a telegraph. Often, at the end of a
road, on a hilltop, in the sunshine, I have seen those folding black
arms extended like the legs of some giant beetle, and I promise you,
never have I contemplated them without emotion, thinking that
those bizarre signals so accurately travelling through the air, carrying the unknown wishes of a man sitting behind one table to another
man sitting at the far end of the line behind another table, three
hundred leagues away, were written against the greyness of the
clouds or the blue of the sky by the sole will of that all-powerful
master. Then I have thought of genies, sylphs, gnomes and other
occult forces, and laughed. Never did I wish to go over and examine
these great insects with their white bellies and slender black legs,
because I was afraid that under their stone wings I would find the
human genie, cramped, pedantic, stuffed with arcane science and
sorcery. Then, one fine morning, I discovered that the motor that
drives every telegraph is a poor devil of a clerk who earns twelve
hundred francs a year and – instead of watching the sky like an
astronomer, or the water like a fisherman, or the landscape like an
idler – spends the whole day staring at the insect with the white
belly and black legs that corresponds to his own and is sited some
four or five leagues away. At this, I became curious to study this
living chrysalis from close up and to watch the dumbshow that it
offers from the bottom of its shell to that other chrysalis, by pulling
bits of string one after the other.'

'So that is where you are going?'

'It is.'

'To which telegraph? The one belonging to the Ministry of the
Interior, or the observatory?'

'No, certainly not. There I should find people who would try to
force me to understand things of which I would prefer to remain

ignorant, and insist on trying to explain a mystery that is beyond their grasp. Come! I want to keep my illusions about insects; it is enough to have lost those I had about human beings. So I shall not go either to the telegraph at the Ministry of the Interior, or to the one at the observatory. What I need is a telegraph in the open countryside, so I can see the fellow fixed in his tower and in his pure state.'

'You are an odd sort of aristocrat,' said Villefort.

'What line do you advise me to examine?'

'Whichever is busiest at the moment.'

'Well, then! The Spanish one?'

'Exactly. Would you like a letter from the minister asking them to explain . . .'

'No, not at all,' said Monte Cristo. 'On the contrary, as I have just told you, I do not wish to understand any of it. As soon as I understood it, there would be no more telegraph, there would just be a signal from Monsieur Duchâtel or Monsieur de Montalivet, en route for the prefect in Bayonne and disguised in two Greek words: τηλε γραφειν.[3] What I wish to preserve, in all its purity and my veneration, is the creature with the black legs and fearful words.'

'You must go then, because it will be dark in two hours and you will see nothing.'

'No! Now I am worried. Where is the nearest?'

'On the Bayonne road, I think.'

'Then let it be the Bayonne road.'

'That would be the one at Châtillon.'

'And after that?'

'The one at the Tour de Montlhéry, I think.'

'Thank you. Farewell! I shall tell you on Saturday what I think of it.'

At the door, the count met the two notaries who had just disinherited Valentine and were leaving, delighted at having completed a piece of business that was bound to do them credit.

LXI

HOW TO RESCUE A GARDENER FROM DORMICE WHO ARE EATING HIS PEACHES

Not the same evening, as he had said, but the following morning, the Count of Monte Cristo left Paris through the gate at Denfert, set off down the Orléans road and drove through the village of Linas without stopping at the telegraph which, at the precise moment when the count went by, was waving its long skeletal arms. Eventually he reached the tower at Montlhéry which, as everyone knows, is situated on the highest point of the plain of that name.

The count dismounted at the foot of the hill and started to climb it by a little winding path, eighteen inches across. When he reached the top, he was confronted by a hedge on which green fruit had come to replace the pink and white flowers. He soon found the gate into the little garden. It was a small wicket, turning on willow hinges and closed with a nail and a piece of string. He lost no time in discovering how it opened.

He was now in a little garden, twenty feet by twelve, enclosed on one side by the part of the hedge in which was set the ingenious mechanism we called a gate; and, on the other, by the old tower wreathed in ivy and strewn with wallflowers and stocks. Seeing it in this way, wrinkled and bedecked with flowers, like an old woman whose grandchildren have just been celebrating her birthday, it was hard to believe that it could have told many awful tales, if its walls had had a voice as well as the ears that an old proverb attributes to them.

The garden was crossed by a path of red sand, bordered with a boxwood hedge, already several years old and forming a contrast of colours that would have delighted the eye of Delacroix,[1] our modern Rubens. The path turned back on itself to form a figure '8', in such a way as to make a walk of sixty feet in a garden of twenty. Never had Flora, the youthful and smiling goddess honoured by Roman horticulturalists, been worshipped with such pure and meticulous devotion as she was in this little garden. Not one leaf on any of its twenty rosebushes bore a trace of greenfly and not a twig housed a little cluster of those aphids which gnaw and lay waste plants growing in damp soil. This did not mean, however, that it was dry here.

On the contrary, the earth as black as soot and the dense foliage of the trees bore witness to a natural humidity, which could always be supplemented by artificial means from a barrel full of stagnant water at one corner of the garden. Here, on the green surface, a frog and a toad had taken up residence, but always on opposite sides of the circle, with their backs turned to one another, owing no doubt to some incompatibility of temperament. There was not a blade of grass on the path and not the shoot of a weed in the flowerbeds. No modish belle would clean and polish the geraniums, cacti and rhododendrons on her china jardinière with as much care as the person, still invisible, who looked after this little patch.

Monte Cristo stopped, after closing the gate by attaching the string to the nail, and looked all about him.

'It would seem,' he said, 'that the gentleman of the telegraph has at least one full-time gardener, or else is himself passionately fond of gardening.'

Suddenly he stumbled over something behind a wheelbarrow full of leaves. The thing in question stood up with an exclamation of surprise, and Monte Cristo was confronted by a man of around fifty who had been collecting strawberries and placing them on vine leaves. There were twelve leaves and almost as many strawberries. As he got up, the man had almost knocked over the fruit, the leaves and a plate.

'Harvest time?' the count asked with a smile.

'Forgive me, Monsieur,' the man replied, touching his cap. 'I am not up there, I know, but I have only just come down.'

'Please do not bother on my account, my friend,' said Monte Cristo. 'Gather your strawberries while ye may, if there are still any left.'

'Ten more,' said the man. 'I have eleven here and there were twenty-one in all, five more than last year. It is not surprising. The spring was warm this year, and what strawberries need, Monsieur, is heat. This is why, instead of the sixteen I had last year, I have this year, as you can see, eleven that I have already picked, twelve, thirteen, fourteen, fifteen, sixteen, seventeen, eighteen . . . Oh, my goodness! I am missing two. They were still here yesterday, Monsieur, I know they were here, I counted them. It must be Mère Simon's son who filched them from me. I saw him lurking around here this morning. Oh, the little devil! Stealing out of someone's garden! Who knows where he will end up?'

'I agree,' Monte Cristo said. 'It's serious, but you must allow for the felon's youth and natural appetite.'

'Certainly, but that makes it no less irritating. However, I beg your pardon once more, Monsieur: am I perhaps keeping one of my bosses waiting like this?' And he looked apprehensively at the count's blue coat.

'Have no fear, my friend,' the count said, with that smile of his which he could make, at will, so benevolent or so fearful and which now expressed only benevolence. 'I am not a superior who has come to inspect you, but a mere traveller, driven by curiosity, who even now is beginning to reproach himself for coming and wasting your time.'

'Oh, my time is not very valuable,' the man said with a melancholy smile. 'However, it is the government's time and I should not waste it, but I received a signal telling me I could take an hour's rest . . .' (at this, he cast a glance towards the sundial – for there was everything in the garden at the tower of Montlhéry, even a sundial) '. . . and, as you see, I still have ten minutes to go. Moreover, my strawberries were ripe and if I had left them a day longer . . . Now, truly, Monsieur, would you believe me if I were to say that the dormice eat them?'

'Goodness, no, I should never have believed it,' Monte Cristo replied gravely. 'They are not good neighbours, dormice, for those who do not eat them, as the Romans did.'

'Oh? Did the Romans eat them?' the gardener asked. 'Dormice?'

'So Petronius tells us,' said the count.

'Really? They can't taste very good, even though people say "plump as a dormouse". And it's not surprising that they are fat, since they sleep all day long and only wake up so that they can spend the whole night gnawing. Last year, now, I had four apricots and they took one from me. I also had a nectarine, just one, though admittedly it's a rare fruit. Well, sir, they ate half of it, on the side nearest the wall – a superb nectarine, with an excellent flavour. I have never eaten a better.'

'You did eat it, then?' Monte Cristo asked.

'The half that remained, you understand. Delicious. Those little robbers don't choose the worst morsels, any more than Mère Simon's son chooses the worst strawberries. Huh! But don't worry,' the gardener continued, 'this is the last time it will happen, even if I have to stay awake all night guarding them when they are nearly ripe.'

Monte Cristo had seen enough. Every man has a passion gnawing away at the bottom of his heart, just as every fruit has its worm. The passion of the telegraph man was gardening. He began to break off the vine-leaves that were hiding the bunches of grapes from the sun and immediately won the gardener's heart.

'Did Monsieur come to look at the telegraph?'

'Yes, provided the rules do not forbid it.'

'Not at all,' said the gardener. 'There is no danger, because no one knows or can know what we are saying.'

'Yes, indeed,' said the count. 'I have even been told that you repeat signals that you do not understand yourselves.'

'Indeed we do, Monsieur, and I much prefer that,' the telegraph man said, laughing.

'Why do you prefer it?'

'Because in that way I have no responsibility. I am a machine and nothing more. As long as I work, no one asks anything more from me.'

'Confound it!' Monte Cristo thought to himself. 'Can I have fallen by chance on one man who has no ambition? Damnation: that would be too unlucky.'

'Monsieur,' the gardener said, glancing at his sundial. 'The ten minutes are almost up and I must go back to my post. Would you like to join me?'

'You lead the way.'

They went into the tower which was divided into three floors. The ground floor was unfurnished except for some gardening tools leaning against the wall: spades, rakes, watering-cans and so on.

The first floor was the man's usual – or, rather, nocturnal – home. It contained a few miserable household utensils, a bed, a table, two chairs and an earthenware sink, as well as some plants hanging from the ceiling, which the count understood to be beans and sweet peas, dried in order to preserve the seeds in their pods. They had been labelled with as much care as the work of a master botanist at the Jardin des Plantes.

'Does it take a long time to learn telegraphy, Monsieur?' he asked.

'Not in itself, but the apprenticeship is long.'

'And how much do you earn?'

'A thousand francs, Monsieur.'

'That's hardly anything.'

'But, as you can see, one is housed.'

Monte Cristo looked around the room and muttered: 'As long as one doesn't mind where one lives.'

They went up to the third floor; this was the telegraph room. Monte Cristo studied each of the two handles which the man used to operate the machine.

'Very interesting,' he said. 'But in the long run, doesn't this life become rather dull?'

'Oh, yes. At first you get a stiff neck from looking; but after a year or two you get used to that. Then we have rest days and days off.'

'Days off?'

'Yes.'

'When do you have those?'

'When it's foggy.'

'Ah! Of course.'

'Those are my holidays. I go down to the garden and plant, cut or prune. In short, time goes by.'

'How long have you been here?'

'Ten years, with five as an apprentice, making fifteen in all.'

'And you are . . . ?'

'Fifty-five.'

'How long do you have to work to earn a pension?'

'Oh! Twenty-five years.'

'And how much does it amount to?'

'A hundred écus.'

'Poor creatures!' Monte Cristo murmured.

'I beg your pardon, Monsieur?'

'I said that it was most curious.'

'What?'

'All this . . . that you have shown me. But you understand nothing of your signals?'

'Absolutely nothing.'

'And you have never tried to understand?'

'Never; why should I?'

'But there must be some signals addressed to you personally?'

'Those ones are always the same.'

'What do they say?'

' "Nothing to report", "Take an hour off" or "Good-night".'

'That's perfectly innocuous,' said the count. 'But, look! Isn't your correspondent starting to move?'

'Oh, yes, that's right! Thank you, Monsieur.'

'What is he saying? Is it something you understand?'

'Yes, he's asking if I'm ready.'

'How do you reply?'

'With a signal that tells the telegraphist to my right that I am ready and at the same time warns the one on my left to get ready in his turn.'

'Very ingenious,' said the count.

'You will see,' the man said proudly. 'In five minutes, he will start speaking.'

'So I have five minutes,' thought Monte Cristo. 'More time than I need.' Then he said aloud: 'My dear sir, let me ask you a question.'

'Please do.'

'Are you fond of gardening?'

'Passionately.'

'So what if, instead of a patch twenty feet long, you could have a garden of two acres?'

'I should make it into an earthly paradise.'

'And you don't live well on your thousand francs?'

'Not very well; but I can survive.'

'Yes, but you only have a tiny garden.'

'That's true: the garden is not very large.'

'And it is full of dormice who eat everything.'

'They are the bane of my life.'

'Tell me, suppose you were unfortunate enough to turn your head away when the telegraphist to your right started operating?'

'Then I wouldn't see his signals.'

'What would happen?'

'I couldn't repeat them.'

'And then?'

'What would happen is that, if I neglected to repeat them, I would be fined.'

'How much?'

'A hundred francs.'

'A tenth of your income! That's nice!'

'Ah, well . . .' the telegraphist said.

'Has that happened to you?'

'Once, Monsieur, once . . . when I was grafting a rose-bush.'

'Very well. Now suppose you were to change something in the signal or to send a different one?'

'That's another matter. I should be dismissed and lose my pension.'

'Three hundred francs?'

'Yes, a hundred *écus*, Monsieur. So you understand, I would never do that.'

'Not even for fifteen years' salary? Come, it's worth considering, I think?'

'For fifteen thousand francs?'

'Yes.'

'Monsieur, you are frightening me.'

'Huh!'

'Monsieur, are you trying to tempt me?'

'Exactly! Fifteen thousand francs, you understand?'

'Please, Monsieur, let me look at my correspondent to the right.'

'No, don't look at him. Look at this.'

'What is it?'

'Do you mean you don't recognize this paper?'

'Banknotes!'

'Square ones, fifteen of them.'

'Whose are they?'

'Yours, if you wish.'

'Mine!' the man cried, in a strangled voice.

'Undoubtedly! Yours and no one else's.'

'But look, Monsieur, my correspondent to the right has started up.'

'Let him carry on.'

'You have distracted me, I'm going to be fined.'

'It will cost you a hundred francs. So, you see, it is in your interest to take my fifteen banknotes.'

'Monsieur, my correspondent on the right is getting impatient. He is repeating his signals.'

'Let him. Take the notes.' And the count put the packet into the telegraphist's hand. 'Now,' he said, 'that's not all. You won't be able to live on fifteen thousand francs.'

'I shall still have my job.'

'No, you'll lose it, because you are going to send a different signal from the one you receive.'

'But, Monsieur, what are you suggesting?'

'Child's play.'

'Monsieur, only if I were forced to . . .'

'That is precisely what I intend.' He took another packet out of his pocket and said: 'Here are ten thousand more francs; with the fifteen thousand you already have, that makes twenty-five thousand. Five thousand is enough to buy a pretty little house and two acres of land; with the remainder, you can have an income of a thousand francs.'

'A garden of two acres?'

'And an income of a thousand francs.'

'Good Lord! Oh, Lord!'

'Take it, then!' And Monte Cristo forced the ten thousand francs into the telegraphist's hands.

'What do I have to do?'

'Nothing very hard.'

'What, then?'

'Repeat these signals.'

Monte Cristo took a sheet of paper out of his pocket on which there were three ready-prepared signals and numbers showing the order in which they were to be sent.

'As you see, it will not take long.'

'Yes, but . . .'

'And for this, you will have nectarines and to spare.'

This was the telling blow. Feverish, red, pouring with sweat, the man sent the three signals he had been given by the count, despite the wild gesticulations transmitted by the telegraphist to his right, who was quite unable to understand the reason for the alteration and had begun to think that the nectarine man was mad. Meanwhile the man to the left conscientiously transmitted the new signals, which finally made their way to the Ministry of the Interior.

'Now you are rich,' Monte Cristo said.

'Yes,' said the telegraphist. 'But at what price!'

'Listen, my friend,' Monte Cristo said. 'I do not want your conscience to suffer. So believe me, I swear to you that you have done no harm to anyone and that you have served God's will.'

The telegraphist looked at the banknotes, felt them, counted them. He went pale, then red. Finally he hurried into his room to drink a glass of water, but he was unable to reach the sink and fainted among the dry beans.

Five minutes after the telegraphic signal had reached the ministry, Debray harnessed his coupé and hurried round to Danglars'.

'Does your husband have Spanish government bonds?' he asked the baroness.

'Yes, indeed he does. Six millions' worth.'

'Tell him to sell them at any price.'

'Why?'

'Because Don Carlos has escaped from Burgos and returned to Spain.'

'How do you know?'

'I have my sources,' said Debray, with a shrug of the shoulders.

The baroness did not need to be told twice. She hastened to tell her husband, and he in turn ran round to his stockbroker and ordered him to sell at any price. When people saw that M. Danglars was selling, Spanish bonds at once began to fall. Danglars lost 500,000 francs, but he liquidated all his stock.

That evening, you could read in *Le Messager*: 'King Don Carlos has escaped from house arrest in Burgos and has crossed the Catalonian border into Spain. Barcelona has risen to support him.'

Throughout the evening, everyone was talking about Danglars' foresight in selling his stock, and the speculator's good fortune in losing only 500,000 francs on the deal. Those who had kept their Spanish stock or bought from Danglars decided they were ruined, and spent a very unpleasant night.

The next day, you could read in *Le Moniteur*: 'Yesterday's article in *Le Messager* announcing Don Carlos' escape and a rebellion in Barcelona was without foundation. King Don Carlos is still in Burgos and the peninsula is entirely tranquil. A telegraphic signal, misread because of the fog, gave rise to this false report.'

Spanish stock rose to double its price before the alarm. In actual losses and loss of profits, it meant a million francs to Danglars.

'Very well!' Monte Cristo said to Morrel, who was at his house when the news arrived of the odd reversal which had struck Danglars at the Exchange. 'I have just paid twenty-five thousand francs for a discovery for which I would willingly have paid a hundred thousand.'

'What have you discovered?' Maximilien asked.

'I have just found out how to rescue a gardener from the dormice who are eating his peaches.'

LXII
GHOSTS

At first sight, on the outside, the house in Auteuil had none of the splendour one would expect from a dwelling intended for the magnificent Count of Monte Cristo. But this simplicity was consistent with the master's wishes: he had given strict instructions that nothing was to be changed on the outside, and one had only to consider the inside to understand why: the door was hardly open before the scene changed utterly.

M. Bertuccio had outdone himself in the good taste shown in the choice of furnishings and in the speed of fitting the house out. Like the Duc d'Antin, who once had a row of trees cut down overnight because King Louis XIV had complained that they interrupted the view, so in three days M. Bertuccio had had an empty courtyard entirely planted, while fine poplars and sycamores, transplanted with their huge mass of roots, gave shelter to the façade of the house in front of which, instead of stones half overgrown with grass, there was a lawn: the turves had been laid that very morning to make a vast carpet still glistening with the water that had been sprinkled over it.

The orders for all this had come from the count. He had given Bertuccio a plan on which he had marked the number and position of the trees that needed planting, and the shape and extent of the lawn that was to take the place of the stone yard. Now that the work was done, the house had become unrecognizable and Bertuccio himself claimed that he could no longer recognize it, nestling as it was into its setting of greenery.

While he was about it, the steward would have liked to make some changes in the garden, but the count had expressly forbidden him to alter anything. Bertuccio made up for the disappointment by filling the antechambers, stairways and mantelpieces with flowers.

In all, this house, which had been empty for twenty-five years and only the day before had been dark and gloomy, impregnated with what might be called the aroma of time, had in a single day recovered an appearance of life, full of the master's favourite perfumes and even his preferred amount of daylight: nothing could

better have illustrated the steward's skill and his master's understanding – the first, in what was needed to serve, the latter in what
was needed to be served. When he came in, the count found his
books and his weapons to hand, and his favourite paintings before
his eyes. In the antechambers were the dogs it pleased him to stroke
and the birds it pleased him to hear sing. Like the Sleeping Beauty's
castle, the whole house had been awakened from its long sleep and
come to life; it sang and blossomed like one of those houses that
we have long cherished and in which, when we are unfortunate
enough to leave them, we involuntarily relinquish a part of our
souls.

Servants were coming and going joyfully in the superb courtyard:
some belonged to the kitchens and they were gliding along the
corridors as if they had always inhabited this place, or up staircases
that had been restored only the day before; others were stationed
in the coachhouse, where the different sets of harness, numbered
and stored, seemed to have been here for fifty years, and the stables,
where the horses in their stalls neighed in answer to their grooms,
who spoke to them with more respect than many servants use in
addressing their masters.

The library was installed in two chambers on two sides of one
wing; it contained roughly ten thousand volumes. A whole section
was devoted to the modern novel and the latest work was already
in its place, showing off its red-and-gold binding.

On the other side of the house, corresponding to the library, was
the conservatory, full of rare plants blooming in wide Japanese
pots. In the middle of this conservatory, which was a delight to
look at and to smell, was a billiard table which seemed to have
been abandoned only an hour earlier by players who had let the
balls lie where they came to rest on the cloth.

The grand Bertuccio had only left one room alone. This was the
bedroom in the left corner on the first floor, reached by the main
staircase but also containing the entrance to the secret stairway into
the garden. When the servants passed in front of this room, they
looked at it with curiosity; Bertuccio looked with terror.

At exactly five o'clock the count arrived at the house, followed
by Ali. Bertuccio had been waiting for his master with impatience
and a measure of anxiety: he hoped for a compliment, but feared a
raised eyebrow.

Monte Cristo got down in the courtyard, then looked around

the house and the garden in silence, giving no sign of either approval or disapproval. However, when he came into his bedroom, which was opposite the locked room, he pointed to the drawer of a little rosewood table that he had picked out on his first visit.

'That can only be for gloves,' he said.

'As you say, Excellency,' Bertuccio replied, delighted. 'If you open it, you will find gloves.'

In the other pieces of furniture the count also found just what he expected: perfume bottles, cigars, jewellery.

'Very good!' he said.

M. Bertuccio withdrew, gratified to the very depth of his soul, so great, so powerful and so real was the influence of the man on everything about him.

At six o'clock precisely, there was the sound of a horse stamping its hoofs in front of the door: the captain of spahis had arrived on Médéah. Monte Cristo was waiting for him at the top of the steps with a smile on his lips.

'I'm the first – certain of it!' Morrel called. 'Deliberately: I wanted to have you to myself for a moment, before the others arrive. Julie and Emmanuel have a million things to tell you. Oh, but it's splendid here, you know! Tell me, Count, can I trust your people to look after my horse for me?'

'Don't worry, my dear Maximilien, they are experts.'

'He needs to be rubbed down, though. If you could only have seen him: he went like a whirlwind.'

'I should think so, dammit,' said Monte Cristo in the sort of voice a father would use to his son. 'A horse costing five thousand francs!'

'Do you regret the money?' Morrel asked, with his candid smile.

'Heavens, no!' the count replied. 'No, I would only be sorry if the horse was no good.'

'So good is he, my dear Count, that Monsieur de Château-Renaud, the best judge of horseflesh in France, and Monsieur Debray, who rides the Arabs belonging to the ministry, are even now chasing after me and lagging a bit behind, as you see. They have Baroness Danglars breathing down their necks, and her horses can manage a steady six leagues an hour.'

'So, they're behind you?' Monte Cristo asked.

'In fact, here they are.' At that very moment, a coupé with a steaming team, then two panting saddle-horses, stopped in front of the gate, which opened to let them in. The coupé drove around and stopped at the foot of the steps, followed by the riders. In a moment, Debray had dismounted and was standing beside the carriage door. He offered the baroness his hand and she, as she stepped down, made a movement that anyone except Monte Cristo would have failed to notice. But the count missed nothing, and he saw, in Mme Danglars' palm, the flash of a little white paper, no more visible than the movement of the hand that held it, which passed between Mme Danglars and the minister's secretary with an ease that suggested the manoeuvre was well practised.

The banker followed his wife, as pale as though he had just stepped from the tomb, instead of from his coupé.

Mme Danglars cast a rapid, exploratory glance about her (which only Monte Cristo could understand), taking in the courtyard, the peristyle and the façade of the house. Then, mastering some slight emotion which would surely have shown on her face had she allowed its colour to change, she walked up the steps, saying to Morrel: 'Monsieur, if you were a friend of mine, I should ask you whether your horse is for sale.'

Morrel gave a pained smile and turned to Monte Cristo, as if to beg him for help in escaping from this dilemma. The count took his meaning.

'Oh, Madame,' he replied. 'Why don't you ask me?'

'With you, Monsieur,' the baroness said, 'one cannot be permitted to wish for anything, because one is too certain of obtaining it. So I asked Monsieur Morrel.'

'Unfortunately,' the count said, 'I happen to know that Monsieur Morrel cannot give away his horse, since honour requires him to keep it.'

'How is that?'

'He wagered that he could break Médéah in within six months. Now, Baroness, you understand that if he were to part with the animal before that time, not only would he lose the bet, but people would also say that he was afraid. A captain of spahis, even to satisfy the whim of a beautiful woman – which, in my view, is one of the most sacred of obligations – cannot allow such a stain on his reputation.'

'So, you see, Madame . . .' Morrel said, turning a grateful smile in the direction of Monte Cristo.

'In any case, I should have thought that you'd had enough of horses for a while,' Danglars said, in a surly manner, ill-concealed behind a coarse smile.

It was not usual for Mme Danglars to let such a sally pass without some retort; yet, much to the surprise of the young men, she pretended not to hear and said nothing.

Monte Cristo smiled at her silence, a sign of unaccustomed humility, while at the same time showing the baroness two vast Chinese porcelain pots, wreathed in marine vegetation of such size and craftsmanship that only nature can possess such richness, vigour and ingenuity. The baroness was amazed.

'But you could plant one of the chestnuts from the Tuileries in there!' she exclaimed. 'How on earth did they ever fire such an enormous object?'

'Don't expect our craftsmen to answer that, Madame,' he said, 'with their Sèvres figurines and fine glass. This is the product of another age, the work, as it were, of the genies of earth and sea.'

'How do you mean? What age?'

'I don't know, but I heard that an emperor of China had a kiln specially built and in it, one after another, they fired twelve pots like this. Two broke in the heat of the fire. The ten remaining ones were sunk three hundred fathoms under the sea. The sea knew what was expected of her: she wrapped her weeds around them, built her corals on them and encrusted them with shells. For two hundred years this decoration was cemented in place at these unheard-of depths, because a revolution overthrew the emperor who thought of the experiment and left only the record of the firing of the pots and their immersion at the bottom of the sea. After two hundred years, this document was discovered and a plan made to recover the vases. Divers were sent down, in specially made engines, to search the bay where the pots had been deposited. Out of the ten, only three were found, the others having been scattered and broken by the waves. I love these vases. Sometimes I imagine that in their depths shapeless, terrifying, mysterious monsters, like those that only divers see, have fastened their cold, flat and astonished eyes, and myriads of fish have slept, finding a refuge from their enemies.'

While the count was speaking, Danglars, who had little interest in curios, had been automatically tearing the leaves off a splendid orange tree; and, when he had dealt with that, turned to a cactus, which he found less compliant than the orange: it pricked him horribly. He shuddered and rubbed his eyes, like someone awaking from a dream.

'Monsieur,' Monte Cristo said to him, 'I know you are a connoisseur of paintings and have magnificent things yourself, so I cannot recommend mine. However, I have here a couple of Hobbemas, a Paul Potter, a Mieris, two Gerrit Dous, a Raphael, a Van Dyck, a Zurbaran, and two or three Murillos, which are worth pointing out to you.'

'Look!' said Debray. 'There's a Hobbema I recognize.'

'Really!'

'Yes, they offered it to the museum.'

'Which doesn't have one, I believe?' Monte Cristo ventured.

'No, but they turned it down, even so.'

'Why?' asked Château-Renaud.

'You're so tactful! Because the government is not rich enough, that's why!'

'Oh, I beg your pardon,' said Château-Renaud. 'I've been hearing this kind of thing for eight years now, and I still can't get used to the idea.'

'You will,' said Debray.

'I doubt it,' said Château-Renaud.

'Major Bartolomeo Cavalcanti, Viscount Andrea Cavalcanti!' Baptistin announced.

With a black satin collar fresh from the tailor's hands, a newly trimmed beard, grey moustaches, a confident eye and a major's uniform with three medals and five ribbons – in short, an impeccable veteran's costume: enter Major Bartolomeo Cavalcanti, the loving father we met a short while ago.

Beside him, in a brand-new outfit and with a smile on his face, walked Viscount Andrea Cavalcanti, that obedient son whom we also know.

The three young men were talking among themselves and they looked from father to son, naturally subjecting the latter to a longer and more detailed examination.

'Cavalcanti!' said Debray.

'Dammit!' said Morrel. 'That's a fine name.'

'Yes,' said Château-Renaud. 'There's no denying it, these Italians have stylish handles – but no dress sense.'

'That's a bit hard, Château-Renaud,' said Debray. 'Those are well-cut clothes, and brand new.'

'Precisely what's wrong about them. The fellow looks as though he had dressed up today for the first time in his life.'

'Who are these gentlemen?' Danglars asked Monte Cristo.

'As you heard, the Cavalcantis.'

'All that tells me about them is their name.'

'Of course! You would not be acquainted with our Italian nobility. Cavalcanti is synonymous with royal blood.'

'Wealthy?' the banker asked.

'Fabulously.'

'What do they do?'

'They try to spend their money, but are unable to exhaust their fortune. Moreover, they have some credits with your bank, according to what they told me when they came to see me a couple of days ago. I even invited them for that very reason. I'll introduce you.'

'They seem to speak French very well,' said Danglars.

'I understand the son was educated in a college in the south, in Marseille or thereabouts. You will find him a great enthusiast.'

'For what?' asked the baroness.

'For Frenchwomen, Madame. He is determined to find a wife in Paris.'

'That's a fine notion!' Danglars said, shrugging his shoulders.

Mme Danglars gave her husband a look that on any other occasion would have preceded an outburst, but for the second time she kept silent.

'The baron seems very gloomy today,' Monte Cristo said to Mme Danglars. 'Are they trying to appoint him minister, by any chance?'

'Not yet, as far as I know. I think he must have been gambling on the Stock Exchange and lost, and doesn't know who to blame.'

'Monsieur and Madame de Villefort!' Baptistin announced.

The two people in question came in. Despite his self-control, M. de Villefort was visibly disturbed. Taking his hand, Monte Cristo noticed that it was trembling.

'Really, only women know how to disguise their feelings,' he thought, looking at Mme Danglars, who was smiling at the crown prosecutor and embracing his wife.

After these first exchanges, the count noticed Bertuccio, who up to then had been busy in the kitchens, and was now slipping into a little drawing-room next to the one where they had gathered.

He went over to him and said: 'What do you want, Monsieur Bertuccio?'

'His Excellency did not tell me the number of his guests.'

'Ah! You're right!'

'How many places should I lay?'

'Count for yourself.'

'Is everyone here now, Excellency?'

'Yes.'

Monte Cristo did not take his eyes off Bertuccio while he glanced through the half-open door.

'Oh, my God!' Bertuccio cried.

'What is it?' the count asked.

'That woman . . . That woman!'

'Which one?'

'In the white dress, with the diamonds . . . the blonde!'

'Madame Danglars?'

'I don't know her name. But that's her, Monsieur, that's her!'

'Who?'

'The woman in the garden! The one who was pregnant! The one walking backwards and forwards . . . waiting! waiting!' Bertuccio was pale and open-mouthed, his hair standing on end.

'Waiting for whom?'

Without replying, Bertuccio pointed to Villefort, with a gesture like Macbeth pointing to Banquo.

'Oh! . . . Oh!' he murmured at length. 'Do you see him?'

'Whom? What?'

'Him.'

'Him! The crown prosecutor, Monsieur de Villefort? Of course I can see him.'

'You mean, I didn't kill him?'

'Come, come! I think you are losing your wits, my good Bertuccio,' said the count.

'But he isn't dead?'

'No, he isn't, as you can very well see. Instead of striking him between the sixth and seventh left rib, as your compatriots usually do, you must have struck higher or lower; and these lawyers, you know, are not easy to kill off. Either that or else everything that you told me is untrue, a product of your imagination, a hallucination of the mind. Perhaps you fell asleep while inadequately digesting your revenge. It weighed down on your stomach and you had a nightmare, nothing more. So recover your wits and count: Monsieur and Madame de Villefort, two; Monsieur and Madame Danglars, four; Monsieur de Château-Renaud, Monsieur Debray, Monsieur Morrel, seven; Major Bartolomeo Cavalcanti, eight.'

'Eight!' Bertuccio repeated.

'Wait! Wait for a moment! You're in a devilish hurry to be gone and you're forgetting one of my guests: Monsieur Andrea Cavalcanti, the young man in the black coat there, looking at the Virgin by Murillo and just turning around . . .'

This time Bertuccio started to give a cry that a look from Monte Cristo froze on his lips.

'Benedetto!' he muttered under his breath. 'Fate!'

'It is just striking half-past six, Monsieur Bertuccio,' the count said severely. 'This is the time for which I ordered dinner to be served, and you know that I don't like to wait.'

At this, Monte Cristo went into the drawing-room where his guests had gathered, while Bertuccio returned to the dining-room, steadying himself against the walls.

Five minutes later, the doors opened. Bertuccio appeared and, making a final heroic effort, like Vatel at Chantilly,[1] he announced: 'Monsieur le Comte is served!'

Monte Cristo offered his arm to Mme de Villefort. 'Monsieur de Villefort,' he said, 'please be good enough to escort Madame la Baronne Danglars.'

Villefort obeyed and they went into the dining-room.

LXIII

DINNER

It was clear that all the guests experienced the same feeling as they went into the dining-room. They were wondering what strange force had brought them together in this house; and yet, puzzled and even, in some cases, nervous though they were, they would not have wished to be anywhere else. Recent connections, the count's unusual and isolated situation, and his unknown, almost fabulous fortune, should have required the men to be cautious and have deterred the women from entering a house where there was no one of their own sex to receive them. Yet the men had been prepared to discard caution and the women, custom: curiosity had pricked them with its irresistible spur and overcome all other feelings.

Only the Cavalcantis – the father despite his starchiness and the son despite his casual manners – seemed uncomfortable at finding themselves in the house of this man whose motives they did not understand, with these other people whom they were meeting for the first time.

Seeing M. de Villefort approach to offer his arm, as Monte Cristo had instructed him, Mme Danglars started and M. de Villefort felt his own expression change behind his gold-rimmed spectacles when he felt the baroness's arm touch his. Neither of these two reactions had escaped the count; there was much to interest an observer of the scene merely in such contact between individuals.

M. de Villefort had Mme Danglars on his right and Morrel on his left. The count was sitting between Mme de Villefort and Danglars. The other places were filled by Debray, sitting between the elder Cavalcanti and the younger, and by Château-Renaud, between Mme de Villefort and Morrel.

The meal was magnificent. Monte Cristo had determined entirely to discard Parisian symmetry and to supply the desired nourishment more to the curiosity than to the appetite of his guests. They were offered an Oriental feast, but more like a repast from the *Arabian Nights* than anything else.

All the fruits that the four corners of the earth can deliver whole and ripe into the European horn of plenty were amassed in pyramids, in Chinese vases and Japanese bowls. Rare birds, with their most brilliant feathers, monstrous fish lying on sheets of silver, all the wines of the Aegean, Asia Minor and the Cape, enclosed in extravagantly moulded vessels, the bizarre form of which seemed to add to the savour of the food, all came past in succession – like one of those reviews in which Apicius invited his guests to participate – before the eyes of these Parisians who could accept an expenditure of a thousand *louis* on a dinner for ten, provided that one ate pearls like Cleopatra or drank molten gold like Lorenzo de' Medici.

Seeing the general amazement, Monte Cristo burst into laughter and began to scoff aloud. 'Gentlemen,' he said, 'you must confess that when one has reached a certain level of prosperity, only the superfluous becomes necessary, just as these ladies will admit that, beyond a certain degree of rapture, only the ideal is tangible. So, let us pursue the same line of argument: what is a marvel? Something that we do not understand. What is truly desirable? A possession that we cannot have. So, my life is devoted to seeing things that I cannot understand and obtaining things that are impossible to have. I succeed by two means: money and will. I am as persevering in the pursuit of my whims as, for example, you are, Monsieur Danglars, in building a railway; or you, Monsieur de Villefort, in condemning a man to death; or you, Monsieur Debray, in pacifying a kingdom; you, Monsieur de Château-Renaud, in finding favour with a woman; or you, Monsieur Morrel, in breaking a horse that no one else can ride. Take these two fish, for example, one of them born fifty leagues from Saint Petersburg, the other five leagues from Naples. Isn't it amusing to bring them together on the same table?'

'What kind of fish are they?' asked Danglars.

'Monsieur de Château-Renaud, who has lived in Russia, will tell you the name of the first, and Major Cavalcanti, who is Italian, can tell you that of the other.'

'I think this one is a sturgeon,' said Château-Renaud.

'Perfect.'

'And that, if I'm not mistaken, is a lamprey,' said Cavalcanti.

'Just so. Now Monsieur Danglars, ask these two gentlemen where these fish are caught.'

'You can only catch sturgeon in the Volga,' said Château-Renaud.

'And I only know of Lake Fusaro where you can find lampreys of this size,' said Cavalcanti.

'Precisely. One comes from the Volga, the other from Lake Fusaro.'

'Impossible!' all the guests exclaimed at once.

'And that is exactly what I find entertaining,' said Monte Cristo. 'I am like Nero: *cupitor impossibilium*;[1] and this is just what is entertaining you at the moment. That's why this fish, which may not in reality be as good as perch or salmon, will seem delicious to you in a short while – because common sense tells you that it is impossible to obtain, and yet, here it is!'

'But how did you manage to have these two fish brought to Paris?'

'Good Lord! Nothing could be more simple. Each of the two fish was brought in a huge cask, the first padded with weeds and rushes from the river, the other with reeds and plants from the lake. They were installed in a specially constructed wagon and lived in this way, the sturgeon for twelve days, the lamprey for a week. Both of them were quite alive when my cook took them out to poach the first one in milk and the other in wine. Don't you believe me, Monsieur Danglars?'

'I still have my doubts,' Danglars replied, with his gross smile.

'Baptistin!' Monte Cristo called. 'Bring the other sturgeon and the other lamprey, would you – you know, the ones in the other barrels that are still alive.'

Danglars' eyes bulged with astonishment and the rest of the company clapped. Four servants brought in two casks, decorated with water-weeds, in each of which was a quivering fish, like the ones lying, cooked, on the table.

'But why two of each kind?' asked Danglars.

'Because one might have died,' Monte Cristo said simply.

'You are without doubt a remarkable man,' Danglars said. 'And, whatever philosophers say, it's marvellous to be rich.'

'And, above all, to have ideas,' said Mme Danglars.

'Oh, don't give me the credit for that one, Madame; it was very popular with the Romans. Pliny tells us that relays of slaves were employed to carry, on their heads, from Ostia to Rome, fish of the kind called *mulus*, which were probably a variety of sea-bream, judging by his description. It was held a luxury to have it alive because when it died the fish changed colour three or four times, like a vanishing rainbow, going through all the colours of the spectrum; then it was sent down to the kitchen. Its death-throes were part of the appeal. If it was not seen alive, it was despised when dead.'

'Yes,' said Debray, 'but it is only seven or eight leagues from Ostia to Rome.'

'That's true,' Monte Cristo replied. 'But what would be the merit in living eighteen hundred years after Lucullus if one could not surpass him?'

The two Cavalcantis stared in astonishment, but had the good sense to keep quiet.

'That is all very fine,' said Château-Renaud, 'but I must admit that what I admire most is the efficiency of the service. Isn't it true,

Monsieur le Comte, that you only bought this house five or six days ago?'

'At the most,' said Monte Cristo.

'Well, I am sure that in a week it has undergone a complete transformation because, if I'm not mistaken, there was another entrance apart from this one, and the courtyard was paved and empty, whereas now it is a splendid lawn fringed with trees that seem to be a century or so old.'

'What do you expect? I like greenery and shade.'

'Yes,' Mme de Villefort said, 'the entrance used to be through a door giving on to the road, and I remember that, on the day of my miraculous rescue, you brought me into the house through that door to the road.'

'Yes, Madame,' said Monte Cristo. 'But since then I have decided to turn the entrance round so that I can see the Bois de Boulogne through my fence.'

'In four days!' Morrel exclaimed. 'It's incredible!'

'Yes, indeed,' said Château-Renaud. 'To make a new house out of an old one is a miracle, because this house was quite old and very gloomy. I remember, my mother got me to look it over, two or three years ago, when Monsieur de Saint-Méran put it on the market.'

'Monsieur de Saint-Méran?' said Mme de Villefort. 'Did this house belong to Monsieur de Saint-Méran before you bought it?'

'It appears so,' said Monte Cristo.

'What! It appears so . . . Don't you know who you bought it from?'

'Well, no. My steward looks after all those details.'

'Admittedly it hadn't been inhabited for at least ten years,' said Château-Renaud, 'and it was very depressing to see it with its shutters down, its doors locked and grass growing in the courtyard. In fact, if it hadn't belonged to the father-in-law of a crown prosecutor, one might have taken it for one of those ill-omened houses in which some great crime was committed.'

Villefort, who until this moment had not touched any one of the three or four glasses full of exceptionally fine wines on the table in front of him, picked one indiscriminately and drained it at a gulp.

Monte Cristo let a moment go by; then, breaking the silence that followed Château-Renaud's words, he said: 'Now that's odd,

Baron, but the same idea struck me, the first time I came here. The house seemed to me so dismal that I should never have bought it if my steward had not chosen it for me. No doubt the fellow got some tip from the solicitor.'

'I expect so,' Villefort stammered, with an attempt at a smile. 'But, believe me, I am not responsible for any of this. Monsieur de Saint-Méran wanted to sell this house, which was part of his granddaughter's dowry, because if it had remained empty for another three or four years it would have fallen into decay.'

Now it was Morrel's face that was drained of colour.

'In particular,' Monte Cristo continued, 'there was one room – oh, quite ordinary to look at! A room like any other, with red damask hangings, which for some reason seemed to me particularly sinister.'

'Why?' asked Debray. 'Why sinister?'

'Can one explain these feelings? Are there not some places where one seems naturally to inhale an odour of sadness? Why? Who can tell? A linking of memories, a chance thought recalling other places and other times, which may perhaps have no connection with the time and place in which we find ourselves. So it was that this room powerfully recalled for me the chamber of the Marquise de Ganges or that of Desdemona.[2] In fact, now that we have finished dinner, I must show it to you. Then we shall come back down and take coffee in the garden; and, after that, the evening's entertainment.'

Monte Cristo made a sign to invite his guests to go with him. Mme de Villefort got up, he did the same and everyone else followed suit. Villefort and Danglars, however, remained for an instant as if glued to their chairs, exchanging a look that was silent and icy cold.

'Did you hear?' said Mme Danglars.

'We must go,' Villefort replied, getting up and offering her his arm.

Everyone was already scattered around the house, driven by curiosity, because they assumed that the visit would not be confined to the single bedroom but would allow them at the same time to wander around the rest of this hovel that Monte Cristo had transformed into a palace. So everyone rushed through one door after another. Monte Cristo waited for the two latecomers and, when they had gone through in their turn, took up the rear with a smile which, if they could have understood its meaning, would have terrified the guests much more than the empty room they were about to enter.

They began by going through the apartments: the bedrooms, which were done out in the Oriental manner with no beds except divans and cushions and no furniture except pipes and swords; the drawing-rooms hung with the finest old master paintings; and the boudoirs in Chinese materials, with fantastical colours, extravagant designs and marvellous silks. Then, finally, they reached the famous room itself.

There was nothing unusual about it except that, although it was growing dark, there were no lights here and, unlike all the other rooms, it had not been refurbished. These two things in themselves were enough to give it a gloomy air.

'Brrr!' said Mme de Villefort. 'It certainly is spooky.'

Mme Danglars tried to stammer a few words that no one heard, and various remarks were passed, all amounting to the opinion that the room with the red damask was truly sinister.

'Isn't it, indeed?' said Monte Cristo. 'Look how oddly that bed is placed, with its sombre, blood-red awning. And those two portraits, in pastel, which have faded because of the damp: do their pallid lips and staring eyes not seem to say: "I saw what happened!"'

Villefort was ashen. Mme Danglars slumped into a chaise-longue beside the fireplace.

'Oh, dear!' Mme de Villefort said. 'You are brave sitting there: it could be the very place where the crime was committed!'

Mme Danglars leapt to her feet.

'And that,' said Monte Cristo, 'is not all.'

'What more is there?' asked Debray, aware of the effect this was having on Mme Danglars.

'Yes, how much more?' asked Danglars. 'I must confess that so far I can't see a lot in it. How about you, Monsieur Cavalcanti?'

'Well, we have Ugolino's tower[3] in Pisa, Tasso's prison in Ferrara and the bedroom of Francesca and Paolo in Rimini,' the Italian replied.

'Yes, but you don't have this little staircase,' said Monte Cristo, opening a door concealed behind the hangings. 'Look at it and tell me what you think.'

'What a sinister style of stairway!' Château-Renaud said with a laugh.

'I don't know if that Chian wine is conducive to melancholy,' Debray said, 'but the fact is that I am starting to see this house in a grim light.'

As for Morrel, ever since the mention of Valentine's dowry, he had remained glum and silent.

'Can you imagine,' Monte Cristo continued, 'an Othello or some Abbé de Ganges, going down this staircase step by step, on a dark and stormy night, carrying some grim burden which he is anxious to conceal from the eyes of men, if not from those of God!'

Mme Danglars almost fainted in the arms of Villefort, who was obliged to support himself against the wall.

'Good Lord, Madame!' Debray exclaimed. 'What has come over you? How pale you are!'

'What's come over her?' said Mme de Villefort. 'What's come over her is quite simply that Monsieur de Monte Cristo is telling us these ghastly stories, no doubt hoping to make us die of fright.'

'Yes, yes,' said Villefort. 'Look, Count, you're terrifying the ladies.'

'What's wrong?' Debray whispered again to Mme Danglars.

'Nothing, nothing,' she answered, making an effort to control her feelings. 'I just need a little air.'

'Would you like to go down to the garden?' Debray asked, offering his arm to Mme Danglars and leading the way towards the hidden staircase.

'No,' she said. 'No. I'd rather stay here.'

'Is that so, Madame?' said Monte Cristo. 'Is this terror serious?'

'No, Monsieur,' said Mme Danglars. 'But you have a way of hypothesizing that gives an appearance of reality to illusions.'

'Good Lord, yes!' Monte Cristo said with a smile. 'All this is a figment of the imagination. Why could one not just as well imagine this room to be the good and respectable bedroom of the mother of a family. The bed with its purple awning, like a bed visited by the goddess Lucina[4] . . . and the mysterious staircase as a passage down which the doctor and the nursemaid might go, so as not to disturb the young mother's restorative slumber, or even the father, carrying the sleeping child?'

This time, instead of being reassured by the evocation of this tender tableau, Mme Danglars gave a groan and fainted completely away.

'Madame Danglars is ill,' stammered Villefort. 'Perhaps we should take her to her carriage.'

'How frightful!' said Monte Cristo. 'And I didn't bring my flask.'

'I have mine,' said Mme de Villefort, giving the count a flask full of a red liquid similar to the one that had so benefited Edouard when the count tried it on him. He took it from Mme de Villefort's hands, raising an eyebrow.

'Yes,' she said. 'On your instructions, I tried it.'

'Successfully?'

'I think so.'

Mme Danglars had been taken into the next room. Monte Cristo let a drop of the red liquid fall on her lips and she revived. 'Oh,' she said, 'what a terrible dream!'

Villefort grasped her wrist to let her know that it had not been a dream. They looked for M. Danglars, but he was not in the mood for poetical reverie and had gone down into the garden, where he was talking to the elder Cavalcanti about a scheme to build a railway from Leghorn to Florence.

Monte Cristo appeared desperate. He took Mme Danglars' arm and led her down into the garden, where they found M. Danglars taking coffee between the two Cavalcantis.

'Tell me, Madame,' Monte Cristo said, 'did I really terrify you?'

'No, Monsieur, but you know our impressions are sometimes amplified by whatever happens to be our state of mind.'

Villefort forced a laugh and said: 'So, you understand, a supposition may be enough, or a chimera . . .'

'Even so,' Monte Cristo told them, 'believe it or not, I am convinced that a crime took place in that room.'

'Beware!' said Mme de Villefort. 'We have the crown prosecutor with us.'

'So we do,' said Monte Cristo. 'Very well, since that is the case, I shall take advantage of it to make my statement.'

'Your statement?' said Villefort.

'Precisely, in front of witnesses.'

'All very interesting, this,' said Debray. 'If there really has been a crime, it should help our digestion no end.'

'There was a crime,' said Monte Cristo. 'Come this way, gentlemen. Come, Monsieur de Villefort. For the statement to be valid it must be made before the proper authorities.'

He took Villefort's arm and, with Mme Danglars' arm beneath the other, led the crown prosecutor under the plane-tree to where the shadows were deepest. All the other guests followed.

'Now then,' said Monte Cristo. 'Here, at this very spot' (he stamped his foot on the ground) 'in order to revive these old trees, I got my men to dig in some leafmould. Well, when they were digging, they uncovered a chest, or the ironwork from a chest, in the midst of which was the skeleton of a new-born child. I hope you don't consider that an illusion?'

He felt Mme Danglars' arm stiffen and a tremor go through Villefort's wrist.

'A new-born child?' Debray answered. 'By Jove! This sounds to me as if it's getting serious.'

'Well, I was right,' said Château-Renaud, 'when I said just now that houses had a soul and a face like people and that their inner-most beings were reflected in their physiognomy. This house was sad because it was full of remorse. It was full of remorse because it was concealing a crime.'

'Who says it was a crime?' Villefort asked, making one final effort.

'What! A child buried alive in a garden! Is that not a crime?' Monte Cristo exclaimed. 'What other name do you have for such an action, crown prosecutor?'

'Who says that he was buried alive?'

'Why bury him there if he was dead? This garden has never been a cemetery.'

'What do they do to infanticides in this country?' Major Caval-canti asked innocently.

'Huh! They simply cut off their heads,' Danglars replied.

'Oh! They cut off their heads,' said Cavalcanti.

'I think so . . . That's right, isn't it, Monsieur de Villefort?' Monte Cristo asked.

'Yes, Count,' he answered, in a voice that was hardly human.

Monte Cristo could see that the two people for whose benefit he had devised this scene could not bear any more of it; so, not wishing to push them too far, he said: 'But, gentlemen, I think we are forgetting the coffee!' And he led his guests over to the table which had been set in the middle of the lawn.

'The truth is, Monsieur le Comte,' said Mme Danglars, 'I am ashamed to admit my weakness, but all those frightful stories have been too much for me. I beg you, let me sit down.' She slumped into a chair.

Monte Cristo bowed and went over to Mme de Villefort. 'I think Madame Danglars needs your flask again,' he said. But before Mme de Villefort could go over to her friend, the crown prosecutor had already whispered in Mme Danglars' ear: 'I must speak to you.'

'When?'

'Tomorrow.'

'Where?'

'In my office . . . At the law courts, if you prefer. That could be the safest place.'

'I shall be there.'

At that moment Mme de Villefort came up.

'Thank you, my dear,' said Mme Danglars, trying to smile. 'It's nothing. I'm quite better.'

LXIV

THE BEGGAR

The evening went on. Mme de Villefort expressed a desire to return to Paris, which Mme Danglars had not yet dared to do, despite the obvious discomfort that she felt. So, at his wife's request, M. de Villefort was the first to make a move to depart. He offered Mme Danglars a place in his landau, so that his wife could look after her. As for M. Danglars, he paid no attention to what was going on, being engrossed in a most absorbing conversation about industrial matters with M. Cavalcanti.

While Monte Cristo was asking Mme de Villefort for her flask, he had noticed M. de Villefort go over to Mme Danglars and, judging by the situation, also guessed what was said between them, even though Villefort had spoken so softly that Mme Danglars herself could hardly hear him.

He made no objection, but let Morrel, Debray and Château-Renaud leave on horseback, while the two ladies got into M. de Villefort's landau. Danglars, for his part, was increasingly delighted with the elder Cavalcanti, whom he invited to join him in his coupé.

As for Andrea Cavalcanti, he took his tilbury, which was waiting at the door with a groom, dressed in an extravagant version of the English fashion, holding the enormous iron-grey horse and standing on tiptoe. Andrea had said little during dinner, precisely because he was an intelligent lad who was afraid of saying something ridiculous in front of these rich and powerful guests among whom his anxious eyes had perhaps been disturbed to find a crown prosecutor. After that, he had been monopolized by M. Danglars who, after a quick glance at the stiff-necked old major and his rather shy son, had weighed up this evidence in the light of Monte Cristo's hospitality and concluded that he was dealing with some nabob who had come to Paris to 'finish' his only son by introducing him to society.

Consequently he had looked with odious complacency at the huge diamond adorning the major's little finger – for the major, as a cautious man of the world, had been afraid that some accident might befall his banknotes and had rapidly converted them into an object of value. Then, after dinner, still on the pretext of industry and travel, he had questioned father and son on their style of life. The pair, knowing that one of them was to have his credit of 48,000 francs, when they arrived, with Danglars' bank, and the other his annual credit of 50,000 *livres*, had both been charming and full of conviviality towards the banker. Indeed, their gratitude felt so urgent a need to express itself that they would even have shaken hands with Danglars' servants, if they had not managed to restrain themselves.

One thing in particular increased Danglars' respect – one might almost say veneration – for Cavalcanti. The latter, obedient to Horace's principle *nil admirari*,[1] had been satisfied as we saw with demonstrating his erudition by naming the lake from which one gets the best lampreys. Then he had eaten his share of the same without uttering another word. Danglars jumped to the conclusion that this kind of feast was quite familiar to the illustrious descendant of the Cavalcantis, who probably dined at his home in Lucca on trout from Switzerland and lobster from Brittany brought to him by the same means as the count had used to fetch lampreys from Lake Fusaro and sturgeon from the Volga. So, when Cavalcanti announced: 'Tomorrow, Monsieur, I shall have the honour of visiting you on a matter of business,' he responded with a marked air of amiability.

'And I, Monsieur,' he replied, 'shall be happy to receive you.'

Whereupon he had offered to drive Cavalcanti back to the Hôtel des Princes, provided (of course) that he could bear to be separated from his son.

Cavalcanti replied that his son had long been accustomed to lead the bachelor life of a young man and consequently had his own horses and carriages; since they had not arrived together, he saw no difficulty in their leaving separately.

So the major got into Danglars' carriage and the banker took his place by his side, ever more charmed by the man's ideas of order and economy, even though he gave his son 50,000 francs a year, which indicated a fortune capable of producing an income of some 5,000 or 6,000 *livres*.

As for Andrea, in order to cut a good figure, he started by scolding his groom for not coming to collect him at the steps instead of at the gate, meaning that he had an extra thirty steps to reach his tilbury. The groom accepted the telling-off with good grace and shifted the bit into his left hand, to restrain the horse, which was stamping its hoof with impatience, and with the other hand gave the reins to Andrea, who took them and lightly set his polished boot on the running-board.

At that moment a hand touched his shoulder. The young man looked around, thinking that Danglars or Monte Cristo must have forgotten to tell him something and wished to catch him as he was leaving. But, instead of either of them, he saw a strange face, tanned by the sun and enclosed in a ready-made beard, with eyes shining like gems and a mocking smile which revealed, inside the mouth, each one in its place and not a single one missing, thirty-two sharp white teeth, as ravenous as those of a wolf or a jackal.

The head, with its dirty greying hair, was covered in a red check handkerchief, and the dirtiest, most ragged workman's smock hung around a frame so fleshless and bony that you half expected the bones to clink like those of a skeleton as it walked. As for the hand which clasped Andrea's shoulder, and the first thing that the young man saw, it seemed to him to be of gigantic size. Did the young man recognize the creature in the light from the lantern on his tilbury, or was he simply struck by his horrible appearance? We cannot say, but he shuddered and started back.

'What do you want with me?' he asked.

'Beg pardon, guv'nor!' the man said, lifting a hand to his red kerchief. 'I may be interrupting, but I must have a word.'

'You shouldn't beg after dark,' the groom said, threatening to drive this trouble-maker away from his master.

'I'm not begging, my fine fellow,' the stranger replied with an ironic smile – a smile so terrifying that the groom shrank back. 'I just want to say two words to your guv'nor, who asked me not a fortnight ago to do something for him.'

'Come, come,' said Andrea, loudly enough to disguise his anxiety from the servant. 'What do you want? Quick now, friend.'

'I want . . . I want . . .' the man in the red kerchief whispered, 'you to spare me the trouble of walking back to Paris. I'm very tired and, not having dined as well as you, I can hardly stand.'

The young man shuddered at this unusual familiarity. 'But what do you want from me?' he asked.

'Well, I should like you to let me get into your fine carriage and to drive me back.'

Andrea's face paled, but he said nothing.

'For heaven's sake!' the man in the red kerchief said, digging his hands into his pockets and giving the young man a challenging look. 'Yes, it's an idea I've got. Do you understand, my little Benedetto?'

At that name, the young man no doubt thought again, with the result that he went over to his groom and said: 'I did indeed give this man a job to do for me and he is going to tell me the outcome. Walk as far as the gate and take a cab there, so as not to be too late home.'

The servant went away, surprised.

'At least let me reach the shadows,' said Andrea.

'As far as that's concerned, I'll find you the perfect spot,' the man said, taking the horse by the bit and leading the tilbury to a place where it was impossible for anyone to see the honour Andrea was according him. 'It's not because I want the glory of getting into your fine carriage,' he continued, 'but simply that I am tired; and also, a bit, because I have business to discuss with you.'

'Come, get in,' said the young man.

It is a great shame that it was not daylight, because the spectacle must have been odd indeed, with the tramp plainly seated on the upholstered seat of the tilbury beside its elegant young driver.

Andrea drove the horse to the last house on the outskirts of the village without saying a word to his companion, who smiled and kept his mouth shut, as if delighted to be travelling in such a fine vehicle. But once they were out of Auteuil, Andrea looked around, no doubt to make sure that they could not be overheard or over-looked, pulled up the horse and said, crossing his arms in front of the man with the red kerchief: 'Damn it! Why have you come to disturb me now?'

'And why do you defy me, my lad?'

'How have I defied you?'

'How? You are asking me how? We separated at the Pont du Var, when you told me you were going to travel through Piedmont and Tuscany, and not a bit of it: you came to Paris.'

'Why should you mind?'

'On the contrary, I don't. Not at all. I even hope it might be useful.'

'Ah! I see!' Andrea said. 'You're speculating on me.'

'There you are! Insults already.'

'I warn you, Master Caderousse, you would be making a mistake.'

'All right, my lad, all right. Don't get angry. But you must know what it's like to fall on hard times. It makes you envious. So there am I, thinking you're roving around Piedmont and Tuscany, forced to work as a *faccino* or a *cicerone*, and feeling sorry for you, as I would for my own child . . . You know I've always called you my child?'

'So? What about it?'

'Hold on! Be patient!'

'I am patient. Just say what you have to.'

'Then all at once I see you riding through the gate at Les Bons-Hommes with a groom, and a tilbury, and brand-new clothes. Brand new! What does it mean? You've discovered a gold mine – or have you bought a place on the Exchange?'

'And the result, you tell me, is that you're envious?'

'No, no, I'm happy; so happy that I wanted to congratulate you, little one! But since I was not formally dressed, I took steps to make sure I didn't compromise you.'

'Some steps!' Andrea said. 'You accosted me in front of my servant.'

'What do you expect! I accosted you when I could. You have a lively horse and a light carriage, you are by nature as slippery as an eel and, if I had missed you this evening, I might never have caught you at all.'

'I'm not hiding, as you can see.'

'Good for you; I wish I could say the same. But I am hiding. Not to mention the fact that I was afraid you would not recognize me – but you did,' Caderousse added, with his evil smile. 'There! You're a kind fellow.'

'So what do you want?'

'You're not polite with me and that's not nice, Benedetto, to an old comrade. Be careful, you may make me very demanding.'

At this threat, the young man's anger subsided: a cold breath of coercion had just blown over it. He whipped his horse back to a trot.

'It's not nice of you, my friend,' he said, 'to take that tone with an old comrade, as you say. You are a Marseillais, I'm . . .'

'Have you found out what you are now?'

'No, but I was brought up in Corsica. You are old and obstinate, I am young and stubborn. It's a bad idea for people like us to threaten one another. We should do business amicably. Is it my fault if luck is still hard on you and has been kind to me?'

'So, your luck's good, is it? Which means it's not some borrowed groom or borrowed tilbury or borrowed clothes that we have here? Fine! So much the better!' Caderousse said, his eyes gleaming with greed.

'You can see that very well and you know it, since you've accosted me,' Andrea said, getting more and more excited. 'If I had a kerchief like yours on my head, a filthy smock on my back and gaping shoes on my feet, you wouldn't recognize me.'

'You see, little one, you do despise me, and you are wrong. Now I've found you, there's no reason why I shouldn't be dressed in fine linen like anyone else, since I know your generosity. If you had two coats, you would give one to me. I gave you my share of soup and beans when you were starving.'

'That's true,' Andrea said.

'What an appetite you had! Do you still?'

'Surely,' Andrea said with a laugh.

'You must have had a good dinner with that prince you have just left.'

'He's not a prince, just a count.'

'A count? Rich, huh?'

'Yes, but don't rely on him. He looks an awkward customer.'

'Oh, don't worry! I've got no plans for your count; keep him for yourself. But,' Caderousse added, the same unpleasant smile hovering about his lips, 'you'll have to pay for it, you know . . .'

'Come on, what do you need?'

'I think that with a hundred francs a month . . .'

'Yes?'

'I could live . . .'

'On a hundred francs?'

'And not very well, as you know. However, with . . .'

'With?'

'A hundred and fifty francs, I should be very happy.'

'Here are two hundred,' said Andrea, putting ten gold *louis* into Caderousse's hand.

'Good,' said Caderousse.

'Come and see the concierge on the first of every month and you will have the same.'

'Come, now! You're humiliating me again!'

'Why?'

'Sending me to deal with the skivvies. No, I want to deal directly with you.'

'Very well, ask for me, and on the first of every month, for as long as I am getting my income, you shall have yours.'

'You see! I was right, you are a fine lad, and it's a blessing when good fortune comes to those like you. So, tell me all about it.'

'Why do you need to know?' Cavalcanti asked.

'There! Hostility again!'

'No, no. Well, I've found my father.'

'A real one?'

'Huh! As long as he pays . . .'

'You will believe in and honour him. That's fair. What's this father's name?'

'Major Cavalcanti.'

'Is he happy with you?'

'For the time being, I seem to fit the bill.'

'And who found this father for you?'

'The Count of Monte Cristo.'

'This count you've just left?'

'Yes.'

'In that case, try to find me a post with him as a grandparent, since he's making a business of it.'

'I'll mention you to him. Meanwhile, what will you do?'

'Me?'

'Yes, you.'

'You're a good lad, to worry about that,' said Caderousse.

'Since you're taking such an interest in me, I can at least find out something about you myself.'

'Very well. I'm going to rent a room in a respectable house, buy myself a decent coat, get a shave every day and go and read the newspaper in a café. In the evenings, I shall go to the theatre with the man who organizes the claque. I'll be taken for a retired baker. That's my dream . . .'

'Excellent! If you follow that plan sensibly, everything will be fine.'

'Listen to Monsieur Bossuet[2] . . . And what are you going to become: a peer of the realm?'

'Uh, uh!' Andrea said. 'Who knows?'

'Perhaps Major Cavalcanti is one. What a shame the hereditary peerage has been abolished.'

'Keep off politics, Caderousse! Now you have what you wanted and we have arrived home, jump down and disappear.'

'Not so, my good friend.'

'What do you mean: not so?'

'Just think, little one: here I am with a red kerchief on my head, virtually no shoes, no documents at all and ten gold *napoleons* in my pocket, quite apart from what was there already, which adds up to a round two hundred francs! They would most certainly arrest me at the gate, and I should be forced, in my own defence, to tell them that you gave me these ten *napoleons*. Then there'd have to be a statement and an enquiry. They would find that I left Toulon without asking for leave and send me back from one police force to the next down to the shores of the Mediterranean. I should quite simply become, once more, Number one hundred and six[3] – and goodbye to my dreams of playing the part of a retired baker! No, no, son, I'd rather stay honestly in the capital.'

Andrea raised an eyebrow. As he had boasted himself, this supposed son of Major Cavalcanti was something of a hothead. He paused, cast a rapid glance around him and, as his eyes completed this circular investigation, innocently let his hand go down to his trouser pocket where it began to fondle the stock of a small pistol. However, during this same time, Caderousse, while not taking his eyes off the other man, put his hands behind his back and gently opened a long Spanish knife which he kept there for any eventuality.

These two friends, as one may see, were well suited to understand one another, and did so. Andrea's hand came empty out of his pocket, went up to his moustache, and stroked it a few times. 'Very well, Caderousse,' he said. 'Will you be content?'

'I shall do my best,' replied the innkeeper from the Pont du Gard, slipping his knife back into its sheath.

'Come on then, back to Paris. But how will you get through the gates without arousing suspicion? Dressed as you are, I think you're even more likely to do so than if you were on foot.'

'Wait. I'll show you.' And Caderousse took Andrea's hat and the broad-collared greatcoat that the groom had left behind on his seat when he was sent away from the tilbury; he put them on and adopted the sullen air of a servant in a good household whose master is driving himself.

'So,' said Andrea, 'am I to go bare-headed?'

'Pah! In this wind, your hat could easily have blown off.'

'Come on then, let's get it over.'

'What's stopping you?' said Caderousse. 'Not me, I hope.'

'Hush!' said Cavalcanti. They had no trouble getting past the gate. At the first side-road Andrea stopped the carriage, and Caderousse jumped down.

'Well, then?' said Andrea. 'What about my servant's coat and my hat?'

'Surely you wouldn't want me to catch cold?' said Caderousse.

'What about me?'

'You're young and I'm starting to grow old. *Au revoir*, Benedetto!' And he disappeared down the narrow street.

'Alas, alas!' Andrea said, with a sigh. 'One can never be completely happy in this world.'

LXV

A DOMESTIC SCENE

The three young men had separated at the Place Louis XV, Morrel going via the boulevards, Château-Renaud crossing the Pont de la Révolution and Debray following the path by the river. It seemed likely that Morrel and Château-Renaud would be returning to the bosom of their families – as they still call it in the House, in well-turned speeches, and at the theatre in the Rue de Richelieu, in well-written plays; but the same was not true of Debray. When he got to the grille at the Louvre, he took a left turn, crossing the Carrousel at the double, slipped down the Rue Saint-Roch, came out at the Rue de la Michodière and arrived finally at M. Danglars' door, just as M. de Villefort's landau, having deposited him and his wife in the Faubourg Saint-Honoré, was pulling up to let the baroness return home.

Debray, as someone who knew the house, was the first to go into the courtyard and he tossed the reins to a footman, then went back to the door of the carriage to help Mme Danglars, offering her his arm so that she could get down and go indoors. As soon as the gate was closed and the baroness and Debray were in the courtyard, he asked: 'What is wrong, Hermine? Why were you ill when the count told that story – or, rather, that fairy tale?'

'Because I was in terrible form this evening, my friend,' the baroness replied.

'No, Hermine,' Debray protested. 'You won't convince me of that. On the contrary, you were in an excellent mood when you got to the count's. I admit, Monsieur Danglars was a trifle gloomy, but I know what importance you attach to his bad tempers. Someone did something to you. Tell me about it. You know that I should never allow anyone to insult you in any way.'

'You are wrong, Lucien, I assure you,' Mme Danglars said. 'It is just as I said, together with the bad temper that you noticed and which I did not think was worth mentioning to you.'

It was clear that Mme Danglars was suffering from one of those nervous irritations which women are often unable to explain even to themselves, or else, as Debray had guessed, that she had experienced some hidden disturbance which she did not want to discuss with anyone. So, as a man who was used to treating 'the vapours' as a part of a woman's life, he did not press the matter, but waited for a suitable opportunity to arise, either for further questioning, or else for a confession *proprio motu*.

At the door of her room, the baroness met Mlle Cornélie. Mlle Cornélie was her chambermaid and confidante.

'What is my daughter doing?' asked Mme Danglars.

'She spent the whole evening studying,' Mlle Cornélie answered. 'Then she went to bed.'

'But isn't that a piano I can hear?'

'It's Mademoiselle Louise d'Armilly playing, while mademoiselle is in bed.'

'Very good,' said Mme Danglars. 'Come and undress me.'

They went into her bedroom. Debray slouched on to a large sofa and Mme Danglars went through to her dressing-room with Mlle Cornélie.

'My dear Monsieur Lucien,' Mme Danglars said through the door, 'are you still complaining that Eugénie doesn't deign to speak to you?'

Lucien was playing with the baroness's lapdog which, acknowledging him as a friend of the house, was responding affectionately to his attentions. 'Madame,' he replied, 'I'm not the only one who has complained about it to you. I think I heard Morcerf telling you only the other day that he could not get a word out of his fiancée.'

'That's true,' said Mme Danglars, 'but I think that all this will change one of these fine mornings, and you'll see Eugénie coming to your chambers.'

'To my own chambers?'

'I mean, the ministerial ones.'

'Why?'

'To ask you to persuade them to take her on at the Opera. I must tell you, I've never seen such an infatuation with music. It's ridiculous in someone of her position.'

Debray smiled. 'If she comes with your consent and that of the baron,' he said, 'we'll have her engaged and try to make the part suitable for her, though we are not really rich enough to pay for a talent such as hers.'

'You may go, Cornélie,' Mme Danglars said. 'I don't need you any more.'

Cornélie vanished, and a moment later Mme Danglars emerged from her dressing-room in a charming négligée and sat down beside Lucien. Then, distractedly, she began to stroke the spaniel. Lucien looked at her for a moment in silence.

'Come now, Hermine,' he said eventually. 'Something is troubling you, isn't it?'

'No, nothing,' said the baroness. And yet, feeling stifled, she got up, tried to recover her breath and went to look at herself in a mirror.

'I'm a real fright this evening,' she said.

Debray was just getting up with a smile to go over and reassure the baroness that this was not the case, when suddenly the door opened and M. Danglars appeared. Debray sat down again.

Mme Danglars had turned around at the sound of the door and was looking at her husband with an astonishment that she did not even attempt to conceal.

'Good evening, Madame,' the banker said. 'Good evening, Monsieur Debray.'

No doubt the baroness thought that this unexpected visit signified something, for example a desire to make up for the bitter words which the baron had uttered during the day, so she took on a haughty air and turned towards Lucien, without answering her husband. 'Read something to me, Monsieur Debray,' she said.

Debray had been slightly uneasy at this visit to begin with, but, seeing the baroness's imperturbability, he recovered his calm and stretched out his hand towards a book, marked in the centre with a mother-of-pearl paperknife inlaid with gold.

'Excuse me, Baroness,' said the baron, 'but you will tire yourself if you stay up so late. It is eleven o'clock and Monsieur Debray lives a long way from here.'

Debray was astonished, though Danglars' voice was perfectly steady and polite; but behind the calm good manners he detected a certain unaccustomed impulse to do something, apart from bowing to the wishes of his wife. The baroness was equally surprised and showed her astonishment with a look that would no doubt have given her husband pause for reflection, if he had not been attentively searching the closing prices in a newspaper. The result was that her arrogant look failed to reach its target and so was completely wasted.

'Monsieur Lucien,' the baroness said, 'I must declare, I have not the slightest desire to sleep and there are a dozen things I want to talk about, so you will stay and listen to me all night, even if you fall asleep on your feet.'

'As you wish, Madame,' Lucien said phlegmatically.

'My dear Monsieur Debray,' the baron said, 'you really must not exhaust yourself, I beg you, in listening to Mme Danglars' nonsense tonight, because you can just as well hear it tomorrow. This evening is mine, and I am reserving it for myself, if you would be so good as to allow me, because I have some grave matters to discuss with my wife.'

This time the assault was so direct and well aimed that Lucien and the baroness were stunned by it. They exchanged a look as if each was trying to find assistance against this attack. But the irresistible power of the master of the house triumphed and the husband was left victorious.

'Don't, please, think that I am driving you away, my dear Debray,' Danglars went on. 'No, not in the slightest. But an un-expected eventuality has made me wish to have a conversation with the baroness this very evening. This is such a rare occurrence that no one could hold it against me.'

Debray stammered a few words, bowed and left the room, knocking against the corners, like Nathan in *Athalie*.[1] 'It's extraordinary,' he said, when the door had closed behind him, 'how easily these husbands, whom we consider so ridiculous, are none the less able to regain the advantage over us!'

When Lucien had gone, Danglars sat down in his place on the sofa, closed the book and, adopting a thoroughly pretentious pose, continued to stroke the dog. However, the animal did not have the same sympathy for him as for Debray and tried to bite him, so he grasped it by the nape of the neck and tossed it across the room on to a chaise-longue. The spaniel yelped on finding itself in mid-air, but on reaching its destination buried itself in a cushion and, stupefied by this unaccustomed treatment, remained silent and motionless.

'Do you know, Monsieur,' said the baroness, without raising an eyebrow, 'you really are excelling yourself. Normally you are merely coarse, but tonight you are behaving like a brute.'

'That's because I am in a worse mood than usual tonight,' said Danglars.

Hermine considered the banker with utter contempt. Normally

Danglars, a proud man, would be infuriated by these looks, but on this occasion he hardly seemed to notice.

'What do I care about your bad moods?' the baroness exclaimed, exasperated by her husband's impassivity. 'Are they anything to do with me? Shut them up in your part of the house or confine them to your offices. Since you have paid clerks, take your foul tempers out on them!'

'No, Madame, not at all,' Danglars replied. 'Your advice is quite misguided and I have no intention of taking it. My offices are my "golden goose", as I believe Monsieur Desmoutiers calls them, and I should not want to upset the bird or ruffle its feathers. My clerks are honest fellows who earn a fortune for me and are paid at a rate considerably below what they are worth, if that is judged according to the profits they bring; so I am not going to lose my temper with them. The people who do put me in a rage are those who eat my dinners, wind my horses and plunder my wealth.'

'And what people are those, who plunder your wealth? Please explain, Monsieur.'

'Oh, don't worry, I may be talking in riddles, but I won't keep you guessing for long. The people who plunder my wealth are the ones who take five hundred thousand francs away from me in an hour.'

'I don't follow you, Monsieur,' said the baroness, trying to disguise the emotion in her voice and the blush on her cheeks.

'On the contrary, you follow me very well,' said Danglars. 'But if you persist in pretending otherwise, I must tell you that I have just lost seven hundred thousand francs on the Spanish loan.'

'Oh, well, I never!' sniggered the baroness. 'Are you trying to blame me for your loss?'

'Shouldn't I?'

'Is it my fault if you lost seven hundred thousand francs?'

'In any case, it's not mine.'

'Once and for all, Monsieur,' the baroness said, sharply, 'I have told you never to talk money to me. It's a language I was not taught either by my parents or in the house of my first husband.'

'I can certainly believe that,' said Danglars. 'Neither of them had a penny to rub together.'

'All the more reason for me not to have learnt your banker's argot, which assails my ears here from morning to night. I am repelled by that sound of coins being counted and recounted;

I don't know if it is not more odious to me than the sound of your voice.'

'How strange, indeed!' said Danglars. 'And I always thought you took a close interest in my business.'

'I! What can have made you think such a thing?'

'You yourself did.'

'How ridiculous!'

'Certainly.'

'I should be pleased to know on what occasion.'

'Oh, that's very easy. Last February, you were the first to mention the Haitian funds to me. You dreamt that a ship was entering the port at Le Havre, with news that a payment, which everyone had thought postponed indefinitely, was about to be made. I know how clear-headed you are when asleep, so I had them buy up all the bonds that they could on the Haitian debt and I made four hundred thousand francs, a hundred thousand of which was duly handed over to you. What you did with it is no business of mine.

'In March, there was a tender on the railways. Three firms bid for it, each offering equally firm guarantees. You told me that your instinct informed you that the contract would be given to a company from the south. Now, even though you pretend to be ignorant, I do believe that sometimes you have a very acute instinct in such matters.

'I immediately bought two-thirds of the stock in that firm. It did indeed win the contract and, as you predicted, the shares tripled in value. I made a million, of which two hundred and fifty thousand francs went to you as pin-money. What did you do with it?'

'But where is all this leading, Monsieur?' the baroness exclaimed, trembling with scorn and impatience.

'Patience, Madame, we are coming to the point.'

'Thank goodness for that!'

'In April, you went to dinner with the minister. There was talk of Spain and you overheard a private conversation about the expulsion of Don Carlos.[2] I bought Spanish stock. The expulsion took place and I earned six hundred thousand francs on the day when Charles V crossed the Bidassoa. Out of that, you had fifty thousand *écus*. They were yours, and you could do as you wished with them; I'm not asking you to account for it. But the fact remains that this year you have had five hundred thousand *livres*.'

'So, Monsieur?'

'Ah, yes, *so*! Well, it was just after that that everything turned sour.'

'You really do have a way of putting it . . .'

'It expresses how I feel, which is all I need . . . "After that" was three days ago. Three days ago you had a discussion on politics with Monsieur Debray and you thought he said that Don Carlos had returned to Spain. As a result, I sold my stock. The news spread, there was a panic and I wasn't able to sell any more, I was giving it away. The next day, the news turned out to have been false, and this false news had cost me seven hundred thousand francs!'

'So, what of it?'

'So, since I give you a quarter when I win, you owe me a quarter when I lose. A quarter of seven hundred thousand francs is one hundred and seventy-five thousand francs.'

'What you are saying is ludicrous. And I really cannot see why you should bring Monsieur Debray's name into all this.'

'Because if you don't happen to have the one hundred and seventy-five thousand francs that I am claiming from you, you can borrow from your friends, of whom Monsieur Debray is one.'

'Fiddle-de-dee!' the baroness exclaimed.

'Oh, let's have no gestures, no cries, no melodrama, Madame, or I shall be obliged to tell you that I can see from here Monsieur Debray sniggering over the five hundred thousand francs or so that you have given him this year, and telling himself that he has at last found what the most skilful gambler has never found, which is a roulette wheel where you can win without playing and don't lose even when you lose.'

The baroness was fit to burst. 'You wretch!' she said. 'Do you dare say that you were not aware of what you now venture to reproach me with?'

'I don't say that I knew or that I didn't; I am just telling you this: consider how I have behaved in the four years since we have ceased to live as man and wife, and you will see that my conduct has always been consistent. Some time before the breach between us, you wanted to study music with that famous baritone who was such a success at the Théâtre Italien, while I wanted to study dancing with that dancer who had been so warmly received when she appeared in London. It cost me, for you and for me, some hundred thousand francs. I did not complain, because one must try to preserve the peace in one's home. A hundred thousand francs for the man and the woman to perfect their dancing and their music is not excessive. Then you soon became bored with singing, and you got the idea that you would like to study diplomacy with one of the minister's secretaries. I let you. You see, it doesn't matter to me, as long as you are paying for your lessons out of your own pocket. But I now see that you are dipping into mine and that your further education might cost me as much as seven hundred thousand francs a month. Whoa, Madame! It can't go on like this. Either the diplomat will have to start giving his . . . lessons for nothing, and I shall put up with him, or he will not be allowed to set foot again in my house. Do you understand?'

'But this is really too much, Monsieur!' Hermine cried, barely able to speak. 'You are exceeding the bounds of ignominy!'

'And I am glad to see,' said Danglars, 'that you are not far behind me, and that you have willingly chosen to obey the legal maxim: "The wife should follow her husband."'

'You insult me.'

'You are right. Let's stop arguing and be reasonable. I have never interfered with your business except to do you good; you do the same. You say that my wealth is none of your business? Very well, look after your own, but don't try to increase or diminish mine. In any case, who can tell if this is not some kind of political chicanery – if the minister, furious because I am with the opposition and jealous of the popular sympathy that I enjoy, has not been in league with Monsieur Debray to ruin me?'

'Very likely, I must say!'

'Why not? Who has ever seen anything like it: a false message on the telegraph, in other words something more or less impossible: different signals given by the two operators! It was done specifically to harm me, that's the truth of it.'

'Monsieur,' the baroness said humbly, 'you must know, I think, that the operator in question was dismissed, there was even talk of bringing him to trial and the order had gone out to arrest him, which would have been done if he had not escaped detection by fleeing in a way that proves his madness, or his guilt . . . There was some mistake.'

'Yes, and one which makes fools laugh, the minister lose a night's sleep and the secretaries of state blacken a lot of paper, but which cost me seven hundred thousand francs.'

'But then,' Hermine said, suddenly, 'if all this, according to you, is Monsieur Debray's fault, why not tell him about it directly, instead of coming to me? Why accuse the man and attack the woman?'

'Do I know Monsieur Debray?' said Danglars. 'Do I want to know him? Do I want to know that he gives advice? Do I want to take it? Do I gamble? No, you do all these things, not I.'

'But I would have thought, since you profit by it . . .'

Danglars shrugged his shoulders.

'What mad creatures they are, these women who think themselves geniuses because they have managed to carry on one or two affairs without everyone in Paris knowing about them! But just consider: even if you had disguised your irregularities from your husband himself – and that is the most elementary skill in the business, because most of the time husbands don't want to see what is going on – you would still only be a pale copy of what most of your society friends are doing. With me it is different: I saw and I have always seen. In roughly the past sixteen years you may have hidden a thought from me, but never a step, an action or a sin. While you were flattering yourself as to your skill and firmly believed that you were deceiving me, what happened? The truth was that, thanks to my turning a blind eye, there has not been one of your friends, from Monsieur de Villefort to Monsieur Debray, who has not been afraid of me. There is not one who has not treated me as the master of the house, which is my only claim on you. In short, not one would have dared say to you the things about myself that I am telling you today. I will let you make me hateful, but I refuse to allow you to make me ridiculous and, above all, I absolutely forbid you to ruin me.'

Until the name of Villefort was mentioned, the baroness had looked fairly confident but, on hearing that name, she paled and, getting up as though driven by a spring, she held out her arms as if to ward off an apparition and took three steps towards her husband, as though trying to extract from him the remains of a secret that he did not know; or which, perhaps, he did not want to reveal altogether, as part of some vile scheme – for all Danglars' schemes were vile.

'Monsieur de Villefort! What is this? What do you mean?'

'What I mean, Madame, is that Monsieur de Nargonne, your first husband, being neither a philosopher nor a banker – or, perhaps, being both – and seeing that there was nothing to be obtained from a crown prosecutor, died of sorrow or of wrath on coming back from a nine months' absence to find you pregnant by six. I am brutal: not only do I know that, I am proud of it: it is one secret of my success in business. Why, instead of killing the other man, did he kill himself? Because he had no fortune to save. But I do, and I have an obligation to my money. My associate, Monsieur Debray, has lost me seven hundred thousand francs. Let him pay for his share of the loss and we shall continue to do business. Otherwise, let him go bankrupt for his hundred and seventy-five thousand *livres* and do what all bankrupts do, which is to disappear. Heavens, he's a charming youth, I know, when his news is accurate; but when it's wrong there are fifty others in society who are worth more than he is.'

Mme Danglars was crushed, but she made one final effort to respond to this last assault. She fell back into a chair, thinking of Villefort, of the scene at the dinner and of the strange series of misfortunes that had fallen, one by one, on her family over the past few days, replacing the comfortable peace of her household with shocking arguments. Danglars was not even looking at her, even though she did all she could to faint. He opened the bedroom door without a further word and went back to his own apartments, so that Mme Danglars, recovering from her half-unconscious state, might even have thought she had suffered a nightmare.

LXVI

MARRIAGE PLANS

The day after this scene, at the time which Debray usually chose to make a brief visit to Mme Danglars on his way to the office, his coupé did not appear in the courtyard. Instead, at this same time, around half-past twelve, Mme Danglars called for her carriage and went out.

Danglars had been expecting this departure and watched it from behind a curtain. He gave orders that he should be told as soon as madame returned, but at two o'clock she had still not done so. He called for his horses and went to the House, where he had his name put down to speak against the budget.

Between midday and two o'clock, Danglars had been in his study, breaking the seals on his dispatches and growing more and more gloomy as he piled one set of figures on another. He also received some visitors, including Major Cavalcanti who, in blue as always, stiff and punctual, arrived at the time appointed on the previous day to complete his business with the banker.

During the debate Danglars had shown signs of violent agitation and, above all, had been more than usually cutting about the government; on leaving the House, he got into his carriage and asked to be driven to No. 30, Avenue des Champs-Elysées.

Monte Cristo was at home, but he had a visitor, so he asked Danglars to wait for a moment in the drawing-room. While he was waiting, the door opened and he saw a man enter, in the dress of an abbé. This person, instead of waiting like Danglars, appeared to be a more familiar visitor at the house: he bowed, went through into the inner room and disappeared.

A moment later, the door through which the priest had entered opened and Monte Cristo appeared. 'Forgive me, dear Baron,' he said, 'but one of my good friends, Abbé Busoni, whom you saw enter, has just arrived in Paris. It is a long time since we last met and I could not tear myself away from him immediately. I hope that this reason will be sufficient to persuade you to excuse me for keeping you waiting.'

'What do you mean?' said Danglars. 'I am the one who chose my time badly. I shall leave at once.'

'Not at all. On the contrary, please sit down. But, my goodness, what is wrong? You seem quite worried. In truth, you alarm me. A crestfallen capitalist is like a comet: he always warns of some great misfortune to come.'

'What's wrong, Monsieur,' said Danglars, 'is that I have been suffering a run of bad luck for the past few days, and all the news I have is bad news.'

'Heaven preserve us!' said Monte Cristo. 'Have you had another loss on the Exchange?'

'No, I'm cured of that, at least for a few days. The latest is a bankruptcy in Trieste.'

'Really? I suppose your bankrupt wouldn't be Jacopo Manfredi by any chance?'

'The very man! Here is someone who – for I don't know how long – has been doing eight or nine hundred thousand francs of business with me a year. Never any mistakes, never any delays: the man used to settle his debts like a prince . . . like a paying prince. I advance him a million and, lo and behold, for the first time the devil stops his remittance.'

'Is that so?'

'It's an extraordinary piece of luck. I drew six hundred thousand *livres* on him, which has been returned, unpaid, and, in addition to that, I hold bills of exchange to the value of four hundred thousand francs, signed by him and payable by his partner in Paris at the end of the month. It is the thirtieth. I send someone for the money and – as you've guessed – the partner is not to be found. With this Spanish business, it's been a good month, I can tell you!'

'But did you really lose on that Spanish business?'

'No doubt about it: I'm not less than seven hundred thousand francs down.'

'How on earth did an old fox like you get caught in that way?'

'There you are! It's my wife's fault. She dreamt that Don Carlos had returned to Spain, and she believes in dreams. It's to do with magnetism, she says, and when she dreams something, it must surely happen. I allow her to gamble on her beliefs: she has her own account and her broker. She gambled and lost. Of course it was her money and not mine that she lost, but you must still see that, when seven hundred thousand francs go out of the wife's pocket, the husband is bound to notice it a little. What! Didn't you know about it? Everyone was talking about what happened.'

'Yes, I did hear tell of it, but I didn't know the details. And then I am utterly ignorant when it comes to anything to do with stocks and shares.'

'You don't gamble on the Exchange?'

'Me? How do you expect me to gamble? I already have enough trouble working out my income. I should be obliged to take on a clerk and an accountant as well as my steward. But, on this matter of Spain, it seems to me that the baroness was not alone in dreaming about the return of Don Carlos. Didn't the papers have something to say about it?'

'Do you believe what you read in the papers?'

'Not in the least, but I did think that *Le Messager* was an exception to the rule, and that it only carried authenticated news, news from the telegraph.'

'And that is precisely what can't be explained,' Danglars

said. 'The news of Don Carlos' return did come through the telegraph.'

'All of which means that you have lost around one million seven hundred thousand francs this month?'

'It's not a matter of "around", that's the figure.'

'The deuce it is!' Monte Cristo said sympathetically. 'For a third-class fortune, that's a hard blow.'

'A third-class fortune!' Danglars exclaimed, slightly insulted. 'What the devil do you mean by that?'

'Oh, yes, no doubt,' said Monte Cristo. 'I divide the rich into three categories: first-class, second-class and third-class fortunes. A first-class fortune, I would call one which is made up of disposable treasures, land, mines and incomes from government bonds in countries like France, Austria or England, provided these treasures, possessions or incomes add up to a total of at least a hundred million. A second-class fortune is one whose owner possesses factories, business interests, viceroyships or principalities yielding under one million five hundred thousand francs, all adding up to a capital of some fifty million. Finally, a third-class fortune would be capital paying compound interest, profits depending on the will of others or on chance, which are liable to be damaged by a bankruptcy or shattered by a telegraph signal; occasional speculation and other operations subject to the whims of a fate which we might call *force mineure*, by analogy with the whims of nature which are *force majeure*; all of it amounting to a real or hypothetical capital of some fifteen million. Isn't that roughly your situation?'

'Good heavens, yes!' said Danglars.

'So that means that six months like the one you have just had would send a third-class firm to its deathbed,' Monte Cristo said imperturbably.

'Huh!' Danglars said, with a very pale smile. 'That's a nice way of putting it.'

'Say seven months,' Monte Cristo continued, in the same tone. 'Tell me, have you ever considered that seven times one million seven hundred thousand francs makes about twelve million? No? Well, you are right, because if one were to reflect on such things, one would never venture one's capital, which is to the financier what his skin is to a civilized man. We have our more or less sumptuous clothes, which are our credit, but when a man dies he has only his skin. Just as, when you leave business, you will have your real wealth – five or six million at most . . . because a third-class fortune barely represents a third or a quarter of what it appears, much as the locomotive of a railway train, amid the steam and smoke that enwraps it and enlarges it, is only at base a more or less powerful machine. Well, of the five million that represent your real capital, you have just lost around two million, which reduces your notional fortune or your credit by the same amount. All this means, my dear Monsieur Danglars, that your skin has just been opened by a wound which, repeated four times, would mean death. Well, well! You must be careful, my dear Monsieur Danglars. Do you need money? Can I lend you some?'

'Your sums are quite wrong!' Danglars exclaimed, summoning up all the philosophy and dissimulation he could muster. 'The way things stand, money has been coming into my account from successful speculation. The blood that flowed out of the wound has been replaced by nourishment. I may have lost a battle in Spain, and I was defeated at Trieste, but my Indian navy should have captured some galleons and my Mexican prospectors have found a mine.'

'Excellent, excellent; but the scar remains. At the first loss it will re-open.'

'No, because my business is founded on certainties,' said Danglars with the glibness of a charlatan whose profession is to extol his own credit. 'For me to be overthrown, three governments would have to fall.'

'Well, it has happened.'

'And for the harvest to fail.'

'Remember the seven fat cows and the seven lean cows.'[1]

'Or for the sea to part, as at the time of the Pharaohs; and even then, there are several seas, and the ships would get by through turning into caravans.'

'So much the better, a thousand times, my dear Monsieur Danglars,' said Monte Cristo. 'I see I was wrong and that yours comes into the category of second-class fortunes.'

'I think I may aspire to that honour,' said Danglars with one of those fatuous smiles which had the same effect on Monte Cristo as the pallid moons that inferior painters plant in the sky above their ruins. 'But since we are talking business,' he continued, delighted at finding this excuse to change the subject, 'can you give me some idea of what I might do for Monsieur Cavalcanti?'

'Give him some money, I suppose, if he has a credit with you and you think it's good.'

'Splendid! He presented himself this morning with a bill for forty thousand francs, drawn on you and payable on sight, signed Busoni and forwarded to me by you with your endorsement. You will appreciate that I gave him his forty notes straight away.'

Monte Cristo gave a nod to signify his full approval.

'But that is not all,' Danglars went on. 'He has opened a credit with us on behalf of his son.'

'If I might venture to ask, how much is he giving the young man?'

'Five thousand francs a month.'

'Sixty thousand a year. I'm not surprised,' Monte Cristo said, shrugging his shoulders. 'They are so timorous, these Cavalcantis. What does he expect a young man to do with five thousand a month?'

'But you know, if the young man should need a few thousand more . . .'

'Don't. The father would leave you to foot the bill. You don't know these Italian millionaires: they are real misers. By whom was the credit opened?'

'By the firm of Fenzi, one of the best in Florence.'

'I'm not saying that you'll lose, far from it. But keep strictly to the letter.'

'Don't you have confidence in this Cavalcanti?'

'Me? I'd give him ten million against his signature. My dear sir, his is one of those second-class fortunes we were just talking about.'

'Yet he is such an ordinary man. I'd have taken him for a major, nothing more.'

'He would have been honoured, because you're right, he's nothing to look at. When I saw him for the first time, he looked to me like an old lieutenant gone to seed. But all Italians are like that: either they look like old money-lenders, or else they dazzle you like Oriental magi.'

'The young man is better,' said Danglars.

'Yes. A trifle shy, perhaps. But all in all he seemed respectable enough to me. I was worried about him.'

'Why?'

'Because when you met him at my house, that was virtually his first encounter with society, or so they tell me. He travelled with a very strict tutor and had never been to Paris.'

'These upper-class Italians, they usually marry among themselves, don't they?' Danglars asked casually. 'They like to unite their fortunes.'

'Usually that's true. But Cavalcanti is an eccentric who does nothing like anyone else. I am convinced that he has sent his son to France to find a wife.'

'Do you think so?'

'I'm sure of it.'

'And you know about his fortune?'

'I hear about nothing else. Except that some people say he has millions, others that he doesn't have a farthing.'

'What's your personal opinion?'

'Just that: personal, so don't rely on it.'

'But . . .'

'My opinion is that all these old *podestas*, the former *condottieri* – because the Cavalcantis used to command armies and used to rule provinces . . . Well, my opinion, as I say, is that they buried millions in nooks and crannies that only their ancestors knew and passed down from eldest son to eldest son through the generations. The proof is that they are all dry and yellow like their florins from the days of the republic: their faces have spent so long looking at the coins that they have come to reflect them.'

'Exactly,' said Danglars. 'All the more so since none of these people seems to own a square inch of land.'

'Very little, at least. In Cavalcanti's case, all I know is his palace in Lucca.'

'Ah, so he does have a palace,' said Danglars, laughing. 'That's something at any rate.'

'Yes, and he rents it to the Minister of Finance, while he himself lives in a cottage. I told you: I think the fellow's tight-fisted.'

'I must say, you don't flatter him.'

'Listen, I hardly know him. I may have seen him three times in my life. What I do know comes from Abbé Busoni and from Cavalcanti himself. He was talking to me this morning about his plans for his son and hinted that he was tired of letting large sums of money sleep idly in Italy, which is a dead country, so he would like to find a way, in either France or Italy, of making his millions bear fruit. However, I must insist that, though I have every confidence in Abbé Busoni himself, I can guarantee nothing.'

'No matter. Thank you for sending me a customer. It's a fine name to write on my register, and my cashier, to whom I explained about the Cavalcantis, is full of self-importance about it all. By the way – just out of idle curiosity – when such people marry off their sons, do they give them a dowry?'

'It depends. I knew one Italian prince, as rich as a gold mine, one of the leading families in Tuscany, who would give millions to his sons when they married as he wished and, when they went against his wishes, cut them off with an income of twenty *écus* a month. Supposing Andrea were to marry someone of whom his father approved, he might give him one, two or three million. If it was with the daughter of a banker, for example, he might take an interest in his son's father-in-law's firm. On the other hand, suppose he was not pleased with his daughter-in-law: well, *slap-bang*, old Cavalcanti grabs the key to his safe, gives a double turn to the lock and Master Andrea is obliged to live like a young Parisian beau, marking cards and loading dice.'

'The boy will find a Bavarian or Peruvian princess: he'll want a closed crown, an Eldorado with the Potosi running through it.'

'No, these transmontane aristos often marry mere mortals: they are like Jupiter, they like mixing species.[2] But tell me, my dear Monsieur Danglars, you're not thinking of marrying Andrea yourself are you, with all these questions?'

'By golly, it might not be a bad investment,' Danglars said. 'And I am a speculator.'

'But surely not Mademoiselle Danglars? Do you want Albert to cut poor Andrea's throat?'

'Albert?' said Danglars with a shrug of the shoulders. 'Oh, he's not worried.'

'But he's engaged to your daughter, I think?'

'The fact is, Monsieur Morcerf and I have spoken a few times about this marriage, but Madame de Morcerf and Albert . . .'

'You're not telling me he isn't a good match?'

'Just a moment! I think Mademoiselle Danglars is worth Monsieur de Morcerf.'

'Mademoiselle Danglars' dowry will certainly be fine, I don't doubt, especially if the telegraph doesn't get up to its tricks again.'

'It's not just the dowry. But tell me, now we mention it . . .'

'What?'

'Why didn't you invite Morcerf and his family to your dinner?'

'I did so, but he said he was going to Dieppe with Madame de Morcerf, who was advised to take some sea air.'

'My word, yes,' said Danglars with a laugh. 'It must be good for her.'

'Why?'

'Because it is the air she breathed when she was young.'

Monte Cristo let the allusion pass without comment. 'But, when all's said and done,' he continued, 'while Albert may not be as rich as Mademoiselle Danglars, you cannot deny that he bears a fine name.'

'Yes, but I like mine too,' said Danglars.

'Agreed, your name is a popular one, and it ennobled the title with which they sought to ennoble it; but you are too intelligent not to realize that, according to certain prejudices which are too deeply ingrained for them to be eradicated, a title five centuries old is better than one of only twenty years.'

'And that,' said Danglars, with an attempt at a sardonic smile, 'is why I should prefer Monsieur Andrea Cavalcanti to Monsieur Albert de Morcerf.'

'Yet I imagine that the Morcerfs do not cede to the Cavalcantis?'

'The Morcerfs! Tell me, my dear Count, you are a noble man, aren't you?'

'I think so.'

'And well versed in heraldry?'

'A little.'

'Well, consider the paint on my coat of arms: it's drier than that on Morcerf's.'

'How can that be?'

'Because, even though I am not a baron by birth, I am at least called Danglars.'

'So?'

'While he is not called Morcerf.'

'What! He is not called Morcerf?'

'Not in the slightest.'

'Come now!'

'I was made a baron by someone, so that is what I am; he made himself a count, so that is what he is not.'

'Impossible.'

'Listen, my dear Count,' Danglars went on. 'Monsieur de

Morcerf has been my friend, or rather my acquaintance, for thirty years. You know that I don't attach much importance to my coat of arms, since I have not forgotten where I came from.'

'That is evidence either of great humility or of great pride,' said Monte Cristo.

'Well, when I was a clerk, Morcerf was a mere fisherman.'

'What was his name then?'

'Fernand.'

'Just "Fernand"?'

'Fernand Mondego.'

'Are you sure?'

'Am I! I ought to know him. He sold me enough fish.'

'So why are you giving him your daughter?'

'Because Fernand and Danglars are two upstarts, both ennobled, both enriched and neither better than the other; except for some things that have been said about him and never about me.'

'What things?'

'Nothing.'

'Oh, I understand. What you have just said has refreshed my memory about the name Fernand Mondego. I heard it in Greece.'

'About the affair of Ali Pasha?'

'Precisely.'

'That's the mystery,' said Danglars. 'I confess, I'd give a lot to find out about it.'

'It wouldn't be hard if you really want to.'

'How could it be done?'

'I suppose you have a correspondent in Greece?'

'Of course.'

'In Janina?'

'I have connections everywhere . . .'

'Well, then. Write to your man in Janina and ask him what part was played in the catastrophe of Ali Tebelin by a Frenchman named Fernand.'

'That's it!' Danglars exclaimed, leaping to his feet. 'I'll write this very day.'

'Do that.'

'I shall.'

'And if you uncover some scandal . . .'

'I'll let you know.'

'I should be glad.'

Danglars rushed out of the apartments and, in one bound, was in his carriage.

LXVII

THE CROWN PROSECUTOR'S OFFICE

Let us leave the banker's horses trotting smartly home with him and follow Mme Danglars on her morning excursion. We said that at half-past twelve she had called for her carriage and gone out.

She set off towards the Faubourg Saint-Germain, went down the Rue Mazarine and called for the driver to halt at the Passage du Pont-Neuf. Here she got down and crossed the street. She was very simply dressed, appropriately for a woman of taste at this time of day. At the Rue Guénégaud, she got into a cab and asked to be driven to the Rue du Harlay.

No sooner was she inside the cab than she took a thick black veil out of her pocket and pinned it on her straw hat. Then she put the hat back on her head and was pleased to see, looking in her little pocket-mirror, that only her white skin and the shining pupils of her eyes were visible.

The cab drove across the Pont Neuf and through the Place Dauphine into the courtyard at Rue du Harlay. Mme Danglars paid the driver as he opened the door and swept towards the stairway, which she lightly mounted, soon reaching the Salle des Pas-Perdus. In the morning there is lots of business and still more busy people in the Palais de Justice. Busy people do not bother much with women, so Mme Danglars crossed the Salle des Pas-Perdus without attracting any more notice than ten other women waiting to see their lawyers.

There was a crowd in M. de Villefort's antechamber, but Mme Danglars did not even have to mention his name. As soon as she appeared, an usher got up, came across to her and asked whether she were not the person who had an appointment with the crown prosecutor. When she replied that she was, he led her along a private corridor into M. de Villefort's study.

The magistrate was sitting in his armchair, writing, with his back towards the door. He heard it open and the usher say: 'This way,

Madame!', then the door close, all without moving; but as soon as he heard the usher's footsteps going away along the corridor, he leapt up, went to draw the curtains, lock the doors and inspect every corner of the study. Only when his mind was at rest and he was certain of not being seen or heard, did he say: 'Madame, thank you for your punctuality,' and he offered Mme Danglars a seat, which she accepted, because her heart was beating so hard that she felt as though she was suffocating.

The crown prosecutor also sat down and turned his chair around to face Mme Danglars. 'Madame,' he said, 'it is a long time since I had the pleasure of speaking to you alone, and I deeply regret that we should be meeting to discuss something so disagreeable.'

'Despite that, Monsieur, you see that I have come as soon as you asked, even though the topic must be still more disagreeable for me than for you.'

Villefort gave a bitter smile and said, in response more to his own thoughts than to Mme Danglars' words: 'So it is true that every one of our actions leaves some trace on our past, either dark or bright. So it is true that every step we take is more like a reptile's progress across the sand, leaving a track behind it. And often, alas, the track is the mark of our tears!'

'Monsieur,' said Mme Danglars, 'you must understand my feelings. I beg you to spare me as much as possible. This room, through which so many guilty men and women have passed, trembling and ashamed ... this chair on which I, in my turn, sit trembling and ashamed ... It takes all the strength of my reason to persuade me that I am not a guilty woman and you a threatening judge.'

Villefort shook his head and sighed: 'I tell myself that my place is not on the judge's bench, but in the dock with the accused.'

'You?' Mme Danglars said in astonishment.

'Yes, I.'

'I think that, so far as you are concerned, Monsieur,' said Mme Danglars, her lovely eyes briefly lighting up, 'you are overscrupulous and exaggerating the situation. The tracks that you mentioned have been made by all hot-blooded youths. Beneath passion and beyond pleasure, there is always a trace of remorse; and that is why the Gospel, that everlasting succour to the unfortunate, has given us poor women as a prop the excellent parable of the sinner and the woman taken in adultery. So, when I consider the follies of my youth, I sometimes think that God will forgive them, because some compensation for them (though not an excuse) is to be found in my sufferings. But what do you have to fear from all this, you men whom everyone excuses and who are elevated by scandal?'

'Madame,' Villefort replied, 'you know me. I am not a hypocrite – or, at least, I never dissemble without some purpose. My brow may be forbidding, but that is because it is darkened by many misfortunes; my heart may be stone, but it needs must be to withstand the blows that have assailed it. I was not like this in my youth, I was not like this at the betrothal feast in Marseille when we all sat at a table in the Rue du Cours. Since then, much has changed, both around me and within me. My life has been worn away in the pursuit of difficult things and in breaking down those who, voluntarily or otherwise, of their own free will or as a result of chance, stood in my way and raised such obstacles. It is rare to feel an ardent desire for something and not find that it is ardently defended by those from whom one would like to take it or seize it. So, most ill deeds present themselves to their perpetrators in the specious guise of necessity; then, when the deed has been committed – in a moment of passion, fear or delirium – one realizes that it might have been avoided. Blind as you were, you did not see the correct course of action, which now appears plainly and simply before you. You think: how can I have done that, instead of this? You ladies, on the other hand, are rarely tormented by remorse, because the decision rarely comes from you. Your misfortunes are almost always imposed on you and your errors almost always another's crime.'

'In any event, Monsieur, you must agree,' Mme Danglars replied, 'if I did make a mistake, I was severely punished for it yesterday.'

'Poor woman!' said Villefort, pressing her hand. 'Too severely, since your strength twice nearly gave way; and yet . . .'

'Well?'

'Well, I must tell you . . . Be brave, Madame, we are not yet at an end.'

'My God!' Mme Danglars exclaimed in terror. 'What is there still to come?'

'You can only see the past, and it is grim, I confess. But imagine a still grimmer future, a future that is sure to be frightful . . . and perhaps stained with blood!'

The baroness knew Villefort's usual restraint and was so horrified by this lurid outburst that she opened her mouth to scream, but the cry was stifled in her throat.

'How has this terrible past been resurrected?' Villefort asked. 'How has it arisen from its sleep in the depths of the tomb and the depths of our hearts, like a ghost draining the blood from our cheeks and making the pulse beat in our temples?'

'Alas!' said Hermine. 'By chance, no doubt.'

'Chance!' said Villefort. 'No, no, Madame, there is no chance.'

'Of course there is. Was it not chance, admittedly a fatal one, but chance none the less that was behind all this? Was it not chance that the Count of Monte Cristo bought that house? That he had the earth dug? And, finally, that the unhappy child was dug up from under the trees? That poor innocent creature, flesh of my flesh, to whom I never gave a kiss, but only tears. Oh, my heart fluttered when I heard the count speak of those cherished remains that were found among the flowers.'

'And yet it is not so, Madame. This is the frightful thing that I must tell you,' Villefort replied, in a stifled voice. 'There were no remains discovered among the flowers, no child unearthed. No! You should not be weeping, you should not moan! You should be trembling with fear!'

'What can you mean?' Mme Danglars exclaimed with a shudder.

'I mean that Monsieur Monte Cristo, had he dug under those trees, would not have found either a child's skeleton or the iron of a box, because neither was there to be found.'

'Neither was there!' Mme Danglars repeated, looking at the prosecutor with eyes of sheer terror, their pupils horribly dilated. Then, like someone trying, in the sound of the words or the voice, to grasp an idea that is about to elude them, she repeated: 'Neither was there!'

'No,' said Villefort, burying his face in his hands. 'A hundred times no!'

'But was it not there that you put the poor child, Monsieur? Why deceive me? Tell me, why should you want to do such a thing?'

'It was there. But listen to me, Madame; hear me out and you will sympathize with me, I who have borne for twenty years the burden of sorrow that I am about to tell you, without shuffling the smallest part of it off on to you.'

'My God! You terrify me! No matter, I am listening.'

'You know the events of that unhappy night when you lay gasping on your bed in that room with the red damask, while I waited for you to be delivered, almost as exhausted as you. The child came and was handed to me, motionless, not breathing or crying. We thought it was dead.'

Mme Danglars made a sudden movement, as though to leap from the chair, but Villefort stopped her, clasping his hands as though begging her to listen.

'We thought he was dead,' he repeated. 'I put him in a box that would serve as a coffin and went down to the garden, where I dug a grave and hastily buried it. I had just finished covering it with earth when the Corsican struck me. I saw a shape rise up and the flash of a blade. I felt a stab of pain and tried to cry out, but an icy shudder ran through my body and stifled the cry in my throat. I fell, dying; I thought I was dead. I shall never forget your sublime courage when, regaining my senses, I dragged myself with one final effort to the foot of the staircase where you, though you were yourself on the brink of death, came over to me. We had to hush up this awful catastrophe. You bravely returned home, supported by your nurse, while I used a duel as an excuse for my wound. Astonishingly, we both managed to keep the secret. I was carried to Versailles and, for three months, fought against death. Finally, when I seemed to be over the worst, I was prescribed the sun and air of the south. Four men carried me from Paris to Chalon, at a rate of six leagues a day. Madame de Villefort followed the stretcher in her carriage. In Chalon, I was put on the Saône, then on the Rhône and, carried by the current, I went down to Arles, where I once more took to my stretcher and continued to Marseille. My convalescence lasted six months. I heard nothing of you and did not dare ask after you. When I returned to Paris, I learned that Monsieur de Nargonne had died and you had married Monsieur Danglars.

'What had been constantly on my mind from the moment I regained consciousness? Always the same thing: the child's body which, every night in my dreams, rose up out of the earth and hovered over the grave, threatening me with its look and gesture. So, no sooner had I returned to Paris than I asked about the house. It had not been inhabited since we left, but it had just been leased for nine years. I went to find the tenant and pretended that I was most anxious that this house, which belonged to my wife's parents, should not fall into the hands of strangers. I offered them compensation in exchange for the lease. They asked for six thousand francs; I would have given ten thousand or twenty thousand. I had the money on me and, there and then, got them to sign the papers. As soon as the lease was in my hands, I set off at a gallop for Auteuil. Since I had last been there, no one had entered the house.

'It was five o'clock in the afternoon. I went up to the red room and waited for nightfall. While I was waiting, everything that I had thought during the past agonizing year rose up in my mind, more threatening than ever.

'The Corsican who had declared a vendetta against me, who had followed me from Nîmes to Paris, who had hidden in the garden and struck me: this man had seen me dig the grave and bury the child. He might discover who you were, perhaps he knew it already. Would he not one day make you pay for his silence in this terrible business? Would that not be a sweet revenge for him, when he learned that I had not died from my wound? So it was urgent for me, first and foremost, to get rid of all traces of the past and destroy any material evidence. The reality was clearly enough present in my mind.

'This is why I had bought the lease, why I had come here, why I was waiting.

'Night fell and I waited until it was quite dark. I had no light in the room, and gusts of wind shook the doors, behind which I constantly thought I could see someone hiding. From time to time I shuddered, thinking that I could hear your groans behind me from the bed, and I dared not turn around to look. My heart beat so fast in the silence that I thought my wound would re-open. Then, finally, I heard all the noises of the country cease, one by one. I realized that I had nothing more to fear, that I could neither be seen nor heard, and I decided to go downstairs.

'Believe me, Hermine, I consider myself as brave as the next man, but when I went to the chain around my neck and took out the little key to the staircase – which was so dear to both of us and which you had attached to a gold ring – when I opened the door and saw a pale moon through the windows casting a long streak of light across the spiralling steps, I had to lean against the wall and I almost cried out. I thought I was going mad.

'At last I managed to control myself. I went down, step by step. The only thing that I was unable to master was a strange trembling in my knees. I clasped the stair-rail: if I had let it go for a moment, I should have fallen.

'I reached the door at the bottom; beyond it there was a spade leaning against the wall. I had a covered lantern and stopped in the middle of the lawn to light it, then went on.

'It was now the end of November and all the greenery of the garden had vanished. The trees were nothing but skeletons with long, bony arms, and the dead leaves crackled like the gravel under my feet. I was so terrified that as I came close to the bushes I took a pistol out of my pocket and primed it. I still expected to see the Corsican emerging from among the branches.

'With the covered lantern, I lit up the cluster of bushes; there was no one there. I looked around and saw that I was indeed alone. No noise broke the silence of night except the sharp, lugubrious cry of an owl, calling up the ghosts of night.

'I hung the lantern on a forked branch that I had already noticed a year earlier, at the very place where I had stopped to dig the grave. During the summer, the grass had grown thickly on the spot and there had been no one there in the autumn to mow it. However, one place where the grass was thinner attracted my attention. This was clearly where I had dug the ground. I set to work. I had at last reached the moment I had been waiting for for over a year!

'So, how I hoped, how I worked and how I sounded out each tuft of grass, expecting to feel something solid beneath my spade. But, nothing! Yet the hole I made was twice as large as the first. I thought I must have been wrong and had mistaken the spot. I took my bearings, looked at the trees, tried to recognize the details that had struck me. A sharp, cold breeze was whining through the naked branches, yet my brow was covered in sweat. I remembered that the dagger had struck me just as I was stamping on the ground to cover the grave. As I did so, I leant against a laburnum-tree, and behind me was an artificial rock intended to serve as a bench, because, when I fell, my hand had gone from the laburnum to the cold of the stone. On my right was this same laburnum and behind me the rock. I fell in the same way, got up and began to dig again, enlarging the hole. Nothing! Still nothing! The box had vanished.'

'The box had vanished?' Mme Danglars muttered, barely able to speak for horror.

'Don't think that I left it at that,' Villefort went on. 'No. I looked all around. I thought that the assassin might have dug the box up and, thinking it was a treasure, wanted to steal it and had carried it off; then, realizing his mistake, had dug another hole and put it inside. But no: nothing. Then I had the idea that he would not have taken such precautions, but purely and simply thrown the box away somewhere. If that was right, I would have to wait for daylight to look for it, so I went back up to the room and waited.'

'Oh, my God!'

'When daylight came, I went down again. I walked directly across to the shrubbery, hoping to find some sign that I might have missed in the darkness. I had dug the earth over an area of more than twenty square feet and to a depth of more than two feet. A hired labourer would have taken at least a day to do what I had done in an hour. Nothing: there was nothing to be seen.

'Consequently I set about looking for the box, on my earlier assumption that it had been discarded somewhere. It would have to be on the path leading to the way out, but this new search was as fruitless as the first and, with a heavy heart, I returned to the shrubbery, though I no longer had any hope even there.'

'That was enough to drive you mad!' Mme Danglars cried.

'I did hope as much for a time,' said Villefort, 'but I did not have that good fortune. However, gathering my strength and my thoughts, I began to wonder why the man should have taken away a body.'

'But you said it yourself: to have proof.'

'No, Madame, that could no longer be it! A person does not keep a corpse for a year. He shows it to a magistrate and makes a statement. But nothing like that had happened.'

'So? Then what?' Hermine asked, trembling all over.

'Then something more awful, more deadly and more terrifying for us, which is that the child may perhaps have been alive and the murderer saved it.'

Mme Danglars gave a fearful cry and grasped Villefort's hands: 'My child was alive!' she said. 'You buried my child alive! Monsieur, you were not sure that my child was dead, and yet you buried it . . . Ah!' She was now standing in almost a threatening way before the crown prosecutor, grasping his wrists in her delicate hands.

'How can I tell? I am telling you this as I might anything else,' Villefort replied, staring in a manner that suggested this powerful man was nearing the limits of madness and despair.

'My child! Oh, my poor child!' the baroness cried, collapsing back into her chair and stifling her sobs in a handkerchief.

Villefort recovered his senses and realized that the maternal tempest gathering about his head could only be warded off by letting Mme Danglars share his own terror. He got up and went over to the baroness so that he could whisper to her: 'Don't you understand that if this is the case, we are lost. The child is alive, and someone knows he is alive, someone shares our secret. And since Monte Cristo was speaking to us about a child dug up at the spot where that child vanished, then he is the one who shares our secret.'

'Oh, God! Just and vengeful God!' Mme Danglars muttered; to which Villefort replied only with a sort of roar.

'But the child, Monsieur, what about the child?' the mother asked obstinately.

'Believe me, I have looked for him,' Villefort said, wringing his hands. 'How many times have I called him in the long sleepless nights. How many times have I wanted a princely fortune to purchase a million secrets from a million men, so that I might discover mine in theirs. So finally, when day came and I picked up the spade for the hundredth time, I asked myself for the hundredth time what the Corsican could have done with the child. A child is burdensome for a fugitive. Perhaps, seeing that it was still living, he threw it in the river.'

'Impossible!' Mme Danglars exclaimed. 'One may murder a man for revenge, but not drown an infant in cold blood.'

'So perhaps,' Villefort went on, 'he put it in the foundling hospital.'

'Yes, yes! Monsieur, my child is there,' the baroness cried.

'I went to the hospital and learned that that very night, the twentieth of September, a child was placed in the tower, wrapped in half a cloth of fine linen, deliberately torn. This piece of cloth bore half a baron's coronet and the letter "H".'

'That's it, that's it!' Mme Danglars exclaimed. 'All my linen has that mark. Monsieur de Nargonne was a baron and my name is Hermine. Oh, God, thank you! My child did not die!'

'No, he didn't die.'

'And you can tell me this. You tell me this without fearing that I shall die of happiness! Where is he? Where is my child?'

Villefort shrugged his shoulders and said: 'How do I know? Do you think that, if I did, I would lead you to the answer inch by inch, like a dramatist or a novelist? No, alas, I can't tell you. About six months before, a woman had come to claim that child with the other half of the cloth. She gave all the guarantees demanded by law, and they handed the child over to her.'

'But you should have enquired after this woman, you should have found her.'

'What do you think I did, Madame? I pretended it was for a criminal investigation and put all the finest sleuths and cleverest bloodhounds in the police force to look for her. She was followed as far as Chalon, then they lost trace of her.'

'Lost trace?'

'Yes, lost; lost for ever.'

Mme Danglars had heaved a sigh, let fall a tear or given a cry for every detail of this story. 'Is that all?' she asked. 'Did you stop there?'

'Oh, no,' said Villefort. 'I have never stopped looking, enquiring, investigating, except that, for the past two or three years, I have relaxed my efforts slightly. From today, I shall resume the hunt with more persistence and determination than ever and I shall succeed, because it is no longer my conscience that drives me, it is fear.'

'But it seems to me that the Count of Monte Cristo can know nothing, or he would not seek our company in the way he does.'

'The wickedness of men runs very deep,' said Villefort, 'since it is deeper than the kindness of God. Did you notice the man's eyes while he was talking to us?'

'No.'

'But have you ever looked closely at him?'

'Of course. He is odd, that's all. I did, however, notice one thing which is that, throughout the whole of that exquisite meal which he gave us, he himself touched nothing from any dish.'

'Yes, I too noticed that. If I had known what I know now, I should not have eaten anything myself. I should have thought he wanted to poison us.'

'But you would have been wrong, as you can see.'

'Certainly, but that man, believe me, has some other plans. This is why I wanted to see you, why I asked to speak to you and why I wanted to warn you against everyone, but especially against him. Tell me,' he said, staring harder at the baroness than ever, 'have you mentioned our affair to anyone?'

'Never, not a soul.'

'You will understand,' Villefort said affectionately, 'if I repeat: no one – forgive me for insisting – no one in the world?'

'Yes, I do fully understand,' the baroness said, blushing. 'Never, I swear.'

'You don't write down every evening what has happened during the day: you don't keep a diary?'

'No. Alas, my life is spent in frivolous trifles, which I even forget myself.'

'And, as far as you know, you don't talk in your sleep?'

'I sleep like a baby. Don't you remember?' The blood rushed to her face and out of Villefort's. 'That's true,' he said in a barely audible voice.

'Well, then?' asked the baroness.

'Well, then, I know what has to be done. Within a week, I shall know what this Monte Cristo is, where he comes from, where he is going and why he tells us about children dug up from his garden.'

Villefort spoke these words in a tone of voice that would have made the count shudder if he could have heard them. Then he shook the hand which the baroness reluctantly gave him and respectfully showed her to the door. Mme Danglars hailed another cab, which took her back to the passage, at the far end of which she found her own carriage and her coachman who had been sleeping peacefully on his seat while waiting for her return.

LXVIII

A SUMMER BALL

The same day, at about the time when Mme Danglars was engaged as we have seen in the study of the crown prosecutor, a travelling coach drove into the Rue du Helder, through the gate of No. 27 and into the courtyard, where it stopped. After a moment the door opened and Mme de Morcerf stepped down, leaning on her son's arm.

Hardly had Albert brought his mother home than he called for a bath and then his horses. After allowing his valet to attend to him, he had himself driven to the Champs-Elysées, to the Count of Monte Cristo's.

The count greeted him with his usual smile. It was a strange thing: one never appeared to take a step forward in the heart or mind of this man. Those who wished, so to speak, to force their way into intimacy with him found the path blocked.

Morcerf was running over to him with open arms, but, on seeing him, despite the count's friendly smile, he let his arms fall and dared at most to offer his hand. The count touched it, as he always did, but without shaking it.

'Well, my dear Count, here I am,' Morcerf said.

'Welcome.'

'I have just got back.'

'From Dieppe?'

'From Le Tréport.'

'Oh, yes. That's right.'

'And you are the first person I have visited.'

'That's charming of you,' said Monte Cristo, as casually as he might have said anything.

'Well, then. What news?'

'News! You are asking me, a foreigner, for news!'

'When I ask for news, I mean: have you done anything for me?'

'Did you give me some job to do?' the count said, with a pretence of concern.

'Come now,' said Albert. 'Don't pretend not to care. They say that there are sympathetic warnings that cross distances: well, in Le Tréport, I had an electric shock. Even if you didn't do anything on my behalf, you did think of me.'

'That's possible,' Monte Cristo said. 'I did, indeed, think of you. But the magnetic current which I served to conduct was, I have to admit, generated independently of my will.'

'Really? Elucidate, I beg you.'

'Easy. Monsieur Danglars had dinner with me.'

'I know, because the reason my mother and I left Paris was to avoid him.'

'And he dined with Monsieur Andrea Cavalcanti.'

'Your Italian prince?'

'Let's not exaggerate. Monsieur Andrea only awards himself the title of viscount.'

'Awards himself?'

'As you say.'

'So he isn't one?'

'How do I know? He awards himself, I award him, they award him: isn't that all the same as if he had it?'

'Come now, you are behaving strangely! So then?'

'Then, what?'

'Monsieur Danglars dined here?'

'Yes.'

'With your Viscount Andrea Cavalcanti?'

'With Viscount Andrea Cavalcanti, his father the marquis, Madame Danglars, Monsieur and Madame de Villefort, and some delightful people: Monsieur Debray, Maxmilien Morrel . . . and who else? Wait . . . Oh, yes, Monsieur de Château-Renaud.'

'Was my name mentioned?'

'Not once.'

'Too bad.'

'Why? I would have thought that, in forgetting you, they did only what you wanted.'

'My dear Count, if they didn't mention me, that means that they must have thought about me a lot, so I'm at my wits' end.'

'What does it matter, since Mademoiselle Danglars was not here among those who were thinking about you? True, she might have thought about you at home.'

'Oh, no. I'm quite sure of that. Or if she did, it was in the same way that I think of her.'

'How charming, this meeting of minds. So you hate one another?'

'Please don't misunderstand me,' said Morcerf. 'If Mademoiselle Danglars were the sort of woman to sympathize with the torments I am not enduring on her behalf and to recompense me outside the provisions of the marriage contract drawn up between our two families, I should be delighted with the arrangement. In short, I think Mademoiselle Danglars would make a charming mistress, but as a wife, good God!'

'So that's how you envisage your future?' Monte Cristo said with a laugh.

'Yes. When all's said and done, it is. Slightly brutal, I realize, but accurate. But, since this dream can never come true and since, for me to reach a particular goal, Mademoiselle Danglars must become my wife – that is to say, live with me, think beside me, sing near me, write verses and make music a few yards away from me, and all this for the rest of my life – then I am appalled at the prospect. You can leave a mistress, Count, but a wife ... Huh! That's a different matter entirely: a wife is for eternity, whether close by or at a distance. The idea of having Mademoiselle Danglars for ever is terrifying – even at a distance.'

'You're fussy, Viscount.'

'Yes, because I dream of something impossible.'

'Which is?'

'Finding a wife for myself like the one my father found.'

The colour drained from Monte Cristo's cheeks and he watched Albert, while toying with some magnificent pistols, rapidly cocking them, then releasing the springs.

'So, your father has been a happy man,' he said.

'You know how I feel about my mother, Count: she is an angel, still beautiful, still witty, finer than ever. I have just come back from Le Tréport. Now, for any other son, just imagine: travelling with his mother would be an act of kindness or an unavoidable burden. Yet I have just spent four days with mine in Le Tréport and I can tell you they were more satisfying, more relaxing and more poetical than if I had been with Queen Mab or Titania.'[1]

'Anyone would despair of rivalling such perfection. You will make anyone who hears you wish seriously to remain a bachelor.'

'Which is precisely why, knowing that there is one accomplished woman in the world, I'm not anxious to marry Mademoiselle Danglars. Have you noticed how our egoism paints everything that belongs to us in brilliant hues? The diamond that sparkled in the windows of Marlé or Fossin becomes much lovelier once it is our diamond; but if circumstances force you to acknowledge that there is still finer one and you are condemned for ever to wear this diamond which is inferior to the other, do you understand what torture that is?'

'Snob!' the count muttered.

'And that's why I shall be jumping for joy on the day when Mademoiselle Eugénie notices that I am only a puny little atom, possessing hardly as many hundreds of thousands of francs as she has millions.'

Monte Cristo smiled.

'I did have another idea,' Albert went on. 'Franz likes odd things, so I tried to make him fall in love with Mademoiselle Danglars, in spite of himself. I wrote him four letters in the most enticing of styles, but he always gave me the same answer: "I may be eccentric, it's true, but my eccentricity does not extend to breaking my word once I have given it."'

'Now, there's what I call true friendship: giving another person as wife the woman one only wants for oneself as a mistress.'

Albert smiled. 'Incidentally,' he said, 'dear Franz is on his way home; but that doesn't bother you. You don't like him, do you?'

'What! My dear Viscount, whatever told you that I don't like Monsieur Franz? I like everybody.'

'I am included in everybody. Thank you.'

'Oh, don't misunderstand me,' said Monte Cristo. 'I like everybody in the way that God ordered us to love our neighbours, that is, in Christian charity. I only bestow true hatred on certain people. But to get back to Franz d'Epinay: he is coming home, you say?'

'Yes, on the instructions of Monsieur de Villefort, who is as mad keen to marry off Mademoiselle Valentine, apparently, as Monsieur Danglars is to marry off Mademoiselle Eugénie. It really does appear that being the father of grown-up girls is one of the most exhausting states. As far as I can see, their temperature soars and their pulses beat ninety to the minute until they have disposed of them.'

'But Monsieur d'Epinay is not like you. He is reconciled to his fate.'

'More than that, he takes it seriously. He puts on white ties and is already talking about his family. And he holds the Villeforts in high esteem.'

'Deservedly, no doubt?'

'I think so. Monsieur de Villefort has always been considered a strict but just man.'

'At last,' said Monte Cristo. 'Here is someone at least whom you do not treat like poor Monsieur Danglars.'

'Perhaps that's because I'm not obliged to marry his daughter,' Albert said, laughing.

'Really, my dear sir,' said Monte Cristo, 'you are disgustingly smug.'

'I? Smug?'

'Yes, you. Have a cigar.'

'Thank you. So why am I smug?'

'Because here you are shielding yourself and struggling not to marry Mademoiselle Danglars. Why not just let things take their course, and perhaps you won't be the first to take back your word.'

'What?' Albert said, gawping.

'Huh, yes, Monsieur le Vicomte! What do you think of that? They won't tie you down by force. But, seriously,' Monte Cristo said, in a different tone of voice, 'do you want to break it off?'

'I'd give a hundred thousand francs if I could.'

'Well, you'll be happy to know that Monsieur Danglars is prepared to give twice that amount to achieve the same end.'

'What happiness! Can it be true?' Albert exclaimed, but was unable, in spite of that, to prevent a faint cloud from passing across his brow. 'My dear Count, does Monsieur Danglars have some reason for that?'

'How typical that is, you proud and self-absorbed creature! This is indeed the man who enjoys taking an axe to the self-esteem of others, but cries out when a needle touches his own.'

'No, no. I just think that Monsieur Danglars . . .'

'Should be delighted to have you as a son-in-law; isn't that it? Well, now, Monsieur Danglars is a man of poor taste, we all know, and he is still more delighted by someone else . . .'

'Who is that?'

'I don't know. Look carefully, catch every hint as it goes past and profit by what you learn.'

'Good! I understand. Listen, my mother . . . No, not my mother, I'm wrong. My father had the idea of giving a ball.'

'A ball at this time of year?'

'Summer balls are in fashion.'

'Even if they weren't, the countess would only have to wish it and they would become so.'

'Not bad . . . You know, these are thoroughbred events: people who stay in Paris in July are real Parisians. Would you be good enough to invite Monsieur Cavalcanti?'

'When will this ball take place?'

'On Saturday.'

'The elder Cavalcanti will have left by then.'

'But not the son, so perhaps you could bring the younger Cavalcanti?'

'Listen, Viscount, I don't know him . . .'

'You don't know him?'

'No. I met him for the first time three or four days ago, and I can't answer for him at all.'

'But you invite him here!'

'That's different. He was recommended to me by a good abbé, who might have been mistaken himself. Invite him indirectly, certainly, but don't ask me to introduce him to you. If he was later to marry Mademoiselle Danglars, you would accuse me of manipulation and you would have a bone to pick with me. In any case, I'm not sure that I'll go myself.'

'Go where?'

'To your ball.'

'Why on earth not?'

'First of all, you haven't invited me yet.'

'I came especially to deliver the invitation.'

'That's too kind. But suppose I have another engagement.'

'I have only to tell you one thing, and I think you will be good enough to forgo any prior engagement.'

'What is that?'

'My mother begs you to come.'

'The Comtesse de Morcerf?' Monte Cristo said with a shudder.

'I warn you, Count, Madame de Morcerf speaks to me quite freely; and if you did not feel those sympathetic fibres I mentioned just now crackling inside you, that means that you are entirely devoid of them, because you were our only subject of conversation in the past four days.'

'I was? I am overwhelmed.'

'Listen, this is a privilege of your profession: when one is a living enigma . . .'

'Ah, so I'm also an enigma for your mother? Quite honestly, I should have thought her too sensible to indulge in such flights of fancy.'

'An enigma, my dear Count, an enigma for everyone, my mother as well as the rest. As long as the mystery has been recognized but not solved, you will remain an enigma, don't worry. My mother is only puzzled by the fact that you seem so young. I think, underneath, that whereas Countess G— thinks you are Lord Ruthwen, my mother takes you for Cagliostro or the Comte de Saint-Germain. The first time you meet Madame de Morcerf, you must confirm her in that impression. It shouldn't be difficult: you have the wit of one and the philosopher's stone of the other.'

'Thank you for warning me,' the count said, smiling. 'I shall try to live up to all expectations.'

'So you will come on Saturday?'

'Since Madame de Morcerf requests my company.'

'You are charming.'

'And Monsieur Danglars?'

'Oh, he's already had a triple invitation. My father looked after that. We shall also try to have The Great Daguesseau, Monsieur de Villefort, but I don't expect we shall succeed.'

'One must never give up hope, the proverb says.'

'Do you dance, my dear Count?'

'Do I dance?'

'Yes, you. Why not?'

'Well, I suppose, while one is still under forty. But no, I don't dance. However, I like to watch others. Does Madame de Morcerf dance?'

'No, never. You can talk. She so much wants to talk to you.'

'Really?'

'I give you my word. And I must tell you, you are the first man about whom my mother has shown such curiosity.'

Albert took his hat and got up. The count accompanied him to the door. Stopping at the top of the steps, he said: 'I was wrong about one thing.'

'What was that?'

'It was indiscreet of me to tell you about Monsieur Danglars.'

'On the contrary, please keep telling me, talk about him as much as you like, as long as the message remains the same.'

'Well, you make me feel better about it. So when is Monsieur d'Epinay arriving back?'

'In five or six days at the latest.'

'And when is he getting married?'

'As soon as Monsieur and Madame de Saint-Méran are here.'

'When he gets to Paris, bring him to see me. Even though you say that I don't like him, I assure you I shall be happy to see him.'

'Very well, m'lud. Your orders shall be carried out.'

'Au revoir!'

'Until Saturday, at least – it's agreed?'

'Of course! I've given my word.' The count watched and waved. Then, when Albert had got into his phaeton, he turned around and saw Bertuccio behind him. 'Well?' he asked.

'She went to the law courts,' the steward answered.

'Did she stay long?'

'An hour and a half.'

'Then returned home?'

'Without stopping.'

'Very good,' said the count. 'And now, my dear Monsieur Bertuccio, if I have a piece of advice for you, it is to go to Normandy and see if you can't find the little estate I mentioned.'

Bertuccio bowed and, the count's command being entirely coincidental with his own wishes, left that very evening.

LXIX

INFORMATION

M. de Villefort kept his word to Mme Danglars (and most of all to himself) by trying to find out how the Count of Monte Cristo could have learnt the story of the house in Auteuil. That same day he wrote to a certain M. de Boville who, after once being an inspector of prisons, had been transferred at a higher rank to the detective branch of the police, enquiring whether he could provide the necessary information. Boville asked for two days to hunt down the best sources. When the two days were up, M. de Villefort received the following note:

The person described as the Count of Monte Cristo is known particularly to Lord Wilmore, a rich foreigner and an occasional visitor to Paris, who is here at the moment; and also to Abbé Busoni, a Sicilian priest who is highly reputed in the East, where he accomplished many good works.

M. de Villefort replied, ordering that the most precise information should be obtained at once on these two persons. By the next evening, his orders had been carried out and he received the following news:

The abbé was only in Paris for one month. He lived behind the church of Saint-Sulpice in a little house consisting of a single storey above the ground floor, the entire accommodation, of which he was the sole tenant, being made up of four rooms altogether, two up and two down. The two downstairs rooms consisted of a dining-room with a table, two chairs and a walnut sideboard; and a drawing-room, painted white, with no ornaments, no carpet and no clock. It could be seen that, for himself, the abbé was content with the bare necessities.

Admittedly, he preferred to live in the first-floor living-room, which was entirely furnished with theological texts and parchments in which, according to his valet, he was accustomed to bury himself for months on end, making this less a living-room than a library.

This valet examined visitors through a kind of judas window. If their faces were unknown or unpleasing to him, he would tell them that M. l'Abbé was not in Paris. Most were satisfied with this reply, knowing that the abbé often travelled and sometimes spent long periods abroad. In any case, whether or not he was at home, whether he was in Paris or in Cairo, the abbé always gave alms, so the little window in his door served as a passage for the gifts that the valet constantly distributed in his master's name.

The other room, close to the library, was a bedroom. The furnishings here were entirely made up of a bed with no curtains, four armchairs and a sofa covered in yellow Utrecht velvet, together with a prie-dieu.

As for Lord Wilmore, he lived in the Rue Fontaine-Saint-Georges. He was one of those touring Englishmen who spend all their inheritance on travel. He rented the apartment, furnished, where he lived, but spent only two or three hours a day there and slept there rarely. One of his eccentricities was that he refused to speak French, even though it was reported that he could write the language very correctly.

The day after the crown prosecutor received this precious information, a man, getting down from his carriage at the corner of the Rue Férou, went and knocked on a door painted in olive green and asked for Abbé Busoni.

'Monsieur l'Abbé went out early this morning,' said the valet.

'I cannot be satisfied by that answer,' the visitor said. 'For I come on behalf of a person to whom everyone is at home. But kindly give Abbé Busoni . . .'

'I already told you: he is not here,' the valet repeated.

'Then when he gets back, give him this card and this sealed paper. Will the abbé be at home this evening at eight?'

'Undoubtedly, Monsieur, unless he is working, in which case it is as if he was out.'

'So I shall come back this evening at the time we mentioned,' the visitor said, then went away.

That evening, at the appointed hour, the same man returned in the same carriage, which this time, instead of stopping on the corner of the Rue Férou, drew up in front of the green door. He knocked, it was opened and he went in. From the valet's obsequious behaviour, he realized that his letter had had the desired effect.

'Is Monsieur l'Abbé at home?' he asked.

'Yes, he is working in his library, but he is expecting you, sir,' the servant replied.

The stranger climbed a fairly rough staircase. Sitting behind a table, the whole surface of which was flooded in the light concentrated on it by a huge lampshade, while the rest of the apartment was in shadow, he saw the abbé, in ecclesiastical dress, his head hooded in one of those hoods with which medieval scholars used to cover their skulls.

'Do I have the honour of speaking to Monsieur Busoni?' the visitor asked.

'Yes, Monsieur,' the abbé replied. 'And you are the person sent to me by Monsieur de Boville, former inspector of prisons, on behalf of the prefect of police?'

'Precisely, Monsieur.'

'One of those agents appointed to look after security in Paris?'

'Yes, Monsieur,' the stranger replied, with momentary hesitation and, above all, a blush.

The abbé adjusted the large glasses that covered not only his eyes but also his temples; and, sitting down again, he motioned to the visitor to do likewise.

'I am listening,' he said, in a marked Italian accent.

'The mission I have to accomplish, Monsieur,' the visitor resumed, weighing each word as though finding it difficult to get it out, 'is a confidential mission, both for the person carrying it out and for the one who will assist him in his enquiries.'

The abbé bowed his head.

'Yes,' the stranger continued. 'Your probity, Monsieur l'Abbé, is so well known to the prefect of police that, as a magistrate, he would like to know something touching that same public safety in the name of which I have been sent to you. Consequently, Monsieur l'Abbé, we hope that neither ties of friendship nor any other human considerations will induce you to hide the truth from the eyes of the law.'

'Monsieur, as long as whatever you wish to know does not affect any scruple of my conscience. I am a priest and the secrets of the confessional, for example, must remain between me and God's justice, not between me and human justice.'

'Oh, Monsieur l'Abbé, you may be quite reassured on that,' said the stranger. 'In any case, we shall ensure that your conscience is protected.'

At this, the abbé leant on his side of the lampshade, raising it on the opposite side, so that it lit fully the face of the stranger, while leaving his own still in shadow. 'I beg your pardon, father,' the other man said. 'This light is terribly tiring for my eyes.'

The abbé lowered the green shade and said: 'Now, Monsieur, I am listening. Speak.'

'I am coming to the point. Do you know the Count of Monte Cristo?'

'I suppose you are speaking of Monsieur Zaccone?'

'Zaccone! So he is not called Monte Cristo!'

'Monte Cristo is the name of an island, or rather of a rock, not of a family.'

'Very well. Let's not argue about words. So, since Monsieur de Monte Cristo and Monsieur Zaccone are the same man . . .'

'Absolutely the same.'

'. . . then let us talk about Monsieur Zaccone.'

'Agreed.'

'I asked if you knew him?'

'Very well.'

'Who is he?'

'The son of a rich shipowner in Malta.'

'Yes, I know that that's what they say. But, as you must realize, the police cannot be satisfied with mere hearsay.'

'And yet,' the abbé said, with a very pleasant smile, 'when hearsay is the truth, everyone must be satisfied with it, the police as well as the rest.'

'But are you sure of what you are saying?'

'What! Am I sure?'

'Please understand me, Monsieur. I do not in any way question your good faith. I am merely asking if you are sure.'

'Come now, I knew Monsieur Zaccone, his father.'

'Ah!'

'And while I was still a child I played a dozen times with his son in their shipyards.'

'But this title: count?'

'That can be bought, you know.'

'In Italy?'

'Everywhere.'

'But this wealth which, still according to rumour, is immense . . .'

'Ah, that!' said the abbé. 'Immense is the word.'

'You know him. How much do you think he owns?'

'Oh, an income of at least a hundred and fifty to two hundred thousand *livres*.'

'That's reasonable,' the visitor said. 'There was talk of three or four million.'

'An income of two hundred thousand *livres*, Monsieur, adds up to a capital of just four million.'

'But there was talk of an income of three or four million!'

'Oh, it's impossible to believe that.'

'Do you know his island of Monte Cristo?'

'Of course. Anyone who has come from Palermo, Naples or Rome to France by sea knows it, since he will have sailed past it and seen it as he went.'

'They say it's an enchanted spot.'

'It's a rock.'

'Why should the count buy a rock?'

'Precisely in order to be a count. In Italy, to be a count, you still need a county.'

'You have doubtless heard of Monsieur Zaccone's youthful adventures?'

'The father's?'

'No, the son's.'

'Ah, this is where I am less certain, because I lost touch with my young friend.'

'Did he fight in the war?'

'I think he served in it.'

'In what force?'

'In the navy.'

'Aren't you his confessor?'

'No, Monsieur. I think he is a Lutheran.'

'How is that? A Lutheran?'

'I say, I think so. I couldn't swear to it. In any case, I thought there was freedom of worship now in France.'

'Indeed there is, and we are not concerned with his beliefs at this moment, but with his actions. In the name of the prefect of police, I request you to tell me whatever you know.'

'He is reputed to be a very charitable man. Our Holy Father the Pope made him a Knight of Christ, a favour that he hardly ever grants except to princes, for his outstanding services to Christians in the East. He has five or six ribbons acquired for services to princes or states.'

'Does he wear them?'

'No, but he is proud of them none the less. He says that he prefers awards given to benefactors of mankind to those given to destroyers of men.'

'Do you mean he is a Quaker?'

'That's right, a Quaker, apart from the broad-brimmed hat and brown coat, of course.'

'Does he have any friends, as far as you know?'

'Yes, everyone who knows him is his friend.'

'And any enemies, then?'

'Only one.'

'Who is that?'

'Lord Wilmore.'

'Where can I find him?'

'He is in Paris at this very moment.'

'Can he give me any information?'

'Yes, very valuable. He was in India at the same time as Zaccone.'

'Do you know where he lives?'

'Somewhere in the Chaussée-d'Antin. I am not sure of the street or the number of the house.'

'Are you on bad terms with this Englishman?'

'I like Zaccone and he detests him, so for that reason we do not get along.'

'Abbé, do you think that the Count of Monte Cristo has ever been to France before the journey that has brought him to Paris?'

'Oh, as far as that is concerned, I do know something to the point. No, Monsieur, he has never been here, because six months ago he asked me for the information he needed. And I, since I did not know precisely when I should be returning to Paris myself, I sent him to see Monsieur Cavalcanti.'

'Andrea?'

'No, Bartolomeo, the father.'

'Very well, Monsieur. I have only one more thing to ask you and I command you, in the name of honour, humanity and religion, to answer me without any attempt at concealment.'

'Ask your question.'

'Do you know for what purpose the Count of Monte Cristo bought a house in Auteuil?'

'Indeed, I do; he told me.'

'So, why?'

'With the idea of turning it into an asylum for lunatics on the model of the one set up in Palermo by Baron de Pisani. Do you know that asylum?'

'Only by reputation, Monsieur l'Abbé.'

'It is a wonderful institution.'

At this, the abbé got up, like a man intimating to his visitor that he would not be sorry to resume his interrupted work. The other did the same, either because he understood what the abbé wanted or because he had run out of questions. The abbé accompanied him to the door.

'You give generously in alms,' the visitor said. 'And, even though they say you are rich, I would like to offer you something for the poor. Would you accept my gift?'

'Thank you, Monsieur, but I boast of only one thing in the world, which is that all the good I do comes from me alone.'

'Yes . . . !'

'My resolve is unwavering. But seek, Monsieur, and you will find: alas, every rich man has more than enough of poverty to pass by on his road through life!'

The abbé bowed once more as he opened the door, and the stranger returned the compliment and left. His carriage took him immediately to Monsieur de Villefort's and, an hour later, it drove out again, this time towards the Rue Fontaine-Saint-Georges. It stopped by No. 5, which was the address of Lord Wilmore.

The stranger had written to Lord Wilmore to request a meeting, which had been fixed for ten o'clock. As the prefect of police's envoy arrived at ten to ten, he was told that Lord Wilmore, who was the soul of punctuality, had not yet returned, but that he would do so on the stroke of ten.

The visitor waited in the drawing-room; there was nothing

remarkable about this room, which was like any other in furnished lodgings: a mantelpiece with two modern Sèvres vases, a clock with Cupid drawing his bow and a mirror, in two sections; engravings on each side of the mirror, one showing Homer carrying his guide, the other Belisarius[1] begging alms; wallpaper, grey on grey; a sofa upholstered in red, and printed in black – this was Lord Wilmore's drawing-room. It was lit by two lamps with shades of frosted glass that gave only a feeble light, as if deliberately designed not to strain the tired eyes of the prefect's emissary.

After he had waited ten minutes, the clock struck ten and, on the fifth stroke, the door opened and Lord Wilmore appeared.

He was a man of more than average height, with thin, reddish side-whiskers, a pale complexion and greying blond hair. He was dressed with typically English eccentricity: that is to say, he wore a blue coat with gold buttons and high piqué collar, of the kind worn in 1811, with a waistcoat of white cashmere and nankeen breeches, three inches too short, restrained by straps under the feet from mounting up to his knees. His first words on entering were: 'You know, Monsieur, that I do not speak French.'

'I certainly know that you do not like to speak our language,' the policeman said.

'But you may speak it,' Lord Wilmore continued. 'For, though I do not speak, I can understand.'

'And I speak English well enough,' said the visitor, changing to that language, 'for us to hold a conversation. So you may feel at ease, Monsieur.'

'Haoh!' Lord Wilmore exclaimed, with an intonation that only a pure-blooded Englishman can achieve.

The other man gave him his letter of introduction, which was perused with peculiarly British phlegm. Then, when he had finished, he said, in English: 'Yes, I quite understand.' So the visitor began his enquiries.

The questions were roughly the same as those that had been asked of Abbé Busoni; but since Lord Wilmore, an enemy of the Count of Monte Cristo, did not show the same discretion as the abbé, his answers were much fuller. He described the count's youth, saying that as a boy of ten he had entered into the service of one of those Indian princelings who make war against the English: this is where he and Lord Wilmore met for the first time and fought one another. In the course of the war, Zaccone was taken prisoner, sent to England and put in the hulks, from which he escaped by jumping into the water. This was the start of his journeys, his duels, his love affairs. When the Greeks rebelled, he fought for them against the Turks and, while in their service, discovered a silver mine in the mountains of Thessaly, about which he was careful to tell no one. When the Greek government was consolidated after the Battle of Navarino, he asked King Otto[2] for a licence to exploit the mine, which was granted. Hence the vast fortune which, according to Lord Wilmore, might yield an income of two million, but which would at the same time dry up overnight, if the mine itself were to do so.

'But do you know why he has come to France?' the visitor asked.

'He wishes to speculate on the railways,' said Lord Wilmore. 'And, being a skilled chemist and no less distinguished physicist, he has invented a new form of telegraph which he is in process of developing.'

'Roughly how much does he spend a year?' the policeman asked.

'Oh, five or six hundred thousand francs, at the most,' said Lord Wilmore. 'He is a miser.'

It was clear that the Englishman was inspired by hatred and, not finding anything else to say against the count, he reproached him with avarice.

'Do you know anything about his house in Auteuil?'

'Yes, indeed.'

'What?'

'Do you mean, his reason for buying it?'

'Yes.'

'Well, the count is a speculator who will certainly ruin himself with experiments and wild dreams. He claims that in Auteuil, close to the house which he had just bought, there is a stream of mineral water which can rival those of Bagnères, Luchon and Cauterets. He wants to make his house into what the Germans call a *badhaus*, and has already dug over the whole of his garden two or three times to discover this famous spring. Since he has been able to find nothing, you will shortly see him buy all the houses around his own. Since there is no love lost between us, I hope that his railways, his electric telegraph and his mineral waters will ruin him. I shall enjoy his discomfiture, which is bound to arrive sooner or later.'

'And why do you dislike him?'

'Because once, when he was in England, he seduced the wife of one of my friends.'

'So why not try to be revenged on him?'

'I have already fought the count three times,' the Englishman said. 'The first time with pistols, the second with foils and the third with sabres.'

'What was the result of these duels?'

'The first time he broke my arm; the second, he ran me through the lung; and the third, he gave me this wound.'

The Englishman turned down the shirt-collar that reached up to his ears and revealed a scar, the redness of which showed that it must have been made recently.

'So I greatly resent him,' the Englishman said. 'Naturally, he will die by no hand except mine.'

'But it seems to me that you are doing nothing to kill him.'

'Haoh!' the Englishman said. 'Every day I go to the shooting range, and every other day Grisier comes here.'

This was all that the visitor wished to know, or, rather, all that the Englishman appeared able to tell him. The agent got up and left, after taking leave of Lord Wilmore, who returned his bow with characteristically English stiffness and politeness.

For his part, Lord Wilmore, on hearing the street-door shut, went back into his bedroom and, in a trice, lost his blond hair, his red sideboards, his false jaw and his scar, to resume the black hair, dark colouring and pearly teeth of the Count of Monte Cristo.

And, as it happened, it was M. de Villefort himself, and not an emissary of the prefect of police, who returned to M. de Villefort's house.

The crown prosecutor was a little easier in his mind after these two visits: he had not learnt anything reassuring from them, but neither had he learnt anything disturbing. As a result, for the first time since the dinner in Auteuil, he slept quite calmly the following night.

LXX

THE BALL

The hottest days of July had come when the calendar arrived at the Saturday appointed for M. de Morcerf's ball. It was ten o'clock in the evening. The large trees in the count's garden were sharply outlined against a sky across which drifted the last tufts of cloud from the storm that had been threatening all day, to reveal an azure field sprinkled with golden stars.

From the ground-floor rooms one could hear the blast of music and the swirling of the waltz and the gallop, while sharp bands of light shone out through the slats of the persian blinds. The garden, for the time being, was solely the province of a dozen or so servants, who had just been ordered to lay out the supper by their mistress, who was reassured at seeing the steady improvement in the weather. Until then, she had been unsure whether to eat in the dining-room or under a long canvas awning, set up above the lawn. But this lovely blue sky, full of stars, had now settled the issue in favour of the awning and the lawn.

The garden paths were lit by coloured lamps, as is the custom in Italy, and the supper table was laden with candles and flowers, as is the custom in all countries where they understand how to dress a table, which when properly done is the rarest of all luxuries.

Just as the Countess de Morcerf had given her last orders and was returning indoors, the drawing-rooms began to fill with guests, attracted more by the countess's charming hospitality than by the distinguished position of the count. Everyone knew in advance that the party would supply them with some details which would either be worth relating or, in the event, copying, thanks to Mercédès' good taste.

Mme Danglars had been so deeply disturbed by the events we have described that she was reluctant to attend; but that morning her carriage had crossed Villefort's. The latter signalled to her, the two carriages pulled up alongside each other and the crown prosecutor said, through the window: 'You are going to Madame de Morcerf's, I suppose?'

'No,' answered Mme Danglars. 'I'm not well enough.'

'That is a mistake,' Villefort said, with a significant look. 'It is important for you to be seen there.'

'Oh, do you think so?' the baroness asked.

'I do.'

'Then I shall go.'

Then the two carriages had continued on their separate ways. However, Mme Danglars did come, looking beautiful not only with her own beauty, but dressed with dazzling extravagance. She was just coming in through one door when Mercédès entered by the other. The countess sent Albert to greet Mme Danglars, and he came forward, offered the baroness some well-deserved compliments on her dress and took her arm to lead her wherever she wanted to go. At the same time, he looked around.

'Are you looking for my daughter?' the baroness asked with a smile.

'I confess I am. Surely you have not been so cruel as to leave her at home?'

'Don't worry. She met Mademoiselle de Villefort, who led her away. Look, they are there behind us, both in white dresses, one with a bouquet of camellias, the other with a bouquet of forget-me-nots . . . But tell me . . .'

'And what are you looking for?' Albert asked, smiling.

'Will you not be having the Count of Monte Cristo this evening?'

'Seventeen!' Albert replied.

'What do you mean?'

'I mean that all is well,' said the viscount, laughing, 'and that you are the seventeenth person to ask me the same question. He's popular, the count! I must compliment him.'

'And do you answer everyone in the same way?'

'Ah! You're quite right! I didn't answer. Have no fear, Madame, we shall be privileged to receive the man of the moment.'

'Were you at the opera yesterday?'

'No.'

'He was.'

'Really? And did the eccentric signore do anything out of the ordinary?'

'Can he appear in public otherwise? Elssler was dancing in *Le Diable boiteux*; the Greek princess was delighted. After the cachu-cha,[1] he slipped a superb ring on the stems of a bouquet and threw it to the delightful ballerina, who reappeared in the third act with the ring on her finger, as a tribute to him. Will his Greek princess be here?'

'No, you must do without her. Her status in the count's entourage is slightly ambiguous.'

'Now, leave me, and go to pay your respects to Madame de Ville-fort,' said the baroness. 'I can see that she's dying to speak to you.'

Albert bowed and went across to Mme de Villefort, whose mouth started to open even as he was approaching her.

'I bet,' he said, interrupting, 'that I can guess what you're going to say.'

'Well, I never!' said Mme de Villefort.

'Will you admit it, if I'm right?'

'Yes.'

'On your honour?'

'On my honour.'

'You were going to ask me if the Count of Monte Cristo had arrived or if he was coming.'

'Nothing of the sort. I'm not concerned with him at the moment. I was going to ask if you had any news of Monsieur Franz?'

'Yes, yesterday.'

'And what did he have to say?'

'That he was leaving at the same time as his letter.'

'Very well. And, now, what about the count?'

'The count will come, have no fear.'

'Did you know he has another name, apart from Monte Cristo?'

'No, I didn't.'

'Monte Cristo is the name of an island, and he does have a family name.'

'I've never heard it.'

'Well, I know more than you do. He's called Zaccone.'

'Possibly.'

'He is a Maltese.'

'That's also possible.'

'The son of a shipowner.'

'Come, now. You should be telling everybody about it. You'd have a huge audience.'

'He served in India, has a silver mine in Thessaly and has come to Paris to set up, selling mineral water in Auteuil.'

'Well, it's about time,' said Morcerf. 'This really is news. Can I repeat it?'

'Yes, but little by little, one item at a time, without saying that it comes from me.'

'Why?'

'Because it's almost a secret I've found out.'

'From where?'

'The police.'

'And where was the news travelling?'

'At the prefect's, yesterday evening. The authorities were put out, you understand, by this unusual ostentation, so the police made some enquiries.'

'Huh! You might as well arrest the count as a vagabond, on the excuse of his being too rich.'

'Which is just what might have happened to him, if the information had not been so much in his favour.'

'Poor count. Does he know the danger he was in?'

'I don't think so.'

'Well, it is only right and proper to let him know. I shall certainly do it as soon as he arrives.'

At that moment a handsome young man with sparkling eyes, black hair and a well-waxed moustache came to pay his respects to Mme de Villefort. Albert held out his hand.

'Madame,' he said, 'I have the honour to introduce Monsieur Maximilien Morrel, captain of spahis, one of our fine and, most of all, brave officers.'

'I have already had the pleasure of meeting this gentleman in Auteuil at the Count of Monte Cristo's,' Mme de Villefort replied, turning away with distinct coldness.

This reply and, most of all, the tone in which it was delivered wrung poor Morrel's heart; but a consolation was in store. Turning around, he saw a beautiful, pale face in the doorway, its wide and apparently expressionless eyes fixed on him, while the bouquet of forget-me-nots was raised to its lips.

This greeting was well enough understood by Morrel for him to lift his handkerchief to his mouth, though with the same blank expression on his face. These two living statues, whose hearts were beating so rapidly despite the marble calm of their faces, separated from one another by the whole length of the room, momentarily forgot themselves; or, rather, momentarily forgot everyone else in their silent contemplation of one another. Indeed, they could have remained for a long time in this way, lost in each other, without anyone noticing their total self-absorption: the Count of Monte Cristo had just come in.

As we have already mentioned, either because of some imagined aura or because of his natural presence, he attracted attention wherever he went. It was not his black coat, superbly though it was cut, simple and without decoration; it was not his plain white waistcoat; nor was it his trousers, fitting over a delicately shaped foot, that attracted attention. It was his dark complexion, his wavy black hair, his pure, calm face, his deep and melancholy eye and, finally, his exquisitely formed mouth which could so easily adopt an expression of sovereign contempt, which drew all eyes to him.

There may have been more handsome men, but there was surely none more *significant*, if we may be allowed to use the word. Everything about the count meant something and carried some weight; for the habit of positive thought had given to his features, to the expression on his face and to the least of his gestures an incomparable strength and suppleness.

Apart from which, our society here in Paris is so strange that it might have paid no attention to all that, were it not that behind it lay a mysterious tale, gilded by a huge fortune.

However it may be, he came forward, running the gauntlet of stares and cursory greetings, towards Mme de Morcerf who, standing in front of the mantelpiece, had observed his entrance in a mirror facing the doorway and was getting ready to receive him. She consequently turned around with a well-judged smile at the very moment when he bowed in front of her.

Doubtless she thought that the count would say something; and doubtless, on his side, he was expecting her to address him. But both remained silent, each surely feeling that a mere commonplace would be unworthy of them, and, after they had exchanged these silent salutations, Monte Cristo turned and began to walk towards Albert, who came to greet him with hand outstretched.

'You saw my mother?' Albert asked.

'I have just had the honour of paying her my respects,' said the count. 'But I did not see your father.'

'There! He is over there, talking politics, in that small circle of great celebrities.'

'Really?' said Monte Cristo. 'Are the gentlemen I can see down there celebrities? I should never have guessed. What kind? There are all sorts of celebrities, you know.'

'First a scientist: that dry old stick. He discovered a species of lizard in the Roman *campagna*, which has one vertebra more than any other, and has come back to inform the Institut[2] of his discovery. There was a long debate on the matter, but the dry old stick won the day. The vertebra attracted a lot of attention in the scientific world; and the old stick, who used to be a knight of the Legion of Honour, is now an officer of the order.'

'Excellent!' said Monte Cristo. 'The decoration seems to me to have been judiciously awarded. And if he finds another extra vertebra, they will make him a commander?'

'Quite probably,' said Morcerf.

'What about that other gentleman who has had the unusual notion of dressing up in a blue coat with green piping. What species can he be?'

'It wasn't his idea to dress up in that coat; it was the republic which, as you know, was something of an artist and thought it would give some kind of uniform to members of the French Academy, so it asked David to design them a coat.'[3]

'Really?' said Monte Cristo. 'You mean the gentleman is an Academician?'

'He has been a member of the learned assembly for a week.'

'And what is his talent, his speciality?'

'His speciality? I think he sticks pins in rabbits' heads, feeds madder to hens and uses whales to cultivate the spinal columns of dogs.'

'And he is in the Academy of Sciences because of that?'

'No, in the French Academy.'

'But what has all that got to do with the French Academy?'

'I'll tell you. It seems . . .'

'His experiments have greatly advanced science, I presume?'

'No, but he writes them up in a very fine style.'

'That,' said the count, 'must be most gratifying for the self-respect of the rabbits into whose heads he sticks pins, the hens whose bones he colours red and the dogs whose columns he cultivates.'

Albert started to laugh.

'What about that other person?' asked the count.

'Which one?'

'The third . . .'

'Ah, the cornflower-blue coat?'

'Yes.'

'A colleague of the count's who has just emphatically opposed a measure in the Upper House to give its members a uniform. His speeches on the topic were warmly applauded. He was in bad odour with the liberal press, but his noble opposition to the wishes of the court has put him back in favour with them, and there is talk that he might be made an ambassador.'

'What entitles him to the peerage?'

'He's written two or three comic operas, fought four or five lawsuits against *Le Siècle* and voted five or six times for the government.'

'Hurrah, Viscount!' said Monte Cristo, with a laugh. 'You are a delightful guide. Now, will you do something for me?'

'What?'

'Don't introduce these gentlemen to me and, if they ask to be introduced to me, give me good warning.' At that moment he felt a hand on his arm. He looked around, to see Danglars. 'Ah, it's you, Baron,' he said.

'Why do you call me baron?' said Danglars. 'You know very well that I care nothing for my title – unlike you, Viscount. You do care for yours, I think?'

'Undoubtedly,' said Albert, 'since, if I were not a viscount, I should be nothing, while you – well, you can give up your title of baron and you would still be a millionaire.'

'And that seems to me the finest of titles under our July Monarchy,'[4] said Danglars.

'Unfortunately,' said Monte Cristo, 'one cannot be a millionaire for life, as one is a baron, a peer of the realm or an academician. Look at the millionaires Frank and Poulmann, of Frankfurt, who have just gone bankrupt.'

'No, really?' said Danglars, going pale.

'Why, yes. I got the news only this evening by courier. I had something like a million with them, but I was given due warning and had myself reimbursed almost a month ago.'

'Oh, good Lord!' said Danglars. 'They drew on me for two hundred thousand francs.'

'Well, you have been warned. Their signature is worth five per cent.'

'But the warning comes too late,' said Danglars. 'I honoured their signature.'

'Well, now,' said Monte Cristo. 'That's two hundred thousand francs which have gone to . . .'

'Hush!' said Danglars. 'Don't speak about such things . . .' Then, coming closer to Monte Cristo, he added: 'Especially not in front of the younger Cavalcanti.' At which he turned around, smiling in the direction of the young man.

Morcerf had left the count to go and talk to his mother. Danglars left him to speak to young Cavalcanti and, for a moment, Monte Cristo found himself alone.

The heat was starting to become unbearable. Valets were walking round the drawing-rooms bearing trays laden with fruit and ices. Monte Cristo took out a handkerchief and wiped a face dripping with sweat, but he shrank back when the tray passed by him and partook of no refreshment. Mme de Morcerf had not taken her eyes off Monte Cristo. She saw the tray pass, untouched, and even noticed his movement away from it.

'Albert,' she said, 'have you noticed something?'

'What, mother?'

'The count has never wanted to accept an invitation to dine with Monsieur de Morcerf.'

'Yes, but he did agree to take lunch at my house, since that is when he made his entrée into society.'

'With you is not the same as with the count,' Mercédès muttered. 'I have been watching him since he arrived.'

'Well?'

'Well, he has not yet taken anything to eat or drink.'

'He is very abstemious.'

Mercédès smiled sadly. 'Go over to him,' she said, 'and, the next time the tray comes round, insist.'

'Why, mother?'

'Just do it for me, Albert,' Mercédès said. Albert kissed his mother's hand and took up his position near the count. Another tray came past, loaded like the rest. She saw Albert pressing the count to take something, and even offering him an ice, but the count obstinately refused.

Albert returned to his mother's side. She was very pale. 'Did you see?' she said. 'He refused.'

'Why are you worried about that?'

'You know, Albert, we women are peculiar. I should have been pleased to see the count take something in my house, if only a pomegranate seed. But perhaps he is not used to French manners, or he might have some preference, for something in particular?'

'No, I'm sure of it. I saw him taste everything in Italy. I expect he is feeling unwell this evening.'

'Since he has always lived in hot countries,' the countess said, 'he may be less sensitive than other people to the heat.'

'I don't think so, because he complained that it was stifling and asked why, since the windows had already been opened, the shutters were not opened as well.'

'Yes,' Mercédès said, 'that's a way of finding out if his abstinence is deliberate.'

She left the room, and a moment later the shutters were opened and, through the jasmine and clematis that hung around the windows, one could see the whole garden lit up with lamps and the supper laid out under the awning.

The men and women on the dance floor, gamblers and talkers, all let out cries of joy – their thirsty lungs drinking in the air which poured into the room. At the same time Mercédès reappeared, paler than when she left, but with a remarkable expression of determination which her face took on in certain circumstances. She went directly to the group around her husband and said: 'Count, please don't keep these gentlemen here. If they are not playing cards, I am sure they would prefer to breathe in the garden than to suffocate here.'

'Oh, Madame,' said a very gallant old general who had sung *Partons pour la Syrie*[5] in 1809, 'we will not go into the garden alone.'

'Very well,' said Mercédès. 'I shall set you an example.' And she turned towards Monte Cristo. 'Monsieur le Comte, please do me the honour of giving me your arm.'

The count seemed almost to stagger on hearing these simple words, then he looked at Mercédès for a moment. The moment lasted as long as a flash of lightning, but to the countess it seemed to last a century, so much intensity of thought did Monte Cristo put into this single glance.

He offered the countess his arm and she leant on it; or, rather, she allowed her little hand to brush against it; and the two of them went down one of the staircases outside the french windows, bordered with rhododendron and camellias. By the other staircase, with noisy cries of delight, some twenty guests hurried along behind them into the garden.

LXXI

BREAD AND SALT

Mme de Morcerf directed her companion under the arbour of linden-trees that led towards a greenhouse. 'It was too hot in the drawing-room, wasn't it, Count?' she said.

'Yes, Madame. It was an excellent idea of yours to open the doors and the shutters.'

As he said these words, the count noticed that Mercédès' hand was trembling. 'But perhaps you are cold, with that light dress and no other protection around your neck except a chiffon scarf?' he said.

'Do you know where I am taking you?' the countess asked, not answering Monte Cristo's question.

'No, Madame,' he replied, 'but, as you see, I am offering no resistance.'

'To the greenhouse down there, at the end of this path.'

The count looked at her questioningly, but she carried on without a word, so he too said nothing.

They arrived at the building, hung with splendid fruit which matured at the beginning of July in this temperature, designed to replace that of the sun which is so unreliable in our climate. The countess let go of Monte Cristo's arm and went to pluck a bunch of grapes from a vine.

'Here, Count,' she said, with such a sad smile that it did not disguise the tears at the corners of her eyes, 'take it. Our French grapes are not, I know, comparable to those you have in Sicily or Cyprus, but I know you will excuse our pale northern sun.'

The count bowed and took a pace backwards.

'Are you refusing me?' said Mercédès, her voice quivering.

'Madame,' Monte Cristo replied, 'I beg you most humbly to forgive me, but I never eat muscat grapes.'

Mercédès let the bunch fall with a sigh. A magnificent peach was hanging from a nearby shrub, espaliered and warmed, like the vine, by the artificial heat of the greenhouse. Mercédès went over to the luscious fruit and picked it.

'Then take this peach,' she said.

But the count made the same gesture of refusal.

'Again!' she said, with such a pained note in her voice that one could feel it covered a sob. 'Truly, I am unfortunate.'

There was a long silence. The peach, like the bunch of grapes, had fallen on the sand.

'Monsieur le Comte,' Mercédès said finally, looking imploringly at Monte Cristo, 'there is a touching Arab custom that promises eternal friendship between those who have shared bread and salt under the same roof.'

'I know it, Madame,' the count replied. 'But we are in France and not in Arabia; and in France there is no more eternal friendship than there is sharing of bread and salt.'

'But we are friends, are we not?' she said, breathing rapidly and looking directly into Monte Cristo's eyes, while clasping his arm with both hands.

The blood rushed to the count's heart and he became as white as death; then it rose from his heart to his throat and spread across his cheeks. For a few moments his eyes would not focus, like those of a man dazzled by a bright light. 'Of course we are friends, Madame,' he replied. 'Why should we not be?'

His tone was so far from the one that Mme de Morcerf desired that she turned away with a sigh that was almost a groan. 'Thank you,' she said, then started to walk on. In this way they went round the whole garden without saying a word.

'Monsieur,' the countess suddenly resumed, after they had walked for ten minutes in silence, 'is it true that you have seen so much, travelled so far, suffered so deeply?'

'Yes, Madame, I have suffered a great deal,' he said.

'But are you happy now?'

'Yes, of course,' the count replied. 'No one hears me complain.'

'And does your present happiness calm your soul?'

'My present happiness equals my past misery,' said the count.

'Have you ever married?'

'Married?' Monte Cristo replied, shuddering. 'Who told you that?'

'No one, but several times you have been seen at the opera with a beautiful young woman.'

'She is a slave whom I bought in Constantinople, Madame, the daughter of a prince whom I took for my own, not having anyone else to cherish.'

'So you live alone?'

'I do.'

'You have no sister . . . son . . . father?'

'No one.'

'How can you live like that, with nothing attaching you to life?'

'It is not my fault, Madame. In Malta I loved a girl and was going to marry her, when the war came and swept me away from her like a whirlwind. I thought that she loved me enough to wait for me, even to remain faithful to my tomb. When I came back, she was married. This is the story of every man who is aged over twenty. Perhaps my heart was weaker than that of others and I suffered more than they would in my place, that's all.'

The countess stopped for a moment, as if needing to recover her breath. 'Yes,' she said, 'and that love has remained in your heart. One is only really in love once . . . Did you ever see her again?'

'Never.'

'Never?'

'I did not go back to the country where she lived.'

'To Malta?'

'Yes, to Malta.'

'So she is in Malta, then?'

'I think so.'

'And have you forgiven her what she made you suffer?'

'Her I have forgiven, yes.'

'But only her. You still hate those who separated you?'

The countess stood in front of Monte Cristo, still holding part of the bunch of grapes in her hand. 'Take it,' she said.

'I never eat muscat grapes, Madame,' the count replied, as if the matter had never been discussed between them before.

'You are quite inflexible,' she muttered. But Monte Cristo remained as impassive as though the reproach had not been addressed to him.

At this moment Albert ran up. 'Oh, mother,' he said. 'A great disaster!'

'What? What has happened?' the countess asked, stiffening, as though she had been recalled to reality from a dream. 'A disaster? Indeed, disasters must happen.'

'Monsieur de Villefort is here.'

'So?'

'He has come to fetch his wife and daughter.'

'Why?'

'Because the Marquise de Saint-Méran has arrived in Paris, with the news that Monsieur de Saint-Méran died on leaving Marseille, at the first post. Madame de Villefort, who was very merry, did not want to understand or believe in this misfortune, but Mademoiselle Valentine guessed everything from the first words, despite her father's attempt to disguise it from her. The blow struck her down like a bolt of lightning and she fell in a dead faint.'

'What is Monsieur de Saint-Méran to Mademoiselle de Villefort?' the count asked.

'Her maternal grandfather. He was coming to Paris to speed up his granddaughter's marriage to Franz.'

'Really?'

'Now Franz is delayed. Why is Monsieur de Saint-Méran not also an ancestor of Mademoiselle Danglars?'

'Albert! Albert,' Mme de Morcerf said, gently reprimanding him. 'What are you saying? Oh, Monsieur le Comte, he has such a great respect for you: tell him he shouldn't say such things.' She took a step forward.

Monte Cristo was looking so oddly at her, with an expression that was at once so abstracted and so full of affectionate admiration, that she advanced again, took his hand and that of her son, and joined them together. 'We are friends, are we not?' she said.

'Well, now, Madame,' said the count. 'Your friend? I should not pretend to that. But, in any case, I am your most respectful servant.'

The countess left with an inexpressible weight on her heart and had not gone more than ten yards when the count even saw her dab her eyes with a handkerchief.

'Have you fallen out over something, my mother and you?' Albert asked with astonishment.

'On the contrary,' the count replied, 'since she has just told me in front of you that we are friends.' And they went back to the drawing-room which Valentine had just left with M. and Mme de Villefort. It goes without saying that Morrel followed them.

LXXII

MADAME DE SAINT-MÉRAN

A mournful scene had just taken place in M. de Villefort's house. After the departure of the two ladies for the ball, all Mme de Villefort's efforts having failed definitely to persuade her husband to accompany her, the crown prosecutor had shut himself up as usual in his study with a pile of dossiers which would have terrified another man but which, in normal circumstances, would hardly have been enough to satisfy his mania for work.

This time, however, the dossiers were merely a façade; Villefort was not shutting himself up to work but to reflect; and, once the door was shut and the order had been given that he should be disturbed only in an emergency, he sat down in the chair and went over in his mind everything that in the past week or so had filled his cup of bitter sorrows and dark memories to overflowing.

Then, instead of starting on the pile of dossiers in front of him, he opened a drawer in his desk, released a secret spring and took out a bundle of personal papers, precious manuscripts which he had put in order and labelled, with figures known only to him, the names of all those who had become his enemies – whether in his political career, his business dealings, his legal practice or his secret love affairs.

By this time the number was so huge that he began to tremble; and yet all these names, powerful and fearful as they were, had often brought a smile to his face, as a traveller may smile when, on reaching the summit of the mountain, he looks at the narrow peaks, impassable trails and steep precipices beneath him, up which he struggled for so long to reach his present station.

When he had gone through all the names in his memory, re-read them, studied them and commented on each list, he shook his head. 'No,' he muttered. 'None of those enemies would have waited and toiled patiently until now to come and crush me with this secret. Foul deeds will rise, as Hamlet[1] says, and sometimes fly through the air like a will-o'-the-wisp, but these are flames that light us a moment to deceive. The story must have been told by the Corsican to some priest, and by him in turn to others. Monte Cristo learned it and wanted to verify it . . .

'But why want to verify?' he wondered after a moment's reflection. 'What interest can a dark, mysterious and inconsequential event like that have for Monsieur de Monte Cristo, Monsieur Zaccone, son of a Maltese shipowner and operator of a Thessalian silver mine, who is paying his first visit to France? Among the jumble of information I obtained from that Abbé Busoni and Lord Wilmore, the friend and the enemy, only one thing stands out clearly and plainly in my view, which is that at no time, in no event and under no circumstances can there have been the slightest contact between him and me.'

But Villefort said this without believing his own words. The worst thing, for him, was not the revelation of what he had done, because he could deny it, or even reply to the accusation. It was not the *Mene, mene, tekel, upharsin*[2] suddenly appearing in bloody letters on the wall; what troubled him was not knowing to what body the hand that traced them belonged.

Just as he was trying to reassure himself – and, in place of the political career which he had sometimes envisaged in his ambitious imaginings, he was resigning himself to a future confined to the joys of family life, for fear of awakening this long-dormant enemy – he heard the sound of a carriage outside, then the steps of an old person on the stairs, followed by sobs and exclamations of 'Alas!', of the kind that servants emit when they want to make themselves interesting because of their masters' sorrows.

He hastened to pull back the bolt on his study door and soon, unannounced, an old woman came in, a shawl on her arm and a hat in her hand. Her white hair disclosed a brow as dull as yellowed ivory and her eyes, in the corners of which age had etched deep wrinkles, had almost vanished, so swollen were they with tears.

'Oh, Monsieur!' she said. 'Oh, Monsieur! What a misfortune! I too shall die of it! Oh, yes, I shall surely die!' And, collapsing into the nearest armchair, she dissolved into tears.

The servants, standing at the door and not daring to advance into the room, turned to look at Noirtier's old manservant who, having heard the noise from his master's room and hurried across, was now standing behind the rest. Villefort got up and ran over to his mother-in-law – for she it was.

'Heaven preserve us, Madame!' he exclaimed. 'What has happened? Who has put you in this state? And is Monsieur de Saint-Méran not with you?'

'Monsieur de Saint-Méran is dead,' the old marchioness said, coming directly to the matter, but without any sign of feeling, in a kind of stupor.

Villefort started back and struck his hands together. 'Dead!' he stammered. 'Dead, like that . . . so suddenly?'

'A week ago,' Mme de Saint-Méran continued. 'We were getting into the carriage after dinner. For some days, Monsieur de Saint-Méran had been unwell, yet the idea of seeing our dear Valentine gave him strength despite his pain. He was just starting out when, six leagues from Marseille, after taking his usual pills, he fell into an unnaturally deep sleep. I was unwilling to wake him, but then his face seemed to go red and the veins in his temples to beat more violently than usual. However, as it was now night and getting too dark to see, I let him sleep. Shortly afterwards he gave a dull, heart-rending cry, like a man tormented by a nightmare, and sharply threw back his head. I called the valet, had the coach stopped, called to Monsieur de Saint-Méran and got him to breathe my sal volatile, but it was all over, he was dead and I journeyed to Aix seated beside his corpse.'

Villefort stood there, thunderstruck, his mouth gaping. 'You called a doctor, I suppose?' he said.

'Immediately, but, as I told you, it was too late.'

'Of course, but at least he could say from what illness the poor marquis died.'

'Yes, Monsieur, he did that. It appears to have been an apoplectic stroke.'

'So what did you do?'

'Monsieur de Saint-Méran always used to say that if he died far from Paris he would like his body to be brought to rest in the family vault. I had it put into a lead coffin and it is on its way, a few days' drive behind me.'

'Oh, poor mother!' said Villefort. 'To be entrusted with such a task, and after such a blow!'

'God gave me strength; and in any case the dear marquis would surely have done for me what I did for him. It is true that, since I left him behind me there, I have felt I am going mad. I can no longer weep, yet I feel that one should do so, as long as one is suffering. Where is Valentine, Monsieur? We were coming for her; I want to see Valentine.'

Villefort thought that it would be frightful to reply that Valentine was at the ball. He simply told the marchioness that her grand-daughter had gone out with her stepmother and that she would be informed.

'Now, Monsieur, at once, I beg you,' said the old lady.

Villefort slipped his arm under that of Mme de Saint-Méran and took her to her apartment. 'Rest, mother,' he said.

At that word, the marchioness looked up and, seeing the man who reminded her of the much-mourned daughter who seemed to live again for her in Valentine, struck by the name of 'mother', she burst into tears and sank to her knees before a chair in which she buried her venerable head. Villefort told the women to look after her, while old Barrois hurried across in a state of consternation to his master: nothing terrifies old people so much as when death leaves their side to strike down another old person. Then, while Mme de Saint-Méran, still kneeling, began to pray from the depths of her heart, Villefort sent for a carriage and took it himself to collect his wife and daughter from Mme de Morcerf's. He was so pale when he got to the door of the drawing-room that Valentine ran across to him, crying: 'Oh, father! Something terrible has happened!'

'Your grandmother has just arrived, Valentine,' he said.

'And grandfather?' the girl asked, trembling.

M. de Villefort's only reply was to give her his arm. He was only just in time because Valentine reeled, nearly fainting. Mme de Villefort hurried over to support her and helped her husband to get her into the carriage, saying: 'How strange! Who would have thought it! This truly is strange!' With that, the stricken family drove off, casting its sadness like a black veil across the rest of the gathering.

Valentine found Barrois waiting for her at the foot of the stairs. 'Monsieur Noirtier would like to see you this evening,' he whispered.

'Tell him to expect me when I have seen my dear grandmother,' Valentine said, her delicate soul having realized that Mme de Saint-Méran was the person who needed her most at that time.

She found her in bed. Silent caresses, painful swelling of the heart, broken sighs and burning tears were the only positive events in what passed between them. Mme de Villefort was also present, on her husband's arm, and was full of respect for the poor widow – or so at least it seemed.

After a short while she leant across to whisper in her husband's ear: 'With your permission, I think I should retire, because the sight of me appears to make your mother-in-law more distressed.'

Mme de Saint-Méran overheard the remark. 'Yes, yes,' she said in Valentine's ear. 'Let her go; but you, stay.'

Mme de Villefort went out and Valentine was left alone at her grandmother's bedside because the crown prosecutor, dismayed by this unexpected death, followed his wife.

Barrois, however, had gone back to Noirtier's side the first time; the old man had heard the commotion in the house and sent his servant, as we said, to find out the cause of it. When he returned, the lively and, above all, intelligent eyes asked for his message.

'Alas, Monsieur,' said Barrois, 'something terrible has happened: Madame de Saint-Méran is here and her husband is dead.'

M. de Saint-Méran and Noirtier had never been close, but the effect on one old man of hearing that another has died is well known. Noirtier let his head fall on his chest, like a man weighed down with sorrow or deep in thought, then shut one eye.

'Mademoiselle Valentine?' Barrois asked.

Noirtier indicated: 'Yes.'

'Monsieur knows very well that she is at the ball, because she came to say goodbye and to show him her dress.'

Noirtier again shut his left eye.

'You want to see her?'

The old man indicated that he did.

'Well, no doubt they are going to fetch her from Madame de Morcerf's. I shall await her on her return and tell her to come up. Is that correct?'

'Yes,' said the paralysed man.

This is why Barrois was waiting for Valentine's return and, as we have seen, informed her of her grandfather's wishes. Consequently, Valentine went up to M. Noirtier's on leaving Mme de Saint-Méran who, despite her distress, had finally succumbed to tiredness and was sleeping feverishly. Within her reach they had put a little table with a carafe of orange juice, her usual drink, and a glass. When that was done, the girl left the marchioness's bedside to go up to Noirtier.

She went to kiss the old man, who looked at her with such tenderness that the young woman felt new tears rising to her eyes from a well that she thought had dried. The old man looked insistently at her.

'Yes, yes,' said Valentine. 'What you are saying is that I still have one good grandfather; is that it?' The old man indicated that this was indeed what his look had meant.

'Luckily, alas!' said Valentine. 'Because, without that, what would become of me?'

It was one o'clock in the morning. Barrois, who wanted to go to bed himself, remarked that after such a painful evening everyone needed rest. The old man did not like to say that rest, as far as he was concerned, was to see his granddaughter. He sent Valentine away; tiredness and sorrow had indeed made her look unwell.

The next day she came in to see her grandmother and found her still in bed. Her fever had not gone down; on the contrary, a dull fire burned in the old marchioness's eyes and she seemed to have been seized by a violent fit of nervous irritation.

'Oh, my dear grandmother! Are you feeling worse this morning?' Valentine exclaimed, seeing these signs of agitation.

'No, no, my girl,' said Mme de Saint-Méran. 'I was waiting for you to come so that I could send you to fetch your father.'

'My father?' Valentine asked anxiously.

'Yes, I want to speak to him.'

Valentine did not dare to object to the old woman's wish – and in any case did not know what was behind it; so a moment later Villefort came in.

'Monsieur,' Mme de Saint-Méran said, without any preliminaries and as though she was afraid of running out of time. 'You wrote to tell me that there were plans to marry your daughter, I believe?'

'Yes, Madame,' Villefort replied. 'It is more than a plan, it is an agreement.'

'And your future son-in-law is Franz d'Epinay?'

'Yes, Madame.'

'Son of General d'Epinay, one of our people, who was assassinated a few days before the usurper returned from Elba?'

'Precisely.'

'The son is not deterred by the idea of marrying the grand-daughter of a Jacobin?'

'Thankfully, mother, our civil strife is ended,' said Villefort. 'Monsieur d'Epinay was little more than a child when his father died. He is not well acquainted with Monsieur Noirtier and will regard him, if not with pleasure, at least with indifference.'

'Is it a good match?'

'In every way.'

'The young man . . .'

'Enjoys general respect.'

'Is he acceptable?'

'He is one of the most distinguished young men I know.'

Valentine had remained silent throughout this conversation.

'Well, Monsieur,' said Mme de Saint-Méran after a few moments' thought. 'You must hurry, because I have little time left to live.'

'You, Madame! You, dear grandmother!' Villefort and Valentine exclaimed together.

'I know what I am saying,' the marchioness went on. 'You must hurry so that, not having a mother, she may at least have a grandmother to bless her marriage. I am the only one remaining to her from the side of my poor dear Renée, whom you so soon forgot, Monsieur.'

'Madame,' said Villefort, 'you forget that I had to give this poor child a mother when she no longer had her own.'

'A stepmother can never be a mother. But we're not talking about that. We're talking about Valentine. Let the dead lie!'

All this was said with such volubility and emphasis that the conversation almost seemed like the beginning of a delirium.

'Everything shall be done according to your wishes, Madame,' said Villefort, 'particularly as they accord with my own; and as soon as Monsieur d'Epinay arrives in Paris . . .'

'Grandmother,' said Valentine, 'think of convention, your recent bereavement . . . Would you wish a marriage to take place under such sad auspices?'

'My dear girl,' said the grandmother, brusquely interrupting her, 'don't give me any of those trite arguments that prevent weak minds from building a solid future for themselves. I too was married at my mother's deathbed, and was no unhappier for that.'

'Again, this idea of death, Madame!' said Villefort.

'Again! Still! I tell you, I am going to die, do you understand? Well, before dying I want to see my grandson-in-law, I want to tell him to make my granddaughter happy, I want to read in his eyes whether he intends to obey me, in short I want to know him,' the old woman continued, with a terrifying look, 'so that I can seek him out from the depth of my tomb if he is not what he should be, if he is not what he must be.'

'Madame,' said Villefort, 'you must put aside such wild fancies, which are close to madness. Once the dead have been laid in their tombs, they sleep there and do not return.'

'Oh, yes, grandmother, calm yourself,' said Valentine.

'Whatever you say, Monsieur,' the marchioness said, 'I have to tell you that things are not as you believe. Last night I slept very badly. I could, as it were, see myself sleeping, as though my soul was already hovering above my body. I struggled to open my eyes, but they refused to obey me. I know that this will seem impossible to you, especially to you, Monsieur, but with my eyes shut, at the very spot where you are now standing, coming from the corner where there is a door leading to Madame de Villefort's dressing-room, I saw a white shape.'

Valentine gave a cry. Villefort said: 'You were feverish, Madame.'

'Doubt me if you wish, but I am sure of what I am saying. I saw a white figure and, as if God were afraid that I might doubt the evidence of any of my senses, I heard my glass move – that glass, on the table.'

'Oh, grandmother, it was a dream!'

'It was so surely not a dream that I reached out for the bell, and upon that the shadow vanished. Then the chambermaid came in with a lantern. Ghosts only appear to those who ought to see them. This was the soul of my husband. Well, if my husband's soul is coming back to call me, why should my soul not come back to defend my granddaughter? I think the tie is even stronger.'

In spite of himself, Villefort was profoundly shaken. 'Madame,' he said, 'do not give way to such mournful ideas. You will live with us, you will live for a long time, happy, loved, honoured, and we shall help you to forget . . .'

'Never! Never! Never!' said the marquise. 'When does Monsieur d'Epinay return?'

'We are expecting him at any moment.'

'Very well. Tell me as soon as he arrives. We must hurry. Then I should like to see a lawyer to ensure that all our property goes to Valentine.'

'Oh, grandmother,' Valentine murmured, pressing her lips to the old woman's burning brow. 'Do you want me to die? You are feverish. It's not a lawyer you need, but a doctor.'

'A doctor?' she said, shrugging her shoulders. 'I am not in pain; a little thirsty, that's all.'

'What would you like to drink?'

'You know what I like: my orange juice. The glass is on that table. Please give it to me, Valentine.'

Valentine poured out the orange juice from the carafe into the glass and forced herself to pick it up and give it to her grandmother: this was the same glass that the ghost was supposed to have touched. The marquise emptied it at a single gulp, then lay back on her pillow, saying: 'A lawyer, a lawyer!'

M. de Villefort went out. Valentine sat down near her grandmother's bed. The poor child herself seemed much in need of the doctor whom she had suggested calling. Her cheeks burned red, her breathing was short and panting, and her pulse was beating as if she had a high temperature. She was thinking of Maximilien's despair when he learned that Mme de Saint-Méran, instead of being an ally, was unconsciously acting as though she were his enemy.

More than once, Valentine had thought of telling her grandmother everything, and she would not have hesitated for a moment if Maximilien Morrel had been called Albert de Morcerf or Raoul de Château-Renaud; but Morrel came from a lower-class family and Valentine knew how much the proud Marquise de Saint-Méran despised everyone who was not well bred. Consequently, whenever her secret had been on the point of coming out, it had been driven back into her heart by the sad assurance that she would reveal it in vain and that, once her father and grandmother shared that secret, all would be lost.

About two hours passed. Mme de Saint-Méran slept fitfully and feverishly. The lawyer was announced.

Even though the servant had spoken very softly, Mme de Saint-Méran sat up in bed. 'The lawyer?' she said. 'Have him brought here!'

He had been standing outside, and came in.

'Go away, Valentine,' Mme de Saint-Méran said, 'and leave me with this gentleman.'

'But, grandmother . . .'

'Go, go.'

The girl kissed her grandmother's forehead and went out, holding a handkerchief to her eyes. At the door she found the *valet de chambre*, who told her that the doctor was waiting in the drawing-room.

Valentine quickly went down. The doctor was a family friend and at the same time one of the most skilled of his profession. He was very fond of Valentine, whom he had seen being born. He had a daughter of roughly Mlle de Villefort's age but whose mother was a consumptive. His life was spent in continual fear for her child.

'Oh, dear Monsieur d'Avrigny,' said Valentine. 'We have been waiting for you. But, first of all, how are Madeleine and Antoinette?'

Madeleine was M. d'Avrigny's daughter, Antoinette his niece.

'Antoinette, very well,' he answered, with a sad smile, 'Madeleine, quite well. But you called for me, my dear child. I hope it is not your father or Madame de Villefort who is ill? As for us, although clearly we have trouble overcoming our nerves, I suppose you have no need of me except to recommend that you don't let your imagination run away with you?'

Valentine blushed. M. d'Avrigny had almost miraculous powers of divination: he was one of those doctors who always treat physical ills through the mind.

'No,' she said, 'it's my poor grandmother. I suppose you know the misfortune that we have suffered?'

'I don't know anything,' said d'Avrigny.

'Alas,' Valentine said, repressing a sob. 'My grandfather is dead.'

'Monsieur de Saint-Méran? Was it sudden?'

'An attack of apoplexy.'

'Apoplexy?' the doctor repeated.

'Yes, and the result is that my poor grandmother has the idea that her husband, whose side she never left, is calling for her and she is going to join him. Oh, Monsieur d'Avrigny! Please go and look at her!'

'Where is she?'

'In her room, with the lawyer.'

'And Monsieur Noirtier?'

'Always the same: perfectly clear in his mind, but still immobile and speechless.'

'And still as affectionate towards you, I imagine, my dear child?'

'Oh, yes, he is very fond of me,' Valentine said with a sigh.

'Who would not be?'

She smiled sadly.

'How does your grandmother's illness manifest itself?'

'Unusual nervous excitement and oddly troubled sleep. This morning she claimed that while she was asleep her soul had hovered above her body and she had seen herself sleeping. She is delirious.

She claimed to have seen a ghost come into her room and heard the noise made by this supposed ghost when it touched her glass.'

'That's odd,' the doctor said. 'I did not know Madame de Saint-Méran was subject to such hallucinations.'

'This is the first time I have seen her like that,' said Valentine. 'This morning she really frightened me, I thought she was going mad. Even my father – and, Monsieur d'Avrigny, you know what a serious-minded man my father is – even my father seemed deeply troubled.'

'Let's go and see. What you tell me is odd.'

The lawyer came down and the servant came to tell Valentine that her grandmother was alone.

'Go up,' she said to the doctor.

'What about you?'

'I dare not. She forbade me to send for you. And then, as you say, I am upset, feverish and unwell. I shall take a walk round the garden to revive myself.'

The doctor shook Valentine's hand and, while he went up to her grandmother, she went down the steps.

We hardly need say what part of the garden was Valentine's favourite walk. After walking twice round the path that encircled the house, and plucking a rose to put in her hair or her belt, she set off down the dark path that led to the bench, then from the bench she went across to the grille.

This time, as usual, she walked two or three times round among her flowers, but without picking any. The mourning in her heart, though it had not yet had time to be reflected in her dress, rejected that simple ornament. Then she went over to the path by the gate. As she was going there, she thought she heard a voice speaking her name. She stopped short in astonishment.

The voice seemed more distinct, and she recognized it as Maximilien's.

LXXIII

THE PROMISE

It was, indeed, Morrel who had been in a frantic state since the previous evening. With that instinct which only lovers and mothers possess, he had guessed that, following Mme de Saint-Méran's return and the death of the marquis, something would happen that affected his love for Valentine. As we shall see, his forebodings had been realized and it was not mere anxiety that brought him in fear and trembling to the gate by the chestnut-trees.

However, Valentine had not been warned of his arrival, since this was not the usual time when he came, and pure chance – or, if you prefer, a sympathetic instinct – had brought her to the garden. When she appeared, Morrel called her and she ran to the gate.

'You! At this time!' she said.

'Yes, my poor friend,' Morrel replied, 'I have come to look for you, bringing bad news.'

'This is the house of ill-fortune,' said Valentine. 'Tell me, Maximilien, even though our cup of sorrows is more than over-flowing.'

'Dear Valentine,' Morrel said, trying to master his own feelings and speak calmly. 'Please listen, because what I have to say is most important. When do they intend for you to marry?'

'Maximilien,' said Valentine, 'I don't want to hide anything from you. They were discussing my marriage this morning, and my grandmother, on whom I had counted as an unfailing support, not only declared herself to be in favour of my marrying Franz d'Epinay, but wants it so much that she is only waiting for his return: the contract will be signed the very next day.'

The young man gave a painful sigh and for a long time stared sadly at the girl. 'Alas,' he said quietly, 'it is terrible to hear the woman one loves say calmly: "The hour of your torment is fixed, it will take place shortly, but no matter, this must be and I shall not make any objection to it." Well, since you tell me that they are only waiting for Monsieur d'Epinay to sign the contract, and since you will be his the day after he arrives home, then you will be engaged to Monsieur d'Epinay tomorrow, because he reached Paris this morning.'

Valentine cried out.

'I was with the Count of Monte Cristo an hour ago,' Morrel continued. 'We were talking, he about the sorrow in your house and I about your sorrow, when suddenly a carriage pulled up in the courtyard. Listen, I have never until now believed in premonitions, Valentine, but henceforth I must. At the sound of that carriage, I began to tremble. Soon I heard footsteps on the stairs. The echoing steps of the Commander did not terrify Don Juan[1] more than those steps terrified me. At length the door opened. Albert de Morcerf was the first to come in and I was about to doubt my own instincts and decide that I had been mistaken, when another young man approached behind him and the count exclaimed: "Ah, Baron Franz d'Epinay!" I had to summon up all the strength and courage in my heart to contain my feelings. I may have gone pale, I may have shuddered, but I certainly kept a smile on my lips. Five minutes later, however, I left without hearing a single word of what had been said in that time. I was totally prostrate.'

'Poor Maximilien!' Valentine muttered.

'Here I am, Valentine. Now, answer me this, as you would answer a man to whom your words are the difference between life and death: what are you going to do?'

Valentine lowered her head. She was overwhelmed.

'Listen,' said Morrel, 'this is not the first time that you have thought about the situation in which we now find ourselves. It is serious, it is pressing, it is crucial. I do not think this is the moment to give way to sterile misery: that may be enough for those who want to suffer at their ease and have time to drink their own tears. There are people like that, and God will no doubt reward them in heaven for their resignation on earth; but anyone who has the will to fight will not lose precious time, but immediately strike back at that Fate which has dealt a blow. Have you the will to fight against ill-fortune, Valentine? Tell me, because that is what I have come to ask you.'

Valentine shuddered and looked at Morrel wide-eyed in terror. The idea of standing up to her father, her grandfather, in short her whole family, had not even occurred to her.

'What are you saying, Maximilien?' she asked. 'What do you mean by "fight"? Rather call it a sacrilege! Am I to struggle against my father's orders and the wishes of my dying grandmother! Impossible!'

Morrel shuffled.

'You are too noble a spirit not to understand me and you do understand me, dear Maximilien, since I have reduced you to silence. I, fight? God forbid! No, no, I must keep all my strength to struggle against myself and drink my own tears, as you say. As for bringing sorrow to my father and disturbing my grandmother's final hours – never!'

'You are right,' said Morrel coolly.

'My God! The way you say that . . .' Valentine cried, wounded.

'I say it as a man who admires you, mademoiselle.'

'Mademoiselle!' Valentine cried. 'Mademoiselle! Oh, the selfish man! He sees I am in despair and pretends he cannot understand me.'

'You are mistaken, I understand you perfectly. You do not want to go against Monsieur de Villefort's wishes, you do not want to disobey the marquise, and tomorrow you will sign the contract binding you to your husband.'

'But what else can I do, for heaven's sake?'

'Don't ask me, Mademoiselle, I am a poor judge in this case and my selfishness would blind me,' said Morrel, his blank voice and clenched fists indicating his growing exasperation.

'What would you have suggested, Morrel, if you had found me ready to accept your proposal? Come, tell me. Instead of telling me that I am doing wrong, advise me.'

'Are you seriously asking me for advice, Valentine?'

'Yes, indeed, dear Maximilien. If it is good, I shall take it. You know that I am devoted to you.'

'Valentine,' Morrel said, taking away an already loose plank, 'give me your hand to show that you forgive me my anger. You understand, my head is reeling and in the past hour the maddest ideas have been whirling around my head. Oh, if you were not to take my advice . . .'

'Which is?'

'This, Valentine.'

The girl raised her eyes to heaven and sighed.

'I am free,' Maximilien continued. 'I am rich enough for both of us. I swear to you that you will be my wife even before my lips have touched your brow.'

'You are making me afraid,' the girl said.

'Come with me,' Morrel said. 'I will take you to my sister, who is worthy of being yours. We shall set off for Algiers, for England or for America, unless you would prefer us to find a place together in the country where we can wait until our friends have overcome your family's objections before we return to Paris.'

Valentine shook her head. 'I was expecting this, Maximilien,' she said. 'This is a mad scheme and I should be madder even than you if I were not to stop you immediately with a single word: impossible, Morrel, it is impossible.'

'So you will follow your fate, whatever it may bring, without even trying to resist?' Morrel said, his face clouding over.

'Yes, even if it kills me!'

'Well, Valentine,' Maximilien continued, 'I can only repeat that you are right. Indeed, I am the madman and you have proved to me that passion can blind the sanest mind. So thank you, thank you for reasoning without passion. Very well, it's agreed then, tomorrow you will be irrevocably engaged to Monsieur Franz d'Epinay, not by that theatrical formality invented for the last act of a comedy, which is called "signing the contract", but by your own free will.'

'Once more, Maximilien, you are driving me to despair! Once more you are turning the knife in the wound! What would you do, if your sister were to listen to the sort of advice you are giving me?'

'Mademoiselle,' Morrel said with a bitter smile, 'I am selfish and an egoist, as you say; and, as such, I do not think of what others would do in my position, only of what I intend to do. I think that I have known you for a year; that, on the day we met, I wagered all my chances of happiness on your love; that the day came when you told me that you loved me; and that from that day forward I have staked all my future on having you. That has been my life. Now, I no longer think anything. All I can tell myself is that fate has turned against me, that I expected to win heaven and I have lost it. It happens every day that a gambler loses not only what he has, but also what he does not have.'

Morrel spoke perfectly calmly. Valentine looked at him for a moment with her large questioning eyes, trying not to let those of Morrel look at the storm already raging at the bottom of her heart. 'So what will you do?' she asked.

'I shall have the honour of bidding you farewell, Mademoiselle, asking God, who hears my words and reads what is in my heart, to witness that I wish you a tranquil life, happy and busy enough for it to hold no place for any memory of me.'

'Oh,' Valentine murmured.

'Farewell, Valentine, farewell!' Morrel said, bowing.

'Where are you going?' the young woman cried, reaching out her hand through the fence and grasping Maximilien by his jacket, realizing from her own inner turmoil that her lover's calm demeanour must be feigned. 'Where are you going?'

'I am going to ensure that I bring no further disruption to your family and to give an example for all honest and devoted men who find themselves in my position to follow.'

'But before you leave, tell me what you are going to do, Maximilien.'

The young man smiled sadly.

'Speak, speak!' Valentine cried. 'I beg you, speak!'

'Has your resolve changed, Valentine?'

'It cannot change. Alas, unhappy man, you know it cannot!' she said.

'Then, Valentine, adieu!'

Valentine shook the grille with a force that one would have thought beyond her and, as Morrel was leaving, put both hands through the fence and clasped them, twisting them together. 'What are you going to do?' she cried. 'Where are you going?'

'Have no fear,' said Maximilien, stopping three yards from the gate. 'It is not my intention to make another man responsible for the harsh fate that is in store for me. Anyone else might threaten to find Monsieur Franz, provoke him and fight with him; but all that would be senseless. What has Monsieur Franz to do with all this? He saw me this morning for the first time, and has already forgotten that he saw me. He did not even know that I existed when an understanding between your two families decided that you would belong to one another. So I have no quarrel to pick with Monsieur Franz, I swear it. I shall not blame him.'

'Whom then? Me?'

'You, Valentine! Oh, God forbid. Woman is sacred, the woman one loves is holy.'

'Yourself then, you unhappy man . . . ? Yourself?'

'I am the guilty one, am I not?' said Morrel.

'Maximilien, come here,' said Valentine. 'I command it!'

Maximilien came over, smiling softly. Had it not been for the pallor of his face, one might have thought he was in his normal state.

'Listen to me, my dear, my beloved Valentine,' he said in his low, melodious voice. 'People like us, who have never had a thought that would have made them blush before others, before their parents or before God, people like us can read one another's hearts like an open book. I have never been a character in a novel, I am not a melancholy hero, I have no pretensions to be Manfred or Antony.[2] But without words, without oaths and protestations, I entrusted my life to you. You are failing me and you are right to do what you are doing, I told you so and I repeat it. But you are failing me and my life is lost. If you go away from me, Valentine, I shall be alone in the world. My sister is happy with her husband, and her husband is only my brother-in-law, that is to say a man who is attached to me by social convention alone; hence, no one on earth has any need of me and my existence is useless. This is what I shall do: I shall wait until the last second before you are married, because I do not wish to lose even the faintest shadow of one of those unexpected twists of fate that chance sometimes has in store for us: between now and then, Franz d'Epinay may die; or, just as you are approaching it, a bolt of lightning may strike the altar. To a condemned man, everything is credible and, when his life itself is at stake, miracles may be counted possible events. So, as I say, I shall wait until the final moment and when my misfortune is certain, without any hope or remedy, I shall write a confidential letter to my brother-in-law and another to the prefect of police to inform him of my intention, and in the corner of some wood, beside some ditch or on the bank of some river, I shall blow out my brains, as surely as I am the son of the most honest man who has ever lived in France.'

Valentine was seized with a violent trembling. She let go of the fence that she had been holding in both hands, her arms fell to her sides and two large tears ran down her cheeks. The young man remained standing before her, sombre and resolute.

'Oh, for pity's sake, for pity's sake,' she said, 'tell me that you will live.'

'No, on my honour,' Maximilien said. 'But what does it matter to you? You will have done your duty and your conscience will be clear.'

Valentine fell to her knees, clasping her breaking heart. 'Maximilien,' she said, 'Maximilien, my friend, my brother on earth, my true husband in heaven, I implore you, do as I shall and live with your suffering. Perhaps one day we shall be reunited.'

'Adieu, Valentine!'

'My God,' Valentine said, raising her two hands to heaven with a sublime expression on her face, 'witness that I have done everything in my power to remain a dutiful daughter: I have begged, prayed and implored, but he has not listened to my entreaties, to my prayers or to my tears. Well, then,' she continued, wiping away her tears and recovering her resolve, 'I do not wish to die of remorse, I should rather die of shame. You will live, Maximilien, and I shall belong to no one except you. When? At once? Speak, order me, I am ready.'

Morrel, who had again taken a few steps away, came back once more, pale with joy, his heart swelling, and, passing both hands through the fence to Valentine, said: 'My dearest friend, you must not speak to me in that way; or else, let me die. Why should I owe my possession of you to force, if you love me as I love you? Are you obliging me to live, out of humanity, and nothing more? In that case, I should prefer to die.'

'In truth,' Valentine murmured, 'who in the world loves me? He does. Who has consoled me in all my unhappiness? He has. Who is the repository of all my hopes, the focus of my distracted eyes, the resting-place of my bleeding heart? He is, none but he. Well, now it is you who are right, Maximilien. I shall follow you, leave my father's house, everything. Oh, how ungrateful I am!' she exclaimed with a sob. 'Everything! Even my dear grandfather – I was forgetting him!'

'No,' said Maximilien. 'You shall not leave him. It appears, as you said, that Monsieur Noirtier feels some sympathy for me; so, before you leave, tell him everything; his consent will be a sanction for you before God. Then, as soon as we are married, he will come with us: instead of one child, he will have two. You told me how he spoke to you and how you answered. Come, Valentine, I shall soon learn this tender language of signs. I swear to you, instead of despair, it is happiness that awaits us.'

'Oh, Maximilien, look, look what power you have over me: you have almost made me believe what you are saying; and yet it is insane, because I shall bear my father's curse. I know him, his heart is stone, he will never forgive. So, listen to me, Maximilien, if by some trick, by prayer, by an accident – I don't know what – I can delay the marriage, you will wait for me, won't you?'

'I swear that I will, as you have sworn to me that this frightful marriage will never take place and that, even if you were to be dragged before a magistrate or a priest, you would say no.'

'I swear it, Maximilien, by all that is most sacred to me in the world, by my mother!'

'Then let us wait,' Morrel said.

'Yes, let us wait,' Valentine repeated. 'There are many things that may save unfortunates like ourselves.'

'I am trusting in you, Valentine,' Morrel said. 'Everything that you do will be well done; but suppose they disregard your prayers, suppose your father and Madame de Saint-Méran were to call tomorrow for Monsieur Franz d'Epinay to sign the contract . . .'

'You have my word, Morrel.'

'Instead of signing . . .'

'I shall come to you and we shall flee. But in the meantime, let's not tempt fate. We must not meet: it is a miracle, a divine gift that no one has yet discovered us. If that were to happen, if anyone knew how we meet, we should no longer have any recourse left.'

'You are right. But, then, how can I find out . . .'

'Through the notary, Monsieur Deschamps.'

'Yes, I know him.'

'And from me, because you may be assured that I myself shall write to you. My God, Maximilien! This marriage is as detestable to me as it is to you.'

'Very well. Thank you, my beloved Valentine,' Morrel continued. 'So we are agreed. Once I know the day and the hour, I shall hurry here and you can leap over this wall into my arms. It will be simple. A carriage will be waiting for us at the gate into the field, you will get in it with me and I shall take you to my sister's. There, incognito if you wish, or ostentatiously if you prefer, emboldened by knowing our own strength and will, we shall not allow ourselves to have our throats cut like lambs, defended only by our sighs.'

'Agreed,' said Valentine. 'And I in turn tell you that whatever you do, Maximilien, will be well done.'

'Oh!'

'Are you happy with your wife?' she said sadly.

'My beloved Valentine, it is too little to say no more than "yes".'

'Say it, even so.'

Valentine had drawn close to the fence, or rather had put her lips to it, and her words, on her sweet-scented breath, drifted across the lips of Morrel, whose mouth was pressed to the other side of the cold and implacable barrier.

'Goodbye,' Valentine said, tearing herself away from this bliss. 'Goodbye!'

'You will send me a letter?'

'Yes.'

'Thank you, my dear wife. Goodbye.'

There was the sound of an innocent lost kiss, and Valentine ran off under the linden-trees.

Morrel listened to the fading sounds of her dress rustling among the bushes and her footsteps on the gravel, raised his eyes to heaven with an indescribable smile of thanks to God for allowing him to be so well loved, then left in his turn. He went home and waited for the remainder of the evening and all the following day, but had no word. It was only on the day after that, at around ten o'clock in the morning, as he was about to set out for M. Deschamps, the notary, that the postman arrived with a little note which he recognized as being from Valentine, even though he had never seen her handwriting. It read as follows:

Tears, entreaties and prayers have all been in vain. Yesterday I spent two hours at the church of Saint-Philippe-du-Roule and for two hours I prayed from the depth of my heart; but God is as indifferent as men. The signing of the marriage contract is to take place this evening at nine o'clock.

I have only one word to give, as I have only one heart; and my word has been given to you, Morrel: my heart is yours.

This evening, then, at a quarter to nine, at the gate.

Your wife,

VALENTINE

P.S. My poor grandmother's state of health gets worse and worse. Yesterday, her excitement became delirium, and today the delirium is almost madness.

You will love me truly, won't you, Morrel, and help me to forget that I abandoned her in this state?

I think they are keeping grandpa Noirtier from learning that the contract will be signed this evening.

Morrel was not simply content with hearing this from Valentine; he went to the notary, who confirmed that the signing of the contract would take place at nine o'clock that evening. Then he went to see Monte Cristo, and there he heard the most detailed account. Franz had been to tell the count of this solemn event, and Mme de Villefort had written to him to apologize for not inviting him, but the death of M. de Saint-Méran and his widow's state of health cast a pall of sadness over the gathering which she could not ask the count to share, wishing him on the contrary every happiness.

On the previous day, Franz had been introduced to Mme de Saint-Méran, who had left her bed long enough for the introduction to take place, then immediately returned to it.

As one may well imagine, Morrel was in a state of agitation that could hardly be expected to escape an eye as perceptive as that of the count. Monte Cristo was consequently more affectionate towards him than ever, to such a point that two or three times Maximilien was on the verge of confessing everything to him. But he remembered his formal promise to Valentine and the secret remained sealed in his heart.

Twenty times during the day the young man re-read Valentine's letter. This was the first time she had written to him – and in such circumstances! Each time he re-read it, Maximilien renewed his promise to himself that he would make Valentine happy. A girl who can take such a courageous decision acquires every right: is there any degree of devotion that she does not deserve from the person for whom she has sacrificed everything! To her lover, she must surely be the first and worthiest object of his devotion, at once the wife and the queen; no soul is vast enough to thank and to love her.

Morrel kept thinking, with unspeakable anxiety, of the moment when Valentine would arrive and say: 'Here I am. Take me!'

He had prepared everything for the escape. Two ladders were concealed among the alfalfa grass in the field. A cab, which would take Maximilien himself, was waiting; there would be no servants and no lights, though, once round the first corner, they would light the lanterns, because it was essential that an excess of precautions should not lead them into the hands of the police.

From time to time a shudder passed right through Morrel's body. He was thinking of the moment when he would be helping Valentine come down from the top of the wall and would feel this girl, whom he had not touched until then except to squeeze her hand and kiss the tips of her fingers, abandon herself, trembling, to his arms.

However, when the afternoon came and Morrel knew that the time was drawing near, he felt a need to be alone. His blood was boiling and the merest question, even the voice of a friend, would have irritated him. He shut himself up at home and tried to read, but his eyes slipped across the pages without taking anything in, and eventually he tossed the book aside and, for the second time, set about drawing his plan, his ladders and his field.

At last, the moment approached.

No man truly in love has ever let the hands of a clock go peacefully on their way. Morrel tortured his so much that finally they showed half-past eight at six o'clock; so he decided that it was time to leave, that nine o'clock might be the hour appointed for signing the contract, but that in all probability Valentine would not wait for this pointless ceremony. Leaving the Rue Meslay at half-past eight on his clock, Morrel went into the field just as eight o'clock was striking at Saint-Philippe-du-Roule. The horse and cab were hidden behind a little ruined hut in which Morrel himself was accustomed to hide.

Little by little, night fell and the trees in the garden merged into deep black clusters. Morrel came out of his hiding-place and, with beating heart, went to look through the hole in the fence. So far, there was no one there.

Half-past eight struck. Half an hour more went by in waiting. Morrel walked up and down; then, at increasingly frequent intervals, went over to press his face against the fence. The garden was growing darker and darker, but he looked in vain for the white dress in the blackness and listened in vain for the footfall on the path.

The house, which could be seen through the leaves, remained dark and there was nothing about it that suggested a house open to celebrate an event as important as the signing of a marriage contract. Morrel looked at his watch, which struck a quarter to ten; but almost at once the church clock, which he had heard already two or three times, corrected the mistake by striking half-past nine. This meant he had already been waiting for half an hour beyond the time Valentine herself had appointed: she had said nine o'clock, before rather than after.

This was the worst moment for the young man, on whose heart each second fell like a lead mallet.

The slightest rustling of the leaves or whisper of the wind would catch his attention and make the sweat break out on his forehead. When he heard these sounds, shivering, he set up his ladder and, not to lose any time, put his foot on the bottom rung. While he was caught between these contraries of hope and despair, in the midst of these swellings and contractions of the heart, he heard ten o'clock strike on the church tower.

'It's impossible,' Morrel muttered in terror, 'that the signing of a contract should take so long, unless something out of the ordinary has happened. I've taken everything into account and worked out how long each part of the ceremony should take: something is wrong.'

Now, alternately, he paced feverishly in front of the gate and stopped to press his burning forehead on the icy metal. Had Valentine fainted after the contract? Had she been stopped while trying to flee? These were the only two conjectures that occurred to the young man, and each was horrifying. Eventually he fixed on the idea that Valentine's strength had given way during her flight and she had fallen, senseless, in the middle of one of the garden paths. 'And if that is so,' he cried, hurrying to the top of the ladder, 'I should lose her, and by my own fault!'

The demon which had whispered this idea to him would not leave him, buzzing in his ear with that persistence which rapidly ensures that some doubts, by the sole force of reasoning, become certainties. Seeking to penetrate the growing darkness, his eyes thought that they could detect something lying on the path under the trees. Morrel even ventured to call and thought he could hear a faint cry carried back to him on the wind.

At length half-past also struck. It was impossible for him to contain himself any longer. Anything might have happened. Maximilien's temples were beating violently and a haze clouded his eyes. He swung his legs over the wall and jumped down on the far side.

He was in the Villeforts' garden; he had just climbed over their wall. He was fully aware of what might be the consequences of such an action, but he had not come this far only to turn back. In a few seconds he had passed the clump of trees and reached a point from which he could see the house.

This confirmed one thing that Morrel had guessed in trying to peer through the trees, which was that instead of the lights that he expected to see shining from every window, as would be normal on such an important occasion, he could see nothing except a grey pile, still further obscured by the great curtain of darkness cast by a huge cloud crossing in front of the moon. From time to time a single light flickered as it crossed in front of three first-floor windows, as if distraught. These three windows belonged to the apartment of Mme de Saint-Méran.

Another light remained motionless behind some red curtains. These were the curtains at the windows of Mme de Villefort's bedroom.

Morrel guessed all these things. Often, trying to follow Valentine in his thoughts at all times of the day, he had asked her to make him a plan of the house, so that now he knew it, without ever having seen it.

The young man felt even more appalled by this darkness and silence than he had been by Valentine's absence. Distraught, wild with grief and determined to brave all in order to see Valentine and discover what was wrong, whatever it might be, Morrel reached the edge of the trees and was about to start crossing the flower garden – as fast as he could, because it was entirely open – when a sound of voices, still quite distant, drifted across to him on the wind.

At this noise, he stepped backwards into the bushes from which he had already half emerged and, concealing himself entirely in them, remained there without moving or making a sound, buried in darkness.

He was now resolved. If it was Valentine alone, he would whisper to her as she went past; if Valentine was accompanied by someone else, he would at least see her and ensure that no misfortune had befallen her; if they were strangers, he might grasp some words of their conversation and manage to understand this mystery, which so far remained impenetrable.

The moon now came out from behind the cloud that had been concealing it and Morrel saw Villefort at the door leading into the garden, followed by a man in black. They came down the steps and began to walk towards where he was hiding. They had only taken a few paces when Morrel recognized the man in black as Dr d'Avrigny. Seeing them approach, he automatically shrank back until he came up against the trunk of a sycamore at the centre of the clump; here he was obliged to stop.

Very shortly afterwards, the sound of the two men's footsteps left the gravel.

'My dear doctor,' the crown prosecutor said, 'heaven is definitely looking with disfavour on my house. What a horrible death! What a terrible blow! Do not try to console me; alas, the wound is too fresh and too deep. Dead! She is dead!'

The young man burst out in a cold sweat and his teeth began to chatter. Who then had died in this house which Villefort himself described as accursed?

'My dear Monsieur de Villefort,' the doctor replied, in tones that only increased the young man's terror. 'I have not brought you here to console you. Quite the opposite.'

'What do you mean?' the crown prosecutor asked, appalled.

'What I mean is that, behind the misfortune that has just befallen you, there may be another, still greater misfortune.'

'My God!' said Villefort, clasping his hands. 'What more have you to tell me?'

'Are we quite alone, my friend?'

'Yes, quite alone. But why these precautions?'

'Because I have a dreadful secret to impart to you,' the doctor said. 'Let's sit down.'

Villefort fell rather than sat down on a bench. The doctor remained standing in front of him, one hand resting on his shoulder. Morrel, chilled with terror, was clasping one hand to his forehead, while the other was pressed against his heart, for fear that they could hear it beating.

'Dead, dead!' he repeated, his thoughts echoed by his heart. And he himself felt as though he would die.

'Speak, doctor, I am listening,' said Villefort. 'Strike. I am ready for anything.'

'Madame de Saint-Méran was certainly very old, but she enjoyed excellent health.'

Morrel breathed again for the first time in ten minutes.

'Sorrow killed her,' said Villefort. 'Yes, doctor, sorrow. After forty years living with the marquis . . .'

'It was not sorrow, my dear Villefort,' the doctor said. 'Sorrow can kill, though such cases are rare, but it does not kill in one day, in one hour, in ten minutes.'

Villefort did not answer, merely raising his head, which had been lowered until then, and looking at the doctor with terrified eyes.

'Did you stay with her in her last moments?' d'Avrigny asked.

'Of course,' the crown prosecutor answered. 'You whispered to
me not to go away.'

'Did you notice the symptoms of the disease to which Madame
de Saint-Méran succumbed?'

'Certainly I did. Madame de Saint-Méran had three successive
attacks, a few minutes apart, the intervals becoming shorter and
the attacks more serious. When you arrived, Madame de Saint-
Méran had already been gasping for breath for some minutes. Then
she suffered what I took to be a simple nervous attack: I did not
start to become seriously concerned until I saw her rise up in her
bed, her limbs and her neck stiffening. At this point, I could see
from her face that it was more serious than I had believed. When
the crisis was over, I tried to catch your eye, but I could not.
You were taking her pulse and counting it when the second crisis
occurred, before you had turned in my direction. The second seizure
was worse than the first, accompanied by the same convulsive
movements, while the mouth contracted and turned purple. At the
third crisis she expired. I had already recognized tetanus from the
first attack, and you confirmed that opinion.'

'Yes,' said the doctor, 'in front of everybody; but now we are
alone.'

'What do you have to tell me, doctor?'

'That the symptoms of tetanus and poisoning by certain vegetable
substances are precisely the same.'

M. de Villefort leapt to his feet; then, after standing for a moment
in silence, he sat back down on the bench.

'My God, doctor,' he exclaimed. 'Have you really considered
what you are saying?'

Morrel did not know if he was awake or dreaming.

'Listen,' the doctor said. 'I know the significance of what I say
and the character of the man to whom I have said it.'

'Are you speaking to the magistrate or to your friend?' Villefort
asked.

'To my friend, and to him alone at the moment. The similarity
between the symptoms of tetanus and those of poisoning by certain
extracts of plants are so similar that, if I had to put my hand to
what I am telling you, I should be reluctant to do so. So, I repeat, I
am addressing you as a friend, not as a magistrate. What I have
to say to this friend is as follows: for the three-quarters of an
hour that it lasted, I studied Madame de Saint-Méran's agony, her

convulsions and her death. I am convinced, not only that Madame de Saint-Méran died of poisoning, but that I can say – I can actually say – what poison killed her.'

'Monsieur!'

'Look, it is all there: drowsiness, broken by nervous fits; over-excitement of the brain; sluggishness of the vital organs. Madame de Saint-Méran succumbed to a massive dose of brucine or strychnine, which was administered to her, no doubt by chance, perhaps by mistake.'

Villefort grasped the doctor's hand.

'Impossible!' he said. 'My God, I must be dreaming! I must be dreaming! It is appalling to hear a man like yourself say such things. In heaven's name, doctor, tell me you may be mistaken.'

'Of course, I may, but . . .'

'But?'

'But I think not.'

'Doctor, spare me. In the last few days, so many unheard-of things have been happening to me that I am beginning to believe in the possibility that I may be going mad.'

'Did anyone apart from me see Madame de Saint-Méran?'

'No one.'

'Were any prescriptions sent out to the chemist's that were not shown to me?'

'None.'

'Did Madame de Saint-Méran have any enemies?'

'I know of none.'

'Did anyone have an interest in seeing her dead?'

'No, good heavens! My daughter is her sole heir. Valentine alone . . . Oh, but if I could ever entertain such a thought I should drive a dagger into my heart to punish it for conceiving the idea.'

'Come!' M. d'Avrigny exclaimed in his turn. 'My dear friend, God forbid that I should accuse anyone; I am only speaking of an accident, you understand, a mistake. But whether accident or mistake, the fact is there, and it whispers to my conscience; so my conscience speaks aloud to you: make enquiries.'

'Of whom? How? What about?'

'Let's see. Perhaps Barrois, the old servant, made a mistake and gave Madame de Saint-Méran a potion which had been prepared for his master.'

'For my father?'

'Yes.'

'But how could a potion that had been prepared for Monsieur Noirtier poison Madame de Saint-Méran?'

'Quite simply. As you know, in some illnesses, poisons become remedies; paralysis is one of those. About three months ago, after trying everything to restore the power of speech and movement to Monsieur Noirtier, I decided to resort to one final remedy; so, as I say, for the past three months I have been treating him with brucine. The last potion that I ordered for him contained six centigrammes. These six centigrammes had no effect on Monsieur Noirtier's paralysed organs; he has in any case become accustomed to them by successive doses; but the same six centigrammes would be enough to kill anyone else but him.'

'But my dear doctor, there is no direct access from Monsieur Noirtier's apartment to that of Madame de Saint-Méran, and Barrois never used to go into my mother-in-law's. So, even though I know you to be the most skilled and, above all, the most conscientious man in the world, and even though your words are on every occasion a guiding light to me, equal to that of the sun, well, doctor, even so and despite my belief in you, I must have recourse to the maxim: *errare humanum est*.'

'Listen, Villefort,' said the doctor, 'is there any of my colleagues in whom you have as much confidence as you do in me?'

'Why do you ask? What are you suggesting?'

'Call him in; I shall tell him what I saw, what I observed, and we shall perform an autopsy.'

'Will you find any traces of poison?'

'No, not of poison, I'm not saying that, but we can establish the exasperation of the nervous system and recognize the obvious and undeniable signs of asphyxia, and tell you: my dear Villefort, if this was caused by negligence, take care for your servants; if by hatred, take care for your enemies.'

'Good Lord, d'Avrigny, what are you suggesting?' Villefort answered despondently. 'If anyone apart from you were to be taken into our confidence, an enquiry would become necessary – an enquiry, in my house! Impossible! But of course,' the crown prosecutor continued, pulling himself up and looking anxiously at the doctor, 'of course, if you want it, if you absolutely insist, I shall have it done. Indeed, it may be my duty to pursue the matter; my character demands it. But you see me already overwhelmed with sadness: to start such a scandal in my house after such sorrow. It would kill my wife and daughter; and I, doctor, I . . . You know, a man does not reach my position, a man cannot be crown prosecutor for twenty-five years, without acquiring a fair number of enemies. I have many of them. If this affair were to come out, it would be a triumph that would make them leap for joy and cover me with shame. Forgive me these base thoughts. If you were a priest, I should not dare to say that to you, but you are a man and you know other men. Doctor, doctor, tell me: you have not told me anything, have you?'

'My dear Monsieur de Villefort,' the doctor replied, shaken, 'my first duty is one of humanity. I would have saved Madame de Saint-Méran, if it had been within the power of science to do so, but she is dead and my responsibility is to the living. Let us bury this terrible secret in the depth of our hearts. If the eyes of anyone are opened to it, I shall allow my silence to be blamed on my ignorance. However, Monsieur, keep on looking, actively, because this may not be an end to it. And when you find the guilty party, if you find him, I shall say: you are the judge, do what you will!'

'Thank you, doctor, thank you,' Villefort said, with inexpressible joy. 'I shall never have a better friend than you.' And, as though afraid that Dr d'Avrigny might change his mind, he got up and led him back towards the house.

They vanished. Morrel, as if needing to breathe, put his head out of the arbour so that the moon shone on a face so pale that it might have been taken for that of a ghost.

'God is protecting me, in an obvious but terrible way,' he said. 'But Valentine, Valentine, my poor friend! Can she withstand so much sorrow?' And he looked alternately from the window with the red curtains to the three with the white ones.

The light had almost entirely disappeared from the red-curtained window. No doubt Mme de Villefort had just put out her lamp and only a night-light cast a flicker on the window-panes. But at the far end of the building he saw someone open one of the three windows with the red curtains. A candle on the mantelpiece cast a few rays of pale light outside and a shadow came and leant over the balcony. Morrel shuddered: he thought he had heard a sob.

It was not surprising that this soul, usually so strong and resolute, now tossed alternately up and down between the two most powerful of human passions, love and fear, should have been weakened to the point where he had begun to have hallucinations.

Although it was impossible for Valentine to see him where he was hiding, he thought he saw the shadow in the window motion to him: his troubled mind told him and his warm heart repeated this to him. The double error became a compelling reality and, with one of those incomprehensible impulses of youth, he leapt from his hiding-place, at the risk of being seen, or of terrifying Valentine and raising the alarm, were she to give an involuntary cry. In two bounds he crossed the flower garden that seemed in the moonlight as broad and white as a lake and, beyond the row of orange trees planted in boxes in front of the house, he reached the steps, ran up them and pushed the door, which opened freely before him.

Valentine had not seen him. Her eyes were lifted upwards, following a silver cloud gliding in front of the deep blue sky, its shape like that of a ghost rising to heaven. Her romantic and poetic nature told her it was her grandmother's soul.

Meanwhile Morrel had crossed the antechamber and found the banisters. A staircarpet muffled his steps. In any event, he had reached such a degree of exultation that not even the presence of M. de Villefort himself would have frightened him. Should M. de Villefort appear in front of him, he had decided what to do: he would go up to him and confess everything, begging his forgiveness and his approval of the love that bound Morrel to his daughter and vice versa.

Morrel was mad. Fortunately he did not see anyone.

Now, most of all, he found a use for Valentine's descriptions of the internal layout of the house. He arrived safely at the top of the stairs and, once there, was taking his bearings when a sob, in tones that he recognized, showed him the way. He turned around. A half-open door gave out a shaft of light and the moaning voice. He pushed it and went in.

At the bottom of an alcove, under a white sheet covering its head and outlining its shape, lay the corpse, still more terrifying in Morrel's eyes now that he had chanced on the secret of her death. Valentine was kneeling beside the bed, her head buried in the cushions of a broad-backed chair, shivering and heaving with sobs, her two hands stiffly joined above her head, which remained invisible.

She had come back here from the still-open window and was praying aloud in tones that would have melted the hardest heart. The words poured swiftly from her lips, made incoherent by the pain that grasped her throat in its burning embrace.

The moon, its light coming in shafts through the blinds, outshone the candle and cast a funereal glow over this scene of desolation.

Morrel was overcome by it. Though he was neither exceptionally pious nor easy to impress, it was more than he could do to remain silent on seeing Valentine suffer, weep and wring her hands in front of him. He sighed and breathed a name; the head, bathed in tears and like marble against the velvet cushion of the chair, the head of a Mary Magdalene by Correggio, was raised and turned towards him.

Valentine gave no sign of astonishment on seeing him there. No halfway emotions can exist in a heart swollen with utmost despair.

Morrel offered her his hand. To excuse herself for not coming to meet him, Valentine showed him the body lying under its shroud and once more began to sob. Neither one of them dared to speak in this room and each was reluctant to break a silence that seemed to have been ordered by some figure of Death standing in a corner with a finger to its lips.

Valentine, at length, was the first to speak.

'My friend,' she said, 'what are you doing here? Alas! I should say welcome to you, if it were not that Death had opened the doors of this house to you.'

'Valentine,' Morrel said in a trembling voice, his hands clasped, 'I have been here since half-past eight. Not seeing you come, I was overwhelmed with anxiety, so I leapt over the wall and entered the garden. Then I heard voices talking about the terrible occurrence . . .'

'What voices?' Valentine asked.

Morrel shuddered, suddenly remembering the whole conversation between the doctor and M. de Villefort; and, through the winding sheet, thought he could see those twisted arms, convulsed neck and violet lips.

'The servants' voices told me everything,' he said.

'But we are lost now that you have come here,' Valentine said, with neither anger nor fear.

'Forgive me,' Morrel replied in the same tones. 'I shall leave.'

'No,' said Valentine. 'They will see you. Stay.'

'Suppose someone comes?'

She shook her head. 'No one will come,' she said. 'Have no fear. This is our safeguard.' And she pointed to the shape of the body under its shroud.

'But what happened to Monsieur d'Epinay? Tell me, I beg you.'

'He arrived to sign the contract at the very moment when my dear grandmother was breathing her last.'

'Alas!' Morrel exclaimed, with a feeling of egoistic joy, thinking in himself that this death would indefinitely delay Valentine's marriage.

'But what increases my sorrow,' the young woman went on – as if his feeling were destined for instant punishment, 'is that my poor grandmother, as she died, ordered the marriage to be concluded as soon as possible. My God! Even she, thinking she was protecting me, acted against my interest!'

'Listen!' Morrel exclaimed. The two young people fell silent.

They could hear a door opening and footsteps along the floor in the corridor and on the staircase.

'It's my father, coming out of his study,' Valentine said.

'And showing the doctor out,' said Morrel.

'How do you know it is the doctor?' she asked in astonishment.

'I assume it must be,' said Morrel.

Valentine looked at him.

Meanwhile they heard the street door shut. M. de Villefort also went to lock the door to the garden and then came back up the stairs. Reaching the antechamber, he paused for a moment, as though hesitating between his own room and that of Mme de Saint-Méran. Morrel hastily hid behind a door. Valentine did not move: it was as though the depth of her sorrow had put her beyond the reach of ordinary fears.

M. de Villefort went into his room.

'Now,' said Valentine, 'you cannot leave either through the garden door or through that leading into the street.' Morrel looked at her in astonishment. 'Now,' she continued, 'there is only one safe way out remaining, which is through my grandfather's apartments.'

She got up. 'Follow me,' she said.

'Where?' Maximilien asked.

'To my grandfather's.'

'Me? To Monsieur Noirtier's?'

'Yes.'

'How can you think of such a thing, Valentine?'

'I have been thinking of it for a long time. He is my only friend in the world, and we both need him. Come.'

'Careful, Valentine,' Morrel said, reluctant to do as she said. 'Take care. The scales have fallen from my eyes and I can see that I was mad to come here. Are you sure that you are acting altogether sensibly, my dearest?'

'Yes,' Valentine said. 'I have no misgivings, except that I must leave the mortal remains of my grandmother alone when I promised to guard them.'

'Death is sacred in itself, Valentine.'

'Yes, and in any case I shall not be away long. Come.'

She crossed the corridor and went down a little staircase that led to Noirtier's. Morrel followed her on tiptoe. As they reached the landing outside Noirtier's rooms, they met the old servant.

'Barrois,' Valentine said, 'shut the door and let no one come in.' And she led the way.

Noirtier, still sitting up in his chair and alert to the slightest noise, knowing everything that went on through his servant, was looking eagerly towards the bedroom door. He saw Valentine and his eyes lit up. But the old man was struck by something grave and solemn in the young woman's approach and manner; and, while continuing to shine, his eye also looked questioningly at her.

'Dear grandfather,' she said briefly, 'listen carefully to what I have to say. You know that grandmother Saint-Méran died an hour ago and that now, apart from yourself, I have no one left who loves me in the world?'

An expression of infinite tenderness passed across the old man's eyes.

'So, if I have any sorrows or any hopes, I must confide them to you alone?'

The invalid answered, yes.

Valentine took Maximilien's hand. 'Well, then,' she said, 'look at this gentleman.'

The old man turned an enquiring and mildly astonished look on Morrel.

'This is Monsieur Maximilien Morrel,' she continued, 'the son of the honest businessman in Marseille whom you have no doubt heard of?'

'Yes,' the old man indicated.

'His is a name beyond reproach, and Maximilien is in process of making it glorious for, at the age of only thirty, he is a captain of spahis and an officer of the Legion of Honour.'

The old man indicated that he recalled Morrel.

'Well, then, grandfather,' said Valentine, kneeling in front of the old man and indicating Morrel with one hand, 'I love him and I shall belong to no one else! If I am forced to marry another, I shall let myself die or kill myself!'

The invalid's eyes expressed the tumult of ideas in his head.

'You love Monsieur Maximilien Morrel, don't you, grand-father?' the young woman asked.

'Yes,' the old man answered, motionless.

'And can you protect us, we who are also your children, against my father's will?'

Noirtier turned his intelligent look towards Morrel, as if to say: 'That depends.'

Maximilien understood. 'Mademoiselle,' he said, 'you have a sacred duty to perform in your grandmother's room. Would you permit me to have the honour of speaking to Monsieur Noirtier for a moment?'

'Yes, yes, that's right!' said the old man's eyes. Then he looked anxiously at Valentine.

'Do you mean: how will he understand you, grandfather?'

'Yes.'

'Oh, don't worry. We have so often spoken about you that he knows very well how I communicate with you.'

Then, turning to Maximilien with a charming smile (though one clouded with inexpressible sadness), she said: 'He knows everything that I do.'

She got to her feet, drew up a seat for Morrel and instructed Barrois not to let anyone in; then, after tenderly embracing her grandfather and sadly saying farewell to Morrel, she left.

As soon as she had gone, Morrel, to prove to Noirtier that he had Valentine's confidence and knew all their secrets, took the dictionary, the pen and paper, and put all of them on a table with a lamp. 'But first, Monsieur,' he said, 'please let me tell you who I am, that I love Mademoiselle Valentine and my intentions towards her.'

'I am listening,' Noirtier indicated.

He made an imposing sight, this old man, in appearance a useless burden, yet who had become the one protector, the sole support and the only judge of two young, handsome, strong lovers on the threshold of life. His face, with its extraordinary nobility and austerity, intimidated Morrel, whose voice trembled as he started to speak. He described how he had met and come to love Valentine, and how Valentine in her loneliness and unhappiness had accepted the offer of his devotion. He described his birth, position and fortune. More than once, when he looked questioningly at the old man, the latter looked back with the reply: 'Very well, continue.'

'Now,' Morrel said, when he had finished the first part of his story, 'having told you about my love and my hopes, Monsieur, should I tell you what we intend to do?'

'Yes,' said the invalid.

'Very well. This is what we have resolved.'

So he described everything to Noirtier: how a cab was waiting near the field, how he meant to elope with Valentine, take her to his sister's, marry her and, after waiting for a respectable period, hope that M. de Villefort would pardon him.

'No,' said Noirtier.

'No?' Morrel repeated. 'This is not what we should do?'

'No.'

'So the plan does not have your approval?'

'No.'

'Well, there is another way,' said Morrel.

The old man's eyes looked at him, asking: 'What way?'

'I shall go and find Monsieur Franz d'Epinay – I am pleased to be able to tell you this in the absence of Mademoiselle de Villefort – and I shall behave towards him in such a way as to oblige him to behave as a gentleman.'

Noirtier's look was still questioning.

'You want to know what I shall do?'

'Yes.'

'This. As I said, I shall go and speak to him and tell him the ties that unite me to Mademoiselle Valentine. If he is a man of feeling, he will prove it by himself renouncing his claim to his fiancée's hand, and from that moment until his death, he will be assured of my friendship and devotion. If he refuses, either out of greed or because of some stupid considerations of pride, after proving to him that he would be forcing himself on my wife, that Valentine loves me and cannot love anyone else, I shall fight with him, giving him every advantage. I shall then kill him or he will kill me. In the former case, he will not marry Valentine; in the latter, I shall be certain that Valentine will not marry him.'

Noirtier gazed with unspeakable pleasure on this noble and sincere countenance, on which were illustrated all the feelings that his tongue expressed, the look on his handsome face adding all that colour can add to a firm and accurate drawing. Yet when Morrel had finished speaking, Noirtier closed his eyes several times which, as we know, was his way of saying: 'No.'

'No?' said Morrel. 'Do you disapprove of this second plan, as you did the first?'

'Yes, I disapprove,' the old man replied.

'So, Monsieur, what can I do?' Morrel asked. 'Madame de Saint-Méran's last words were to hasten her granddaughter's marriage. Should I let things take their course?'

Noirtier remained motionless.

'Yes, I understand,' said Morrel. 'I must wait.'

'Yes.'

'But any delay may be fatal, Monsieur. Alone, Valentine is power-less and she will be forced to submit like a child. Having miracu-lously entered this house to find out what was happening and miraculously finding myself in your presence, I cannot reasonably expect such good fortune to recur. Believe me, and forgive this youthful vanity on my part, but only one or other of the courses that I have suggested can work. Tell me which you prefer: do you authorize Mademoiselle Valentine to entrust herself to my honour?'

'No.'

'Would you prefer me to go and speak to Monsieur d'Epinay?'

'No.'

'But, for heaven's sake, who will give us the help that we are praying for?'

The old man's eyes smiled, as usual when heaven and prayer were mentioned: the old Jacobin had retained some of his atheistic ideas.

'From chance?' said Morrel.

'No.'

'From you then?'

'Yes.'

'From you?'

'Yes,' the old man repeated.

'You do understand what I am asking, Monsieur? Forgive my asking you yet again, but my life depends on your reply: will our salvation come from you?'

'Yes.'

'Are you sure?'

'Yes.'

'Do you promise it?'

'Yes.'

There was such strength in the look that gave this affirmative reply that it was impossible to doubt the man's will, even if one might doubt his power to carry it out.

'Oh, thank you, Monsieur! Thank you a hundred times! But, unless a divine miracle restores your power of speech and movement, how can you, chained to that chair, dumb and motionless . . . how can you oppose the marriage?'

The old man's face lit up with a smile: it is a strange thing, a smile in the eyes on an unmoving face.

'So, I must wait?' the young man asked.

'Yes.'

'And the contract?'

The same smile reappeared.

'Are you telling me that it will not be signed?'

'Yes,' said Noirtier.

'So, not even the contract will be signed!' Morrel exclaimed. 'Forgive me, Monsieur! One may be forgiven for doubting such happiness. The contract will not be signed?'

'No,' said the invalid.

Despite this assurance, Morrel was reluctant to believe. Such a promise from a powerless old man was so strange that, instead of emanating from a powerful will, it might indicate a weakening of the faculties: is it not normal for a madman who does not know his own folly to claim that he can accomplish things that are beyond his power? A weak one speaks of the weights he can lift, a timorous one of the giants he can confront, the poor of the treasures he possesses and the most humble peasant, on account of his pride, is called Jupiter.

Whether it was that Noirtier understood the young man's uncertainties or that he did not completely trust in the docility that he had shown, he stared hard at him.

'What do you want, Monsieur?' Morrel asked. 'That I should repeat my promise to do nothing?'

Noirtier's look remained fixed and firm, as if to say that a promise was not enough; then it was lowered from Morrel's face to his hand.

'You want me to swear?' Maximilien asked.

'Yes,' the invalid replied with the same solemnity. 'I do.'

Morrel understood that the old man attached a great deal of importance to this oath. He held out his hand.

'On my honour,' he said, 'I swear to you that I shall await your decision before I do anything against Monsieur d'Epinay.'

'Very good,' said the old man's eyes.

'Now, Monsieur,' Morrel asked, 'do you wish me to leave?'

'Yes.'

'Without seeing Mademoiselle Valentine?'

'Yes.'

Morrel indicated that he was ready to obey. 'But first, Monsieur,' he said, 'will you allow your son to embrace you as your daughter did a moment ago?'

There was no mistaking the expression in Noirtier's eyes.

The young man put his lips on the old man's forehead at the very same place where the young woman had put hers. Then he bowed once more and went out.

Outside, in the hall, he found the old servant, who had been told by Valentine to wait for him. He guided him down a dark winding corridor to a little door leading into the garden. Once there, Morrel went back to the gate past the arbour and, in a moment, was on top of the wall. A second later, thanks to his ladder, he was in the alfalfa field, where the cab was still waiting for him.

He got in and, exhausted by all the day's emotions, but lighter in heart, he got home to the Rue Meslay at around midnight, threw himself on his bed and slept as deeply as though he were blind drunk.

LXXIV
THE VILLEFORT FAMILY VAULT

Two days later, a considerable throng gathered at around ten in the morning at M. de Villefort's door and watched a long line of funeral carriages and private coaches extending the whole length of the Faubourg Saint-Honoré and the Rue de la Pépinière. Among them there was one of peculiar shape which seemed to have travelled a long way. It was a sort of waggon, painted black, which had been one of the first to arrive for this sad appointment. On enquiry it had been learnt that, by a strange coincidence, this carriage contained the body of M. de Saint-Méran, so those who had come for a single funeral would find themselves following two bodies.

Their number was considerable. The Marquis de Saint-Méran, one of the most zealous and faithful dignitaries in the courts of King Louis XVIII and King Charles X,[1] had kept a good number of friends, and these, together with people who were socially acquainted with Villefort, made up a large crowd.

The authorities were immediately informed and it was agreed that the two processions could take place at once. A second hearse, decked out with the same funereal trimmings as the first, was brought to M. de Villefort's door and the coffin transferred to this funeral car from the waggon in which it had travelled.

The two bodies were to be buried in the cemetery of Père-Lachaise, where M. de Villefort had long ago inaugurated the vault ultimately intended for his whole family. Already, poor Renée's body had been laid to rest there, ten years later to be joined by those of her father and mother.

Paris, always curious and fascinated by the spectacle of a funeral, watched in solemn silence the passing of this magnificent procession which bore to their last resting-place two names of that old aristocracy who more than any others were celebrated for their traditional spirit, reliability in their dealings and obstinate devotion to principle.

Beauchamp, Albert and Château-Renaud were in the same funerary carriage, discussing this almost sudden death.

'I saw Madame de Saint-Méran only last year in Marseille,' said Château-Renaud, 'on my way back from Algeria. She was a woman fated to live to a hundred, thanks to her excellent health, sound mind and undiminished energy. How old was she?'

'Sixty-six,' Albert replied, 'at least, so Franz assures me. It was not old age that killed her, though, but grief at the death of the marquis. It appears that she was completely shattered by his death and never really recovered her wits.'

'Even so, what did she die of?' asked Beauchamp.

'A stroke, apparently, or an apoplexy. It's the same thing, isn't it?'

'More or less.'

'Apoplexy?' said Beauchamp. 'Now that's hard to believe. I too saw Madame de Saint-Méran a couple of times: she was petite, slightly built and much more of a nervous than a sanguine temperament. It's very rare for grief to produce apoplexy in a person of Madame de Saint-Méran's constitution.'

'In any event,' said Albert, 'whatever the illness or the doctor who killed her, this means that Monsieur de Villefort – or rather, Mademoiselle Valentine – or, again, rather, our friend Franz – can enjoy a splendid inheritance: an income of eighty thousand *livres*, isn't it?'

'What's more, it will be almost doubled when that old Jacobin, Noirtier, dies.'

'Now there's a tenacious old bird,' said Beauchamp. '*Tenacem propositi virum*.[2] I do believe he has wagered with death that he will bury all his heirs, and, by heaven, he'll do it. He really is the old Conventionnel[3] of '93, who told Napoleon in 1814: "You are going down because this empire of yours is a young shoot exhausted by its own growth. Take the republic as your guide, let's go back to the battlefield with a good constitution and I promise you five hundred thousand soldiers, another Marengo and a second Austerlitz.[4] Ideas never die, Sire, and, though they may slumber for a time, they wake up stronger than when they fell asleep." '

'It appears that for him men are like ideas,' said Albert. 'There's only one thing bothering me, which is how Franz d'Epinay will get on with a grandfather-in-law who cannot do without Franz's wife. By the way, where is Franz?'

'In the front carriage with Monsieur de Villefort, who already considers him one of the family.'

More or less similar conversations were taking place in each of the carriages in the funeral procession. People were amazed at these two deaths, so sudden and so close together, but no one suspected the terrible secret which M. d'Avrigny had revealed to M. de Villefort in their midnight walk.

After a drive of about an hour they reached the cemetery gates. The weather was calm but overcast, and so quite appropriate for the dismal ceremony that they had come to perform. Among the groups going towards the family vault Château-Renaud recognized Morrel, who had come alone and in a cab. He was walking by himself, very pale and silent, along the little path lined with yews.

'You – here!' Château-Renaud said, slipping his arm into the captain's. 'Do you know Monsieur de Villefort, then? And in that case, how is it that I have never seen you in his house?'

'It's not that I know Monsieur de Villefort, but that I knew Madame de Saint-Méran,' said Morrel.

At that moment Albert joined them with Franz.

'Here's not a good place to make introductions,' said Albert. 'But who cares? We're not superstitious, are we? Monsieur Morrel, let me introduce Monsieur Franz d'Epinay, a splendid travelling companion with whom I toured Italy. My dear Franz: Monsieur Maximilien Morrel, an excellent friend whom I have acquired in your absence and whose name you will hear coming up in the conversation every time I want to speak of heart, spirit and pleasant companionship.'

Morrel hesitated for a moment. He wondered if it was not disgraceful hypocrisy to address an almost friendly greeting to a man whose interests he was secretly undermining; but he recalled his oath and the solemnity of the occasion and made an effort to let nothing appear on his face. He contained himself and bowed.

'Mademoiselle de Villefort appears to be very sad,' Debray said to Franz.

'Yes,' said Franz. 'So much indeed that her sadness is inexplicable. This morning she was so overcome that I could hardly recognize her.'

These apparently simple words broke Morrel's heart. Had this man seen Valentine, had he spoken to her? The ardent young officer needed all his strength to resist the desire to break his vow. Instead he took Château-Renaud's arm and led him quickly towards the vault, in front of which the undertakers had just put down the two coffins.

'Fine dwelling,' said Beauchamp, glancing at the mausoleum.

'Summer palace, winter palace. You'll live there yourself in the end, my dear d'Epinay, as you're soon going to be one of the family. As for me, philosopher that I am, I should like a little country house, a cottage far away under the trees, with less hewn stone on my poor corpse. When I die, I shall say to those about my deathbed what Voltaire wrote to Pirron: *eo rus*;[5] and that will be it. Dammit, Franz, cheer up! Your wife's an heiress.'

'I must say, Beauchamp,' said Franz, 'you are impossible. Politics have accustomed you to laugh at everything, and men who administer affairs usually don't believe in anything. But, I must ask you, Beauchamp, when you have the honour to find yourself in the company of ordinary men and the good fortune to be out of politics for a moment, please try to pick up the heart that you leave behind at the cloakroom of the Lower and Upper House.'

'By God!' said Beauchamp. 'What is life except a pause in the antechamber of death?'

'Beauchamp's getting on my nerves,' Albert said, dropping behind four paces with Franz and leaving Beauchamp to continue his philosophical discussion with Debray.

The Villefort family vault consisted of a square of white stones, rising to a height of about twenty feet. An inner wall divided the families of Saint-Méran and Villefort into two compartments, each with its own entrance. Inside, there were none of those base drawers, one above the other, as in other tombs, which allow the dead to be packed in economically with an inscription like a label on each one. All that one could see at first through the bronze door was an austere, dark antechamber, separated from the tomb itself by a wall. It was in the middle of this wall that the two doors we mentioned were set, giving entrance to the Villefort and Saint-Méran family sepulchres.

Here, sorrow could have free rein without the silent contemplation or tearful prayers of the visitor to the tomb being disturbed by the songs, shouts or gallivanting of those merry passers-by who make a visit to the Père-Lachaise into a picnic or a lovers' meeting.

The two coffins were taken into the right-hand vault, which was that of the Saint-Méran family. They were placed on trestles that had been prepared in advance to receive these mortal remains. Only Villefort, Franz and a few close relatives entered the sanctuary.

Since the religious ceremony had been carried out at the door, and there were no speeches to be made, the mourners dispersed immediately, Château-Renaud, Albert and Morrel going off in one direction, Debray and Beauchamp in another. Franz remained at the gate of the cemetery with M. de Villefort. Morrel stopped on the first excuse and saw the two of them leaving in one of the funerary carriages; he found this tête-à-tête ominous. Then he returned to Paris and, though he was in the same carriage as Château-Renaud and Albert, did not hear a word of what the two young men said.

In fact, as Franz had been about to take his leave of M. de Villefort, the latter had asked: 'Tell me, Baron, when shall I see you again?'

'When you wish, Monsieur,' Franz replied.

'As soon as possible.'

'I am at your disposal. Do you wish us to return together?'

'If it does not inconvenience you.'

'Not at all.'

This was why the future father-in-law and future son-in-law got into the same carriage and Morrel, seeing them go by, was rightly disturbed. So Villefort and Franz returned to the Faubourg Saint-Honoré together.

The crown prosecutor, without going to see anyone or speaking to his wife and daughter, showed the young man into his study and, motioning him to a chair, said, 'Monsieur d'Epinay, I must remind you . . . and this is not such an inappropriate moment as it seems, because obedience to the dead is the first offering that one should place on their tombs . . . I must remind you of the wish that Madame de Saint-Méran expressed two days ago on her deathbed, namely that Valentine's marriage should not be delayed. You know that the affairs of the deceased are entirely in order and that her will bequeaths to Valentine the entire fortune of the Saint-Mérans. The notary showed me yesterday the documents that will allow us to draw up a definitive contract of marriage. You can see him and ask him on my behalf to show you these papers. His name is Monsieur Deschamps, Place Beauveau, Faubourg Saint-Honoré.'

'Monsieur,' d'Epinay replied, 'this may not be the moment for Mademoiselle Valentine, plunged as she is in grief and mourning, to think about getting married. In fact, I would be afraid that . . .'

M. de Villefort interrupted him. 'Valentine,' he said, 'will have no more urgent desire than to fulfil her grandmother's last wishes. I guarantee there will be no objection from that side.'

'In that case, Monsieur,' Franz replied, 'as there will be none from mine, you can go ahead at your own convenience. I have given my word and I shall keep it not only with pleasure but also with happiness.'

'Then nothing is stopping us. The contract was to have been signed three days ago, so we shall find it completely drawn up. We can sign it this very day.'

'But what about the period of mourning?' asked Franz.

'Don't worry,' said Villefort. 'You will not find that in this house convention is disregarded. Mademoiselle de Villefort can retire for the appropriate three months into her estate at Saint-Méran – I say, her estate, because from now on it belongs to her. There, in a week if you wish, quietly and with a minimum of ceremony, we can conduct the civil wedding. It was Madame de Saint-Méran's desire that her granddaughter should be married on the estate. Once the marriage has been concluded, Monsieur, you can return to Paris, and your wife will spend the period of mourning with her step-mother.'

'As you wish, Monsieur,' said Franz.

'Well, then,' Villefort continued, 'please be good enough to wait for half an hour. Valentine will come down to the drawing-room. I shall send for Monsieur Deschamps, we can read and sign the contract on the spot and, this evening, Madame de Villefort will take Valentine down to her estate, where we shall go and join them in a week's time.'

'Monsieur,' said Franz, 'I have only one thing to ask you.'

'What is that?'

'I should like Albert de Morcerf and Raoul de Château-Renaud to be present at the signature of the contract. As you know, they are my witnesses.'

'Half an hour will be enough to inform them. Would you like to go for them yourself? Or would you prefer me to have them sent for?'

'I would rather go myself, Monsieur.'

'So, I shall expect you in half an hour, Baron, and in half an hour Valentine will be ready.'

Franz bowed and left the room.

Hardly had the street-door closed behind him than Villefort sent one of the servants to ask Valentine to come down to the drawing-room in half an hour, because they were expecting the

notary and M. d'Epinay's witnesses. This unexpected news produced a great commotion in the house. Mme de Villefort refused
to believe it and Valentine was struck down as if by a bolt of
lightning. She looked frantically around her as if searching for
someone whom she could beg for help.

She tried to go down to find her grandfather, but on the stairs
she met M. de Villefort, who took her arm and led her into the
drawing-room. In the antechamber she passed Barrois and gave
the old servant a look of desperation.

A moment after Valentine, Mme de Villefort entered the drawing-
room with little Edouard. It was clear that the woman had been
affected by the family misfortunes: she was pale and seemed desperately tired. She sat down and took Edouard on her knees, occasionally hugging this child convulsively to her breast. He seemed to
have become the centre of her entire life.

Soon they heard the sound of two carriages entering the courtyard. One belonged to the notary, the other to Franz and his friends.
In a moment they were all gathered in the drawing-room.

Valentine was so pale that one could see the blue veins from her
temples standing out around her eyes and running the length of
her cheeks. Franz too was overcome with powerful feelings. As
for Château-Renaud and Albert, they looked at one another
with astonishment: the ceremony that had just finished did not
seem to them to have been sadder than the one that was about
to begin.

Mme de Villefort was in shadow, behind a velvet curtain and,
since she was constantly bent over her son, it was hard to tell
what was going on in her mind. M. de Villefort, as always, was
impassive.

The notary set out the papers with a lawyer's habitual precision,
sat down on his chair, raised his glasses and then turned to Franz.
'Are you Monsieur Franz de Quesnel, Baron d'Epinay?' he asked,
perfectly aware of the answer.

'I am,' Franz replied.

The notary bowed. 'I must inform you, Monsieur,' he said, 'as I
am requested to do by Monsieur de Villefort, that your intended
marriage with Mademoiselle de Villefort has altered the terms of
Monsieur Noirtier's will towards his granddaughter and that he is
withdrawing entirely the fortune that he intended to bequeath to
her. Let me at once add,' the notary continued, 'that the testator

has the right to alienate only a portion of his wealth and that, since he has withdrawn all of it, the will can successfully be contested, whereupon it will be declared null and void.'

'Yes,' Villefort said, 'though I must warn Monsieur d'Epinay in advance that my father's will is not to be contested in my lifetime, since my position does not allow me to suffer even the hint of a scandal.'

'Monsieur,' said Franz, 'I regret that it has been found necessary to raise such a question in front of Mademoiselle Valentine. I have never tried to discover the amount of her fortune which, even reduced, will be much larger than mine. What my family sought in my marriage to Monsieur de Villefort's family was rank; what I am seeking is happiness.'

Valentine made a barely perceptible sign of thanks, while two silent tears ran down her cheeks.

'In any event, Monsieur,' Villefort said to his future son-in-law, 'apart from the loss of this portion of your expectations, there is nothing in this unexpected will which is to your discredit; it may be explained by Monsieur Noirtier's weakness of mind. What displeases my father is not that Mademoiselle de Villefort is marrying you, but that she is marrying at all. Her marriage to any other man would have caused him equal displeasure. Old age is selfish, Monsieur, and Mademoiselle de Villefort was a devoted companion to Monsieur Noirtier in a way that the Baroness d'Epinay can no longer be. My father's unfortunate state means that people seldom discuss serious matters with him, the feebleness of his wits not allowing him to follow such conversations. I am quite convinced that at the moment, while he is aware that his granddaughter is getting married, Monsieur Noirtier has even forgotten the name of the man who is to become his grandson.'

Hardly had M. de Villefort spoken these words, to which Franz replied with a bow, than the door of the room opened and Barrois appeared.

'Gentlemen,' he said, in a voice that was strangely firm for a servant speaking to his masters on such a solemn occasion. 'Gentlemen, Monsieur Noirtier de Villefort wishes to speak immediately with Monsieur Franz de Quesnel, Baron d'Epinay.' Like the notary, and so that no one could be mistaken, he gave the fiancé his full title.

Villefort started, Mme de Villefort let her son slip down from her knees and Valentine got up, as pale and silent as a statue. Albert and Château-Renaud exchanged a second glance which was even more astonished than the first.

The notary looked at Villefort.

'Impossible,' said the crown prosecutor. 'In any event, Monsieur d'Epinay cannot leave the drawing-room at this moment.'

'It is precisely at this moment that my master, Monsieur Noirtier, wishes to speak of important matters with Monsieur Franz d'Epinay,' said Barrois, with equal firmness.

'Is grandpa Noirtier talking now?' Edouard asked, with his usual impertinence. But Mme de Villefort did not even laugh at this quip, so much was everyone preoccupied and so solemn did the occasion seem.

'Tell Monsieur Noirtier that it is impossible to do as he asks,' Villefort went on.

'Then Monsieur Noirtier would like to inform these gentlemen that he will have himself brought in person to the drawing-room,' said Barrois.

The astonishment reached its height. A sort of smile crept over Mme de Villefort's face. Valentine, as if involuntarily, looked towards the ceiling in gratitude to heaven.

'Valentine,' Villefort said, 'please be so good as to go and find out what this new whim of your grandfather's is.'

She hurried towards the door, but then M. de Villefort thought better of it and said: 'Wait, I shall come with you.'

'Excuse me, Monsieur,' said Franz, in his turn. 'It seems to me that, since I am the one whom Monsieur Noirtier is asking to see, it is above all up to me to do as he wishes. In any case, I shall be happy to pay my respects, since I have not yet had the opportunity to request the favour of doing so.'

'Oh, come, come!' said Villefort, clearly uneasy. 'Don't put yourself out.'

'Excuse me, Monsieur,' Franz said, in the voice of a man who has made up his mind. 'I should not like to miss this opportunity to prove to Monsieur Noirtier how wrong he would be to harbour any hostility towards me – and I am determined to overcome it, whatever the cause may be, by showing him my profound devotion.'

Without allowing Villefort to detain him any longer, Franz got up and followed Valentine, who was already going down the stairs

with the joy of a drowning person whose hand has touched a r[c]
M. de Villefort followed them.

Château-Renaud and Morcerf exchanged a third look which was
even more astonished than the first two.

LXXV

THE JUDICIAL ENQUIRY

Noirtier was waiting, dressed in black and seated in his chair.

When the three people he was expecting to see had entered, he
looked at the door, which his valet immediately closed.

'Mind what I say,' Villefort whispered to Valentine, who could
not disguise her joy. 'If Monsieur Noirtier wants to tell you something that will prevent your marriage, I forbid you to understand
him.'

Valentine blushed but did not reply. Villefort went across to
Noirtier. 'Here is Monsieur Franz d'Epinay,' he said. 'You asked
to see him, Monsieur, and he has acceded to your wishes. We have
all doubtless wanted this interview to take place for a long time
and I shall be delighted if it proves to you how ill-founded was your
opposition to Valentine's marriage.'

Noirtier replied only with a look that turned Villefort's blood to
ice. Then the same eyes asked Valentine to come over to him. In a
moment, thanks to the means which she usually employed in her
conversations with her grandfather, she had found the word 'key'.
Then she looked at the invalid, who was staring hard at the drawer
in a little table between the two windows. She opened the drawer
and did indeed find a key inside it.

Once she had the key and the old man had shown her that it
was the right one, his eyes turned towards an old, long-forgotten
writing-desk which everyone assumed to be full of useless papers.

'Should I open the writing-desk?' Valentine asked.

'Yes,' the old man indicated.

'Should I open the drawers?'

'Yes.'

'The ones at the side?'

'No.'

e middle?'

...e opened it and took out a bundle. 'Is this what you
...randfather?' she said.

'No.'

She took out all the other papers in turn, until there was absolutely nothing left in the drawer. 'It's empty now,' she said.

Noirtier's eyes were fastened on the dictionary.

'Yes, grandpa, I understand,' the young woman said. And she repeated each letter of the alphabet, one after another. At the letter 'S', Noirtier stopped her. She opened the dictionary and went down to the word 'secret'.

'Ah, there's a secret!' said Valentine.

'Yes,' Noirtier replied.

'Who knows it?'

Noirtier looked towards the door, through which the servant had just left.

'Barrois?' she asked.

'Yes,' said Noirtier.

'Should I call him?'

'Yes.'

She went to the door and called Barrois.

Meanwhile Villefort was sweating with impatience and Franz was struck dumb with astonishment.

The old servant appeared.

'Barrois,' said Valentine, 'my grandfather has asked me to take the key out of this console, open the desk and pull out this drawer. Now there is some secret compartment to this drawer which, it appears, you know; please open it.'

Barrois looked at the old man.

'Obey,' said Noirtier's intelligent eye. Barrois did so. A hidden compartment opened and revealed a bundle of papers, tied with a black ribbon.

'Is this what you want, Monsieur?' Barrois asked.

'Yes,' said Noirtier.

'To whom should I give these papers? To Monsieur de Villefort?'

'No.'

'To Mademoiselle Valentine?'

'No.'

'To Monsieur Franz d'Epinay?'

'Yes.'

Franz, in astonishment, took a step backwards. 'To me, Mo sieur?' he asked.

'Yes.'

Barrois handed him the papers and, looking at the cover, Franz read:

To be entrusted after my death to my friend General Durand, who will himself, when he dies, bequeath this packet to his son, with instructions to keep it, since it contains a document of the greatest importance.

'Well, then, Monsieur,' Franz asked, 'what would you like me to do with this document?'

'To preserve it, sealed, as it is, no doubt,' said the crown prosecutor.

'No, no,' Noirtier replied vigorously.

'Perhaps you would like the gentleman to read it?' Valentine asked.

'Yes,' the old man replied.

'Did you understand, Baron? My grandfather is asking you to read the paper,' Valentine said.

'In that case, let's sit down,' Villefort said impatiently. 'This will take some time.'

'Sit down,' said the old man's eye.

Villefort did so, but Valentine remained standing beside her father and leaning on the back of his chair, with Franz in front of him. The mysterious piece of paper was in his hand.

'Read,' said the old man's look.

Franz unwrapped the envelope and everything in the room fell silent. In the midst of this, he read: 'Abstract of the proceedings of the session of the Bonapartist Club in the Rue Saint-Jacques, held on February the fifth, 1815.' At that, Franz paused and exclaimed: 'February the fifth, 1815! That is the day on which my father was assassinated!'

Valentine and Villefort said nothing; only the old man's eye clearly commanded him to read on.

'But it was after he left this very club that my father disappeared,' Franz said.

Noirtier's look still said: 'Read!'

Franz continued: 'We, the undersigned Louis-Jacques Beau-

t-colonel in the artillery, Etienne Duchampy,
Claude Lecharpal, director of forestry,

declare that on February the fourth, 1815, a letter
as from the island of Elba, recommending to the members
Bonapartist Club, General Flavien de Quesnel who, having
ved the emperor from 1804 to 1815, was worthy of their trust
and goodwill, as being entirely devoted to the Napoleonic dynasty,
despite the title of baron with which King Louis XVIII had just
endowed his estate of Epinay.

'A letter was consequently sent to General de Quesnel inviting
him to take part in the following day's session, February the fifth.
This letter did not inform the general of either the street or the
number of the house in which the meeting was to be held, but asked
him to be ready for someone to collect him at nine o'clock in the
evening. Meetings were held between nine and midnight.

'At nine o'clock the president of the club called on the general.
The latter was ready. The president told him that one condition of
his admission was that he should always remain ignorant of the
venue for the meeting, and that he should allow his eyes to be
bound, swearing that he would not try to raise the blindfold.
General de Quesnel accepted this condition and promised on his
honour not to try to see where he was to be led.

'He had asked for his carriage to be prepared, but the president
told him that it could not under any circumstances be used, since
there was no sense in blindfolding the master if his coachman was
to keep his eyes open and recognize the streets through which they
drove.

' "What is to be done, then?" asked the general.

' "I have my own carriage," said the president.

' "Are you then so sure of your coachman that you would confide
in him a secret that you consider unwise to impart to mine?"

' "Our coachman belongs to the club," said the president. "We
are to be driven by a member of the council of state."

' "In that case," the general said, laughing, "We are running a
different risk, which is that we shall end in the ditch!"

'We cite this pleasantry as evidence that the general was in no
way obliged to take part in the meeting, but attended it of his own
free will.

'Once they had got into the coach, the president reminded the
general of his promise to let his eyes be bound. The general made

no objection to this formality and it was carried out with a scarf, left ready for the purpose in the coach. As they were driving, the president thought he observed the general trying to look under his blindfold and again reminded him of his oath. "Of course," said the general.

'The carriage stopped in a driveway off the Rue Saint-Jacques. The general got down, guided by the hand of the president, without being aware of the latter's eminence: he took him to be a simple member of the club. Crossing the drive, they went up to the first floor of the house and into the council chamber.

'The meeting had already begun. The members of the club, informed of the person who was to be introduced that evening, were all present. The general was led to the centre of the room and asked to take off his blindfold. He immediately complied and seemed very astonished at finding so many well-known faces in an organization, the very existence of which until then he had not even suspected.

'He was questioned about his loyalties, but contented himself with the answer that the letters from Elba must have made clear . . .'

Franz stopped reading. 'My father was a Royalist,' he said. 'There was no need to ask him about his loyalities, which were well known.'

'Hence my own attachment to him,' said Villefort. 'When two people share the same ideas, my dear Franz, they easily become attached to one another.'

'Read!' the old man said with a look.

Franz continued: 'Here, the president requested the general to explain himself more fully, but Monsieur de Quesnel replied that his chief wish was to know what they wanted of him.

'He was then acquainted with the contents of the letter from the island of Elba, recommending him to the club as a man whose help and co-operation could be counted on. One paragraph dealt at length with the emperor's probable return from Elba and promised a further letter with more details on the arrival of the ship *Pharaon*, belonging to the shipowner Morrel, of Marseille, whose captain was entirely devoted to the imperial cause.

'Throughout the time that this was being read, the general, on whom the company had thought they could rely as on a brother, gave on the contrary visible signs of disgust and dissatisfaction.

When the letter had been read, he remained silent, with lowered brow.

' "Well?" the president asked. "What do you say to this letter, Monsieur le Général?"

' "I say that it is a little soon," he replied, "since we gave our oaths to King Louis XVIII, for us to violate them on behalf of the former emperor." This time the reply was too unambiguous for there to be any mistake about his feelings.

' "General," the president said, "for us there is no present King Louis XVIII any more than there is any former emperor. There is only His Majesty the King and Emperor, who for ten months has been exiled from France, his state, by violence and treachery."

' "Excuse me, gentlemen," said the general. "It may be that for you there is no King Louis XVIII, but there is one for me, since it was he who made me baron and brigadier. I shall never forget that I owe these two titles to his fortunate return to France."

' "Monsieur," the president said, in the gravest tones, rising to his feet, 'beware of what you are saying. Your words clearly demonstrate that our friends on Elba were mistaken about you and that they misled us. What you have been told depended on the confidence we had in you and, consequently, on a belief that did you honour. Now it appears we were wrong: a title and a military rank have led you to transfer your loyalty to the new government that we wish to overthrow. We shall not oblige you to assist us: we would not enrol anyone against his conscience and his will; but we shall oblige you to behave as a man of honour, even if you should not be inclined to do so."

' "By man of honour you mean knowing of your conspiracy and not revealing it! I for my part should describe this as being your accomplice. You see that I am even more open than you are." '

'Oh, father,' said Franz, pausing. 'Now I understand why they killed you.'

Valentine could not help glancing at Franz: the young man was truly handsome in his filial devotion. Villefort was pacing up and down behind him, and Noirtier's eyes searched the face of everyone there, while the man's attitude remained stern and dignified.

Franz went back to the manuscript and continued: ' "Monsieur," the president said, "we asked you to come to this meeting, we did not drag you here by force. When we suggested blindfolding you, you did not demur. By agreeing to these two requests, you knew perfectly well that we were not concerned with bolstering up the throne of King Louis XVIII, because in that case we should not have taken so much trouble to hide from the police. Now, you understand, it would be too convenient if one could put on a mask in order to uncover people's secrets and then have simply to take off that mask to destroy those who have trusted in you. No, no, you must first of all say frankly if you support this present fortuitous monarch or His Majesty the Emperor."

'"I am a Royalist," the general replied. "I have sworn an oath to Louis XVIII and I shall keep it."

'At these words a murmur ran round the room and, from the looks exchanged between several members of the club, it was evident that they were debating the question of whether Monsieur d'Epinay should be made to regret these rash words.

'The president rose once more and called for silence. "Monsieur," he said, "you are too serious and sensible a man not to realize the consequences of the situation in which we stand towards one another. Your very frankness dictates the conditions that we must now impose on you: you must therefore swear on your honour that you will reveal nothing of what you have heard."

'The general reached for his sword: "Since you mention honour, then at least start by not ignoring the rules of honour, and do not attempt to impose anything by violence."

'"And you, Monsieur," the president went on, with a calm that was perhaps more awful than the general's anger, "I advise you not to touch your sword."

'The general looked around him with an expression which betrayed a hint of anxiety. However, he still did not give way but, on the contrary, summoning up all his strength, he said: "I shall not swear!"

'"In that case, Monsieur, you will die," the president replied calmly.

'Monsieur d'Epinay became very pale. Once more he looked all around him. Several members of the club were muttering and searching for weapons under their cloaks.

'"Calm yourself, general," the president said. "You are among men of honour who will try every means to persuade you, before turning to the last resort. But, as you said, you are also among conspirators and in possession of our secret, so you must restore it to us."

'A highly charged silence followed these words and, since the general did not reply, the president ordered the footmen to close the doors. The same deathly silence followed this order. Then the general came forward and, making a violent effort to control his feelings, said: "I have a son, and I must think of him, now that I find myself among murderers."

'"General," the leader of the assembly said, with dignity, "a single man always has the right to insult fifty: that is the privilege of weakness. However, he is wrong to exercise that right. Believe me, you would do better to swear and not to abuse us."

'Once more reduced to silence by the other's moral superiority, the general hesitated for a moment; then, at last, he walked across to the president's desk and asked: "What is the form of words you require?"

'"The following: I swear on my honour never to reveal to anyone in the world what I saw and heard on February the fifth, 1815, between nine and ten o'clock in the evening, and I declare that I deserve the punishment of death if I should violate this oath."

'The general appeared to suffer a nervous tremor that for some seconds prevented him from replying. At length, overcoming his obvious reluctance, he did utter the words required of him, but in such a low voice that it could hardly be heard. Several members therefore demanded that he should repeat it more loudly, and this was done.

'"Now I wish to leave," the general said. "Am I free at last?"

'The president stood up, nominated three members of the group to accompany him and, after blindfolding the general, got into the carriage with him. One of the three members was the coachman who had brought them. The other members of the club dispersed in silence.

'"Where would you like us to take you?" the president asked.

'"Wherever I can be delivered from your presence," Monsieur d'Epinay answered.

'"Take care, Monsieur," the president warned. "You are no longer in a large company – you are dealing with individuals. Don't insult them unless you wish to take responsibility for your remarks."

'But, instead of taking his meaning, Monsieur d'Epinay replied: "You are still as bold in your carriage as you were in your club, for no other reason, Monsieur, than that four men are always stronger than one."

'The president called on the driver to stop the carriage. They had just arrived at the end of the Quai des Ormes, where there is a stairway leading down to the river.

'"Why have you pulled up here?" Monsieur d'Epinay asked.

'"Because you have insulted a man, Monsieur," said the president, "and this man does not want to take a step further without demanding that you make honourable amends."

'"Here is yet another method of assassination," said the general, shrugging his shoulders.

'"Silence!" the president replied. "Unless you wish me to consider you as one of those people you referred to a short while ago, that is to say, as a coward who uses his weakness as a shield. You are alone, and one man alone will answer you. You have a sword at your side, and I have one in this cane. You have no second, but one of these gentlemen will serve you. Now, if you are agreeable, you can take off your blindfold."

'The general at once tore off the handkerchief around his eyes, saying: "At last, I shall find out whom I am dealing with."

'The carriage door was opened and the four men got down . . .'

Once more Franz paused. He wiped the sweat from his brow: there was something fearful in the sight of this son, pale and trembling, reading aloud these previously unknown details of his father's death.

Valentine clasped her hands as if in prayer. Noirtier looked at Villefort with an almost sublime expression of contempt and pride.

Franz continued: 'As we mentioned, it was February the fifth. For the past three days the temperature had fallen to five or six degrees below freezing. The stairway was coated with ice, the general was tall and fat, so the president offered him the side nearest the rail to go down. The two seconds followed behind.

'The night was dark, the quayside between the stairway and the river was damp with snow and frost, and a few blocks of ice flowed past in the deep, black water. One of the seconds went to fetch a lantern from a coal barge and by the light of it they examined the weapons.

'The president's sword, which he said was a simple swordstick, was shorter than that of his opponent and had no handguard. General d'Epinay suggested that they should draw lots for the two

swords, but the president replied that he had provoked the duel
and that by so doing he had implied that each of them should use
their own weapon. The seconds tried to persuade him, but the
president told them to desist.

'The lantern was set on the ground, the two adversaries stood on
either side of it and the duel began. The light transformed the two
swords into shafts of lightning, but the men could hardly be seen,
so dark was it.

'The general had the reputation of being one of the best blades
in the army. But, from the first passes, he was harried so hard that
he gave ground and, in doing so, he fell.

'The seconds thought he was dead, but his opponent, who knew
that he had not hit him, offered his hand to help him back to his
feet. This gesture, instead of calming the general, annoyed him and
he threw himself in his turn against his opponent.

'The latter, however, did not give an inch, blocking him against
his sword. Three times the general retreated, finding he was too
hard-pressed, then returned to the fray. On the third occasion, he
fell once more.

'They thought that he had slipped, as before; but, since he did
not get up, the witnesses went over to him and tried to lift him to
his feet. Then the man who had taken hold of his shoulders felt
something wet beneath his hands. It was blood.

'The general, who had more or less lost consciousness, recovered
his senses and said: "Ah, they sent me some swordsman, some
fencing master from the army."

'Without replying, the president went over to the second who
was holding the lantern and, rolling back his sleeve, showed two
wounds that had pierced his arm and then, opening his coat and
unbuttoning his waistcoat, he pointed to a third wound in his side.
Yet he had not uttered a sigh.

'General d'Epinay was in his death-agony. He expired five
minutes later.'

Franz read these last words in such a choking voice that they
could hardly be heard. After reading them, he stopped, passing his
hand across his eyes as if to dispel a cloud. But after a moment's
silence, he went on:

'The president went back up the stairway, after replacing his
sword in its stick. A trace of blood in the snow marked his passage.
He had not yet reached the top of the stairs when he heard the dull

sound of something hitting the water: it was the general's body which the seconds had just thrown into the river after confirming that it was dead.

'Consequently, the general died as the result of an honourable duel and not, as might be supposed, in an ambush.

'In witness of which we have signed the present account to establish the true facts, so that none of the participants in these terrible events should ever be accused of premeditated murder or of failing to respect the laws of honour. Signed: Beaurepaire, Duchampy and Lecharpal.'

When Franz had finished this account, so terrible for a son to read; when Valentine, pale and tense, had wiped away a tear; and when Villefort, trembling in a corner, had tried to avert the storm with a look of entreaty towards the pitiless old man, d'Epinay turned to Noirtier and said: 'Monsieur, since you know every detail of this frightful story, since you have had it witnessed by honourable men, and finally since you seem to take an interest in me, even though so far your interest has only been a source of pain, do not deny me one last satisfaction: tell me the name of the president of the club, so that I may at last know who killed my poor father.'

Villefort, as though distracted, was groping for the handle of the door. Valentine shrank back a pace: she had guessed the old man's reply before anyone, having often noticed the scars of two sword-wounds on his forearm.

'In heaven's name, Mademoiselle,' Franz said, turning to his fiancée, 'assist me, so that I may discover the name of the man who made me an orphan at the age of two.'

Valentine remained silent and motionless.

'Come, Monsieur,' said Villefort. 'Take my advice, do not prolong this frightful scene. In any case, the names were concealed deliberately. Even my father does not know this president; or, if he does, he would not be able to tell us. There are no proper names in the dictionary.'

'Alas, no!' said Franz. 'The one hope that sustained me throughout the account and gave me the strength to read it to the end, was that I should at least learn the name of the man who killed my father. Monsieur!' he cried, turning to Noirtier, 'In heaven's name, do what you can . . . I beg you, try to show me, to let me know . . .'

'Yes,' said Noirtier.

'Ah, Mademoiselle!' said Franz. 'Your grandfather indicated that he can tell me . . . the man's name . . . Help me . . . You understand him . . . Give us your aid.'

Noirtier looked towards the dictionary. Franz picked it up with a nervous shudder and said the letters of the alphabet until he reached 'M'. Here the old man signalled 'Yes'.

'M!' Franz repeated. The young man's finger ran down the words but, at every one, Noirtier replied in the negative. Valentine's head was buried in her hands.

At last Franz reached the word: 'MYSELF'.

'Yes,' the old man said.

'You!' Franz cried, his hair rising on his head. 'You, Monsieur Noirtier! Did you kill my father?'

'Yes,' Noirtier replied, fixing the young man with an imperious look.

Franz's feet could no longer support him and he slumped into a chair. Villefort opened the door and fled, for he had just had an impulse to stifle the last dregs of life still remaining in the old man's fearsome heart.

LXXVI

THE PROGRESS OF THE YOUNGER CAVALCANTI

During this time, M. Cavalcanti the elder had left to resume his post, not in the army of His Majesty the Emperor of Austria, but at the roulette tables of Bagni di Lucca, where he was one of the most loyal courtiers. It goes without saying that he had taken with him the amount allocated for his journey – and as a reward for the solemn and dignified way in which he had played his role of father – scrupulously counted down to the last *paul*.

On his departure, M. Andrea had inherited all the papers affirming that he had the honour to be the son of the Marquis Bartolomeo and the Marchioness Leonora Corsinari. He was thus more or less established in Parisian society, which is so open to receiving strangers and treating them, not as what they are, but as what they wish to be. In any case, what is required of a young man in Paris? To speak the language, more or less; to be acceptably turned out; to be a good sport; and to pay cash.

It goes without saying that still more indulgence is shown to foreigners than to Parisians.

As a consequence, within a fortnight Andrea had acquired a reasonably good standing. He was addressed as 'Monsieur le Comte', it was said that he had an income of 50,000 *livres* and there were rumours of an immense fortune belonging to his noble father, which was allegedly buried in the quarry at Saravezza. This last detail was stated as a fact in the presence of a scientist, who announced that he had seen that very quarry; this added a great deal of weight to statements that had, until then, been dubious and insubstantial, but henceforth took on the solidity of fact.

This was the state of things in that portion of Parisian society to which we have introduced our readers when, one evening, Monte Cristo went to visit M. Danglars. Danglars himself was out, but the count was invited to visit the baroness, who was at liberty to receive guests, and he accepted.

Since the dinner at Auteuil and the subsequent events, Mme Danglars could not hear Monte Cristo's name without a sort of nervous twitch. If the mention of his name was not followed by the count's physical presence, this painful sensation intensified. On the other hand, if the count appeared, his open features, his shining eyes, his friendliness and his gallantry towards Mme Danglars very rapidly dispelled all traces of anxiety. It seemed to the baroness impossible that a man so charming in appearance could have any evil designs against her. In any case, even the most corrupt of us finds it hard to believe in evil unless it is based on some interest. We reject the idea of harm done for no cause and without gain as anomalous.

When Monte Cristo entered the boudoir into which we have already once introduced our readers – and where the baroness was casting an anxious eye over drawings handed to her by her daughter after she had looked at them with the younger Cavalcanti – the count's presence produced its usual effect and the baroness received him with a smile, though she had been somewhat troubled at the sound of his name.

He took in the whole scene at a glance. Beside the baroness, Eugénie was sitting, almost recumbent, on a sofa, with Cavalcanti standing. He was dressed in black like a hero from Goethe, with highly polished shoes and white silk stockings, running a white, well-manicured hand through his blond hair in the midst of which could be seen the flicker of a diamond: despite Monte Cristo's advice, the vain young man had not been able to resist slipping this stone on to his little finger. The hand movement was accompanied by provocative glances at Mlle Danglars and sighs dispatched in the same direction as the glances.

Mlle Danglars was still the same: that is to say, beautiful, cold and contemptuous. Not a single glance or sigh from Andrea escaped her, but they appeared to be deflected by the breastplate of Minerva, which philosophers sometimes say in fact covered the breast of Sappho.[1]

Eugénie greeted the count coldly and took advantage of the earliest opportunity in the conversation to take herself off to her study, whence two voices could shortly be heard, merry and boisterous, accompanied by the first chords on a piano, informing Monte Cristo that Mlle Danglars had just preferred the company of Mlle Louise d'Armilly, her singing instructor, to his own and that of M. Cavalcanti.

Most of all, even as he was talking to Mme Danglars and appeared entirely absorbed in the conversation, the count noticed M. Andrea Cavalcanti: his anxiety, his way of going over to the door to listen to the music (without daring to go through it), his way of expressing his admiration.

Shortly afterwards, the banker himself came in. His first look was towards Monte Cristo, the second towards Andrea. As for his wife, he greeted her as certain husbands do greet their wives, a thing that bachelors will be able to imagine only when someone has done a very profound analysis of the conventions of married life.

'Haven't these young ladies invited you to make music with them?' Danglars asked Andrea.

'Alas, no, Monsieur,' Andrea replied, with an even more perceptible sigh than the earlier ones.

Danglars at once went across to the door between the two rooms and opened it, to reveal the two young women sitting on the same piano seat in front of the same piano. Each was playing the part for one hand, an exercise that they had practised to amuse themselves and at which they had become remarkably proficient.

Framed in this way by the door, Mlle d'Armilly could now be

seen with Eugénie forming one of those *tableaux vivants* which are often exhibited in Germany. She was of quite exceptional beauty – or, rather, of exquisite sweetness. She was a small woman, as slender and blonde as a fairy, with eyes heavy with tiredness and long hair falling in ringlets across an excessively long neck, of the sort that Perugino sometimes gives to his virgins. It was said that she had a weak chest and that, like Antonia in the *Violon de Crémone*,[2] she would one day die singing.

Monte Cristo took in this female group in a single, rapid, searching glance. It was the first time he had seen Mlle d'Armilly, though he had often heard her mentioned in this house.

'Well, then?' the banker said to his daughter. 'Are you trying to keep us out?' And he led the young man into the small drawing-room. Whether by chance or intentionally, the door was pushed to behind Andrea so that, from where they were sitting, neither Monte Cristo nor the baroness could see anything. But, as the banker had followed Andrea, Mme Danglars did not appear to notice this fact.

Shortly afterwards the count heard Andrea's voice harmonizing with the sound of the piano which accompanied a Corsican song. As he listened to this with a smile – forgetting Andrea and recalling Benedetto – Mme Danglars was boasting to Monte Cristo of her husband's strength of character, since that very morning he had again lost three or four hundred thousand francs in a Milanese bankruptcy. Indeed, the praise was well merited: if the count had not known of it through the baroness, or perhaps through one of those means he had of knowing everything, the baron's face would have told him nothing.

'Good!' Monte Cristo thought. 'He is already at the stage where he is concealing his losses. A month ago he was boasting of them.' Then, aloud, he said: 'Oh, Madame! Monsieur Danglars knows the Exchange so well that he is sure to regain there what he loses elsewhere.'

'I see that you share a common misconception,' said Mme Danglars.

'What is that?' asked Monte Cristo.

'That Monsieur Danglars gambles on the Stock Exchange – when in fact, on the contrary, he never does any such thing.'

'Ah, of course not! I recall now that Monsieur Debray told me … By the way, Madame, what has become of Monsieur Debray? I have not seen him for three or four days.'

'Nor have I,' said Mme Danglars, with astonishing self-control. 'But you began to say something . . .'

'What was that?'

'That Monsieur Debray, you said, told you . . .'

'That's right: Monsieur Debray told me that you were the one who is addicted to gambling on the Exchange.'

'I did have a taste for it, I admit,' said Mme Danglars, 'for a while, but no longer.'

'Then you are wrong, Madame. Heavens! Chance is so uncertain a thing that, if I were a woman and fate had made me the wife of a banker, however much faith I had in my husband's good luck – because, as you know, everything in speculation depends on good or bad luck – however much, I say, I were to trust in my husband's good luck, I should make certain of acquiring some independent means, even if to do so I had to entrust my interests to a stranger.'

Mme Danglars blushed, despite herself.

'Now, for example,' said Monte Cristo, as if he had noticed nothing, 'people are speaking of a splendid killing that was made yesterday on Neapolitan bonds.'

'I don't have any of those,' the baroness interjected, 'and I never did. But that's enough of the Exchange now, Monsieur le Comte. We must sound like a couple of stockbrokers. What about the poor Villeforts, who are having such bad luck at present?'

'What has happened to them?' Monte Cristo asked quite innocently.

'But you know very well: after losing Monsieur de Saint-Méran three or four days[3] after his departure, they have just lost the marchioness three or four days after her arrival.'

'So they have. I did hear that. But, as Claudius says to Hamlet[4], such is the law of nature: they lost their fathers, and mourned them; they will die before their sons, who will mourn them in turn.'

'But that's not all.'

'How do you mean, it's not all?'

'No. You know they were going to marry their daughter . . .'

'To Monsieur Franz d'Epinay . . . Has the marriage fallen through?'

'Yesterday morning, apparently, Franz released them from their obligations.'

'Really? Does anyone know the reason for this upset?'

'No.'

'Good Lord! What are you telling me, Madame? And how is Monsieur de Villefort facing up to all this misfortune?'

'Philosophically, as always.'

At that moment Danglars returned, alone.

'Well!' said the baroness. 'Have you left Monsieur Cavalcanti with your daughter?'

'What about Mademoiselle d'Armilly?' the banker said. 'Doesn't she count?' Then he turned to Monte Cristo. 'A charming young man, don't you think, Monsieur le Comte, this Prince Cavalcanti? The only question is: is he really a prince?'

'I can't guarantee it,' Monte Cristo said. 'His father was introduced to me as a marquis, he could be a count; but I think that he doesn't even make any great claim to the title himself.'

'Why not?' said the banker. 'If he is a prince, he is wrong not to boast of it. Every man has his rights. Personally, I don't like those who renounce their origins.'

'You are a perfect democrat,' Monte Cristo said with a smile.

'Just consider the risk you are taking,' said the baroness. 'If Monsieur de Morcerf were to come here by chance, he would find Monsieur Cavalcanti in a room where he, Eugénie's fiancé, has never been permitted to enter.'

'You are right to say "by chance",' said the banker, 'because, in truth, we see him so rarely that one could indeed say that he comes by chance.'

'Well, no matter: if he were to come, and find this young man with your daughter, he might be displeased.'

'He? Huh! You are mistaken. Monsieur Albert does not do us the honour of being jealous of his fiancée – he doesn't love her enough for that. In any case, what do I care if he is displeased or not?'

'Even so, at the stage we have reached . . .'

'Yes, at the stage we have reached. Shall I tell you what stage we have reached? The stage is that at his mother's ball he only danced with my daughter once, while Monsieur Cavalcanti danced with her three times, and Albert didn't even notice.'

'Viscount Albert de Morcerf!' the footman announced.

The baroness leapt to her feet. She was about to go through to the little drawing-room to warn her daughter, but Danglars put his hand on her arm. 'Leave it,' he said.

She looked at him in astonishment.

Monte Cristo pretended not to have seen this little piece of stage business. Albert came in, very handsome and very pleased with life. He greeted the baroness in an easy manner, Danglars in a familiar one and Monte Cristo with affection. Then, turning to the baroness, he asked: 'May I be permitted to enquire after the health of Mademoiselle Danglars?'

'Excellent, Monsieur,' Danglars replied sharply. 'At the moment she is music-making in her private study with Monsieur Cavalcanti.'

Albert preserved his air of calm indifference. He may perhaps have felt some inner annoyance, but he felt Monte Cristo's eyes on him.

'Monsieur Cavalcanti has a very fine tenor voice,' he said, 'and Mademoiselle Eugénie a superb soprano, not to mention the fact that she plays the piano like Thalberg.[5] It must be a delightful concert.'

'The fact is,' Danglars said, 'that they harmonize wonderfully well together.'

Blatant though it was, Albert pretended not to have noticed the ambiguity in this remark, but Mme Danglars blushed.

'I am a musician myself,' the young man went on; 'or, at least, so my teachers say. So it's an odd thing, but I have never yet been able to make my voice harmonize with any other – and with soprano voices least of all.'

Danglars gave a little smile that meant: but why aren't you annoyed? And, doubtless hoping to achieve his goal, he said: 'Which is why the prince and my daughter were universally admired yesterday. Weren't you there yesterday, Monsieur de Morcerf?'

'What prince is that?' Albert asked.

'Prince Cavalcanti,' Danglars said, still persisting in giving the young man this title.

'Oh, I beg your pardon,' said Albert. 'I was not aware that he was a prince. So! Prince Cavalcanti sang with Mademoiselle Eugénie yesterday? It must have been truly delightful to hear and I am very sorry to have missed it. I could not accept your invitation; I had to accompany Madame de Morcerf to the Baroness de Château-Renaud – the mother, that is – where the Germans were singing.' Then, after a short pause, he added, quite casually: 'Might I be allowed to present my respects to Mademoiselle Danglars?'

'Oh, wait, wait, I beg you,' said the banker, putting a hand on his arm. 'Can't you hear: what an exquisite cavatina? Ta, ta, ta, ti, ta, ti, ta, ta! Charming! Just a moment, and they will have finished . . . Perfect! Bravo! Bravi! Brava!' Danglars launched into a frenetic round of applause.

'Truly delightful,' said Albert. 'No one could understand the music of his country better than Prince Cavalcanti. You did say "prince", didn't you? In any case, even if he isn't a prince, he can be made one: it's easy in Italy. But to come back to our delightful songsters – you should do something for us, Monsieur Danglars: without telling them that there is a stranger here, you should ask Mademoiselle Danglars and Monsieur Cavalcanti to begin another piece. It is such an exquisite pleasure to enjoy music from a distance, in the shadows, without seeing or being seen, and so without embarrassing the musician, who can thus abandon himself or herself to all the impulses of genius and the transports of the heart.'

This time, the young man's sang-froid left even Danglars speechless. He drew Monte Cristo aside. 'Well, I never. What do you think of our lover?' he asked him.

'I have to admit, he does seem a trifle cold. But what can you do? You're committed.'

'Certainly, I'm committed, to give my daughter to a man who loves her, not to one who doesn't. Just look at him: cold as marble, arrogant like his father . . . If only he were rich, if he had a fortune like the Cavalcantis, then one might overlook it. As yet I have not spoken to my daughter, but if she has any taste . . .'

'Oh, come!' said Monte Cristo. 'I may be blinded by my friendship for him, but I assure you that Monsieur de Morcerf is a delightful young man, who will make your daughter happy and eventually make something of himself. After all, his father moves in the highest circles.'

'Hum!' Danglars said.

'Why these reservations?'

'There is still his past . . . shrouded in obscurity . . .'

'But the father's past does not affect the son.'

'No, no, indeed!'

'Come now, don't be carried away. A month ago you thought it was a splendid match. You understand, I'm deeply mortified: it was at my house that you met young Cavalcanti – and, as I told you, I do not know him.'

'I do,' said Danglars. 'That's all I need.'

'You know him? Have you made enquiries into his background?' asked Monte Cristo.

'Do I need to? Can't you tell what kind of a man he is just by looking at him? To start with, he's rich.'

'I can't swear to it.'

'But you're standing surety for him, even so?'

'For fifty thousand *livres*; a mere trifle.'

'He is well educated.'

It was Monte Cristo's turn to say: 'Hum!'

'He's a musician.'

'Just like all Italians.'

'Come now, Count, you are not fair to the young man.'

'Well, no, I confess I am sorry to see that, knowing your arrangement with the Morcerfs, he should interfere with it in this way and take advantage of his wealth.'

Danglars began to laugh. 'What a Puritan you are!' he said. 'It happens every day in society!'

'But, my dear Monsieur Danglars, you cannot just break it off like that: the Morcerfs are counting on the match.'

'They're counting on it?'

'Absolutely.'

'Then let them explain what's going on. You should have a word about this with the father, my dear Count, since you are such a good friend of the family.'

'Me? What on earth made you think that?'

'Their ball, I think. I mean to say: the countess, the proud Mercédès, the haughty Catalan, who barely deigns to open her mouth to her oldest acquaintances, took your arm and went out into the garden with you, led you off to the far corner and only reappeared half an hour later.'

'Please, Baron, please!' said Albert. 'We can't hear a thing. What an outrage – from a music-lover like yourself, too!'

'Oh, yes, very witty! Young Mister Sarcasm!' he said; then, turning back to Monte Cristo: 'Would you be good enough to say that to the father?'

'Certainly, if you wish.'

'And this time let's have it all done clearly and definitely: he can ask me for my daughter's hand, set a date, talk about the dowry ... In short, let's shake hands on it or shake fists, but no more delays; you understand ...'

'Very well, I'll talk to him for you.'

'I'm not saying that I await the outcome with pleasure, but I shall expect to hear from him. As you know, a banker is bound by his word.' And he gave one of those sighs that had been heard from the younger Cavalcanti half an hour earlier.

'Bravi! Bravo! Brava!' Morcerf yelled, applauding the end of the piece, in parody of the banker.

Danglars was starting to bristle at this when a footman came and whispered in his ear.

'I'll be back shortly,' he said to Monte Cristo. 'Wait for me: I may have something to tell you before you leave.' And he went out.

The baroness took advantage of her husband's absence to throw open the door to her daughter's study and they saw M. Andrea, who had been seated at the piano with Mlle Eugénie, leap to his feet as if powered by a spring. Albert smiled and bowed to Mlle Danglars, who did not appear in the slightest embarrassed but returned her usual cold curtsey.

Cavalcanti, on the other hand, did show signs of evident embarrassment. He greeted Morcerf, who returned the greeting with a look of the utmost impertinence, then started to pour out a torrent of praise for Mlle Danglars' voice, saying how much he regretted not having been able to attend the previous evening's soirée, having heard an account of it . . .

Cavalcanti, left to himself, took Monte Cristo aside.

'Now then,' said Mme Danglars, 'that's enough music and compliments. Let's take a cup of tea.'

'Come on, Louise,' Mlle Danglars said to her friend, and they all went into the drawing-room next door, where tea was indeed waiting. Just as they were beginning, in the English manner, to leave their spoons in their cups, the door opened and Danglars reappeared, evidently very upset. Monte Cristo particularly noticed it and gave the banker an enquiring look.

'I have just received my dispatches from Greece,' he said.

'Oh?' said the count. 'Is that why you were called away?'

'Yes.'

'And how is King Otto keeping?' Albert asked, in his jolliest tone of voice. Danglars looked askance at him without replying, and Monte Cristo turned away to hide a look of pity that had appeared on his face, and which almost immediately vanished.

'We shall leave together, shan't we?' Albert asked the count.

'Yes, if you wish,' he replied.

Albert could not understand anything in the expression on the banker's face; so, turning to Monte Cristo, who understood perfectly well, he said: 'Did you see how he looked at me?'

'Yes,' said the count. 'Did you find something odd in this look?'

'I certainly did. But what is all this about news from Greece?'

'How should I know?'

'Because I assume you have spies in the country.'

Monte Cristo smiled, as one does when one has no intention of replying.

'Look, he's just coming over to you,' said Albert. 'I'm going to compliment Mademoiselle Danglars on the cameo she is wearing. Meanwhile the father will have time to tell you all about it.'

'If you do compliment her, let it be for her voice, at least,' said Monte Cristo.

'Not at all: anyone could do that.'

'My dear Viscount, you have the conceit of impertinence,' Monte Cristo said.

Albert crossed over to Eugénie with a smile on his lips.

Meanwhile Danglars bent over the count's ear. 'You gave me excellent advice,' he said, 'and there is a frightful story behind those two words: Fernand and Janina.'

'No, really?' said Monte Cristo.

'Yes, I'll tell you about it. But take the young man away. For the moment I should be too embarrassed to stay in the room with him.'

'That's just what I'm going to do; he's coming with me. And do you still want me to send the father to you?'

'More than ever.'

'Very well.'

The count signalled to Albert, both of them said goodbye to the ladies and left – Albert treating Mlle Danglars' scorn with utter indifference, Monte Cristo repeating to Mme Danglars his advice on the wisdom for a banker's wife of ensuring her future.

M. Cavalcanti remained master of the field.

LXXVII

HAYDÉE

Hardly had the count's horses rounded the corner of the boulevard than Albert turned to him and burst out into a peal of laughter, a little too loud not to be slightly forced.

'Well, now,' he said, 'I might ask you, as King Charles IX asked Catherine de' Medici after the Saint Bartholomew's Day massacre: "How do you think I played my little part?"'

'In what connection?' asked Monte Cristo.

'Why, in connection with setting up my rival with Monsieur Danglars . . .'

'What rival?'

'What rival! Your protégé, Monsieur Andrea Cavalcanti, of course!'

'You must be joking, Viscount. I do not in any way protect Monsieur Andrea, at least not where Monsieur Danglars is concerned.'

'That's a criticism I should make of you, should the young man need protection; but, luckily for me, he doesn't.'

'Why? Do you think he's courting?'

'I guarantee it. He rolls his eyes and groans like a lover. He aspires to the hand of the proud Eugénie. Huh! That's a perfect anapaestic line! I promise you, it was unintentional. No matter, I'll repeat it: he aspires to the hand of the proud Eugénie.'

'What matter, since you are the only suitor under consideration?'

'Don't say that, my dear Count. I'm spurned from both sides.'

'How do you mean: from both sides.'

'Of course! Mademoiselle Eugénie hardly spoke to me and her confidante, Mademoiselle d'Armilly, not at all.'

'Yes, but the father adores you,' said Monte Cristo.

'Really? On the contrary, he thrust a thousand daggers into my heart; admittedly they were stage daggers, with disappearing blades, but he thought they were real enough.'

'Jealousy implies affection.'

'Yes, but I am not jealous.'

'However, he is.'

'Of whom? Of Debray?'

'No, of you.'

'Me? I guarantee that in a week he will have barred his door to me.'

'You are wrong, Viscount.'

'Prove it.'

'Do you want me to?'

'Yes.'

'I have been asked to request Monsieur de Morcerf to make some definite proposal to the baron.'

'Who asked you?'

'The baron himself.'

'Oh, now,' Albert said, in the most wheedling tone he could summon. 'You wouldn't do that, would you, my dear Count?'

'That's where you're wrong, Albert. I have promised and I shall do it.'

'Well, then,' Albert said with a sigh, 'it appears you are determined to see me married.'

'I am determined to stay on the right side of everyone. But, speaking of Debray, I haven't seen him recently at the baron's.'

'There has been a disagreement.'

'With Madame?'

'With Monsieur.'

'Did he notice something going on?'

'Huh! That's a good one!'

'Do you really think he suspected?' Monte Cristo asked, with charming innocence.

'Did he, indeed. Where do you come from, my dear Count?'

'The Congo, if you wish.'

'Still not far enough.'

'What do I know about your Parisian husbands?'

'Husbands, my dear Count, are the same everywhere. Once you have seen one specimen in a given country, you know the whole breed.'

'So what can have come between Danglars and Debray? They seemed to get on so well,' Monte Cristo said, still feigning innocence.

'Now, there we are talking about one of the mysteries of Isis, and I am not an initiate. When the young Cavalcanti is part of the family, you can ask him that.'

The carriage halted.

'Here we are,' said Monte Cristo. 'It is only half-past ten, why don't you come up?'

'I should like to.'

'My carriage can take you home.'

'Thank you, but I think my coupé will have followed us.'

'Yes, here it is,' said Monte Cristo, jumping down. Both men entered the house where the drawing-room was already lit.

'Make us some tea, Baptistin,' Monte Cristo said.

Baptistin went out without a sound. Two seconds later, he reappeared with a plate ready laid which, like a meal in one of those magical entertainments, seemed to have risen out of the ground.

'I must admit, my dear Count,' Morcerf said, 'that what I admire in you is not your wealth, because there may be people richer than you are; it is not your wit, because although Beaumarchais' was not greater, it was as great; but it is your way of obtaining service, without any answering back, to the minute, no, to the second, as if your people had guessed from the manner of your ring, just what you wanted, and as if what you wanted was always ready waiting.'

'There is some truth in what you say. They know my habits. For example: isn't there something you would like to do while you are drinking your tea?'

'Why, yes: I should like to smoke.'

Monte Cristo went over to the bell-push and sounded it once. A second later, a concealed door opened and Ali appeared with two chibouks, already filled with excellent Latakia.

'Extraordinary!'

'No, no: elementary, my dear Morcerf,' said Monte Cristo. 'Ali knows that, when I take tea or coffee, I usually smoke. He knows that I have called for tea and that I came back with you. He hears me ring for him, guesses the reason and, since he is a native of a country where hospitality is expressed chiefly around the pipe, he brings two chibouks, instead of one.'

'Agreed, that is as good an explanation as any other, but the fact remains that only you . . . Ah! What's that I hear?' And Morcerf bent his head towards the door, through which wafted sounds which were similar to those of a guitar.

'There, my dear Viscount: you are condemned to have music this evening. No sooner have you escaped from Mademoiselle Danglars' piano than you are entrapped by Haydée's *guzla*.'

'Haydée! What a delightful name! Are there really women called Haydée outside the poems of Lord Byron?'[1]

'Indeed there are. Haydée may be a rare name in France, but it is common enough in Albania and Epirus. It is as though you were to say: chastity, modesty or innocence. It is a kind of baptismal name, as you Parisians call them.'

'That's utterly charming!' said Albert. 'How I should love to see our Frenchwomen called Mademoiselle Silence, Miss Goodness, or Miss Christian Charity! Just suppose that Mademoiselle Danglars, instead of being called Claire-Marie-Eugénie, as she is, was named Miss Chastity-Modesty-Innocence Danglars, dammit ... Think how that would sound when they published the banns!'

'Idiot!' the count said. 'Don't joke so loudly; Haydée might hear you.'

'Would it upset her?'

'Not at all,' the count replied haughtily.

'Good-natured, is she?' Albert asked.

'It's nothing to do with goodness, but with duty. A slave does not get upset with her master.'

'Come, come! Don't joke yourself. Are there still slaves?'

'Of course, since Haydée is mine.'

'I must say, you do nothing and possess nothing as other people do. Slave to Monsieur le Comte de Monte Cristo – that's a rank in France! The way you shift gold, it must be worth a hundred thousand *écus* a year.'

'A hundred thousand *écus*! The poor girl used to own more than that: she came into the world with a fortune beside which those in the *Thousand and One Nights* are a trifle.'

'She must be truly a princess, then?'

'As you say – and, moreover, one of the greatest in her country.'

'I thought as much; but how did a great princess become a slave?'

'How did Denys the Tyrant[2] become a schoolmaster? The fortunes of war, my dear Viscount, and the whims of fate.'

'Is her name a secret?'

'For everyone else, it is, but for you, dear Viscount, since you are a friend and know how to keep quiet, don't you, if I ask you not to tell anyone ... ?'

'On my honour!'

'Do you know the story of the pasha of Janina?'

'Ali Tebelin?[3] Certainly, since it was in his service that my father made his fortune.'

'Of course it was; I had forgotten.'

'So what is Haydée to Ali Tebelin?'

'Quite simply his daughter.'

'What! The daughter of Ali Pasha?'

'And the beautiful Vasiliki.'

'And now she is your slave?'

'She most certainly is.'

'How did it happen?'

'Why! One day when I was strolling through the market in Constantinople, I bought her.'

'Magnificent! One does not live with you, dear Count, one dreams! Now, listen . . . But I am going to be very presumptuous . . .'

'Tell me anyway.'

'Since you go out with her and take her to the opera . . .'

'What then?'

'Could I be bold enough as to ask this of you?'

'Be bold enough to ask me whatever you wish.'

'Well, then, Count: will you introduce me to your princess?'

'Certainly, on two conditions.'

'I accept without hearing them.'

'The first is that you never tell anyone that you have met her.'

'Very well.' Morcerf held out his hand. 'I swear.'

'The second is that you will not tell her that your father served hers.'

'I swear that, too.'

'Excellent, Viscount; you will remember these two oaths, won't you?'

'*Please!*' said Albert.

'Very well. I know you are a man of honour.'

The count rang the bell again and Ali reappeared. 'Tell Haydée,' the count said, 'that I shall be taking coffee in her room and inform her that I should like her to permit me to introduce her to one of my friends.'

Ali bowed and went out.

'Are we agreed then, Viscount? No direct questions. If you wish to know something, ask me and I shall ask her.'

'That's agreed.'

Ali reappeared for a third time and kept the door open to indicate to his master and Albert that they could go through.

'Come in,' said Monte Cristo. Albert ran a hand through his hair and curled his moustache, while the count took his hat, put on his gloves and preceded his guest into the apartment that was guarded by Ali like an advance sentry, and protected by the three French maids, under Myrto.

Haydée was waiting in the first room, the drawing-room, her eyes wide with astonishment: this was the first time that any man other than Monte Cristo had come into her quarters. She was seated on a sofa, in a corner of the room, her legs crossed under her, having built as it were a nest for herself in the richest striped and embroidered materials of the East. Near her was the instrument, the sound of which had betrayed her presence. It was a delightful picture.[4]

When she saw Monte Cristo, she raised herself up with a smile that was at once that of a daughter and a lover, unique to herself. Monte Cristo went over and offered his hand, to which as usual she pressed her lips. Albert had stayed by the door, enraptured by this strange beauty, impossible to imagine in France, which he was seeing for the first time.

'Whom have you brought me?' the young woman asked Monte Cristo in Romaic. 'A brother, a friend, a mere acquaintance or an enemy?'

'A friend,' Monte Cristo replied, in the same language.

'Called?'

'Count Albert. He is the one I rescued from the bandits in Rome.'

'In what language would you like me to address him?'

Monte Cristo turned to Albert. 'Do you know modern Greek?' he asked.

'Alas, no!' said Albert. 'Not even ancient Greek, my dear Count. Never have Homer and Plato had such a poor – I might even say such a disdainful student as I was.'

'In that case,' Haydée said, showing that she had understood Monte Cristo's question and Albert's reply, 'I shall speak French or Italian – if my master wishes me to speak, of course.'

Monte Cristo thought for a moment. 'Speak Italian,' he said. Then, turning to Albert: 'It's a pity you don't understand either modern or ancient Greek, both of which Haydée speaks exceptionally well. The poor child will have to talk to you in Italian, and this may give you a wrong idea of her.' And he motioned to Haydée.

'Welcome, friend, since you come with my lord and master,' the young woman said, in excellent Tuscan, with that gentle Roman accent that gives the language of Dante a richer sound than that of Homer. 'Ali, bring us coffee and pipes.' She gestured to Albert to come over, while Ali left to carry out his young mistress's orders.

Monte Cristo showed Albert two folding stools, and each of them went to take one and draw it up to a kind of pedestal table, with a hookah as its centrepiece, surrounded by natural flowers, drawings and albums of music.

Ali returned, bringing the coffee and the chibouks. As for M. Baptistin, this part of the house was off limits to him. Albert declined the pipe that the Nubian offered him.

'Take it, do,' said Monte Cristo. 'Haydée is almost as civilized as a Parisian woman. She dislikes havana tobacco, because she is not fond of foul odours, but Oriental tobacco, as you know, is a perfume.'

Ali went out. The cups of coffee were standing ready with, for Albert, a bowl of sugar. Monte Cristo and Haydée took their mocha in the Arabic manner, that is, unsweetened.

Haydée reached out and took the Japanese porcelain cup in the tips of her long, pink fingers, raising it to her lips with the innocent pleasure of a child drinking or eating something that she likes. At the same time two women came in carrying more trays, laden with ices and sorbets, which they set down on two small tables waiting there especially for that purpose.

'My dear host,' said Albert in Italian, 'and you, Signora, forgive my astonishment. I am naturally amazed: here in the heart of Paris I find the Orient, the true Orient, not unfortunately as I have experienced it, but as I have dreamed it; and only a moment ago I could hear the sound of a passing omnibus and the lemonade-sellers ringing their bells. Oh, Signora! If only I could understand Greek; your conversation, in these enchanted surroundings, would make this an evening that I would always remember.'

'I speak Italian well enough to converse with you, Monsieur,' Haydée said calmly. 'I shall do my best, if you like the East, to help you discover it here.'

'What can I talk about?' Albert whispered to Monte Cristo.

'Whatever you wish: about her country, her childhood, her memories. Then, if you prefer, about Rome, Naples or Florence.'

'Oh, no,' Albert said. 'There is no point in meeting a Greek if one is merely going to talk to her about all the things one would discuss with a Parisienne. Let me ask her about the East.'

'Go on, then, my dear Albert. She likes nothing better than to talk of that.'

Albert turned to Haydée. 'At what age did the signora leave Greece?' he asked.

'At the age of five,' Haydée replied.

'And do you recollect your homeland?' Albert asked.

'When I close my eyes, I can again see everything that I used to see. There are two ways of seeing: with the body and with the soul. The body's sight can sometimes forget, but the soul remembers for ever.'

'What is your earliest memory?'

'I could hardly walk. My mother, who is called Vasiliki – in Greek, Vasiliki means "royal",' the young woman added, tossing back her head, '. . . my mother took my hand and, both covered in a veil, after putting all the gold we had into the bottom of a purse, we went to beg for alms for prisoners, saying: "He that hath pity upon the poor, lendeth unto the Lord".[5] Then, when the purse was full, we went back to the palace and, saying nothing to my father, we sent all the money that people had given us, thinking we were poor women, to the *hegumenos*[6] of the monastery, who divided it among the prisoners.'

'How old were you at that time?'

'Three,' said Haydée.

'So you can remember everything that happened around you since the time when you were three?'

'Everything.'

'Count,' Morcerf whispered to Monte Cristo, 'please allow the signora to tell us something about her history. You forbade me to talk to her about my father, but perhaps she would say something about him, and you cannot imagine how happy I should be to hear his name on such lovely lips.'

Monte Cristo turned to Haydée and, furrowing his brow in a way that warned her to pay the closest attention to what he was about to tell her, said in Greek: 'Πατρος μεν ἀτην, μηδε ὀνομα τροδοτου και προδασιαν, είπε ήμιν.' [Literally: 'Tell us your father's fate, but not the traitor's name or his treachery.']

Haydée gave a deep sigh and a dark cloud passed across her pure brow.

'What did you tell her?' Morcerf asked, under his breath.

'I repeated that you are a friend and that she has no cause to hide anything from you.'

'So,' Albert went on, 'this distant pilgrimage on behalf of the prisoners was your first memory. What is the next?'

'The next? I see myself in the shade of some sycamore-trees, near a lake whose shimmering reflection I still glimpse between the branches. My father was sitting on cushions against the oldest and most leafy of them, and my mother lying at his feet, while I, a weak child, am playing with the white beard that falls upon his chest and the *cangiar*[7] with the diamond hilt that hung in his belt. Then, from time to time, an Albanian would come to him and say a few words, which I ignored; and he would reply, without any alteration in his voice, either "Kill!" or "Spare".'

'It's strange,' Albert said, 'to hear such things from the lips of a young woman, other than in the theatre, and to tell oneself: "This is not an invention." With such a poetic horizon, such a wondrous past, how do you find France?'

'I think that it's a beautiful country,' Haydée said. 'But I see France as it is, because I see it with the eyes of a grown woman, while I have only ever seen my own country with the eyes of a child, so that it seems to me always enwrapped in a mist that is either luminous or dark, depending on whether my eyes perceive it as a sweet homeland or a place of bitter suffering.'

'How can someone as young as you, Signora, have known suffering?' Albert asked, succumbing despite himself to the force of banality.

Haydée turned to Monte Cristo who, with a barely perceptible gesture, murmured: *'Ειπε!'* ['Speak.']

'More than anything else, it is one's first memories that furnish the depths of the soul and, apart from the two that I have just told you, all my childhood memories are sad.'

'I beg you to continue, Signora,' said Albert. 'I assure you that I am quite enchanted to listen to you.'

Haydée smiled sadly. 'Would you like me to recall my other memories?' she said.

'Please do,' said Albert.

'I was four years old when, one evening, I was woken by my mother. We were in the palace at Janina. She lifted me off the cushions where I was lying and, when I opened my eyes, I saw that hers were full of large tears.

'She took me away, saying nothing. But when I saw her cry, I started to do the same. "Silence, child!" she said.

'Often, capricious like all children, I would carry on crying despite my mother's consolation or her threats; but this time there was such a note of terror in her voice that I instantly fell silent.

'She hurried away with me. I saw that we were going down a wide staircase. In front of us, all my mother's maidservants were going or, rather, rushing down the same staircase, carrying boxes, bags, ornaments, jewels and purses of gold. Behind them came a guard of twenty men, armed with long rifles and pistols, dressed in a costume that has become familiar to you in France since Greece regained its nationhood.

'I assure you,' Haydée said, shaking her head and paling at the mere memory, 'there was something sinister in this long procession of slaves and women half drugged with sleep – or so I thought at least, perhaps believing that others were sleeping because I was only partly awake myself. Gigantic shapes hurried down the stairway, their shadows cast on the ceiling by pine torches.

'"Hurry!" cried a voice at the end of the gallery. At the sound, every head was bent, as the wind blowing over the plains bends a field of corn. But I shuddered to hear it, because it was the voice of my father. He was walking behind us all, dressed in his finest attire, holding a carbine that your emperor gave him; and, his free hand resting on his favourite, Selim, he drove us before him like a shepherd with a frightened flock.

'My father,' Haydée said, looking up, 'was an illustrious man, known in Europe as Ali Tebelin, Pasha of Janina, who made the Turks tremble before him.'

Without knowing why, Albert shuddered on hearing these words spoken in tones of such pride and dignity. It seemed to him that something dark and fearful shone from the young woman's eyes when, like a pythoness[8] calling up a ghost, she re-awoke the memory of this bloodstained figure whose awful death made him loom gigantic in the eyes of modern Europe.

'Shortly afterwards,' Haydée continued, 'the procession halted.

We were at the foot of the steps on the edge of a lake. My mother pressed me to her beating breast and, two paces behind us, I saw my father who was casting anxious glances to all sides.

'In front of us were four marble steps, with a boat bobbing at the last of them. From where we were we could see a black shape in the middle of the lake: this was the pavilion for which we were heading. Perhaps because of the darkness, it seemed a long way away to me.

'We stepped down into the boat. I remember that the oars made no noise as they touched the water. I looked over the side at them: they were wrapped in the belts of our Palicares.[9] In the boat, apart from the oarsmen, there were only some women, my father, my mother, Selim and I. The Palicares had stayed at the edge of the lake, kneeling on the bottom step and using the other three as a rampart, in case they had been followed. Our boat was flying like the wind.

' "Why is the boat going so fast?" I asked my mother.

' "Hush, child!" she said. "We are fleeing."

'I could not understand. Why was my father fleeing – my father, the all-powerful, before whom others normally would flee, my father whose motto was: "They hate me, and that is why they fear me"? Yet he was indeed fleeing across the lake. He has since told me that the garrison of the castle at Janina, tired of long service . . .'

Here Haydée turned meaningfully towards Monte Cristo, whose eyes did not leave hers. Consequently, she continued slowly, like someone inventing or disguising the details of the story.

'You were saying, Signora,' Albert said, paying close attention to her account, 'that the garrison at Janina, tired of long service . . .'

'Had negotiated with the *seraskier* Kurchid,[10] who was sent by the sultan to kidnap my father. At this, my father decided to retire into a hiding-place that he had long kept prepared for himself (called *kataphygion*, which means "refuge"), after sending the sultan a Frankish officer, in whom he trusted utterly.'

'Do you remember the name of this officer, Signora?' Albert asked.

Unseen by Morcerf, Monte Cristo exchanged a look with the young woman.

'No,' she said. 'I cannot remember it but I may do so later, and then I shall tell you.'

Albert was about to mention his father's name when Monte Cristo quietly raised his finger to call for his silence. The young man remembered his vow and said nothing.

'We were rowing towards this pavilion. It had a ground floor with arabesque ornamentation, and a first floor overlooking the lake. As far as could be seen, that was all. But beneath the ground floor was an underground passage extending beneath the island – a vast cavern into which I, my mother and her women were led. Here, piled into a single heap, were sixty thousand purses and two hundred barrels. In the purses were twenty-five million in gold coin and in the barrels thirty thousand pounds of powder.

'Selim, the favourite of my father's whom I mentioned, was standing by the barrels. He would watch day and night, holding a stave at the end of which was a burning wick. He had orders to blow everything up – the pavilion, the guards, the pasha, the women and the gold – at the slightest sign from my father. I remember that our slaves, knowing they were in such fearful company, spent their days and nights in praying, weeping and moaning. As for myself, I can still see the young soldier with his pale skin and black eyes. When the angel of death comes down to take me, I am certain I shall recognize Selim.

'I cannot say how long we remained thus. In those days I did not know what time was. At intervals, though rarely, my father had us brought up to the terrace of the palace. These were moments of delight for me, since there was nothing to look at underground except the groaning figures in the darkness and Selim's burning stave. Sitting in front of a large opening, my father would look grimly towards the depths of the horizon, studying every black dot that appeared on the lake, while my mother, half sitting, half lying beside him, rested her head on his shoulder and I played at his feet. With that wonder of childhood which magnifies things, I would admire the escarpments of Pinde, looming on the horizon, the castles of Janina, rising white and angular from the blue waters of the lake, and the huge tufts of black foliage, clinging like lichens to the mountainside, which from afar look like tufts of moss, and from close to are tall fir-trees and immense myrtle bushes.

'One morning my father sent for us. We found him quite calm, but paler than usual.

' "Be patient, Vasiliki, for today all will be over. Today, the master's *firman*[11] arrives and my fate will be sealed. If there is a complete pardon, we shall return in triumph to Janina. If the news is bad, we shall flee tonight."

' "But suppose they do not let us flee?" said my mother.

' "Have no fear on that score," Ali answered, smiling. "Selim and his burning stave guarantee that. They might wish me dead, but not if it is a matter of dying with me."

'These words of consolation did not come from my father's heart, and my mother answered them only with sighs. She prepared the iced water that he continually drank; because, from the moment when he retired into the pavilion, he had been seized with a burning fever. She perfumed his white beard and lit the chibouk, the smoke of which, as it curled into the air, he would watch abstractedly, sometimes for hours on end.

'Then, suddenly, he made a brusque movement which startled me. Without taking his eyes away from what had attracted his attention, he asked for his telescope. My mother gave it to him, whiter than the balustrade against which she was leaning. I saw my father's hand shake. "One boat . . . two . . . three," he murmured. "Four . . ." And he got to his feet, grasped his weapons and, I remember, emptied some powder into the pan of his pistols.

' "Vasiliki," he told my mother, with a visible shudder, "this is the moment that will decide our fate. In half an hour we shall know the response of the sublime emperor. Return underground with Haydée."

' "I do not wish to leave you," Vasiliki said. "If you die, my master, I want to die with you."

' "Go to Selim!" my father cried.

' "Farewell, my Lord," my mother muttered obediently, bent double as if by the approach of death.

' "Take Vasiliki!" my father told his Palicares. But I was forgotten. I ran to him and reached out my hands. He saw me and, leaning over, pressed his lips to my forehead.

'Oh! That kiss! It was the last, and it is still on my brow.

'On the way down, through the vines on the terrace, we saw the boats getting larger as they approached across the lake: at first they had been merely black dots; now they were already like birds skimming across the surface of the waters.

'Meanwhile, in the pavilion, twenty Palicares, seated at my father's feet and hidden by the wooden panelling, were watching the arrival of these boats with angry eyes, their long guns, encrusted with silver and mother-of-pearl, held at the ready; a large number of cartridges were spread around the floor. My father looked at his watch and walked anxiously back and forth.

'This is the scene that I saw as I left my father, taking with me the last kiss that I ever received from him.

'My mother and I went down the underground passage. Selim was still at his post. He smiled at us sadly. We went to search for cushions on the other side of the cavern and came to sit close to him: in times of great danger, loyal hearts seek one another and, though I was only a child, I felt instinctively that a great misfortune was hovering above our heads.'

Albert had often heard tell of the last moments of the vizier of Janina – not from his father, who never spoke of it, but from strangers. He had also read different accounts of the man's death; but this story, brought to life in the person and the voice of this young woman, these living tones and this mournful elegy, struck him with both an inexpressible charm and an inexpressible feeling of horror. As for Haydée, she had paused for a moment, caught up in her dreadful memories. Her head, like a flower bending on a stormy day, had fallen forward on to her hand; and her eyes, lost in the distance, still seemed to see the green slopes of Pinde on the horizon and the blue waters of the lake of Janina, a magic mirror reflecting the dark scene that she had described. Monte Cristo was looking at her with an indefinable look of concentration and pity. 'Carry on,' he said to her in Romaic.

Haydée looked up, as though Monte Cristo's sonorous voice had woken her from a dream, and continued her story: 'It was four o'clock in the evening; but even though it was a pure and brilliant day outside, we were plunged in the darkness of the underground tunnel. A single light was burning in the cave, like a star trembling against a black sky: this was Selim's taper. My mother was a Christian and she was praying, while from time to time Selim repeated the hallowed formula: "God is great!"'

'Even now my mother retained some hope. As she came down, she thought she recognized the Frank who had been sent to Constantinople and in whom my father had every confidence, knowing that the soldiers of the French sultan are usually noble and generous. She took a few steps towards the staircase and listened. "They are coming," she said. "Let us pray that they are bringing peace and life."'

' "What are you afraid of, Vasiliki?" Selim replied, in a voice that was at once so soft and so proud. "If they do not bring peace, we shall give them death." And he stirred the embers with his lance, in a gesture like that of an antique Cretan Dionysus. But, being an innocent child, I was afraid of his courage, which seemed to me savage and senseless, and I shrank from the terrible death that flared up in the air and the flames.

'My mother experienced the same fear, because I felt her shudder.

' "My God, my God, mother!" I cried. "Are we going to die?" '

'When they heard this, the cries and lamentations of the slaves redoubled.

' "Child," Vasiliki said, "pray God you may not come to desire the death that you fear so much now." Then, under her breath, she said: "Selim, what are the master's orders?"

' "If he sends me his dagger, then the sultan refuses him mercy and I must light the fire; if he sends me his ring, then the sultan has pardoned him and I hand over the powder store."

' "Friend," my mother said, "when the master's order comes, if it is the dagger that he sends, instead of you subjecting us to that death which so terrifies us both, we shall offer you our throats and you can kill us with the dagger."

' "Yes, Vasiliki," Selim answered calmly.

'Suddenly we heard loud cries. We listened. They were cries of joy. The name of the Frank who had been sent to Constantinople echoed backwards and forwards between our Palicares. It was clear that he had brought the reply of the sublime emperor and that the reply was favourable.'

'You don't remember his name?' Morcerf asked, ready to prod the storyteller's memory. Monte Cristo made a sign to her.

'No, I don't remember it,' said Haydée.

'The noise increased. Footsteps approached: someone was coming down the steps into the underground shelter.

'Selim prepared his lance.

'Shortly afterwards, a shape appeared in the bluish half-light of the sun's rays which penetrated right down to the door of the cavern.

' "Who are you?" Selim asked. "Whoever you are, do not take another step."

' "Glory to the sultan!" the shape said. "A full pardon has been granted to the Vizier Ali. Not only is his life spared, but his fortune and his possessions are returned to him."

'My mother gave a cry of joy and pressed me to her heart.

'"Stop!" Selim said to her, seeing that she was already preparing to run out. "You know that I need the ring."

'"That is true," my mother said, falling to her knees and raising me towards the heavens as if, since she was praying to God on my behalf, she actually wanted to lift me towards Him.'

Once more Haydée paused, overcome with such emotion that the sweat ran down her pale brow and her strangled voice seemed unable to emerge from her dry throat.

Monte Cristo poured a little iced water into a glass and gave it to her, saying: 'Be strong!' in a gentle voice beneath which there was the hint of an order.

Haydée wiped her eyes and her forehead and went on: 'Meanwhile our eyes, getting used to the dark, had recognized the Pasha's envoy. He was a friend. Selim had recognized him, but the noble young man knew only one thing: how to obey!

'"In whose name do you come?" he asked.

'"In the name of our master, Ali Tebelin."

'"If you come in Ali's name, do you know what to give me?"

'"Yes," said the envoy. "I bring you his ring." And as he said this he held his hand above his head. But he was too far away, and from where we were standing it was not light enough for Selim to distinguish what he was holding up, and recognize it.

'"I cannot see what you are holding," said Selim.

'"Then come over here," said the messenger, "or I shall come over to you."

'"Neither," the young soldier replied. "Put whatever you are showing me down on the spot where you are, under that ray of light, and go away until I have examined it."

'"Very well," said the messenger, and he retired after putting down the token in the place where he had been told.

'Our hearts were beating fast. The object did indeed appear to be a ring; but was it my father's?

'Selim, still holding his burning torch, went over to the doorway, bent down beneath the ray of light and picked up the token. "The master's ring," he said, kissing it. "All is well." Then he turned the torch earthwards and extinguished it with his feet.

'The messenger gave a cry of joy and clapped his hands. At the signal, four soldiers of *seraskier* Kurchid dashed forward and Selim fell beneath the wounds of five daggers, each man having smitten him with his own. Yet, drunk with their crime, though still pale with fear, they rushed into the cavern, searching everywhere for any sign of fire and rolling among the sacks of gold.

'Meanwhile my mother seized me in her arms and, nimbly hurrying through meandering passages that only we knew, she came to a concealed staircase up to the pavilion, where the most frightful tumult reigned. The lower rooms were entirely occupied by Kurchid's Tchodoars, that is, by our enemies. At the moment when my mother was about to push open the little door, we heard the pasha's voice, terrible and threatening. My mother pressed her eye to an opening in the wall and it happened that there was another gap, at my own eye level, so I also looked.

'"What do you want?" my father was saying to some men holding a sheet of paper with gold lettering on it.

'"What do we want? We want to inform you of His Highness's wishes. Do you see this *firman*?"

'"I do," said my father.

'"Read it, then; it calls for your head."

'My father gave a shout of laughter more terrifying than any threat. It had not ended before two pistol-shots erupted from each of the pistols in his hands and he had killed two men. At this, the Palicares, who were lying all around my father, face down on the floor, leapt to their feet and began firing. The room filled with noise, flames and smoke. At the same moment, firing began from the other side and shots whistled through the wooden planks all around us.

'Oh, how handsome he was and how great he was, my father, the vizier Ali Tebelin, in the midst of this gunfire, his scimitar in his hand and his face black with gunpowder! How his enemies fled before him!

'"Selim, Selim!" he cried. "Keeper of the fire, do your duty!"

'"Selim is dead," replied a voice which seemed to come from the depths of the pavilion. "And you, my lord Ali, you are lost!"

'At the same moment there was a dull thud and the floor burst into pieces around my father's feet. The Tchodoars were firing upwards through it. Three or four Palicares fell, rent from head to foot by wounds that traversed their whole bodies.

'My father roared, plunged his fingers into the bullet-holes and pulled up an entire floorboard. But at that moment, through the hole he had made, twenty shots rang out and a sheet of flame, rising as though from the crater of a volcano, lit the hangings and devoured them.

'In the midst of all this dreadful noise, in the midst of all these fearful cries, two shots rang clearer than any of the rest and two cries more heart-rending than any around them. The two shots had delivered a mortal wound to my father and it was he who had cried out. Yet he still remained standing, clasping on to a window-frame. My mother beat on the door, wanting to enter and die with him, but the door was locked from the inside.

'Around him the Palicares were writhing in their death-throes. Two or three who were unharmed or only lightly wounded dived out of the windows. At the same time the whole floor cracked open, shattered from below. My father fell to one knee and, as he did so, twenty arms reached up, holding sabres, pistols and daggers; twenty blows struck that one man simultaneously; and my father vanished in a maelstrom of fire, fanned into life by these roaring demons, as if hell itself had opened beneath his feet. I felt myself pulled to the ground: my mother had fainted.'

Haydée let fall her arms, groaning and looking at the count as though to ask if he was satisfied with her obedience. He got up, came across to her, took her hand and said to her in Romaic: 'Rest, my dear child, and console yourself with the thought that there is a God to punish traitors.'

'This was a dreadful story, Count,' Albert said, alarmed at Haydée's pallor. 'I reproach myself now for having been so indiscreet.'

'You have no need to,' Monte Cristo replied. Then, putting his hand on her head, he continued: 'Haydée is a brave woman and she has sometimes found relief in describing her misfortunes.'

'Because, my Lord,' the young woman exclaimed, 'the tale of my sufferings reminds me of your goodness towards me.'

Albert looked at her curiously. She had not yet told him what he most wanted to know: how she had become the count's slave. Haydée saw the same wish in his eyes and the count's, so she went on:

'When my mother came to herself, we were both in front of the *seraskier*. "Kill me," my mother said, "but spare the honour of Ali's widow."

' "It is not I with whom you should plead," said Kurchid.

' "With whom, then?" '

' "With your new master." '

' "And who is that?" '

'Kurchid showed us one of the men who had most contributed to my father's death,' the young woman said, with brooding anger.

'So did you become this man's property?' Albert asked.

'No,' Haydée replied. 'He did not dare keep us, but sold us to some slave-dealers on their way to Constantinople. We crossed through Greece and were almost dead on arriving at the imperial gate, which was crowded with onlookers who stepped aside to let us pass, when suddenly my mother follows their eyes, cries out and falls to the ground, showing me a head impaled above the gate. Beneath it were the words: "This is the head of Ali Tebelin, Pasha of Janina." '

'Weeping, I tried to raise my mother to her feet; but she was dead!

'I was taken to the bazaar. A rich Armenian bought me, educated me, gave me teachers and, when I was thirteen, sold me to Sultan Mahmoud.'

'And from him,' Monte Cristo said, 'I bought her, as I told you, Albert, for that stone equal to the one in which I keep my lozenges of hashish.'

'Oh, my lord, how good and great you are,' said Haydée, kissing Monte Cristo's hand. 'How fortunate I am to belong to you!'

Albert was dumbstruck at what he had heard.

'Finish your coffee,' the count said to him. 'The story is over.'

LXXVIII

A CORRESPONDENT WRITES FROM JANINA

Franz had staggered out of Noirtier's room in such a confused state that even Valentine felt sorry for him. Villefort merely muttered some incoherent phrases and fled to his study where, two hours later, he received the following letter:

After what was revealed this morning, Monsieur Noirtier de Villefort cannot imagine any alliance to be possible between his family and that of

Monsieur Franz d'Epinay. Monsieur Franz d'Epinay is appalled when he
considers that Monsieur Villefort, who appeared to know about the events
that were described this morning, did not anticipate his reaction.

Anyone who could have seen the magistrate at that moment,
stricken as he was, would not have believed that he had foreseen it.
Indeed, he would never have thought that his father would be so
frank – or so brutal – as to recount such a story. True, M. Noirtier,
contemptuous of his son's opinion, had never taken the trouble to
elucidate the matter for Villefort and the latter had always assumed
that General Quesnel – or Baron d'Epinay, according to whether
one prefers to call him by the name he made for himself or the
one that was made for him – had been assassinated, rather than
honourably killed in a duel.

   This harsh letter, from a young man who until then had been so
respectful, was devastating to the pride of someone like Villefort.
Hardly had he entered his study than his wife followed. Franz's
disappearance, at M. Noirtier's summons, had so astonished everyone that the position of Mme de Villefort, who had remained alone
with the notary and the witnesses, had become more and more
embarrassing. Eventually she made up her mind and left, announcing that she was going to find out what had happened.

   Villefort told her only that, after a dispute between himself, M.
Noirtier and M. d'Epinay, Franz's engagement to Valentine had
been broken off. This was not easy to relay to the people who were
still waiting, so Mme de Villefort went back and said simply that
M. Noirtier had suffered some kind of apoplectic seizure at the
start of the meeting, so the signature of the contract had naturally
been postponed for a few days. This news, false though it was, made
such a singular impression, coming after two other misfortunes of
the same kind, that all of them looked at one another in astonishment, then left without a word.

   Meanwhile Valentine, at once happy and appalled, after embracing and thanking the weak old man who had with just a single blow
shattered a bond that she had already come to consider indissoluble,
asked if she could retire so that she could recover, and Noirtier,
with a look, gave her permission to do so. However, instead of
going up to her room, Valentine went out and down the corridor,
then, leaving by the little door, ran into the garden. In the midst of
all the events that had taken place, one after the other, her mind

had been constantly tormented by a vague apprehension: from one moment to the next, she expected to see Morrel burst in, pale and threatening like the Laird of Ravenswood at the betrothal of Lucy of Lammermoor.[1]

As it happened, she reached the gate just in time. Maximilien, guessing what was about to take place when he saw Franz leave the cemetery with M. de Villefort, had followed him. Then, after seeing him enter, he saw him come out again, then return with Château-Renaud. He could no longer have any doubt. He hurried to his field, ready for anything, sure that Valentine would come there to him as soon as the opportunity presented itself.

He had been right. His eye pressed to the fence, he saw the young woman run towards the gate, without taking any of her usual precautions. At first glance, Maximilien was reassured, and at her first word he leapt with joy.

'Saved!' Valentine said.

'Saved!' Morrel repeated, unable to believe such good fortune. 'By whom are we saved?'

'By my grandfather. Oh, Morrel! Love him dearly!'

Morrel swore to love the old man with all his soul; and the oath cost him nothing, for at that moment he did not merely love him like a friend or a father: he adored him as a god.

'But how did it happen?' Morrel asked. 'What strange means did he employ?'

Valentine opened her mouth to tell him everything, but then considered that there was a dreadful secret behind all this that did not belong only to her grandfather.

'Later,' she said. 'I shall tell you everything later.'

'When?'

'When I am your wife.'

This put the conversation on a plane which made it easy for Morrel to understand anything; so he understood that he must be content with what he knew and that this was enough for one day. However, he agreed to leave only on the promise that he would see Valentine the following evening.

She gave him her promise. Everything had changed in her eyes and it was certainly easier for her now to believe that she would marry Morrel than it had been an hour earlier to believe that she would not marry Franz.

While this was going on, Mme de Villefort had gone up to see

Noirtier. The old man looked at her with the stern, dark eye that he usually turned on her.

'Monsieur,' she said, 'I do not need to tell you that Valentine's engagement has been broken off, because this is where the breach occurred.'

Noirtier gave no sign of emotion.

'But,' Mme de Villefort went on, 'what you do not know, Monsieur, is that I was always opposed to the match, which was to take place in spite of my objections.'

Noirtier looked enquiringly at his daughter-in-law.

'Well, now that the engagement is broken off – and I was always aware of your distaste for it – I have come with a request that neither Monsieur de Villefort nor Valentine could make.'

Noirtier's eyes asked what this could be.

'I have come, Monsieur,' Mme de Villefort went on, 'as the only person who has a right to do so, being the only one who has nothing to gain from it, to beg you to restore to your granddaughter, not your goodwill, since she has always had that, but your fortune.'

Noirtier's eyes remained unsure for an instant, clearly seeking the motives behind this demand and unable to find them.

'Am I right to hope, Monsieur,' Mme de Villefort said, 'that your intentions were in harmony with the request I have just made?'

'Yes,' said Noirtier.

'In that case, Monsieur,' she concluded, 'I shall leave you with both gratitude and contentment.' And, bowing to him, she went out of the room.

The following day, Noirtier duly called for the notary. The first will was torn up and a new one made under which he left his entire fortune to Valentine, on condition that she was not separated from him. Some people in society therefore calculated that Mlle de Villefort, heiress to the Marquis and Marquise de Saint-Méran and now restored to her grandfather's favour, would one day have an income of nearly 300,000 *livres*.

While the engagement was being broken off at the Villeforts', the Comte de Morcerf received a visit from Monte Cristo and, to show Danglars how eager he was, he put on his lieutenant-general's dress uniform – the one he had had decked out with all his decorations – and called for his best horses. In this finery, he trotted round to the Rue de la Chaussée-d'Antin and had himself announced to

Danglars, who was going over his end-of-the-month accounts. In recent weeks this had not been the best time to meet the banker if one wanted to find him in a good mood. So, at the sight of his old friend, Danglars put on his most majestic air and drew himself up in his chair.

Morcerf, contrary to his usual strait-laced manner, was wearing a jolly, affable smile. Since he was more or less certain that his suit would be received favourably, he did not bother with diplomatic niceties, but came straight to the point: 'Here I am, Baron,' he said. 'For a long time we have been beating about the bush over what we said . . .'

As he began speaking, Morcerf expected the banker's face to relax, attributing its lowering expression to his silence; but, on the contrary, the face became still more cold and impassive (though one would hardly have deemed this possible). This was why Morcerf had stopped in the middle of his sentence.

'What did we say, Monsieur le Comte?' the banker asked, as if searching his memory for an explanation of the general's meaning.

'Ah, I see!' the count said. 'You are going to respect the formalities, my dear sir, and want to remind me that protocol requires us to follow the proper procedure. Very well, so be it! You must forgive me: I only have one son and this is the first time I have considered marrying him, so I am still a novice in these matters. Right, I'll do as you wish.' And, with a forced smile, he got up, made a deep bow to Danglars and said: 'Baron, I have the honour to ask for the hand of Mademoiselle Eugénie Danglars, your daughter, for my son, Viscount Albert de Morcerf.'

However, instead of receiving these words in the favourable manner that Morcerf would have expected, Danglars raised an eyebrow and – without inviting the count, who was still standing, to sit down – said: 'Monsieur le Comte, I shall have to consider the matter before giving you a reply.'

'Consider!' Morcerf exclaimed with mounting astonishment. 'Haven't you had time to consider in the eight years since we first mentioned this match?'

'Every day, Count,' Danglars said, 'we find that we are obliged to reconsider things in the light of new considerations.'

'What do you mean?' Morcerf asked. 'I don't follow you, Baron.'

'I mean, Monsieur, that in the past fortnight certain new circumstances . . .'

'One moment, I beg you,' said Morcerf. 'Are you serious, or is this some game we are playing?'

'What game?'

'Yes, let's put our cards on the table.'

'That's all I ask.'

'You have seen Monte Cristo!'

'I see him quite often,' said Danglars, tugging his chin, 'he's a friend of mine.'

'Well, last time you saw him, you told him that I seemed vague and uncertain where this match is concerned.'

'Quite so.'

'Well, here I am, neither vague nor forgetful, as you can see, since I have come to ask you to keep your promise.'

Danglars said nothing.

'Have you changed your mind,' Morcerf added, 'or are you forcing me to make an explicit request just for the pleasure of humiliating me?'

Danglars realized that, if the conversation were to continue along these lines, it would be to his disadvantage, so he said: 'Monsieur le Comte, you must be justifiably surprised by my coolness; I understand that; so, believe me, you cannot regret it more than I do myself; but, I assure you, it is required by circumstances beyond my control.'

'That's all very well, my dear sir,' said the count. 'And your average visitor might be satisfied with such mumbo-jumbo. But the Comte de Morcerf is not your average visitor and, when a man like myself comes to see another, when he reminds him of a promise and the other fails to keep his word, then he has the right to demand on the spot that he at least be given a good reason.'

Danglars was a coward, but he did not wish to appear one. He was irritated by Morcerf's tone.

'I have plenty of good reasons,' he answered.

'And what do you mean by that?'

'That there is a good reason, but not one that I can easily give you.'

'I suppose you must realize, however,' said Morcerf, 'that your reservations are of little use to me; and, in any event, one thing seems clear, which is that you are rejecting the match.'

'No,' said Danglars. 'I am postponing a decision, that's all.'

'You surely cannot be expecting that I should submit to your whim and wait, quietly and humbly, until you are more favourably disposed?'

'Very well then, Count, if you cannot wait, consider our arrangement annulled.'

The count bit his lip until it bled in order to restrain himself from the outburst that his proud and irascible temperament urged him to make. Realizing, however, that in these circumstances he was the one who would appear ridiculous, he was already making his way to the door of the room when he changed his mind and returned. A cloud had passed across his brow, replacing injured pride with a hint of uncertainty.

'Come, my dear Danglars,' he said. 'We have known one another for many years and should consequently show some consideration for one another. You owe me an explanation and the least I can ask is that you should tell me what unfortunate event has caused my son to forfeit your good intentions towards him.'

'It is nothing personal to the Viscount, that's all I can tell you, Monsieur,' Danglars replied, becoming impertinent again when he saw that Morcerf was giving ground.

'So to whom is it personal?' Morcerf asked in a strangled voice, the colour draining from his face.

Danglars noted each of these symptoms and stared at the count with unusual self-confidence. 'You should be grateful to me for refusing to clarify the matter,' he said.

A nervous shudder, doubtless the product of repressed anger, shook Morcerf. He made a supreme effort to contain himself. 'I have the right,' he said, 'and the intention of requiring the satisfaction of an explanation. Do you have something against Madame de Morcerf? Is it that my wealth is insufficient? Or my political opinions, the contrary of yours . . .'

'None of that, Monsieur,' said Danglars. 'In those cases, it would be unforgivable since I knew all that when I entered the agreement. No, look no further. I am truly ashamed of having made you suggest such things. Believe me, we should leave it there. Let's settle for a simple delay, which will be neither an engagement nor a breach. For heaven's sake, there is no hurry! My daughter is seventeen and your son twenty-one. Time will move on, even as we pause, and events will occur . . . Things that appear obscure one day are sometimes only too clear the next; in that way, the cruellest slanders can vanish from one day to the next.'

'Slanders! Did you say slanders, Monsieur!' Morcerf cried, white as a sheet. 'Someone is slandering me!'

'I tell you, Count, look no further.'

'So I must accept this rejection without a murmur?'

'It is above all painful for me. Yes, more than for you, because I was counting on the honour of a match with you, and a broken engagement always looks worse for the girl than for her fiancé.'

'Very well, Monsieur, let's say no more,' Morcerf muttered and, angrily slapping his gloves, left the room. Danglars noticed that not once had Morcerf dared to ask if it was because of him – Morcerf – that Danglars was withdrawing his consent.

That evening, he had a long meeting with several of his friends and M. Cavalcanti, who had remained constantly in the salon with the ladies, was the last to leave the banker's house.

The next day, when he woke up, Danglars asked for the papers and they were brought to him at once. He put three or four aside, and picked up *L'Impartial*. This was the one managed and edited by Beauchamp. He quickly tore off the wrapper, opened it with nervous haste, cast a contemptuous eye over the home news and came to the 'news in brief', where he stopped with a malicious grin at an item beginning with the words: 'A correspondent writes from Janina . . .'

'Very well,' he said, after reading it. 'There is a little piece on Colonel Fernand which will quite probably relieve me of the obligation to give the Comte de Morcerf any further explanation.'

At this same moment, which is to say just as nine o'clock was striking, Albert de Morcerf, dressed in black and neatly buttoned up, arrived at the house in the Champs-Elysées in a state of some agitation and curtly asked for the count.

'Monsieur le Comte went out some half an hour ago,' said the concierge.

'Did he take Baptistin with him?' Morcerf asked.

'No, Monsieur le Vicomte.'

'Call Baptistin, I wish to speak with him.'

The concierge went to look for the valet himself and came back with him a short time later.

'My friend,' said Albert, 'I beg you to forgive me for asking, but I wanted to find out from you whether your master is really not at home.'

'No, Monsieur, he is not,' Baptistin replied.

'Even to me?'

'I know how happy my master is to receive Monsieur and I should be careful to exclude him from any general instruction.'

'You are right, because I have a serious matter to discuss with him. Do you think he will be long?'

'No, he ordered breakfast for ten o'clock.'

'Very well, I shall take a walk along the Champs-Elysées and be here at ten. If Monsieur le Comte returns before I do, ask him to be so good as to expect me.'

'I shall, Monsieur may be sure of that.'

Albert left his hired cab at the count's door and went off on foot. Walking past the Allée des Veuves, he thought he recognized the count's horses standing at the door of Gosset's shooting gallery. He went over and, having recognized the horses, now recognized the driver.

'Is the count shooting?' he asked him.

'Yes, Monsieur,' the coachman replied.

Several shots had rung out at regular intervals since Morcerf had approached the shooting gallery. He went in. The attendant was standing in the little garden.

'I beg the vicomte's pardon,' he said, 'but would you mind waiting for a moment?'

'Why is that, Philippe?' Albert asked: being a regular visitor, he was astonished at this incomprehensible barrier.

'Because the gentleman who is practising at the moment hires the whole range for himself and never shoots in front of anyone.'

'Not even you, Philippe.'

'As you see, Monsieur, I am standing by the door to my office.'

'And who loads his pistols?'

'His servant.'

'A Nubian?'

'A negro.'

'That's what I mean.'

'Do you know the gentleman, then?'

'I have come to find him. He is a friend.'

'Oh, that's a different matter. I'll go in and tell him.' And Philippe, driven by curiosity, went into the shooting gallery. A moment later Monte Cristo appeared at the door.

'Please forgive me for following you here, my dear Count,' said Albert, 'and I must start by telling you that it was not the fault of your servants; I alone have been indiscreet. I went to your house and was told that you were out walking, but that you would return at ten o'clock for breakfast. I also went out for a walk to pass the time and it was then that I saw your horses and your carriage.'

'What you say leads me to hope that you have come to invite me to breakfast.'

'No, thank you, there's no question of dining for the moment. Perhaps we may lunch together later, but I shall be poor company, confound it.'

'What on earth is the matter?'

'My dear Count, I am going to fight today.'

'You! How on earth is that?'

'In a duel, of course.'

'Yes, I realize that, but for what reason? You understand, people fight for all sorts of reasons.'

'On a point of honour.'

'Ah, now. That's serious.'

'So serious that I have come to ask a favour of you.'

'Which is?'

'To be my second.'

'Then it's really serious. Let's not discuss it here, but go home. Ali, some water!'

The count rolled up his sleeves and went into the little hallway outside the shooting ranges where the marksmen are accustomed to wash their hands.

'Come in, Monsieur le Vicomte,' Philippe whispered. 'I've got something to show you.'

Morcerf followed him. Instead of targets, playing cards had been fixed to the board. From a distance, Morcerf thought it was a complete pack from the ace to the ten.

'Huh!' he said. 'Were you playing piquet?'

'No,' said the count. 'I was making a pack of cards.'

'What do you mean?'

'Those are aces and twos that you see; my bullets made them into threes, fives, sevens, eights, nines and tens.'

Albert went over to look and saw that, indeed, the bullets had replaced the absent symbols with perfectly precise holes at perfectly equal distances, passing through each card at the points where it should have been painted. As he was walking across to the board, Morcerf also picked up two or three swallows that the count had shot when they were rash enough to fly within range of his pistol.

'I'll be damned!' said Albert.

'What do you expect, my dear Viscount?' Monte Cristo said, wiping his hands on a towel that Ali brought. 'I must fill in my idle moments. Come, now, let's go.'

They both got into Monte Cristo's coupé and a few minutes later it put them down at the door of No. 30. Monte Cristo showed Morcerf into his study and offered him a seat. They sat down.

'Now, let's discuss this calmly,' the count said.

'As you see, I am perfectly calm.'

'Who are you going to fight?'

'Beauchamp.'

'But he's a friend of yours!'

'It's always one's friends that one fights.'

'But you must at least have a reason.'

'I do.'

'What has he done to you?'

'In last night's newspaper, there was . . . But read it for yourself.' And Albert handed Monte Cristo a paper in which he read the following:

A correspondent writes from Janina:

We have learned a fact which has remained unknown, or at least unpublished up to now. The castles defending the town were betrayed to the Turks by a French officer in whom the vizier, Ali Tebelin, had placed all his trust. His name was Fernand.

'Well?' said Monte Cristo. 'What have you found in that to shock you?'

'What have I found!'

'Yes. What does it matter to you that the castles of Janina were betrayed to the Turks by an officer called Fernand?'

'It matters because my father, the Comte de Morcerf, was christened Fernand.'

'And your father served under Ali Pasha?'

'He fought for the independence of Greece; that is the slander.'

'Come now, my dear Viscount, be reasonable.'

'I ask nothing better.'

'So tell me: who the devil in France knows that this officer

Fernand is the same as the Comte de Morcerf, and who today cares at all about Janina, which was captured in 1822 or 1823, I believe?'

'This is precisely what is so perfidious: they have let time pass, and only now do they dig up these forgotten events to turn them into a scandal that might tarnish a man in a prominent position. Well, as the heir to my father's name, I should not like even the shadow of a doubt to hang over it. I shall send two seconds to Beauchamp, whose paper published this article, and he will retract it.'

'Beauchamp will retract nothing.'

'Then we must fight.'

'No, you will not, because he will retort that there were perhaps fifty officers with the name Fernand in the Greek army.'

'We shall fight for all that. Oh, how I wish all this could go away! My father ... such a noble soldier, such an illustrious career ...'

'Or else he can write: "We have every reason to believe that the Fernand in question has nothing to do with Monsieur le Comte de Morcerf, whose given name is also Fernand."'

'I must have a full and total retraction; that would not be enough.'

'So you are going to send him your seconds?'

'Yes.'

'You are wrong.'

'That is to say, you refuse me the service I asked you?'

'Oh, you know what I think about duels. I explained my ideas to you in Rome, don't you remember?'

'Despite which, my dear Count, I found you just now, this very morning, engaged in a pastime that seems to accord ill with those ideas.'

'Because, you must understand, my dear friend, one should never be exclusive. When one lives among madmen, one should train as a maniac. From one minute to the next, some hothead, with no greater reason to seek a quarrel with me than you have to seek one with Beauchamp, will come and hunt me out on the first flimsy pretext he can find, or send me his seconds, or insult me in a public place. Well, I shall be obliged to kill him.'

'So you admit that you would fight?'

'Heavens, yes!'

'So why do you want to prevent me from doing the same?'

'I'm not saying that you should not fight, I'm just saying that a duel is a serious matter which demands reflection.'

'Did he reflect, do you think, before insulting my father?'

'If he didn't, and he admits as much, you should not hold it against him.'

'My dear Count, you are too indulgent by half.'

'And you are too stringent by half. Come now, just imagine . . . Listen: just imagine . . . Now don't be angry with what I am about to say . . .'

'I'm listening.'

'Just suppose the fact he published was true.'

'No son should admit such a supposition touching his father's honour.'

'Good Lord! But we live in times when so many things are allowed.'

'Which is precisely the vice of the times.'

'Are you attempting to reform them?'

'Yes, when it affects me.'

'What a moralist you are, dear boy!'

'That's the way I am made.'

'Are you beyond the reach of good advice?'

'No, not when it comes from a friend.'

'Do you count me as one?'

'Yes.'

'Then before sending your seconds to Beauchamp, discover the facts.'

'From whom?'

'Well, for example, from Haydée.'

'Involve a woman in this! What could she do?'

'Tell you that your father had nothing to do with the overthrow or death of her father, for example, or enlighten you on the subject, if by chance your father did have the misfortune . . .'

'I have already told you, my dear Count, that I cannot admit such a possibility.'

'So you refuse to adopt this solution.'

'I do.'

'Absolutely?'

'Absolutely.'

'Then, one last piece of advice.'

'Yes, but let it be the last.'

'Don't you want it?'

'On the contrary, I ask you to give it to me.'

'Don't send your seconds to Beauchamp.'

'Why?'

'Go and see him yourself.'

'That's not done. It would be most unconventional.'

'Your affair is not a conventional one.'

'So why must I go myself then?'

'Because in that way the matter will remain between you and Beauchamp.'

'Explain.'

'Of course. If Beauchamp is inclined to retract, you must leave him with the merit of his goodwill. The retraction will be made just as surely. If he refuses, on the contrary, it will be time to confide your secret to two strangers.'

'They will not be strangers, but friends.'

'Today's friends are tomorrow's enemies.'

'What a thing to say!'

'Look at Beauchamp.'

'So . . .'

'So, I advise caution.'

'So you think I should go and see Beauchamp myself.'

'Yes.'

'Alone?'

'Alone. When you want to obtain something touching a man's self-respect, you must spare his pride even the appearance of suffering.'

'I think you are right.'

'I'm very glad to hear it.'

'I shall go alone.'

'Good; but you would do better not to go at all.'

'That's impossible.'

'So do as you say. It is still preferable to what you intended.'

'In that case, tell me: if, despite all my efforts and all my approaches, I still have a duel, will you serve as my second?'

'My dear Viscount,' Monte Cristo said, with the utmost gravity, 'you must have seen that I am devoted to you at any time or place, but the service you ask of me falls outside the range of those that I can perform for you.'

'Why is that?'

'You may perhaps find out one day.'

'And meanwhile?'

'I beg your indulgence for my secret.'

'Very well, I shall take Franz and Château-Renaud.'

'Do so: they will suit perfectly.'

'But at least, if I do have to fight, you will at least give me a little training with the épée or the pistol?'

'No, that too is impossible.'

'What an odd fellow you are, indeed! So you don't want anything to do with it.'

'Absolutely nothing.'

'Very well, we'll say no more. Farewell, Count.'

'Farewell, Viscount.'

Morcerf took his hat and went out. At the door, he picked up his cab and, repressing his anger as best he could, asked to be driven to Beauchamp's. Beauchamp was at his newspaper, so Albert had the driver proceed there.

Beauchamp was in an office which was dark and dusty, as newspaper offices are from the day they open for business. Albert de Morcerf was announced. He had the name repeated twice; then, still incredulous, called out: 'Enter!'

Albert appeared. Beauchamp gave a cry as he saw his friend struggling over bundles of paper and stubbing his unpractised toes against the newspapers of every size that littered, not the wooden, but the red-tiled floor of his office.

'This way, this way, my dear Albert,' he said, offering the young man his hand. 'What the devil brings you? Are you lost like Tom Thumb? Or have you just come to invite me to lunch? Try to find a chair. Look, there's one, over there by the geranium: the plant alone persuades me that there are leaves in the world that are not leaves of paper.'

'It's about your paper, Beauchamp, that I have come to talk to you,' Albert said.

'You, Morcerf? What do you want?'

'A retraction.'

'You? A retraction? About what, Albert? Do sit down.'

'Thank you,' Albert said for the second time, with a slight nod.

'Now, explain.'

'A retraction on a matter that sullies the honour of a member of my family.'

'Come, come!' Beauchamp said in surprise. 'What matter? It's not possible.'

'The matter that your correspondent writes from Janina.'

'Janina?'

'Yes, Janina. You really do seem not to know why I am here.'

'I swear I do not ... Baptiste! Yesterday's paper!' Beauchamp shouted.

'No need, I've brought my own copy.'

Beauchamp read the passage, muttering: 'A correspondent writes from Janina . . .'

'You see that it is a serious matter,' Morcerf said, when Beauchamp had finished.

'This officer is a relation of yours?' the journalist asked.

'Yes,' Albert replied, blushing.

'So what would you like me to do for you?' Beauchamp asked gently.

'What I want, my dear Beauchamp, is for you to print a retraction.'

Beauchamp looked at Albert attentively and visibly with a great deal of goodwill. 'Let's see, now,' he said. 'This is going to be a long discussion, because a retraction is always a serious matter. Sit down and I shall read the three or four lines again.'

Albert sat down and Beauchamp re-read the offending words more attentively than the first time.

'There,' said Albert, firmly, and even roughly. 'You see: someone of my family has been insulted in your newspaper and I want a retraction . . .'

'You . . . *want* . . .'

'Yes, I want!'

'May I point out, my dear Viscount, that you are not addressing the House.'

'I have no wish to do so,' the young man retorted, standing up. 'I am seeking retraction of an item that you published yesterday, and I shall obtain it. You are enough of a friend,' Albert went on through clenched teeth, seeing that Beauchamp was also beginning to adopt an air of injured pride, 'you are enough of a friend, and consequently know me well enough, I hope, to understand my tenacity in such circumstances.'

'I may be your friend, Morcerf, but eventually you will make me forget it, with words such as those you have just used. Come now, let's not get angry with one another – at least, not yet. You are upset, annoyed, irritated . . . So tell me, who is this relation called Fernand?'

'My father, no less,' Albert said. 'Fernand Mondego, Count of Morcerf, an old soldier who fought on twenty battlefields, whose noble scars are now being spattered with filthy mud from the roadside.'

'Your father?' Beauchamp said. 'That's another matter. I can understand your indignation, my dear Albert . . . So, let's have another look at this . . .' And he re-read the note, this time weighing each word.

'But how do you know that this Fernand in the paper is your father?' Beauchamp asked.

'I don't, of course, but others will. That is why I want the item to be denied.'

At those words 'I want', Beauchamp looked at Morcerf, then almost at once looked down again and thought for a moment.

'You will retract it, won't you, Beauchamp?' Morcerf went on, with still-contained but increasing anger.

'Yes,' said Beauchamp.

'At last!' Albert exclaimed.

'But only when I am certain that the allegation is false.'

'What!'

'The matter is worth clarifying, and I shall do so.'

'But what is there to clarify in all this, Monsieur?' said Albert, beside himself. 'If you do not believe it is my father, say so at once. If you do believe it was him, then prepare to answer to me for that belief!'

Beauchamp looked at Albert with his own particular smile, that could accommodate itself to every emotion.

'Monsieur,' he continued, ' – since we are on such terms – if you came here to challenge me, then you should have done so straight away and not started talking about friendship and other tiresome matters of that kind which I have been patiently listening to for the past half-hour. If this is how things are to be between us from now on, tell me.'

'They will, unless you retract that infamous slander!'

'One moment! No threats, please, Monsieur Albert Mondego, Vicomte de Morcerf. I won't stand for them from my enemies, still less from my friends. So you want me to deny the report about Colonel Fernand, a report in which, on my honour, I had no part?'

'Yes, that is what I want!' said Albert, his head starting to spin.

'Otherwise, we fight?' Beauchamp went on as calmly as before.

'Yes!' Albert repeated, his voice rising to a crescendo.

'Very well,' said Beauchamp. 'Here is my reply, my dear sir. This report was not published by me and I had no knowledge of it; but you yourself have brought it to my attention and now I am interested. So the report will stand until it is either confirmed or denied by the proper authorities.'

'In that case, Monsieur,' Albert said, 'I shall have the honour to send you my seconds. You may discuss the place and weapons with them.'

'Precisely, my dear sir.'

'And we shall meet this evening, if you wish, or at the latest tomorrow.'

'No, no, not so fast! I shall be here when the time comes, and in my opinion – which I have the right to give, since I am the one who has been provoked – in my opinion, as I say, the time is not yet. I know that you are a good swordsman, and I am a fair one. I know that you can hit three bull's-eyes out of six, which is roughly my own score. I know that a duel between us will be a serious matter, because you are a brave fellow and . . . well, I am too. Consequently I do not want to risk killing you or being killed by you for no reason. Now, I shall in turn ask you the question, and quite cat-eg-or-ic-al-ly: are you so set on this retraction that you will kill me if I do not make it, even though I have told you, and repeat to you, and swear on my honour, that I was not aware of this report; and even though it would be impossible for anyone except a Don Japhet like yourself to guess that Monsieur le Comte de Morcerf might be referred to under that name, Fernand?'

'I am absolutely set on it.'

'Very well, my good sir, I agree to cut my throat with you, but I want three weeks. In three weeks, come back and I shall either tell you: yes, the report is false, I shall annul it; or else, yes, the report is true, and I get the swords out of their scabbards, or the pistols from their cases, as you wish.'

'Three weeks!' Albert cried. 'But three weeks are three centuries in which I shall be dishonoured!'

'If you had remained my friend, I should say to you: Patience, friend. You have made yourself my enemy and I say to you: What do I care, Monsieur!'

'Very well, in three weeks, agreed,' said Morcerf. 'But consider this: in three weeks, there will be no more delays and no subterfuge that you can use to avoid . . .'

'Monsieur Albert de Morcerf,' Beauchamp said, getting up in his turn, 'I cannot throw you out of the window for another three weeks, that is to say, twenty-four days, and you will only have the right to assault me at that time. It is now August the twenty-ninth, so on the twenty-first of September . . . Until then – and this is a piece of advice from a gentleman – please let us spare one another the barking of bulldogs who cannot reach each other because they are chained.' And, bowing to the young man, he turned his back on him and went through into the printing works.

Albert took out his feelings on a pile of newspapers which he spread across the room with sweeping blows from his stick. After that he left, but not without two or three backward glances towards the door of the printing works.

After crossing the boulevard, Albert began whipping the front of his carriage, just as he had whipped the innocent papers, black with ink, which could do nothing to ease his frustration. At that moment he noticed Morrel who, head held high, with sparkling eyes and freely swinging arms, was walking along in front of the Chinese Baths from the direction of the Porte Saint-Martin and going towards the Madeleine.

'Ah,' Albert thought, with a sigh, 'there is a contented man!'

As it happens, he was not wrong.

LXXIX

LEMONADE

Morrel was indeed very contented. M. Noirtier had just sent for him, and he was in such a hurry to know why that he had not taken a cab, trusting his own two legs more than those of a hired horse. He had set out at a fair pace from the Rue Meslay and was on his way to the Faubourg Saint-Honoré. He was proceeding at a jog, while poor Barrois followed on as best he could. Morrel was thirty-one, Barrois sixty; Morrel was drunk with love, Barrois faint with heat. The two men, so different in age and interests, were like two sides of a triangle: separated at the base, meeting at the apex; the apex was Noirtier.

He had told Morrel to make haste, and Morrel, much to the despair of Barrois, was following this instruction precisely. When they arrived, Morrel was not even out of breath – love gives wings – but Barrois, who had not been in love for a long time, was pouring with sweat.

The old servant showed Morrel in by the side entrance and closed the study door. Soon the sound of a dress brushing against the floor announced the arrival of Valentine. She was ravishingly beautiful in her mourning clothes. The dream was becoming so sweet that Morrel would almost have done without talking to Noirtier; but the old man's wheelchair could soon be heard outside, and he came in.

With a benevolent smile Noirtier accepted the thanks which Morrel heaped upon him for the miraculous intervention that had saved Valentine and himself from despair. Then Morrel's look turned towards the young woman, enquiring of her the reason why he was newly in favour. She, shyly sitting at some distance from Morrel, was waiting to speak until she was obliged to. Noirtier looked at her in turn.

'Must I say what you told me to, then?' she asked.

'Yes,' Noirtier indicated.

'Monsieur Morrel,' Valentine said, addressing the young man who was devouring her with his eyes. 'My grandpapa Noirtier had a thousand things to tell you, and he has told them to me in the past three days. Today, he has sent for you so that I can repeat them. I shall do so, since he has chosen me as his interpreter, without changing a word of his meaning.'

'I am impatient to hear,' the young man replied. 'Please speak, Mademoiselle, speak.'

Valentine lowered her eyes. This was a sign that seemed to Morrel to augur well: Valentine was weak only when she was happy.

'My grandfather wants to leave this house,' she said. 'Barrois is trying to find him suitable lodgings.'

'What about you, Mademoiselle,' said Morrel, 'you, who are so dear and so essential to Monsieur Noirtier?'

'I shall not abandon my grandfather,' the young woman said.

'This has been agreed between us. My apartment will be near his. Either I shall have Monsieur de Villefort's consent to go and live with grandpapa Noirtier, or it will be refused. In the first case, I shall leave at once; in the second, I shall await my majority, which falls in eighteen months. Then I shall be free, I shall have independent means and . . .'

'And?' said Morrel.

'And, with my grandfather's permission, I shall keep the promise that I made to you.'

Valentine spoke these last words so softly that Morrel would have been unable to hear them, had they not meant as much to him as they did.

'Isn't that your opinion, grandpa?' she added, turning to Noirtier.

'Yes,' said the old man.

'Once I am settled in at my grandfather's,' Valentine added, 'Monsieur Morrel will be able to come and visit me in the presence of this good and worthy protector. Our hearts may be ignorant or capricious; but if the bond that they have started to form seems respectable and gives some guarantees of future happiness to our endeavour – though, alas, they do say that hearts which are fired to overcome obstacles go cold when these are removed – then Monsieur Morrel can ask me for my hand; I shall wait for him.'

'Oh!' cried Morrel, tempted to kneel in front of the old man as before God, and in front of Valentine as before an angel. 'Oh! What have I done in my life to deserve such happiness?'

'Until then,' the young woman continued, in her clear, strict voice, 'we shall respect the conventions, and even the will of our parents, provided that will does not attempt to separate us for ever. In a word, and I repeat it, because it says everything, we shall wait.'

'I swear to carry out the sacrifices that the word imposes, Monsieur,' Morrel said, 'not with resignation, but with joy.'

'So,' Valentine went on, with a look that was very dear to Maximilien's heart, 'no more rash deeds, my friend. Do not compromise one who, from today onwards, considers herself destined to bear your name with purity and dignity.'

Morrel put his hand to his heart.

During this time, Noirtier was watching them both tenderly. Barrois, who had stayed at the back of the room, as someone from whom they had nothing to hide, was smiling and wiping the huge beads of sweat that coursed across his bald head.

'Heavens above, look how hot he is, poor Barrois,' said Valentine.

'That's because I had a good run, Mademoiselle,' Barrois said. 'But I must grant him this, Monsieur Morrel ran even faster than I did.'

Noirtier's eyes turned towards a tray on which were a carafe of lemonade and a glass. Half an hour earlier, Noirtier himself had drunk what was missing from the jug.

'Go on, my dear Barrois,' the girl said. 'Have it: I can see that you are casting envious looks at that half-empty jug.'

'The fact is,' he replied, 'I am dying of thirst and I should dearly like to drink a glass of lemonade to your health.'

'Go on, then,' said Valentine. 'Come back in a moment.'

Barrois took the tray and no sooner was he in the corridor than they saw him, through the door that he had forgotten to close, toss back his head to empty the glass that Valentine had filled.

Valentine and Morrel were exchanging farewells in Noirtier's presence when they heard the bell ring in Villefort's staircase. It was the signal that someone was coming to visit. Valentine looked at the clock.

'It is midday,' she said. 'And as today is Saturday, grandpapa, this must be the doctor.'

Noirtier made a sign confirming that he agreed with her.

'Since he is going to come here, Monsieur Morrel must leave, mustn't he, grandpapa?'

'Yes,' the old man replied.

'Barrois!' Valentine called. 'Barrois, come here!'

They heard the voice of the old servant answer: 'I'm coming, Mademoiselle.'

'Barrois will take you to the door,' Valentine said to Morrel. 'Now, Captain, remember one thing, which is that my grandfather advises you not to do anything which might threaten out future happiness.'

'I promised to wait,' said Morrel, 'and I shall.'

At this moment, Barrois came in.

'Who rang?' Valentine asked.

'Doctor d'Avrigny,' Barrois said, staggering.

'What's wrong, Barrois?' Valentine asked. The old man did not reply. He was looking at his master with panic-stricken eyes, while his hand grasped for something to hold on to, to keep him upright.

'He's going to fall!' Morrel cried.

The trembling in Barrois' limbs was increasing at an alarming rate and his expression was contorted by the contractions of the muscles, suggesting a violent nervous seizure. Noirtier, seeing Barrois' distress, gave a succession of looks that clearly and plainly expressed all the emotions that he was feeling. Barrois took a few steps towards his master. 'Oh, my God! My God!' he exclaimed. 'What is wrong with me? I am in such pain. I can no longer see. There are a thousand burning embers in my brain. Oh, don't touch me! Don't touch me!'

His eyes began to bulge, distraught, and his head fell backwards, while the rest of his body stiffened. Valentine gave a cry of terror and Morrel took her in his arms, as though to defend her against some unknown danger.

'Monsieur d'Avrigny! Monsieur d'Avrigny!' she cried in a strangled voice. 'Come here! Help!'

Barrois wheeled around, took three steps backwards, staggered and fell at Noirtier's feet, resting his hand on his knee and gasping: 'My master! My good master!'

At that moment, M. de Villefort appeared on the threshold of the room, attracted by the commotion.

Morrel let go of the half-unconscious Valentine and leapt back, hiding in a corner of the room where he was partly concealed by a curtain. Pale, as if he had seen a snake rearing up before him, he stared in horror at the dying man.

Noirtier was burning with impatience and terror; his soul flew to the aid of the poor old man – a friend rather than a servant. One could see the life-and-death struggle on his brow by the bulging of the veins and the contraction of the few muscles that were still living around his eyes.

Barrois, with a tortured expression, bloodshot eyes and head thrown back, was lying on the floor, beating it with his hands, while his legs, on the contrary, were so stiff that they seemed liable to break rather than bend. Traces of foam had appeared around his lips and he was gasping painfully.

Villefort, astonished, remained for a moment staring at this scene, which is what had drawn his attention as soon as he entered. He had not seen Morrel. After an instant of mute contemplation, in which his face paled and his hair stood on end, he cried: 'Doctor! Doctor! Come quickly!' as he rushed to the door.

'Madame! Madame!' Valentine cried, calling her stepmother and dashing herself against the walls of the stairway. 'Come! Come quickly, and bring your smelling-salts!'

'What is the matter?' asked the self-possessed, metallic voice of Mme de Villefort.

'Oh, please come! Quickly!'

'But where is the doctor!' Villefort cried. 'Where has he gone?'

Mme de Villefort came slowly down; they could hear the boards creaking under her feet. In one hand she held a handkerchief with which she was wiping her face, in the other a flask of English smelling-salts. Her first glance, as she reached the door, was for Noirtier, whose face showed his condition was unaltered, apart from the anxiety natural in such circumstances. Only then did she turn to look at the dying man.

She went pale and her eyes flashed as it were from the servant to the master.

'But in heaven's name, Madame, where is the doctor? He went into your apartments. It's an apoplexy, as you can see, and if he is bled we can save him.'

'Has he eaten anything recently?' Mme de Villefort asked, evading the question.

'He has had nothing to eat, Madame,' said Valentine, 'but he ran very hard this morning on an errand for grandpapa. The only thing he had, on his return, was a glass of lemonade.'

'Oh?' said Mme de Villefort. 'Why not wine? Lemonade is very bad for you.'

'The lemonade was right here, in grandpapa's jug. Poor Barrois was thirsty, so he drank what he had to hand.'

Mme de Villefort shuddered. Noirtier fixed her with his penetrating eyes.

'His neck is so short!' she said.

'Madame,' said Villefort, 'you must tell us where Monsieur d'Avrigny is. In heaven's name, answer!'

'He is with Edouard, who is slightly unwell, in his room,' she said, unable to evade the question any longer.

Villefort dashed to the stairs himself to fetch the doctor.

'Here,' the young woman said, giving her flask to Valentine. 'I expect they will bleed him. I'll go back to my room: I can't stand the sight of blood.' And she followed her husband.

Morrel emerged from the dark corner where he had concealed himself and remained unseen during the commotion.

'Go quickly, Maximilien,' Valentine said, 'and wait until I call for you. Go.'

Morrel made a gesture to ask Noirtier's opinion and the old man, who had kept himself under control, indicated that he should do as she said. He pressed Valentine's hand to his heart and went out through the hidden passage. As he was doing so, Villefort and the doctor came in through the opposite door.

Barrois was starting to regain his senses: the crisis had passed, he could groan a few words and he raised himself on one knee. D'Avrigny and Villefort carried him to a chaise-longue.

'What do you prescribe, doctor?' asked Villefort.

'Bring me water and ether – do you have some in the house?'

'We do.'

'Go and fetch me some oil of terebinth and an emetic.'

'Go on!' Villefort commanded.

'Now, everyone must leave.'

'Including me?' Valentine asked timidly.

'Yes, Mademoiselle, especially you,' the doctor said harshly. Valentine looked at him in astonishment, kissed M. Noirtier on the forehead and went out. The doctor emphatically closed the door behind her.

'There now, doctor. He's coming round. It was only some mild seizure.'

M. d'Avrigny gave a grim smile. 'How do you feel, Barrois?' he asked.

'A little better, Monsieur.'

'Can you drink this glass of etherized water?'

'I can try, but don't touch me.'

'Why not?'

'Because I feel that, if you were to touch me, even with the tip of a finger, I should suffer another attack.'

'Drink it.'

Barrois took the glass, lifted it to his purple lips and drank about half of what was in it.

'Where is the pain?' asked the doctor.

'Everywhere. It is like frightful cramps.'

'Do you feel dizzy?'

'Yes.'

'Is there a ringing in your ears?'

'Dreadful.'

'When did it start?'

'Just a short while ago.'

'Very suddenly?'

'Like a thunderbolt.'

'Nothing yesterday, or the day before?'

'Nothing.'

'No sleepiness? No lassitude?'

'No.'

'What have you eaten today?'

'Nothing. I just took a glass of Monsieur's lemonade, that's all.'
And Barrois nodded towards Noirtier, sitting motionless in his
chair and watching this dreadful scene without missing a movement
or a word.

'Where is this lemonade?' the doctor asked urgently.

'Outside, in the jug.'

'What do you mean by "outside"?'

'In the kitchen.'

'Would you like me to fetch it, doctor?' Villefort asked.

'No, stay here and try to make the patient drink the rest of this
glass of water.'

'But the lemonade . . .'

'I'll go myself.'

D'Avrigny leapt up, opened the door and ran out on to the service
stairs, where he almost knocked over Madame de Villefort. She,
too, was going down to the kitchen.

She cried out. D'Avrigny took no notice; his mind fixed on one
single idea, he jumped the last three or four stairs, hurried into the
kitchen and, seeing the little jug standing there, three-quarters
empty, pounced on it like an eagle on its prey. Panting for breath,
he went back to the ground floor and into M. Noirtier's room.

Mme de Villefort slowly went back up the stairs towards her
apartment.

'Is this the jug?' d'Avrigny asked.

'Yes, doctor.'

'And this lemonade is the same that you drank?'

'I think so.'

'How did it taste?'

'Bitter.'

The doctor poured a few drops of lemonade into the palm of his hand, sniffed it and, after washing it round his mouth as one does when tasting wine, spat the liquid into the fireplace.

'It must be the same,' he said. 'Did you also drink it, Monsieur Noirtier?'

'Yes,' said the old man.

'And you noticed this same bitter taste?'

'Yes.'

'Oh, doctor!' Barrois cried. 'It's starting again! Oh, God! Oh, Lord, have pity on me!'

The doctor hurried across to the sick man. 'Villefort,' he said, 'see if the emetic is coming.'

Villefort hurried out, shouting: 'The emetic! Has anyone brought the emetic?' There was no answer. The whole house was gripped with a profound sense of terror.

'If I had some means of getting air into his lungs,' d'Avrigny said, looking round about him, 'there might perhaps be some hope of avoiding asphyxia. But there is nothing! Nothing!'

'Oh, Monsieur,' Barrois cried, 'will you let me die without aid? Oh, I am dying! My God, I am dying!'

'A quill! A quill!' said the doctor, then he noticed a pen on the table. He tried to force it into the patient's mouth; Barrois, in his convulsions, was vainly trying to vomit. His jaw was so rigid that the quill could not pass through it. He was now in the grip of a nervous attack even more powerful than before; he slid from the chaise-longue to the floor and lay there, rigid.

The doctor, powerless to relieve his agony, left him and went over to Noirtier.

'How do you feel?' he said to him in an urgent whisper. 'Well?'

'Yes.'

'Does your stomach feel heavy or light? Light?'

'Yes.'

'As it does when you take the pill I make for you every Sunday?'

'Yes.'

'Did Barrois make your lemonade?'

'Yes.'

'And did you urge him to drink some of it?'

'No.'

'Was it Monsieur de Villefort?'

'No.'

'Madame?'

'No.'

'Valentine, then?'

'Yes.'

D'Avrigny's attention was drawn by a sigh from Barrois, a yawn that seemed to make his jawbone crack. He left Noirtier and hurried to the patient's side. 'Barrois,' he said, 'can you speak?'

Barrois muttered a few unintelligible words.

'Try to speak, my friend.'

Barrois re-opened his bloodshot eyes.

'Who made the lemonade?'

'I did.'

'Did you take it to your master as soon as it was made?'

'No.'

'So you left it somewhere, then?'

'In the scullery. I was called away.'

'And who brought it here?'

'Mademoiselle Valentine.'

D'Avrigny beat his brow. 'Oh, my God,' he murmured. 'My God!'

'Doctor, doctor!' Barrois cried, feeling the onset of another attack.

'Will no one bring that emetic?' the doctor shouted.

'Here is a glass of it ready prepared,' said Villefort, coming back into the room.

'By whom?'

'By the pharmacist's apprentice who came with me.'

'Drink.'

'I can't, doctor. It's too late. My throat is so tight. I am suffocating! Oh, my heart! Oh, my head! Oh, what hell! Must I suffer this for much longer?'

'No, no, my friend,' the doctor said. 'Soon you will suffer no longer.'

'Ah, I understand,' said the unfortunate man. 'My God! Have pity on me.' And, with a cry, he fell back as though struck by lightning.

D'Avrigny put a hand to his heart and held a mirror to his lips.

'Well?' asked Villefort.

'Go to the kitchen and ask them to bring me some syrup of violets.'

Villefort left at once.

'Don't worry, Monsieur Noirtier,' d'Avrigny said. 'I am taking the patient into another room to bleed him. This kind of attack is truly awful to see.' Taking Barrois under the arms, he dragged him into the next room, but returned almost immediately to where Noirtier was, to fetch the rest of the lemonade. Noirtier closed his right eye.

'Valentine? You want Valentine? I'll tell them to send her to you.'

Villefort was coming back up, and d'Avrigny met him in the corridor.

'Well?' he asked.

'Come with me,' said d'Avrigny, leading the way into the bedroom.

'Is he still unconscious?' the crown prosecutor asked.

'He is dead.'

Villefort stepped back, put his hands to his head and, with unfeigned pity, looked at the corpse and said: 'So suddenly!'

'Yes, very sudden, wasn't it?' d'Avrigny said. 'But you shouldn't be surprised at that: Monsieur and Madame de Saint-Méran died just as suddenly. People die quickly in your family, Monsieur de Villefort.'

'What!' the magistrate exclaimed, in tones of horror and consternation. 'Are you still pursuing that awful notion?'

'Yes, Monsieur, I still am,' d'Avrigny said solemnly. 'I have not had it out of my mind for an instant. And so that you can be quite convinced this time that I am not mistaken, listen carefully, Monsieur de Villefort.'

Villefort gave a convulsive shudder.

'There is a poison that kills almost without leaving any trace. I am well acquainted with this poison; I have studied all the effects that it produces and every symptom that results. I recognized this poison just now in poor Barrois, as I also recognized it in Madame de Saint-Méran. There is a way of detecting its presence: when litmus paper has been reddened by an acid, it will restore its blue colour; and it will give a green tint to syrup of violets. We do not have any litmus paper – but here they are with the syrup of violets that I asked for.'

There was a sound of footsteps in the corridor. The doctor

opened the door and took a cup from the chambermaid; in it were two or three spoonfuls of syrup.

As he closed the door, 'Look,' he said to the crown prosecutor, whose heart was beating so hard as to be almost audible. 'Here in this cup I have some syrup of violets and in this jug the remains of the lemonade, part of which was drunk by Barrois and Monsieur Noirtier. If the lemonade is pure and harmless, the syrup will not change colour. If the lemonade is poisoned, the syrup will turn green. Watch!'

The doctor slowly poured a few drops of lemonade from the jug into the cup, where a cloudy liquid instantly formed at the bottom. At first this cloud had a bluish tinge, then it turned to sapphire and opal, and finally from opal to emerald. When it reached this last colour, it settled, so to speak. The experiment was incontrovertible.

'Poor Barrois was poisoned with false angostura or Saint Ignatius' nut,'[1] d'Avrigny said. 'I will swear to it before God and man.'

For his part, Villefort said nothing, but raised his hands to heaven, opened wide his distraught eyes and fell senseless on to a chair.

LXXX

THE ACCUSATION

The magistrate seemed like a second corpse in this funerary chamber, but d'Avrigny soon brought him back to his senses.

'Death is in my house!' Villefort cried.

'You should rather say: crime,' said the doctor.

'Monsieur d'Avrigny!' Villefort exclaimed, 'I cannot tell you all that is going on in my mind at this moment: there is terror, pain, madness . . .'

'Yes,' M. d'Avrigny said, with impressive calm, 'but I think it is time to act; I think it is time we raised some barrier to stem this rising tide of mortality. For my part, I do not feel capable any longer of carrying the burden of such secrets, without any prospect of immediate vengeance for society and the victims.'

Villefort cast a grim look around him.

'In my house,' he muttered. 'In my house!'

'Come, judge,' said d'Avrigny. 'Be a man. As the interpreter of the law, your honour demands a total sacrifice.'

'I am horrified at what you say, doctor: sacrifice!'

'That's what I said.'

'Do you suspect someone?'

'I suspect nobody. Death knocks at your door, he enters and, intelligent as he is, does not go blindly from one room to the next. Well, I follow his footsteps, I recognize where he has passed by. I draw on the wisdom of the ancients, but I can only feel my way because my friendship for your family and my respect for you are like two blindfolds for me . . . Well . . .'

'Carry on, doctor, I shall have strength.'

'Well, Monsieur, there is in your house, perhaps even in your family, one of those monstrous creatures which appear only once in a hundred years. Locusta and Agrippina,[1] living in the same century, were the exception that proved the determination of Providence to destroy the Roman Empire, which was sullied by so many crimes. Brunhaut and Fredegonde were the product of a civilization painfully struggling to be born, at a time when mankind was learning to master the spirit, even were it to be by the emissary of darkness. Well, all these women had been or still were young and beautiful. On their brows had been seen, or still blossomed, that same flower of innocence that is to be found also on the guilty party who is in your house.'

Villefort gave a cry, clasped his hands and looked imploringly at the doctor; but the latter went on pitilessly: 'There is an axiom of jurisprudence that tells us to look for the one who profits from the crime . . .'

'But, doctor!' Villefort cried. 'Alas, doctor, how often has human justice not been deceived by those grim words! I do not know, but it seems to me that this crime . . .'

'So you admit that the crime exists?'

'Yes, I do. I must: what alternative is there? But let me continue. I was saying: it seems to me that this crime falls on me alone and not on the victims. I suspect that some disaster for me is intended behind all these strange disasters.'

'Oh, what is man!' d'Avrigny muttered. 'The most egoistical of all animals, the most personal of all creatures, who cannot believe otherwise than that the earth revolves, the sun shines and death reaps for him alone – an ant, cursing God from the summit of a blade of grass! And did those who lost their lives lose nothing, then? Monsieur de Saint-Méran, Madame de Saint-Méran, Monsieur Noirtier . . .'

'What! Monsieur Noirtier!'

'Why, yes. Do you imagine that this unfortunate servant was the intended victim? No, no: like Polonius in Shakespeare,[2] he died on behalf of another. It was Noirtier who was meant to drink the lemonade. It was Noirtier who did drink it, according to the logical expectation that he would; the other man drank only by chance. And, even though it was Barrois who died, it was Noirtier who should have done so.'

'But then how did my father manage not to succumb?'

'I already told you why, one evening, in the garden, after the death of Madame de Saint-Méran: because his body has become accustomed to the use of this very poison; because a dose that was trivial to him was fatal to anyone else; and finally because no one, not even the murderer, knows that for the past year I have been treating Monsieur Noirtier's paralysis with brucine – though the murderer does know, and has proved, that brucine is a very effective poison.'

'My God!' Villefort muttered, wringing his hands.

'Follow the criminal's path: he kills Monsieur de Saint-Méran.'

'Oh, doctor!'

'I would swear it. What I was told of the symptoms fits too well with the evidence of my own eyes.'

Villefort groaned, but ceased to argue.

'He – or she – kills Monsieur de Saint-Méran,' the doctor repeated. 'She kills Madame de Saint-Méran: a double legacy to collect.'

Villefort wiped the sweat that was pouring down his brow.

'Listen . . .'

'Alas,' Villefort stammered, 'I am not missing a word, not a single word.'

'Monsieur Noirtier's previous will,' M. d'Avrigny continued unsparingly, 'was against you, against your family and, in short, in favour of the poor. Monsieur Noirtier was spared: nothing was expected of him. But no sooner has he destroyed his first will, and no sooner has he made a second one, than he is struck, doubtless because of fear that he will make a third. The will dates from yesterday, I believe. You see, there is no time to be lost.'

'Oh, spare us!'

'Spare no one, Monsieur. The doctor has a sacred mission on earth; to fulfil it he must go back to the well spring of life and descend into the mysterious darkness of death. When a crime has been committed and God, horrified no doubt, turns his face away from the criminal, it is the doctor's duty to say: Here she is!'

'Spare my daughter, Monsieur!' Villefort muttered.

'You see: you it was who named her – you, her own father!'

'Spare Valentine! Listen, it cannot be so. I would rather accuse myself. Valentine, that flower of innocence, that heart of diamond!'

'Spare no one, Monsieur le procureur. The crime is blatant. Mademoiselle de Villefort herself wrapped up the medicine that was sent to Monsieur de Saint-Méran, and Monsieur de Saint-Méran died. Mademoiselle de Villefort prepared Madame de Saint-Méran's tisanes, and Madame de Saint-Méran died. When Barrois was sent outside, it was Mademoiselle de Villefort who took from him the jug of lemonade that the old man usually drank to the last drop of during a morning, and M. Noirtier only escaped by a miracle.

'Mademoiselle de Villefort is the guilty party! She is the poisoner! Monsieur le procureur du roi, I denounce Mademoiselle de Villefort to you: do your duty!'

'Doctor, I cannot offer any further resistance, I cannot deny anything, I believe you; but for pity's sake, spare my life and my honour!'

'Monsieur de Villefort,' the doctor said, with increasing energy, 'there are some circumstances in which I must break all the bounds of foolish human caution. If your daughter had only committed one first crime, and I were to see her contemplating a second, I should say to you: warn her, punish her, let her spend the rest of her life in some cloister, some convent, in prayer and lamentation. If she had committed a second crime, I should say to you: "Here, Monsieur de Villefort: here is a poison which has no known antidote, which is as quick as thought, as rapid as a bolt of lightning and as deadly as a thunderbolt; give her this poison, recommending her soul to God, and so save your honour and your life, because you are the one she hates." And I can see her creeping up to your bedside with her hypocritical smiles and her sweet exhortations! Woe betide you, Monsieur de Villefort, if you do not hasten to strike the first blow! That is what I should tell you if she had killed only two people. But she has contemplated three death agonies, she has considered three dying souls, she has knelt beside three bodies. To the scaffold with the poisoner! To the scaffold with her! You speak about your honour: do what I tell you, and immortality awaits!'

Villefort fell to his knees. 'Listen,' he said. 'I do not have your strength – or rather the strength that you would have if, instead of my daughter Valentine, we were speaking of your daughter Madeleine.'

The doctor went pale.

'Doctor, every man who is the son of woman is born to suffer and die. I shall suffer, doctor, and I shall wait for death.'

'Beware,' said M. d'Avrigny. 'It will be slow, this death. You will see it come after it has struck down your father, your wife, perhaps your son . . .'

Villefort clasped the doctor's arm, gasping for breath. 'Listen!' he said. 'Pity me! Help me! No, my daughter is not guilty. Drag us before a court and I shall say again: "No, my daughter is not guilty." There is no crime in my house. Do you hear me: I do not want there to be crime in my house, because when crime enters somewhere, it is like death, it does not come alone. Listen: what does it matter to you if I die poisoned? Are you my friend? Are you a man? Have you a heart? No, you are a doctor! Well, I say to you: "My daughter will not be dragged out by me to be delivered into the hands of the executioner!" The very idea eats into my brain and urges me to tear my heart out with my fingernails! And suppose you were wrong, doctor! Suppose it was someone other than my daughter? Suppose, one day, I were to come to you, white as a ghost, and say: "Murderer! You killed my daughter . . . !" If that were to happen, even though I am a Christian, Monsieur d'Avrigny, I should kill myself.'

'Very well,' the doctor said after a moment's silence. 'I shall wait.'

Villefort looked at him as though still doubting his words.

'There is just one thing,' M. d'Avrigny went on, in a slow and solemn voice. 'If anyone in your house should fall ill, if you yourself should be smitten, do not call me, because I shall not come. I agree to share this dreadful secret with you, but I do not want shame and remorse to come into me, growing and multiplying in my conscience, as crime and misfortune will grow and multiply in your house.'

'Are you abandoning me, then, doctor?'

'Yes, because I cannot go further with you down this road, which leads only to the foot of the scaffold. Some other revelation will bring this dreadful tragedy to an end. Farewell!'

'Doctor, I beg you!'

'All the horrors that besmirch my thoughts make your house odious and fatal to me. Adieu, Monsieur.'

'Just one final word, doctor! You are leaving me to the full horror of this situation, a horror that has been increased by what you revealed to me. But how are we to explain the sudden death that struck down that poor servant?'

'That's true,' said M. d'Avrigny. 'Show me out.'

The doctor left first, with Villefort following. The servants were anxiously lining the corridors and stairways along which the doctor had to pass.

'Monsieur,' he said to Villefort, in a loud voice so that everyone could hear, 'poor Barrois had been too sedentary for some years. At one time, he used to love riding with his master or travelling by coach to the four corners of Europe, and this monotonous attendance beside a chair killed him. His blood thickened, he was stout, with a short, fat neck: he died of an apoplectic fit and I was sent for too late.

'By the way,' he added, in a whisper, 'make sure you throw that cup of violets into the fire.' With that, not shaking Villefort's hand or revising any of his conclusions, the doctor left amid the tears and lamentations of all the family servants.

That very evening, all the Villeforts' domestic staff met in the kitchen and talked for a long time among themselves, then came to ask Mme de Villefort for permission to leave. No entreaty and no promise of an increase in wages could change their minds; to every offer, they replied: 'We wish to go because there is death in this house.'

So leave they did, in spite of pleading, and expressed deep regret at leaving such good employers, above all Mlle Valentine, who was so kind, so generous and so sweet. At these words, Villefort looked at Valentine. She was weeping.

How odd it was! For all the confused feelings that he experienced on seeing those tears, he also managed to observe Mme de Villefort; and it seemed to him that a faint, dark smile passed briefly across her thin lips, like one of those sinister meteors that can be glimpsed as they fall between two clouds against a stormy sky.

LXXXI

THE RETIRED BAKER'S ROOM

On the evening of the day when the Comte de Morcerf came away from Danglars' with the shame and fury that one can imagine, given the banker's cold reception, M. Andrea Cavalcanti, with his hair curled and shining, his moustaches waxed, and closely fitting white gloves, drove into the banker's courtyard at the Chaussée-d'Antin, almost standing upright on his phaeton.

After ten minutes' conversation in the drawing-room, he managed to take Danglars aside into a bay window and there, after a cleverly worked preamble, spoke about the torments of his existence since the departure of his noble father. Since this departure, he said, the banker had been kind enough to welcome him into his family like a son and there he had found all those guarantees of happiness that a man ought to look for in preference to the vagaries of passion; though, as far as passion was concerned, he had been fortunate enough to encounter it in the eyes of Mlle Danglars.

Danglars listened very closely to this declaration, which he had been expecting for two or three days. Now that it had come, his eyes shone, just as they had darkened and narrowed while he listened to Morcerf. Even so, he did not want to accept the young man's proposal without making some conscientious observations.

'Monsieur Andrea,' he said, 'aren't you a little young to be thinking of marriage?'

'Not at all, Monsieur,' Cavalcanti replied. 'Or at least, not in my view. In Italy, noblemen generally marry young; it is a reasonable custom: life is so uncertain that one should grasp happiness as soon as it comes within reach.'

'Very well, Monsieur,' said Danglars. 'Let us suppose that your proposal, which honours me, is acceptable to my wife and daughter; then with whom shall we discuss terms? It seems to me that this is an important matter which only fathers can properly negotiate in the interests of their children's happiness.'

'Monsieur, my father is a wise man, possessing much reason and a good sense of propriety. He anticipated that I might well feel some desire to settle in France, so, as he was going, he left me – as well as all the papers which confirm my identity – a letter in which he guarantees me an income of one hundred and fifty thousand *livres*, from the day of my marriage onwards, provided I make a choice acceptable to him. As far as I can tell, this is one-quarter of my father's own income.'

'It was always my intention,' Danglars said, 'to give my daughter five hundred thousand francs when I married her. In any event, she is my only heir.'

'Very well,' Andrea said, 'as you see, it would be for the best, always assuming that my proposal is not rejected by Madame the Baroness and Mademoiselle Eugénie. This would give us an income of one hundred and seventy-five thousand *livres*. Now let us further suppose that I were to persuade the marquis that, instead of paying me the income, he were to give me the capital – it will not be easy, I know, but it could be done – then you would invest these two or three millions for us; and two or three millions in skilled hands can bring in a good ten per cent.'

'I never take money at more than four,' said the banker, 'or even three and a half; but for my son-in-law, I would agree to five, and we could share the profits fifty-fifty.'

'That's perfect, father-in-law,' said Cavalcanti, letting himself be carried away by the slightly vulgar instincts which, despite his efforts, occasionally cracked the aristocratic varnish beneath which he attempted to conceal them. But he at once remembered himself and said: 'Oh, please forgive me, Monsieur! You see, hope itself is enough to drive me almost mad; what will be the effect of the reality?'

'But surely, there is a part of your fortune that your father cannot refuse you?' said Danglars, not noticing how quickly this conversation, which had started so disinterestedly, had turned to the management of business matters.

'What is that?' the young man asked.

'Why, the part that comes from your mother.'

'Ah, yes, indeed; that which comes from my mother, Leonora Corsinari.'

'And what might be the amount of this portion?'

'My goodness, Monsieur,' said Andrea, 'I must confess that I've never thought much about it, but I would judge it to be at least two million.'

Danglars felt that suffocating sense of joy that is experienced either by a miser unearthing a lost treasure or by a drowning man whose feet touch solid ground instead of the emptiness that was about to engulf him.

Andrea bowed to the banker with warm respect: 'Then, Monsieur, may I hope . . .'

'Monsieur Andrea,' Danglars said, 'hope on and believe that, provided no obstacle from your side halts the progress of the matter, it is signed and sealed.' Then he continued thoughtfully: 'Why is it that the Count of Monte Cristo, your patron in our Parisian society, did not accompany you to make this request?'

Andrea blushed imperceptibly. 'I have just come from the count's, Monsieur,' he said, 'and he is undoubtedly a charming man, but also unbelievably eccentric. He approved of my plan; he even said that he did not think that my father would hesitate for a moment to give me the capital instead of the income; and he promised me to use his influence to that end; but he told me that personally he had never taken on himself – and never would take on – the responsibility of being the bearer of a proposal of marriage. I must grant him this, however: he was kind enough to add that, if he had ever deplored his prejudice in the matter, it was in my case, since he thought that we would be happy and well matched in our union. Moreover, while he does not want to do anything in an official capacity, he told me that he fully expected to answer any of your questions, when you wished to discuss them with him.'

'Ah, that's very good.'

'And now,' Andrea said, with his most charming smile, 'I should like to turn from the father-in-law to the banker.'

'And what do you want with him, then?' said Danglars, laughing.

'The day after tomorrow I am to draw something like four thousand francs on your bank, but the count realized that the coming month might bring an excess of expenditure which would not be covered by my small bachelor's income, so here is a bill for twenty thousand francs which he gave me, more as a present than as a contribution to expenses. It is signed by him, as you see. Will that do?'

'Bring me one like this for a million and I'll cash it for you,' said Danglars, putting the bill into his pocket. 'Give me a time tomorrow, and my cashier will come to you with a bond for twenty-four thousand francs.'

'At ten in the morning then, if you don't mind. The earlier, the better; I should like to go to the country tomorrow.'

'Very well, ten o'clock; still at the Hôtel des Princes?'

'Yes.'

The next day, with a punctuality that was a tribute to the banker's conscientiousness, the twenty-four thousand francs were in the young man's hands and he went out, as he had said, leaving two hundred francs for Caderousse.

As far as Andrea was concerned, the main aim of this excursion was to avoid meeting his dangerous friend, so he came home as late as possible. But no sooner had he set foot on the flagstones of the courtyard than he found the concierge of the building waiting for him, cap in hand.

'Monsieur,' he said, 'that man called.'

'What man?' Andrea asked – casually, as if he had forgotten someone whom in fact he remembered only too well.

'The man to whom Your Excellency gave that little subscription.'

'Ah, yes,' Andrea said. 'That former servant of my father's. Well, did you give him the two hundred francs I left for him?'

'Yes, Excellency.' (Andrea demanded to be addressed as 'Excellency'.) 'Just as you said,' the concierge went on, 'but he refused to take them.'

Andrea paled but, since it was dark, no one saw the colour drain from his face.

'What! He wouldn't take them?' he said, a slight quaver in his voice.

'No, he wanted to speak to Your Excellency. I told him that you had gone out, but he insisted. Eventually, he did seem to let himself be persuaded and he gave me this letter, which he had brought, already sealed.'

'Let me see,' said Andrea; and by the lamp on his phaeton, he read: 'You know where I live. I shall expect you tomorrow morning at nine o'clock.'

Andrea looked at the seal to see if it had been tampered with, and if any prying eyes could have seen inside the letter; but it was folded in such a way, with so many wafers and overlaps, that it could not have been read without breaking the seal, and this was quite intact.

'That's very good,' he said. 'Poor man! He's such a fine creature.' And he left the concierge to digest these edifying words, not knowing whom he admired the most: the young master or the old retainer.

'Quickly attend to the horses, then come up and see me,' Andrea said to his groom. Then, in two bounds, he was inside his room, where he burned Caderousse's letter, even disposing of the ashes. He was just completing this task when the servant came in.

'Pierre, you are about my size, aren't you?' he said.

'I do have that honour, Excellency,' the man answered.

'You must have fresh livery which was given to you yesterday?'

'Yes, Monsieur.'

'I'm involved with a pretty little creature, but I don't want her to know my title or my position. Lend me your livery and your papers so that, if necessary, I can sleep at an inn.'

Pierre did as he was asked. Five minutes later, Andrea, completely disguised, left the house without being recognized, took a cab and had himself driven to the inn of the Cheval-Rouge in Picpus. The next day he left the inn as he had left the Hôtel des Princes (that is, unnoticed), followed the boulevard to the Rue Ménilmontant and, stopping at the door of the third house on the left, looked around to see where he could get information, there being no concierge.

'What are you looking for, luv?' asked the woman from the fruiterer's opposite.

'Monsieur Pailletin, if you please, grandma?' Andrea answered.

'Is it a retired baker?' she asked.

'That's right, the very one.'

'Bottom of the yard, door on the left, third floor.'

Andrea followed her directions and on the third floor found a bell-pull that he tugged with a feeling of ill-temper which communicated itself to the bell. A moment later, Caderousse's face appeared at a grilled spyhole cut in the door.

'You're punctual,' he said, drawing back the bolts.

'Damnation!' said Andrea, going in and throwing his livery cap ahead of him. It missed the chair, fell to the floor and rolled round the room on its edge.

'Come, come, now,' said Caderousse. 'Don't get angry, dear boy! There now, I've thought of you: just look what a good breakfast we'll have; all things that you like!'

Breathing in, Andrea could indeed detect the smell of cooking, its gross odours not without charm for a hungry stomach: there was that mixture of fresh oil and garlic which indicates the inferior breed of provençal cuisine, with additionally a hint of breaded fish and, above all, the acrid scent of nutmeg and cloves. All this was exhaled from two covered tureens keeping hot on two stoves and a dish bubbling in the oven of an iron cooker.

In the adjoining room Andrea also observed a moderately clean table with two places laid; two bottles of wine, one with a green and the other with a yellow seal; a good measure of spirits in a decanter; and a fruit salad in a large cabbage leaf, artistically displayed on a porcelain dish.

'What do you think, dear boy?' said Caderousse. 'Smells good, doesn't it? Ah, by God, I was a good cook in those days! Do you remember how people would lick their fingers – and you most of all. You've tried a few of my sauces and not spat them out, I warrant!' And he began to peel some more onions.

'Yes, yes, we know all that,' Andrea said irritably. 'Huh! If you've brought me all this way just to have lunch, then to hell with you!'

'My son,' Caderousse said pompously, 'as one eats, one may speak; and anyway, you ungrateful boy, aren't you a little pleased to see your old friend? Look: I'm overjoyed.'

Caderousse was actually weeping, though it was hard to tell whether it was joy or onions that had affected the lachrymal glands of the former innkeeper from the Pont du Gard.

'Get away with you, you hypocrite,' said Andrea. 'Are you that fond of me?'

'Yes, indeed I am, or may the devil take me,' said Caderousse. 'I know it's a weakness on my part, but I can't help it.'

'And in spite of it you brought me here for some treachery.'

'Now, now!' Caderousse said, wiping his broad knife on his apron. 'If I wasn't fond of you, would I put up with the miserable life you make me lead? Just look around: you are wearing your servant's coat, and that means you have a servant; I have none, so I'm forced to peel my own vegetables. You scoff at my cooking because you dine at the table d'hôte at the Hôtel des Princes or the Café de Paris. Well, now, I too could have a servant, I could have a tilbury and I could dine wherever I wished. And why don't I? So as not to cause any distress to my poor Benedetto, that's why. Come on, you must admit that I could, huh?' And Caderousse gave a perfectly clear look to underline his meaning.

'Very well, then,' said Andrea. 'Let's accept that you are fond of me; then why have you asked me to lunch?'

'To see you, of course, dear boy.'

'Why do you want to see me? We've already agreed our terms.'

'Ah now, dear friend,' said Caderousse. 'Was there ever a will without a codicil? But you came to have lunch, first of all, didn't you? So sit down and let's start with these sardines and fresh butter, which I put out on vine-leaves especially for you, ungrateful child. I see you're looking round my room: my four straw-seated chairs, my pictures at three francs apiece . . . It's not exactly the Hôtel des Princes here, is it?'

'So, you're discontented now, are you? You're not happy any more, yet at one time you asked nothing better than to live like a retired baker.'

Caderousse sighed, so Andrea continued: 'Well, what have you to say? Your dream has come true.'

'I'll say it's a dream. A retired baker is rich, my dear Benedetto, he has an income.'

'So do you, by God.'

'I do?'

'Yes, since I'm bringing two hundred francs with me, right now.'

Caderousse shrugged. 'It's humiliating,' he said, 'to get money in this way, money that is given reluctantly, ephemeral money, that may cease between one day and the next. You must see how I am forced to economize, to insure against your prosperity failing one day. Well, my friend, fortune is a fickle jade, as the regimental . . . chaplain said. I know that you're prospering, you rascal. You are going to marry Danglars' daughter.'

'What! Danglars' . . . ?'

'Yes, of course, Danglars'. Do I have to call him Baron Danglars? It would be like saying Count Benedetto. He's an old friend, Danglars, and if his memory were not so short he'd be inviting me to your wedding . . . since he came to mine. Yes, yes, yes, to mine! My God, he wasn't so proud in those days. He was a clerk at good Monsieur Morrel's. I've dined more than once with him and the Comte de Morcerf. There! You see what fine friends I have, and if I were to cultivate them a little we should be meeting in the same drawing-rooms.'

'Come on now, your jealousy is putting rainbows in your head, Caderousse.'

'Very well, Benedetto mio, but I know what I'm saying. Perhaps one day we'll put on our Sunday best and go to address some door: "Bell-pull please!" But until then, sit down and eat.'

Caderousse set a good example, lunching hungrily and putting in a good word for each dish as he offered it to his guest. The latter seemed to resign himself to making the best of it, bravely uncorking bottles and tucking into the bouillabaisse and the cod in bread-crumbs with garlic and oil.

'There now, mate,' said Caderousse. 'You seem to be reconciled with your old landlord?'

'Yes, I suppose so,' Andrea replied, his youthful and vigorous appetite taking precedence at that moment over everything.

'Are you enjoying it, you rogue?'

'So much so that I can't understand how a man who can fry and eat such good things can possibly be disillusioned with life.'

'Well, now,' said Caderousse, 'the trouble is that all my happiness is ruined by a single thought.'

'What can that be?'

'That I am living at the expense of a friend, when I have always sturdily struggled to earn my own bread.'

'Oh, don't fret over that,' said Andrea. 'I've got plenty for two, don't you worry.'

'No, no, it's the truth: believe me or not, but at the end of every month, I feel guilty.'

'My dear Caderousse!'

'So much so that yesterday I didn't want to take the two hundred francs.'

'Yes, you wanted to talk about it; but did you really feel guilty, then?'

'Really! And then I had an idea.'

Andrea shuddered. He always shuddered at Caderousse's ideas.

'It's a miserable business,' Caderousse went on, 'always having to wait until the end of the month.'

Andrea shrugged philosophically, deciding to see where this was leading. 'Isn't life spent waiting?' he asked. 'Look at me: what do I do but wait? Well, I'm patient, aren't I?'

'Yes, because instead of waiting for two hundred miserable francs, you are waiting for five or six thousand, perhaps ten, or even twelve. You're a sly one, you are. Even in the old days you always had your little purses or money-boxes that you tried to hide from your poor friend Caderousse. Luckily, the said Caderousse had a way of sniffing them out.'

'There you go again, wandering off the subject and turning the past over and over. I ask you, what's the use of harping on like that?'

'Oh, you say that because you're twenty-one; you can forget the past. I'm fifty and obliged to remember it. But no matter, let's get back to business.'

'Yes, let's.'

'I was saying that in your place . . .'

'What?'

'I should cash in . . .'

'What! You'd cash in . . .'

'Yes, I'd ask for a six-month advance, on the grounds that I wanted to go into politics and I was going to buy a farm; then, once I had the money, I'd be off.'

'Well, well, well,' said Andrea. 'That's perhaps not such a bad idea after all.'

'My dear friend,' said Caderousse, 'eat my cooking and digest my words; you won't be any the worse for it, physically or otherwise.'

'Well, in that case,' said Andrea, 'why don't you take your own advice? Why not cash in a half-year, or even a whole one, and retire to Brussels? Instead of looking like a retired baker, you would seem like a fully active bankrupt: that's a step up.'

'And how the devil do you expect me to retire on twelve hundred francs?'

'Now, then, Caderousse,' said Andrea. 'You're getting fussy! Two months ago you were starving to death.'

'The more you eat,' said Caderousse, baring his teeth like a laughing monkey or a growling tiger, 'the more you want. Moreover, I've got a plan,' he added, biting off a huge mouthful of bread with those same teeth, which were sharp and white, despite the man's age.

Caderousse's plans terrified Andrea even more than his ideas: the ideas were only the seed, the plan was the full fruit.

'Tell us this plan,' he said. 'It must be a good one!'

'Why not? Who had the plan that got us out of Monsieur Thingummy's place? I did, it goes without saying. And it wasn't a bad plan, after all, since we're both here.'

'I'm not denying it,' said Andrea. 'You do sometimes have a good one. So, let's hear it.'

'In that case,' Caderousse continued, 'can you, without paying a *sou*, get me fifteen thousand francs . . . ? No, fifteen thousand is not enough, I don't want to become an honest man for less than thirty thousand.'

'No,' Andrea replied drily, 'I can't.'

'I don't think you can have understood me,' Caderousse replied, coldly and calmly. 'I said: without paying a *sou*.'

'I suppose you're not asking me to steal, so that I can ruin everything for myself, and you with me, and have both of us taken back where we came from?'

'Oh, as far as I'm concerned,' said Caderousse, 'I don't mind either way if I'm caught. I'm an odd fish, you know: I sometimes miss the company . . . I'm not heartless like you, happy if you never see your old friends again!'

This time Andrea did more than shudder: he went pale. 'Come now, Caderousse,' he said, 'don't do anything foolish.'

'Don't worry, I won't, my little Benedetto. Just show me the means to make thirty thousand francs. You don't have to be involved. Just let me get on with it.'

'All right, I'll see, I'll look for something,' said Andrea.

'Meanwhile, you can increase my allowance to five hundred francs a month. I've got this idea in my head that I'd like a maid.'

'Very well, you shall have your five hundred,' said Andrea. 'But it's not going to be easy for me, Caderousse. You're starting to take advantage . . .'

'Huh!' said Caderousse. 'You get it from a bottomless chest.'

Andrea seemed to be expecting this, because his eye shone with a brief flame, though one that was immediately extinguished. 'That's true,' he replied. 'My protector is very good to me.'

'Your dear protector!' said Caderousse. 'How much does he give you every month?'

'Five thousand francs.'

'A thousand for every hundred you will be giving me,' Caderousse said. 'As they say, only bastards know real good fortune. Five thousand francs a month . . . What the devil can you do with it all?'

'Believe me, it soon goes! So, like you, I would prefer a lump sum.'

'A lump sum . . . Yes, I understand. Everyone would like a lump sum.'

'And I am going to get one.'

'Who will give it to you, then? Your prince?'

'Yes, my prince; but unfortunately I have to wait.'

'What for?' asked Caderousse.

'His death.'

'Your prince's death?'

'Yes.'

'Why?'

'Because he has provided for me in his will.'

'Is that so?'

'On my word.'

'How much?'

'Five hundred thousand.'

'Is that all? Thanks a lot.'

'I'm telling the truth.'

'Come on, it's impossible.'

'Caderousse, are you my friend?'

'Of course: in life, to the death!'

'I'm going to tell you a secret.'

'Go on.'

'Listen, then.'

'Right, then! Not a word.'

'Well, I think . . .' Andrea stopped and looked around.

'You think . . . ? Don't worry, we're alone.'

'I think I have found my father.'

'Your real father?'

'Yes.'

'Not Father Cavalcanti?'

'No. Anyway, he's gone. No, the real one . . .'

'Who is it?'

'Caderousse, it's the Count of Monte Cristo.'

'Huh!'

'Yes. Don't you see, it explains everything. Apparently he cannot admit to me openly, but he has had me recognized by Monsieur Cavalcanti and given him fifty thousand francs for doing so.'

'Fifty thousand francs, to be your father! I would have done it for half as much; or even for twenty, no, fifteen! Why didn't you think of me, ungrateful wretch!'

'How did I know, since it all happened while we were inside?'

'So it did. And you say that in his will . . . ?'

'He leaves me five hundred thousand *livres*.'

'Are you sure?'

'He showed it to me; but that's not all.'

'There is a codicil, as I just said.'

'Probably.'

'And in it . . . ?'

'He acknowledges me.'

'Oh, what a good father! A fine father! A most excellent father!' Caderousse said, twirling a plate in the air between his hands.

'Now tell me that I keep any secrets from you!'

'No, and in my view your trusting nature does you credit. And this prince of fathers, is he rich . . . ultra-rich?'

'I think so. He doesn't know his own wealth.'

'I can't believe it!'

'Dammit, I can see as much, since I'm admitted to his house at all hours. The other day, a boy came from the bank with fifty thousand francs in a portfolio as big as your briefcase. Yesterday, a banker brought him one hundred thousand francs in gold.'

Caderousse was stunned. It seemed to him that the young man's words rang like metal and he could hear showers of gold coins. 'And you go into that house?' he exclaimed naïvely.

'Whenever I want.'

Caderousse reflected for a moment. It was easy to see that his mind was turning over some deep thought. Then suddenly he exclaimed: 'Wouldn't I love to see all that! It must be lovely!'

'In fact, it's magnificent,' Andrea said.

'Doesn't he live in the Avenue des Champs-Elysées?'

'At number thirty.'

'Ah, number thirty?' said Caderousse.

'Yes. A fine house, standing alone in its own grounds, which is all you can see.'

'Perhaps, but it's not the outside that interests me; it's indoors. There must be some fine furniture, huh?'

'Have you ever seen the Tuileries?'

'No.'

'Well, this is better.'

'Tell me, Andrea, when this good Monte Cristo drops his purse, it must be worth stooping to pick it up?'

'Oh, heavens! No need to wait for that,' said Andrea. 'Money lies around in that house like fruit in an orchard.'

'Now, you really should take me there one day.'

'How can I? As whom?'

'You're right, but you've made my mouth water. I really must see it. I'll find a way.'

'Don't do anything silly, Caderousse.'

'I'll introduce myself as a polisher.'

'They have carpets everywhere.'

'That's a pity. I'll just have to imagine it.'

'Believe me, that's the best way.'

'At least help me to guess what it must be like.'

'How can I do that?'

'Nothing simpler. Is it big?'

'Neither too large, nor too small.'

'What is the general layout?'

'Hell! I'd need ink and paper to draw a plan for you.'

'Here you are!' Caderousse said at once, going over to his writing-desk to fetch some white paper, ink and a quill. 'There, now, put it all down on paper, my lad.'

Andrea took the pen with a faint smile and began. 'As I told you, the house is in its own grounds; do you see? Like this.' He drew the outline of the garden, the courtyard and the house.

'High walls?'

'No, eight or ten feet at most.'

'That's risky,' said Caderousse.

'In the courtyard, tubs for orange-trees, lawns and flowerbeds.'

'Any mantraps?'

'No.'

'And the stables?'

'On either side of the fence, you see: there.' Andrea went on with his plan.

'Let's see the ground floor,' said Caderousse.

'On the ground floor there's a dining-room, two drawing-rooms, a billiard-room, a stairway from the hall and a little hidden staircase.'

'Windows?'

'Splendid windows, so beautiful and so wide that I honestly do believe a man of your size could climb through a single pane.'

'Why on earth do they have stairways, with such windows?'

'What do you think! Extravagance!'

'But there are shutters?'

'Yes, there are, but they are never used. He's eccentric, this Count of Monte Cristo, and likes to see the sky, even at night.'

'So where do the servants sleep, then?'

'Oh, they have their own house. Picture a fine storeroom on the right as you go in, where they keep the ladders. Well, on top of that there is a collection of rooms for the servants, with bells corresponding to the rooms.'

'Hell's bells!'

'What was that?'

'Nothing. I was just saying that they're expensive to install, bells. And what use are they, I ask you?'

'At one time there was a dog which used to walk around the courtyard at night, but they've taken him to the house in Auteuil – you know, the one you visited?'

'Yes.'

'And I was saying only yesterday: "It's unwise of you, Monsieur le Comte, because when you go to Auteuil, and take your servants, the house remains empty."

' "What about it?" he asked.

' "What about it? Well, one day someone will burgle you." '

'What did he say to that?'

'What did he say?'

'Yes.'

'What he said was: "What if I am burgled?" '

'Andrea, he must have some mechanical bureau.'

'What do you mean?'

'Yes, something that traps the thief in a cage and plays a tune. I'm told there was something of the sort at the last Exhibition.'

'He just has a walnut bureau and I've always seen the key in it.'

'And no one steals from it?'

'No, his servants are all devoted to him.'

'There must be something inside that bureau, mustn't there? Coin?'

'Perhaps; there's no way of telling.'

'And where is it?'

'On the first floor.'

'So, make me a plan of the first floor, dear boy, as you did of the ground floor.'

'That's easy.' Andrea took the pen. 'On the first floor, as you see, there's an anteroom, a drawing-room, then on the right of that, a library and study, while on the left we have a bedroom and dressing-room. The famous bureau is in the dressing-room.'

'Is there a window in this dressing-room?'

'Two: one here, and one here.' Andrea drew two windows in the room which, on the plan, stood in a corner of the house, like a shorter rectangle joined to the long rectangle of the bedroom.

Caderousse was deep in thought. 'So, does he often go to Auteuil?' he asked.

'Two or three times a week. Tomorrow, for example, he is due to spend the day and the following night there.'

'Are you sure?'

'He invited me to dinner.'

'Wonderful! That's the way to live!' said Caderousse. 'A house in town, a house in the country.'

'That's what it means to be rich.'

'And will you go to dinner.'

'Probably.'

'When you dine there, do you stay the night?'

'If I want to. I'm quite at home in the count's house.'

Caderousse looked at the young man as if to tear the truth from the depths of his heart; but Andrea took a cigar case out of his pocket, extracted a Havana, calmly lit it and began to smoke with an entirely natural air.

'When would you like the five hundred francs?' he asked.

'Straight away, if you have them.'

Andrea took twenty-five *louis* out of his pocket.

'Gold coins?' said Caderousse. 'No, thanks!'

'Why not? Do you despise them?'

'On the contrary, I have a high regard for them, but I don't want any.'

'You'll gain on the exchange, idiot. Gold is worth five *sous*.'

'That's right, and then the dealer will have your friend Caderousse followed, a hand will fall on his shoulder and he'll have to explain who these farmers are, paying him his fees in gold coin. Let's not be silly, dear boy. Just give me my money: round coins with the head of some monarch or other. Anyone can come by a five-franc coin.'

'You must realize, I don't have five hundred on me. I would have needed to bring a broker with me to carry it.'

'In that case, leave it with your concierge; he's a good man, I'll come and pick it up.'

'Today?'

'Tomorrow. I won't have time today.'

'As you say, then. Tomorrow, as I'm setting out for Auteuil, I'll leave them for you.'

'Can I count on it?'

'Absolutely.'

'Because I'm going to hire my maid in advance.'

'Do it. But that will be the end, won't it? You won't torment me any longer?'

'Never again.'

Caderousse had become so moody that Andrea was afraid he might be obliged to notice the change, so he pretended to be even merrier and more insouciant.

'You're full of beans,' Caderousse said. 'Anyone would think you'd already come into your inheritance.'

'No, alas. But the day when I do . . .'

'What?'

'I'll remember my friends. I'll say no more.'

'Yes, and you have such a good memory, too.'

'What do you expect? I thought you wanted to turn me in for the reward.'

'Me? What an idea! On the contrary, as a friend, I'm going to give you another piece of advice.'

'Which is?'

'To leave the diamond you've got on your finger here. I never! Do you want us to be caught? Do you want to do for the pair of us with such idiocies?'

'How do you mean?' Andrea asked.

'What! You put on livery, to disguise yourself as a servant, yet you keep a diamond worth four or five thousand francs on your finger!'

'Well I'll be damned! That's a good estimate. You should be an auctioneer.'

'I know about diamonds. I used to have some.'

'I advise you not to boast about it,' said Andrea; and, without losing his temper, as Caderousse had feared he might at this new piece of extortion, quietly handed over the ring. Caderousse examined it so closely that Andrea realized he was looking to see if the edges of the cut sparkled.

'It's a fake,' said Caderousse.

'Come, come,' said Andrea, 'you must be joking.'

'Oh, don't worry about it; we'll soon see.' He went across to the window and ran the diamond across the pane. The glass screeched.

'*Confiteor!*'[1] Caderousse said, slipping the ring on his little finger. 'I was wrong, but those thieving jewellers are so clever at imitating stones that one no longer dares to go and steal from one of their shops. That's another branch of the industry paralysed.'

'Well, is that it?' Andrea said. 'Do you have anything else to ask me? Don't hesitate, while I'm here.'

'No, you're a good fellow underneath. I won't keep you any longer and I'll try to cure myself of my ambition.'

'But be careful that the same doesn't happen when you sell the diamond as you feared might happen with the gold.'

'I shan't sell it, don't worry.'

'No, not between now and the day after tomorrow, at least,' the young man thought.

'You lucky devil!' said Caderousse. 'You're going back to your lackeys, your horses, your carriage and your fiancée.'

'So I am,' said Andrea.

'Here, I hope you'll make me a good wedding present the day you marry the daughter of my friend Danglars.'

'I told you: that's some nonsense you've dreamed up.'

'What kind of dowry?'

'I told you already . . .'

'A million?'

Andrea shrugged his shoulders.

'Let's say a million,' said Caderousse. 'You'll never have as much as I'd wish for you.'

'Thank you,' said the young man.

'Don't mention it,' Caderousse said, giving a raucous laugh. 'Wait, I'll show you the way out.'

'Don't bother.'

'I must.'

'Why?'

'Because there's a little secret on the door, a precautionary measure that I thought I should take: a lock by Huret et Fichet, specially adapted by Gaspard Caderousse. When you're a capitalist, I'll make you one.'

'Thank you,' said Andrea. 'I'll give you a week's notice.'

They took their leave of one another. Caderousse remained on the landing until he had seen Andrea go down the three flights, and also cross the courtyard. Only then did he hurry back inside, carefully shutting the door and, like a practised architect, started to study the plan that Andrea had left him.

'Dear Benedetto,' he said. 'I don't think he'll be sorry to inherit; and the person who brings the day closer when he is to get his hands on five hundred thousand francs will not be his worst enemy, either.'

LXXXII

BREAKING AND ENTERING

The day after the conversation that we have just recorded, the Count of Monte Cristo did indeed leave for Auteuil, with Ali, several servants and some horses which he wanted to try out. The main reason for his departure – which he had not even considered on the previous day and about which Andrea knew no more than he did – was the arrival of Bertuccio, who had come back from Normandy with news about the house and the boat. The house was ready – and the corvette, delivered a week before and anchored in a small bay where it remained with its six-man crew, after completing all the necessary formalities, was already fully prepared to set sail.

The count praised Bertuccio's fine efforts and told him to stand by to depart soon, since he did not intend to stay longer than a month in France.

'Now,' he said, 'I may need to go in a single night from Paris to Tréport. I want eight relays at intervals along the route which will allow me to cover fifty leagues in ten hours.'

'Your Excellency already expressed that desire,' Bertuccio replied, 'and the horses are ready. I bought them and stationed them at the most convenient points, that is to say in villages where normally no one stops.'

'That's very good,' said Monte Cristo. 'I shall be staying here a day or two, so do whatever you need to.'

As Bertuccio was going out to order everything necessary for this stay, Baptistin opened the door. He was carrying a letter on a gilt bronze tray.

'What are you doing here?' the count asked, seeing him covered in dust. 'I don't think I called for you, did I?'

Without replying, Baptistin went over to the count and gave him the letter. 'Urgent and in haste,' he said.

The count opened it and read:

Monsieur de Monte Cristo is warned that tonight a man will break into his house in the Champs-Elysées, in order to purloin some papers that he believes to be hidden in the bureau in the dressing-room. The Count of Monte Cristo is known to be brave enough not to turn for help to the police, whose involvement might seriously compromise the person who is giving this warning. Monsieur le Comte can administer his own justice, either by entering the dressing-room through an opening from the bedroom, or by lying in wait in the dressing-room. A lot of people and obvious precautions would surely scare away the burglar and deprive the count of this opportunity to discover an enemy who became known by chance to the writer of this warning – a warning which he may not have the opportunity to repeat if this first attempt should fail and the wrongdoer attempt another.

The count's first impulse was to think that this must be a thieves' trick, a crude trap warning him of a slight danger in order to expose him to a more serious one; so he was going to have the letter taken to a police commissioner – despite (or, perhaps, because of) the instruction from his anonymous friend – when he suddenly thought that there might, in fact, be some enemy peculiar to him, whom he alone could recognize and, in that event, take advantage of him as Fiesco[1] did of the Moor who tried to assassinate him. The reader knows the count, so there is no need to mention that he was athletic and daring, and that his mind rebelled against the impossible with that energy peculiar to superior beings. Because of the kind of life he had led, and because of the resolve he had made – and kept – not to shrink from anything, the count had managed to enjoy unknown pleasures in the struggle against nature, which is God, and against the world – which is, near enough, the Devil.

'They don't want to steal my papers,' Monte Cristo said. 'They want to kill me: these are not thieves, but murderers. I do not want the prefect of police to meddle with my private affairs. Why, I am rich enough to cover the entire budget of his force.'

The count recalled Baptistin, who had left the room after bringing the letter. 'Go back to Paris,' he told him, 'and bring all the remaining servants here. I need everyone in Auteuil.'

'But will no one be left in the house, Monsieur le Comte?' Baptistin asked.

'Yes, there will: the concierge.'

'Monsieur le Comte will reflect that it is a long way from the porter's lodge to the house.'

'Well?'

'Well, the whole house could be burgled and no one hear a sound.'

'Who would do that?'

'Why, thieves!'

'You are an idiot, Monsieur Baptistin. If thieves were to ransack the whole house, they would not cause me as much displeasure as a service poorly carried out.'

Baptistin bowed.

'You heard me,' said the count. 'Take your fellow-servants, from the first to the last, and leave everything in its usual state. Close the ground-floor windows, that's all.'

'And those on the first floor?'

'You know that they are never closed. Now go.'

The count gave instructions that he would dine alone and wished to be served only by Ali.

He dined with his usual calm and sobriety and, after dinner, motioning to Ali to follow him, he left by the side-door, went to the Bois de Boulogne as though going for a walk, unobtrusively took the road for Paris and by nightfall was standing in front of his house in the Champs-Elysées.

Everything was dark except for a faint light burning in the porter's lodge which, as Baptistin had said, was some forty yards from the house.

Monte Cristo leant against a tree and, with an eye that was rarely deceived, tested the double pathway, examined the passers-by and looked up and down the neighbouring streets, to see if anyone was waiting in ambush. After ten minutes he was convinced that no one was waiting for him. He at once ran to the little side-door with Ali, hurried in and, using his key to the back stairs, reached his bedroom without opening or stirring a single curtain, so that the concierge himself could not have guessed that the house, which he thought to be empty, was once more occupied by its principal inhabitant.

916 THE COUNT OF MONTE CRISTO

When he got to the bedroom, the count signalled to Ali to stop there, then went into the dressing-room, which he examined. Everything was in its usual state: the precious bureau was in its place and the key in the bureau. He double-locked it, took the key, came back to the bedroom door, removed the double tumbler on the bolt and returned.

Meanwhile Ali had laid out on a table the weapons which the count had asked for: a short carbine and a pair of double pistols with superimposed barrels that allowed the user to aim as accurately as with a target pistol. Thus armed, the count held the lives of five men in his hands.

It was about half-past nine. The count and Ali quickly ate a piece of bread and drank a glass of Spanish wine. Then Monte Cristo slid back one of the moving panels that allowed him to see from one room into the next. His pistols and his carbine were within reach, and Ali, beside him, held one of those little Arab axes that have not changed in design since the Crusades. Through one of the bedroom windows, parallel to that in the dressing-room, the count could see into the street.

Two hours passed in this way. It was completely dark, and yet, through this darkness, Ali, thanks to his savage nature, and the count, no doubt thanks to an acquired ability, could distinguish even the slightest rustle of the trees in the courtyard. The little light in the porter's lodge had long since been extinguished.

Presumably the attack, if one was really planned, would take place by the staircase from the ground floor and not through a window. In Monte Cristo's mind, the criminals were after his life, not his money, so they would attack the bedroom, reaching it either by the hidden staircase, or through the dressing-room window. He placed Ali in front of the door to the staircase and continued his own watch on the dressing-room.

A quarter to twelve rang on the Invalides clock, the west wind carrying the dreary resonance of the three blows[2] on its moist breath. As the last one faded, the count thought he could hear a faint noise from the dressing-room. This first sound – to be precise, this first scraping sound – was followed by another, then a third. At the fourth, the count knew what was going on. A firm and skilled hand was engaged in cutting the four sides of a window-pane with a diamond.

The count felt his heart beat faster. However much a man is

inured to taking risks, however well prepared he is for danger, the fluttering of his heart and the pricking of his skin will always let him know the vast difference that lies between dream and reality, planning and execution.

However, Monte Cristo only made a sign to alert Ali; and the latter, realizing that the danger came from the direction of the dressing-room, stepped over, closer to his master.

Monte Cristo was anxious to know what enemies and how many he had to deal with.

The window that was the object of attention was opposite the opening through which the count had been staring into the dressing-room. His eyes consequently focused on this window. He could see a thicker shadow against the darkness. Then one of the panes became entirely opaque, as if a sheet of paper had been stuck on to it from outside, and the glass cracked without falling. Through the opening a hand groped for the catch. A second later the window was opening on its hinges and a man entered.

The man was alone.

'Here is a bold scoundrel,' the count muttered.

At that moment he felt Ali touch his shoulder. He turned around. Ali was pointing to the window of the room where they were, which looked out on the street. Knowing the superb delicacy of his faithful servant's senses, Monte Cristo went across to the window and there saw another man emerging from the shelter of a doorway and climbing on a boundary stone, apparently so that he could see what was happening in the count's house.

'So!' he said. 'There are two of them: one to act, the other to keep watch.' He motioned to Ali to keep his eyes on the man in the street and returned to the one in his dressing-room. The glass-cutter had got inside and was taking his bearings, his arms extended in front of him. Finally he appeared to have understood everything. There were two doors in the dressing-room; he bolted each of them.

When he came across to the door into the bedroom, Monte Cristo thought he was about to enter, and raised one of the pistols; but he heard simply the noise of the bolts sliding in their bronze rings. It was merely a precaution: the nocturnal visitor, not realizing the care with which the count had removed the tumblers, could now consider himself at home and in safety.

Alone and free to act, the man now took something out of his pocket which the count could not make out in the darkness, put it on a small table, then went directly over to the bureau and felt around the lock, only to find that, contrary to his expectations, the key was not in place.

But the glass-cutter was a resourceful fellow, who had made provision for every eventuality. The count soon heard the clink of iron on iron made by the rustling of that bunch of shapeless keys that locksmiths bring when you call for them to open a door, and which thieves call skeleton keys; or, if they are French thieves, *rossignols*, which means 'nightingales', no doubt because of the pleasure they experience on listening to their nocturnal song when they grate against the bolt of a lock.

'Oh, oh!' Monte Cristo murmured with a disappointed smile. 'It's only a thief.'

But the man, in the darkness, could not find the right key; so he reached for the object which he had placed on the table, and worked a spring. At once a pale light (though bright enough to see by) cast a golden hue across the man's hands and face.

'Well, I never!' said Monte Cristo, starting back in surprise. 'It's . . .'

Ali raised his axe.

'Don't move,' the count whispered. 'And leave your axe here, we won't need to be armed.'

He added a few more words in an even lower voice, because (stifled though it had been) the count's involuntary exclamation of surprise had been enough to startle the man, who had remained in the pose of the antique knife-grinder.[3] What the count had said to Ali was an order, because he at once tiptoed away and took down a black cloak and a three-cornered hat from the wall of the alcove. Meanwhile Monte Cristo rapidly removed his frock-coat, his waistcoat and his shirt. Now, by the ray of light glowing through the hole in the panelling, you could see that the count was wearing on his chest one of those finely woven and pliable tunics of mail; in a France where people are no longer afraid of being knifed, the last person to wear one of these was probably Louis XVI[4], who did fear a dagger in his chest – but died from an axe to the head.

The mail-coat soon vanished under a long soutane, as the count's hair did under a tonsured wig. The triangular hat, on top of the wig, completed the count's transformation into an abbé.

Meanwhile the man had heard nothing more, so he got up and,

while Monte Cristo was changing his appearance, went back to the bureau and began to crack the lock with his 'nightingale'.

'Very well,' the count muttered, doubtless aware of some secret of the lock-smith's art unknown to the lockpick, skilled though he was. 'You'll be at it for a few minutes.' And he went to the window.

The man whom he had seen climb on to a boundary stone had got down and was still walking up and down in the street; but oddly, instead of watching for anyone who might come, either along the Avenue des Champs-Elysées or down the Faubourg Saint-Honoré, he appeared to be concerned only with what was happening at the count's: all his movements were designed to let him see what was going on in the dressing-room.

Suddenly Monte Cristo struck his forehead and allowed a silent laugh to play across his lips. Then he went over to Ali and whispered: 'Stay here, hiding in the dark, and, whatever noise you may hear or whatever may happen, do not come in and show yourself unless I call you by name.'

Ali nodded to show that he had heard and that he would obey.

At this, Monte Cristo took a ready-lighted candle out of a cupboard and, at the moment when the thief was concentrating most attentively on his lock, quietly opened the door, making sure that the light in his hand completely illuminated his face. The door opened so quietly that the thief did not hear it. But, to his amazement, he suddenly saw the room light up. He swung around.

'Well, good evening, dear Monsieur Caderousse,' Monte Cristo said. 'What the devil are you doing here at this hour?'

'Abbé Busoni!' cried Caderousse. And, quite at a loss to explain how this strange apparition had reached him, since he had locked the doors, he dropped his bunch of skeleton keys and remained motionless, as though struck dumb with astonishment. The count stepped between Caderousse and the window, cutting the terrified thief off from his only route of escape.

'Abbé Busoni!' Caderousse repeated, staring at the count in horror.

'Yes, indeed, Abbé Busoni,' Monte Cristo went on. 'In person; and I am glad that you recognize me, Monsieur Caderousse, because it shows you have a good memory. If I'm not mistaken, it's nearly ten years since we met.'

This calm, this irony, this power filled Caderousse with a dizzying sense of terror. 'The abbé! The abbé!' he muttered, his hands clasped and his teeth chattering.

'So, are we trying to rob the Count of Monte Cristo?' asked the counterfeit abbé.

'Monsieur l'Abbé,' Caderousse muttered, trying to reach the window, while the count pitilessly barred his way. 'Father, I don't know . . . Please believe me . . . I swear that . . .'

'A broken window-pane,' the count went on, 'a dark lantern, a bunch of skeleton keys, a lock half forced . . . It seems clear enough.'

Caderousse was knotting his cravat around his neck, looking for a corner to hide in or a hole down which he might vanish.

'Come, now,' said the count. 'I see you have not changed, my fine murderer.'

'Monsieur l'Abbé, as you seem to know everything, you must know that it was not me; it was La Carconte. That was acknowledged at the trial, since they only sentenced me to the galleys.'

'So, did you serve your time, since here you are trying to have yourself sent back for another term?'

'No, father, someone released me.'

'Whoever it was did society a rare favour.'

'Ah!' said Caderousse. 'But I did promise . . .'

'So, you're breaking your parole?' Monte Cristo interrupted.

'Alas, yes,' said Caderousse, deeply unsure of himself.

'An unfortunate lapse which, if I'm not mistaken, will lead you to the block. Too bad, too bad, *diavolo*! – as worldly folk say in my country.'

'Father, I gave way to temptation . . .'

'All criminals say that.'

'And necessity . . .'

'Spare me that,' Busoni said with contempt. 'Necessity may make a man beg for alms or steal a loaf at the baker's door, but not come and crack the lock of a bureau in a house that he thinks is uninhabited. When the jeweller Joannès had just paid you forty-five thousand francs in exchange for the diamond that I gave you, and you killed him so that you could have both the diamond and the money, was that also necessity?'

'Forgive me, Monsieur l'Abbé,' said Caderousse. 'You saved me once, save me a second time.'

'I'm not tempted to.'

'Are you alone, father?' Caderousse asked, clasping his hands. 'Or do you have the police waiting, ready to take me in?'

'I am entirely alone,' said the abbé. 'And I still feel pity for you. I shall let you go, at the risk of whatever new misfortune my weakness may bring, if you tell me the whole truth.'

'Oh, Monsieur l'Abbé!' Caderousse cried, clasping his hands and coming towards the count. 'I can tell you, you are my saviour!'

'You claim you were released from hard labour?'

'Oh, yes, father. I swear on my honour!'

'Who did that?'

'An Englishman.'

'What was his name?'

'Lord Wilmore.'

'I know him, so I shall know if you are lying.'

'Monsieur l'Abbé, I'm telling you the absolute truth.'

'So this Englishman protected you?'

'Not me, but a young Corsican who was my fellow convict.'

'What was this Corsican's name?'

'Benedetto.'

'That's a Christian name.'

'He had no other; he was a foundling.'

'So the young man escaped with you?'

'Yes.'

'How?'

'We were working at Saint-Mandrier, near Toulon. Do you know Saint-Mandrier?'

'I do.'

'Well, while we were sleeping, from twelve to one . . .'

'Convicts taking a siesta! Poor creatures!' said the abbé.

'Dammit,' said Caderousse. 'No one can work all the time. We are not dogs.'

'Fortunately for dogs,' said Monte Cristo.

'So, while the others were taking a siesta, we went a little way off, sawed through our leg-irons with a file that the Englishman had got to us and escaped by swimming.'

'What became of this Benedetto?'

'I have no idea.'

'But you must know.'

'Truly, I don't. We parted company at Hyères.' And, to give more force to his words, Caderousse took another step towards the abbé, who remained calm and questioning, not moving from the spot.

'You are lying!' Abbé Busoni said, in tones of unmistakable authority.

'Monsieur l'Abbé!'

'You are lying! The man is still your friend, and perhaps you may even be using him as your accomplice?'

'Oh, Monsieur l'Abbé . . .'

'How have you managed to survive since you left Toulon? Answer me!'

'As best I could.'

'You're lying!' the abbé said for the third time, in an even more compelling voice. Caderousse looked at him in terror. 'You have been living on the money he has given you,' the count continued.

'Yes, it's true,' said Caderousse. 'Benedetto became the son of a great nobleman.'

'How can he be the son of a great nobleman?'

'The illegitimate son.'

'And what is this nobleman's name?'

'The Count of Monte Cristo, the same in whose house we are.'

'Benedetto is the count's son?' Monte Cristo asked, astonished in his turn.

'By God, he must be, since the count has found him a false parent, the count gives him forty thousand francs a month and the count is leaving him five hundred thousand francs in his will.'

'Ah! Ah!' said the fake abbé, starting to understand. 'And what name is this young man using in the meantime?'

'He is called Andrea Cavalcanti.'

'So, he is the young man whom my friend, the Count of Monte Cristo, receives in his home, and who is engaged to Mademoiselle Danglars?'

'The very same.'

'And you would allow this, you wretch! Knowing his life and his crimes?'

'Why should I stand in the way of a comrade's success?'

'You are right. It is not your place to warn Monsieur Danglars, but mine.'

'Don't do that, father!'

'Why not?'

'Because you would lose us our living.'

'Do you think that, in order to ensure a living for wretches like you, I should become a party to their deception and an accomplice in their crime?'

'Monsieur l'Abbé!' Caderousse said, coming still closer.

'I shall tell everything.'

'To whom?'

'To Monsieur Danglars.'

'By the devil and all his works!' cried Caderousse, taking an open knife from under his coat and striking the count full in the chest. 'You will say nothing, Abbé!'

To his great astonishment, instead of burying itself in the count's chest, the dagger glanced off, blunted. At the same time, the count grasped the murderer's wrist in his left hand and twisted it with such force that the knife fell from his numbed fingers and Caderousse gave a cry of pain. But instead of stopping at this cry, the count continued to twist the bandit's wrist until he fell to the ground, at first on his knees, and then face downwards, his arm dislocated. The count put his foot on the man's head and said: 'I don't know what is stopping me from breaking your head, scoundrel!'

'Mercy, mercy!' cried Caderousse.

The count took away his foot. 'Get up!' he said. Caderousse did as he was told.

'Begorrah, what a grip you have, father!' he said, rubbing an arm bruised by the sinewy vice that had gripped it. 'By God, what a grip!'

'Be quiet. God gives me the strength to tame a wild beast like yourself. I act in His name. Remember that, wretch; sparing you at this moment is also in accordance with the will of God.'

'Ouch!' said Caderousse, still in pain.

'Take this pen and paper and write what I tell you.'

'I can't write, Monsieur l'Abbé.'

'You are lying. Take the pen and write.'

Caderousse, overwhelmed by this superior power, sat down and wrote:

Monsieur, the man whom you are receiving in your house and to whom you intend to give your daughter's hand, is a former convict, who escaped with me from the prison at Toulon. His number was 59 and mine 58. He

was called Benedetto, but he does not himself know his real name, having
never known his parents.

'Sign!' the count ordered.

'But do you want to ruin me?'

'If I wanted to ruin you, idiot, I should take you to the first officer
of the watch. In any case, it is likely that by the time the letter
reaches the person to whom it is addressed, you will have nothing
more to fear. So sign it.'

Caderousse signed.

'The address: *To Monsieur le Baron Danglars, banker, rue de la
Chaussée-d'Antin.*'

Caderousse wrote the address.

The abbé took the letter. 'That's good,' he said. 'Now, go.'

'Which way?'

'The way you came.'

'Are you asking me to leave by this window?'

'You came in by it.'

'Are you planning something against me, father?'

'You fool, what could I be planning?'

'Then why not open the door to me?'

'What is the point in waking the concierge?'

'Monsieur l'Abbé, tell me that you don't want me dead.'

'I want what God wants.'

'But swear to me that you will not strike me while I am going
down.'

'You are an idiot and a coward.'

'What do you want to do with me?'

'I'm asking you. I tried to make you into a happy man, and I
only created a murderer!'

'Monsieur l'Abbé,' said Caderousse. 'Try one last time.'

'Very well,' said the count. 'You know I am a man of my word?'

'Yes,' said Caderousse.

'If you return home safe and sound . . .'

'Whom do I have to fear, except you?'

'If you return home safe and sound, leave Paris, leave France;
and wherever you are, as long as you live an honest life, I shall
ensure that you receive a small salary. Because, if you get home
safe and sound, well, then . . .'

'Well, then?' Caderousse asked, trembling.

'Well, I shall think that God has pardoned you and I shall do the same.'

'As true as I'm a Christian,' Caderousse stammered, shrinking back, 'you're scaring me to death!'

'Go!' said the count, pointing to the window. Though still not entirely reassured by the promise, Caderousse climbed out of the window and put his foot on the ladder. There he paused, shivering.

'Now, go down it,' said the abbé, folding his arms. Caderousse started to realize that he had nothing to fear from that side, and went down. As he did so, the count held up the candle, so that from the Champs-Elysées one could see this man coming out of the window, lit by another.

'But what are you doing, father?' Caderousse said. 'Suppose the watch were to go past.' And he blew out the candle. Then he continued to go down the ladder, but it was not until he felt the earth of the garden under his feet that he felt truly secure.

Monte Cristo went back into his bedroom and glanced quickly from the garden to the street. First of all he saw Caderousse, after reaching the ground, walk around the garden and place his ladder at the far end of the wall, so as to leave by a different place from the one where he had entered. Then, looking from the garden to the street, he saw the man, who had seemed to be waiting there, run along the street on the far side of the wall and station himself at the very corner near which Caderousse was about to descend.

Caderousse slowly climbed the ladder and, reaching the top rungs, put his head above the parapet to make sure that the street was empty. No one was to be seen, no sound to be heard. One o'clock struck at the Invalides.

At that, Caderousse sat astride the top of the wall and, drawing the ladder up, passed it over to the other side and prepared to go down; or, rather, to slide down the two uprights, which he did with a degree of skill that proved how accustomed he was to the operation.

However, once he had started to let himself slide, he was unable to stop. When he was half-way down, he saw a man dash out of the shadows – but to no avail; he saw an arm raised at the very moment he reached the ground – but to no avail: before he could defend himself, the arm struck him so savagely in the back that he let go of the ladder and he cried out: 'Help!' A second blow followed almost immediately, striking him in the side, and he fell down, crying: 'Murder!' And finally, as he writhed on the ground, his adversary grasped his hair and struck him another blow on the chest. This time Caderousse tried to cry out again, but could do no more than groan: he groaned, and three streams of blood flowed from his three stab wounds.

The murderer, seeing that he could no longer cry out, lifted his head by the hair. Caderousse's eyes were closed and his mouth twisted. The murderer, thinking he was dead, let his head fall back and vanished.

Caderousse, hearing the footsteps fade in the distance, lifted himself on his elbow and, making one final effort, cried faintly: 'Murder! I am dying! Help me, Monsieur l'Abbé!'

This mournful cry pierced the darkness. The door to the hidden stairway flew open, then the little door into the garden, and Ali and his master hurried out, carrying lights.

LXXXIII

THE HAND OF GOD

Caderousse continued to cry out in a pitiful voice: 'Monsieur l'Abbé, help me! Help me!'

'What's the matter?' asked Monte Cristo.

'Help,' said Caderousse. 'I've been murdered.'

'We're here. Don't worry.'

'No, it's all over. You've come too late, in time only to see me die. What wounds! What blood!' And he passed out.

Ali and his master lifted the wounded man and carried him inside. There, Monte Cristo signed to Ali to undress him and they found the three dreadful wounds that had struck him down.

'Oh, God,' said Monte Cristo, 'your vengeance may sometimes be slow in coming, but I think that then it is all the more complete.'

Ali looked at his master, as if to ask what should be done.

'Go and find the crown prosecutor, Villefort, who lives in the Faubourg Saint-Honoré, and bring him here. On the way, wake up the porter and tell him to go and fetch a doctor.'

Ali obeyed and left the false abbé alone with Caderousse, who was still unconscious. When the unfortunate man re-opened his

THE HAND OF GOD

eyes, the count, seated a short distance away from him, was giving him a sombre, pious look, his lips moving, apparently muttering a prayer.

'A doctor, Monsieur l'Abbé! Fetch a doctor!' said Caderousse.

'Someone has already gone for one,' said the abbé.

'I know that it is too late to save my life, but he might perhaps give me the strength to make my statement.'

'About what?'

'About my murderer.'

'Do you know who it was?'

'Of course I do! Yes, I know him: it was Benedetto.'

'The young Corsican?'

'The same.'

'Your comrade?'

'Yes. After giving me plans of the count's house, no doubt expecting that I would kill him and so allow Benedetto to inherit, or else that he would kill me and Benedetto would be rid of me, he waited for me in the street and killed me himself.'

'As well as the doctor, I sent for the crown prosecutor.'

'He will be too late, too late . . .' said Caderousse. 'I can feel my life's blood running out.'

'Wait,' said Monte Cristo. He left then returned, five minutes later, with a flask. While he was away, the dying man, his eyes staring horribly, had not taken them off the door through which he instinctively guessed that help would come.

'Hurry, father, hurry!' he said. 'I feel myself fainting again.'

Monte Cristo bent down and poured two or three drops of the liquid in the flask on to the wounded man's purple lips. Caderousse sighed. 'Oh, that is life you are giving me. More, more . . .'

'Another two drops would kill you,' the abbé replied.

'If only someone would come so that I could denounce the wretch!'

'Would you like me to write out your statement?'

'Yes, yes,' said Caderousse, his eyes shining at the idea of this posthumous revenge.

Monte Cristo wrote: 'I die, murdered by the Corsican Benedetto, my fellow-prisoner in Toulon under the number 59.'

'Hurry, hurry!' said Caderousse. 'Or I shall not be able to sign.'

Monte Cristo gave him the pen, and Caderousse gathered all his strength, signed it and fell back on the bed, saying: 'You can tell them the rest, father. Say that he is calling himself Andrea Cavalcanti, that he is living at the Hôtel des Princes, that . . . Oh, God! Oh! I am dying!' And once more he fainted. The abbé made him breathe the scent from the flask, and the wounded man opened his eyes. The desire for revenge had not left him while he was unconscious.

'You will say all that, won't you, father?'

'All that and much more.'

'What more?'

'I shall say that he doubtless gave you the plan of this house in the hope that the count would kill you. I will say that he sent a letter to the count to warn him, and I shall say that, in the count's absence, I received this letter and lay in wait for you.'

'And he will be guillotined, won't he?' said Caderousse. 'Promise me he will be guillotined. I die in that hope; it will help me to die.'

'I shall say,' the count continued, 'that he followed you here, that he watched you all the time and that when he saw you coming out, he ran up and hid behind a corner of the wall.'

'Did you see all that, then?'

'Remember what I said: "If you return home safe and sound, I shall believe that God has pardoned you and I shall do the same."'

'And you didn't warn me?' Caderousse cried, trying to lift himself on his elbow. 'You knew that I would be killed when I left here, and you didn't warn me?'

'No, because I saw the hand of Benedetto as the justice of God, and I thought I should be committing a sacrilege if I were to interfere with Fate.'

'The justice of God! Don't speak to me of that, Monsieur l'Abbé. If there was any divine justice, you know as well as anyone that there are people who would be punished but who are not.'

'Patience!' said the abbé, in a tone of voice that made the dying man shudder. 'Be patient!' Caderousse looked at him in amazement.

'And then,' the abbé continued, 'God is full of mercy for everyone, as He has been towards you. He is a father before He is a judge.'

'Oh, so you believe in God, do you?' Caderousse asked.

'Even if I were so unfortunate as not to have believed in Him up to now, I should do so on looking at you.'

Caderousse raised his clasped hands to heaven.

'Listen,' the abbé went on, extending a hand above the wounded man as if ordering him to believe. 'Here is what He did for you, this God whom you refuse to recognize even in your last hour. He gave you health, strength, secure work and even friends; in short, life as it must appear sweet to a man, offering an easy conscience and the satisfaction of his natural desires. But, instead of making use of these gifts of the Lord, which He so rarely grants in all their fullness, what did you do? You abandoned yourself to idleness and drunkenness, and in your drunkenness you betrayed one of your best friends.'

'Help!' cried Caderousse. 'It's not a priest I need, but a doctor. Perhaps I am not mortally wounded, perhaps I am not yet going to die, perhaps I can be saved!'

'You are mortally wounded, and so much so that, without the three drops of liquid which I gave you just now, you would already be dead. So listen.'

'Oh!' groaned Caderousse. 'What a strange priest you are, who puts despair instead of comfort into a dying man's heart.'

'Listen,' the abbé continued. 'When you had betrayed your friend, God began, not by striking you down, but by warning you. You lapsed into poverty and you knew hunger. You had spent half a life in envy that you could have spent in profitable toil, and you were already thinking about crime when God offered you a miracle, when God, by my hands, sent you a fortune in the midst of your deprivation – a fortune that was splendid for you, who had never possessed anything. But this unexpected, unhoped-for, unheard-of fortune was not enough for you, as soon as you owned it. You wanted to double it. How? By murder. You did double it, and God took it away from you by bringing you to human justice.'

'I didn't want to kill the Jew,' said Caderousse. 'It was La Carconte.'

'Yes,' Monte Cristo replied. 'So God, who is always – I shall not say "just" this time, because His justice would have awarded you death; but God, who is always merciful, allowed your judges to be touched by your words and let you live.'

'Huh! To condemn me to prison for life! A fine pardon that was!'

'You wretch: you did at least consider it a pardon when it was given. Your cowardly heart, trembling at the prospect of death, leapt with joy at the announcement of your perpetual shame because, like all convicts, you said to yourself: prisons have doors, the tomb has none. You were right, because the door to your prison opened unexpectedly. An Englishman, visiting Toulon, has made a vow to free two men from infamy. He chooses you and your companion. A second fortune drops on you from heaven, you regain both money and ease, and you can once more live the life of other men, after having been condemned to live that of a convict. And at this, you wretch, you begin to tempt God for a third time. "I haven't got enough," you say, when you have more than you ever possessed, and you commit a third crime, motiveless, inexcusable. But God had grown tired; He has punished you.'

Caderousse was weakening visibly. 'Water,' he said. 'I'm thirsty, I'm burning.'

Monte Cristo gave him a glass of water.

'That scoundrel Benedetto,' Caderousse said, giving back the glass, 'he'll get away with it, even so!'

'No one will escape: I am telling you that, Caderousse. Benedetto will be punished.'

'Then you too will be punished,' said Caderousse. 'Because you did not do your duty as a priest. You should have stopped Benedetto killing me.'

'I!' said the count, with a smile that made the dying man shudder with fear. 'I, stop Benedetto killing you, just after you had broken your dagger on the mail-coat protecting my chest! Yes, perhaps, if I had found you humble and repentant, then I should have stopped Benedetto killing you. But I found you arrogant and bloodthirsty, so I let God's will be done!'

'I don't believe in God!' Caderousse shouted. 'Nor do you ... You are lying ... lying ... !'

'Be quiet,' said the abbé. 'You are urging the last drops of blood out of your body. Oh, so you don't believe in God – yet you are dying at His hand! Oh, so you don't believe in God; yet God only asks for a single prayer, a single word, a single tear to forgive you. God could have guided the murderer's dagger so that you would die immediately, yet He gave you a quarter of an hour to reconsider. So look in your heart, you wretch, and repent!'

'No,' said Caderousse. 'No, I do not repent. There is no God, there is no Providence. There is only chance.'

'There is both Providence and God,' said Monte Cristo. 'The proof is that you are lying there, desperate, denying God, and I am standing before you, rich, happy, healthy and safe, clasping my hands before the God in whom you try not to believe and in whom, even so, you do believe in the depths of your heart.'

'But who are you then?' asked Caderousse, turning his dying eyes towards the count.

'Look carefully at me,' Monte Cristo said, taking the candle and putting it next to his face.

'Well: the Abbé . . . Busoni.'

Monte Cristo took off the wig that was disguising his features and let down the fine black hair that so harmoniously framed his pale face.

'Oh!' Caderousse exclaimed in terror. 'If it were not for that black hair, I would take you for the Englishman, I would take you for Lord Wilmore.'

'I am not Abbé Busoni, or Lord Wilmore,' said Monte Cristo. 'Look more carefully; go back further; look into your earliest memories.' These words were spoken by the count with such a magnetic vibrancy that the man's exhausted senses were awakened for one last time.

'Yes,' he said. 'Yes, I think I did see you, I did know you once.'

'Yes, Caderousse, you saw me. Yes, you did know me.'

'Who are you then? And, if you saw me, if you knew me, why are you letting me die?'

'Because nothing can save you, Caderousse: your wounds are mortal. If you could have been saved, I would have seen that as one last act of God's mercy and, I swear it on my father's grave, I should have tried to bring you back to life and to repentance.'

'On your father's grave!' said Caderousse, fired by one last flickering spark of life and raising himself to look more closely at this man who had just made an oath sacred to all men. 'Who are you, then?'

The count had watched every stage of Caderousse's agony. He realized that this burst of life was the last. He bent over the dying man and, with a look that was both calm and sad, he said, whispering in his ear: 'I am . . .' And his lips, barely parting, let fall a name spoken so low that the count himself seemed to fear the sound of it.

Caderousse, who had pulled himself up to his knees, reached out his arms, made an effort to shrink back, then clasped his hands and raised them in one supreme final effort: 'Oh, God,' he said. 'Oh, God, forgive me for denying You. You do indeed exist, You are the father of men in heaven and their judge on earth. Oh, my Lord, I have long mistaken You! My Lord God, forgive me! My God, my Lord, receive my soul!' And, closing his eyes, Caderousse fell backwards with a last cry and a final gasp.

At once the blood stopped on his lips and ceased to flow from his wounds. He was dead.

'One!' the count said, mysteriously, staring at the corpse already disfigured by its awful death.

Ten minutes later the doctor and the crown prosecutor arrived, the first with the concierge, the other with Ali. They found Abbé Busoni praying beside the body.

LXXXIV

BEAUCHAMP

For a whole fortnight, no one in Paris spoke of anything except this daring attempted robbery at the count's. The dying man had signed a statement naming Benedetto as his murderer. The police were asked to put all their agents on the criminal's trail.

Caderousse's knife, his shrouded lantern, his bunch of keys and his clothes, except for the waistcoat, which could not be found, were handed over to the clerk of the court, and the body was taken to the morgue.

The count told everyone that this adventure had happened while he was in his house in Auteuil and that, consequently, he knew only what he had been told by Abbé Busoni. By sheer chance, the abbé had asked the count if he might spend the night at his house in order to do some research into one or two of the precious volumes in his library.

Only Bertuccio went pale every time the name of Benedetto was mentioned in his presence, but there was no reason for anyone to notice the pallor on Bertuccio's cheeks.

Villefort, called in to establish the facts of the crime, had allocated the case to himself and was pursuing the investigation with all the passionate enthusiasm that he gave to every criminal case in which he was involved. But three weeks had already elapsed without the most active enquiries bringing any result; and society gossips were starting to forget about the attempted robbery at the Count of Monte Cristo's and the murder of the thief by his accomplice, turning instead to the forthcoming marriage of Mlle Danglars to Count Andrea Cavalcanti.

The marriage was more or less arranged and the young man received at the banker's as a future son-in-law.

The elder Cavalcanti had been contacted by letter and had warmly approved of the match. Expressing deep regret that his duties absolutely forbade him to leave Parma, where he then was, he stated his intention of releasing a capital sum sufficient to give an income of 150,000 *livres*. It was agreed that the three million would be entrusted to Danglars, who would invest them. Some people had tried to sow doubt in the young man's mind about the solidity of his future father-in-law's position: Danglars had recently been making repeated losses on the Exchange; but the young man, with sublime confidence and disinterestedness, dismissed all these vain murmurings, and had the tact to say nothing about them to the baron.

The baron, consequently, adored Count Andrea Cavalcanti.

The same could not be said of Mlle Eugénie Danglars. Having an instinctive horror of marriage, she had welcomed Andrea as a means of repelling Morcerf; but now that Andrea was coming too close, she began to feel a visible repulsion towards him. The baron may perhaps have noticed it but, as he could only attribute this feeling to a whim, he had pretended not to notice it.

Meanwhile, the period of grace that Beauchamp had asked for had almost passed. During it, Morcerf had come to appreciate the value of Monte Cristo's advice when he told him to let the matter clear itself up. No one had remarked on the note about the general and no one had thought to identify the officer who had betrayed the castle of Janina with the noble count who sat in the Upper House.

Even so, Albert felt insulted, because the intention to offend was quite obviously there, in the few lines that had wounded his honour. Moreover, the manner in which Beauchamp had ended their meeting had left a bitter taste in his mouth. For these reasons, he still harboured the idea of a duel but hoped, if Beauchamp would agree, that they might be able to disguise the real reason for it, even from their seconds.

As for Beauchamp, he had not been seen since the day of Albert's visit and, whenever anyone asked for him, the reply was that he had left for a few days' journey. Where was he? Nobody knew.

One morning Albert was awoken by his valet, announcing Beauchamp. He rubbed his eyes and asked for the visitor to be shown into the little smoking parlour on the ground floor. Then he dressed quickly and went down.

Beauchamp was pacing up and down, but he stopped when he saw Albert.

'Your decision to come and see me yourself, instead of waiting for the visit that I intended to pay on you today myself, seems to me like a good omen,' said Albert. 'Come, tell me straight away, can I offer you my hand and say: "Beauchamp, admit your mistake and keep your friend," or should I simply instruct you to choose your weapons?'

'Albert,' Beauchamp said with an expression of grief that astonished the young man, 'let's first sit down and talk.'

'Come, Monsieur: it seems to me that, before we sit down together, you must answer me.'

'There are occasions,' the journalist said, 'when the difficulty lies in the answer itself.'

'Let me make it easier for you then, by repeating my question: do you retract – yes or no?'

'Morcerf, one cannot answer yes or no to a question that touches on the honour, the social standing and the life of a man like Lieutenant-General the Comte de Morcerf, peer of the realm.'

'So what can one do?'

'One can do what I did, Albert, which is to say: money, time and effort are nothing when it is a matter of the reputation and interests of an entire family. One says: more than probability is needed, we must have certainty if we are to accept a duel to the death with a friend. One says: if I cross swords or pull the trigger against a man whose hand I have shaken over the past three years, I must at least know why I am doing such a thing, so that I may arrive at the appointed place with my mind at rest and the easy conscience which a man needs when he must use his arm to save his life.'

'Very well, then,' Morcerf asked impatiently, 'what does all this mean?'

'It means that I have just come back from Janina.'

'From Janina? You!'

'Yes, I.'

'Impossible!'

'My dear Albert, here is my passport. Look at the visas: Geneva, Milan, Venice, Trieste, Delvino, Janina. Do you believe the authorities of a republic, a kingdom and an empire?'

Albert looked at the passport, then again, with astonishment, at Beauchamp. 'You went to Janina?' he said.

'Albert, if you had been a foreigner, a stranger, or a mere lord like that Englishman who came to challenge me three or four months ago, and whom I killed to stop him bothering me, you will realize that I would not have taken such trouble. But I thought I owed you this mark of my consideration. I spent a week on the outward journey, a week on the return, plus four days in quarantine and forty-eight hours when I arrived: that adds up to my three weeks. I got back last night, and here I am.'

'My God! My God, what a roundabout story, Beauchamp, and still you won't tell me what I am waiting to hear.'

'The truth is, Albert . . .'

'You seem reluctant.'

'Yes, I'm afraid.'

'Afraid of admitting that your correspondent deceived you? Now, now, Beauchamp, don't be proud! Admit it: no one can doubt your courage.'

'Oh, it's not that,' the journalist muttered. 'On the contrary . . .'

Albert went deathly pale. He tried to speak but the words failed on his lips.

'My friend,' Beauchamp said, in the most affectionate tone, 'believe me, I should be delighted if I could apologize to you, and I should do so with all my heart; but alas . . .'

'But what?'

'The report was correct, my friend.'

'What! The French officer . . .'

'Yes.'

'This Fernand?'

'Yes.'

'The traitor who delivered the castles of the man in whose service he was . . .'

'Forgive me for saying this, my friend: that man was your father!'

Albert leapt up furiously to throw himself on Beauchamp, but he was restrained more by the other's compassionate look than by his outstretched hand.

'Here,' he said, taking a sheet of paper out of his pocket. 'My dear friend, here is the proof of it.'

Albert unfolded the sheet of paper. It was a sworn statement by four leading inhabitants of Janina, confirming that Colonel Fernand Mondego, army instructor in the service of the Vizier Ali Tebelin, had betrayed the castle of Janina for a payment of two thousand purses.

The signatures had been validated by the consul.

Albert staggered and fell, dumbstruck, into a chair. This time there could be no doubt: the family name was there. And, after a moment of painful silence, his heart swelled, the veins bulged on his neck and a stream of tears burst from his eyes.

Beauchamp, who had looked with the utmost compassion on the young man as he gave way to his grief, came over to him and said: 'Do you understand, now, Albert? I wanted to see everything and to judge everything for myself, in the hope that the explanation would be favourable to your father and that I could do full justice to him. But on the contrary the information that I obtained stated that the instructing officer, Fernand Mondego, promoted by Ali Pasha to the rank of governor-general, was none other than Count Fernand de Morcerf. So I returned, reminding myself of the honour you had done in admitting me to your friendship, and I hastened round to see you.'

Albert, still stretched out in the chair, was covering both eyes with his hands, as if to prevent the daylight reaching him.

'I hastened round to see you,' Beauchamp continued, 'to say this to you: Albert, the sins of our fathers, in these times of action and reaction, cannot be visited on their children. Albert, few men have gone through the revolutions in which we were born, without some spot of mire or of blood staining their soldier's uniform or their judge's robe. No one in the world, Albert, now that I have all the proof, now that I am the master of your secret, can force me to engage in a combat that your conscience, I am sure, would tell you was a crime. But I have come to offer you what you no longer have the right to demand of me. This proof, these revelations, these statements that I alone possess – would you like me to make them disappear? Would you like this terrible secret to remain between the two of us? Protected by my word of honour, it will never cross my lips. Tell me, Albert: would you like that? Is that what you want, my friend?'

Albert fell on Beauchamp's neck. 'Oh, noble heart,' he cried.

'Here, then,' said Beauchamp, handing the papers to him. Albert seized them convulsively, crumpled them, twisted them and considered tearing them up; but, fearing that the smallest scrap might be blown away in the wind and come back to haunt him one day, he went across to the candle which he kept burning continually to light cigars, and let the flames devour them to the last fragment.

'Dear friend, best of friends!' he muttered, as he burned the papers.

'Let all this be forgotten like a bad dream,' Beauchamp said. 'Let it vanish like those last sparks flickering on the blackened paper, and let all fade like that wisp of smoke drifting away from those silent ashes.'

'Yes, yes,' said Albert. 'Let nothing remain except the eternal friendship that I owe to my saviour, a friendship that my children will transfer to yours, a friendship that will always remind me that I owe you the blood in my veins, the life in my body and the honour of my name . . . For, if such a thing were to be known, oh, Beauchamp! I am telling you, I would blow my brains out. Or else, no, my poor mother! I should not wish to kill her at the same time – otherwise, I should go abroad.'

'My dear Albert!' Beauchamp said.

But the young man's unexpected and somewhat artificial joy was short-lived, and he soon relapsed into an even deeper melancholy.

'What is it, dear friend?' Beauchamp asked. 'What is it?'

'What it is,' Albert said, 'is that something is broken in my heart. You must understand, Beauchamp, that one cannot in an instant abandon that feeling of respect, of confidence and pride, that a father's spotless name inspires in his son. Oh, Beauchamp! How shall I face him? Shall I shrink back when he puts his lips to my forehead or withdraw my hand from his touch? Beauchamp, I am the most wretched of men. Oh, my mother, my poor mother!' he said, looking through tear-filled eyes at her portrait. 'How you would have suffered, had you witnessed all this!'

'Come, come,' Beauchamp said, clasping him by both hands. 'Take heart.'

'But that first note that you printed in your paper: where did it come from?' Albert exclaimed. 'There is some secret hatred, some invisible enemy behind all this.'

'All the more reason, then,' said Beauchamp. 'Courage, Albert! Let nothing show on your face. Carry your sorrow inside you as the cloud conceals ruin and death like a deadly secret that is understood only when the storm breaks. Come, my friend, gather strength for the moment when the storm will break.'

'What! You don't think it's over yet?' Albert said in horror.

'I don't think anything, but everything is possible. By the way . . .'

'What?' Albert asked, seeing Beauchamp hesitate.

'Are you still going to marry Mademoiselle Danglars?'

'What makes you ask that now, Beauchamp?'

'Because, to my mind, the match may depend on the question that is uppermost in our thoughts just now.'

'What!' Albert exclaimed, reddening. 'Do you think Monsieur Danglars . . .'

'I'm merely asking how your marriage plans stand. For heaven's sake, don't try to read anything more into my words than I intend, and don't give them more significance than they actually have!'

'No,' Albert said. 'The engagement has been broken off.'

'Good,' said Beauchamp. Then, seeing that his friend was about to relapse into melancholy, he said: 'Come on, Albert, take my advice and let's go out. A ride round the Bois in a phaeton or on horseback will take your mind off things. Then we'll come back and have lunch somewhere, you can go off to your business and I'll go back to mine.'

'Good idea,' said Albert. 'But let's walk. I think it would do me good to tire myself out a little.'

'Certainly,' said Beauchamp; and the two friends set out, on foot, down the boulevard. When they got to the Madeleine, Beauchamp said: 'Why, since we're going in this direction, let's go and see the Count of Monte Cristo. He'll take your mind off things. He's a wonderful person for raising one's spirits, because he never asks questions: in my opinion, people who don't ask too many questions give the best consolation.'

'Yes,' said Albert, 'let's go and see the count. I like him.'

LXXXV

THE JOURNEY

Monte Cristo gave a cry of joy on seeing the two young men together. 'Ah, ah!' he said. 'Well, now, I hope that it's all over, cleared up and settled?'

'Yes,' said Beauchamp. 'Some ridiculous rumours which came from nowhere and which, if they were to be repeated now, I should be the first to challenge. So, let's say no more about it.'

'Albert will tell you that that was my advice to him,' said the count, before adding: 'Now, as it happens, you find me after what I think is the most detestable morning I've ever spent.'

'What are you doing?' Albert asked. 'Arranging your papers, apparently?'

'My papers! Thank heavens, no! My papers are always perfectly arranged, since I have none. I'm putting some order into the papers of Monsieur Cavalcanti.'

'Monsieur Cavalcanti?' Beauchamp asked.

'Yes, don't you know?' said Morcerf. 'He's a young man the count is launching.'

'Not at all,' said Monte Cristo. 'Let's be quite clear about it, I'm not launching anyone, least of all Monsieur Cavalcanti.'

'And he's going to marry Mademoiselle Danglars in my stead and place – which,' Albert continued, forcing a smile, 'as you can well imagine, my dear Beauchamp, is a cruel blow to me.'

'What! Cavalcanti to marry Mademoiselle Danglars?' Beauchamp asked.

'What do I hear?' said Monte Cristo. 'Have you been away in the back of beyond? And you a journalist, the bedfellow of Rumour? Parisian society is talking of nothing else.'

'Were you responsible for this marriage, Count?' Beauchamp asked.

'I? Hush, scribbler, don't even whisper such a thing! I go a-match-making? Never! You don't know me. On the contrary, I opposed it as strongly as I could; I refused to make the formal request.'

'Oh, I understand,' said Beauchamp. 'For the sake of our friend Albert, here?'

'For my sake!' said the young man. 'Oh, no, not a bit of it! The count will support me when I say that I always begged him, on the contrary, to break off the engagement, which has now fortunately been broken off. The count claims that he is not the person I should thank, so, like the ancient Romans, I'll raise an altar "To the Unknown God".'

'Listen,' said Monte Cristo, 'so little is this to do with me that I have fallen out both with the father-in-law and with the young man. The only one still to hold me in some affection, when she saw the extent to which I was disinclined to make her renounce her precious liberty, is Mademoiselle Eugénie, who doesn't appear to me to have a marked vocation for the married state.'

'And you say this marriage is about to take place?'

'Yes, in spite of everything I could say. I don't know the young man myself, though they say he is rich and comes from a good family; but that's just hearsay as far as I'm concerned. I repeated all this, time and again, to Monsieur Danglars but he is besotted with his Luccan. I even told him about what seems to me a more serious fact, namely that the young man was kidnapped, carried off by gypsies or mislaid by his tutor, I'm not sure which. What I do know is that his father lost sight of him for ten years, and God only knows what he did during that time. Well, none of that made any difference. I have been asked to write to the major, to request some papers from him: here they are. I'm sending them on, but at the same time, like Pilate, I wash my hands of it.'

'What about Mademoiselle d'Armilly?' Beauchamp asked. 'How does she feel about you, now that you're taking her pupil away?'

'I really can't tell, though it seems she is leaving for Italy. Madame Danglars mentioned her to me and asked me for some letters of recommendation to impresarios. I gave her a note for the director of the Teatro Valle, who owes me a favour. But what's wrong, Albert? You seem quite miserable. Could you perhaps be in love with Mademoiselle Danglars without realizing it?'

'Not as far as I know,' Albert said with a melancholy smile. Beauchamp began to study the pictures.

'You're certainly not in your usual good humour,' Monte Cristo went on. 'Come, now: what's the matter?'

'I've got a headache,' Albert said.

'In that case, my dear Viscount, I have an infallible remedy to suggest, one that has always worked for me whenever I have suffered some annoyance or other.'

'What is that?' the young man asked.

'Travel.'

'Really?' Albert said.

'Really. And since at the moment I have a lot that is bothering me, I'm going to travel. Would you like us to go together?'

'You, Count?' said Beauchamp. 'Something bothering you? What can it be?'

'Huh! You speak very lightly about it, as you may; but I'd like to see you with a judicial enquiry going on in your house!'

'An enquiry! What enquiry?'

'The one that Monsieur Villefort is engaged in against my lovable assassin, some kind of bandit who had escaped from prison, it seems.'

'That's right,' said Beauchamp. 'I read about it in the papers. Who is this Caderousse?'

'Pooh! It appears he is a Provençal. Monsieur de Villefort had heard speak of him when he was in Marseille, and Monsieur Danglars recalls seeing him. The result is that the crown prosecutor is taking the matter very much to heart and that the prefect of police is apparently extremely interested in it; and the result of all this interest, for which no one could be more grateful than I am, is that for the past fortnight they have rounded up every bandit they could find in Paris and its suburbs, and sent them here, alleging that they are Monsieur Caderousse's murderers. And the result of *that* will be that in three months, if it continues, there will not be a thief or an assassin in the whole fine kingdom of France who does not know the plan of my house like the back of his hand. So I've decided to abandon it to them entirely and go as far away as the earth can carry me. Come on, Viscount, I'm taking you with me.'

'Certainly.'

'So, it's agreed?'

'Yes, but where?'

'I told you: where the air is pure, noise sleeps and, however proud one may be, one feels humble and small. It pleases me to be humbled in that way, since like Augustus they call me master of the universe.'[1]

'So, to cut a long story short, where are you going?'

'To the sea, Viscount, to the sea. You must understand, I'm a sailor. As a child I was rocked in the arms of the old ocean and on the breast of the beautiful Amphitrite. I played with the green robe of the first and the azure robe of the second. I love the sea as one may love a mistress, and when I have not seen her for a long time I pine for her.'

'Let's go, Count, let's go!'

'To the sea?'

'Yes.'

'You accept, then?'

'I do.'

'Well, Viscount, this evening in my courtyard there will be a *britzka*[2] in which one can lie flat out, as on a bed. Four post-horses will be harnessed to this *britzka*. Monsieur Beauchamp, it will easily hold four. Would you like to join us? Let me take you!'

'No, thank you. I have just come back from the sea.'

'What? From the sea?'

'Yes, more or less. I've just been on a little journey to the Borromean islands.'

'Well? Come, even so,' said Albert.

'No, my dear Morcerf, you must realize that if I refuse, it's because it cannot be done. In any case,' he said, lowering his voice, 'I must stay in Paris, if only to keep an eye on the newspaper's postbox.'

'Oh, you're a fine and good friend,' Albert said. 'Yes, you're right. Watch and wait, Beauchamp, and try to find out who was responsible for this revelation.' The two friends took leave of one another; their final handshake implied all that their lips could not express in front of a third person.

'Excellent young man, Beauchamp!' Monte Cristo exclaimed after the journalist had left. 'Don't you think so, Albert?'

'Oh, yes, a man of heart, I can vouch for it. I love him with all my soul. But, now we are alone, though I'm not bothered too much one way or the other, where are we going?'

'To Normandy, if you agree.'

'Perfect. Well out in the country? No visitors, no neighbours?'

'We shall have the company of horses for riding, dogs for hunting and a boat for fishing, that's all.'

'Just what I need. I must inform my mother, and then I'm all yours.'

'But will they let you?' Monte Cristo asked.

'Let me what?'

'Come to Normandy.'

'Why? Aren't I free?'

'Free to go where you wish, alone, I know, since I met you on an escapade in Italy.'

'Well, then?'

'But are you free to come with the man called the Count of Monte Cristo?'

'You have a short memory, Count.'

'Why is that?'

'Didn't I tell you how much my mother likes you?'

'Woman is often fickle, said François I; and woman is like the waves, said Shakespeare.[3] One was a great king, the other a great poet, so they must have known women.'

'Yes, women. But my mother is not "women", she is a woman.'

'A poor foreigner might perhaps be forgiven his failure to understand all the subtleties of your language . . .'

'What I mean is that my mother is not prodigal with her feelings, but, once she has given them, it is for ever.'

'Oh, really?' said Monte Cristo, with a sigh. 'And do you think she does me the honour of granting me any feeling other than entire indifference?'

'Listen! I've said it before, and I repeat: you must really be a very unusual and superior being.'

'Oh?'

'Yes, because my mother is captivated – I won't say, by curiosity, but by the interest you have aroused in her. When we are together, you are the only subject of our conversation.'

'And did she tell you to beware of this Manfred?'

'No, on the contrary, she told me: "Morcerf, I think the count is a noble creature; try to win his affection."'

Monte Cristo turned away and sighed. 'Really?' he asked.

'So you understand,' Albert continued, 'far from disapproving of my journey, she will applaud it with all her heart, since it conforms with her daily instructions to me.'

'Very well, then,' said Monte Cristo. 'We'll meet this evening. Be here at five o'clock. We'll get there at midnight, or one.'

'What! To Le Tréport?'

'There or near it.'

'It only takes you eight hours to cover forty-eight leagues?'

'That's a lot, even so.'

'You most certainly are a man of miracles, and you will not only succeed in going faster than the railway, which is not too difficult, especially in France, but even go faster than the telegraph.'

'However that may be, Viscount, it will still take us seven or eight hours to get there, so be on time.'

'Don't worry. I've nothing else to do between now and then, except to get ready.'

'Five o'clock, then?'

'Five o'clock.'

Albert left. Monte Cristo, after having nodded to him with a smile, remained for a moment lost in thought, as though meditating profoundly. At last, passing a hand across his forehead, as if to brush away his reverie, he went to the bell and rang it twice. At this signal, Bertuccio came in.

'Monsieur Bertuccio,' the count said, 'it will not be tomorrow, or the day after, as I originally thought, but this evening that I leave for Normandy. From now until five o'clock gives you more time than you need. Alert the ostlers at the first relay. Monsieur Morcerf will accompany me. Now, go!'

Bertuccio obeyed and a groom sped towards Pontoise with a warning that the post-chaise would be coming by at exactly six o'clock. The ostler at Pontoise sent an express messenger to the next relay, and so on. Six hours later, every relay along the route was prepared.

Before leaving, the count went up to see Haydée and announced his departure; he told her where he was going and put his whole household under her orders.

Albert arrived on time. The journey, gloomy at first, was lightened by the physical effects of speed. Morcerf had never imagined travelling so fast.

'I must agree,' said Monte Cristo, 'that it is impossible to move forward at all, when your mail travels at two leagues an hour, and you have this ridiculous law that forbids one traveller to overtake another without asking his permission – which means that a sick or ill-humoured traveller has the right to hold up any number of light-hearted and healthy persons on the road behind him. I avoid these handicaps by travelling with my own postilion and my own horses – don't I, Ali?'

At this the count, leaning out of the window, gave a little shout of encouragement which lent wings to the horses: they were no longer galloping, they flew. The carriage thundered along the regal highway and every head turned to watch this flaming meteor go by. Ali, repeating the shout, showing his white teeth and wrapping his powerful hands around the reins flecked with foam, spurred on the horses, whose fine manes were spreading in the wind. Ali, child of the desert, was here in his element and, through the dust he stirred up around him, with his black face, shining eyes and snow-white burnous, he seemed like the genie of the simoun and the god of the whirlwind.

'This is a pleasure I had not previously experienced,' said Morcerf. 'The pleasure of speed!' And the last trace of gloom vanished from his brow, as though the air that they were cleaving in their path had brushed the clouds aside.

'Where in the world did you find such horses?' Albert asked. 'Did you have them bred specially?'

'Just so,' the count replied. 'Six years ago, I came across a stallion in Hungary, famous for its speed. I bought it, I don't know how much it cost; Bertuccio paid for it. In that same year, it had thirty-two offspring. We shall be able to inspect that entire generation of children from the one father. Each one is alike, black, without a single blemish except a star on the forehead: this privileged member of the stud had his mares chosen for him, like the favourites of a pasha.'

'Admirable! But tell me, Count, what do you do with all these horses?'

'As you see, I travel with them.'

'But you won't always be travelling?'

'When I have no further need of them, Bertuccio will sell them. He claims he will make thirty or forty thousand francs on the deal.'

'There won't be a king in Europe rich enough to buy them from you!'

'Then he must sell them to some simple vizier in the East, who will empty his treasury to pay for them and restock it by bastonading his subjects.'

'Count, might I tell you something that has occurred to me?'

'What is it?'

'That, after you, Monsieur Bertuccio must be the richest individual in Europe.'

'Well, there you are wrong, Viscount. I am sure that if you were to turn out Bertuccio's pockets, you wouldn't find two *sous* to rub together.'

'Why's that?' the young man asked. 'Is this Monsieur Bertuccio such a prodigy? Please, my dear Count, don't test my credulity too far or, I warn you, I shall cease to believe you.'

'There are never any prodigies with me, Albert. Figures and facts, that's all. So, consider this puzzle: a steward steals, but why does he steal?'

'Pooh! It's in his nature, I think,' said Albert. 'He steals because he has to.'

'No, you're wrong. He steals because he has a wife and children, and ambitions for himself and his family. Above all, he steals because he is never quite sure that he will not leave his master and he wants to provide for the future. Now, Monsieur Bertuccio is alone in the world. He dips into my purse without telling me, and he is sure that I shall never dismiss him.'

'How can he be sure?'

'Because I shall never find anyone better.'

'You're going round in circles, all based on supposition.'

'Not at all: these are certainties. To me, a good servant is one over whom I have the power of life or death.'

'And do you have the power of life or death over Bertuccio?' Albert asked.

'Yes,' the count said curtly. Some words end a conversation like a steel door falling. The count's 'Yes' was one of those words.

The remainder of the journey continued at the same pace. The thirty-two horses, divided into eight relays, covered the forty-eight leagues in eight hours. In the middle of the night they arrived at the gateway to a fine park. The porter was awake and holding the gates open. He had been alerted by the ostler from the last relay.

It was half-past two in the morning. Morcerf was shown to his rooms. He found a bath and supper ready for him. The servant who had travelled on the rear box of the carriage was at his disposal, while Baptistin, who had travelled in front, was to serve the count.

Albert took his bath, had supper and went to bed. All night he was rocked by the melancholy sound of the waves. Getting up the next morning, he went over to the window, opened it and found himself on a little terrace, with the vastness of the sea in front of him and, behind, a pretty park adjoining a small wood.

A little corvette was bobbing in a fairly large cove; it had a narrow hull and tall mast with a flag flying from the lateen yard and bearing Monte Cristo's coat of arms: a mountain on a field

azure with a cross gules at the chief, which could also have been an
allusion to his name (evoking Calvary, which Our Saviour's passion
has made a mountain more precious than gold, and the infamous
cross which his divine blood made holy) as much as to any personal
memory of suffering and regeneration buried in the mysterious
night of the man's past. Around the schooner were several little
boats belonging to the fishermen in the surrounding villages, which
seemed like humble subjects awaiting the orders of their queen.

Here, as wherever Monte Cristo stopped, even if only for two
days, the temperature of life was raised to a high degree of comfort,
which meant that life immediately became easy. Albert found two
guns and every other piece of equipment necessary for hunting in
a small room beside his bedroom. A more lofty room on the ground
floor was given over to all those ingenious devices that the English
– who are great fishermen, because they have both patience and
leisure – have so far not managed to persuade the more workaday
fishermen of France to adopt.

All their time was spent in these different pursuits, at which
Monte Cristo excelled: they killed a dozen pheasants in the park,
caught the same number of trout in the streams, dined in a pergola
overlooking the sea and took tea in the library.

Around the evening of the third day, Albert, worn to a thread by
the exertions of this life, which seemed to be a game for Monte
Cristo, was sleeping at a window while the count and his architect
ran over the plan of a conservatory that he wanted to build in his
house, when the sound of a horse's hoofs crushing the gravel on
the path made the young man sit up. He looked out of the window
and was extremely and unpleasantly surprised to see his valet in
the courtyard, having left the man behind to save embarrassment
to Monte Cristo.

'Florentin!' he exclaimed, leaping up from his chair. 'Can my
mother be ill?' He ran to the door of the room.

Monte Cristo looked after him and saw him in conversation with
the valet who, still out of breath, took a small sealed packet from
his pocket. The packet contained a newspaper and a letter.

'Who is this letter from?' Albert asked urgently.

'From Monsieur Beauchamp,' Florentin replied.

'So did Monsieur Beauchamp send you?'

'Yes, Monsieur. He called me to his house, gave me the money
for my journey, summoned a post-horse for me and made me

promise not to stop until I reached Monsieur. I covered the distance in fifteen hours.'

Albert opened the letter, trembling. At the first lines, he gave a cry and grasped the newspaper, a visible shudder running through his frame. Suddenly his eyes clouded, his knees seemed to buckle and, as he was on the point of falling, he leant against Florentin, who reached out to support him.

'Poor young man!' Monte Cristo muttered, so low that even he could not hear these words of compassion as he spoke them. 'It is written that the sins of the fathers shall be visited on the sons, even to the third and fourth generation.'

Meanwhile Albert's strength had returned and he went on reading, while shaking the hair on a head drenched in sweat. Then, crumpling both the paper and the letter, he said: 'Florentin, is your horse in any condition to return to Paris?'

'It's a lame old post-horse.'

'Oh, good Lord! And how was the house when you left?'

'Quite calm. But when I returned from Monsieur Beauchamp's, I found madame in tears. She called me to ask when you would return, so I told her that I was going to fetch you, at Monsieur Beauchamp's request. Her first impulse was to reach out as if to restrain me, but after thinking for a moment, she said: "Yes, go, Florentin. Let him come back."'

'Yes, mother, yes,' said Albert. 'Have no fear, I am coming – and a curse on the vile slanderer! But, first of all, I must get started.' And he set off towards the room where he had left Monte Cristo.

He was no longer the same man. Five minutes had been enough to accomplish a pitiful change in Albert. He had left, his usual self; and now he returned, his voice strangled, his face blotched with feverish flushes, his eyes glistening beneath blue-veined lids and his walk unsteady like that of a drunken man.

'Count,' he said, 'thank you for your excellent hospitality, which I should like to have enjoyed longer, but I have to go back to Paris.'

'What has happened?'

'A great misfortune; but please let me leave: this is something more important than life itself to me. No questions, Count, I beg you; just a horse!'

'My stables are at your disposal, Viscount,' Monte Cristo said. 'But you will drop dead of exhaustion if you go by post-horse. Take a brougham, a coupé, some sort of carriage . . .'

'No, that would take too long, and in any case I need the fatigue that you fear for me: it will do me good.'

Albert took a few steps, reeling like a man with a bullet wound, and slumped into a chair near the door. Monte Cristo did not see this second moment of dizziness; he was already at the window, shouting: 'Ali, a horse for Monsieur de Morcerf! Hurry, he has no time to lose!'

These words brought Albert back to his senses. He ran out of the room, followed by the count. 'Thank you,' he muttered, bounding into the saddle. 'Come back as soon as you can, Florentin. Is there any password I need to get horses?'

'None. Simply hand over the one you are riding and another will instantly be saddled up for you.'

Albert was about to gallop off, but paused.

'You may find my departure odd, even senseless,' he said. 'You may not realize how a few lines in a newspaper can drive a man to despair. Well,' the young man added, throwing the paper to the count, 'read this, but only after I have left, so that you do not see my shame.'

While the count was picking up the paper, he dug the spurs that had just been attached to his boots into the horse's flanks and the animal, astonished at coming across any rider who thought he needed such encouragement, went off like a shot from a sling.

The count looked after him with a feeling of infinite compassion. Only when he had altogether disappeared did he turn back to the newspaper, where he read as follows:

The French officer in the service of Ali, Pasha of Janina, who was mentioned three weeks ago in the newspaper *L'Impartial*, and who not only betrayed the castles of Janina, but also sold his benefactor to the Turks, was indeed at that time named Fernand, as stated by our honourable colleagues in that newspaper. Since then, as well as his Christian name, he has acquired a title of nobility and the name of a landed estate.

Today, he calls himself Monsieur le Comte de Morcerf and is a member of the chamber of peers.

So the dreadful secret which Beauchamp had so generously buried had reappeared like an armed phantom; and, on the day after Albert's departure for Normandy, another newspaper had been maliciously informed and had published these few lines that drove the unfortunate young man to the brink of insanity.

LXXXVI

JUDGEMENT IS PASSED

At eight o'clock in the morning, Albert stormed into Beauchamp's like a thunderbolt. The valet had been forewarned and showed Morcerf into his master's room, where Beauchamp had just got into his bath.

'Well?' Albert asked.

'Well, my poor friend,' Beauchamp replied, 'I was expecting you.'

'Here I am. I don't need to say, Beauchamp, that I consider you too good and loyal a friend to have spoken of this to anyone; no, my dear fellow. In any case, the message you sent me is proof of your affection. So let's lose no time in preliminaries: do you have any idea where this blow comes from?'

'I'll say something about that later.'

'Yes, and first, my friend, you must tell me that story of this abominable treachery in all its details.'

Beauchamp told the young man, who was crushed with shame and anguish, the following simple facts.

Two days earlier, in the morning, the article appeared in a newspaper other than *L'Impartial* and (something which made the matter even more serious) in a paper well known for supporting the government. Beauchamp was having lunch when the passage leapt out at him. He immediately ordered a cab and, without finishing his meal, hurried round to the paper. Although his professed political opinions were diametrically opposed to those of the managing editor of the paper making the accusation, Beauchamp and he were close friends, something that happens occasionally – or even, we might say, quite often.

When he arrived, the editor was holding a copy of his own paper and apparently admiring a leader on sugar beet, probably of his own composition.

'Good!' said Beauchamp. 'As I see you have a copy of your paper, my dear chap, I don't need to tell you what brings me.'

'Are you by any chance an advocate of cane sugar?' asked the editor of the government paper.

'No,' Beauchamp replied. 'In fact I have absolutely no ideas on the matter. I'm here for another reason.'

'So why are you here?'

'About the Morcerf article.'

'Oh, yes. Yes, indeed. Odd, isn't it?'

'So odd that you are in danger of a libel case, I would think, and a very risky trial.'

'Not at all. With the note, we received all the supporting evidence, and we are quite convinced that Monsieur de Morcerf will keep quiet. Anyway, it's a service to the country to denounce these wretches who don't deserve the honours they have received.'

Beauchamp was astonished. 'But who gave you all this information?' he asked. 'My paper, which first raised the matter, had to hush it up for lack of proof, even though we have more interest than you do in unmasking Monsieur de Morcerf, since he's a peer of the realm and we belong to the Opposition.'

'Heavens, it's very simple. We didn't go looking for scandal, it came and found us. A man came yesterday from Janina, bringing the incriminating dossier and, since we were still slightly unwilling to make the accusation, he told us that if we refused, the article would appear in another paper. Come on now, Beauchamp: you know what important news is; we didn't want to let this slip through our fingers. Now it's out, there'll be terrible repercussions to the ends of Europe.'

Beauchamp realized that there was nothing more to be done, so he left in despair and dispatched a message to Morcerf.

What he had not been able to tell Albert, because it took place after his letter had left, was that the same day there had been a great commotion in the Upper House which had broken out and spread among the ordinarily tranquil groups that made up the assembly. Everyone had arrived almost before time and was discussing the grim news that was to preoccupy public opinion and turn every eye on one of the most prominent members of that illustrious body.

The article was read in a whisper, followed by an exchange of comments and recollections which gave more details about the facts. The Comte de Morcerf was not liked by his colleagues. Like all those who have risen in the world, he had been obliged to behave with a degree of hauteur, in order to maintain his rank. Great aristocrats laughed at him, talented men rejected him and those whose reputations were justly pure instinctively despised him. The count was in the unhappy situation of a scapegoat: once he had been designated by the Lord's finger to be the sacrificial victim, everyone was prepared to cry him down.

The Comte de Morcerf alone knew nothing of this. He did not receive the newspaper in which the defamatory article had appeared, and he had spent the morning writing letters and trying out a horse.

He arrived at his usual hour, his head held high, with a proud look and insolent manner, got down from his carriage, and strode along the corridors and into the chamber, not noticing the sidelong glances of the ushers or the grudging nods of his colleagues. When he came into the chamber, it had already been in session for more than half an hour.

Though the count, as we have said, ignorant of what had happened, made no change in his look or manner, this look and this manner seemed to everyone even more arrogant than usual, and his presence on this occasion appeared such an act of aggression in this assembly that was jealous of its honour, that everyone considered it a breach of etiquette, while several thought it an act of bravado, and a few took it as an insult. Clearly, the whole chamber was burning with eagerness to begin the debate.

The accusing newspaper could be seen in everyone's hands but, as is always the case, no one was keen to take on the responsibility of opening the attack. Finally one honourable peer, a declared enemy of the Comte de Morcerf, mounted the tribune with a solemnity that proclaimed the long-expected moment had come.

There was a fearful silence. Only Morcerf remained unaware of the reason for this awed attention, paid for once to an orator who was seldom accorded such an attentive audience.

The count sat, unruffled, through the preamble in which the speaker announced that he was going to speak of something so serious, so solemn and so vital to the House that it demanded the full attention of his colleagues.

At the first mention of the words 'Janina' and 'Colonel Fernand', however, Morcerf went so horribly pale that the whole assembly was convulsed by a single shudder and all eyes turned on the count.

Moral wounds have the peculiarity that they are invisible, but do not close: always painful, always ready to bleed when touched, they remain tender and open in the heart.

When the article had been read in the midst of this silence, which was then ruffled by a stir that ceased as soon as the speaker indicated that he was about to continue, the accuser described his misgivings and began to suggest what a hard task he had taken on. It was M. de Morcerf's honour and that of the whole House that he sought to defend, by initiating a debate that would deal with these still controversial personal questions. Finally, he concluded by asking for an inquiry to be set up, rapidly enough to nip this slander in the bud and avenge M. de Morcerf by restoring him to the position that public opinion had for so long accorded him.

Morcerf was shaking, smitten by this enormous and unexpected calamity to the point where he could barely stammer out a few words, while casting a haggard look at the faces of his colleagues. His diffidence, which could equally well indicate the astonishment of an innocent man as the shame of a guilty one, gained him some sympathy. Truly generous men are always ready to feel compassion when their enemy's misfortune exceeds the bounds of their hatred.

The chairman asked for a vote on the inquiry, which was held by members rising or remaining seated. The result was that the inquiry would be held. The count was asked how long he would need to prepare his defence.

Morcerf's strength had returned as soon as he realized he had survived this terrible blow. 'Gentlemen and fellow peers,' he said, 'time is not what one needs to repel an attack such as that which is here being directed against me by unknown enemies, who are no doubt hiding in the shadows of their own obscurity. I must reply instantly, like a thunderbolt, to this flash of lightning that for an instant dazzled me. How I wish that, instead of such self-justification, I could spill my blood to prove to my colleagues that I am worthy to be counted as one of their peers.'

These words made a favourable impression.

'Consequently,' he continued, 'I request that the inquiry should be held as soon as possible and I shall give the House all the documents necessary to facilitate it.'

'When would you like the inquiry to begin?' asked the chairman.

'I am at the disposal of the House immediately,' the count replied.

The chairman rang his bell. 'Is the House of the opinion that this inquiry should take place today?' he asked.

'Yes!' came the unanimous reply from the assembly.

A twelve-member commission was chosen to decide what documents Morcerf should be required to provide. The first session of this commission was to convene at eight o'clock in the evening in the offices of the House. If several sessions were needed, they would be held at the same time, in the same place.

Once this had been decided, Morcerf asked permission to retire. He had to collect the documents that he had long been gathering, to brave a storm that his cunning and indomitable character had warned him would eventually descend upon him.

Beauchamp told the young man everything that we have just told the reader, with the difference that his account enjoyed the immediacy of a living thing, as compared to a dead one.

Albert listened, trembling now with hope, now with anger, at times with shame – for, from what Beauchamp had confided to him, he knew that his father was guilty and wondered how, in that case, he could succeed in proving his innocence.

When he got to this point, Beauchamp paused.

'And then?' Albert asked.

'And then . . .' Beauchamp repeated.

'Yes.'

'My friend, that word imposes a dreadful compulsion upon me. Do you wish to know what happened next?'

'There is absolutely no alternative; and I should prefer to learn it from your lips, my friend, than from any others.'

'Very well,' said Beauchamp. 'Prepare your courage, Albert, because you will never have had greater need of it.'

Albert drew a hand across his forehead to reassure himself as to his own strength, like a man preparing to defend his life who tests his armour and flexes the blade of his sword. He felt strong, mistaking his fever for energy.

'Go on!' he said.

'The evening came,' Beauchamp continued. 'All Paris was on tenterhooks. Many people said that your father had only to show himself for the charges to collapse, while many others said that he would not appear. Some claimed they had seen him leaving for Brussels, and a few went to the police to ask if it was true, as they had heard, that the count had collected his passport.

'I admit that I did everything I could,' Beauchamp went on, 'to get a member of the commission, a young peer who is a friend of mine, to gain admission for me to some kind of gallery in the chamber. At seven o'clock he came to fetch me and, before anyone else had arrived, handed me over to an usher who shut me into a sort of box, like a box in the theatre: I was concealed by a pillar and wrapped in total darkness, so I could reasonably hope to see and hear each of the terrible events that were about to take place. By eight o'clock exactly, everyone had assembled.

'Monsieur de Morcerf came in as the clock had just finished striking. He had some papers in his hands and his face appeared calm. For him, his manner was unusually simple, and his dress studied and severe. In the manner of an old soldier, he wore his coat buttoned from top to bottom.

'His entrance was very favourably received. The commission was certainly not ill-disposed towards him, and several of its members came over to offer him their hands.'

Albert felt that his heart would break on learning these details, yet in the midst of his pain he experienced a feeling of gratitude: he would like to have been able to embrace these men who had given his father this sign of their esteem when his honour had been so gravely challenged.

'At that moment an usher came in and gave the chairman a letter. "You have the floor, Monsieur de Morcerf," he said, as he was breaking the seals.

'The count began his defence and, I assure you, Albert,' Beauchamp went on, 'he spoke with extraordinary eloquence and skill. He produced documents to prove that the vizier of Janina, to his very last hour, had honoured him with his entire confidence, since he had entrusted him with a life-and-death mission to the emperor himself. He showed the ring, a token of authority which Ali Pasha commonly used to seal his letters, and which he had given him so that when he returned, he could have access to him, at whatever hour of the day or night, even if he was in his harem. Unfortunately, he said, his mission had failed and, when he returned to defend his benefactor, Ali was already dead. But as he died, the count said, so great was Ali Pasha's confidence in him that he had entrusted his favourite mistress and their daughter to him.'

Albert shuddered at these words because, even while Beauchamp was speaking, the young man was recalling the whole of Haydée's story and he remembered what the beautiful Greek girl had said about that message, that ring and how she was sold into slavery.

'What was the effect of the count's speech?' Albert asked anxiously.

'I must admit I found it moving, and so did the whole commission,' said Beauchamp.

'However, the chairman casually glanced at the letter that had just been brought to him. But as he read the first lines, his interest was awakened. He read it once, then again and said, looking hard at Monsieur de Morcerf: "Count, you have just told us that the vizier of Janina entrusted his wife and daughter to you?"

' "Yes, Monsieur," Morcerf replied. "But here, as in the rest, I was pursued by misfortune. On my return, Vasiliki and her daughter, Haydée, had vanished."

' "Did you know them?"

' "The confidence that the pasha placed in my loyalty and the intimate nature of our relationship meant that I was able to see them more than twenty times."

' "Have you any idea what became of them?"

' "Yes, Monsieur. I heard that they succumbed to their grief and perhaps to poverty. I was not rich, my own life was in serious danger and, to my great regret, I was not able to look for them."

'The chairman frowned imperceptibly. "Gentlemen," he said, "you have heard what Monsieur le Comte de Morcerf has said and followed his explanation. Now, Count, can you bring forward any witness in support of the account you have just given us?"

' "Alas, no, Monsieur," the count replied. "All those around the vizier who knew me at his court are either dead or scattered across the world. I believe that I am alone among my compatriots to have survived that frightful war. I have the letters of Ali Tebelin which I have shown you; I have the ring which was the token of his authority – here it is; and finally I have the most convincing refutation that I can supply to this anonymous attack, which is the absence of any witness against my word as an honourable man and the unblemished record of my military career."

'A murmur of approval ran through the assembly. At that moment, Albert, if nothing had intervened, your father's case was won.

'All that was left was to proceed to a vote, when the chairman asked to be heard. "Gentlemen," he said, "and you, Count, I suppose you will not be displeased to hear someone who claims to be a very important witness and who has just presented himself here of his own accord. Having listened to our colleague, we cannot doubt that this witness will prove his entire innocence. Here is the letter that I have just received on the matter. Would you like it to be read out, or will you decide to discard it and ignore this incident?"

'Monsieur de Morcerf paled and gripped the papers he was holding even tighter, so that they rustled audibly in his hands.

'The commission decided to hear the letter. As for the count, he was thoughtful and offered no opinion one way or the other. So the chairman read the following.

'"Monsieur le président,

'"I can supply the most definite information to the commission of enquiry which has been charged with examining the conduct in Epirus and Macedonia of Lieutenant-General, the Comte de Morcerf . . ."

'Here the chairman paused. The colour drained from the count's face and the chairman looked enquiringly around the assembly.

'"Carry on!" they cried in every part of the room. The chairman continued:

'"I was present at the death of Ali Pasha. I witnessed his final moments. I know what became of Vasiliki and Haydée. I am at the disposal of the commission, and even demand the honour of being heard. I shall be in the hall of the House at the moment when this letter is given to you."

'"And who is this witness – or, rather, this enemy?" the count asked in a voice which was audibly and profoundly distorted by his feelings.

'"That we shall discover, Monsieur," the chairman replied. "Does the commission agree that we should hear this witness?"

'"Yes, yes," every voice cried simultaneously.

'The usher was recalled. "Usher," the chairman asked, "is there someone waiting in the hall?"

'"Yes, Monsieur le président."

'"Who is this person?"

'"A lady accompanied by a servant."

'Everyone exchanged glances.

'"Bring her in," said the chairman.

'Five minutes later, the usher reappeared. Every eye was fixed on the door. And I too,' Beauchamp added, 'shared in the general mood of expectation and anxiety.

'Behind the usher walked a woman wrapped in a large cloak which entirely concealed her. Under it, from the shape it outlined and the perfumes that it exhaled, one could guess at the presence of an elegant young woman, but no more.

'The chairman asked the stranger to remove her veil and it could then be seen that she was dressed in Greek costume; and, in addition to that, she was of outstanding beauty.'

'Ah,' said Morcerf. 'Her.'

'Whom do you mean: her?'

'Haydée.'

'Who told you?'

'Alas, I guessed it. But, Beauchamp, please continue. You can see that I am calm and strong. We must be coming to the end.'

'Monsieur de Morcerf,' Beauchamp continued, 'looked at the woman with a mixture of surprise and alarm. For him, it was life or death that hung on those charming lips, while, for everyone else, this was such a strange and curious adventure that the loss or salvation of Monsieur de Morcerf had become a secondary consideration.

'The chairman gestured the young woman towards a seat, but she indicated that she would remain standing. As for the count, he had fallen back into his chair and it was clear that his legs would no longer carry him.

' "Madame," the chairman said, "you wrote to the commission to offer some information about the affair at Janina and you claim that you were an eye-witness of the events."

' "Indeed I was," the stranger replied with a voice imbued with a delightful sadness and stamped with that sonorousness peculiar to Oriental voices.

' "However," the chairman said, "permit me to remark that you were very young at that time."

' "I was four years old but, since the events were of supreme significance to me, not a single detail has left my mind and not one circumstance has escaped my memory."

' "What significance can these events have had for you? Who are you, for this great catastrophe to have produced such a profound impression on you?"

' "It was a matter of the life or death of my father," the young woman replied. "My name is Haydée, daughter of Ali Tebelin, Pasha of Janina, and Vasiliki, his well-beloved wife."

'The blush, at once modest and proud, that spread across the young woman's cheeks, the flame in her eyes and the solemnity of her revelation produced an indescribable effect on the assembly. As for the count, he could not have been more smitten if a thunderbolt had fallen, opening a pit at his feet.

' "Madame," the chairman continued, after bowing respectfully, "allow me to ask one simple question, without casting doubt on your words, which will be the last: have you any proof of what you say?"

' "I do, Monsieur," Haydée said, taking from under her cloak a sachet of perfumed satin. "Here is the certificate of my birth, drawn up by my father and signed by his principal officials; and here, with the certificate of my birth, is that of my baptism, my father having agreed that I might be brought up in the religion of my mother: this certificate bears the seal of the great primate of Macedonia and Epirus. Finally – and this is doubtless the most important – here is the bill for the sale of my person and that of my mother to the Armenian merchant, El Kobbir, by this Frankish officer who, in his infamous dealings with La Porte, had reserved as his share of the booty the wife and daughter of his benefactor, and sold them for the sum of a thousand purses, that is to say for approximately four hundred thousand francs."

'A greenish pallor spread across the Comte de Morcerf's cheeks and his eyes became shot with blood as these terrible charges were spelled out, to be greeted by the assembly in melancholy silence.

'Haydée, still calm, but far more threatening in her calm than another might have been in anger, passed the bill of sale across to the chairman. It was written in Arabic; but since it had been anticipated that some of the documents produced might be in Arabic, Romaic or Turkish, the parliamentary interpreter had been asked to stand by, and he was called. One of the peers, who knew Arabic, having learned the language during the glorious Egyptian campaign,[1] followed the words on the parchment as the translator read them aloud:

I, El Kobbir, slave dealer and supplier of His Royal Highness's harem, acknowledge having received from the Frankish lord, Count of Monte Cristo, for delivery to the most glorious emperor, an emerald valued at 2,000 purses, in payment for a young Christian slave aged eleven years, by name Haydée, legitimate daughter of the late lord Ali Tebelin, Pasha of Janina, and Vasiliki, his favourite, the same having been sold to me seven years ago, with her mother, who died on arrival at Constantinople, by a Frankish colonel in the service of the vizier Ali Tebelin, named Fernand Mondego.

The above-mentioned sale was made on behalf of His Royal Highness, by whom I was mandated, for the amount of one thousand purses.

In Constantinople, with authorization from His Royal Highness, year 1274 of the hegira.

Signed: EL KOBBIR

The present deed is fully and properly authenticated by the imperial seal, which the vendor must ensure is attached.

'Near the merchant's signature one could indeed see the seal of the august emperor.

'A dreadful silence followed the reading of the letter and the sight of the seal. The count was powerless to do anything but stare. His eyes, fastened as though involuntarily on Haydée, were shot with blood and flames.

' "Madame," the chairman said, "can we not speak to the Count of Monte Cristo, who is in Paris together with you, I believe?"

' "Monsieur," Haydée replied, "the Count of Monte Cristo, my second father, has been in Normandy for the past three days."

' "In that case, Madame," the chairman said, "who advised you to take this step – though the court thanks you for it, and it was quite natural in view of your birth and your misfortunes?"

' "This was dictated to me by my respect and my sorrow, Monsieur," Haydée replied. "God forgive me: though I am a Christian, I have always thought to avenge my illustrious father. After I set foot in France and learned that the traitor lived in Paris, my eyes and my ears remained constantly open. I lived in seclusion in the house of my noble protector, but I live thus because I love obscurity and silence, which allow me to inhabit my own thoughts and meditations. The Count of Monte Cristo surrounds me with his paternal care and I am aware of all that goes on in the world, but I only hear distant echoes of it. I read all the newspapers, just as I am sent all the albums and all the new music. Because I follow the lives of others, without taking part in them, I learned of what happened this morning in the House and what was to take place here this evening; and I wrote to you."

' "So the Count of Monte Cristo is not involved in what you have done?" the chairman asked.

' "He is quite unaware of it, Monsieur, and I am afraid of only one thing, which is that he will disapprove when he finds out about it. However," the young woman went on, looking with burning eyes towards heaven, "it is a fine day for me, now that I have at last the opportunity to avenge my father."

'Throughout all this, the count had not spoken a single word. His colleagues were looking at him and, no doubt, pitying this greatness that had been blown away by the scented breath of a woman. The dreadful marks of his misfortune were little by little appearing on his face.

'"Monsieur de Morcerf," said the chairman, "do you recognize this lady as the daughter of Ali Tebelin, pasha of Janina?"

'"No," Morcerf said, attempting to rise. "This is a tissue of lies, woven by my enemies."

'Haydée, who had been looking intently towards the door as if expecting someone, turned sharply and, seeing the count on his feet, gave an awful cry. "You do not recognize me," she said. "Well, fortunately I recognize you! You are Fernand Mondego, the Frankish officer who was instructor to the troops of my noble father. You it was who betrayed the castles of Janina! You it was who, having been sent by your benefactor to deal directly on the matter of his life or death with the emperor, brought back a false *firman* giving him a complete pardon! You it was who with this *firman* obtained the pasha's ring which would command the obedience of Selim, keeper of the fire! You it was who stabbed Selim! You it was who sold us, my mother and me, to the merchant El Kobbir! Assassin! Assassin! Assassin! Your master's blood is still on your brow! Let it be seen by all!"

'These words were spoken with such passionate conviction that all eyes turned towards the count, and he even put his hand to his forehead as if he had felt Ali's blood on it, still warm.

'"So do you positively identify Monsieur de Morcerf as this same officer Fernand Mondego?"

'"Indeed I do recognize him!" Haydée exclaimed. "Oh, my mother! You told me: 'You were free, you had a father whom you loved, you were destined to be almost a queen! Look well on this man: he it is who has made you a slave, who raised your father's head on the end of a pike, who sold us, who betrayed us! Look well on his right hand, the one that bears a broad scar; should you forget his face, you would recognize him by that hand into which, one by one, fell the coins of the merchant El Kobbir!' Indeed, I do recognize him! Oh, let him say now that he does not recognize me!"

'Each word fell like the blow of a cutlass on Morcerf and drained a part of his energy. At the last words, he involuntarily hastened to conceal his hand in his coat: it was indeed disfigured by a wound; then he fell back into his seat, plunged into the desolation of utter despair.

'This scene had caused a commotion among the minds of all those present which swirled like the leaves torn from a tree by the powerful north wind.

' "Monsieur de Morcerf," said the chairman, "do not let your courage fail you; reply. The justice of the court is supreme and equal for all, like that of God. It will not let you be crushed by your enemies without providing you with the means to combat them. Would you like further enquiries to be made? Do you wish me to order two members of the commission to visit Janina? Speak!"

'Morcerf said nothing.

'At this, all the members of the commission looked at one another with a sort of horror. They knew the count's powerful and aggressive character. It would take the most terrible blow to overwhelm this man's defences; it must be that this silence, which was like a slumber, would be followed by an awakening that would be like thunder.

' "Well, then?" asked the chairman. "What have you decided?"

' "Nothing!" the count said in a toneless voice, rising to his feet.

' "Then has the daughter of Ali Tebelin really told us the truth?" said the chairman. "Is she really the awful witness to whom the guilty man never dares to answer: *no*? Did you really do all these things that she accuses you of doing?"

'The count looked around him with an expression that would have melted the heart of a tiger but which could not disarm a judge. Then he raised his eyes towards the vaulted ceiling as if fearing that it might open to reveal that second tribunal which is called heaven and that other judge who is called God.

'At last, with a sudden movement, he tore open the tightly buttoned coat that seemed to stifle him and left the room like a disconsolate madman. For a short while his footsteps echoed lugubriously down the passage, and soon the rumbling of the carriage as it galloped away with him shook the portico of the Florentine building.

' "Gentlemen," said the chairman, when the sounds had died

away, "does Monsieur de Morcerf stand convicted of felony, treason and conduct unworthy of a member of this House?"

'"Yes!" replied all the members of the commission of inquiry with one voice.

'Haydée had stayed until the very end of the session. She heard the count's guilt pronounced without a single muscle on her face expressing either pity or joy. Then, once more covering herself with her veil, majestically she took her leave of the counsellors and walked out with that bearing which Virgil described as the walk of a goddess.'[2]

LXXXVII

PROVOCATION

'So I took advantage of the silence and darkness in the room,' Beauchamp went on, 'to leave without being seen. The usher who had brought me in was waiting for me at the door. He conducted me through the corridors to a little door opening on to the Rue de Vaugirard. I left with my heart at once shattered and enchanted – Albert! Forgive me for saying it: shattered with regard to you, but enchanted by the nobility of that young woman seeking to avenge her father. Yes, Albert: wherever this revelation came from – and I grant you that it may have been from an enemy – I swear that that enemy was an agent of Providence.'

Albert was holding his head in both hands. He raised a face that was red with shame and bathed in tears, and grasped Beauchamp's arm.

'Friend,' he said, 'my life is over. All that remains for me is not to say, as you do, that Providence dealt me this blow, but to seek out the man who has been pursuing me with his hatred. Then, when I know his name, I shall kill him, or else he will kill me. I am counting on your friendship to assist me, Beauchamp, provided that contempt has not driven friendship from your heart.'

'Contempt, my dear friend? How can this misfortune affect you? No, thank God! We no longer live in a time when children were blindly and unjustly made responsible for the deeds of their fathers. Recall your whole life, Albert. It has been brief, but was the dawning of a summer's day ever purer than your beginning? No, Albert, take my advice, you are young, you are rich: leave France. Everything is soon forgotten in this Babylon with its tumultuous life and changing fashions. Come back in three or four years' time, when you have married some Russian princess, and no one will recall what happened yesterday, still less what happened sixteen years ago.'

'Thank you, my dear Beauchamp, thank you for the excellent intentions that inspire your words, but it cannot be. I have told you my wish; and now, if necessary, I shall change the word "wish" to "will". You must understand that, being involved as I am in the matter, I cannot see it in the same light as you do. What appears to you to have some celestial origin, seems to me to come from an impurer source. I have to admit that Providence appears to me to have nothing to do with all this; and fortunately so because, instead of an invisible and intangible messenger bringing celestial rewards and punishments, I shall find a tangible and visible being on whom I may be avenged – oh, yes, I swear to you that I shall – for all that I have suffered over the past month. Now, Beauchamp, I repeat: I want to return to the solid reality of human life and, if you are still the friend you say you are, help me to find the hand that struck this blow.'

'Very well, then,' said Beauchamp. 'If you are determined to bring me back to earth, back I must come. If you are set upon hunting down an enemy, I shall hunt with you. And I shall find him, for my honour is almost as much implicated as yours.'

'Then let's start our enquiries now, without delay. Every moment that we do delay is an eternity for me. The author of this denunciation has not yet been punished. He may hope that he will not be; but on my honour, if he does hope so, he is mistaken!'

'Listen to me, Morcerf.'

'Beauchamp, I can see that you know something. You restore me to life!'

'I am not saying that this is the answer, Albert, but I can see a light in the darkness and we may follow it to our goal.'

'Tell me! You can see, I'm boiling over with impatience.'

'This is something that I did not want to let you know when I returned from Janina.'

'Tell me!'

'Here is what happened. Naturally, I went to the first banker in the town to obtain information. As soon as I mentioned the matter, and even before your father's name was spoken, he said: "Ah, I can guess why you are here."

' "How can you, and why?"'

' "Because barely a fortnight ago I was questioned on the same subject."'

' "By whom?"'

' "By a banker in Paris, an associate of mine."'

' "Whose name is?"'

' "Monsieur Danglars." '

'Him!' Albert cried. 'He has long pursued my poor father with jealous hatred; supposedly a man of the people, he cannot forgive the Count de Morcerf for being a peer of the realm. And what about that marriage, broken off for no specific reason? It must be him!'

'Find out, Albert, but don't get carried away until you know. Find out, I tell you, and, if it proves to be the case . . .'

'Oh, yes, if it proves to be the case!' the young man exclaimed. 'He will repay me for all I have suffered.'

'Be careful, Morcerf. He is already an old man.'

'I shall take heed of his age as he took heed of my family's honour. If he had a quarrel with my father, why did he not strike him? Oh, no: he was afraid to confront the man!'

'I'm not criticizing you, Albert, but I do want to restrain you. Be cautious.'

'Don't worry. In any case, Beauchamp, you will come with me: such solemn matters must be dealt with in front of witnesses. Before the end of today, if Monsieur Danglars is guilty, Monsieur Danglars will have ceased to live, or I shall be dead. By heavens, Beauchamp, I want to bury my honour with all due ceremony!'

'Very well. When one has taken such a resolve, Albert, it must be carried out at once. Do you want to visit Monsieur Danglars? Then let's go.'

They sent out for a hired cab. As they turned into the drive of the banker's house, they noticed Andrea Cavalcanti's phaeton and servant at the door.

'Well, I never! There's a stroke of luck,' said Albert in a grim voice. 'If Monsieur Danglars does not want to fight with me, I shall kill his son-in-law. A Cavalcanti must fight, surely?'

The young man was announced to the banker who, knowing what had happened the previous evening, heard Albert's name and forbade him entry. But it was too late: he had followed the lackey, heard the order being given, pushed open the door and went through into the banker's study, followed by Beauchamp.

'But, Monsieur, what is this?' Danglars exclaimed. 'Can one no longer be allowed to choose whom one shall or shall not receive in one's home? I think you are forgetting yourself.'

'No, Monsieur,' said Albert. 'There are some circumstances – yours included – when one must be at home, at least to certain people, unless one pleads cowardice. You may choose that alternative.'

'So what do you want with me, Monsieur?'

'I want,' said Morcerf, coming over to him without appearing to pay any attention to Cavalcanti, who was leaning against the mantelpiece, 'I want to suggest a meeting with you, in a quiet spot, where no one will trouble you for ten minutes – I ask no longer – and where, of two men who have met there, one will remain among the leaves.'

Danglars went pale and Cavalcanti started. Albert turned to the young man and said: 'Why, do come if you wish, Count, you have the right to be there, you are almost one of the family. When I give this kind of invitation, it is open to as many people as there may be to accept it.'

Cavalcanti looked dumbfounded at Danglars who, with an effort, got up and came to stand between the two young men. Albert's attack on Andrea had put the matter on a different footing, and he began to hope that his visit had a different motive from the one he had supposed.

'Ah, I understand, Monsieur,' he said to Albert. 'If you have come here to pick a fight with this gentleman because I preferred him over you, I must warn you that it will be a matter for the public prosecutor.'

'You are mistaken, Monsieur,' said Morcerf with a grim smile. 'I am not speaking at all about marriage and I only addressed myself to Monsieur Cavalcanti because it appeared that he might momentarily have considered intervening in our discussion. But then, on the other hand,' he added, 'you are right: today I am ready to pick a fight with everybody. But have no fear, Monsieur Danglars, you shall have priority.'

'Monsieur,' Danglars said, white with anger and fear, 'I warn you that when I have the misfortune to come across a rabid mastiff blocking my path, I kill it; and, far from thinking myself guilty, I consider I have done a service to society. So I warn you, if you are rabid and try to bite me, I shall strike you down without pity. I ask you! Is it my fault if your father has been dishonoured?'

'Yes, you wretch!' cried Morcerf. 'It is your fault!'

Danglars stepped backwards. 'My fault!' he said. 'Mine! Do I know anything about Greek history? Have I travelled in those countries? Did I advise your father to hand over the castles of Janina? To betray . . .'

'Silence!' Albert said in a stern voice. 'No, it was not you directly who created this scandal and caused this misfortune, but you it was who hypocritically initiated it.'

'I!'

'Yes, you! Where else did the revelation come from?'

'But the newspaper told you that: from Janina, of course!'

'And who wrote to Janina?'

'To Janina?'

'Yes. Who wrote to ask for information about my father?'

'I suppose that anyone can write to Janina.'

'Yet only one person did write.'

'Only one?'

'Yes, and that person was you!'

'Certainly, I did write. It seems to me that when you are marrying your daughter to a young man, you should obtain some information about his family. To do so is not only one's right but one's duty.'

'You wrote, Monsieur,' said Albert, 'knowing perfectly well what reply you would receive.'

'What! Ah, now, I swear to you,' Danglars exclaimed, with a certainty and confidence that may perhaps have come even less from his fear than from the interest he felt in his heart for the unfortunate young man. 'I swear to you that I should never have considered writing of my own accord. Whatever did I know about the catastrophe that befell Ali Pasha?'

'So did anyone suggest that you write?'

'Indeed they did.'

'Someone encouraged you to do it?'

'Yes.'

'Who did? Tell me! Go on!'

'But nothing could be easier. I was speaking of your father's past and saying that the origin of his fortune had always remained a mystery. This person asked me where your father had made his fortune, so I replied: "In Greece." And he said: "Then, write to Janina."'

'Who gave you this advice?'

'It was the Count of Monte Cristo, your friend.'

'The count told you to write to Janina?'

'Yes and I did so. Do you want to see the letters? I can show them to you.'

Albert and Beauchamp exchanged looks.

'Monsieur,' Beauchamp said, up to this point having taken no part in the conversation, 'it appears that you are accusing the count when he is away from Paris and cannot answer the charge.'

'I am accusing no one, Monsieur,' said Danglars. 'I am telling you, and I shall repeat in front of the Count of Monte Cristo what I have just said before you.'

'Does the count know what reply you received?'

'I showed it to him.'

'Did he know that my father's Christian name was Fernand and his surname Mondego?'

'Yes, I told him that a long time ago. Moreover, I only acted in all this as anyone else would, and I may perhaps have done less than many others. When, on the day after this reply, at the instigation of Monsieur de Monte Cristo, your father came to ask me for my daughter officially, as one does when one wants to conclude a match, I refused. I refused outright, it's true, but without giving an explanation and without making a stir. Why should I cause any trouble? What do I care for the honour or dishonour of Monsieur de Morcerf? There's no percentage in it for me either way.'

Albert felt himself blush. There could be no further doubt: Danglars was defending himself basely, but with the confidence of a man who is speaking, if not the whole truth, at least a part of it – not for motives of conscience, admittedly, but through fear. In any case, what did Morcerf want? It was not either the greater or lesser guilt of Danglars or Monte Cristo; it was a man who would answer for the offence, whether great or small, a man who would fight; and it was clear that Danglars would not.

Then, one by one, certain things that he had forgotten or failed to notice became visible to his eyes and present in his memory: Monte Cristo knew everything, since he had bought the daughter of Ali Pasha; and, knowing everything, he had advised Danglars to write to Janina. Once he knew the reply, he had granted Albert's wish to be introduced to Haydée; and, once in her presence, he had allowed the conversation to turn to the death of Ali, not objecting to Haydée's story – but no doubt instructing the young woman, in the few words of Romaic that he spoke to her, not to allow Morcerf to recognize his father. Moreover, had he not requested Morcerf to avoid mentioning his father's name in front of Haydée? Finally he had taken Albert to Normandy at the very moment when he knew that the scandal would break. There could no longer be any doubt: all this was part of a plot and, without any doubt, Monte Cristo was in collusion with his father's enemies.

Albert led Beauchamp into a corner and told him what he thought. 'You are right,' Beauchamp said. 'Monsieur Danglars is only implicated in the crude, operational part of what has happened. If you want an explanation, you must ask Monte Cristo for it.'

Albert turned around. 'Monsieur,' he said to Danglars, 'you will understand that I am not definitively taking my leave of you. I still need to confirm that your charges are correct and I shall go at once to do so from the Count of Monte Cristo.' And, bowing to the banker, he left with Beauchamp, without appearing to pay any further heed to Cavalcanti.

Danglars accompanied them to the door and there repeated his assurance to Albert that he felt no personal animosity towards the Comte de Morcerf.

LXXXVIII

THE INSULT

As they were leaving the banker's, Beauchamp stopped Morcerf. 'Listen,' he warned, 'just now I said, while we were at Monsieur Danglars', that the person you should ask for an explanation was Monsieur de Monte Cristo.'

'Yes, and we are going to see him.'

'One moment, Morcerf. Think before you go to the count's.'

'What do you want me to think about?'

'The seriousness of this step.'

'Is it more serious than going to see Monsieur Danglars?'

'Yes. Monsieur Danglars was a man of money and, as you know, men of money have too precise an idea of the capital they are risking to fight easily. The other, on the contrary, is a gentleman, at least in appearance. Are you not afraid of discovering the bravo beneath the gentleman?'

'I am afraid of only one thing, which is to discover a man who will not fight.'

'Have no fear,' said Beauchamp. 'This one will fight. I am even afraid of something, namely that he will fight too well. Take care!'

'My friend,' Morcerf said, with a fine smile, 'that's all I ask. And the best that could happen to me is to be killed for my father: that would save all of us.'

'Your mother would die of grief!'

'Yes, my poor mother,' said Albert, putting a hand to his eyes. 'I know. But it is better for her to die of grief than of shame.'

'So you have really made up your mind, Albert?'

'Yes.'

'Come on, then. But do you think we will find him?'

'He was due to return a few hours after me and will certainly have done so.'

They got into the cab and ordered the driver to take them to No. 30, Avenue des Champs-Elysées.

Beauchamp wanted to go in alone, but Albert pointed out to him that this affair was so unusual that it allowed them to ignore the usual duelling etiquette. The young man was acting in this case in such a sacred cause that Beauchamp could do nothing except bow to his will, so he did as Morcerf said and agreed to follow him.

Albert covered the distance between the concierge's lodge and the front steps in a single bound. Baptistin came to greet him. The count had indeed returned, but he was in the bath and had forbidden him to admit anyone at all.

'And after the bath?' Morcerf asked.

'Monsieur will take dinner.'

'And after dinner?'

'Monsieur will sleep for an hour.'

'And then?'

'And then he will go to the opera.'

'Are you sure of that?' Albert asked.

'Absolutely sure. Monsieur ordered his horses for eight o'clock precisely.'

'Very well,' said Albert. 'That is all I wanted to know.' Then, turning to Beauchamp, he added: 'If you have anything to do, Beauchamp, do it at once. If you have any appointment for this evening, postpone it until tomorrow. You realize that I am counting on you to come to the opera. If you can, bring Château-Renaud with you.'

Beauchamp took advantage of the leave he was granted and left Albert, promising to collect him at a quarter to eight.

As soon as he got rid of him, Albert informed Franz, Debray and Morrel of his wish to see them that evening at the opera. Then he went to see his mother who, since the events of the previous day, had barred her door to visitors and remained in her room. He found her in bed, overwhelmed by this public humiliation.

The sight of Albert produced the effect one might imagine on Mercédès. She clasped her son's hand and burst into tears; but the tears relieved her.

Albert remained standing silently for a moment beside his mother. From his pale face and furrowed brow one could see that the edge was gradually wearing off the thirst for vengeance in his heart. 'Mother,' he asked, 'do you know any enemies of Monsieur de Morcerf's?'

Mercédès shuddered; she noticed that the young man did not say: 'of my father's'.

'My dear,' she said, 'people of the count's standing have many enemies whom they do not even know. In any case, the enemies whom one does know are clearly not the most dangerous.'

'Yes, I know that, so I am appealing to all your perspicacity. Mother, you are a woman of such superior intellect, that nothing escapes you!'

'Why do you say that?'

'Because you will have noticed, for example, that on the evening of our ball Monsieur de Monte Cristo did not want to take any refreshment in our house.'

Mercédès raised herself on one arm, trembling with fever. 'Monsieur de Monte Cristo!' she exclaimed. 'What has he to do with your question to me?'

'You know, mother, Monsieur de Monte Cristo is almost a man of the East and an Oriental; in order not to interfere with his freedom to take revenge, he never eats or drinks in his enemy's house.'

'What are you saying, Albert?' Mercédès asked, turning whiter than the sheet that covered her. 'Monsieur de Monte Cristo – one of our enemies? Whoever told you such a thing? Why? You are mad, Albert. Monsieur de Monte Cristo has shown nothing but courtesy towards us. He saved your life and you yourself introduced him to us. Oh please, my son, if you have any such ideas, discard them; and if I have anything to say to you – even more, if I have any prayer to make to you – it is that you should remain in good standing with him.'

'Mother,' the young man said, glowering, 'you have your own reasons for telling me to remain on good terms with this man.'

'I!' Mercédès cried, blushing as rapidly as she had previously gone pale, then almost immediately turning even whiter than before.

'Yes, certainly; and the reason must surely be that he can only do us harm?'

Mercédès shuddered and, looking enquiringly at her son, said: 'You are speaking strangely and it seems to me that you have some odd prejudices. What has the count done to you? Three days ago you were with him in Normandy. Three days ago, I considered him, as you also did, your best friend.'

An ironic smile flickered across Albert's lips. Mercédès saw it and, with the combined instincts of a wife and a mother, she guessed everything; but, strong and prudent, she hid her anxiety.

Albert fell silent, and a moment later the countess resumed the conversation. 'You came to ask me how I was,' she said. 'And I will tell you frankly, my dear, that I am not feeling well. You should stay here, Albert, and keep me company. I have a need not to be alone.'

'Mother,' the young man replied, 'I should obey you, and you know how happily, if urgent and important business did not oblige me to leave you for the whole evening.'

'Very well, Albert,' she replied, sighing. 'I should not like to make you a slave to your filial duty.'

Albert pretended not to have heard, kissed his mother and left. Hardly had he closed the door, however, than Mercédès called a trusted servant and ordered him to follow Albert wherever he went and to report back to her immediately. Then she rang for her chambermaid and, weak as she felt, had herself dressed to be prepared for any eventuality.

The task she had given the servant was not hard to carry out. Albert returned home and got dressed, in clothes that were somehow stylish, but not ostentatious. At ten to eight Beauchamp arrived. He had seen Château-Renaud, who had promised to be in the stalls before the curtain went up. Both got into Albert's coupé and he, having no reason to hide where he was going, said aloud: 'To the opera!'

In his impatience he arrived before the curtain went up. Château-Renaud was in his seat and, as he had been told everything by Beauchamp, Albert had no need to explain anything to him. The idea of a son seeking revenge for his father was so natural that Château-Renaud made no attempt to dissuade him, but merely repeated his assurance that he was at Albert's disposal.

Debray had not yet arrived, but Albert knew that he rarely missed a performance at the opera. Albert wandered around the theatre, waiting for the curtain to rise. He did hope to meet Monte Cristo, either in the corridor or on the staircase. The bell called him to his seat and he went to sit in the stalls between Château-Renaud and Beauchamp, but his eyes remained fixed on the side box, which remained obstinately closed throughout the first act.

Finally, at the start of the second act, as Albert was looking at his watch for the hundredth time, the door of the box opened and Monte Cristo, dressed in black, came in and leant on the rail while he looked round the auditorium. Morrel followed him, searching for his sister and brother-in-law. He saw them in a box on the second level and waved.

As the count was running his eyes over the audience, he noticed a pale head and shining gaze that seemed eager to draw his attention; and he did indeed recognize Albert, but the expression he saw on that devastated face must have warned him to give no sign that he had seen him. Without any indication of what he was thinking, he sat down, took his glasses out of their case and turned them in another direction.

However, even though he appeared not to see Albert, the count did not lose sight of him; and when the curtain fell at the end of the second act, his eagle eyes followed the young man as he left the stalls with his two friends. Then he saw the same head appear in a box on the balcony, opposite his own. He anticipated the approaching storm and, when he heard the key turn in the door of his box, even though he was at that moment speaking to Morrel with his most cheerful expression, he knew what to expect and was ready for it.

The door opened. Only then did Monte Cristo turn around and see Albert, white and trembling. Behind him were Beauchamp and Château-Renaud.

'Well, now!' he exclaimed, with the benevolent courtesy that usually distinguished his greeting from the banal politeness of social convention. 'Here is my horseman, at the end of his ride! Good evening, Monsieur de Morcerf.' And the man, so utterly in command of himself, wore an expression of the utmost cordiality.

Only now did Morrel remember the letter that the viscount had sent him in which the latter, with no further explanation, had asked him to come to the opera; and he realized that something dreadful was about to take place.

'We have not come to exchange hypocritical courtesies or pretensions of friendship,' the young man said. 'We have come to ask you for an explanation, Monsieur le Comte.' His trembling voice was loath to emerge from between his clenched teeth.

'Explanation? At the opera?' said the count with his calm voice and penetrating gaze, two signs that infallibly indicate a man who is utterly sure of himself. 'Unfamiliar though I am with Parisian manners, I should not have thought, Monsieur, that this is where one would go to explain oneself.'

'Yet when someone hides away,' Albert retorted, 'when one cannot reach him, on the grounds that he is in the bath, at table or in bed, one must repair to wherever he can be met.'

'I am not hard to find, Monsieur,' said Monte Cristo. 'Only yesterday, unless my memory deceives me, you were staying in my house.'

'Yesterday, Monsieur,' said the young man, whose head was starting to spin, 'I was in your house because I did not know who you were.'

As he spoke these words, Albert raised his voice so that he could be heard by the people in the neighbouring boxes and those passing along the corridor. At the sound of the argument, the people in the boxes turned around and those passing along the corridor stopped behind Beauchamp and Château-Renaud.

'Where have you come from, Monsieur!' Monte Cristo said, without giving the slightest appearance of any emotion. 'You do not appear to be in your right mind.'

'I shall always be sensible enough,' Albert said furiously, 'if I can understand your perfidy and manage to make you understand that I want revenge for it.'

'I don't understand a word of what you are saying,' Monte Cristo retorted. 'Even if I did, you would still be saying it too loudly. I am at home here, Monsieur, and only I have the right to raise my voice above the rest. So kindly leave!' And he showed him the door with a splendidly imperative gesture.

'Oh, I'll get you out of your home all right!' said Albert, convulsively twisting a glove in his hands, while Monte Cristo kept his eyes firmly fixed on it.

'Very well, very well,' he said resignedly. 'You want an argument with me, Monsieur, I can see that. But let me just give you one word of advice, Viscount, and don't forget it: it is a bad habit to shout it from the rooftops when one challenges a person. Not everyone benefits from attracting attention, Monsieur de Morcerf.'

At the name, a murmur of astonishment passed like a shiver among all those who had been observing the scene. Since the previous day the name of Morcerf had been on everyone's lips.

Albert understood the implication of the quip sooner and better than anyone, and made to throw his glove in the count's face; but Morrel grasped his wrist, while Beauchamp and Château-Renaud, fearing that the incident might develop into something more than a challenge, restrained him from behind.

Monte Cristo, without getting up, tipped his chair back and reached out to snatch the damp, crumpled glove from the young man's hand. 'Monsieur,' he said in a terrifying voice, 'I will consider your gauntlet thrown down and send it back wrapped around a bullet. Now leave me or I shall call my servants to throw you out.'

Intoxicated, horrified, wild-eyed, Albert took two steps back, and Morrel seized the opportunity to shut the door.

Monte Cristo took up his lorgnette and went back to his survey of the theatre, as if nothing out of the ordinary had happened. The man had a heart of bronze and a face of marble. Morrel leant over and whispered: 'What did you do to him?'

'I? Nothing, at least nothing personal,' the count replied.

'But there must be some reason for this peculiar incident?'

'The young man is enraged by the Comte de Morcerf's misfortune.'

'Did you have anything to do with that?'

'Haydée was the one who told the House of his father's treachery.'

'Indeed,' said Morrel, 'I was told, though I couldn't believe it, that the Greek slave I saw with you in this very box was the daughter of Ali Pasha.'

'It's absolutely true.'

'Good heavens! Now I understand everything. The incident was premeditated.'

'How is that?'

'Yes, Albert wrote to me to come to the opera this evening. He wanted me to witness his insult to you.'

'Probably,' said Monte Cristo with his imperturbable calm.

'But what will you do with him?'

'With whom?'

'Albert.'

'With Albert?' Monte Cristo replied, in the same voice. 'What will I do with him, Maximilien? Why, as surely as you are here and I am shaking your hand, I shall kill him tomorrow before ten in the morning. That's what I'll do with him.'

Morrel took Monte Cristo's hand in both of his and shuddered to feel how cold and steady it was.

'Oh, Count,' he said. 'His father loves him so much!'

'Don't tell me that!' said Monte Cristo with the first sign of anger that he had allowed himself to show. 'I would make him suffer!'

Morrel dropped the count's hand in amazement. 'Count!' he exclaimed.

'My dear Maximilien,' the count interrupted, 'listen to how admirably Duprez sings that phrase: O, Mathilde, idole de mon âme![1] Now I was the first to spot Duprez in Naples and the first to applaud him. Bravo! Bravo!'

Morrel understood that there was no more to be said, and he waited.

The curtain, which had risen at the end of the incident with Albert, fell shortly after. There was a knock on the door. 'Come in,' said Monte Cristo, his voice not betraying any emotion.

Beauchamp appeared.

'Good evening, Monsieur Beauchamp,' said Monte Cristo, as if meeting the journalist for the first time that evening. 'Do sit down.'

Beauchamp bowed, came in and sat down.

'Monsieur,' he said to Monte Cristo. 'A short time ago, as you will have observed, I accompanied Monsieur de Morcerf.'

'That probably means,' Monte Cristo said with a laugh, 'that you had just had dinner together. I am happy to see that you are more sober than he was, Monsieur Beauchamp.'

'I admit, Monsieur, that Albert was wrong to lose his temper and I have come on my own account to make my excuses to you. But now that my excuses have been made – and mine only, you understand, Count – I have come to tell you that I consider you too honourable a man to refuse to give me some explanation of your relations with the people in Janina; and I shall add a few words about that young Greek woman.'

With a gesture of the lips and eyes, Monte Cristo ordered silence. 'Well now,' he said with a laugh, 'all my expectations are disappointed.'

'What do you mean?' Beauchamp asked.

'No doubt you were in a hurry to give me a reputation for eccentricity: according to you, I am a Lara, a Manfred, a Lord Ruthwen.[2] Then, once the time for seeing me as eccentric has gone, the image is spoiled and you try to turn me into an ordinary man. You want me to be commonplace and vulgar. You even ask me for explanations. Come, come, Monsieur Beauchamp! You are joking!'

'And yet,' Beauchamp replied haughtily, 'there are some occasions when honesty commands us . . .'

'What commands the Count of Monte Cristo,' the strange man interrupted, 'is the Count of Monte Cristo. So, not a word of all this, I beg you. I do what I wish, Monsieur Beauchamp, and believe me, it is always very well done.'

'Sir,' said the young man, 'an honourable person cannot be paid in such coin. One must have guarantees of honour.'

'I am a living guarantee,' said Monte Cristo, imperturbably, but with a threatening light in his eyes. 'We both have blood in our veins which we wish to spill, there is our mutual guarantee. Take that reply back to the viscount and tell him that tomorrow, before ten o'clock, I shall have seen the colour of his.'

'So there is nothing left for me but to make arrangements for the duel.'

'All that is a matter of perfect indifference to me, Monsieur,' said the count. 'There was no need to come and interrupt the performance for such a slight thing. In France, one fights with sword or pistol; in the colonies they take carbines; in Arabia, a dagger. Tell your client that, though I am the injured party, to keep my eccentricity to the very end I shall let him have the choice of weapons and will accept any, without discussion or argument. Any, do you understand? Even a duel by drawing lots, which is always stupid. But with me, it is a different matter: I am sure of winning.'

'Sure of winning!' Beauchamp repeated, looking at the count with alarm.

'Yes, indeed,' said Monte Cristo, lightly shrugging his shoulders. 'Otherwise, I should not fight Monsieur de Morcerf. I shall kill him, I must do it and so it will be. Simply send round to my house this evening to tell me the weapon and the place. I do not like to be kept waiting.'

'Pistols, eight in the morning, in the Bois de Vincennes,' said Beauchamp, somewhat put out, not knowing whether he was dealing with an impudent braggart or a supernatural being.

'Perfect, Monsieur,' said Monte Cristo. 'And now that we have settled that, I beg you, let me watch the performance and ask your friend Albert not to come back this evening: he would do himself no good with all his ill-mannered aggression. Tell him to go home and get some sleep.'

Beauchamp left in astonishment.

'And now,' Monte Cristo said, turning to Morrel, 'I can call on you, can't I?'

'Certainly, Count; I am at your disposal. Yet . . .'

'What?'

'It is important for me to know the true cause . . .'

'Does this mean you are refusing me?'

'Not at all.'

'The cause, Monsieur Morrel?' said the count. 'The young man himself is going forward blindly, without realizing it. The true cause is known only to myself and to God; but I give you my word of honour that God, who does know it, will be on our side.'

'That is enough, Count,' said Morrel. 'Who is your other second?'

'I know no one in Paris whom I would wish to honour in that way apart from yourself, Morrel, and your brother-in-law, Emmanuel. Do you think he would perform this service for me?'

'I can answer for him as for myself, Count.'

'Good! That's all I need. Tomorrow at seven o'clock, at my house then?'

'We shall be there.'

'Hush! the curtain is just rising. Listen. I never miss a note of this opera. It's such wonderful music, *William Tell*!'

LXXXIX

NIGHT

Monte Cristo waited, as he usually did, until Duprez had sung his famous *'Suivez-moi!'*,[1] and only then did he get up and leave.

Morrel left him at the door, repeating his promise to be at the count's, with Emmanuel, the next morning at exactly seven o'clock. Then the count got into his coupé, still calm and smiling. Five minutes later he was home. But one would have not to know the man to mistake the tone in which he said to Ali, as he came in: 'Ali, my ivory-handled pistols!'

Ali brought his master the box, and the count started to examine the weapons with the natural concern of a man who is about to entrust his life to some scraps of lead and metal. These were private weapons that Monte Cristo had had made for target practice in his apartments. A percussion cap was enough to fire the bullet, and from the adjoining room no one could doubt that the count, as they say on the firing ranges, was engaged in getting his eye in.

He was just fitting the weapon in his hand and looking for the bull on a small metal plaque that served him as a target, when the door of his study opened and Baptistin came in. But, even before he had opened his mouth, the count noticed through the still-open door a veiled woman standing in the half-light of the next room. She had followed Baptistin.

She saw the count with a pistol in his hand, she had seen two swords on the table and she ran forward.

Baptistin looked enquiringly at his master. The count gestured to dismiss him and Baptistin left, closing the door behind him.

'Who are you, Madame?' the count asked the veiled woman.

The stranger looked all around her to make sure that she was quite alone then, bending forward as if she wanted to kneel down and clasping her hands, she said in a desperate voice: 'Edmond! You must not kill my son!'

The count took one pace backwards, gave a faint cry and dropped the pistol he was holding.

'What name did you say, Madame de Morcerf?' he asked.

'Yours!' she cried, throwing back her veil. 'Yours, which perhaps I alone have not forgotten. Edmond, it is not Madame de Morcerf who has come to you, it is Mercédès.'

'Mercédès is dead, Madame,' said Monte Cristo. 'I do not know anyone of that name.'

'Mercédès is alive, Monsieur, and Mercédès remembers, for she alone recognized you when she saw you, and even without seeing you, by your voice, Edmond, by the mere sound of your voice. Since that time she has followed you step by step, she has watched you and been wary of you, because she did not need to wonder whose was the hand that has struck down Monsieur de Morcerf.'

'Fernand, you mean, Madame,' Monte Cristo said, with bitter irony in his voice. 'Since we are remembering one another's names, let's remember all of them.'

Monte Cristo had spoken Fernand's name with such hatred that Mercédès felt a shudder of fear run through her whole body.

'You see, Edmond, I was not mistaken!' she cried. 'I was right to say to you: spare my son!'

'Whoever told you, Madame, that I had any quarrel with your son?'

'No one! A mother has second sight. I guessed everything. I followed him to the opera this evening and, from the ground-floor box where I was hiding, I saw everything.'

'If you saw everything, Madame, then you will have seen that Fernand's son insulted me publicly,' Monte Cristo said with dreadful impassivity.

'Oh, have pity!'

'You saw,' he went on, 'that he would have thrown his glove in my face if one of my friends, Monsieur Morrel, had not stayed his arm.'

'Listen to me. My son also guessed what is going on and attributes his father's misfortunes to you.'

'You are confused, Madame,' Monte Cristo said. 'These are not misfortunes, they are a punishment. I am not the one who has struck Monsieur de Morcerf: Providence is punishing him.'

'So why do you take the place of Providence?' Mercédès cried. 'Why do you remember, when it has forgotten? What do they matter to you, Edmond – Janina and its vizier? What wrong did Fernand Mondego do to you by betraying Ali Tebelin?'

'So, Madame,' Monte Cristo replied, 'all this is an affair between the Frankish captain and Vasiliki's daughter. You are right, it does not concern me, and, if I have sworn to take my revenge, it is not on the Frankish captain or on the Count of Morcerf, but on the fisherman Fernand, husband of Mercédès the Catalan.'

'Oh, Monsieur!' the countess exclaimed. 'What a dreadful revenge for a sin which fate drove me to commit – because I am the guilty party, Edmond! If you must take revenge on anyone, let it be on me, because I did not have the strength to withstand your absence and my loneliness.'

'And why was I absent? Why were you all alone?' Monte Cristo cried.

'Because you were arrested, Edmond, and taken prisoner.'

'Why was I arrested? Why was I imprisoned?'

'I don't know,' said Mercédès.

'Yes. You do not know, Madame, or at least I hope you do not. Well, I will tell you. I was arrested and imprisoned because in the café of La Réserve, the very day before I was due to marry you, a man called Danglars wrote this letter which the fisherman Fernand personally took it upon himself to post.' And, going to his bureau, Monte Cristo took out a faded piece of paper, written on in ink the colour of rust, which he handed to Mercédès.

It was the letter from Danglars to the crown prosecutor which the Count of Monte Cristo had removed from the dossier of Edmond Dantès on the day when, disguised as an agent of the house of Thomson and French, he had paid the 200,000 francs to M. de Boville.

Appalled, Mercédès read the following lines:

The crown prosecutor is advised, by a friend of the monarchy and the faith, that one Edmond Dantès, first mate of the *Pharaon*, arriving this morning from Smyrna, after putting in at Naples and Porto Ferrajo, was entrusted by Murat with a letter for the usurper and by the usurper with a letter to the Bonapartist committee in Paris.

Proof of his guilt will be found when he is arrested, since the letter will be discovered either on his person, or at the house of his father, or in his cabin on board the *Pharaon*.

'Oh, God!' said Mercédès, wiping the sweat from her forehead. 'And this letter . . .'

'It cost me two hundred thousand francs to obtain it, Madame,' said Monte Cristo. 'But it was cheap at the price, since it has allowed me today to exonerate myself in your sight.'

'What was the outcome of this letter?'

'That, as you know, was my arrest; what you do not know is how long my imprisonment lasted. What you do not know is that I stayed for fourteen years a quarter of a league away from you, in a dungeon in the Château d'If. What you do not know is that every day during those fourteen years, I repeated the vow of revenge that I made on the first day, even though I did not know that you had married Fernand, the man who denounced me, and that my father was dead, starved to death!'

'By God's law!' Mercédès exclaimed, staggering.

'That, I learned when I left prison, fourteen years after I went in, and this is why I swore, on the living Mercédès and on my dead father, to be avenged on Fernand and . . . I am avenged . . .'

'Are you sure that the unhappy Fernand did this?'

'By my soul, Madame, and in the way I told you. In any case it is not much more disgraceful than having gone over to the English, when he was a Frenchman by adoption; having fought against the Spaniards, when he was one by birth; having betrayed and killed Ali, when he was in Ali's pay. What was the letter that you have just read, compared with such things? An amorous ploy which, I confess and I can understand, might be forgiven by the woman who married the man, but which cannot be forgiven by the lover who was to marry her. Well, now: the French have not had vengeance on the traitor, the Spaniards did not shoot the traitor; and Ali, lying in his tomb, left the traitor unpunished; but I, who have also been betrayed, assassinated and cast into a tomb, I have emerged from that tomb by the grace of God and I owe it to God to take my revenge. He has sent me for that purpose. Here I am.'

The poor woman let her head fall into her hands, her legs gave way beneath her and she fell to her knees.

'Forgive, Edmond,' she said. 'For my sake, forgive, for I love you still.'

The dignity of the wife reined back the impulse of the lover and the mother. Her forehead was bent nearly to the carpet. The count ran over to her and raised her up.

Then, seated on a chair, through her tears, she was able to look at Monte Cristo's masculine features, still imprinted by sorrow and hatred with a threatening look.

'Not crush this accursed race?' he muttered. 'Disobey God, who roused me up to punish it! Impossible, Madame, impossible!'

'Edmond,' the poor mother said, trying everything in her power. 'My God, when I call you Edmond, why do you not call me Mercédès?'

'Mercédès,' Monte Cristo repeated. 'Mercédès! Ah, yes, you are right, this name is still sweet to me when I speak it, and this is the first time for many years that it has sounded so clear as it left my lips. Oh, Mercédès, I have spoken your name with sighs of melancholy, with groans of pain and with the croak of despair. I have spoken it frozen with cold, huddled on the straw of my dungeon. I have spoken it raging with heat and rolling around on the stone floor of my prison. Mercédès, I must have my revenge, because for fourteen years I suffered, fourteen years I wept and cursed. Now, I say to you, Mercédès, I must have my revenge!' And, fearful that he might give way to the prayers of the woman whom he had loved so much, the count summoned up his memories in the service of his hatred.

'Take your revenge, Edmond,' the poor woman said. 'But take it on those who are guilty. Be avenged on him, on me, but not on my son!'

'It is written in the Holy Book that the sins of the fathers shall be visited upon the children even unto the third and fourth generation,' Monte Cristo replied. 'Since God dictated those very words to his prophet, why should I be better than God?' And he gave a sigh that was like a roar, and clasped his fine hair in his hands.

'Edmond,' Mercédès went on, holding out her hands to him. 'As long as I have known you, I have worshipped your name and respected your memory. My friend, do not ask me to tarnish that noble and pure image which is constantly reflected in the mirror of my heart. Edmond, if you knew all the prayers that I have offered up to God on your behalf, as long as I hoped you were still living and since I believed you were dead; yes, alas, dead! I thought that your corpse was buried beneath some dark tower or cast into one of those depths into which jailers throw the bodies of dead prisoners; and I wept! But what could I do for you, Edmond, except pray or weep? Listen to me. Every night for ten years, I had the same dream. They said that you had tried to escape, that you had taken the place of another prisoner, that you had climbed into a dead man's shroud and that then they had flung the living corpse from the top to the bottom of the Château d'If, and that only the cry which you gave on crashing against the rocks revealed the substitution to your burial party, who had become your executioners. Well, Edmond, I swear on the head of the son on whose behalf I now beseech you, Edmond: for ten years every night I saw men throwing something shapeless and nameless from the top of a rock; and every night, for ten years, I heard a dreadful cry that woke me up, shivering and icy cold. Oh, believe me, Edmond, I too, wrongdoer though I was, I too have suffered!'

'Did you experience your father's death in your absence? Did you see the woman you loved hold out her hand to your rival, while you were croaking in the depths of the abyss?' Monte Cristo plunged his hands deeper into his hair.

'No,' Mercédès said, interrupting him. 'But I have seen the man I loved preparing to become the murderer of my son!'

She said these words with such overwhelming grief, in such a desperate voice, that when he heard it a sob rose in the count's throat. The lion was tamed, the avenging angel overcome.

'What do you want?' he said. 'Your son's life? Well, then: he shall live.'

Mercédès gave a cry that brought two tears to Monte Cristo's eyes, but these two tears disappeared almost immediately, God doubtless having sent some angel to gather them as being more precious in His eyes than the richest pearls of Gujarat or Ophir.

She clasped the count's hand and raised it to her lips. 'Oh, Edmond!' she cried, 'Thank you, thank you! You are as I have never ceased to think of you, as I have never ceased to love you. Oh, now I can say it!'

'So much the better,' Monte Cristo replied, 'that poor Edmond will not have long to be loved by you. The corpse is about to return to its tomb and the ghost into the darkness.'

'What are you saying, Edmond?'

'I am saying that, since you command me to do so, Mercédès, I must die.'

'Die! Whoever said such a thing? Who speaks of dying? Where do you get such ideas?'

'Surely you don't imagine that, having been publicly insulted, in front of a theatre full of people, in the presence of your friends and those of your son, provoked by a child who will boast of my forgiveness as a victory . . . you do not imagine, I say, that I have any desire to live for a moment longer. What I have loved most after you, Mercédès, is myself, that is to say my dignity, that is to say the strength that made me superior to other men. That strength was my life. You have shattered it with a word. I die.'

'But the duel will not take place, Edmond, since you have forgiven him.'

'It shall take place, Madame,' Monte Cristo said solemnly. 'But my blood will slake the earth instead of your son's.'

Mercédès gave a great cry and rose to her feet. Then suddenly she stopped.

'Edmond,' she said. 'There is a God above us, since you are alive and I have seen you again, and I trust in Him in the very depths of my heart. In expectation of His aid, I shall rely on your word. You said that my son will live: this is true, isn't it?'

'Yes, he shall, Madame,' Monte Cristo said, astonished that, without any further exclamation or other sign of surprise, Mercédès had accepted the heroic sacrifice he was making for her.

She offered him her hand. 'Edmond,' she said, her eyes filling with tears as she looked at the man before her, 'how fine it is of you, how great what you have just done, how sublime to have had pity on a poor woman who put herself at your mercy, when everything seemed to be contrary to her hopes. Alas, I have been aged more by sorrow than by the years and I can no longer recall to my Edmond's memory, even by a look or a smile, that Mercédès whom he once gazed on for so many hours on end. Believe me, Edmond, I told you that I too have suffered much. I repeat, it is dreary indeed to see one's life pass without recalling a single joy or retaining a single hope; but this proves that all is not finished on this earth. No! All is not finished: I feel it from what still remains in my heart. Oh, Edmond, I say again: it is fine, it is great, it is sublime to forgive as you have just done!'

'You say that, Mercédès. What would you say if you knew the

extent of the sacrifice I am making for you? Suppose that the Lord God, after creating the world, after fertilizing the void, had stopped one-third of the way through His creation to spare an angel the tears that our crimes would one day bring to His immortal eyes. Suppose that, having prepared everything, kneaded everything, seeded everything, at the moment when He was about to admire his work, God had extinguished the sun and with His foot dashed the world into eternal night, then you will have some idea ... Or, rather, no ... No, even then you cannot have any idea of what I am losing by losing my life at this moment.'

Mercédès looked at the count with an expression that showed her combined astonishment, admiration and gratitude.

Monte Cristo put his head into his burning hands, as if no longer able to support the weight of his thoughts.

'Edmond,' said Mercédès, 'I have only one more word to say to you.'

The count gave a bitter smile.

'Edmond,' she went on, 'you will see that even though my brow has paled, my eyes have lost their sparkle, my beauty is gone and, in short, Mercédès no longer looks like herself, as far as her face is concerned ... you will see that her heart is still the same! Farewell, then, Edmond. I have nothing further to ask of God ... I have rediscovered you as noble and as great as ever. Adieu, Edmond, thank you and farewell!'

The count did not reply.

Mercédès opened the door of the study, and had vanished before he emerged from the deep and painful reverie into which his lost vengeance had plunged him. One o'clock was striking on the clock on the Invalides when the carriage bearing away Madame de Morcerf, as it rolled across the paving-stones of the Champs-Elysées, made Monte Cristo look up. 'Senseless!' he said. 'The day when I resolved to take my revenge ... senseless, not to have torn out my heart!'

XC
THE ENCOUNTER

After the departure of Mercédès, everything in Monte Cristo's house lapsed into darkness. Around him and within him his thoughts ceased, and his energetic mind slumbered as the body does after a supreme effort.

'What!' he thought, while the lamp and the candles burned sadly away and the servants waited impatiently in the antechamber. 'What! The structure that was so long in building, which demanded so much anxious toil, has been demolished at a single blow, a single word, a breath of air! What, this "I" that I thought was something; this "I", of which I was so proud; this "I" that I saw so small in the dungeons of the Château d'If and managed to make so great, will be, tomorrow, a speck of dust! Alas, it is not the death of the body that I mourn: is not that destruction of the vital spark the point of rest towards which everything tends, for which every unfortunate yearns, that material calm which I have so long sighed for and towards which I was proceeding by the painful road of hunger when Faria appeared in my cell? What is death? One step further into calm and two perhaps into silence. No, it is not life that I regret, but the ruin of my plans, which were so long in devising and so laborious to construct. Providence, which I thought favoured them, was apparently against them. God did not want them to come to fruition!

'This burden which I took on, almost as heavy as a world, and which I thought I could carry to the end, was measured according to my desire and not my strength. I shall have to put it down when my task is barely half completed. Ah, I shall have to become a fatalist, after fourteen years of despair and ten years of hope had made me a believer in Providence!

'And all this, good Lord, because my heart, which I thought was dead, was only numbed; because it awoke, it beat; because I gave way to the pain of that beating which had been aroused in my breast by the voice of a woman!

'And yet,' the count went on, lapsing more and more into antici-pation of the dreadful future that Mercédès had made him accept, 'and yet it is impossible that that woman, with such a noble heart, could for purely selfish reasons have agreed to let me be killed, when I am so full of life and strength! It is not possible that she should take her maternal love or, rather, her maternal delirium, that far! Some virtues, when taken to the extreme, become crimes. No, she will have imagined some touching scene in which she will come and throw herself between our swords, and what was sublime here will become ridiculous in the field.' And a blush of pride rose to his cheeks.

'Ridiculous!' he repeated. 'And the ridicule will rebound on me! I, ridiculous! Never! I would rather die!' And by exaggerating in advance the worst possible outcome on the morrow, which he had called down on himself by promising Mercédès to let her son live, the count eventually told himself: 'Folly, folly, folly! To place oneself as a sitting target in front of that young man's pistol! He will never believe that my death is suicide, and yet it is important for the honour of my memory . . . This is not vanity, is it, God? Rightful pride, nothing more . . . It is important for the honour of my memory that the world knows that I myself agreed, of my own will, by my own free choice, to stay my arm when it was raised to strike; and that I struck myself down with that hand so powerfully protected against others. I shall do it. I must.' And, grasping a pen, he took a sheet of paper from the secret drawer in his bureau and, at the bottom of this sheet, which was the will that he had drawn up on arriving in Paris, added a sort of codicil that would make his death clear to the least perceptive reader.

'I am doing this, God, as much for your honour as for mine,' he said, raising his eyes to heaven. 'For the past ten years, I have considered myself as the emissary of your vengeance, God; and, apart from this Morcerf, there are other wretches – Danglars, Villefort – who must not imagine that chance has rid them of their enemy; and nor should Morcerf himself. On the contrary, let them know that Providence, which had already pronounced sentence on them, has been revised by the sole power of my will, that the punishment that awaited them in this world, now awaits them in the next, and that they have merely exchanged time for eternity.'

While he was hovering amid these uncertainties, the nightmare of a man kept awake by pain, daylight began to whiten the window-panes and shed its light on the pale-blue paper under his hands, on which he had just written this supreme justification of Providence. It was five o'clock.

Suddenly, a faint sound reached his ears. Monte Cristo thought he had heard something like a muffled sigh. He turned around, looked about him and saw no one; but the noise was repeated so clearly that doubt became certainty.

He got up and quietly opened the drawing-room door. On a chair, her arms hanging over the sides and her beautiful pale head leaning back, he saw Haydée, who had placed herself in front of the door so that he could not leave without seeing her – but sleep, which is so potent to subdue youth, had surprised her after the exhaustion of the previous day. Even the sound of the door opening could not rouse her from her sleep.

Monte Cristo turned on her a look full of tenderness and regret. 'She remembered that she had a son,' he said, 'but I forgot I had a daughter!' Then, sadly shaking his head: 'Poor Haydée! She wanted to see me and talk to me; she must have feared or guessed something. Oh, I cannot go without saying farewell to her. I cannot die without entrusting her to someone.'

He returned quietly to his desk and wrote beneath the first lines:

'I bequeath to Maximilien Morrel, captain of spahis and son of my former master, Pierre Morrel, shipowner of Marseille, the sum of twenty million francs, a part of which he will give to his sister Julie and to his brother-in-law Emmanuel, provided he does not think that this excess of wealth might threaten their happiness. These twenty millions are buried in my caves on Monte Cristo, the secret of which is known to Bertuccio.

'If his heart is free and he wishes to marry Haydée, daughter of Ali Pasha of Janina, whom I have brought up with the love of a father and who has shown the affection of a daughter towards me, then he will carry out, if not the last impulse of my will, at least the last desire of my heart.

'The present will has already appointed Haydée heiress to the rest of my fortune, consisting of lands, liquid assets in England, Austria and Holland, and movable property in my different palaces and houses; and which, after these twenty millions have been subtracted, could still amount to sixty million francs.'

He had just finished writing this last line when a cry behind him made the pen fall from his hand. 'Haydée,' he said. 'Did you read it?'

The young woman, awakened by the daylight falling on her

eyelids, had got up and come in to the count without him hearing her light steps, muffled by the carpet.

'Oh, my lord,' she said, clasping her hands. 'Why are you writing at such an hour? Why are you bequeathing me all your fortune, my lord? Are you leaving me?'

'I am going on a journey, my angel,' Monte Cristo said with an expression of infinite melancholy and tenderness. 'And if some misfortune should befall me . . .' He paused.

'Well?' the young woman asked in an authoritative voice that the count had not heard before. It made him shudder.

'Well, if some misfortune should befall me,' he continued, 'I want my girl to be happy.'

Haydée smiled sadly and shook her head. 'Are you thinking about death, my Lord?' she asked.

'It's a salutary thought, my child, the sages say.'

'Well, then, if you die,' she said, 'leave your wealth to someone else, because if you die . . . I shall no longer need anything.' Taking the paper, she tore it into four parts, which she scattered in the middle of the room. After that, exhausted by this expenditure of energy, so unusual for a slave girl, she fell to the ground, not asleep this time, but in a faint.

Monte Cristo bent over her and lifted her in his arms. Seeing her pale complexion, her lovely closed eyes, this beautiful body, senseless, as though in abandon . . . for the first time it occurred to him that she might perhaps love him in some way other than that in which a daughter loves her father. 'Alas!' he murmured, with profound despondency. 'So I might yet have been happy!'

He carried Haydée into her apartments, entrusted her, still sense-less, to the care of her women, and, returning to his study (and this time locking the door behind him), he recopied the torn will.

Just as he was coming to the end, he heard the noise of a cab driving into the courtyard. He went over to the window and saw Maximilien and Emmanuel getting out. 'Good – about time!' he said. And he sealed his will with three seals.

A moment later he heard the sound of footsteps in the drawing-room and went to open the study door himself. Morrel appeared on the threshold. It was twenty minutes before the appointed time.

'I may be early, Count,' he said. 'But I admit frankly that I have been unable to sleep for a minute, and the same was true of everyone in our house. I needed to see you, strengthened by your courage and confidence, to recover myself.'

Monte Cristo could not let this proof of affection go unacknowledged, and it was not his hand but both arms that he opened to greet him, saying, in a voice full of emotion: 'Morrel, it is a fine day for me when I feel myself to have gained the affection of a man such as you. Good morning, Monsieur Emmanuel. So, Maximilien, are you coming with me?'

'By heaven!' said the young captain. 'Did you ever doubt it?'

'But suppose I were in the wrong . . .'

'Listen: I watched you yesterday throughout that incident when you were provoked, and all last night I was thinking of your self-confidence. I decided that justice must be on your side, or else one can no longer trust in the look on a man's face.'

'Yet Albert is your friend, Morrel.'

'A mere acquaintance, Count.'

'Did you meet him for the first time on the day we met?'

'Yes, that's right. Well, then, you see? You had to remind me before I remembered it.'

'Thank you, Morrel.' Then, striking the bell, he said, when Ali at once answered the call: 'Take this to my notary. It's my will, Morrel. When I am dead, please go and consult it.'

'What do you mean,' said Morrel, '. . . when you are dead?'

'Oh, one must prepare for any eventuality, dear friend. But what did you do yesterday after you left me?'

'I went to Tortoni's where, as I expected, I found Beauchamp and Château-Renaud. I must admit I was looking for them.'

'Why, since everything was settled?'

'Come, Count, this matter is serious, unavoidable.'

'Did you ever doubt that?'

'No. The insult was public and everyone was already talking about it.'

'So?'

'So, I hoped to have a change of weapons and substitute swords for pistols. Pistols are blind.'

'Did you succeed?' Monte Cristo asked, with an imperceptible glimmer of hope.

'No, because they know your skill with the sword.'

'Pah! Who gave my secret away?'

'The fencing masters who were worsted by you.'

'So you failed?'

'They refused outright.'

'Morrel,' the count said, 'have you ever seen me fire a pistol?'

'No, never.'

'Well, we have time. Watch.'

Monte Cristo took the pistols that he had been holding when Mercédès came in and, sticking an ace of clubs to the board, he shot off each of the four points of the club. Morrel went paler with every shot. He examined the bullets with which Monte Cristo had achieved this *tour de force* and saw that they were no larger than buckshot.

'It's terrifying,' he said. 'Look, Emmanuel!' Then, turning back to Monte Cristo, he said: 'Count, in heaven's name, don't kill Albert. The wretch has a mother!'

'Indeed he has,' said Monte Cristo. 'And I have none.'

Morrel shuddered at the voice in which these words were spoken.

'You are the injured party, Count.'

'Certainly. What does that mean?'

'It means that you will fire first.'

'I will?'

'Oh, yes. That much I did manage to obtain or, rather, I insisted on it. We are making enough concessions to them: they had to agree to that.'

'From how many paces?'

'Twenty.'

A terrible smile passed over the count's lips. 'Morrel,' he said, 'don't forget what you have just seen.'

'So I am counting on your human feelings to save Albert,' the young man said.

'My feelings?' said the count.

'Or your generosity, my friend. Since you are so sure of hitting your mark, I can say something to you that would be ridiculous if I said it to anyone else.'

'Which is?'

'Break his arm, wound him, but don't kill him.'

'Now listen to this, Morrel,' said the count. 'I need no encouragement to deal gently with Monsieur de Morcerf. Indeed Monsieur de Morcerf, I can tell you now, will be treated so kindly that he will go home quietly with his two friends, while I . . .'

'You will . . . what?'

'That's another matter. I shall be brought back.'

'Come, come!' cried Maximilien, beside himself.

'It's as I am telling you, my dear Morrel. Monsieur de Morcerf will kill me.'

Morrel looked at the count like a man who no longer understands what is being said.

'What has happened to you since yesterday evening, Count?'

'What happened to Brutus on the eve of the Battle of Philippi:[1] I have seen a ghost.'

'And this ghost?'

'This ghost, Morrel, told me that I had lived long enough.'

Maximilien and Morrel exchanged looks.

Monte Cristo took out his watch. 'Let's go,' he said. 'It is five to seven, and the appointment is for exactly eight o'clock.'

A carriage was waiting, ready harnessed. Monte Cristo got into it with his two seconds.

Crossing the corridor, he paused to listen by a door. Maximilien and Emmanuel, who had tactfully carried on for a few steps, thought they heard a sigh answering a sob.

As the clock struck eight, they arrived at the meeting-place. 'Here we are,' said Morrel, putting his head out of the window. 'We are the first.'

'The gentleman will excuse me,' said Baptistin, who had accompanied his master, in a state of unspeakable terror, 'but I believe I can see a carriage over there, under the trees.'

'So there is,' said Emmanuel. 'I can see two young men walking together. They seem to be waiting.'

Monte Cristo jumped lightly down from his barouche and offered Emmanuel and Maximilien his hand so that they could follow. Maximilien kept the count's hand in his. 'That's better,' he said. 'There's the sort of hand I like to see on a man whose life depends on the rightness of his cause.'

Unobtrusively Monte Cristo held Morrel back a few paces behind his brother-in-law. 'Maximilien,' he said, 'is your heart pledged to anyone?'

Morrel looked at him with astonishment.

'I'm not asking you to confide any secrets in me, my good fellow. It is a simple question, and all I ask is that you should answer yes or no.'

'I am in love with a young woman, Count.'

'Very much in love?'

'More than life itself.'

'Ah, well,' said Monte Cristo. 'That's another hope gone.' Then he added under his breath, with a sigh: 'Poor Haydée!'

'I must say, Count, if I didn't know you so well, I should think you less resolute than you are!' said Morrel.

'Because I am sighing at the thought of someone I must leave behind? Now, now, Morrel, does a soldier know so little about courage? Do I mind losing my life? What can it mean, to live or die, to me, who have spent twenty years hovering between life and death? In any case have no fear, Morrel: even if this were a weakness, it would be for your eyes alone. I know that the world is a drawing-room from which one must retire politely and honourably, that is to say, with a bow, after paying one's gaming debts.'

'That's better,' said Morrel. 'Now you're talking. By the way, have you brought your weapons?'

'Why should I? I hope that these gentlemen will have theirs.'

'I shall find out,' said Morrel.

'Yes, but no negotiation, you understand?'

'Oh, rest assured of that.'

Morrel crossed over to Beauchamp and Château-Renaud. The latter, seeing Maximilien coming, advanced to meet him. The three young men greeted one another, if not with warmth, at least politely.

'I beg your pardon, gentlemen,' said Morrel. 'I don't see Monsieur de Morcerf.'

'He sent a message to us this morning,' Château-Renaud replied, 'saying that he would join us here.'

'Ah!' said Morrel.

Beauchamp took out his watch. 'Five past eight: no time has been lost, Monsieur Morrel,' he said.

'That was not why I remarked on it,' Maximilien replied.

'In any event,' said Château-Renaud, interrupting, 'here is a carriage.'

A carriage was proceeding at a full trot down one of the avenues leading to the crossroads at which they were standing.

'Gentlemen,' said Morrel, 'you have doubtless brought some pistols with you. Monsieur de Monte Cristo has said he is ready to waive his right to use his own weapons.'

'We anticipated this courteous gesture by the count,' Beauchamp replied. 'I have brought some pistols which I purchased a week or ten days ago, thinking I might need them for an affair such as this one. They are entirely new and have never been fired. Would you like to inspect them?'

'Oh, Monsieur Beauchamp,' said Morrel, bowing. 'Since you assure me that Monsieur de Morcerf is unacquainted with these weapons, I suppose you must realize that your word is enough?'

'Gentlemen,' said Château-Renaud. 'It was not after all Morcerf whom we saw arriving in that carriage. It was, believe it or not, Franz and Debray!'

As he said it, the two young men in question were coming over to them. 'You here, gentlemen!' Château-Renaud said, shaking hands with each of them. 'What brings you?'

'Albert does,' said Debray. 'He sent a message this morning for us to be here.'

Beauchamp and Château-Renaud looked at each other in astonishment.

'Gentlemen,' said Morrel, 'I may have the answer.'

'Tell us!'

'Yesterday afternoon, I received a letter from Monsieur de Morcerf asking me to be at the opera.'

'So did I,' said Debray.

'So did I,' said Franz.

'And so did we,' said Château-Renaud and Beauchamp.

'He wanted you to be present at the provocation,' said Morrel. 'Now he wants you to be present at the duel.'

'Yes,' the young men said. 'That must be it, Monsieur Maximilien. You are quite probably right.'

'But, in spite of all that,' Château-Renaud muttered, 'Albert hasn't arrived. He is ten minutes late.'

'Here he is!' said Beauchamp. 'On horseback. Look: he's galloping along, with his servant behind him.'

'How rash and foolish of him,' Château-Renaud said. 'To come on horseback when he is going to fire a pistol. I thought I had trained him better than that!'

'Just look,' said Beauchamp. 'He's wearing a collar, his coat open, a white waistcoat ... Why didn't he draw a target on his stomach? It would have been quicker and easier altogether!'

While they were talking, Albert had come within ten yards of the group. He pulled up his horse, jumped down and threw the reins to his servant. Then he began to walk over to them.

He was pale, his eyes red and swollen. It was clear that he had not slept a wink the whole night. His whole face was imprinted with an air of grave sadness that was uncommon in him.

'Thank you, gentlemen,' he said, 'for being so kind as to accept my invitation. Believe me, I am most grateful for this mark of friendship.'

As Morcerf approached, Morrel had stepped back some ten yards and was standing apart from the rest.

'And also to you, Monsieur Morrel,' said Albert. 'I owe you my thanks. Please come over, you are welcome here.'

'Monsieur,' said Maximilien, 'perhaps you are not aware that I am here as a second to the Count of Monte Cristo?'

'I was not sure of it, but I suspected as much. So much the better. The more honourable men there are here, the happier I shall be.'

'Monsieur Morrel,' said Château-Renaud, 'you can tell Monsieur de Monte Cristo that Monsieur de Morcerf has arrived and that we are at his disposal.'

Morrel was on the point of fulfilling his mission, while Beauchamp fetched the box of pistols from the carriage.

'Wait, gentlemen,' said Albert. 'I have something to say to the Count of Monte Cristo.'

'In private?' asked Morrel.

'No, Monsieur. In front of everyone.'

Albert's seconds looked at one another in surprise. Franz and Debray whispered a few words to one another; and Morrel, delighted by this unexpected occurrence, went to find the count, who was walking along a side-path with Emmanuel.

'What does he want with me?' he asked.

'I don't know, but he wishes to speak to you.'

'I hope to heaven that he will not tempt Fate with some new insult!'

'I don't believe that is his intention.'

The count came over, with Maximilien and Emmanuel. His face, entirely calm and serene, contrasted strangely with the shattered features of Albert, who also advanced from his side, with the other four young men following. When they were three yards from one another, Albert and the count stopped.

'Gentlemen,' said Albert, 'please come closer. I should not like you to miss a word of what I am about to have the honour to say to Monsieur le Comte de Monte Cristo, because I want you, who will hear it, to repeat what I shall say, however odd my speech may sound to you.'

'I am waiting, Monsieur,' said the count.

'Monsieur,' said Albert, in a voice that was unsteady at first, but which became more confident as he went on, 'I reproached you for having divulged the conduct of Monsieur de Morcerf in Epirus because, however guilty the Count of Morcerf might have been, I did not think you had the right to punish him. Now, Monsieur, I realize that you do have that right. It is not Fernand Mondego's treachery towards Ali Pasha that makes me so willing to forgive you, it is the treachery of the fisherman Fernand towards you and the unimaginable misfortunes that followed on that treachery. So I say, and I proclaim it aloud: yes, Monsieur, you were right to take your revenge on my father; and I, his son, thank you for not having done more!'

If a thunderbolt had fallen among the witnesses to this unexpected scene, it could not have left them more astonished than they were by Albert's statement.

As for Monte Cristo, his eyes had slowly been raised to the heavens with an expression of infinite gratitude; and he was full of admiration for the way in which Albert's fiery temperament – and he had had ample opportunity to observe his courage when faced by the Roman bandits – had immediately bowed to this sudden humiliation. In this, he saw the influence of Mercédès and understood now why her noble heart had not tried to prevent him from making a sacrifice which she knew in advance would be unnecessary.

'Now, Monsieur,' said Albert, 'if you consider that the excuses I have just made are sufficient, I beg you to give me your hand. After the most rare virtue of infallibility, which you seem to possess, the greatest virtue of all in my opinion is to be able to admit when one is wrong. But this confession only concerns me. I acted properly in the eyes of men, but you did so in the eyes of God. Only an angel could save one of us from death, and that angel came down from heaven, if not to make us friends (alas! fate has made that impossible), at least two men who respect one another.'

Monte Cristo, with damp eyes, his chest heaving and his mouth half open, offered Albert a hand which the latter grasped and pressed with a feeling that was akin to awestruck terror.

'Gentlemen,' he said, 'Monsieur de Monte Cristo has been good enough to forgive me. I acted hastily towards him. Haste is a poor counsellor: I acted wrongly. Now my fault is repaired. I hope that the world will not consider me a coward because I have done what my conscience ordered me to do. But, in any case, if people were to be mistaken about me,' the young man said, raising his head proudly, and as if throwing down the gauntlet to his friends and enemies, 'I should try to correct their opinions.'

'What can have happened last night?' Beauchamp asked Château-Renaud. 'It seems to me that we have had a sorry part to play here.'

'Indeed. What Albert has just done is either quite wretched or very noble,' the baron answered.

'Come now, tell me,' Debray asked Franz, 'what does all this mean? What! The Count of Monte Cristo dishonours Monsieur de Morcerf, and the man's son thinks he is in the right! Well, if I had ten Janinas in my family, I should consider myself under only one obligation, and that would be to fight ten duels.'

As for Monte Cristo, with his head bent and his arms hanging by his side, weighed down under twenty-four years of memory, he was not thinking of Albert, or Beauchamp, or Château-Renaud, or any of those around him. He was thinking about that courageous woman who had come to beg him for her son's life, and to whom he had offered his own, and who had just saved him by the awful confession of a family secret which might have killed for ever in this young man the feeling of filial piety. 'Once more, Providence!' he muttered. 'Ah, only now, from this day onwards, am I really certain of being the emissary of God!'

XCI

MOTHER AND SON

With a smile full of melancholy and dignity, the Count of Monte Cristo bowed in farewell to the five young men, then got back into his carriage with Maximilien and Emmanuel. Albert, Beauchamp

and Château-Renaud remained alone on the field of battle. The
young man gave his two seconds a look that, without being timid,
seemed to be asking for their opinion on what had just taken place.

Either because he was the more sensitive or less hypocritical,
Beauchamp was the first to speak. 'Well, well, my dear friend,' he
said, 'let me congratulate you. This is an unexpected conclusion to
a very unpleasant affair.'

Albert remained deep in thought and said nothing. Château-
Renaud just tapped his boot with his cane.

'Are we going, then?' he asked, after an embarrassing silence.

'Whenever you wish,' Beauchamp replied. 'Just give me time to
congratulate Monsieur de Morcerf. He has today demonstrated
such chivalrous . . . and such rare generosity.'

'Ah, yes,' said Château-Renaud.

'It is quite splendid,' Beauchamp went on, 'to be able to keep
such mastery over oneself!'

'Yes, indeed it is,' Château-Renaud said, with a highly significant
chill in his voice. 'I, for my part, would never have managed it.'

'Gentlemen,' Albert interrupted, 'I don't think you have understood that something very serious happened between Monsieur de
Monte Cristo and myself . . .'

'Yes, I'm sure you're right,' Beauchamp said at once, 'but not
every idle young blade will be capable of understanding your
heroism and, sooner or later, you will find yourself having to
explain it to them more forcefully than may be good for the health
of your body or the length of your life. Can I give you some advice,
as a friend? Set off for Naples, the Hague or Saint Petersburg: these
are tranquil spots whose inhabitants are more sensible about a
point of honour than our hotheaded Parisians. Once you are there,
get in plenty of target practice and train yourself with an endless
number of quarte parries and tierce parries. Either be well enough
forgotten to come quietly back to France in a few years, or command enough respect by your gymnastic exercises to ensure your
peace of mind. Aren't I right, Monsieur de Château-Renaud?'

'My opinion entirely,' the nobleman said. 'Nothing attracts a
serious duel like an inconclusive one.'

'Thank you, gentlemen,' Albert answered, with a cold smile. 'I
shall take your advice, not because you are giving it to me, but
because it was already my intention to leave France. I thank you
too for the service you have done me by acting as my seconds. It is

deeply engraved on my heart because, after the words that I have just heard, I can still only remember that service.'

Château-Renaud and Beauchamp looked at one another. The impression on both of them was the same and the tone of voice in which Morcerf had expressed his thanks was so resolute that the position would have become awkward for all of them if the conversation had been prolonged.

'Adieu, Albert,' Beauchamp suddenly said, casually offering the young man his hand, though it did not seem to stir the other from his lethargy. Indeed, he made no response to the proffered hand.

'Adieu,' Château-Renaud said in turn, keeping his little cane in his left hand while giving a wave with the right.

Albert's lips barely muttered, 'Adieu!' His face was more explicit: it expressed a whole symphony of repressed anger, proud disdain and generous indignation.

When his two seconds had left in their carriage, he remained for a while in the same motionless and melancholy pose. Then suddenly, untying the reins of his horse from the little tree around which his servant had knotted them, he leapt lightly into the saddle and galloped back towards Paris. A quarter of an hour later, he was going back into the house in the Rue du Helder.

As he dismounted, he thought he saw his father's pale face looking out from behind the bedroom curtains. Albert turned his head away with a sigh and went into his little pavilion.

Once inside, he cast a final glance at all the luxury that had made his life so pleasant and happy since childhood. He took one final look at the paintings whose faces seemed to smile at him and whose landscapes seemed alive with bright colours. Then he took down the portrait of his mother, removed the canvas from its oak stretcher and rolled it up, leaving the gold frame that had surrounded it black and empty.

After that he put his fine Turkish swords in order, and his fine English guns, his Japanese porcelain, his mounted dishes, his artistic bronzes, signed by Feuchères or Barye,[1] went to the cupboards and put the keys in each one. He threw all the loose change that he had on him into a drawer of his bureau, leaving it open, and followed it by all the ornamental jewels which he had in goblets and boxes or on shelves. He made a precise inventory of everything, putting it at the most visible spot on a table, after removing the books and papers that were cluttering it up.

As he was just starting to do this, despite Albert's order that he wanted to be left alone, his servant came into the room.

'What do you want?' Morcerf asked him, in a voice more of sorrow than of anger.

'I beg your pardon, Monsieur,' said the valet. 'I do know that Monsieur told me not to disturb him, but Monsieur le Comte de Morcerf has just called for me.'

'Well?' Albert asked.

'I did not want to go to the count's without getting my instructions from Monsieur.'

'Why?'

'Because the count no doubt knows that I went with Monsieur to the field.'

'I would imagine so,' said Albert.

'And if he has called for me, it is most probably to question me on what happened. What should I tell him?'

'The truth.'

'So I shall say that the encounter did not take place?'

'Tell him that I made my excuses to the Count of Monte Cristo. Now go!'

The valet bowed and left. Albert returned to his inventory.

Just as he was completing it, his attention was attracted by the noise of horses' hoofs in the courtyard and the wheels of a carriage rattling the windows. He went over to the window and saw his father get into his barouche and drive away.

No sooner had the gate closed behind the count than Albert went up to his mother's apartment and, since no one was there to announce him, went directly to Mercédès' room. There, his heart swelling at what he saw – and what he guessed – he stopped on the threshold.

As if a single soul had inhabited the two bodies, Mercédès was doing in her apartment just what Albert had been doing in his. Everything had been put in order: lace, trimmings, jewels, linen, money, all to be carefully put away in the bottom of drawers, to which the countess was carefully collecting the keys.

Albert saw all these preparations. He knew what they meant and, crying, 'Mother!' threw his arms round Mercédès' neck. The painter who could capture the expression on those two faces would surely have created a fine picture.

All the material evidence of firm determination, which had not worried Albert for himself, made him deeply anxious for his mother. 'What are you doing?' he asked.

'And what were you doing?' she replied.

'Oh, mother!' Albert cried, almost speechless with emotion. 'It is not the same for you as for me. No, you cannot have come to the same decision as I have, because I am here to tell you that I am bidding farewell to your house . . . and to you.'

'So am I, Albert,' Mercédès replied. 'I, too, am leaving. But I confess, I had been counting on my son's going with me. Was I wrong?'

'Mother,' Albert said firmly, 'I cannot make you share the fate that I intend for myself. Henceforth I must live without a name and without a fortune. So as to begin learning this hard existence, I shall have to borrow from a friend the bread that I shall eat between now and the time when I have earned more. That is why, my dearest mother, I was going to see Franz, to ask him to lend me the small sum which I have calculated I shall need.'

'You, my poor child!' Mercédès cried. 'You! Suffer poverty, suffer hunger . . . Oh, don't say that, or you will shatter all my resolutions.'

'But not mine, mother,' Albert replied. 'I am young, I am strong, I believe that I am courageous. Since yesterday, I have learnt what willpower can achieve. Alas, mother, there are people who have suffered greatly, and who did not die, but raised a new fortune on the ruins of all those promises of happiness that heaven had made to them, and on the debris of all the hopes that God had given them! I learned as much, mother, I have seen these men. I know that from the depths of the abyss into which their enemies plunged them, they have risen with such strength and glory that they have overcome their former vanquisher and cast him down in his turn. No, mother, no. From today, I have broken with the past. I accept nothing of it, not even my name, because you understand . . . you do understand this, mother, don't you? Your son cannot bear the name of a man who ought to blush before another.'

'Albert, my child,' said Mercédès, 'if my heart had been stronger, that is the advice I should have given you. Your conscience spoke when my exhausted voice was hushed. Listen to your conscience, my son. You had friends, Albert; break with them for the time being, but do not despair, for your mother's sake. At your age, life is still sweet, my dear Albert: you are barely twenty-two; and since a heart as pure as yours needs a spotless name, take that of my father: he was called Herrera. I know you, Albert. Whatever path you follow, you will soon make this name illustrious in it. So, my friend, come back to the world, made still more brilliant by your past misfortunes; and, if that is not to be, despite all my expectations, at least leave me that hope: from now on, I shall have only that thought, since I have no future and the tomb awaits me on the threshold of this house.'

'I shall do everything, just as you wish, mother,' the young man said. 'Yes, I share your hope: the wrath of heaven will not pursue us, you who are so pure and I so innocent. But since we are resolved, let us act promptly. Monsieur de Morcerf left the house around half an hour ago; so, as you see, we have a good opportunity to avoid scandal or explanations.'

'I shall wait for you, my son,' said Mercédès.

Albert hurried on to the boulevard and brought back a cab which would pick them up outside the house. He recalled a little boarding-house in the Rue des Saints-Pères, where his mother could find simple but decent lodgings. He came back to fetch her.

Just as the cab stopped in front of the door and Albert was getting down, a man came over to him and gave him a letter. Albert recognized him; it was Bertuccio. 'From the count,' he said.

Albert took the letter, opened it and read. After reading it, he looked around for Bertuccio, but the steward had vanished. So Albert, with tears in his eyes and a lump in his throat, went back to Mercédès and, without a word, handed her the letter. She read:

ALBERT,

By showing you that I have guessed the plan that you are about to adopt, I hope also to show you that I understand tact. You are free, you are leaving the count's house and you are going to take your mother, who is as free as you are. But consider, Albert, you owe her more than you can ever repay, poor noble soul though you are. Keep the struggles for yourself, demand suffering for yourself, but spare her the first destitution that must inevitably accompany your first efforts; for she does not even deserve to partake indirectly of the misfortune that has befallen her, and Providence does not wish the innocent to pay for the guilty.

I know that you are both going to leave the house in the Rue du Helder, taking nothing with you. Don't attempt to discover how I found this out. I know it: that's all.

So listen to me, Albert. Twenty-four years ago I returned home to my own country, joyful and proud. I had a fiancée, Albert, a pious young woman whom I adored, and I was bringing back to my fiancée one hundred and fifty *louis* which I had managed to save with much difficulty through continual labour. I intended this money for her and, knowing how treacherous the sea is, I had buried our treasure in the little garden of the house that my father inhabited in Marseille, on the Allées de Meilhan.

Your mother, Albert, knows that dear little house well.

Recently, on my way to Paris, I came through Marseille. I went to see that house with its painful memories. And in the evening, with a spade, I probed the corner where I had buried my treasure. The iron box was still in the same place, no one had touched it. It is in the corner shaded by a fine fig-tree, which my father planted on the day of my birth.

Well, Albert, this money, which was once intended to secure the life and tranquillity of the woman I loved, has now, by a strange and painful twist of fate, returned to its former use. Oh, please understand how I feel – I who could offer millions to that poor woman, and who am merely returning to her a scrap of black bread which has been hidden under my humble roof since the day when I was separated from her whom I loved.

You are a generous man, Albert, but perhaps despite that you are blinded by pride or resentment. If you refuse me, if you ask someone else to do what I have the right to offer you, then I shall say that it was cruel of you to refuse the offer of life to your mother, from a man whose father was driven to starvation, despair and death by your father.

When she had finished reading, Albert remained pale and motionless, waiting for his mother to make up her mind. She looked up to heaven with an indescribable expression and said: 'I accept. He has the right to pay the dowry that I shall take into a convent.' And putting the letter to her heart, she took her son's arm and walked towards the stairs, perhaps with a firmer step than even she had expected.

XCII

SUICIDE

Meanwhile Monte Cristo had also gone back into town with Emmanuel and Maximilien. Their return was merry. Emmanuel did not disguise his joy at seeing war replaced by peace and loudly proclaimed his philanthropic feelings. Morrel, seated in a corner of the carriage, let his brother-in-law's merriment evaporate in words and kept his own joy to himself, allowing it to shine only in his look, though it was no less sincere.

At the Barrière du Trône they met Bertuccio, who was waiting there as motionless as a sentry on duty. Monte Cristo put his head out and exchanged a few words with him; then the steward disappeared.

'Count,' said Emmanuel when they got to the Place Royale, 'please drop me off at my front door, so that my wife will not have a single unnecessary moment of anxiety for either of us.'

'If it was not ridiculous to go around proclaiming one's triumph,' said Morrel, 'I should invite the count into our home. But he too has no doubt some anxious minds to put at rest. Here we are, Emmanuel. Let's say goodbye to our friend and allow him to go on his way.'

'One moment,' said Monte Cristo. 'Don't deprive me in this way of both my companions together. Go in and see your wife, and give her my respects; and you, Morrel, come with me to the Champs-Elysées.'

'Perfect,' said Maximilien. 'Particularly since I have something to attend to in your part of town, Count.'

'Can we expect you for lunch?' asked Emmanuel.

'No,' Morrel replied.

The door closed and the carriage went on its way.

'You see: I brought you good luck,' said Morrel when he was alone with the count. 'Did that occur to you?'

'Certainly,' said Monte Cristo. 'That's why I always want to keep you by me.'

'It's a miracle!' said Morrel, in answer to his own thoughts.

'What is?' asked Monte Cristo.

'What has happened.'

'Yes,' the count said, smiling. 'That's the right word, Morrel: a miracle!'

'Because Albert is brave enough.'

'Very much so,' said Monte Cristo. 'I've seen him sleeping with a dagger hanging over his head.'

'And I know that he has fought twice already, and very well,' Morrel said. 'So how does that square with his behaviour this morning?'

'Your influence, again,' said Monte Cristo, still smiling.

'Lucky for Albert he's not a soldier,' said Morrel.

'Why?'

'Excuses on the field!' the young captain said, shaking his head.

'Now, now,' the count said gently. 'Don't let's give way to these prejudices of ordinary people, Morrel. You must agree that, since Albert is brave, he cannot be a coward, so he must have had some reason to act as he did this morning; and that consequently his behaviour was more heroic than otherwise?'

'No doubt,' said Morrel. 'But, like the Spaniard, I would say: He was not as brave today as he was yesterday.'

'You'll take lunch with me, won't you, Morrel?' the count said, to change the subject.

'No, I'm afraid I must leave you at ten o'clock.'

'So your appointment is for lunch?'

Morrel smiled and shook his head.

'But you must eat somewhere.'

'But suppose I am not hungry?'

'Ah,' said the count, 'I know of only two things which can spoil one's appetite like that: pain – and since, I'm pleased to say, you seem very happy, it can't be that – and love. Moreover, in view of what you told me about your affections, I may perhaps surmise . . .'

'I won't deny it, Count,' Morrel said merrily.

'But you're not telling me about it, Maximilien?' the count said, in a tone of voice that showed how curious he was to learn the secret.

'Didn't I show you this morning that I have a heart?'

In reply, Monte Cristo offered the young man his hand.

'Well,' he continued, 'as that heart is no longer with you in the Bois de Vincennes, it is somewhere else, and I am going to recover it.'

'Go on, then,' the count said slowly. 'Go, my dear friend, but do this for me: if you should encounter any obstacle, remember that I have some power in this world, that I am happy to use it for the benefit of those I love, and that I love you, Morrel.'

'Thank you,' the young man said. 'I shall remember it as selfish children remember their parents when they need them. When I need you, Count – and that time may come – I shall ask for your help.'

'Very well, I have your word. Goodbye, now.'

'Au revoir.'

They had reached the door of the house on the Champs-Elysées. Monte Cristo opened the door and Morrel jumped on to the pavement. Bertuccio was waiting at the steps. Morrel vanished down the Avenue de Marigny and Monte Cristo walked quickly over to Bertuccio. 'Well?' he asked.

'Well, she is leaving her house,' said the steward.

'And her son?'

'Florentin, his valet, thinks he will do the same.'

'Come with me.'

Monte Cristo took Bertuccio into his study, wrote the letter that we have already seen and gave it to the steward. 'Go, and go quickly,' he said, adding: 'Oh, and have Haydée told that I am back.'

'I am here,' said the girl, who had already come down at the sound of the carriage, her face shining with joy at seeing the count safe and sound. Bertuccio went out.

In the first moments after this return which she had awaited with such impatience, Haydée experienced all the emotion of a daughter reunited with a dear father and all the delirium of a mistress greeting an adored lover. And Monte Cristo's joy, though less expansive, was no less great. For hearts which have long suffered, happiness is like dew on soil parched by the sun: both heart and earth absorb this beneficial rain as it falls on them, and nothing appears on the surface. For some days, Monte Cristo had realized something that for a long time he had not dared to believe, which is that there were two Mercédès in the world, and he could once more be happy.

His eyes, burning with gladness, were eagerly fixed on those of Haydée, when suddenly the door opened. The count frowned.

'Monsieur de Morcerf!' said Baptistin, as if the name itself were enough to excuse the interruption. And the count's face did, indeed, lighten. 'Which one?' he asked. 'Viscount or Count?'

'The count.'

'My God!' Haydée exclaimed. 'Is it not over yet?'

'I do not know if it is finished, my dearest child,' Monte Cristo said, taking the young woman's hands. 'What I do know is that you have nothing to fear.'

'But this is the wretch . . .'

'The man is powerless against me, Haydée,' Monte Cristo said. 'The time to fear was when I had to deal with his son.'

'You will never know, master, how I suffered,' she said.

He smiled and put a hand on her head. 'I swear on my father's grave,' he said, 'that if anyone is to suffer, it will not be me!'

'I believe you, my Lord, as if God were speaking to me,' she said, offering him her forehead. Monte Cristo gave her pure and beautiful brow a kiss that made two hearts beat together, one urgently, the other in silence.

'Oh, God!' the count murmured. 'Will you then let me love again . . .' He took the young Greek woman towards a concealed staircase and said to Baptistin: 'Show the Comte de Morcerf into the drawing-room.'

A word of explanation may be needed: this visit, though Monte Cristo had expected it, will no doubt come as a surprise to our readers.

While Mercédès, as we mentioned, was in her apartments making the same sort of inventory as Albert had done in his house, sorting through her jewels, closing her drawers and collecting her keys, so as to leave everything in perfect order, she did not notice a sinister bloodless face appear in the glass window of a door designed to let light enter the corridor; from that point, one could hear as well as see. So it seems more than likely that the person who was watching there, without himself being seen or heard, saw and heard all that went on in Mme de Morcerf's.

From the glass door the pale-faced man went into the Comte de Morcerf's bedroom and, once there, restively lifted the curtain on a window overlooking the courtyard. He stayed there for ten minutes, motionless, silent, listening to the beating of his own heart. It was a long time for him, ten minutes.

It was at this point that Albert, returning from his appointment, saw his father watching for him to return behind the curtain, and turned his head.

The count's eyes opened wide. He knew that Albert's insult to Monte Cristo had been fearful and that, in every country in the world, such an insult would be followed by a duel to the death. So, if Albert was returning safe and sound, then he was avenged.

An unspeakable ray of joy lit his dreary face, like a last ray of sunshine from the sun disappearing into clouds which seem less like its bed than its tomb. But, as we said, he waited in vain for the young man to come up to his apartments to proclaim his triumph to his father. It was understandable that his son, before going out to fight, had not wanted to see the father whose honour he was to avenge; but, once that had been done, why did the son not come and throw himself into his arms?

At this point, since he could not see Albert, the count sent for his servant. As we know, Albert told the servant to hide nothing from him.

Ten minutes later, General de Morcerf appeared on the front steps wearing a black coat, with a military collar, black trousers and black gloves. It appears that he had already given orders because he had hardly put his foot on the last step when his carriage appeared, fully harnessed, out of the coachhouse and drew up in front of him. His valet then arrived with a military cloak, stiffened by the two swords wrapped inside it, which he threw into the carriage; then he closed the door and sat down beside the coachman.

The latter bent over the side of the barouche to take his orders. 'To the Champs-Elysées!' the general said. 'To the Count of Monte Cristo's. Hurry!'

The horses leapt forward under the whip and, five minutes later, pulled up in front of the count's house.

M. de Morcerf opened the door himself and, while the carriage was still moving, jumped down like a young man on to the path, rang, then vanished with his servant through the open door. A second later, Baptistin was announcing him to Monte Cristo and the latter, after showing Haydée out, gave the order to let M. de Morcerf into the drawing-room. The general had paced three times the full length of the room when he turned around and saw Monte Cristo standing on the threshold.

'Oh! It's Monsieur de Morcerf,' Monte Cristo said, calmly. 'I thought I had misheard.'

'Yes, it is I,' the count said with a frightful contraction of the mouth that prevented him from pronouncing the words clearly.

'Now all I need to know,' Monte Cristo said, 'is what brings me the pleasure of seeing the Comte de Morcerf at such an early hour.'

'Did you have a meeting with my son this morning, sir?' the general asked.

'So you know about that?' the count replied.

'I also know that my son had good reason for wishing to fight you and doing his best to kill you.'

'Indeed, Monsieur, he had very good reason. But you see that, even so, he did not kill me, or even fight me.'

'Yet he considered you to be the cause of his father's dishonour and of the frightful catastrophe that is at the moment afflicting my house.'

'That is so, Monsieur,' said Monte Cristo with dreadful imperturbability. 'A secondary cause, perhaps, and not the main one.'

'So you must have made some excuse to him or given some explanation?'

'I gave him no explanation and he was the one to make his excuses.'

'How do you explain that behaviour?'

'Probably by his conviction that there was a more guilty man in all this than I.'

'Who was that man?'

'His father.'

'Yes,' said the count, blanching. 'But you know that the guilty man does not like to hear himself convicted of his crime?'

'I do . . . So I was expecting what has happened.'

'You were expecting my son to prove himself a coward!' the count exclaimed.

'Monsieur Albert de Morcerf is not a coward,' said Monte Cristo.

'A man who has a sword in his hand and, within reach of that sword, his mortal enemy . . . If such a man does not fight, he is a coward! If only he were here for me to tell him so!'

'Monsieur,' the Count of Monte Cristo replied coldly, 'I assume that you did not come to see me to inform me of these trifling family matters. Go and tell Monsieur Albert; he will know how to answer you.'

'Oh, no,' the general said, with a smile that vanished as soon as it had appeared. 'No, you are right, I did not come here for that! I came to tell you that I too regard you as my enemy. I came to tell you that I hate you instinctively, that it seems to me that I have always known you, and always hated you! And finally, since the young people of today do not fight, then we shall have to. Do you agree, Monsieur?'

'Absolutely. So when I said that I was expecting what has happened, I was referring to the honour of your visit.'

'So much the better, then. Your preparations are made?'

'They always are, Monsieur.'

'You know that we shall fight until one of us is dead?' the general said, his teeth clenched with rage.

'Until one of us is dead,' the Count of Monte Cristo repeated, gently nodding his head.

'Come on, then. We need no witnesses.'

'Indeed, no,' said Monte Cristo. 'We know one another so well!'

'On the contrary,' said the count. 'We don't know one another at all.'

'Come now,' Monte Cristo replied, with the same infuriating lack of emotion. 'Aren't you the soldier Fernand who deserted on the eve of the battle of Waterloo? Aren't you the Lieutenant Fernand who served as a guide and spy for the French army in Spain? Aren't you the Colonel Fernand who betrayed, sold and murdered his benefactor, Ali? And all these Fernands, did they not finally amount to: Lieutenant-General, Comte de Morcerf, peer of France?'

'Ah!' the general cried, the words striking him like a hot iron. 'You wretch! Do you reproach me with my shame at the moment when you may be about to kill me? No, I did not say that I was unknown to you. I know very well, demon, that you have penetrated the darkness of the past and read every page of my life – though I cannot tell by the light of what torch! But perhaps there is still more honour in me, in my disgrace, than in you, for all your arrogant exterior. No, no, I admit that I am known to you, but I do not know you, you adventurer, smothered in gold and precious stones! In Paris you call yourself the Count of Monte Cristo. In Italy, Sinbad the Sailor. In Malta – who knows what? I have forgotten. What I ask from you is your real name. I want to know your true name, in the midst of these hundred false names, so that I can say it on the field of combat as I plunge my sword in your heart.'

The Count of Monte Cristo went terribly pale; his wild eyes burned with angry fire. He rushed out into the study adjoining his bedroom and, in less than a second, tearing off his cravat, his coat and his waistcoat, he put on a small sailor's jacket and a sailor's hat, only partly covering his long black hair.

Dressed in this way, he returned, fearful, implacable, walking in front of the general with his arms crossed. The other had understood nothing of his disappearance, but was waiting for him and, feeling his teeth chatter and his legs give way under him, took a step back and stopped only when he reached a table which provided some support for his clenched hands.

'Fernand!' Monte Cristo cried. 'Of my hundred names, I shall need to tell you only one to strike you down. But you can already guess that name, can't you? Or, rather, you can recall it. For in spite of all my woes, in spite of all my tortures, I can now show you a face rejuvenated by the joy of revenge, a face that you must have seen often in your dreams since your marriage . . . your marriage to my fiancée, Mercédès!'

The general, his head thrown back, his hands held out, his eyes staring, watched this dreadful spectacle in silence. Then, reaching out for the wall and leaning on it, he slid slowly along it to the door, out of which he retreated backwards, giving this one, single, lugubrious, lamentable, heart-rending cry: 'Edmond Dantès!'

Then, with sighs in which there was nothing human, he dragged himself to the front porch of the house, crossed the courtyard like a drunken man and fell into the arms of his valet, simply muttering in an unintelligible voice: 'Home, home!'

On the way, the fresh air and the shame he felt at the stares of his servants restored him to a state in which he could gather his thoughts, but the journey was short and, the nearer he got to his home, the more the count felt all his agony returning.

At a short distance from the house he told them to stop the carriage and let him out. The door to the house was wide open; a cab, astonished at being called to this magnificent mansion, was standing in the middle of the courtyard. The count looked anxiously at this cab, but did not dare ask anyone about it and ran up to his apartments.

Two people were coming down the stairs. He just had time to slip into a small room to avoid them. It was Mercédès, leaning on her son's arm; both were leaving the house. They passed a few inches away from the unfortunate man who, hiding behind a damask curtain, was practically brushed by the hem of Mercédès' silk dress and felt on his face the warm breath of these words which his son spoke: 'Have strength, mother. Come, come, we are no longer at home here!'

The words died, the footsteps faded.

The general drew himself up by his hands clasping the damask curtain. He was repressing the most frightful sob that ever rose from the breast of a father, abandoned at one and the same time by his wife and by his son.

Soon he heard the iron door of the cab slam shut, then the voice of the driver, then the clattering of the heavy vehicle which rattled the windows. At that he flung himself into his bedroom to see once more everything that he had loved in this world. But the cab left without Mercédès' head, or Albert's, appearing at the window to give one last glance at the solitary house, at the abandoned father and husband . . . one last glance of farewell and regret, that is to say, of forgiveness.

So, at the very moment when the wheels of the cab were clattering over the cobbles under the archway, a shot rang out and a whiff of dark smoke curled out through one of those bedroom windows, shattered by the force of the detonation.

XCIII

VALENTINE

The reader will have guessed where Morrel's business was and whom he was due to meet. On leaving Monte Cristo, he made his way slowly towards the Villefort house. If he went slowly, it is because he had more than half an hour to cover a distance of five hundred yards; but he had still hastened to take his leave of Monte Cristo, even though the time was more than enough, because he wanted to be alone with his thoughts.

He knew the time – the time when Valentine, after seeing Noirtier have lunch, was sure that she would not be disturbed in this pious duty. Noirtier and Valentine had allowed him two visits a week and he was going to take advantage of his right.

Valentine was waiting for him when he arrived. Anxious, almost distracted, she grasped his hand and led him in to her grandfather's.

Her anxiety, as we said, had risen almost to the pitch of distraction, the result of the rumours that were circulating about Morcerf's adventure: people knew (as people in society always do) about what had happened at the opera. At the Villeforts', no one doubted that a duel would inevitably result from this scandal. Valentine, with her woman's instinct, had guessed that Morrel would be Monte Cristo's second and, knowing the young man's courage and his firm friendship with the count, she was afraid that he would not have the strength to confine himself to the passive role implied by this.

So one can well understand how eagerly the story was asked for, told and heard; and Morrel read unspeakable joy in his beloved's eyes when she knew that this dreadful business had ended in a way that was as fortunate as it was unexpected.

'Now,' Valentine said to Morrel, motioning him to sit beside the old man, and herself sitting on the stool on which he was resting his feet, 'now, let's talk a bit about our own business. You know, Maximilien, that my grandfather was thinking for a time of leaving this house and taking an apartment somewhere else?'

'Yes, I do,' said Maximilien. 'I remember the plan very well and I strongly approved of it.'

'Well, you can continue to approve, Maximilien, because my grandfather has come back to the idea.'

'Bravo!' said Maximilien.

'And do you know why he says he is leaving this house?'

Noirtier looked at his granddaughter to urge her to silence, but Valentine was not looking at Noirtier. Her eyes, her look, her smile were all for Morrel.

'Oh, whatever reason Monsieur Noirtier gives,' Morrel said, 'I'm sure it is good.'

'Very good,' said Valentine. 'He says that the air of the Faubourg Saint-Honoré is not beneficial to me.'

'Perhaps so,' said Morrel. 'Listen, Valentine, Monsieur Noirtier could be right. I feel that you haven't been well for the past two weeks.'

'Yes, not very, it's true,' Valentine answered. 'So grandfather has become my doctor and, as he knows everything, I have great confidence in him.'

'But is it true then that you are not well, Valentine?' Morrel asked anxiously.

'Oh, heavens, no. It's not what you would call being ill. I just don't feel very well, that's all. My appetite has gone and I feel that my stomach has to struggle to take anything in.'

Noirtier did not miss one of Valentine's words.

'And what course of treatment are you following for this unknown illness?'

'Very simple,' said Valentine. 'Every morning I drink a spoonful of the potion they bring for grandfather. When I say a spoonful, I started with one, and now I have reached four. My grandfather pretends it's a panacea.'

Valentine smiled, but there was something sad and pained in her smile.

Maximilien, intoxicated with love, looked at her in silence. She was very beautiful, but her pallor had a duller tone, her eyes shone with a less ardent flame than usual and her hands, normally white like mother-of-pearl, looked like wax hands which, with time, were acquiring a hint of yellow.

From Valentine, the young man looked at Noirtier. The latter was staring at the young woman (who was absorbed in her love) with that strange and deep understanding that he had; but he too, like Morrel, was examining these traces of silent suffering, even though they were so faint as to have escaped every eye except those of the lover and the grandfather.

'But this medicine, of which you are now taking four spoonfuls,' said Morrel, 'wasn't it prescribed for Monsieur Noirtier?'

'I know it is very bitter,' said Valentine. 'So bitter that anything I drink afterwards seems to have the same taste.'

Noirtier looked at her questioningly.

'Yes, grandfather,' said Valentine. 'That's how it is. Just now, before coming down to see you, I drank a glass of sugar water and had to leave half of it, so bitter did it seem to me.'

Noirtier went pale and indicated that he wished to speak. Valentine got up to look for the dictionary, and Noirtier's eyes followed her with obvious anxiety.

And, indeed, the blood was rising to the young woman's head and her cheeks were flushed. 'That's odd!' she said, as light-hearted as ever. 'Very odd: I feel faint! Have I caught the sun?' And she supported herself on the window-catch.

'There is no sun,' Morrel said, more worried by the expression on Noirtier's face than by Valentine's indisposition in itself. He ran across to her.

She smiled. 'Don't worry, dear grandfather,' she said. 'And you, Maximilien, don't worry. It's nothing, I feel better already. But listen: isn't that the sound of a carriage coming into the court-yard?'

She opened Noirtier's door and went quickly over to a window in the corridor, then hurried back. 'Yes,' she said, 'it's Madame Danglars and her daughter who have come to visit us. Goodbye, I must go or they will come and look for me here. Or, rather, au revoir: stay with grandfather, Maximilien. I promise not to keep them long.'

Morrel watched her go out and close the door, then heard her going up the little staircase which led to both Mme de Villefort's room and her own. As soon as she had vanished, Noirtier indicated to him that he should take down the dictionary. Morrel did so; under Valentine's guidance he had quickly learnt to understand the old man.

Yet, despite his familiarity with the procedure, since it was neces-sary to go through some at least of the twenty-four letters of the alphabet and find each word in the dictionary, it was ten minutes before the invalid's thoughts had been translated into these words: 'Fetch the glass and the jug from Valentine's room.' Morrel immedi-ately rang for the servant who had replaced Barrois and gave him the order in Noirtier's name. The man came back a moment later. The jug and glass were entirely empty.

Noirtier showed that he wanted to speak. 'Why are the glass and jug empty?' he asked. 'Valentine said that she had only drunk half a glass.'

This new enquiry took a further five minutes to convey.

'I don't know,' the servant said. 'But the chambermaid is in Mademoiselle Valentine's apartments; perhaps she emptied them.'

'Ask her,' Morrel said, this time translating Noirtier's thoughts from a look.

The servant went out and returned almost immediately. 'Madem-oiselle Valentine went through her room on her way to Madame de Villefort's,' he said. 'As she went, because she was thirsty, she drank what remained in the glass. As for the jug, Master Edouard emptied it to make a pond for his ducks.'

Noirtier turned his eyes to heaven as a player might when he is staking his all on a single throw. After that, he looked at the door and remained staring in that direction.

As Valentine had thought, it was Mme Danglars and her daughter whom she had seen arriving. They were shown into Mme de

Villefort's room, where she had said she would receive them. This is why Valentine went through her own apartments: her room was on a level with her mother-in-law's, the two being separated only by that of Edouard.

The women came into the drawing-room with that sort of formal stiffness that presages an announcement. This kind of nuance is quickly picked up by those who move in the same circles, and Mme de Villefort replied to their solemnity in kind. Then Valentine came in and the curtseys were performed over again.

'My dear friend,' the baroness said, while the two girls took each other's hands, 'I have come with Eugénie to be the first to announce to you my daughter's forthcoming marriage with Prince Cavalcanti.'

Danglars had clung to the title of 'prince': the People's Banker felt that it sounded better than 'count'.

'Then allow me to compliment you most sincerely,' Mme de Villefort replied. 'Prince Cavalcanti seems to be a young man of many rare qualities.'

The baroness smiled. 'Talking as friend to friend,' she said, 'I have to tell you that the prince does not yet seem to us what he will eventually become. He has some of that strangeness that allows us French to recognize an Italian or German aristocrat at first glance. Yet he appears to have a very good heart and a ready wit. As for compatibility, Monsieur Danglars claims that his fortune is "majestic" – that's his own word.'

'And then,' Eugénie said, leafing through Mme de Villefort's album, 'you must admit, Madame, that you have yourself taken a fancy to the young man.'

'I don't have to ask if you share that predilection?' said Mme de Villefort.

'Huh!' said Eugénie with her usual self-assurance. 'Not in the slightest, Madame. It never was my vocation to tie myself down to household chores or the whim of a man, whoever he might be. My vocation was to be an artist, free in heart, body and thought.'

Eugénie spoke these words in such firm and ringing tones that Valentine blushed. The timid young woman could not comprehend this energetic creature who seemed to have none of the diffidence of a woman.

'In any case,' she went on, 'since I am destined to be married, whether I like it or not, I can thank Providence for showering me with the contempt of Monsieur Albert de Morcerf, because without it I should now be the wife of a dishonoured man.'

'That's true enough,' said the baroness with that odd naïvety that is sometimes found among aristocratic women and which even associating with their inferiors does not entirely dispel. 'It's true. If the Morcerfs had not held back, my daughter would have married that Monsieur Albert. The general was very keen on it; he even came to compel Monsieur Danglars to conclude the match. We had a narrow escape.'

'But surely,' Valentine said shyly, 'does all the shame of the father rebound on the son? Monsieur Albert seems to me quite innocent of the general's treachery.'

'Oh, please, my dear friend,' said the inflexible young woman. 'Monsieur Albert claims his share and deserves it. It appears that after provoking Monsieur de Monte Cristo yesterday at the opera, he this morning apologized to him on the field.'

'Impossible!' said Mme de Villefort.

'Oh, my dear, no,' said Mme Danglars, with the same naïvety we mentioned. 'It's an established fact. I have it from Monsieur Debray, who was there when the confrontation took place.'

Valentine also knew the truth, but she did not reply. A word had taken her back into her own thoughts and she was imagining herself in Noirtier's room where Morrel was waiting for her. For some time, lost in this sort of inner meditation, she ceased to take any part in the conversation. It would even have been impossible for her to repeat what had been said over the past few minutes, when suddenly Mme Danglars' hand, touching her arm, shook her out of her reverie.

'What is it, Madame?' Valentine said, shuddering at the touch of Mme Danglars' fingers as she might at an electric shock.

'It's you, my dear Valentine,' said the baroness. 'You are feeling ill?'

'I am?' The young woman touched her burning forehead.

'Yes, look at yourself in that mirror. In the last minute you have blushed, then paled, three or four times.'

'Yes, indeed,' Eugénie exclaimed. 'You're very pale!'

'Oh, don't worry, Eugénie. I've been like this for some days.' And, guileless though she was, she guessed that this might be an opportunity to leave. In any event, Mme de Villefort came to her assistance, saying: 'You had better go and lie down, Valentine. As you really are ill, these ladies will excuse you. Have a glass of pure water and it will make you feel better.'

Valentine kissed Eugénie, curtseyed to Mme Danglars, who had already got up to leave, and went out.

'Poor child,' Mme de Villefort said when Valentine had gone. 'I'm very concerned about her. I should not be surprised if there were not something seriously wrong with her.'

However, Valentine, in a sort of exhilaration of which she was barely aware herself, had passed through Edouard's room without replying to some spiteful remark from the child, and hurried through her own room to the little staircase. She had gone down all the steps but the last three and could already hear Morrel's voice when suddenly her eyes clouded, her foot stiffened and missed the step, her hands no longer had the strength to support her and, leaning against the wall, she fell rather than walked down the last three steps.

Morrel rushed to the door, opened it and found Valentine stretched out on the landing. In an instant he lifted her under her arms and put her down in a chair. Her eyes opened.

'How clumsy I am!' she said, the words tumbling feverishly out. 'Don't I know how to stand up? I forgot there were three steps to the landing.'

'Oh, my God! Heavens above, Valentine, have you hurt yourself?' Morrel cried.

Valentine looked around. She saw the most profound anxiety in Noirtier's eyes.

'Have no fear, grandfather,' she said, trying to smile. 'It's nothing, it's nothing . . . I just felt a little faint, that's all.'

'Another dizzy spell,' Morrel said, clasping his hands. 'Please take heed, Valentine, I beg you.'

'No, no,' said Valentine. 'No, I told you, it has gone and it was nothing. Now, let me give you some news. In a week Eugénie is getting married, and in three days there will be a kind of great feast to celebrate the betrothal. We are all invited: my father, Madame de Villefort and I . . . at least, as I understand . . .'

'So when will it be our turn to think about that sort of thing? Oh, Valentine, you have so much influence with your grandfather; try to make him say *Soon*!'

'You expect me to hurry things along and awaken grandfather's memory?' she asked.

'Yes,' Morrel said. 'Oh, for goodness' sake, be quick. Until the moment when you are mine, Valentine, I shall always be afraid of losing you.'

'Oh, truly, Maximilien,' she said, with a convulsive movement, 'you are too fearful, for an officer, for a soldier who, they say, has never known fear. Ha, ha! Ha, ha!' And she burst into a strident and painful laugh. Then her arms stiffened and turned, her head fell back in the chair and she remained motionless.

The cry of terror that God brought to Noirtier's lips blazed out from his eyes. Morrel understood: they must call for assistance. He tugged at the bell, and the chambermaid who was in Valentine's apartments and the servant who had replaced Barrois hurried in simultaneously.

Valentine was so pale, so cold and so lifeless that, without listening to what they were told, seized by the terror that constantly hovered about that accursed house, they rushed out into the corridors, crying for help.

Mme Danglars and Eugénie were just leaving, but they still had time to discover the cause of all the commotion.

'Just as I said!' Mme de Villefort exclaimed. 'Poor child!'

XCIV

A CONFESSION

At the same moment, M. de Villefort's voice was heard shouting from his study: 'What's the matter?'

Morrel exchanged glances with Noirtier, who had recovered his composure and, with a glance, pointed him towards the closet in which he had already concealed himself on a similar previous occasion. He just had time to pick up his hat and jump inside, panting for breath. The crown prosecutor's footsteps could be heard in the corridor.

Villefort hurried into the room, ran over to Valentine and took her in his arms. 'A doctor! A doctor!' he cried. 'Get Monsieur d'Avrigny! Or, rather, I'll go myself.' He hurried out of the apartment.

Morrel hastened out through the other door. He had just been struck by the most appalling recollection: he remembered the conversation between Villefort and the doctor, which he had overheard on the night when Mme de Saint-Méran died. The symptoms, though in a milder form, were the same as the ones that had preceded the death of Barrois.

At the same time he heard Monte Cristo's voice in his ear, saying, as he had barely two hours earlier: 'Whatever you need, Morrel, come to me; I have a great deal of power.' So, swifter than thought, he hurried from the Faubourg Saint-Honoré to the Rue Matignon, and from the Rue Matignon to the Avenue des Champs-Elysées.

In the meanwhile M. de Villefort had arrived, in his hired cab, at M. d'Avrigny's door. He rang so violently that the concierge ran to open with a look of terror. Villefort rushed up the stairs without being able to say anything. The concierge knew him and let him go by, merely shouting after him: 'In his consulting-room, Monsieur, in his consulting-room!'

Villefort was already opening – or, rather, crashing through – the door of the room.

'Ah, it's you!' the doctor said.

'Yes, doctor,' Villefort said, closing the door behind him. 'Now it's my turn to ask you if we are quite alone. Doctor, my house is accursed!'

'What!' the doctor said, disguising the welter of feelings inside him under an appearance of calm. 'Has someone else been taken ill?'

'Yes, doctor,' Villefort cried, plunging his hands with a convulsive movement into his hair. 'Yes!'

D'Avrigny's look said: 'I warned you.'

Then his lips slowly spoke these words: 'So who is going to die in your house, and what new victim will accuse us of weakness before God?'

Villefort gave a painful sob. He went over to the doctor and clasped his arm. 'Valentine,' he said. 'It's the turn of Valentine!'

'Your daughter!' d'Avrigny exclaimed, overcome with distress and surprise.

'You see: you were wrong,' the lawyer muttered. 'Come and see her, on her bed of pain, ask her forgiveness for suspecting her.'

'Every time you have called me in, it has been too late,' said M. d'Avrigny. 'No matter, I'm on my way. But, Monsieur, we must hurry. With the enemies who strike at your family, there is no time to be lost.'

'Ah, this time, doctor, you will not reproach me for my weakness. This time I shall find the murderer and strike.'

'Let us try to save the victim before we think about revenge,' said d'Avrigny. 'Come on!' And the cab that had brought Villefort took him and d'Avrigny back at full speed, at the very moment when Morrel, for his part, was knocking at Monte Cristo's door.

The count was in his study. Bertuccio had just sent him a note and he was reading it with some anxiety. When the valet announced Morrel, who had left him barely two hours earlier, the count looked up.

Clearly a good deal had happened to him, as it had to the count, in those two hours, because the young man, who had left with a smile on his lips, was returning in a state of visible disarray. The count got up and hurried to meet him.

'What is wrong, Maximilien?' he asked. 'You are quite pale and your forehead is bathed in sweat.'

Morrel fell rather than sat down in a chair. 'Yes,' he said. 'I have been hurrying. I needed to speak to you urgently.'

'Is everyone well in your family?' the count asked with an unmistakably sincere note of affectionate goodwill.

'Yes, thank you, Count, thank you,' the young man replied, clearly at a loss to know how to open the conversation. 'Yes, in my family everyone is well.'

'Good. But you have something to tell me?' the count asked, more and more anxious.

'Yes, and it's true I have just hurried to see you from a house which has been touched by the arrival of death.'

'Have you been to Monsieur de Morcerf's, then?' Monte Cristo asked.

'No,' Morrel said. 'Has someone died at Monsieur de Morcerf's?'

'The general has just blown his brains out.'

'Oh, what a terrible thing!' Maximilien exclaimed.

'Not for the countess or for Albert,' Monte Cristo said. 'Better a husband and father dead than a husband and father dishonoured. The blood will wash away the shame.'

'Poor countess! She is the one I pity most: such a noble woman!'

'Pity Albert as well, Maximilien. Believe me, he is a worthy son of his mother. But let's return to you. You have hurried round to see me, you say. Might I have the happiness of being able to help you?'

'Yes, I need you; that is to say, like a madman, I believed that you could help me in a case where in fact only God can do so.'

'Tell me, even so,' said Monte Cristo.

'I don't know if I am entitled to reveal such a secret to human ears,' said Morrel. 'But fate drives me to it and necessity obliges me, Count . . .' He hesitated.

'Do you believe in my affection for you?' Monte Cristo said, clasping the young man's hand in his.

'Oh, you are encouraging me. And something here' (Morrel put his hand on his heart) 'tells me that I should have no secrets from you.'

'You are right, Morrel, God speaks to your heart and your heart to you. Tell me what your heart is telling you.'

'Count, will you let me send Baptistin to ask, on your behalf, for news of someone you know?'

'I have put myself at your disposal, so my servants are all the more yours to command.'

'I shall not live until I am certain that she is recovering.'

'Shall I ring for Baptistin?'

'No, let me talk to him myself.' Morrel went out, called Baptistin and whispered a few words to him. The valet left at the double.

'Well, is that done, then?' Monte Cristo asked when he returned.

'Yes, and I can breathe a little easier.'

'You know I am waiting,' Monte Cristo said with a smile.

'Yes, and I will tell you. Listen: one evening I was in a garden, hidden by a clump of trees so that no one guessed I was there. Two people walked close to me – please allow me not to tell you their names for the time being. They were talking very quietly together, but I was so interested to hear what they were saying that I did not miss a word.'

'This is not going to be a happy tale, to judge by the colour of your cheeks and the shudder you gave.'

'No, it is a dismal one, my friend. Someone had just died in the house of the man who owned the garden where I was hiding. The owner was one of the two people whose conversation I heard, the other was the doctor. The former was telling the latter about his anxieties and his fears, because this was the second time in a month that death had struck, speedily and unexpectedly, in this family.

You might think it had been singled out by an exterminating angel to suffer the wrath of God.'

'Ah, ha!' said Monte Cristo, staring at the young man and imperceptibly turning his chair so that he was in shadow, while the light shone full on Maximilien's face.

'Yes,' the latter went on. 'Death had struck this family twice within a month.'

'And what was the doctor's reply?' Monte Cristo asked.

'He replied . . . he replied that the death was not natural . . . that it was attributable to . . .'

'To what?'

'To poison!'

'Really!' said Monte Cristo, with a little cough that, at times when he was profoundly moved by something, allowed him to disguise a blush, a loss of colour, or even the attention with which he was listening. 'Really, Maximilien. Did you hear that?'

'Yes, my dear Count, I did hear it; and the doctor added that, if such a thing should occur again, he would feel himself obliged to call in the law.'

Monte Cristo listened (or appeared to do so) with the greatest calm.

'Then,' said Maximilien, 'death struck a third time, and neither the master of the house nor the doctor said anything. Death may strike a fourth time, perhaps. Count, what obligation do you think knowing this secret imposes on me?'

'My dear friend,' Monte Cristo answered, 'you seem to be telling a story that each of us knows by heart. I know the house where you overheard that conversation, or at least one very similar: a house with a garden, a father and a doctor, a house in which there have been three peculiar and unexpected deaths. Well, consider me. I have not overheard any confidences, yet I know all of this as well as you do; do I have any scruples of conscience? No, it doesn't concern me. You say that an exterminating angel seems to have designated this family for the wrath of God; well, who tells you that what seems to be is not the case? You should not see things that those who have good reason to see them fail to see. If it is justice and not God's wrath that hovers about that house, Maximilien, turn away and let divine justice proceed.'

Morrel shuddered. There was something at once dismal, solemn and fearsome in the count's voice.

'In any case,' he said, with such a sudden change in his tone that one would not have thought the words came from the same man's lips, 'who tells you that it will occur again?'

'It has, Count!' Morrel cried. 'That is why I have come to see you.'

'Well, what can I do, Morrel? Do you by any chance want me to inform the crown prosecutor?' These last words were spoken with such clarity and emphasis that Morrel leapt to his feet and exclaimed: 'Count! You know whom I mean, don't you?'

'Of course I do, my dear friend, and I will prove it to you by dotting the *i*'s and giving names to the people. You were walking one evening in Monsieur de Villefort's garden. According to your account, I suppose it must have been on the evening when Madame de Saint-Méran died. You heard Monsieur de Villefort speaking to Monsieur d'Avrigny about Monsieur de Saint-Méran's death and the no less unexpected death of the marquise. Monsieur d'Avrigny said that he believed one, or even both of them, had been poisoned; and you, the most law-abiding of men, have been wondering ever since, searching your heart and sounding your conscience to decide whether you should reveal the secret or not. We are no longer in the Middle Ages, my dear fellow, and there is no longer any holy Vehme or *francs-juges*.[1] What the devil are you going to ask those people? "Conscience, what do you want of me?" as Sterne says. No, my friend, let them sleep if they are sleeping, let them go grey with insomnia, and you, for the love of God, sleep, since you have no pangs of conscience to keep you awake.'

A look of unspeakable anguish appeared on Morrel's face. He grasped Monte Cristo's hand. 'But it has started again, I tell you!'

'So?' said the count, astonished at this insistence, which he could not understand, and looking closely at Maximilien. 'Let it start again. It's a family of Atreides.[2] God has condemned them and they will suffer their fate. They will disappear like the houses of cards that children set up, which fall one by one when their builders blow on them – and would do so even if there were two hundred of them. Three months ago it was Monsieur de Saint-Méran; two months ago, Madame de Saint-Méran; the other day it was Barrois, and today it will be old Noirtier or young Valentine.'

'You knew?' Morrel cried in such a paroxysm of terror that even Monte Cristo, who would have watched the sky fall without blanching, shuddered. 'You knew and said nothing!'

'Why? What does it matter to me?' the count said, shrugging his shoulders. 'Do I know those people? Must I destroy one to save another? Good Lord no, because between the guilty party and the victim I have absolutely no preference.'

'But I do!' Morrel shouted in agony. 'I do! I love her!'

'Whom do you love?' cried Monte Cristo, leaping to his feet and clasping the two hands which Morrel was lifting, entwined, to heaven.

'I love passionately, I love madly, I love like a man who would give his life's blood to spare her a tear, I love Valentine de Villefort who is being murdered at this moment, do you understand? I love her and I beg God and you to tell me how I can save her.'

Monte Cristo gave a savage cry which can only be imagined by those who have heard the roar of a wounded lion.

'Wretch!' he cried, wringing his hands in his turn. 'Wretch! You love Valentine! You love that daughter of an accursed race!'

Morrel had never seen such an expression. Never had such a fearful eye blazed up before his face and never had the spirit of terror which he had so often seen appear, either on the battlefield or in the murderous Algerian night, fanned such sinister flames around him. He shrank back in horror.

As for Monte Cristo, after this outburst he closed his eyes for a moment as if dazzled by some inner lightning. During that moment he collected himself with such force that one could gradually see his chest cease to heave with the inner storms that shook it, as the raging and foaming of the sea is appeased when the clouds disperse and the sun shines out again.

This silence, this inner struggle, lasted for some twenty seconds. Then the count raised his pale face. 'You see,' he said in a strained voice. 'See how, my dear friend, how God punishes the most boastful and the most detached of men for their indifference to the frightful scenes that He displays before them. I, who was watching the unfolding of this dreadful tragedy as an impassive and curious spectator; I, who, like the fallen angel, laughed at the evil that men do when they are sheltered by secrecy – and secrecy is easy to preserve for the rich and powerful – now I myself am bitten by that serpent whose progress I was observing – bitten to the heart!'

Morrel gave a dull moan.

'Come now,' the count said. 'No more sighs. Be a man, be strong, be full of hope, for I am here, watching over you.'

Morrel sadly shook his head.

'Don't you understand: I told you to hope!' cried Monte Cristo.
'Learn this: I never lie, I am never wrong. It is mid-day, Maximilien.
Give thanks to heaven that you came at mid-day and not this
evening or tomorrow morning. Listen to what I am about to tell
you, Morrel: it is mid-day and, if Valentine is not dead now, she
will not die.'

'Oh my God! My God!' Morrel cried. 'And I left her dying!'

Monte Cristo put a hand to his forehead. What was going on
inside that head, so heavy with its terrible secrets? What were the
angel of light and the angel of darkness saying to that mind, at once
implacable and humane? Only God knew.

Monte Cristo looked up once more, and this time he was as calm
as a child waking from sleep. 'Maximilien,' he said, 'go quietly
back home. I order you not to do anything, not to try any approach,
not let the shadow of a single worry cloud your face. I shall have
news for you. Now go.'

'My God!' said Morrel. 'You terrify me, Count, with your lack
of emotion. Have you some remedy for death? Are you more than
a man? Are you an angel? A god?' And the young man, who had
never flinched from any danger, shrank away from Monte Cristo,
seized with unspeakable terror.

However, Monte Cristo was looking at him with a smile that
was at once so melancholy and so tender that Maximilien felt the
tears filling his eyes.

'I can do many things, my friend,' the count replied. 'Go now; I
need to be alone.'

So Morrel, subjugated by the powerful ascendancy that Monte
Cristo exercised over everything around him, did not even try to
object. He shook the count's hand and left. But at the door he
stopped to wait for Baptistin, whom he had just seen running round
the corner of the Rue Matignon.

In the meantime Villefort and d'Avrigny had hurried home.
When they got there, Valentine was still unconscious, and the
doctor examined his patient with the care demanded by the circumstances and an attentiveness made all the more minute by his
knowledge of the secret. Villefort, hanging on his every look and
word, awaited the outcome of the examination. Noirtier, paler than
the girl herself, even more eager to find a solution than Villefort, was
also waiting, everything about him expressing intelligence and
sensitivity.

At last d'Avrigny said slowly: 'She's still alive.'

'Still!' Villefort exclaimed. 'Oh, doctor, what a dreadful word that is.'

'Yes,' the doctor said, 'and I repeat: she is still alive and I am very surprised by it.'

'But is she saved?' the father asked.

'Yes, since she is alive.'

At that moment, d'Avrigny's eye caught that of Noirtier, which shone with such astonishing joy and such a rich abundance of ideas that the doctor was quite struck by it.

He lowered the girl on to the chair. Her lips were so pale and white, like the rest of her face, as to be barely distinguishable. Then he stayed motionless, watching Noirtier, who was waiting and observing each of the doctor's movements.

'Monsieur,' d'Avrigny said to Villefort, 'call Mademoiselle Valentine's chambermaid, if you please.'

Villefort laid down his daughter's head, which he had been supporting, and went in person to call the chambermaid. As soon as he had closed the door, d'Avrigny went over to Noirtier. 'Do you have something to tell me?' he asked.

The old man blinked expressively; it was, as we have said, the only affirmative sign that he had at his disposal.

'To me alone?'

'Yes,' Noirtier affirmed.

'Very well, I shall remain with you.'

At that moment Villefort returned, followed by the chambermaid. Behind her came Mme de Villefort.

'But what has happened to this dear child?' she asked. 'She has just left me and she did complain that she was not feeling well, but I could not believe it was serious.' And, with tears in her eyes and with every mark of affection of a true mother, the young woman crossed to Valentine and took her hand.

D'Avrigny was still watching Noirtier. He saw the old man's eyes dilate and grow round, his cheeks drain of colour and start to tremble. There was sweat on his brow. 'Ah!' d'Avrigny said involuntarily, following Noirtier's eyes towards Mme de Villefort, who was saying: 'This poor child will be better lying down. Come, Fanny, we must take her to her bed.'

M. d'Avrigny saw in this suggestion a means to stay alone with Noirtier and nodded to show that this was indeed the best thing to do, but forbade them to give the patient anything at all except what he would prescribe for her.

Valentine was taken away, having regained consciousness but still unable to make any movement or virtually to speak, so grave had been the effect of the shock on her limbs. However, she did muster the strength to greet her grandfather with a look; and, as they took her away, it seemed as though they were tearing out his soul.

D'Avrigny followed the patient, finished giving his instructions and told Villefort to take a cab and go in person to the pharmacist's to have the preparations made up in front of him, then to bring them back and wait for him in his daughter's room. Finally, after repeating his order that Valentine should not be allowed to take anything, he went back down to Noirtier's, carefully closed the doors and, after making sure that they could not be overheard, said: 'Now, do you know something about your granddaughter's illness?'

'Yes,' the old man affirmed.

'Listen, we have no time to lose. I am going to question you and you will answer me.'

Noirtier indicated that he was ready to reply.

'Did you foresee what happened to Valentine today?'

'Yes.'

D'Avrigny thought for a moment, then came closer to Noirtier and added: 'Excuse me for what I am about to say, but no clue must be overlooked in the present frightful circumstances. Did you see poor Barrois die?'

Noirtier looked heavenwards.

'Do you know what he died of?' d'Avrigny asked, putting a hand on Noirtier's shoulder.

'Yes,' the old man replied.

'Do you think his death was natural?'

Something like a smile appeared on Noirtier's paralysed lips.

'So the idea has occurred to you that Barrois was poisoned?'

'Yes.'

'Do you think that the poison that killed him was intended for him?'

'No.'

'Now do you think that the same hand which struck Barrois down, intending to strike at someone else, has now struck Valentine?'

'Yes.'

'Will she also succumb to it?' d'Avrigny asked, looking attentively at Noirtier. He was waiting to see the effect of the question on the old man.

'No,' the latter replied, with an air of triumph that could have refuted the prophecies of the most skilled soothsayer.

'So you are hopeful?' d'Avrigny said in surprise.

'Yes.'

'What are you hoping for?'

The old man indicated with a look that he could not reply to such a question. 'Ah, of course,' d'Avrigny muttered. Then, turning back to Noirtier, he said: 'Do you hope that the murderer will give up trying?'

'No.'

'Then you hope that the poison will not affect Valentine?'

'Yes.'

'Because I am not revealing anything to you, am I, when I tell you that someone has tried to poison her?'

The invalid showed that he had no doubt on that subject.

'So how do you hope that Valentine will escape?'

Noirtier kept his eyes obstinately fixed in one direction. D'Avrigny followed them and saw that they were settled on the bottle containing the potion that he brought every morning.

'Ah! I see!' said d'Avrigny, suddenly understanding. 'Did you have the idea . . .'

Noirtier did not let him finish.

'Yes,' he said.

'The idea of forearming her against the poison . . .'

'Yes.'

'By accustoming her little by little . . .'

'Yes, yes,' said Noirtier, delighted at being understood.

'In short, you learned that there was brucine in the potions which I have been giving you?'

'Yes.'

'So, by accustoming her to this poison, you hoped to neutralize the effects of the poison?'

The same triumphant joy on Noirtier's face.

'Well, you succeeded!' d'Avrigny exclaimed. 'Without that, Valentine would be dead today, murdered without any possible protection, murdered without mercy; the shock was considerable, but she has only been shaken, and this time at least Valentine will not die.'

A supreme ray of joy lit the old man's eyes, which he turned heavenwards with a look of infinite gratitude.

At that moment Villefort returned. 'Here you are, doctor,' he said. 'This is what you requested.'

'Was it prepared in front of you?'

'Yes,' the crown prosecutor replied.

'It has not left your hands?'

'No.'

D'Avrigny took the bottle and poured out a few drops of the liquid it contained into the palm of his hand, then swallowed it.

'Very well,' he said. 'Let's go up to Valentine's. I shall give my instructions to everyone and you will be personally responsible, Monsieur de Villefort, for ensuring that no one disobeys them.'

As d'Avrigny was entering Valentine's room, accompanied by M. de Villefort, an Italian priest, stern in manner, calm and firm of speech, rented the house next door to the mansion inhabited by M. de Villefort.

It was impossible to know exactly what persuaded the three tenants of the house to move out two hours later; but the rumour that went round the district was that the house was not solidly fixed on its foundations and was threatening to collapse. However, this did not prevent the new tenant from settling in, with his modest furnishings, at around five o'clock on the very same day.

A lease was taken out for three, six or nine years by the new tenant who, in accordance with a custom established by the landlords, paid six months in advance. This new tenant – who, as we have said, was Italian – was named Signor Giacomo Busoni.

Workmen were immediately summoned and the very same night the few passers-by who stopped at the top end of the Faubourg were surprised to see carpenters and builders shoring up the foundations of the unsteady building.

XCV

FATHER AND DAUGHTER

In the previous chapter we heard Mme Danglars officially announce to Mme de Villefort the forthcoming marriage of Mlle Eugénie Danglars with M. Andrea Cavalcanti.

This formal announcement, which indicated (or appeared to do so) a resolution taken by all parties involved in this great matter, had however been preceded by a scene which we owe it to our readers to inform them about.

We beg them in consequence to step back in time with us and to transport themselves, on the very morning of this day which was to be marked by such great catastrophes, to the finely gilded drawing-room to which we have already introduced them, the pride and joy of its owner, Baron Danglars.

At around ten o'clock in the morning, the baron himself was pacing up and down in this drawing-room, thoughtful and visibly anxious, pausing at every sound and looking at every door. When his store of patience was exhausted, he called the valet.

'Etienne,' he said. 'Pray go and enquire why Mademoiselle Eugénie asked me to wait in the drawing-room and discover why she is making me wait so long.'

The baron calmed down a little after blowing off this petulant blast.

Mlle Danglars, after waking up, had indeed sent to ask for an audience with her father, appointing the gilt drawing-room as the venue for this meeting. The banker was not a little surprised by the oddness of the request, particularly by its formal nature, but immediately complied with his daughter's wishes by being the first to arrive in the room.

Etienne soon returned from his mission. 'Mademoiselle's chambermaid,' he said, 'informed me that Mademoiselle was completing her toilet and would not be long in coming.'

Danglars nodded to show he was satisfied. In the eyes of the world, and even in those of his servants, Danglars played the indulgent father and good-natured fellow; this was one side of the part he had chosen for himself in the popular comedy he was playing: an appearance he had taken on, which seemed to suit him as it suited the right profile of one of those masks worn by the fathers of the theatre in Antiquity to have the lips turned upwards and smiling, while on the left side the lips were turned down and sorrowful. We might add that, in his family circle, the smiling, up-turned lips dropped and became down-turned and dismal ones, so that most of the time the good-natured fellow vanished, giving way to a brutal husband and tyrannical father.

'Why the devil, if the silly goose wants to talk to me, as she claims,' Danglars muttered, 'can't she just come to my study? And why does she want to talk to me?'

He was turning this irksome question around in his head for the twentieth time when the door opened and Eugénie appeared, wearing a dress of black satin embroidered with velvety flowers of the same colour, with her hair put up and her arms encased in gloves, as though she were going to her box in the Théâtre Italien.

'Now, Eugénie, what's the matter?' her father exclaimed. 'And why do we have to be formal in the drawing-room, when it's so much more comfortable in my private study?'

'You are perfectly right, Monsieur,' said Eugénie, motioning to her father that he could sit down. 'You have just asked two questions which sum up the whole of the conversation we are about to have. I shall therefore answer both of them and, contrary to custom, the second first, since it is the simpler. I chose the drawing-room, Monsieur, as the venue for our meeting, to escape from the disagreeable impressions and the atmosphere of a banker's study. Those account registers, however well gilded; those drawers, shut tight like the gates of a fortress; those piles of banknotes that come from heaven-knows-where; those masses of letters from England, Holland, Spain, the Indies, China or Peru ... all have a peculiar effect on the mind of a father and make him forget that there is in the world something greater and more sacred than social standing or the opinion of his investors. So I chose this drawing-room, where you can see your portrait, mine and my mother's, smiling and happy, in their magnificent frames, as well as all sorts of pastoral landscapes and charming scenes of shepherds and shepherdesses. I attach great importance to the effect of external impressions. This may perhaps be a mistake, especially where you are concerned, but what do you expect? I should not be an artist if I did not indulge in a few fancies.'

'Very well,' said M. Danglars, who had been listening to this diatribe with utter imperturbability but not understanding a word of it because, like every man who is full of ulterior motives, he was preoccupied with finding his own train of thought in the speaker's ideas.

'So, there we have the second point more or less cleared up,' said Eugénie, quite undisturbed, expressing as usual an entirely masculine composure in her words and gestures. 'And you appear to be satisfied with the explanation. Now to return to the first point. You ask me why I wanted this talk. Let me put it very briefly, Monsieur: I do not want to marry Count Andrea Cavalcanti.'

Danglars leapt out of his seat. The shock of his descent back threw his arms in the air and cast his eyes heavenwards.

'Yes, Monsieur, there you have it,' said Eugénie, still quite unmoved. 'I can see you are surprised because, since this whole business started, I have not shown the slightest objection, being sure that, when the moment came, I would always frankly and absolutely express my opposition to people who do not consult me and things which I do not like. This time, however, this calm, this passivity, as philosophers say, originated elsewhere. It came from the fact that, as a submissive and devoted daughter' (a faint smile appeared on the young woman's crimson lips) 'I was trying the path of obedience.'

'Well?' said Danglars.

'Well, Monsieur,' Eugénie went on, 'I tried; I tried with all my strength and, now that the moment has come, despite all the efforts I have made over myself, I feel unable to obey.'

'But, tell me,' said Danglars, an inferior mind who seemed at first quite bewildered by the weight of this pitiless logic, stated with a coolness that argued so much premeditation and strength of will, 'what is the reason for this refusal, Eugénie; what is the reason?'

'The reason?' the young woman replied. 'Good Lord, it's not because the man is uglier, stupider or more disagreeable than any other. No, for those who consider a man from the point of view of his face and figure, Monsieur Andrea Cavalcanti might even pass as quite a fine model. And it's not because my heart is any less moved by him than by another: that sort of answer would do for a schoolgirl, but I consider it quite beneath me. I love absolutely no one, Monsieur: you know that, don't you? So I cannot see why, unless forced to do so, I should wish to encumber my life with an eternal companion. Didn't the sage say somewhere: "Nothing in excess"; and elsewhere: "Carry everything with you"? I was even taught those two aphorisms in Latin and Greek: one is from Phaedrus, I believe, the other from Bias.[1] Well, my dear father, in the shipwreck of life – for life is an eternal shipwreck of our hopes – I throw all my useless baggage in the sea, that's all, and remain with my will, prepared to live entirely alone and consequently entirely free.'

'You wretched creature!' Danglars muttered, the blood draining from his face, for he knew from long experience the solidity of the obstacle he had suddenly run up against.

'Wretched?' Eugénie repeated. 'Did you say wretched, Monsieur? Not at all, I assure you, and the exclamation seems altogether too theatrical and pretentious. On the contrary, I am anything but wretched: I ask you, what more could I want than I have? People consider me beautiful, which is enough to be favourably received. I like to be received with a smile which is becoming to a face and which makes those around me appear less ugly than usual. I have some wit and a certain relative sensitivity that allows me to extract what I find acceptable from the generality of existence and bring it into my own, like a monkey cracking a green nut to take out what is inside. I am rich because you have one of the finest fortunes in France, I am your only child and you are not obstinate like the fathers in plays at the Porte Saint-Martin or the Gaîté,[2] who disinherit their daughters because they refuse to give them grandchildren. In any case, the law in its wisdom has deprived you of the right to disinherit me – at least, entirely – just as it has deprived you of the power to force me to marry some monsieur or other. So, beautiful, witty and blessed with some talent, as they say in the comic operas – and rich! Why! That's happiness, Monsieur! So how can you call me wretched?'

Danglars, seeing his daughter smiling and proud to the point of insolence, could not suppress a surge of aggression which expressed itself as a sharp cry; but that was all. Before his daughter's quizzical look, confronted by this fine black eyebrow, raised interrogatively, he turned around cautiously and immediately got his anger under control, repressing it with the iron hand of circumspection.

'Indeed, my girl,' he replied, smiling, 'you are everything that you boast of being, except one thing; I don't want to tell you too directly what that is. I should prefer to let you guess.'

Eugénie looked at Danglars, very surprised that he could challenge one of the jewels in the crown that she had so arrogantly just placed on her head.

'My daughter,' the banker went on, 'you have explained to me quite clearly the feelings which guide the resolve of a girl such as yourself when she has decided not to get married. Now it is my turn to tell you what are the motives of a father such as myself when he has decided that his daughter will get married.'

Eugénie bent her head, not like an obedient daughter listening to her father, but like an adversary in waiting, ready to answer back.

'My dear,' said Danglars, 'when a father asks his daughter to take a husband, he always has some reason for wishing to see her married. Some fathers suffer from the folly you just mentioned, that of wanting to live again through their grandchildren. I'll tell you straight away, I do not have that weakness and I am more or less indifferent to the joys of family life. This I can confess to a daughter whom I know to be detached enough herself to understand my feeling and not to reproach me with it.'

'Good!' said Eugénie. 'Very good. Let's be frank. I like that.'

'Oh, as you see, without as a general rule sharing your partiality for frankness, I do resort to it when I think the circumstances require it. So, let me continue. I offered you a husband, not for your sake, because I honestly was not thinking about you at all at the time. You like frankness: I hope that is frank enough for you. The reason was that I needed you to marry that husband as soon as possible, for the sake of some commercial transactions that I am currently engaged in.'

Eugénie started.

'That's how it is, my girl, and you must not mind, because you are obliging me to speak in this way. You understand: I regret having to go into these questions of arithmetic with an artist such as yourself, who is afraid to go into a banker's study in case she encounters some unpleasant and anti-poetic feelings.

'However, you should know that there are lots of things to be learnt, even to the advantage of young women who do not wish to get married, inside that banker's study – where, incidentally, you were willing enough to risk setting foot yesterday, to ask me for the thousand francs which I give you every month to amuse yourself. For example – it is out of consideration for your nervous susceptibilities that I say this here, in the drawing-room – one may learn that a banker's credit is his whole life, physical and moral: credit sustains the man as breath sustains a body; and Monsieur de Monte Cristo made a pretty little speech to me on the subject one day and I have never forgotten it. One may learn that, when credit is withdrawn, the body becomes a corpse and that this can happen very quickly to a banker who has the honour to be the father of a girl with such an excellent command of logic.'

Eugénie, instead of bowing under the blow, rose to meet it. 'Ruined!' she said.

'You have hit on the very word, my dear girl, the right word,' said Danglars, rummaging around his chest with his hands, while his coarse features kept the smile of a man who might be deficient in heart but not in wit. 'Ruined! Precisely.'

'Ah!' said Eugénie.

'Yes, ruined! Well, now the dreadful secret's out, as the tragic poets say. So listen here, my dear girl, while I tell you how the disaster can be reduced, not for me, but for you.'

'Oh, you know very little about the human face, Monsieur,' Eugénie exclaimed, 'if you imagine that I deplore the catastrophe you are describing for my own sake.

'What does it matter if I am ruined? Haven't I still got my talent? Why should I, like Pasta, Malibran or Grisi,[3] not make for myself what you could never have given me, however great your fortune: an income of one hundred or one hundred and fifty thousand *livres* that I owe to myself alone and which, instead of reaching me like the miserable twelve thousand francs that you used to give me, with sour looks and reproachful reflections on my prodigality, will come with clapping, cheers and flowers? And even if I do not have this talent – your smile suggests you doubt that I do – shall I not still have that passionate love of independence which will always be more important to me than any treasure and which with me even takes precedence over the instinct of self-preservation?

'No, I am not sorry for myself, because I shall always manage to get by: I shall still have my books, my pencils and my piano, things which are not expensive and which I shall always be able to obtain. And if you think I am sorry for Madame Danglars, then there too you can think again. Either I am very mistaken, or my mother has taken every necessary precaution to ensure that the catastrophe threatening you will pass her by. I hope she has managed to protect herself; she was certainly not distracted in her fortune-hunting by her concern for me because, thank heaven, she left me all my independence on the excuse that I liked my freedom.

'Oh, no, Monsieur, since my childhood I have seen too many things going on around me, and understood them too well, for misfortune to make any more impression on me than it ought. Ever since I can remember, no one has loved me – too bad! And this has naturally led me to love nobody – so much the better! There you have my credo.'

'In that case,' Danglars said, pale with an anger which did not originate in injured paternal love, 'Mademoiselle . . . In that case, do you persist in wishing to bring about my ruin?'

'Your ruin!' said Eugénie. 'I, bring about your ruin? What do you mean? I don't follow you.'

'I'm glad to hear it: that leaves me a ray of hope. Listen.'

'I'm listening,' said Eugénie, staring so hard at her father that he had to make an effort not to lower his eyes beneath the young woman's powerful gaze.

'Monsieur Cavalcanti is marrying you,' Danglars went on. 'And in doing so he will bring a dowry of three million which he will invest with me.'

'Splendid,' said Eugénie with utter contempt, smoothing her gloves against one another.

'Do you think I would hold those three million against you?' said Danglars. 'Not at all. Those three million are intended to produce at least ten more. With another banker, a colleague of mine, I have obtained a concession on a railway, the only industry which nowadays offers those fabulous chances of immediate success that Law managed to convince the good people of Paris, who are always enchanted by speculation, were to be found in some imaginary Mississippi.[4] By my estimate, a millionth of a rail should yield the same as formerly an acre of fallow land on the banks of the Ohio. It's a mortgage investment, which is progressive, as you see, since one will obtain at least ten, fifteen, twenty or a hundred pounds of iron in exchange for one's money. Well, a week from now, I have to put in four millions in my name. As I have said, these four millions will produce ten or twelve.'

'But when I visited you, the day before yesterday, Monsieur, as you must remember,' Eugénie went on, 'I saw you cashing in – that is the term, I believe? – five and a half million. You even showed

me it in two treasury bonds, and you were surprised that a piece
of paper which was so valuable didn't dazzle me like a flash of
lightning.'

'Yes, but those five and a half million are not mine; they are
simply a proof of the confidence that people have in me. My title
as a people's banker has gained me the confidence of the hospitals,
and those five and a half million belong to them. At any other time
I should not hesitate to make use of them, but today people know
the great losses I have made and, as I told you, credit is starting to
pull away from me. At any moment the authorities could reclaim
the deposit and, if I have spent it on something else, I shall be forced
into a shameful bankruptcy. Believe me, I have no objection to
bankruptcy, as long as it makes a man richer and doesn't ruin him.
Either you marry Monsieur Cavalcanti and I get the three million
from the dowry, or else people will think that I am to get them;
then my credit will strengthen and my fortune, which for the past
month or two has been slipping into a bottomless pit in front of
me, because of some incredible ill-luck, will be re-established. Do
you follow me?'

'Yes. You are pawning me for three million: am I right?'

'The larger the sum, the more flattering it is. It gives you some
idea of your value.'

'Thank you. One final word, Monsieur. Do you promise me to
use the amount of this dowry that Monsieur Cavalcanti is to bring,
for as long as you wish, but not to touch the capital? This is not a
matter of selfishness, but of scruple. I am quite willing to serve as
the instrument for rebuilding your fortune, but I don't wish to be
your accomplice in the ruin of others.'

'But I'm telling you that with these three million . . .'

'Do you think you can get by, Monsieur, without having to touch
the three million?'

'I hope so, provided that the marriage strengthens my credit.'

'Could you pay Monsieur Cavalcanti the five hundred thousand
francs that you are giving me for my contract?'

'He will get them when he comes back from the town hall.'

'Good!'

'Why, good? What do you mean?'

'I mean that, while asking me for my signature, you will leave
me entirely free in myself?'

'Absolutely.'

'Then, "good". As I told you, Monsieur, I am ready to marry Monsieur Cavalcanti.'

'But what do you have in mind?'

'That's my secret. Where would I get my superiority over you if, knowing your secret, I were to entrust you with mine?'

Danglars bit his lip. 'So,' he said, 'you are prepared to carry out the few official visits that are absolutely necessary?'

'Yes,' Eugénie replied.

'And to sign the contract in three days?'

'Yes.'

'Then I must say "good" in my turn.' And he took his daughter's hand and pressed it between his own.

However, what was extraordinary was that, while their hands were joined, the father did not dare to say: 'Thank you, my child.' And the daughter had no smile for her father.

'Is the meeting over?' Eugénie asked.

Danglars nodded to show that he had nothing more to say.

Five minutes later the piano was sounding under the fingers of Mlle d'Armilly, and Mlle Danglars was singing Brabantio's curse from Desdemona.[5]

At the end of the piece, Etienne came in and told Eugénie that the horses were harnessed and that the baroness was waiting for them to go visiting. We have already seen how the two women went to the Villeforts', then left to continue their rounds.

XCVI

THE MARRIAGE CONTRACT

Three days after the episode that we have just described, that is to say at around five o'clock in the afternoon on the day appointed for signing the contract of marriage between Mlle Eugénie Danglars and Andrea Cavalcanti, whom the banker insisted on entitling 'Prince', a fresh breeze rustled all the leaves in the little garden in front of the Count of Monte Cristo's house. He was getting ready to go out. His horses were waiting for him, pawing the ground with their hoofs, restrained by the coachman who had already been sitting on his box for a quarter of an hour. At this moment, the elegant phaeton which we have already had occasion to meet several times, particularly during the evening at Auteuil, swung rapidly round the gatehouse and ejected (rather than deposited) on the steps leading up to the house Monsieur Andrea Cavalcanti, as gilded and radiant as if he, for his part, were on the point of marrying a princess.

He enquired after the count's health with his usual familiarity and, bounding lightly up to the first floor, met Monte Cristo himself at the top of the stairs. When he saw the young man, the count stopped. As for Cavalcanti, he was in full flight and when he was launched nothing would stop him.

'Ah, good day, my dear Monte Cristo,' he said.

'Monsieur Andrea!' the other said, in his half-mocking tone. 'How are you?'

'Excellent, as you see. I have come to tell you lots of things – but, first, are you coming in or going out?'

'I was going out, Monsieur.'

'Well, then, so as not to delay you, I'll get into your coach, if I may, and Tom will follow behind, with my phaeton in tow.'

'No,' the count said, with an imperceptible smile of contempt, not wanting to be seen in the young man's company. 'No, I prefer to listen to what you have to say here, my dear Monsieur Andrea. One can speak better in a room where there is no coachman to catch what you say.'

The count led the way into a little drawing-room on the first floor, sat down, crossed his legs and motioned to the young man to take a seat.

Andrea adopted his most jovial expression. 'You know, Count,' he said, 'the ceremony takes place this evening. The contract will be signed at the father-in-law's, at nine o'clock.'

'Really?' Monte Cristo asked.

'What! Is this news to you? Didn't Monsieur Danglars inform you of this solemn occasion?'

'Yes, he did,' the count said. 'I had a letter from him yesterday, but I don't think any time was mentioned in it.'

'That's possible. I suppose my father-in-law was relying on word getting around.'

'Well, now,' Monte Cristo said, 'you're happy then, Monsieur Cavalcanti. That's a very desirable match you are entering; and Mademoiselle Danglars is pretty.'

'She is,' Cavalcanti replied, with a good deal of modesty.

'And most of all, she is very rich, or at least so I understand,' said Monte Cristo.

'Very rich, do you think?' the young man repeated.

'No doubt of it. They say that Monsieur Danglars hides at least half his wealth.'

'And he admits to fifteen or twenty million,' Andrea said, his eyes shining with joy.

'Besides which,' Monte Cristo added, 'he is on the point of engaging in a form of speculation that is already a bit overdone in the United States and in England, but quite new in France.'

'Yes, yes, I know what you mean: it's the railway for which he has just been awarded the contract, I suppose?'

'Precisely! The general view is that he will make at least ten million on the affair.'

'Ten million? Do you really think so? Marvellous . . .' said Cavalcanti, intoxicated by the metallic sound of these golden words.

'Not to mention,' Monte Cristo went on, 'that this whole fortune will revert to you, which is only right, since Mademoiselle Danglars is an only child. In any case, your own fortune is almost as great as that of your fiancée, at least, so your father told me. But let's put aside these money matters. Do you know, Monsieur Andrea, that you have managed this business quite neatly and skilfully?'

'Not bad,' said the young man. 'Not bad at all: I am a born diplomat.'

'Well, you shall be one. You know, diplomacy is not learnt; it's a matter of instinct . . . So, this is a love match for you?'

'Indeed, I fear it is,' Andrea replied, in the tone of voice he had heard Dorante or Valère using to answer Alceste in the Théâtre Français.[1]

'And does she love you a little?'

'She must,' Andrea said, with a victor's smile, 'since she's marrying me. But let's not forget one very important thing.'

'Which is?'

'That I was greatly helped in all this.'

'Pooh!'

'But, certainly.'

'By events?'

'No, by you.'

'By me? Come, come, Prince,' Monte Cristo said, ironically stressing the title. 'What could I do for you? Were not your name, your social standing and your personal qualities enough?'

'No,' said Andrea, 'they weren't. And, Monsieur le Comte, whatever you say, I maintain that the position of a man such as yourself did more than my name, my social standing and my personal qualities.'

'You are utterly mistaken, Monsieur,' Monte Cristo said, grasping the young man's treacherous skill and the implication of his words. 'You gained my protection only after I had enquired into the influence and wealth of your respected father. For who allowed me the honour of knowing you, when I had never seen you in my life, either you or your illustrious sire? It was two close friends of mine, Lord Wilmore and Abbé Busoni. What encouraged me, not to serve as a guarantor for you, but to support you? Your father's name, which is so well known and honoured in Italy. Personally, I don't know you.'

The count's calm and easy manner gave Andrea to understand that for the time being he was in the grasp of a stronger hand than his own and that its grip would not easily be broken.

'Tell me,' he said. 'Does my father really have a huge fortune, Count?'

'It appears so, Monsieur,' Monte Cristo answered.

'Do you know if the dowry he promised me has arrived?'

'I have received the advice note.'

'And the three million?'

'In all probability the three million are on their way.'

'So I shall really have them?'

'Dammit!' the count said. 'It doesn't seem to me, Monsieur, that you have lacked for money so far!'

Andrea was so surprised that he could not prevent himself from pausing to think for a moment. Then, coming out of his reverie, he said: 'Monsieur, I have just one request left to make of you, and this one you will understand, however disagreeable it may be.'

'Tell me,' said Monte Cristo.

'Thanks to my wealth, I have been brought into contact with many distinguished people and, for the time being at least, I have a host of friends. But in marrying as I shall do, before all of Parisian society, I should be sponsored by someone with a famous name and, failing my father's hand, it should be that of some powerful man who will lead me to the altar. My father never comes to Paris, does he?'

'He is old, covered in wounds and, he says, suffers mortal agonies every time he travels.'

'I understand. Well, I have a request to make of you.'

'Of me?'

'Yes, you.'

'Good Lord, what is it?'

'That you should take his place.'

'What! My dear fellow, after the various contacts that you have had with me, do you know me so little that you could make such a request?

'Ask me for the loan of half a million and, though it's an unusually large sum, I swear that the request would be less of a burden to me. You should know – I thought I had already told you – that when the Count of Monte Cristo is involved in any of the things of this world, particularly in spiritual matters, he has never ceased to regard them with the scruples, I might even say the superstitions, of an Oriental.

'I have a seraglio in Cairo, another in Smyrna and another in Constantinople ... And you ask me to preside at a wedding! Never!'

'So you are refusing me?'

'Outright. Even if you were my son, or my brother, I should refuse in the same way.'

'Well, I never!' Andrea said, disappointed. 'So what is to be done?'

'You have a hundred friends, as you said yourself.'

'Yes, but you were the person who introduced me to Monsieur Danglars.'

'Not at all! Let's get the facts straight: I arranged for you to have dinner with him in Auteuil, and you introduced yourself. Why, it's entirely different!'

'Yes, but my marriage ... you helped ...'

'I did? In no way, believe me. Remember what I said to you when you came to ask me to make the proposal: I never matchmake, my dear Prince, it's an absolute rule with me.'

Andrea bit his lips. 'But you will at least be there?'

'All of Parisian society will be coming?'

'Certainly.'

'Then I shall be there with the rest,' the count said.

'Will you sign the contract?'

'I see no objection; my scruples don't extend that far.'

'Well, then, if you will not agree to anything more, I shall have to make do with what you will give me. But one final word, Count.'

'What's that?'

'I need some advice.'

'Beware! A piece of advice is worse than a helping hand.'

'Oh, you can give me this without compromising yourself.'

'Tell me, then.'

'My wife's dowry is five hundred thousand *livres*.'

'That's the figure that Monsieur Danglars told me himself.'

'Should I take it or deposit it with the lawyers?'

'Here is how things are usually done, when the parties want to show some gallantry: at the time of the contract, your two notaries agree to meet the following day or the one after. On the appointed day, they exchange the two dowries, each giving the other a receipt. Then, once the marriage has been celebrated, they put the millions at your disposal, as the one in charge of the joint estate.'

'The reason I ask,' Andrea said, with ill-disguised unease, 'is that I thought I understood my father-in-law to say that he intended to invest our funds in the famous railway that you were speaking about a little while ago.'

'So?' said Monte Cristo. 'Everyone agrees that it should allow you to triple your capital in a year. Baron Danglars is a good father and knows how to add up.'

'Very well, then,' said Andrea. 'Everything's fine except your refusal, which wounds me deeply.'

'Just put it down to what are, in the circumstances, quite natural scruples.'

'As you wish, then,' said Andrea. 'This evening at nine?'

'Until this evening.' And, though the count shrank back slightly and his lips paled, while still preserving his polite smile, Andrea seized his hand, pressed it, leapt into his phaeton and rode off.

He spent the last four or five hours until nine o'clock in shopping and in visits to drum up interest among the friends whom he had asked to appear at the banker's in their finest carriages, dazzling them with the promise of shares – which were later to turn every head, but in which for the time being Danglars had the initiative.

At half-past eight, accordingly, Danglars' main reception room, the gallery leading to it and the three other reception rooms on the same floor were full of a crowd of scented people, very few of whom were attracted by sympathy, and very many by an irresistible urge to be where they knew something was going on. A self-conscious stylist would say that society receptions are a bed of flowers that attracts capricious butterflies, hungry bees and buzzing hornets.

Needless to say, the rooms were resplendent with candles and light poured from the gilt mouldings on to the silk hangings; and all the bad taste of furnishings which expressed nothing but wealth shone out in its full glory.

Mlle Eugénie was dressed with the most elegant simplicity: a white silk dress embroidered in white, and a white rose half hidden in her jet-black hair, made up her entire costume, enriched by not a single jewel. Yet her eyes shone with perfect self-assurance, contradicting what she saw as the vulgarly virginal significance of this outfit.

Thirty yards away, Mme Danglars was talking to Debray, Beauchamp and Château-Renaud. Debray had made his entry into the house for this solemn occasion, but like everyone else and with no special privileges.

M. Danglars, surrounded by members of parliament and men of money, was explaining a new theory of taxation which he intended to introduce when circumstances compelled the government to call him to ministerial office.

Andrea, arm-in-arm with one of the most dashing young dandies from the opera, was explaining his future plans to him – somewhat impertinently, given that he needed to be bold to appear at ease – and how he intended to advance the cause of Parisian fashions with his income of 75,000 *livres*.

The main crowd was ebbing and flowing around the rooms, like a tide of turquoises, rubies, emeralds, opals and diamonds.

As always, it was the oldest women who were the most heavily adorned and the ugliest who were most determined to make an exhibition of themselves. If there was any fine white lily, or any sweet-scented, velvety rose, she had to be hunted down and revealed, hidden in a corner behind a mother in a turban or an aunt with a bird of paradise.

At intervals, above this crush, this hum, this laughter, the voices of the ushers could be heard announcing the name of someone well known in the financial world, respected in the army or illustrious in the world of letters; and, at that, a faint movement in the clusters of people would greet the name. But for each one who had the privilege of causing a stir in this ocean of human waves, how many were greeted with indifference or a snigger of contempt!

Just as the hand of the massive clock – of the clock showing the sleeping Endymion – reached nine on the gold face and the bell, faithfully translating the thought of the machine, struck nine times, the Count of Monte Cristo's name rang out in its turn and everyone in the crowd, as if drawn by an electric flash, turned towards the door.

The count was dressed, with his usual simplicity, in black. A white waistcoat covered his broad and noble chest and his black collar seemed unusually neat, outlined against the masculine pallor of his complexion. His only ornament was a watch-chain so fine that the slender band of gold was barely visible against the white stitching.

A crowd immediately assembled round him. At a glance, the count observed Mme Danglars at one end of the room, Monsieur Danglars at the other and Mlle Eugénie in front of him.

He went across, first of all, to the baroness, who was talking to Mme de Villefort, who had come alone, Valentine still being unwell. Without deviating from his course, the crowd parting before him, he went from the baroness to Eugénie, whom he complimented in a few concise and restrained words which impressed the proud artist.

Mlle Louise d'Armilly was standing close by her; she thanked the count for the letters of recommendation that he had so kindly given her for Italy and which, she said, she intended to make use of very shortly.

On leaving these ladies, he turned around and found himself close to Danglars, who had come over to offer him his hand.

After completing these three social duties, Monte Cristo stopped and looked around him with that self-confident look which bears the stamp of an expression peculiar to people who belong to a particular rank in society and, above all, to those who enjoy a certain influence in it; a look that seems to imply: 'I have fulfilled my obligations; now let others pay their dues to me.'

Andrea, who was in an adjoining room, felt the sort of shiver that Monte Cristo sent through the crowd and hastened to pay his respects. He found him entirely surrounded. People were hanging on his every word, as is always the case with those who say little and never waste words.

At that moment the notaries entered and set up their scrawled signs on the gold-embroidered velvet covering on the table that had been prepared for the signing, a table of gilded wood. One notary sat down, the other remained standing.

They were about to proceed to the reading of this contract which half of Paris would sign, having gathered for the occasion.

Everyone took their place; or, rather, the women clustered round while the men, less moved by what Boileau[2] calls the 'energetic style', commented on Andrea's nervous agitation, M. Danglars' concentration, Eugénie's impassivity, and the lively and casual way in which the baroness was treating this important business.

There was total silence while the contract was read, but, as soon as the reading was over, the noise resumed in every room, twice as loud as before: the jealous gathering had been deeply impressed by these marvellous amounts, these millions paving the future path of the young couple, complemented by the exhibition of the bride-to-be's trousseau and diamonds in a room entirely set aside for them. All this doubled Mlle Danglars' charms, blotting out the light of the sun, in the eyes of the young men. As for the women, it goes without saying that, jealous though they were of the millions, they did not believe them necessary to appear beautiful. Andrea, hemmed in by his friends, complimented, adulated, was beginning to believe in the reality of the dream he was having; Andrea was about to lose his head.

The notary solemnly took the quill, raised it in the air and said: 'Gentlemen, the contract is about to be signed!'

The baron was to sign first, then the proxy for M. Cavalcanti the elder, then the baroness, then the 'future spouses' (as they say in that abominable style commonly used on stamped paper). The baron took the quill and signed, followed by the proxy. The baroness approached, on Mme de Villefort's arm.

'My friend,' she said, taking the quill, 'isn't it just too much? An unexpected incident, connected with that business of murder and theft of which the Count of Monte Cristo was so nearly a victim, has deprived us of Monsieur de Villefort's company.'

'Oh, good Lord!' Danglars exclaimed, with no more emotion than he might have said: 'What? I really couldn't care less!'

'Oh, dear,' Monte Cristo said, coming over. 'I am very afraid I may be the involuntary cause of his absence.'

'What, Count? You?' said Madame Danglars as she signed. 'If that is so, beware, because I shall never forgive you.'

Andrea pricked up his ears.

'It is not at all my fault,' said the count, 'so I wish it to be put on record.'

Everyone was listening eagerly. Monte Cristo, who so rarely opened his mouth, was about to speak.

'You remember,' the count said, in the midst of the most complete silence, 'that it was in my house that he died, that wretch who came to rob me and who was killed as he left the house, as they believe, by his accomplice?'

'Yes,' said Danglars.

'Well, in order to assist him, they undressed him and threw his clothes into a corner where the police came and collected them. But the police, while taking the coat and jacket as evidence, forgot the waistcoat.'

The colour drained visibly from Andrea's face and he edged towards the door. He could see a cloud looming on the horizon, and this cloud seemed to be drawing a storm along behind it.

'So, this miserable waistcoat was found today, covered in blood, with a hole above the heart.'

The ladies cried out and one or two got ready to faint.

'It was brought to me. No one could guess where the rag came from; only I thought that it probably belonged to the victim. Then suddenly my valet, gingerly and with some disgust looking over this lugubrious relic, felt a piece of paper in the pocket. He took it out and found a letter – addressed to whom? Why, Baron, to you.'

'To me?' Danglars exclaimed.

'Yes, by heaven, to you. Yes, I managed to read your name under the blood with which the paper was stained,' Monte Cristo replied, in the midst of a general gasp of surprise.

'But how has this prevented Monsieur de Villefort from being here?' Mme Danglars asked, looking anxiously at her husband.

'Quite simple, Madame,' Monte Cristo replied. 'The waistcoat and the letter were what are called exhibits in evidence. I sent both of them to the crown prosecutor. You understand, my dear Baron, the legal process is the most reliable in criminal cases. There may be some plot against you.'

Andrea stared hard at Monte Cristo and vanished into the second drawing-room.

'It could be,' said Danglars. 'Was this murdered man not a former convict?'

'Yes,' said the count. 'A former convict named Caderousse.'

Danglars went a little pale. Andrea left the second drawing-room to go into the antechamber.

'But sign, sign!' said Monte Cristo. 'I see that my story has upset everyone and I most humbly beg your pardon, Madame la Baronne, and that of Mademoiselle Danglars.'

The baroness, who had just signed, handed the quill to the notary.

'Prince Cavalcanti,' the lawyer said. 'Prince Cavalcanti, where are you?'

'Andrea! Andrea!' repeated several voices of young people who were already on terms of such intimacy with the noble Italian that they called him by his first name.

'Call the prince! Tell him it's his turn to sign!' Danglars shouted to an usher. But at the same moment the crowd of onlookers swept back into the main reception room, terrified, as if some dreadful monster had entered the apartments, *quaerens quem devoret.*[3]

Indeed, there was reason to shrink back and cry out in fear.

An officer of the gendarmerie stationed two gendarmes at the door of each drawing-room, then marched over toward Danglars, preceded by a commissioner of police decked out in his scarf of office. Mme Danglars gave a cry and fainted. Danglars, who felt himself under threat – some consciences are never at rest – presented his guests with a face contorted by terror.

'What is the matter, Monsieur?' asked Monte Cristo, going to meet the commissioner.

'Which of you gentlemen is named Andrea Cavalcanti?' the commissioner asked, without replying to the count's question.

A cry of amazement rose from every corner of the room. Everyone looked around and asked questions.

'Who is this Andrea Cavalcanti, then?' Danglars enquired, in a state of near distraction.

'A former convict who escaped from the penitentiary of Toulon.'

'What crime has he committed?'

'He is accused of the murder of one Caderousse,' the commissioner said, in his impassive voice, 'formerly his fellow-inmate, as the said Caderousse was leaving the house of the Count of Monte Cristo.'

Monte Cristo looked quickly around him. Andrea had vanished.

XCVII

THE ROAD FOR BELGIUM

A few minutes after the scene of confusion produced by the sudden appearance of the brigadier of the gendarmerie in M. Danglars' house, and the revelation that followed, the vast mansion had emptied with much the same haste as would have followed the announcement of a case of the plague or cholera among the guests. In a few minutes, everyone had hurried to leave, or, rather, to flee, by every door, down every stairway, out of every exit. This was one of those circumstances in which one should not even try to offer the trite consolations that make the best of friends so unwelcome in the event of a great catastrophe.

No one remained in the banker's mansion except Danglars, shut up in his study with the officer of gendarmes; Mme Danglars, terrified, in the boudoir with which we are already acquainted; and Eugénie who, with her proud eyes and scornfully curled lips, had retired to her room with her inseparable companion, Mlle Louise d'Armilly.

As for the many servants, even more numerous that evening than usual because they had been joined for the occasion by the ice-cream chefs, cooks and maîtres d'hôtel of the Café de Paris, they were standing around in groups in the pantries and the kitchens, or in their rooms, turning against their masters the anger they felt at what they called this 'affront' to them and not at all bothered about their domestic duties – which had, in any case, naturally been suspended.

In the midst of these various people, all agitated by their own interests, only two deserve our attention: Mlle Eugénie Danglars and Mlle Louise d'Armilly.

The young fiancée, as we mentioned, had retired with a haughty air and a curled lip, and with the bearing of an insulted queen, followed by her companion who was paler and more disturbed than she was.

When they got to her room, Eugénie locked the door from the inside, while Louise slumped into a chair.

'Oh, my God! My God! What a dreadful thing!' said the young musician. 'Whoever could have imagined it? Monsieur Andrea Cavalcanti . . . an assassin . . . an escaped convict . . . a criminal!'

An ironic smile formed on Eugénie's lips. 'I really am fated,' she said. 'I escape from Morcerf and find Cavalcanti!'

'Oh, Eugénie, don't confuse one with the other.'

'Be quiet. All men are scoundrels and I am happy to be able to do more than hate them: now I despise them.'

'What can we do?' Louise asked.

'What shall we do?'

'Yes.'

'The very thing we should have done three days ago: leave.'

'So, as you are not getting married, you still want to?'

'Listen, Louise, I abhor this society life, ordered, measured and ruled out like our sheets of music paper. What I've always wanted, aspired to and yearned for is an artist's life, free, independent, where one depends only on oneself and is responsible only to oneself. Why should we stay? So that they will try, in a month's time, to marry me off again? To whom? Perhaps to Monsieur Debray: they did consider it for a while. No, Louise, no. This evening's adventure will be my excuse. I didn't look for it, I didn't ask for it. God sent it, and I welcome it.'

'How strong and courageous you are!' the fragile young blonde said to her dark-haired companion.

'Surely you know me by now? Come, Louise, let's discuss the whole matter. The carriage . . .'

'Was purchased three days ago, luckily.'

'Did you have it taken where we are to join it?'

'Yes.'

'And our passport?'

'Here it is!'

And Eugénie, with her usual sang-froid, unfolded the document and read: 'Monsieur Léon d'Armilly, twenty years old, an artist by profession, black hair, black eyes, travelling with his sister.'

'Wonderful! How did you obtain this passport?'

'I went and asked Monsieur de Monte Cristo for letters to the directors of the theatres in Rome and Naples, telling him that I was afraid to travel as a woman. He quite understood my feelings and offered to get me a man's passport. Two days later, I received this one and added, with my own hands, "travelling with his sister".'

'Fine!' Eugénie said merrily. 'Now all that's left is to pack our trunks. We'll leave on the evening of signing the contract, instead of leaving on the wedding night, that's all.'

'Think carefully, Eugénie.'

'Oh, I've thought about it. I'm tired of hearing about nothing but reports, ends of the month, rises, falls, Spanish funds, Haitian paper. Instead of that, Louise, don't you see: the air, freedom, the song of the birds, the plains of Lombardy, the canals of Venice, the palaces of Rome, the beach at Naples. How much have we got, Louise?'

The young woman answered by taking a little locked wallet out of an inlaid bureau, opening it and counting twenty-three banknotes. 'Twenty-three thousand francs,' she said.

'And at least as much again in pearls, diamonds and jewels,' said Eugénie. 'We are rich. With forty-five thousand francs, we can live like princesses for two years, or more modestly for four. But in less than six months, you with your music and I with my voice, we shall have doubled our capital. Come, you take the money, I'll look after the jewel box, so that if one of us is unlucky enough to lose her treasure, the other will still have hers. Now the suitcase! Quickly, the suitcase!'

'Wait,' Louise said, going to listen at Mme Danglars' door.

'What are you afraid of?'

'Being surprised.'

'The door's closed.'

'Suppose they tell us to open it.'

'Let them say what they like, we won't open.'

'You're a real Amazon, Eugénie!'

With a prodigious show of activity, the two girls began to throw everything they thought they would need on their journey into a trunk.

'There,' said Eugénie. 'Now, while I get changed, you close the case.'

Louise pressed with all the strength of her little hands on the lid of the trunk. 'I can't do it,' she said. 'I'm not strong enough. You close it.'

'Of course,' Eugénie said with a laugh. 'I was forgetting that I'm Hercules and you're just a feeble Omphale.'[1] And, putting her knee on the trunk, she stiffened her two white muscular arms until the two halves of the case met and Mlle d'Armilly had slid the bar of the padlock through the two hooks. When this was done, Eugénie opened a cupboard with a key she had on her and brought out a travelling cloak in quilted violet silk. 'Here,' she said. 'You can see I've thought of everything. With this on, you won't be cold.'

'What about you?'

'Oh, I don't feel the cold, as you know. In any case, dressed as a man . . .'

'Are you going to dress here?'

'Certainly.'

'But will you have time?'

'Don't worry, chicken-heart. No one is thinking of anything except the great affair. And what is there so surprising about my shutting myself in my room, when you think of how desperate I must be?'

'No, that's true. You've reassured me.'

'Come on, give me a hand.'

And from the same drawer out of which she had taken the cloak that she had just given Mlle d'Armilly (and which the latter had put around her shoulders), she took a complete set of men's clothes, from the boots to the frock-coat, with a supply of linen which included all the essentials, but nothing unnecessary.

Then, with a rapidity that showed this was surely not the first time that she had, for fun, put on the clothes of the other sex, Eugénie pulled on the boots, slipped into the trousers, rumpled her cravat, buttoned a high-necked waistcoat up to the top and got into a frock-coat that outlined her slender, well-turned waist.

'Oh, that's very good! It's truly very good indeed!' Louise said, looking admiringly at her. 'But what about your lovely black hair, those splendid locks that were the envy of every woman: will they fit under a man's hat like the one I see there?'

'You'll see,' said Eugénie. And with her left hand she grasped the thick plait of hair which her slender fingers could barely reach around, while with the right she took a pair of long scissors. Very soon the steel blades were squeaking in the midst of the magnificent and luxuriant head of hair, which fell in tresses around the young woman's feet as she bent backwards to prevent it covering her coat.

Then, when the hair on the crown of her head was cut, she turned to the sides, shearing them without the slightest sign of remorse. On the contrary, her eyes shone, more sparkling and joyful than usual under her ebony-black brows.

'Oh, your lovely hair!' said Louise, regretfully.

'Don't I look a hundred times better like this?' Eugénie asked, smoothing down the few curls left on her now entirely masculine haircut. 'Don't you think I'm more beautiful as I am?'

'Oh, you are beautiful, beautiful still,' Louise cried. 'Now, where are we going?'

'To Brussels, if you like. It's the nearest frontier. We'll travel through Brussels, Liège and Aix-la-Chapelle, then up the Rhine to Strasbourg, across Switzerland and into Italy by the Saint Gothard pass. Agreed?'

'Of course.'

'What are you looking at?'

'You. You truly are adorable like that. Anyone would say you were abducting me.'

'By God, they'd be right!'

'Oh, Eugénie! I think you swore!'

And the two girls, whom anyone would have expected to be plunged in misery, one on her own account, the other out of devotion to her friend, burst out laughing while they set about clearing up the most obvious signs of the mess that had naturally accompanied the preparations for their flight.

Then the two fugitives blew out their lights and, with eyes peeled, ears pricked and necks craned, they opened the door to a dressing-room which gave access to the service stairs leading down to the courtyard. Eugénie went first, holding the suitcase in one hand, while Mlle d'Armilly struggled with the opposite handle in both of hers.

The courtyard was empty. Midnight had just struck. The concierge was still on duty.

Eugénie crept up and saw the trusty guard asleep at the back of his lodge, spread out across a chair. She went back to Louise, picked up the case which she had put down for a moment, and the two of them, keeping to the shadow cast by the wall, reached the porch.

Eugénie got Louise to hide behind the door so that the concierge, if he should chance to wake up, would see only one person. Then, herself standing in the full glare of the lamp lighting the courtyard, she cried: 'Door!' in her finest contralto voice, knocking on the window.

The concierge got up, as Eugénie had anticipated, and even took a few steps to try to recognize the person who was going out but, seeing a young man impatiently tapping his trouser-leg with his cane, he opened immediately.

Louise at once slid like an adder through the half-open door and lightly bounded outside. Eugénie followed, apparently calm, though it is quite probable that her heart was beating faster than it usually did.

A delivery man was passing, so they asked him to take charge of the trunk, and the two young women told him they were going to the Rue de la Victoire and to Number 36 in that street; then they followed behind the man, whose presence Louise found reassuring. As for Eugénie, she was as strong as a Judith or a Delilah.

They arrived at the door of Number 36. Eugénie told the delivery man to put the trunk down, gave him a few small coins and, after knocking at the shutter, sent him on his way. The shutter on which Eugénie had tapped belonged to a little washerwoman who had been forewarned of their arrival. She had not yet gone to bed, so she opened up.

'Mademoiselle,' Eugénie said, 'have the concierge bring the barouche out of the coachhouse and send him to fetch horses from the post. Here are five francs for his trouble.'

'I do admire you,' Louise said. 'I might even say that I respect you.'

The washerwoman looked on in astonishment, but, as it was agreed that she should have 20 *louis* for herself, she did not pass any remark on the matter.

A quarter of an hour later, the concierge came back with the postilion and the horses. The latter were immediately harnessed to the carriage, on which the concierge fastened the trunk with a rope and a clasp.

'Here's the passport,' said the postilion. 'Which route does the young gentleman wish to take?'

'To Fontainebleau,' Eugénie replied in an almost masculine voice.

'What did you say?' Louise asked.

'I'm putting them off the scent,' Eugénie said. 'That woman took twenty *louis* from us, but she could betray us for forty. When we reach the boulevard, we'll change course.' And, hardly touching the running board, she leapt into the *britzka*,[2] which had been fitted out as an excellent sleeping compartment.

'You are always right, Eugénie,' the singing teacher said, taking her place next to her friend.

A quarter of an hour later, the postilion had been put back on the correct road and was cracking his whip as he drove through the barrier at Saint-Martin. 'Ah,' Louise said with a sigh. 'We're out of Paris!'

'Yes, my sweet; and the abduction has been well and truly accomplished,' Eugénie replied.

'But without violence,' said Louise.

'I'll offer that in mitigation,' said Eugénie; but her words were drowned in the noise made by the carriage as it rumbled across the cobbles at La Villette.

Monsieur Danglars had a daughter no longer.

XCVIII

THE INN OF THE BELL AND BOTTLE

Let us leave Mlle Danglars and her friend bowling along the Brussels road, and return to poor Andrea Cavalcanti, who had been so inopportunely halted in his bid for fortune.

Despite his tender years, Monsieur Andrea Cavalcanti was a most adept and intelligent young man. So, as we saw, when the very first rumours began to filter into the drawing-room, he gradually made his way to the door, then through one or two rooms, and finally vanished.

One thing that we forgot to add, though it deserves to be mentioned, is that one of the rooms through which Cavalcanti passed was that in which the bride's trousseau was exhibited: caskets of diamonds, cashmere shawls, lace from Valenciennes and English veils – in short, everything that goes to make up that mass of tempting objects, the wedding presents that are known as *le corbeille*: the word alone is enough to make a young girl's heart flutter.

What shows that Andrea was not only a very intelligent and very adept, but also a most provident young man, is that, as he ran through the room, he seized the most valuable of the jewels on display. Then, with this provision for his journey, he felt himself lighter by half as he jumped out of the window and slipped between the fingers of the gendarmes.

Tall and well built like a Greek wrestler, muscular as a Spartan warrior, Andrea sped on for a quarter of an hour without knowing where he was heading, his one aim being to put as much distance as possible between himself and the place in which he had nearly been caught. He had set off from the Rue du Mont-Blanc and, with that instinct for barriers that thieves possess in the same way that a hare knows the way to its form, he found himself at the end of the Rue Lafayette. Here, panting for breath, he stopped.

He was entirely alone, with the vast desert of the Clos Saint-Lazare on his left and, on the right, the full extent of Paris itself.

'Am I lost?' he wondered. 'No, not if I can achieve a greater burst of activity than my enemies. So my salvation boils down to a simple matter of kilometres.'

At that moment he observed a licensed cab coming up the Boulevard Poissonnière: its driver, glumly smoking his pipe, seemed bent on reaching the outer limits of the Faubourg Saint-Denis, which was no doubt the place where he was normally stationed.

'Hello, my friend!' Benedetto called.

'What is it, my good sir?' the coachman asked.

'Is your horse tired?'

'Tired? Very funny! He's done nothing all day. Four miserable fares and twenty *sous* in tips; that's seven francs in all, and I have to give ten to my boss.'

'Would you like to add these twenty francs to the seven you have?'

'Only too happy, sir. Twenty francs are not to be sniffed at. What do you want me to do for them?'

'Something very simple, if your horse is not too tired.'

'I tell you, he'll go like the wind. All we need is to know which way he has to go.'

'Towards Louvres.'

'Yes, yes, I know: the place where the ratafia comes from?'

'That's it. All we have to do is to catch one of my friends with whom I'm due to go hunting tomorrow at La Chapelle-en-Serval. He was to have waited for me here with his cab until half-past eleven. It's midnight now, so I suppose he got tired of waiting and set off on his own.'

'Quite likely so.'

'Well, can you try to catch him up?'

'I'd be only too delighted.'

'If we don't catch him between here and Le Bourget, you'll have twenty francs. If we don't catch him before Louvres, thirty.'

'And if we do catch him?'

'Forty!' Andrea said, after hesitating a moment, then realizing that he was quite safe in promising.

'Done!' said the driver. 'Hop in and we'll be off! Prroom!'

Andrea jumped into the cab and they sped rapidly across the Faubourg Saint-Denis, down the Faubourg Saint-Martin, through the barrier and into the endless suburbs of La Villette.

He made sure that they didn't meet up with the mythical friend, but from time to time he would ask after a green cab with a piebald horse from late passers-by or at still-open cabarets. As there are a good number of carriages on the road to the Netherlands, and nine-tenths of cabs are green, there was no shortage of information: the coach had always just passed; it was 500 or 200 or a hundred yards ahead. Then they overtook it; it was the wrong one.

On one occasion their cab itself was overtaken – by a barouche swept along at a gallop by two post-horses. 'Ah,' Cavalcanti thought. 'If only I had that barouche, those two good horses and, most of all, the passport one would need to obtain them.' And he gave a deep sigh.

The barouche was the one carrying Mlle Danglars and Mlle d'Armilly.

'Forward!' Andrea said. 'Keep going! We must catch him soon.' And the poor horse resumed the furious trot that it had maintained since they left Paris and arrived, steaming, in Louvres.

'Decidedly,' said Andrea, 'I can see that I am not going to catch up with my friend and that I shall kill your horse. Better stop now. Here are your thirty francs. I'll sleep at the Cheval Rouge and take the first coach where I can find a spare seat. Good-night, friend.'

He pressed six five-franc pieces into the driver's hand and jumped lightly on to the pavement.

The coachman joyfully put the money in his pocket and set off at a walk down the Paris road. Andrea pretended to go to the inn; but, after stopping for a moment by the door and hearing the sound of the cab fading into the distance, he carried on and, at a brisk trot, covered two leagues before stopping to rest. By this time he must have been very close to La Chapelle-en-Serval, where he had said he was going.

It was not tiredness that stopped Andrea. It was the need to take a decision, the need to fix on a plan.

It was impossible for him to get into a stagecoach, and equally impossible to take the mail: for either, a passport was essential.

It was also impossible, especially for a man as expert as Andrea was in criminal matters, to imagine staying in the *département* of the Oise, which is one of the most exposed and closely watched in France.

Andrea sat down on the edge of a ditch, put his head between his hands and thought.

Ten minutes later, he looked up. He had come to a decision.

He was wearing a sleeveless jacket which he had managed to seize from its hanger in the antechamber and button over his evening dress; and this he smeared with dust down one side. Then, marching into La Chapelle-en-Serval, he boldly went up to the door of the only inn in the village and knocked on the door. The landlord opened.

'My friend,' Andrea said, 'I was on my way from Mortefontaine to Senlis when my horse, which is a troublesome beast, shied and threw me. I must get to Compiègne tonight or my family will be very worried about me. Do you have a horse I could hire?'

Good, bad or indifferent, an innkeeper always has a horse.

This particular one called his stableboy, ordered him to saddle 'The Grey' and woke up his son, a child of seven years old, who would mount up behind the gentleman and bring the animal back. Andrea gave the innkeeper twenty francs and, as he was taking them from his pocket, let fall a visiting card.

This card belonged to one of his friends from the Café de Paris. The result was that the innkeeper, when Andrea had gone and he picked up the card that had fallen from his pocket, was convinced he had hired his horse to Monsieur le Comte de Mauléon, of 25, Rue Saint-Dominique – this being the name and address on the card.

The Grey was not a fast mover but steady and conscientious. In three and a half hours Andrea had covered the nine leagues separating him from Compiègne. Four o'clock was striking on the town hall clock when he came into the square where the stagecoaches drew up.

There is an excellent hostelry in Compiègne which even those who have stayed there only once will remember.[1]

Andrea had stopped here on one of his excursions around Paris and he recalled the Bell and Bottle. He took his bearings, saw the inn sign by the light of a streetlamp and, after sending the boy away with all the small change he had on him, knocked at the door, rightly judging that he had two or three hours in front of him and that the best thing was to prepare for future exertions with a good sleep and a good supper.

A young lad opened the door. 'My friend,' Andrea said, 'I have just come from Saint-Jean-au-Bois, where I had dinner. I was counting on taking the coach that goes through here at midnight but, like an idiot, I got lost and have been wandering around the woods for the past four hours. So, would you be kind enough to give me one of those pretty little rooms overlooking the courtyard and send up a cold chicken, with a bottle of claret.'

The boy was quite unsuspecting. Andrea's voice was completely composed, he had a cigar in his mouth and his hands in the pockets of his jacket; his clothes were smart, his beard fresh and his boots beyond reproach. He looked like a gentleman up late, nothing more.

While the boy was preparing Andrea's room, the hostess got up. Andrea greeted her with his most charming smile and asked if he might have Number 3, which he had occupied last time he was here in Compiègne. Unfortunately, Number 3 was already occupied, by a young man travelling with his sister.

Andrea seemed utterly downcast and was only consoled when the hostess assured him that Number 7, which was being got ready for him, had precisely the same outlook as Number 3. Warming his feet and chatting about the latest Chantilly races, he waited for them to announce that his room was ready.

Andrea had had good reason to talk of those pretty rooms overlooking the yard. The courtyard of the Bell and Bottle, with the three tiers of galleries which make it seem like a theatre, with the jasmine and clematis which lightly entwine its pillars like a natural decoration, is one of the most lovely inn yards anywhere in the world.

The chicken was fresh, the wine was old, the fire crackled brightly.

Andrea was surprised to find himself dining as heartily as though nothing had happened. Then he went to bed and fell asleep almost immediately with that relentless sleep that a man always has at twenty years old, however much his conscience troubles him. Though we are forced to confess that while Andrea's conscience had good reason to trouble him, it did nothing of the sort.

This is Andrea's plan, which accounted for most of his feeling of security: when day broke, he would get up and leave the hotel, after scrupulously settling his bill. He would make for the forest and, on the pretence of a desire to do some studies in oils, he would rent a room from a peasant. He would obtain a woodcutter's costume and an axe, exchanging the lion's clothes for those of a peasant; then, with his hands covered in earth, his hair coloured by using a lead comb and his complexion darkened by a dye prepared to a recipe given him by his former comrades, he would go from one stretch of woodland to the next until he reached the nearest frontier, walking by night and sleeping by day in the woods or quarries, and not going near any human habitation except to buy a loaf of bread from time to time.

Once he was across the frontier, he would convert his diamonds into cash and consolidate the money into a dozen bank drafts, which he would always carry on him in case of accident. He would once more be the possessor of some 50,000 *livres*, which, to his mind, did not seem too bad a second best.

Apart from that, he was counting on the interest that the Danglars would have in hushing up their misfortune. This is why, apart from sheer tiredness, Andrea went to sleep so quickly and slept so well.

As an additional precaution, Andrea had not closed his shutters, so that the light would wake him. Otherwise he had merely bolted the door and left open on his bedside table a certain very sharp knife which he knew to be of excellent quality and which never left him.

At about seven o'clock, Andrea was woken by a bright, warm ray of sunshine which settled on his face.

In every well-organized mind the dominant idea – and there always is a dominant idea – is the one which, being the last to go to sleep, is also the first to shine among the newly awakened thoughts.

Andrea had not fully opened his eyes before the dominant idea seized him, telling him that he had overslept. He leapt out of bed and ran over to the window.

A gendarme was crossing the yard.

A gendarme is one of the most striking objects there is, even in the eyes of a man whose conscience is untroubled; but for a timid soul or one which has some reason for anxiety, the yellow, blue and white of a gendarme's uniform take on a terrifying hue.

'Why this gendarme?' Andrea wondered. Then he answered his own question with the logic that the reader will already have noticed in him: 'There is nothing surprising about a gendarme in an inn; but let's get dressed, even so.' And he dressed with a speed that the possession of a valet had not diminished in the few months of fashionable life he had led in Paris.

'Good,' Andrea said, as he dressed. 'I shall wait for him to leave and, when he does so, I shall sneak out.' As he said these words, freshly booted and cravated, Andrea quietly went across to the window and once more lifted the net curtain.

Not only had the first gendarme not left, but the young man saw a second blue, yellow and white uniform at the foot of the staircase – the only one down which he could go – and a third, on horseback, with a carbine in his hand, was doing sentry duty at the main door, the only one through which he could reach the road. This third gendarme was highly significant, because behind him stood a semi-circle of onlookers blocking the door.

'They're after me!' was Andrea's first thought. 'Damnation!' The colour drained from his face and he looked around anxiously.

His room, like all those on that floor, only gave on to the external gallery, which was open to all eyes.

'I am lost!' was Andrea's second thought.

In reality, for a man in Andrea's situation, arrest meant the assizes, sentencing and death – death without mercy and without delay. For a moment he crushed his head convulsively between his hands; and in that moment he nearly went mad with fear.

Soon, however, from the host of thoughts milling around in his head, one hope emerged. A pale smile appeared on his wan lips and his taut cheeks.

He looked around. The things he was looking for were on the marble top of a bureau: a pen, paper and ink.

He dipped the pen in the ink and wrote, in a hand which he forced to remain firm, the following lines, on the first leaf of the pad: 'I have no money to pay you, but I am not a dishonest man. As security I am leaving this pin which must be worth ten times my bill. Please forgive me for leaving at daybreak: I was ashamed!'

He took out his tiepin and put it on the sheet of paper.

Having done this, instead of leaving the room locked, he drew back the bolts and even left the door ajar, as if he had gone out of the room and forgotten to shut it behind him. Then, like a man who was used to this kind of exercise, he slipped into the chimney, pulling to behind him the paper screen representing Achilles with Deidamia,[2] rubbing out with his feet even the traces of his footprints in the ashes, and began to climb up the arching tube that offered him the only means of escape in which he could still trust.

At that very moment, the first gendarme whose appearance had struck Andrea was climbing the staircase, preceded by the commissioner of police and covered by the second gendarme who was guarding the bottom of the stairs and could himself call for reinforcements from the one at the door.

Here are the circumstances to which Andrea owed this visit – and the considerable efforts he was making to receive his guests.

At first light the telegraphs had come into operation in all directions. In every locality, almost immediately informed, the relevant authorities had been woken up and the forces of law and order launched in pursuit of Caderousse's murderer.

Compiègne, as a royal residence, a hunting town and a garrison town, has an abundance of officials, gendarmes and police commissioners. Consequently, as soon as the telegraph order arrived, the searches began; the Bell and Bottle Inn is the main hotel in town, so naturally that is where they started.

Moreover, reports from the sentries who that night were on guard outside the town hall – which is adjacent to the inn – stated that several travellers had arrived during the night at the hostelry.

The sentry who had been relieved at six in the morning even recalled, the moment after he had taken up his post, that is to say at a few minutes past four, having seen a young man riding a white horse with a little peasant boy behind him, the said young man dismounting in the main square and sending away the boy and his horse, then going and knocking at the door of the Bell and Bottle, which opened, then shut behind him. This young man, who was up at that late hour, was the object of suspicion; and this young man was none other than Andrea.

On the basis of this information, the commissioner of police and the gendarme, who was a brigadier, were proceeding towards Andrea's door. They found it ajar.

'Oh, ho!' said the brigadier, a wily old fox skilled in the tricks of his trade. 'Bad sign, an open door. I'd rather see it triple-locked.'

Indeed, the little note and the pin which Andrea had left on the table confirmed the sad fact – or at least tended to so do: Andrea had gone. I say 'tended', because the brigadier was not a man to close a case on one piece of evidence.

He looked around him, under the bed, behind the curtains, in the cupboards, and finally stopped at the chimney. Thanks to Andrea's precautions, there was no sign of his footsteps in the ashes. However, this was still a way out, and in the present circumstances every exit had to be seriously investigated. So the brigadier called for some wood and some straw, stuffed it into the chimney as he might a mortar, and lit it.

The fire made the brick walls crack, and a thick column of smoke rose through the passages and towards the sky like a dark plume from a volcano; but it did not bring down the prisoner as the brigadier expected.

The reason was that Andrea, having been at war with society all his life, was at least a match for a gendarme, even one who had risen to the respectable rank of brigadier. Anticipating the fire, he had climbed out on to the roof and was hiding behind the chimney stack.

For a moment he hoped he might be saved, because he heard the brigadier calling the two gendarmes and shouting to them: 'He's gone!' But, craning his neck, he saw that the men, instead of going away, which would be the normal thing as soon as they heard this, in fact, on the contrary, doubled in vigilance.

He in turn looked around him. On his right, like a dark rampart, was the town hall, a huge sixteenth-century building, and from the windows and openings of this pile you could see every nook and cranny on the roof, just as you can see into a valley from a mountain. Andrea realized that at any moment he would see the head of the brigadier of the gendarmerie appear at one of those openings.

If he was seen, he was lost. He had no hope of escaping in a rooftop chase.

He therefore resolved to get down, not through the chimney by which he had come up, but by some similar path. He looked for a chimney from which no smoke was rising, crawled across the roof to it and vanished down it without anyone seeing him.

At the same moment, a little window in the town hall opened and the brigadier of gendarmerie poked his head out of it. For a short while the head remained motionless like one of the stone gargoyles decorating the building. Then, with a long sigh of disappointment, it vanished.

The brigadier, impassive and upright as the law he represented, walked through the crowd that had gathered on the square without replying to any of the thousand questions flung at him, and went back into the inn.

'Well?' the two gendarmes asked in turn.

'Well, lads,' the brigadier replied, 'the bandit must have got well away early this morning; but we shall send out along the roads to Villers-Cotterêts and Noyon, and scour the forest, and that is where, incontrovertibly . . .'

The worthy officer had just given birth to this high-sounding adverb, with the intonation peculiar to those of his kind, when a long cry of terror, accompanied by the frantic ringing of a bell, shook the courtyard of the inn.

'Huh!' the brigadier cried. 'What's that?'

'There's a guest who seems in a great deal of a hurry,' said the innkeeper. 'What number is ringing?'

'Number three.'

'So go there, boy!'

At that moment the cries and the sound of the bell increased in intensity. The boy started to run.

'No, stop!' said the brigadier, halting him. 'It sounds to me as if the person ringing needs more than a waiter. We'll serve him a gendarme. Who's staying in number three?'

'The little young man who arrived with his sister last night in a post-chaise and asked for a room with two beds.'

The bell rang again, with an anguished tone.

'Here, follow me!' the brigadier called to the commissioner. 'Follow me and hurry.'

'One moment,' said the innkeeper. 'There are two staircases to room number three: internal and external.'

'Very well,' the brigadier said, 'I'll take the inside: internal affairs are my department. Are the carbines loaded?'

'Yes, brigadier.'

'Well, keep watch outside, the rest of you, and if he tries to escape, shoot. He's a master criminal, the telegraph says.'

The brigadier, followed by the commissioner, at once disappeared up the inside staircase, leaving a hum of excitement that his revelations about Andrea had awakened in the crowd.

Here is what had happened:

Andrea had very nimbly descended two-thirds of the way down the chimney, but when he got to that point he lost his footing and, though he pressed with his hands, he came down faster and, in particular, more noisily, than he would have wished. This would not have mattered if the room had been empty but, as ill-luck would have it, it was occupied.

Two women were sleeping in one bed and the noise woke them up. They looked in the direction from which it had come and saw a man appear in the fireplace. One of the women, the blonde, gave the dreadful cry that echoed through the whole house, while the other, who was a brunette, grasped the bell-cord and gave the alarm by tugging it as hard as she could.

Andrea, as one can see, was dogged by misfortune.

'For pity's sake!' he cried, pale and distraught, without seeing whom he was addressing. 'For pity's sake, don't call anyone. Save me! I don't mean you any harm.'

'Andrea the murderer!' one of the young women exclaimed.

'Eugénie! Mademoiselle Danglars!' Cavalcanti muttered, going from terror to amazement.

'Help! Help!' cried Mlle d'Armilly, seizing the bell-pull from Eugénie's lifeless hand and ringing even more energetically than her companion.

'Save me, they're after me!' Andrea said, clasping his hands. 'For pity's sake, spare me, don't turn me in.'

'Too late. They're coming up,' said Eugénie.

'Then hide me somewhere. Say that you were afraid for no reason. You can allay suspicion and you will save my life.'

The two women, clasped in each other's arms, their blankets wrapped around them, remained deaf to this pleading voice. Every kind of apprehension, every sort of repugnance, struggled in their minds.

'All right then,' said Eugénie. 'Go back the way you came, wretch. Leave, and we shall say nothing.'

'There he is! There he is!' cried a voice on the landing. 'There he is: I can see him!'

The brigadier had put his eye to the keyhole and had seen Andrea standing and begging. A heavy blow from the butt of a rifle broke the lock, two more loosed the bolts, and the door fell inwards.

Andrea ran to the opposite door, which overlooked the gallery above the courtyard, and opened it, ready to jump. The two gendarmes were there with their carbines levelled at him.

He stopped dead. Standing, his face pale, his body bent slightly backwards, he clasped his useless knife tightly in his hand.

'Run!' said Mlle d'Armilly, pity filling her heart as fear drained from it. 'Oh, run, do!'

'Or kill yourself!' said Eugénie, adopting the voice and posture of one of those vestals who, in the circus, would motion with their thumbs to order the victorious gladiator to finish off his stricken adversary. Andrea shuddered and looked at the young woman with a smile of contempt, proving that his corrupt nature did not understand this sublime ferocity of honour. 'Kill myself?' he said, throwing down his knife. 'What is the point of that?'

'But you said it yourself!' said Mlle Danglars. 'You'll be condemned to death and executed like a common criminal.'

'Huh!' Cavalcanti replied, folding his arms. 'One has friends.'

The brigadier came towards him, holding his sabre.

'Come, come,' said Cavalcanti. 'Put up your sword, my good fellow; there's no sense in getting so worked up about it. I'll come quietly.' And he held out his hands for the handcuffs.

The two young women looked in horror at the hideous transformation taking place before their eyes, as the man of the world shuffled off his outer shell and became once more the convict.

Andrea turned around to them and, with an impudent smile, said: 'Do you have any message for your father, Mademoiselle Eugénie? Because, in all probability, I shall be returning to Paris.'

Eugénie buried her head in both hands.

'Oh, come, now!' said Andrea. 'There's no need to be ashamed. I don't blame you for catching the mail coach to chase after me . . . Why! I was almost your husband!' And with this quip he went out, leaving the two fugitives a prey to the agonies of shame and the remarks of the crowd.

An hour later, both dressed in women's clothes, they climbed into their travelling barouche. The door of the inn had been shut to keep them from constant scrutiny; but when the door was opened they still had to pass along a double line of onlookers, muttering and staring with eager eyes.

Eugénie lowered the blinds but, even though she could no longer see, she could still hear, and the sound of sniggering reached her. 'Oh, why is the world not a desert!' she exclaimed, throwing herself into the arms of Mlle d'Armilly, her eyes blazing with that fury which made Nero wish that the Roman world had one neck, so that he could cut it with a single blow.

The following day they arrived at the Hôtel de Flandre, in Brussels. By then, Andrea had already spent one night as a prisoner in the conciergerie.

XCIX

THE LAW

We have seen how Mlle Danglars and Mlle d'Armilly were left in peace to undergo their transformation and make their escape: the reason is that everyone was too preoccupied with his or her own affairs to bother with theirs.

We shall leave the banker in a cold sweat as he drew up the huge columns of his liabilities to confront the spectre of bankruptcy, and follow the baroness who, after remaining momentarily crushed by the blow that had fallen on her, had gone to seek advice from her usual counsellor, Lucien Debray.

The baroness had been counting on the marriage to give up finally a guardianship which, with a daughter of Eugénie's character, could not be anything but a burden; because, in those sorts of tacit agreements that establish the hierarchical links in a family, the mother is only truly able to command her daughter when she can offer her a continual example of wisdom and a model of perfection.

Now Madame Danglars was in awe of Eugénie's perspicacity and the advice of Mlle d'Armilly. She had intercepted certain contemptuous looks cast by her daughter in the direction of Debray – looks which seemed to indicate that Eugénie knew all about her amorous and financial relations with the private secretary. In fact, a better-informed and closer examination would have told her that

Eugénie detested Debray, not as a cause of disruption and scandal in her father's house, but quite simply because she classed him among those bipeds whom Diogenes tried to avoid describing as 'men' and Plato designated under the circumlocution 'two-footed animals without feathers'.

From her own point of view – and unfortunately in this world everyone has his or her own point of view which obscures that of others – from her point of view, then, Mme Danglars regretted infinitely that Eugénie's marriage had been broken off, not because the match was suitable, compatible and destined to make her daughter happy, but because it would have given her back her own freedom.

Consequently, as we have said, she hurried round to Debray's. Like everyone else in Paris, he had been present on the evening of the contract and had witnessed the scandal that followed, and had now lost no time in retiring to his club, where he was discussing with a few friends the event which was by now a subject of conversation for three-quarters of the inhabitants of the supremely talkative town, known as the capital of the world.

Just as Mme Danglars, dressed in a black robe and hidden behind a veil, was climbing the stairs to Debray's apartment, despite the concierge's assurance that the young gentleman was not at home, Debray was engaged in refuting the arguments of a friend who had tried to persuade him that, after the dreadful scandal that had taken place, it was his duty as a friend of the house to marry Mlle Eugénie Danglars and her two million francs.

Debray was defending himself like a man who asks nothing better than to be defeated. The idea had often occurred to him of its own accord. But then from time to time, knowing Eugénie, with her independent and haughty character, he would adopt a completely defensive attitude, saying that the match was impossible; yet meanwhile allowing himself to be secretly titillated by the wicked thought that (if moralists are to be believed) incessantly worries at the most honest and the purest of man, lurking in the depth of his soul like Satan behind the Cross. The conversation, as one can see, was interesting, since it involved matters of such gravity and, with tea and gambling, lasted until one in the morning.

Meanwhile the valet had shown Mme Danglars into Lucien's apartment, where she waited, veiled and tremulous, in the little green drawing-room between two baskets of flowers that she herself had sent that morning and which Debray, it must be said, had trimmed and set in tiers with a care that made the poor woman forgive his absence.

At twenty to twelve, Mme Danglars grew tired of waiting, got back in her cab and had herself driven home.

Society women have this in common with successful courtesans: they do not usually return home after midnight. The baroness slipped back into the house as unobtrusively as Eugénie had left it: her heart beating, she tiptoed up the stairs to her apartment which, as we know, was next to Eugénie's. She was so afraid of causing tongues to wag and, poor woman – respectable at least in this respect – believed so firmly in her daughter's innocence and attachment to the paternal home!

When she got in, she listened at Eugénie's door and then, hearing no sound, tried to open it; but the bolts were shut.

Mme Danglars assumed that Eugénie, exhausted by the dreadful emotions of the evening, had gone to bed and was sleeping. She called the chambermaid and questioned her.

'Mademoiselle Eugénie went to her room,' the chambermaid said, 'with Mademoiselle d'Armilly. Then they took tea together and after that sent me away, saying that they had no further need of me.'

Since then the chambermaid had been in the servants' quarters and, like everyone else, thought that the two young ladies were in their room. So Mme Danglars went to bed without the slightest suspicion; but, though her mind was at rest as far as the participants were concerned, it worried about the events.

As her ideas became clearer, the significance of the incident grew larger. It was no longer a mere scandal, it was a pandemonium; it was no longer a matter of shame, but of ignominy. Now the baroness involuntarily recalled how pitiless she had been towards poor Mercédès, recently afflicted with as great a misfortune through her husband and her son.

'Eugénie,' she thought, 'is ruined, and so are we. The affair, in the way it will be represented, covers us with opprobrium: in a society such as ours, certain forms of ridicule are open wounds, bleeding and incurable.'

'How fortunate,' she murmured, 'that God gave Eugénie that strange character which has so often been a cause of concern to me!' And she looked gratefully up towards heaven from which some mysterious Providence arranges everything in advance according to what will occur and sometimes transforms a defect, or even a vice, into a piece of good fortune.

Then her thoughts soared through space, like a bird extending its wings to cross an abyss, and alighted on Cavalcanti. 'That Andrea was a wretch, a thief, an assassin; yet the same Andrea had manners which indicated at least a half-education, if not a complete one; this same Andrea presented himself to society with an appearance of great wealth and the support of honourable names.'

How could she see her way through this puzzle? Whom could she ask for help in this cruel dilemma?

As a woman, her first instinct, which sometimes proves fatal, had been to look for help from the man she loved, but Debray could only offer advice. She must turn to someone more powerful.

This was when the baroness thought of M. de Villefort.

It was M. de Villefort who had wanted to have Cavalcanti arrested; it was M. de Villefort who had pitilessly brought discord into the heart of her family, as if it had been foreign to him.

But no, on reflection, the crown prosecutor was not a pitiless man. He was a judge and the prisoner of duty, a firm and loyal friend who, with an unrelenting but practised hand, had applied a scalpel to corruption. He was not an executioner but a surgeon, a surgeon who wanted to cut Danglars' honour free from the ignominy of that irredeemable young man whom they had introduced to society as their son-in-law.

If M. de Villefort, a friend of the Danglars family, acted in that way, there was no further reason to suppose that the crown prosecutor had known anything in advance or had any complicity in Andrea's intrigues. So, on reflection, Villefort's conduct still appeared to the baroness in a light that showed it to their mutual advantage. But here his inflexibility must stop. She would go and see him the next day and persuade him to agree, not to fail in his judicial duties, but at least to make full allowances for them.

She would appeal to the past. She would refresh his memories and beg him in the name of a time that was guilty, but happy. M. de Villefort would be flexible about the matter, or at least – for this, he would only need to turn a blind eye – at least he would let Cavalcanti escape and prosecute the crime only against that shadow of a criminal who can be tried *in absentia*.

Then, only then, would she sleep easily.

The following day she got up at nine o'clock and, without ringing for her chambermaid or giving any sign of life to anyone, she dressed, with the same simplicity as on the previous evening, then went down the stairs and out of the Danglars residence, walked as far as the Rue de Provence, got into a cab and had herself driven to M. de Villefort's house.

For the past month this accursed place had had the mournful appearance of a lazaretto during an outbreak of the plague. Some of the rooms were closed, inside and out. The closed shutters would only open to let in air; and then one might see a lackey's terrified face at the window, which would then shut like a tombstone falling back on a sepulchre, while the neighbours were whispering: 'Shall we see another coffin come out of the crown prosecutor's house today?'

Mme Danglars shuddered at the appearance of this desolate house. She got out of her cab and, her knees giving way beneath her, went up to the closed door and rang the bell.

It was only at the third ring of the bell, whose mournful tinkling seemed to participate in the general sadness, that a concierge appeared, opening the door just wide enough to let out his words.

He saw a woman, a lady, elegantly dressed; but despite this the door remained almost shut.

'Come on!' said the baroness. 'Open up.'

'Firstly, Madame, who are you?' the concierge asked.

'Who am I? But you know me perfectly well.'

'We don't know anyone any more, Madame.'

'But, my good fellow, you're mad!' exclaimed the baroness.

'Where do you come from?'

'This really is too much!'

'Excuse me, Madame, it's orders. Your name?'

'Baroness Danglars. You've seen me twenty times.'

'Quite possibly, Madame. Now what do you want?'

'Oh! What a cheek! I'll complain to Monsieur de Villefort about the impertinence of his staff.'

'Madame, it's not impertinence, it's a precaution. No one comes in here without a word from Monsieur d'Avrigny or without having business with the crown prosecutor.'

'Well, as it happens I do have business with the crown prosecutor.'

'Urgent business?'

'As you must see, since I have not yet got back into my carriage. But let's make an end of this: here is my card; take it to your master.'

'Will Madame wait here?'

'Yes. Go on.'

The concierge closed the door, leaving Mme Danglars in the street.

Admittedly she did not have to wait long. A short time later the door opened wide enough to admit her. She went through and it closed behind her. Once they were in the courtyard, the concierge, without for a moment losing sight of the door, took a whistle out of his pocket and blew it. Monsieur de Villefort's valet appeared on the steps.

'Madame must forgive that good fellow,' he said, coming down to meet her. 'He has precise orders and Monsieur de Villefort asked me to tell Madame that he could not have done otherwise.'

Also in the courtyard there was a supplier, who had been admitted only after the same precautions and whose merchandise was being examined.

The baroness went up the steps. She was deeply affected by the prevailing mood which seemed, as it were, to extend the circle of her own melancholy. Still guided by the valet, she was shown into the magistrate's study without her guide once losing sight of her.

Preoccupied though she was by what had brought her here, the reception she had been given by all these underlings seemed to her so undeserved that Mme Danglars started to complain. But Villefort raised a head so bowed down with sorrow and looked at her with such a sad smile that the complaint died on her lips.

'Please excuse my servants for a regime of terror for which I cannot blame them. Suspect themselves, they have become suspicious.'

Mme Danglars had often heard people speak of this regime of terror which the judge mentioned, but if she had not seen it with her own eyes she could never have believed that it could have been taken to this point.

'So you too are unhappy?' she said.

'Yes, Madame,' the judge replied.

'Then you must feel for me?'

'I do, Madame, sincerely.'

'And you understand why I'm here?'

'You want to talk to me about what is happening to you, I suppose?'

'Yes, Monsieur. A terrible disaster.'

'You mean, a mishap.'

'A mishap!' the baroness cried.

'Alas, Madame,' the crown prosecutor replied imperturbably, 'I have reached the point where I only describe what is irreparable as a disaster.'

'Ah, Monsieur! Do you think people will forget . . . ?'

'People forget everything, Madame,' said Villefort. 'Your daughter's marriage will take place tomorrow, if not today; or in a week, if not tomorrow. And as for regretting Mademoiselle Eugénie's intended spouse, I can't imagine you would do that.'

Mme Danglars stared at Villefort, amazed by this almost mocking imperturbability. 'Am I in the presence of a friend?' she asked in a voice full of pained dignity.

'You know you are,' Villefort replied, blushing as he gave this assurance. In fact it alluded to events other than the ones that were on his mind and that of the baroness at that moment.

'Well then, my dear Villefort,' the baroness said, 'be more affectionate. Speak to me as a friend and not as a judge; and when I am deeply unhappy, don't tell me I should be joyful.'

Villefort bowed. 'When I hear tell of misfortunes, Madame,' he said, 'I have, in the past three months, acquired the unfortunate habit of thinking about my own; this selfish comparison takes place in my mind in spite of myself. This is why, beside my misfortunes, yours seemed to me a mishap; this is why, beside my dreadful situation, yours seemed to me something to envy; but it upsets you, so let's forget it. You were saying, Madame?'

'I have come to ask you, my friend,' the baroness resumed, 'how the affair of this impostor stands at present.'

'Impostor!' Villefort repeated. 'Assuredly, Madame, you are determined to extenuate certain things and exaggerate others. Monsieur Andrea Cavalcanti – or, rather, Monsieur Benedetto – an impostor! You are mistaken, Madame: Monsieur Benedetto is nothing more or less than a murderer.'

'Monsieur, I don't deny that you are right to correct me; but the more harshly you arm yourself against this unfortunate, the harder you will strike our family. Come, forget him for the moment. Instead of pursuing him, let him escape.'

'You have come too late, Madame. The orders have been given.'

'Well, if he is arrested . . . Do you think they will arrest him?'

'I hope so.'

'If he is arrested . . . listen, I hear that the prisons are overflowing – well, leave him in prison.'

The crown prosecutor shook his head.

'At least until my daughter is married,' the baroness added.

'Impossible, Madame. The law has its procedures.'

'Even for me?' the baroness asked, half joking, half serious.

'For everyone,' Villefort replied. 'And for me as for everyone else.'

'Ah!' the baroness exclaimed, without putting into words what her thoughts had revealed by this exclamation.

Villefort looked at her with the look he used to sound out a person's thoughts. 'I know what you mean,' he said. 'You are referring to those dreadful rumours that are circulating, that there is something unnatural about all those deaths which over the past three months have clothed me in mourning, and the death from which Valentine has just escaped, as if by a miracle.'

'I was not thinking of that,' Mme Danglars hastened to say.

'Yes, Madame, you were, and it's only fair, because you could not do otherwise than to think of it; and you were saying to yourself: you hunt out crime, so why are there crimes in your house that go unpunished?'

The baroness blushed.

'You were thinking that, were you not, Madame?'

'I confess, I was.'

'Then I shall answer you.'

Villefort drew his chair up close to that of Mme Danglars and, resting both hands on his desk and adopting a more subdued tone than usual, he said: 'There are crimes that go unpunished because the criminals are not known and one is afraid of striking an innocent head instead of a guilty one; but when these criminals are discovered –' here Villefort reached out his hand towards a crucifix hanging opposite his desk and repeated ' – when these criminals are discovered, by the living God, Madame, whoever they are, they shall die! Now, after the oath I have just sworn, and which I shall keep, do you dare, Madame, to ask my pardon for that wretch?'

'Well, now, Monsieur,' said Mme Danglars, 'are you sure that he is as guilty as they say?'

'Listen: here is his record. Benedetto, sentenced first of all to five years in the galleys for forgery, at the age of sixteen. As you can see, the young man showed promise. Then an escaped convict, then a murderer.'

'And who is he, the wretch?'

'Who knows? A tramp, a Corsican.'

'He has not been claimed by anyone?'

'No one. His parents are unknown.'

'But the man who came from Lucca?'

'Another crook, his accomplice perhaps.'

The baroness clasped her hands. 'Villefort,' she began, in her sweetest and most cajoling tone.

'For God's sake, Madame,' the prosecutor replied, with a resolve that was somewhat unfeeling. 'For God's sake, never ask me to pardon a guilty man. What am I? The law. Does the law have eyes to see your sorrow? Does the law have ears to hear your soft pleadings? Does the law have a memory to make itself the conduit for your tender thoughts? No, Madame, the law orders and when it orders, it strikes.

'You will tell me that I am a living being and not a book of laws; a man, not a rule. Look at me, Madame; look around me: have men treated me as a brother? Have they loved me? Have they considered me? Have they spared me? Has anyone ever begged pardon for Monsieur de Villefort, and has anyone ever granted a pardon to Monsieur de Villefort? No, no, no! Struck, struck and struck again!

'You insist, woman, siren that you are, in speaking to me with that charming and expressive look that reminds me I should blush. Yes, yes, blush for what you know about, and perhaps for other things as well.

'But in the end, since I myself failed and was found wanting – more profoundly perhaps than other men; well, since that time I have shaken out their clothes to discover a blemish, and I have always found it; I will say more: I have found it with joy, this evidence of human weakness and perversity.

'Every man that I found guilty, every guilty man that I punished, seemed to me a living proof, a proof constantly renewed, that I was not some hideous exception! Alas, alas, alas! The whole world is wicked, Madame, so let us prove it and strike down the wicked man!'

Villefort uttered these final words with a feverish vehemence that gave them a kind of savage eloquence.

Madame Danglars decided to try one last effort. 'But,' she said, 'you tell me this young man is a tramp, an orphan, abandoned by everyone?'

'Too bad, too bad – or, rather, so much the better. Providence has ensured that no one will weep for him.'

'But this is striking at the weak, Monsieur.'

'A weak man who kills!'

'His dishonour will reflect on my house.'

'Do I not have death in mine?'

'Ah, Monsieur,' cried the baroness, 'you have no pity for your fellow man. Well, I tell you now: there will be no pity for you!'

'So be it!' said Villefort, raising his hands in a threatening gesture towards heaven.

'At least put back this wretch's case, if he is arrested, until the next assizes. This will give us six months for people to forget.'

'No, I cannot,' said Villefort. 'I still have five days. The charge has been made; five days is more time than I need. And, don't you realize, Madame, that I too need to forget? Well, when I work – and I work night and day – there are moments when I no longer remember; and when I no longer remember, I am happy as the dead are happy; but that is far better than suffering . . .'

'Monsieur, he has fled. Let him escape. To do nothing is the simplest kind of mercy.'

'But I told you! It is too late! The telegraph was in operation at daybreak and by now . . .'

'Monsieur,' said the valet, coming in, 'a dragoon has brought this dispatch from the Ministry of the Interior.'

Villefort seized the letter and hastily broke the seals. Mme Danglars shivered with terror, Villefort trembled with joy.

'Arrested!' he cried. 'He has been arrested at Compiègne. It's over!'

Mme Danglars got up, cold and pale.

'Farewell, Monsieur,' she said.

'Farewell, Madame,' the crown prosecutor replied, almost joyful, as he showed her to the door. Then, returning to his desk, he struck the letter with the back of his right hand and said: 'There now! I had a fraud, I had three thefts, I had three cases of arson, all I lacked was a murder. And here it is: it will be a fine session.'

C

THE APPARITION

As the crown prosecutor had told Mme Danglars, Valentine had not yet recovered. In fact, quite exhausted, she was keeping to her bed and it was there, in her room, from Mme de Villefort, that she learned of the events which we have just described, namely the flight of Eugénie and the arrest of Andrea Cavalcanti, or rather Benedetto, as well as the charge of murder against him.

But Valentine was so weak that the story did not perhaps have as much effect on her as it would have done had she been in her normal state. There were only a few vague notions and blurred images, and even these mingled with odd ideas and fleeting spectres born of her sick mind or drifting before her eyes; and soon even they vanished so that her personal feelings could resume with all their force.

During the day Valentine was still kept close to reality by the presence of Noirtier, who had his granddaughter brought to him and stayed with her, brooding over her with paternal eyes. Then, when he came back from court, Villefort in turn spent an hour or two with his father and his child.

At six o'clock he retired to his study. At eight o'clock, Monsieur d'Avrigny would arrive, personally delivering the night-time medicine that had been prepared for the young woman. Then Noirtier was taken away, a night nurse chosen by the doctor replaced everyone and she herself retired only when, at around ten or eleven o'clock, Valentine had fallen asleep.

On her way down, this person gave the keys of Valentine's room to Monsieur de Villefort himself, so that no one could reach the patient except through Mme de Villefort's apartments and little Edouard's room.

Every morning, Morrel came to Noirtier for news of Valentine; but, astonishingly enough, Morrel seemed less anxious as the days went by. Firstly, although subject to extreme nervous excitement, Valentine improved day by day – and then, had Monte Cristo not told him, when he rushed round to see him, that if Valentine was not dead in two hours she would be safe? Well, she was still alive, and four days had passed.

The nervous excitement pursued Valentine even into her sleep; or rather into the state of drowsiness that, for her, followed wakefulness. It was now that, in the silence of night and the half-dark created by the night-light burning in its alabaster stand on the mantelpiece, she would see those passing shades that haunt the rooms of the sick and which fever shakes with its quivering wings.

At such times she would imagine she saw either her stepmother, threatening her, or Morrel, opening his arms, or beings who were almost strangers in her ordinary life, like the Count of Monte Cristo. In such moments of delirium, even the furniture seemed to move and wander about the room. This would last until two or three in the morning, when a deep sleep would overtake her and last until daybreak.

It was on the evening after the morning when Valentine learned of the flight of Eugénie and Benedetto's arrest – and when, after being confused for a moment with the sensations of her own life, these events began bit by bit to leave her thoughts – and following the successive withdrawal of Villefort, d'Avrigny and Noirtier, while eleven o'clock was striking on the clock of Saint-Philippe-du-Roule and after the night nurse had given her patient the medicine prepared by the doctor and shut the door of her room, and retired to the servants' quarters where she was now shuddering as she listened to what the servants had to say, furnishing her memory with the dreary tales which for the past three months had passed back and forth in the antechamber of the crown prosecutor's house – that a peculiar incident happened in that carefully closed and guarded room.

It was about ten minutes since the night nurse had left. Valentine, a prey for the past hour to the fever which resumed every night, let her head continue beyond her control the active, monotonous and implacable operation of the brain, which exhausts itself by constantly reproducing the same thoughts or giving birth to the same images.

Thousands upon thousands of rays were leaping from the wick of the night-light, all imbued with strange meanings; but suddenly Valentine thought that in its quivering light she could see her bookcase, which stood beside the chimney in a recess in the wall, open slowly, without the hinges on which it appeared to be turning making the slightest sound.

At any other time Valentine would have grasped her silk bell-pull and tugged it, calling for help; but in her present situation nothing surprised her any longer. She was aware that all these visions around her were the product of her delirium, and she was convinced of it by the fact that in the morning no trace had ever remained of all those spirits of the night, which vanished with the coming of day.

A human figure appeared behind the door.

Thanks to her fever, Valentine was only too familiar with this kind of apparition to feel afraid. She merely opened her eyes wide, hoping to recognize Morrel.

The shape continued to approach her bed, then stopped and seemed to be listening attentively. At that moment a ray of light from the night-light played across the nocturnal visitor's face. 'It's not him,' she muttered; and she waited, convinced that she was dreaming and that the man, as happens in dreams, would disappear or change into someone else.

However, she felt her pulse and, feeling it beating rapidly, she remembered that the best way of making such unwanted visions disappear was to drink something. The coolness of the drink, which had been prepared specifically with the aim of calming such agitation, after Valentine had complained of it to the doctor, brought down her temperature and so revived the normal operation of the brain. For a short time, after drinking, she felt better.

For this reason, Valentine reached out to take the glass on the crystal saucer on which it was standing. But while she was extending her shaking arm outside the bed, the apparition took two steps towards the bed, with more determination than ever, and came so close to the young woman that she could hear his breath and thought she could feel the touch of his hand.

This time, the illusion – or, rather, the reality – went beyond anything that Valentine had experienced so far. She began to think she must really be awake and alive. She realized that she was in full possession of her faculties and began to tremble.

The purpose of the touch that Valentine had felt was to stop her hand. Valentine slowly brought it back towards her.

At this, the figure took the glass, went over to the night-light and looked at the potion, as if trying to assess its clarity and transparency. Valentine was unable to take her eyes off him, though he seemed protective rather than threatening.

The preliminary evidence given by the light was not enough. The man – or, rather, the ghost, for he walked so softly that the carpet muffled the sound of his steps – took a spoonful of the drink out of the glass and swallowed it. Valentine watched what was happening before her eyes with a deep feeling of astonishment. She was sure that all this would vanish and give place to another scene; but the man, instead of fading away like a ghost, came over to her, and held the glass out to her, saying in a voice that was full of emotion: 'Now, drink!'

Valentine shuddered. This was the first time that one of her visions had spoken to her in this vibrant tone. She opened her mouth to cry out, but the man put a finger to his lips.

'Monsieur le Comte de Monte Cristo!' she muttered.

In the terror evident in the young woman's eyes, in the trembling of her hands, in the rapid movement that she made to hide herself under the sheets, one might have seen the last struggle of doubt against certainty. However, the presence of the Count of Monte Cristo in her room at such an hour and his mysterious, fantastic, inexplicable entrance through one of the walls, seemed impossible to Valentine's understanding.

'Don't call out, don't be afraid,' said the count. 'Don't even have the glimmer of a suspicion or the shadow of a doubt in your heart. The man whom you see before you, Valentine – and this time you are right, it is not an illusion – the man whom you see is the tenderest father and most respectful friend you could ever dream of . . .'

Valentine could not think of anything in reply. She was so frightened by the voice, which assured her of the real presence of the speaker, that she was afraid of adding her own to it. But her terrified look meant: if your intentions are pure, why are you here?

With his extraordinary wisdom, the count understood everything that was going on in the young woman's heart. 'Listen to me,' he said. 'Or, rather, look at me. See my red eyes and my face, which is even paler than usual. This is because for the past four nights I have not slept for a single moment. For the past four nights I have been watching over you, protecting you, guarding you for our friend, Maximilien.'

A rush of blood suffused the patient's happy cheeks, for the name that the count had just uttered removed the last trace of suspicion that he had inspired in her.

'Maximilien!' Valentine repeated, so sweet did the name seem to her. 'Maximilien! Has he confessed everything to you, then?'

'Everything. He told me that your life was his and I promised him that you would live.'

'You promised him that I should live?'

'Yes.'

'Monsieur, you have spoken of watching and protection. Are you a doctor, then?'

'Yes, the best that heaven could send you at this moment, believe me.'

'You say that you kept watch?' Valentine said anxiously. 'Where? I didn't see you.'

The count waved towards the bookcase. 'I was hidden behind that door, which leads into the house next door which I have rented.'

Valentine, overcome with pride and modest shame, turned away her eyes and said, in high alarm: 'Monsieur, what you did was unexampled folly, and the protection you gave me is very like an insult.'

'Valentine,' he answered, 'in all the long time that I watched, this is all that I saw: the people who came into your room, what food was prepared for you, what drinks were served to you. Then, if the drinks seemed dangerous to me, I entered as I have just done, emptied your glass and substituted a health-giving beverage for the poison; and that, instead of the death that had been prepared for you, made life run in your veins.'

'Poison! Death!' Valentine cried, once more imagining herself to be possessed by some feverish hallucination. 'What are you saying?'

'Hush, child!' said Monte Cristo, putting his finger to his lips. 'I said poison, yes . . . I said death, and I repeat it; but first drink this.' He took out of his pocket a phial containing some red liquid and poured a few drops into the glass. 'And when you have drunk it, don't take anything else this night.'

Valentine reached out her hand, but hardly had she touched the glass than she pulled back in terror.

Monte Cristo took the glass, drank half of the liquid in it, and offered it to Valentine, who smiled before drinking the remainder. 'Oh, yes,' she said. 'I recognize the taste of my night-time drinks, that water which helped to cool my chest and calm my mind. Thank you, Monsieur, thank you.'

'This is how you managed to live for four nights, Valentine,' the count said. 'But how did I manage? Oh, what painful hours I have spent! Oh, what dreadful torture you put me through, when I saw the deadly poison poured into your glass and was terrified lest you should have time to drink it before I could empty it into the fireplace.'

'Monsieur,' said Valentine, at the height of terror, 'so you were tormented by the sight of the deadly poison being poured into my glass? But if you saw the poison being poured, then you must have seen the person who poured it?'

'Yes.'

Valentine sat upright in bed and, drawing the embroidered lawn nightdress up over her breast (which was whiter than snow), still damp from the cold sweat of her delirium, now starting to mingle with the still icier sweat of terror, she said: 'You saw this person?'

'Yes,' the count repeated.

'What you are telling me, Monsieur, is frightful: you want me to believe in something hellish. What! In my father's house, in my room, on my bed of pain, someone is still trying to kill me? No, Monsieur, begone! You tempt my conscience and blaspheme against the goodness of God! It is impossible! It cannot be!'

'But are you the first person this hand has struck, Valentine? Did you not see Monsieur de Saint-Méran, Madame de Saint-Méran and Barrois all succumb? Would you not have seen Monsieur Noirtier follow them, if the treatment which he has been receiving over the past three years had not protected him, overcoming poison by the habit of poison?'

'Good heavens!' said Valentine. 'That is why over the past month my dear grandfather has insisted on my sharing all his drinks?'

'Those drinks,' Monte Cristo asked urgently, 'do they have a taste like that of partly dried orange peel?'

'Bless us! Yes, they do!'

'That explains everything,' said Monte Cristo. 'He, too, knows that there is a poisoner here – and perhaps who that poisoner is. He protected you, his dearly beloved grandchild, against the deadly substance, and this substance lost its power when it met this initial defence. That is why you are still alive, which I could not understand, after you were subjected four days ago to a poison which is usually unrelenting.'

'But who is the poisoner, the murderer?'

'I might ask you in your turn: have you never seen anyone come into your room at night?'

'Yes, I have often thought I saw shadows pass, come close, go away, disappear. I thought they were hallucinations produced by my fever; just now when you came in, well . . . for a long time I thought I was delirious or dreaming.'

'So you do not know who is trying to take your life?'

'No,' said Valentine. 'Why should someone wish me dead?'

'You will find out,' Monte Cristo said, listening carefully.

'How?' Valentine asked, looking around in terror.

'Because this evening your fever and delirium are gone, you are entirely awake and midnight is striking. This is the murderer's hour.'

'My God!' Valentine said, wiping the sweat from her brow.

Midnight was indeed striking slowly and mournfully. It was as though each blow of the bronze hammer struck the young woman's heart.

'Valentine,' the count went on, 'call up all your strength, control your heart in your breast and your voice in your throat; pretend to be asleep, and you will see! You will see!'

Valentine grasped his hand. 'I think I can hear a noise,' she said. 'Hide yourself!'

'Farewell – or, rather, au revoir!' the count replied. Then, with such a sad, fatherly smile that the young woman's heart was filled with gratitude, he slipped back on tiptoe to the door in the book-case. But, as he turned before closing it behind him, he said: 'Not a movement, not a word. You must seem to be asleep, or you will be killed before I can reach you.'

And with this terrible warning, the count disappeared through the door, which closed silently behind him.

CI

LOCUSTA

Valentine was left alone. Two other clocks, lagging behind that on Saint-Philippe-du-Roule, again struck midnight at different intervals. Then, apart from the noise of a few distant coaches, all was quiet once again.

Now Valentine's attention was entirely concentrated on the clock in her room, as its pendulum marked off the seconds.

She began to count these seconds and noticed that they were only half as rapid as the beating of her heart. Yet she still had doubts. Inoffensive as she was herself, Valentine could not imagine that anyone wanted her dead. Why? To what end? What harm had she done that could have earned her an enemy?

There was no fear of her falling asleep.

One idea, one terrible idea, kept her mind on edge: there was in the world someone who had tried to kill her and would try again.

Suppose this time the person, tired of seeing the ineffectiveness of the poison, decided as Monte Cristo said to have recourse to cold steel! Suppose the count did not have enough time to reach her! Suppose her last moment had come and she would never again see Morrel!

At this thought, which made the blood drain from her face and covered her in a cold sweat, Valentine was ready to grasp the bell-pull and call for help. But it seemed that, through the door in the bookcase, she could see the count's eyes shining; and the eyes weighed on her memory: when she thought about them, she was overwhelmed with such shame that she wondered whether gratitude could ever manage to efface this unfortunate aspect of the count's indiscreet friendship.

Twenty minutes, twenty eternities passed in this way, then ten minutes more. Finally the clock, one second early, struck against the bell. At that moment, the faintest scratch on the wood of the bookcase told Valentine that the count was watching and advised her to do the same.

Now, indeed, from the opposite side, that is towards Edouard's room, Valentine thought she heard the floor creak. She listened carefully, holding her breath. The door-handle squeaked and the door opened on its hinges.

Valentine had raised herself up on her elbow and only just had time to fall back into bed and hide her eyes under her arm. Then, trembling, anxious, her heart seized with unspeakable fear, she waited.

Someone was coming over to the bed and touching the curtains. Valentine gathered all her strength and gave out that regular breathing that is the sign of untroubled sleep.

'Valentine!' a voice whispered.

The young woman shuddered to the depths of her heart, but did not reply.

'Valentine!' the same voice repeated.

The silence continued: Valentine had promised not to wake up. Then nothing moved. The only sound that Valentine could hear was the almost inaudible one of a liquid filling the glass that she had just emptied.

At this she dared to half-open her eyelids, behind the protection of her outstretched arm. She saw a woman in a white robe who was pouring a liquid out of a phial into her glass.

For that brief moment Valentine may have held her breath or made some movement, because the woman anxiously stopped and leant over the bed to see if she was really sleeping. It was Madame de Villefort.

When she recognized her stepmother, Valentine was unable to repress a shudder that made the bed move. Mme de Villefort immediately slipped along the wall and there, hidden by the bed-curtain, silent, attentive, she watched Valentine's every movement.

Valentine herself recalled Monte Cristo's dreadful words. In the hand that was not holding the phial she thought she had seen a sort of long, sharp knife shining. So, summoning up all the power of her will, she tried to shut her eyes; but this operation of the most fearful of our senses, an operation that is normally so simple, at that moment became almost impossible to carry out, so strongly did eager curiosity struggle to push back her eyelids and discover the truth.

However, reassured by the silence in which she could again hear, by Valentine's regular breathing, that she was asleep, Mme de Villefort once more reached out and, half hidden behind the curtains which were drawn back to the head of the bed, finished emptying the contents of her phial into Valentine's glass. Then she left, without the slightest noise to tell Valentine that she was no longer there. She had seen the arm vanish, that's all – the fresh, plump arm of a woman of twenty-five, young and beautiful, who was pouring out death.

It is impossible to express what Valentine had felt for the minute and a half that Mme de Villefort was in her room.

The scratching of a fingernail on the bookcase roused the young woman from the state of torpor into which she had lapsed, and which seemed like the numbness of sleep. She had difficulty in raising her head. The door, still silent, opened again on its hinges and Monte Cristo reappeared.

'Well?' he asked. 'Do you still doubt?'

'Oh, my God!' she muttered.

'Did you see?'

'Alas, yes!'

'Did you recognize her?'

Valentine groaned. 'Yes,' she said, 'but I cannot believe it.'

'Would you rather die, then, and kill Maximilien?'

'My God, my God!' the young woman repeated, almost distracted. 'Can't I leave the house and escape?'

'Valentine, the hand which is pursuing you will reach you wherever you go; it will bribe your servants with gold and death will reach out to you under every disguise: in the water you drink from the spring, or the fruit you pluck from the tree.'

'But surely you said that my grandfather's precautions had given me immunity against poison?'

'Against one poison and, even then, only if given in a small dose. The poison will be changed or the quantity increased.'

He took the glass and touched the liquid against his lips. 'There you are,' he said. 'It's already being done. She is no longer using brucine to poison you, but a simple narcotic. I recognize the taste of the alcohol in which it has been dissolved. If you had drunk what Madame de Villefort has just poured into this glass, Valentine, you would have been lost.'

'But why in heaven's name is she hounding me like this?' she cried.

'What! Are you so sweet, so good, so immune to thoughts of evil that you do not know, Valentine?'

'No,' the girl said. 'I have never done her any harm.'

'But you are rich, Valentine. You have an income of two hundred thousand *livres* and you are taking this money away from her son.'

'What! My fortune is not his. It comes from my parents.'

'Indeed. That is why Monsieur and Madame de Saint-Méran died: so that you would inherit from your parents; that is why, on the day he made you his heir, Monsieur Noirtier was condemned; and that is why you, too, must die, Valentine – so that your father can inherit from you, and your brother, now an only child, can inherit from your father.'

'Edouard! Poor child! Is it for his sake that all these crimes are being committed?'

'Ah, you do understand at last.'

'My God! As long as it does not all rebound on him!'

'You are an angel, Valentine.'

'But she has given up trying to kill my grandfather, then?'

'She considered that, if you were dead, except in the event of disinheritance, the fortune would naturally revert to your brother; and that, when it came down to it, the crime was pointless and doubly dangerous to commit.'

'How could such a plot have been hatched in the mind of a woman! Oh, my God!'

'Remember Perugia, the arbour at the post-house and the man with the brown cape whom your stepmother was asking about *aqua tofana*. Well, it was at that time that this whole infernal plot was born in her head.'

'Oh, Monsieur!' the sweet young woman cried, bursting into tears. 'I can see, in that case, that I am condemned to die.'

'No, Valentine, no. I have provided against every intrigue. Our enemy is vanquished, now that we know her. No, Valentine, you will live . . . live to love and be loved, to be happy and to make a noble heart happy. But if you are to live, you must trust in me.'

'Tell, me, Monsieur: what must I do?'

'You must blindly follow my instructions and take what I tell you.'

'As God is my witness,' Valentine exclaimed, 'if I were alone, I should prefer to let myself die.'

'Don't confide in anyone, even your father.'

'My father is not a part of this frightful plot, is he, Monsieur?' Valentine said, clasping her hands.

'No, yet your father, as a man used to juridical accusations, must suspect that all these deaths in his family are not natural. It is your father who should be watching over you, who should now be here in my place, who should already have emptied this glass and have taken action against the murderess. A spectre against a spectre,' he murmured, completing his sentence aloud.

'Monsieur,' Valentine said, 'I will do anything to live, because there are two beings in the world who love me enough to die if I should die: my grandfather and Maximilien.'

'I shall watch over them as I have watched over you.'

'Very well, then, do what you will with me,' said Valentine; then she added, more softly: 'Oh, my God, my God! What is to become of me?'

'Whatever happens, Valentine, have no fear. If you are in pain, if you lose your sense of sight, hearing or touch, fear nothing. If you should wake up without knowing where you are, do not be afraid, even if when you awoke you were to find yourself in some tomb-like crypt or nailed into some coffin. Summon your strength and think: at this moment, a friend, a father, a man who wants my happiness and Maximilien's, is watching over me.'

'Alas, alas, what a dreadful extremity!'

'But Valentine, would you prefer to denounce your stepmother?'

'I'd rather die a hundred times! Oh, yes, I'd rather die.'

'You shall not die; and promise me that, whatever should happen to you, you will not complain, you will have hope?'

'I shall think of Maximilien.'

'You are my dear child, Valentine. Only I can save you, and I shall.'

Valentine, at the height of terror, realizing that the moment had come to ask God for strength, put her hands together and sat up to pray, muttering a jumble of words and forgetting that her white shoulders had no covering other than her long hair, and that her heart could be seen beating under the fine lace of her nightdress.

The count gently touched the young woman's arm, drew the velvet counterpane up to cover her neck and said, with a paternal smile: 'My child, believe in my devotion, as you believe in the goodness of God and the love of Maximilien.'

Valentine gave him a look full of gratitude and remained as docile as a child under the bedclothes.

The count took his emerald pillbox out of his waistcoat, raised the golden lid and emptied a little pastille the size of a pea into Valentine's right hand.

She took it in her other hand and looked closely at the count. The face of her fearless protector wore a look of divine majesty and power, while on Valentine's there was clearly a question. 'Yes,' he told her. Valentine put the pastille to her lips and swallowed it.

'And now, goodbye, my child,' he said. 'I am going to try to sleep, because you are saved.'

'Do,' said Valentine. 'Whatever happens to me, I promise I shall not be afraid.'

Monte Cristo remained looking at the young woman for a long time as she gradually fell asleep, overcome by the power of the drug that the count had just given her. Then he took the glass, emptied three-quarters of it into the fireplace, so that it would seem as though Valentine had drunk the missing portion, and put it back on the bedside table. Finally he went back to the door behind the bookcase and disappeared, after a final glance towards Valentine, who was sleeping with the confidence and candour of an angel lying at the feet of the Lord.

CII

VALENTINE

The night-light continued to burn on Valentine's mantelpiece, exhausting the last drops of oil still floating on the water. Already the alabaster of the shade was reddening and a brighter flame flared up, crackling with those last sparks that represent, in inanimate objects, the final death throes, so often compared to those of poor human creatures. A faint, sinister light cast an opal hue over the white curtains and the sheets on the young woman's bed. All sound from the street, for once, was hushed and the silence was dreadful.

Now it was that the door to Edouard's room opened and a head which we have already seen appeared in the mirror opposite the door: it was Mme de Villefort, coming to see the effect of her potion.

She stopped on the threshold, listened to the crackling of the lamp, the only sound audible in this room which appeared to be unoccupied; then she went cautiously over to the bedside table to see if Valentine's glass was empty.

It was still one-quarter full, as we said.

Mme de Villefort took it and emptied it into the fireplace, stirring the ashes to ensure that the liquid was absorbed. Then she carefully washed the glass, wiped it with her own handkerchief and put it back on the bedside table.

If anyone had been watching and able to see inside the room, they would have observed Mme de Villefort's reluctance to look at

Valentine or to go over to the bed. The gloomy light, the silence and the awful poetry of night had no doubt combined with the fearful poetry of her conscience: the poisoner was afraid to see her work.

At length she did pluck up courage, drew back the curtain, leant on the head of the bed and looked at Valentine.

The young woman was no longer breathing and her teeth, half-clenched, did not give out a single trace of that respiration which indicates life. Her pale lips had ceased to tremble; her eyes, drowning in a violet mist that seemed to have seeped beneath the skin, formed a whiter protuberance where the orb swelled beneath the lid; and her long black lashes were outlined against skin that was already as dull as wax.

Mme de Villefort looked at this face with an expression that was eloquent in its passivity. Then she grew bolder and, lifting the blanket, put her hand to the young woman's heart.

It was silent and icy cold. All that she could feel beating was the pulse in her own fingers. She shuddered and drew back her hand.

Valentine's arm was hanging out of the bed. This arm, from the shoulder to the elbow, appeared to have been modelled on that of one of Germain Pilon's three Graces,[1] but the forearm was slightly deformed by a contraction of the muscles and the wrist, so pure in shape, was resting on the walnut table, slightly stiffened, with the fingers spread.

There was a bluish tinge at the base of the fingernails.

For Mme de Villefort there could be no further doubt. Everything was over: the dreadful task, the last she had to carry out, had finally been accomplished.

There was nothing further for the poisoner to do in the room. She withdrew with such care that it was evident she was afraid of the sound of her feet on the carpet; yet even as she went she still kept the curtain lifted, taking in the scene of death, which exercises an irresistible attraction when death is not decomposition but only immobility and, so long as it remains a mystery, does not yet inspire disgust.

The minutes passed. Mme de Villefort could not let go of the curtain which she was holding like a shroud above Valentine's head. She was paying her tribute to reflection: but reflection, in the case of crime, should be remorse.

At that moment the spluttering of the night-light doubled. At the noise, Mme de Villefort shuddered and let the curtain fall. The night-light went out and the room was plunged into terrifying darkness.

The poisoner, fearful at these successive disturbances, groped her way to the door and returned to her own room with her forehead bathed in anxious sweat.

Darkness continued for a further two hours. Then, bit by bit, pallid daylight entered into the room, filtering through the slats of the blinds; and, still bit by bit, it filled out and restored colour and shape to objects and bodies.

It was at this moment that the nurse could be heard coughing on the stairway and the woman came into Valentine's room, carrying a cup.

To a father or a lover, the first glance would have been enough: Valentine was dead. But to this hired servant, she seemed merely asleep. 'Good,' she said, going over to the bedside table. 'She's drunk part of her medicine; the glass is two-thirds empty.' Then she went to the fireplace, relit the fire, settled into her chair and, although she had just got out of bed, took advantage of Valentine's sleep to catch a few more minutes of slumber herself.

She was woken by the clock striking eight.

It was only now that she felt surprised at the young woman's persistent sleep, and frightened by the arm hanging out of the bed, which was still in the same position as before. She went over to the bed and noticed the cold lips and icy breast.

She tried to put the arm next to the body, but the arm only responded with a dreadful stiffness that was unmistakable for someone accustomed to caring for the sick. She gave a horrid cry, then ran to the door, shouting: 'Help! Help!'

'Help? Why help?' M. d'Avrigny's voice replied from the foot of the stairs.

This was the time when the doctor usually arrived.

'What? Why help?' Villefort's voice exclaimed as he hurried out of his study. 'Doctor, did you hear someone shout "Help"?'

'Yes, yes. Let's go up,' d'Avrigny said. 'Quickly, to Valentine's room!'

But before the doctor and the father had entered, the servants (who were on the same floor, in the rooms or the corridors) had rushed into the room and, seeing Valentine pale and motionless on her bed, threw up their hands and staggered as if overcome by dizziness.

'Call Madame de Villefort! Wake up Madame de Villefort!' the crown prosecutor cried at the door of the room, apparently not daring to enter. But the servants, instead of replying, were watching M. d'Avrigny, who had come in, rushed over to Valentine and lifted her in his arms.

'Now her . . .' he muttered, letting her fall back on the bed. 'Oh God, oh God, when will you tire of this?'

Villefort rushed into the room.

'What are you saying! My God!' he cried, raising both hands to heaven. 'Doctor . . . doctor . . . !'

'I am saying that Valentine is dead,' d'Avrigny replied in a solemn voice, and one that was dreadful in its solemnity. M. de Villefort went down as though his legs had been broken under him and fell with his head on Valentine's bed.

At the doctor's words and the father's cry, the servants fled in terror, muttering oaths. Down the stairs and along the corridors one could hear their running steps, followed by a commotion in the courtyard, then silence. The noise faded: from the highest to the lowest, they had deserted the accursed home.

At this moment, Mme de Villefort pushed back the door-curtain, her arm half inside her morning robe. For a moment, she remained on the threshold, looking questioningly at those around and summoning a few reluctant tears to her aid.

Suddenly she took a step, or, rather, she leapt forward, her arms extended towards the table. She had just seen d'Avrigny bending curiously over it and picking up the glass which she was sure she had emptied during the night. But the glass was one-third full, just as it had been when she emptied the contents into the fireplace.

The spectre of Valentine herself rising up before her poisoner would have produced a less startling effect on her.

It was indeed a liquid of the same colour as the one she had poured into Valentine's glass, and which Valentine drank; it was indeed that poison which could not deceive M. d'Avrigny, which M. d'Avrigny was examining attentively. It was undoubtedly a miracle performed by God so that, despite the murderess's precautions, a trace, a proof should remain to denounce her crime.

However, while Mme de Villefort had remained motionless like a statue of Terror and Villefort, his head buried in the sheets of the death-bed, saw nothing of what was happening around him, d'Avrigny went across to the window to make a closer ocular examination of the contents of the glass and to taste a drop on the end of his finger.

'Ah, it's not brucine any more,' he muttered. 'Let's see what this is!' He went over to one of the wardrobes in Valentine's room, which had been converted into a medicine chest, and, taking a phial of nitric acid out of its little silver compartment, he poured a few drops into the opal liquid, which immediately changed into half a glass of crimson blood.

'Ah!' said d'Avrigny, with the horror of a judge learning the truth and, at the same time, the joy of the scientist who elucidates a problem.

For a moment Mme de Villefort staggered, her eyes at first darting fire then becoming dull. She reached unsteadily for the door-handle and went out. A moment later, there was the distant sound of a body falling to the ground. But nobody took any notice of it. The nurse was examining the chemical sample, while Villefort was still insensible. Only d'Avrigny had watched Mme de Villefort and noticed her hurried exit.

He raised the curtain in front of the door to Valentine's room and, looking through that of Edouard, he could see into Mme de Villefort's apartment. He saw her stretched, motionless, on the floor.

'Go and see to Madame de Villefort,' he said to the nurse. 'She is unwell.'

'But what about Mademoiselle Valentine?' she asked.

'Mademoiselle Valentine has no further need of help,' d'Avrigny said. 'Mademoiselle Valentine is dead.'

'Dead! Dead!' Villefort exclaimed in a paroxysm of suffering all the more acute for being quite new, unknown and unexpected in this heart of bronze.

'Dead, you say?' cried a third voice. 'Who said that Valentine was dead?'

The two men turned around and, at the door, saw Morrel standing, pale, frightful, devastated with horror.

This is what had happened. Morrel had arrived, at his usual time, through the little door leading to Noirtier's. Unusually, he found the door open and, not needing to ring, came in. In the hall, he waited for a moment, calling for a servant who would show him up to old Noirtier's rooms. But no one replied: as we know, the servants had deserted the house.

That day, Morrel had no particular reason for anxiety. He had Monte Cristo's promise that Valentine would live, and up to now that promise had been faithfully kept. Every evening the count had given him good news, which was confirmed the next day by Noirtier himself.

However, on this morning the silence seemed odd. He called a second, then a third time, but there was no reply, so he decided to go up.

Noirtier's door was open, like the rest.

The first thing he saw was the old man in his armchair. His dilated pupils seemed to express an inner terror that was confirmed by the strange pallor that had spread across his face.

'How are you, Monsieur?' the young man said, not without some sinking in his heart.

'Well!' the old man replied with a wink. 'Well!' But the anxiety on his face seemed to increase.

'You are worried,' Morrel went on. 'Do you need something? Shall I call one of your people?'

'Yes,' Noirtier went.

Morrel hung on the bell-pull but, even though he tugged it to breaking point, no one came. So he turned back to Noirtier. The pallor and anguish had increased on the old man's face.

'My God!' said Morrel. 'Why does no one come? Is someone sick in the house?'

Noirtier's eyes seemed to be bulging out of their sockets.

'But what is wrong?' Morrel went on. 'You are frightening me . . . Valentine, Valentine!'

'Yes, yes!' Noirtier indicated.

Maximilien opened his mouth to speak, but his tongue could not form any sound. He staggered and held on to the panelling to support himself. Then he reached out towards the door.

'Yes, yes, yes!' the old man continued.

Maximilien plunged down the little staircase, covering it in two leaps, while Noirtier's eyes seemed to shout at him: 'Faster, faster!'

It took the young man only a minute to cross through several rooms, empty like the rest of the house, and reach Valentine's apartments. He did not need to push the door to her room, which was already wide open. The first sound that he heard was a sob. As if through a cloud, he saw a black shape kneeling and buried in a confused mass of white linen. Fear, a dreadful fear, kept him frozen at the door.

It was then that he heard a voice say: 'Valentine is dead!' and a second voice, like an echo, reply: 'Dead! Dead!'

CIII

MAXIMILIEN

Villefort got up, almost ashamed at being discovered in this extremity of grief. The awful profession he had exercised for the past twenty-five years had made him more, or less, than a man.

His eyes, after wandering for a moment, settled on Morrel.

'Who are you, Monsieur?' he asked. 'Have you forgotten that one does not enter a house that is occupied by death? Begone, Monsieur! Begone!'

But Morrel remained motionless, unable to take his eyes off the frightful spectacle of the rumpled bed with the figure lying on top of it.

'Go, do you hear!' Villefort cried, while d'Avrigny came forward to oblige Morrel to leave.

Morrel looked in distraction at the body, the two men, the whole room ... He seemed to hesitate for a moment and opened his mouth. Then, finding no word to say, despite the vast swarm of deadly thoughts swirling in his brain, he retreated, plunging his fingers through his hair, so that Villefort and d'Avrigny, momentarily distracted from the matter uppermost in their minds, looked after him with an expression that meant: 'He is mad!'

However, in less than five minutes they heard the staircase creak beneath some considerable weight and saw Morrel who, with superhuman strength, was lifting Noirtier's chair in his arms, bringing the old man up to the first floor of the house.

When he got to the top of the stairs, Morrel put the chair down and pushed it quickly into Valentine's room. The whole of this operation was carried out with a strength increased ten times by the young man's frenzied hysteria. But the most terrifying thing was Noirtier's face as it advanced towards Valentine's bed, pushed by Morrel: Noirtier's face in which the intellect exerted every means within its power and the eyes concentrated all their strength to compensate for the loss of the other faculties. This pale face with its blazing look was a terrifying apparition to Villefort.

Each time that he found himself in contact with his father, something dreadful happened.

'See what they have done!' Morrel cried, one hand still resting on the back of the chair which he had just pushed up to the bed, and the other outstretched towards Valentine. 'Look, father, look!'

Villefort shrank back a step and stared with amazement at this young man, who was almost unknown to him, yet who called Noirtier his father.

At that moment the old man's whole soul seemed to rise into his eyes, which were shot with blood. Then the veins on his neck swelled and a bluish tint, like that which suffuses the skin of an epileptic, spread across his neck, his cheeks and his temples. The only thing that was missing from this internal explosion of the whole being was a cry.

But that cry seemed to emerge as it were from every pore, terrifying in its dumbness, heart-rending in its silence.

D'Avrigny rushed over to the old man and made him sniff a powerful revulsive.

'Monsieur,' Morrel exclaimed, grasping the paralysed man's inert hand. 'They ask me what I am and what right I have to be here. You know the answer. Tell them! Tell them . . .' And his voice was drowned in sobs.

As for the old man, his chest heaved as he gasped for breath. One might have imagined that he was prey to the convulsions that precede the death agony. Finally, tears poured from his eyes: he was more fortunate than the young man, who could only sob without weeping. His head could not bow, so he closed his eyes.

'Tell them,' he said, in a strangled voice. 'Tell them I was her fiancé. Tell them that she was my noble friend, my only love on this earth! Tell them . . . Tell them that this body belongs to me!'

The young man, presenting the awful spectacle of some great

force breaking, fell heavily to his knees beside the bed while his fingers clasped it convulsively.

His grief was so touching that d'Avrigny turned away to hide his emotion and Villefort, asking for no further explanation, drawn by the magnetism that drives us towards those who have loved those for whom we grieve, offered the young man his hand.

But Morrel could see nothing. He had grasped Valentine's ice-cold hand and, unable to weep, was groaning and biting the bed-clothes.

For some time nothing could be heard in the room other than this conflict of sobs, oaths and prayers. Yet one noise rose above all, and that was the harsh, harrowing sound of breathing which, at each gulp of air, seemed to break one of the springs of life in Noirtier's chest.

Finally, Villefort, the most self-possessed of all, after having as it were ceded his place for some time to Maximilien, began to speak.

'Monsieur,' he told Maximilien, 'you loved Valentine, you say. You were her fiancé. I must admit I was unaware of this love and of the engagement. Yet, as her father, I forgive you for it, since I can see that your grief is great, true and real.

'Moreover my own grief is too great to leave room in my heart for anger.

'But, as you see, the angel for whom you longed has left this earth. She no longer needs the adoration of men – she, who, at this moment, is adoring the Lord. So say your farewells, Monsieur, to these sad remains that she has left behind among us. Once more take the hand that you were expecting to take in other circumstances and part from her for ever. Valentine no longer has need of anyone except the priest who will bless her.'

'You are wrong, Monsieur,' Morrel exclaimed, rising on one knee, his heart smitten by a pain sharper than any he had yet felt. 'You are wrong. Valentine, having died as she has, needs not only a priest but an avenger. You send for the priest, Monsieur de Villefort; I shall be her avenger.'

'What do you mean, Monsieur?' Villefort murmured, quaking at this new product of Morrel's delirium.

'What I mean,' Morrel continued, 'is that there are two men in you, Monsieur. The father has wept enough; let the crown pros-ecutor resume his duties.'

Noirtier's eyes shone, and d'Avrigny came over to them.

'Monsieur,' the young man went on, his eyes picking up every feeling that was expressed on the faces of those around him, 'I know what I am saying and you all know as well as I do what I mean. Valentine was murdered!'

Villefort bent his head. D'Avrigny took another step. Noirtier moved his eyes.

'So, Monsieur,' Morrel continued, 'nowadays when a creature, even one less young, even one less beautiful, even one less adorable than Valentine . . . such a creature does not disappear violently from the earth without someone asking for a reason. Come, Monsieur,' Morrel added, with growing vehemence, 'no pity – Prosecutor! I am reporting the crime to you, find the murderer!'

And his implacable eyes were fixed on Villefort, while he, for his part, looked from Noirtier to d'Avrigny and back.

'Yes,' went the old man.

'Yes, indeed,' said d'Avrigny.

'Monsieur,' Villefort replied, trying to struggle against these three wills and against his own feelings, 'you are wrong. No crimes are committed in my house. Fate has struck, God is trying me, which is horrible to believe; but no one is being murdered!'

Noirtier's eyes flashed and d'Avrigny opened his mouth to speak. But Morrel lifted his hand to order silence.

'I tell you that people are being murdered here!' he cried, his voice lowered without losing any of its dreadful power. 'I tell you that this is the fourth victim struck down in four months. I tell you that four days ago someone already tried to poison Valentine and that the attempt only failed because of the precautions taken by Monsieur Noirtier . . .

'I tell you that the dose was doubled, or that the type of poison was changed. And this time the attempt succeeded!

'And, finally, I tell you that you know all this as well as I do, because this gentleman warned you, as a doctor and as a friend.'

'Oh, you are delirious!' Villefort cried, vainly trying to escape from the trap that he felt closing in on him.

'I am delirious?' Morrel cried. 'Well, then, I appeal to Monsieur d'Avrigny himself. Ask him, Monsieur, if he still remembers the words he spoke in your garden, the garden of this very house, on the evening when Madame de Saint-Méran died and when the two of you, thinking yourselves alone, were discussing that tragic death

– in which the fate you mentioned, and God, whom you unjustly accuse, could only have played one part, that is, in creating Valentine's murderer.'

Villefort and d'Avrigny looked at one another.

'Yes, yes, remember,' said Morrel. 'Those words, which you thought you entrusted to silence and solitude, reached my ears. Certainly, that very evening, seeing Monsieur de Villefort's culpable leniency towards his own family, I should have revealed everything to the authorities. I should not then be an accomplice in your death, Valentine! My beloved Valentine! But the accomplice will become the avenger. This fourth murder is flagrant and visible to all; and, Valentine, even if your father abandons you, I swear that I shall pursue your murderer.'

This time, as though nature had finally taken pity on this strong constitution about to be crushed by its own strength, Morrel's last words were stifled in his throat, his chest heaved with sobs, and tears, which had for so long refused to come, poured from his eyes. He could no longer support himself but fell on his knees, weeping, beside Valentine's bed.

Now it was the turn of d'Avrigny. 'I, too, add my voice to that of Monsieur Morrel to demand justice for this crime,' he said emphatically. 'My heart rebels at the idea that my cowardly indulgence encouraged the murderer.'

'Oh, my God!' Villefort muttered, overwhelmed.

Morrel raised his head and, looking at the old man, whose eyes were blazing with a superhuman light, he said: 'Monsieur Noirtier has something to say.'

'Yes,' Noirtier went, with an expression all the more dreadful in that all the poor man's faculties were concentrated in that look.

'Do you know the murderer?' Morrel asked.

'Yes,' Noirtier replied.

'And you will direct us to him?' the young man exclaimed. 'Listen! Monsieur d'Avrigny, listen!'

Noirtier gave the unhappy Morrel a melancholy smile, one of those sweet smiles in his eyes that had so often made Valentine happy, then he concentrated his attention. Having so to speak fastened the other man's eyes on his, he then turned them towards the door.

'Do you wish me to go out, Monsieur?' Morrel asked, in a pitiful tone of voice.

'Yes,' Noirtier said.

'Alas, Monsieur, have pity on me!'

But the old man's eyes remained implacably fixed on the door.

'May I at least return?' asked Morrel.

'Yes.'

'Must I go out by myself?'

'No.'

'Whom should I take with me? The crown prosecutor?'

'No.'

'The doctor?'

'Yes.'

'You wish to remain alone with Monsieur de Villefort?'

'Yes.'

'Will he be able to understand you?'

'Yes.'

'Oh, yes,' Villefort said, almost happy now that the investigation was to take place between the two of them. 'Have no fear, I can understand my father very well.' But even though he said this with an expression of relief, the crown prosecutor's teeth were chattering violently.

D'Avrigny took Morrel's arm and led the young man into the next room. Then the house lapsed into a silence deeper than the silence of death.

Finally, after a quarter of an hour, an unsteady step could be heard and Villefort appeared on the threshold of the drawing-room in which d'Avrigny and Morrel were waiting, one absorbed in his thoughts, the other sunk in grief.

'Come in,' Villefort said; and he led them back to where Noirtier was sitting.

Morrel examined Villefort closely. The crown prosecutor's face was livid. Huge patches of reddish colour had appeared on his forehead while, between his fingers, a quill was falling to pieces after being bent and twisted in a hundred different ways.

'Gentlemen,' he said to Morrel and d'Avrigny in a strangled voice, 'your word of honour that this dreadful secret will remain buried among us!'

The two men started.

'I beg you!' said Villefort.

'But the guilty person,' said Morrel. 'The murderer! The assassin!'

'Have no fear, Monsieur, justice shall be done,' said Villefort.

'My father has told me the name of the guilty person; he is as thirsty as you are for revenge; yet, like me, he implores you to keep the secret – don't you, father?'

'Yes,' Noirtier went, firmly.

Villefort continued: 'He knows me, and I have given him my word. Rest assured, gentlemen. Three days: I ask you for three days, which is less than the law would demand, and in three days the revenge that I shall have exacted from the murderer of my child will make the most impassive of men shudder to the depths of his heart. Am I not right, father?'

As he spoke, he ground his teeth and shook the old man's numbed hand.

'Will all these promises be kept, Monsieur Noirtier?' Morrel asked, while d'Avrigny put the same question with a look.

'Yes,' Noirtier answered, with a sinister joy in his eyes.

'So, gentlemen, swear,' Villefort said, joining d'Avrigny and Morrel's hands. 'Swear that you will take pity on the honour of my family and leave me to avenge it?'

D'Avrigny turned away and muttered a barely audible 'Yes', but Morrel tore his hand away from the judge, dashed over to the bed, pressed his lips to the icy lips of Valentine, and fled with the long-drawn-out groan of a soul plunged in despair.

We have already mentioned that all the servants had left. As a result, Monsieur de Villefort was obliged to ask d'Avrigny to take care of the proceedings, so delicate and so many, which must follow a death in one of our large towns, especially when it takes place in suspicious circumstances.

As for Noirtier, his motionless grief, his frozen despair and his noiseless tears were something terrible to behold.

Villefort returned to his study. D'Avrigny went to fetch from the town hall the doctor who fulfils the office of coroner and is quite unambiguously designated 'doctor of the dead'.

Noirtier did not want to leave his granddaughter.

After half an hour d'Avrigny returned with his colleague. The street door had been closed and, since the concierge had left with the rest of the staff, Villefort himself came to open it. But he stopped on the landing; he no longer had the courage to go into the death chamber, so the two doctors went in alone.

Noirtier was close to the bed, as pale as the corpse, as motionless and as silent.

The coroner approached the body with the indifference of a man who spends half his life in the presence of corpses, lifted the sheet covering the young woman and partly opened her lips.

'Don't worry, she's quite dead,' said d'Avrigny. 'Poor girl.'

'Yes,' the doctor replied laconically, letting the sheet fall back on to Valentine's face. Noirtier gave a dull croak.

D'Avrigny turned around: the old man's eyes were shining. The good doctor understood that Noirtier was asking to see his child. He brought him closer to the bed and, while the coroner was dipping the fingers that had touched the dead woman's lips into some chlorinated water, he uncovered the calm, pale face which looked like that of a sleeping angel. A tear once more appearing in Noirtier's eye expressed his gratitude to the doctor. The 'doctor of the dead' wrote his report on the corner of a table in Valentine's room and, when this last formality was completed, d'Avrigny showed him out.

Villefort heard them descend and came to the door of his study. He briefly thanked the doctor and said, turning to d'Avrigny: 'And now, the priest?'

'Do you have a clergyman whom you would particularly like to have pray beside Valentine?' D'Avrigny asked.

'No,' Villefort said. 'Fetch the nearest one.'

'The nearest one,' the doctor said, 'is a good Italian abbé who has come to live in the house next to yours. Shall I go and see him on my way?'

'D'Avrigny,' Villefort said, 'please would you go with this gentleman? Here is a key so that you can come and go as you wish. Bring back the priest and take charge of settling him in my poor child's room.'

'Would you like to speak to him, my friend?'

'I want to be alone. Please forgive me. A priest must understand every kind of sorrow, including a father's.' And M. de Villefort, giving d'Avrigny a master key, once more took leave of the unknown doctor and returned to his study, where he began to work.

For some constitutions work is the cure for all ills.

Just as the doctors were going out into the street, they noticed a man, dressed in a soutane, standing on the threshold of the house next door. 'There is the person I mentioned,' the coroner told d'Avrigny. D'Avrigny went over to the priest.

'Monsieur,' he said, 'would you be willing to do a great service for an unfortunate father who has just lost his daughter, the crown prosecutor, Villefort?'

'Yes, Monsieur, I know,' the priest answered, in a pronounced Italian accent. 'I know that death is in his house.'

'Then I do not need to tell you what he would like you to do for him.'

'I was going to volunteer my services, Monsieur,' the priest said. 'It is our mission to exceed our duties.'

'It is a young woman.'

'I know. I learned that from the servants whom I saw fleeing the house. I learned, too, that she was called Valentine, and I have already prayed for her.'

'Thank you, Monsieur, thank you,' said d'Avrigny. 'And since you have already started to perform your holy office, please be good enough to continue. Come and sit with the dead woman, and the whole family will be grateful to you in its grief.'

'I am going, Monsieur,' the abbé replied. 'And I may say that never will prayers have been more ardent than mine.'

D'Avrigny took the abbé's hand and, without meeting Villefort, who was shut up in his study, he led him up to Valentine's room, which the undertakers were to occupy only on the following night.

When he entered the room, Noirtier's eyes met those of the abbé and they must doubtless have read something particular in them, because they remained fixed on the priest. D'Avrigny entrusted him not only with the dead woman but also with the living man, and the priest promised d'Avrigny that he would give his prayers to Valentine and his care to Noirtier.

He made this solemn promise and, doubtless to avoid being interrupted in his devotions and so that Noirtier would not be disturbed in his grief, as soon as M. d'Avrigny had left the room, he went to draw not only the bolts on the door through which the doctor had just left but also those on the door leading to the apartments of Mme de Villefort.

CIV

THE SIGNATURE OF BARON DANGLARS

The following day dawned sad and overcast.

During the night the undertakers had accomplished their dismal task and sewn the body, as it lay on the bed, in that shroud which gloomily enfolds the dead, supplying (whatever is said about the levelling effect of death) a last sign of the luxury that they enjoyed in their lifetimes.

In this case the shroud was a magnificent piece of cambric lawn that the young woman had bought a mere fortnight earlier.

During the evening, some men who had been brought in for this purpose transported Noirtier from Valentine's room to his own and, against all expectation, the old man made no objection to being taken away from his grandchild's body.

Abbé Busoni watched until daybreak and then went back to his house without calling anyone.

At about eight in the morning, d'Avrigny returned. He had met Villefort, who was going to see Noirtier, and accompanied him in order to discover how the old man had spent the night. They found him in the large armchair that served as his bed, enjoying a gentle sleep and almost smiling.

They both stopped on the threshold in astonishment. 'You see,' d'Avrigny said to Villefort, who was looking at his sleeping father. 'See how nature is able to assuage the most awful pain. Surely, no one would have said that Monsieur Noirtier did not love his granddaughter, yet he is asleep.'

'Yes, you are right,' Villefort replied, in surprise. 'He is sleeping; and that is very strange, because the slightest upset used to keep him awake for nights on end.'

'He is exhausted by grief,' d'Avrigny replied. And the two men returned thoughtfully to the crown prosecutor's study.

'Now, I didn't sleep,' Villefort said, showing d'Avrigny his untouched bed. 'Grief has not exhausted me and I have not been to bed for two nights. On the other hand, look at my desk: good Lord, what I have written over those two days and nights! How I have perused that dossier, how I have annotated that indictment against the murderer Benedetto! Work, work! My passion, my joy, my fury: it is for you to exhaust all my griefs!' And he seized d'Avrigny's hand in a convulsive grip.

'Do you need me?' the doctor asked.

'No,' Villefort said. 'But, I beg you, come back at eleven o'clock. It is at twelve that . . . oh, my poor child! The departure . . . My God, my poor child!' And the crown prosecutor, a man again, raised his eyes to heaven and heaved a great sigh.

'Will you be receiving in the drawing-room then?'

'No, I have a cousin who has agreed to undertake that sad honour. I shall work, doctor; when I work, everything vanishes.'

And, indeed, the doctor had hardly reached the door before the crown prosecutor was once more immersed in his labours.

On the steps d'Avrigny met the relative whom Villefort had mentioned, an insignificant personage both in the family and in this story, one of those beings who are born to play a purely utilitarian role in the world.

He was punctual, dressed in black, with a crêpe armband, and he had come round to his cousin's with his face composed into a suitable expression, which he intended to keep for as long as need be and then put aside.

At eleven o'clock the funerary carriages were clattering over the paved courtyard, and the Rue du Faubourg-Saint-Honoré filled with the murmur of the crowd, equally hungry for the joys and the griefs of the rich, and hurrying to a fine funeral with the same haste as it would to a duchess's wedding.

Little by little the drawing-room filled up with mourners. Among the first to arrive were some of our old acquaintances: Debray, Château-Renaud and Beauchamp; then all the luminaries of the bench, of letters and the arts, because Monsieur de Villefort, less by reason of his social standing than for his personal qualities, occupied one of the highest ranks in Parisian society.

The cousin stood at the door and showed everyone in; and it must be said that it was a great relief for the indifferent to see a neutral face who did not require the guests to produce any hypocritical expression or false tears, as a father, brother or fiancé would have done. Those who knew one another exchanged looks and gathered in groups, one of which was made up of Debray, Château-Renaud and Beauchamp.

'Poor girl!' Debray said, acknowledging this sad occasion (as, incidentally, everyone else was quite spontaneously doing).

'Poor girl! So rich and beautiful! Would you have thought it, Château-Renaud, when we came here, when was it – three weeks or a month ago at the most – to sign that contract that was not signed?'

'Heavens, no,' said Château-Renaud.

'Did you know her?'

'I spoke to her once or twice at Madame de Morcerf's ball. She seemed charming, if a trifle melancholic. Where is the stepmother? Do you know?'

'She has gone to spend the day with the wife of the worthy gentleman who greeted us as we came in.'

'And what might he be?'

'Who?'

'The gentleman at the door: a member of parliament?'

'No,' said Beauchamp. 'I am condemned to see those honourable gentlemen daily, and I don't know his face.'

'Did you mention this death in your newspaper?'

'I didn't write the piece myself, but it was mentioned. I doubt if it will please Monsieur de Villefort. I believe the writer remarked that if four successive deaths had occurred anywhere except in the crown prosecutor's house, the crown prosecutor would certainly have more to say about it.'

'For all that,' Château-Renaud said, 'Doctor d'Avrigny is my mother's doctor, and says he is quite distraught.'

'Who do you keep looking for, Debray?'

'The Count of Monte Cristo,' the young man replied.

'I met him on the boulevard on my way here. I think he was just leaving, going to his banker,' Beauchamp said.

'His banker? Isn't that Danglars?' Château-Renaud asked Debray.

'I think so,' the private secretary answered, with some faint signs of unease. 'But Monte Cristo is not the only person I can't see here. Where is Morrel?'

'Morrel! Did he know them?' asked Château-Renaud.

'I think he had been introduced to Madame de Villefort only.'

'No matter, he should have come,' said Debray. 'What will he have to talk about this evening? This burial is the main news of the day. But hush, say no more: here is the Minister of Justice and Religion. He will feel obliged to make his little speech to the mournful cousin.' And the three young people went over to the door to hear the minister's speech.

THE SIGNATURE OF BARON DANGLARS

What Beauchamp had said was true: on his way to the funeral he had met Monte Cristo who was going to see Danglars at his home in the Rue de la Chaussée-d'Antin.

From his window the banker had seen the count's carriage turning into the courtyard. He came to meet him with a sad but welcoming face.

'Well, Count,' he said, offering Monte Cristo his hand. 'You have come to offer me your condolences. In truth, my family is plagued by misfortune – to the point where, when I saw you coming, I was just asking myself whether I might have harboured some uncharitable thoughts against those poor Morcerfs, to justify the proverb: Let ill befall him that wishes ill. Well, no, on my honour, I did not wish any ill on Morcerf. He may perhaps be a little proud for a man who has come up from nothing, like me, and owes everything to himself, like me; but we all have our faults. Ah, mark this, Count, men of our generation . . . But, forgive me, you aren't of our generation, you're a young man . . . Those of our generation are not having a good year, this year: take our puritanical crown prosecutor, take Villefort, who has just lost his daughter. Why, in sum, there is Villefort, as I said, losing all his family in mysterious circumstances; Morcerf, dishonoured and dead; myself, dishonoured by the villainy of that Benedetto, and then . . .'

'Then, what?' the count asked.

'Alas, don't you know?'

'Some new misfortune?'

'My daughter . . .'

'Mademoiselle Danglars?'

'Eugénie has left us.'

'Good heavens, what are you saying?'

'The truth, my dear Count. You don't know how lucky you are, not having a wife or children!'

'Do you think so?'

'Oh, my God.'

'You said that Mademoiselle Eugénie . . .'

'Was unable to bear the indignity to which that wretch subjected us and asked my permission to travel.'

'Has she left already?'

'A few nights ago.'

'With Madame Danglars?'

'No, with a relative . . . But we are still losing her, dearest Eugénie, because, knowing her proud character, I doubt if she will ever consent to return to France.'

'What can be done, my dear Baron?' said Monte Cristo. 'These are family sorrows, which would be devastating for some poor devil whose child was his whole fortune, but are bearable for a millionaire. Whatever philosophers say, a practical man will always contradict them on this: money is a great consolation; and you should be more easily consoled than anyone, if you will admit the virtues of this sovereign remedy – you, the king of finance, at the crossroads of power . . .'

Danglars looked sideways at the count to see if he was mocking him or speaking seriously.

'Yes,' he said. 'The fact is that if wealth is a consolation, I should feel it, because I am rich.'

'So rich, my dear Baron, that your fortune is like the pyramids: even if anyone should wish to demolish them, he would not dare; and if he dared, he could not.'

Danglars smiled at this confident bonhomie. 'That reminds me,' he said, 'when you came in I was making out five little bills. I had already signed two of them; would you permit me to do the other three?'

'Of course, my dear Baron, of course.'

There was a moment's silence, broken only by the scratching of the banker's quill, while Monte Cristo stared at the gilt mouldings on the ceiling.

'Spanish bonds?' Monte Cristo asked. 'Haitian bonds, bonds from Naples?'

'No,' Danglars said, giving one of his self-satisfied laughs. 'Bearer bonds, drawn on the Bank of France. Here, Count,' he added, 'you who are the emperor of finance as I am the king, have you seen many scraps of paper of this size, each worth a million?'

Monte Cristo took the five paper bills that Danglars proudly tendered him, as if to weigh them in his hand, and read: 'May it please the Governor of the Bank to pay on my order, from the funds deposited by me, the sum of one million, value in account. Baron Danglars.'

'One, two, three, four, five,' Monte Cristo counted. 'Five million! Damnation! There's no stopping you, Milord Croesus!'

'That's how I do business,' said Danglars.

'Marvellous, especially since, as I have no doubt, the sum is to be paid in cash.'

'It will be,' said Danglars.

'It is wonderful to have such credit. In truth, one only finds such things here in France: five scraps of paper worth five million; it has to be seen to be believed.'

'Do you doubt it?'

'No.'

'You say that in a certain kind of voice . . . Go on, try it: drive my clerk to the bank and you will see him come out with treasury bonds for the same amount.'

'No,' Monte Cristo said, folding the bills. 'No, it's too amazing; I'll test it for myself. My credit with you was six million. I have drawn nine hundred thousand francs, so you still owe me five million, one hundred thousand francs. I'll take your five scraps of paper, which I will accept on the sole guarantee of your signature, and give you, here, a receipt for the whole of the six million, which will settle our account. I prepared it in advance because, I have to tell you, I am in great need of money today.' And with one hand Monte Cristo put the five bills in his pocket, while with the other he handed his receipt to the banker.

If a thunderbolt had fallen at Danglars' feet, he could not have been stricken with such terror.

'What!' he stammered. 'What! What! Count, are you taking that money? Excuse me, please, that's money I owe to the hospice, a deposit, and I promised to pay it this morning.'

'Oh, that's another matter,' said Monte Cristo. 'I'm not particular about these five bills exactly. Pay me with some other bonds. It was out of sheer curiosity that I took these, so that I could tell everyone that, with no prior warning, without asking me to wait even for five minutes, the firm of Danglars paid me five million in cash! It would have been quite exceptional! But here are your bonds. As I say, give me some others.'

He handed the five bills to Danglars who, white as a sheet, at first put out his hand, like a vulture reaching out his claw beyond the bars of his cage to pull back the meat that someone was trying to wrench from him. Then, suddenly, he changed his mind, making a violent effort to contain his feelings.

'In point of fact,' he said, 'your receipt is currency.'

'Of course it is! If you were in Rome, the house of Thomson and

French would not make any more difficulty about paying you against my receipt than you have done yourself.'

'Forgive me, Monsieur le Comte, forgive me.'

'So: can I keep this money?'

'Yes,' said Danglars, wiping away the sweat that had gathered along his hairline. 'Keep it, keep it.'

Monte Cristo put the five notes into his pocket with that untranslatable expression on his face that says: 'Come now, think again: there is still time if you want to change your mind!'

'No,' said Danglars, 'no. Really: keep my bills. You know, there is no one so much a stickler for formality as a moneyman. I meant to give that money to the hospice and I would have thought myself a robber if I didn't give them those very bills, as if one *écu* were not worth the same as any other. Forgive me.' And he burst into a loud, nervous laugh.

'I forgive you,' Monte Cristo replied graciously. 'There!' And he put the bills into his portfolio.

'But that leaves one hundred thousand francs,' said Danglars.

'Oh, a mere trifle,' said Monte Cristo. 'The charges must amount more or less to that amount. Keep it and we'll be quits.'

'Count, are you serious?' said Danglars.

'I never joke with bankers,' Monte Cristo said, with a gravity bordering on impertinence. He was just going towards the door when the valet announced: 'Monsieur de Boville, receiver-general for hospices.'

'Well, well,' said Monte Cristo. 'It seems I came just in time to benefit from your bills: everyone's after them.'

Danglars went pale again and hurried to take his leave of the count.

Monte Cristo exchanged courteous greetings with Monsieur de Boville, who was standing in the waiting-room; as soon as Monte Cristo had gone, he was shown into Monsieur Danglars' study. One might have seen the count's grave features light up with a fleeting smile at the sight of the portfolio that the receiver-general was carrying in his hand.

At the door, he got into his carriage and asked to be driven immediately to the Bank of France.

Meanwhile, repressing his feelings, Danglars came forward to greet the receiver. It goes without saying that the smile on his lips and the courteous manner were purely for show.

'Good morning, dear creditor,' he said. 'For I am prepared to wager that it is the creditor who has come to see me . . .'

'Quite so, Baron,' Monsieur de Boville said. 'You see before you, in my person, the hospices whose widows and orphans hold out their hands in mine to ask for alms of five million francs.'

'And they say orphans are to be pitied!' Danglars said, carrying on the pleasantry. 'Poor mites!'

'So I have come in their name. Did you get my letter of yesterday's date?'

'I did.'

'Here is my receipt then.'

'My dear Monsieur de Boville,' Danglars said, 'perhaps your widows and orphans would be good enough to wait for twenty-four hours, since Monsieur de Monte Cristo, whom you have just seen leaving here . . . you did see him, I suppose?'

'Yes, I did. What about it?'

'Well, Monsieur de Monte Cristo was taking away the five million!'

'How do you mean?'

'The count has an unlimited credit with me, a credit opened by the House of Thomson and French in Rome. He came to ask me for the sum of five million in a single payment. I gave him a draft on the bank: that is where my funds are deposited and, you understand, I am afraid it might seem rather strange to the governor if I were to draw ten million on him in one day. In two days,' Danglars added, 'that's a different matter.'

'Come, come!' Monsieur de Boville exclaimed in tones of utter incredulity. 'Five million to that gentleman who was just leaving and who greeted me as he went, as though I knew him?'

'Perhaps he does know you, without you knowing him. The Count of Monte Cristo knows everybody.'

'Five million!'

'Here is his receipt. Be like Saint Thomas: see and touch!'

M. de Boville took the paper that Danglars gave him and read: 'Received of Baron Danglars, the sum of five million one hundred thousand francs, to be reimbursed to him on demand by the House of Thomson and French, in Rome.'

'Good Lord, it's true!' he said.

'Do you know the firm of Thomson and French?' Danglars asked.

'Yes,' said Monsieur de Boville. 'I did once do business with them for two hundred thousand francs, but I have not heard anything of them since then.'

'It's one of the finest houses in Europe,' Danglars said, lightly tossing down the receipt that he had just taken from Monsieur de Boville's hands.

'And so he had five million, just with you? Well I never! Is he a nabob, this Count of Monte Cristo?'

'To be honest, I don't know what he is. But he had three unlimited credits: one with me, one with Rothschild, and one with Laffitte; and,' Danglars added casually, 'as you see, he gave me precedence, leaving a hundred thousand francs for bank charges.'

M. de Boville gave every sign of extreme admiration. 'I must go and call on him,' he said, 'and get some pious bequest for us.'

'You can count on it: his donations to charity alone amount to more than twenty thousand francs a month.'

'Splendid! And I would offer him the example of Madame de Morcerf and her son.'

'What example?'

'They gave all their money to almshouses.'

'What money?'

'Their wealth, General de Morcerf's, the deceased.'

'Why?'

'Because they did not want a fortune that had been so dishonourably acquired.'

'What will they live on?'

'The mother is to retire to Provence and the son is going to enlist.'

'Well, well,' said Danglars. 'What fine scruples!'

'I registered the donation yesterday.'

'How much do they have?'

'Oh, not much: twelve or thirteen hundred thousand francs. But let's get back to our millions.'

'Certainly,' Danglars said, as naturally as could be imagined. 'So, are you in a hurry for this money?'

'Yes, I am. The accountants check our assets tomorrow.'

'Tomorrow! Why didn't you say so at once? But it's ages until tomorrow. What time does the check take place?'

'At two o'clock.'

'Send someone round at midday,' Danglars said with a smile. M. de Boville did not answer anything much. He nodded and shuffled his portfolio.

'Ah, but I've just thought of a better idea!' said Danglars.

'What should I do?'

'Monsieur de Monte Cristo's receipt is worth money. Take it to Rothschild or Laffitte; they will take it from you immediately.'

'Even though it's reimbursable in Rome?'

'Of course. It will just cost you a discount of five or six thousand francs.'

The receiver started back. 'Oh, no! No, indeed; I'd rather wait until tomorrow. Whatever next!'

'I beg your pardon,' Danglars said, with supreme insolence. 'I thought for a moment that you had a little deficit to make up.'

'Huh!' said the receiver.

'Listen, this kind of thing happens and, in such cases, one must make a small sacrifice.'

'No, thank you!' said M. de Boville.

'Then, until tomorrow, my dear friend?'

'Yes, until tomorrow – without fail, I hope?'

'Of course! You're joking! Send someone at midday, and the bank will have it ready.'

'I'll come myself.'

'Even better, since that will give me the pleasure of seeing you again.' They shook hands.

'By the bye,' said M. de Boville, 'aren't you going to the funeral of that poor Mademoiselle de Villefort, which I passed on my way here?'

'No,' the baron said. 'I am still made to feel a little ridiculous since the matter of that Benedetto, so I'm keeping my head down.'

'Come now, you're quite wrong. Was any of that your fault?'

'Well, my dear friend, you know, when one has a name as spotless as mine, one is vulnerable.'

'Believe me, everyone feels sorry for you and, most of all, for your poor daughter.'

'Yes, poor Eugénie!' Danglars said with a deep sigh. 'Did you know she was taking the veil, Monsieur?'

'No.'

'Alas, yes, it's only too true. The very next day after all that, she decided to set off with one of her friends, who is a nun. She's gone to look for a convent of some very strict order in Italy or in Spain.'

'But that's dreadful!' And M. de Boville bowed himself out with a flood of condolences to the father.

No sooner was he outside, however, than Danglars, with an emphatic energy that will be understood only by those who have seen a performance of Robert Macaire by Frédérick,[1] exclaimed: 'Imbecile!' And, slipping Monte Cristo's receipt into a little port-folio, he added: 'Come at midday – I'll be a long way off!'

Then he double-locked his door, emptied all the drawers of his cash desk, amassed some fifty thousand francs in banknotes, burned various papers, put others where they could clearly be seen, and began to write a letter which he eventually sealed, marking it on the outside: 'To Madame the Baroness Danglars'.

'This evening,' he muttered, 'I shall leave it myself on her dressing-table.'

Then he took a passport out of the drawer. 'Good,' he said. 'It is still valid for another two months.'

CV

THE PÈRE LACHAISE CEMETERY

M. Boville had indeed crossed the route of the funeral procession leading Valentine to her final resting-place.

The weather was dark and cloudy. A wind, still warm but fatal to the yellowed leaves, was whipping them off the branches, which were gradually stripped clean, and making them flutter above the heads of the vast crowd filling the boulevards.

M. de Villefort, a pure Parisian, considered the Père-Lachaise cemetery the only one worthy of receiving the mortal remains of a Parisian family. The others appeared to him like country cemeteries, death's lodging-houses. Only in the Père-Lachaise could the respect-able departed be accommodated at home.

There, as we have seen, he had bought a perpetual lease on the plot above which rose the monument which was being so swiftly occupied by all the members of his family. The pediment of the mausoleum bore the inscription: FAMILIES OF SAINT-MÉRAN AND VILLEFORT, such having been the last wish of poor Renée, Valentine's mother.

So it was towards the Père-Lachaise that the magnificent cortège wended its way from the Faubourg Saint-Honoré. They crossed all Paris, following the Faubourg du Temple and then the outer boulevards as far as the cemetery. More than fifty private carriages followed behind twenty funerary coaches and, behind these, more than five hundred more people were following on foot.

Almost all were young men who had been forcibly struck by Valentine's death and who, despite the cold mists of the century and the prosaic spirit of the age, felt the elegiac poetry of this beautiful, chaste, adorable young woman, struck down in her prime.

As they were leaving Paris, they saw a speedy team of four horses drawing a coach which suddenly halted as they stiffened their hocks, which were as nervous as steel springs. It was Monte Cristo.

The count got down from his barouche and joined the crowd following the hearse on foot. Château-Renaud noticed him. He at once got out of his coupé and came over to his side. Beauchamp also left the hired cab in which he had been riding.

The count was searching carefully through every gap in the crowd. Obviously he was looking for someone. Eventually he could contain himself no longer. 'Where is Morrel?' he asked. 'Does any one of you gentlemen know where he is?'

'We were already wondering that at the house,' said Château-Renaud. 'No one has seen him.'

The count said nothing, but continued to search around him.

Finally they reached the cemetery.

Suddenly Monte Cristo's sharp eyes penetrated the clumps of yews and pinetrees and soon he lost all anxiety: a shape had glided under the dark walkways and Monte Cristo had doubtless seen what he was looking for.

Everyone knows what a burial is like in this magnificent necropolis: dark groups scattered around the white walkways, the silence of sky and earth broken by the sound of some snapping branches or a hedge trampled around a tomb. Then the melancholy chanting of the priests, mingled here and there with a sob rising from beneath a cluster of flowers, behind which one can see a woman, overcome, her hands clasped . . .

The shadow that Monte Cristo had noticed was quickly moving through the quincunx of trees behind the tomb of Héloïse and Abélard[1] as he stood with the undertakers at the head of the horses drawing the hearse, and a moment later was at the place chosen for the sepulchre.

Each one was looking at something, but Monte Cristo looked only at the shadow which had hardly been noticed by those around it. Twice he came out of the crowd to see if the man's hands were feeling for something hidden under his clothes.

When the cortège halted, the shadow could be recognized as Morrel, with his black coat buttoned right up to the neck, his ashen forehead, his hollow cheeks and his hat crumpled in his hands. He was standing with his back to a tree, on a mound above the mausoleum, so that he would lose none of the details of the funeral ceremony that was about to take place.

Everything went off according to custom. A few men – and, as always, the least impressive – made speeches. Some regretted this premature death, others expatiated on her father's grief. Some had been found who were ingenious enough to have discovered that the young woman had more than once implored M. de Villefort on behalf of guilty men over whose head the sword of justice was suspended. Finally, every flowery metaphor and tortuous syntactical device was exhausted in every type of commentary on the lines written by Malherbe to du Périer.[2]

Monte Cristo heard and saw nothing; or, rather, he saw nothing except Morrel, whose calm immobility was a terrifying sight for the only person able to read what was going on in the depths of the young officer's heart.

'Look!' Beauchamp suddenly said to Debray. 'There's Morrel! Why the devil has he planted himself over there?' And they pointed him out to Château-Renaud.

'How pale he is,' Château-Renaud said with a shudder.

'He's cold,' said Debray.

'Not so,' Château-Renaud said slowly. 'I think it's the emotion. Maximilien's a very impressionable man.'

'Pah!' Debray retorted. 'He hardly knew Mademoiselle de Villefort. You said so yourself.'

'That's true, but I remember that at Madame de Morcerf's ball he did dance with her three times; you know, that ball where you made such an effect.'

'No, I don't know,' Monte Cristo answered, without knowing either to whom or about what he was speaking, so much was he preoccupied with watching Morrel, whose cheeks were moving like those of someone who is gasping or holding his breath.

'The speeches are over. Farewell, gentlemen,' the count said brusquely. And he gave a signal for departure by vanishing, though no one knew where.

The funerary spectacle being over, the audience turned back towards Paris.

Only Château-Renaud for a moment looked around for Morrel; but, while his eyes were following the disappearing figure of the count, Morrel had left his place and Château-Renaud, after looking for him in vain, followed Debray and Beauchamp.

Monte Cristo had slipped into a thicket and, hidden behind a wide tomb, was watching Morrel's every movement. The young man had gradually gone over towards the mausoleum, from which the onlookers and then the workmen were drifting away. He looked around him slowly and vaguely. But just as his head was turning towards the point on the horizon opposite him, Monte Cristo took advantage of this to come forward another ten yards without being seen.

Morrel was kneeling.

The count, arching his neck, his eyes staring and the pupils dilated, his knees flexed as if to jump at the merest signal, came closer and closer.

Morrel bent his forehead until it touched the stone, grasped the iron railings with both hands and murmured: 'Oh, Valentine!'

The count's heart was rent by the shattering effect of these two words. He took another step and said, touching Morrel on the shoulder: 'It's you, dear friend! I was looking for you.'

He expected some outburst, reproaches or recriminations, but he was wrong. Morrel turned around and with an appearance of calm said: 'You see: I was praying.'

The count scrutinized the young man from head to toe and seemed more at ease after this examination. 'Would you like me to take you back to Paris?' he asked.

'No, thank you.'

'Do you need anything?'

'Please leave me to pray.'

The count went away without any objection, but only to take up a new station from which he could see everything that Morrel did. The latter finally got up, wiped his knees where they had been whitened by the stones and set off towards Paris without looking around. He was walking slowly down the Rue de la Roquette.

The count, sending on his carriage which had been waiting at the cemetery, followed a hundred yards behind him. Maximilien crossed the canal and returned to the Rue de Meslay by the boulevards. Five minutes after the door had shut behind him, it re-opened to admit Monte Cristo.

Julie was at the entrance to the garden, where she was entirely absorbed in watching Maître Penelon: with the utmost seriousness concerning his profession as a gardener, he was taking cuttings from some Bengal roses.

'Ah, Monsieur le Comte de Monte Cristo!' she exclaimed with the joy that every member of the family usually displayed when the count visited the Rue Meslay.

'Maximilien has just come home, I believe, Madame?' the count said.

'I think I saw him go past, yes . . .' the young woman said. 'But, please, call Emmanuel.'

'No, Madame, you must excuse me: I have to go up immediately to Maximilien's,' Monte Cristo replied. 'I have something of the utmost importance to tell him.'

'Then go,' she said, following him with her delightful smile until he had vanished up the stairs.

Monte Cristo soon went up the two floors between the ground and Maximilien's room. On the landing he stopped to listen. Not a sound could be heard. As in most old houses inhabited by a single master, the landing was closed off only by a glazed door. However, there was no key on the outside. Maximilien had shut himself inside, but it was impossible to see through the glass, because there was a red silk curtain across the door.

The count's anxiety showed itself in a reddening of the face, a quite unusual sign of emotion in this impassive man. 'What should I do?' he muttered, and thought for a moment.

'Should I ring? No, no! The sound of a bell, that is to say of a visitor, often precipitates the resolve of those in Maximilien's situation, and then another sound follows that of the bell.'

He shuddered from head to toe; then, since he was a man whose decisions are made with the swiftness of lightning, he struck one of the panes of glass in the door with his elbow. It shattered and he lifted the curtain to see Morrel in front of his desk, a quill in his hand, having just leapt up at the sound of the breaking glass.

'Nothing!' the count said. 'A thousand apologies, my dear friend. I slipped, and my elbow went through your glass door. But now, since it is broken, I shall take advantage of that to come in. Please don't disturb yourself, I beg you.' And, putting his hand through the broken pane, he opened the door.

Morrel got up, evidently irritated, and came across to Monte Cristo, less to greet him than to bar his way.

'I do declare, it's your servants' fault,' Monte Cristo said, rubbing his elbow. 'The floors here shine like mirrors.'

'Have you hurt yourself, Monsieur?' Morrel asked coldly.

'I don't know. What were you doing there? Writing?'

'What was I doing?'

'Your fingers are all ink-stained.'

'That's true,' Morrel replied. 'I was writing. It does happen sometimes, even though I'm a soldier.'

Monte Cristo took a few steps into the apartment. Maximilien was obliged to let him pass, but he followed behind.

'You were writing, then?' Monte Cristo said, with a daunting stare.

'I've already had the honour to answer yes,' said Morrel.

The count took another look around him. 'And your pistols are beside the writing table!' he said, pointing to the weapons on Morrel's desk.

'I am leaving on a journey,' Maximilien answered.

'My dear fellow!' Monte Cristo said, with infinite tenderness.

'Monsieur!'

'My friend, my dear Maximilien, I beg you, do nothing irrevocable.'

'Irrevocable?' Morrel said, shrugging his shoulders. 'How can a voyage be irrevocable, I wonder?'

'Maximilien,' Monte Cristo said, 'let's both drop the masks we are wearing. You no more deceive me with that appearance of calm than I do you with my light-hearted concern. You realize, don't you, that to do what I have just done, to have broken your door and violated the privacy of a friend's room, you realize, I say, that to do such a thing, I must be harbouring some serious anxiety, or rather a dreadful certainty. Morrel, you want to kill yourself!'

'Well, now,' Morrel said, shaking. 'Where did you get that idea, Monsieur le Comte?'

'I say that you want to kill yourself,' the count went on in the same tone of voice. 'And here is the proof!' Going over to the desk, he picked up the white sheet of paper that the young man had thrown over the letter he had been writing, and took the letter.

Morrel rushed forward to snatch it from his hands. However, Monte Cristo had anticipated the gesture and grasped Maximilien by the wrist, halting him like a steel chain halts an unfolding spring.

'You see,' said the count. 'You do want to kill yourself: here it is in black and white!'

'Very well,' Morrel exclaimed, instantaneously switching from an appearance of calm to one of extreme violence. 'Very well, suppose that is so, suppose I have decided to turn the barrel of this pistol against myself, who will stop me? Who will have the courage to stop me? Suppose I should say: all my hopes are dashed, my heart is broken, my life is extinguished, there is nothing about me except mourning and horror, the earth has turned to ashes and every human voice is tearing me apart . . . Suppose I should say: it is only humane to let me die because, if you do not, I shall lose my reason, I shall become mad . . . Tell, me, Monsieur, if I should say that, and when it is seen that it is voiced with the anguish and the tears of my heart, will anyone answer me: "You are wrong"? Will anyone prevent me from being the most unhappy of creatures? Tell me, Count, would you have the courage to do so?'

'Yes, Morrel,' Monte Cristo said, in a voice so calm that it contrasted strangely with the young man's excited tones. 'Yes, I am the one.'

'You!' Morrel cried, with a growing expression of anger and reproach. 'You, who deceived me with absurd hopes; you, who restrained me, lulled me, deadened me with vain promises when, by some dramatic stroke or extreme resolve, I might have been able to save her, or at least to see her die in my arms; you, who pretend to have all the resources of intelligence and the powers of matter; you, who play – or appear to play – the role of Providence and don't even have the power to give an antidote to a young girl who has been poisoned . . . ! Oh, Monsieur, I swear it, you would inspire pity in me if you did not inspire horror!'

'Morrel . . .'

'Yes, you told me to lay down the mask. Well, you may have your wish: I shall lay it down.

'Yes, when you followed me to the cemetery, I still answered you, out of the goodness of my heart; when you came in here, I allowed you to do so . . . But now that you are taking advantage of my goodness, and challenging me even here in this room, to which I had retired as if to my tomb; since you are inflicting a new torment on me, when I thought I had exhausted every form of torment . . . Count of Monte Cristo, my supposed benefactor, Count of Monte Cristo, universal saviour, then be satisfied! You will witness the death of your friend!' And, with a mad laugh on his lips, Morrel threw himself once more towards the pistols.

Monte Cristo, pale as a ghost but with his eyes flashing, reached out for the weapons and said to the frenzied man: 'I repeat that you will not kill yourself!'

'Just try to stop me!' Morrel said, making a final grasp which, like the previous one, exhausted itself against the count's steely arm.

'I will prevent you!'

'But who are you, then, after all, to dare claim this tyranny over free, intelligent creatures!'

'Who am I?' Monte Cristo repeated. 'Let me tell you . . .' And he continued: 'I am the only man in the world who has the right to say to you: Morrel, I do not want your father's son to die this day!'

Monte Cristo, majestic, transfigured, sublime, advanced with arms folded towards the trembling young man who, overcome despite himself by the near divinity of the man, shrank back a step.

'Why do you mention my father?' he stammered. 'Why involve the memory of my father in what is happening to me now?'

'Because I am the man who has already saved your father's life, one day when he wanted to kill himself as you do today; because I am the man who sent the purse to your young sister and the *Pharaon* to old Morrel; because I am Edmond Dantès, who dandled you on his knees when you were a child!'

Morrel shrank back again, staggering, panting, speechless, overwhelmed. Then all his sense failed him and he fell prostrate at Monte Cristo's feet. But then, at once, just as suddenly and completely, there was a surge of regeneration in that admirable constitution. He got up, leapt out of the room and dashed to the top of the stairs, crying at the top of his voice: 'Julie, Julie! Emmanuel, Emmanuel!'

Monte Cristo also tried to follow, but Maximilien would have died rather than release the hinges of the door which he thrust back against the count.

At the sound of Maximilien's cries, Julie, Emmanuel, Penelon and some servants ran up in fright. Morrel took them by the hands and, re-opening the door, gasped out in a voice stifled by sobs: 'On your knees, on your knees! This is the benefactor, this is our father's saviour, this is . . .'

He was about to say: 'This is Edmond Dantès!'

The count stopped him by grasping his arm.

Julie seized the count's hand, Emmanuel embraced him as he would a guardian angel and Morrel again fell to his knees, dashing his forehead against the ground.

At this, the man of bronze felt his heart swell in his breast, a devouring flame shot from his throat to his eyes, and he lowered his head and wept.

For a few moments the room was full of a chorus of tears and sublime sobs that must have seemed harmonious even to the dearest angels of the Lord!

Scarcely had Julie recovered from the deep emotion that had overwhelmed her than she rushed out of the room, went down one floor and ran into the drawing-room, with childish glee, to lift the glass dome protecting the purse given by the stranger in the Allées de Meilhan.

Meanwhile Emmanuel said to the count, in a voice choking with emotion: 'Oh, Count, how – when you heard us so often speak of our unknown benefactor, when you saw us surround his memory with such gratitude and adoration, how could you wait until today to reveal yourself? Oh, this is cruel towards us – and, I might almost say, towards yourself.'

'Listen, my friend,' the count said. 'And I can call you that because, without realizing it, you have been my friend for eleven years: the revelation of this secret has come about by a great event that you cannot know. God is my witness that I wished to conceal it for ever in my soul, but your brother Maximilien forced it out of me by violence which, I am sure, he now regrets.'

Then, seeing that Maximilien had thrown himself sideways on to a chair while still remaining on his knees, he said softly, squeezing Emmanuel's hand in a significant manner: 'Take care of him.'

'Why?' the young man asked in astonishment.

'I cannot tell you; but watch over him.'

Emmanuel looked around the room and saw Morrel's pistols. His eyes settled in alarm on the weapons, which he pointed out to

Monte Cristo by slowly raising his arm towards them. Monte Cristo nodded, and Emmanuel made a movement in the direction of the pistols. 'Leave them,' said the count.

Then, going to Morrel, he took his hand. The tumult that had briefly racked his heart had given way to a profound stupor.

Julie came back upstairs, holding the silk purse in her hands, and two shining and happy tears ran down her cheeks like two drops of morning dew.

'Here is the relic,' she said. 'Do not think that it is any less dear to me since our saviour was revealed.'

'My child,' Monte Cristo said, blushing, 'allow me to take back that purse. Now that you know the features of my face, I should not want to be recalled to your memory except by the affection that I beg you to give me.'

'Oh, no!' Julie said, pressing the purse to her heart. 'No, I beg you, because one day you might leave us . . . because one day, alas, you will leave us, won't you?'

'You are right, Madame,' Monte Cristo replied, smiling. 'In a week, I shall have left this country where so many people who deserved the vengeance of heaven were living happily while my father was dying of hunger and grief.'

As he was announcing his forthcoming departure, Monte Cristo kept his eyes on Morrel and noticed that the words 'I shall have left this country' passed without rousing the young man from his lethargy. He realized that he must engage in a further bout against his friend's grief and, taking the hands of Julie and Emmanuel and clasping them in his own, he told them, with the gentle authority of a father: 'My dear friends, please leave me alone with Maximilien.'

For Julie this was an excuse to take away the precious relic which Monte Cristo had forgotten to mention again. She pulled her husband after her, saying: 'Come, let's leave them.'

The count remained alone with Morrel, who was as motionless as a statue.

'Come, now,' the count said, touching his shoulder with his fiery hand. 'Are you once more becoming a man, Maximilien?'

'Yes, because I am starting to suffer again.'

The count frowned, seemingly a prey to some grave dilemma.

'Maximilien, Maximilien!' he said. 'The thoughts that obsess you are unworthy of a Christian.'

'Have no fear, my friend,' Morrel said, looking up with a smile of infinite sadness. 'I shall no longer seek for death.'

'So: no more weapons, no more despair?'

'No, for I have something better than the barrel of a gun or the point of a knife to cure me of my grief.'

'You poor, crazed man: what do you have?'

'I have my grief itself: that will kill me.'

'My friend,' Monte Cristo said, in tones as melancholy as those of the man he was addressing, 'listen to me. One day, in a moment of despair equal to your own, since it induced me to take a similar resolution, I too wanted to kill myself; and one day, your father, equally desperate, also wanted to do the same.

'If anyone had said to your father, at the moment when he was lifting the barrel of the pistol to his head, and if anyone had said to me, at the moment when I was thrusting away from my bed the prison bread that I had not touched for three days, I say, if anyone had said to us at that climactic moment: Live! Because the day will come when you will be happy and bless life; then, wherever that voice had come from, we would have answered it with a smile of scepticism or with pained incredulity; and yet, how many times, when he embraced you, has your father not blessed life and how many times have I . . .'

'Ah!' Morrel cried, interrupting him. 'But you only lost your freedom; my father only lost his fortune. I have lost Valentine.'

'Look at me, Morrel,' Monte Cristo said, with the solemnity that on certain occasions made him so great and so persuasive. 'Look at me. I have no tears in my eyes, or fever in my veins, or dread beatings in my heart; yet I am watching you suffer, you, Maximilien, whom I love as I should my own son. Well, Maximilien, does that not tell you that grief is like life and that there is always something unknown beyond it? So, if I beg you, if I order you to live, Morrel, it is in the certainty that one day you will thank me for saving your life.'

'My God!' the young man exclaimed. 'My God, what are you telling me, Count? Take care! Perhaps you have never been in love?'

'Child!' the count replied.

'About love,' Morrel said, 'I do understand.

'You see, I have been a soldier for as long as I have been a man. I reached the age of twenty-nine without ever being in love, because none of the feelings that I experienced up to then deserved the name of love. Then, at twenty-nine I saw Valentine. For almost two years I have loved her, for almost two years I have been able to read the virtues of womanhood, inscribed by the hand of the Lord on that heart which was as plain to me as a book.

'Count, for me with Valentine there could be an infinite, immense, unknown happiness, a happiness too great, too complete and too divine for this world. Since this world has not given it to me, Count, that means that there is nothing for me on earth except despair and desolation.'

'I told you to hope, Morrel,' the count repeated.

'Then I too shall repeat: take care,' said Morrel, 'because you are trying to persuade me, and if you do persuade me, you will make me lose my mind, because you will make me believe I can see Valentine again.'

The count smiled.

'My friend, my father!' Morrel cried, in exultation. 'For the third time I must tell you: take care, because I am terrified at the power you have over me. Beware of the meaning of your words, because my eyes are lighting up again, my heart is being born anew. Beware, or you will make me believe in the supernatural.

'I should obey if you were to order me to raise the stone of the sepulchre in which the daughter of Jairus[3] is entombed, I should walk on the water, like the apostle, if your hand were to signal to me to step on the waves. Take care: I should obey.'

'Hope, my friend,' the count repeated.

'Oh!' Morrel cried, crashing from the highest point of his exultation to the depths of sorrow. 'Oh, you are toying with me: you are like one of those good mothers or, rather, like one of those selfish mothers who calm their children's sorrows with honeyed words, because they are tired of hearing them cry.

'No, my friend. I was wrong to tell you to beware. Fear nothing. I shall bury my grief with so much care in the depth of my heart, I shall make it so dark, so secret, that it will not even try your sympathy any more. Farewell, my friend! Adieu!'

'On the contrary,' the count said. 'From this moment onwards, Maximilien, you will live near me and with me. You will not leave my side and in a week we shall have left France.'

'Do you still tell me to hope?'

'I do because I have the means to cure you.'

'Count, you are making me even sadder, if that were possible. All you can see, after the blow that has struck me, is an ordinary grief, which you intend to console by ordinary means – by travel.' And Morrel shook his head, in contemptuous disbelief.

'What can I say?' Monte Cristo replied. 'I have faith in what I promise, so let me try the experiment.'

'Count, you are prolonging my agony, nothing more.'

'So, feeble spirit that you are,' said the count, 'you do not even have strength enough to allow your friend a few days for the experiment he is trying. Come, do you know what the Count of Monte Cristo can do? Do you know that he commands many powers on earth? Do you know that he has enough faith in God to obtain miracles from Him who said that if a man has faith he can move mountains? Well, wait for the miracle I am hoping for, or . . .'

'Or . . . ?' Morrel repeated.

'Or beware, Morrel, I shall call you ungrateful.'

'Have pity on me, Count.'

'I do, Maximilien, so much so that if I have not cured you in a month, day for day, hour for hour – do you hear? – I shall put you myself in front of those pistols, fully loaded, and a glass of the most deadly of Italian poisons, one more certain and quicker than the one that killed Valentine; remember that!'

'Do you promise?'

'Yes, for I am a man and I too, as I told you, wished to die. Ever since misfortune has deserted me, I have often dreamed of the delights of eternal sleep.'

'Oh, surely, do you promise me this, Count?' Maximilien asked, intoxicated.

'Not only do I promise, I swear it,' Monte Cristo said, extending his hand.

'In a month, on your honour, if I am not consoled, you will leave me free to take my life and, whatever I do, you will not call me ungrateful?'

'In a month, day for day, Maximilien; in a month, to the hour. The date is sacred: I don't know if you have realized, but today is the fifth of September. Ten years ago today, I saved your father, who wanted to die.'

Morrel grasped the count's hands and kissed them. The count accepted the homage as if such adoration were his due.

'In a month,' he went on, 'you shall have, on the table in front of which we shall both be sitting, fine weapons and an easy death. But, in exchange, do you promise me to wait until then?'

'Oh, yes!' cried Morrel. 'In my turn, I swear it!'

Monte Cristo clasped the young man to his heart and held him there for a long time.

'And now,' he said, 'from this day forth you will come and live with me. You will take Haydée's rooms and my daughter will at least be replaced by my son.'

'Haydée?' Morrel said. 'What has happened to her?'

'She went away last night.'

'To leave you?'

'To wait for me . . . So be ready to join me in the Champs-Elysées, and smuggle me out of here without anyone seeing.'

Maximilien bent his head and obeyed, like a child or a disciple.

CVI

THE SHARE-OUT

The first floor in the house on the Rue Saint-Germain-des-Prés[1] which Albert de Morcerf had chosen for his mother and himself consisted of a little, self-contained apartment which was rented to a very mysterious character.

Not even the concierge had seen the man's face, either when he was coming in or going out. In winter he buried his chin in one of those red scarves that high-class coachmen wear while they are waiting for their masters to leave the theatre; in summer he was always blowing his nose just at the moment when he might have been seen going in front of the lodge. It must be said that, contrary to all usual practice, this inhabitant was not being spied on by anyone and that the rumour going around that his alias disguised a most eminent personage – and one who could pull lots of strings – had led people to respect the mystery of his comings and goings.

His visits were usually at fixed times, though sometimes delayed or brought forward: but almost always, winter and summer, he took possession of the apartment at four o'clock, but never stayed the night there.

At half-past three, in winter, the fire was discreetly lit by the servant who had charge of the little apartment; and at half-past three, in summer, the same girl would bring up ices.

At four o'clock, as we have said, the mysterious character would arrive.

Twenty minutes later, a carriage would stop in front of the house. A woman in black or dark blue, always wrapped in a huge veil, would get out, drift like a shadow in front of the concierge's lodge and go up the stairs, though no one ever heard a single board creak under her light footsteps. Nor had anyone ever asked her where she was going.

Her face, like the stranger's, was thus entirely unknown to the two door-keepers, model concierges and perhaps the only ones in the vast brotherhood of the capital's watchdogs who would have been capable of such discretion.

Needless to say, she went up only as far as the first floor. She scratched in a special way on the door, which opened then closed tightly, and that's all.

To leave the building, the same procedure was followed. The woman would go out first, always veiled, and get back into her carriage, which vanished sometimes down one end of the street, sometimes the other. Then, twenty minutes later, the stranger would go out in his turn, buried in his scarf or hidden behind his handkerchief, and he too would disappear.

The day after the one on which Monte Cristo had paid his visit to Danglars, the day of Valentine's funeral, the mysterious occupier came in at around ten o'clock in the morning, instead of his usual time of four in the afternoon. Almost at once, without leaving the usual space of time, a hired cab arrived and the veiled lady quickly went up the stairs. The door opened and closed. But, even before the door had closed, the lady exclaimed: 'Oh, Lucien! Oh, my friend!' – with the result that, for the first time, the concierge who had overheard the exclamation was made involuntarily aware that his tenant was called Lucien; but, being a model doorkeeper, he resolved not to mention it, even to his wife.

'What is it, my dearest?' asked the man whose name the veiled lady had revealed, in her anxiety or her haste. 'Tell me.'

'My dear, can I count on you?'

'Of course, as you very well know. What is wrong? Your note this morning was quite bewildering: the haste and disorder in your handwriting . . . Come, reassure me or terrify me entirely!'

'Lucien, something of great importance!' she replied, scrutinizing him closely. 'Monsieur Danglars left last night!'

'Left! Monsieur Danglars! Where has he gone?'

'I don't know.'

'What do you mean, you don't know? Has he gone for good?'

'Certainly. At ten in the evening, his horses took him to the barrier at Charenton. There, he found a coach ready harnessed. He got in with his valet and told his coachman he was going to Fontainebleau.'

'So, what did you mean . . . ?'

'One moment, dear. He left me a letter.'

'A letter?'

'Yes. Read it.' And she reached in her pocket for an unsealed letter which she gave Debray.

Before reading it, he hesitated, as if seeking to guess what it contained; or, rather, as if, whatever it contained, he had decided to make up his mind in advance. After a few moments, his decision had no doubt been reached, because he began to read.

The following were the contents of the letter that had so disturbed Mme Danglars:

Madame, My Most Faithful Wife . . .

Unconsciously, Debray stopped and looked at the baroness, who blushed to the roots of her hair. 'Read it,' she said.

Debray went on:

When you receive this letter you will no longer have a husband! Oh, don't be too alarmed: you will not have a husband in the sense that you no longer have a daughter, by which I mean that I shall be on one of the thirty or forty roads leading out of France.

I owe you an explanation and, since you are a woman who will understand it perfectly, I shall give it to you. Here it is:

This morning I received a demand for payment of five million, and I honoured it. Another for the same amount followed almost immediately. I adjourned it until tomorrow, and I am leaving today to avoid that tomorrow which would be too unpleasant for me to bear.

You do understand, do you not, Madame and most precious wife? If I say 'you do understand', it is because you know my affairs as well as I do myself. You may even know them better than I do, since I should be unable

to say, if anyone were to ask me, where at least half of my fortune has
vanished, though it was once quite considerable; while I am certain that
you, on the contrary, would be entirely capable of doing so.

Women have infallible instincts and can explain even miracles by an
algebra of their own devising. I know only my figures, and I knew nothing
from the day when my figures began to deceive me.

Have you ever admired the rapidity of my fall, Madame? Have you been
slightly dazzled by the bright flame that has devoured my ingots? I must
confess that I saw only fire, but let's hope that you managed to find some
gold in the ashes.

It is with that consolation that I depart, Madame, my most prudent
spouse, without the slightest pricking of conscience at abandoning you.
You still have your friends, the ashes I mentioned and, to complete your
happiness, the freedom that I hasten to give you.

However, Madame, the moment has come to introduce a word or two
on more intimate matters.

As long as I hoped you were working for the good of our family and the
prosperity of our daughter, I philosophically turned a blind eye; but since
you have brought our house to ruin, I do not wish to provide a foundation
for another man's wealth.

I took you rich, but with little honour.

Forgive me for speaking so frankly but, since it is probable that only we
will read these words, I do not see why I should mince them.

I increased our wealth, which continued to grow for more than fifteen
years, until the moment when these unknown catastrophes, which I am
still unable to comprehend, arrived to seize it and cast it down – without
my being to blame, I might say, for any of it.

You, Madame, have been working solely to increase your own wealth
and that, I am certain in my own mind, you have managed to do. So I shall
leave you as I found you, rich, but scarcely honourable.

Adieu.

From now on, I too shall start to work for my own benefit.

Accept the assurance of my gratitude for the example which you have
given me, and which I shall follow.

Your most devoted husband.
BARON DANGLARS

The baroness had been watching Debray during the long and
painful reading of this letter and, despite his well-known self-
control, she had seen the young man change colour once or twice.

When he had finished, he slowly refolded the paper and resumed his pensive attitude.

'Well?' Mme Danglars asked, with understandable anxiety.

'Well, Madame?' Debray repeated mechanically.

'What do you think of this letter?'

'Very simple. I think Monsieur Danglars was suspicious.'

'Of course he was; but what do you have to tell me?'

'I don't follow you,' Debray said, icy cold.

'He has left, altogether gone! Left, never to return!'

'Oh,' Debray said, 'don't think that, Baroness.'

'I tell you, he will never come back. I know him: he is quite unshakeable in any resolution that reflects his own interests. If he had thought me of any use to him, he would have taken me. If he has left me in Paris, it is because the separation can serve his own ends: this means that he will never change his mind and that I am free for ever,' Mme Danglars added, with the same pleading expression. But Debray, instead of answering, left her poised in the same anxious and questioning state of mind and posture.

'What!' she said finally. 'Do you not even answer me, Monsieur!'

'I have only one question to ask of you: what do you expect will become of you?'

'I was going to ask you,' the baroness replied, her heart pounding.

'Oh?' said Debray. 'Are you asking for my advice, then?'

'Yes, I would like your advice,' the baroness said through dry lips.

'Well, if you're asking my advice,' the young man said, 'I would advise you to travel.'

'Travel!' muttered Mme Danglars.

'Yes, indeed. As Monsieur Danglars said, you are rich and quite free. It will be absolutely necessary for you to leave Paris in any case, I should have thought, after the double scandal of Mademoiselle Eugénie's broken engagement and Monsieur Danglars' disappearance. All that matters is that everyone should know that you have been abandoned and should think you poor, because a bankrupt's wife would not be forgiven her opulent style of life.

'To achieve this, all you need do is to remain a fortnight in Paris, repeating to everyone that you have been abandoned and telling your closest friends, who will repeat it to everyone, exactly how the desertion took place. Then you must move out of your mansion, leaving behind your jewels and relinquishing your dowry, and everybody will admire your disinterestedness and sing your praises.

'Then it will be known that you have been abandoned and people will think you are poor. Only I know your true financial situation and will be willing to account to you for it as your loyal associate.'

Pale, devastated, the baroness had listened to this speech with as much dread and despair as Debray had shown calm and indifference in delivering it. 'Abandoned!' she repeated. 'Oh, yes, indeed abandoned. Yes, you are right, Monsieur: no one will doubt my abandonment.'

These were the only words that a proud woman, deeply in love, could reply.

'But rich, very rich,' Debray continued, opening his wallet and spreading the few papers it contained across the table.

Mme Danglars ignored him, being entirely taken up with quelling the beating of her heart and holding back the tears which she felt pricking at the corners of her eyes. Finally her sense of self-respect got the upper hand and, though she could not suppress the beating of her heart, she did at least manage to avoid shedding a tear.

'Madame,' Debray said, 'we have been associated for some six months. You contributed funds to the value of one hundred thousand francs.

'Our association dates from April this year. Our speculations began in May.

'In that month we made four hundred and fifty thousand francs. In June, profits amounted to nine hundred thousand. In July, we added a further one million seven hundred thousand francs: that, as you know, was the month of the Spanish bonds.

'In August, at the start of the month, we lost three hundred thousand, but by the fifteenth we had recovered our losses and by the end of the month we had our revenge. Our accounts, brought up to date from the time when we formed our partnership to yesterday, when I closed them, give us assets amounting to two million four hundred thousand francs, that is to say, twelve hundred thousand francs each.

'Now,' he continued, slamming his account book shut with the steady and methodical hand of a stockbroker, 'we find eighty thousand francs for the compound interest on that sum which has remained in my hands.'

'But what is this interest?' the baroness interrupted. 'What does it mean, since you never invested the money?'

'I beg your pardon, Madame,' Debray said coldly. 'I had your authority to exploit it and I took advantage of it. This means forty thousand francs in interest for your half, plus the hundred thousand francs of the original capital sum, that is to say thirteen hundred and forty thousand francs for your share.

'Well, Madame,' he continued, 'I took the precaution of cashing your money in yesterday – not long ago, as you see: anyone would think I had been expecting at any moment to be asked to account to you for it. It is there, half in banknotes, half in bills, payable to the bearer.

'I say "there", and it's true. As I thought my house was not sufficiently secure and a notary not discreet enough, and property speaks even louder than a notary ... In short, since you do not have the right to buy or possess anything apart from the joint property of the marriage, I kept this entire sum, which is today your only fortune, in a safe at the bottom of this wardrobe and, to be even more secure, I did the carpentry myself.

'Now,' he went on, opening first the wardrobe, then the safe, 'here are eight hundred notes of one thousand francs each, which, as you can see, resemble a thick, iron-bound volume. To that I have added a bond for twenty-five thousand francs and finally, to make up the sum, which amounts, I believe, to something around a hundred and ten thousand francs, here is a demand note on my banker – and since my banker is not Monsieur Danglars, the note will be honoured, I can assure you.'

Mme Danglars mechanically took the demand note, the bond and the sheaf of banknotes.

This vast fortune seemed to amount to very little, laid out in that way on a table. Mme Danglars, dry-eyed but with her breast swelling with sobs, picked it up and shut the steel-bound pouch in her case, put the bond and the demand note in her portfolio and stood, pale and silent, waiting for one kind word that might console her for being so rich. But she waited in vain.

'Now, Madame,' Debray said, 'you have a splendid living, an income of something like sixty thousand *livres*, an enormous sum for a woman who will not be able to set up house for at least a year from now. This will allow you to indulge whatever notion may pass through your head; apart from which, if you should find your share inadequate, in consideration of the past that is now fading away from you, you may dip into mine. I am prepared to offer you

– oh, as a loan, naturally! – all that I possess, that is to say, one million sixty thousand francs.'

'Thank you, Monsieur,' the baroness replied. 'Thank you; but you will appreciate that what you have given me here is far more than could be required by a poor woman who does not envisage reappearing in society, at least for a long time hence.'

For a moment Debray was astonished, but he recovered and made a gesture that might most politely be interpreted as: 'Do as you please.'

Up to then, Mme Danglars had perhaps continued to hope for something, but when she saw the casual gesture that Debray had just unconsciously made, and the sidelong glance that accompanied it, as well as the deep bow and significant silence that followed them, she raised her head, opened the door and, with no outburst of anger or nerves, but also without hesitation, she swept down the stairs, not even deigning to address a nod of farewell to the man who was allowing her to leave in this manner.

'Pooh!' Debray said, when she had gone. 'Fine plans! She will stay in her house, read novels and play lansquenet, since she cannot play on the Exchange any longer.' And he took up his notebook, carefully crossing out the amounts he had just paid.

'I have one million sixty thousand francs left,' he said. 'What a pity Mademoiselle de Villefort is dead! There's a woman who would have suited me in every respect; I should have married her.'

Phlegmatically, as usual, he waited for twenty minutes after Mme Danglars' departure before leaving himself. During these twenty minutes, he did his accounts, with his watch on the table beside him.

Asmodée, that diabolical personage whom any adventurous imagination might have created with a greater or lesser degree of felicity, had Le Sage[2] not already established priority with his masterpiece, Asmodée, then, who lifted the roofs off houses in order to see inside, would have enjoyed a remarkable scene if, at the moment when Debray was doing his accounts, he had raised the top of the little boarding-house in the Rue Saint-Germain-des-Prés.

Above the room in which Debray had just shared out two and a half million francs with Mme Danglars, there was another room, also occupied by people we know, people who played an important enough role in the events which have just been described for us to take a continuing interest in them.

In this room were Mercédès and Albert.

Mercédès had changed a great deal in the past few days. It was not that, even at the time of her greatest wealth, she had ever displayed the proud luxury that visibly marks a person out from other ranks in society and means that one can no longer recognize her when she appears in more simple attire; nor was it that she had fallen into that state of depression where one is driven to wear an outward appearance of misery. No, Mercédès had changed because her eyes no longer shone, her mouth no longer smiled and a perpetual sense of constraint froze on her lips the quick retort formerly thrown up by an ever-ready wit.

It was not poverty that had withered Mercédès' intelligence or lack of courage that made her poverty burdensome to her.

Stepping down from the sphere in which she had lived, lost in the new sphere which she had chosen for herself, Mercédès was like those people who suddenly emerge out of a splendidly illuminated salon into darkness. She seemed like a queen who had left her palace for a cottage and who, reduced to the absolute essentials, cannot recognize herself either in the earthenware dishes that she is obliged to carry to the table in her own hands, or in the straw mattress that has replaced her feather bed.

Neither the beautiful Catalan nor the noble countess had preserved her proud look or her charming smile, because when her eyes rested on what was around her the only objects they met were distressing: the room was papered in one of those grey-on-grey papers that thrifty landlords choose because they show the dirt least; there was no carpet on the floor, and the furniture attracted attention, obliging one to contemplate the poverty in affected luxury; in short, these were all things that clashed and were liable to upset eyes accustomed to harmony and elegance.

Mme de Morcerf had been living here ever since she had left the family mansion. She found the silence dizzying, like a traveller reaching the edge of a precipice. Noticing that Albert was constantly looking at her surreptitiously to judge her state of mind, she had forced herself to wear an unchanging smile on her lips which, since it was not accompanied by that gentle glow of a smile in the eyes, produced the same effect as simple luminescence, that is to say light without warmth.

Albert, for his part, was preoccupied, ill at ease, embarrassed by the remnants of a lifestyle that prevented him from belonging to his present state. He wanted to go out without gloves, and considered his hands too white. He wanted to walk everywhere and thought his boots were too well-polished.

However, these two noble and intelligent creatures, indissolubly linked by ties of maternal and filial love, could understand one another without speaking and economize on all the niceties required between friends to accept the material truth on which life depends. At last, Albert was able to say to his mother, without frightening her: 'Mother, we have no money left.'

Mercédès had never really known destitution. Often, in her youth, she had herself spoken of poverty, but that is not the same thing: 'need' and 'necessity' are synonyms, but there is a world of difference between them.

In the Catalan village, Mercédès had needed for many things, but she never went without certain others. As long as the nets were in good repair, they caught fish; as long as the fish were sold, they had rope to repair the nets. And then, isolated from friendship, only having a love that had nothing to do with the material details of the situation, one thought of oneself, each for oneself, only oneself.

From the little that she had, Mercédès used to make her share as generously as possible. Now she had two shares to make, and from nothing.

Winter was coming on. Mercédès, in this bare room, already cold, had no fire – though once she had had a boiler which had heated the whole house from the halls to the bedrooms; she did not even have one miserable little flower, though her rooms had once been a hothouse which cost a king's ransom to furnish with plants. But she did have her son . . .

Up to then, the joy of fulfilling, perhaps over-fulfilling, their duty had kept them in a state of exultation. Such a state is close to enthusiasm and that makes one insensible to the things of this earth. But their enthusiasm had died down, and they had had gradually to return from the land of dreams to the world of reality.

When the ideal was exhausted, they had to talk of practicalities.

'Mother,' Albert said, just as Mme Danglars was coming down the stairs, 'let's just count all our wealth, if you don't mind. I need a total on which to build my plans.'

'Total: nothing,' Mercédès said with a pained smile.

'On the contrary, mother, total: three thousand francs, first of all, and then I intend with those three thousand francs to give us a truly delightful life.'

'My child!' Mercédès sighed.

'Alas, my dear mother,' the young man said, 'I have unfortunately spent enough of your money to know its worth. You see, now, three thousand francs is a vast sum: I have built a miraculous future on it, one of everlasting security.'

'You say that, my dear,' the poor mother said, blushing, 'but can we even accept these three thousand francs?'

'I think it's agreed we can,' said Albert in a firm voice. 'We accept them all the more readily since we do not have them, for as you know they are buried in the garden of the little house in the Allées de Meilhan, in Marseille. With two hundred francs,' he continued, 'we shall both go to Marseille.'

'For two hundred francs!' said Mercédès. 'Do you really think that, Albert?'

'Oh, I'm absolutely sure of it. I've enquired about coaches and steamships and done my sums. You hire your seats in the coach for Chalon: you see, mother, I'm treating you like a queen; that's thirty-five francs . . .'

He took a pen and wrote:

> Coach, 35 francs 35
> From Chalon to Lyon, steamship 6
> From Lyon to Avignon, again steamship 16
> From Avignon to Marseille, seven francs 7
> Travelling expenses, 50 francs 50
> Total . . . . . . 114 Frs.

'Let's say one hundred and twenty,' Albert said, with a smile. 'See how generous I am, mother?'

'But what about you, my poor boy?'

'Me! Don't you see that I've left eighty francs for myself? A young man does not need a good deal of comfort. In any case, I know what it means to travel.'

'With your post-chaise and your valet.'

'However it may be, I know, mother.'

'Very well,' said Mercédès. 'But the two hundred francs?'

'Here they are, and another two hundred. I sold my watch for a hundred francs and the chain and trimmings for three hundred.

Isn't that splendid: a watch-chain worth three times as much as the watch! A matter of sheer excess again. So we are rich since, instead of the hundred and fourteen francs you needed for the journey, you now have two hundred and fifty.'

'But do we owe something for our rent here?'

'Thirty francs, which I can take out of my hundred and fifty. So it's agreed. And, since I only need eighty francs myself for the journey, if it comes down to it, you can see we're in the lap of luxury. But that's not all; what do you say to this, mother?'

And, out of a little wallet with a gold lock – the remnant of some past self-indulgence or perhaps a tender souvenir of one of those mysterious, veiled women who used to knock at the little door – Albert took a thousand-franc note.

'What is that?' Mercédès asked.

'A thousand francs, mother. Oh, it's perfectly in order.'

'But where did it come from?'

'Now listen to me, mother, and don't get too excited.' Albert stood up, went over to kiss his mother on both cheeks, then paused to look at her.

'You have no idea, mother, how beautiful I think you are!' he said, with profound feelings of filial love. 'You really are the most beautiful woman I have ever seen, and the most noble.'

'Dear child!' Mercédès said, trying unsuccessfully to hold back the tears that were forming in the corners of her eyes.

'I do think that you needed only to be unhappy for my love to change to adoration.'

'I am not unhappy while I have my son,' Mercédès said. 'I never shall be, as long as I have him.'

'Oh, yes, now,' said Albert. 'That's where the trying times will begin. You know what is agreed?'

'Have we agreed something?' Mercédès asked.

'Yes, it is agreed that you will live in Marseille and I shall leave for Africa. There, instead of the name I have given up, I shall make for myself the name I have adopted.'

Mercédès sighed.

'Well, mother, yesterday I enrolled in the spahis,' the young man said, lowering his eyes with some feeling of shame, not realizing how sublime his humiliation was. 'Or, rather, I thought that my body was mine and that I could sell it; since yesterday I have replaced someone. I have sold myself, as they say, and . . .' he added, forcing a smile, 'dearer than I ever expected, that is to say for two thousand francs.'

'So this thousand francs?' Mercédès said, shuddering.

'Half of the amount, mother; the rest in a year's time.'

Mercédès raised her eyes heavenwards with an expression beyond the power of any artist to depict. Her inner feelings overflowed and the two tears poised on the rim of her eyelids ran silently down her cheeks. 'The price of his blood,' she murmured.

'Yes, if I should be killed,' said Morcerf, with a laugh. 'But I assure you, dear mother, that I have every intention of defending myself savagely. I have never felt such a strong desire to live.'

'My God, my God!' Mercédès said.

'Anyway, mother, why should I be killed? Was Lamoricière killed, that second Ney from the south? Was Changarnier killed? Or Bedeau?[3] Has our friend Morrel been killed? Just think how pleased you will be when you see me come home in my uniform with the braid on it! I do assure you, I intend to look quite magnificent in it; I only chose that regiment for the sake of the uniform.'

Mercédès sighed, while attempting to smile. The saintly woman realized that it was wrong for her to let her son bear all the weight of their sacrifice.

'So, you see, mother,' Albert said, 'you are already guaranteed more than four thousand francs. With that you can live for at least two years.'

'Do you think so?' said Mercédès.

The words had slipped out, and the pain behind them was so real that Albert could not help grasping their real meaning. He felt a lump in his throat and, taking his mother's hand, clasped it tenderly in his and said: 'Oh, yes, you shall live!'

'I shall,' Mercédès exclaimed. 'But you will not go, will you, my son?'

'Mother, I must,' Albert said, firmly and calmly. 'You love me too much to keep me beside you in fruitless idleness. In any case, I have signed my name.'

'You must do what you will, my son. I shall do what God wills.'

'Not what I will, mother, but what reason and necessity dictate. We are two desperate creatures, aren't we? What is life for you now? Nothing. What is life for me? Very little indeed without you, mother, believe me. Without you, I swear, my life would have ended on the day when I first doubted my father and renounced his name. But I shall live, if you promise me that you will continue to hope. If you leave your future happiness in my care, you will double my strength. When I arrive there, I shall go and see the governor of Algeria. He is a fine man and, above all, a true soldier. I will tell him my sad story and beg him to watch me from time to time. If he does so, and sees how I manage, in six months I shall be an officer or dead. If I am an officer, mother, then your future is assured, because I shall have enough money for both of us and a new name of which we can both be proud, since it will be your true name. If I am killed . . . Well, if I am killed, then, mother dear, you will die, if you please, and our misfortunes will be ended by their own excess.'

'Very well,' said Mercédès, with her noble and eloquent look. 'You are right, my son. Let us prove to certain people who are watching us and waiting to see what we will do to criticize us, and let us at least prove to them that we deserve their sympathy.'

'But let's have no funereal thoughts, mother: I swear to you that we are, or at least can be, very happy. You are a woman who is both full of wit and resigned; I have become simple in my tastes and, I hope, without passion. Once I am in the army, I shall be rich; once you are in Monsieur Dantès' house, you will be at peace. Let's try, mother, I beg you, let's try.'

'Yes, my son, you must live, you must be happy,' Mercédès replied.

'So, we each have our shares,' the young man concluded, giving an appearance of being utterly at ease. 'We can leave today. Come then, I shall reserve your place, as they say.'

'And yours?'

'I must stay here two or three days more. This is a first separation and we must get used to it. I need a few letters of recommendation and some information about Africa; then I shall join you in Marseille.'

'Very well then, let's go!' Mercédès said, wrapping herself in the only shawl she had brought with her, which happened to be a very expensive black cashmere. 'Let's go!'

Albert hurriedly collected his papers, rang to pay the thirty francs he owed the owner of the boarding house, and offered his mother his arm to go down the stairs.

Someone was going down in front of them and this someone, hearing the rustling of a silk dress on the banisters, turned around.

'Debray!' Albert muttered.

'You, Morcerf!' the minister's secretary answered, stopping on the stair where he was standing.

Curiosity overcame Debray's wish to remain incognito; in any event, he had been recognized. There was something very intriguing about discovering the young man whose misfortune was the talk of the whole town in this obscure boarding-house.

'Morcerf!' Debray repeated. Then, noticing Mme de Morcerf's still youthful figure in the half-light and her black veil, he added, smiling: 'Oh, I beg your pardon, Albert! I shall leave you.'

Albert understood what he was thinking. 'Mother,' he said, turning to Mercédès, 'this is Monsieur Debray, secretary to the Minister of the Interior, and one of my former friends.'

'What do you mean, "former"?' Debray spluttered.

'I say that, Monsieur Debray,' Albert went on, 'because today I have no more friends and must have none. I thank you very much, Monsieur, for being so good as to recognize me.'

Debray ran up the two steps and shook Albert's hand earnestly. 'Believe me, my dear Albert,' he said, with all the feeling of which he was capable, 'I sympathized deeply in the misfortune that has befallen you and I am at your disposal for anything you should need.'

'Thank you, Monsieur,' Albert said, smiling. 'But, despite our misfortunes, we have remained rich enough not to need to apply to anyone. We are leaving Paris and, after paying for our journey, we shall have five thousand francs left.'

Debray blushed. He had a million in his portfolio. However little poetry there was in that mathematical soul, he could not escape the reflection that the same house had only a short while before contained two women, one of whom, justly dishonoured, had left poverty-stricken despite the fifteen hundred thousand francs under her cloak; while the other, unjustly struck down, sublime in her misfortune, considered herself rich with a few pence. The comparison deflected his polite platitudes and the force of the example crushed every argument. He muttered a few more or less civil words and hastened to the bottom of the stairs.

That day, the clerks in the ministry who worked for him had to put up with a good deal of irritation. In the evening, however, he purchased a very fine house, situated on the Boulevard de la Madeleine, which brought in 50,000 francs a year.

The following day, at the time when Debray was signing the deeds, that is to say at about five o'clock in the evening, Mme de Morcerf tenderly embraced her son and was tenderly embraced by him, then got into the stagecoach, the door of which shut behind her.

A man was hidden in the courtyard of the Messageries Laffitte, behind one of those arched mezzanine windows above each of the offices. He saw Mercédès get into the coach and saw it drive off. He watched Albert walk away. Then he drew his hand across a brow furrowed with doubt and said: 'Alas! How can I give those two innocent people back the happiness I have taken away from them? God will help me.'

CVII

THE LIONS' PIT

One sector of La Force,[1] the one that contains the most dangerous prisoners and those accused of the worst crimes, is called Saint Bernard's Court. But the prisoners have renamed it – in their expressive slang – 'The Lions' Pit', probably because the captives' teeth often gnaw the bars and sometimes the warders.

This is a prison within a prison: the walls are twice as thick as elsewhere. Every day a doorkeeper carefully tests the massive railings, and one can see from the Herculean stature and cold, penetrating eyes of the warders here that they have been chosen for their physical and mental ability to inspire fear.

The exercise yard for this section is enclosed in vast walls across which the sun shines obliquely when it deigns to penetrate into this gulf of spiritual and physical ugliness. It is on these stones that, from dawn onwards, careworn, wild-eyed and wan, like ghosts, those men wander whose necks justice has bent beneath the sharpening blade.

They can be seen crouching, hugging whichever wall holds most warmth. There they remain, talking in pairs, but more often alone, constantly glancing towards the door which opens to call one or other inhabitant forth from this grim place, or to fling into the gulf some new piece of detritus thrown out of the melting pot of society.

St Bernard's Court has its own visiting-room: a long rectangle, divided in two by two parallel grilles set three feet apart, so that the visitor cannot shake hands with the prisoner or pass him anything. The interview room is dark, dank and in every way repellent, especially when one considers the appalling secrets that have passed between the grilles and rusted the iron bars. But this place, ghastly though it is, is a paradise in which men whose days are numbered come to recall a society that they long for and savour: so rare is it for anyone to emerge from the Lions' Pit to go anywhere except to the Barrière Saint-Jacques,[2] to the penal colony or to the padded cell!

In the courtyard we have just described, dripping with dank humidity, a young man was walking, with his hands in the pockets of his coat – a young man who was looked on by the inhabitants of the pit with a good deal of curiosity.

He would have passed for something of a dandy, thanks to the cut of his clothes, if these clothes had not been in rags. However, they were not worn out: the cloth, fine and silken where it still remained intact, would soon regain its lustre when the prisoner stroked it with his hand, trying to restore his coat.

He applied the same care to holding together a lawn shirt that had considerably faded in colour since he entered the prison, and rubbed his polished boots with the corner of a handkerchief which was embroidered with initials under a heraldic crown.

Some detainees in the Lions' Pit showed a marked interest in the prisoner's attention to his dress.

'Look there: the prince is smartening himself up,' one of the thieves said.

'He is naturally very smart-looking,' another said. 'If only he had a comb and some pomade, he would outshine all those gentlemen in white gloves.'

'His coat must have been brand new and his boots have a lovely polish on them. It's an honour for us to have such respectable colleagues; and the gendarmes are a real bunch of hooligans. What envy! To destroy a set of clothes like that!'

'They do say he's a celebrity,' another added. 'He's done the lot, and in style. And he's come in so young. Oh, it's marvellous!'

The object of this frightful admiration seemed to be savouring the praise – or the whiff of praise, because he could not hear the words.

His toilet complete, he went over to the window of the canteen against which a warder was leaning. 'Come, Monsieur,' he said. 'Lend me twenty francs. I'll return them very soon: you need not worry about me. Just think: some of my relatives have more millions than you have farthings. So, a matter of twenty francs, if you please, so that I can get a pistol and buy a dressing-gown. I can't bear always being in a coat and boots. And what a coat! Monsieur! For Prince Cavalcanti!'

The warder turned his back on him and shrugged his shoulders. He didn't even laugh at these words, which would have brought a smile to anyone's lips, because he had heard many variations on the theme; or, rather, the same thing over and over.

'Very well,' Andrea said. 'You are a man without feeling and I shall get you sacked.'

The last remark made the warder turn around, and this time he did respond, with a huge burst of laughter. At that, the other prisoners gathered around.

'I am telling you,' Andrea said, 'that with this paltry sum I could buy myself a coat and dressing-gown, so that I shall be able to receive the illustrious visitor I am expecting, any day now, in an appropriate manner.'

'He's right! He's right!' the prisoners cried. 'Damnation! You can see he's a proper gentleman.'

'Well, then, you lend him the twenty francs,' said the warder, shifting his weight to his other, enormous shoulder. 'Don't you owe that to a comrade?'

'I am not the comrade of these people,' the young man said proudly. 'Don't insult me. You have no right to do that.'

The thieves looked at one another, muttering under their breath; and a storm, raised by the warder's provocation even more than by Andrea's words, began to rumble around the aristocratic prisoner.

The warder, sure of doing a *quos ego*[3] when the waves began to rise too high, let the storm brew a little to play a trick on the man who had been importuning him and to give himself a little light relief in a tedious day's work.

The thieves had already come close to Andrea, and some were shouting: 'The slipper! The slipper!'

This is a cruel game which consists in attacking a colleague who has fallen foul of these gentlemen, not with a slipper, but with a hobnailed boot.

Others suggested the eel: this is a different type of entertainment, consisting in filling a twisted handkerchief with sand, pebbles or coins (when they have any), and beating the victim around the head and shoulders with it.

'Let's whip the fine fellow,' some said. 'The real gent!'

But Andrea, turning around towards them, winked, put his tongue in his cheek and gave a clicking of the lips that meant a host of things to these bandits, who fell silent. These were masonic signs that Caderousse had shown him, and the hooligans recognized one of their own.

The handkerchiefs dropped at once and the hobnailed slipper went back on the head executioner's foot. Some voices muttered that the gentleman was right, that he could be honest in his own way and that the prisoners ought to set an example of freedom of thought.

The riot receded. The warder was so amazed that he immediately took Andrea's hands and began to search him, attributing this sudden change in the inhabitants of the Lions' Pit to something other than mere hypnotism. Andrea let him, but not without protest.

Suddenly there was a shout from the gates. 'Benedetto!' an inspector called. The warder gave up his prey.

'Someone wants me?' said Andrea.

'In the visitors' room,' said the voice.

'You see, someone to visit me. Oh, my dear friend, you'll soon see if a Cavalcanti is to be treated like an ordinary man!'

Hurrying across the courtyard like a black shadow, Andrea swept through the half-open door, leaving his fellow-prisoners and even the warder looking after him admiringly.

He had indeed been called in to the visitors' room, and one should not be any less surprised at this than Andrea himself, because the clever young man, since he had first been put in La Force, instead of following the custom of ordinary prisoners and taking advantage of the opportunity to write to have visitors come and see him, had kept the most stoical silence.

'Obviously,' he thought, 'I have some powerful protector. Everything goes to prove it: my sudden fortune, the ease with which I overcame every obstacle, a ready-made family, an illustrious name which was mine to use, the gold showered upon me, the splendid matches offered to satisfy my ambition. My good luck unfortunately failed me and my protector was away, so I was lost, but not entirely, not for ever! The hand was withdrawn for a moment, but it must now reach out to me again and catch me just as I feel myself about to fall into the abyss.

'Why should I risk doing something unwise? Perhaps I would alienate my protector. There are two ways to get out of this spot: a mysterious escape, expensively paid for, or pressure on the judges to dismiss the case. Let's wait before speaking or acting, until it is proved that I have been utterly abandoned, then . . .'

Andrea had worked out a plan which some might consider clever; the rascal was bold in attack and tough in defence. He had put up with the wretchedness of prison and every form of deprivation. But, little by little, nature (or, rather, habit) regained the upper hand. He was suffering from being naked, dirty and hungry, and time was hanging heavy on his hands. It was when he had reached this point of boredom that the inspector called him to the visitors' room.

Andrea felt his heart leap with joy. It was too early for a visit from the investigating magistrate and too late for a call from the prison director or the doctor. It must therefore be the visit he was expecting.

He was introduced into the visiting-room. There, behind the grille, his eyes wide with hungry curiosity, he saw the dark and intelligent face of M. Bertuccio, who was also looking, though with painful astonishment, at the iron bars, the bolted doors and the shadow moving behind the iron lattice.

'Ah!' Andrea exclaimed, deeply touched.

'Good day, Benedetto,' Bertuccio said, in his resounding, hollow voice.

'You!' the young man exclaimed, looking around in terror. 'You!'

'You don't recognize me,' said Bertuccio. 'Wretched child!'

'Be quiet!' said Andrea, knowing that these walls had very sharp ears. 'Do be quiet! My God, don't talk so loudly!'

'You would like to speak to me, wouldn't you?' said Bertuccio. 'A tête-à-tête?'

'Yes, certainly,' said Andrea.

'Very well.' After feeling around in his pocket, Bertuccio motioned to a warder who could be seen in his box behind a glass screen. 'Read this,' he said.

'What is it?' Andrea asked.

'An order to take you into a room, to leave you there, and to let me converse with you.'

'Oh!' Andrea said, leaping for joy. And immediately, in his inner thoughts, he told himself: 'Once more, my unknown protector! I have not been forgotten! He is trying to keep it quiet because we are to talk alone in a room. I've got them! Bertuccio has been sent by my protector.'

The warder briefly consulted his superior, then opened the two barred doors and led Andrea, beside himself with joy, to a room on the first floor with a view over the courtyard.

The room was whitewashed, as prison rooms usually are. It had a pleasant appearance, which seemed delightful to the prisoner: a stove, a bed, a chair and a table made up its luxurious furnishings.

Bertuccio sat down on the chair; Andrea threw himself on the bed. The warder left the room.

'Now, then,' said the steward. 'What have you to say to me?'

'And you?'

'You speak first . . .'

'Oh, no. You have a lot to tell me, since you came to find me.'

'Very well. You have continued to pursue your criminal career: you have stolen, you have committed murder . . .'

'Pooh! If it was to tell me that that you had me brought to a private room, you might have saved yourself some time. I know all those things; but there are others that I do not know. Let's start with those, if you don't mind. Who sent you?'

'Oh! You're going very fast, Monsieur Benedetto.'

'I am, and straight to the point. Let's not waste words. Who sent you?'

'No one.'

'How did you know that I was in prison?'

'I recognized you a long time ago in the insolent dandy who was so elegantly driving his horse down the Champs-Elysées.'

'The Champs-Elysées! Ah, we're getting warm, as they say in hunt the slipper. The Champs-Elysées . . . So, let's talk about my father, shall we?'

'Who am I, then?'

'You, my good sir, are my adoptive father. But I don't suppose it was you who put at my disposal some hundred thousand francs, which I spent in four or five months. I don't suppose it was you who forged an Italian father for me – and a nobleman. I don't suppose you were the one who introduced me to society and invited me to a certain dinner, which I can still taste, in Auteuil, with the best company in Paris, including a certain crown prosecutor whose acquaintance I was mistaken not to cultivate; he could be useful to me at this moment. In short, you are not the one who stood guarantor for me for two million when I suffered the fatal accident of the revelation of the truth. Come, my fine Corsican, say something . . .'

'What can I say?'

'I'll help you. You were talking about the Champs-Elysées just now, my dear adoptive father.'

'Well?'

'Well, in the Champs-Elysées lives a rich, a very rich man.'

'You committed burglary and murder at his house?'

'I do believe I did.'

'The Count of Monte Cristo?'

'You were the one who mentioned him, as Monsieur Racine says.[4] Well, should I throw myself into his arms, press him to my heart and cry: "Father, father!!" as Monsieur Pixérécourt does?'

'Don't joke,' Bertuccio answered. 'Such a name should not be spoken here in the tone in which you dare to speak it.'

'Huh!' said Andrea, a little stunned by the gravity of Bertuccio's demeanour. 'Why not?'

'Because the man who bears that name is too favoured by heaven to be the father of a wretch like yourself.'

'Fine words!'

'With fine consequences, if you are not careful.'

'Threats! I'm not afraid of them . . . I'll say . . .'

'Do you imagine you are dealing with pygmies like yourself?' Bertuccio said, so calmly and with such a confident look that Andrea was shaken to the core. 'Do you imagine you are dealing with one of your ordinary convicts or your weak-minded society gulls? Benedetto, you are in dreadful hands. These hands are ready to open for you: take advantage of it. But don't play with the lightning that they may put down for a moment but will pick up again if you try to hamper their freedom of movement.'

'My father! I want to know who my father is,' Andrea said obstinately. 'I'll die in the attempt if I must, but I will find out.

What does a scandal mean to me? Good, reputation, "publicity", as Beauchamp the journalist says. But the rest of you, who belong to society, always have something to lose by scandal, for all your millions and your coats of arms . . . So, who is my father?'

'I have come to tell you.'

'Ah!' Benedetto cried, his eyes shining.

At that moment the door opened and the keeper said to Bertuccio: 'Excuse me, Monsieur, but the investigating magistrate is waiting for the prisoner.'

'That's the end of the enquiry into my case,' Andrea told the good steward. 'Damn him for disturbing us.'

'I'll come back tomorrow,' said Bertuccio.

'Very well,' Andrea replied. 'Gentlemen of the watch, I am all yours. Oh, my good sir, please leave the guard ten *écus* or so, for them to give me what I need in here.'

'It will be done,' Bertuccio replied.

Andrea offered his hand. Bertuccio kept his in his pocket and merely jingled a few coins with it.

'That's what I meant,' Andrea said, forcing a smile, but in fact quite overwhelmed by Bertuccio's calm manner.

'Could I have been wrong?' he wondered, getting into the oblong vehicle with its barred windows, which is called the Black Maria. 'We'll see! So, until tomorrow,' he added, turning to Bertuccio.

'Until tomorrow!' said the steward.

CVIII

THE JUDGE

It will be recalled that Abbé Busoni had remained alone with Noirtier in the funerary chamber and that it was the old man and the priest who had taken on the task of watching over the young girl's body.

Perhaps the abbé's Christian exhortations, or his gentle charity, or his winning words had restored the old man's courage because, as soon as he had the opportunity to confer with the priest, instead of the despair that had at first overwhelmed him, everything in Noirtier spoke of great resignation; and this calm was all the more surprising to those who remembered the deep affection that he felt for Valentine.

M. de Villefort had not seen the old man since the morning of her death. The whole household had been renewed: another valet was hired for himself, another servant for Noirtier; two women had come into Mme de Villefort's service; and all of them, right down to the concierge and the chauffeur, provided new faces which had, so to speak, risen up between the different masters in this accursed household and interposed themselves in the already quite cold relationships between them. In any case, the assizes opened in three days and Villefort, shut up in his study, was feverishly working on the indictment against Caderousse's murderer. This affair, like all those in which the Count of Monte Cristo was involved, had caused a great stir in Paris. The evidence was not conclusive, since it relied on a few words written by a dying convict, a former fellow-inmate of the man he was accusing, who might be acting out of hatred or for revenge. The magistrate was morally certain, but nothing more. The crown prosecutor had eventually succeeded in acquiring for himself the dreadful certainty that Benedetto was guilty, and this difficult victory was to reward him with one of those satisfactions to his vanity which were the only pleasures that still touched the fibres of his icy heart.

So the trial opened, thanks to Villefort's unending work. He wanted to make it the first case to be heard at the next assizes, so he had been obliged to hide himself away even more than usual in order to avoid answering the huge number of demands for tickets to the hearing that were addressed to him.

Moreover, so little time had passed since poor Valentine had been laid to rest. The family's grief was still so recent that no one was surprised to see the father so totally absorbed in his duties, that is to say in the only thing that might take his mind off his sorrow.

Only once, the day after Benedetto had received a second visit from Bertuccio, the one when he was to tell him the name of his father, in fact the day after that, which was Sunday – only once, as we say, did Villefort notice his father. This was at a moment when the magistrate, overcome with tiredness, had gone down into the garden of his house and, dark, bent beneath some implacable thought, like Tarquin[1] cutting the heads off the tallest poppies with his cane, M. de Villefort was knocking down the long, dying stems of the hollyhocks that rose on either side of the path like the ghosts of those flowers that had been so brilliant in the season that had just passed away.

He had already more than once reached the end of the garden, that is to say the famous gate overlooking the abandoned field, from which he would always return by the same path, resuming his walk at the same pace and repeating the same gestures, when he looked up, mechanically, towards the house, where he could hear his son playing noisily. The boy had come home from boarding school to spend Sunday and Monday with his mother.

At that moment, he saw M. Noirtier at one of the open windows. The old man had had his chair brought up to that window to enjoy the last rays of the still warm sun as it came to bid farewell to the dying convolvulus flowers and the reddened leaves of the vines entwined around the balcony.

The old man's eye was fixed as it were on a point which Villefort could only imperfectly distinguish. His look was so full of hatred and savagery, and burned with such impatience, that the crown prosecutor, accustomed to interpreting every nuance of the features that he knew so well, stepped aside from his route to see who could have attracted such a powerful look.

Under a group of lime-trees, almost entirely bare of leaves, he saw Mme de Villefort, sitting with a book in her hand and looking up from her reading at intervals to smile at her son or to throw back the rubber ball which he insisted on throwing from the drawing-room into the garden.

Villefort paled, knowing what the old man wanted.

Noirtier was still looking at the same spot, but his eyes often turned from the wife to the husband, and then Villefort himself had to suffer the onslaught of those devastating eyes which, as they switched from one object to another, also changed in meaning, though without losing any of their threatening expression.

Mme de Villefort, quite unaware of these passions beamed back and forth above her head, was at that moment holding her son's ball and motioning him to come and fetch it with a kiss; but Edouard took a lot of persuading: a kiss from his mother probably seemed insufficient reward for the trouble he would have to take. Finally he made up his mind, jumped out of the window into a bed of asters and heliotropes and ran over to Mme de Villefort, his forehead bathed in sweat. Mme de Villefort wiped it dry, put her lips to the damp ivory and sent the child off with his ball in one hand and sweets in the other.

Villefort, drawn by an invisible magnet, like a bird fascinated by a snake, came towards the house. As he approached, Noirtier's eyes were lowered to follow him and the fire in his pupils seemed to reach such a degree of incandescence that Villefort felt it eating into the depths of his heart. There was indeed a fearsome reproach to be read in those eyes, as well as a dreadful threat. Then Noirtier's eyes and eyelids were raised towards heaven, as if reminding his son of a forgotten oath.

'Very well, Monsieur!' Villefort replied, stepping into the court-yard. 'Very well! Be patient for one day more. I shall do as I said.'

Noirtier seemed to be calmed by these words and his eyes turned indifferently away. Villefort swiftly unbuttoned the frock-coat that was stifling him, passed a pale hand across his brow and went back into his study.

The night passed, cold and calm. Everyone went to bed and slept as usual in the house. Only Villefort (as usual) did not go to bed with the rest but worked until five in the morning, running over the last interrogations carried out the day before by the investigating magistrates, studying the evidence of witnesses and clarifying the language of his own opening speech, one of the most powerful and subtly written that he had ever made.

The first session of the assizes was to take place on the following day, Monday. Villefort saw that day dawn, sinister and sickly pale, its bluish light reflecting off the lines on the paper, written in red ink. The judge had fallen asleep for a moment while his lamp burned itself out. He was woken by its spluttering, his hands damp and ink-stained as if he had dipped them in blood.

He opened his window: a wide orange band crossed the distant horizon, cutting across the slender poplars outlined in black against the sky. In the field of alfalfa, beyond the wall by the chestnut-trees, a skylark winged its way into the heavens, followed by its clear morning song. The damp air of dawn flooded over Villefort's head, awakening his memory.

'Today will be the day,' he forced himself to say. 'Today the man who is to hold the sword of justice must strike wherever the guilty one may be.'

Involuntarily his eyes turned towards Noirtier's window, which was at right angles to his: the window where he had seen the old man the evening before. The curtain was drawn. Yet the image of his father was so clear in his mind that he spoke to the closed window as if it had been open, and through the opening he could see the threatening old man. 'Yes,' he muttered. 'Don't worry.'

His head fell back on his chest and, with it bowed, he walked a few times round his study before finally throwing himself, fully dressed, on a sofa, not so much to sleep as to loosen his limbs which were stiff with tiredness and the chill of work which reached right to the marrow of the bones.

Little by little, everyone woke up. Villefort, in his study, heard the successive noises that, as it were, made up the life of the house: the doors opening and closing; the ringing of Mme de Villefort's bell, summoning her maid; the first cries of the child, who got up merrily as one does at that age.

Villefort himself rang. His new valet came in, bringing the newspapers together with a cup of chocolate.

'What's that you're bringing me?' Villefort asked.

'A cup of chocolate.'

'I didn't ask for it. Who is taking such care of me?'

'Madame. She said that Monsieur would no doubt have to speak a good deal today in that matter of the murder and that he needed to build up his strength.' And the valet put down the vermeil cup on the table beside the sofa – a table which, like the rest, was covered in papers. Then he went out.

Villefort looked grimly for a moment at the cup, then suddenly grabbed it and drank down the contents in a single draught. It was as though he hoped that the liquid was some deadly poison and that he was calling on death to release him from a duty that was ordering him to do something much more difficult than dying. Then he got up and walked round his study with a sort of smile which would have been terrible to see, had there been anyone to see it.

The chocolate was harmless and M. de Villefort felt no ill-effects.

When breakfast time arrived, M. de Villefort did not appear at table. The valet came back to the study. 'Madame wishes to inform Monsieur that eleven o'clock has just struck,' he said, 'and that the session opens at midday.'

'So?' said Villefort.

'Madame's toilet is complete. She is quite ready and wishes to know if she will be accompanying Monsieur?'

'Where?'

'To the law courts.'

'What for?'

'Madame says that she would very much like to be present at the session.'

'Ah!' Villefort said, in almost terrifying tones. 'Does she really!'

The servant shrank back and said: 'If Monsieur would like to go out alone, I shall inform Madame.'

For a moment Villefort said nothing, but scratched his cheek – pale, in contrast to his ebony-black beard.

'Tell Madame,' he said finally, 'that I should like to speak to her and that she should expect me in her rooms.'

'Yes, Monsieur.'

'Then come back to shave and dress me.'

'Immediately.'

The valet disappeared briefly, then returned to shave Villefort and solemnly dress him in black. When he had finished, he said: 'Madame says that she will expect Monsieur as soon as he is ready.'

'I am going.' With his dossiers under his arm and his hat in his hand, Villefort set off towards his wife's apartments.

At the door, he stopped for a moment and wiped away the sweat that was running down his livid white forehead. Then he pushed open the door.

Mme de Villefort was sitting on an ottoman, impatiently leafing through some newspapers and brochures that young Edouard was tearing in pieces even before his mother had had time to finish reading them. She was completely dressed to go out. Her hat was waiting for her on a chair and she had her gloves on.

'Ah! Here you are, Monsieur,' she said quite calmly, in her ordinary voice. 'Good heavens, how pale you are! Have you been working all night again? Why didn't you come to have luncheon with me? So, are you going to take me, or shall I go on my own with Edouard?'

As one can see, Mme de Villefort had asked one question after another, in order to get some response; but M. de Villefort remained cold and silent as a statue at every enquiry.

'Edouard,' he said, fixing the child with a commanding look. 'Go and play in the drawing-room. I have something to say to your mother.'

This cold stare, resolute voice and unexpected introduction made Mme de Villefort shudder. Edouard had looked up at his mother and, when she did not confirm M. de Villefort's orders, went back to cutting the heads off his lead soldiers.

'Edouard!' M. de Villefort shouted, so harshly that the child leapt up on the carpet. 'Do you hear me? Go!'

The child, unaccustomed to such treatment, got up, ashen-faced – though it was hard to say whether from anger or fear. His father went over to him, took his arm and kissed his forehead. 'Go on, child,' he said. Edouard went out.

M. de Villefort walked over to the door and locked it.

'My heavens!' the young woman said, looking deep into her husband's soul and starting to form a smile, which was frozen by Villefort's impassive stare. 'What is the matter?'

'Madame, where do you keep the poison that you habitually use?' the magistrate said, clearly and unambiguously, standing between his wife and the door.

Mme de Villefort felt what a lark must feel when it sees the tightening circle of the kite above its head. A harsh, broken sound, somewhere between a cry and a sigh, burst from her chest and she went as white as a sheet. 'Monsieur,' she said. 'I . . . I don't understand.'

She had leapt up in a paroxysm of terror and now, in a second paroxysm that seemed even stronger than the first, she collapsed back on to the cushions on the sofa.

'I asked you,' Villefort said in a perfectly calm voice, 'where you keep the poison with which you killed my father-in-law, Monsieur de Saint-Méran, my mother-in-law, Barrois and my daughter, Valentine.'

'Oh, Monsieur!' Mme de Villefort cried, clasping her hands. 'What are you saying?'

'It is not your place to question me, but to reply.'

'To the husband or the judge?' Mme de Villefort stammered.

'To the judge, Madame; to the judge!'

The woman's pallor, her anguished expression and the trembling that shook her whole body were dreadful to behold.

'Oh, Monsieur,' she muttered. 'Oh, Monsieur . . .' Nothing more.

'You do not answer me, Madame!' said her terrible questioner. Then he added, with a smile that was even more terrifying than his anger: 'It is true that you don't deny it!'

She shrank back.

'And you cannot deny it,' Villefort added, stretching his hand towards her as if to seize her in the name of justice. 'You carried out these different crimes with impudent skill, though it could only have deceived those whose affection for you predisposed them to blindness where you were concerned. After Madame de Saint-Méran's death, I knew that there was a poisoner in my house. Monsieur d'Avrigny had warned me of it. After the death of Barrois, God forgive me, my suspicions turned towards someone, towards an angel . . . those suspicions which, even when no crime has been committed, are always smouldering in the depth of my heart. But after Valentine's death, I could have no further doubt, Madame. And not only I, but others. So your crime, which is known now to two people and suspected by many, will be made public. As I said to you a moment ago, Madame, it is no longer your husband who is speaking to you, but your judge!'

The young woman hid her face in both hands. 'Oh, Monsieur,' she stammered, 'I beg you, don't be misled by appearances!'

'Can you be a coward?' Villefort cried, in a contemptuous voice. 'I have indeed always noticed that poisoners are cowards. But are you a coward, who had enough frightful courage to watch two old people and a girl die in front of you, when you had killed them?

'Can you be a coward?' he continued, in growing excitement. 'You, who have counted out one by one the minutes of four death agonies? You who have concocted your infernal plans and your criminal potions with such miraculous skill and precision? You who have so devised all that so well, could you have forgotten to calculate one thing: namely, where the revelation of your crimes might lead? No, that's impossible! You must have kept some sweeter, subtler and more lethal poison to escape from your just deserts . . . I hope at least you have done that?'

Mme de Villefort wrung her hands and fell to her knees.

'I know, I know,' he said, 'you confess. But a confession made in court, a last-minute confession, a confession when the facts can no longer be denied: such a confession does not in any way mitigate the punishment inflicted on the guilty party.'

'Punishment!' Mme de Villefort cried. 'Punishment! Monsieur, this is twice that you have spoken that word, I think?'

'Indeed so. Is it because you are four times guilty that you thought you would escape scot-free? Is it because you are the wife of him who demands punishment that you thought to evade it? Whoever she may be, the scaffold awaits the poisoner, especially, as I have just said, if she did not take care to reserve a few drops of her most lethal poison for herself.'

Mme de Villefort gave a wild cry, and hideous and uncontrollable terror swept over her ravaged features.

'Oh, do not fear the scaffold, Madame,' the magistrate said. 'I do not wish to dishonour you, because that would be to dishonour myself. No, on the contrary, if you have fully understood what I said, you will realize that you cannot die on the scaffold.'

'No, I have not understood. What do you mean?' the unhappy woman stammered, completely aghast.

'I mean that, by her infamy, the wife of the chief magistrate of Paris will not soil a name which has so far been without blemish, or dishonour her husband and her child.'

'No! Oh, no!'

'Very well, Madame. That will be a fine action on your part, and I thank you for it.'

'Thank me? What for?'

'For what you have just said.'

'What I have said! My head is reeling! I don't understand anything any more! Oh, my God! My God!' And she looked up, her hair dishevelled, her lips foaming.

'You have not replied, Madame, to the question which I put you on entering this room: where is the poison which you habitually use, Madame?'

Mme de Villefort raised her arms towards heaven and convulsively wrung her hands.

'No!' she cried. 'No! You cannot want that!'

'What I do not want, Madame, is for you to perish on the scaffold,' said Villefort. 'Do you understand that?'

'Oh, Monsieur, spare me!'

'What I do want is for justice to be done. I have been put on earth to punish, Madame,' he added, his eyes blazing. 'To any other woman, even a queen, I should send the executioner. But on you I shall have mercy. To you, I shall say: is it not true, Madame, that you have kept a few drops of your gentlest, quickest and most infallible poison?'

'Oh, forgive me, Monsieur! Let me live!'

'She was a coward!' said Villefort.

'Consider that I am your wife!'

'You are a poisoner.'

'In heaven's name . . . !'

'No!'

'In the name of the love you once had for me!'

'No! No!'

'In the name of our child! Oh, for our child's sake, let me live!'

'No, no, no, I tell you! One day, if I should let you live, you might kill him as you did the others.'

'I! Kill my son!' the mother cried, wildly hurling herself on Villefort. 'I, kill my Edouard! Oh, oh!' And the sentence ended in a terrible laugh, a demonic laugh, the laugh of a madwoman, and was drowned by a bloody croak. Mme de Villefort had fallen at her husband's feet.

Villefort went over to her. 'Consider this, Madame,' he said. 'If, on my return, justice has not been done, I shall denounce you with my own lips and arrest you with my own hands.'

She listened, panting, exhausted, crushed. Only her eye still lived, smouldering with an awful fire.

'Do you hear me?' Villefort asked. 'I am going there to demand the death penalty against a murderer . . . If I come back to find you still alive, you will sleep in the conciergerie this evening.'

Mme de Villefort gave a sigh, her nerves gave way and she fell, a broken woman, on the carpet.

The crown prosecutor seemed to feel a pang of pity. He looked at her less severely and, bending gently over her, said slowly: 'Adieu, Madame! Adieu!'

This last farewell fell like the fatal blade on Mme de Villefort. She fainted. The crown prosecutor left the room and, after doing so, double-locked the door.

CIX

THE ASSIZES

The Benedetto Affair, as it was called in the courts and in society, had created an enormous sensation. A frequenter of the Café de Paris, the Boulevard de Gand and the Bois de Boulogne, the pseudo-

Cavalcanti, while he had been in Paris and for the two or three months that his glory had lasted, had met a host of people. The newspapers had described the accused in his different incarnations, in society and in prison, so there was tremendous curiosity on the part of everyone who had personally been acquainted with Prince Andrea Cavalcanti. It was these above all who had decided to risk anything to get a glimpse of M. Benedetto, murderer of his fellow-convict, while he stood in the dock.

To many people, Benedetto was, if not a victim of the law, at least of a judicial error. M. Cavalcanti, the father, had been seen in Paris and they expected him to appear once more to claim his illustrious offspring. Several people, who had never heard speak of the famous Polishwoman with whom he arrived at the Count of Monte Cristo's, had been struck by the imposing air, perfect good manners and urbanity shown by the old nobleman who, it must be admitted, appeared a flawless aristocrat, provided he was not doing his sums or talking about them.

As for the accused man himself, many people remembered him as so pleasant, so handsome and so generous that they preferred to believe in some machination by an enemy of the kind that is found in that portion of society where great wealth increases the means to do ill or to do good to such a fabulous extent, and the power to do these things to an unheard-of degree.

So everyone was hastening to the assizes, some to enjoy the spectacle, others to comment on it. A queue started to form outside the gates at seven o'clock in the morning and, one hour before the session began, the courtroom was already full of those who had some leverage there.

Before the judge enters, and often even afterwards, a courtroom on the day of some great trial resembles a drawing-room in which a lot of people recognize one another, meet when they are close enough not to lose their seats or make gestures at each other when they are separated by too many spectators, lawyers or gendarmes.

It was one of those splendid autumn days that sometimes compensate for the lack of the preceding summer, or its brevity. The clouds that M. de Villefort had seen passing in front of the sun had dispersed as though by magic and allowed one of the last and sweetest September days to shine in all its purity.

Beauchamp was one of the kings of the press and consequently had his throne everywhere. Eyeing the crowd to right and left, he noticed Château-Renaud and Debray, who had just won the favour of a sergeant-at-arms, who had decided to stand behind them instead of blocking their view, as was his right. The good fellow had scented the presence of a secretary at the ministry and a millionaire, and was showing himself full of consideration for his fine neighbours, even allowing them to go and see Beauchamp, while promising to keep their places.

'Well, then,' Beauchamp said, 'have we come to see our friend?'

'Heavens, yes, we have!' Debray replied. 'A fine prince he was! Devil take these Italian princes!'

'A man who had Dante for his genealogist and could trace his line back to the *Divine Comedy*.'

'The nobility of the rope,' Château-Renaud said coolly.

'He will be condemned, I suppose?' Debray asked Beauchamp.

'My dear fellow,' the journalist replied, 'I should think you were the person one should ask about that. You know the political climate better than we do. Did you see the president at the last soirée in your ministry?'

'Yes.'

'What did he say?'

'Something that will surprise you.'

'Well, then, do tell me, quickly, my dear chap. It's so long since I heard anything that did that.'

'Well, he told me that Benedetto, who's considered a firebird of subtlety and a giant of cunning, is only a very subordinate, very naïve rogue, quite undeserving of the experiments which will be made on his phrenological organs once he is dead.'

'Pooh!' Beauchamp said. 'He played the prince well enough for all that.'

'For you, perhaps, Beauchamp: you hate those poor princes so much that you are delighted if they misbehave. But I can sniff out a true gentleman straight away and spring an aristocratic family, whatever it may be, like a heraldic bloodhound.'

'So, you never believed in his principality?'

'In his principality, yes; but in his princedom? No.'

'Not bad,' said Debray. 'But I assure you that he could get by with anyone else . . . I saw him with the ministers.'

'Oh, yes,' said Château-Renaud. 'For all that your ministers know about princes!'

'There are some good things in what you have just said,' Beauchamp answered, bursting into laughter. 'The phrase is short, but rather fine. I ask your permission to use it in my report.'

'Take it, my dear Monsieur Beauchamp,' said Château-Renaud. 'You can have my phrase, for what it's worth.'

'But if I spoke to the president,' Debray said to Beauchamp, 'you must have spoken to the crown prosecutor.'

'Impossible: Monsieur de Villefort has locked himself away for the past week; it's quite natural, after that odd series of domestic misfortunes, culminating in the strange death of his daughter.'

'The strange death! What do you mean, Beauchamp?'

'Oh, yes, pretend to know nothing, on the grounds that all this is taking place among the peerage,' Beauchamp said, putting his pince-nez to his eye and forcing it to stay up by itself.

'My dear sir,' said Château-Renaud, 'let me tell you that, as far as the pince-nez is concerned, you cannot hold a candle to Debray. Debray, do give Monsieur Beauchamp a lesson.'

'Look,' Beauchamp said. 'I'm sure I'm not mistaken.'

'What about?'

'It's her.'

'Her, who?'

'They said she had gone.'

'Mademoiselle Eugénie?' Château-Renaud asked. 'Is she back already?'

'No, not her; her mother.'

'Madame Danglars?'

'Come, come!' said Château-Renaud. 'It can't be. Ten days after her daughter has run off and three days after her husband's bankruptcy?'

Debray blushed slightly and followed Beauchamp's eyes. 'Come on,' he said. 'That's a veiled woman, a stranger, some foreign princess, perhaps Prince Cavalcanti's mother. But you were saying, or rather about to say, something really interesting, I think, Beauchamp.'

'I was?'

'Yes, you were talking about Valentine's strange death.'

'Yes, so I was. But why isn't Madame de Villefort here?'

'Poor woman!' said Debray. 'No doubt she is making balm for the hospitals and inventing cosmetics for herself and her friends. You know she spends two or three thousand *écus* at that game, so they assure me. And you're right: why isn't she here? I should have been very pleased to see her. I like her very much.'

'And I hate her,' said Château-Renaud.

'Why?'

'I don't know. Why does one love or hate? I hate her for reasons of antipathy.'

'Or instinctively, of course . . .'

'Perhaps. But let's get back to what you were saying, Beauchamp.'

'Well, are you not curious to know, gentlemen, why they are dying so repetitiously in the Villefort family?'

'I like that "repetitiously",' said Château-Renaud.

'You'll find the word in Saint-Simon.'[1]

'And the thing in Monsieur de Villefort's house; so tell us about it.'

'Good Lord!' Debray said. 'I must confess I have not taken my eyes off that house which has been dressed in mourning for three whole months, and only the day before yesterday, on the subject of Valentine, Madame was saying . . .'

'Madame is who precisely?' Château-Renaud asked.

'Why, the minister's wife, of course!'

'Oh, I beg your pardon,' said Château-Renaud. 'I do not frequent ministers. I leave that to princes.'

'You used merely to be handsome, but now you are starting to blaze with glory. Have pity on us, Baron, or you will burn us like a second Jupiter.'

'I shall not say another word,' said Château-Renaud. 'But for God's sake, have pity on me. Don't cap every remark I make.'

'Come, come, let's try to finish what we were saying, Beauchamp. Now I was telling you that Madame asked me about the matter the day before yesterday. You tell me, I'll tell her.'

'Well, gentlemen, if people are dying in the Villefort family so repetitiously – and I stick by the word – that means there is a murderer in the house!'

The two young men shuddered, because the same idea had struck them more than once.

'And who is the murderer?' they asked.

'Young Edouard.'

The speaker was not at all put out by a burst of laughter from his audience, but went on: 'Yes, gentlemen, young Edouard, an infant phenomenon, who is already killing as well as his parents ever did.'

'This is a joke?'

'Not in the slightest. Yesterday I took on a servant who has just left the Villeforts'. And listen to this . . .'

'We're listening.'

'I shall sack him tomorrow, because he eats a vast quantity to make up for the terrified abstinence that he imposed on himself while he was there. Well, it appears that the dear child got his hands on some flask of a drug which he uses from time to time against those who displease him. Firstly, it was grandpa and grandma Saint-Méran who annoyed him and he poured them three drops of his elixir. Three were enough. Then it was good old Barrois, grandpa Noirtier's old servant, who would occasionally scold the dear little imp, so the little imp gave him three drops of the elixir. The same was the fate of poor Valentine, not because she scolded him – she didn't – but because he was jealous of her. He gave her three drops of his elixir and her day was done, as it was for the rest.'

'What fairy story is this you are telling us?' Château-Renaud asked.

'Yes,' Beauchamp said. 'A tale of the Beyond.'

'It's absurd,' said Debray.

'There!' Beauchamp said. 'You see? You're already playing for time. Dammit! Ask my servant; or, rather, the man who won't be my servant tomorrow. Everyone in the family talked about it.'

'But where is this elixir? What is it?'

'Of course, the child hides it.'

'Where did he get it?'

'In his mother's laboratory.'

'Does his mother have poisons in her laboratory?'

'How do I know! You're interrogating me like the crown prosecutor. All I can say is what I've been told, and I'm giving you my source: I can't do better than that. The poor devil was too terrified to eat.'

'Incredible!'

'No, my good chap, not incredible at all. You saw that child in the Rue Richelieu last year who entertained himself by killing his brothers and sisters by sticking a pin in their ears while they were asleep. The generation after our own is very precocious, old boy.'

'I am prepared to bet that you don't believe a word of it,'

Château-Renaud said. 'But I don't see the Count of Monte Cristo. How can he not be here?'

'He's blasé,' Debray said. 'He wouldn't want to appear here in front of everyone, after he'd been taken in by all these Cavalcantis who came to him, apparently, with false letters of credit, with the result that he has a mortgage of a hundred thousand francs on the principality.'

'By the way, Monsieur de Château-Renaud,' Beauchamp asked, 'how is Morrel?'

'Do you know,' he answered, 'I've been round to his house three times, and found neither hide nor hair of Morrel. But his sister didn't seem too worried about it and told me, quite calmly, that she had not seen him for two or three days either, but that she was sure he was well.'

'I've just thought: Monte Cristo can't be here,' said Beauchamp.

'Why not?'

'Because he's part of the case.'

'Has he killed someone?' Debray asked.

'No. On the contrary, he's the one somebody tried to kill. You know that it was while he was coming out of Monte Cristo's that that fine fellow Caderousse was murdered by young Benedetto. Moreover it was in the count's house that they found the famous waistcoat in which there was the letter that interrupted the signing of the marriage contract. Can you see the famous waistcoat? There it is, all bloody, on the desk, as evidence.'

'Oh, wonderful!'

'Hush! Gentlemen, the court is in session. Take your places.'

There was some commotion in the court. The sergeant-at-arms called his two protégés with a loud *hem*! And the usher, appearing on the threshold of the counsel chamber, cried out – in that yelping voice that ushers had already acquired in Beaumarchais' time: 'Gentlemen! All rise!'

CX

THE INDICTMENT

The judges took their seats in the midst of utter silence. The jury filed into their places. M. de Villefort, in his ceremonial headgear, the object of general attention and, one might almost say, admiration, sat down in his chair, looking around him imperturbably.

Everyone was astonished to see this grave and severe face, which seemed immune in its impassivity to a father's grief, and there was a sort of awe as they considered this man who was a stranger to human emotions.

'Gendarmes!' said the presiding judge. 'Bring up the accused.'

At this, the public became more alert and all eyes turned towards the door through which Benedetto would enter. Soon the door opened and the accused appeared. The impression was the same on everyone, and no one mistook the look on his face.

His features bore no sign of that deep emotion that drives the blood back to the heart and discolours the forehead and cheeks. His hands, elegantly posed, one on his hat, the other in the opening of his white quilted waistcoat, did not shake; his eyes were calm and even bright. Hardly was he in the chamber than the young man began to examine the ranks of the judges and the rest of the crowd in court, pausing longer on the presiding judge and longer still on the crown prosecutor.

Beside Andrea was his lawyer, who had been appointed by the court, since Andrea had not bothered to concern himself with such details, apparently attaching no importance to them. This lawyer was a young man with lustreless blond hair, his face reddened with an inner turmoil that was a hundred times more evident than the defendant's.

The presiding judge asked for the indictment to be read; as we know, it had been composed by M. de Villefort's adroit and implacable pen.

The reading lasted a long time. The effect on anyone else would have been devastating, and, throughout, every eye was on Andrea, who bore the weight of the charges against him with the merry indifference of a Spartan warrior.

Never, perhaps, had Villefort been more pithy or more eloquent. The crime was described in the liveliest colours, while the accused man's antecedents, his transformation and his progress, step by step, since quite an early age were deduced with all the talent that experience of life and a knowledge of the human heart could supply in a mind as elevated as that of the crown prosecutor.

This indictment itself was enough to damn Benedetto for ever in public opinion, leaving nothing for the law except to punish him in a more tangible way.

Andrea did not pay the slightest attention to the succession of charges raised, then laid on his head. M. de Villefort, who frequently studied his reaction, no doubt continuing the psychological analyses that he had so often had the opportunity to make of men in the dock, could not once persuade him to lower his eyes, however fixedly and penetratingly he stared at him.

Finally the reading was concluded. 'Defendant,' the presiding judge said, 'what is your name?'

Andrea rose to his feet. 'Forgive me, Monsieur le Président,' he said, in the purest and clearest of tones, 'but I see that you are going to pursue an order of questioning which I shall not be able to follow. I claim that it is up to me, later, to justify being considered an exception to the general run of accused persons; so I beg you to let me reply to your questions in a different order, though I shall in fact answer all of them.'

The presiding judge looked in astonishment at the jury, who looked at the crown prosecutor. A wave of surprise ran through the whole assembly; but Andrea did not seem in the slightest bit concerned.

'How old are you?' the presiding judge asked. 'Will you answer that question?'

'Like the rest, I shall, Monsieur, but in its turn.'

'How old are you?' the judge repeated.

'Twenty-one; or, rather, I shall be in just a few days, since I was born on the night of September the twenty-seventh and twenty-eighth, 1817.'

M. de Villefort, who was taking notes, looked up on hearing the date.

'Where were you born?' the presiding judge continued.

'In Auteuil, near Paris,' Benedetto answered.

M. de Villefort looked up again and gave Benedetto the sort of look he might have given the head of Medusa. The colour drained from his face.

As for Benedetto, he passed the embroidered corner of a fine lawn handkerchief across his lips with an elegant gesture.

'What is your profession?' the judge asked.

'Firstly, I was a counterfeiter,' Andrea said, as cool as a cucumber. 'Then I took up the profession of thief and quite recently I have become a murderer.'

A murmur, in fact a storm of indignation and astonishment, erupted from every corner of the room. Even the judges exchanged looks of amazement, while the jury exhibited the most profound disgust for such cynicism, which was not what it expected from a well-turned-out man.

M. de Villefort put a hand to his forehead which, having been pale, was now red and feverish. He leapt abruptly to his feet and looked around him like a man who had lost his way. He was gasping for breath.

'Are you looking for something, prosecutor?' Benedetto asked, with his most obliging smile.

M. de Villefort said nothing but sat down – or, rather, fell back into his chair.

'Prisoner, will you now agree to tell us your name?' asked the presiding judge. 'The brutal manner in which you have enumerated your various crimes which you describe as professions, making it as it were a point of honour, something for which, in the name of morality and respect for humankind, the court must severely reprimand you, all these may well be the reason why you have so far declined to give us your name. You wish to enhance the name by first giving your titles.'

'It's extraordinary, Monsieur le Président,' Benedetto said, in the most condescending tone of voice and with the politest of manners, 'how clearly you have read my mind. That was indeed precisely why I asked you to change round the order of questions.'

The amazement was at its height. The accused's words showed no trace of boasting or cynicism, and a stunned audience sensed that there was some burst of lightning gathering in the depths of this dark cloud.

'Very well,' said the judge. 'What is your name?'

'I cannot tell you my name, because I do not know it; but I know the name of my father and I can tell you that.'

Villefort was blinded by a flash of pain. Bitter drops of sweat could be seen falling rapidly from his cheeks on to the papers which he was shuffling with distraught and convulsive hands.

'Then tell us the name of your father,' the judge said.

Not a breath or a sigh broke the silence: the whole of this vast assembly was hushed and waiting.

'My father is a crown prosecutor,' Andrea replied calmly.

'A crown prosecutor!' the judge said in astonishment, without noticing the shocked expression on Villefort's face. 'A crown prosecutor!'

'Yes, and since you ask me his name, I shall tell you. His name is de Villefort.'

The outburst that had for so long been contained by the respect that is paid to the law while a court is in session erupted, like a peal of thunder, from every breast. The court itself did not even consider trying to repress this movement in the crowd. There were interjections, insults shouted at Benedetto (who remained impassive), violent gestures, commotion among the gendarmes and the sniggering of that baser element which in any crowd rises to the surface in times of disturbance or scandal. All this lasted five minutes, before the judges and ushers could manage to restore calm.

In the middle of all this noise, the presiding judge's voice could be heard shouting: 'Prisoner! Are you making fun of the law? Do you dare to give your fellow citizens the spectacle of a degree of corruption which is hitherto unequalled even in an age which has had more than its fair share of the same?'

Ten people flocked round the crown prosecutor, who was sitting, completely overwhelmed, and offered him consolation, encouragement and assurances of their entire sympathy.

Order was finally restored, except at one place in the room where a fairly large group continued to call out and agitate. It appeared that a woman had fainted. She was offered smelling salts and came back to her senses.

Throughout all this commotion, Andrea had turned a smiling face on the crowd. Then, at last resting one hand on the oak handle of his bench, in the most elegant posture, he said: 'Gentlemen, God forbid that I should try to insult the court or, before such an august company, try to cause any unnecessary scandal. I was asked what age I am, and I answered; I was asked where I was born, and I replied; I was asked my name, and I cannot say it, because my parents abandoned me. But, even without saying my name, since I have none, I can say that of my father; so, I repeat, my father is called Monsieur de Villefort and I am ready to prove it.'

The young man's voice carried a certainty, a conviction and a power that reduced everyone to silence. For a moment every eye turned towards the crown prosecutor who remained as motionless in his seat as a man who had just been struck dead by lightning.

'Gentlemen,' Andrea said, with a tone and a gesture that demanded silence, 'I owe you proof of my words and an explanation for them.'

'But,' snapped the presiding judge, 'you declared in the preliminary hearings that you were called Benedetto and that you were an orphan, describing Corsica as your homeland.'

'I said at that hearing what was convenient for me to say then, because I did not want anyone to weaken or even prevent the solemn repercussions of my words – and this would surely have been done.

'I now repeat that I was born in Auteuil, in the night of September the twenty-seventh to the twenty-eighth, 1817, and that I am the son of Crown Prosecutor de Villefort. Now, do you want some details? Here they are.

'I was born on the first floor of Number twenty-eight, Rue de la Fontaine, in a room hung with red damask. My father took me in his arms, telling my mother that I was dead, wrapped me in a towel marked with an "H" and an "N", and carried me down to the garden, where he buried me alive.'

A shudder went through the whole room when they saw that the prisoner's confidence was growing, to keep pace with M. de Villefort's horror.

'But how do you know all these details?' the judge asked.

'I shall tell you, Monsieur le Président. That very same night, in the garden where my father had just buried me, a man who was his mortal enemy had entered, having long waited and watched in order to carry out an act of Corsican vengeance against him. The man had hidden himself in a clump of bushes. He saw my father bury something in the ground and struck him with a knife while he was still engaged in the operation. Then, thinking that the object must be some treasure, he dug up the hole and found me, still alive. The man took me to the orphanage, where I was admitted under the number fifty-seven. Three months later, his sister travelled from

Rogliano to Paris to fetch me, claimed me as her son and took me away. This is how, even though I was born in Auteuil, I was brought up in Corsica.'

There was a moment's silence, but a silence so profound that, had it not been for the tension that seemed to be exhaled from a thousand breasts, you would have thought the room empty.

'Continue,' said the presiding judge.

'No doubt,' Benedetto went on, 'I could have been happy with these good people who adored me; but my perverse nature gained the upper hand over all the virtues that my adoptive mother tried to instil in my heart. I grew up badly and turned to crime. One day, when I was cursing God for making me so wicked and giving me such a dreadful fate, my adoptive father said: "Don't blaspheme, you wretch! God was generous in giving you life. The evil comes not from you but from your father – the father who doomed you to hell should you die, and to misery if some miracle should give you life!"

'From then on, I ceased to blaspheme God, but I cursed my father. That is why I have come here and spoken the words for which you have reproached me, Monsieur le Président. That is why I caused the commotion from which this gathering has still not recovered. If that is a further crime, punish me for it. But if I have convinced you that from the day of my birth my fate has been mortal, tormented, bitter and lamentable, then pity me!'

'And what about your mother?' the judge asked.

'My mother thought me dead; my mother is not guilty. I have never wanted to know my mother's name, and I do not know it.'

At that moment, a shrill cry, ending in a sob, rang out from the midst of the group which, as we have said, included a woman. She fell to the ground in a violent fit of hysteria and was taken out of the room. As she was being helped out, the thick veil hiding her face slipped aside and they recognized Mme Danglars. Though nearly paralysed by nervous exhaustion, and despite the humming in his ears and the sort of madness that had seized his brain, Villefort too recognized her and rose to his feet.

'Proof!' cried the presiding judge. 'Proof! Prisoner, do you realize that this tissue of horrors must be supported by the most incontrovertible proof?'

'Proof?' Benedetto said, with a laugh. 'Do you want proof?'

'We do.'

'Then look at Monsieur de Villefort, and ask me for further proof.'

Everyone turned towards the crown prosecutor who, beneath the weight of a thousand eyes turned towards him, stepped forward into the well of the court, staggering, his hair awry and his face blotchy from the pressure of his fingernails.

The whole room heaved a long murmur of astonishment.

'Father, they are asking me for proof,' said Benedetto. 'Do you wish me to provide it?'

'No,' M. de Villefort stammered, in a strangled voice. 'No, there is no need.'

'What do you mean, no need?' cried the judge.

'I mean,' said the crown prosecutor, 'that I should struggle in vain against the deadly fate that holds me in its grasp. Gentlemen, I realize that I am in the hands of a vengeful God. No proof, there is no need. Everything this young man has just said is true!'

A dark and heavy silence, such as precedes some natural catastrophe, wrapped its leaden cloak around all those who heard these words, and the hair stood up on their heads.

'What! Monsieur de Villefort,' the judge cried, 'are you sure you are not dreaming? Are you really in full command of your faculties? One might believe that such a strange accusation, so dreadful and so unexpected, must have troubled your mind. Come, now, pull yourself together.'

The crown prosecutor shook his head. His teeth were chattering violently like those of a man eaten up with fever; and yet he was deathly pale.

'I am in full command of my faculties, Monsieur,' he said. 'Only my body is unwell, as you may well understand. I admit my guilt for everything that the young man has accused me of, and I shall henceforth remain at home at the disposal of the crown prosecutor, my successor.'

After saying which, in a dull and almost inaudible voice, M. de Villefort staggered towards the door, which the duty usher automatically opened for him.

The whole company was left speechless and appalled by this revelation and this confession, making such a dreadful conclusion to all the various incidents that had shaken Parisian society over the preceding fortnight.

'Well!' Beauchamp said. 'Let anyone now deny that drama is only in art and not in nature!'

'Good Lord,' said Château-Renaud. 'I'd really much rather end like Monsieur de Morcerf: a pistol-shot is a kindness beside such a disaster.'

'And it does kill you,' said Beauchamp.

'Just think! I briefly considered marrying his daughter,' said Debray. 'Poor child: my God, she did well to die!'

'The session is ended, gentlemen,' said the presiding judge. 'The case will be adjourned to the next assizes. The matter must be investigated afresh and entrusted to another counsel.'

As for Andrea – calm as ever and much more interesting – he left the room, escorted by the gendarmes, who involuntarily showed him some sign of respect.

'So, what do you think of that, my good man?' Debray asked the sergeant-at-arms, slipping a *louis* into his hand.

'They'll find extenuating circumstances,' he answered.

CXI

EXPIATION

The crowd, closely packed though it was, opened to let M. de Villefort pass. Great sorrow is so august that, even in the most unfortunate times, there is no case recorded when the first reaction of the mass has not been to sympathize with a great catastrophe. Many hated people have been killed by the mob, but rarely has anyone unfortunate, even a criminal, been attacked by the men who were present when he was condemned to death.

Thus Villefort was able to pass through the ranks of spectators, guards and officials of the courts, and to walk away, having admitted his guilt but protected by his grief.

There are some situations which men instinctively comprehend but are unable to comment on intellectually. In such cases, the greatest poet is the one who emits the most powerful and the most natural cry. The crowd takes this cry for a complete story, and it is right to be satisfied with that, and still more so to find it sublime when it is truthful.

In any case, it would have been impossible to express the state of stupefaction in which Villefort found himself on leaving the courts, or to describe the fever that made every artery throb, tensed every fibre, swelled every vein to bursting and dissected every point of his mortal body in millions of agonies.

He dragged himself along the corridors, guided solely by habit. He threw the magistrate's gown off his shoulders, not because he felt it was proper for him to quit it, but because it had become an overwhelming burden, a shirt of Nessus,[1] full of torments.

Staggering, he reached the Cour Dauphine, saw his carriage, woke the coachman by opening the door himself and slumped back against the cushions, while pointing towards the Faubourg Saint-Honoré. The coachman set off.

The full weight of his devastated fortune had come down upon his head and this weight was crushing him. He did not know what the outcome would be, he had not measured it; he felt it, but did not assess the legal consequences like a cold murderer commenting on the letter of the law.

God was in the depth of his heart.

'God!' he murmured, without even knowing what he was saying. 'God, God!'

He could only see the hand of God behind the maelstrom that had overwhelmed him.

The carriage sped along. Writhing on his cushions, Villefort felt something underneath them.

He reached for it: it was a fan that Mme de Villefort had lost between the cushion and the back wall of the carriage. The fan woke some memory, and the memory was like a flash of lightning in the dark.

Villefort thought of his wife.

'Oh!' he cried, as if a hot iron had traversed his heart.

For the past hour he had had only one side of his misfortune before his eyes; now, suddenly, his mind saw another, and one no less terrible than the first.

He had just assumed the role of implacable judge with this woman, condemning her to death; and she, stricken with terror, crushed with remorse and sunk beneath the shame that he had aroused in her with the eloquence born of his own spotless virtue, she, a poor, feeble woman, defenceless against this absolute and supreme authority, might perhaps at this very moment be preparing to die.

An hour already had elapsed since her condemnation: no doubt she was going over all her crimes in her memory, asking for God's mercy and writing a letter to humbly beg forgiveness of her virtuous husband, a favour that she would purchase at the cost of her life . . . Villefort gave another roar of pain and fury.

'Oh!' he cried, writhing on the satin upholstery of his carriage. 'This woman only became a criminal because she touched me. I am oozing with crime. She caught it off me as one may catch typhus, or cholera, or the plague! And I am punishing her! I dared to tell her: "Repent and die . . ." I! No, no, she shall live! She will follow me. We will flee, leave France, wander as far as the earth will carry us. I spoke to her of the scaffold! Good Lord! How did I dare utter the word! The scaffold waits also for me. We shall flee . . . I shall confess all to her. Yes, every day I shall tell her, prostrating myself, that I too have committed a crime. What a marriage of the tiger and the snake – worthy wife of a husband such as I! She must live! My infamy must make hers pale into insignificance!'

And Villefort slammed down the window in the front of the carriage, rather than opening it, crying: 'Faster! Faster!' in a voice that made the coachman leap up on his seat. The horses, carried forward by fear, flew to the house.

'Yes, yes,' Villefort repeated as he drew closer to home. 'The woman must live; she must repent and bring up my son, my poor child, the only one apart from the indestructible old man, who has survived the destruction of the family. She loved him: everything she did was for him. One must never despair of the heart of a mother who loves her child; she will repent. No one will know that she was guilty: the crimes that were committed in my house, which now trouble people's thoughts, will be forgotten in time; or, if some enemies of mine do remember them, they will add them to the list of my crimes. One, two, three more: what does it matter! My wife will escape, taking some money with her or, and above all, taking my son, far from the abyss into which I feel everyone must tumble with me. She will live, she will be happy again, since all her love is invested in her son and her son will never leave her. I shall have done a good deed; my heart grows lighter at the thought.' The crown prosecutor breathed more freely than he had for a long time.

The carriage drew up in the courtyard of the house. Villefort leapt from the running board on to the steps. He saw that the servants were surprised at his early return. He read nothing else on their faces; no one said anything to him. They stopped in his path, as usual, to let him pass; nothing more.

He passed Noirtier's room and, through the half-open door, he saw as it were two shadows; but he did not concern himself about the other person who was with his father: all his thoughts were drawing him somewhere else.

'Come,' he said, climbing the little stairway leading to his wife's apartments and Valentine's empty room. 'Come, nothing here has changed.'

He took particular care to close the landing door.

'No one must bother us here,' he said. 'I must be able to speak freely to her, to accuse myself before her, to tell her everything . . .'

He approached the door and reached out for the glass handle. The door opened.

'Not locked! Oh, good, very good,' he muttered, entering the little drawing-room where in the evenings they would put up Edouard's bed. Though he was at a boarding school, the child returned home every evening: his mother did not want to be separated from him.

In a single glance, he took in the little drawing-room.

'No one,' he said. 'She must be in her bedroom.'

He rushed to the door, but this one was locked. He stopped, trembling.

'Héloïse!' he shouted, and thought he heard a piece of furniture move.

'Héloïse!' he said, a second time.

'Who is there?' said the voice of the woman he was calling. It seemed to him that this voice was weaker than usual.

'Open up! Open up!' Villefort cried. 'It is I.'

Despite the anguished tone in which this order was given, the door did not open. Villefort broke the lock with a kick.

Mme de Villefort was standing in the doorway to her boudoir, pale, drawn, looking at him with a terrifying stare.

'Héloïse, Héloïse!' he said. 'What is it? Speak to me!'

She held out a rigid, ghastly white hand towards him. 'It is done, Monsieur,' she said, with a croaking sound that seemed to tear her throat. 'What more do you want?' And she fell full length on the carpet.

Villefort ran to her and grasped her hand. The hand was convulsively clasping a crystal flask with a gold stopper.

Mme de Villefort was dead.

Senseless with horror, Villefort shrank back to the door of the room and looked at the body. Then suddenly he cried: 'My son! Where is my son? Edouard, Edouard!' And he rushed from the room, shouting the boy's name in such anguished tones that the servants came running.

'My son! Where is my son?' Villefort asked. 'Someone must take him away . . . Don't let him see . . .'

'But Monsieur Edouard is not downstairs, Monsieur,' the valet replied.

'He must be playing in the garden. Go and find him!'

'No, Monsieur. Madame called her son about half an hour ago. Monsieur Edouard went into Madame's room and has not come down since then.'

An icy sweat poured across Villefort's brow, his feet stumbled on the floor and his thoughts began to whirl in his head like the disordered works of a broken watch. 'To Madame's room!' he muttered. 'To Madame's . . .' And he slowly retraced his steps, wiping his forehead with one hand and supporting himself with the other against the wall.

Going back into the room meant once more seeing the unhappy woman's body. Calling Edouard meant reawakening the echo of this room which had become a coffin: to speak was to violate the silence of a tomb. Villefort's tongue seemed to be paralysed in his throat.

'Edouard,' he stammered. 'Edouard . . .'

The child did not reply. So where was he if, as the servants said, he had gone into his mother's room and not come out?

Villefort stepped forward.

Mme de Villefort's body was lying across the doorway to the boudoir in which Edouard must be: the body seemed to be keeping watch on the threshold with staring, open eyes and with a frightful and mysterious look of irony on the mouth.

Behind the body, the curtain was lifted to reveal part of the boudoir, a piano and the end of a blue satin sofa.

Villefort took three or four steps forward and saw his child lying on the divan. No doubt the boy was sleeping.

The unfortunate man had a sudden feeling of unspeakable joy. A ray of pure light had shone into the hell in which he was writhing. It was merely a matter of stepping over the body into the boudoir, taking the child in his arms and fleeing with him a long, long way away.

Villefort was no longer the man whose exquisite corruption made a model of civilized man. He was a mortally wounded tiger leaving its broken teeth in its last wound. He was no longer afraid of prejudice, but of ghosts. He took a running jump over the body, as if he had been leaping across a blazing fire.

He picked the child up in his arms, holding him close, shaking him, calling to him; the child did not reply. He pressed his eager lips to his cheeks, but the cheeks were livid and ice-cold. He massaged his stiffened limbs, he put his hand to his heart, but the heart was no longer beating.

The child was dead.

A sheet of folded paper fluttered from Edouard's breast. Devastated, Villefort dropped on his knees. The child fell from his lifeless arms and rolled over towards his mother. Villefort picked up the paper, recognized his wife's handwriting and perused it eagerly. This is what he read:

'You know that I was a good mother, since it was for the sake of my child that I became a criminal. A good mother does not go away without taking her son with her!' Villefort could not believe his eyes; Villefort could not believe his own reason. He dragged himself towards Edouard's body and examined it with the minute attention that a lioness gives to the study of a dead cub. Then he gave a heart-rending cry.

'God!' he cried. 'As ever, God!'

The two victims appalled him. Within himself he could feel rising the horror of a solitude peopled by two corpses.

A moment before, he had been sustained by fury, that huge resource for a strong man; and by despair, the supreme virtue of grief, which drove the Titans to climb the heavens and Ajax to brandish his fist at the gods.[2]

Villefort bent his head under the weight of sorrows, rose up on his knees, shook his hair, which was damp with sweat and standing on end with horror, and this man, who had never had pity on anyone, went to seek out the old man, his father, just so that in his weakness he might have someone to whom to tell his misfortune and someone with whom to weep.

He went down the staircase that we already know and came into Noirtier's.

When Villefort entered, Noirtier seemed to be listening, attentively and as affectionately as his paralysis allowed, to Abbé Busoni, who was as calm and emotionless as ever.

Seeing the abbé, Villefort put his hand to his forehead. The past returned to him like one of those waves which in its rage raises more foam than any of its fellows. He recalled the visit that he had paid to the abbé the day after the dinner in Auteuil and the visit that the abbé had paid him on the day of Valentine's death.

'Are you here, Monsieur!' he said. 'And do you never appear except in the company of Death?'

Busoni rose to his feet. Seeing the look on the lawyer's face and the fierce light burning in his eyes, he realized, or thought he realized, that the events at the assizes had taken place. He knew nothing of the rest.

'I came to pray over the body of your daughter,' Busoni replied.

'And today? Why are you here today?'

'I have come to tell you that you have paid your debt to me and that from now on I shall pray God that He will be satisfied, as I am.'

'My God!' Villefort cried, shrinking back with a horrified look on his face. 'That voice! It is not Abbé Busoni's!'

'No.'

The abbé tore off his tonsured wig and shook his head, so that his long black hair fell freely across his shoulders, framing his masculine features.

'That is the face of Monte Cristo!' Villefort exclaimed, looking aghast.

'Not quite, Monsieur. Look harder, and further back.'

'That voice! That voice! Where did I hear it for the first time?'

'You heard it first in Marseille, twenty-three years ago, on the day of your wedding to Mademoiselle de Saint-Méran. Look in your files.'

'You are not Busoni? You are not Monte Cristo? My God, you are that hidden enemy, deadly and implacable! I did something to harm you, something in Marseille! Oh, woe is me!'

'Yes, you are right, you are absolutely right,' the count said, crossing his arms over his broad chest. 'Think! Think!'

'But what did I do to you?' Villefort cried, his mind already hovering on the borderline between reason and madness, in that mist which is no longer a dream but not yet wakefulness. 'What did I do to you? Tell me! Speak!'

'You condemned me to a slow and frightful death, you killed my father and you deprived me of love at the same time as you deprived me of freedom, and of fortune as well as love!'

'Who are you? Then who are you? My God!'

'I am the spectre of an unfortunate man whom you locked up in the dungeons of the Château d'If. When this spectre finally emerged from its tomb, God put on it the mask of the Count of Monte Cristo and showered it with diamonds and gold so that you should not recognize it until today.'

'Ah! I recognize you, I do recognize you!' the crown prosecutor said. 'You are . . .'

'I am Edmond Dantès!'

'You are Edmond Dantès!' cried the crown prosecutor, grasping the count by the wrist. 'Then, come with me!'

He dragged him down the staircase, and Monte Cristo followed him, amazed, not himself knowing where he was being taken, but with a premonition of some further catastrophe.

'There, Edmond Dantès!' he said, showing the count the bodies of his wife and child. 'There! Look! Are you fully avenged?'

Monte Cristo paled at this terrible spectacle. He realized that he had exceeded the limits of vengeance, he realized that he could no longer say: 'God is for me and with me.'

With an inexpressible feeling of anguish, he threw himself on the child's body, opened the eyes, felt the pulse and dashed with it into Valentine's room, double-locking the door behind him . . .

'My child!' Villefort cried. 'He is stealing my child's body! Accursed man! Woe betide you!'

He tried to rush after Monte Cristo but, as if in a dream, felt his feet rooted to the ground, his eyes bursting out of their sockets and his fingers gradually burying themselves in his chest until blood reddened his nails. The veins of his temples swelled with boiling ferments that tried to burst the narrow vault of his skull and drown his brain in a deluge of fire. This paralysis lasted for several minutes, until the frightful commotion in his mind was stilled.

Then he gave a great cry, followed by a long burst of laughter, and dashed down the stairs.

A quarter of an hour later, the door to Valentine's room opened and Monte Cristo reappeared, pale, leaden-eyed and heavy in heart.

All the features of his face, which was usually so calm and noble, were distorted with pain. In his arms he held the child whom no measure had succeeded in restoring to life. Monte Cristo knelt on one knee and reverently set him down beside his mother, his head resting on her breast.

After that, he got up and went out. Coming across a servant, he said: 'Where is Monsieur de Villefort?'

The servant did not answer but merely pointed towards the garden.

Monte Cristo went down the steps and proceeded towards the place where the man had pointed. There, with his servants making a circle around him, he saw Villefort, a spade in his hand, digging the ground in a kind of fury. 'It's not here,' he was saying. 'And it's not here, either.' After which he would dig a little further on.

Monte Cristo went over to him and said quietly, in what was almost a humble voice: 'Monsieur, you have lost a son, but . . .'

Villefort interrupted. He had neither listened nor heard. 'Oh, I'll find him,' he said. 'Even though you say he's not here, I'll find him, even if I have to look until Judgement Day.'

Monte Cristo shrank back in horror, exclaiming: 'He is mad!' And, as if fearing that the walls of the accursed house might fall in on him, he rushed out into the street, wondering for the first time whether he had had the right to do what he had done.

'Enough!' he said. 'Let that be enough, and we will save the last one.'

On arriving home, Monte Cristo met Morrel, who was wandering around the house in the Champs-Elysées, silent as a ghost waiting for the moment appointed by God for it to return to the tomb.

'Get ready, Maximilien,' the count said, smiling. 'We're leaving Paris tomorrow.'

'Have you nothing more to do here?' Morrel asked.

'No,' Monte Cristo replied. 'Pray God that I have not already done too much.'

CXII
DEPARTURE

All Paris was engrossed in what had just taken place. Emmanuel and his wife discussed it, with quite understandable surprise, in their little house on the Rue Meslay; and they drew comparisons between the three disasters, all as sudden as they were unexpected, that had struck Morcerf, Danglars and Villefort.

Maximilien, who had come to visit, listened to their conversation; or, at least, he was present while they talked, plunged into his usual state of insensibility.

'Really, Emmanuel,' said Julie, 'wouldn't you think that all these rich people, so happy only a short while ago, had built their fortunes, their happiness and their social position, while forgetting to allow for the wicked genie; and that this genie, like the wicked fairy in Perrault's stories[1] who is not invited to some wedding or christening, had suddenly appeared to take revenge for that fatal omission?'

'So many disasters!' Emmanuel said, thinking of Morcerf and Danglars.

'So much suffering!' said Julie, remembering Valentine, though her woman's instinct told her not to mention the name in front of her brother.

'If God did strike them,' Emmanuel said, 'that's because God, who is goodness itself, could find nothing in the past life of these people which would justify a mitigation of sentence: it means that they were indeed damned.'

'Isn't that a rather rash judgement?' said Julie. 'When my father had a pistol in his hand and was ready to blow out his brains, if someone had said, as you are now doing, "That man deserves his punishment", wouldn't that person have been wrong?'

'Yes, but God did not allow our father to succumb, just as he did not allow Abraham to sacrifice his son. He sent the Patriarch – and us – his angel, who cut the wings of Death in mid-flight.'

He had just said this when the bell rang. This was the signal from the concierge that a visitor had arrived. Almost at the same instant the drawing-room door opened and the Count of Monte Cristo appeared on the threshold. The two young people gave a double cry of joy.

Maximilien looked up, then let his head fall back.

'Maximilien,' the count said, apparently unaware of the different reactions of his hosts to his arrival, 'I have come to look for you.'

'For me?' said Morrel, as if waking from a dream.

'Yes,' said Monte Cristo. 'Didn't we agree that I should take you, and did I not ask you to be ready to leave?'

'Here I am,' said Maximilien. 'I had come to say goodbye to them.'

'Where are you going, Count?' Julie asked.

'First of all, to Marseille, Madame.'

'To Marseille?' both the young people said together.

'Yes, and I'm taking your brother.'

'Alas, Count, bring him back to us, cured!'

Morrel turned his blushing face away from them.

'Did you notice that he was unwell?' asked the count.

'Yes,' the young woman replied. 'I am afraid that he is not happy with us.'

'I shall distract him,' said the count.

'I am ready, Monsieur,' said Maximilien. 'Farewell, my good friends! Adieu, Emmanuel! Julie, adieu!'

'What: adieu?' Julie exclaimed. 'Are you leaving like that, at once, with no preparations and no passports?'

'Delays double the pain of parting,' said Monte Cristo. 'And Maximilien, I am sure, must have prepared everything in advance. I advised him to do so.'

'I have my passport, and my trunks are packed,' Morrel said, in a dull monotone.

'Excellent,' said Monte Cristo with a smile. 'That is the punctiliousness of a good soldier.'

'So you are leaving us like that?' said Julie. 'Immediately? Won't you give us another day, or an hour?'

'My carriage is at the door, Madame. I must be in Rome in five days.'

'Surely Maximilien isn't going to Rome?' said Emmanuel.

'I shall go wherever it pleases the count to take me,' Morrel said, with a sad smile. 'I belong to him for another month.'

'Oh, my God! He says that in such a voice, Count!'

'Maximilien is accompanying me,' the count said in his reassuringly pleasant manner. 'Don't worry about your brother.'

'Farewell, sister,' Morrel repeated. 'Farewell, Emmanuel.'

'He worries me so much with his nonchalance,' said Julie. 'Oh, Maximilien, Maximilien, you are hiding something from us.'

'Pooh!' said Monte Cristo. 'When you see him again, he will be happy, smiling and joyful.'

Maximilien gave the count a look that was almost contemptuous, and almost irritated.

'Let's go,' said the count.

'Before you do, Count,' said Julie, 'will you let me tell you that the other day . . .'

'Madame,' the count said, taking both her hands, 'anything that you might have to say to me will never be worth what I can read in your eyes, what your heart has thought and mine felt. Like a benefactor in a novel, I should have left without seeing you again; but such conduct was beyond my feeble powers, because I am a weak and vain man, and because a joyful and tender look from one of my fellow-creatures does me good. Now I am leaving, and I shall take selfishness to the point of saying to you: Don't forget me, my friends, because you will probably never see me again.'

'Not see you again!' Emmanuel cried, while two large tears rolled down Julie's cheeks. 'Not see you again! This is not a man, but a god who is leaving us, and this god will return to heaven after appearing on earth to do good.'

'Don't say that,' Monte Cristo said urgently. 'My friends, don't ever say that. Gods never do ill, gods stop when they want to stop. Chance is not stronger than they are and it is they, on the contrary, who dictate to chance. No, Emmanuel, on the contrary, I am a man and your admiration is as unjust as your words are sacrilegious.'

He pressed Julie's hand to his lips and she fell into his arms, while he offered his other hand to Emmanuel. Then, tearing himself away from this house, a sweet and welcoming nest, he made a sign to Maximilien, who followed him, passive, unfeeling and bewildered as he had been since the death of Valentine.

'Make my brother happy again!' Julie whispered in Monte Cristo's ear. He pressed her hand, as he had done eleven years earlier on the staircase leading to Morrel's study.

'Do you still trust Sinbad the Sailor?' he asked, smiling.

'Oh, yes.'

'Well, you may sleep in peace and trust in the Lord.'

As we have said, the post-chaise was waiting. Four lively horses were shaking their manes and impatiently pawing the road.

At the bottom of the steps, Ali waited, his face shining with sweat. He looked as though he had just run a long way.

'Well?' the count asked, in Arabic. 'Did you go to the old man's?'

Ali nodded.

'And you showed him the letter, in front of his eyes, as I told you?'

'Yes,' the slave repeated, respectfully.

'And what did he say – or, rather, do?'

Ali stood under the light, so that his master could see him and, with his intelligent devotion, imitated the old man's face, closing his eyes as Noirtier did when he meant 'yes'.

'Very good, he accepts,' said Monte Cristo. 'Let's go.'

Hardly had he said the words than the carriage began to move and the horses' hoofs struck a shower of sparks from the cobbles. Maximilien settled into his corner without saying a word.

After half an hour, the coach suddenly stopped: the count had just tugged on the silver thread attached to Ali's finger. The Nubian got down and opened the door.

The night was shining with stars. They were at the top of the Montée de Villejuif, on the plateau from which Paris is a dark sea shimmering with millions of lights like phosphorescent waves; and waves they are, more thunderous, more passionate, more shifting, more furious and more greedy than those of the stormy ocean, waves which never experience the tranquillity of a vast sea, but constantly pound together, ever foaming and engulfing everything!

The count stayed alone and motioned for the carriage to come forward. Then he stood for a long time with his arms crossed, contemplating this furnace in which all the ideas that rise, boiling, from the depths to shake the world melt, twine and take shape. Then, when he had turned his powerful gaze on this Babylon which inspires religious poets as it does materialistic sceptics, he bent his head and clasped his hands as if in prayer, and murmured: 'Great city, it is less than six months since I came through your gates. I think that the spirit of God brought me here and takes me away triumphant. To God, who alone can read my heart, I confided the secret of my presence within your walls. He alone knows that I am leaving without hatred and without pride, but not without regret. He alone knows that I employed the power with which He had entrusted me, not for myself, nor for any idle purpose. O great city!

In your heaving breast I found what I was looking for; like a patient miner, I churned your entrails to expel the evil from them. Now my work is complete, my mission accomplished; now you can offer me no further joys or sorrows. Farewell, Paris! Farewell!'

His eyes, like those of some spirit of the night, swept once more across the vast plain. Then, mopping his brow, he got back into the carriage, closing the door behind him, and they had soon vanished down the far side of the hill in a welter of dust and noise. They covered two leagues in utter silence. Morrel was dreaming, Monte Cristo watching him dream.

'Morrel,' the count asked, 'do you regret coming with me?'

'No, Count; but leaving Paris, perhaps . . .'

'If I had thought that happiness awaited you in Paris, Morrel, I should have left you there.'

'But it is in Paris that Valentine rests, and leaving Paris is to lose her for the second time.'

'Maximilien,' the count said, 'the friends whom we have lost do not rest in the earth, they are buried in our hearts, and that is how God wanted it, so that we should always be in their company. I have two friends who are always with me, in that way: one is the man who gave me life, the other is the one who gave me understanding. The spirit of both lives in me. I consult them when I am in doubt and, if I have done any good, I owe it to their advice. Look into your heart, Morrel, and ask it if you should continue to show me that sorry face.'

'My friend,' said Maximilien, 'the voice of my heart is sad indeed and promises only misfortune.'

'Only a weak spirit sees everything from behind a dark veil. The soul makes its own horizons; your soul is overcast, and that is why the sky seems stormy to you.'

'That may be true,' Maximilien said, then he reverted to his reverie.

The journey was accomplished with that astonishing speed that was a peculiar talent of the count's. Towns passed by like shadows on the road; the trees, shaken by the first winds of autumn, seemed to rise up before them like dishevelled giants and fled rapidly into the distance as soon as they had caught up with them. The next morning they arrived at Chalon, where the count's steamship was waiting. Without wasting an instant, the carriage was put on board and, even before that, the two travellers had embarked.

The ship was built for speed, like an Indian dugout. Its two paddle-wheels were like two wings on which it skimmed the water – a migrating bird. Morrel himself experienced that heady intoxication of speed, and at times the wind, lifting his hair, seemed also for a moment nearly to lift the cloud from his brow.

As for the count, the further he moved away from Paris, the more a sort of inhuman serenity appeared to envelop him like an aura. It was as though an exile was returning home.

Soon Marseille – white, warm, throbbing with life; Marseille, twin sister of Tyre and Carthage, their successor as ruler of the Mediterranean; Marseille, ever younger, the older she grows – Marseille appeared before them. For both men the scene was rich in memories: the round tower, the Fort Saint-Nicholas, Puget's town hall and the port with its brick quays where both of them had played as children.

So, by common agreement, they stopped on the Canebière.

A ship was leaving for Algiers. The packages, the passengers crowded on the deck, the host of friends and relations saying goodbye, shouting, weeping, made a spectacle that is always moving, even for those who see it every day; but even this commotion could not take Maximilien's mind off something that had struck him as soon as he set foot on the broad stones of the quay.

'Look,' he said, taking Monte Cristo's arm. 'This is the place where my father stopped when the *Pharaon* came into port. Here the good man whom you saved from death and dishonour threw himself into my arms. I can still feel his tears on my face – and he did not weep alone. Many other people were in tears when they saw us.'

Monte Cristo smiled.

'I was there,' he said, showing Morrel the corner of a street.

As he said this, from the direction towards which the count was pointing they heard a painful groan and saw a woman waving to a passenger on the boat that was about to leave. The woman was veiled. Monte Cristo watched her with an emotion that Morrel would easily have perceived if, unlike the count's, his eyes had not been fixed on the boat.

'Oh, my God!' he cried. 'I'm right! That young man waving his hat, the one in uniform: it's Albert de Morcerf!'

'Yes,' said Monte Cristo. 'I recognized him.'

'How could you? You were looking in the opposite direction.'

The count smiled, as he did when he did not want to reply; and his eyes turned back to the veiled woman, who disappeared round the corner of the street. Then he turned back to Morrel.

'Dear friend,' he said. 'Don't you have something to do in town?'

'I must go and weep on my father's grave,' Morrel replied softly.

'Very well. Go, and wait for me there. I shall join you.'

'Are you leaving me?'

'Yes. I too have a pious duty to perform.'

Morrel placed a limp hand in the one the count offered him. Then, with an indescribably melancholy movement of the head, he left his companion and walked towards the east of the town. Monte Cristo let him go, remaining on the same spot until he had disappeared, before turning towards the Allées de Meilhan, going back to the little house that our readers must remember from the start of this story.

The house was still standing in the shadow of the great avenue of lime-trees which serves idle Marseillais as a place to stroll, furnished with huge curtains of vines which cross their arms, blackened and shredded by age, on stones turned yellow by the burning southern sun. Two stone steps, worn down by passing feet, led to the door, which consisted of three planks, repaired every year but never touched by putty or paint, patiently waiting for the damp to reunite them.

Old as it was, the house was charming, joyful despite its evident poverty, and still the same as the one where Old Dantès had once lived. The difference was that the old man used to occupy the attic, and the count had put the entire house at Mercédès' disposal.

The woman whom Monte Cristo had seen leaving the departing ship came here and was shutting the door just as he appeared at the corner of the street, so that he saw her vanish almost as soon as he caught up with her. The worn steps were old acquaintances and he knew better than anyone how to open the old door, its inner latch raised by a broad-headed hook. He went in without knocking or calling, like a friend, like a guest.

At the end of a passage paved in brick lay a little garden, bathed in warmth, sun and light. Here, at the place he had mentioned, Mercédès had found the money that the count had considerately put there twenty-five years earlier. The trees of this garden could be seen from the street door. As he reached the threshold, Monte Cristo heard a sigh which was like a sob. This sigh guided his eyes to a leafy arbour of jasmine with long purple flowers, where he saw Mercédès sitting, weeping.

She had raised her veil and, alone in the sight of heaven, her face hidden in her hands, she freely abandoned herself to the sighs and tears that she had repressed for so long in her son's presence.

Monte Cristo took a few steps forward, the sand crunching under his feet. Mercédès looked up and cried out in terror at seeing a man in front of her.

'Madame,' the count said, 'I am no longer able to bring you happiness, but I can give you consolation. Would you accept it, as from a friend?'

'Indeed,' said Mercédès, 'I am very unhappy, and alone in the world. I only had my son and he has left me.'

'He did the right thing,' the count replied. 'He has a noble heart. He realized that every man owes some debt to his country: some give their talents, others their hard work; some watch, others bleed. Had he stayed with you, he would have wasted a life that had become useless to him and would have been unable to accustom himself to your grief. The frustration would have filled him with hatred. Now he will become great and strong by struggling against adversities that he will change into good fortune. Let him rebuild the future for both of you, Madame. I can promise that he is in good hands.'

'Alas,' the poor woman murmured, sadly shaking her head, 'I shall not enjoy this good fortune that you speak of and which with all my heart I pray God to give him. So much has been broken in me and around me that I feel I am near to my grave. You did well, Count, in bringing me close to the place where I was so happy: one should die in the place in which one was happy.'

'Madame!' Monte Cristo exclaimed. 'Every one of your words falls, bitter and burning, on my heart, and all the more so since you have cause to hate me. I am responsible for all your misfortunes. Why do you not pity me instead of accusing me? You would make me still more unhappy . . .'

'Hate you, Edmond! Accuse you! Am I to hate the man who saved my son's life – because it was your deadly and bloody intent, was it not, to kill the son of whom Monsieur de Morcerf was so proud? Oh, look at me and see if there is the glimmer of a reproach in me.'

The count looked up and fixed his eyes on Mercédès who, half standing, was holding both hands towards him.

'Look at me,' she went on, with a feeling of profound melancholy. 'Today, a man can bear to see the sparkle in my eyes. The days have gone when I used to smile at Edmond Dantès, as he waited for me up there, by the window of the garret where his old father lived . . . Since then, many sad days have gone by, digging a gulf between me and that time. Accuse you, Edmond! Hate you, my friend! No, it is myself that I accuse and hate! Oh, wretch that I am!' she cried, clasping her hands and raising her eyes to heaven. 'Have I been punished enough! I had religion, innocence and love, the three gifts that make angels, and, wretch as I am, I doubted God.'

Monte Cristo took a step towards her and silently offered his hand; but she gently drew back her own. 'No,' she said. 'No, my friend, do not touch me. You have spared me, but of all those whom you have struck, I was the most guilty. The others acted out of hatred, greed or selfishness, but I was a coward. They wanted something, I was afraid. No, don't squeeze my hand, Edmond. I can see that you are about to say something kind; but don't . . . Keep it for someone else, I no longer deserve your affection. See . . .' (she completely removed her veil) 'See: misfortune has turned my hair grey and my eyes have shed so many tears that there are dark rings round them; and my forehead is furrowed. But you, Edmond, you are still young, still handsome and still proud. You did have faith, you had strength, you trusted in God, and God sustained you. I was a coward, I denied Him, so God abandoned me; and here I am!'

Mercédès burst into tears, her heart breaking under the weight of memory.

Monte Cristo took her hand and kissed it respectfully, but she herself felt that the kiss was passionless, as if his lips were pressing the marble hand of the statue of some saint.

'Some lives,' she continued, 'are predestined, so that a single error destroys all that is to come. I thought you dead, I should have died. What was the sense in eternally mourning for you in my heart? Nothing, except to make a woman of fifty out of one of thirty-nine. What good did it do that, once I had recognized you, of everyone I managed to save only my son? Should I not also have saved the man, guilty though he was, whom I had accepted as my husband? Yet I let him die – oh, God! What am I saying! I contributed to his death by my cowardly insensitivity and my contempt, forgetting, or not wanting to remember, that it was for my sake that he became a perjurer and a traitor. Finally, what is the use in my having accompanied my son here if I let him leave alone, if I abandon him, if I deliver him to the hungry land of Africa? Oh, I tell you, I was a coward. I disowned my love and, like a turncoat, I bring misfortune to all those around me.'

'No, Mercédès,' Monte Cristo said. 'No, think better of yourself. You are a noble and devout woman, and your grief disarmed me. But behind me was God, an invisible, unknown and jealous God, whose envoy I was and who did not choose to restrain the lightning bolt that I unleashed. Oh, I implore that God, at whose feet I have prostrated myself every day for ten years, and I call on Him to witness that I did sacrifice my life to you and with it all the plans that depended on it. But – and I say this with pride, Mercédès – God needed me, and I lived. Look at the past, look at the present, try to divine the future and consider whether I am not the instrument of the Lord. The most frightful misfortunes, the most cruel suffering, the abandonment of all those who loved me and persecution by those who did not know me: this was the first part of my life. Then, suddenly, after captivity, solitude and misery, air, freedom and a fortune so brilliant, so imposing and so extravagant that, unless I was blind, I must have thought that God had sent it to me for some great purpose. From then on, that fortune seemed to me a holy vocation; from then on, there was not one further thought in me for that life, the sweetness of which you, poor woman, have sometimes partaken. Not an hour of calm, not a single hour. I felt myself driven like a cloud of flame through the sky to destroy the cities of the plain. Like those adventurous captains who set off on some dangerous voyage or prepare for a perilous expedition, I got together my supplies, I loaded my weapons and I gathered the means of attack and defence, making my body used to the most violent exercise and my soul to the roughest shocks, teaching my arm to kill, my eyes to see suffering and my mouth to smile at the most dreadful of spectacles. Kind, trustful and forgiving as I was, I made myself vengeful, secretive and cruel – or, rather, impassive like fate itself, which is deaf and blind. Then I launched myself down the road that I had opened, plunging forward until I reached my goal. Woe betide whomsoever I met on my path!'

'Enough!' Mercédès cried. 'Edmond, enough! You may believe that the only person to recognize you was also the only one who could understand. But, Edmond, the woman who recognized and understood you, even if you had found her standing in your way and broken her like glass, would have had to admire you, Edmond! Just as there is a gulf between me and the past, so there is a gulf between you and other men, and my most painful torture, I can tell you, is to make comparisons. There is no one in the world your equal; there is nothing that resembles you. Now, say farewell to me, Edmond, and let us be parted.'

'Before I go, what do you want, Mercédès?' Monte Cristo asked.

'Only one thing, Edmond: for my son to be happy.'

'Pray God, who alone holds the lives of men in His hands, to spare him from death, and I shall take care of the rest.'

'Thank you, Edmond.'

'And you, Mercédès?'

'I need nothing. I am living between two tombs. One is that of Edmond Dantès, who died so long ago – I loved him! The word is no longer appropriate on my shrunken lips, but my heart still remembers and I would not exchange that memory of the heart for anything in the world. The other is that of a man whom Edmond Dantès killed. I approve of the murder, but I must pray for the dead man.'

'Your son will be happy, Madame,' the count repeated.

'Then I shall be as happy as I can be.'

'But . . . what will you do?'

Mercédès smiled sadly.

'If I were to tell you that I should live in this place as Mercédès once did, that is to say by working, you would not believe me. I can no longer do anything except pray, but I do not need to work. The little treasure that you buried was still in the place that you mentioned. People will wonder who I am, and ask what I do, and have no idea how I live; but that is of no significance! It is between God, yourself and me.'

'Mercédès,' the count said, 'I am not reproaching you, but you did make too much of a sacrifice when you gave up the whole of the fortune that Monsieur de Morcerf had accumulated: at least half of it was rightly yours, because of your good management and your vigilance.'

'I know what you are about to suggest, but I cannot accept, Edmond. My son would forbid me.'

'And I will be careful not to do anything for you that would not have Monsieur Albert de Morcerf's approval. I shall find out what he intends and act accordingly. But, if he accepts what I want to do, would you cheerfully do the same?'

'You know, Edmond, I am no longer a thinking creature. I have no further resolve except that of never again being resolved about anything. God has so shaken me with storms that I have lost all willpower. I am in His hands, like a sparrow in the claws of an eagle. Since I am alive, He does not want me to die. If He sends me any succour, it will be because He wants it, and I shall accept.'

'Take care, Madame,' said Monte Cristo. 'That is not how God should be worshipped. He wants us to understand and debate His power: that is why He gave us free will.'

'Wretch!' Mercédès cried. 'Don't speak like that to me. If I believed that God had given me free will, what would remain to save me from despair!'

Monte Cristo paled slightly and bowed his head, overwhelmed by the extremity of her suffering.

'Don't you want to say goodbye to me?' he asked, holding out his hand.

'Yes, indeed,' Mercédès said, solemnly pointing to heaven. 'I will say au revoir, to prove to you that I still hope.'

She touched the count's hand with her own, trembling, then ran up the stairs and vanished from his sight.

Monte Cristo slowly left the house and turned back towards the port. Mercédès did not see him leave, even though she was at the window of the little room that had been his father's. Her eyes were searching the distant horizon for the ship taking her son across the open sea. But her voice, almost involuntarily, muttered softly: 'Edmond, Edmond, Edmond!'

CXIII

THE PAST

The count came away heavy-hearted from this house where he was leaving Mercédès, in all probability never to see her again.

Since the death of little Edouard, a great change had overtaken Monte Cristo. Having reached the summit of his vengeance by the slow and tortuous route that he had followed, he had looked over the far side of the mountain and into the abyss of doubt.

There was more than that: the conversation that he had just had with Mercédès had awoken so many memories in his heart that these memories themselves needed to be overcome.

A man of the count's stamp could not long exist in that state of melancholy which may give life to vulgar souls by endowing them with an appearance of originality, but which destroys superior beings. The count decided that if he had reached the stage where he was blaming himself, then there must be some mistake in his calculations.

'I think ill of the past,' he said, 'and cannot have been mistaken in that way. What! Could the goal that I set myself have been wrong? What, have I been on the wrong road for the past ten years? What, can it be that in a single hour the architect can become convinced that the work into which he has put all his hopes was, if not impossible, then sacrilegious?

'I cannot accept that idea, because it would drive me mad. What my thinking today lacks is a proper assessment of the past, because I am looking at this past from the other end of the horizon. Indeed, as one goes forward, so the past, like the landscape through which one is walking, is gradually effaced. What is happening to me is what happens to people who are wounded in a dream: they look at their wound and they feel it but cannot remember how it was caused.

'Come, then, resurrected man; come, extravagant Croesus; come, sleepwalker; come, all-powerful visionary; come, invincible millionaire, and, for an instant, rediscover that dread prospect of a life of poverty and starvation. Go back down the roads where fate drove, where misfortune led and where despair greeted you. Too many diamonds, gold and happiness now shine from the glass of the mirror in which Monte Cristo gazes on Dantès. Hide the diamonds, dull the gold, dampen the rays. Let the rich man redis-cover the poor one, the free man the prisoner, and the resurrected man the corpse.'

Even as he was saying this to himself, Monte Cristo went down the Rue de la Caisserie. This was the same street down which, one night twenty-four years before, he had been led by a silent guard. These houses, now bright and full of life, had then been dark, silent and shuttered.

'Yet they are the same,' Monte Cristo muttered. 'The difference
is that then it was night and now it is full daylight. It is the sun that
brings light and joy to all this.'

He went down on to the quays along the Rue Saint-Laurent and
walked towards the Consigne. This was the point on the port from
which he had been brought to the ship. A pleasure-boat was going
past with its superstructure covered in cotton twill. Monte Cristo
called the master, who immediately turned the boat towards him
with the eagerness shown in such circumstances by a boatman who
senses a good tip in the offing.

The weather was splendid, the journey a delight. The sun was
setting on the horizon, blazing red in the waters that caught fire as
it descended towards them. The sea was flat as a mirror, but
wrinkled from time to time by leaping fish, chased by some unseen
enemy, that jumped out of the water to look for safety in another
element. Finally, on the horizon could be seen the fishing boats on
their way to Les Martigues or the merchant ships bound for Corsica
or Spain, passing by as white and elegant as travelling gulls.

Despite the clear sky and the finely shaped ships, despite the
golden light flooding the scene, the count, wrapped in his cloak,
recalled one by one all the details of the dreadful journey: the lone
light burning in Les Catalans, the sight of the Château d'If that told
him where he was being taken, the struggle with the gendarmes
when he tried to jump into the water, his despair when he felt
himself overcome, and the cold touch of the muzzle of the carbine
pressed to his temple like a ring of ice.

Little by little, just as the springs that dry up in the summer heat
are moistened bit by bit when the autumn clouds gather and begin
to well up, drop by drop, so the Count of Monte Cristo also felt
rising in his breast the old overflowing gall that had once filled the
heart of Edmond Dantès.

From now on there was no more clear sky, or graceful boats, or
radiant light for him. The sky was clouded over with a funereal veil
and the appearance of the black giant known as the Château d'If
made him shudder, as though he had suddenly seen the ghost of a
mortal enemy.

They were about to arrive. Instinctively the count shrank to the
far end of the boat, even though the master told him in his most
unctuous voice: 'We are about to land, Monsieur.'

Monte Cristo recalled that on this same spot, on this same rock, he had been violently dragged by his guards, who had forced him to go up the ramp by digging him in the side with the point of a bayonet.

The journey seemed long then to Dantès. Monte Cristo had found it quite short: every stroke of the oars threw up a million thoughts and memories in the liquid dust of the sea.

Since the July Revolution[1] there had been no more prisoners in the Château d'If. Its guardhouse was inhabited only by a detachment of men who were meant to discourage smugglers, and a concierge waited for visitors at the door to show them round this monument of terror which had become a monument of curiosity.

Yet, even though he knew all this, when he passed under the vault, went down the dark staircase and was taken to see the dungeons that he had asked to visit, a cold pallor swept across his brow and its icy sweat flowed back into his heart.

The count asked if any former doorkeeper remained from the time of the Restoration. All had retired or gone on to other work. The concierge who showed him round had been there only since 1830.

He was taken to see his own dungeon.

He saw the pale light seeping through the narrow window; he saw the place where the bed had stood (though it had since been removed); and, behind the bed, now blocked, but still visible because of the newness of the stones, the opening made by Abbé Faria. Monte Cristo felt his legs give way under him. He took a wooden stool and sat down.

'Do they tell any stories about this castle, apart from those to do with Mirabeau's imprisonment[2] here?' he asked. 'Is there any tradition connected with these dismal haunts in which one can hardly believe that men once shut up their fellow creatures?'

'Yes, Monsieur,' said the concierge. 'The doorkeeper Antoine even told me one story about this very cell.'

Monte Cristo shuddered. This doorkeeper Antoine was his doorkeeper. He had almost forgotten the name and the face but, on hearing the name, he saw the face, its features ringed by a beard, and the brown jacket and the bunch of keys: it seemed to him that he could hear them rattle still. He even turned around and thought he could see the man in the corridor, in shadows made even darker by the light of the torch that burned in the concierge's hands.

'Would the gentleman like me to tell him the story?' the man asked.

'I would,' said Monte Cristo. 'Tell me.' And he put a hand on his chest to repress the beating of his heart, terrified at hearing his own story.

'Tell me,' he repeated.

'This dungeon,' the concierge said, 'was inhabited by a prisoner, a long time ago, who was a very dangerous man and, it appears, all the more dangerous since he was very industrious. Another man was held in the château at the same time as him, but he was not a wicked man, just a poor priest, and mad.'

'Yes, I see. Mad,' Monte Cristo repeated. 'What form did his madness take?'

'He offered millions to anyone who would give him his freedom.'

Monte Cristo raised his eyes heavenwards but could not see the heavens: there was a veil of stone between him and the firmament. He considered that there had been no less impenetrable a veil between the eyes of those to whom Abbé Faria had offered his treasures and the treasures which he was offering them.

'Could the prisoners meet one another?' he asked.

'Oh, no, Monsieur, that was expressly forbidden. But they got round the prohibition by digging a tunnel between one dungeon and the other.'

'And which of the two dug this tunnel?'

'Oh, it must surely have been the young one,' said the concierge. 'He was industrious and strong, while the poor abbé was old and weak. In any case, his mind wandered too much for him to concentrate on one idea.'

'How blind!' Monte Cristo murmured.

'So it was,' the concierge went on, 'that the young man drove this tunnel – how, no one knows – but he did drive it through, and the proof is that you can still see the marks: there, do you see?' And he brought his torch up to the wall.

'Ah, yes, indeed,' said the count, his voice choked with emotion.

'The outcome was that the two prisoners could communicate with one another, no one has any idea for how long. Then, one day, the old man fell ill and died. And guess what the young one did?' he said, interrupting his narrative.

'Tell me.'

'He took away the body of the dead man, put him in his own

bed with his face turned towards the wall, then returned to the empty dungeon, blocked the hole and slipped into the dead man's winding-sheet. Can you imagine such a thing?'

Monte Cristo closed his eyes and felt again every sensation that he had undergone when the rough cloth rubbed against his face, still cold from the corpse.

The keeper went on: 'You see, this was his plan: he thought that they buried dead bodies in the Château d'If and, as he guessed that they would not go to the expense of a coffin for the prisoners, he imagined he would be able to lift up the earth with his shoulders. But unfortunately there was a custom here on the island that upset his plans: the dead weren't buried, they just had a cannonball fastened around their legs and were thrown into the sea. And that's what happened. Our man was thrown into the water from the top of the gallery. The next day, they found the real body in his bed and guessed everything, because the burial party said something that they had not dared to admit up to then, which was that at the moment when the body was thrown out into the void, they heard a dreadful cry, instantly smothered beneath the water into which he was thrown.'

The count had difficulty breathing; sweat was pouring down his forehead and his heart was gripped with anguish.

'No!' he muttered. 'No! That doubt which I experienced was the sign that I was starting to forget; but here the heart is mine once more and feels once more a hunger for revenge.

'And this prisoner,' he asked, 'did anyone hear of him again?'

'Never, not a word. You see, there are only two possibilities. Either he fell flat and, since he was falling from fifty feet, he would have been killed instantly . . .'

'You said that they tied a cannonball to his feet: in that case, he would have fallen standing up.'

'Or else he fell standing up,' the concierge went on, 'and in that case the weight on his feet would have dragged him to the bottom, and there he stayed, poor fellow.'

'Do you pity him?'

'Good heavens, yes, even though he was in his element.'

'Why do you say that?'

'The rumour was that the poor man had once been a naval officer, arrested for Bonapartism.'

'Ah, Truth,' the count muttered, 'God made you to float above the waves and the flames. So the poor sailor does live in the memory of some storytellers; they retell his dreadful tale at the fireside and shudder at the moment when he flew through the air and was swallowed up by the sea.

'Did they ever know his name?' he asked aloud.

'What?' said the keeper. 'Oh, yes. He was only known as number thirty-four.'

'Villefort, Villefort!' Monte Cristo muttered. 'That is what you must often have told yourself when my spectre haunted your sleepless nights.'

'Would the gentleman like to continue the tour?' the concierge asked.

'Yes, and I'd particularly like to see the poor abbé's room.'

'Ah, number twenty-seven?'

'Yes, number twenty-seven.' It seemed he could still hear Abbé Faria's voice when he asked him his name, and the abbé called back that number through the wall.

'Come.'

'Wait,' said Monte Cristo. 'Let me cast a final glance over every aspect of this dungeon.'

'Just as well,' said the guide. 'I forgot to bring the key to the other.'

'Then go and fetch it.'

'I'll leave you the torch.'

'No, take it with you.'

'But you will have to stay here without a light.'

'I can see in the dark.'

'Why, just like him!'

'Like whom?'

'Number thirty-four. They say he was so used to the dark that he could have seen a pin in the darkest corner of his cell.'

'It took him ten years to reach that point,' the count muttered as the guide went off, carrying the torch.

The count was right. He had hardly been a few moments in the dark before he could see everything as if in broad daylight. So he looked all round him and truly recognized his dungeons.

'Yes,' he said, 'there is the stone on which I used to sit. There is the trace of my shoulders where they have worn their imprint in the wall. There is the mark of the blood that flowed from my forehead, the day when I tried to dash out my brains against the wall. Oh, those figures! I remember! I made them one day when I was calculating the age of my father to know if I would find him alive, and the age of Mercédès to know if I should find her free . . . I had a moment's hope after doing those sums . . . I had not counted on starvation and infidelity.'

A bitter laugh escaped him. As if in a dream, he had just seen his father being taken to the tomb and Mercédès walking to the altar!

He was struck by an inscription on the far wall. Still white, it stood out against the greenish stones: 'My God!' he read. 'Let me not forget!'

'Yes, yes,' he said. 'That was my only prayer in my last years. I no longer asked for freedom, I asked for memory, and was afraid I should become mad and forget. My God, you did preserve my memory and I have not forgotten. Thank you, God, thank you.'

At that moment the light of the torch was reflected off the walls: the guide had returned.

Monte Cristo went to meet him. 'Follow me,' the man said; and, without needing to return to the daylight, he took him down an underground corridor which led to another entrance.

Here, too, Monte Cristo was overwhelmed with a host of thoughts. The first thing that struck him was the meridian on the wall by which Abbé Faria counted the hours. Then there were the remains of the bed on which the poor prisoner died.

At the sight of this, instead of the anguish he had felt in his own dungeon, a sweet and tender feeling, a feeling of gratitude, filled his heart, and two tears rolled down his cheeks.

'Here,' said the guide, 'is where they kept the mad priest. And there is the place through which the young man came to join him.' And he showed Monte Cristo the opening to the tunnel which, on this side, had been left uncovered. 'By the colour of the stone,' he went on, 'a scientist realized that they must have been in communication with each other for about ten years. Poor folk, how miserable they must have been, those ten years!'

Dantès took a few *louis* from his pocket and handed them to the man who, for the second time, had felt sorry for him without knowing who he was.

The concierge accepted the money, thinking that it must be a few small coins; then, in the light of the torch, he realized how much the visitor had given him.

'Monsieur,' he said, 'you've made a mistake.'

'What do you mean?'

'You have given me gold.'

'I know that.'

'What! You know?'

'Yes.'

'And you intended to give me this gold?'

'Yes.'

'So I can keep it in all conscience?'

'Yes.'

The concierge looked at Monte Cristo in amazement.

'And honesty,' the count said, like Hamlet.[3]

'Monsieur,' the concierge said, not daring to believe in his good fortune, 'I do not understand your generosity.'

'It's simple enough, my friend,' said the count. 'I used to be a sailor, and your story touched me more than it might another person.'

'So, Monsieur,' the guide said, 'as you are so generous, you deserve a present.'

'What can you give me, friend? Seashells, straw dolls? No thank you.'

'Not at all, Monsieur; something that has to do with the story I just told you.'

'Really?' the count exclaimed. 'What is it?'

'Listen,' the concierge said. 'Here's what happened. I thought to myself, there's always something to be found in a room where a prisoner has lived for fifteen years, so I began to tap the walls.'

'Ah!' Monte Cristo said, remembering the abbé's double hiding-place. 'As you say . . .'

'So by looking,' the concierge went on, 'I discovered that there really was a hollow sound at the head of the bed and under the hearth.'

'Yes,' Monte Cristo said. 'Yes . . .'

'I lifted the stones, and I found . . .'

'A rope ladder and tools?' the count cried.

'How did you know that?' the concierge asked in astonishment.

'I don't know; I guessed,' the count said. 'Those are the sort of things that one usually finds in prisoners' hiding-places.'

'Yes, Monsieur,' the guide said. 'A rope ladder and some tools.'

'Do you still have them?' Monte Cristo asked eagerly.

'No, Monsieur. I sold the various things, which were very unusual, to visitors. But I do have something else.'

'What is that?' the count asked impatiently.

'I have a sort of book, written on strips of cloth.'

'Oh!' Monte Cristo cried. 'You have such a book?'

'I don't know if it is a book,' said the concierge. 'But I do have what I told you.'

'Go and fetch it, my friend,' said the count. 'Go, and if it's what I think, don't worry.'

'I'm going, Monsieur.' And the guide left.

At this, the count went to kneel piously in front of the remains of the bed which death had made an altar for him. 'Oh, my second father,' he said. 'You who gave me liberty, knowledge, riches; you who, like those beings of some higher essence than ourselves, had an understanding of good and evil, if in the depths of the tomb something remains of us which still shudders to hear the voices of those who have remained on earth; if in the transfiguration undergone by the body in death, something animate remains in the places where we have greatly loved or greatly suffered, noble heart, supreme spirit, profound soul, I beg you by some word, some sign or some revelation, in the name of the paternal love which you gave me and the filial respect that I returned to you, take away this remaining doubt that, if it does not become a certainty, will turn into remorse.'

The count bent his head and clasped his hands.

'Here, Monsieur!' said a voice behind him. He started and turned around. The concierge was holding out the strips of cloth to which Abbé Faria had entrusted all the fruits of his wisdom. This was the manuscript of Abbé Faria's great work on the monarchy in Italy.

The count seized it eagerly and the first thing his eyes met was the epigraph, which read: 'You will pull the dragon's teeth and trample the lions underfoot, said the Lord.'

'Ah!' he cried. 'There is my answer! Thank you, father, thank you.'

Taking out of his pocket a small wallet containing ten banknotes of a thousand francs each, he said: 'Here, take this.'

'Are you giving it to me?'

'Yes, on condition that you do not look inside it until after I have gone.'

Placing the relic which he had just found against his chest – a relic which for him was worth the most precious treasure – he hurried out of the underground tunnel and stepped back into the boat, with the order: 'To Marseille!'

As they were pulling away, he looked back towards the grim fortress and said: 'Woe betide those who had me shut up in that awful place and those who forgot that I was imprisoned there.'

As they sailed back past Les Catalans, the count turned away, wrapped his head in his cloak and muttered a woman's name. The victory was complete. Twice he had driven away his doubts. And the name which he spoke with an expression of tenderness that was close to love, was that of Haydée.

On reaching land, Monte Cristo set off for the cemetery where he knew he would find Morrel. Ten years earlier, he too had piously searched out a tomb in this graveyard, but he had searched in vain. Returning to France a millionaire, he had been unable to find the tomb of his father, who had starved to death. Morrel had indeed arranged for a cross to be raised, but the cross had fallen and the gravedigger had burned it, as gravediggers do with old pieces of wood lying around in cemeteries.

The worthy merchant had been luckier. He died in the arms of his children, who laid him to rest beside his wife, who had preceded him by two years into eternity.

Two large slabs of marble bearing their names lay, one beside the other, in a little plot surrounded by an iron railing, in the shade of four cypress-trees. Maximilien was leaning against one of these, staring at the two graves but seeing nothing. His agony was profound and he was in almost a state of distraction.

'Maximilien,' the count said, 'that is not where you should be looking, but there!' And he pointed to heaven.

'The dead are all around us,' said Morrel. 'Isn't that what you told me yourself when you took me away from Paris?'

'Maximilien,' the count said, 'during the journey you asked me to stop for a few days in Marseille: is that still what you want?'

'I no longer want anything, Count. But I feel that I shall wait with less displeasure here than elsewhere.'

'So much the better, Maximilien, because I am leaving you, but taking your word of honour with me, I think?'

'Oh, I shall forget it, Count,' said Morrel. 'I shall forget it.'

'No, you will not forget, because before all else you are a man of honour, Morrel, because you have sworn and because you must swear again.'

'Please, Count, have pity on me! I am so unhappy!'

'I once knew a man who was more unhappy than you, Morrel.'

'Impossible!'

'Alas,' said Monte Cristo, 'our poor species can pride itself on the fact that every man thinks himself unhappier than another unfortunate, weeping and moaning beside him.'

'What can be more unhappy than a man who had lost the only thing in the world that he loved and desired?'

'Listen, Morrel,' Monte Cristo said, 'and concentrate for a moment on what I am about to tell you. I knew a man who, like you, placed all his expectations of happiness in a woman. He was young and had an old father whom he loved and a fiancée whom he adored. He was about to marry her when suddenly one of those twists of fate – which would make us doubt the existence of God if God did not reveal himself later by demonstrating that everything is to Him a means by which to lead us to His infinite oneness . . . when suddenly a twist of fate took away his freedom, his fiancée, and the future he dreamed of, which he believed was his (blind as he was, he could only read the here-and-now), and threw him in the depths of a dungeon.'

'Oh, yes,' Morrel said. 'But people come out of dungeons – after a week, or a month, or a year.'

'He stayed there for fourteen years, Morrel,' the count said, putting his hand on the young man's shoulder.

Maximilien shuddered. 'Fourteen years!' he murmured.

'Fourteen years,' the count repeated. 'And he too, in those fourteen years, had many moments of despair. He too, like you, Morrel, thinking himself the most unhappy of men, wanted to kill himself.'

'And?' Morrel asked.

'And at the very last moment God revealed himself to him by human means; because God no longer performs miracles. Perhaps at first (because eyes clouded by tears need some time to clear entirely), he did not understand the infinite mercy of the Lord. But he was patient and waited. One day he miraculously emerged from his tomb, transfigured, rich, powerful, almost a god. His first thought was for his father, but his father was dead.'

'My father too is dead,' said Morrel.

'Yes, but he died in your arms, loved, happy, honoured, rich and full of years. This man's father died poor, desperate, doubting God; and when, ten years after his death, his son looked for the grave, even that had vanished, and no one could tell him: "Here is where the heart that loved you so sleeps in the Lord." '

'Oh,' said Morrel.

'So, as a son, he was unhappier than you are, Morrel; he did not even know where to find his father's grave.'

'Yes,' said Morrel, 'but he did still have the woman whom he loved.'

'You are wrong, Morrel. The woman . . .'

'Was she dead?' Maximilien cried.

'Worse. She had been unfaithful and married one of her fiancé's tormentors. So you see, Morrel, the man was more unfortunate even than you are.'

'And did God send him consolation?' Morrel asked.

'He did at least send him tranquillity.'

'And might he still be happy one day?'

'He hopes so, Maximilien.'

The young man bowed his head and, after a moment's silence, said: 'You have my promise; but, remember . . .' And he offered Monte Cristo his hand.

'On October the fifth, Morrel, I shall expect you on the island of Monte Cristo. On the fourth a yacht will be waiting for you in the port at Bastia. The yacht will be called the *Eurus*. You will tell the master your name and he will bring you to me. That's agreed, isn't it, Maximilien?'

'Agreed, Count, and I shall do as we have agreed. But remember that on October the fifth . . .'

'Child, who does not yet know what a man's promise means! I have told you twenty times that on that day, if you still want to die, I shall help you. Now, farewell.'

'Are you leaving me?'

'Yes, I have business in Italy. I am leaving you alone, alone with your grief, alone with that powerful eagle which the Lord sends to his elect to transport them to his feet. The story of Ganymede[4] is not a fable, Maximilien, but an allegory.'

'When will you leave?'

'Immediately. The steamship is waiting for me, and in an hour I shall already be far away. Will you come with me to the port?'

'I am entirely at your disposal, Count.'

'Embrace me.'

Morrel walked with the count down to the port. Already a huge plume of smoke was pouring out of the black tube which cast it upwards towards the skies. Shortly afterwards the boat set out, and an hour later, as Monte Cristo had said, the same trail of smoke was barely visible, streaking an eastern horizon darkened by the first shades of night.

CXIV

PEPPINO

At the very same moment as the count's steamship was vanishing behind the Cap Morgiou, a man, travelling by the mail on the road from Florence to Rome, had just left the little town of Aquapendente. Doing some of the journey on foot, he covered a lot of ground without attracting suspicion.

Dressed in a frock-coat or, rather, an overcoat, much worn by travel but showing the ribbon of the Legion of Honour sewn on to it, still bright and shining, the man was recognizably French, not only by his dress and his decoration, but also by the accent in which he addressed the postilion. Another proof that he had been born in that land, with its universal language, was that he knew no other Italian words except those pertaining to music which, like Figaro's 'goddam',[1] can stand in for all the subtleties of a particular tongue.

'Allegro!' he cried to the coachmen as they went up a hill. 'Moderato!' he cried every time they went down.

God knows, there are plenty of hills, up and down, between Florence and Rome along the road through Aquapendente.

The two words, of course, caused enormous hilarity among the good fellows to whom they were addressed.

Once in the presence of the Eternal City, that is to say on arriving at La Storta, the point from which one may catch sight of Rome, the traveller did not experience the feeling of fervent curiosity that impels every foreigner to rise from his seat in an attempt to see the famous dome of Saint Peter's, which can be glimpsed long before anything else. No. He merely took a portfolio from his pocket and, from the portfolio, a piece of paper folded four times, which he unfolded and refolded with an intensity that was close to respect, saying only: 'Good, I still have it.'

The carriage entered through the Porta del Popolo, turned left and stopped at the Hôtel de Londres.

Our old friend Signor Pastrini greeted the traveller on the door-step, cap in hand. The traveller got down, ordered a good dinner and asked for the address of the firm of Thomson and French, which was instantly pointed out to him, since the firm was one of the best known in Rome. It was situated in the Via dei Banchi, near Saint Peter's.

In Rome, as anywhere else, the arrival of a stage-coach is an event. Ten young descendants of Marius and the Gracchi,[2] barefoot and with holes at their elbows, but with one hand on their hip and the other arm picturesquely bent above their head, watched the traveller, the post-chaise and the horses. These typical Roman *ragazzi* had been joined by some fifty idlers from the Papal States, of the sort who make rings on the water by spitting into the Tiber from the Ponte Sant' Angelo, when there is water in the river.

Now since the *ragazzi* and street urchins of Rome, unlike the *gamins* of Paris, understand every language, especially French, they heard the traveller ask for rooms, order dinner and finally enquire as to the address of Thomson and French.

The result was that, when the new arrival came out of the hotel with his inevitable guide, a man emerged from the group of onlookers and, without being observed by the traveller (or, apparently, by the guide), walked a short distance behind the foreigner, tailing him with as much skill as a Parisian detective.

The man was in such a hurry to visit Thomson and French that he had not bothered to wait for the horses to be harnessed. The carriage was to pick him up on the way or wait for him at the door of the bank. He got there before the coach reached him.

The Frenchman went in, leaving his guide in the antechamber, where he immediately got into conversation with two or three of those businessmen who have no business (or, if you prefer, have a thousand businesses), who in Rome hang around at the doors of banks, churches, ruins, museums or theatres.

At the same moment, the man who had left the group of onlookers at the hotel also went in. The Frenchman rang at the window in the front office and came through into the first room. His shadow did likewise.

'Messrs Thomson and French?' the foreigner asked.

A sort of lackey got up at a sign from a confidential clerk, the solemn guardian of the first office.

'Whom should I announce?' asked the lackey, preparing to precede the foreigner.

'Baron Danglars,' the traveller replied.

'Follow me,' said the lackey.

A door opened. The lackey and the baron vanished through it. The man who had come in behind Danglars sat down on a bench to wait.

The clerk went on writing for roughly five minutes. During this time the seated man remained absolutely still and silent.

Then the clerk's quill stopped scratching across the paper. He looked up, searched carefully all around him and, after reassuring himself that they were alone, said: 'Ah! So there you are, Peppino.'

'Yes,' the man replied laconically.

'Did you see the chance of anything good from that fat man?'

'There's not much to be had out of him: we've been informed.'

'So you know what he's here for, snooper?'

'Why, he's come to make a withdrawal; the only thing is, we don't know how much.'

'You'll find out soon enough, my friend.'

'Good, but don't do as you did the other day and give me misinformation.'

'What do you mean? What are you thinking of? Is it the Englishman who went away with three thousand *écus* a few days ago?'

'No, he really did have three thousand *écus* and we found them. I'm talking about that Russian prince.'

'What of him?'

'Well, you told us thirty thousand *livres* and we only found twenty-two.'

'You probably didn't look hard enough.'

'Luigi Vampa did the search in person.'

'In that case, either he had paid his debts . . .'

'A Russian?'

'Or spent the money.'

'I suppose that's possible.'

'It's definite. But let me go to my post, or the Frenchman will have done his business before I can discover the precise amount.'

Peppino nodded and, taking a rosary out of his pocket, began to mutter some prayer or other, while the clerk vanished through the same door that had opened for the lackey and the baron.

Ten minutes later, he reappeared, with a broad smile.

'Well?' Peppino asked.

'Stand by! It's a princely sum.'

'Five or six millions, I believe?'

'Yes. How do you know the figure?'

'Against a bill signed by His Excellency, the Count of Monte Cristo?'

'You know the count?'

'Credited on Rome, Venice and Vienna.'

'Just so!' the clerk exclaimed. 'How are you so well informed?'

'I told you that we had advance information.'

'So why did you come to me?'

'To be sure that this is really our man.'

'It's him all right. Five million . . . A fine sum, eh, Peppino?'

'Yes.'

'We'll never have as much for ourselves.'

'At least we'll get some crumbs of it,' Peppino said philosophically.

'Hush! Here he comes.'

The clerk took up his pen and Peppino his rosary. When the door opened, the one was writing and the other praying. Danglars appeared, in fine spirits, together with the banker, who accompanied him to the door.

As agreed, the carriage that was to meet Danglars was waiting in front of the House of Thomson and French. The guide held the door open: a cicerone is a very accommodating creature, who can be put to all sorts of uses.

Danglars leapt into the carriage with the spring of a twenty-year-old. The guide shut the door and got up beside the driver. Peppino climbed on to the rear box.

'Would Your Excellency like to see Saint Peter's?' the guide asked.

'What for?' the baron replied.

'Why, just to see it!'

'I didn't come to Rome to see anything,' Danglars said aloud; then, with an avaricious smile, he said under his breath: 'I came to touch.' And he meaningfully touched his portfolio, in which he had just enclosed a letter.

'So, Your Excellency is going . . .'

'To the hotel.'

'Casa Pastrini,' the guide said to the coachman, and the carriage set off as briskly as a racing gig.

Ten minutes later, the baron had returned to his rooms and Peppino had taken up his place on the bench running along the front of the hotel, after whispering a few words to one of those descendants of Marius and the Gracchi whom we noted at the start of this chapter, the boy in question setting off down the road for the Capitol as fast as his legs could carry him.

Danglars was weary, satisfied and sleepy. He went to bed, put his pocket-book under the bolster and fell asleep.

Peppino had plenty of time, however. He played *morra*[3] with some porters, lost three *écus* and in consolation drank a flagon of Orvieto.

The next day, Danglars woke late, even though he had gone to bed early. For the previous five or six nights he had slept badly, if at all. He had an ample breakfast and not being, as he had said, much inclined to enjoy the beauty of the Eternal City, he asked for his post-horses to be brought at noon.

However, Danglars had not counted on the formalities of the police and the idleness of the postmaster. The horses arrived only at two o'clock and the guide did not bring back the passport, with its visa, until three.

All these preparations had drawn a fair crowd of onlookers to the door of Signor Pastrini's, and there was no lack of descendants of the Gracchi and Marius among them. The baron walked in triumph through these groups of idlers who called him 'Excellency', to get a *baiocco*.

Danglars, who was a very democratic fellow as we know, had up to then been content to be addressed as 'Baron', and had not yet been called 'Excellency'; he found the title flattering and threw a few *pauls* to the mob, which was quite ready, for a further dozen or so of the same, to nominate him 'Your Royal Highness'.

'What road?' the postilion asked in Italian.

'To Ancona,' the baron replied.

Signor Pastrini translated the request and the reply, and the carriage set off at a gallop.

Danglars intended to go to Venice and draw out part of his fortune, then from Venice to Vienna, where he would withdraw the rest. Then his idea was to settle in the latter city which, he had been assured, was one offering many pleasures.

Hardly had they done three leagues through the Roman campagna than night began to fall. Danglars had not realized that they were leaving so late; otherwise he would have stayed in Rome. He asked the postilion how long it would be before they arrived in the next town.

'*Non capisco*,' the man replied.

Danglars nodded, to indicate 'Very good', and the carriage drove on.

'I can stop at the first post,' Danglars thought.

He still felt some traces of that well-being which he had experienced on the previous day and which had given him such a good night's sleep. He was comfortably installed in a solid English coach with double springs. He felt himself being pulled forward at a gallop by two strong horses, and he knew that the relay was seven leagues on. What is one to do when one is a banker and one has successfully gone bankrupt?

For ten minutes he thought of his wife, who was still in Paris; and for another ten minutes he considered his daughter, who was running round the globe with Mlle d'Armilly. He devoted a further ten minutes to his creditors and how he would spend their money. Then, having nothing left to think about, he closed his eyes and fell asleep.

From time to time, however, shaken by a jolt which was harder than the rest, Danglars would momentarily re-open his eyes and feel himself carried along at the same speed through the same Roman campagna, among a scattering of broken aqueducts which looked like granite giants petrified as they ran. But the night was cold, dark and rainy, and it was far better for a man who was half asleep to stay at the back of the coach, with his eyes closed, than to put his head out of the door and ask where he was – from a postilion whose only answer would be: '*Non capisco.*' So Danglars went on sleeping, thinking that it would be time enough to wake up when they arrived at the relay.

The carriage stopped. Danglars thought he had at last reached his much-desired goal.

He opened his eyes and looked through the glass, expecting to find himself in the middle of some town, or at least of some village. But he could see nothing except a kind of isolated hovel, with three or four men coming and going like shadows.

He waited for a moment, expecting the postilion who had finished his relay to come and ask him for his pay. He thought he could take advantage of the opportunity to ask for some information from his new driver. But the horses were unharnessed and replaced without anyone coming to ask the traveller for money. Astonished, Danglars opened the door, but a firm hand immediately slammed it shut, and the carriage set off again.

The baron woke up completely at this, and in some astonishment.

'Hey!' he called to the postilion. 'Hey, *mio caro!*'

This was more bel canto Italian that he had learnt when his daughter used to sing duos with Prince Cavalcanti. But *mio caro* did not reply. So Danglars opened the window.

'I say, my good friend! Where are we going?' he said, putting his head out.

'*Dentro la testa!*' cried a serious and commanding voice, accompanied by a threatening gesture.

Danglars understood *dentro la testa*: 'put your head in!' As we can see, he was making rapid progress in Italian. He obeyed, but with some misgivings. And, since his anxiety was increasing minute by minute, after a few moments his mind, instead of the void that it had contained on setting out, which had brought sleep . . . his mind, as we say, filled with a large quantity of thoughts, each more likely than the previous one to keep a traveller on his toes, especially one finding himself in Danglars' situation.

In the darkness his eyes took on that degree of acuity that strong emotions tend to give them at first, only for the effect to be reversed later through overuse. Before one is afraid, one sees clearly; while one is afraid, one sees double; and after being afraid, one sees dimly.

Danglars saw a man wrapped in a cloak galloping beside the right-hand door.

'Some gendarme,' he said. 'Have I been denounced to the pontifical authorities by the French telegraph?'

He decided to resolve his uncertainties. 'Where are you taking me?' he asked.

'*Dentro la testa!*' the same voice repeated, in the same threatening tone.

Danglars looked over at the left-hand door. Another man on horseback was galloping alongside it.

'Definitely,' said Danglars. 'I have definitely been arrested.' And he slumped back into the seat, this time not to sleep but to think.

A moment later the moon rose.

From the back of the carriage he looked out at the countryside and saw the huge aqueducts, stone phantoms which he had noticed in passing; but now, instead of being on his right, they were on the left.

He realized that the carriage had turned round and that he was being taken back to Rome.

'Oh, wretch that I am,' he muttered. 'They must have obtained an order for my extradition.'

The carriage continued to dash forward at a terrifying speed. A dreadful hour went by, because every new indication that appeared proved beyond doubt that the fugitive was being taken back the way he had come. Finally, he saw a dark mass against which it seemed that the carriage was about to crash; but it turned aside and continued parallel to the dark shape, which was nothing other than the ring of ramparts encircling Rome.

'Oh, oh!' Danglars muttered. 'We're not going into the city, so I am not being arrested after all. Good heavens, I've just thought: could it be . . .'

His hair stood on end, because he recalled those interesting stories of Roman bandits which were taken with such a large pinch of salt in Paris. Albert de Morcerf had told some of them to Mme Danglars and Eugénie when it had been a matter of the young viscount becoming the son-in-law of the first and the husband of the latter.

'Perhaps they are thieves!' he thought.

Suddenly the carriage was running over something harder than a sanded roadway. Danglars ventured to look out on both sides of the road and saw oddly shaped monuments. Thinking about Morcerf's story, which was now coming back to him in every detail, he thought that he must be on the Appian Way.

On the left of the carriage, in a sort of dip, could be seen a circular excavation. It was the Circus of Caracalla.[4]

At a word from the man who was galloping by the right-hand door the carriage stopped. At the same time the left-hand door opened and a voice ordered: '*Scendi!*'

Danglars got down without further ado. He could still not yet speak Italian, but he was already understanding the language. More dead than alive, he looked around him. He was surrounded by four men, apart from the postilion.

'*Di quà,*' one of the four said, going down a little path that led from the Appian Way to the middle of the irregular mounds that break up the topography of the Roman campagna. Danglars followed his guide without debate, and did not need to turn around to confirm that the other three men were following him. But it seemed to him that these men were stopping like sentries at more or less equal distances.

After they had walked for some ten minutes, in which Danglars did not exchange a single word with his guide, he found himself standing between a small hillock and a tall bush. Three silent men standing around him formed a triangle, with himself at its centre. He tried to speak, but his tongue refused to obey.

'*Avanti,*' said the same sharp and commanding voice.

This time Danglars doubly understood. He understood both by word and by gesture, because the man who was walking behind him pushed him forward so roughly that he nearly collided with his guide. The guide was our friend Peppino, who advanced into the high bushes along a winding track that only the ants and the lizards could have recognized as a pathway.

Peppino stopped in front of a rock surmounted by a thick bush. This rock, half open like an eyelid, swallowed up the young man, who disappeared into it like a devil into the pit in one of our fairy tales.

The voice and gestures of the man behind Danglars ordered him to do the same. There could be no further doubt: the French bankrupt was in the hands of Roman bandits.

Danglars did as he was told like a man caught between two frightful perils, made brave by fear. Despite his stomach, which was not built for wriggling through cracks in the Roman campagna, he slipped in behind Peppino and, letting himself drop with his eyes closed, he fell on his feet. As he did so, he re-opened his eyes.

The track was wide but dark. Peppino, making no effort to conceal himself now that he was at home, struck a flame from a tinder box and lit a torch. Two other men came down behind Danglars, taking up the rear, and, pushing Danglars if he ever happened to stop, drove him down a gentle slope to the centre of a sinister-looking crossroads.

Here were white stone walls, hollowed out to make coffins, superimposed one above the other, which seemed like the deep black eyes of a skull. A sentry was tapping the barrel of his carbine against his left hand. 'Friend or foe?' he asked.

'Friend,' said Peppino. 'Where is the captain?'

'There,' the sentry said, indicating over his shoulder a sort of large room hollowed out of the rock, its light shining into the corridor through wide arched openings.

'Good prey, Captain, good prey,' Peppino said in Italian, seizing Danglars by the collar of his frock-coat and dragging him towards an opening like a door, through which one could gain access to the room in which the captain appeared to have made his lodging.

'Is this the man?' he asked, looking up from Plutarch's *Life of Alexander* which he had been reading attentively.

'That's him, Captain, that's him.'

'Very well. Show him to me.'

On this rather impertinent order, Peppino brought his torch so sharply up to Danglars' face that he leapt back, afraid of having his eyelashes burned. His face, pale and distraught, showed all the signs of frightful terror.

'This man is tired,' the captain said. 'Let him be shown to his bed.'

'Oh!' Danglars murmured. 'This bed is probably one of the coffins around the walls, and that sleep is the sleep of death that one of the daggers I can see shining in the darkness will bring me.'

Indeed, in the black depths of the vast hall, rising off their beds of dry grass or wolf's skin, one could see the companions of the man whom Albert de Morcerf had found reading Caesar's *Commentaries* and whom Danglars found reading *The Life of Alexander*.

The banker emitted a dull groan and followed his guide. He did not try either to pray or to cry out. He was without strength, will, power or feeling. He went because he was taken.

He tripped against a step and, realizing that there was a stairway in front of him, he bent down instinctively so as not to strike his head and found himself in a cell cut out of the sheer rock. It was clean, if bare, and dry, even though situated an immeasurable depth below the surface of the ground. A bed of dry grass, covered with goatskins, was not standing, but spread out in a corner of this cell. Seeing it, Danglars thought he saw the glowing symbol of his salvation.

'Oh, God be praised!' he murmured. 'It's a real bed!'

This was the second time in the last hour that he had called on the name of God, something that had not happened to him for ten years.

'*Ecco,*' the guide said. And, pushing Danglars into the cell, he shut the door behind him. A bolt grated and Danglars was a prisoner.

In any case, even if there had been no lock, it would have taken Saint Peter, guided by a heavenly angel, to pass through the midst of the garrison which guarded the Catacombs of Saint Sebastian, camped around its leader, in whom the reader will surely have recognized the celebrated Luigi Vampa.

Danglars had most certainly recognized the bandit, though he had not wanted to believe in the man's existence when Morcerf had tried to introduce him in France. He had recognized not only him but also the cell in which Morcerf had been imprisoned and which, in all probability, was a lodging reserved for foreigners.

These memories which, as it happened, Danglars recalled with some joy brought back a feeling of calm. Since they had not killed him at once, the bandits did not intend to kill him at all. They had captured him in order to rob him, and since he had only a few *louis* on him, he would be ransomed.

He recalled that Morcerf had been taxed at around 4,000 *écus*. As he considered himself a good deal more important than Morcerf, he mentally settled his own price at 8,000 *écus*. And 8,000 *écus* was equivalent to 48,000 *livres*.

He would still be left with something in the region of 5,050,000 francs. With that, he could manage anywhere.

So, feeling more or less sure that he would survive the adventure, especially since there was no case in which a man had ever been held for a ransom of 5,050,000 *livres*, Danglars lay down on his bed and, after turning around two or three times, fell asleep, as easy in his mind as the hero whose story Luigi Vampa was reading.

CXV

LUIGI VAMPA'S BILL OF FARE

Every sleep – apart from the one that Danglars feared – ends with an awakening.

Danglars woke up. For a Parisian who was accustomed to silk curtains, velvet hangings on the walls and the scent that rises from wood whitening in the chimney-piece or is wafted back from a ceiling lined in satin, to wake up in a chalky stone grotto must be like a dream in the worst possible taste. As he touched the goatskin curtains, Danglars must have thought he was dreaming about the Samoyeds or the Lapps. But in such circumstances it is only a second before the most intractable doubt becomes certainty.

'Yes,' he thought. 'Yes, I'm in the hands of the bandits about whom Albert de Morcerf was telling us.'

His first impulse was to breathe, to make sure that he was not wounded: this was something that he had come across in *Don Quixote*, not perhaps the only book he had read, but the only one of which he could remember something.

'No,' he said. 'They have not killed me or wounded me, but they may perhaps have robbed me . . .'

He quickly felt in his pocket. It had not been touched. The hundred *louis* that he had put aside for his journey from Rome to Venice were still in his trouser pocket, and the pocket-book with the letter of credit for five million, fifty thousand francs was still in the pocket of his frock-coat.

'These are strange bandits,' he thought, 'to have left me my purse and my pocket-book. As I said yesterday when I went to bed, they will try to ransom me. Well, well! I still have my watch. Let's see what time it is.'

Danglars' watch, a masterpiece by Breguet which he had carefully wound up the previous day before setting out, sounded half-past five in the morning. Without it, Danglars would have had no idea of the time, since there was no daylight in his cell.

Should he ask the bandits to explain themselves? Should he wait patiently until they asked for him? The second alternative seemed the wiser, so Danglars waited.

He waited until noon.

Throughout this time a sentry had been stationed at his door. At eight in the morning, the guard was changed; and at this moment, Danglars felt a desire to find out who was guarding him.

He had noticed that rays of light – lamplight, not daylight – were managing to make their way through the ill-fitting planks of the door. He went across to one of these openings just at the moment when the bandit took a few gulps of brandy which, because of the leather bottle that contained it, exuded an odour that Danglars found quite repellent. 'Ugh!' he exclaimed, retreating to the far corner of the cell.

At noon the man with the brandy was replaced by another operative. Danglars was curious to see his new keeper, so he once more crept over to the gap in the boards. The new man was an athletic bandit, a Goliath with large eyes, thick lips, a broken nose and red hair which hung over his shoulders in twisted locks like vipers.

'Oh, my God!' Danglars said. 'This one is more like an ogre than a human being. In any case, I am old and quite gristly: a fat white, not good to eat.'

As we may see, Danglars still had enough wits about him to joke.

At the same moment, as if to prove that he was no ogre, his guard sat down in front of the cell door, took a loaf of black bread out of his haversack, with some onions and cheese, which he forthwith began to devour.

'Devil take me,' Danglars said, observing the bandit's dinner through the gaps in his door. 'Devil take me if I can understand how anyone could eat such filth.' He went and sat down on the goatskin, which reminded him of the smell of the first sentry's brandy.

However, it was all very well for Danglars to think that, but the secrets of nature are beyond our understanding and it may be that the crudest of victuals can address a tangible invitation in quite eloquent terms to a hungry stomach.

Suddenly Danglars felt that at this moment his was a bottomless pit: the man seemed less ugly, the bread less black and the cheese less rancid.

Finally, those raw onions, the repulsive foodstuff of savages, began to evoke certain *sauces Robert*,[1] certain dishes of boiled beef and onions which his cook had adapted to more refined palates

when Danglars would tell him: 'Monsieur Deniseau, give us a spot
of plain home cooking today.'

He got up and went to bang on the door. The bandit looked up.
Danglars saw that he had been heard and banged louder.

'*Che cosa?*' the bandit asked.

'I say, I say, my good fellow,' Danglars said, tapping his fingers
against the door. 'Isn't it about time someone thought of feeding
me as well, eh?'

But either because he did not understand or because he had no
orders regarding Danglars' breakfast, the giant went back to his
meal.

Danglars' pride was wounded and, not wishing to compromise
himself any further with this brute, he lay down once more on the
goatskin without uttering another word.

Four hours went by. The giant was replaced by another bandit.
Danglars, who was suffering dreadful stomach cramps, quietly got
up, put his eye to the door and recognized the intelligent face of his
guide. It was indeed Peppino who was preparing to enjoy his guard
duty in as much comfort as possible, sitting down opposite the
door and placing between his legs an earthenware casserole which
contained some chick peas tossed in pork fat, hot and redolent.
Beside these chick peas, Peppino set down another pretty little
basket of Velletri grapes and a flask of Orvieto wine. Peppino was
something of a gourmet.

Danglars' mouth began to water as he watched these gastronomic
preparations. 'Ah, ha,' he thought. 'Let's see if this one is any more
amenable than the last.' And he hammered gently on his door.

'*On y va,*' the bandit said. Thanks to his association with Signor
Pastrini's house, he had eventually learned even idiomatic French;
so he came and opened the door.

Danglars recognized him as the man who had shouted at him in
such an enraged tone: 'Put your head in!' However, this was no
time for recriminations. On the contrary, he adopted his most
pleasant manner and said, with a gracious smile: 'I beg your pardon,
Monsieur, but am I not also to be given some dinner?'

'What!' Peppino exclaimed. 'Is Your Excellency hungry, by any
chance?'

'I like that "by any chance",' Danglars thought. 'It is now fully
twenty-four hours since I last ate anything.' And he added aloud,
shrugging his shoulders: 'Yes, I am hungry; in fact, very hungry.'

'So would Your Excellency like to eat?'

'Immediately, if possible.'

'Nothing simpler,' said Peppino. 'Here one can get whatever one wishes, if one pays, of course, as is customary among honest Christians.'

'Of course,' said Danglars. 'Though the fact is that people who arrest you and throw you in jail should at least feed their prisoners.'

'Oh, Excellency,' Peppino replied, 'that's not customary.'

'That's no argument,' Danglars said, hoping to tame his keeper with his good humour. 'But I shall have to make do with it. Now then, let me have something to eat.'

'At once, Excellency. What is your pleasure?' And Peppino put his bowl on the ground so that the fumes found their way directly into Danglars' nostrils. 'Give me your order.'

'Do you have kitchens here, then?' the banker asked.

'What! Do we have kitchens? The finest kitchens.'

'And cooks?'

'Superb cooks.'

'Well, then: fowl, fish or flesh – anything, as long as I can eat.'

'As Your Excellency pleases. Shall we say a chicken?'

'Yes, a chicken.'

Peppino drew himself up and cried as loudly as he could: 'A chicken for His Excellency!' His voice was still echoing under the vaults when a young man appeared, handsome, slim and half naked, like a fish porter in Antiquity. He bore in the chicken on a silver plate, balancing it on his head.

'This is just like the Café de Paris,' Danglars muttered.

'Here we are, Excellency,' Peppino said, taking the chicken from the young bandit and putting it down on a worm-eaten table which, with a stool and the goatskin bed, made up the entire furniture of the cell.

Danglars asked for a knife and fork.

'There you are, Excellency,' Peppino said, offering him a little knife with a rounded end and a boxwood fork. Danglars took the knife in one hand and the fork in the other, and set to work cutting up the piece of poultry.

'Excuse me, Excellency,' Peppino said, putting a hand on the banker's shoulder. 'Here we pay before eating: the customer may not be happy when he leaves . . .'

'Oh, I see,' thought Danglars. 'It's not like in Paris, quite apart from the fact that they are probably going to fleece me; but let's do things in style. Come now, I've always been told how cheap it is living in Italy. A chicken must be worth some twelve *sous* in Rome.'

'Here you are,' he said, throwing a *louis* to Peppino.

Peppino picked up the *louis*, and Danglars again put the knife on the bird.

'One moment, Excellency,' said Peppino, getting up. 'Your Excellency still owes me something.'

'Didn't I say they would fleece me?' Danglars muttered. But, resolving to make the best of this extortion, he asked: 'So, how much do I still owe you for this skinny old boiler?'

'Your Excellency has given me a *louis* on account.'

'A *louis*, on account, for a chicken?'

'Yes, indeed.'

'Come, you're joking.'

'That leaves only four thousand, nine hundred and ninety-nine *louis* that Your Excellency still owes me.'

Danglars stared wide-eyed at the announcement of this enormous pleasantry. 'Oh, very funny,' he muttered. 'Very funny indeed.' He was about to go back to cutting up the chicken, but Peppino grasped his right hand with his own left hand, while holding out the other.

'Come,' he said.

'You're not joking?' Danglars asked.

'We never joke, Excellency,' said Peppino, as serious as a Quaker.

'What! A hundred thousand francs for this chicken!'

'Excellency, you wouldn't believe how hard it is to raise poultry in these confounded caves.'

'Come, come,' said Danglars. 'I find this very entertaining ... Very amusing, I must say. But, as I'm hungry, let me eat. Here, there's another *louis* for yourself, my friend.'

'Then that will be only four thousand, nine hundred and ninety-eight *louis*,' Peppino said, with unaltered equanimity. 'If we are patient, we'll get there in the end.'

'Now, see here,' said Danglars, disgusted by this persistent determination to make fun of him, 'as far as that goes, never. Go to hell! You don't know the person you're dealing with.'

Peppino made a sign, and the young boy reached out and snatched away the chicken. Danglars threw himself back on the goatskin bed and Peppino shut the door, then went back to eating his chick peas.

Danglars could not see what Peppino was doing, but the clatter of the bandit's teeth left the prisoner in no doubt as to the nature of the exercise he was engaged in. It was quite clear that he was eating, and even that he was eating very noisily, like a badly brought-up young man.

'Brute!' Danglars said. Peppino pretended not to hear. Without even turning around, he went on eating at a very sensible pace. Danglars' stomach seemed to have as many holes in it as the barrel of the Danaids.[2] He couldn't believe that he would ever manage to fill it. However, he lasted for another half-hour, though it is true to say that that half-hour seemed to him like a century.

Then he got up again and went to the door.

'Come, Monsieur,' he said. 'Don't keep me on tenterhooks like this any longer. Just tell me straight away what you want of me.'

'But, Excellency, why not rather say what you want of us? Give us your orders and we shall carry them out.'

'Well, first, open the door.'

Peppino opened it.

'I want,' Danglars said, 'by God, I want to eat!'

'You're hungry?'

'As you very well know.'

'What would Your Excellency like to eat?'

'A piece of dry bread, since chicken is priceless in these accursed caves.'

'Bread! Very well,' said Peppino. And he called out: 'Ho, there, bring some bread!'

A young boy brought a roll.

'There you are,' said Peppino.

'How much?' Danglars asked.

'Four thousand, nine hundred and ninety-eight *louis*: You have two *louis*' credit.'

'What! A bread roll is a hundred thousand francs?'

'A hundred thousand,' said Peppino.

'But you asked me the same price for a chicken.'

'We don't offer an *à la carte* menu; only *prix fixe*. Whether you eat a lot or a little, ask for ten dishes or just one, it's still the same amount.'

'This joke again! My good friend, I tell you, this is absurd, it's ridiculous! Why not tell me at once that you want me to die of starvation: it would be quicker.'

'No, Excellency. You are the one who wants to commit suicide. Pay up and eat up.'

'What can I pay with, you frightful creature?' Danglars said in exasperation. 'Do you think I carry a hundred thousand francs around in my pocket?'

'You have five million and fifty thousand francs in your pocket, Excellency,' said Peppino. 'That is a hundred chickens at a hundred thousand francs and half a chicken at fifty thousand.'

Danglars shuddered and the scales fell from his eyes. It was still a joke, but he understood it at last. It is even true to say that he found it more piquant than he had a moment before.

'Come, come, now,' he said. 'If I give you those hundred thousand francs, will you at least consider us quits and let me eat in peace?'

'Of course,' said Peppino.

'But how can I give them to you?' Danglars asked, breathing more freely.

'Nothing could be easier. You have a credit with Messrs Thomson and French, Via dei Banchi, in Rome. Give us a bill for four thousand nine hundred and ninety-eight *louis* on those gentlemen, and our banker will cash it for us.'

Danglars at least wanted to show willing. He took the pen and paper which Peppino offered him, wrote out the order and signed it.

'There,' he said. 'That's a bill, payable to bearer.'

'And that's your chicken.'

Danglars cut into the fowl with a sigh. It seemed to him very thin for such a large sum of money. As for Peppino, he read the paper carefully, put it in his pocket and went on eating his chick peas.

CXVI

THE PARDON

The next day, Danglars was hungry again. The air of this cave was decidedly stimulating to the appetite, but the prisoner thought that today he would have no further expense. Being a thrifty man, he had hidden half of his chicken and a piece of his bread in the corner of the cell. But no sooner had he eaten them than he was thirsty. He had not thought of that.

He struggled against his thirst until he felt his parched tongue sticking to his palate. Then, unable to resist the fire devouring him, he called out.

The sentry opened the door; it was a new face. Danglars felt that it would be better to deal with a more familiar one and called for Peppino.

'Here I am, Excellency,' the bandit said, arriving promptly (which seemed a good omen to the banker). 'What would you like?'

'Something to drink,' the prisoner said.

'Excellency, you know that wine is ridiculously expensive in the region around Rome.'

'Then give me water,' said Danglars, trying to parry the blow.

'Oh, Excellency, water is even scarcer than wine. The drought has been so bad!'

'I see,' said Danglars. 'It appears that we are going to start that again.' Though he was smiling, to give the impression that he was joking, the wretch felt sweat beading on his forehead.

'Now, now, friend,' he continued, when Peppino made no response. 'I'm asking you for a glass of wine. Will you refuse me?'

'I've already told Your Excellency that we don't sell retail or by the glass,' said Peppino.

'Very well, give me a bottle.'

'Of which?'

'The cheaper.'

'They are both the same price.'

'Which is . . . ?'

'Twenty-five thousand francs a bottle.'

'Tell me,' said Danglars, with a bitterness that only Harpagon[1] could have noted on the scale of the human voice, 'Tell me that you want to skin me alive, it would be quicker than devouring me piecemeal.'

'Perhaps that is what the master intends,' said Peppino.

'Who is the master?'

'The one to whom you were taken the day before yesterday.'

'And where is he?'

'Here.'

'Let me see him.'

'That's easy.'

A moment later, Luigi Vampa was standing in front of Danglars. 'Did you call for me?' he asked his prisoner.

'Are you the leader of those who brought me here, Monsieur?'

'Yes, Excellency.'

'What ransom do you want from me? Tell me.'

'Just the five million you have on you.'

Danglars felt a dreadful shudder run through his heart. 'That is all I have in the world, Monsieur,' he said, 'and the remains of a vast fortune. If you take that away from me, take my life.'

'We have been forbidden to shed your blood, Excellency.'

'By whom?'

'By the person whom we obey.'

'So you do obey somebody?'

'Yes, a leader.'

'I thought that you yourself were the leader.'

'I am the leader of these men, but another is my leader.'

'And does this leader obey anyone?'

'Yes.'

'Whom?'

'God.'

Danglars thought for a moment. 'I don't understand,' he said.

'Possibly.'

'Did the leader tell you to treat me in this way?'

'Yes.'

'Why?'

'I don't know.'

'But my money will run out.'

'Probably.'

'Come, come,' said Danglars. 'Would you like a million?'

'No.'

'Two?'

'No.'

'Three million? Four? Come now, four million? I'll give it to you on condition you let me go.'

'Why do you offer us four million for something that is worth five?' said Vampa. 'That's usury, Signor Banker, if I'm not mistaken.'

'Take it all! Take it all, I say!' Danglars said. 'And kill me!'

'Come, come, Excellency, calm yourself. You will whip up your blood, and that will give you an appetite to eat a million a day. Be more economical, please!'

'But when I have no more money to pay you . . . !' Danglars said in exasperation.

'Then you'll go hungry.'

'Go hungry?' said Danglars, turning pale.

'Quite probably,' said Vampa with admirable equanimity.

'But you said you did not wish to kill me?'

'No.'

'Yet you do want to let me starve to death?'

'That's different.'

'Well, you wretches,' Danglars cried, 'I shall foil your vile schemes! If I have to die, I should rather get it over at once. Make me suffer, torture me, kill me, but you shall not have my signature again!'

'As you wish, Excellency,' said Vampa. And he left the cell.

With a roar of frustration Danglars threw himself down on his goatskin.

Who were these men? Who was their invisible leader? What plan were they carrying out against him? And when everyone else was able to buy freedom, why could he not do the same?

Oh, certainly, death, sudden and violent, was a good way to foil his implacable enemies, who seemed to be pursuing him with some incomprehensible desire for vengeance. Yes, but that meant dying! Perhaps for the first time in his long career, Danglars thought of death with a simultaneous desire and a fear of dying: the moment had come for him to look directly at the implacable spectre which hovers over every living creature and which, at every heartbeat, says to itself: You will die!

Danglars was like one of those wild animals that at first are excited by the hunt, then are driven to desperation and which sometimes, in their very desperation, manage to escape. It was of escape that Danglars was thinking.

But the walls were solid rock and in front of the only entrance to the cell a man was reading. Behind him could be seen the shapes of others with rifles, passing back and forth.

His determination not to sign lasted for two days, after which he asked for food and offered a million. He was served a magnificent dinner and they took his million.

From then on the unfortunate prisoner's life was one of continual rambling. He had suffered so much that he no longer wished to expose himself to suffering and he gave in to every demand. After twelve days, one afternoon when he had just eaten as he used to in the days when he had been rich, he did his accounts and discovered that he had signed so many bills to bearer that he had only 50,000 francs left.

His reaction to this discovery was an odd one. Having just given up five million, he tried to save these last 50,000 francs. Rather than give up his 50,000 francs, he resolved to suffer a life of privation; he had glimmers of hope that were close to madness. Having long forgotten God, he recalled only that God had some-times performed miracles: that the cave might collapse, that the pontifical *carabinieri* might discover this accursed retreat and come to his aid; that then he would have 50,000 francs left and that this was enough to prevent a man dying of hunger. He begged God to let him keep these 50,000 francs and, as he prayed, he wept.

Three days passed in which the name of God was constantly, if not in his heart, at least on his lips. From time to time he had moments of delirium in which he thought he could see, through the window, a miserable room in which an old man lay, dying, on a straw pallet. The old man too was dying of starvation.

On the fourth day he was no longer a man but a living corpse. He had grubbed up from the earth the smallest crumb from his previous meals and began to devour the matting which covered the earth.

Then he begged Peppino, as one might beg a guardian angel, to give him some food. He offered him a thousand francs for a mouthful of bread, but Peppino did not answer.

On the fifth day, he dragged himself to the door of the cell. 'Aren't you a Christian?' he said, hauling himself to his knees. 'Do you wish to murder a man who is your brother before God? Oh, my former friends, my former friends!' he muttered. And he fell, face down, on the ground.

Then, raising himself with a sort of despair, he cried: 'The leader! The leader!'

'Here I am,' said Vampa, suddenly appearing. 'What do you want now?'

'Take the last of my gold,' Danglars stammered, offering his pocket-book. 'And let me live here, in this cave. I am not asking for freedom, I am only asking to live.'

'So are you really suffering?' Vampa asked.

'Oh, yes! I am suffering, cruelly!'

'But there are men who have suffered more than you have.'

'I cannot believe it.'

'It is so! Those who died of hunger.'

Danglars thought of the old man whom he had seen through the windows of his mean room in his hallucinations, groaning on his bed. He beat his forehead against the ground, moaning: 'It's true, there are those who have suffered more than I do, but they at least were martyrs.'

'Do you at least repent?' asked a dark and solemn voice which made the hair stand up on Danglars' head. His weakened eyes tried to make out things in the darkness, and behind the bandit he saw a man wrapped in a cloak and half hidden by the shadow of a stone pillar.

'Of what must I repent?' Danglars stammered.

'Of the evil you have done,' said the same voice.

'Oh, yes, I do repent! I do!' Danglars cried, and he beat his breast with his emaciated fist.

'Then I pardon you,' said the man, throwing aside his cloak and taking a step into the light.

'The Count of Monte Cristo!' Danglars said, terror making him more pale than he had been a moment before from hunger and misery.

'You are mistaken. I am not the Count of Monte Cristo.'

'Who are you then?'

'I am the one whom you sold, betrayed and dishonoured. I am the one whose fiancée you prostituted. I am the one on whom you trampled in order to attain a fortune. I am the one whose father you condemned to starvation, and the one who condemned you to starvation, but who none the less forgives you, because he himself needs forgiveness. I am Edmond Dantès!'

Danglars gave a single cry and fell, prostrate.

'Get up,' said the count. 'Your life is safe. The same good fortune did not attend your two accomplices: one is mad, the other is dead. Keep your last fifty thousand francs, I give them to you. As for the five million you stole from the almshouses, they have already been returned by an anonymous donor.

'Now, eat and drink. This evening you are my guest.

'Vampa, when this man has had his fill, he will be free.'

Danglars remained prostrate, while the count walked away. When he looked up, he saw only a sort of shadow disappearing down the corridor, while the bandits bowed as it passed.

As the count had ordered, Vampa served Danglars: he brought him the best wine and finest fruits of Italy and, having put him into his post-chaise, left him on the road, with his back to a tree.

He stayed there until dawn, not knowing where he was.

When day broke, he found that he was near a stream. He was thirsty, so he dragged himself over to it. Leaning over the water to drink, he observed that his hair had turned grey.

CXVII

OCTOBER THE FIFTH

It was around six in the evening, and light the colour of opal, pierced by the golden rays of the autumn sun, spread over a bluish sea.

The heat of the day had gradually expired and one was starting to feel that light breeze which seems like the breath of nature awaking after the burning midday siesta: that delicious breath that cools the Mediterranean coast and carries the scent of trees from shore to shore, mingled with the acrid scent of the sea.

Over the huge lake that extends from Gibraltar to the Dardanelles and from Tunis to Venice, a light yacht, cleanly and elegantly shaped, was slipping through the first mists of evening. Its movement was that of a swan opening its wings to the wind and appearing to glide across the water. At once swift and graceful, it advanced, leaving behind a phosphorescent wake.

Bit by bit, the sun, whose last rays we were describing, fell below the western horizon; but, as though confirming the brilliant fantasies of mythology, its prying flames reappeared at the crest of every wave as if to reveal that the god of fire had just hidden his face in the bosom of Amphitrite, who tried in vain to hide her lover in the folds of her azure robe.

Though there was apparently not enough wind to lift the ringlets on a girl's head, the yacht was travelling fast. Standing in its bow, a tall, bronzed man was staring wide-eyed at the dark, conical mass of land rising from the midst of the waves like a Catalan hat.

'Is that Monte Cristo?' asked the traveller, who appeared to be in command of the yacht, in a grave and melancholy voice.

'Yes, Excellency,' said the master. 'We are just reaching the end of our journey.'

'The end of our journey!' the traveller muttered, with an indefinable note of dejection. Then he added under his breath: 'Yes, this is port.' And he relapsed into thoughts that expressed themselves in a smile sadder than tears.

A few minutes later he saw an onshore light that was immediately extinguished, and the sound of a gunshot reached the yacht.

'Excellency,' the master said, 'that is the signal from onshore. Would you like to reply?'

'What signal?' he asked.

The master pointed towards the island, from the side of which a single whitish plume of smoke was rising, spreading and breaking up as it mounted into the sky.

'Oh, yes,' the traveller said, as if waking from a dream. 'Give it to me.'

The master offered him a ready-loaded carbine. He took it, slowly raised it and fired into the air.

Ten minutes later they were furling the sails and dropping anchor five hundred yards outside a little port. The boat was already in the sea, with four oarsmen and a pilot. The traveller got in, but instead of sitting in the prow, which was furnished with a blue carpet, he remained standing with his arms crossed. The oarsmen waited, with their oars poised above the water, like birds drying their wings.

'Go!' said the traveller.

The eight oars dipped into the sea simultaneously without a single splash and the boat, driven forward, began to glide rapidly across the water. In no time they were in a small bay, formed by a natural fold in the rock. The boat grated on a fine sandy bottom.

'Excellency,' the pilot said, 'climb on the shoulders of two of our men; they will take you ashore.'

The young man replied to the invitation with a gesture of complete indifference, put his legs over the side of the boat and slid into the water, which came up to his waist.

'Oh, Excellency,' the pilot muttered, 'you are wrong to do that. The master will tell us off.'

The young man continued to plough forward towards the shore, following two sailors who chose the best route. After thirty paces they had landed. He shook his feet on dry land and looked around for the path that he would probably be told to follow, because it was quite dark.

Just as he was turning his head, a hand rested on his shoulder and he shuddered at hearing a voice say: 'Good day, Maximilien. You are punctual. Thank you.'

'It's you, Count,' the young man exclaimed, with a movement which could have been one of joy, grasping Monte Cristo's hand in both of his.

'Yes; as you see, as punctual as you. But you are soaking wet, my dear fellow. You must get changed, as Calypso used to say to Telemachus.[1] Come, I've got rooms all ready for you where you can forget tiredness and cold.'

Monte Cristo saw that Morrel was looking around. He waited. Indeed the young man was surprised that he had not heard a word from those who had brought him; he had not paid them, and yet they had left. He could even hear the plashing of the oars on the little boat taking them back to the yacht.

'Ah, you're looking for your sailors?' said the count.

'Yes, of course. They left without me giving them anything.'

'Don't bother about that, Maximilien,' Monte Cristo said with a laugh. 'I have a deal with the navy, so that there is no charge for passage to my island. I'm an account customer, as they say in civilized countries.'

Morrel looked at him with astonishment.

'Count,' he said, 'you are not the same as you were in Paris.'

'In what way?'

'Why, here you laugh.'

Monte Cristo's brow clouded immediately. 'You are right to recall me to myself,' he said. 'Seeing you again was a pleasure for me and I forgot that every pleasure is transitory.'

'Oh, no, no, Count!' Morrel exclaimed, once more grasping his friend's hand with both of his. 'Please do laugh. Be happy and prove to me by your indifference that life is only a burden for those who suffer. Oh, you are generous, you are kind, you are good, my friend; and you pretend to be happy only to give me strength.'

'You are wrong, Morrel,' said Monte Cristo. 'I really was happy.'

'Then you have forgotten me. So much the better!'

'What do you mean?'

'Because you know, my dear friend, I say to you, as the gladiator would say to the sublime emperor on entering the arena: "Those who are about to die salute you!" '

'You are not consoled, then?' Monte Cristo asked, with a strange look.

'Oh, did you really think I could be?' Morrel answered, with one full of reproach.

'Listen,' the count said, 'and listen carefully to what I am about to say. You don't think I am some vulgar babbler, a rattle that gives out a crude and meaningless sound. When I asked you if you were consoled, I was speaking to you as a man for whom the human heart holds no secrets. Well, then, Morrel, let us sound the depths of your heart. Is it still that ardent impatience of pain that makes the body leap like a lion bitten by a mosquito? Is it still that raging thirst that can be sated only in the tomb? Is it that ideal notion of regret that launches the living man out of life in pursuit of death? Or is it merely the prostration of exhausted courage, the ennui that stifles the ray of hope as it tries to shine? Is it the loss of memory, bringing an impotence of tears? Oh, my friend, if it is that, if you can no longer weep, if you think your numbed heart is dead, if you have no strength left except in God and no eyes except for heaven – then, my friend, let us put aside words that are too narrow to contain the meanings our soul would give them. Maximilien, you are consoled, pity yourself no longer.'

'Count,' Morrel said, in a voice that was at once soft and firm. 'Count, listen to me, as you would listen to a man pointing towards the earth and with his eyes raised to heaven. I came here to join you so that I might die in the arms of a friend. Admittedly there are those whom I love: I love my sister Julie, I love her husband, Emmanuel. But I need someone to open strong arms to me and smile at my last moments. My sister would burst into tears and faint; I should see her suffer and I have suffered enough. Emmanuel would seize the weapon from my hands and fill the house with his cries. You, Count, have given me your word; you are more than a man: I should call you a god if you were not mortal. You will lead me gently and tenderly, I know, to the gates of death . . .'

'My friend,' said the count, 'I have one lingering doubt. Will you be so weak as to pride yourself on the exhibition of your grief?'

'No, no, I am a plain man,' Morrel said, offering the count his hand. 'See: my pulse is not beating any faster or slower than usual. No, I feel I am at the end of the road; I shall go no further. You told me to wait and hope. Do you know what you have done, wise as you are? I have waited a month, which means I have suffered a month. I hoped – man is such a poor and miserable creature – I hoped, for what? I don't know: something unimaginable, absurd, senseless, a miracle . . . but what? God alone knows, for it was He who diluted our reason with that madness called hope. Yes, I waited; yes, Count, I hoped; and in the past quarter of an hour, while we have been speaking, you have unwittingly broken and tortured my heart a hundred times, for each of your words proved to me that I have no hope left. Oh, Count! Let me rest in the sweet and voluptuous bosom of death!'

Morrel spoke the last words with an explosion of energy that made the count shudder.

'My friend,' he continued, when the count did not reply, 'you named October the fifth as the end of the reprieve that you asked me to accept . . . And, my friend, this is the fifth . . .'

Morrel took out his watch. 'It is nine o'clock. I have three hours left to live.'

'Very well,' Monte Cristo replied. 'Come with me.'

Morrel followed mechanically, and they were already in the grotto before Morrel had realized it. He found carpets under his feet. A door opened, he was enveloped in perfumes and a bright light dazzled him. He stopped, reluctant to go on. He was wary of being weakened by the delights around him.

Monte Cristo pulled him gently forward. 'Is it not appropriate,' he said, 'for us to spend the three hours we have left like those ancient Romans who, when they were condemned to death by Nero, their emperor and their heir, would sit at a table decked with flowers and breathe in death with the scent of heliotropes and roses?'

Morrel smiled and said: 'As you wish. Death is still death, that is to say forgetfulness, rest, the absence of life and so the absence of pain.'

He sat down and Monte Cristo took his place in front of him.

They were in the wonderful dining-room that we have already described, where marble statues carried baskets full of fruit and flowers on their heads. Morrel had looked vaguely at all this, and had probably seen nothing of it.

'Let's speak man to man,' he said, staring hard at the count.

'Go on,' the latter replied.

'Count, you are an encyclopedia of all human knowledge, and you strike me as someone who has come down from a more advanced and wiser world than our own.'

'There is some truth in that, Morrel,' the count said with a melancholy smile that transfigured his face. 'I have come from a planet called sorrow.'

'I believe whatever you tell me, without trying to elucidate its meaning, Count. The proof is that you told me to live, and I have lived. You told me to hope, and I almost hoped. So I shall dare to ask you, as if you had already died once before: Count, does it hurt very much?'

Monte Cristo looked at Morrel with an infinite expression of tenderness. 'Yes,' he said. 'Yes, no doubt, it does hurt, if you brutally shatter the mortal envelope when it is crying out to live. If you make your flesh scream under the imperceptible teeth of a dagger; if you drive an insensitive bullet, always ready to meander on its way, through your brain – which suffers from the merest jolt; yes, indeed, you will suffer and leave life in the most horrifying way, in a desperate agony that will make you ready to think it better than rest bought at such a price.'

'I understand,' said Morrel. 'Death has its secrets of pain and pleasure, like life; it is just a question of knowing what they are.'

'Precisely, Maximilien: you have hit the nail on the head. Death, according to the care we take to be on good or bad terms with it, is either a friend which will rock us as gently as a nursing mother or an enemy which will savagely tear apart body and soul. One day, when our world has lived another thousand years, when people have mastered all the destructive forces of nature and harnessed them to the general good of mankind, and when, as you just said, men have learnt the secrets of death, then death will be as sweet and voluptuous as sleep in a lover's arms.'

'And you, Count, if you wanted to die, would you know how to die in that way?'

'I should.'

Morrel reached out his hand. 'Now I understand,' he said, 'why you have brought me here to this desolate island, in the midst of the ocean, to this subterranean palace, a tomb that a Pharaoh would envy. It was because you love me, wasn't it, Count? You love me enough to give me one of those deaths that you spoke of just now, a death without agony, a death that will allow me to expire with Valentine's name on my lips and your hand in mine?'

'You are right, Morrel,' the count said, simply. 'That's how I see it.'

'Thank you. The idea that tomorrow I shall no longer suffer is like balm to my heart.'

'Is there nothing you will miss?' Monte Cristo asked.

'No,' Morrel replied.

'Not even me?' the count asked, with deep feeling.

Morrel stopped, his clear eye suddenly clouded, then shone with even greater brilliance. A large tear rolled from it and left a silver trace across his cheek.

'What!' the count exclaimed. 'There is something you will regret leaving on earth, yet you want to die!'

'Oh, I beg you,' Morrel cried in a weak voice. 'Not a word, Count, do not prolong my agony.'

The count feared that Morrel was weakening, and this belief momentarily revived the terrible doubt that had already once struck him in the Château d'If. 'I am engaged in giving this man back his happiness,' he thought. 'I consider that restitution is a weight thrown back into the scales in the opposite tray from the one where I cast evil. Now, suppose I am wrong and this man is not unhappy enough to deserve happiness. Alas, what would happen to me – I, who am unable to atone for evil except by doing good?'

'Listen to me, Morrel,' he said. 'Your grief is immense, I can see that; but you believe in God; perhaps you do not wish to risk the salvation of your soul?'

Morrel smiled sadly: 'Count,' he said, 'you know that I do not exaggerate; but, I swear, my soul is no longer my own.'

'Listen, Morrel,' the count said. 'I have no living relative, as you know. I have grown accustomed to thinking of you as my son. Well, to save my son, I would sacrifice my life and, even more readily, my fortune.'

'What do you mean?'

'I mean, Morrel, that you want to leave life because you do not know all the pleasures that life gives to the very rich. Morrel, I possess nearly a hundred million; you can have it. With that much money you could achieve anything you desire. Are you ambitious? Every career is open to you. Stir up the world, change it, commit any kind of folly, be a criminal if you must, but live!'

'Count, I have your word,' the young man replied coldly. 'And,' he added, taking out his watch, 'it is half-past eleven.'

'Could you do such a thing, Morrel, in my house, before my eyes?'

'Then let me leave,' Maximilien said, his face clouding. 'Or I shall think you don't love me for myself, but for you.' And he got up.

'Very well, then,' said Monte Cristo, his face lightening at these words. 'You want it, Morrel, and you are immovable. Yes, you are profoundly unhappy and, as you said, only a miracle could cure you. Sit down, and wait.'

The young man obeyed. Monte Cristo got up in his turn and went to open a carefully locked cupboard, the key to which he wore on a gold chain. He took out a little silver casket, magnificently sculpted and modelled with four arched figures at the four corners, like pining caryatids, shaped like women, symbols of angels reaching for heaven.

He put the casket down on the table, then opened it, taking out a little gold box, the lid of which was raised by pressure on a hidden spring.

This box contained a half-congealed, oily substance, its colour indefinable because of the shining gold and the sapphires, rubies and emeralds encrusting it. It was like a shimmering mass of blue, purple and gold.

The count took a small quantity of the substance on an enamelled spoon and offered it to Morrel, fixing his eyes on him. Only now could it be seen that the substance was green in colour.

'This is what you asked me for,' he said. 'This is what I promised you.'

'While I still have life,' the young man said, taking the spoon from Monte Cristo's hands, 'I thank you from the bottom of my heart.'

The count took a second spoon and dipped once more into the gold box.

'What are you doing, my dear friend?' Morrel asked, grasping his hand.

'Why, Morrel,' the other said, with a smile. 'God forgive me, but I think that I am as weary of life as you are, and while the opportunity presents itself . . .'

'Stop!' the young man cried. 'Oh, you who love and are loved, you who can trust in hope, oh, don't you do what I am about to do. For you, it would be a crime. Farewell, my noble and generous friend. I shall tell Valentine all that you have done for me.' And slowly, without any more hesitation than a pressure on the left hand which he was holding out to the count, Morrel swallowed – or, rather, savoured – the mysterious substance that Monte Cristo had offered him.

Then both men fell silent. Ali, noiseless and attentive, brought tobacco and pipes, served coffee and then vanished.

Little by little the lamps paled in the hands of the marble statues holding them and the perfume from the censers seemed less pervasive to Morrel. Opposite him, Monte Cristo was watching him through the dark, and he could see nothing except the burning of the count's eyes.

The young man was overwhelmed with an immense pain. He felt the hookah fall from his hands and the objects around him gradually lost their shape and colour. His clouded eyes seemed to see doors and curtains opening in the walls.

'My friend,' he said, 'I feel I am dying. Thank you.'

He made one last effort to hold out his hand, but it fell, powerless, beside him.

And now it seemed to him that Monte Cristo was smiling, no longer with that strange and terrifying smile that had several times allowed him to glimpse the mysteries of that profound soul, but with the tender compassion of a father towards the follies of his child.

At the same time the count was growing before his eyes. His figure almost doubled in size, outlined against the red hangings; he had thrown back his black hair and stood proudly like one of those avenging angels with which the wicked are threatened on Judgement Day.

Morrel, beaten, overwhelmed, slumped back in his chair. A silky torpor filled his every vein. His mind was refurnished, as it were, by a change of thoughts, just like a new pattern appearing in a kaleidoscope. Lying back, panting, excited, he felt nothing more living in him apart from this dream. He seemed to be plunging directly into the vague delirium that precedes that other unknown, called death.

Once again he tried to reach out to take the count's hand, but this time his own would not even budge. He tried to utter a last goodbye, but his tongue turned heavily in his mouth, like a stone blocking the entrance to a sepulchre. Hard as he tried, he could not keep his languid eyes open; yet behind their lids there was an image that he recognized despite the darkness which he felt had enveloped him. It was the count, who had just opened the door.

At once, an immense burst of light flooded from an adjoining room – or, rather, a wonderful palace – into the room where Morrel was abandoning himself to his gentle death-throes. And then, on the threshold of that other chamber, between the two rooms, he saw a woman of miraculous beauty. Pale and sweetly smiling, she seemed like an angel of mercy casting out the angel of vengeance.

'Is heaven already opening its gate to me?' thought the dying man. 'This angel is like the one I lost.'

Monte Cristo pointed the young woman to the sofa where Morrel was lying, and she stepped forward with her hands clasped and smiling lips. 'Valentine! Valentine!' Morrel cried, in the depths of his soul. But his throat did not utter a sound and, as though all his strength had been concentrated on that inner feeling, he gave a sigh and closed his eyes.

Valentine dashed forward. Morrel's lips moved again.

'He is calling you,' said the count. 'He is calling you from the depth of his sleep, the man to whom you have entrusted your fate and from whom death tried to separate you; but fortunately I was there and I overcame death. Valentine, from now on you must never be separated on this earth because, to rejoin you, he would leap into his grave. Without me, you would both have died. I give you back to one another; may God credit me with these two lives that I have saved!'

Valentine clasped Monte Cristo by the hand and, with an irresistible burst of joy, put it to her lips.

'Yes, yes,' he said. 'Thank me. Oh, tell me over and over again, never tire of telling me that I have made you happy. You do not know how much I need the certainty of that!'

'Oh, yes, I thank you with all my soul!' Valentine said. 'And if you doubt the sincerity of my thanks, ask Haydée, ask my dear sister Haydée, who has made me wait patiently since our departure from France, talking to me of you, until this happy day that has now dawned.'

'Do you love Haydée?' Monte Cristo asked, with ill-disguised emotion.

'Oh, yes, with all my heart!'

'Then, Valentine, listen to me,' said the count. 'I have a favour to beg of you.'

'Of me! Good heavens, am I fortunate enough for that?'

'You called Haydée your sister. Let her be your sister indeed, Valentine. Give her everything that you think you owe to me. Protect her, you and Morrel, because . . .' (and here the count's voice was almost stifled in his throat) '. . . because from now on she will be alone in the world.'

'Alone in the world!' repeated a voice from behind the place where the count was standing. 'Why?'

Monte Cristo turned and saw Haydée, pale and ice-cold, giving him a look of utter disbelief.

'Because tomorrow, my child, you will be free,' he replied. 'Because you will resume your proper place in the world and because I do not want my fate to cloud your own. You are the daughter of a prince: I am restoring your father's wealth and your father's name to you!'

Haydée's face was drained of colour. She opened her translucent hands like a virgin recommending her soul to God, and said, in a voice harsh with tears: 'So, my Lord, you are leaving me?'

'Haydée, Haydée, you are young and beautiful. Forget even my name, and be happy.'

'Very well,' said Haydée. 'Your orders will be carried out, my lord. I shall forget even your name, and I shall be happy.' And she took a pace backwards, to leave the room.

'Oh, my God!' cried Valentine, who was supporting Morrel's numbed head on her shoulder. 'Can't you see how pale she is? Don't you realize what she is suffering?'

Haydée addressed her with a heartrending expression on her face: 'How do you expect him to understand me, my sister? He is my master, and I his slave. He has the right to see nothing.'

The count shuddered at the tone of this voice, which awoke the deepest fibres of his being. His eyes met those of the young woman and could not bear to look into them. 'My God, my God!' he said. 'Can what you hinted to me be true? Haydée, would you be happy then not to leave me?'

'I am young,' she answered softly. 'I love life, which you have always made so pleasant for me. I should be sorry to die.'

'Do you mean that if I were to leave you, Haydée . . .'

'Yes, my Lord, I should die!'

'Do you love me, then?'

'Oh, Valentine, he asks if I love him! Tell him: do you love Maximilien?'

The count felt his breast swell and his heart fill. He opened his arms and Haydée threw herself into them with a cry. 'Oh, yes! Oh, yes I love you!' she said. 'I love you as one loves a father, a brother, a husband! I love you as one loves life, and loves God, for you are to me the most beautiful, the best and greatest of created beings!'

'Let it be as you will, my sweet angel!' said the count. 'God, who roused me against my enemies and gave me victory, God, I can see, does not wish my victory to end with that regret. I wished to punish myself, but God wants to pardon me. So, love me, Haydée! Who knows? Perhaps your love will make me forget what I have to forget.'

'What are you saying, my Lord?' the young woman asked.

'I am saying that a word from you, Haydée, enlightened me more than twenty years of sage wisdom. I have only you left in the world, Haydée. It is through you that I am attached to life; through you I can suffer and through you I can be happy.'

'Do you hear that, Valentine?' Haydée cried. 'He says that through me he can suffer! Through me, when I would give my life for him!'

The count thought for a moment. 'Have I understood the truth? Oh, God! What matter! Reward or punishment, I accept my fate. Come, Haydée, come . . .' And putting his arm round the young woman's waist, he pressed Valentine's hand and disappeared.

About an hour passed in which, breathing heavily and staring, unable to speak, Valentine remained by Morrel's side. Finally she felt his heart beat, a barely perceptible breath passed his lips and the young man's whole body was shaken by that slight shudder which indicates returning life. Finally his eyes opened, though at first they stared wildly. Then sight returned, sharp and true, and, with it, feeling; and, with feeling, pain.

'Oh!' he wailed in a desperate voice. 'I am still alive! The count deceived me!' And his hand reached for a knife on the table.

'My friend,' said Valentine, with her irresistible smile, 'wake up and look towards me.'

Morrel gave a great cry and, delirious, full of doubt, dazzled as though by some celestial vision, he fell on both knees . . .

The next day, with the first rays of sunlight, Morrel and Valentine were walking arm in arm on the shore, Valentine telling Morrel how Monte Cristo had appeared in her room, how he had revealed everything to her, how he had made her unveil the criminal and, finally, how he had miraculously saved her from death, while letting everyone believe that she was dead.

They had found the door to the grotto open and had gone out. The last stars were still shining in the blue of the morning sky. And, in the half-light of a cluster of rocks, Morrel saw a man waiting for a sign to come over to them. He pointed him out to Valentine.

'Oh, that's Jacopo,' she said, motioning to him to join them. 'The captain of the yacht.'

'Do you have something to tell us?' Morrel asked.

'I have this letter to give you on behalf of the count.'

'From the count!' the two young people exclaimed in unison.

'Yes, read it.'

Morrel opened the letter and read:

MY DEAR MAXIMILIEN,

There is a felucca lying at anchor for you. Jacopo will take you to Leghorn where Monsieur Noirtier is awaiting his granddaughter, whom he wishes to bless before she follows you to the altar. Everything that is in this grotto, my friend, my house in the Champs-Elysées and my little country house in Le Tréport are a wedding present from Edmond Dantès to the son of his master, Morrel. Mademoiselle de Villefort must have half of it, because I beg her to give the poor people of Paris whatever money she has coming to her from her father, who has become mad, and her brother, who died last September with her stepmother.

Tell the angel who will watch over your life, Morrel, to pray sometimes for a man who, like Satan, momentarily thought himself the equal of God and who, with all the humility of a Christian, came to realize that in God's hands alone reside supreme power and infinite wisdom. These prayers may perhaps ease the remorse that he takes with him in the depth of his heart.

As for you, Morrel, this is the whole secret of my behaviour towards you: there is neither happiness nor misfortune in this world, there is merely the comparison between one state and another, nothing more. Only someone who has suffered the deepest misfortune is capable of experiencing the heights of felicity. Maximilien, you must needs have wished to die, to know how good it is to live.

So, do live and be happy, children dear to my heart, and never forget that, until the day when God deigns to unveil the future to mankind, all human wisdom is contained in these two words: 'wait' and 'hope'!

Your friend

EDMOND DANTÈS

Count of Monte Cristo.

While he was reading this letter, which informed her of her father's madness and the death of her brother, neither of which she had known until then, Valentine went pale and gave a painful sigh; tears, no less touching for being silent, ran down her cheeks. She had purchased her happiness at a high price.

Morrel looked around him anxiously. 'But the count really is being too generous,' he said. 'Valentine will be happy with my modest fortune. Where is the count, my friend? Take me to him.'

Jacopo pointed to the horizon.

'Why! What do you mean?' Valentine asked. 'Where is the count? Where is Haydée?'

'Look,' said Jacopo.

The two young people looked in the direction towards which the sailor was pointing and, on the dark-blue line on the horizon that separated the sky from the Mediterranean, they saw a white sail, as large as a gull's wing.

'He is gone!' cried Morrel. 'Gone! Farewell, my friend! My father!'

'Yes, he is gone,' Valentine muttered. 'Farewell, my friend! Farewell, my sister!'

'Who knows if we shall ever see them again?' Morrel said, wiping away a tear.

'My dearest,' said Valentine, 'has the count not just told us that all human wisdom was contained in these two words – "wait" and "hope"?'

Notes

I
MARSEILLE – ARRIVAL

1. *Fort Saint-Jean*: The entrance to the old harbour at Marseille is guarded by two forts, the Fort Saint-Jean on the north and the Fort Saint-Nicholas on the south. The Pharo lies west of the Fort Saint-Nicholas, and Les Catalans south-west. In the standard text, some place-names are misspelt ('Morgion' for 'Morgiou', etc.). These have been corrected, to accord with Schopp (1993).

The new harbour was under construction, north of Fort Saint-Jean, at the time when the novel was published. The city rises away from the old harbour, or Vieux Port, forming – in the words of *Murray's Handbook for Travellers in France* (London, 1847) 'a basin or amphitheatre, terminating only with the encircling chain of hills. From this disposition of the ground, the port becomes the sewer of the city – the receptacle of all its filth, stagnating in a tideless sea and under a burning sun . . . The stench emanating from it at times is consequently intolerable, except for natives . . .'

On the whole, Marseille was not considered attractive for tourists, and Dumas' novel did a good deal to enhance its image.

2. *supercargo*: On a merchant ship, the officer in charge of the cargo and of finances.

3. *for Marshal Bertrand*: Marshal Bertrand (1773–1844) was one of Napoleon's marshals. He followed the emperor to exile on Elba.

4. *the Italian proverb: chi ha compagno, ha padrone*: 'Whoever has a partner, has a master'.

II
FATHER AND SON

1. *a hundred louis*: All sums of money have been left as in the original text. The *louis* was a gold coin worth 24 francs: the franc had become the

standard unit of currency after 1795, divided into 100 *centimes* (or 10 *décimes*). However, a number of denominations continued in circulation, including the *louis*, the *livre* (equal to the franc), the *écu* and others.

Equivalents are hard to assess. The exchange rate, in the first half of the nineteenth century, was 25 francs to the pound sterling (so one *louis* was worth just under a pound). The fare by mail coach from Paris to Marseille, via Lyon, was around 145 francs, or nearly 6 pounds (though, as we see in Chapter CVI, Albert manages to do it for 114 francs, by using river transport for part of the journey). This may sound like a bargain to travellers on French Railways, but one must remember (as Coward points out in his edition of the 1846 translation) that a curé's stipend was only 1,000 francs (£40) a year.

IV

THE PLOT

1. *The Flood . . . water drink*: A couplet from Louis-Philippe de Ségur's *Chanson morale*.
2. *crown prosecutor*: There is no English equivalent to the office of *procureur du roi*, who was, broadly speaking, the officer responsible for investigating crimes and instituting criminal proceedings on behalf of the state. In the early nineteenth century, the *procureur* in Marseille was assisted by five deputies, or *substituts*.
3. *Murat*: Joachim Murat (1767–1815), one of Napoleon's marshals.

V

THE BETROTHAL

1. *commissioner of police*: The *commissaire de police* was responsible for policing in a given administrative district.

VI

THE DEPUTY CROWN PROSECUTOR

1. *a god*: Napoleon Bonaparte (1769–1821) was an officer in the pre-revolutionary army, commissioned lieutenant in 1785. After the abolition of the Bourbon monarchy and the execution of King Louis XVI in 1793, he had a spectacular career in the revolutionary army, becoming a general by the age of twenty-seven and leading the French armies in Egypt in 1798.

In the following year, he organized the coup d'état that made him First Consul, then Consul for life (1802) and finally Emperor (1804).

To some, Napoleon's foreign conquests and grandiose style seemed to herald a new era of glory for France; to others, including some in the countries annexed to France, he appeared to be carrying forward the revolutionary ideals of liberty and equality; to French liberals, he appeared an increasingly autocratic tyrant; and by monarchists, of whatever country, he was seen as merely an upstart and a usurper. His disastrous Russian campaign (1812) led ultimately to his abdication in April 1814 and his exile on the Mediterranean island of Elba, where he was allowed to retain his title of Emperor and sovereignty over its inhabitants. Meanwhile the Bourbon king, Louis XVIII, was restored to the throne.

In March 1815 (the time when the novel begins), Napoleon escaped from Elba. The army rallied to him, the king fled and the empire was restored for the brief period known as the Hundred Days, which ended (18 June 1815) with the victory of the allied coalition at Waterloo. Napoleon again abdicated and was exiled to the Atlantic outpost of St Helena.

Louis XVIII regained his throne and was succeeded on his death (1824) by his brother, Charles X. This undistinguished Second Restoration ended in 1830 with the July Revolution, which installed another branch of the royal family, under King Louis-Philippe. Most of those who lived through this period found it stale and inglorious after the excitements of the Revolution and the victories of the empire, and its writers (Stendhal, Musset, Vigny, Lamartine, Hugo) reflect this sense of disillusionment in various ways. In fact, the Restoration was a time of considerable intellectual ferment, from the realm of academic, scientific and historical enquiry to the expansion of the periodical press, theatres and other forms of popular entertainment, and the ideological battles over Romanticism in literature and the arts.

2. *Joséphine*: Joséphine de Beauharnais (1763–1814), Napoleon's first wife, whom he divorced in 1809 because she could not bear him an heir.

3. *the Cross of Saint Louis*: Under the royalist regime, the state decoration equivalent to the orders of the Legion of Honour (which Napoleon instituted in 1802).

4. *the exile of Hartwell*: Louis XVIII, as Count of Provence, lived at Hartwell in Buckinghamshire from 1809 to 1814. Dumas portrays him (in the next chapter) as a pedantic classical scholar, incapable of managing his country's affairs.

5. *the 9th Thermidor and the 4th April 1814*: The first of these dates, given according to the republican calendar which replaced the Christian calendar in France from 1703 to 1806, was the day on which Robespierre fell; the second was that of Napoleon's abdication. To a monarchist, both would have been happy events.

6. *a Girondin*: A member of the moderate party under the Revolution, which was opposed to the Terror and was overthrown by Robespierre in

June 1793. This seems to be an error by Dumas: elsewhere, it is made clear that Noirtier is a member of the more extreme sect, the Jacobins.

7. *two thousand leagues*: Approximately 8,000 kilometres. A league is about 4 kilometres (or 2½ miles).

8. *the poor Duc d'Enghien*: Louis-Antoine-Henri de Bourbon, Duc d'Enghien (1772–1804), went into exile at the time of the Revolution and lived in Germany as one of the leaders of the anti-revolutionary armies. In 1804 he was kidnapped (almost certainly on Napoleon's order and in contravention of international law), tried in Vincennes on a charge of conspiracy, and shot. He became a martyr of the opposition to Napoleon.

9. *Aesculapius*: Roman god of healing and medicine.

VII

THE INTERROGATION

1. *carbonari*: Members of a secret society formed to combat the annexation of northern Italy by France under Napoleon and, later, to struggle for freedom from Austria. A meeting (of twenty members) was called a *vente*.

VIII

THE CHÂTEAU D'IF

1. *the Château d'If*: The island fortress, made famous by Dumas' novel, had in reality only one notorious prisoner, the Comte de Mirabeau, who was sent there under the Royalist regime for debt.

2. *the abbé*: Originally (like the English 'abbot') this meant the head of a monastery; but after the Middle Ages it came to be used of any ecclesiastic, usually one who had not taken priestly vows.

IX

THE EVENING OF THE BETROTHAL

1. *the fatal stamp of which Virgil speaks*: Virgil, *Aeneid*, IV, ll. 70–74, referring to a deer wounded by a hunter's arrow.

2. *Hoffmann*: Ernst Theodor Amadeus Hoffmann (1776–1822), German author and composer, the writer of a series of fantastic tales which greatly influenced the Romantic movement (and inspired Offenbach's opera, *Tales of Hoffmann*).

X

THE LITTLE CABINET IN THE TUILERIES

1. *Louis-Philippe*: Louis-Philippe, Duc d'Orléans (1773–1850), became king after the Revolution of July 1830 (see note 1 to Chapter VI).
2. *Gryphius*: An edition of Horace's poems published in Lyons in 1540. The details are supposed to reinforce the idea of Louis as a pedantic old man, more interested in his books than in affairs of state.
3. *'Canimus surdis'*: 'We sing for the deaf'. A misquotation of Virgil, *Eclogues*, X, 8: 'We do not sing for the deaf'.
4. *Pastor quum trahiret*: 'As the shepherd was hurrying'; Horace, *Odes*, I, 15, line 1. This refers to Paris' abduction of Helen, Paris having been brought up by shepherds.
5. *'Mala ducis avi domum'*: 'Under evil auspices you are leading home'; Horace, *Odes*, I, 15, line 5. Again, this refers to Paris carrying Helen off to Troy (her abduction being the cause of the Trojan War).
6. *bella, horrida bella*: 'Wars, frightful wars'; Virgil, *Aeneid*, IV, line 86. Like the previous quotations, this is an indirect comment on the political situation and the threat of war, perhaps suggesting that Louis has a better understanding of events than it appears.
7. *prurigo*: Various types of skin disease, characterized by intense itching, are known under this name.
8. *two Virgilian shepherds*: Some of the *Eclogues* (or *Bucolics*), Virgil's pastoral poems, are written as dialogues between shepherds (e.g. the first, fifth, seventh, eighth and ninth), with the speakers responding to one another in carefully balanced passages.
9. *grognards*: 'Grumblers', 'gripers', 'grousers'; the name given to the loyal old guard of Napoleon's army.
10. *Molli fugiens anhelitu*: 'Thou shalt flee, panting and weak'; Horace, *Odes*, I, 15, line 31. Nereus is prophesying that Paris will flee from the Greek hero Diomedes.
11. *'Justum et tenacem propositi virum'*: 'The man who is firm and just in his intentions', Horace, *Odes*, III, 3, line 1.

XII

FATHER AND SON

1. *Arcole, Marengo and Austerlitz*: Battles in which Napoleon defeated the successive coalitions against him.

XIII
THE HUNDRED DAYS

1. *the Hundred Days*: See note 1 to Chapter VI.

XIV
THE RAVING PRISONER AND THE MAD ONE

1. *one of Marcellus' soldiers*: The geometer Archimedes directed the defence of his native city of Syracuse against the Romans, led by Marcellus. When Syracuse fell (212 BC), 'the Roman general gave strict orders to his soldiers not to hurt Archimedes, and even offered a reward to him who brought him alive and safe into his presence. All these precautions were useless: he was so deeply engaged in solving a problem, that he was even ignorant that the soldiers were in possession of the town; and a soldier, without knowing who he was, killed him . . .' (Lemprière, *Classical Dictionary*, 1828).

2. *Abbé Faria*: In creating this fictional character, Dumas has drawn on the personality of a real Portuguese cleric, José-Custodio de Faria (1756–1819), an eccentric figure in Parisian society in the early years of the century because of his experiments with hypnotism and magnetism. A student of Swedenborg and Mesmer, he lectured on hypnotism in Paris from 1813 onwards.

XV
NUMBER 34 AND NUMBER 27

1. *Martin's Babylonian scenes*: The English artist John Martin (1789–1854) specialized in vast and spectacular canvases of biblical subjects, including *The Fall of Babylon* (1819). They were well known from lithographs.

2. *Ugolino*: Dante's *Inferno*, XXXII, 124–9. Count Ugolino Della Gherardesca was the leader of the Guelph (pro-papal) faction in Pisa, but fell victim to a conspiracy led by Archbishop Ruggieri. In 1289, with his sons and grandsons, he was walled up in the Torre della Fame in the Piazza dei Cavalieri where, according to Dante, he resorted to cannibalism and as a punishment was condemned for eternity to gnaw at Ruggieri's skull.

3. *Belshazzar's feast*: Interrupted by a mysterious hand, writing the three fateful words on the wall, which the prophet Daniel interpreted as meaning the end of Belshazzar's reign as King of Babylon. See Daniel 5. The feast was another of John Martin's subjects, in a painting of 1821 (see note 1).

XVI

AN ITALIAN SCHOLAR

1. *Duc de Beaufort ... Latude from the Bastille*: Dumas used the escape of the Duc de Beaufort from Vincennes (1643) in his novel *Twenty Years After*. Abbé Dubuquoi escaped from the Bastille after being imprisoned in 1706, and Jean-Henri Latude twice escaped from the prison at Vincennes, after being arrested in 1749 for sending a box of powder to Madame de Pompadour, but was recaptured and spent a total of thirty-five years in prison. On his release, he wrote his memoirs, which made him famous.

2. *Lavoisier ... Cabanis*: Antoine-Laurent Lavoisier (1743–94) was a celebrated chemist. The physician Pierre-Jean-Georges Cabanis (1757–1808) influenced a number of writers, including Stendhal, with his theories on the nature of human psychology.

XVII

THE ABBÉ'S CELL

1. *lead us to wrongdoing*: Dumas shows Faria as essentially a follower of Jean-Jacques Rousseau (1712–78), who believed that human beings are born free and virtuous, but are corrupted by society.

2. *Descartes*: The philosopher René Descartes (1596–1650), who developed a pre-Newtonian theory of physics based on vortices of material particles, an extension of the atomic theories found in classical writers from Epicurus to Lucretius.

XVIII

THE TREASURE

1. *Cardinal Spada*: Cesare Spada, who purchased his cardinal's hat from Pope Alexander IV, was poisoned with his nephew Guido by the pope in 1498. The sinister byways of Italian history held a peculiar fascination for French writers at the start of the nineteenth century, particularly for liberals who saw political capital to be made out of relating past papal misdeeds. But there is more to it than that: Stendhal, who tells similar stories in his *Chroniques italiennes* and *Promenades dans Rome*, admired the mixture of refinement and savagery that he perceived in Italian culture, and was fascinated by its reversals of expectations (noble bandits, degenerate nobles). The Italian scenes in Dumas' novel are an interesting reflection of

the image of Italy in his time and suggest the appeal of a country that French visitors often found liberating after Restoration France.

XXI
THE ISLAND OF TIBOULEN

1. *alguazils*: Policemen, constables.
2. *a Genoese tartan*: A small, single-masted boat.
3. *Phrygian cap*: The red cap, a symbol of liberty during the Revolution, was modelled on the Phrygian cap worn by freed slaves in antiquity.

XXII
THE SMUGGLERS

1. *Doctor Pangloss*: The optimistic philosopher in Voltaire's novel *Candide*, ridiculed because of his belief that we live in 'the best of all possible worlds' – and consequently that progress is impossible.

XXIII
THE ISLAND OF MONTE CRISTO

1. *this other Pelion*: A mountain in Thessaly which the giants, in their war against the gods, heaped up on Mount Ossa so that they could scale the heavens more easily.

XXIV
DAZZLED

1. *Alaric*: Visigoth king (d. 410), who died after sacking Rome. To ensure that his grave would not be violated, it was placed in the course of the River Busento and the slaves who had dug it were executed.

XXV

THE STRANGER

1. *a double napoléon*: A gold coin worth 40 francs.

XXVI

AT THE SIGN OF THE PONT DU GARD

1. *ferrade . . . tarasque*: Provençal festivities. The *ferrade*, held in Arles, Nîmes and the Camargue, marked the branding of horses and cattle. The *tarasque* is a monster which reputedly emerged from the Rhône at Tarascon and devoured children, until subdued by St Marthe. The ceremonies associated with it, held at Whitsun, were described by Dumas in his book, *Le Midi de la France* (1841).
2. *the Second Restoration*: That of 1815. See note 1 to Chapter VI.

XXVII

CADEROUSSE'S STORY

1. *the war in Spain*: In 1822 France intervened in support of the autocratic King Ferdinand against the Spanish constitutionalists.
2. *the capture of the Trocadero*: On 7 April 1823, French forces under the Duc d'Angoulême captured the fort from the constitutionalists.
3. *Ali Pasha*: Ali Pasha, 'the Lion' (1741–1822), was a brigand who rose to power in Greece and Albania, being made pasha of various provinces in the Ottoman Empire, including (in 1788) Janina. He attracted support from both France and Britain, who saw him as a relatively enlightened ruler. In 1820, Sultan Mahmud II turned against him and, though he was promised safe conduct if he surrendered, he was put to death in 1822.

   The fame of Ali Pasha was propagated notably by Victor Hugo, in his early collection of poems, *Les Orientales* (1829). In the preface to the first edition he writes that 'Asian barbarism' cannot be so lacking in great men as civilized Europe would like to imagine: 'One must remember that it [i.e. Asia] has produced the only colossus that this century can offer who will measure up to [Napoleon] Bonaparte, if anyone can be said to do so: this man of genius, in truth a Turk and a Tartar, is Ali Pasha, who is to Napoleon as the tiger to the lion or the vulture to the eagle' (see *Preface*, p. xi).
4. *'Frailty, thy name is woman'*: Shakespeare, *Hamlet*, I, 2.

XXIX
MORREL AND COMPANY

1. *Montredon*: Either La Madrague-de-Montredon, east of Marseille, or possibly Montredon-Labessonie, in south-west France, which was dusty because of its sawmills.

XXXI
ITALY – SINBAD THE SAILOR

1. *Signor Pastrini*: Pastrini, proprietor of the Hôtel de Londres in the Piazza di Spagna, is a historical personage, mentioned by Dumas in *Le Speronare* (1842). Dumas stayed at his hotel in 1835 and records that rooms there cost between 2 and 20 francs.

2. *Algiers*: Using as its excuse the long history of piracy from the port, France sent an expedition which in 1830 captured Algiers and exiled the bey to Naples. It marked the start of the French colonial empire in Africa and a love–hate relationship with Arab North Africa that was to last for the next 130 years. But in the early nineteenth century the conquest would not have posed any moral dilemma, even for a liberal like Dumas. It is clear from the novel that he sees Algeria as an outlet for France's youthful energies after the end of the Napoleonic empire.

3. *Adamastor*: A giant who guarded the Cape of Good Hope, invented by the Portuguese poet Camöes in his epic, *The Lusiads* (V, 39–40).

4. *Bourgeois Gentilhomme*: A reference to Molière's play, *Le Bourgeois gentilhomme* (IV, 3), where the central character, Monsieur Jourdain, is amazed when confronted by a man, supposed to be a Turk, who says the words '*bel-men*', which are interpreted as meaning: 'You must go with him to prepare for the ceremony and then see your daughter and conclude her marriage.' 'What!' Jourdain exclaims. 'All that in two words!'

5. *The Huguenots*: An opera, with music by Meyerbeer and libretto by Eugène Scribe and Emile Deschamps (1836).

6. *yataghan*: A Turkish sword.

7. *Appert*: Benjamin-Nicholas-Marie Appert (1797–?), whom Dumas had known in the early 1820s, when both were employed by the Duc d'Orléans, and a philanthropist who devoted himself to aiding convicts; not the now better-known Nicholas Appert (1750–1841), inventor of a process for preserving food. The man in the blue cloak is Edmé Champion (1764–1852), a diamond merchant who devoted his later years to relief of the poor.

XXXIII
ROMAN BANDITS

1. *moccoletti*: Little candles.
2. *affettatore*: Rogue, swindler.
3. *Corneille's 'Qu'il morût . . .'*: In Pierre Corneille's play *Horace* (III, 4), where the hero's old father says unhesitatingly that his son should have died rather than (as he believes) sacrifice his honour – in the event, the younger Horace turns out to have had a cleverer plan than his father gave him credit for.
4. *Florian*: Jean-Pierre Claris de Florian (1755–94), the author of sentimental romances.
5. *Léopold Robert or Schnetz*: Both the Swiss artist Léopold Robert (1794–1835) and the French painter Jean-Victor Schnetz (1787–1870) were pupils of David and painted scenes of the Roman countryside.
6. *Avernus*: The entry to Hell, according to Virgil (see *Aeneid*, VI, line 126).

XXXIV
AN APPARITION

1. *Martial*: Roman poet (*c.* AD 40–104), famous for his epigrams. The reference here is to his *De Spectaculis*: his praise of the Colosseum was well rewarded by the Emperors Titus and Domitian.
2. *Parisina*: From a poem by Byron, with music by Gaetano Donizetti (1797–1848), who was also the composer of *Lucia di Lammermoor*, from Scott's novel, *The Bride of Lammermoor*. *Parisina* (1833) tells of the love of Parisina (sung by La Spech) for Ugo (Napoleone Moriani), the illegitimate son of her husband, Azzo (Domenico Coselli). Dumas met Coselli in Naples in 1835.
3. *Countess G—*: It is clear from the manuscript that Dumas is thinking of Byron's mistress, Countess Teresa Guiccioli.
4. *Lord Ruthwen*: The short novel, *Lord Ruthwen, or The Vampire* (first published in 1819 in the *New Monthly Magazine*), was written by Byron's companion and physician, Dr Polidori, who did not discourage the attribution to the poet himself. It was soon translated into French by Henri Faber (1819) and again by Amédée Pichot (1820), and helped to fuel an extraordinary vogue for vampire stories and melodramas, including Cyprien Bérard's *Lord Rutwen*, and the melodrama *Le Vampire* (1820), co-authored by Charles Nodier. Dumas saw this in 1823 and devoted several chapters to it in his memoirs (3rd series, 1863).
   Nodier's play was promptly re-translated into English by James Planché, as *The Vampire, or The Bride of the Isles* (1820), and before the end of the

same year in France there had been at least five other vampire productions on the Parisian stage: a burlesque, a farce, a comic opera, a vampire Punch and a 'vaudeville folly' in which one character says: 'Vampires! They come from England . . . That's another nice present those gentlemen have sent us!' Nodier observed that 'the myth of the vampire is perhaps the most universal of our superstitions'. It revived, of course, with Bram Stoker's *Dracula* (1899); and lives on in our own century in a medium which might be said to feature only the shadowy figures of the Undead – the cinema.

5. *the Do-Nothing Kings*: 'Les Rois Fainéants', the name given to a succession of minors in the Merovingian dynasty, during the seventh and eighth centuries, who ruled through regents.

6. *guzla*: A Balkan musical instrument, like a violin with only one or two strings. The writer Prosper Mérimée (1803–70) published a collection of supposedly Illyrian songs, *La Guzla* (1827), under the pseudonym Hyacinthe Maglanowich, both as a satire and as a tribute to the vogue for the East and its folklore.

XXXV

LA MAZZOLATA

1. *Comte de Chalais*: Chalais was beheaded in 1626 for plotting against Cardinal Richelieu. The execution was carried out, very inexpertly, by another condemned man.

2. *Castaing*: The poisoner Dr Edmé-Samuel Castaing was executed in 1823; Dumas attended the trial (and may have used some details of the evidence in Chapter LII), but he did not watch the execution. In fact, neither did Albert, since, according to the internal evidence of the book, he would only have been six years old at the time (and not, as he claims here, leaving college).

XXXVI

THE CARNIVAL IN ROME

1. *Callot*: Jacques Callot (1592–1635), painter and engraver.

2. *The Bear and the Pasha*: The actor Jacques-Charles Odry (1779–1853) played the role of Marécot in Scribe's vaudeville *The Bear and the Pasha* (1820).

3. *L'Italiana in Algeri*: Rossini's opera, first performed in 1813.

4. *Didier or Antony*: Didier is the hero of Victor Hugo's *Marion Delorme*, which was first performed in 1831, at the same theatre as Dumas' own

play *Antony*. Though Dumas himself defended Hugo against the charge, Hugo was accused by some of imitating Dumas' play, since both central characters are characteristic examples of the doomed Romantic hero.

5. *Gregory XVI*: Pope from 1831 to 1846. Dumas was granted an audience with him in 1835 and (as this passage and his account elsewhere show) was favourably impressed.

6. *Manfred . . . Lara's head-dress*: Manfred and Lara are two of the most Romantic figures in Byron's work.

7. *forty at least*: Dumas is sometimes inaccurate about dates, and also deliberately vague about the count's age. In fact, on the evidence of the novel, Monte Cristo was born in 1796. It is now 1838, so he is forty-two.

8. *Aeolus*: God of storms and winds.

XXXVIII

THE RENDEZ-VOUS

1. *Aguado . . . Rothschild*: Alejandro-Maria Aguado, Marquis of Las Marimas del Guadalquivir (1784–1842), was a Spanish financier who opened a bank in Paris in 1815. The French branch of the Rothschild family was founded by James de Rothschild, but Dumas might be thinking of Charles de Rothschild (1788–1855), whom he had met.

2. *Colomba*: A novel by Prosper Mérimée, the author of *Carmen* and one of the writers who had done most to popularize Spanish and Corsican subjects, in which the local colour is provided mainly by the characters' fierce courage and sense of honour. *Colomba* was not published until 1840, so Morcerf's reference to it in 1838 is an anachronism.

3. *Prix Montyon*: A prize for virtuous conduct awarded by the Institut de France.

XXXIX

THE GUESTS

1. *Grisier, Cooks, and Charles Leboucher*: Auguste-Edmé Grisier ran a fencing school; Dumas wrote the preface to his *Les Armes et le duel* (1847). Cooks had a gymnasium, and Leboucher was a boxing master.

2. *Don Carlos of Spain*: Claimant to the Spanish throne, on the death of his brother, Ferdinand VII, in 1833. He and his followers (the Carlists) fought against Isabella II but were defeated; Carlos fled to France in 1839 and was interned in Bourges. In 1844 he renounced his own claim in favour of his son and spent the remaining eleven years of his life in Austria.

3. *Béranger*: Pierre-Jean de Béranger (1780–1857) was the author of

light-hearted and mildly satirical songs and verses, who succeeded in upsetting the Restoration government. The phrase Lucien has just used is taken from his *Chansons*.

4. *Constantine*: The Algerian city was captured in 1837, after an unsuccessful attempt in the previous year.

5. *yataghan*: See note 6 to Chapter XXXI.

6. *Klagmann ... Marochetti*: Jean-Baptiste-Jules Klagmann (1810–67) was a sculptor who helped Dumas to decorate his Théâtre Français in 1846–7. Charles Marochetti (1805–62) was a well-known sculptor.

7. *Prix Montyon*: See note 3 to Chapter XXXVIII.

8. *Mehmet Ali*: Mehmet Ali (1769–1849), an Albanian officer, was sent to Egypt to oppose the French in 1798 and was later made viceroy. His rebellion against the Turks during the 1830s was supported by France but not by Britain.

9. *the Casauba*: The Casbah, a fortified citadel.

10. '*Punctuality ... sovereigns claimed*': The remark is attributed to Louis XVIII.

XL

BREAKFAST

1. *eighty-five départements*: The administrative districts into which France was divided after 1790. To begin with there were eighty-three, later increased by the addition of Corsica and three *départements* in Algeria. By the late twentieth century, after various administrative reorganizations and the loss of Algeria and other former colonies, the number stood at ninety-six in Metropolitan France and five overseas *départements* (Martinique, Guyane, Guadeloupe, Réunion and St Pierre-et-Miquelon).

XLI

THE INTRODUCTION

1. *Dupré ... Delacroix ... vanished with earlier centuries*: Apart from Eugène Delacroix (1798–1863), these artists are now largely forgotten. However, most were friends or acquaintances of Dumas, so the list is intended to demonstrate Morcerf's good taste in his choice of contemporary art.

2. *Léopold Robert*: See note 5 to Chapter XXXIII. Incidentally, according to the internal chronology of the novel, Mercédès would have been thirty-two, not 'twenty-five or twenty-six' in 1830, when Albert says the portrait was made.

3. *Gros*: Jean-Antoine Gros (1771–1835), also a pupil of David, specialized in historical and battle scenes.

4. *d'Hozier and Jaucourt*: Two genealogists known for their encyclopedic learning and erudite industry. Pierre d'Hozier (1592–1660) wrote a genealogy of leading French families in 150 volumes, which was continued by his son and grand-nephew. Louis de Jaucourt (1704–79) wrote on genealogy for the *Encyclopédie*.

XLII
MONSIEUR BERTUCCIO

1. *'I was almost made to wait'*: Louis XIV's famous rebuff to a courtier who arrived insufficiently early.

XLIV
THE VENDETTA

1. *the Hundred Days*: See note 1 to Chapter VI.

XLVI
UNLIMITED CREDIT

1. *Albano and Fattore*: The Italian painters Francesco Albano (1488–1528) and Giovanni Francesco Penni, known as 'Il Fattore' (1578–1660).
2. *Thorwaldsen, Bartolini, or Canova*: Neo-classical artists, who were not in favour with the Romantics: Bertel Thorwaldsen (1768–1844) was Danish, Lorenzo Bartolini (1777–1850) and Antonio Canova (1757–1822) were Italians.

XLVII
THE DAPPLE-GREYS

1. *Antiquity – as interpreted by the Directoire*: The Directoire was the regime in power from 1795 to 1799, in which executive power was exercised by a five-member 'directorate', elected by the legislature. As a whole the revolutionary period saw a succession of attempts to discover aesthetic styles appropriate to a non-monarchical regime, usually by adapting motifs

from republican Greece or Rome. Like the Neo-classicism of Thorwaldsen and Canova, this had gone out of fashion by the 1830s, and Danglars' enjoyment of it is a sign of his lack of taste.

2. *Rousseau*: The philosopher Jean-Jacques Rousseau (1712–78) was the author of an enormously influential treatise on education, *Emile* (1762). He recommended a method that both relied on the influence of nature and required a fairly strict regime. He would not have approved of Madame de Villefort's mollycoddling of her obnoxious son.

3. *Ranelagh*: A public dance-hall, opened in 1774.

XLVIII
IDEOLOGY

1. *the senior or junior branch of the royal family*: The Bourbon dynasty reigned in France up to the Revolution and was the branch of the royal family restored in 1815. The younger princes of the royal blood had been Dukes of Orléans since the fourteenth century and, under the Revolution, one of these, Louis-Philippe-Joseph, known as Philippe-Egalité, supported the revolutionary cause. Philippe-Egalité died on the scaffold in 1793, but his son, also Louis-Philippe, remained a supporter of a moderate, liberal monarchy. At the Revolution of July 1830, the Bourbon king, Charles X, abdicated in his favour, and Louis-Philippe's accession was greeted as heralding a new, constitutional monarchy (though, in the event, these expectations were disappointed). It is to this junior, Orléanist branch that the present pretenders to the French throne belong.

2. *Harlay . . . Molé*: Two leading magistrates and presidents of the Paris *parlement* in the early seventeenth century.

3. *four revolutions*: Villefort was born just before the Revolution of 1789, so he had lived through the revolutionary period, the Napoleonic Empire, the Restoration and the July Revolution of 1830. It is not clear whether Dumas counts the Napoleonic coup of 1799 as a 'revolution' or whether he means the First Restoration (1814) and the Second Restoration (1815) to be counted separately. The implication is clear: that Villefort has managed to benefit from every change of government.

4. *pede claudo*: The full phrase is *pede poena claudo*; 'punishment comes limping', Horace, *Odes*, III, 2. That is: retribution will come slowly but surely – a good motto for Monte Cristo.

5. *Tobias*: See Tobit 7:15, where the angel reveals himself.

6. *non bis in idem*: The principle that a person cannot be tried twice for the same offence.

7. *carbonaro*: See note 1 to Chapter VII.

XLIX
HAYDÉE

1. *say tu to me*: Every European language except English (in which 'thee' and 'thou' have long been archaic except in some dialects) has kept the second person singular for use with intimates, close friends and relatives. English translations usually try to get round this in some way: ' "Why do you address me so coldly – so distantly?" ' is the version given in the 1852 translation, but it makes very little sense here, because Monte Cristo has said only three words (four in the translation) since entering the room, which is frankly not enough to provide grounds for her accusation. The point is that one of the three words is the formal, second person plural, *vous*.

L
THE MORRELS

1. *Presse ... Débats: La Presse*, founded in 1836 by Emile de Girardin, was a liberal, popular newspaper, to which Dumas contributed. *Le Journal des Débats* (1789–1944) is one of the great newspapers in the history of French nineteenth-century journalism. *The Count of Monte Cristo* first appeared in it in serial form.

LI
PYRAMUS AND THISBE

1. *aristocracy of the lance ... nobility of the cannon*: That is to say, the pre-revolutionary aristocracy and those ennobled under Napoleon because of their service to the empire.

LII
TOXICOLOGY

1. *Mithridates, rex Ponticus*: Mithridates VII (123–63 BC), King of Pontus in Asia Minor, who fought to defend his kingdom against the Romans, 'fortified his constitution by drinking antidotes against the poison with which his enemies at court attempted to destroy him' (Lemprière, *Classical Dictionary*). However, Monte Cristo is wrong in attributing this information to the historian Cornelius Nepos.

2. *Flamel, Fontana or Cabanis*: Nicholas Flamel (1330–1418) was reputed to be an alchemist. Félix Fontana (1730–1805) studied poisons and the doctor Pierre-Jean-Georges Cabanis (1757–1808) gave the philosopher Condorcet the poison he used to escape the guillotine in 1794.

3. *Galland*: Antoine Galland (1646–1715) made a celebrated translation of *The Thousand and One Nights* (1704–11).

4. *Desrues*: Antoine Desrues (1734–77), a famous poisoner. A. Arnould told his story in the series of *Crimes célèbres* (1839–40), to which Dumas contributed.

5. *Borgias ... Baron de Trenk*: Famous poisoners, spies or adventurers. The Italian perfumer René was accused of poisoning the Prince de Condé; he and Ruggieri were agents of Catherine de' Medici, and both feature in historical novels by Dumas. Friedrich von der Trenck was guillotined as an Austrian spy in 1794.

6. *Magendie ... Flourens*: François Magendi (1783–1855) and Marie-Jean-Pierre Flourens (1794–1867) were, respectively, a well-known anatomist and a well-known doctor.

7. *that paradox of Jean-Jacques Rousseau*: Rastignac, in Balzac's novel *Le Père Goriot* (Chapter II), puts the question: 'What would you do if you could become rich by killing an old mandarin in China, by the sole force of your will, without leaving Paris?' He wrongly attributes the idea to Rousseau.

LIII
ROBERT LE DIABLE

1. *Mlles Noblet, Julia and Leroux*: Three dancers who performed the 'Ballet des Nonnes' in Jacques Meyerbeer's opera *Robert le Diable* (1831).
2. *Ali Tebelin*: See note 3 to Chapter XXVII.

LIV
RISE AND FALL

1. *Danaro e ... della Metà*: Dumas translates, in a note: 'Money and sanctity – half of the half' – in other words, both lend themselves to exaggeration.
2. *Henri IV ... Pont Neuf*: A reference to King Henri IV's affair with his mistress, Gabrielle d'Estrées. The reason the king did not leave the Pont Neuf is that his statue stands at one end of the bridge.
3. *Dante ... d'Hozier*: The genealogist (see note 4 to Chapter XLI). Dante acted as genealogist to the Cavalcantis by including Cavalcante Cavalcanti, father of his friend Guido, in Book X of the *Inferno*, ll. 52–72.

LVI

ANDREA CAVALCANTI

1. *Antony*: Another reference to Dumas' play, in which the central character (II, 5) boasts of being a bastard.

LVII

THE ALFALFA FIELD

1. *eventually revert to her son*: It was not unheard of for girls to be put into convents in order to concentrate the family wealth; above all, this discussion illustrates how few options a girl in Valentine's position could have, despite her apparent wealth and privilege, and how powerless she is to decide her future. It also throws a new light on the behaviour of Eugénie Danglars, the unfeminine counterpart to Valentine (the latter being presented as the ideal, submissive, caring, modest, timid, selfless young woman).

LX

THE TELEGRAPH

1. *the Montagne*: The name given to the radical, Jacobin group in the revolutionary Convention.

2. *A telegraph*: The telegraph, introduced in 1793 and using a form of semaphore, was considered one of the great inventions of the age; by the 1840s there were over 3,000 miles of communication lines, all belonging to the War Department. It was superseded in 1845 by the electric telegraph, using Morse Code.

3. *τηλε γραφειν*: *Tele graphein*; 'distance writing'. Montalivet was Minister of the Interior from 1837 to 1839, succeeded by Duchâtel.

LXI

HOW TO RESCUE A GARDENER FROM DORMICE
WHO ARE EATING HIS PEACHES

1. *Delacroix*: See note 1 to Chapter XLI.

LXII
GHOSTS

1. *like Vatel at Chantilly*: Vatel was chef to the Prince de Condé, and committed suicide in 1671 because, one fast day when the prince was playing host to the king, the fish for dinner failed to arrive.

LXIII
DINNER

1. *cupitor impossibilium*: 'One who desires the impossible'. In fact, what Tacitus says of Nero (*Annals*, XV, 42) is *cupitor incredibilium* – 'one who desires the incredible'.
2. *the Marquise de Ganges . . . Desdemona*: The Marquise de Ganges was assassinated in 1667 by her two brothers-in-law; another of Dumas' *Crimes célèbres*. Desdemona was strangled by Othello (*Othello*, V, 2).
3. *Ugolino's tower*: For Ugolino, see Chapter XV, note 2. The poet Torquato Tasso spent seven years in prison, after a bout of madness. Francesca da Rimini married Giovanni Malatesta, but fell in love with her husband's younger brother, Paolo. Giovanni ran them through with a single thrust of his sword. They figure among those tossed on the winds of passion in a celebrated passage in Dante's *Inferno* (Canto V).
4. *Lucina*: Goddess of childbirth.

LXIV
THE BEGGAR

1. *nil admirari*: 'Not to be impressed by anything'. See Horace, *Epistles*, I, 6.
2. *Bossuet*: Jacques-Bénigne Bossuet (1627–1704), an eminent orator and theologian.
3. *Number one hundred and six*: In Chapter LXXXII, however, Caderousse says that his number was 58 and Andrea's 59.

LXV
A DOMESTIC SCENE

1. *like Nathan in Athalie*: In Racine's tragedy (III, 5), the character shows his inner turmoil by his inability to find the way out. Debray's actions,

bumping into the wall, are not in Racine's text and must reflect a memory of the play in performance.

2. *Don Carlos*: See note 2 to Chapter XXXIX.

LXVI
MARRIAGE PLANS

1. *fat cows . . . lean cows*: See Pharaoh's dream in Genesis 41.

2. *Jupiter . . . mixing species*: The Roman god 'became a Proteus to gratify his passions. He introduced himself to Danae in a shower of gold, he corrupted Antiope in the form of a satyr and Leda in the form of a swan. He became a bull to seduce Europa, and he enjoyed the company of Aegina in the form of a flame of fire. He assumed the habit of Diana to corrupt Callisto, and became Amphitryon to gain the affections of Alcmena . . .' (Lemprière, *Classical Dictionary*).

LXVIII
A SUMMER BALL

1. *Queen Mab . . . Titania*: See Shakespeare, *A Midsummer Night's Dream* and *Romeo and Juliet* (I, 4).

LXIX
INFORMATION

1. *Homer . . . Belisarius*: The engravings of works by Gérard and Morel both in fact represent the Byzantine general, Belisarius.

2. *Battle of Navarino . . . King Otto*: The Greek war of independence against the Turks began in 1821. It was supported by Britain, France and Russia, who defeated the Egyptian and Turkish fleets at the Battle of Navarino (1827). In 1832, Frederick of Bavaria was appointed King of Greece, under the name Otto I. He ruled until 1862.

LXX
THE BALL

1. *the cachucha*: An Andalusian dance, very popular in the early part of the nineteenth century. The scene in which the two leading female characters dance the cachucha, in Coralli and Burat de Gurgy's ballet *Le Diable boiteux* (1836), had been made famous by Fanny Elssler's performance.

2. *the Institut*: Set up in 1795 to combine the functions of the two major existing learned societies, the Académie Française and the Académie des Inscriptions. In 1803, the two académies were reinstated, together with the Académie des Sciences and the Académie des Beaux-Arts, under the umbrella of the Institut.

3. *to design them a coat*: Morcerf is quite right about the republican period: it did like dressing up. In fact, it was not the painter David but the more humble embroiderer Picot who designed the Academician's dress, a frock-coat heavily embroidered in gold.

4. *July Monarchy*: See note 1 to Chapter XLVIII.

5. *Partons pour la Syrie*: A song, with music by Philippe Droult and words variously attributed to Queen Hortense and to Count Alexandre de Laborde, which became a Bonapartist anthem.

LXXII
MADAME DE SAINT-MÉRAN

1. *Hamlet*: In Shakespeare's play, Act I, Scene 2.

2. *Mene, mene, tekel, upharsin*: See note 3 to Chapter XV.

LXXIII
THE PROMISE

1. *Don Juan*: At the end of the story (eg. in Molière's play, *Don Juan*, Act V, Scene 5) the statue of the Commander comes to lead Don Juan down to hell.

2. *I have no pretensions to be Manfred or Antony*: See note 6 and note 4 to Chapter XXXVI.

LXXIV

THE VILLEFORT FAMILY VAULT

1. *King Louis XVIII and King Charles X*: The two kings who reigned during the Restoration, from 1815 to 1830. See note 1 to Chapter VI.

2. *Tenacem propositi virum*: 'A man who is firm in his intentions'; Horace, *Odes*, III, 3, line 1. Already quoted (see note 11 to Chapter x).

3. *Conventionnel*: A member of the revolutionary Convention.

4. *Marengo . . . Austerlitz*: Scenes of Napoleon's great victories in 1800 and 1805.

5. *eo rus*: 'I am going to the country.' No letter of Voltaire's using this phrase has been identified, but Schopp, in his edition of the novel, points to an anecdote in Voltaire's *Le Siècle de Louis XIV* in which Voltaire recalls having asked the Abbé de Saint-Pierre how he considered his impending death, to which the abbé replied: 'Like a journey to the country.'

LXXVI

THE PROGRESS OF THE YOUNGER CAVALCANTI

1. *Sappho*: Greek poet of the sixth century BC, born on Lesbos, whose name has long been associated with female homosexuality: 'Her tender passions were so violent, that some have represented her attachment with three of her female companions, Telesiphe, Atthis and Megara, as criminal . . . The poetess has been censured for writing with that licentiousness and freedom which so much disgraced her character as a woman' (Lemprière, *Classical Dictionary*). Minerva was the goddess of wisdom, noted for her chastity: her breastplate would ward off tender looks and protect against desire. The references confirm the interlinked notions of Eugénie's lesbianism and her 'masculine' independence.

2. *Antonia in the Violon de Crémone*: A tale by E. T. A. Hoffmann. Antonia has a sublimely beautiful voice, but is forbidden to sing by her doctor, who says that it will kill her. She takes up the violin instead. One night, her father dreams that he hears the sound of his daughter's voice, singing to the violin. The next morning, he finds her dead.

3. *three or four days*: According to Chapter LXXII, M. de Saint-Méran had covered only 6 leagues (about 25 kilometres); 'three or four hours' seems more plausible.

4. *as Claudius says to Hamlet*: See *Hamlet*, Act I, Scene 2.

5. *Thalberg*: Sigismund Thalberg (1812–71), pianist, made his Paris début in 1835.

LXXVII

HAYDÉE

1. *Haydée . . . Lord Byron*: See Byron's *Don Juan*, Canto II.
2. *Denys the Tyrant*: Denys the Younger, fourth-century tyrant of Syracuse, who was said to have become a teacher after being expelled from the city in 343 BC.
3. *Ali Tebelin*: See note 3 to Chapter XXVII.
4. *a delightful picture*: A direct reference to the similarity of the scene evoked by Dumas and paintings of Oriental subjects.
5. *'He that hath pity upon the poor, lendeth unto the Lord'*: Dumas notes the origin of this in Proverbs 19.
6. *hegumenos*: The bursar.
7. *cangiar*: A scimitar, or curved sword.
8. *pythoness*: A female soothsayer or prophetess.
9. *Palicares*: Greek soldiers during the War of Independence (modern Greek: *palikaris*, 'brave').
10. *seraskier Kurchid*: A *seraskier* is a commander-in-chief under the Turks. Kurchid gave Ali Tebelin his assurance that, if he surrendered, his life would be spared, but broke his word.
11. *firman*: An edict of the sultan.

LXXVIII

A CORRESPONDENT WRITES FROM JANINA

1. *Lucy of Lammermoor*: A reference to Walter Scott's novel, *The Bride of Lammermoor* (Chapter XXXIII).

LXXIX

LEMONADE

1. *false angostura or St Ignatius' nut*: The Indian tree *Strychnos nux-vomica*, the seeds of which contain strychnine and other poisons.

LXXX
THE ACCUSATION

1. *Locusta ... Agrippina*: Locusta was employed by Nero to poison Britannicus, then was executed for trying to poison Nero himself. Agrippina, Nero's mother, poisoned her husband, the emperor Claudius, then, 'after many cruelties and much licentiousness' (Lemprière, *Classical Dictionary*) was assassinated by her son. Brunhaut and Fredegonde were rival Frankish queens in the sixth century. Fredegonde seems to have had a particularly murderous career: her rivalry with Brunhaut began when she had Brunhaut's husband done to death.
2. *like Polonius in Shakespeare*: Killed accidentally while hiding behind the arras. See *Hamlet*, Act III, Scene 4.

LXXXI
THE RETIRED BAKER'S ROOM

1. *'Confiteor'*: 'I confess': the start of a prayer in the Latin mass.

LXXXII
BREAKING AND ENTERING

1. *Fiesco*: A reference to Schiller's play, *Die Verschwörung des Fiesco zu Gena*, which Dumas had adapted as *Fiesque de Lavagna*, a five-act historical drama turned down by the Comédie-Française in 1828.
2. *the three blows*: In French theatres, before the curtain goes up, the stage manager demands the audience's attention by knocking three times on the floor with a rod. The phrase, *frapper les trois coups* (here applied to the striking of the clock), indicates the hush before the action starts.
3. *the antique knife-grinder*: A marble statue which Dumas saw in Florence and which intrigued him because the pose of the figure suggests that he is preoccupied with something other than grinding his knife.
4. *Louis XVI*: Guillotined in January 1793.

LXXXV
THE JOURNEY

1. *Augustus . . . master of the universe*: A reference to Corneille's play, *Cinna* (Act V, Scene 3).
2. *britzka*: A light horse-drawn carriage with a covered rear seat.
3. *François I . . . Shakespeare*: François I wrote a couplet on the fickleness of women. Othello says of Desdemona: 'She was false as water' (Act V, Scene 2); and Hamlet exclaims: 'Frailty, thy name is woman!' (Act I, Scene 2).

LXXXVI
JUDGEMENT IS PASSED

1. *the glorious Egyptian campaign*: One of Napoleon's earliest successes was the conquest of Egypt in 1798 (though it was abandoned after Nelson's victory over the French fleet at Aboukir).
2. *Virgil . . . goddess*: 'Her walk revealed a true goddess . . .'; Virgil, *Aeneid*, Book I, lines 404–5.

LXXXVIII
THE INSULT

1. *Duprez . . . O, Mathilde, idole de mon âme*: Gilbert Duprez, tenor, whom Dumas had met in Naples in 1835. The phrase is sung by Melchthal in Rossini's opera *William Tell* (Act I, Scene 5).
2. *Lara . . . Manfred . . . Lord Ruthwen*: See note 4 to Chapter XXXIV and note 6 to Chapter XXXVI.

LXXXIX
NIGHT

1. *'Suivez-moi!'*: In *William Tell*, Act II, Scene 2.

XC

THE ENCOUNTER

1. *Brutus . . . Philippi*: 'Plutarch mentions that Caesar's ghost made its appearance to Brutus in his tent and told him that he would meet him at Philippi' (Lemprière, *Classical Dictionary*). Brutus and Cassius were defeated by Antony and Octavian at Philippi in 42 BC.

XCI

MOTHER AND SON

1. *Feuchères . . . Barye*: The Romantic sculptor Jean-Jacques Feuchère (1807–52) and the animal specialist Antoine-Louis Barye (1796–1875).

XCIV

A CONFESSION

1. *holy Vehme or francs-juges*: The *vehme* was a church court in medieval Germany which, like the courts of the *francs-juges*, held its sessions in secret and gave account to no one for its judgements. The reference to Sterne seems to refer to Yorick's sermon in *Tristram Shandy*, Book II, Chapter 17.
2. *Atreides*: Members of the accursed family of Atreus in Greek myth.

XCV

FATHER AND DAUGHTER

1. *Phaedrus . . . Bias*: The maxim is found in Plato's *Philebus* and is sometimes attributed to Solon, rather than to the Latin translator of Aesop's *Fables*. Bias was one of the seven wise men of Greece.
2. *at the Porte Saint-Martin or the Gaîté*: The sites of popular theatres showing the kind of melodrama in which fathers would behave in this way.
3. *Pasta, Malibran or Grisi*: Famous opera singers.
4. *Law . . . Mississippi*: John Law (1671–1729) was a Scotsman who played an important role in French finances in the early eighteenth century, firstly as controller of finances, then as the creator of the Compagnie d'Occident which for a long time had a monopoly on trade with North

America. His plans to raise money to colonize Louisiana led to the collapse of the scheme and caused many bankruptcies.
5. *Desdemona*: From Rossini's *Otello* (1816).

XCVI
THE MARRIAGE CONTRACT

1. *Dorante . . . Valère . . . Alceste . . . Théâtre Français*: Lovers in plays by Molière (*Le Misanthrope, Le Bourgeois gentilhomme* and *Tartuffe*). The Théâtre Français is another name for the Comédie-Française, the leading French classical theatre, which originated in Molière's own company.
2. *Boileau*: Nicolas Boileau (1636–1711), a literary critic who offered the most consistent formulation of the theory underpinning French literary classicism.
3. *quaerens quem devoret*: The Devil, 'seeking whom he may devour' (I Peter 5:8).

XCVII
THE ROAD FOR BELGIUM

1. *Hercules . . . Omphale*: Omphale, Queen of Lydia, bought Hercules as a slave, not knowing who he was, and fell in love with him. The pair were also in the habit of cross-dressing: 'As they [Hercules and Omphale] once travelled together, they came to a grotto on Mount Tmolus, where the queen dressed herself in the habit of her lover, and obliged him to appear in a female garment . . .' (Lemprière, *Classical Dictionary*). However, by casting herself in the role of Hercules, Eugénie is simply indicating that she is the dominant partner, and physically the stronger.
2. *britzka*: See note 2 to Chapter LXXXV.

XCVIII
THE INN OF THE BELL AND BOTTLE

1. *excellent hostelry . . . remember*: The building that once housed the Hôtel de la Cloche et de la Bouteille still exists in Compiègne. Dumas greatly admired the proprietor, Vuillemot, and often stayed here. It was in Compiègne, he tells us, that he finished writing *The Count of Monte Cristo*.
2. *Achilles with Deidamia*: The print could be from a painting by either Rubens or Teniers, both of whom depicted Achilles at the court of

Lycomedes, King of Scyros, whose daughter was seduced by Achilles. In order to win her favours, he came to her father's court disguised in women's clothes.

CII
VALENTINE

1. *Germain Pilon's three Graces*: The group, *The Three Graces*, was commissioned from the sculptor Germain Pilon (1528–90) to support the funerary urn of King Henri II. It is now in the Louvre.

CIV
THE SIGNATURE OF BARON DANGLARS

1. *Robert Macaire . . . Frédérick*: 'Robert Macaire' was the central character in Antier, Saint-Amant and Paulyanthe's melodrama, *L'Auberge des Adrets* (1823) and its sequel *Robert Macaire* (1834). It was famously played by Frédérick Lemaître (1800–76), who features in this role in Marcel Carné's film, *Les Enfants du paradis* (played by Pierre Brasseur).

CV
THE PÈRE LACHAISE CEMETERY

1. *Héloïse and Abélard*: A monument to the twelfth-century lovers, made to cover their tomb after Héloïse's death in 1164, was eventually transferred to the Père Lachaise cemetery in the early nineteenth century.
2. *Malherbe . . . du Périer*: A celebrated poem to console du Périer on the death of his daughter, by François de Malherbe (1555–1628).
3. *the daughter of Jairus*: The story of how Jesus resurrected the daughter of Jairus is told in three gospels (Matthew 19: 18–26; Mark 5: 22–43; and Luke 8: 40–56). The story of Jesus walking on the water is in Matthew, 14: 28–9.

CVI
THE SHARE-OUT

1. *Saint-Germain-des-Prés*: Chapter XCI puts the house in the Rue des Saint-Pères (which is in the district of Saint-Germain-des-Prés).
2. *Asmodée . . . Le Sage*: In Le Sage's play, *Le Diable boiteux* (1707).
3. *Lamoricière . . . Changarnier . . . Bedeau*: Christophe-Louis-Léon Juchault de Lamoricière (1806–65), Nicholas-Anne-Théodule Changarnier (1793–1877) and Marie-Alphonse Bedeau (1804–63) were officers who distinguished themselves in the conquest of Algeria.

CVII
THE LIONS' PIT

1. *La Force*: The building, originally a thirteenth-century royal mansion, became a prison in 1782, housed political prisoners during the Revolution and was demolished in 1850.
2. *Barrière Saint-Jacques*: After 1832, the place where executions were carried out.
3. *quos ego*: 'You, whom I . . .' the start of Neptune's reprimand to the disobedient winds in Virgil's *Aeneid*, Book II, l. 135.
4. *as Monsieur Racine says*: In his play *Phèdre*, Act I, Scene 3.

CVIII
THE JUDGE

1. *Tarquin*: Tarquin the Proud (534–510 BC), King of Rome, who indicated to his son, Tarquinius Sextus, how he wanted him to treat the leading citizens of the beseiged town of Gabii by knocking the heads off some flowers.

CIX
THE ASSIZES

1. *Saint-Simon*: Louis de Rouvroy, Duc de Saint-Simon (1675–1755) was the celebrated author of memoirs on the court of Louis XIV. The reference has not been traced, and could be an invention of Dumas'.

CXI

EXPIATION

1. *a shirt of Nessus*: The garment, poisoned with the blood of the centaur Nessus, which caused the death of Hercules.
2. *Titans . . . Ajax . . . at the gods*: In Greek mythology, the Titans were giants who challenged the gods. Ajax, son of Oileus, was saved from drowning and boasted that he had survived without the help of the gods; for this impiety, Neptune cast him back into the water.

CXII

DEPARTURE

1. *Perrault's stories*: Charles Perrault (1628–1703) was the author of the original versions of many of the best-known fairy-tales. In this case the reference is to *Sleeping Beauty*.

CXIII

THE PAST

1. *Since the July Revolution*: In 1830. See note 1 to Chapter XLVIII.
2. *Mirabeau's imprisonment*: See note 1 to Chapter VIII.
3. *like Hamlet*: Shakespeare, *Hamlet*, Act III, Scene 1.
4. *Ganymede*: A Trojan youth who 'became the cup-bearer of the gods in the place of Hebe. Some say that he was carried away by an eagle, to satisfy the shameful and unnatural desires of Jupiter' (Lemprière, *Classical Dictionary*).

CXIV

PEPPINO

1. *Figaro's 'goddam'*: In Beaumarchais' *Le Mariage de Figaro*, Act III, Scene 5.
2. *Marius and the Gracchi*: Gaius Marius (155–86 BC) was a Roman general; the two Gracchi were political reformers who tried to redistribute wealth, but were murdered successively in 133 BC and 121 BC. Dumas seems to be using the names simply as representative early citizens of Rome.
3. *morra*: A game in which one player tries to shout out the number of

fingers shown on the hand of the other, who quickly raises and lowers them.

4. *Circus of Caracalla*: The baths and circus of the Emperor Caracalla (188–217) still survive on the outskirts of Rome.

CXV
LUIGI VAMPA'S BILL OF FARE

1. *sauces Robert*: An onion sauce which Dumas, in his *Grand dictionnaire de cuisine*, describes as highly appetizing, as well as highly flavoured.

2. *the barrel of the Danaids*: The fifty daughters of the king of Argos were betrothed to the fifty sons of Aegyptus, but their father, to avert a prophecy that he would be killed by one of his sons-in-law, made them promise to murder their husbands. They were condemned to spend eternity in hell filling barrels full of holes.

CXVI
THE PARDON

1. *Harpagon*: The central character in Molière's play *L'Avare*.

CXVII
OCTOBER THE FIFTH

1. *Calypso . . . Telemachus*: In Fénélon's novel *Télémaque*, Calypso welcomes the hero to her island and seems in effect to be telling him to slip into something more comfortable.

PENGUIN ⟨Ⓟ⟩ CLASSICS

The Classics Publisher

'Penguin Classics, one of the world's greatest series' JOHN
KEEGAN

'I have never been disappointed with the Penguin Classics. All
I have read is a model of academic seriousness and provides
the essential information to fully enjoy the master works that
appear in its catalogue' MARIO VARGAS LLOSA

'Penguin and Classics are words that go together like horse and
carriage or Mercedes and Benz. When I was a university teacher
I always prescribed Penguin editions of classic novels for my
courses: they have the best introductions, the most reliable
notes, and the most carefully edited texts' DAVID LODGE

'Growing up in Bombay, expensive hardback books were
beyond my means, but I could indulge my passion for reading
at the roadside bookstalls that were well stocked with all the
Penguin paperbacks ... Sometimes I would choose a book just
because I was attracted by the cover, but so reliable was the
Penguin imprimatur that I was never once disappointed by the
contents.

   Such access certainly broadened the scope of my reading,
and perhaps it's no coincidence that so many Merchant Ivory
films have been adapted from great novels, or that those novels
are published by Penguin' ISMAIL MERCHANT

'You can't write, read, or live fully in the present without knowing the literature of the past. Penguin Classics opens the door
to a treasure house of pure pleasure, books that have never
been bettered, which are read again and again with increased
delight' JOHN MORTIMER

PENGUIN CLASSICS

DON QUIXOTE   MIGUEL DE CERVANTES

'Didn't I tell you they were only windmills? And only someone with windmills on the brain could have failed to see that!'

Don Quixote has become so entranced by reading romances of chivalry that he determines to become a knight errant and pursue bold adventures, accompanied by his squire, the cunning Sancho Panza. As they roam the world together, the ageing Quixote's fancy leads them wildly astray. At the same time the relationship between the two men grows in fascinating subtlety. Often considered to be the first modern novel, *Don Quixote* is a wonderful burlesque of the popular literature its disordered protagonist is obsessed with.

John Rutherford's landmark translation does full justice to the energy and wit of Cervantes's prose. His introduction discusses the traditional works parodied in *Don Quixote*, as well as issues surrounding literary translation.

'John Rutherford . . . makes *Don Quixote* funny and readable . . . His Quixote can be pompous, imposingly learned, secretly fearful, mad and touching' Colin Burrow, *The Times Literary Supplement*

Voted greatest book of all time by the Nobel Institute

Translated with an introduction and notes by John Rutherford

PENGUIN CLASSICS

THE DEATH OF KING ARTHUR

'Lancelot has brought me such great shame as to dishonour me through my wife, I shall never rest till they are caught together'

Recounting the final days of Arthur, this thirteenth-century French version of the Camelot legend, written by an unknown author, is set in a world of fading chivalric glory. It depicts the Round Table diminished in strength after the Quest for the Holy Grail, and with its integrity threatened by the weakness of Arthur's own knights. Whispers of Queen Guinevere's infidelity with his beloved comrade-at-arms Sir Lancelot profoundly distress the trusting King, leaving him no match for the machinations of the treacherous Sir Mordred. The human tragedy of *The Death of King Arthur* so impressed Malory that he built his own Arthurian legend on this view of the court – a view that profoundly influenced the English conception of the 'great' King.

James Cable's translation brilliantly captures all the narrative urgency and spare immediacy of style. In his introduction, he examines characterization, narrative style, authorship and the work's place among the different versions of the Arthur myth.

Translated by James Cable

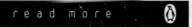
PENGUIN CLASSICS

DEERBROOK
HARRIET MARTINEAU

'If you do a thing which a village public does not approve, there will be offence in whatever else you say and do, for some time after'

When the Ibbotson sisters, Hester and Margaret, arrive at the village of Deerbrook to stay with their cousin Mr Grey and his wife, speculation is rife that one of them might marry the village apothecary, Edward Hope. Although he is immediately attracted to Margaret, Edward is persuaded to wed the beautiful Hester, and becomes trapped in an unhappy marriage. But his troubles are compounded when he becomes the victim of a malicious village gossip, whose rumours threaten his entire career. A powerful exploration of the nature of ignorance and prejudice, *Deerbrook* proved an inspiration for both Charlotte Brontë and Elizabeth Gaskell. It may be regarded as one of the first Victorian novels of English domestic life.

New to Penguin Classics, this edition of *Deerbrook* contains the full text of the original three-volume novel. Valerie Sanders's introduction outlines the novel's themes and considers its unique position in nineteenth-century women's literature. This volume also contains a chronology, further reading and detailed notes.

Edited with an introduction and notes by Valerie Sanders

read more

PENGUIN CLASSICS

THÉRÈSE RAQUIN
EMILE ZOLA

'It was like a lightning flash of passion, swift, blinding, across a leaden sky'

In a dingy apartment on the Passage du Pont Neuf in Paris, Thérèse Raquin is trapped in a loveless marriage to her sickly cousin Camille. The numbing tedium of her life is suddenly shattered when she embarks on a turbulent affair with her husband's earthy friend Laurent, but their animal passion for each other soon compels the lovers to commit a crime that will haunt them forever. *Thérèse Raquin* caused a scandal when it appeared in 1867 and brought its twenty-seven-year-old author a notoriety that followed him throughout his life. Zola's novel is not only an uninhibited portrayal of adultery, madness and ghostly revenge, but is also a devastating exploration of the darkest aspects of human existence.

Robin Buss's new translation superbly conveys Zola's fearlessly honest and matter of fact style. In his introduction, he discusses Zola's life and literary career, and the influence of art, literature and science on his writing. This edition also includes the preface to the second edition of 1868, a chronology, further reading and notes.

Translated with an introduction and notes by Robin Buss

PENGUIN CLASSICS

THREE TALES
GUSTAVE FLAUBERT

'When she went to church, she would sit gazing at the picture of the Holy Spirit and it struck her that it looked rather like her parrot'

First published in 1877, the *Three Tales*, dominated by questions of doubt, love, loneliness and religious experience, form Flaubert's final great work. 'A Simple Heart' relates the story of Félicité – an uneducated serving-woman who retains her Catholic faith despite a life of desolation and loss. 'The Legend of Saint Julian Hospitator', inspired by a stained-glass window in Rouen cathedral, describes the fate of Julian, a sadistic hunter destined to murder his own parents. The blend of faith and cruelty that dominates this story may also be found in 'Herodias' – a reworking of the tale of Salome and John the Baptist. Rich with a combination of desire, sorrow and faith, these three diverse works are a triumphant conclusion to Flaubert's creative life.

Roger Whitehouse's vibrant new translation captures the exquisite style of the original prose. Geoffrey Wall's introduction considers the inspiration for the tales in the context of Flaubert's life and other work. This edition includes a further reading list and detailed notes.

Translated by Roger Whitehouse

Edited with an introduction by Geoffrey Wall

PENGUIN CLASSICS

MADAME BOVARY   GUSTAVE FLAUBERT

'Oh, why, dear God, did I marry him?'

Emma Bovary is beautiful and bored, trapped in her marriage to a mediocre doctor and stifled by the banality of provincial life. An ardent devourer of sentimental novels, she longs for passion and seeks escape in fantasies of high romance, in voracious spending and, eventually, in adultery. But even her affairs bring her disappointment, and when real life continues to fail to live up to her romantic expectations the consequences are devastating. Flaubert's erotically charged and psychologically acute portrayal of Emma Bovary caused a moral outcry on its publication in 1857. It was deemed so lifelike that many women claimed they were the model for his heroine; but Flaubert insisted: 'Madame Bovary, c'est moi'.

This modern translation by Flaubert's biographer, Geoffrey Wall, retains all the delicacy and precision of the French original. This edition also contains a preface by the novelist Michèle Roberts.

'A masterpiece' Julian Barnes

'A supremely beautiful novel' Michèle Roberts

Translated and edited with an introduction by Geoffrey Wall
With a Preface by Michèle Roberts

THE STORY OF PENGUIN CLASSICS

Before 1946 ...'Classics' are mainly the domain of academics and students, without readable editions for everyone else. This all changes when a little-known classicist, E. V. Rieu, presents Penguin founder Allen Lane with the translation of Homer's *Odyssey* that he has been working on and reading to his wife Nelly in his spare time.

1946 *The Odyssey* becomes the first Penguin Classic published, and promptly sells three million copies. Suddenly, classic books are no longer for the privileged few.

1950s Rieu, now series editor, turns to professional writers for the best modern, readable translations, including Dorothy L. Sayers's *Inferno* and Robert Graves's *The Twelve Caesars*, which revives the salacious original.

1960s The Classics are given the distinctive black jackets that have remained a constant throughout the series's various looks. Rieu retires in 1964, hailing the Penguin Classics list as 'the greatest educative force of the 20th century'.

1970s A new generation of translators arrives to swell the Penguin Classics ranks, and the list grows to encompass more philosophy, religion, science, history and politics.

1980s The Penguin American Library joins the Classics stable, with titles such as *The Last of the Mohicans* safeguarded. Penguin Classics now offers the most comprehensive library of world literature available.

1990s The launch of Penguin Audiobooks brings the classics to a listening audience for the first time, and in 1999 the launch of the Penguin Classics website takes them online to a larger global readership than ever before.

The 21st Century Penguin Classics are rejacketed for the first time in nearly twenty years. This world famous series now consists of more than 1300 titles, making the widest range of the best books ever written available to millions – and constantly redefining the meaning of what makes a 'classic'.

The Odyssey continues ...

The best books ever written

PENGUIN 🐧 CLASSICS

SINCE 1946

Find out more at www.penguinclassics.com